The Temple Of The EXPLODING HEAD OMNIBUS

THE DEAD HELD HANDS THE MACHINE
THE TEMPLE OF THE EXPLODING HEAD

REN GARCIA

The Temple of the Exploding Head Omnibus

This book is a work of fiction. The names, characters, places, and events in this novel are either fictitious or are used fictitiously. Any resemblance to actual events or persons is entirely coincidental.

ISBN: 978-1-940466-73-6

Hydra
Publications

ST. G

Published by Hydra Publications
Prepared by St G
Printed in the United States of America
First Hydra edition: May 2018
Visit our website: www.hydrapublications.com

Also by Ren Garcia

The League of Elder Series:
Sygillis of Metatron
The Hazards of the Old Ones

The Temple of the Exploding Head Trilogy:
The Dead Held Hands
The Machine
The Temple of the Exploding Head

The Belmont Saga
Sands of the Solar Empire
Against the Druries

Turns of the Shadow tech Goddess
The Shadow tech Goddess
Stenibelle
Kat
Melazarr (coming soon)
Taara (coming soon)

The House of Bloodstein
Perlamum
Mentralysis

Non-Fiction by Ren Garcia
10 Weeks at Chanute

For more please visit: www.thetempleoftheexplodinghead.com

Table of Contents

Book 1
The Dead Held Hands

Prologue

Part I
Kay and Sam

Part II
The Invisible World

Lord Kabyl of Blanchefort

Book 2
The Machine

Book 3
The Temple of the Exploding Head

League of Elder
The Temple of the Exploding Head

Book One

The Dead Held Hands

The Vith have a saying that the Dead hold hands and lend the living their power.
With the Dead, the Living are Invincible,
Without the Dead, the Living can do nothing.

Prologue

I—The Temple

The latest round of Faithful filed into the huge temple complex. The temple was vast and stony, washed in dark shadows and unseen reaches. It was deep underground and, like a cave, was bereft of sunlight. Pillars, covered with lurid painted glyphs and symbols, lined the distant walls, and pagan idols lurked in the shadows like predatory beasts. Brass braziers on thin, stilt-like legs created fitful pockets of jumpy orange light. The light from the braziers did little except throw the huge space into a mass of flickering mystery.

The whole place seethed with energy, enough to light a thousand cities, but the temple needed more. It had to have more energy, much more, and the Faithful were there to give it just that.

Rugs of various types and materials were thrown out on the gritty stone floor, looking like a patchwork of cancerous skin. Incense burners in the shape of squat, angry gods filled the dank air with a heavy smell.

The Faithful made their way into the interior and took their places. They were naked. Their golden bodies of various shapes and configurations were washed and oiled—they glistened in the feeble brazier light.

They quivered in anticipation. If they lived through what was to come, they could expect to indulge in each other's flesh after it was over.

If they lived— and that was very much in question.

Far away, at the front of the complex, a naked priestess, her golden body dripping with oil and wearing a feathered headdress, climbed up onto a dirty stone platform. The steps leading up to the platform were dented in the center, from the slow wear of passing feet up and down through the ages. The Priestess was one of 10,000 who served the temple. She would stand there on the platform and lead the Faithful until she collapsed from exhaustion, and then the next one would take her place.

She lightly tapped a small tambourine-like instrument. Though small and lightly played with slim, oiled fingers, its tinkling sounds filled the vast temple from one end to the other. From the unseen sides of the temple to the right and left, throaty drums beat in answer.

Behind the priestess, ten nude figures were chained to several posts. Either drugged or tormented into a trance, they hung in their chains and vibrated with the drumbeats, insensate and mumbling in their obscure language. Several reeking creatures with no skin tended to the chained figures; they washed their pale flesh and tenderly stroked their long masses of black hair.

The chained people didn't have long to live.

The Faithful, spaced out on their motley rugs, fell to their knees (if they had knees, for some did not—some had no knees at all, and others had many more than just two) and abased themselves.

The ceremony continued, and would last for as long as this batch of Faithful held out. It was exhausting and would possibly be fatal for some in attendance, but they lived for this. There was no other place they wanted to be. To die here, to have their flesh consumed here in the dark, would be a blessing.

The brutal rituals taking place in the temple had been going on, without stop, for ages. The 10,000 feathered priestesses of golden skin presided over the temple, each stepping alone onto the platform, each playing the tambourine, one after the next, daughters and granddaughters of priestesses before them. Likewise, the Faithful, in shifts, took their turn exploring the wonders and facing the consequences of the temple—such was the price it exacted. It was a like roaring fire that needed constant tending; otherwise, it would go out. The priestesses made sure that didn't happen.

That would ruin everything.

This temple was the anchorage. This was their portal and place of power supreme granting them mastery over time and distance, and they, in their depravity, gave it life, gave it power. Their age-old rule depended on the temple. They fed upon the riches the temple granted them, and, in turn, the temple fed upon them –a closed circle.

In an alien language, they began afresh.

"Bathloxi, hear our prayer ..." the priestess sang.

"Enemies of old, feel despair ..." the Faithful replied.

"Bathloxi, dance of light ..." the priestess sang.

"God of gods, invincible knight ..." the Faithful, entranced, mumbled.

"Bathloxi, our faith is sold ...

"Give to us what was foretold ..."

And on and on, over and over, through the hours, through the buried night, they concentrated. The temple needed strong emotion to function, and that's exactly what the Faithful were going to give it.

The Faithful focused on all sorts of strange feelings—though what they were truly feeling was known only to them. They felt something similar to hatred. It could be said they lusted. They might have envied, and probably they despised. Whatever they were feeling, it was passionate, and all of that heated energy condensed into a visible spark that danced off their prostrate backs and went to the nearest pillar like a leash of blue flame.

Eventually, a cloud of condensed energy filled the heights of the temple like an angry fog and became dense enough for the temple to feed upon it. Some of the Faithful strangled in the cloud, choked on its vapors and died where they were. The temple soaked the cloud up and converted it into raw, bestial power. Gouts of lightning from this newly collected energy sparked across the heights of the temple every so often, charging the humid air with static. Sometimes, the lightning came down fast in belching strokes, hitting select pockets of the Faithful, killing them by the score. If that happened, then so be it; again, the temple exacted its price.

If they managed to survive the noxious, energy-rich cloud and the random lightning hits, a further horror vexed the Faithful. Every so often, some of the Faithful, clutching their heads (if they had a head, for some did not), suddenly stood in a panic. Spinning around in the fog, their bodies bulged, losing their shapes, and spread out in gold-flecked masses, enveloping those around.

And their heads (if applicable) exploded in a spray. The effort, the strange feelings they generated, and the greedy temple itself had been too much for them.

The rest continued, having survived the cloud, the lighting and, so far, the exploding head chanting until their alien voices were ragged.

A few more fell apart in an endoplasmic gel and head spray.

Another lightning hit—more dead. More blood. The temple gorged itself on death.

As the pagan night wore on, their prayers appeared to be answered. A strange creature appeared near the priestess. Four-legged, hoofed, antlered, it looked like a deer, though its sylvan eyes were flickering with bad intentions.

Slowly the deer began dancing to the drums and the tambourine. It reared up on its hind legs, and, when it did, its deer-like body transformed into a shaggy, man-like shape with horns.

A continual bolt of lightning came down and struck the deer in the antlers—apparently causing it no harm. It wore the lightning like a bright, spindly hat.

Bathloxi, a mixture of man, animal and pure energy, he had come at last.

The priestess presented the ten chained figures as an offering. Having total mastery over her body, she gave herself many arms. They grew gracefully out of her body. With hardly an effort, she broke their chains and picked them up by the throat, holding all ten victims aloft as easily as new born babies. She presented them, dangling, to the god.

Bathloxi regarded them with nostalgia and a bit of longing; then, he sprang with passion. After a howling moment, some were consumed, others were electrocuted, and a few were burned.

The chained people with pale skin and thick black hair were dead. They were merely the latest victims of the temple.

"*I am here; my body is bathed, my hunger is slaked. My conditions are met. I will do as you ask,*" Bathloxi said, blood drenched, energy crackling. "*My blood shall give this place of worship continued life ...*"

And energy flowed from the god to the Temple—the priestess and her Faithful successful once again in currying favor from Bathloxi, and that meant renewed energy for the temple—much, much more than they had been able to generate on their own.

Victorious, the surviving Faithful, as a reward for their efforts, fell upon each other and engaged in any number of travesties in the moaning dark. They copulated and fed upon their flesh. They tore each other's skin, gouged eyes, ripped hair and bathed in the flowing juices in an orgy of pain and ecstasy. To cause pain gave them ecstasy—the whole process sustaining itself. Eventually, they had no more bodies. They fell apart and flowed together as one prodding, jabbing mass creating a vast stagnant pool on the temple floor.

For ages the temple had stood there buried deep in the ground and exacted its tribute. For ages the golden priestesses, the Faithful, the sacrificial victims and their bloody god had fueled it.

Soon, very soon, their patience was to be rewarded.

II—Lady Poe's Birthday

Lady Poe of Blanchefort's birthday was on February 14, apparently the date of an ancient holiday proclaiming love and togetherness; although, by the Kanan calendar, February had thirty-four days instead of the ancient count of twenty-eight.

Still, it was appropriate for Lady Poe was such a kind, loving person adored by all who knew her. As the month of February sat toward the very end of the cold winter season in the Vithlands of Kana, Poe and her family lived in their warmer southern residence, the Duke of Oyln's Grand Manor outside the city of Effington in the Estherlands. Her husband, Lord Peter, being in service to and good friends with the Duke of Oyln, was invited to live there with his family as he pleased. They had a whole wing to call their own.

To celebrate her birthday every year, the Duke and his Duchess, Lady Torrijayne, threw a large party with Poe as the guest of honor. Poe's brother and his wife, Lord Davage and Countess Sygillis of Blanchefort, helped in the planning and financing of the party and were always in attendance. Unfortunately, Countess Sygillis and Duchess Torrijayne hated each other. Their long running feud went back to their sordid days as Black Hats and was a constant source of A-List news and gossip around the League. Socialites were always eagerly curious to see which of the two would make a fresh snide remark or fire a sarcastic quip about the other. There was even talk of heated private meetings and secluded hair-pulling fist-fights conducted between the two. However, for Lady Poe's birthday party, they mutually agreed to a truce and behaved themselves.

Lady Poe certainly loved grand parties and spared no expense, but, truth be told, it was the quiet, private celebration she enjoyed with her family that was her favorite birthday treat of all.

Her husband, Lord Peter of Blanchefort (formerly of Ruthven) usually had a surprise or two cooked up for her— a little something that he had baked himself or possibly a clever trinket that he made, something quaint and hand-crafted. Lord Peter had skilled hands, and Lady Poe loved receiving hand-made gifts from her husband. Coming from a House Minor, Lord Peter was out-ranked by the House of Blanchefort and took its name by tradition upon their union. The often caustic social scene on Kana was a-buzz with the union, and a few Great Houses tried to block it through legal channels stating such a mismatched marriage in status violated League law. Others speculated that it would never last; however, Peter and Poe shared a loving relationship that held fast and grew through the years.

Their children also came up with something neat for their mother on her birthday.

Milos, their eldest son, sometimes wrote her a poem or a story which she listened to, eyes closed, hand in hand with Peter. Milos was so bright and creative that it was easy for him to come up with such things and captivate his mother.

The twins, Sarah and Phillip, had a harder time. They couldn't simply go out and buy mother something for Lady Poe of Blanchefort already had everything she wanted. They weren't quite as artistic as their older brother Milos, so they would knock heads for weeks, trying to come up with something witty and charming to present to her. Fortunately for them, Sarah was the spitting image of her late grandmother, Countess Hermilane (Lady Poe's mother), and usually Sarah and Phillip acted out a scene from Hermilane's past, which many times involved some sort of sword fight or duel, as the late countess had been a known pugilistic hot-head in her day. Lady Poe watched their performance and clapped, giving the twins a big kiss on the cheek when they were finished. Also, if they really got desperate, all Sarah had to do to make her mother happy was put on a gown, which, being a proto-typical tomboy, was a tough chore for her.

Their fourth child Millicent, or just Millie for short, got a pass up to this point. She was still babbling in a high chair and couldn't actively participate, not for a few years yet.

There was a final child of sorts who always showed up on Poe's birthday, the one who brought with him the most surprises and jokes of all—Carahil.

Lady Poe, being a mighty Silver tech female, had made Carahil in a Vith fountain at Castle Blanchefort some twenty-five years prior. Her brother, Lord Davage, often told dinner-time stories of a saintly silver seal he'd befriended in the Xaphan city of Metatron, and Poe, listening, was inspired and re-created Carahil in Silver tech. She put a lot of effort into it, spending months of exhausting work until the fountain was overflowing with silver. When Carahil opened his eyes, he was wise and powerful in the form of a silver seal. As such, Carahil soon became a full member of the Celestial Arborium, and he soared over the cosmos defending balance and righting wrongs.

In short, Lady Poe of Blanchefort, using her Silver tech, had created a god and was its mother. Such was the extent of her power and the width of her character—to be content as an unassuming wife and mother rejoicing in the simple things, her vast power kept in check by her love for her husband and her children.

Carahil was so busy spanning the heavens far from home that he rarely saw his mother anymore, but, like a good son, he always remembered to visit Lady Poe on her birthday. He usually tried to sneak up on Poe and scare her—Carahil's love of pranks still knew no end. He'd jump out from behind a huge potted plant (Duchess Torrijayne loved plants and Grand Effington was a literal botanical garden in certain places), or he'd cut the lights and appear out of nowhere. Carahil loved making a grand entrance.

Everybody loved Carahil, and, once everybody recovered from their shock, they'd give him a huge hug. He reveled with his family for a time, telling stories, playing with the children and basking in his mother's presence. After a bit the Duke and Duchess Torrijayne would come out and sit with Carahil as well, for they were his friends, too.

✶ ✶ ✶ ✶ ✶

On this particular occasion, Carahil seemed a bit off-put. He wasn't quite his normal, happy self. He twitched his whiskers and asked if the children could give himself and his mother a few minutes in private. With a cry of displeasure they exited the area, the Duchess promising to give them all a treat from the kitchen.

Lord Peter also took his leave along with the rest. "Please, Lord Peter, stay," Carahil said. "You need to hear this, too."

Alone in the room, just the three of them, Lady Poe looked at Carahil, that happy faced, silver seal. She sensed danger. "Is there something wrong, Carahil?"

He twitched his whiskers. "Yes, Mother, there is."

Poe was shocked. Carahil usually didn't just come right out and say something. He enjoyed making people coax information out of him. His stark, concise answer alarmed her.

She gently placed her hands on the dome of his smooth silver head. "What is it?" she asked.

"I've come to you for advice, Mother, and for help. I need your help, and yours as well, Lord Peter."

"Anything, Carahil. Anything we can do," Lady Poe said.

Carahil reveled in her touch. Though he was a god with power supreme, he found comfort and solace in the soothing touch of his mother's hand, as any child did.

Finally, he spoke.

"I need you to help me save the League, Mother."

And Carahil told them.

Carahil and the Tree of Life

III—Born in a Jar

Her family didn't often come out of the fog; that was a sure way to bring the demons.

She had seen the Kanan sun many times, a lot more than her brothers and sisters ever had, though she was a girl not ten years old yet, the youngest of her large family by far. She was born in a jar, a blessed birth by any measure. Her ancient home on the black hill by the lake was thick in perpetual fog. Even the brightest noon was little more than a dull gray twilight at Castle Astralon. To see the sun meant to venture a distance from the lakeshore where the fog ended, but few ever wanted to do that. Again, fear of the demons ruled everything they did.

But that was they, her family and neighbors, not her. Fearless, she often traveled far enough from the fog near the lake to see the sun, to marvel at it, to feel its warmth. She had done it lots of times and never once encountered a demon.

That's where *He* was, out there in the sun somewhere. The little boy she'd fallen in love with.

Great fecundity was a common feature of her people. All the tribes multiplied with abandon. She had twenty four brothers and forty seven sisters. She was the youngest of the bunch by three months. She was born in a clutch of twelve, a rather standard amount in her family. The Searchers discovered her tiny, partially developed embryo mixed in with the others who were fully formed and ready to be born.

"An Anuian is born to us! We are blessed!" they cheered as she was whisked away and placed into the brine filled jar. There she stayed for another three months, completing her development in the warm water and 'knocking' when she was ready to come out.

As she grew, it became clear she was slightly different from the rest of her family. Though still only a girl, she was fuller, sturdier than others her age with larger eyes than usual, long eyelashes and 'notched' lips. She was stronger and faster than the rest. It was clear she was a rare birthing among the Monamas; she was an Anuian, a Greater Monama, and a treasure for Castle Astralon.

The Anuians, she was told, rebelled and fought the demons long ago and were hunted down and wiped out for their temerity, leaving the smaller, more docile Conox, or Lesser Monamas for the demons to torture. Though gone, occasionally, an Anuian was born amongst the Conox and placed in a jar, and was a jewel for their House. Already, the tribes offered their sons to her, to the girl born in a jar.

With all those brothers and sisters every generation, one should expect her family to be massive, getting exponentially larger with every generation until they filled a hundred Castle Astralons.

Such was not the case.

The demons kept them thinned out. Every year, and with greater frequency, she lost aunts, uncles, cousins, brothers and sisters to the demons. Sometimes they vanished in the night. Sometimes they would be sitting right there, getting dressed, eating their breakfast or telling a story; then, in a Flash! they were gone, their utensils clattering out of air to the table below. Vanishing into thin air wasn't an overly unusual thing; her people could disappear and travel great distances at will—it was a talent they all shared. But this was different. This was for good.

The demons had gotten them.

According to their ancient stories, they as a people had been evil once, long ago in the mists of time, and the gods would not allow them to forget it.

The demons …

When the demons came, one never returned. Such was the sadness her people had endured for ages. Sudden death was something they lived with, both from the demons that tormented them, to the sundry wounds they chose to inflict upon themselves. There were the duels they fought, sometimes over petty arguments and misunderstandings. When her people fought, it wasn't a pretty thing to see. They were strong, and they had nails that could scratch iron.

And there were the Trials. One could not even enjoy the act of falling in love without the prospect of death lingering. One of her brothers had been killed while at Trial. He had fallen in love with a girl from Nebulon on the other side of the lake, and the Trials for her love had killed him. One of her sisters had committed suicide after her love, a boy from the Zerb tribe, had been killed while at Trial for her. Unwilling to live without him, she soon followed him in death.

She had lost thirty brothers and sisters to the demons, and she had lost her parents as well in such a fashion—they kissed her to bed one night, and in the morning they were gone, never to be seen again. She was raised mostly by her grandmother, a large and bold woman, an Anuian, born in a jar just like she had been. All she had left of her mother and father was the jar she had been born in, which she kept on her window sill. Sometimes she grieved so much for her lost family that she forgot who she was and could do nothing but sit there, eyes blank, staring at ghosts. Her grandmother sang to her at such times with her magical voice to pull her back from her delirium.

Her name was Sammidoran. In her native Anuie tongue, *sammidoran* meant The Far One (female case), and she lived up to her name, for she was young and rather impulsive, doing things Astralon girls usually didn't do. That was the Anuian in her coming out defiant and strong.

She loved to run with the wild herds of gazelle and other grassland animals that grazed beyond the perimeter of her fog-bound home. With them she bounded through the grasslands, easily keeping up with the herd, running in the sun that she cherished so much. She ran all the way to the forest, and sometimes to the sea, reveling in all the things her family feared.

An odd paradox, she sometimes thought. Her people, even the common lesser ones, were mighty, gifted, swift and strong, yet they were powerless against the demons. The demons could not be met. The demons could not be crossed. The demons could not be fought.

So she was told ...

Sammidoran had no friends to speak of. Some of the children of Castle Cardinal whom she knew were all taken by the demons. So were the Nebulons and the young Minzer children. The others who were left were afraid of her. The animals she ran with and the golden sun high above were her only sure companions. The demons could never take those from her.

* * * * *

She began having visions when she was five years old. All of her kind had visions, and hers were especially vivid. She could see the future, and she didn't want to. Many of her family saw their deaths in their visions, at the hands of the demons, and they crumpled up in sadness and waited for it to happen—waited for the end to come. She watched one of her brothers waste away in such a state. She went to her grandmother and pleaded

"Why, why does this have to be?"

And her grandmother calmed her as only she could and said: "Nothing has to be. Nothing is indelibly etched. If you see bad future, or you see a darkness coming, then make it better. Keep your head clear and fight for what you want, as I have done. How do you think I've lasted so long?"

Her aunts and uncles didn't like that sort of talk. What sort of thing was that to tell a child? Filling her head with dreams and impossibilities. Their motto was simpler and much more stark: Live your life while you can and hope for the best, and, when the end comes, let your head swarm and take you to places where there is no pain and sadness, where the demons can't hurt you.

As if such a place could exist.

Though she was just a little girl, she took exception to her aunts' and uncles' advice. To give up and fade away? To be so frightened that the only place to hide was deep within oneself? What sort of life was that? On her runs far from home, she sometimes saw her gazelle being chased by predators. They didn't just give up, lay down and be eaten; they ran. They ran until they could run no more, often times eluding the predators that stalked them. Mostly, the predators went home hungry.

There was a lesson to be learned in that, she thought. Just because a monster was chasing close behind that meant to do harm did not mean it was going to get you. She kept that thought in her heart.

Her visions began in the smoky pools of her dreams, and there was no denying them. She had visions of the people beyond the fog: the Elders who had come from the sky. The people with hair of differing colors. The people with the alluring eyes the color of sky, forest and earth.

She often heard her brothers and sisters talking about dreaming of Elders in their faraway cities, their *Arin-Dans* and *Cerri-Telas*, and how sad the dreams made them. She'd thought it was a lot of nonsense. Why would a mere dream make them so sad?

But now she was dreaming of Elders herself, and experiencing it was quite a bit different from merely hearing about it.

It was overwhelming.

She saw herself as a grown woman, tall and thin, standing on a hillside. She wore a black Bronta-covered gown with the usual Astralon bustle. Next to her was a man, with oddly colored hair (even for an Elder), a tailed coat, and a black, three-pointed hat. A long silver weapon hung at his side. Somehow, she got the impression that the silver weapon at his side was *her* weapon—that it belonged to her. In the future, he gave it to her on his knees, and she accepted it, writing her name into the shaft with her claw-like fingernails: SAMMIDORAN. It was cold where they were standing. Cold was bad. Cold hurt and could quickly end her life as surely as the demons could. For some reason, the cold was not bothering her; she was resisting it. A special charm at her neck kept her warm. Where did she get such a thing she wondered?

She saw a great castle in the cold mountains. She saw her grandmother at the castle talking to the Elder lord and countess. She appeared to be friends with those people. Her folk rarely bothered much with the people beyond the fog, except for the occasional fortune-telling and prostitution that provided them with their meager income. Her grandmother, however, was an exception.

As night after night unfolded, she saw the man younger and younger each time. Most often she dreamed of the man with the weapon as a little boy, far away, living in that castle in the mountains. He was a boy with a perfect face and strangely-colored hair.

His eyes, look at his eyes, like the forest-colored pebbles on the lakeshore ... They melted her. The things his eyes could see.

At first, she tried to distance herself from the image of the boy, to watch him impassively. She didn't want to become enraptured by her Elder vision, as her brothers and sisters before her had. But every night, there he was, emerging from the shadows, drawing her ever closer to him, lured in by wondrous things that he wanted to share with her. She was haunted by the little boy. Even as she opened her eyes in the first moments of morning, she could still hear his laughter.

A word began to enter her thoughts, one that she had previously thought silly and quaint: *Arin-Dan*. It meant 'beloved' and 'dreamed of.' As with her brothers and sisters, this little boy was, more and more, becoming her *Arin-Dan.*

He was bright and cheerful. He had an inviting smile. And he was loving and kind, making her laugh, showing her interesting Elder things in his castle and inviting her to sample delights from their kitchen. Her visions were so real that, in the morning, she often forgot the things she experienced were merely parts of a dream. It was heartbreaking sometimes to wake up and not have him there and to know that all the wonderful things she'd seen and tasted were not real.

She saw moments of sadness when he was hurting. His people were cruel to him. They thought him flawed and weak. She wanted to reach out and comfort him. If they didn't see the value in him, she did.

Don't weep, my Arin-Dan ...

There was yet another thing he introduced her to: desire. He was handsome, even as a little boy, and he had that Elder belly button that her people found so attractive. Trying to be coy, she ran from him through the corridors of her dreams, and he chased her. When she could stand it no longer, she allowed him to catch up, and together they fell into a feathery pile of bliss. Invariably, the dream ended, and she would awake, her thin body alone and aching. “Come back here!” she’d say. “Finish what you started!”

Still, he wasn’t perfect by any means. He was a bit spoiled and self-indulged. He was loathe to take action, to be as great as he could. He was a loafer; she hated that, it infuriated her, but that stage wouldn’t last. She saw him transform from a loaf to a great Vith lord, mighty and brave. All he needed was a push. She saw him taking her into his arms—she could feel his embrace. Once there, she felt safe and content. In his arms, nothing else mattered, not her family, not even the demons.

That was where she wanted to be, safe and sound, with him ...

She told her brothers and sisters about her visions, and they understood. They, too, had had dreams of their *Arin-Dans* and *Cerri-Telas*. They told her such dreams were dangerous and would bring the demons. She must be rid of them for her sake and for his as well.

They advised her on what needed to be done. Pick a ceremonial White Emilia flower from the wild and go to the blackened Mourning Wall near the lake and plant it there. They told her that, once she completed the task, the vision will fade, and it will hurt for a while, terribly, but then it will be gone, and she will be all right.

She took their advice, went out and picked a single White Emilia flower and took it to the Mourning Wall, which was just a blackened fragment of an old Anuian castle that the demons had destroyed centuries earlier. Around the base of the wall was a dense bed of White Emilia flowers, all planted there by her kin hoping to rid themselves of their visions. Holding her flower, she thought of the little boy somewhere out there beyond the fog. She thought of his laughter and his arms around her and what it would be like to not have that any more.

All those forsaken dreams growing there in a carpet of white.

The Anuian in her spoke. She did not want the dream to end. She wanted it to be real.

She wanted her *Arin-Dan.*

Turning, she walked back home and

planted the White Emilia in her jar, a reminder to her of what she almost let go.

Time passed. Her dreams continued and became more and more vivid. Her *Arin-Dan* was powerful—could do many things. She saw him turning invisible. Mouth open, heart fluttering, she watched him... *flying* ... through the sky in blasts of wind. And his lovely eyes ...

His Sight, splendid in time, can save both of your souls ...

All he needed was a little push, and he could be great.

But there was darkness too—horrible things lurking in the distance like an afternoon thunderstorm.

She saw the demons coming to her *Arin-Dan* and crawling into bed with him.

She saw the silver weapon with her name on it crossing with a demon's blade shaped like a phallus, the two weapons ringing as they clashed.

She saw him in a life or death struggle with a demon, covered in giant insects.

She saw him lying on the ground in a terrible place, the demons around him ... *eating him.*

No, no, no! Please! My life for his! My soul for his!

And, worst of all, she saw clawed hands around his throat, trying to wring the life out of him. The hands were chalk white, delicately formed with long fingers, and ended in a stout set of black, claw-like fingernails.

Those hands... could they be... HER hands?

She forced the thoughts from her head where they simmered for a time, grew dark and came again.

And, strangest of all, she saw herself doing the unthinkable. She saw herself one day going against the demons, running from them, plotting their ruin, and it would begin with her walking into an Elder den full of mystery: THE MYSTERY DEN.

Sammidoran told her grandmother of her visions.

"Who is this boy? What is his name?"

"I don't know. I want him. I love him. He's my *Arin-Dan*."

"*Arin-Dan*?" her grandmother replied, shocked. "Have you not gone to the Wall? Have you not been instructed to do that?"

"I did, and I chose not to plant my flower there. I didn't want it to end."

"Anuians!" she spat. "You understand you are condemning yourself to a bitter end? The demons will come for you and for your *Arin-Dan,* too."

"I won't let them. You taught me to fight. I won't let that happen."

Despite her better judgment, her grandmother admired her spirit, very courageous for such a young person. Her grandmother buried herself near the lake and had visions. She saw the demons taking an interest in her granddaughter, to take the love she felt for this Elder boy and twist it into a tragedy. The demons were always waiting to pounce upon Monama love and use it for their own ends. But, she also saw her granddaughter having great resolve, and with this Elder boy at her side, what possibilities ...

Sammidoran described the castle in the mountains, the cold, and her grandmother's frequent presence there. She described the weapon that hung at his side. A long sword-like weapon. But it wasn't a sword; it was a metal tube with a handle.

Her grandmother smiled. "That is a CARG. That's what it is called," she said. “You are having visions of Castle Blanchefort far to the north. You are seeing the son of Lord Davage and Countess Sygillis of Blanchefort. He is not yet born, even now. He still rests in his mother’s womb.”

Sammidoran had been dreaming of a boy not yet a minute old.

She was intrigued. She spent much of her time thinking about this unborn boy—this Lord Blanchefort. A boy who, one day, was to do great things. A boy who one day will hold her in his arms.

A boy who will be eaten by demons, or, worse, be torn to shreds ... by her own hands

She sat there in the fog, lost in a dream, addicted to it like a narcotic. She talked to him, though he wasn’t there. She’d laugh; sometimes, she’d argue with him—he was so stubborn! Why did he have to be so stubborn?

She said his name, for she now knew it, too; it echoed to her from future’s maelstrom: Kay. Lord Kabyl. Lord Kabyl of Blanchefort.

This unborn boy was her only friend, her confidant and her lover.

Living up to her name, she began using her power to ‘Blink’ far to the north to Castle Blanchefort. There she prowled the castle and gazed out the windows to the majestic scenery outside. She tried going outside to the wondrous Grove behind the castle to look around, but it was so cold. She could feel her skin freezing and her throat tightening. She could only withstand it for a few minutes before having to go back inside the castle.

In a dusty corner of the southern wing of the castle, she located the currently unused tower where the boy will one day live, and she walked around investigating it—haunting the place as an invisible little ghost. Although now a quiet and unused place, one day it will be brimming with life, for not only will Kay live in this wing, but so, too, his sisters and brothers and cousins, each getting their own colossal tower to grow up in.

Zorn tower—here was Kay’s tower. That was its name.

Her Kay ...

Rolling around in its darkened interior, she wrote her name on the walls in several select spots with her long, sharp fingernail. She explored the tower from top to bottom. It was a huge place, over one hundred, fifty stories high, bigger all by itself than the whole of Castle Astralon. She went to the dusty, disused places in the tower and sometimes visited the rooms and galleries where she would one day pass her time with Kay, acting out scenes from the future to herself.

She was very excited when the Lord and Countess Blanchefort began getting the tower ready for the new arrival. Though his birth was still months away, she felt the wheels were in motion, that things were finally starting to happen. Seeing the Countess, a beautiful, red-headed Elder woman with her pregnant belly, she was desperate to reach out and touch it. It drove her mad. She sometimes considered presenting herself to Countess Blanchefort and demanding to touch her belly. That was Kay resting within, her *Arin-Dan.*

He belonged to her. She felt entitled.

Patience, patience ...

Soon, her love will be born.

They had their staff clean the one-hundred, fifty story tower from top to bottom, and a team of skilled craftsmen were there building the furniture Kay would one day use.

She watched as they skillfully built Kay's bed. She was breathless as she watched them work.

Kay's bed. The things she and Kay will share there, do there. She sat in the corner and trembled.

She didn't want to wait. If only she could travel through time.

Kay's room and new nursery will be on the terraced levels, and Sammidoran helped get his room ready. Not an idler by any means, she tried to help the staff out when she could. One day she picked up a sponge when the staff went down for lunch and scrubbed the walls. She was shocked when Lord Blanchefort came in.

He knelt down and smiled. "Well hello," he said as she stood there holding the sponge. He spoke in Elder, which her grandmother had taught her to speak. "Are you Lady Sammidoran? You must be. Your grandmother has told me all about you, and I've been eager to make your acquaintance," he said.

He told her that, as she was the granddaughter of Countess Hortensia of Monama, she was always welcome there. He then grabbed another sponge and, together, the Lord and the pale little girl, finished scrubbing the walls.

✶ ✶ ✶ ✶ ✶

She had a strange vision one night, and unlike the visions she had of Kay, she never had that particular vision again—but she remembered it. She never forgot a single detail.

The *Olonol* ... She dreamed of the *Olonol.*

It was a vision that could possibly change everything.

✶ ✶ ✶ ✶ ✶

The day before Kay was born was when she saw her first demon in the flesh. She had run out to the sea with a basket full of stuffing and thread. There, out in the sun, she put the finishing touches on a little stuffed animal she had been working on. Her basket was open and all her materials were carefully arranged in front of her. It was a gazelle made of a colorful patchwork of red, blue, green and gold fabrics. It had green buttons for eyes—just like his eyes will be. Her grandmother had gotten her all the components for its making, and she'd spent weeks working on it. Like all of her people, she had strong, dexterous hands and, though she had never made a stuffed animal before, it was quite accomplished; a master toy-maker couldn't have done better.

She was going to give it to Kay, as a gift from her to him. It was a modest gift. He was a Great Elder Lord, born into money and power and technological items that she could only wonder over. But, she had made this little gazelle all on her own and had poured every bit of care and love she had into its making. She hoped one day that it might mean something to him. She dreamed of talking to him about it one day: "Kay, I made that little gazelle for you before you were born. I made it just for you."

I hope you come to love it, Arin-Dan. Just like I love you ...

She was restless and impatient. She wanted Kay. She wanted him born. She wanted him out in the world ... with her.

And then, she could feel eyes all over her. Watching, laughing.

Demons! There they were, staring at her from behind a tree: leering, bleeding, skinless.

"Hi ya, Sam," they hissed. *"What're you doing?"*

Terrified, she dropped everything and turned to run home.

Wait! The gazelle! She left it there. She turned to grab it and then run away as fast as she could.

A demon stood there holding the gazelle by the neck, squeezing it in her bloody fist. The demon was female, miserably thin, and dripping half-clotted blood. She was horribly bent at the torso.

She stank, as she heard demons always do.

"You forget this?" the demon said in a callow voice holding up the stuffed gazelle.

Sammidoran stood there powerful but helpless before the demon who could not be fought.

She'd worked so hard on that little gazelle.

That was for Kay. She hated the demon! She hated them all!

Moving like an uncoiling serpent, she tore off across the grassland leaving the demons behind in a hurry.

"HAHAHAHAHA! Run! Run, Sam!" they called to her. *"Run all you want ... we've got plans for you ... All in good time!"*

✶ ✶ ✶ ✶ ✶

She sat by a favored tree later that afternoon and wept, her hands to her face. She'd always considered herself so bold and brave. She'd thought herself fearless. Yet, when standing face-to-face with the hated demons at last, she found herself powerless.

She had been afraid. She had been wracked with fear, and she lost Kay's toy gazelle. She felt herself a failure, and so she wept.

As she sat there and cried, she became aware of something creeping through the grass toward her.

The demons!

She stood and made to run away. Approaching the tree, low in the grass, was an odd sort of animal. It was small and shiny with a smooth-domed head and a set of long whiskers. It didn't have legs, but rather flippers, like the turtles that swam in the lake water. It seemed like it belonged in the water, or in the air, or anywhere else it wished to go. It was a beautiful little animal, and she didn't feel afraid any longer.

It held something in its mouth. It set whatever it was holding down and backed away. It looked at her expectantly with bright eyes and twitched its whiskers. She almost felt as if the shiny animal wished to talk to her. It seemed to be smiling.

The toy gazelle she had lost to the demons lay in the grass. There it was, unharmed, unblemished by the demon's hand, a patchwork of colorful cloth.

She was elated as she picked it up. She wished to bow and thank the little animal for delivering it to her. Surely he was a messenger of the gods sent to uplift her spirits. Perhaps he was a god himself. Now, she'd have a gift to give to Kay.

The animal was gone, as quickly as it had come. Cradling the gazelle, she ran home. She was bursting with joy.

As she ran, she thought she heard a kind voice say: *"You worked so hard on that, Sam, seems a shame to lose it ..."*

✶ ✶ ✶ ✶ ✶

The next day, Sammidoran and her grandmother went north to Castle Blanchefort. She had been invited to be in attendance as the next Lord of Blanchefort was born. Many people were there—all Elders. She had never seen so many at once before. She stood there in her black gown next to her grandmother holding her hand as many came to peer into Lord Kabyl's crib. As they waited for their turn, she held the little gazelle to her.

It took some time, but, eventually, they arrived at the front of the line. Countess Hortensia picked her up and allowed her to look down into his crib.

There he was, mere hours old, yet she had known him for years. *"Such kind fate,"* she said to her grandmother in her Anuie tongue as she stared at him, her heart racing.

As she took in the sight of this newly born baby, whom she had seen in her dreams, she made a promise to herself.

She would ignore and abjure what her aunts and uncles said about life, about fate. About giving up when things looked bad.

The things she'd seen: the goodness, the love, the laughs, his arms around her …

And the darkness waiting for her that she tried to ignore. "*We've got plans for you ...*" the demon said. *A dark future is coming.*

She would follow her grandmother's advice. If the future looked bad, then do something about it … change it. Fight for it. The things she had seen regarding this tiny baby who was now right in front of her, both the good and the bad, were worth it.

What will be created between them was worth it.

I'm going to be strong for you, Kay. I am going to watch over you. I am going to be there when you need me. I am going to keep the other girls away, for there is only me. Me!

She then took the stuffed gazelle she'd made and gave it to Kay as a gift. She propped it up against the side of his crib and was led away.

Part One:

Kay and Sam

1—The Pale Ghost

Crash! Thump!

Lady Kilos of Blanchefort sat properly on the stone wall and watched with passing disinterest.

Her older brother was on the leafy ground, trying to stand. A tall woman in a Fleet coat stood over him.

"Ok, so all that pretty Vith fighting is nice for show, but, if you really want to win a fight, you do it street style, and you do it dirty, too. Right? And, don't ever hesitate to cheat. All that Vith honor I hear so much about—leave it for the dinner table," Lt. Kilos said, lending Kay a hand while pulling him out of the leaves.

They were out in the cold of the Telmus Grove surrounded by old, gnarled trees and fallen leaves. Kilo's silver Tweeter bird bounced around in the branches and fussed with the other birds.

She was showing Kay how to street fight, Onaris style.

Lord Kabyl of Blanchefort, or 'Kay' as everybody called him, had had a crush on Lt. Kilos for as long as he could remember. She was an old friend of the family, his father's first officer and a trusted mentor to Old Dav's kids. There she was: tall, a lot taller than his rather tiny mother, wiry and lean in her ever-present Fleet uniform with a thick head of long brown hair that touched the small of her back. Kay had always thought she was so pretty.

"Let's go again," Kay said, raising his fists.

She laughed. "I think you've had enough for today, but you're doing well. Just get a little more meat on your bones, and you'll be tough as nails. Promise."

Kay reached down behind the wall and put his purple and black coat on. His younger sister, Lady Kilos, sat nearby in a minty blue gown watching them spar, her whitish blue hair done up in the Blanchefort style. She had been named in honor of Lt. Kilos, which got a little confusing sometimes with both of them running around. The Lady was growing up to be much more prissy and girlie than the brusque tom-boyish Lt.

"Lt., I'd like to try," she said standing up. If she'd had sleeves to roll up, she would have.

"I like your spirit, Bottle, but you're too much of a lady to do things like fighting. Your cousin Sarah, on the other hand, oh boy, I think she's going to be in quite a few of them before she's done—the kid's a real blue-haired hothead." Lt. Kilos always called his sister "Bottle." Since they both had the same name, a nick-name was a must. Lady Kilos used to have a habit of throwing her bottle around, which Lt. Kilos thought was funny.

"I don't like Sarah," Lady Kilos said. "She's mean to me."

"She is not," Kay said.

"She does have a big mouth," Lt. Kilos agreed, "and that never gets you anywhere, but I think she means well."

Ki stared hard at Kay. "Come here, kid. Let me have a look at you."

Kay stepped in front of her, and she placed her strong hands on his shoulders. "You're getting so big. How old are you now, Kay?"

"I'm twelve."

"Twelve? Oh Creation, where's the time go? I still remember when you were bouncing off Syg's lap. I'm only a hundred and four, and you're making me feel like an old maid." She took a hard look at his eyes. "You've got the coolest eyes, Kay. What are they, sort of a jade color, creamy jade?"

"I guess. I don't know. All the bloody lords and ladies who come in to stare at me don't like them much."

"What is the deal with that? Every Tuesday, Dav and Syg have you downstairs standing there in the gallery, and all these stuffy blue folk come in and start pawing you like a mannequin at the stores holding a tray of free samples. What is that?"

"It's called 'The Review'. It's a Vith tradition. All the various Houses that think they might wish to ally themselves with the House, or arrange a marriage or do business with the House, come and have a look at the eldest children up until we turn fifteen. And we have to stand there and not move or say a word. I moved once to scratch my nose, and one of them wanted to cane me for moving, but Father wouldn't let them."

"Cane you? I wouldn't think so."

"I hate it," Kay said.

"I have to do it, too," Lady Kilos said.

"Yes, but they love you, don't they? They love your blue hair and your blue eyes and everything about you. Me? They say a green-eyed Vith lord is no Vith at all. They talk about me like I'm not even there. They say I'm too short, and they don't like my hair either. And I just have to stand there, lock still, like a bloody statue for hours sometimes and take it."

Lt. Kilos ruffled his hair. "I guess being a peasant like I am has its advantages sometimes. I couldn't put up with all that rigid society stuff. I'd have knocked somebody's damn teeth out by now."

She squinted and looked at Kay's hair. It was dark purple, like a grape-flavored popsicle, long, wavy, tied-up in a tail.

"You know, I guess I'm used to seeing it this shade by now. I mean, you Blancheforts come in all sorts of cool colors, don't you? Your dad with his blue hair, Bottle over there with her whitish-blue, and Hathaline and your baby brother Maser—boy, those two have a carrot-top going, don't they?"

"I used to chase Kay around and try to put his hair in my mouth. I thought it would taste like grape," Lady Kilos said.

"Yuck!" Lt. Kilos replied. "I'll bet it doesn't taste like grape, does it, Bottle?"

"No."

"You don't have any kids, do you, Ki?" Kay asked.

"Me? No, sure don't. I've never had time for it. My husband brings it up every so often, but I'm not ready. I'm having too much fun hanging out with your mom and dad. I don't even have my womb turned on—Elder Women can do that, you know. If you leave it turned on, it gets messy."

"Really? You'd be a good mother, Lt.," Kay said.

"Think so?" She checked the time. "We'd best be getting back to the castle.

It's getting late and your mom will have my head. Come on."

"You've been in fights with mother before, haven't you, Ki?" Kay asked.

"Fights? Yeah, yeah we used to fight all the time. That was before we became friends. She hits pretty hard for such a tiny squirt. She's a great lady, your mom. Great lady."

They got their stuff together, hats and coats, and headed back, crunching through the leaves and stepping up onto the cobbled path. It was a long walk back to Castle Blanchefort.

Lt. Kilos suddenly stopped and checked her coat pockets, slapping them frantically with her hands. "Damn! I think my flask fell out somewhere back there while we were sparring. It's missing. I've got it topped-off with some good stuff, and I don't want to lose it. Tweeter, find me my flask!"

Tweeter, glowing like a silver candle-flame, hopped off her shoulder and flapped back the way they came, ready for her to follow. "You two, wait here, ok? I'll be right back. I'm just going to get it."

She headed into the trees. "Don't move!" she called back one last time.

Kay and Lady Kilos stood still on the path as asked. She smiled. "I wouldn't listen to those stupid lords and ladies," she said. "I wish I had your eyes and hair, and I wish my face wasn't so puffy. You're so pretty, and I look like a marshmallow," she said, touching her swollen eyes with her hand. "I hate my face right now."

Kay made to respond when a noise came from the trees ahead of him.

"*Kay!*" he heard.

Kay gazed into the trees. "Who's there?"

He saw a tan, brown-haired face peek out from around a tree. "It's me, Kay. It's Kilos."

Kay stepped forward. "Lt.? Where'd you come from?" She had previously disappeared through the trees to the east but was now peering out at him from due west.

Kilos' voice was trembling. "Can you come here?" she said at a whisper. "Please?"

Leaving Lady Kilos behind, Kay stepped into the trees. There was Ki, leaning against a stump.

Ki?

Her clothes were different. She was wearing a crinkled black gown covered with intricate black-on-black designs, low cut, showing off arms and shoulders and a fair amount of her cleavage, pulled tight into an hour-glass shape. Odd—Lt. Kilos didn't have a girly figure; she had more of an up-and-down tom-boy body like Sarah's, only taller. Kay, also, had never seen her wear anything other than her Fleet uniform, and seeing her in this black getup was a little disconcerting.

The final strange touch on her clothes was a chain wrapping around the skirt portion of her gown and dragging on the ground.

"What happened to your clothes?" Kay asked.

"My clothes? I lost them," she said, her whispered voice trembling.

"Lost them? What's with the chain?"

"Oh, it's a tradition. Don't pay it any mind."

She advanced on him, her large brown eyes wide and rather intense. Her lips and hands were shaking uncontrollably. Her hair was rather wooly and down to her ankles.

"And what happened to your hair?"

"My hair?"

"It's really long. Why are you shaking?"

"It's so cold. Aren't you cold? You fought well today, and I wanted to offer you a kiss as a reward. Would you like that?"

Kay's insides bloomed. A kiss from Lt. Kilos?

"Umm, sure."

She came forward and put her trembling hands on his shoulders. "You're so handsome, I've always thought so. Such colors."

Kay had thought she was going to give him a friendly peck on the cheek like mother often did, but, no, she lifted his chin and parted her lips to give him a kiss. As she came in, he noticed her fingernails were long, pointed, almost claw-like.

The kiss she gave him was like none he'd ever received before, slow and warm, moving and moist, and full of passion. He felt the tip of her tongue come wandering into his mouth.

"Kay!" came a voice. He surfaced from the kiss and craned his neck. Lt. Kilos was standing a distance away on the path next to his sister, hat on and blue coat parted, booted, holding her newly recovered flask.

There was a rustling and rattling of a chain, and the "Kilos" he'd been kissing was gone. He caught his breath. "I'm here, Lt.!" he said coming out of the trees.

The two Kilos' came running up. "I thought I asked you not to move!"

"I saw you bade me go into the trees," he replied.

"You what?"

"Yes. I heard you call my name, and then I saw you beckon from the trees. Right over there! It looked like you, only you were wearing a low-cut black gown, like for a funeral. You also had really long fingernails, kind of scary."

Kilos drew her gigantic Marine SK pistol from its holster. "Show me," she said.

Kay led them over to where the other "Kilos" had been standing. She leaned down and inspected the grass. "Right here," he said. "She gave me a kiss, tongue and all."

Ki looked up, open-mouthed. "What?"

"Yes. She wanted a kiss, or, I should say, 'you' wanted a kiss."

"Listen, I love you, kid, but you're a little young for me, right? And, by the way, when I want a kiss, I don't ask, I take, so it wasn't me."

"Did you give it to her, Kay?" Lady Kilos asked.

"Yeah."

Ki blushed a little and began inspecting the ground again. "Tweeter, was there someone standing here with Kay?"

He hopped a little and rustled his wings. "Hmmm, he says, 'yes'. I see a trail. Wait here." She stood and followed it back into the trees, SK at the ready. "And," she called back, "if you see me again, and I want another kiss, it's not me, ok?" She disappeared into the trees.

Kay and Lady Kilos stood there. "It might have been Sarah playing a joke on you," she said. "I think she's been developing the Gift of Cloak. Maybe it was Sarah."

"Sarah can't Cloak. Besides, she's not here. She's south for the winter with her mom and dad and Phillip; and, even if she were here, Sarah would rather punch me than kiss me."

"It was just a thought." Another idea came into her head. "You know, Kay, it might have been the ghost!"

"What ghost?"

"I see a pale ghost all the time in the castle. It's a girl ghost, I think. She's always off hiding in a corner. I see her peeking out all the time when your back is turned."

"It felt too solid to be a ghost."

"Ghosts can feel solid. Father told me."

"What does this 'pale ghost' look like?"

"I think she's a kid, like us. A bit bigger than we are perhaps. She wears black, just like what you described, and her hair is black. She has a lot of hair, all the way down past her knees. Her skin is really pale, chalky white almost. That's why I call her the Pale Ghost, because she's pale, see? And she follows you around everywhere. I went to mother, and I said: 'Mother, how come Kay gets a ghost following him around, and I don't have one?'"

"And what did mother say?"

"She didn't say anything. Oh, and the Pale Ghost's fingernails are *really* long—I mean this big!" Ki lifted her hands and held them out several inches apart.

Kay considered the thought and shuddered. "That's creepy. What does she want?"

"I don't know. I've seen her coming out of your room, and once, when I was in the village with mother, I saw her standing on your balcony."

"Oh, Creation ..."

"I don't think she's a bad ghost. I don't think she means you any harm."

Lt. Kilos returned. "I found a fresh trail in the woods. It went back near to the clearing where we were sparring."

"You mean the ghost was watching us?"

"Ghost? Are we calling this kiss-seeking, gown-wearing manifestation a ghost? Well then, yes, the ghost was watching us. Come on, we're heading back."

✶ ✶ ✶ ✶ ✶

When they returned to the castle, Lady Kilos followed Kay to his tower, Zorn Tower, one of the larger ones on the western face, southern wing. "Hey, you know what we can do, Kay?" she asked. "We can do an exorcism. Yeah. I have a book I inherited from Aunt Pardock that shows you how to do it. Let me go get it, and I'll meet you upstairs. Leave your door open." She stood straight up and concentrated. After a minute or so, she Wafted away. Ki's Gifts, at only eight years old, were manifesting quite well. Kay felt a little jealous as his Gifts weren't doing anything yet, and he was four years older.

He went inside and took the lift up. The floors, mostly empty, whizzed by as he climbed.

He got out and went into his bedroom. While not feeling scared, per se, he was feeling a bit anxious. Perfectly understandable seeing how a ghost just tried to put its tongue in his mouth.

He got his toy gazelle down from its shelf. It was his favorite toy; he'd had it forever. It always helped calm him on nights when he was certain there were monsters in the room with him. He swore it had a voice. He swore it sang to him sometimes.

As he waited for Ki, he sat to check his holo-mail. There were several new posts, mostly from Sarah.

His cousin Sarah, two years younger than he and the daughter of his aunt, Lady Poe of Blanchefort, had a love of the bizarre and the grotesque. She lived there in the castle in Xyotel Tower during the summer and went south with her parents in the winter. Every day she trawled the Posts looking for lurid headlines and sordid articles, looking for stories of monsters and murder, never failing to find them in abundance. When she was there in the summer, she assailed Kay and her twin brother Phillip with all the sensational stories she'd found. When she was gone in the winter, she'd holo-post them to Kay's account every day. Sarah and Phillip, by all accounts, were Kay's best friends, their friendship growing with each passing year.

He'd get items from her like:

"DEMONS TERRORIZE CHRISTOPHER PARK!"
or:
"WRAITH OF GASTON' STRIKES."

He read the posts as Ki Wafted in with a crash of wind and noise. She was holding a huge book.

"Where did you get that?" he asked.

"I said I inherited it from Aunt Pardock. It belonged to our great grandmother!" Kilos put her hand to her mouth and whispered. "... And she was a Bloodstein Witch. Yeah."

"Oh," Kay said, impressed.

Ki flopped down cross-legged in the massive inverted funnel of her gown and opened the book, flipping through the creaky pages.

"Ah!" she cried. "Here it is. Ritual to perform an exorcism. It says the three points of a triangle are very important. It says the top of the triangle represents the present, the left side the past and the right side the future. It says that, if we can surround something of the Pale Ghost on three sides, then we can wish it away or do whatever we want. Oh wait! We don't have anything of it, do we?"

"I've got some of its slobber in my mouth."

"Good idea! Spit on the floor."

"Really?"

"It can't hurt."

Kay leaned forward and spat on the floor. Reading her book, Ki drew some symbols on the floor in chalk, front, left and then right. "There!" she said happily. That takes care of the Pale Ghost."

"Is that all?"

"Yep." She yawned. "I'm going to bed. Performing exorcisms makes me sleepy."

She Wafted away.

Kay looked at the little three-sided design Ki had made on the floor with his spit in the middle of it.

A Pale Ghost had come to him for a kiss. Why? Thinking back on it, he hadn't felt scared or put off; her clothes were a little strange and she had seemed a little intense, but that was all.

"Hey, if you can hear me, thank you for the kiss. I wish you hadn't run away. Why do you hide? What's your name? Hello?"

No answer. Oh, wait—Ki's exorcism. Did it really work? Was the Pale Ghost no longer able to reach him in his room?

He debated it in his mind and then went to his bathroom and fetched a towel. He got down on his knees and rubbed out Ki's markings and his blob of spit.

He had decided to welcome the Pale Ghost and not shun her.

Kay sat up for a bit longer, wondering if she'd show. Not seeing anything, he went out onto his terrace. Across the way was Harkness Tower, where his sister Kilos, the exorcist-in-waiting, lived. The lights in her room were on. They went out a moment later; Ki must have just gone to bed.

Feeling sleepy himself, he undressed and crawled into bed. As he ventured into the warming realms of sleep, he heard a tiny voice.

That was the worst exorcism I've ever seen. It wouldn't have worked, but I'm proud of you for getting rid of it anyway. Don't be afraid of what's on the other side of the door. You might be surprised by what's there ...

St Vith Cathedral, Blanchefort Village

2—The Last Day of His Life

Kay had spent a lot of time finding the perfect spot where he would take his own life. He was now thirteen, and he couldn't handle it anymore.

The constant failure. The disappointment and blank stares as he stood there in the gallery, lock still.

The great lords and ladies chiding him in review.

Look at his eyes. Look at his hair.

It's his mother's fault.

His mother's fault!

Lord Davage chose poorly, and here's the result.

Ah no, his sister; now she's a classic Blanchefort and Vith. Too bad she's not a man.

Crying? He's crying!

His father coming up and whispering in telepathy. <*You ... need to be strong.*> Even his telepathic voice rang with anger.

Lord Davage's flawed, non-Vith son.

It wasn't just the Reviews that had him down. It was everything. Everything he tried, it seemed, he failed at.

Space:

His father was a great captain in the Stellar Fleet and commanded a star-faring vessel called the *New Faith* that he and mother were often away on. His father took him up in the ship several times, to help him get his 'legs.' He'd hoped Kay might one day follow him to the stars as father and son.

Each trip had been a disaster. Kay had been badly sick the entire time. Once, they even had to turn back and send him home he was so sick.

The King CARG:

His father carried a CARG, the LosCapricos weapon of his House. His father's was a huge, coppery weapon called the King CARG that was monstrously heavy. Davage often talked loudly of how he planned to give it to Kay one day.

"It's very heavy. It's seventy-seven pounds, and I had to work up to lifting it when I was your age, Kay, so don't be put off if you find it too heavy to lift now," he said. "I have this—it's a mockup CARG called, the 'Runvanion'. It's the same size and nearly the same weight. When you can lift the Runvanion, you may have my King CARG. I shall leave it in the west wing library on a stand. Try it as you will."

And Kay tried it. It was like the Runvanion was nailed to the floor. He couldn't budge it. It was rather embarrassing. His cousin Phillip could lift it, and Sarah could, too, but he couldn't do a thing with it.

Kay's Skills:

He found a list one day, written by his father and Lady Poe, detailing his various strengths and failings. The list wasn't pretty:

Physical Strength	Poor to Average
Appearance:	Exceptional (No childhood puffiness present)
Speed/Agility:	Fair
Dirge:	undetermined
Waft:	undetermined
Stare:	undetermined
Cloak:	undetermined
Piloting Skills:	Nil
Penmanship:	Exceptional
Linguistics:	Exceptional
General Aptitude:	Exceptional
Sight:	???????????

Kay's Piloting Skills:

Kay clearly had inherited his mother's skills as a pilot, and that was a terrible thing. His mother had wrecked a number of Ripcars, leaving them battered and dented into shapelessness. His father Davage was an incredible pilot and was keen to teach Kay how to fly; however, Kay had zero instincts, feel or aptitude for flying. His cousin Phillip was a wonderful budding pilot; he and Davage would stand and watch as Phillip and his father, Lord Peter, cavorted across the sky over the castle in their sleek *Goshawk* ship. Even his seven year old baby sister, the red-headed Hathaline, could fly a level simulator better than he could. Much better. She showed real promise while Kay had none.

Kay's Gifts:

"Kay," his father Davage often said. "We selected Zorn Tower just for you before you were born. It is, by far, the most haunted, phantom-riddled, chain-rattling place in the castle. We selected it for you as a test, for your Gift of Sight. The Gift of Sight is a proud Blanchefort tradition going back over a thousand years, and you, as our son and first-born, no doubt have a tremendous Sight. You will, most likely, have more than just one Gift, but the Sight is the most important. You shall see all sorts of things roaming about your tower, and, truth be told, not all will be pleasant. It's just part of the experience. Be bold and face your Gift with courage and a spirit of adventure. Feel free to share your experiences with your mother and me. We are always available to give ear and lend advice."

But, Kay never saw anything beyond the mundane. No Sight. He had strange dreams, always tinted in Amber. He had lots of those. He often dreamed of himself bearing a mark around his right eye, like mother had. But dreaming strange things apparently didn't have the same import as seeing them.

And he saw nothing.

He also heard plenty of things, such as His name whispered or shouted, strange titterings and the occasional rattling of chains. He heard laughing and chiding. He heard something speaking in a strange language.

Tena mortza, Arin-Dan.

Arin-Dan. He heard that word a lot but didn't know what it meant. It wasn't Vith; he didn't know what it was, perhaps some old ghost language or Haitathe. He'd research it later.

He also heard a friendly, jovial voice mixed into the rest, one that comforted him. It said things like: "*Hey kid, don't let them get you down*". He actually looked forward to hearing that voice. He thought the voice came from his gazelle.

But he saw nothing. Not even the Pale Ghost that Ki had mentioned, which was sort of a relief.

✶ ✶ ✶ ✶ ✶

And then there was the humiliation with the Stertors.

"The Stertors are coming to pay us a visit, Kay," his father said, calling him into his study. "It's a rather odd name and perhaps a bit sinister as well, but the Stertors are a branch of the Sisterhood of Light, and they are our friends. They visit all the great Houses, and they shall observe you and proclaim what Gifts you have."

And the Stertors came wrapped up in their white robes and winged headdresses. They came in the summer when Sarah and Phillip and the rest were present in the castle, and all the children were tested and proclaimed, starting at the lowest rank, moving to highest. Between Lord Davage/Countess Sygillis, and Lady Poe/ Lord Peter, there were quite a few children to sort through, the Stertor scribe noting them on an official parchment:

Name	Rank	Age	Registered Gifts
Millicent	Daughter of Lady Poe	6	Gifts: Sight, Stare
Phillip	Son of Lady Poe	11	Gifts: Sight
Sarah	Daughter of Lady Poe	11	Gifts: Sight, Strength
Milos	Son of Lady Poe	12	Gifts: Sight, Dirge
Maser	Son of Lord Davage	3	Gifts: Sight, Strength
Hathaline	Daughter of Lord Davage	7	Gifts: Sight, Stare, Dirge
Kilos	Daughter of Lord Davage	9	Gifts: Stare, Dirge, Waft
Kabyl	Son of Lord Davage	13	Gifts: Cloak, Waft

The Stertors reviewed the list with Davage, Sygillis, Lady Poe and Lord Peter, her husband. Very impressive, they noted. A great diversity of Gifts, and most of the children had at least two. Look at all the Sighters present. The House of Blanchefort was well-favored.

Davage read the list. "There must be a mistake. Lord Kabyl and Lady Kilos are not listed with Sight," he said.

"They do not have the Sight, my lord," the Stertor replied.

Kay remembered the expression of hopeless shock on his father's face.

No Sight. A Blanchefort heir with no Sight ... Thousands of years of tradition lost.

* * * * *

So, he planned his death, to rid the House of his imperfect green-eyed, purple-haired self. He put a lot of thought into it. He didn't want to leave his House in danger of extinction without an heir. His little brother Maser, three years old and redheaded like a ruby, would grow to become Lord of the House. Kay was replaceable. Not having Kay around would mean nothing, and his sister Ki would hold rule as House Regent until Maser grew old enough.

Ki would do a good job. She was a proper Vith. The House would be fine.

He picked a high balcony in westward-facing Pendar Tower, one of the smaller towers in the castle that Lt. Kilos often used as a guest tower. It was high up, and he would fall to the crags four thousand feet below. The crags had drainage access to the Bay of Bloodstein, so, after a little rain, all the blood and gore of his dead body would be neatly washed away; there would be no mess to clean up.

No fuss. Perhaps his little corpse would wash away, too.

Certainly mother and father and Sarah and Phillip and Ki, too, would feel a little sad, but they'd get over it. They were Vith and understood such things. And there were others to take his place. This House was secure and better off without him.

* * * * *

Today was to be the last day of his life. It was raining and the water would be up in the crags beneath Pendar Tower. Sarah and Phillip were away, gone south to spend the winter in Grand Oyln Manor with their parents. Ki was away on an outing to the south with father.

Pretty empty in the castle today. Perfect. Now, all he had to do was let the water accumulate, go up to the balcony and simply step off, and it would be like he never existed at all.

Castle Blanchefort

3—Sam

He stepped out onto the balcony in the wind and pelting rain. The stone was wet and slippery. Just over the rail was four thousand feet straight down to the flooded crags. He climbed up onto the railing, the strong wind ready to blow him off, and stood up straight.

This was it.

"Hey, kid," he heard a voice in his thoughts. *"Where's your note? You can't have a suicide without a note; why, that wouldn't be good form, would it? Why, they'd say, 'He threw himself off a balcony, and he didn't leave a note explaining his actions. Apparently, everything we thought about him was true.' Better come down and write your note."*

Kay climbed back down. What had he heard? Was that his conscience? In any event, the voice was right. What was he thinking? No note? That would be rude, so he looked around for paper and a writing implement. Not finding any, he exited the tower and went to his favorite reading room. There he sat down to compose his note.

He'd written a few lines when his mother appeared at the door, body-suited and barefoot as always when not in a gown. "Here you are, Kay; I've been looking all over for you." Standing at her side was his little sister, Hathaline. Mother was carrying his little brother Maser—the heir to the House after he was gone. At seven years old, Hathaline was still barely larger than a toddler, her curled red hair a scarlet carpet spilling over her little girl's gown. Her thumb was in her mouth.

"It's been a while since we've done any exploring of the castle, and I thought I'd give you a task to perform on this rainy afternoon. You must be lonely without your cousins."

She glanced at the note. "Your penmanship is coming along. Is that a note for your cousins or for a lucky lady out there somewhere?"

"No, mother, just a few musings."

"Ah. Well, come on, Kay. Let's go on an adventure."

Kay stood and followed his mother out of the room leaving the suicide note on the table.

His mother had many interests. She loved bowling in the secret Blanchefort alley, and she loved crawling in the dark reaches of the castle. She had personally mapped and re-discovered many hidden places under the castle, covered up by the newer sections and forgotten over time. Now that Kay and his cousins were getting older and more able to cope with the rigors of 'castle-caving', she came to them more and more to share her passion. No doubt, bowling would soon follow.

"Have you ever heard of Countess Fercandia, Kay?" she asked as they walked down the corridor heading toward the eastern section of the castle, Kay's boots clicking on the tiles, his mother's bare feet making no sound.

"No, mother, I'm sorry I haven't."

"She's an old countess from long ago when the Vith still had to fight the Haitathe to survive. Countess Fercandia was a warrior who fought at her lord's side, and she fought with a CARG, just like he did. Her CARG wasn't big and heavy like her lord's. It was smaller and lighter, something that she could use. It was still a CARG, just different. I wanted you to see it. I thought you might be inspired." Her face filled with motherly love and pride. She touched his cheek. "And, maybe you wouldn't be so hard on yourself. Look at you, just a little boy, yet so burdened. I can sense it, Kay. I know you've been hurting."

"I'm fine, mother," he lied.

"You take things upon yourself that you shouldn't, Kay. Take your father's CARG for instance. Your father specifically told you that you wouldn't be able to lift the Runvanion right away; it's just too heavy. He told you you'd have to work up to it, but you didn't listen. You can't lift it now and, therefore, you consider yourself a failure now. Don't feel that way, Kay. All in good time. So, I wanted you to spend a moment or two with one of your ancestors who also used a CARG, just a different kind of CARG."

She pointed at a stone bench. "Look under the bench. You'll see a small grate. The grate trails off into a crawlspace, at the end of which you'll find the hidden chapel of Countess Fercandia. I want you to go there now and pay your respects. The going will be tight, and this is a four-out-of-five stone crawl, so it's a difficult one. But, if you stay small and take your time, you'll be fine."

Sygillis seated herself on the bench and bounced the tiny Maser on her knee. Little Hathaline stood to the side, still sucking her thumb. Kay took off his coat and laid it on the bench. "I don't like how this coat fits on you," she said. "I'm starting to take an interest in the doings at our factories, and I want to design you some clothes myself. I have all sorts of ideas and those people down there better start listening to me, or else."

Kay thought about wearing his mother's clothes, but, of course, he wasn't going to be wearing anything much longer. He would be dead soon. "Thank you, Mother. I look forward to it."

"Oh, wait," Sygillis said. She removed her pouch and held it out. "Take this. You'll need it."

Kay took the pouch. Inside there were two sweet pastries within to tide him over if he got hungry, a telecom should telepathy fail, and a never-dim neon flash-light.

A flashlight. He picked the flashlight up and looked at it in dismay.

What a disgrace he was.

Mother detected his distress. "It's just a flashlight, Kay. Use it if you can't see. It's all right."

He put the flashlight back into the pouch and stuffed the whole thing into the grate.

"You know," Sygillis said as he wiggled headfirst into the hole. "Your sister, Kilos, the one whom all the lords and ladies can't get enough of, couldn't do this."

"Couldn't do what?" Kay asked, his baggy white shirt clinging to the grate in a frustrating manner.

"This. Crawling into tiny places. She's claustrophobic, Kay. She doesn't like small spaces."

"She doesn't?"

"No. You see, even a perfect Vith like your sister isn't perfect at everything. She fails and feels fear every now and again. Being afraid sometimes isn't a weakness. Take what makes you afraid and learn from it. That's what a great man or a great woman would do. Go on, the countess awaits."

He crawled into the tight dusty space. The way was rough going—mother certainly didn't give him overly-easy tasks, and, even he, with his tiny body, got stuck once or twice. The musty space was only twelve inches high at most. He lay there on his stomach, his head cranked to one side because he couldn't hold it out straight, and he crawled on his elbows in jerky stages, dragging his legs and boots along. He came to and S-bend and got stuck, his knees getting wedged. He was in a real fix. Suddenly, the cool open space of the long fall off the balcony he was soon to take seemed very free and inviting.

He tried to look around, but his head was stuck in a cranked position. Despite the confines, he remained perfectly calm and collected in the tight uterine fold. If his sister Kilos suffered from claustrophobia, then this straitjacket-like situation would probably stop her heart with fear.

<How're you doing, Kay?> his mother sent.

<I'm fine.>

<If you get stuck at the S-bend, you'll need to turn around and go in feet first. It's too small, and you'll get pretty stuck going headfirst. Going in feet first will allow you to bend your knees and twist with the contours. It's much easier that way. Trust me.>

<Thank you, Mother,> he sent. He pulled himself free and, balled up into the fetal position, wiggled around and plunged into the bend feet-first. Sure enough, he slid through like a bullet being stuffed through the barrel of a crooked gun.

Beyond the bend was what appeared to be a dead end. It was horribly dark, and he couldn't see much of anything. With chagrin he got the flashlight out and waved it around. Webs and old stone, a solid wall ahead of him. Where was the chapel? Had he taken a wrong turn?

He spied a crack in the stone face. It was small, very small—only about nine inches wide at its maximum. Peering in, he could see hints of a murky room beyond.

Must be the chapel.

Puzzling it out, the only way he could figure to enter the chapel without using the Waft—which he was still trying to master at thirteen—was to plunge in feet first again, a courageous thing to do not knowing what was waiting for him on the other side. The squeeze was harrowingly tight, even for a small boy like himself, and he had to control the urge to panic as the uterine stone caught and held on his clothes.

He paused and allowed the momentary hand of panic to go elsewhere. Fully composed, he stuffed himself through the hole into the waiting room on the other side.

<How are you doing, Kay?> his mother telepathied again.

<Fine, Mother, I just got through into the chapel.>

<Very good!! I'm so proud of you!! Do you know how hard that squeeze is to get through? See how fearless you are—let the Vith lords choke on that! Take your time and look around, and don't forget to offer a blessing—you're in the presence of your ancestor.>

<I won't.>

He thought a moment and prevented a tear from coming. He would miss his mother.

Don't cry for me, Mother. I'm sorry I had to be a bother.

The room was bathed in a wash of lamp-black. He sat there trying to allow his flawed green eyes to adjust to the lightless surroundings. His hearing was rather acute, and he could hear minute little things going on around him, but he couldn't see a thing. He turned his neon flashlight on and waved it around.

The chapel beyond the squeeze was fairly small and dusty, mostly a faded blue color with complicated stained-glass windows dotting the walls which now looked out on packed earth and masonry; apparently, this chapel had once faced an outside wall and had been built over in the many years since its construction. That was a usual feature of Castle Blanchefort, the new covering up the old.

He panned around with the flashlight. A few ancient pews emerged in the dusty beam, as well as a life-sized marble statue of the Countess that was partially buried in the far wall. There she was. Pretty lady, he thought, admiring the serene-looking woman, a carved CARG resting in her left hand; her right hand open and inviting. The tiled floor was strewn with dried leaves—ancient and brittle. He picked one up and immersed it in the flashlight's beam; no, not leaves, they were roses! Dried roses littered the floor. He made his way to the statue to have a good look at her CARG. He was careful not to step on the roses as he made his way, he thought she might not like that. Those were her flowers, mummified or not, and he didn't want to hurt them.

The CARG in her hand was tapered and dainty, like a rapier. It was quite a bit smaller and lighter than his father's accursed King CARG, which was like a lead club in comparison. He'd never thought of a CARG being dainty and light—it hadn't occurred to him.

There was Vith writing carved into the hilt of the countess's CARG, which Kay, from his lessons, could read.

Putting his 'exceptional' linguistic skills to work, it said:

Killed one hundred Haitathe with Windamere

That must be her CARG's name. Windamere. And, it had killed a hundred Haitathe. He was impressed.

An image came to his mind of going to the castle smithy by the lake and forging a CARG similar to this one, something small and light that he could use without effort. He imagined the excitement, the heat and smoke, the sizzling of the molten raw materials. Perhaps his mother could add a bit of Silver tech to the forging, to make it stronger, make it glow. He imagined presenting it to his father, allowing him to see what he had made.

He had a momentary dream in amber where he saw it in his hand, real and solid. It glowed with Silver tech power. There was something that he couldn't see clearly etched in the hilt: -AM-ID-RA-

The amber faded and he was back in the dark looking at the countess's CARG. All sorts of ideas entered his head. He could have a CARG just like this one. It could be real.

But no, it was too late for all that.

The balcony awaited him.

Recalling his mother's task, he approached the statue and bowed, head down, offering a simple prayer to her memory and thanks for this lesson, though it had come too late, he had already made up his mind and was walking dead.

Just then, the statue spoke to him.

<Hi!> it said in a cheerful female voice.

Kay looked up, startled. He thought, at first, it was his mother playing a trick on him, but no, mother was nowhere around.

One of his sisters perhaps? Ki was too haughty to play childish games and Hathaline couldn't really talk yet.

Who had spoke?

"Ummm, hello," he responded, holding the flashlight up to the statue's face in the gloom.

<What's your name?> the statue said, again in a pleasing, cheerful voice. The statue didn't move, its mouth didn't open and close, but its voice was plain as day.

"Kabyl, my name is Kabyl." He had a thought. "Countess Fercandia, is that you?"

<Kabyl's a very lovely name. And no … what name did you say? Fer—what?>

"Countess Fercandia."

<That's not my name, and I'm not a countess. Maybe someday I'll be one, but not now. My name is Sammidoran. That's kind of hard to say isn't it, so you can just call me Sam, or Sammi, or Dora. Or, if you feel brave, you can call me Sammidoran, whatever you like. May I call you Kay? Do you mind so much if I call you that? That's your nick-name, isn't it?>

"Sure … I mean, no, I don't mind. Everybody calls me Kay."

<Oh, thank you, Kay, you're a nice fellow, I can tell that already.>

Kay waved his flashlight around, trying to find the source of the voice. It seemed to be coming directly from the statue.

<Why are you using a flashlight, Kay?> Sam asked.

"Because it's dark, and I can't see."

<Oh, you must be pulling my leg. You don't need a flashlight—use your Sight.>

Kay stood there before the statue, feeling a fresh wave of embarrassment trickle over him. "I … don't have the Sight," he said quietly.

<Sure you do!> Sam's voice shot back. Her voice was heavily accented with a trilling burr, and it sounded vaguely familiar, though Kay couldn't place it. It wasn't like a Remnath accent, or Esther, or Zenon either. It was most similar to Hala, like what his aunt, Countess Pardock, spoke, though Sam's voice was more musical and friendly in tone.

"Sam," Kay asked. "Your voice—it has an interesting sound to it."

<It does?> Sam replied. <You'll have to pardon me, Kay. Your language isn't what I normally speak. My grandmother taught it to me. I worked extra hard to learn it. I ... I hope I'm doing all right.>

"I can understand you just fine," Kay said. "What language do you normally speak, if I may ask?"

<Which one? Well, let's just say maybe I'll teach it to you here and there. A little at a time. I'd love to speak to you in my own language. Do you pick up languages fast?>

"I'm told I do."

<Well, great! I'm sure you'll be a natural.>

Sam was about to say something else but then paused. <Kay, I don't mean to sound rude, but do I smell something good in your pack? It smells like something to eat. It smells really good, and I'm so very hungry. I've not lunched yet today.>

Kay opened his pack and pulled out one of the pastries. "You mean this? It's a fresh pastry from the kitchens; the cooks make them every day. My mother loves them."

<I can see why; they smell just wonderful. Is it be possible … I mean, could I possibly ask you to share one with me? I hate to ask because I really don't have anything to share with you in return.>

"That's … that's all right. I'll give you one, and you needn't give me back anything. I've always been taught to share."

<Oh!> Sam exclaimed, <you're so very kind.>

"Where should I go to give you this?" he asked.

<Ummm, simply place it in the statue's hand. I'll be able to get it there.>

Kay, without really thinking about it, stepped forward and placed the pastry into the old statue's open hand. "There, I hope you enjoy it."

After a moment, as he watched, the pastry vanished. <Ohhh!!> Sam exclaimed. <That was soooooo good!! Thank you so very much! You're such a nice fellow, Kay!>

Kay looked into his pack. "I have another one, Sam. I offer it to you, if you want it."

<You … you don't want it?>

<No, Sam, you can have it. I offer it to you.>

Sam was quiet for a moment. Then, <Yes, Kay, I would like it very much. Thank you.> Her voice sounded strained as if she were on the verge of tears. Kay placed the pastry in the statue's hand, and again it vanished.

He backed away and sat down in one of the old pews, the dusty yew wood groaning as he did. He trained his dusty flashlight beam on the statue. "Sam, where are you?"

Sam stayed silent for a moment. <Well …we've only just met, and I don't want you to think ill of me or anything. Let's just say that I'm pretty far away.>

"Far away?" he said, repeating. "So, how is it that I am speaking to you?"

<Ohhh, I can do lots of things, Kay. I was poking around and saw you.>

Sam again paused. <I think you're cute, Kay. I hope that doesn't intimidate you.>

"No, it doesn't," he said feeling a little bashful. "Can you see me?"

<I'm looking right at you. I like your hair. I like the color. Please, what do you call it?>

"My hair? It's purple. It's not a usual sort of hair color."

<Purple,> Sam repeated. <It's so lovely.>

"The great lords and ladies who come to gawk at me every week certainly don't like it."

<Who cares what they think? I like it. Your parents like it.>

"No, they don't. It needs to be blue."

<Blue? Is that a color?>

"Yes."

<Like your sister's hair? Your dad's hair? Sort of like the sky?>

Kay laughed. "Yes."

<Well, I think purple is very pretty. It sets you apart and makes you who you are. I saw you the other day standing there like a statue while all the people passing by made mean remarks. I wanted to reach out and cheer you up. I saw you were upset, and who wouldn't be? I'd be upset, too. Your dad really got mad.>

"He got mad at me because the people made me cry."

<No! No, he didn't. He was mad at the people, for the things they said about you and about your mother. He'd had enough. Do you know what your father said? He said to them: 'Leave my home and never return. Should I catch you on our holdings ever again, it shall mean war'. What does 'war' mean?>

Kay shrugged. "Fighting. Killing, with armies."

<Oh. I wouldn't want to 'war' with your father; he's a great warrior. If he's willing to 'war' with the other lords over you, he must love you a lot.>

"I guess so. I'm sort of a disappointment around here."

<Why?>

"I can't fly, and I can't pick up father's CARG, and going into space makes me sick. And, I can't see anything. I can't Sight."

<And you consider yourself a failure?>

Kay thought about his response. "Yes."

<But you can see, and you can fly. You can't fly machines the way your father does, but you can fly none-the-less. You can't see the way your father sees, but you can see such things. Maybe you're just not looking in the right way. Your eyes are green and your hair is ... purple ... maybe your ability to see is different, too. Have you ever thought of that?>

No, he hadn't.

Sam continued. <I can't fly, and I can't see, and I've never been to space, but it would probably make me sick, too. I can't do all those things, but I can talk to you from far away through the mouth of a statue, and I can lift your father's CARG. Hey, Kay, maybe we can help each other.>

"How so?"

<I can lift your father's CARG. I can help you to lift it, too, or come up with a suitable solution around it. Perhaps once you've lifted it, you'll figure out how to properly see, too. You never know.>

"You'll help me lift father's CARG? I suppose you saw me trying and failing? Is that right?"

<Yes.>

"Are you the Pale Ghost, Sam?"

<Pardon? Am I the what?>

"There is a ghost that's been following me around. A pale ghost with really long fingernails. Is that you?"

Sam laughed. <I'm not a ghost, Kay. My heart beats. My skin is warm. At night, I go to bed. And, there's nothing unusual about my fingernails. In our culture, ghosts are evil. I'm not evil.>

"Well, I'm sorry. I didn't mean to call you a ghost. So, you want to help me lift the Runvanion?"

<Runvanion? What's that?>

"It's the mock-up of my father's CARG in the library—the one I can't lift. You'll help me?"

<Oh! Oh, yes, I'd love to help you.>

"Wait. The Runvanion is seventy-seven pounds. I can't budge it, and you sound like a girl."

<I am a girl. So?>

"A girl couldn't lift the Runvanion."

<I can lift it. I'm stronger than all my brothers and sisters. Shall I prove it to you?>

"Yes. Please, prove it."

<Then turn off your flashlight and close your eyes.>

"Turn off my flashlight?"

<No peeking. Promise?>

"I promise."

He turned off the flashlight and couldn't see a thing. A moment later, he felt a soft hand touch his shoulder. The hand moved down his arm until it got to his, where it gently raised it aloft. He felt the cold, smooth shaft of the Runvanion fall softly into his palm. Feeling with his fingers, he followed the shaft down to the hilt. There, he felt a warm hand gripping the handle. The hand was soft and small. "Is that you, Sam?" he asked.

He heard her voice. "Yes, Kay, that's my hand." He heard the pew groan a little as she leaned over. He couldn't see her leaning over, but he sensed it. She whispered into his ear, so close he could feel her breath. He could smell the soft notes of her skin.

"See, nothing to it."

"How are you able to do this?"

She took his hand and moved it slowly up the length of her arm. Her arm was soft and girl-like in feel. He felt the bend of her elbow go by and then the jack-in-the-box of her upper arm. She flexed, and he felt a machine-like network of muscle rise-up through the softness like a submarine ship bursting out of a calm stretch of water. Then, without effort, she lifted him up off the pew, cradling him to her breast—and all while still holding the Runvanion.

She whispered into his ear. "So, have I proved my point? Perhaps you'd like to wrestle as well."

"I-I'm sure there's no need for that. So, what do you want in return?"

"In return? I don't want anything in return. Wait! I take that back. There is something I want."

"What is it?"

"I've always liked reading the news posts in the morning, but they don't come where I live. We don't have the holonet here. Will you read them to me?"

"Read you the morning posts? Is that all you want?"

"Yes, I would like that very much."

"All right then, I agree. I will read you the posts and you'll help me lift the Runvanion. Please put me down."

"You promise?" Sam asked.

"Yes, I promise."

She set him back on the pew. He felt the cool Runvanion gently touch the side of his face, guided by Sam's hand. "You aren't just saying what I want to hear, are you, Kay? A promise is very important to my people, just as it is to yours. You've made me a promise, and now you're obligated to keep it. I don't want you, once we're done here, to go upstairs and do anything silly. Right? That would break everyone's heart here; it would never be the same. And, it would hurt me, too, as you just made me a promise that you didn't keep. I'm eager to hear you read me the posts."

Kay shuffled uncomfortably. "I don't know what you mean. I'm not going to do anything silly."

The balcony and the long drop to the crags hung in his thoughts.

"All right. When may I expect you to read to me?"

"Tomorrow."

Sam's voice brightened, and the Runvanion fell away. The pew groaned again as Sam stood up and was gone. <Tomorrow it is,> came her voice from the statue. <You promised.>

He turned the flashlight back on. He was alone in the old chapel as before. They talked a bit more, then Kay thought he'd better be getting back to his mother.

<Kay … I've greatly enjoyed meeting you today.>

"And so have I. Err, can you see me anywhere I am in the castle?"

Sam laughed. <You mean, can I see you in the bathroom and in the shower? Yes, I could if I wanted, but I promise I won't do that. Here is where we'll meet. This will be our special place, *zemfa*?>

"What?"

<Oh, sorry. What's the word I want? Ummm, oh!> She repeated herself: <This will be our special meeting place, *okay*? I think that's the right word.>

"All right."

<Until tomorrow, Kay ...>

Kay left the chapel and returned to his mother. He told her about what he had experienced, and she quickly went into the chapel to see for herself. When she emerged, she said she had heard nothing. She pummeled him with questions, then apparently satisfied that it was a standard, run-of-the-mill ghost the castle teemed with and nothing more, they returned to the central castle and had lunch.

✶ ✶ ✶ ✶ ✶

Kay went back up to his reading room. It was raining hard, and the water would be way up in the crags below Pendar Tower. He could just head to the balcony and step off; there was nothing stopping him.

Only a strange promise he'd just made to a voice in a chapel.

He decided to postpone the suicide. He'd first keep his promise, read the posts to the voice named Sam, and then, once the conditions of the promise were fulfilled, he'd kill himself. He figured the afterlife might be pretty tough on those who didn't keep their promises.

Yes, he'd kill himself later.

4—Forging his CARG

Kay didn't kill himself that day, or the next, or any day after that. In fact, he forgot all about it.

True to his promise, he returned to the hidden chapel and read Sam the posts with a tiny portable terminal. Nearly every day he went there. Sam wasn't a passive listener. She asked frequent questions and even liked to forcefully share her opinion on things, even if she didn't really know what she was talking about. Sometimes they argued about the posts.

Kay began to consider Sam a close friend, someone with whom he could share his deepest secrets.

And she loved to flirt. She loved to tell him how cute she thought he was, and every so often he'd feel a warm kiss on his cheek.

"Show yourself, Sam!" Kay often said, but Sam refused. She said she wasn't allowed.

True to her word, she helped him lift the Runvanion, mostly through encouragement, though she also taught him a few simple techniques for clearing his mind and focusing. He would sit on the floor in the chapel cross-legged, and, in the dark, he could sense Sam sitting next to him in a similar manner. Before the winter was out, he was able to lift the Runvanion off its stand, though the effort took everything he had, let alone trying to use it to fight with.

He could now lift it, and he should, by rights, inherit his father's King CARG, but, what good would that do? He couldn't fight with it; he couldn't even lift it up to level.

To that end, Sam had a much better idea. <You should forge your own CARG. Is there any rule against that?>

"No, but my father was hoping to pass his CARG down to me so that I'd carry it with me, as he's done."

<Well, you're not your father—and he's not you. Did he never forge his own CARG?>

"No, I don't think so. He just uses my grandfather's. The King CARG was created by my grandfather back in the day."

<Just think how proud he'd be if you walked up to him one day and said, 'Look, father, I made this with my own two hands, and it'll serve me and the House well for years to come.' I think he'd be really impressed.>

Kay thought about it. It seemed to make sense. "You really think so?"

<I do.>

Kay was bursting with excitement and ideas. "All right. Let's do it! But, wait! One second here! I don't know the first thing about making a CARG."

<Well ... let's start with the basics. What is a CARG?>

"It's the traditional weapon of our House, designed to fight the Haitathe, the giants of old. It's a tubular shaft with a hilt, usually straight, and anywhere from three to eight feet long, the shaft being adjustable in length."

<Is it a club?>

"No, you use it like a sword, sort of. It cuts like a sword with the tube being micro faceted to cut. There are drums, I think, in the old smithy by the lake that machine-in the correct grooves and facets that allow it to work." He approached the statue of Countess Fercandia and pointed at her CARG. "Something like hers. Something small and fairly light, though I don't like her hilt. My father's CARG has an X-shaped hilt, with each arm of the X being dedicated to a different season. I should have a similar X-shaped hilt for my CARG as a tribute to his."

<That's a great idea. I think he'd like that.>

Kay was buzzing with ideas. "I'm going to get some books on the various kinds of metals to use, and I'm going to have to draft a design of some sort."

<Can I do that, Kay? I'm pretty good at drawing and inscribing things. I mean, it won't have any technical details, but I would like to contribute something if I could.>

"Sure, Sam, sure."

Kay left the chapel and got out as many books as he could find on the subject of blade smithing, including several arcane Blanchefort texts on the subject of CARG-making, which was quite a bit different. He read all about drop-forging and casting and creating the machining for the various links that would compose the CARG's expandable shaft.

Look at all the math! Equations for calculating correct diameter and circumference. Equations for determining the center of balance, metal thickness, link weighting and on and on. It was rather overwhelming. His cousin Phillip was quite good with math, and Kay sent him several holos asking for help. Phillip responded and got him started. Phillip was curious what Kay was doing, and he replied:

It's a surprise. See you in a few months.

Phillip must have told Sarah, as she sent Kay a basket full of mail demanding to know what he was doing. She even requested that he stop whatever he was up to and wait for them to return in April; then, they could help him.

Sorry, Sarah. Thanks for the offer, but he wanted to do this alone.

The next morning, he awoke to find a packet of papers lying on his bed. It was a draft design for a CARG, hand drawn but laid out with incredible skill and detail. A professional draftsman couldn't have done better. There was a note attached to it.

What do you think?
—S

There it was—a beautiful facsimile of Countess Fercandia's CARG. The hilt was X-shaped, like his father's, with some exquisite design work decorating each arm. Sam had done a wonderful job. She was a true artist.

It was Tuesday, and that meant it was time to go down with Lady Kilos and be Reviewed by the great lords and ladies. He normally dreaded those days, but today he stood like a statue without a care as his mind was elsewhere, turning on his CARG.

People came by, and he barely noticed or heard what they said. At some point during the afternoon a smallish man with a round belly and a garish plumed hat came up. He smiled and stood there for a while. He whispered in Kay's ear.

"Hello, Kay, well met. I am Milos, Lord of Probert, a good friend of the family. I designed the ship your father flies around in. I've known your father since I was a just boy about your age. What a fine son Dav and Syg have. I have a son who's about your age as well. His name is Lon. I brought him today and hope you two might become friends, keep the tradition going."

After the Review had concluded, Davage and Sygillis led Kay into a ground floor reading room. Sitting within was a small, round boy wearing a long coat, knee-britches and buckle shoes. He'd pulled down a few books and was reading them, two at a time. The remains of a bowl of ice cream sat in front of him.

Must be that Lon kid Lord Probert had mentioned. The door closed, and Kay and Lon were stuck in there.

There was a lot of silence as the two boys gawked at each other.

Eventually, Kay, feeling rather uncomfortable, found a few books himself and decided to take advantage of the time to continue designing his CARG, the two boys sitting opposite at the table and saying nothing. He pulled Sam's drawing from his coat pocket and began trying to calculate the various lengths of the pieces using Phillip's equations as a guide.

He'd written out several pages of notes, when:

"Are you working on something?"

There was Lon, sitting there on the other side of the table, trying to see what he was doing. He was clearly quite curious. A touch of chocolate stained his lips.

"Just a project."

"Oh." Lon stared at him. "Is your hair purple?"

"Yes. What of it?"

"Nothing. Just asking."

More silence. Lon's stomach rumbled.

"Can I see?"

"Why?"

"Just curious. My father's a great engineer. I'm going to be an engineer too, or maybe a scientist. My mother's a great scientist."

"It's a secret project."

Lon seemed impressed. "Oh, well, I'm great at keeping secrets. My mother's shared all sorts of secrets with me, and I've never told a soul. Not even the Sisters can Stare them out of me."

"Really?" Kay sized the tiny Lon up. "What if I came over there and beat them out of you? What then?"

"Oh, well, I wouldn't like that much, but you'd still not get anything of use out of me. I'm sure I'd say something, but you'd never know if I was secret-telling or not. I've memorized volumes of convincing-sounding fake secrets."

Kay laughed and showed Lon his drawings.

Lon looked them over. "Oh, you're designing a weapon?"

"I am."

"Very interesting. The most important thing is your center of balance." He came over to Kay's side and pointed at the design. "See, this length here is too long; your equation isn't quite correct, I think. It'll be top-heavy how you've got it. There are a few changes we can apply to this to right the balance. Here ..."

And soon Kay of Blanchefort and Lon of Probert were sitting side by side with their coats off pouring over the details. Trays of snacks were sent into the room as they worked. They started the day uncomfortable strangers and ended it great friends.

✶ ✶ ✶ ✶ ✶

A month later, Kay was nearly ready. He stood in the old smithy where his ancestors used to smelt bullets and other such things. It had fallen into disuse after the Blancheforts switched from arms-making to fabric-making as a family trade. The last thing forged there many years ago was, oddly enough, the King CARG.

The kettle high overhead was bubbling with molten metal, kept hot by the ceramic furnace, spewing steam and heat. His father, seeing the plume of smoke coming from the smithy, had wanted to know what was going on. Thinking fast, Kay mentioned he was creating a cast statue of Mother to present to her on her birthday. Davage was excited about the idea and was happy with Kay's initiative. To keep from making himself into a liar, Kay also was going to pour a statue of Sygillis. Once again, Sam, proving herself a wonderful artist, created the drawings of it. Davage came out every so often to see how he was progressing, and Kay showed him the drawings. He was pleased.

Standing before Kay was a vat of wet silica sand thirty feet wide and ten feet deep. Resting inside the wet sand was a form of his CARG, along with four pieces of what would become his mother's statue. The forms were made of springcyst—a polymer that would be evaporated by the molten metal. When the metal was poured in, it would destroy the springcyst and occupy the space in the sand, assuming the precise shape of the CARG and his mother's statue pieces.

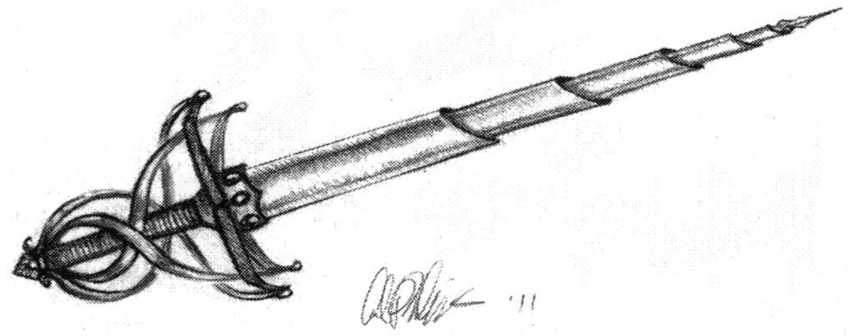

With the help of the staff, Kay had made several mock-ups of the CARG and the statue pieces, starting with clay and finishing with a fired ceramic. He then gave the mock-ups to Lon, who, using his father's resources, had them scanned and recreated as the springcyst blanks.

Originally, Kay had planned on making a CARG the way his grandfather had, with billets of hammered metal creating each link, then machining them into a shaft. To that end, he'd acquired a raw consignment of carbon steel, titanium, vanadium, aluminum, molybdenum, tungsten, antimony, gold and lead. The steel was mostly for the statue pieces. All that changed when his mother Sygillis came down to see what he was doing. He decided to share with her his plans and showed her all he'd done, with the exception of the statue.

"This is wonderful, Kay. Truly. I'm so amazed by what you've done. The drawings, the metals, I'm so proud! I'd like to contribute something, if I may."

And Sygillis filled a kettle full of glowing Silver tech straight from her hands. "Heat this for a month, keep it hot, add the other metals, and you'll be amazed by the results. You won't need to create links. Just pour it into a form. Trust me."

She kissed him and left.

After a month of keeping the Silver tech molten hot and adding the other metals, the smithy masters from the village poured the concoction into the sand, down the shaft and into the form of his CARG, the noise and smoke terrific as they did so. The form didn't fill up and burst out in a fan of sparks like he thought it would. Instead, the masters drained the kettle and then opened the gate admitting the waters of the Bloodstein Run into the vat. A clamor of steam escaped as the metal was quenched. They then reset the vat and repeated the process with the steel for his mother's statue.

After it had cooled, there it was, his CARG, perfectly formed. With the infusion of Silver tech, it did some amazing things that were readily apparent. It glowed, just like Lt. Kilos' Tweeter bird, making a soft whitish light. It was lighter than anything, not even ten pounds, and it could change its size longer and shorter as needed without having to manually adjust it. All he had to do was want it to change, and it did.

Running outside, he found a tree and swung, hoping to chop it in two.

WHOK!!

The CARG shook the tree and vibrated out of his hand. It took great skill to use the CARG in a cutting manner, a skill he didn't possess.

✶ ✶ ✶ ✶ ✶

"What's this?" Davage said as Kay entered his study.

Davage was sitting behind his desk. He was wearing his usual Fleet coat and frilly shirt, exactly what Lt. Kilos always wore. His blue hair appeared black in the quiet light of the study. Kay came in, got on one knee and held out his CARG. "I made this, Father."

He put down his pen and stood, taking the CARG from Kay's hands, turning it over, inspecting it. "Kay, you made this?"

"Yes, Father."

"All on your own, with no help?"

"Oh, I had lots of help. Phillip and Lon helped me work out the math, and I had help with the design, and mother contributed Silver tech in its making."

"I see that. Creation, what a thing. Look at it, so light. Balance perfect." Davage tried to bend the shaft. "Strong too. The general shape reminds me of Windamere, Countess Fercandia's CARG of long ago."

Kay nodded. "I used Windamere as a starting point. I can lift the Runvanion now, Father, but it's so heavy, I don't think I'll ever be much use with it. I thought a smaller, lighter weapon would serve me better. I hope you're not disappointed."

"Disappointed?" Davage gasped. "Look at this, look what you've done here. What about your mother's statue that you told me about? Was that just a cover to prevent me from discovering what you were doing?"

"Yes, Father, although, I didn't want to disappoint or lie to you, and I created a statue of mother as well, cast in four pieces. It's not completed yet. It needs to be welded and finished."

Davage, gazing at the CARG, pushed his hat back and smiled, ear to ear. "God's Bodkins. See, this is what those lords and ladies miss in Review—that there's a heart in there, character and a soul to match. This is what it means to be a Vith, Kay, not your hair color or how tall you are or the shade of your eyes. It's how you overcome an obstacle, and it's keeping the promises you make—even those made in passing. I'm not dismissing your accomplishment with your CARG here, but I think keeping the statue part of your promise shows just what sort of man you're going to become, and I'm very proud of you." Davage looked at the CARG in his hands. "Look at this. Look at what my son has done," he said over and over. "I'd like your mother's statue completed and ready to present to her by her birthday. I think I know of a wonderful spot in the Grove where we can place it. Do you need help?"

"No, Father."

Davage gave the CARG back to Kay and unsaddled his King CARG, a giant in comparison.

"Well now, Kay, you have your weapon, and a fine one it is. Now it's time you learned how to use it. Are you ready to begin your learning? There's much to train."

"I am, Father."

5—Five Questions

As time passed, Kay grew. He had shot up over the years and added a nice coating of lean muscle. He carried his saddled CARG at his side all the time, and, after four years of training, was quite good with it.

At seventeen, he was done with The Review. Now he could mingle in social circles and his purple hair and green eyes, once his bane, were now his greatest assets. Young ladies came up to him fascinated, and his mother often told him that his pile of correspondence should be getting quite big soon. It never seemed to happen, though. His pile remained small and uninteresting.

He developed a core group of friends. His best friends were his twin cousins Sarah and Phillip, they being of fairly similar age and disposition, but every winter Sarah and Phillip left to go to Grand Oyln Manor in the south with their mother and father, and Kay was left on his own in the castle. He had his sisters and brother, and Lady Kilos wasn't bad to hang out with, though she enjoyed the social battlefield much more than Kay did. Lady Hathaline tended to do her own thing and was a growing pilot, flying across the sky with father, showing great talent for it. Maser was still so young and chained to their mother's side. Lord Lon of Probert was also a good friend, but he was usually in Arden with his parents and was only around occasionally.

Kay still had a few mandatory duties to perform. The worst of these duties came when the The Witch was in attendance for a visit. 'The Witch,' as Sarah called her, was the Countess Hortensia of Monama, a close personal friend of his parents. She often came, apparently to tell their fortunes, as Monamas were adept at that. When she did come, Lord Davage and Countess Sygillis were always keen for Kay to visit with her in private, to get to know the Countess on a more personal level. On such occasions, Sarah relentlessly filled his ear.

"The Witch is here," she'd say. "She's going to cast a spell, or throw you into a pot—look how big she is; her belly's full of little boys just like you. She might turn into a Berserkacide and eat you whole!"

With that in mind, Kay went to sit in attendance with her in the Firth House, a tearoom where guests were entertained. The Countess was a strange sight—a big, girthy woman, covered up with a blanket and sitting by a heater to ward off the northern chill. She had coal black hair, chalk-white skin and sinister black eyes that didn't seem human to him. That marked her as a Monama, those black eyes. But, instead of acting like a witch who wanted to eat him as Sarah had said, she seemed very friendly and kind and had a wry wit and easy manner. She told him stories and sang to him with her soothing Monama voice. Though Kay was hesitant at first because of the Countess's appearance, by the end of the session, this Monama had won him over. Her voice was strikingly similar in inflection to Sam's voice.

Monamas, if she was any indicator, weren't all that bad. But, the moment she left, Sarah, avid consumer of lurid Posts and cheap horror vids, relentlessly filled his ear afresh.

Witch …

Berserkacide …

Eater of children …

And then the Countess Hortensia of Monama died, of long old age, and was buried by their lake in the far south. No more visits. No more singing in his ear.

Only Sarah's voice remained.

✶ ✶ ✶ ✶ ✶

In the winter, with Sarah and Phillip gone, Kay often crawled into the old chapel to speak to Sam. He usually brought her food, for which she was always very appreciative, desserts being her favorite. He also continued bringing a terminal into the chapel with him and read to her from the Posts. Kay considered Sam a close personal friend, his secret friend.

As the years went by, the obvious questions began to be posed with more and more frequency and force.

"Who are you, Sam?"

"Where are you, Sam?"

"What are you, Sam?"

Always, in a very polite tone, she skirted around the question. Always, she said she was afraid that, if she told him, he might not want to be her friend, or come and read to her anymore.

And she told him that she couldn't bear that.

Kay had to take Sam at her word, that she was a person from far away who could, obviously, do a number of very powerful things, spoke an odd language, and was too bashful to meet him in person, though Sam, safely hidden behind her mystical veils, was certainly not a bashful person at all. Kay liked to imagine that Sam was a Sister hidden away in one of their mysterious research centers. Sisters were told to be incredibly strong, and Sam was very strong, so she must be a Sister, perhaps yearning for something beyond the cloister.

Or, better yet, that she was one of those pretty, golden-haired Zenon-girls he'd seen at a recent ball, girls so pretty they made him blush and feel small.

Maybe Sam was a Zenon-girl who was also a Sister. Wouldn't that be neat?

✶ ✶ ✶ ✶ ✶

Kay sat alone in Sam's chapel—he had come to think of Countess Fercandia's chapel as Sam's chapel. It was chilly with winter in full force.

He had been talking and laughing with Sam all afternoon. They argued over a post that they disagreed on.

"Sam," Kay said on a more serious note. "What am I to you?"

Sam was silent a moment. <You're my friend, Kay … you're my best friend.>

"And how long have we been friends?"

<Four years now.>

"Yes, four years, and I've never seen your face. I know almost nothing about you. It's not fair."

<I know, Kay. It's just … I don't want to lose you … as a friend. I'm afraid, if you saw me, that you won't want to be my friend anymore.>

"Why, are you a monster of some sort?"

Sam paused a moment. <No, I'm not a monster, silly.>

"Are you a Sister?"

Sam seemed astonished. <No, Kay, I'm not a Sister either.>

"Then I want to meet you in person."

<You must know I consider you my secret boyfriend.>

"You consider me your boyfriend?"

<I do. I've had a thing for you for some time now, Kay. And don't say you didn't know that—I can't possibly be any more obvious about it. Do you think of me as your girlfriend?>

"Well, no Sam. You're a voice in a chapel."

<You don't ... > Sam sounded a little hurt.

"I've never had a girlfriend. My parents have tried to set up meetings for me with various girls from around Kana, but they never seem to make it here."

<How sad,> Sam said with a tiny hint of elation in her voice. <They don't know what they're missing.>

"And, I don't get a whole lot of correspondence from girls either, so, if you were my girlfriend, you'd probably just vanish on me and not write."

Sam laughed. <You're so cute, Kay. I'm not going anywhere. So, do I get to be your girlfriend?>

"I don't know. You're just a voice."

Kay felt something tap him on the shoulder. He turned, and nothing was there.

<I'm not a voice, Kay. I'm a full-fledged person.>

"Then let's meet. Let me see you."

<I'm not going to risk it.>

Kay crossed his arms, and they were silent for a bit. "I know, Sam," he said finally, "how about we play Five Questions? I'll ask you five questions, and I'll bet I can guess where you are within a hundred miles. Can we do that? And if I can guess where you are, then you have to agree to meet."

<Five questions? Well, all right, Kay. Let's do that; it sounds like fun. I'm ready for your first question.>

Kay thought a moment. "Look out the nearest window; is it cloudy or sunny right now?"

Sam chuckled. <I really don't need to look. It's cloudy—foggy actually. That's one question. You get four more.>

Foggy, eh? Kay smiled. His thoughts turned. Now he would see how well he had absorbed all of his sessions with his father. Five questions should be more than enough to zero in on the unsuspecting Sam. "Okay, next question. Is it cold or warm where you are?"

<Warm.>

"Warm, all right. My third question: If you look out your window, in the direction of the sun, do you see any mountains or hills?" This was the key question.

<Hold on.> She was silent for a minute or two. <Nope, no mountains or hills.>

A flatland, huh? "Fourth question: Is there a sizable amount of water near where you are?"

<Yes.>

"Last question: Are you on the southern continent?"

<Yes.>

Kay smiled. "Sam, you're in the southern highlands, near or in the Zenon region. Am I right?"

He heard Sam giggle. <I'm impressed, Kay! You know your geography, but you're not quite close enough, so no deal.>

"I'm plenty close, Sam. Don't lie. You're in Zenon; that makes you a Zenon girl! I'll bet you're very good looking."

<Sorry, no deal, and, for the thousandth time, I'm not a Zenon girl. However, I have been told many times that I'm very attractive. I've had lots of potential boy suitors. I could have any of them I wanted, but I turned them away.>

"Why?"

<They're not you, Kay.>

Kay stood up and closed his terminal. "So, Sam, are we going to meet or not?"

<No, I'm sorry.>

"In that case, Lady Sammidoran, I bid you good day."

<Kay, where are you going?>

"I'm leaving, and I shan't be back."

<Why?> Sam shrieked.

"I just told you why."

<Kay, don't go!>

As he slowly Wafted away—he was too large now to squeeze through the hole—he heard Sam cry out for him.

✶ ✶ ✶ ✶ ✶

Several days later Kay received a strange letter on his pillow. It had been a rough few days, and several times he found himself heading to Sam's Chapel. He missed Sam. He missed her quite a bit, but, through sheer will, he put her out of his mind.

His name was written out on the envelope in a thin, twisting script written in black ink. It was something a skilled engraver might produce. There was no return mark or other indication where the letter came from.

He took the letter out—the paper was stark white against the flowing black lettering.

It said:

I've decided not to be mad at you anymore. If you insist that we meet, then let us meet. Just remember—I warned you.

Walk to the Grove tomorrow at noon, and I will be there.

Your girlfriend,

S

PS—I'm actually very excited. I've been eager to stand before you for some time.

6—Meet Sam

The next morning Kay got up and dressed in his best. He wore the purple and black coat that his mother had made for him, and his favorite boots. He made sure his boots were nicely shined. He saddled his silver CARG and popped on his black triangle hat. He had thought to wear his usual black fencer's gloves but thought better of it.

So attired, he strode out into the Grove, not really knowing where he was going. He wandered around for a bit and intentionally hid from Lady Hathaline as she passed by yelling his name. She was holding a snowball and apparently wanted to dash it into his face. He'd get her later. For now, he wanted to be alone.

As the morning settled into afternoon, Kay ended up in the Holt courtyard near the statue of his mother he had created years prior. Larger than life, streaked in green patina, the statue loomed over the courtyard. He was nervous. What if Sam was morbidly ugly or somehow deformed? Why else should she act in such a mysterious fashion?

She was from the south, near Zenon; she had to be. The Zenon girls were usually very pretty with tawny or auburn hair. In the past he had tried to zero in on her by the few words of her native tongue that she slipped out every so often. She was very careful about letting him hear too much of her language, and he made sure to write down as best he could the few words that got through. Clearly, Sam wanted to share it with him but was preventing herself. Sitting at a holo-terminal, he plugged the words in to see if he got any matches. Nothing ever came up—he was probably spelling them incorrectly. He recalled one word that she'd uttered on their very first meeting, *zemfa,* that apparently meant 'okay.' He hit the holo-net with gusto, trying every way he could think of to spell it:

zamfas
zambas
zembas
zimbas

Finally, a hit:

zemfa: (adj, adv, interj): 1:—All right; permissible, meeting standards.
Language: Anuie
Region: South Kana, Zenon Midlands
Addendum: Anuie. Regional language based on a family of similar tongues hailing from the south of Kana, west of Zenon, by the ...

Zenon!!

Kay read no further. Zenon! That was all he needed to know. Sam must be a Zenon girl. Great! Yes, yes, that was just fine.

Sam was a Zenon girl.

So, where was she?

As he waited, his mind began turning. How was Sam just going to 'appear' in the Grove? For her arrival, certainly, there had to be a retinue of ships, coming from wherever. Certainly, the ship's occupants had to announce themselves, and, certainly, the staff would have a proper reception ready for them.

How had she done any of the things she was apparently able to do?

As Kay's thoughts turned, he barely heard a soft voice coming from behind him.

"Kay?"

He spun around. Standing in a thick copse of trees behind the statue was a figure.

Kay smiled and took a step forward. "Sam, is that you?"

The figure nodded. "Yes, yes it's me, Kay."

"Why are you standing in that growth of trees? You could hurt yourself. You could twist your ankle. Come out here."

Tentatively, the figure emerged. She was hunched over a little, wearing a thick overcoat covered with a fur over top of it. She held the opening of the coat tightly shut.

She had a long wave of curly blonde hair that went down to her knees. There was a flower nestled in the mass of her hair. She had sparkling blue eyes. She was trembling and seemed to be in some discomfort.

"Where did you come from?"

"Like I told you before, I can do a lot of things, Kay. You should know that by now."

"Did you Waft in here?"

"Sort of."

"Are you all right? Why are you trembling?"

"C-cold—freezing actually, and I'm a little n-nervous, too. I've waited a long time for this meeting."

Kay held out his hand. "Cold? Oh, this is nothing, you big baby. You should be here when it's really cold. Well, it's probably a lot colder than you're used to in Zenon. Come, let's get inside."

Sam took Kay's hand. He noted her hand was elegant and slim. They made their way to the castle. Sam was moving slowly, bent over.

"Are you injured, Sam? Did you hurt your ankle?"

She spoke in a stutter, her breath coming out in a cloud. "I-I am s-so cold. This was a m-mistake, Kay. I should g-go home and come back when it's a little warmer, or we should have met inside. I didn't think it would b-be this c-cold."

She put her hand on his cheek and approached to give him a kiss.

The hand transformed. It was chalk white, ghastly of pallor, like that of a corpse, and her fingernails were like black daggers.

Sam fell over struggling for breath. Kay rushed to her side. "Sam, let me help you! The castle's just this way!"

When she looked up, the blonde hair and blue eyes were gone. In their place was a giant shock of black hair dark as midnight. It wasn't simply very dark brown hair as most black-haired people had. It was coal black, matte black.

Her face— it was chalk white without a hint of color except for her lips, which were black.

And her eyes—huge, black, like two great holes in her head.

Monama! Creation! She was a Monama!

Sarah's voice filled his head.

Freaks! Witches! Berserkacides going on murderous rampages. She's probably here to kill you—to eat you!

All this time … a Monama.

He jumped away, and she feebly reached out for him. Her coat and fur fell away. Underneath was a rail thin body wrapped up in a black gown with black-on-black designs stitched in the fabric, and there was a chain on her skirt.

A chain?

"Creation! You're the Pale Ghost! You lied to me!"

"Kay ... I didn't lie, I ..."

Kay lurched back instinctively and unsaddled his CARG. "Witch!" he cried. "Slavering beast!"

Sam pleaded with him, her black eyes large and strange. "Kay," she said, her voice strangled with emotion. "Kay, please …"

Kay leveled his CARG at her throat, the same CARG she had helped him create four years ago. Her black lips pulled back in anguish.

"So that's why all the secrecy; that's why all the hiding and lying! Have you been laughing at me all this time? Be gone … be gone from here and trouble me no more!"

Sam's face crumpled up in sadness. A tear fell from her black eye—a plain old tear. She crawled away, summoning whatever strength she had left and was gone in a blink.

Only her coat and fur lying on the frozen cobbles bore proof that she had ever been there.

✶ ✶ ✶ ✶ ✶

Several days later, the whole family was taking a speed barge to Saga, a large city on the windy western island of Barrow. It was a long way to go, but, once out in open water, the barge could move fast. Countess Sygillis had transacted a large sale of new fabrics to the House of Cotten, which was located in the south of Saga, and was headed there to complete the sale in person. The whole family came to see the sights. As usual, Lord Davage piloted the vessel, which could fly and submerge if need be. Countess Sygillis, her dark red hair flying in the breeze, sat at his side. Kay and Lady Kilos sat behind them, and, in the back seat, all bundled up was Lady Hathaline and Lord Maser, locked in his little seat.

One of the children was in trouble. Hath was salty and had been punished by her mother—she had wanted to stand in the front with her father, as always, and help pilot the ship, and she raised a fuss when she hadn't been allowed to do so.

Finally, Lord Davage gave in. "Come on up here, Hath, and help me steer this leviathan," he said to her as the barge came around Mt. Holly Cape, picking up speed. All smiles, Lady Hathaline went to the front, standing there like a pint-sized version of the Countess. Everybody looked around admiring the scenery, except for Kay, who sat in his seat and sulked, the point of his triangle hat aimed at the floor, and Maser, who babbled and drooled.

Sam, a Monama witch, all this time. All the stories Sarah told—of the strange, lonely people hiding by the banks of their black lake, casting spells, seeing the future.

Freaks.

Monsters that sometimes went mad with rage. Berserkacides.

He hated her.

He missed her. He couldn't even go into the eastern wing of the castle where their chapel was. It hurt too much.

Their chapel—what a sad joke.

Sygillis looked back, making sure that Maser wasn't trying to wiggle out of his seat, and saw Kay.

"Kay, why the long face? You've not been yourself the past few days. Is everything all right?" Sygillis tapped him on the hat.

"He's never all right, Mother," Lady Kilos said out of the corner of her mouth, trying to get a response out of him, her whitish-blue hair flying in the breeze.

Davage looked back when he could; Hath was holding the barge's controls in her eleven year old hands. "Well, Kay, out with it. You're depressing me. Perhaps we can help."

Kay shrugged, ready to sit there and sulk, and then changed his mind. "Mother, I've acted out of turn."

"And how so?"

"I have maintained a close communication with a voice for the last four years. I should have made that known to you."

"A voice?" Lady Kilos said. "Are you a nutter, Kay? Do you require a bib to drool on?"

Sygillis smiled. "I see. Please go on."

"I should not have allowed it. I should have gathered more information."

"Why, Kay?"

"Because the voice turned out to be that of a Monama witch."

"A witch?"

Davage let off the throttle a bit.

"Yes. She appeared to me a few days ago, and she was a Monama. I thought she was a Zenon girl, but she was a Monama."

"What would a Zenon girl possibly want with you?" Kilos asked, chiding. "How dumb can you ..."

"Ki," Sygillis said. "That's enough. Please leave your brother alone."

Lady Kilos sat back and turned her attention to the passing seascape.

Sygillis turned back to Kay. "Go on, Kay. So, she revealed herself as a Monama, and then what did you do?"

"I unsaddled my CARG and told her to leave at once. I told her I never wished to speak to her again."

The barge slowed. Davage turned. "Kay," he said. "In seventeen years, you have been our pride and joy. You have always been such a wonderful, mature boy—we have been fortunate to have a son like you. All of our children are special, but you, Kay, are truly unique. I must say, however, I have never been so disappointed in you."

The words stung Kay. "Disappointed?"

"We have tried to teach you better, have we not?" Davage said.

"But a Monama … Sarah has said—"

"Your cousin Lady Sarah needs to grow up a bit, and, apparently, so do you."

His mother came back and sat down next to him. "Kay, how wet do you think your father and I are in our own home? A secret communication with a 'voice' from nowhere? Kay, we granted Lady Sammidoran permission to contact you in her special way four years ago. Countess Hortensia of Monama was our good friend, and Lady Sammidoran, her youngest granddaughter, was there the day you were born. She was just a girl about Hath's age at the time. I remember her grandmother lifting her up so that she could peer down into your crib, the wonder on her face. Her gift to you that day was that little gazelle."

"She gave me my gazelle?"

"Yes. She made it herself, just for you. She was so lonely—she didn't have a friend in the world, Kay, and for the very reasons you just mentioned. She was so excited when we gave her permission to speak to you as only Monamas can—to try and strike up a friendship. We had hoped that you would be you, Kay, that you might choose to be her friend."

"Her eyes, her claws ..."

Sygillis smiled. "That's why we were always so keen on you spending time with Countess Hortensia before she passed away—to show you that Monamas are good people, kind people. Elders, rest her soul. But, you always seemed to harbor the same feelings most others do about Monamas, so Lady Sammidoran hid herself, waiting for the day that you might accept her for what she is. Yes, they are a little different. Yes, many, like your cousin, are afraid of them. Yes, many hate them as well, and that is their loss. Just remember, different doesn't mean bad, Kay. You, of all people, should know that well."

"Their rages, their madness."

"Propaganda," Davage said with bile. "There's no such thing as a Berserkacide."

"And, do you know what she told me, Kay?" Sygillis said. "I hate to pile on right now, but she said she thought that she was falling in love with you. I must admit, I thought that was a bit premature. I mean, you're only seventeen after all and yet to explore all of your possibilities, but I was flattered for you. As a mother, it's flattering for me to know that my son has affected someone in such a profound way. She was your friend for four years, Kay. Discard her if you wish, but please consider just who it is that you'll be hurting in the end."

Sygillis kissed him on the cheek and resumed her seat.

"Good going, Kay," Lady Kilos mumbled, and Sygillis didn't bother to correct her.

Kay said nothing for the rest of the day.

✶ ✶ ✶ ✶ ✶

Kay appeared in the chapel. It was dark and lonely. He sat down in a pew. The chapel was quiet, but full of small, unseen sounds and fleeting murmurs.

"Sam!" he called out into the hollow air. "Sam, I know you can hear me."

Silence. The statue of Fercandia stared at him, reproaching.

He'd struggled the last few days with his conscience. What he did to Sam was wrong, and he knew it.

The look on her face, the anguish. His CARG at her throat.

She gave him his gazelle—made it herself. The toy he cherished. He'd had it since before he could remember.

Sam, the Pale Ghost, watching him from afar since he was a boy. Why?

The days rolled by, and he stayed away from the chapel. He remembered her standing in the Grove under his mother's statue, freezing, her blonde-haired disguise falling away.

The lies. Perhaps that is what had made him so angry. Why didn't she just tell him—tell him that she was a Monama? Would his reaction have been any different?

He went back to the holo-net and looked up the word *zemfa* again. It came up:

zemfa: (adj, adv, interj): 1:—All right; permissible, meeting standards.

Language: Anuie

Region: South Kana, Zenon Midlands

Addendum: Anuie. Regional language based on a family of similar tongues hailing from the south of Kana, west of Zenon, by the Monama tribes of Astralon, Zerb and Nebulon. Known as "Monama Noble" it is ...

Monama. All he had to do was read, and there it was. Ki was right—he was dumb.

So, how was he going to do it? How was he going to say he was sorry?

Completely devoid of a plan, he had grabbed her coat and fur and headed into the chapel.

"Sam, I'm sorry," he said in the echoing dark. "You were right. I'm an idiot. Come on Sam, I want to apologize."

Nothing.

"Sam, in the last few days I've been told, in no uncertain terms, that I have wronged you, and I acknowledge that. Maybe you should have just told me that you are a Monama. That would have given me a moment to ... be ready." He winced. "Oh, that didn't come out right. That didn't sound good—I'm sorry."

Nothing.

Kay held up Sam's fur. "You ... you forgot your fur, and your coat, and I want to give them back. And, in any event ... I miss you, Sam. Creation I miss you. How can I tell you such a thing without sounding like a total fool? I'll just lay it out. The day we started talking, I was going to kill myself. The only reason I'm alive today is because of the promise I made to you. I can't even look at the damn posts without thinking of you. I can't enjoy anything without you. Are you happy?"

He cleared his throat. "Here, how about if I say it like this: *Enier ane mirada.* That's Anuie, right? That's what you speak, I looked it up. That's Anuie for 'Will you forgive me?'"

Silence.

"At least get the last word in; tell me how stupid I am."

"You're stupid ..." he heard a quiet voice say from behind.

Kay turned, and sitting a few pews back was Sam, once again in black, all hair. Black eyes. Her clawed hands placed neatly in her lap. This time, no hiding, no covering her face. There she was ghastly white and matte black, hair all over the place. She looked like a ghost. Her mouth was small and sad. Her downcast eyes were huge, her eyelashes long and feathery.

Even ready for her appearance, Kay found himself choking back a hint of

revulsion.

Why? She wasn't ugly; rather, she was quite pretty. She was beautiful in fact now that he looked at her—perfect. Just those huge eyes, those black holes in her head.

"You called me a witch," she said softly. "I've heard it before, I've heard it lots of times. But coming from you … it really hurt."

"I'm sorry, Sam. I didn't mean it."

"Yes, you did."

"You're right, I did at the time, I didn't know what to think. But I've learned the error of my statement, and I have missed you. I didn't fully understand what you meant to me until you were gone. I'm asking you to forgive me."

Sam sighed. "Before she died, I went to my grandmother after her visits to your castle and asked her if she thought you were ready to see me … I mean really see me. Always, she would say 'Almost, almost.' And I waited for the day when I could come to you as I am, unafraid, and you would take my hand. I was so eager for it." She paused and sat silent for a moment. "I guess 'Almost' was as close as I ever came. I'm going to leave now, Kay, and I'll not be back. I'm sorry I'm not what you were hoping for. I'm sorry I'm not some golden-haired beauty. I'm sorry I'm not a Sister or a Zenon girl that you talk about all the time. I'm sorry I disappointed you—I think that's what hurts the most. I just wanted to say goodbye." She looked utterly miserable.

"Were you the Pale Ghost that used to follow me around and hide my things?"

"Yes."

"Why did you do that?"

"I've done lots of things, Kay, and all for you." She turned to leave. She moved in a haggard fashion. "Goodbye."

"Do you want to say goodbye to me, Sam?"

She didn't answer.

Kay stood and unsaddled his CARG. "Sam wait … before you go, the last time we met, I pointed this at you, I leveled it at your throat. I keep seeing the look on your face in my head, over and over. Please, take my CARG. You helped me create it, and I'm giving it to you as a token of my shame. I want you to have it."

Sam stood there and looked at the gleaming CARG.

"I made this with my own hands, Sam, just like you made my gazelle with yours. I've cherished that little toy that you made for me. It kept me safe when I was a little boy. Take my CARG, and let it keep you safe, too."

Sam reached out and took the CARG, holding it with both hands, her fingernails interlacing.

"Don't go, Sam… I'm begging you. I'm asking you to forgive me. I've learned my lesson. Let me prove it to you. I don't want this to be goodbye. *Enier ane mirada!*"

"You're not saying that right. It's *Enies ane mirada.*"

Kay stepped around the pews and approached her. "What do you say, Sam? If I am as important to you as you've always said, then don't punish yourself. Forgive me and let us move on."

"Do you know how long I've waited to hear you say a few words in my language? I've wanted to share it with you for so long. Was it hard for you to learn?"

"I just practiced until I thought it right. I'm sorry I mispronounced *enies*. It means that what follows will be a question, right? I had trouble understanding that at first."

Sam smiled a little. "That's right. That's what it means. How do you ask a question without it? That was hard for me." She looked at his CARG. "I accept your gift."

With her black fingernail she scratched her name into the shaft of the CARG near the hilt, curled tendrils of silver twisting away as she worked. When she was done, she held it out. "*Ane forstas hithroe CARG ag-ane*," she said. "Do you know what that means?"

Kay struggled. "It means you want ... something. I—"

"It means I wish you to keep my CARG for me, Kay, and maybe you'll use it to defend me someday, to keep me safe."

"I'd like that, Sam. If you can deal with my purple hair, I can deal with anything you have to offer."

Sam laughed. "I love your hair, I think it's neat. And, keep the coat; I was wanting to give it to you as a memento."

Kay took her by the hand. "I'll always treasure it, Sam." He kissed her hand, long and soft, except for the black talon-like nails that were apparently hard enough to etch his CARG.

Sam took a deep breath and threw her long arms around him. "Oh, Kay—Kay … I've missed you, too. I've missed you terribly! The past few days have been like a nightmare. I haven't been able to eat or sleep—I've felt so empty without you. If I had left just now, I don't know what I might have done. You have been my only friend, but you were all I needed." Tears dripped down her pale face. "And I'm sorry, too, that I presented myself as something I'm not, The Gods in Jade and Sapphire punished me. Does this mean that you don't care that I'm a *yendod* Monama?"

"A what?"

"A 'scary' Monama."

"If you'll have me, Sam," Kay said, wiping the tears away with a soft cloth.

She squeezed him tightly, their bodies fitting together nicely. "I've more surprises that you might, one day, discover. Are you willing to explore them with me? Are you going to freak on me again?"

"I won't, Sam." He kissed her on the cheek. "Have you lunched?"

"No, and I'm starving."

They Wafted out of the chapel—Kay's Waft still slow and blustery. Sam 'Blinked' without noise or wind and waited for him to finish his Waft. Kay offered Sam his arm, which she took. "Well, come on. Let's get some lunch and say hello to my parents. They'll be happy to see you."

7—A Silver Hummingbird

Kay and Sam transformed each other over the winter. They saw each other every day, Sam appearing in the Grove in the morning. She still had no tolerance for the cold of the north, but, if she bundled up, she could withstand it for short periods of time. She wore a thick, fur-lined coat with furry mittens and ear muffs, all black of course. They would go into the castle and have breakfast, then make their way to some quiet place, usually a library or comfortable study in Kay's Zorn tower and read or look at the posts together via the Holo-net. Sam was fascinated by the Holo-net. She said she didn't have it at her home, and they spent hours toying around with it. She almost became as bad as his cousin Sarah, who was a true Holo-net/Airenet junkie.

Though elegant and somewhat frail-looking in her black gown, Sam was a lot more rough and tumble than she first let on. She loved to run and climb. She was much faster than Kay, even in a thick coat, gown and heeled shoes. She could run like a deer and had the endurance of a championship athlete. She was a heck of a tree-climber and could scale the largest of trees in the Grove in a matter of moments, a feat that would have Sarah, a champion tree-climber, drooling. Sam used her nails; as he thought, they were every bit as formidable as they appeared. Once she got to the top, she could jump all the way back down and not hurt herself, her hair trailing behind her plummeting body like a black comet as she fell.

Sam flooded Kay with Anuie, her native language, often switching back and forth in mid-sentence. Sometimes she refused to speak anything else, forcing Kay to listen and try to mimic her speech. Speaking in her language was rather important for her. Soon he was babbling away in a rudimentary fashion. Sam was delighted.

✶ ✶ ✶ ✶ ✶

One morning, after they'd argued about an article in the posts, she shocked Kay by challenging him to a wrestling match to settle the matter. Kay tried to get out of it by stating that he didn't want to damage her gown. Sam, however, was determined and she made Kay take her to the laundry room, where she found one of his mother's Hospitaler body suits, cleaned and pressed. They then made their way back to the reading room and moved the furniture aside, giving them plenty of room to wrestle. Sam pulled her shoes off and changed into the suit behind a screen.

Then they went at it. Monamas, as a rule, were incredibly strong, and Sam had proved that. They were once prized on Hoban as arena fighters, and Sam, though quite thin and gangly, was, indeed, as strong as a bull. As they rolled around on the floor, a very real concern Kay had was with Sam's nails—he had thoughts of getting his throat accidentally cut, but Sam appeared adept at using her hands and not cutting him. They were both quite shy at first, confining themselves to headlocks and arm bars, but soon they relaxed and wrestled as hard as they could. Throwing each other around the room, grunting and straining, pretzeled-up in impossible holds, they wrestled for a good hour. Sam wasn't the first girl Kay had wrestled—he and tomboy

Sarah often locked up in the Grove, but Sarah, unless she cheated and used her Gift of Strength, wasn't nearly as solid and tough as Sam was.

Finally, exhausted, they stopped, lay there for a moment and laughed. Then, they went down for some refreshments.

Wrestling Sam became a regular thing, and they did it almost every day.

Kissing Sam soon followed, their matches quickly fading into make out sessions. Sam was quite hot and slithery as they kissed, her long body all over him. She was unabashedly passionate. She seemed all hands, like she had more than just two, and often times they went places Kay felt they ought not to go. She also seemed to have quite a fascination with his bellybutton—she constantly touched it and caressed it with her fingernails. Sometimes she stared at it, and even licked it once, making him lurch with surprise.

✶ ✶ ✶ ✶ ✶

"It's like my whole body just stops working," Sam said, lying next to Kay. "My heart, all of a sudden, slows way down, and I can't breathe. The cold air going into my lungs is like swallowing a razor blade. And I can't see. Even if I bundle up with my coat and furs, it doesn't help much. I feel it coming in through my feet. How do you stand it?"

"The cold? I don't feel it. None of us do. It can be below zero, and I can walk around outside in my shirt-sleeves and not be troubled in the least. They say the Vith are immune to the cold. The reason my cousins go south to Esther every winter is because my uncle, Lord Peter, hates the cold and he can't take it. He's an Esther, and I suppose they're not immune to cold."

Sam rolled on top of him. "What does snow feel like Kay? I can't touch snow without going into shock."

"Well, it depends. It can feel powdery, like sugar, or kind of crunchy, like wet sand. Here, I'll be right back." Kay left the reading room. Several minutes later he returned with a bowl of snow from outside. Sam sat up and looked at it with wonder. Just sitting next to the cold bowl gave her goose bumps.

"Watch," he said. He plunged his hand into the bowl and kept it there.

Several minutes elapsed. "You don't feel that, Kay?" Sam asked.

"No." He pulled his hand out and showed it to Sam.

"Oh, I can feel it radiating off your hand."

"Do you think you can condition yourself to it, little by little?"

Sam stared at the bowl of snow. She rubbed her hands together and then dipped her pinky into the bowl.

She gasped, open mouthed, throwing her head back. Kay pulled her hand out. Immediately, her whole hand turned blue, with her veins popping out in a spidery configuration. It took several minutes before Sam fully recovered, Kay holding her as if she had just been through a terrible ordeal.

✶ ✶ ✶ ✶ ✶

Gazing out of a terrace halfway up Kay's tower, Sam could see the village down below by the sea and wanted to go there and explore. She was bundled up in her coat and muffler as usual. They spoke in Anuie, Kay having developed a fair understanding of the language and a short vocabulary to go with it.

"What is that road there to the south?" Sam asked, leaning over the rail and pointing down from the terrace.

"Bloodstein Road."

"And those smaller buildings south of it?"

Kay looked. "Cyantown. *That's where most of the villagers live. Quiet place."*

"And that pretty domed structure over there?"

"That's St Vith. It's a cathedral. We go there for service from time to time."

She panned her gaze farther north. *"What are those buildings there by the bay?"*

"That's Sarfortnim College. See that horseshoe-shaped structure down there? That's where they play Brandtball."

"What is Brandtball?"

"It's a game, Sam, played with three teams. Wish I could take you down there to see a match. I think you might enjoy it."

Sam shielded her eyes and stared at the arena. *"I want to go there and see, Kay. You'll teach me?"*

"It's too cold for you. You can take it for fifteen minutes at most, and Brandtball games last several hours. You'll freeze to death before the first set is out."

"Isn't there anyplace indoors we can watch from?"

"Nope." Kay thought a moment and switched back to standard Elder. "It's too dangerous. And, I don't want all those people gawking at you bundled up like a coal-black polar bear."

"I know, Kay. I'll disguise myself… I'll make myself look like a Zenon girl that you were so eager for. It'll be hard because of the cold, and I won't be able to wear shoes while I'm doing it, but I'll do it for you. I can be anything you want me to be."

"But, Sam, let's think about that for a second, assuming you could survive out in the cold for an extended time. If we go to the village to watch a match, and you're Cloaked to look like a Zenon girl with no shoes on, people will, no doubt, have all sorts of questions. They'll want to know who was with me at the match. I am the next Lord of Blanchefort, and they're going to be curious."

"Well, let's make up a story."

"That's the worst thing we could do. Say we do that. People will still check into the matter and will soon discover that we were lying; then, it'll blow up into a full-fledged scandal. You watch."

Sam went on a short rant, trucking away in Anuie, but going so fast and using such complex words that Kay couldn't follow her.

"I don't understand," he said.

"Why are people so nosy?" she said. "We mind our own business in the Monamalands"

"That's just the way it is in League Society—gossip's a big thing. It's one of the drawbacks of coming from a big Blue family. Besides, if I let you Cloak yourself to look a different way, that might mean that I tacitly wished you to be something you're not. I like you just the way you are. Look, you're the one who insists on secrecy, not me."

"Our relationship cannot generally be known," she said.

"Why not?

"Because it can't, Kay. Trust me."

Sam was sad. She leaned on the railing and stared at the village. Then she got cold and went inside.

* * * * *

Kay wracked his brains in the following weeks. Every two weeks, and on Tuesdays, Sam had to attend some sort of family function that she kept rather quiet about and stayed away. During that time, he walked the Grove alone moving off the paths and going knee-deep into the snow. He didn't feel the biting cold at all just the delicate lattice-work of the snow, a lovely feeling all in all. Vith must be impervious to cold, as was sometimes said. He recalled his lessons as a boy given by Lady Poe out in the Grove, no coat needed. He used to like throwing snowballs at Sarah while Lady Poe's back was turned, but her familiar Silver tech hound 'Bark' always ratted him out.

"Lord Kabyl, you may sit in the corner for the rest of the lesson," Lady Poe used to say.

Hmmm, Lady Poe ...

His aunt was known for her skill with creating Silver tech animals that could do all sorts of miraculous things. There was Bark and Shadow the cat, and her little bird Tweeter was a marvel, as was Fins the fish who could heal most any injury in a matter of moments. And Lady Poe had more, many more. Perhaps she could help. He had to remember, though, that Lady Poe knew nothing of his relationship with Sam, and she couldn't know. It was a secret Sam insisted upon. He'd have to pick his words carefully.

He went inside and Commed her up, reaching her at her winter home in Esther. As usual, Lady Poe was an affable, smiling lady with her short blonde hair and gigantic Shadowmark, much larger than his mother's. She was sitting in a lovely, terraced garden, a sweating summer drink sitting on the table top next to her.

"Kay," she said. "How goes it? My, I'm certain you've grown over the winter. Look at you!"

"I'm fine, Aunt Poe. How's the south?"

"Warm as always. I'm afraid the duchess isn't too happy with your mother right now, Kay. Something about an attack of cloth-eating StT's at a recent ball that forced her to retire before her gown fell off her body in tatters. I know nothing. I try not to get involved with those things, you see." She leaned toward the screen. "I think the duchess is preparing a revenge of some sort. Don't ask me what it is. I know nothing."

His mother and the duchess, always at each other's throats. He had to laugh a little. "And, Sarah and Phillip?"

"They are eager to return and see you. Sarah prepared a small bedroom that she calls 'Kay's Bedroom' that she's set aside should you ever choose to visit. The duke and duchess would love to see you."

"I will, Aunt Poe, I promise."

"Now, Kay, while I love speaking with you, the proper method for a Great Lord such as yourself in communicating with his peers is via long-hand letter. We are Vith, Kay, and that's how we do it."

"I know, Aunt Poe; however, a situation has occurred that requires prompt action, and I was wondering if I might ask a novel favor of you?"

Poe appeared concerned. "Certainly, Kay, anything I can do."

"Doubtless you know my friend, Lord Lon of Probert."

Lady Poe thought a moment and lit up. "Oh, yes, the son of Lord Milos and Lady Branna! What a delightful young fellow, very intelligent if I recall."

"Yes, that's him. He confessed to me in private that the climate here in Blanchefort is much too frigid for his south-Vithland tastes and finds he can barely stand it."

"Oh," Poe replied. "Many of my friends have mentioned the same thing, though I think the climate is just right." She lowered her voice and leaned into the screen again. "I think your Uncle Peter also has issues with it from time to time."

"I was hoping that you might be able to assist Lord Lon and make his visits a bit more comfortable. I was hoping you might be able to create some sort of Silver tech device that will keep him warm and toasty."

Poe thought about it. "A Silver tech device that will create heat? Well, I ..."

"Is that possible, Aunt Poe?"

Her large Vith blue eyes floated about her head, lost in thought. "Well, certainly anything is possible. Hmmm, I hadn't considered ..." She took a sip from her glass. "Allow me a day or two to prepare something. I think we'll be able to assist Lord Lon nicely. Shall I send my Silver tech device directly to Lon at his home in Arden? It is still Arden, correct?"

"Yes, it is, but you needn't send it there. Please send it to me here in Blanchefort, and thank you very much in advance, Aunt Poe, for your kind help."

In the background Kay could hear Sarah and Phillip running around.

"You're very welcome, Kay. Yes, I think we'll be able to help Lord Lon stay warm. Please give your parents my best."

"I will, and well met, Aunt Poe."

Sarah's blue-haired head popped up in the background. "Is that Kay? Wait!"

"Yes, it is, but if you wish to communicate with your cousin, young lady, you must write him a letter."

"Mother!" Sarah shrieked. "Wait! Kay, did you get my ... "

Lady Poe smiled and screened down, cutting Sarah off in mid-rant.

Kay was hopeful. Lady Poe could always be counted on to go out of her way for a person.

✶ ✶ ✶ ✶ ✶

A few days later Kay received a post from the south. Sam had returned to the castle, and they quickly went up to their favorite haunt high up in his tower to open it.

"What is it, Kay?" Sam asked, looking at the drab brown box.

"It's something I've been expecting from my aunt. It's for you."

"*Prenta aine*?" she exclaimed, meaning, "for me?"

He searched around for a paper knife, and Sam took action cleanly cutting open the package with her fingernail. She was eager to get it open.

"*Bende*," Kay said in Anuie, meaning "thanks."

"*Bende-Bende*," Sam replied, loving to speak in her language. She kissed him on the cheek.

Kay and Sam opened the box and peered inside.

Wrapped up in blue tissue paper was a small silver medallion of a happy-faced hummingbird on a long silver chain. Kay took it out and examined it; clearly, its happy face gave it away as a Lady Poe creation. On the back side was Lady Poe's coat-of-arms, an assurance that the item would work as intended.

There was a note inside:

Kay

This is Snugs. I have a little workshop here at Grand Oyln Manor, and I whipped him up in an afternoon or two. An excellent idea, Kay. I'd not thought of it myself. Now, I can give one to your uncle and a few to some of my friends who are rather shy about visiting Blanchefort due to the climate. Now they have no excuse.

Snugs comes in two forms. My favorite is a full-formed hummingbird which can warm up a whole room, and this one as a mere medallion. Your uncle Peter suggested it. The medallion is not as potent as the full-formed one and must be worn to feel its effects. If you wish to have the full-formed Snugs, please let me know.

Give all my love to your sisters and your little brother, and to your parents, and we'll see you in a few months. Sarah and Phillip are dying to be reunited with you again—they miss you so.

Love

Aunt Poe

PS—Sarah wanted me to tell you she helped out making the medallion and gave it its name.

Sam gazed at the medallion with wonder. "This will keep me warm?"

"So she says. My aunt can do anything with her Silver tech."

Sam got up and bounced up and down. "Let's go see!"

They went down and out into the Grove, Kay carrying Sam's coat, mittens and hat just in case they were needed. Instantly, Sam recoiled a little bit as they stepped into the outdoor air, her skin turning to rapid gooseflesh. She closed her eyes and held her breath. The lattice-work of her veins came to the surface.

Kay clasped the medallion around Sam's neck. A moment or two elapsed as the medallion swung on its chain. As the temperature dropped, the little hummingbird's wings began to flap in fluid movement; up, down, up down, flush across the face of the medallion.

Sam straightened up and looked around.

"How do you feel, Sam?" he asked.

Still holding her breath, she nodded. Her veins vanished, and her gooseflesh flattened out.

"Sam, breathe normally."

Carefully Sam breathed out in a cloud. "This is amazing, Kay. I don't feel a thing." As she stood there, her body literally began to steam slightly in the cold air.

"You're steaming, Sam."

"Am I?"

"You don't feel cold?"

"No, I feel fine! I feel fine!" She took a deep breath and blew a cloud of steam. "I'm a dragon!" she cried. Off came her shoes, and she padded into the snow, whirling around, dancing in it.

Kay dropped her stuff and pawed up a large snowball. Before Sam could react, he pegged her with it in the face. Previously, any contact with snow was enough to put Sam into palpitations. She reached into the snow and scooped up a massive handful, throwing and missing. Kay ran and Sam tackled him, rolling through the snow, laughing.

As always, Lady Poe had created a marvelous Silver tech device that worked flawlessly. With this wondrous charm, Sam was free. The Grove was no longer a dangerous place where Sam could fall into distress at any moment. Now she could run outside in her gown as far as she wanted. Now she could touch the snow and marvel at its structure. She wore the medallion all the time, for she had always found the interior of the castle a bit chilly as well. One day, once they were duly announced, she wanted to approach Lady Poe and properly thank her for this remarkable gift.

"This won't be mine until I've thanked her," she said. "I must thank her as is proper."

8—Lady Kilos

With the problem of the cold defeated came another persistent and possibly more daunting issue. While Snugs did a great job of keeping Sam warm, it had an unexpected side-effect. Snugs totally fouled her ability to disguise herself and change shape. In fact, Sam couldn't do any of her remarkable abilities with it on.

So the fight to go to the village was on again in earnest.

"Sam, there aren't a whole lot of Monamas walking around in Blanchefort village. You're the one who says we have to keep our relationship a secret, not me, and you will stick out down there like nobody's business. Rest assured people are going to talk. Even your grandmother who was here fairly regularly never went to the village. Father tells me that, at their wedding, she nearly collapsed from the cold."

"So, how are we going to do this, Kay? *Ane-te-samma-ventinos!"*

"I know you want to go down there, Sam, but, things will be bad. Trust me. We have to think this out first!"

Kay and Sam wracked their brains. Sam had all sorts of ideas, most of which dealt with using Gifts and other outworldly powers. At one point, she got angry and insisted that he Cloak her himself.

"Cloak me, Kay. You can do it! Cloak me!"

"I can't Cloak you, Sam," he said. "I can't Cloak myself yet."

Sam had a bad moment—she lost her temper. She stood up. "Kay, I am so tired of your lousy Gifts! I can see the future, right? I see you doing such amazing things *but always in the future!* I'm tired of you being great in the future! I want you to be great *now*!!"

She picked him up by the collar. "You could Cloak me to look like whatever you wanted to without half trying if you only applied yourself. Do you know how frustrating that is? You know, Kay, I wonder if I were to throw you off this terrace, would you be able to Waft yourself to safety?"

"Waft? It takes me forever to Waft!"

"Sink or swim, Kay. I'm really thinking about doing it. I certainly hope you choose to swim, but I don't know. Sometimes you are maddeningly content being a do-nothing, and that makes me crazy!!"

"Sam, put me down!"

A voice came from the doorway. "Am I interrupting something? You left your door open."

Sam and Kay were caught, mouths open. Standing there in the threshold to the reading room was Lady Kilos, blue hair up, dressed in a minty gown. She was carrying a few parcels from the village. Sam dropped Kay and made to Blink away. It failed. She ripped Snugs off her neck and recoiled from the cold as if punched in the gut.

"There's really no need to be alarmed, I've known about you two for a long time. Please."

Kay came to Sam's side and put the medallion back on her neck. Sam exhaled harshly as her body warmed.

"Is she all right?" Ki asked.

"She's fine. It's the cold; she can't take it."

"Oh," Ki said.

They spent an uncomfortable moment. "Ki, how did you ..."

"You two really don't hide things well, do you? And you make a remarkable amount of racket up here when you're rolling around on the floor as you tend to enjoy doing. I also managed to worm a few things out of Mother the other day. Not much goes on around here without me knowing about it. I'm very happy Kay chose to come to his senses and make up with you, Lady Sammidoran."

Kay was dumbfounded. His sister Ki was a noted gossiper and social want-to-be. If she knows, how long will it be before the rest of the League knows?

She appeared to read his troubled thoughts to some extent. She smiled and seated herself, placing her packages on the table. Sam slowly seated herself and looked at them with longing.

"Oh, go ahead if you like. Just some sundries that caught my eye."

Sam peered into one of the bags with wonder. "You were just in the village?"

"Yes. It's small, but it's actually a lot of fun. Father's warbird and other Fleet shipping help attract merchants from all over. Rundle Way is lined with wonderful shops; some are even from Bazz."

"Rundle Way is a dilapidated row of old buildings Father was going to have torn down," Kay said.

"Seems you've not been there in a while. It's completely rebuilt and occupied and is screaming to be explored."

Sam listened and was enthralled.

"I think you two are going about this matter wholly wrong-footed," Ki said. "You want to visit the village, but you don't want to create a stir—yes? And, if I heard you correctly, you've been trying to puzzle this out using Gifts and other various feats of mind and body to either hide, Cloak, or move about invisibly. Why not simply go the most pragmatic and obvious route?"

Kay and Sam looked at each other, the two of them not having any thought as to what that route might be.

Lady Kilos smiled. "Lady Sammidoran, come here, please."

Dubiously, Sam stood and approached, still holding one of Ki's bags. "Please, call me Sam."

"Thank you, Sam, I will. And you may call me Ki. My, such lovely eyelashes. May I ask, are those real?"

"Yes," Sam said with a bit of uncertainty.

"There are ladies I know who would collapse for eyelashes like those. Turn around, please, if you will." Sam complied.

"Such lovely, thick hair. Why do you wear a chain on your skirt?"

"It's a tradition."

"Ah. May I see your hands, please?"

Sam slowly raised her hands. Pale, delicate. Her black fingernails, sharp as knives, glinted in the light.

"Thank you. Yes, this puzzle is much simpler than the two of you have considered. I can help."

Kay was dubious. He liked his sister Lady Kilos well enough. Sarah couldn't stand her much, too prissy. Too girlie. Those two attributes were bad black strikes in Sarah's tomboy book. "So, if I am to understand, Ki, you'll help us and keep our secret?"

"Why is it a secret? I'm just asking."

Sam jumped in. "I have insisted on the secrecy, Ki. It's our way in the Monamalands. If it were to become publically known that Kay and I are seeing each other, well, Kay is not ready for what would have to happen after that. Nor am I. It is for his sake that I require our relationship remain a secret. I cannot say anything more."

Ki thought about it for a moment. "Well, that's good enough for me then. You may count on my discretion. I haven't said anything yet, have I? I could have ratted you two out years ago, but, Kay's my brother, and I'm not going to spread rumors about my own kin, except, maybe, Sarah. You know, Sam, Kay is considered bad luck with the ladies around Kana. Oh, they like him well enough. They fawn over him, and they ask me all sorts of things, but few, it seems, have any luck striking up a connection. Do you know anything about that?"

Sam blushed a slight bit. "No. How would I know anything about that? Their misfortune is my gain. Perhaps the gods are involved."

Ki smiled. "The gods ... Perhaps. Fine then. So, if I'm understanding properly, you two want to go to the village and explore, but you're concerned about the gossip that'll no doubt be created. That is a good thought, as Kay correctly anticipated people's understandable reaction. Actually, I'm a little surprised he thought ahead far enough to recognize the problem. The only girl they ever see Kay running around with is Lady Sarah, and you do not look much like Sarah. And, if I heard you correctly, then you cannot use Gifts or sorcery to change your appearance."

Sam held out her medallion. "This keeps me warm, but it disrupts my ability to change my shape."

"You can do that?"

"I can, but not with this medallion on. I trade warmth and safety for my skills."

"Turn around again, please, Sam."

Sam held her arms out and turned around, the bustle of her gown rustling and her chain rattling. Ki laughed. "Yes, I'm fairly certain I can help you. I'll make it so you needn't fear in the village."

Kay wasn't sure. "You're going to help us?"

"That's what I just said."

"What do you want in return?"

Ki rolled her eyes up and thought a moment. "In return, I'd like to come with you. I won't be a third wheel. We can go and have some fun in the village—there are actually a lot of interesting shops and cafes down there, like I said. Good food, and, when we're done and you two want to start rolling around again, I'll leave you alone. I just want to be friends. So, what do you say?"

Kay thought about it. "And our secret is safe with you? No tricks?"

"No tricks, Kay. I'm not Sarah, always looking to get out of a promise like she does. You can count on me. I just want to be part of the gang for a change."

"Sounds fair enough. What do you say, Sam?"

"Oh yes," she replied. "Thank you, Ki. *Bende*. Your offer is most reasonable, and I look forward to becoming good friends with you."

Ki leapt to her feet. "Well then, Sam, please come with me to my tower, and we'll get started. You stay here, Kay, or go do what you want. Give me a few hours; then, you can come up and see. We'll be in my boudoir, 93rd floor. Let's go, Sam."

They left, and Kay stewed alone for an hour or two wondering what was going on over there. He could see Ki's Harkness Tower a fair distance away butted up next to the grand main entrance to the castle. Her tower, structurally, was identical to his. He burned with curiosity as to what was going on within. As he waited, a post came in from Sarah. More ghastly stuff as usual:

"BERSERKACIDE NEST DISCOVERED IN CLOVIS RUINS."

She also left a note asking how Snugs was working.

Fine, just fine, he replied to her. A few more months and she would return with Phillip as always. She and Phillip shared Xyotel Tower just a ways down off the East Wing. The guy wire they had setup from their tower to his for the purposes of sliding back and forth in dramatic style was still there, taut in the wind.

Kay couldn't wait any longer. He went down to the foyer and entered Ki's Tower, up the lift and out on the 93rd floor. The whole floor and the two above it were designated as Ki's gigantic closet, and it was a wonderland of the frilly and the feminine. He'd only been in it once or twice previously. Sarah considered the place a purgatory for the living—a house of horrors containing all the girly things she despised. The layout of the floors were set up museum style, with a winding central path snaking its way past a number of vast display areas and eventually going up a floor to begin again. Ki had it very well organized: first unmentionables, then gowns, then shoes, then accessories, then an area for make-up and so on. Along the way, Ki had little holo-terminals going, chattering and caged to items of interest for her, like the latest fashion milestones from Hoban, Remnath, and Zenon. Other terminals played music, and others flashed postings from her friends so that she would have instant news. Something was always flying by from her friends. Ki also had a number of Perlamum boards set up in alcoves so that she could keep track of the more notable games taking place around the League as they happened.

Kay moved down the path winding through Ki's closet. A chorus of animated mannequins wearing Ki's gowns danced about, whirling as he passed by. Many wore a variety of fashionable hats from the far corners of Kana and Hoban. Ki loved Hoban fashion. How she managed to pick what she wanted to wear every morning was surely a major labor.

Others carried pots of creams and trays of fruit, and they wore a bewildering array of shoes from all over.

He went up a level and moved into Ki's makeup area. Going through a vast pallet of watercolors shaded in every imaginable hue, he located the heart of Ki's boudoir. It was a large open terrace looking down on the village, situated in such a way that there was plenty of natural light coming in.

There was quiet chatter and laughter coming from just ahead accented by a little light music. Surrounded by colors and earthen pots full of powders and oils and a host of animated mannequins were Sam and Ki.

"Hi, Kay, come on over!" Ki said, holding a make-up brush. "You two had a problem, and your problem is now solved!"

"What did you do?" Kay made his way out onto the terrace pushing past a few whirling mannequins. Sam was sitting in a vast chair.

She appeared a little nervous. "Hi, Kay," she said softly.

"You two seem to be getting on well," Kay said.

"We have. Sam's a wonderful lady. You have fine taste, Kay. Notice anything different?" Ki asked.

Sam sat meekly in the chair as Kay looked her over. Firstly, she was wearing a red dress instead of her black Monama gown, which was nearby on a waiting mannequin, chain and all. Another mannequin was holding her black Monama shoes on a platter. Sam was wearing a stylish pair of knee-high black boots. "I had my mannequins whip up a quick dress for Sam. Looks lovely, I think. The boots are Esther. Esthers, short of Hoban, make great boots." Ki leaned down and gently brushed Sam's face. "I love those eyelashes. Now, I've applied a good layer of make up to Sam's face. Coming here as often as she does, she has taken on the slightest bit of blush. She's still very pale, but not anything so much as to create a stir. I've painted her lips a smashing color of red to highlight the rose in her skin, and I've added a gentle bit of azure eye shadow to give her a bit of depth."

Sam looked a bit odd. No black gown, no black lips. She appeared rather festive. She had her hands in her lap hidden under a cloth.

"What do you think, Kay?" she asked. "Do you like it?"

"You look very good. Great in fact."

Kilos beamed, proud of her work. "So, you wish to hide? Hiding in plain sight is always best and most effective."

A few problems quickly entered Kay's mind. "What about her eyes, Ki?"

"I was wondering when you'd ask me that." Ki put her brush down on a vanity and summoned a mannequin holding a fancy cardboard box. She opened the lid and pulled out a copper and silver pair of goggles. Ki put the goggles on Sam's face, carefully placing the stems around her ears.

"What in the name of Creation are those?" Kay asked.

"Gretnas," Ki replied, "from Hoban. They're all the rage over there. Everybody's wearing them."

The goggles contained an intricate set of interlocking lenses and silver and copper disks that were geared to move together like the mechanism of an old-fashioned watch. With them on, Kay couldn't see Sam's eyes, just the complex layers of gears all nested together and sparkling. "Can you see, Sam?" he asked.

Ki adjusted the lenses and Sam looked around. "I can! Actually, I can see better than I normally do! It's so bright here, and I must be a bit nearsighted and didn't know any better. *Cul-lenor*!"

"What does that mean?" Ki asked.

"It means 'amazing' in Anuie," Kay replied.

"You speak Anuie, Kay?"

Sam beamed. "Kay has picked up the basics of my language very quickly. I am so proud of him."

"I'm impressed," Kilos said. "So, with these Gretnas on, nobody will be the wiser. Sam will look like any stately lady about the League, no doubt of a high circle with money to afford these goggles. And, with those on, people will probably be more interested in them than in her, per se."

Kay nodded. He remembered something. "What about her fingernails?"

Sam blushed.

"Show him, Sam," Ki said. "Go on, show him."

"Kay, I hope you're not angry with me," Sam said, squirming in her chair.

"Angry about what?"

"About this." Sam cast her towel aside. Her Monama fingernails, once impossibly long and sharp, were now trimmed down to a very manageable length and were painted red like her lips.

"I had to get a file from the smithy. Her nails are hard as iron," Ki remarked.

"Our nails are a mark of beauty—we treasure them. I hope you don't mind me without them, Kay. Is it all right?" Sam was a bit panicked.

"It's fine, Sam. They look good." Sam got up out of the chair and gave him a hug. The boots she was wearing made her even taller than normal.

Kilos admired her work and then began putting her things away. "So, here's our story. Sam is the daughter of a prominent League House here for a visit and seeing the sights."

"And when they ask what House she's from?" Kay asked. Sam was still holding onto him. The gears inside her goggles clicked a little.

"We say her House is in the middle of a large business transaction with Father, and we can't disclose it until the matter is settled. Happens all the time. They will understand that sort of thing in the village, and the matter will be settled."

Sam gazed at Kay, still wearing the goggles. "Do you think it'll work, Kay?"

"I think so. Ki knows her stuff."

✶ ✶ ✶ ✶ ✶

With goggles, red lips and nails, they finally went down to the village, Sam wearing nothing over her red dress but a light shawl. As they plunged into the maze of shops and eateries, the locals were every bit as nosy and full of questions as Kay had predicted. He simply said she was a guest from the south, which was true. As Lady Kilos was present, the locals took it at that, though a few pressed the question as to which House she was from. Kay said that he was not at liberty to say—due to a pending business transaction. As Ki had predicted, that appeased them.

The three enjoyed the afternoon. Sam liked the shops and waterfront pubs in the village, and she positively loved trying the food, stopping at every eatery to sample the fare. She especially liked the view of the castle from down there. Once or twice Sam pulled Kay into a quiet alley, pushed her goggles aside and kissed him with her hummingbird-heated lips.

Lady Sammidoran of Monama

9—The Future-Telling

As the winter wore on, Sam, Kay and Lady Kilos became good friends. They often went to the village, Sam in colorful dresses provided by Ki and wearing the Gretna goggles from Hoban to cover her eyes. As their friendship grew, Ki told Sam she could have the goggles, as they tended to make her dizzy when she wore them anyway, but Sam wouldn't hear of it. She insisted on paying for them in some way, but Sam didn't have much money.

"I know," Ki said. "You can look into the future for me and give me a reading. How about that?"

Sam was dubious. "The future isn't a place I like to see, Ki," she said.

"Oh, come on. It'll be fun."

It took some convincing, as Sam clearly didn't want to do it; however, after a bit of talking, Sam relented.

They dressed down in sturdy clothing and went out into the Grove. Sam said she needed to be as close to the earth as possible in order to see. Being under the earth was even better. Kay had planned to crash into the vast underworld of Castle Blanchefort; however, Lady Kilos was too claustrophobic to follow them. She didn't like small spaces.

The best place to go, then, would be out in the Grove near the Holt courtyard. There were a number of easy, roomy tunnels to move through in that area, so Ki should be fine. As they trudged out to the Holt courtyard, Sam was wearing one of her permanently appropriated bodysuits and a pair of sandals along with her usual Snugs medallion, the little wings flapping steadily. Her body steamed a bit in the cold air, especially from her head. Kay and Kilos wore smithy-style clothing that they didn't mind getting dirty. The Holt courtyard was wreathed in giant oak and Nadine trees in the shadow of Dead Hill, the old Blanchefort necropolis atop the mushroom-shaped hill to the south. The low-slung confusion of tombs and vaults were spread out across the top of Dead Hill like a layer of gray frosting on a cake. At the west end of the courtyard, Mother's beloved statue loomed, dappled with snow and accented in lights.

They got to the courtyard, and Kay plunged off the trail. Moving through the trees, he located a heavy metal hatch half-buried in snow. "Here it is!" He tried the hatch and it wouldn't turn; rusted shut, it seemed. "This happens every winter." He struggled with it.

"Sam," he said, and she knelt down and gripped the handle. She struggled a moment, then the handle broke loose with a clank.

"That was really rusted shut," she said spinning the hatch open.

"We don't use this tunnel much anymore. It's for kids."

Ki looked within the dark hole with some trepidation as Sam cleared away the rest of the snow.

"Are you sure this is safe, Kay? I just don't like small spaces."

He held his hand out. "It's fine, Ki. This tunnel is big and straight, and it isn't very long. These tunnels here are pretty easy. This tunnel goes under the oak tree and comes back out on the other side near the feet of Mother's statue. Mother doesn't even rate this one with her stone system. It's a 0-stoner, as Sarah calls it."

Ki, carrying a light, took his hand and entered slowly, carefully feeling her way with every step. The tunnel within went down about ten feet in an easy slope and then leveled out. The tunnel was about four feet high and made of hard-packed earth. It ran into the bowers of the oak tree above. The tangled, old-growth roots created a

large, dry vault where they could stand straight.

"This used to be one of my, Sarah, and Phillip's favorite hideouts when we were younger. We trucked all sorts of stuff in here for our adventures. Some of it is probably still lying around if you look for it." Sam quickly found an empty can of red Gasol—left there years ago by Sarah no doubt as red Gasol was her drink of choice.

Kay found a good spot in the roots and seated Ki.

"You ok, sis?" he asked. She was sweating, just on the verge of panicking. After a minute or two, she swallowed and composed herself.

"See, it's not so bad under here, right?"

She nodded tentatively. Kay set the light down as Sam removed her sandals and began digging at the ground.

"Why are we under here again, please?" Ki asked as Sam dug.

"You wanted me to see the future for you. I have to be near the ground to see the future. The gods are in the earth, and I must revel in it."

Kay set up several heaters, directed them at Sam and turned them on, the vault quickly becoming very warm.

Sam sat down and took the loose dirt she'd dug up and rubbed herself with it. "Can you help me, Kay?" she asked. He came over and rubbed dirt into her back. He rubbed a little on her cheeks and she gave him a kiss. "Ki, are you sure you wish this? Sometimes, knowing a thing ahead of time makes the thing much worse than it actually is. Worrying about the future can be terrible. I'll ask one last time. Are you certain you wish this?"

"Yes, Sam, I do."

"All right." She removed her medallion and handed it to Kay. She instantly clenched up a bit even though she was centered in the heater's beam.

"You ok, Sam?"

She took a moment and slowly recovered. "Yes, I'm fine. So cold in here. Now, the future will come upon me, and I will fall into a trance. You may ask me specific questions, and I will answer. I will probably speak in Anuie; Kay will translate. These visions can go out of control, I want you to know that. I might start saying things that don't make sense. Just talk to me, say my name, and I will recover. *Zemfa*?"

"Sure, Sam, sure," Ki replied.

Kay seated himself next to Ki. Sam sat there in the middle of the vault, cross-legged, covered in dirt, trembling slightly.

"Now what?" Ki asked.

"Now, we wait," Sam said. "The future is here with us. It won't be long now."

Sam sat there motionless for awhile. Lady Kilos forgot about her discomfort at being in the tunnel a bit. "Kay," she whispered into his ear, "I have to go to the bathroom."

"Shhh," Kay said.

Then Sam stirred. She said a few things in Anuie.

"What did she say, Kay?"

"I think she said you're not going to the bathroom."

Ki laughed. "Sure I am. Really, I need to pee."

Sam said a few more things. "Ki, Sam wants you to ask her something."

"Oh, Creation—what do I ask?" She thought a moment. "Ok, Sam, when will I get rid of my damn Puffies?"

Sam replied in Anuie. "I think she said five years from now," Kay translated.

"*Five years*?" Ki was beside herself. "Is she sure? Are you translating that right?"

Sam responded. "Yes, and yes, she's sure."

"Oh Feature! Five damn more years of this? Will I be beautiful once it's gone?"

Again in Anuie. "She says you will be considered to be very beautiful. She also says Lady Togstra will not be happy about your beauty."

"Oh, she's a bitch." Ki smiled and sat back down, forgetting about her need to visit the bathroom. "Well, that's something anyway. Will I be prettier than her? No wait—when is she going to be married?"

Sam said something. Kay was confused. "What? Sam, I didn't understand that."

"What did she say?"

"She said something about Lady Togstra of Miles being taken in 003245."

"Really?" Ki said. "That long before she gets married? She's got awhile to go then. Ok, ok, Sam—who's she going to marry? Who's the unlucky fellow?"

Kay was a bit exasperated. "Ki, we came out here to explore the future and all you're worried about is who your friends are going to marry? Is that all you want to know?"

"Yes, Kay, that's what I want to know."

More Anuie. "She said Cogster of Whalen."

Ki laughed out loud. "Lord Cogster of Whalen? The fellow from Esther with the fungal problem? Perhaps when they get married in 003245, he'll have cleared up a bit. Oh, this is great. He's a Shocktyte Jo-Boy!"

"Ki, watch your language," Kay said.

Sam mumbled. "She says they will be married in 003222."

"You said they will be married in 003245," Ki returned.

"She said Lady Togstra will be *taken* in 003245. Not married—taken."

"What does that mean? Where's she going?"

More mumbling. Kay was confused.

"What did she say?" Ki asked.

"I think she said Lady Togstra will die in 003217."

Ki was confused. "Die? Well, how can she be married in 003222, be taken twenty-three years later in 003245 and be killed in 003217? That's just three years from now. I must say, though, that prospect doesn't really bother me much. I really don't like Lady Togstra."

Kay rubbed Sam's shoulders. "I think she's starting to skip around a bit. She warned us that might happen."

"Ok, Sam, who am I going to marry?" Ki asked wringing her hands.

Sam began to speak, but Ki shot up and stopped her. "Oh—no! No! I changed my mind. I don't want to know. You were right!"

She stood and made to exit the tunnel. "I'm done, guys. Thanks, Sam, you've paid for the goggles in full. Seriously, I have got to go pee."

Sam's arm shot out and grabbed her by the wrist, holding her fast.

"Oww!" Ki cried. "Sam, that hurts!"

"003256," Sam said.

"What?"

"003256 is when they take you, too."

"Who takes me?"

Sam grimaced. "Hathaline."

"Lady Hathaline takes me? Where does she take me?"

"Tank," Sam said in League Common. "She takes you to the Tank, where they all go."

Sam seemed lost. She switched back and forth in time. She spoke in Anuie.

"Kay, what did she say?"

"She said you and Sarah get into a fight."

"A fight? Me and Sarah? Well, fighting is so unlady-like. But, I hope I win. Sarah's mean."

"She is not," Kay said.

"Not to you, but to me she's nothing but nasty. I get a little tired of it sometimes."

Sam was deep in a funk. She spoke again in Anuie.

"What, Sam?" Kay said. "What was that?"

"What did she say?"

"I think she said something about bowling?"

"Bowling?"

Sam began a long drone in Anuie, Kay following along as best he could.

"She says we bowl in a hidden place. Very dark. Somebody is there. They are there."

"Who's there?"

"I don't know. She says people I know are there waiting for us." Kay shook Sam a little. "Sam, Sam wake up."

Sam didn't stir.

"Sam! Wake up!"

Her eyes snapped open. She was panicked. In terror, she babbled in Anuie.

"Sam, I can't understand. What are you saying? Sam!"

She tore out of the tunnel, holding her face in her hands. "Sam, where are you going? You need your medallion!"

Kay ran out after her with Ki trailing. Sam moved like a streak to the northeast, deep into the dense oak trees of the Grove. Kay followed as fast as he could, but soon she was out of sight. Fortunately, she left an obvious trail of deep footprints in the snow, appearing to stumble several times.

"Kay, wait!" Ki cried from well in the rear.

Sam's footprints meandered through the trees, moving past an ancient Vith amphitheater, and continued on. The Ten Gardens was just ahead through the oak trees.

In a small oak clearing, he saw Sam slumped on her knees. She was holding a handful of snow, cradling it to her, turning her hands blue. Kay plunged in and came to her side. Her skin was spider-webbed with veins. She gasped for air. He fumbled with the medallion for a moment then got it safely around her neck, great clouds of steam quickly working their way out of her hair.

"Sam! Sam, what's wrong?"

"*Olonol!*" she said. "*Olonol!*"

"What's that word? I don't know that word!"

"It will stand here!" Sam cried, her voice a mixture of triumph and cold-induced shock. "The *Olonol* will one day stand here!"

10—Kay's Gifts

"So, what exactly is this?" Sam asked holding the parchment.

"It's the official pronouncement of my Gifts by the Stertors. They're a branch of the Sisterhood of Light. The Stertors go around and determine what Gifts you have, and, if you start developing Gifts not on the official list, you can get in trouble with the Sisters."

Sam put the parchment down. "We don't think much of the Sisters in the Monamalands. They seem rather off-putting."

"So, it says here I have the Gift of Cloak and the Gift of Waft. My profile, as listed by the Stertors, makes me look more like a Remnath than a Vith."

"This paper is meaningless. You also have the Gift of Sight."

Kay and Sam were underneath the castle, in the labyrinthine quiet spaces. They crawled a long way. The passes weren't heated and were formerly too cold for Sam to enter, but with her medallion, she could follow Kay, her gown shed in favor of a bodysuit. They'd crawled a long way and had made their way into a dusty space just high enough for them to sit up. Kay's flashlight made a laser beam of yellow light contaminated with passing stars of dust.

"So, you say that you've had visions of me and that you've seen me having the Sight?"

Sam snuggled up against him, steam coming off her body. "Yes," she said. Her hand wandered into his bellybutton as it usually did when she was feeling amorous, and that was happening more and more.

Perhaps it was Vith ego speaking from somewhere deep inside or possibly his personal pride, but he didn't feel it was right to go much further with Sam other than innocent kissing because, at this stage of his life, Sam was a much more formidable person than he was.

She was incredibly strong.

She was impossibly fast.

Her senses, especially her nose and sense of smell, were highly acute.

She could Blink away and send herself virtually anywhere on Kana.

She could transmute her thoughts.

She could change her shape.

And, she could see the future.

What could Kay do? He just didn't feel he measured up, and, therefore, never allowed himself to share a bed with her, though that's what she expected of him with growing force. She had a favorite saying in Anuie that she said when she was feeling particularly frustrated: *Te mare Vith consomo!,* which meant: *The Vith are so damn demure!*

"So, what did you see specifically?" Kay asked. "What did you see me doing?"

Sam's hand went into his shirt and farther down. "I saw you seeing things far into the future and the past."

"Perhaps you misinterpreted what you were seeing."

"I did not."

"I mean, you said some very strange things during the Future-Telling."

"Did I?"

"You said my sister was going to be 'taken' in 003256. You said my little sister Hathaline takes her somewhere. Where does she take her? Why?"

"I don't remember any of that. That's not uncommon with future tellings, which is why I hesitated to perform it for her. The future has a tendency to sound very ominous, and I can't really shed any light on what I said because I can't remember it."

"And you mentioned something about *Olonol.* I don't know that word, and you won't tell me what it is. What is it?"

Sam, stopped, considered her response, and then abruptly changed the subject. "That chain that I wear on my gown, do you know why I wear it?"

"You've never said."

"It's for you, Kay. To protect yourself ..."

"From what?"

"From me. Monama women tend to get a little overly excited when the time comes. I want that time to be now."

She crawled on top of him.

"I don't have the chain here."

"I won't hurt you ... much. I've waited for this for years."

Sam was all over him, and Kay couldn't move. She was like an impossibly strong octopus.

Kay felt waves of pleasure come over him. He was on the verge of giving in when a final bit of Vith pride spoke and prevented him from losing himself. "Sam, wait!"

She coiled up a little bit, her black eyes intense.

"Let's have a contest first."

"I'm in no mood for contests, Kay."

"Oh, it'll be fun."

"What sort of contest?"

"I'll find a place to hide, and you come and find me."

She snorted. "We've played this game before. You can't hide from me. Hide anywhere you want, and I can find you like that!" She snapped her fingers. "And ..." she took a deep whiff, "I can smell you, Kay." She licked her lips.

"I think this time you'll be a bit more challenged."

She got off and huddled up on the dusty ground. "Fine then. Go hide, Kay. Hide anywhere in the castle you want. You have an hour. Oh, and Kay?"

"Yes?"

She seized a piece of old mortar and shattered it in her hand. "You best get that chain and don't be afraid to use it when I find you. My gown is in the reading room. Oh, while you're there, take a close look at my gown—take a very close look. Those little designs on the fabric of my gown— they're called 'Bronta'. We put Bronta on our clothes, on our architecture and pottery. Everything. Take a look, and that should spell it out for you. Better get moving. Your time starts now."

Kay moved down the crawlway. Behind him, Sam was huddled up like a wolf ready to spring. "See you soon, Kay," she whispered, waving.

Kay continued down the crawl and emerged in the east wing. He quickly went into their favorite reading room. There was her gown, neatly folded on the arm of the chair, and her shoes. He pulled the chain off her skirt. It wasn't a light chain by any stretch. It was fairly dense and could do some damage. He took it and readied to leave the room.

He recalled what she said and took a look at her gown. Stitched onto the black fabric were bands of intricate black swoops and whorls, very detailed and finely crafted. Other than being pretty designs, he couldn't make much out of them.

He left the reading room and checked his time piece. He had about forty minutes left. As he moved down the corridor, he felt that giddy, tingly feeling of being pursued, like when he hid from Sarah when they used to play hide and seek. Certainly, the consequences of being caught were not unpleasant.

The chain rattled in his hand.

Kay wasn't really in a hurry. He knew exactly where he wanted to hide, and it wasn't all that far from where he started. He walked into the west wing and entered Cathomere's Cathedral—an old chapel dedicated to Lord Cathomere of long ago. It was one of the larger chapels in the castle; it was even presided over by a rector from the village. Kay entered, offered a blessing and then sat down in one of the pews, setting the chain aside. He enjoyed the vast quiet of the place, the smell of age-old incense and the lofty splendor of the stained glass windows. At the far end of the cathedral, standing in a dark corner, a bronze statue of Lord Cathomere stood proud, a slight smile hammered into his metallic face.

He checked his time piece. He had a while to go. He got comfortable and put his hat down over his eyes.

His thoughts raced. Sam was out there pursuing him, chasing him like a game animal.

... Like an animal.

He slept and had amber dreams, like he sometimes did. His thoughts wandered. He saw Sam's gown in an amber hue. There were the designs on her gown, the Bronta designs Sam had mentioned. He saw them greatly magnified. The designs were made up of minute male and female forms in the act of having contorted sex. Apparently, as Sam said, sex made up a large portion of Monama culture.

He saw other things

He saw himself lying in bed, and there was a woman in bed with him. Not Sam—it was a glistening woman with red, twisted hair. She wore a golden mask covering the top portion of her face. She seemed somehow disfigured.

He saw that same woman watching him eat in the Capricos Hall, and watching him at CARG practice with father, and looking out at him from the boat house. He saw her whispering in Sam's ear.

There she was, inside some sort of glass coffin full of noisome brown fluid. She was beating on the glass, begging to get out.

He saw Sam wearing a thorny necklace of crystal spikes.

He saw himself in his bedroom sitting on the floor. A small, silvery creature sat next to him. Outside was Sam, beating on the door trying to get in, splintering the wood. Through his terrace, he saw a strange light coming from the west, low on the horizon.

And there were bugs, swarms of them. Giant bugs from a dream. Buzzing wings.

Forty minutes came. His time piece chimed, and he woke up, the amber fading.

The dreams he just had jostled in his head. What strange things he saw. This cathedral did that if you allowed yourself to fall sleep in here—gave one odd dreams.

Things came into clarity. He was sitting alone in the cathedral, the old smells and empty space filling him up.

Checked his timepiece.

One after.

Normally, Sam should have caught him by now, for she was that fast zeroing in on him. But he was still alone in the cathedral. No Sam.

He wondered what he'd just seen, those visions in amber. What did they mean? He tried to reflect on them, but the visions quickly faded from his memory like a dream that was soon forgotten upon waking.

He heard a commotion out in the hallway. Through the crack of the open door leading out into the corridor, he saw Sam go streaking past, moving like a black and white panther.

The cathedral really works. Sam passed right by and couldn't detect him. There was no way she could find him in here unless she actually poked her head in and looked.

This cathedral was a sort of safe area, a quiet place. Many castles of the north had them, Castle Blanchefort being no exception. Here, within the serene confines of the cathedral, one could sit with one's thoughts and be assured of privacy. No eyes from afar could see, and no ears listening in could hear. No clairvoyance or clairaudience. No nothing. Here, one could be alone with one's thoughts. Even his father said he couldn't Sight into the cathedral. Kay had no idea how it worked; it just did.

More time passed—the rector even tried to evict Kay, but he could not as Kay's rank outstripped his.

At some point he again heard Sam go clattering down the hallway. "Kay?" she yelled, a hint of concern in her voice, "Kay?"

He allowed her to run past. Apparently, she wasn't close enough to sniff him out.

He stayed in the cathedral determined to wait it out a few more minutes. He tried to ponder the meaning of his dream in amber, but so much of it had faded in his mind.

He remembered something about a golden mask and buzzing wings. Didn't make any sense.

"KAY!" came an enraged voice from the door.

Standing there was Lady Kilos and a positively livid Sam. She leapt over the pews, launching herself into the air, landing in front of him.

She seized him by the shirt and lifted him like a doll. "Kay! What are you doing? Do you know how concerned I was?"

"Sorry, Sam. I thought the object of the game was to keep you from finding me."

She cursed in Anuie.

"If Kay was hiding from you in here, Sam, then he was cheating. In this cathedral, you cannot be spied upon or located via technological or mystical means.

She was astounded, and her fury faded. She gently set Kay down. "You mean you can come in here and nobody watching you or listening to you can follow?"

"Nope—you couldn't find me, could you?"

She looked around at the place with wonder. She saw the bronze statue in the shadows and was startled. "Who's that?" she asked pointing.

"It's just a statue of Lord Cathomere, my great, great, great, great grandfather, I think, give or take a 'great' or two."

"Yeah," Ki said in agreement.

Mouth open in awe, her mind seemed to fill up with possibilities. "I had no idea. I had no idea. No visions, nothing. I didn't see this place."

The three of them sat in there for the rest of the afternoon until the rector demanded they leave.

Blanchefort Family Portrait
Lady Hathaline (seated), Lord Kabyl, Lady Kilos, Lord Maser

11—The Pool

The next day, Sam, full of energy, wanted to take a walk. Ki was away visiting friends in Remnath, and Kay's parents were off in their starship, the *New Faith*. They were, for the most part, alone. They waded into the deepest part of the Grove, not another soul around.

When they were assured of privacy, they fell into each other's arms, the cloud-covered cone of Mt. Vith visible in the distance.

Losing control of herself, Sam became like a wild animal, eyes wide, growling slightly. She slammed Kay into a tree and held him there with one arm. "I've been waiting for this for years, Kay," she said breathlessly in an odd voice, ripping his coat off. "You don't know… how hard it's been to… contain myself, to be so polite and proper when I've wanted to tear you apart!" Her voice was flecked with passion. "Kay... Kay! It's time that I showed you how I want you! It's time you discover what Monama women do to their men!"

She pulled the chain off her skirt. "You're going to need this." She threw the chain over her shoulder. Kay made to get past her and grab it, and she tackled him.

Kay struggled with the ravenous Sam. His clothes in tatters, her claws drawing blood, she picked him up and threw him down to the leafy ground, throwing herself on top of him. He was in the fight of his life. She loosened her gown by the straps and wiggled out of it.

Kat reached out and got hold of the chain. He wrapped it around her neck and wrenched her light body off him. She landed in the leaves and patches of snow, freeing herself from the chain.

They circled. Sam tensed up and moved on all fours like an animal. *"Use the chain. Hit me with it,"* she growled, her voice unrecognizable.

She sprang, and he lashed her across the back with the chain raising an angry welt. She roared with passion, and he lashed her again and again. He got the chain around her neck once more and tied her to a Vith stone.

Sam tied up, the both of them bloody, he fell into her embrace, and they made love for the first time, drifting in and out of delirium for what seemed like hours, the afternoon turning to early evening unnoticed.

* * * * *

Another dream in amber as Kay, exhausted and slightly wounded, lay in Sam's arms.

Gonna' have some fun ...

He saw a woman leaning down over him, the top of her face covered with a golden mask, her chin bumpy and glistening.

Gonna' make me jealous ...

He saw her standing there twirling Sam's medallion around on her finger. She hauled back and threw it somewhere into the trees.

Have fun ...

Just another dream in amber.

* * * * *

Sam screamed! Kay awoke. Chained to the stone, Sam clenched up and stopped breathing. Her naked body was racked with convulsions. Kay gawked at her in a panic as her convulsing body broke the chain in several places.

"Sam! Sam, what's wrong?"

She didn't answer. Her veins rose to the surface in a blue web.

Snugs! Her medallion was missing from around her neck!

Where was it?

Frantically, he looked around but didn't see it.

Have fun... came a laughing voice from his dream, Sam's medallion spinning on the woman's finger.

Was that just a dream or ...?

She threw it off into the trees somewhere. Where was it?

Without Snugs, naked and out in the open, Sam didn't have long. Not knowing what else to do, Kay picked up her convulsing, nude body and ran with her to the nearby Ten Gardens, lost somewhere in the depths of the Grove.

In the center of the Lily Garden was a good-sized bath house featuring a large heated pool, partially under the bath house's stone roof, partially open to the elements. Countess Sygillis had put it in years ago; it was one of her favorite places to sit and meditate. The children also used it quite often—Sarah often bemoaning the fact that Grand Oyln Manor didn't have a similar pool. During the winter it was a big hit. Lady Kilos used it just about every day to soak in the steaming water.

Now that heated pool was Sam's only chance.

In his fear and agitation, Kay's thoughts spun, his heart pounded.

Panic! Things began to turn amber around him.

As he ran with Sam, he had a vague thought wondering what might happen should somebody—like Ki or his parents—be using the pool. But, no, they were all gone. What if Lady Hathaline was using it, or what if one of the staff was there enjoying the pool on his or her time off? Seeing the naked Kay, torn and bloodied as he was, come running in holding the equally naked and bloody Sam would, no doubt, create a huge stir, and he and Sam's secret would be lost.

He couldn't worry about that—Sam was about to die!

He saw the familiar stone walls and billowing plumes of steam from the bath house approaching as he ran, and, for a brief second, he thought he could see through the stone walls and into the lavish interior.

"Creation!" There were two people in the bath house! A man and a woman. He didn't recognize them. They must be some of the staff. Whoever they were, they were about to get a catastrophic bit of gossip to spread around. What if they had a holomon or some other type of photographic equipment? Images of he and Sam could be floating around the League in a matter of moments.

He saw them casually watch as he approached. "You there in the bathhouse!" he yelled. "I order you to look away! Look away or face my punishment!" Kay usually tried not to order the staff around much; that's what his sister Lady Kilos and Sarah were for, and he never threatened them with punishment, but, this situation was dire.

He looked down at Sam.

He was shocked. For a moment, he thought he saw some sort of strange, fibrous collar around her neck—one he'd never seen before. Interlaced in the folds of the collar were a host of small, diamond-shaped crystals etched with odd writing. The crystals were pointed and sharp, and the collar they were mounted in seemed somehow stuck to Sam's flesh like it was fused to her skin, or possibly stitched in place.

He blinked to get a better look, and the image in amber was gone, just Sam's perfect neck as usual. He must have been seeing things. He must!

He leapt over the low stone gate and neared the pool, running through the vast garden of lilies. There were a number of hot springs near the surface in this area of the Grove, and the ground felt warm under his feet.

There was the open end of the pool just ahead! Out of breath, Kay slid to the poolside and placed her into the steaming water. Her rigid body wanted to float at the surface like a log. He jumped in with a splash and held her body down. Her head with its mane of black hair refused to submerge, floating like a buoy.

She seemed dead, her face locked in a grimace. "Sam, wake up! Sam!" He splashed the hot water on her face. Nothing.

"You there!" he called to the people he'd seen in the bath house. "I need you to get help at once! My friend is dying! Make haste!"

No answer. The interior of the bath house appeared to be empty. He was certain he'd seen two people within. "Hello!" he said again. "Come out and get help or, by Creation, I'll have the two of you in irons!"

No answer.

Sam coughed, and he turned his attention back to her. The warm water of the pool was having an effect, and she was coming to. She thrashed a bit in confusion, and he continued to hold her body down. She began kicking and nearly pummeled Kay to death as he doggedly held her down.

After a few minutes more, Sam was breathing normally again, her mass of black hair spreading out like an oil slick around her in the steaming water. She calmed and relaxed.

Finally, she opened her eyes and seemed no worse for her adventure. Kay sighed with relief.

"Gods, Sam, are you all right?"

"I think so. What happened? I thought I was going to die of the cold. It was overwhelming." She looked down. "Oh, my medallion, it's gone. What happened?"

"I'm not sure really. I had an odd dream where someone took it from around your neck."

"Who would do that?"

"I don't know. It was just a dream. Perhaps it came unclasped. We're going to have to do something about that, and get a second and third one available as backups to prevent this sort of thing. I'll go back and find it, Sam. You stay put, ok? You'll be safe in the water. Also, I thought I saw somebody in here before we arrived. Call them if you need help while I'm gone."

Sam squinted. "I don't see anybody. Kay, don't go. Where are we?"

"That is a bath house in the Ten Gardens. It's a place my mother had built to take refuge from the daily grind. There are no terminals here, no Holo-nets or any other sort of technological contrivances."

"This water, it's so much like home. And look, I can sit here and enjoy the evening without my medallion." She kicked with her foot and made a splash.

Kay saw the welts on her back and felt the scratches on his begin to sting.

"Are you all right, Sam? Did I hurt you with that chain?"

"I'm fine. I should have given you more preparation. When we get really aroused, that's how we are. Does that prospect give you pause?"

"No." He felt his back sting.

Sam was overjoyed. "Here, I don't need the medallion. Here, I can be anything you want me to be, Kay. Tell me, and I'll be it for you."

"You're fine as is, Sam. Just relax and stay put. I'm going back to fetch your medallion."

She put her arms and legs around him. He tried to pull free, but couldn't budge. "Don't go, Kay. Don't go. I nearly died just now, and I don't want to be alone. You'll find it later. My medallion's not going anywhere. Look for it later."

"But it's getting dark."

"Then wait until morning."

She drew him in tighter.

Night was falling, snow fell, the open-air bath house lit up in soft blue light, the large snowflakes sizzling when they hit the water, pillars of steam rising up into the darkening sky.

"Kay, why have you never brought me here before?" Sam asked basking in the warmth. "This is enchanting, the hot steaming water, the snow. Look at it snow. Now that I can properly appreciate it, it's so pretty. We have nothing like this." The sky was interlaced with bloated clouds lazily dropping snowflakes amid broken cracks revealing stars. "I love it. I could sit in this pool all day with you."

"I never really thought about it, I suppose. I'm still getting used to you being free to move about."

She kissed him. "I'll expect you to bring me here often, Kay. We can make this our place, where I can be anything you want me to be."

"Why do you want to change your image?"

"That's what Monama women do for their men. I want to make you happy."

Kay pulled away a bit and looked at her—he was completely used to her white pallor and her eyes by now; she was a beautiful young woman with a soul to match. He noticed something.

"Sam, where's your bellybutton?"

"I don't have a bellybutton. No Monama does. That's why we like yours so much, I guess. We love bellybuttons. We think they're so neat. I got hold of a picture of you several years ago swimming at the beach on Onaris or somewhere with no shirt on. *You have a great bellybutton, Kay,*" she said with passion. "Do you think less of me for not having one?"

"No, Sam, it's just a bellybutton."

She looked down at his and probed it with her fingers. "Is that mine ... is that my bellybutton?"

A tiny little bit of logic somewhere in his mind took exception.

Wait a second! If you don't have a bellybutton, how are you ... born? How were your sustained during your maturation in your mother's womb?

She snuggled in close, her finger in his bellybutton, and whispered into his ear. "And, there's one more thing ..."

Oh, here it comes, he thought. "What is it, Sam?"

"We, also have something we call *Veda-mena*, the 'Glory Hands'. They are a pair of extra arms that our old ancestors used to have. Old Monamas, centuries ago, used to have four arms, but that trait is mostly gone. Modern Monamas only have two fully developed arms. The second pair is still there, but in a tiny, vestigial state."

She lifted her left arm. There, under her armpit, was a tiny bump. Kay examined it closely.

"Sometimes, if we get very old, the arms sprout and develop, but that only happens every so often. My grandmother's sprouted in the last few years of her life."

Kay continued to examine the bump. "Why did you lose your extra set of arms?"

"I'm not certain. We have old stories of a time long ago when we were four-armed and evil and worshipped a Horned God deep in the ground. And then the Gods of Jade and Sapphire came from the sky and took the evil from us. In payment, they took our second pair of arms. I'm glad they're gone."

She took him by the chin. "There is a word in my language that I've wanted to say to you for a long time. It's a word we don't utter lightly. I've said it to you before, but you weren't listening. When I made your little toy gazelle, I said it. When you were a little boy, I sang it to you. Now, I want to say it to your face, and I want you to understand. How many of my people long for this moment, and how few actually get to live it."

Kay settled into Sam's arms. She cradled him, savoring the warmth of the water.

"*Arin-Dan*," she said. "You are my *Arin-Dan*."

"What does it mean?"

"It means a lot of things. It means, most literally, 'beloved'. It also means 'dreamed of' and 'sacred'. It means that I love you, Kay; that I've dreamed of you my whole life." She grew misty. "I don't know how Elder girls are with the language they use. I don't know if there's a word in your tongue that means as much to them as *Arin-Dan* means to us. *Arin-Dan*, I've always loved you, since I was a little girl haunting your room, afraid to present myself. The first day we spoke in the chapel, I was so happy that I cried myself to sleep that night. I told my grandmother that I finally spoke to my *Arin-Dan*. I've done some things that I'm not particularly proud of through the years. Everything I've done, I've done for you, for my *Arin-Dan*."

The water steamed, and the snow fell.

"Why, Sam? Why me?"

"Because I saw you, and me, in future's night. It happens sometimes. Monamas often see Elders in their dreams, but mostly we just stay by our lake and hide in the fog, wishing we weren't so afraid. And then we go to the wall and plant our flower, and the dream fades leaving us with sadness and regret. We wear black to match the sadness in our souls. I didn't want to stay away, Kay. I didn't want to be afraid. I wanted the dream to become real, and I wanted to give you some of what you've given me."

"You said you and your people are afraid of something. What is it?"

Sam paused and considered her response. "Like I said, we were evil once, and we're still being punished for it."

She waited for a response from Kay. She had just bared her soul. Her heart was out in the open, to either be anointed in love or ripped out and burned.

"Sam," Kay said, "In Anuie, words often have a male and female version, right? Is there a female version of *Arin-Dan*?"

"*Cerri-Tela*. It's *Cerri-Tela*."

"And, if I were to say that to you, how would it make you feel?"

"Like nothing else in the world matters. All my troubles gone."

"Then, you are my *Cerri-Tela*, Sam, no bellybutton and all."

"Say it again."

"Cerri-Tela."

She smiled and pulled him down, and they made love again and again.

Anuian Monamas in tribal garb

12—IN LOCK

Now that they were lovers, Sam often visited Kay at night—something she'd never done before. Kay lay in his huge bed, and then there was Sam, appearing from nowhere, quickly donning her medallion. The interlude in the Grove and the bathhouse truly opened the floodgates, for Sam now loved to have sex—she was crazed for it, and she wasn't gentle either, often scratching and bruising him. Sometimes when she appeared, she had on a thin nightgown, or, when she was more ravenous, she appeared naked, quietly climbing into bed and attacking him.

Sometimes, Kay needed the chain.

Trips to the bath house became frequent, usually late at night so that they could have it to themselves. At Sam's insistence, Kay began picking forms into which Sam would transform. He was shy at first, picking simple things like blonde hair and swarthy skin, though eventually things took an exotic turn. Sam insisted he open up and share his soul with her, to let out all the things that were there deep down inside.

Shame, she said, had no place with his *Cerri-Tela.*

There was a cook in the kitchens with a 4-D tattoo who was rather ugly, but whom Kay found oddly seductive.

Sam became her for him, tattoo and all.

Admitting to his old childhood crush on Lt. Kilos, Sam became Kilos for him, a passionate, ravenous Kilos nude in his arms. Then he chose a Sister, and, another time, she became a demon for him from the pit of his nightmares, winged, fanged and hoofed. Those encounters were truly memorable.

Digging into the deepest corners of his fantasies, just to see what it would be like, Sam became Sarah for him once, her Vith blue eyes alight with passion. Making love to the image of his cousin was strange in the extreme, though, just that one time it gave him unheard of pleasure.

✶ ✶ ✶ ✶ ✶

They conducted themselves in such a way for nearly five years—a secret couple, married in all but name. The only people, other than Kay's parents, knowing about their relationship were his sisters and the staff. Lady Kilos was a friend and proved remarkably good at keeping secrets. Lady Hathaline did her own thing and didn't give a hoot, the House staff minded their own business, and Maser was still too young to really know what was going on.

Sam sometimes had terrible nightmares, usually late in the night. She screamed and spoke Anuie too fast for him to understand. She pleaded and begged before some unseen tormentor. Then, she would cry in her sleep, her whole body shaking. Kay always woke her, and she never recognized him at first. Then she'd embrace him and continue weeping until she cried herself back to sleep. In the early morning he always asked her what she dreamt of, and she wouldn't tell him. She refused to tell. She often said she couldn't remember what had upset her so, but Kay could tell she was lying.

She knew exactly what it was.

Their relationship was still mostly a winter event. Come summertime, with his cousins, Sarah and Phillip, dominating Kay's time, Sam had to stay away, and, though she rarely complained, Kay knew with each passing year she began to resent it more and more. Not having the Holo-net at her home in Castle Astralon, they communicated solely via correspondence in the summertime and with occasional conversations in Sam's chapel. Talking to Sam in the chapel was, frankly, an unpleasant experience as she was often surly, bemoaning the fact that she had to stay away. The letters she wrote him in the summer weren't much better, hinting at her growing impatience.

It was her choice—she insisted on secrecy, so she had to live with it.

✶ ✶ ✶ ✶ ✶

He received a strange correspondence during the summer when he was twenty. Kay's correspondence pile generally shrank in the summer, drying up to only the most droll and uninteresting of letters to which he had no choice but to respond. He got letters from Sarah and Phillip and correspondence from his aunt, the Duchess of Oyln, a forbidden person around the castle, his mother hating her with a passion.

However, he got few letters from prospective ladies.

Seemed odd. That was rather opposite of how it should be. In the winter with Sam around, his pile of letters generally grew, including even a few letters from various ladies from around Kana, though he had little time to answer them properly; Sam made sure of that.

The letter received was hand delivered to Kay by courier. It had no return label. The letter had a small notice stamped where the return address normally went. It said: HELD IN LOCK with the current date, meaning that the letter had been mailed at some unknown time in the past but was held at the sender's request at the Vithland Delivery Center until just the day before. People sometimes mailed letters IN LOCK to ensure that a letter was delivered at a certain desired time and date. People most often sent Dear John letters IN LOCK to ensure that they were far away, possibly on another planet, when the letter was finally delivered.

Inside the envelope was a folded, two page note and a single dried flower, rather like a small daisy with fewer petals. The note was written in red paint and was hopelessly smeared—apparently the letter had been IN LOCK for quite some time and had gotten either wet or had been stored in a humid location. The flower was white with a black button in the center. He didn't know what sort of flower it might be, or what meaning it had. He sent the flower to his aunt, Duchess Torrijayne of Oyln, who was a noted expert on Kanan flowers and knew their lore. Several days later he got the flower back from the Duchess, along with a short note.

It's called, in the common vernacular, White Emilia, a hearty flower hailing from the south of Kana—a near relative of the common daisy. Likes lots of shade. Its nectar is rich in sugar, but can be poisonous to many species of insect if the flower isn't fully matured.

You need to come down here and visit more often.

Signed—Dimples

The Duchess always used the code name 'Dimples' when she corresponded with Kay—just in case his mother got hold of the letter.

Sam swore she had nothing to do with either the letter or the flower. Kay liked a good mystery as well as anybody. He hoped that Sam would one day fess up to sending the note and flower, and reveal what was on her mind. He showed it to his father, hoping he, with his Sight, could make something out of it, but, no, the note had been written in brush-strokes and had no pen scoring marks on the paper that might be followed. The only way to read this note was to go back in time and read it before it had bled into illegibility. He stuck the note up on his bedroom mirror and let the matter drop.

Lady Sammidoran of Monama

13—The Falling in Love Ball

"You wanna' step outside?" Sarah of Blanchefort said, throwing down her napkin and standing up, knocking her chair over.

Kay sat there at the table and shook his head.

Oh, this was a bad idea.

✶ ✶ ✶ ✶ ✶

"So, what is this event that's coming up?" Sam asked as she watched the workmen haul in float-loads of supplies from the village.

"It's a ball. Every so often my mother and my aunt, Lady Poe, talk my father into hosting a lavish ball. My father hates big society functions, but he can't say no to my mother, and she just loves them."

"A Vith party? When will it take place?"

"Next week, on the full moons. Mother and my aunt always pick a theme for their balls, and 'Falling in Love' is the theme for this one."

Sam watched dreamily. "May I come?"

"Certainly you can come if you want, Sam. Of course, nobody knows we're seeing each other, so we couldn't present as a couple."

"We could pretend we don't know each other. My grandmother was your father's seeress, so my having an invitation won't be so unusual. It'll be fun to pretend we don't know each other."

Kay thought about it. "All right, but there's a few things you'll need to be aware of."

Sam was leaning over the rail of his terrace watching the staff haul the supplies in, her medallion dangling.

"Are you listening?"

"I'm sorry, Kay. What is it?"

"As we're both under thirty, we'll be consigned to the children's area. Under thirty is always considered a child in League Society. Also, you're going to notice most of the children in the hall with us shall look a little strange."

"Strange?"

"Puffy faces, like Lady Kilos's. It's just something we Elders have to go through. We live well past our two-hundreds and generally live disease and age-free; however, the trade-off is a rather malformed childhood. Some have it worse than others. I always keep it to myself, but I think Ki looks rather like an unbaked biscuit right now."

"That's mean. Your face isn't puffy."

"I never had it. I don't know why. So, with that in mind, it's a tradition to keep the children separated in their own little area at special functions such as a ball. We'll be seated in the Capricos Hall with the others."

"That's fine."

"Now, there are going to be several people seated with us at our table. One will be my friend, Lord Lon of Probert."

"Who's he?"

"Oh, he's a delightful young fellow from Arden. He helped me work out the technical details of my CARG a few years back. I think you'll like him just fine. Also, there'll be my cousin Phillip. He's coming up from the south specifically for this event."

"I've always wanted to meet your cousins. What is he like?"

"He's a good fellow. He's quiet and rather cerebral, like his father, Lord Peter. He's a natural pilot and can fly the *Goshawk* ship like anything. He and my sister Hathaline are both great pilots—they must have inherited all the piloting skill that I didn't."

"Do you think Phillip will like me?"

"Certainly Phillip will like you; there's no doubt. The problem isn't Lon or Phillip—the problem is Sarah."

"Oh! The blue-haired one who dresses like a boy?"

"That's her. I think she's ten minutes older than Phillip is." Kay struggled for words. "Sarah ... is ..."

"She's the one Ki doesn't like, right?"

"Yes, that's her. Sarah prides herself on being a loudmouth and something of a bully, too. She's quick to judge, quick to jump to conclusions, hotheaded, pugnacious and rather stubborn as well. I'm told by my father that Sarah is the spitting image of my grandmother, Countess Hermilane of Hannover. My grandmother was known about society as a particularly nasty Black Widow, and Sarah is every bit as nasty. Ki just can't stand her."

Sam was perplexed. "I don't think I blame her. She doesn't sound like a very pleasant person, Kay."

"It's mostly a lot of bluster, and Ki can't get past it. Deep down, Sarah is a lot more like her matronly mother, Lady Poe, than she cares to let on. She's a devoted sister and a loyal friend and there's nothing she wouldn't do for you once you have her trust. The big problem with Sarah is that she does not like Monamas at all."

"Why not?"

"Sarah has a big imagination and she loves the lurid and the bizarre. She has a library taking up the entire 50th floor of Xyotel Tower where she keeps all the creepy stuff she's collected, and it's a lot. She has a fascination with Berserkacides most of all. I think she's actually frightened of them a little, and, when she sees a Monama, all she sees is a Berserkacide hiding within."

"I see," Sam said quietly.

"So, she probably isn't going to trust you much and might even go out of her way to be nasty. One thing to keep in mind with Sarah is that she values strength above all else. If she gets in your face, don't back down. Don't overdo it, but don't be meek either."

"Perhaps I should teach her a lesson in humility. Perhaps such a thing might do her some good."

"I'd appreciate it if you didn't, Sam. Sarah's a blowhard, and no doubt she'd have it coming to her, but as she's my friend and my cousin, just let it go and be bigger than she is. All right?"

"Fine," she said. "I promise. Oh, one thing to be aware of. Will there be alcohol?"

"Doubtless. Some light stuff for toasting."

"I cannot drink alcohol. We don't handle it very well."

"That's fine. Just request some Gasol or whatever you want from the servers. It won't be a problem."

Sam put her head down on the rail and watched the staff haul crate after crate of supplies into the castle.

✶ ✶ ✶ ✶ ✶

Sarah of Blanchefort had been giving Sam the evil eye all evening. She was sitting across from Kay in a lemon-colored Blanchefort gown. Sarah detested gowns and was clearly uncomfortable in it. Her royal blue hair was also done up high, and she fussed with it constantly.

She had been talking with Kay about some of the new places she wanted to explore in the summer. " ... And there's this thing I heard about down south haunting the Gaston Way pass called the Wraith of Gaston. I want to do some investigating and catch this entity cold."

Her brother Phillip stirred. "The Gaston Way doesn't sound like any fun to me, Sarah," he said. "Just a lot of nothing out in the mountains."

She was on a roll. "Oh, yeah? The stories coming out of there say there's this freakin' monster that chases down passersby in the wild where there's no help. Then, it disables their transports, hauls them out … and murders them."

Sam sat at her seat at the far end of the table and rustled uncomfortably. She'd been very quiet all evening, getting a constant angry eye from Sarah. "Your pardon," she quietly said. "I don't believe this creature has hurt anyone."

Sarah's gaze snapped to Sam. "What did you say? Speak up!"

"I said, I don't believe that creature you speak of has harmed anybody."

"Yeah? What do you know about it?"

"Well, I ..."

"I can't understand you!" Sarah yelled in her loud voice. "What's with your accent? Don't they teach you how to talk down there?"

Phillip, wearing a lovely green and black tailed coat, spoke up. "Sarah, you're being very rude." Phillip turned to Sam. "Apologies, Lady Monama."

"Don't apologize for me, Phillip! She needs to get the marbles out of her mouth, or, better yet, move to another table! She ought to be apologizing to me for damaging my calm!"

Lady Kilos was sitting next to Kay in a white gown. "I can understand her just fine, Sarah. Perhaps you've got cotton in your ears."

"Who's talking to you, *Tez*?" Sarah said in an ugly voice.

Sarah loved calling Ki 'Tez,' which was an Esther word for 'cheap prostitute'. The Duke of Oyln had taught it to her, and she loved using it, finding it a particularly demeaning name to call a person.

Kay, sitting opposite of Ki, had heard enough. He and Sam shared a few glances here and there. He could see Sarah's sour attitude was wearing on her. "Sarah," he said. "Your enthusiasm is appreciated, but you need to tone it down a little, right? All guests in attendance are welcome here. And, don't call my sister Tez. You know I don't like that."

Sarah usually listened to Kay, and she quieted down for a time, toying at her plate of food with her fork. Still, she kept a mistrusting eye on Sam. *"She could go Berserkacide on us at any moment, Kay,"* she whispered.

"Shhhh," he responded.

Lord Lon seemed to be having no trouble speaking to Sam. He sat next to her in his ill-fitting blue coat and buckle shoes, chattering away. "... and this pin here, my lady, I won at the annual Science and Space Jamboree the Sisters hold every year in Arden," he said pointing at a collection of pins stuck to his coat breast.

"Congratulations, my lord," she said. "You must be very intelligent."

"Oh, ho, ho, well ..."

The staff came by with a tray of watered down kid's wine for a toast. They set a goblet of the purple drink in front of Sam. "*Sen-tre*," she said in Anuie, "may I have a glass of green Gasol instead, please?" The staff member bowed and went to get it for her.

Sarah watched her with interest. "What's the matter, our wine not good enough for you?"

Kay was about to shush Sarah up again when Countess Sygillis came rushing into the hall. "Kay, there you are! Can you come with me, please? Lady Hamilton would like to see your coat and pattern I designed. She might wish to make a sizable purchase." Sygillis had designed Kay's clothes, Phillip's too. Kay stood and Syg adjusted his lapels, looking him over, hands on. "You look wonderful. You, too, Phillip. Come with me, please. It'll only take a moment."

Phillip stood and she took both of them by the arm and led them out of the hall.

Alone at the table, Sarah wasted no time. "Aren't you a little old for green Gasol?" she asked Sam.

Sam sat properly as her glass arrived and was placed on the table, frothing with whitish-green bubbles. "We enjoy such things," she said.

"What? I can't understand you!"

"I said that we like Gasol in the Monamalands."

The time for the toast came, and all stood and raised their glasses. Sam stood with her Gasol.

"What's the matter?" Sarah said, holding her glass. "Can't take it, can you? What a little peasant you are."

"Lady Blanchefort, you are ..."

"Blah, blah, blah ..." Sarah interrupted. "Can't understand a word you say. By the way, I thought I caught you making eyes at Kay. Do it again and I'll have you flogged out of the castle, understand?"

"Not while I out-rank you in this household!" Ki said, jumping in.

"We'll see what Kay has to say about that. He'll listen to me."

"You really are incredibly stupid, aren't you?" Ki shouted.

"Shut up, Tez, this is between me and her anyway. Butt out!" She turned back to Sam. "Now, you speck of Monama trash, pick up the wine and drink it. Pick it up!"

Lon spoke up. "Now, see here, Lady Blanchefort, you are behaving most inconsiderately."

"Lon, when she goes Berserkacide, you're going to be the first one she guts!" Sarah responded.

The word 'Berserkacide' seemed to bother Sam. She pushed her glass of Gasol aside and tentatively picked up the glass of wine. She sniffed it.

"That's right," Sarah said. "Drink it."

"Sam, don't!" Ki said.

"Lady Monama," Lon said. "If you don't want it, don't drink it. Don't listen to Sarah."

Sarah was unrelenting. "No, no Lon, I think she wants to prove she's not a Berserkacide. Go ahead, Monama, drink it down," Sarah said. "You watch. She's going to go 'nuts' on us."

There was a wave of clapping and a tinkling of crystal as the toast filtered through the hall.

Sam closed her eyes and drank a few swallows and clanged her goblet with Lon's.

"Drink it all, peasant, don't be rude!" Sarah said.

Sam emptied her glass and sat down. Sarah watched her eagerly, waiting to see some outworldly transformation take place.

"So, how many people have you killed, Monama?" she asked.

"I've had it with your mouth, Sarah!" Ki yelled.

"Yeah? Want to do something about it, Tez?"

"Sure. I could Stare you down into a pulp, right now! How would you like that?" Ki responded.

Sarah was shocked. "You wouldn't dare use your Gifts on me! We're family! Who's side are you on?"

"Not on yours, that's for sure, and try me. You've had it coming to you for years."

As Ki and Sarah faced off, Sam shrunk in her chair and leaned over, threatening to fall face first to the table. Ki was alarmed. "Sam!—I mean, Lady Monama, are you all right?"

Sam didn't respond.

Ki stood and went to Sam. "Lord Lon, Can you help me with her? I think she's sick!"

As she reached Sam, her eyes snapped up and gave Sarah a withering stare. "So, you love the horrid and the bizarre, do you, Lady Sarah? Shall I tell you about this creature in the Gaston Way you so crave?"

Sarah sat there, fully convinced Sam was about to change into a Berserkacide.

Sam spoke, droning in an odd voice. "It knows the future and sees danger and possible complications from afar. It's afraid of what it sees."

"What's afraid?" Sarah asked.

"It waits for them in the lonely passes, where it knows there's no help. It uses NIGHTMARE magic and makes itself more than what it is. And, when they pass by in their transports, it comes upon them. They think they are safe in their transport. They are frightened when it catches them, running along the ground wreathed in smoke. It attacks their craft, fouling its works and forces them to flee the pass."

"And then it kills them," Sarah added.

"It frightens them and allows them to flee."

"How do you know this?"

Sam narrowed her eyes and ground her teeth. "I can see the future."

✶ ✶ ✶ ✶ ✶

Kay and Phillip returned to the table and seated themselves. "Been behaving yourself, Sarah?" Kay asked.

He saw Ki and Lon standing next to Sam. He saw the empty glass and residue of wine.

"What happened?"

"Sarah goaded Lady Monama into drinking some wine," Ki said.

Kay was furious. "Sarah!" he said, "Monamas can't drink wine! I think we should fetch a Hospitaler! I think I saw Beth in the main ballroom!"

"No, watch!" Sarah said. "Watch. She's predicting the future and is going to change on us any moment, and we need to rush her when she does! Watch!"

Sam sat there wobbling a little.

Lon put a protective hand on her shoulder. "Lady Monama, may I help you to a washroom?"

Sam belched and pushed his hand away. "So, Lord Kabyl, our gracious host," she said, her words slightly slurred, "I've listened to your friend here discuss his accomplishments. What are your plans, sir, if I may be so bold?"

"My lady, we should find you medical assistance, just for in case the wine makes you sick."

"I don't need medical assistance. I'm fine. I'm fine, so my question, please. I'd like an answer." She stood up unsteadily.

"I've currently no plans, my lady. I'm only twenty-two, after all." His jade-colored eyes met her black.

"Are you going to join the Fleet, soar the stars with your mother and father?"

"No, my lady, I find that space travel does not agree with me, I'm sorry to say."

"I see, and you've given no further thought to the future?"

"No, my lady."

Sam smiled. She had big teeth, accentuated by her black lips. "Come now, you are twenty-two in age, but look at you—no trace of puffiness or swelling. You look a man already."

"Thank you, my lady."

Sam gazed at him. "Is he not handsome, Lord Lon?"

Lon was startled by the question. "Well, certainly, I suppose."

Sarah began to get tense and hiked up her gown. "What did I tell you before, Monama? Don't look at him, don't speak to him."

Sam turned back to Lord Kabyl. "And you're certain that you've no plans then, Lord Kabyl? No thoughts for the future?" she asked again, pressing the matter.

Lord Lon brightened and spoke up. "Lady Monama, I am planning to attend the Sister's Twilight 4 technical seminary this summer. I was one of only ten students to be selected."

She turned her head and looked at him for a moment. She gave him a wry smile and patted him on the cheek. "*Sen-tre.* Quite an honor." She loosed another belch then quickly turned back to Kay. "I am still awaiting your answer, my lord."

"No, my lady, and I do not intend to have any for the time being."

Sarah rustled in her chair. "And what about you? You're soon to be of age officially. What are your plans, other than dying and freaking out?"

Phillip gave her a kick under the table, knocking her heeled shoe off.

Sam grabbed a piece of meat off the table, her claw-like fingernails glinting in the hall light as she picked it apart and ate it. "I am to be married, Lady Blanchefort. Yes, I am."

"That's wonderful, Lady Sammidoran," Lord Lon said. "Will you share with us right now who your future Lord might be?"

She sighed. "Oh, let's just say my future husband is sitting here at this very table."

Everybody looked around at each other. The temperature most certainly seemed to drop at the table.

Phillip, brave and empirical as ever, spoke up. "Lady Monama, I congratulate you and Lord Lon for your upcoming union. I must say, I had no idea."

"Me?" he squeaked.

Sammidoran appeared off put and turned to Phillip. "*Mundi-ner-a!*" she exclaimed. "And why, Lord Blanchefort, do you say that I am to be wed to Lord Lon, charming and brilliant though he may be?" she said dryly. She tented her greasy fingers and clacked her long black fingernails together as she awaited his answer.

Phillip paused a moment and responded. "Certainly we've just met, so it cannot be me, and as I know most of the doings of Lord Kabyl here, it cannot be he either. Therefore, it must be Lord Lon, as I am not as aware of his doings."

Lord Lon swallowed.

Sam gave Phillip a hard, squinting stare with her piercing black eyes. "Are you so certain that it cannot be you, Lord Blanchefort? Are you so certain that you have not been … *kranti-gomi?*"

"What does that mean, my lady?" he asked.

"*Promised* to me?" she said in a sly voice. "Are you certain that hasn't happened?" She waved her fingers at him. Her black nails were long and dotted with hanging pieces of meat, and she made sure to let Phillip admire them.

Lady Kilos raised an eyebrow and smiled. *<I think Sam's really drunk,>* she sent to Kay.

<She needs a Hospitaler. I'm going to find Beth or Ennez.>

<No, he's drunk, too. I saw him passed out in the foyer.>

Phillip was clearly shocked. "Yes, Lady Monama, I am quite certain. My mother and father would never do such a thing, and, in any event, my mother cannot keep a secret and would have—"

"She'd have let something like that slip a long time ago," Sarah said interrupting, ready to defend her brother to the death. She fished around under the table for her shoe that Phillip had knocked off.

Sam laughed boldly. "In any event, Lord Blanchefort, rest assured, it is not you. You may breathe easy, sir," she said cheerfully.

Phillip, though he tried to hide it, was visibly relieved.

Lord Lon, after some thought, appeared agreeable to get to know Sam a bit more. Apparently, after a bout of inner turmoil, he'd gotten used to the idea. "Lady Sammidoran," he said in a shy voice lost in the blueness of his large coat, "have you ever attended the annual science and technology exposition in Arden?"

She looked at him for a moment and smiled. "No, my lord, I have not."

"Oh, well, it's a wonderful event and I would love to show you the …"

"Lord Kabyl," Sam said, teetering a little. "You are looking particularly handsome this evening. I approve of your attire. It pleases me. Your mother is a genius."

"Thank you, Lady Monama."

Lon was small in his blue coat that matched Lady Sarah's hair. It was an off-the-rack House Probert creation, not nearly as stylish and well-fitted as Kay's. "Do … do you like my coat, Lady Sammidoran? It's new."

She ignored him. "And what shall we name our first child, sir?" she asked Kay abruptly. "Will you invite me to sit closer to you, sir, as we shall soon be very close."

Everyone was silent.

"You're fine where you are," Sarah said after a moment. "Kay's not marrying you."

"Oh, and I didn't think you were his keeper, Lady Sarah."

Sarah began to get annoyed. "I'm not, but Kay is my cousin, and he's my best friend as well. He's not getting pushed into anything he doesn't want to do. You're not his type, Monama."

"Think so? You'd throw down the baton, Lady Sarah?"

"It would never get that far. I'll throw you down first."

Sam leaned forward, displaying her handsome bosom to Kay. She locked eyes with him. "And what do you say, Lord Kabyl? Would you not want me as a wife and countess?"

Kay swallowed hard, not quite sure where to go with this. Sam, when not drunk, demanded secrecy. He had to be careful. "My lady," he said. "You are a beautiful young woman and doubtless have many gifts with which to share. However, as I have said, I'm merely twenty-two years old and haven't considered courting as of yet."

"You didn't answer my question, sir."

Kay looked at the table. "I really don't know what to say, my lady."

Sam saw Lon's half-finished glass of wine, picked it up and drank it down. She staggered and fell laughing, her pointed Monama shoes flying into the air over the tabletop.

"Sam!" Kay cried.

Lon and Ki knelt down and helped her. "It's all right, my love," she said as they hauled her light body back up. "I expected your reaction, and I forgive you, but you might as well know that, one day, you shall love me like no other."

She made drunken eyes at him relentlessly.

Lord Lon was a little deflated. Sarah fumed.

"Quit looking at him!" Sarah said. "Why don't you go and freak out like your countryman in Calvert did last month and go Berserkacide. That's all you Monamas do, isn't it?"

"Sarah!" Kay said. "Be quiet!"

Sarah stood up, wobbling slightly as she was still missing a shoe. "She's trying to bewitch you, Kay! Can't you see it? I'm trying to help you out here!"

Sam turned and glared at Sarah. "Oh ... if you only knew what I've done with Kay. Up and down, back and forth, sideways and forwards. You don't know your cousin as well as you think you do. You're really not all that bright are you?"

"Oh, yeah? Want to step outside and discover just how smart I am, Berserkacide, I mean Lady Monama?" Sarah yelled, kicking her chair aside.

"Sarah," Kay ordered, "sit down!"

"I've *been* you, Sarah, for K—"

"She needs a Hospitaler!" Kay said cutting her off.

Sarah was frothing mad. "You and your pack of grave-loving freaks are the bane and laughing stock of the League, and the only reason you've been invited to this ball is because my uncle Lord Davage had a fondness for your late grandmother. Otherwise, he'd have nothing to do with the lot of you!"

Sam's normally white complexion turned bloody red. "Bold words," she said at last. "Coming from the daughter of a pirate," she said referring to her father's former, and alleged, membership in the Black Goshawk gang.

Sarah screwed her eyes up and leaned forward. "Better a pirate than a stinking fortune-teller waiting to soak your claws in Elder blood."

Lord Lon struggled to hold Sam up. "Now see here, Lady Blanchefort, that was ..."

"And," Sarah began, on a roll, "if you think you're good enough for Kay, you're as blood-simple and freaked-out as the rest of your family. You're a useless peasant not worth half a hader, and that's all you'll ever be!"

Sam went to say something, then put her hands to her face. She jerked free from Lon and Ki and staggered out of the room toward the noise and pomp of the ball, her black gown and bustle trailing like a shroud.

Kay stood, fuming. "I appreciate your looking out for me, Sarah, but that was exceedingly rude and uncalled for," he said. He saw her elusive missing shoe on the floor near his chair. He picked it up and tossed it to her. "You're lucky I don't floor you right now!"

"Me? Look, I'm sorry, but she's a freak," she said catching the yellow shoe in the mid-riff. "And, what did she mean when she said she's been me? That gives me the creeps."

"I don't know," Kay said.

"I don't think she's a freak," Lon said defiantly.

"Kay," Phillip said. "Where are you going?"

"Lady Monama is a guest of our home, a guest who has just been insulted by my idiotic cousin here. I am going to find her and offer my apologies."

He stormed away to find Sam.

14—The Library

A few weeks after the big Falling in Love ball with winter in full swing, Sam became fascinated with libraries. After watching a Brandtball match at Sarfortnim College, she and Kay toured the campus and ended up in the college's main library. Sam was astounded by all the information that was kept in books. She noted that many of the books in the library were dedicated to engineering and machines of various types. She has always assumed that all archived information in Elder country was stored via holo-node.

"No, Sam, on other League worlds, holo-node is the favored medium to preserve information, but, here in the north of Kana, we still use books and vellum quite often. Not always, but it's a tradition we have."

When they returned to the castle, Sam went on a quest. She insisted Kay show her all of the various libraries scattered throughout the castle. It was a tough task, as there were over a hundred, all in all. Some were fairly small, like the reading rooms in his Tower, while others were quite astounding in size.

"What are you looking for?" he asked.

"A device. One that we have at our home by the lake and doesn't work. I was hoping to discover how to repair it."

Kay wasn't certain he bought her response, but he left it at that.

They combed the castle seeking out and going through every library and reading room they could find. Some of the libraries Sam discounted right away—Lady Poe's favorite library in her tower was stocked mostly with romance novels and horticultural books. The massive library near the kitchen contained nothing but cookbooks, and Countess Sygillis' personal library in her study were mostly self-help and sewing books.

Here and there, Sam found books that interested her—mostly of a technical nature regarding exotic machines. Lord Davage's huge collection in his study provided a healthy cache of interesting reading that Sam devoured—she took over fifty books out of there, each she promised to return. Kay had tried to collect as much information as he could, but so far he had nothing. Whatever machine Sam was searching for eluded the both of them.

And she didn't confine herself to old books. Some nights Kay woke to find her sitting at his desk using the Holo-net. She appeared frustrated, as using the Holo-net could be a tricky, and was a maddeningly quirky method to access information that you wanted. Sarah was probably the best person he knew at using the Holo-net. Eventually, Sam became quite proficient, moving the floating holographic controls about with ease.

Sam was consumed with something, and it occupied her days and nights. At night, Kay often woke to find her sitting up in bed lost in thought, or sometimes she paced about, her mind absorbed in what apparently was a difficult puzzle. He spoke to her, and she didn't hear him at first. Then, she'd turn to him and smile, totally mum on whatever it was that was riveting her.

They eventually exhausted every library in the castle, Sam becoming rather sad that her mysterious search had been in vain.

"There's one more, library, Sam, though you have to promise never to tell."

"Of course, Kay. Where is it?"

Kay led her into the north wing to an innocent looking bench. There, under the bench was a nine-inch high hole hidden behind a vent.

"We can't Waft or Blink in, we're going to have to crawl." They squeezed through it twisting and turning for about a hundred feet until they got to the library, lost in stone—the passage never more than twelve inches high. It was a tough crawl, probably one of the hardest in the castle, Countess Sygillis giving it five full stones out of five. They struggled to get through. They inched along, their progress painfully slow, but they made it.

Once inside, Sam was fascinated by the tempting shelves full of the arcane. "Why is this place so hidden?"

"It's where we keep most of our more forbidden tomes and documents. It's a Blanchefort secret, and it's protected from Wafting and other arcane methods to enter it. You also can't Sight the walls and see it through the stone, not even Father."

The library was fairly small and eight-sided. Shelves full of documents, scrolls and old books lined the walls.

They went through the books, Sam carefully going through each, using her nails to turn the pages. Her nails were back to long and sharp; she had grown them back for the ball to keep up with appearances. Lady Kilos was going to bust them back down tomorrow, which was always a difficult task.

And then she stopped. She cried out in Anuie. She sat there looking at a full-page picture of several legendary machines from the antiquity of Kana. Kay glanced over her shoulder, trying to determine which one had caught her eye.

The machines on the page were all old and fancy, brimming with gems and twisted silver, nearly magical in the abilities they were purported to have. He was familiar with some of them. "Which one are you looking at, Sam?"

Absently, she pointed at the mirror-like machine in the center of the page.

"That's the Mallus Mirror," Kay said. "Supposedly it transverses the planes of dreams and reality. You have one of those at your home?"

"What," she said, preoccupied. "Oh, yes, yes. It's very nice." Kay had the distinct feeling she wasn't focusing on the Mallus Mirror, but rather another machine on the page.

"These machines actually exist?" she asked breathless, holding the book with shaking hands. "This isn't a fantasy book?"

"Yes, these machines are all said to be real. I've actually seen the Mallus Mirror on display at Fleet in Armenelos. If you have one at your home, it must be very valuable, even broken."

"What?" she said, preoccupied. "Oh, yes, that's right."

She stared at the page, her expression lost in thought. She closed her eyes and smiled and, after a moment, a tear leaked down her face.

"Sam? You all right?" Kay asked her. He placed his hand on her back and her heart was racing, beating like only a Monama heart could.

Without answering, she greedily read the book, asking him questions about this and that. "May I borrow this, Kay? Please, I promise I'll return it undamaged."

"Of course, but, are you really interested in the Mallus Mirror, or something else on the page?"

Sam didn't answer. With book in hand, she quickly exited the library, Kay crawling after her as fast as he could. When he exited the crawlspace, she was there in the corridor with the book, removing Snugs from her neck. "I shall return shortly, Kay. I love you! I love you so much, *Arin-Dan!* This is wonderful!"

"What is, Sam? Sam?"

And she was gone.

✶ ✶ ✶ ✶ ✶

She returned later in the day, breathless and preoccupied. She stared off into space and only half-heard when Kay tried to talk to her. That night after bed, Kay watched Sam fooling around with the Holo-net terminal, a vast number of holographic displays danced about her head. She masterfully manipulated the holographic controls. She seemed to come to a dead end, and, frustrated, she gave up in a huff, shut off the terminal, and crawled back into bed.

When she was asleep, he worked himself free of her arms and opened the terminal, curious as to what she was so interested in. The usual holographic gentleman in the black coat appeared with his staff of knowledge.

The last thing she had accessed was a visual history of the House of Want.

The House of Want? That was an odd thing to call up. Recalling his lessons with Lady Poe, the House of Want was an old Remnath House that actually left the League several centuries back. Why they left the League and where they went, nobody really knew. The forlorn ruins of their old castle still stood in the hills north of St. Paris. The House had been known for their incredible technological creations, especially their wondrous, arcane machines. It was sometimes said that their knowledge, especially that of their patriarch, Lord Revis, surpassed even the Elders, and the Sisters were jealous, giving them no peace. It was said they left the League to get away from the Sisters.

Obviously, whatever machine Sam was interested in, it wasn't the Mallus Mirror as she said earlier; it was something created by the House of Want. A quick search brought up literally hundreds of machines created by them, all amazing and well-crafted. There were too many to choose from and he'd probably never be able to guess which one it was, and he couldn't remember what other machines were on the page Sam had been so interested in.

He shut down the terminal and got back into bed, Sam quickly enveloping him. He was determined to know what she was up to. He'd have to sly it out of her.

✶ ✶ ✶ ✶ ✶

Just as Sam couldn't get him to improve his Gifts, he couldn't get her to talk. During this odd period, Kay often asked her what she was looking for and, smiling, she'd simply say that she was working on a project for her household. Her story held no water, as what would her Monama Household need with arcane House of Want creations, machines that, in many ways, replicated mechanically what she and her people could do naturally? It was maddening.

Her demeanor during her nocturnal visits also changed. Instead of wanting to go to the bath house and make love, she, instead, asked him about machines and technical detail, but nothing so detailed that he could draw out of her what she was up to. She had all sorts of questions for Kay and was somewhat annoyed when he couldn't provide her with a lot of good information. Kay wasn't into technical matters. His uncle, Lord Peter, was a great technical resource, as was Phillip, his cousin. Lord Lon of Probert—now, there was a technical whiz. A real chip off the old block was Lon, as his mother, Lady Branna of Probert, was one of the League's top scientists, and his father, Lord Milos of Probert, was the Fleet's lead engineer.

"Lord Lon, the cute little fellow in blue at the ball? Yes, I believe I recall him talking about fairs and the sciences and the like."

"That's him. He's a good friend and smart as a whip."

Sam sat there … her brain wheels apparently spinning. "Lord Lon ..." she repeated, then dropped the matter.

Back Cover, unlettered, by Carol Phillips

Part Two

The Invisible World

1—The *Olonol*

I had a vision when I was a little girl. I had it just once, and never again, but I never forgot a single detail. Through the years, my vision stayed in the back of my thoughts, simmering and waiting to come out.

I had a vision of the *Olonol* ...

And it could change everything.

I dreamed of a strange workshop. All manner of swirling metal gadgets clicked and bobbed about. There were unique tools hanging on the walls, and shelves were lined with ... *things.* I'd never seen such *things*. Elder things. Elder machines.

In the center of the workshop, a man wearing Elder clothing was working on some type of twisting, silver sculpture. He had arms and legs that were long and skinny, and his *frondont*-shaped head sat on the end of a bent *vembla* neck. He wore a little Elder hat, giving him a rather pin-headed look. I thought he looked funny. I wanted to laugh, though I'd been taught not to do such things, so I just stayed quiet.

The sculpture he was working on was beautiful—so pretty, so wonderful, something only an Elder could create. I complimented him on his work. I don't know if he understood.

He looked at me.

"So, you're here," he said. "They say I'm crazy. They say I'm full of it, but don't you believe a word. This machine, this one right here, is my greatest piece of work yet! This thing does what they say is impossible."

"What machine?" I wanted to know.

"This one right here!" he said rapping the sculpture with his tools. "Those headdressed zipheads from Valenhelm will say it doesn't work. They'll scavenge it out of here when I'm gone, wonder about it and scratch their noggins and, eventually, they'll write it off as a bit of failed genius and forget all about it. They'll put it on display and truck it around like a prize trophy. They'll lose it." He pointed toward a window. "See them out there?"

Outside in the afternoon sun, I could see a number of robed forms wearing stiff white headdresses dancing on a nearby hillside. They bobbed around with lots of arm waving and spinning, something a child would do. I laughed; I couldn't help it.

"See them dancing around out there like idiots. Those fools won't give me a minute's worth of peace. Anyway, don't you believe their guff! This machine works! It works every single time." He gave 'The Machine' another loving rap with his tools. "All you have to do is know how to use it. That's all."

I squinted and studied it in detail. The Machine was a type of silver archway, standing about seven *verdits* tall, maybe three *verdits* wide, easily tall and wide enough for a large man to walk comfortably through. It was constructed in a sinewy, organic style. It looked like a living thing, like a partially dissected tree trunk in all its various layers. Such incredible complexity and workmanship. I wanted to look at it for a while. I wanted to touch it.

If I quieted my thoughts, I could hear The Machine talking to me. In the

center of the arch was a large, dark purple stone of some sort. Its color reminded me of my *Arin-Dan's* hair.

The man looked at the whole thing lovingly. "We're leaving. Going to Emmira. Ever heard of it?"

"No, no, I'm sorry I haven't."

"Great place, Emmira. It's a shame I'll have to leave this baby behind. This machine, this one right here, can save your soul if you let it. Do you hear me?"

"Yes, sir, I hear you."

The man looked at me with a walleyed Elder gaze. "So, you want to know what it does? I'm dying for somebody—anybody—to properly appreciate it. For lack of anyone else, you'll do."

"Yes, I want to know." I wanted to know very much.

"Well, sit back and I'll tell you."

He then started. "Now pay attention! I'm only going to go over this with you once, right."

And I did. I listened. I hung on every word he said.

Gods! Can it be true? Can this be real?

I never had that vision again, but I never forgot a moment of it. I set it in stone in my memory. I often thought about it at night, replaying the dream in my thoughts trying to sift hidden meaning out of any small detail.

I never forgot The Machine I'd seen and the wondrous thing it could do. The man told me what it did in exacting detail.

Could such a thing actually exist? The silver machine was the key, a miracle—something beyond the demons that tormented us. It could, indeed, change everything.

The only thing the man didn't tell me was its name or where it could be found. It was the *Olonol,* a machine of riches, a machine of lore. I've been looking for it ever since, and I swore if I ever did find it, nothing would stop me in making use of it.

Nothing.

And now, here it is, drawn on the page of Kay's book exactly as I recalled it! Exact in every detail.

And, what I've been waiting for: a name to go along with it!

Oberphilliax, designed by Lord Revis, House of Want, who left the League in 000011AX.

Just like he said in my dream, he left the League, and he used the *Oberphilliax* to do it. This machine exists, and it works as well.

It does something even the gods cannot do.

And it'll work for me and my *Arin-Dan,* too. All I have to do is find it.

✶ ✶ ✶ ✶ ✶

I like to think that, if this somehow works out, we shall use the machine on a carefree day sometime in the future and go to this man, this Lord Revis, House of Want, and stand before him as man and woman, and thank him as he is due.

Thank him for his genius and his machine that he left behind.

Olonol.

Oberphilliax. Right there on the page.

2—A Pewter Pistol

Sam fell into a genuine funk as winter faded, going through bouts of sadness alternating with euphoria, and then delirium.

Kay asked her what was wrong, and she would say nothing. Nothing's wrong.

She became watchful, looking over her shoulder, always aware of what she said and did, carefully considering every word she spoke. Sometimes she jumped back, startled. Sometimes she fled from nothing as if pursued, and then she wept.

* * * * *

One day, they were out wandering in the Grove and came into a clearing. Sam found one of the ancient oak trees that was so old it had reached giant proportions. There were lots of those old giants scattered about. She saddled up to the tree and began happily carving their initials into the ancient bark with her fingernail. Kay looked over her shoulder to see what she was doing. She turned, smiling, wanting him to see what she'd drawn; then, her smile faded.

She turned, picking up the folds of her gown, and ran from him, chain rattling, covering the ground as only she could.

"Sam!" Kay cried taking off after her.

He might have been imagining it, but Kay thought he'd seen a ghostly hand reaching out for her just before she took off.

* * * * *

Given Sam's odd behavior, Kay began to think that she was sick or addled by some sort of malady. He wondered if the wine she'd had at the Falling in Love ball was having some lingering effects. When she wasn't around, mostly on Tuesdays when she had familial duties to attend, he began doing research on the House of Monama, but there wasn't much out there other than the usual postings and inquiries for fortune-tellers, prostitutes and seers. Their ability to see the future and their skills as prostitutes seemed all they contributed to the general populace; they didn't appear to be part of the League at all other than those select occupations. The lack of solid information was maddening.

He tried inquiring with Samaritan Ennez of the Hospitalers regarding Monamas, and he wasn't much help. Apparently, they knew little about them as well.

Pacing about in his tower one afternoon when Sam was gone, he had a sudden brainstorm.

Sarah, his cousin! Sarah had all sorts of information she'd collected on Monamas and Berserkacides, one of her favorite lurid topics. Sarah was quite meticulous in the documentation of her passions. Of course, being gone for the winter in Esther, Sarah's tower was locked up tight, and the exterior was proofed against the Waft as were all the towers at Castle Blanchefort. Once inside a tower, one could

Waft all they wanted, but one could not Waft from outside to inside. However, Kay didn't need to Waft in; he had the zip line running from his tower all the way to Sarah's bedroom on the 42nd floor.

He got his dusty zip liner out of the closet (he really didn't use it much—it was Sarah who did most of the zipping back and forth with her zip liner) and fastened it to the line. He turned it on and engaged the servo motors, and soon he was dangling in mid-air by the handles, thousands of feet above the distant rocks below. The zip liner was fast in covering the distance; after only a second or two, he was standing on Sarah's balcony. The bedroom within was much neater and more girly than one might expect from the rough and tumble tomboy she liked to present herself as. It was done up in teals and yellows (Sarah secretly favored yellow) and had white provincial furniture, again of a distinctly girlish flavor. Her closet doors were open and mostly empty—quite different from Ki's three-story closet. There were stuffed toys from her childhood arraigned here and there along with a wall full of pictures: many of her parents, Lady Poe and Lord Peter, many of his father and mother and many of the Duke and Duchess Torrijayne. There were also photos of her older brother Milos, whom Kay barely knew, her baby sister Millie, and a healthy amount of pictures of Phillip, Kay, and her. Clearly, Sarah liked keepsakes, and she obviously cherished her family, Phillip and Kay especially.

Kay exited her bedroom and entered the tower's main corridor. Kay knew that Sarah's favorite place to practice her love of the sensational was in the Mystery Library on the 50th floor, an equal distance from Phillip's bedroom on the 58th floor. Everything was locked, so Kay settled back to Waft up. It took forever, his Waft really quite terrible.

How angry Sam would be at such a display.

After a few minutes, he appeared on the 50th floor. The entrance to the library had a large slate over the door stating who was welcome to enter and who was not.

On the WELCOME side was:
SARAH
PHILLIP
KAY
MILOS
MOTHER/FATHER
On the FORBIDDEN side was:
LADY KILOS
BATHLOXI
and, recently added,
LADY SAMMIDORAN OF MONAMA.

Kay chuckled and entered.

Sarah's Mystery Library was well-stocked with books of monsters, ghosts, urban legends and local lore, all carefully shelved, categorized, and perfectly taken care of. The large room was a paradise of comfortable, over-stuffed chairs, a Nadinewood table from Castle Durst, several older model terminals and a cooler always stocked with drinks and snacks, (though it was empty now with Sarah away for the winter). It was a perfect hang-out area. Sarah would make a wonderful librarian. Her collection was truly quite impressive, and the organization of it all was a sight to behold. Unlike many girls who were difficult to buy a gift for, Sarah was easy. A well appreciated birthday gift idea for Sarah was always a new book of the lurid. Against the north wall was a detailed relief map of the winding Gaston Way, haunted, the lair of another of Sarah's favorite new monsters—the Wraith of Gaston. Recorded in holographic projections were Sarah's meticulous notes on locations of various sightings and places where she hoped the three of them would investigate this coming summer. There were even names of people she wanted to interview regarding the haunting.

At the other end of the library in a cozy nook surrounded by shelved books, she kept much of her Monama/Berserkacide materials. Sitting on one of the shelves was a bleached, partially fossilized skull, supposedly of a Berserkacide, though Kay doubted it was real. It had a round hole placed between its eye sockets rubbed smooth by Sarah constantly sticking her fingers in it. The skull also sported a fearsome set of overly-large sharpened teeth there were quite hideous to look at. It was Sarah's prize possession and was, according to her, a gift from Carahil, an elemental spirit created by her mother some years ago. She said she promised Carahil she'd keep it safe here in the Mystery Library. Looking around in the quiet, orderly splendor of the library, Kay saw little images of Carahil all over the place, as wall decorations, as book-stops on the shelves, and as little smiling plushies pushed against the wall. Seeing him was comforting, like he was here protecting the place.

Grabbing as much as he could carry off the shelves, he sat down at the table and started reading, though he dreaded what he might find.

Berserkacides seemed creatures right out of a horror vid or cheap, scary book, but yet, there they were. Berserkacides were Monama men, women, or children who had gone mad and become deformed. With four-arms, they shrieked with rage and killed any who crossed their path. They were said to appear in people's homes, in people's bedrooms, naked and glistening, black claws flashing. They were said to be unreasonable, unstoppable and could absorb massive amounts of damage before dying. There were three topics that Sam refused to talk about. These included her home by the shores of Lake Monama, some of the more detailed aspects of Monama life, and the Berserkacides, whose name she rarely uttered.

Clearly they were monsters for a stormy night and a vivid imagination. His father believed that they didn't exist at all and were products of either a hoax or hysteria.

Kay sometimes had a nightmare in which he would wake one morning and find that Sam had become a Berserkacide, her claws reaching for his throat.

It was a dream he was ashamed of and pushed away, but still, the how's and why's were endless.

If real, how did one become a Berserkacide?

If real, why did one become a Berserkacide?

Sam was mum.

He found all sorts of collected information on Berserkacides in Sarah's books and documents, but scant little on standard, healthy Monamas—apparently that didn't interest her as much. As he sorted through the documents, he tried to bypass the ones regarding Berserkacides, but eventually his curiosity got the better of him:

BERSERKACIDE:

... bestial rage ...

... extremely violent and dangerous ...

...four-armed, extremely powerful ...
... exposed and enlarged pineal gland to aid in ...
... rush of anger, followed by great cunning and cruelty ...
...death of personality ...
...permanent ...
... no known cure, no known cause ...
...Monamas mistrusted in many quarters due to Berserkacide events ...
...Monamas often escorted out of many Remnath cities ...
...Under Sisterhood surveillance ...

Death of personality. Death of soul
... Death of his Sam.

Shuddering, he continued on.

Finally, he found something which seemed promising and didn't involve Berserkacides.

It read:

HEAD SWARM:

A semi-catatonic condition entered into by members of the House of Monama, highlighted by extreme apathy and delirium, lack of recognition and place, lack of muscular control, general weakness and listlessness. Head Swarm is entered into when a Monama believes that he or she is about to die and is...

He put the document down and sat there.

Head Swarm. About to die ...

Sam seemed to be exhibiting some of these symptoms, but not all of them. Even in her blackest and most sullen of moods, Sam recognized Kay and knew where she was.

He read on, but those words kept popping into his brain:

Head Swarm...

... about to die.

Berserkacide...

... death of personality...

...no known cure. No known cause...

...Monamas mistrusted... Monamas detained and escorted away...

He saw one more thing that caught his interest, a short entry reading:

WHITE EMILIA

Herbaceous flowering plant of family Asteraceae, common in the Lake Monama region of Kana that thrives well in shade and low light. Often used symbolically in Monama mating rituals, especially the Nebulon, Astralon and Minzer tribes.

That was the white flower he'd received in the IN LOCK letter. Mating rituals? That was interesting. Sam hadn't mentioned anything about that. He found little else of use. He put everything back where he got it, knowing that the anal Sarah would no doubt discover it and make a fuss when she returned.

Berserkacide ...

Head Swarm ...

White Emilia ...

These names floated through his head for the rest of the afternoon.

✶ ✶ ✶ ✶ ✶

Winter moved on.

Kay tried to ease Sam's flagging spirits by taking her to the village one day when she was in a particularly sad mood. Lady Kilos tagged along as well. Trips to the village usually made Sam happy, but not today. They strolled the vast maze of shops and emporiums—Ki always wanting to stop in the more expensive stores. Quietly, Sam looked around, and Kay offered to get her anything she wanted. Sometimes she wanted certain things, but today she wasn't interested enough to want anything. Ki certainly had no qualms about buying—she soon had an armload of bags and packages.

Sam, in her usual red dress and goggles, seemed determined to be dour.

Head Swarm ... lack of recognition.

"Sam, Sam ..." Kay kept saying, trying to see if she recognized him.

"What, Kay?" she slowly replied, and he'd be appeased for a while. He also recalled from his reading:

Head Swarm ... lack of reflex.

He tried poking her in the shoulder and back every so often to see how she'd react. She got annoyed after a bit and poked him back in the sternum, hard.

"Oww!" he cried.

Ki became quite hungry as the afternoon of shopping wore on. As they walked toward a nice café, they passed a small curio shop near the waterfront called THE MYSTERY DEN. The window of the shop was cluttered with a vaudevillian arrangement of cheap and poorly made trinkets, bathed in flake copper and sprayed-on pewter. It was a classic souvenir shop, clearly a place for tourists and new Fleet crew arrivals to buy inexpensive items to send home to their families.

Kay and Ki didn't look twice at the place.

Sam, though, took one look at the eclectic and rather seedy offerings crowded in the window and immediately became interested. She put her pale hands against the glass and peered in; the intricate and expensive goggles she wore stood out in stark contrast to the crap items on display. The heat from her medallion quickly steamed the window.

Whatever funk she had been in seemed to be gone in a moment.

"Kay," she said, excitedly, "may we go in?"

"You're not serious, are you?" Ki said in a prissy voice.

Sam didn't answer. She went to the door and flew inside, ringing the bell. Looking around to make sure that not too many people were about, Kay and Ki followed her in—they felt a bit sullied, like they were walking into a dirty courtesan's den.

Inside, surrounded by the seedy claptrap, moribund intaglio, and shelf-lined standard trinket fare, Sam seemed intoxicated. Mouth open, she browsed around the semi-lit shop, picking up a whole armful of tacky things best left un-selected.

When the shopkeeper saw Kay and Ki, he was thrilled. "My lord! My lady!" he exclaimed throwing his hands up. "This is a great day! How may I humbly assist you?"

Kay was mortified. "My friend here from the south seems keen on purchasing a memento," he stammered.

"Ah, I have many to choose from. Please, may I point out a new shipment of wonderful commemorative garments that have only recently arrived?"

He pointed to a far wall, and, there, neatly folded, was a hideous assortment of workmen's clothing all stamped BLANCHEFORT VILLAGE somewhere on the cloth. A few had poorly constructed holo pictures of Lord Davage's and Countess Sygillis' smiling faces. Kay wondered if his father was aware that these items—or this wretched store for that matter—existed.

"Ah ... yes, if my friend wishes, we might select some of those later," Kay said wanting to get out of the premises immediately.

Sam appeared to have made up her mind on something. She approached Kay. "May I have this, Kay? Will you buy it for me, please?"

She had discarded most of what she had been holding and was apparently settled on a positively grotesque pewter casting of a long barreled pistol mounted on a flimsy stand. It was clearly one of the most garish and unsightly desk ornaments ever

conceived. The base of the stand had a plaque reading:

BLANCHEFORT PtVa: The Old "Poltava"

Apparently, this grim trinket was supposed to be a likeness of the famous Blanchefort PtVa pistol, once made right there in the village in the factories now churning out his mother's fabrics. His grandfather, Lord Sadric, had abolished the practice of producing firearms, and the weapon immediately fell into lore as a prized collector's item. This brutally ugly piece of pewter-cast gimcrack, long barreled and ungainly, looked nothing like the PtVa, but rather like a dueling pistol. The Poltava was a short-barreled, elegant gun. Kay could easily imagine this same image—most likely having been stamped out in some sweaty shop in Calvert— being passed off as a Grenville 40, or a Dare 88 or an Inseroth D4. Depending on where you were when you bought it, the plaque changed accordingly.

"Sam," Kay asked, "you want … this?"

"Yes, please, Kay, may I have it?"

"But Sam, it doesn't even look like a Poltava."

"Please, Kay, I really want it."

Thoughts of *Head Swarm* again entered his mind. Without another word, Kay, holding the mounted pistol as if it were soaked in urine, walked to the shopkeeper and put it on the counter, the mounted pistol wobbling slightly on its flimsy, soldered metal legs.

"Oh, that's a true beauty sir—the old Poltava; nothing like it will ever be made again," the excited shopkeeper said.

Ki selected a shirt with a hideous holo-picture of Countess Sygillis stamped on the breast and tossed it onto the counter. "I'm going to blackmail mother with this later," she whispered happily.

Kay looked at the shirt and had to laugh a bit. There was a terrible picture of his mother on the breast, truly terrible. Her hair was not set correctly, her smile was goofy and unready to be taken, and her finger was precariously close to her nose; in fact, it was in her nose, truth be told. He wondered how and why such a thing had been mass-produced and put out for sale in the first place.

He read the tag: It had been made by the D of O Clothiers. D of O? The Duchess of Oyln? Dimples, his mother's constant nemesis, had struck again. Kay shook his head and smiled. Dimples was a relentless prankster. No harm done.

The shopkeeper told Kay the price for these two items, and he was appalled.

"Four haders?" These things combined weren't worth a quarter of a hader, but, with Sam and Ki standing there smiling and watching, Kay paid him the money. The shopkeeper put the items into a bag, and then the three shoppers exited the store, Kay very thankful to do so.

The purchase made Sam's day. She cast aside her previous funk and walked happily at Kay's side. Once or twice she pulled him into an alcove and passionately kissed him, whispering of the chain and the things she was going to turn into for him later. They went to lunch and all through the meal, Sam kept peeking into the bag, as if some rare treasure rested inside. It was the happiest he'd seen her in a while, so, ugly or not, he was glad he bought it for her.

✶ ✶ ✶ ✶ ✶

If that was strange, the next day Sam did something even stranger. They went deep into the Grove toward the back quarter past the Ten Gardens, a walk of several miles, Sam chattering happily as they walked. She was carrying the pewter pistol that he had bought her the day before. They entered a huge oak clearing somewhere in the far depths of the Grove, and Sam stopped. "Will you give me a few moments, Kay?" Sam asked. She gave him a kiss and walked away. Mt. Vith rose majestically in the distance. That huge volcanic mountain, the 'Old Man,' of the north looked marvelous from here.

Kay admired the mountain for a bit. Sam had wandered far from him. She stood about a hundred feet away, busy doing something with the ground. She was leaning over, her hands digging into the dirt. Humorously, her rear end and bustle stuck up in the air as she worked.

"Sam, what are you doing?" he asked, nearing her. She had dug a hole in the dirt and had partially buried the ugly pistol he'd bought her in the village. "Are you a dog burying a bone, Sam?"

"*Sala*," she said in Anuie, meaning "hush" as she patted the dirt down, stood up, and examined her work. She looked at it and tapped her chin with her finger. She spoke in Anuie, something she often did when she was preoccupied "*Hmmm, do you think this will be safe out here, Kay? Do you think anybody will accidentally kick it or uncover it?*"

He responded in Elder. "Well, you never know, but I doubt it. It's a big Grove, and nobody comes out here too often. If you really wanted to get rid of that ugly thing, I suggest a trash bin."

Sam clapped the dirt off her hands and put her arms around him. "*No, no—it's fine where it is.*"

"Why did you bury it—other than for obvious reasons?"

"*I put it here as a reminder.*"

"A reminder of what?"

"*A reminder that here it begins.*"

Kay laughed and spun her around. "Okay, Sam, thanks. I'll make a note of it."

They moved out of the clearing, Sam looking back over her shoulder several times as they walked.

3—Hiei

The Sisterhood of Light, the oldest Vith sect in the League, maintained twenty five strongholds across Kana. They also had a few on Hoban, Onaris, Bazz and Planet Fall, Tubruk and Carina, but Kana was their true bastion. These strongholds were, of course, much more than just places of worship or faith—they were research centers and repositories of great knowledge and learning. These centers were solemn and guarded places seldom seen by any outside of the Sisterhood.

There was the great bastion at Pithnar: a lovely Vith ruin on the surface, but a vast complex below where the Sisters continued to experiment and test the Gifts, a task they had been performing for ages. Testing the Gifts was their founding mission. There was the monastery of Attilan where the Sisters tended to their young and trained them for decades. There was the tall tower of Twilight 4 on the southern shores of the lower continent in Remnath where the Sisters researched the odd assortment of weapons the Xaphans and other enemies tended to use against the League (the infamous Fanatics of Nalls were taken to Twilight 4 and never seen again—their secrets removed from them by methods unknown and unspoken of). Some League circles insisted the Sisters had vivisected the Fanatics to get at their secrets, while other, more charitable ones, claimed the Fanatics had cooperated with the Sisters and lived at Twilight 4 in well-cared for splendor.

Either dispassionate, probing monsters or benevolent hosts, the Sisters were easily moldable to match the needs and expectations of any who observed them.

Their places were strongholds, places of impenetrable security. The Sisters were, if anything, jealous of their sundry secrets; that much was perfectly clear. Though always presenting themselves as polite and shy, they quickly could become bitter and spiteful to any who might choose to cross them, especially to those who might wish to tap their secrets; those were enemies to be dealt with swiftly. The Sisters had, at various times in the past, captured and executed various foolish Lords who tested them too much. They had also dissolved whole Houses in a process they called *Shuw-shun*—the old House of Mutt being a notorious example, their holdings dispersed, their patents burned and their progeny lost to the ages in a blast of fire and smoke.

It was an unspoken understanding that the Sisters were the true ruling power in the League.

✶ ✶ ✶ ✶ ✶

The central repository at Hiei, north of Esther, was a quiet and dreary place. As typical for a Sisterhood stronghold, it was located in an out-of-the-way area rife with old stories of ghosts and monsters. The Sisters liked using superstition and local folklore as a first defense in the security of their places. The ground Hiei sat on was craggy Haitathe land—the giants of old. It was situated near the northern sea, not another village or settlement for hundreds of miles.

All things being equal, Hiei was probably one of the more accessible Sisterhood strongholds, if one could call it that. The Grand Abbess of Hiei, a progressive and somewhat radical abbess, openly allowed those not of the Sisterhood to visit the stronghold and make use of *some* of its resources. Some of its resources were available for research, while some were not permitted to be viewed, *ever*, that being the capricious and heavy-handed nature of the Sisters—take it or leave it.

Hiei was a tall castle-like structure built of black rock and weathered masonry. It was an old Haitathe fort, and, as such, it was over-sized and rather bleak of appearance. It was once safely perched a fair pace from the crashing waves and cold water of the Sea of Elder, but with time and erosion pulling back the coastline, the storm-driven waves often rode up its sheer black sides.

It was notable as being one of the larger book repositories in the League. Books, nothing else, were kept there at Hiei, and usually the books were of an old and unique bearing. Even in the technological and modern League, with its Holo-net and imprinted data, books were still an important method of collecting and preserving information. Books were silent and covert and didn't corrupt or crash. Scanned databases could be hacked, could be uncovered by the Gifted and exploited, so information kept in books was usually sensitive, inflammatory or arcane in the extreme. The cache of books stored at Hiei contained information that the Sisterhood considered too sensitive to be allowed to be copied and placed in the Holo-net for general use. Still, the information kept there was not considered *overly*-dangerous or *overly*-critical to the well-being of the League, and, if the proper channels were met and one was well-favored, outsiders could come and perform research there. The ground level of the castle was set up as a massive library. Readers came, made their request, and, if granted, the book was brought to the reader where they could study it at their leisure. Books could never leave Hiei, and the Sisters, kind and smiling but tirelessly vigilant, always watched. They allowed no holos, photographs or scans of the material, but users could make hand-written notes, provided the Sisters look over and approve the content.

✶ ✶ ✶ ✶ ✶

A typical day at Hiei was nearing an end. The readers, coming from all over, had conducted themselves properly and, after the tenth bell, were kindly asked to leave for the day.

The readers gave their books back, exited, and the grand, over-sized doors were closed and locked.

None, not even the Sisters, noticed the dark figure crouching in the heights of the library. The Sisters, blazing with thought and mentality, should have instantly detected it, but, for some reason, they did not.

They were oblivious to its smoldering presence.

After they were satisfied that the library was empty and secure, they retired to their chambers and warm beds in the towers above, leaving only two sentinels to guard the premises. The sentinels sat down at one of the reading tables and tucked into a simple meal of unidentifiable food.

The figure, moving with speed and silent grace, came down from the heights and hid for a moment in the shadows by the door. It could feel that, not only was the door locked, it was girded with the Sister's power—nothing, either by opening it or by Wafting, was getting through that door, in or out.

It considered this for a moment. Perhaps it had over-estimated its own abilities. Maybe it shall die here today.

✶ ✶ ✶ ✶ ✶

One of the sentinels was startled as she ate.

She heard something.

Not getting up to investigate, not even putting her fork down, she reached out with her mind, inquisitively seeking whatever was there. Her mind was all she needed. With it she should instantly determine what it was that was hiding in the shadows. If it were a patron, that person was to be immediately interrogated, mentally and verbally, and a determination would be made as to why that person was still there. Perhaps the person was in the bathroom or something of that nature when the library closed. If that was the case, then no harm done. That patron would be escorted to a room with a bed and, under observation, be allowed to spend the night.

If, however, the person was sneaking around for other reasons, then that would be immediately discovered and that person set to tribunal. And if the person was determined to be a clear threat with sinister motives, then that person would be killed.

What the sentinel sensed in the reaching tentacles of her mind confused her. It seemed that *something* was there by the door, but what it was, she couldn't tell—that was odd. She got the impression of desperation and longing laced with a hint of fear. And, above all else, there was determination, backed with steel.

But that was all. Nothing more could be gleaned. The sentinel should know not only what it was, but who it was as well—the person's hidden thoughts and feelings made available to her like an open scroll.

Stymied, the sentinel put down her fork, got up from the table, calmly walked over to the door and looked with her under-used eyes.

She found nothing there, just the huge door, the tiled floor and the steps leading in. Perhaps she was simply tired. Soon, her duty would be done for the day, and she could go to her modest room in the tower high above and sleep. She walked quietly back to the table and continued her meal.

✶ ✶ ✶ ✶ ✶

But, something had been there. It smoothly crept from the door, across the open tiles to the narrow staircase heading down into the vast, book-filled vaults below. Moving like a patch of excited darkness, it skittered down the stairs.

Perhaps it had expected to meet some resistance along the way—a roaming Sister or two, and it was tensed and ready. It had not planned to fight and kill, but it could not be caught and detained—it would not. If fighting a Sister was required, then it will fight to incapacitate. If that was not possible, then it will fight to kill, and it was more than capable of doing just that.

Fortunately, the stone stairwell, emptying out into a pool of waiting darkness below, was not occupied.

The vaults of Hiei were vast in the extreme and forever plunged in a cave-like dark. The Sisters didn't use their eyes for much of anything, and artificial lights were not required. The thick darkness also helped to preserve the books stored there.

The intruder could also see in the dark, and the ocean of black before it meant nothing. Still, the sheer size of the place took it off guard for a moment. If it hadn't had a good starting place, it would never find what it was searching for.

It turned to the right, moving silently at speed along the floor. Even though the vault was pitch black, it could see patches of darker darkness, like shadows existing within shadows. It moved from one shadow patch to the next. It had a map clutched in its hands that it could clearly see. Following the map, it made its way into the interior one shadow at a time.

It was headed for a restricted section—a collection of books not seen by any eyes other than the Sisters for centuries. Just a little farther in, and it would be there.

Then, it happened. In a crossroad it encountered a Sister who was busy returning large books to their shelves—it came upon her suddenly, literally bumping into her and knocking a book from her hand. They stood there face to face for a moment—the Sister trying to coil it in mentality, confused, and the intruder, tensed and ready.

Then they engaged, the two of them suddenly locked at arms. The Sister tried to open her mouth and wail an aural and mental alarm. The Sisters were thought to be massively strong—where this supposed strength came from was not known. It was possibly an adaptation of the Gift of Strength turned on permanently. The attacker, though, was strong, too, and had the advantage of surprise for a Sister never expected to be forced to physically subdue an opponent.

They grappled for a moment; then, with a devastating blow, the attacker flattened the Sister to the ground, their battle having lasted little more than a second. Dragging the unconscious Sister out of the way, it continued. It must hurry. It could not be captured. Being captured meant pain, death or worse—prolonged torment.

Moving on, it finally found the section it was looking for: a row of shelves about twenty feet high stocked with a multitude of books. It set to work, its eyes quickly scanning. It bounded up the shelves, one after the other, desperately searching, knocking the unwanted books aside as it did.

A few minutes later, it found what it wanted—a large tome bound with a blue cover sitting on the uppermost shelf. It pulled the ancient book down and looked at it for a second, thick and old, pages yellowed, the blue leather cover smelling of age.

This had better be worth it, it thought. It double checked to make sure this was the correct book; then, it made its way back to the stairs.

The Sisters were now aroused. They entered the vault in force. They shrieked a horrible drone that filled its ears and caused it fear. It even thought it saw the Sisters growing in size as they filtered in, becoming monstrous in their anger as they searched.

Calm, be calm. It waited for a clear moment, and then made a break for it.

It wound its way through the maze of corridors and then up the stairs, passing a slew of enraged Sisters as it went.

Again, they appeared to be having issues detecting it. Such an advantage would not last and would not be protection for much longer. They turned to pursue, still clearly having no idea what it was they were up against. No matter, for soon they would have it cornered—there was no way out of Hiei.

It moved at speed across the open floor of the library. Behind, it heard the shrieking mass of giant-sized Sisters pursuing. It could feel the pincers of TK trying to grab hold of it, but slipping off.

It reached the door, but it was TK'ed shut and proofed against Waft. The Sisters might have issues seeing it, but they could hold the door shut without hope of it being opened.

Seeing one chance, it scaled the wall to a tiny window about a hundred feet off the ground, barely larger than the width of the book it was carrying. Breaking out the glass, it stuffed the book through and then it shoved itself in, its body compressing down to allow itself to squeeze through the small space.

And it was through to the dreary night outside.

When the Sisters threw open the door, it was gone, having vanished into the night, leaving no trace.

Duchess Torrijayne of Olyn and Countess Sygillis of Blanchefort

4—Strange Doings

As the winter wound down and Sarah and Phillip's annual return loomed larger and larger, Sam was mysteriously absent for a few days. Normally, at the end of winter, Sam was loathe to be away, so her absence was markedly strange. Kay waited for her in the Grove, and she would not show. He'd lie awake at night waiting for her to appear—no trace.

He went to their chapel several times and tried to communicate. He never got Sam to answer, though, on one occasion, he did get something else.

He heard a whisper that he strained to hear: "*Hiya', Kay. Where's your girlfriend? She's being bad.*"

"Who is this?" Kay asked.

He heard a small laugh in response. "*Who do you think?*"

Unlike Sam's voice, which always appeared to come from the statue of Countess Fercandia, the whisper sounded like it came from behind him, from the back of the chapel. He turned and thought he saw something moving in the dark near the corner. He drew his CARG, its light clearing away the shadows.

Nothing was there, thankfully.

He heard nothing more in the chapel, but the whisper unsettled him. He avoided the chapel after that.

He wondered if he had angered Sam somehow, or that she found someone else. She had been acting awfully strange.

Couldn't be. Not Sam.

✶ ✶ ✶ ✶ ✶

He lay there in bed dead tired, though his mind was racing. His heart was pounding, close to hyper-ventilating.

Where was Sam?

Worry and dread. Uncertainty.

Things became odd around him, and he had no idea if he was awake or partially buried in an uncomfortable dream. The starlight coming into his room was very bright, it kept him from sleeping. Lots of light was coming from the distant ruin of Castle Durst, too. He wanted it dark so that he could quiet his thoughts.

As he lay in bed, he became aware of somebody in the room with him. There was a figure in the corner near the window staring at him, giggling.

"Sam?"

In silhouette, the figure raised a flask to its mouth and tossed back a large drink. It raised a finger to its lips. *"Shhhhh ..."* It came forward. He saw a slender female form approach the bed, staggering a bit, as if drunk.

It didn't look like Sam. She must have transformed herself for him again. "Where've you been?" he asked, his voice hazy with sleep. She began singing a soft song, filling his head with it. His limbs grew heavy, and he couldn't move. He could only lay there.

She stood over the bed. She was wearing a costume or beaded dress, she was also wearing a backpack or some sort of lumpy device on her back that made her stoop a bit. She stripped off the dress and let it fall to the floor with a beady fuss, though she left her backpack on. Still singing her song, she pulled the covers back and got on top of him. She was lathered in some sort of warm oil. Her body was slick with it. She was also wearing a brassy or golden mask that covered the upper half of her face—Kay could see it glinting in the light from his window. This was the oddest thing Sam had ever changed herself into.

"Just want a taste ... " she whispered.

Before he knew what was happening, he was inside her, feeling the roiling heat of her body and rolls of her muscles tightening. Sitting up she rode up and down, her slick body glistening, warm oil all over him. She grunted in an unfamiliar voice. As she came to a peak, she fell forward putting her slick arms around him, kissing his neck.

Kay became aware of something—a wretched odor, an overpowering reek.

What was that? He tried to recoil but couldn't move. Her song filled his head, keeping him still.

Wait, was it a song she was singing? Was it Anuie? It didn't seem to be Anuie. It seemed to be some kind of scream, perhaps?

Yes. It was a scream, terrible to hear. He wanted to shut it out, but it was impossible.

He felt her teeth probe the soft skin of his neck, then she latched onto a tiny piece and bit down, tearing it off. Pain surged through his neck.

She sat back up and stuck her tongue out, the little bit of skin she'd bitten off resting on the tip. Then she put her tongue back into her mouth and swallowed. "*Mmmm.*"

She got off him and picked her dress up, staggering away. "*I'll be watching you. You'll see me again soon, I'll be the last thing you ever see,"* she whispered as she glided away and was gone in a greenish flash.

His neck was stinging. After a few minutes, her scream left his head, and he could move again. He got up and went into the bathroom to run some water on it. When he turned the lights on, he was horrified.

He was covered with sticky blood: his chest, his neck, his face, and other more private parts. Blood was in his mouth.

But wait; he blinked, and a moment later, it was gone. He must have been seeing things. He checked himself, and there was nothing there. He checked his bed, and it was clean as normal. The whole landscape of his bedroom took on a very unreal sort of quality.

Confused and exhausted, he stumbled back to bed and collapsed.

He woke in the morning, his neck fine and unblemished. He must have dreamed the whole thing.

Yes, that's what it was.

A dream...

✶ ✶ ✶ ✶ ✶

On the third day of Sam's long absence, Kay sat in his reading room checking his Holo-mail. He had a lot of the usual correspondence from Sarah and Phillip.

Sarah, always with an eye for lurid and sensational postings, sent him a stack that had caught her attention.
One said:

BERSERKACIDE FIEND TERRORIZES LORD CHRISTOPHER PARK
Synthnet—MERCIA. Chaos reigned as a quiet day at the park turned into a bloody spectacle as a four-armed Berserkacide maniac ran free through Christopher Park in central Lyra. Singled out in the attack was Lord Torval of Clarence and his family as they attempted to enjoy a lovely afternoon. The Berserkacide was killed at length by the local militia after a brief but intense skirmish. Fortunately, Lord Clarence and his family were not injured in the attack. The militia commander had no comment.

Another curious posting read:

PARAFLY INFESTATION SPREADING THROUGHOUT KANA
Synthnet—ARDEN. The Science Ministry has posted a general warning regarding a planet-wide infestation of a large, previously unidentified species of winged insect being called 'Parafly' by Ministry entomologists, who believe the insect is a stowaway from another world. The Science Ministry wishes it to be noted that these insects, though large and swarming, do not appear to pose an immediate threat to the general public. Paraflies, appear similar to an ordinary dragonfly, and may easily be identified by their large size (twice that of a standard dragonfly), and a furtive buzzing sound they create. The Science Ministry advises, should a swarm of Paraflies be encountered, that they be avoided and that the local Ministry chapters be informed of their presence as soon as possible. At present, standard anti-insect agents appear to have little effect upon them.

Sarah and her posts. The girl loved the lurid.

Moving on, he finished a few letters when, suddenly, in a blast of air, there was Lady Kilos, his correspondence scattering. She had Wafted in, her white gown settling at her feet. Her icy blue hair was perfect as ever. Her blast even knocked down some of the trinkets Kay had arranged on his bookshelves.

His favorite toy since he was a small kid, the little patchwork gazelle Sam had made for him, fell to the floor.

Lady Kilos picked the gazelle up, her puffy cheeks flush with excitement. "Kay," she said ready to burst, "Do you know what I just heard?"

"What, Ki?" he said a little perturbed, and slightly worried. Her news had to be regarding Sam, and it probably wasn't good. He stood and took the gazelle from Ki's grasp. He brushed it off and put it back up on the shelf where it belonged.

"I heard that Sam—our Sam—was seen having lunch the other day with … another man!" She panted, having a hard time catching her breath.

"Who told you such a silly thing?" he asked trying to sound disinterested, but the heavy hand of worry was building up inside him, fast.

"I don't reveal my sources—not to you or anybody else. But, there's no doubt about it. Sam was caught red handed— lunching. What are we going to do?"

"It's lunch, Ki—it's not a crime."

"Yes, but lunch … with a guy—who's not you! I thought you two were supposed to be tight. We're buddies the three of us."

"We are tight, you know that." Kay returned to his letter-writing, trying to not appear interested.

"Well, Kay?" she said standing there. "Don't you want to know who it was?"

Kay was burning to know. "Not really," he said, trying to be coy.

Lady Kilos glared at him. "Well then, I'll be off." Kilos, practicing her Wafting skills began to Waft from the room, her wind scattering his pile of letters about a second time.

"Wait a minute, Ki. I know you're dying to tell me, so out with it. Who was it?"

As the Waft coiled up around her, she yawned and vanished.

Only ten seconds to Waft—she was way better at it than he was. His took a whole minute. He was impressed, despite himself.

Damn her and her gossip! Now, he had to know. He tore out of his reading room and combed the castle looking for her. He finally caught up with her later on the main terrace. After following her around the castle, practically begging her to tell, she appeared suitably gratified. Gossip was a powerful weapon. They got lunch and sat down in the Capricos Hall to eat it.

"Ok," Kilos said, bursting to finally tell him. "Sam was caught red handed eating lunch in Arden."

Kay chewed his food and thought a bit. "Arden?"

"Yes, Kay, Arden. Who do you know in Arden?"

Kay thought but couldn't think of anybody. Lord Lon was from Arden, but there was no way. "Will you just tell me, Ki!"

"Lord Lon, you bag!" she said yelling. "She was lunching with Lord Lon. And, of course, Lon, all suave and sophisticated, managed to spill his whole drink on her at some point during the meal."

Kay felt a wash of relief pass over him. "Lon, Ki? Are you kidding me? Lord Lon of Probert? Creation, you had me worried there for a second."

"You're not mad?"

"No, I'm not mad. Lon is my friend, and he's not exactly known for his lady-killing ways, is he? Sam's been obsessed with machines lately, ever since the Future-Telling, and even mentioned Lon to me by name. She was probably discussing some technical matters with him."

"Machines?" Ki said with a bit of distaste. "What sort of machines?"

"I don't know, and she won't say. Says she has some machines around her home that she needs help with, but I don't buy it. Since I don't really have a lot of technical knowledge, she probably went to Lon with her questions. That's all, perfectly innocent."

Ki was a bit deflated. "Maybe, but my sources tell me that Lon looked rather smitten. He seems to like her." She finished up her lunch. "So, are you going to have it out with her? Is there going to be a big fight?"

"No, Ki, there isn't going to be a fight. I trust Sam, and Lon is my friend."

"Lord Lon doesn't know you're seeing Sam… remember?"

Damn her!

5—Lost in the Fog

The Ripcar fell through the heights in a mad half-roll. The pilot surely was either dead at the controls or suicidal. As the ground approached, the Ripcar leveled out, spun once or twice and set down on the flatlands, gentle as a baby.

Lady Hathaline adjusted the controls and the Ripcar's motor revved a bit before settling into a more sedate, idle condition. After all that wind and commotion, Hath's red hair, a molten river, seemed hardly out of place.

Kay's hair, on the other hand, was a mess. He ran a hand through it to salvage a bit of order and popped his hat on. He jumped out.

Four days since Sam had disappeared. Kay could not handle it anymore. He needed answers.

"Thanks for the ride, sis," he said. "I appreciate it." He reached into the back and got his CARG, which he saddled into place at his hip.

Typically a quiet kid, Hath simply smiled back at him. Her blue Ripcar coughed a little in the warm air. Her name 'HATH' was spelled out in glittery letters across the hood.

Kay looked around at the lonely landscape. "I shouldn't be too long, but I'm told that it's best to do this alone. The city of Blue Pierce isn't far to the north. Why don't you get some lunch and then come back for me later." Kay checked his timepiece. "It's ten bells; can you come back for me at twelve bells? I should be done by then. That ok with you?"

Hath nodded and held out her hand.

"Oh," Kay said. He reached into his coat and pulled out a small moneybag. "Here, use what you need."

Hath took the money and pointed at Kay's timepiece. She asked a question.

"No, thank you, I don't want anything. Go on, have some fun, but don't forget about me, right? Twelve bells."

She then grabbed the controls and hauled the rumbling Ripcar into the sky, tearing off to the north, its shiny blue panels looking like a bluebottle fly as it climbed skyward.

Wow, she could pilot a ship. Sixteen years old and look what she was doing. Kay was a bit envious.

With Hath now miles away, Kay took stock of his situation. He was standing alone on a warm flatland, grassy and somewhat forlorn. Far away to his left was the long green line of the Great Armenelos Forest, stretching back for thousands of miles. Every so often, a high-flying vessel came down into the forest, no doubt heading for the Zenon city of Armenelos, which was at the tangled heart of the forest.

To his right were the rolling, bubbly scallops of Remnath with its gentle hills.

Dead ahead was a towering wall of churning fog like a great bag of cotton perpetually draped over the landscape. The fog rose sharply from ground level, up into the heights where it flattened out like an anvil several thousand feet up. Occasional flashes of lightning back-lit the fog in strokes of cherry red. At the very center of this morass was Lake Monama, the largest lake on Kana, going southward for a thousand miles until it ran into the southern Sea of Elder.

Somewhere on the shores of this imposing lake was Castle Astralon, Sam's home—a place he had never been to or seen. He was going to plunge into the fog, find the castle and talk to Sam. He needed answers.

He started walking south, into the fog. It wasn't like any fog he'd ever seen before. It had a definite boundary between clear, warm air and dank impossible murk. The billowing clouds within the boundary rotated in a slow counter-clockwise movement. He reached the edge, took a deep breath and entered.

Immediately, day changed to a shapeless darkness. He was instantly lost. What was he thinking? How far was it to the lakeshore? He knew Sam's home was foggy, but he hadn't expected this. What had Sam told him once, that bright light hurt her eyes? That she could see much better in muted light? Those black eyes of hers were, no doubt, able to see perfectly in this soup.

His lackadaisical attitude toward planning this trip was clear. Sarah would have carefully scouted out such a mission and would have been fully prepared.

He turned to go back the way he came.

More fog. More murk. After just a few steps, he was hopelessly lost. Kay unsaddled his CARG and shined it about. Its silvery light was pinned in by the fog, creating little more than a fitful halo around its shaft. He fought the urge to panic, to lose all sense of decorum and dignity and start screaming for help.

He had to relax. This was Sam's home. She was here somewhere. Revel in her goodness.

Yes, but Sam had told him outsiders weren't welcome. She had never let him come down to the lake, had never invited him. Though this was Sam's home, it was an utterly hostile place.

He paused and knelt to the ground to collect his thoughts. He couldn't be far from the edge. It had to be near.

Calm. Be calm.

Slowly getting hold of himself, he heard the faint but steady flow of voices moving along the ground. It was Monamas talking to each other in Anuie and in another tongue that he didn't know. Just like Sam could speak to him in the chapel, here they used their abilities in place of technology.

He listened intently, and a pair of voices became clearer and clearer though the chatter. It was definitely Anuie.

<You forgot to pack my lunch again, bitch!>

<Call me that again, and I'll slice you in two right here and now! I'm in no mood.>

<Come on, hurry up! I want to be in the Elder city by late day! We've no money to feed our children or ourselves, or have you forgotten?>

<I'm pulling as fast as I can! You need to get these wheels fixed. They stick.>

<We don't have the money to fix the wheels, dumbass! You know I should have sold you to the arena on Hoban years ago!>

<Yes, and the first person I would have fought and killed there would have been you, slor-mouth! Now make yourself useful and get out here and help me pull!>

<I don't pull the cart, remember? You pull the cart! That's what you do, you pull the cart! Now put your back into it before I pull my finger and unleash a fart!>

The voices began laughing. They seemed to be coming from somewhere just ahead. Kay stood and moved in that direction.

Something massive appeared in the fog as a great, darker patch, conical and rumbling along the ground. It was a transport of some kind, about three stories tall and sixty feet long, craggy and hissing with steam issuing from geared engines strapped at the top. As it approached, lights mounted to its side blinked. Squinting, Kay could make out faded, once gaudy writing on the side of the transport:

The Amazing Clatera & Wife—Fortune-teller Extraordinaire: Fates Thwarted, Mysteries De-Mystified and Pleasures Explored.

The transport had eight spindly wheels, each at least twelve feet in diameter, spinning on delicate axels. Harnessed at the front of the transport by a single heavy chain, dwarfed by its mass, was a barefoot Monama woman. She was leaning in the harness, bending over, apparently pulling the massive transport all by herself across the ground. She dug in and set herself with each step.

Kay watched the odd procession go by; then, he called, "Hello!" with his hand cupped against his mouth.

<*What was that?*>

<*Who's out there?*>

The woman stopped pulling and stepped out of the chain where it fell to the ground with a heavy clink. She went to the transport and drew out a massive, spiked club from a sheath, wielding it with one hand. She sniffed the air and instantly locked on to Kay.

<*It's a bloody Elder!*> she said.

<What's an Elder doing in here? Sniff again! Your nose is as wrong and used up as your twat!>

She took a deep breath. *<Smells like an Elder to me. Smells like a rich one, too. It's a male, he's recently bathed, and he's wearing scented oils of some sort. Huzzah! I smell silver on him!>*

<He's bathed? He's got Silver? He can't be a damn Calvert then; they rarely bathe, and they never have money. Maybe he's from Zenon or Remnath. Maybe we've lucked onto our first customer of the day! What in the name of the gods are you doing? Get yourself prettied up in case he wants to screw! I'm coming down!>

The woman sighed. *<I'm too tired to screw! I've been pulling this cart for hours!>*

<You pull the cart. You screw the customers, while I bring you the customers, got it?> She put her club back in its place and disappeared around the back of the transport.

"I say!" Kay called out. "Can you help me, please?"

"Are you lost?" came a sly voice heavy with an Anuie accent from behind. Kay turned.

Standing behind him was a Monama male wearing a black suit and waistcoat with baggy white sleeves. Like Sam, he was skinny with a bursting head of black hair; however, he was thinner than Sam, much shorter and daintier. His eyes were much smaller than Sam's, and he lacked the long feathery lashes that he'd come to associate Monamas with. He smiled. "We don't see many Elders here in the fog."

Kay held his glowing CARG up. "Well met, sir. Well met. I am Lord Kabyl of Blanchefort. I am on my way to Castle Astralon."

The Monama man gave a short snicker. "That a fact? On foot? You understand it's about ninety miles that way?" He pointed with his right hand, his fingernails long and black. "Did you hear that, Mitz? He said he's going to Castle Astralon."

The woman who had been pulling the transport appeared over Kay's right shoulder. She was now wearing a slinky black dress showing off a generous portion of her pale legs and a pair of towering pumps. She smelled of Monama perfume, scented hair oils, and sweat. Like the man, she seemed smaller and less-full than Sam, a lesser version of her. "I wouldn't expect a warm welcome if I were you. They don't like unannounced visitors," she said.

"No," the man agreed. "Astralons don't like anybody."

The two Monamas stood very close to him, invading his personal space. Kay felt ill at ease. "Would you care to introduce yourselves, please?"

"Certainly. I am the Amazing Clatera, and this is my assistant Mitzilaran. Would you care to have your fortune told? As you are lost in the fog ninety miles from your rather prickly destination, you could probably use a Future-Telling."

"Thank you, no. If I may, what tribe are you from?"

The man smiled. "Cardinal, actually. We like the Elders in Cardinal. You're lucky. If we'd been Minzers or Zerbs, we probably wouldn't have stopped."

'Mitz' walked around and began toying with the fabric of his shirt in the region of his bellybutton. "Perhaps you would be interested in something more ... exotic, good sir? I can be anything you want me to be."

Kay wanted away. He began a Waft. Slowly, the twisting column of air began swirling around him. "Thank you, no," he said.

Clatera laughed and put his hand on Kay's shoulder. His Waft sputtered and died. Kay knew a Monama's touch had the odd effect of disrupting his Gifts, just like Snugs disrupted Sam's ability to perform many of her skills. Whenever Sam touched him, his Gifts went chaotic and uncontrollable. She thought it was very funny.

Apparently this Clatera character knew that, too. "You wouldn't be trying to disappear on us, would you? Come now, we mean you no harm. We're simply two traveling merchants from Cardinal trying to get by."

"And you with all that silver," Mitz said. "Certainly there's some service we could offer to earn a few pieces of it."

Kay lifted his CARG and pushed Clatera's hand away. He tried to go on the offensive. "Why were you pulling that transport?"

They both looked back at the hulking shape in the fog. "Because Mitz needs the exercise," Clatera said.

Mitz's feet appeared to be hurting in her high-heeled shoes. She lifted her leg and rotated her foot. "Our steam engine broke. Been like that for awhile."

Kay had a thought. "Well then, sure, I'll buy a service or two. Do you take Blanchefort haders?"

"Haders? I've never seen a hader before," Clatera said. "I'm used to seeing solaris and rubicons and sesterces. Can we exchange them for solaris in the towns?"

"Haders are Vith currency."

"Vith?" Clatera said with a bit of shock. "My, you're far from home, that quaint freezing cold place you come from."

"Yes, and I'll have you know haders enjoy a very favorable rate of exchange."

Clatera made a few fists and spoke to Mitz in rapid Anuie. <*The gods are smiling, Mitz. I'll speak his fortune, predict his death and then take his money. We were due a bit of good luck.*> He switched back to common Elder. "Then, shall we step inside where we can sit?"

Kay laughed. "I don't plan on dying, sir. And, I do not wish a Future-Telling. I simply have a few questions I wish answered that have nothing to do with the future."

Clatera was astonished. "You speak our language?"

Kay responded in Anuie, albeit with a bad accent. *"I do."*

He shook his mane of black hair. "An Elder in the fog who speaks Anuie. This is, in fact, a rare event. Who taught you our language?"

"My *Cerri-Tela*."

Again, Clatera was astonished. "Really? Your *Cerri-Tela* taught you? And who, pray, might that be?"

"A princess of Castle Astralon."

Mitz approached and gave him a good long sniff. "I do smell a Monama woman on him. They've been having a lot of sex. She's even transformed for him."

"Goodness, this Monama woman must just love you to death," Clatera said. "I can only imagine what she's changed herself into for you. You're just full of surprises, Lord Kabyl of Blanchefort. So, shall we go inside where you may ask your questions."

They strode through the fog and approached the transport. It was big and heavy-looking. It hissed and sputtered with a regular beat. The fact that Mitz could pull it all by herself said something about Monama strength.

"Those are the small secondary motors running, for the lights and accessories inside. The large drive motor at the top is dead as a knocker," Clatera said. A door opened, and Kay stepped inside.

The main area of the transport was hollowed out, granting a very open sort of feel. It looked like a little terraced cafe with tables arraigned on the open main floor centered around a babbling fountain. At the far end was a curtained stage. Above was a terrace lined with a number of doors. As they walked in, Mitz removed her shoes.

"Put those back on!" Clatera scolded her in Anuie. "*They make your legs look better.*"

"*I don't think he wants to screw; besides, my feet hurt. And remember, he can understand us.*"

Clatera gestured. "Seems we're a little low on customers today; just grab a seat. On good days in a bustling Zenon town, we have this place full. Those can be tough days for Mitz, what with pulling the cart, serving the drinks and screwing the customers—she's got much on her plate."

"Seems to me she's doing everything. What do you do, sir?"

"I get the customers, and I predict the future. That's the hard job. Sometimes we bring some of our children, and they put on little shows, dancing and changing their form. You people just love that."

Kay found a table near the fountain and sat. Clatera pulled a chair opposite him. "Would you like something to drink? Elder coffee perhaps?"

"That's fine, thanks," Kay replied. Mitz padded away and disappeared through a beaded archway.

Clatera rapped his long fingernails on the metal surface of the table. "So, what sort of questions do you have for me? It's your silver."

Kay cleared his throat. "My *Cerri-Tela* is a very secretive person. There are many things she keeps to herself. She cries in her sleep. She looks over her shoulder and minds what she says. I want to know why?"

Clatera considered his answer. "First, let me ask you something. How did this happen? An Elder and a Monama? *Arin-Dan, Cerri-Tela*. How?"

"She says she's dreamed of me since she was a little girl. As she's several years older than I am, I assume she was seeing me before I was born."

"Possible. All Monamas dream of Elders at some point or another. Did she tell you that? We find you very beautiful. Your interesting hair, your jewel-like eyes, it's all very appealing for us. I'm certain your lady is quite fascinated with your belly-button, isn't she?"

"She is."

"Do you find us attractive as well? We don't come in neat colors like you do."

"Obviously. I think she's beautiful."

"Transformed, or in her natural state?"

"I have never asked her to change her shape, though she herself is rather keen on it. I fancy her as she is. She's a little different from you and your wife."

Clatera raised an eyebrow. "Really? How so?"

Mitz returned through the beads with a tray containing several brass cups hammered with distinctive Monama designs and a pot of steaming coffee.

She poured three cups and passed them out. She finally seated herself and took her cup.

"*Bende, Hosfra,*" Kay said, thanking her and adding a respectful lady's name.

"*Bende-bende*," she replied in response, lifting her cup. As with Sam, speaking Anuie seemed to put her at ease a bit. She drank her coffee down.

Kay studied her as she drank.

"You were saying," Clatera said, "that we are different from your Monama woman. In what way?"

"She's bigger than you both are, a lot bigger. Her eyes are very different. They're much larger, longer lashes."

Clatera and Mitz looked at each other. "Does she have little dashes on her lips, sort of like little notches?" Clatera asked.

"She does."

"Hmmm, seems your woman is an Anuian Monama. Very rare these days. Rare indeed. Most of us, present company included, are Conox. We're not as big and strong and fast as the Anuians, but we're still a lot stronger and faster than you are."

"Clatera!" Mitz scolded. "You needn't be rude. Sir, the Anuians don't exist much anymore. They were killed off, hunted down ages ago and wiped out; though, occasionally, Anuians, like your *Cerri-Tela*, pop up in Conox bloodlines. Doesn't happen much, but still."

"Yes, your Anuian should be doing her civic duty and mating with Monama men, not Elders, creating Monama offspring. Who knows how many more Anuians she could parent," Clatera said.

Kay ignored Clatera. He considered Mitz's words. "You said the Anuians were hunted down. Hunted down by whom?"

Clatera took a drink and changed the subject. "So, yes, as I was saying, dreaming of Elders is not uncommon amongst our people; however, nothing good usually comes out of it. It's best to keep it a dream and nothing more, and that's normally what we do. There is a ritual we have where we try to purge ourselves of our Elder dreams. I had my *Cerri-Tela*, and I planted my flower and never met her."

"Is Lady Mitzilaran not your *Cerri-Tela*?"

"Mitz is my wife, and I love her very much. She is not, however, my *Cerri-Tela*, and I am not her *Arin-Dan*."

"I don't understand."

Clatera's expression drifted into nostalgia for a moment, and then returned. "Of course you don't. Let me make it plain. Your lady, by doing what she's done, by not planting her flower and by coming out of the fog, is risking not only her life but yours as well."

"How so?"

"Those of us who leave the safety of our little place here in the fog tend to become Berserkacides."

Berserkacides? Ah, Kay thought, now we're getting somewhere. "How? Why? Is it a reaction? An infection of some sort that creates a Berserkacide?"

Clatera considered his answer. "You don't have enough silver for me to answer that. Suffice to say there are certain truths to the world, and you're better off not knowing what they are. Ignorance is bliss, right? Isn't that what they say?"

Mitz spoke up. "Anyone of us, at anytime, can become a Berserkacide. Your lady, in seeking you out, has almost guaranteed that she will become a Berserkacide at some point."

"You talk too much, Mitz," Clatera scolded.

"So, you're saying as we sit here that the two of you could suddenly become Berserkacides?" Kay asked. "What sort of malady is that? It doesn't sound real."

"Oh, it's real," Clatera said. "And there are no guarantees. The best way to keep from becoming one is to stick to ourselves and keep our mouths shut. Makes it hard to do business though. There are some centuries that pass where not a single Berserkacide is seen, and there are others, like this one, where they are quite frequent. More and more."

"You see a red light, you best run," Mitz said, shuddering a little.

"Shhht!" Clatera scolded.

"What? A red light? I don't understand."

Clatera finished his coffee. "Like I said, you don't have enough silver. Next question."

Kay pressed the topic. "This Berserkacide business seems very odd to me. It seems to behave with a sort of intelligence behind it from what I can gather, almost like a punishment of some kind."

"Next question. We're done talking about Berserkacides."

Kay wanted to continue, but Clatera clearly wasn't going to budge. He would try to reintroduce the topic again later. "All right. *Olonol.* What does that word mean? I don't know it, and she won't tell me."

"It means 'machine'."

"Machine? What sort of machine? Does it carry any sort of special significance?"

"None that I can think of. It means 'machine'; that's it. You're sitting in an *olonol* right now."

Kay wouldn't let it drop. "She was pointing at the ground after a Future-Telling yelling, *Olonol! Olonol!* What did she mean?"

"Who was?"

"My *Cerri-Tela!*"

"She was probably out of her head with the Future-Telling. It happens a lot."

"You have no stories, no lore regarding machines?" he asked, frustrated.

Clatera responded. "Only that we like them and usually can't afford the more interesting ones you Elders make. Listen, Future-Tellings can get a little muddled. She probably saw some sort of interesting machine standing there in the future and was all spun-up about it. You'll have to ask her."

"I have, and she won't answer."

"Well, there you go. Next question."

"Wait!" Kay said. "This *Olonol* is important. Can you, perhaps, tell my future and determine if you see a machine there at some point?"

Clatera thought about it a moment. He put his cup down, leaned forward and sniffed Kay. He sat back. "I'm going to be honest with you, Elder, because I think I like you ..."

"If you like me, then quit calling me 'Elder'. My name is Lord Kabyl, or just Kay if you wish."

"All right. A future reading on you, Kay, wouldn't be safe."

"Why not?"

Mitz spoke up before Clatera could stop her. "Because you have the demon all over you."

Kay sat there a moment, trying to process.

Demon?

"What? What does that mean?"

Mitz made to say something, and Clatera cut her off. "Nothing. It's just an expression we use. The future isn't with you. I'd just be making it up. I do that. In business, that's what you have to do sometimes because, occasionally, I look into the future and see nothing. I don't want to rob you. You've earned a bit of honesty."

"But, what is this 'demon' bit? I don't understand."

Mitz looked down at the table, and Clatera cleared his throat. "As I said, just a figure of speech. Pay it no mind."

They sat in silence a minute or two, the babbling fountain breaking the silence.

Kay didn't know if he believed Clatera, but would probably get nothing more out of him with further questioning. He decided to move on and try to backtrack to the topic later.

"All right," Kay said. "What is Head Swarm?"

Clatera laughed. "Full of novel questions, aren't you, Kay? When you said you had questions, I thought you'd want to know where to grab a Monama woman to really make her squeal. All right, what's Head Swarm? A choice, that's what Head Swarm is. It's a choice."

"I'd read it was a sickness."

"If you knew something unpleasant was going to happen, and you could either endure it, or place yourself into a peaceful state where you would suffer no anguish and feel no pain, wouldn't you choose the latter?"

"Not if my duty demanded I stay and endure."

"Ah," Clatera said, skeptical. "See that, Mitz? You talk like a Vith after all, sir. Talk is cheap. Sitting here safe and sound is one thing, but, I promise, when the moment you've dreaded is upon you, you'll take the easy way out every time. That's Head Swarm."

Mitz had a question. "Your *Cerri-Tela*? Has she spoken of this? Of Head Swarm?"

"No. But I've seen her do odd things and act with a considerable melancholy. I thought she was falling into Head Swarm."

Mitz shook her head. "No, if she was in Head Swarm, she wouldn't be doing anything other than sitting and staring. You could plunge a knife into her belly, and she'd hardly flinch."

"How do you roust one who is in Head Swarm out of it?"

"You don't," Clatera said. "You let them go and be at peace. They are at a dreaded moment, and you'd best leave them to it."

"I won't let that happen to her," Kay said, resolute.

"Ahhh, and what can you possibly offer that Head Swarm cannot?" Clatera wanted to know.

"So that's the whole of it?" Kay said. "You just give up when things look bad, do you? Is that a Monama-thing? My *Cerri-Tela* is strong and fast. If something terrible has come upon her, why doesn't she stand and fight?"

"Some things cannot be fought," Mitz said. "Some truths cannot be avoided, and some evils cannot be defeated. The invisible world is all around you, and it is not kind."

Kay continued. "Sam often says that you, as a people, were evil once and that the gods are punishing you, even today."

Clatera laughed. "That's right. We were predators long ago, savage and proud. And the gods won't let us forget it."

They sat by the fountain in silence for a few minutes, both Clatera and Mitz appearing quite sad. Clatera was uninterested in talking any further. "I think we're finished here, Kay. Five silver pieces sounds fair to me."

Kay stared at his cup. "What is it that hovers over you? You said there are truths to the world that I'm not aware of, so what are they? I'm listening. What are you so afraid of?"

Clatera stood up. "I said we're done. The exit is that way." He pointed.

"I am here for my *Cerri-Tela*. I want to understand. Whatever it is, I want to face it with her."

"Ah," Clatera said. "You want to face 'It', whatever 'It' is, do you? You Vith. Of all tribes on Kana, you always have your monsters to fight, don't you? Your battles to win. Have you ever considered, Vith, that we are the monsters, that we are the enemy? I'm no Anuian like your woman, yet I could still kill you right now and it would be so easy. What could you do to stop me?"

Kay stood. "Were you to do that, you'd face my CARG."

"I'd be around it in a moment, and at your throat."

"Perhaps and perhaps not. In any event, at least I'd face my death like a man. I wouldn't stick my head in the sand and wait for the end to come like a scared rabbit." He reached into his coat and pulled out his remaining moneybag. "Here's your money, five haders and more. Much more." He set it down and made to walk away. "Thank you for not answering most of my questions."

"Wait!" Mitz said. "Please, don't go!"

"Let him go, Mitz. He needs to go and be away from here, and perhaps he'll return to his land of killing chill and forget all about this, and us. It's for the best."

"But, his *Cerri-Tela*?"

"She should not have come out of the fog. She is doomed, and so is he!"

"But, she did, and here he is." Mitz scooted around the table and stopped Kay. "Please, sir, come and sit."

She seated Kay and pulled up a chair next to him, holding his hand. She looked at his face, taking in his features. She smiled. "Oh, you Elders are so beautiful. Such amazing colors." She reached out and touched his purple hair. "I can imagine what your *Cerri-Tela* feels when you hold her in your arms and look at her with those eyes. She came out of the fog, testing fate, for you—that was probably the Anuian in her speaking. Tell me, when you say that word, *Cerri-Tela*, what emotions does it make you feel?"

"Love, devotion. Heartache, confusion, pain ... sadness."

She closed her eyes. "You have chosen to give your heart to a Monama. And with that comes a great deal of peril, but you must know that by now."

"Why? What peril? Why does she cry? Why does she look over her shoulder? What is it that I don't know?"

Clatera responded. "You can't answer those questions, Mitz, and you know it. You'll condemn him to death and us into Berserkacides."

Mitz was defiant. "We're doomed anyway, whether we hide in the fog or not. They'll come for us sooner or later." She squeezed Kay's hand. "I remember the Elder boy I dreamed of when I was a girl, staring out from the battlements of my crumbling home. Somewhere in Zenon, I think he was, not too far away. I mean, I am devoted to my husband, but I sometimes wonder what might have happened had I come out and searched for him."

"Mitz…"

"There are things he needs to know, Clatera! And he will know. I do this not just for him, but for her, too; for that Monama girl who came out of the fog." Mitz turned to Kay. "There are eyes on us, all the time. We call them Demons—I don't know what else to call them. And they take us and hurt us and make us do things we don't want to do. As my husband said, the gods are punishing us. When the demons come for us, take us screaming from our beds, we fall into Head Swarm to make our suffering less. You asked how to defeat Head Swarm. The only way to do it is to make the here and now, the real world with all its troubles, more attractive than the serene space of her own mind. If you are her *Arin-Dan,* then make her remember that, and she will return."

Mitz continued. "Now, tell me, she has insisted you keep your relationship a secret, am I correct?"

"Yes."

"And she's never told you why? Why the secrecy?"

"No. Again, just one of the many secrets she has."

Mitz leaned down and picked a white flower from a nearby plant stand. She held it up. It resembled a daisy with a black button in the center. Kay recognized it from the odd letter he received, only instead of being dried, this one was fresh and alive.

"This is *Zoznol-Gera*. You call it 'White Emilia'. It's a symbolic flower to us, and we use them in our jars—just like the one your woman was no doubt born in. There might come a day when your Monama girl presents you with a necklace of White Emilia. If you take it, if you let her put it on your neck, you will be at Trial," Mitz said.

"What does that mean?"

Something stirred from above. A door in the upper terrace slammed shut. Clatera and Mitz looked at each other. They appeared terrified. "We've said too much, more than any Monama should," Clatera admitted.

Kay looked up at the terrace and saw nothing. "What? What is it?"

"I'm sorry! I'm sorry!" Mitz said, backing away. "Show her! Show her the White Emilia, and she will have to tell you. I'm sorry!" She Blinked away.

Clatera moved away from the table and pointed. "The edge of the fog isn't far in that direction. Go. We've said too much. Go, keep your silver. Just go!" he said. He then Blinked away leaving Kay alone at the table.

Slowly, Kay stood and lifted his moneybag into the air. "Here, use this to repair your transport and to buy something nice for your wife. She deserves it." He set it back down on the table.

Kay made to exit the transport. "Thank you, once again, and be well. I'll not forget the pair of you." He marked his bearings and plunged into the fog. After a bit of stumbling, he emerged into the sunlight. Sometime later, Hath plunged down from the clouds in her rumbling Ripcar and picked Kay up.

The Ripcar screaming into the heavens, Hath asked him a question. She had to shout over the rushing wind.

"Not really," Kay said looking down at the flickering wall of fog. "I didn't learn much of anything."

✶ ✶ ✶ ✶ ✶

Two nights later, as Kay lay in bed, his thoughts were a carousel of motion and activity. He thought of Sam, and machines, and secret trials. He thought of Lord Lon of all people, his friend since childhood. Was the dumpy and unassuming Lon suddenly a rival for Sam's attention? A bitter bloom of jealousy and a general feeling of dread filled him up. With Sam not being around, not being able to confront her and know the truth, he felt even worse.

Eventually, he drifted off to a shallow, unfulfilling sleep.

Mitz's words banged around in his head: *"you will be at Trial..."*

He woke up some time later and there, wrapped around him, was a sleeping Sam, nude as usual.

She had finally returned.

He thought to wake and confront her.

Why do you keep looking over your shoulder?

What are the Trials?

Who are these 'Demons' I've heard of?

What are you so afraid of?

Tell me, Cerri-Tela. Tell me.

And, he wanted to know about this 'lunch' she had been caught having with Lon and thoroughly interrogate her, but he decided to wait until morning.

She seemed so peaceful, and he was just glad that she was back.

6—And The Dead Held Hands

With the morning came the inevitable slew of questions. Sam, as usual, was evasive and didn't answer.

This time, Kay was not going to be denied. He fetched his dried White Emilia flower, approached Sam, and held it up. "Tell me about the Trials, Sam."

She looked at the flower and took it from him. She was devastated. Sam stood there holding the flower for a long time.

Finally: "The cathedral," she whispered into his ear as she removed Snugs and vanished.

Kay dressed and went down to Cathomere's Cathedral. Inside the twilight interior, Sam was sitting near the front. She had on her goggles and was admiring the statue. The rector was standing near her, asking that she remove her goggles.

"Good sir," Kay said. "Will you give us this space?"

"I've a sermon to prepare," he said.

"I really don't care. Please leave us. We shan't be long," Kay said with a tone of finality as the rector stomped away.

Kay seated himself next to Sam. She sat there small and rather deflated in her gown. She stared at the floor. "I so love this place," she quietly said. "I'm going to miss it."

"Are you going someplace, Sam?"

Sam took a deep breath. "You have shown me the White Emilia, I wonder who told you about that? I am therefore compelled to tell you of the Trials. When a Monama girl gives her heart publically, and her love is known to all, she must put her Love to Trial. This is what the Gods in Jade and Sapphire demand." Sam spoke so softly, Kay had difficulty hearing her.

"A test of some sort? A contest?"

Sam was utterly defeated. "Yes, and I'm not referring to a mere foot face, or a wrestling match." She wept. Her voice was down to a whisper. "Just what sort of contest do you think I'm talking about, Kay? Don't make me say it, please."

The silence of the cathedral around them was profound. Kay shuffled. "Are you saying you're going to have to try and kill me Sam?"

She removed her goggles, her black eyes heavy with tears. "That's right," she said, her voice lost in the vastness around them. "That's right."

Sam sat there, contemplative and bitter. "That's why I've wanted you advancing your Gifts, so that you'd be more ready. I thought …"

"You thought I'd stand a better chance of surviving?"

"Yes, of course." She hesitated and was desperate. "I won't give you any trouble, Kay. I swear. Just tell me to go away, and I won't be a bother."

Kay put his arms around her and she pulled away. "Why would I do that, Sam?"

"Kay, do you have any doubt that, if I wished, I could kill you? Do you?"

"I'm strong, too. I'm fast."

She savored his face and took it into her hands. "Yes, yes you are, Kay, but, in all honesty, if I were to come at you, as in the Trials, you wouldn't last long. That's just the reality of it, and so I'm asking you to tell me to leave and never return. Be done with me."

Sam put her face into her hands and started sobbing. Kay put his arm around her, feeling her body convulsing with her crying.

There she was, her arms skinny and wiry, yet impossibly strong. There were her slender hands ended with a set of deadly claws.

An odd thing happened. Sam had just admitted that she, one day, might have to try and kill him, and given her incredible strength, her wind-like speed and her gut-rending claws, she was easily capable of doing so.

He should have been terrified. He should be fleeing from her side and calling out the castle guard, but Kay did none of those things.

Kay was the son of a Vith Household, but, up to this point in his short life, he had never felt much like a Vith lord. Vith were proud and strong. Vith were fearless and eager to meet any challenge, like his father had. Kay, so far, had been an aloof, castle-bound vagabond who couldn't fly, couldn't manage League Society and couldn't Sight. He was a talentless, purple and green oddity.

But, being with Sam had taught him several things about himself, that he was much more capable than even he had given himself credit for. He had allowed himself to fall in love with a Monama girl, looking past all of their strangeness and social stigmas. He had embraced her ways and tried to understand them, even picking up the basics and a decent vocabulary of Sam's language, which was not easy by any means. He created his own CARG and built a statue of his mother. He did these things all on his own.

And now, here was Sam admitting that she would be compelled to attempt his bloody murder. He didn't feel a hint of fear. He wasn't shocked either. He drew from an unexpected well-spring of courage he didn't know he had, just like his father before him facing his evil Black Hat mother alone for the first time, and just like his little sister Hathaline fearlessly flying her Ripcar.

Just like a Vith.

Sam stared at him, holding her goggles, the fear and despair clear in her large black eyes.

"There's a saying we have, Sam. They say the Vith feel no cold and feel no fear, either, because our ancestors sit in the Gallery of the Dead and hold hands, lending the living their power. It's through the living that the memory of the dead is passed on, and, so, they help us when we are worthy of help, and they take our fear from us. You have just told me you shall have to try and kill me someday. If you expected me to be frightened, I'm not frightened, Sam. If you thought I'd be shocked, I'm not really shocked either. I am Vith—I might not act like it most of the time, but I am. We have faced many perils through the ages, and we have endured. As my father did before me, somehow, someway, I will discover a way to survive. The Dead have held their hands for me, and I am not afraid."

Sam sat there, open-mouth shocked. She wiped her eyes and put her arms around him. "And, you still wish me at your side? How many Elder men have to worry about such things?"

"I'm not other Elder men. My family isn't destined to walk the same trodden path as everybody else. Look at my father; he had to stare into the eyes of death to court my mother. Also, my grandmother was a deadly duelist, and my great grandmother was a Bloodstein witch. And there's more, many more going back into antiquity. Had I selected to court some tea-drinking lady from Zenon, I'd surely be letting a lot of dead ancestors down. Maybe, in such a case, they wouldn't have held hands for me. There is a challenge to be faced, and I will face it when the time is right."

Sam laughed a little. She burst with joy. "Kay! Kay! I've underestimated you then. How could I? Shame on me. I should have told you long ago and anticipated that you'd take it in stride. You are such a remarkable young man. It's fortunate for me that I lost my heart to a Vith Lord."

"Couldn't you have just consulted the future to see what I would have said?"

"Things like this can go many ways, Kay—there are many futures. Besides, as we are sitting in here, I don't think I could see this conversation anyway—blacked out. This cathedral truly is a place of wonder."

"So, you've revealed one secret; what about the other ones? Am I ready to hear those as well? Have I not earned your trust?"

Sam darkened a little. "Kay, if I have other secrets, and I'm not saying I do—I keep them because there are things all around us that you don't understand. I don't understand them either; please, I'm not trying to be condescending. There are things that are beyond me, Kay, things that I'm afraid of—things that I have no control over and nether do you. You might feel no fear, but I do. I'm afraid of many things, and I don't want to burden you with my fears that are mostly silly anyway. My people have a lot of primitive beliefs, and none that have any place out here in the world."

They stood and made to exit the cathedral, Sam holding onto Kay as they walked. She clung to him.

"I don't know if I buy all that, Sam. There is something that not only you but other Monamas shrink from, something that makes you hold your tongue and look over your shoulder. I'd like you to tell me what it is."

"I will make this pact with you, Kay. I have often spoken of you as being great in the future, and I'm ashamed for saying that. You are great now, and I love you so. Study your Gifts—with heart and effort this time, for you now know what's at stake. Develop them, and, when I'm satisfied, I'll tell you all my silly beliefs. It won't be long, I promise. Can you live with that?"

"Do I have a choice?"

Sam didn't answer. As they exited the cathedral, she quickly reverted to darting eyes and glances over her shoulder.

And, after lunch, she was gone again, vanished to who knows where.

7—The Invisible World

Lord Davage of Blanchefort's study was in the northern wing of the castle near the large Palantine Courtyard. It was a spacious, multi-storied edifice adjacent to Mother's study, which was of a similar size and configuration. As Lord Davage was usually away in his starcraft, the *New Faith*, the study was normally locked up.

"Well, Kay," Davage said, "this is a surprise. You've never taken an assertive interest in your Gifts before. I'm very pleased."

Davage sat behind his ancient desk, going over any number of forms and obligations of the House that backed up while he was away. Mother was sitting in her favorite chair next to the desk. She was wearing a vermillion gown of fine fabric. She held a steaming coffee cup.

"What's brought this on, Kay?" she asked.

"I believe it's time I took an interest in such things, Mother. I'm not a child anymore."

"Well, fine then. Well done!" Mother said.

Davage set his papers aside and smiled. He was in his usual Fleet uniform with its embroidered collar and black sash. His hair, aside from its blue color, was near identical to Kay's and was pulled into a tail. "Indeed. Well, let's to it, then. This is most convenient, as there is a ledger I need up on the third balcony."

He pointed. High above the floor of the study was a third-story balcony lined with shelves and books. A large portrait of mother was also up there, framed and lit up. "Can you get it for me? I wish to observe your technique."

Davage and Sygillis watched with interest as Kay stood and centered himself. After about a minute, he appeared on the balcony with a crash of wind. He searched around and pulled a ledger off one of the shelves. "Not this one?" he asked, showing it to Davage.

"That's the very one, in fact," Davage said. Kay straightened and again began the long, unwieldy process of Wafting, eventually appearing with the usual fuss of wind and scattering papers. He handed Davage the book.

"How was that?"

Davage and Sygillis looked at each other. "Well, Kay," he said. "Perhaps you ..."

"What your father is trying to say, Kay, is your form is appallingly bad," Mother said. "I don't mean to be harsh or critical, but that was the worst Waft I've ever seen. Even worse than that Shocktyte Duchess Torrijayne of Oyln. Your sister is much faster and much more accomplished at this stage."

Kay felt a little embarrassed. "What did I do wrong, Mother?"

Davage answered. "Well, 'wrong' isn't really the correct word, Kay. You did everything required to Waft; however, you took a number of pedestrian steps to accomplish the act. First, you stood and centered yourself which isn't required, you waited until the wind started blowing before you really put an effort into it, and then you half-Wafted at the end there, further delaying your appearance. All you need to

work on is your form, and eliminate some of your odd habits."

Kay seated himself. "Could you show me, Father?"

"Certainly, Syg, let's have a race to the top and back and show Kay how it's done."

Mother took a sip from her coffee cup and set it aside. "Oh, you'll beat me, Dav, but fine. I'm ready." A moment later they blasted away and promptly appeared at the top. With another blast they reappeared where they were by the desk, with Davage appearing a moment before Sygillis. The whole thing didn't take more than a second.

"Did you see that, Kay?" Mother asked. "Did you see how fast your father is?"

"He didn't arrive more than a hair before you did, Mother."

"That 'hair' makes all the difference, Kay. That little bit can be the deciding factor between life and death, should things come to that."

"Did you see how we didn't make a big production of performing the Waft?" Davage asked. "With minimal preparation, we quickly Wafted to the top and back down. Less is certainly more in this case. That's the key. Don't think about it as much. Wind and noise, Kay, is a byproduct of the Waft, not a required component of it."

Mother picked her coffee cup back up. "You just have to practice, Kay. We know you have it in you to be a fine Wafter."

"Is there anything you can do to help me along in the process?"

Davage thought for a moment. "Well, I could punch you in the nose. Pain, it seems, helps the Waft along—why I don't know. Your grandfather used to put me and your Aunt Pardock to the cane as we practiced our Waft, and it did yield results. However, I am not going to resort to such draconian measures on you or your sisters. We live in a much more civilized society these days. Just practice hard, try from a seated position even though it's counter-intuitive, and, in time, you'll improve. Work with your sister and don't hesitate to ask her questions."

Kay seated himself and tried to absorb what he'd seen. "What about the Sight? The Stertors said I don't have the Sight."

Davage's ears pricked up. "I'm convinced the Stertors are incorrect."

"Does pain enhance one's use of the Sight as well?"

"No."

Kay blurted out a question he had. "Father, could there be invisible things all around us, even as we speak? I don't mean micro-organisms and such, but hidden sentient beings?"

Davage re-seated himself behind his desk. "Hidden sentient beings? What brings this question?"

"I think Sam believes that something watches her all the time. She refuses to say, but that's what I have come to believe. Other Monamas that I've spoken to imply the same thing. They speak of demons and being punished by the gods."

"Countess Hortensia of Monama never mentioned anything about 'invisible creatures'," mother said.

"No," Davage replied. "But, there was always an air of sadness about her and a certain 'rehearsed' quality about the things she said and did. The Sight, Kay, is a bewildering thing. I see all sorts of things all the time, and this castle has its share of ghosts. So, to answer your question, yes, I do see things here in the castle all the time." Davage was hopeful. "Are you seeing things, Kay?"

"No, Father."

"Kay, it's not possible that you don't have The Sight. Whatever the Stertors say or do not say, it's not relevant. It's passed down. I have it, your grandfather and great-grandfather had it; therefore, you should as well. Your cousins have it, and your sister and little brother have it."

"I know, and I've tried, and Sam insists I have it. But, I've never seen anything."

"Kay, close your eyes, please."

He sat back and closed his eyes, seeing the reddish interior of his closed eyelids.

"All right," came his father's voice. "I'm now holding up an object. I'd like you to tell me what it is, please, and no peeking. Just relax. Be at ease and see."

Kay took a deep breath and tried to get comfortable.

"The Sight, of all Gifts, is an outward Gift. Let it flow out of you. Be unbound. See what there is to see."

"No peeking, Kay," came his mother's cheerful voice.

"I'm not."

He tried his best and, as usual, saw nothing.

"Anything?" Davage asked.

"No, Father." Kay opened his eyes. Davage was standing behind his desk holding a small box. The disappointment on his face was clear.

"Father, I'm sorry."

He was silent for a moment. "No, no, Kay. It's all right. Truly."

The three of them were silent for a moment. "What's in the box, Father?" Kay asked, trying to change the subject.

"Oh, it's a small trinket I bought your mother on Bazz last time out."

Sygillis reached for it. "Well, Dav, may I have my present?"

"Oh, yes. Yes." He gave her the box, and she opened it, pulling out a lovely jade ring. "To match your eyes, Syg," he said.

"Dav ..." She put the ring on, and they kissed. Even after twenty years of marriage, mother and father still behaved as though they were newly in love.

Kay stood and felt utterly defeated. He kissed his mother on the cheek and made to leave, wanting to be away from the study.

"Kay," Davage said. "You are our son, and we love you very much. What you can and can't do is not relevant. Be the best man you can be, and that will make us happy."

Kay nodded and left the study. He had never felt like such a failure.

✶ ✶ ✶ ✶ ✶

He knew of a small bend in the Blanchefort Run creek flowing with black water where Lt. Kilos kept a stash of hard spirits in a flask. She said the cold water kept the spirits at just the right temperature for good drinking. He walked to the Ishtar courtyard in the Grove and stumbled off the path through the tangled growth to the fast-flowing creek. He walked up to the bank and fished around for the rope held in place with a peg.

There it was. He fished it out and, sure enough, there was Ki's trusty flask. It felt full, too. He'd make sure to pay Lt. Kilos back later.

He took the flask and went to Cathomere's Cathedral. The rector was gone, no doubt sleeping in his small home in the Cyantown district of the village at that time of night. Kay walked into the vast open space, hearing his booted footfalls echo about. He found a cozy pew, sat down and tossed back a healthy swig from Ki's flask.

He immediately spat it out. Wow—like drinking freezing cold acid! Spirits dripped down his chin and dribbled onto his clothes. It burned his face, too, and he wiped it off.

Ha! Couldn't Sight, and couldn't drink either. He held his nose and forced down a coughing swig or two, gagging most of it back up. The spirits were way too strong for him. He had hoped to get roaring drunk and wallow in his self pity. He'd come into the cathedral for privacy—he wanted to be alone. He didn't even want to see Sam, should she appear.

Fortunately, though he coughed most of the spirits back up, the little he managed to swallow was more than enough to accomplish his goal of getting drunk. Sarah liked, on occasion, to sneak booze out of the bars and drink it down, but, instead of getting drunk, she usually just passed out to the floor, so it was rather a downer. Kay quickly got dizzy and felt the cavernous cathedral around him spinning in a lazy manner. He closed his eyes and was exhausted, possibly doing a 'Sarah' and quickly ready to pass out where he sat. His mind encapsulated itself into a troubled package and withdrew deep into the recesses of his own consciousness.

Though he was sitting in the pew, he felt himself moving in a sickening ball. He couldn't determine if he was standing or sitting, or flat on the ground. Actually, it made no difference. He thought he opened his eyes, but couldn't see. Everything was a sort of muddled amber color, as if he were on the bottom of a muddy lake looking up at the sun.

He thought he felt something nudge him.

There was a noise. Something spoke. "*Hey! Hey, you awake?*"

Kay felt his mouth moving. He made a noise.

"Wow, you are really drunk. Maybe you should try a nice fruity wine or watered-down ale next time. Might do you a little better. That hard stuff's pretty rad."

He wanted to know to whom he was speaking.

"Oh, you know me, buddy. Look, since you're here, I want to show you a few things. Ok? I hope you're not in a hurry or anything."

Kay felt something soft but strong prop him up.

"*Look over there. Just there, please.*"

Fighting the urge to get sick, Kay's vision came into a confused, amber sort of clarity. He saw a group of staff members assisting somebody from their bed and taking them out into the tower hall.

"Look a little closer," the voice said.

Kay squinted and choked back a wave of vomiting.

Wait. Those staff members? What ... were they? They were hunched and misshapen. Some looked to be nude; others were wearing yellow armor of some sort. They glistened and seemed to be missing their skin. Things were attached to their bodies, horns or something. And, the person they'd assisted from the bedroom—no, they weren't assisting this person. They were dragging the struggling body out by the arms.

Who was that? It was a young lady with long, whitish blue hair. She was terrified, her face locked into a scream. Some sort of greenish gate or doorway opened in front of them in mid air. They stepped through and were gone.

Somebody needed help! Kay tried to move. Must help! "My ... sister ..."

"*Yes,*" came the voice. *"What you just saw was your sister Ki being abducted by demons in the year 003256. Does that year sound familiar? It should. Your girlfriend, during her Future-Telling, said your sister would be taken in 003256—and you just saw it happen."*

"Must ... help ..."

"*What you just saw hasn't happened yet. Ok? That scene of your poor sister getting abducted is something that* can *happen,* might *happen. It might happen to ladies all over the place. Or, it might not. It's something still in the crap-shoot known as The Future. Ok? Depending on a few things, it might not have to happen at all. Do you understand?"*

Kay didn't understand.

"Look, there are some bad things floating around in the world, Kay. Sound familiar? There are things that have always been here, content through the millennia to just sit back and passively watch. But, anymore, they are no longer happy to just watch. I don't know why. I don't claim to understand their motives, but, one thing's clear—they are actively moving at last. They have been at the Xaphans for ages, and now they're coming for you, for the League. Your Monama girlfriend knows all about them, and she knows what the penalty is for opening her mouth."

Kay reacted. "Ber ... Ber ..."

"You mean Berserkacides? If that's what you're trying to say, you're right. Just like you and your people were engineered long ago by the Elders to remain young and healthy throughout your lives, the Monamas were engineered, too. In fact, they've been engineered many times. Long ago, right here on Kana, they were a pretty horrific people, killing and eating everything, and they worshipped an equally horrific god in a temple in the ground. They called this place 'Tevlapradah'. You know Anuie pretty well, right? There's another language the Monamas speak called Systerel. It's a religious language they use. Tevlapradah in Systerel means 'Hell', and that's what this place was. The four-armed Monamas long ago were the dark angels of the Horned God and did his bidding, and that's how it was for a long time, this whole planet dripping in blood. But, nothing's forever, and the Horned God lost his dark angels. I'm a little fuzzy on the details, and I'm still trying to work that out, but, somehow, the Monamas were transformed into what you see today, two-armed and much more civilized. They turned their backs on the Horned God in his temple in the ground and forgot about him. He wasn't too happy about that, and he found others to follow him—new dark angels. These 'newbies' are the demons that haunt the Monamas to this very day. They took the Monamas and sort-of figured out how to turn them back into what they once were—Berserkacides, and they have inflicted great suffering on them over the ages. They now are turning their sights on you."

The voice paused. *"Those skinless creatures you saw taking your sister are called 'Killanjo'. They are mere foot soldiers of the Horned God's dark angels. See, the Monamas are at the bottom of the list, just the blunt instruments, the rabid dogs to be unchained upon command. Then there's the skinless Killanjo doing most of the dirty work. They are the 'demons' tormenting the Monamas. Then, running it all, are the Golden People—people who have no shape, who can be whatever they want to be. Monamas can change their shapes in a small, topical sort of way, but not like this. The Golden People can be literally anything they want: tiny, huge, powerful, whatever. The Golden People are the new disciples of the Horned God—his 'dark angels'. I really don't know what they're doing or why; their motives don't make a lot of sense to me, but, it seems clear they are planning the death of the League. An important initial phase of their plan appears to be to strike at the Vith, as the Vith will be most able to defend themselves against their preferred method of attack. I don't want to go into it, but it's horrible. Trust me.*

"Now, I'm on your side, you know that, right? Just like I'm on your side, the Golden People got the Horned God on theirs, so we're sort of working against each other, he and I. Therefore, I can only do so much. I'm going to need you to take action for me."

Kay tried to talk, but the voice kept on. *"Shhh. Just listen. There's going to be an attack soon, against your House and many other Vith Houses all at once. I think their goal is to try and remove the fighting heart of the Vith and get them out of the way right off the bat. I've done something to your room, Kay, up in your tower. I'm not supposed to, but I did it anyway. They won't be able to get to you in your room, unless they climb in through the window, but it'll be awhile before they figure that out, and that should give you all the time you need. Here's what you're going to do. You'll head out to Castle Durst and go to the top. There, you'll encounter a device emitting light, like a searchlight. Your task will be to destroy that light at all costs. All right? Nothing else matters. Get rid of that damn light. That's the main thing."*

Kay felt himself being lifted away. *"I'm taking you back to your room to sleep it off. When you wake, you'll not remember any of this that I've told you, right? I have to take all of this from your memory, least the Horned God gets wise and take steps. But, when the time is right, you will remember, and you'll know what you have to do."*

He was surrounded by warm sheets and a soft pillow under his head. He thought he saw a small, silvery form leaning over him. "*There's probably going to come a time, Kay, when you feel like you're all alone. You're never alone. I'm never too far away, all right?"*

Who are you?

The figure retreated. *"A friend. Oh, don't worry about Lt. Kilos' flask. I'll put it back in the creek for you. I'll even top it off, `cause I'm a nice guy and all. Oh! Look who's back."*

Kay felt someone crawl into bed with him. It was Sam. He felt her warm body all around him. Sam leaned over him and sniffed, smelling the spirits on his face. She got up and soon returned with a wet cloth from the bathroom. She dabbed his face, softly singing a Monama song. She sang in Anuie, of love and home. The sound of her voice slowly pulled Kay back from wherever he was.

As things became clear, the silvery form he'd been talking to seemed to drift out of the room and hang in the night sky like a silver star. *"Night, Kay. Rest easy, and kiss your lady for me."*

When Sam was done, she set her washcloth aside and curled up in his arms. The two of them slept.

8—The End of Winter

The next morning, as Kay and Sam ate breakfast in the Capricos Hall, they had a blow out fight, but not over Death Trials and secrets, or even lunches with Lon—it was over Sarah and Phillip.

"Kay, I am no longer content to lose you to your cousins in the summertime any more. I'm sorry, but our relationship has matured to the point that your future wife's needs outstrip those of your friends—and, yes, I am assuming that I am going to be your future wife. Therefore, it is *Me* first, *Them* second," she said, rather rank as she ate her food.

He had a wracking headache from the booze, and was still reeling from a night full of odd dreams. "Well, Sam, it's you who insist that we maintain our secret relationship, though I am willing to present ourselves to the League and have told you so many times."

"You now know why I keep us a secret."

"And, as Sarah and Phillip live in this castle in the summertime, I don't see how we are to conduct ourselves without them becoming wise to our activities."

"Avoid them."

"I can't avoid them. This is a big castle, but they'll seek me out. The three of us are normally inseparable in the summer. If I suddenly started avoiding them, they'd instantly know something was up." Kay glared at her. "Where have you been? Where do you keep going?"

"I've been busy. I had to attend to some business. I returned as soon as I could. I didn't want to be away, but I had to."

Sam stewed, clearly upset. "So, I cannot have you in the summer? At least we have the evenings."

"No Sam, we won't have the evenings either; you know that. Sarah and Phillip are known to barge in on me at all hours. Imagine the scene if you were there, all naked, and in they come."

Sam slammed her fork down. "Lord Blanchefort, it appears you are in quite a situation! I am to the point where you need to make a choice right here and now between them and me, and I will advise you that choosing them over me would be a bad, and possibly painful mistake for you!" She seized a large walnut from a nearby basket and shattered it in her pale fist.

Kay was unimpressed. "Really? I hear tell that you have been enjoying lunches in Arden with Lord Lon. What's that all about?"

"How did you find out about that?"

"Never mind. The point is that I know. Where have you been, and what were you discussing with Lon, if I might ask?"

"As I have said, I've been busy, and, regarding my lunch with Lord Lon, you may not ask, Kay. We were discussing a private matter, nothing that would interest you."

Kay was incensed. "Is that a fact? Sam, I want to know what you were talking about with Lon, and I want to know where you've been—now!"

"Or what?" she said rolling up her sleeves.

"Or, start eating this table, plates and all!"

And before another moment had passed, Kay and Sam were locked in a full-fledged fight/wrestling match. They were all over the place, throwing each other around, rocking the huge table in the hall. They hit the floor and started rolling around.

Soon, Kay had Sam by the head, and she had him by the waist, her legs squeezing the daylights out of him, her crossed shoes sticking up in the air.

As they struggled for position, Lord Davage and Countess Sygillis came into the hall with Lady Kilos walking behind. They'd come for breakfast.

Ki looked at them on the floor and shook her head.

✶ ✶ ✶ ✶ ✶

A few hours later, they were up in Kay's reading room. Kay had a scratched face and a few bruised ribs. Sam was doing all right. She treated his scratch with a damp cloth.

"I'm sorry about this morning, Sam," he said.

"It's all right, Kay. If you can't get into the occasional brawl with the person you love, who can you?"

She put the cloth down and settled into his arms.

"I'm sorry I've been so strange and moody lately, Kay, and I'm sorry that I was absent over the last few days. There are things that I can't tell you. I want to—I'm dying to, but I can't. Just know that everything I do, I do for you—for us. You mean everything to me, *Arin-Dan*. And, most of all, I'm sorry about this morning. Not about our little tussle—which I thought was kind of fun—but about almost making you choose between me and your cousins. That was very selfish and unfair of me."

Kay kissed her. "Sam, I think it's time we told Sarah and Phillip about us. They're trustworthy—they won't give up our secret."

"They won't accept me. Sarah hates me, and, after the ball, I don't think I like her much, either."

"She'll just have to see reason. Phillip will be fine. For Sarah, just remember, she values strength. If she gets in your face, don't back down no matter what."

✶ ✶ ✶ ✶ ✶

The sun set on winter. Tomorrow, Sarah and Phillip would return with their mother and father for yet another summer.

That evening Sam, true to her word, returned all of the books she had borrowed, and there were a bunch of them. They went to Lord Davage's study and put back the fifty or so books she'd borrowed. They went to the garden library in the west quarter and put back three books. In the big reading room in Countess Pardock's old tower, they put back ten books. Finally, they went to the hidden eight-sided library. They put back several books she had taken out.

"Did these books help you, in whatever you were looking for?" Kay asked.

"I hope so," she said vacantly as she fiddled with a huge blue book that didn't seem to fit properly on the shelf. She had to adjust several books and lay one on top of the others to make room.

Odd, Kay didn't recall any trouble fitting the books in before.

A large blue book?

"Hey," Kay said, "have I told you how much I love you lately?"

She didn't answer. "Sam?"

She lay there, unmoving, almost like she was dead.

* * * * *

The thing she had feared for years was nigh at hand. The thunderstorm she had foreseen and tried to ignore was ready to darken the skies at long last. She couldn't hold it back—it was here.

The demons were coming, and she wasn't ready.

She wasn't ready!

All the knowledge she had gathered, all her preparations— too late.

Her *Arin-Dan,* dying ...

The sadness that flowed through her was too much. It was just too much.

She saw her death, four armed, enraged. The demons watching and laughing, victorious as always. Her clawed hands at Kay's throat.

She wasn't ready.

She felt her mind detaching from her body, drifting away to quiet places. All the fear she felt, all the dread began to fall to the wayside, replaced with a pall of sweet indifference. In this lukewarm state, nothing mattered.

Head Swarm. She was falling into Head Swarm to protect herself from the unbearable torrent to come.

She casually noted that this was a big Head Swarm. Once in it, she probably couldn't be pulled out, ever. She would wither away over time and die, lost and content.

As she drifted away, she heard a voice in the distance. She heard singing. It was a song she'd never heard, sung with love and care. It was a song that tempted her, prompted her to stay, to come down from the inviting paradise of Head Swarm and return to the fear and troubles of the real world and listen.

Who was singing? Where did it come from?

She fell back into her body and listened.

It was Kay. In the hidden library, he was holding her limp body and was singing an Elder tune. He sang it softly into her ear. She felt his arms around her and listened to the song. She fell into a contented state, a much more blissful one than even the fields of Head Swarm could offer.

Kay's touch and his loving voice kept her from Head Swarm, gave her the strength to fight it off, and the courage to remain in the real world with a clear head, though the real world was soon to offer little but pain and sorrow.

How few Monamas had chosen pain over forgetfulness?

She couldn't have made that choice on her own—Kay helped her make it. She'd forgotten how strong Kay would one day be. Up until this point, it had been Sam who was the strong one, and Kay, blissfully unaware, the weak one. She and Kay were about to enter a new phase of their lives, where she would be in need, and he would have to be strong, where he would have to face the demons that were about to fall upon him all alone.

Was he up to what was coming? She had to have faith that he was.

"Don't let me go away, *Arin-Dan,*" she finally said, her eyes opening.

"I won't, *Cerri-Tela*. I want you here, with me."

He held her for the rest of the night and sang in her ear.

Despite the storm that was about to rage, it was the most contented and safe she had ever felt.

✶ ✶ ✶ ✶ ✶

The following afternoon was the usual cool, deep blue affair common in Blanchefort. Lord Davage and Kay were completing his afternoon CARG practice in the Holt courtyard in the Telmus Grove. The larger-than-life statue of mother that Kay had made for her birthday stood in a pebbled nook overlooking the courtyard. Kay had sheathed it in copper, and the statue had developed a nice greenish patina over the years. The statue bore a water jug on her shoulder, for the coming of Sygillis of Metatron to the House of Blanchefort breathed new life into the old House, which Kay symbolized with the water jug. Mother loved the statue, showed it to all her friends and spent a lot of time in the courtyard admiring it. "My son made this for me," she'd proudly say. She even used the jug as part of her design logo.

A close-knit family, everybody was nearby doing their own thing in the statue's shadow. Countess Sygillis and Lady Kilos were sitting on the low stone wall, arguing as usual. This time, their fight was centered on the cut of a new gown his mother was designing.

A fabric dummy floated in front of mother draped with a new gown she was working on. Lady Hathaline sat nearby, quiet as usual. Lord Davage had promised to go flying with her as soon as he was finished with Kay's lesson. Maser was playing on a little mound of dirt under a huge tree with Lt. Kilos.

A member of the House staff arrived in the courtyard and approached Countess Sygillis. She halted her argument with Lady Kilos and turned to her.

"I am here, my countess, as you requested," the staff member said.

Sygillis held up a novelty shirt with a terrible holopicture of herself on the front—similar to the one Ki had made Kay buy in the village.

"You are to prowl every shop in the village, and, if you discover any more of these shirts, you are to confiscate them at once on my orders, am I clear?"

"Yes, my countess. And if I happen to see anybody wearing the offending shirts, my countess?"

"You are to reimburse the person and seize the shirt off his or her protesting back if need be. If anyone gives you misery, you are to advise them to see me personally. Off you go."

The staff member ran off. Ki had a devilish grin on her face, as she had stockpiled quite a few of the shirts to use for any number of nefarious purposes. No doubt, they would come in handy.

Sygillis turned to Davage. "Dav, I'm at my wits end with that woman."

"To whom are you referring?" Davage asked, as if he didn't know.

"Her—the Duchess of Oyln. I am ready to challenge her to a fight to the death in the arena with the whole League watching; winner take all. The loser dies."

Davage laughed. "Isn't Duchess Oyln ready to deliver another child?"

"I don't care. I'll fight the both of them."

"Syg, you promised you'd quit fighting with Torri," Davage said.

Sygillis wadded up the shirt and threw it at Davage. "I'm not the one who keeps launching attacks of humiliation."

Davage was having a hard time keeping from laughing. "Well, Syg, after you 'bare-assed' the duchess at the Hubert ball, you had to expect some sort of revenge coming your way, yes? Instead of wanting to get the poor, and, might I say, rather pregnant duchess in the arena, why don't you try using your wits? Get even. If she's circulating shirts with an ugly picture of you on the breast, then why don't you circulate a shirt with an even uglier picture of her on it? Fair's fair, I suppose."

"Mother, I think I can get hold of some naked and grotesquely pregnant pictures of the duchess if you want them," Ki said.

Sygillis appeared inspired, then shook her head and turned to Ki, resuming their previous argument.

"Lady Kilos," Sygillis spoke in a firm, impatient voice, "I am not creating clothing for a courtesan. The neckline shall plunge no further, and that is final!" She adjusted and pinned the fabric.

"Mother," Ki replied tartly, "the fashions coming out of Armenelos are much more courageous regarding the display and wear of cleavage this year, and I insist our Blanchefort fashions meet the challenge. I am trying to do you a favor."

Ki, frustrated, turned to Davage. "Father, will you please talk some sense into Mother?"

Davage put his CARG down and took them both by the chin. "Oh, you two clucking hens, always pecking away at each other."

Syg turned the dummy to face Davage. "What do you think, love? Do you like it?"

Davage looked at the gown. "I love it, darling. Very nice shape. Nice colors."

"Father, the neckline is unacceptable," Ki stated firmly. "You shall not catch me wearing that gown."

Syg turned to her. "You'll not be wearing such a thing until you are thirty years old, am I understood?"

"Why not? Kay's allowed to get into a twisting, rolling fight on the floor with his girlfriend, so why can't I wear an interesting gown."

"You shall be involved in a fight here in a moment sure enough, young lady."

Davage looked at it again. "Well, Syg, perhaps you could be a bit more daring, perhaps a tad lower."

Kay, watching, smiled and put his coat back on and saddled his CARG, the lesson over.

"So, Dav, how's my son coming along here in his training?" Sygillis asked tossing Kay's hair and giving him a kiss on the cheek.

"He's got a fine sword arm, and he uses that CARG like he's done it all his life. Though, you shouldn't hold it one-handed like a rapier. It's a CARG, Kay. Use both hands. I keep telling you that, and you keep ignoring my advice."

Kay leveled it, holding it like a fencer. "But Father, like this I can easily cross any incoming attack, while leaving my open hand free to brandish a pistol perhaps."

"A pistol?" Davage smiled, and in a blazingly fast move crossed Kay's CARG with his own. Kay's silver CARG flew out of his hand and spiraled off into the trees landing at the feet of the statue.

"You see, Kay, now you have both hands free. Just imagine if I were an enemy. You need both hands on your weapon at all times."

Kay turned to his brother Maser. "Maser, can you go get my CARG, chief?"

Maser said something inaudible and scurried off into the trees, returning a moment later holding Kay's CARG.

Overhead, a familiar black ship streaked across the sky, heading toward the farther reaches of the Grove.

Davage watched it pass. "Ah, looks like your aunt, uncle and cousins have returned." He checked his timepiece. "Right on time, too."

"Father," Kay asked, "may I be off? I'd like to greet them." He was excited.

Davage pushed his hat back and checked his timepiece again. "Certainly. If you see your aunt and uncle, tell them we'll be along shortly. It's good to have them back."

"Ki," Kay asked, saddling his CARG, "Want to come with me?"

"And get yelled at by Sarah? No thanks. Creation it's going to be a long summer."

"Suit yourself." Kay gave his mother a kiss on the cheek and tore off into the trees.

Lord Phillip and Lady Sarah of Blanchefort

9—Sarah and Phillip of Blanchefort

Kay roughly met up with his cousins Sarah and Phillip, and after a brief laughing melee, they were all hugs and smiles.

Sarah and Phillip were a perfect blend of Blanchefort and Ruthven. They were both tall and thin, like a standard Blanchefort, and they had the thoughtful yet rugged look of the Ruthvens. Unlike her genial mother and father, Sarah, with her rolled, tailed blue hair was a real firecracker and the spitting image of her grandmother, Countess Hermilane, also a firecracker in her day. Sarah had inherited every bit of her grandmother's rather pugnacious temperament. Sarah never met a fight she didn't like: words, fists, sticks or whatever. It didn't matter; she was always ready. Phillip, her younger brother of ten minutes, was the recreation of their father, Lord Peter. He was handsome and auburn-headed and had fully inherited his father's hands and thoughtfulness as well. Rather like his older brother Milos, he was highly intelligent and studious, but, unlike his scholarly brother, he had a love of fun and adventure, and hanging out with Sarah and Kay gave him more than he could manage.

The two of them tended to wear Ruthven garb: white linen shirts, brown pants and tall boots with the long black duster their father used to wear during his pirating days as a member of the Duke of Oyln's Black Goshawk gang. Lady Poe had long given up trying to get Sarah to wear a Blanchefort gown—she wasn't having any of it. "Peter!" she would complain to her husband, "will you please ask your daughter to wear her beautiful gown?" But Sarah, stubborn unless it was a special occasion or Lady Poe's birthday, wouldn't budge. Lady Poe, in frustration, often said, "Young lady, it's a good thing for you that I am your mother, and not your aunt, Countess Pardock, for she would slap your bottom and stuff you into one without mercy!"

✶ ✶ ✶ ✶ ✶

After they finished beating each other up in greeting, they immediately decided to go to Subra Courtyard, a secluded and somewhat remote courtyard in the Grove near Carahil's Walk where they often went. It was their place, their secret spot where there was nobody but the three of them. Here they came to practice with their CARGs and SAPPs; they'd lugged in several practice ones which they stacked in a trunk behind the wall. Phillip had brought in a telescope, a hammock, a portable terminal and a small cooler in which to put snacks— a veritable home away from home. It was a place to simply to relax and share their thoughts, at ease to say whatever came into their heads.

Sarah was walking around with Kay's silver CARG. "So, there was this lunatic threatening the village of Green Sabre, right, and the locals came to the Duke for help. He and Uncle Johnnie went to investigate, and you know what they found?"

Kay was flopped in the hammock, and Phillip sat nearby typing into the portable terminal. "What did they find, Sarah?" Kay asked indulging her. The three of them were already well into summer mode.

"They found a demon with no skin. The demon was the lunatic, and the Duke and Father and Uncle Johnnie pursued it through Green Sabre." Sarah spoke with relish; she loved this sort of thing.

"Then, they cornered it at the gravesite of Junius, a great Esther hero, where the demon summoned a host of Berserkacides to fight the Duke. They met the Berserkacides and killed the demon. Creation, I wish I'd been there."

Kay shook his head. "Well, maybe next time."

"Did you get my posts, Kay? I've got all sorts of new places to investigate along the Gaston Way near the old Tardy ruins. I got a few tips. We're going to have a busy summer."

"Sounds grand," Kay replied.

Phillip was still typing away on the terminal.

"Who are you talking to, Phillip?" Kay asked.

Sarah replied. "He's got himself a new girlfriend. She's a Paulie-girl from Conwell."

"Not true," Phillip said, still staring into the terminal. "She's too tame. I happen to like them a little wild."

Sarah approached Kay. "Have you been practicing with your Sight over the winter? You said you would."

"I have, Sarah, but it didn't do any good. I don't have it."

Sarah lit her Sight, her eyes glowing a soft blue to match her hair. "Now, Kay, all you have to do is relax and let it flow. See, look at me. See how it works?"

Kay lay there on the hammock. "I am relaxed, Sarah. No good. I got nothing."

She knocked him on the shoulder with his CARG. "Come on, Kay, give it a try. Just think how happy it'll make your dad." Though Sarah tried to hide it with a lot of bluster, she was just as matronly as her mother, Lady Poe, though if one mentioned it to her, she would get rather rank.

Kay took a deep breath. "Nothing."

"You're not even trying, are you, you bag?"

Phillip smiled and closed his terminal. "Don't let her put you off, Kay. You should see her. She's got eyes for that Lord Posey fellow from Bern. She's probably just missing him right now."

Sarah quieted her Sight and shot Phillip a deadly look. "I told you not to say anything about that, Phillip! Besides, I'll not marry a guy named Posey. I am not a Posey. Do I look like a Posey? I'll marry into House Champion, or Colt or Midnight, something that sounds cool. Sarah of Colt—yes, I like that."

Sarah went to the cooler and got out something to drink. "So, Kay, how's your correspondence? You got anybody floating around out there? Lady Krista of Gamboa wanted me to ask. She's all keen on you. Says she's written to you."

"I don't recall getting any letters from Gamboa."

Phillip laughed. "Lady Krista of Gamboa is rather ugly, Kay, in case you're wondering."

"She is not."

Kay shrugged. "Well, I've been wanting to share something with you two for awhile now actually."

Sarah took a drink. "What is it?"

Kay got off the hammock and kicked at the ground. "What if told you that

I've been seeing someone for about five years running? Somebody whom I feel very serious about. What if I told you that?"

"Five years?" Sarah repeated finishing her drink. "You've been seeing someone for five years, and you've not said anything?"

"Yes."

"How'd you manage that?"

"Well, it's pretty easy in the winter since you're not here, and in the summer, we just take a step back and cool it. But, it's gotten to the point where we don't want to cool it anymore."

Phillip was curious. "Why've you hidden her from us, Kay? Are you feeling shy?"

"No."

Sarah was getting perturbed. "Well, who is it? Who's this lady? You shouldn't keep secrets from us—we're your pals."

Kay sighed. "Sam, come on out. I'd like to properly introduce you to my cousins."

After a moment, Sam came walking out of the trees. "Hello," she said softly, all smiles.

Sarah reacted violently. "Her? Kay, you've been seeing … *her?"*

"I have, Sarah. I wanted to tell you two before, but it didn't seem the right time."

"What about the scene at the ball? You looked like you were going to be sick when she started making advances toward you!"

"That was just an act."

Sarah was incensed. "You don't know how to act, Kay, and, of all people, why her? For Creation's sake, if you're that desperate, I'll marry you myself—anything but her!" Sarah cried. "She's a pre-berserk Berserkacide!"

"Sarah …"

Sam interrupted. "Lady Blanchefort, Kay told me that you might object."

"You bet I'll object! Kay's my best friend. He's like a brother to me, and it's my duty to knock him in the head when he puts two feet wrong!"

Sarah cuffed Kay in the back of his head, knocking his hat off. "What are you thinking?" She turned to Sam. "What have you done to my cousin? You've bewitched him!"

"You're right; I have bewitched him. And he has bewitched me. It took years. We started off as friends, and it grew from there. He's my *Arin-Dan*, Lady Sarah. *'My love'*. Monama women do not use that term lightly."

"Talk normal!" Sarah shouted.

"We were hoping that you would wish to be my friend."

Phillip spoke up. "You know, Lady Sammidoran, Lord Lon has not stopped talking about you since the ball."

Sam smiled. "Has he? He is adorable—truly. But, I am in love with your cousin. I've loved him my whole life, truth be told. I will be his countess some day."

Sarah turned red. "The flaming hell you will! Kay, if you're hot for a lady, I've got a bunch of friends that I could introduce you to, namely Lady Krista of Gamboa! Anything but this Monama, Berserkacide scum!"

"Sarah, that's enough!"

"Where's your four arms, *Sam*?" she asked. "Don't all you Berserkacides have four arms?"

Sam approached and stood nose-to-nose with her. "I don't have four arms, Lady Sarah. Kay has told me you are a fiery person, and I can see that. Kay has also told me that you admire strength above all else. Tell you what, why don't we step away into the woods and have a private chat, just you and me? I think you've got a bit of honesty coming to you." The nervous energy between the two of them was thick. Sam was spoiling for a fight.

"You'll use your claws on me!"

Sam showed Sarah her nails—they had been trimmed down and painted red. "For my Kay, I have shortened my beloved fingernails to a more Vith-like length."

Sarah poked her in the chest. "If we go into the trees, we're not going to be talking much!"

Sam dropped a few inches as she removed her Monama shoes. "That's fine; any way you want. I do not intend to come between you and Kay, Sarah; nor will I allow you to come between Kay and me. I want us all to be friends. I don't wish to make *Arin-Dan* choose between us."

"You'll use some sort of Monama magic against me! You'll go Berserkacide on me!"

"I will not. Come on, what are we waiting for?"

"It'll take me a minute or two to power up so I can pound you."

"Take all the time you need."

Sam held out her shoes. "Will you hold these for me, please?" she said to Kay. He took them, and Sarah huffed.

"Be careful," Kay said.

"Thanks!" both Sam and Sarah replied. Together they walked out of the courtyard into the trees.

Kay and Phillip stood there. Phillip was gob smacked. "Well, Kay, this is a surprise. You keep a secret well. I had no idea, and there's been no gossip, which is strange. In fact, I heard Lady Sammidoran recently lunched with Lord Lon in Arden. I was happy for him."

"Boy, word gets around. She did. She's working on some sort of project that Lon's helping her with."

"A project? What sort of project?"

"Don't know—she won't tell me."

Phillip was still trying to absorb all of this information. "And Lady Kilos. Is she aware of this?"

"She is."

"And she's not said anything? I'd think she, of all people, an avid gossiper..."

"She's actually quite stalwart at keeping secrets when she wants to. She's been a big help and has welcomed Sam."

Kay stood there holding Sam's shoes and looked to the trees. "I don't like this, Phillip. Sarah doesn't know what she's getting into. Sam's pretty strong."

"Sarah can handle herself. I suppose if anything gets her respect, this will."

Dimly, they could hear a struggle in the distance. Leaves rustled, dry tree limbs snapped. Clearly, Sam and Sarah were going at it.

"And what do you think, Phillip? What's your reaction to all of this?"

"I think Lon's going to be pretty disappointed; that's my reaction. I don't mind Lady Sammidoran. I think she's very beautiful; I noticed her at the ball myself. Again, I'm mostly shocked that you kept quiet about it for so long."

"I wanted to tell you guys, but Sam has insisted on keeping it a secret—it's a Monama tradition, so let's leave it at that."

There was a cry and the sound of bodies falling on top of each other coming from the trees.

"I think I should go over there."

"No, no, Kay, let them finish. So, Kay, do you really have feelings for Lady Monama?"

"Yes, Phillip, I do. I love her."

"Well, that's good enough for me. As long as you're happy, that's all I care about. And don't listen to Sarah. Lady Krista of Gamboa looks like a man in a gown. I suppose I should start poking around, too. We're not kids anymore, are we?"

"Anybody interest you? That Paulie lady Sarah mentioned, perhaps?"

"No, she seems fairly keen to begin something with me, but I'm not really interested. I have come to the conclusion that I like a rather wild woman—like those urchins trawling the streets of Calvert. Sort of like Lt. Kilos, or Sarah—I like that kind of spirit. Most ladies of standing are too tame. The Duke introduced me to Lady Spree of Conwell last winter, and I found that she didn't interest me in the least. Too quiet and shy. I like an element of danger. I like to run and be chased. Ladies of standing don't chase after anybody. Maybe I should hunt down a Black Hat like your dad and the Duke did."

Phillip looked up at the sky. "I've had an image in my thoughts for some time, an image in green and brown of a lady—a fierce one. I suppose I compare all the ladies I meet to this image in my head, to this woman who doesn't exist."

"You dream of a lady, Phillip?" Kay asked.

He laughed. "I suppose so. This lady, though quite pretty, is crass and rough—a real handful. I have no idea what I'd do if I actually met up with someone like that."

Sam and Sarah emerged from the trees. They were both a little mussed up. Sam had the skirt of her gown knotted and hiked up between her pale legs. She pulled the knot, and it came down like a stage curtain. Kay handed Sam her shoes back.

"Lady Sarah and I have been talking. I think we've come to an understanding," Sam said leaning against him as she put them back on. A slight mouse was forming in purples on her lip.

Kay looked at Sarah. "Sarah, are you all right?"

"I'm fine," she said gruffly. Her tightly rolled up and pulled back blue hair was all over the place. Dry leaves hung limply on her duster.

Kay went to the cooler and pulled out two cold drinks, handing one to Sam and a red one to Sarah. Sarah took hers and held it against her right eye. She was sure to have a shiner by morning. She probed her teeth with her tongue.

Sam took a drink and approached Kay. "Lady Sarah is very strong. She is a fine fighter. She can fight every bit as well as you can, Kay."

The compliment appeared to make her brighten a bit. "You've been fighting with Kay?"

"We fight all the time. We had a big one the other day, didn't we, Kay?"

Kay nodded. "So, what do you say, Sarah?" Kay asked. "Are we all friends? Can you deal with this? And you better say 'yes,' otherwise, it'll be you and I walking into the trees next."

She looked at the ground and toyed with her drink. "I still don't know if I trust her. I'm going to be watching you, *Sam*, and, if I seeing anything funny, I'm coming after you." She popped her can open with a gassy rush.

"Funny?" Sam said. "You mean like this?" Sam grabbed Kay and gave him a huge kiss.

Sarah stepped in between them. "Yes, like that. By Creation, no kissing when I'm around. That's the first rule! And no touching, and no talking either!"

Phillip laughed.

"No kissing, oh that's going to be a tough one," Sam said.

Phillip smiled and clapped Sam on the shoulder. "Well, Lady Sammidoran, welcome to our little troupe. I guess the first order of business is to see if we can select somebody for poor Lon. He's going to be heartbroken when he finds out."

"Kay has told me that I can count on your discretion. Our relationship must be kept secret for now—even from Lord Lon. Will you promise?"

"I promise," Phillip said. "You needn't worry about me, or Sarah either. Right, Sarah?"

She grumbled something and looked at the ground again.

"Wonderful," Sam said, "but that doesn't mean we can't find a lucky lady for Lord Lon. Whom do you suggest, Phillip?"

Unused cover concept by Carol Phillips

10—What Sam Did

Summer was a busy time at the castle, full of noise and fighting. Kay's cousins, Sarah and Phillip, absolutely dominated his time, giving him little peace, day or night. Sarah was well known for using the zip line from her tower, shooting across in her pajamas and barging right in through his 89th floor window whenever she had a thought for a crazy new scheme.

And Sarah had lots of crazy schemes, so she was zipping in all the time. Sarah was *slowly* accepting Sam into the group, though she still watched her with a dubious eye.

The only time Kay was separated from Sarah and Phillip was when he had an official duty to perform, as the next heir to the House. Sarah and Phillip, being ranked much farther down the order, got out of all those things, Sarah often snickering as Kay was led away to do whatever. "Try to stay awake," she'd whisper.

✶ ✶ ✶ ✶ ✶

Tuesday. Sam, as usual on Tuesdays, had gone home attending to her own required duties to the south. She would be back in the morning. Kay, Sarah and Phillip had gone to the bath house for a nice soak.

Before long, Kay was summoned via telepathy by his mother.

<Kay, you're needed in the castle. You have a visitor.>

<I do?> Kay was shocked. He never had visitors. *<Who is it?? Is it Sam?>*

<It is not, Sam; however, a young lady is here to see you.>

<Me? But I'm here at the bath house with Sarah and Phillip. We were planning an outing later.>

<You can play with your cousins another time. Come along. She's waiting for you in the Firth House.>

Kay dressed and popped his hat on. "Got to go," he told Sarah and Phillip.

"Where are you off to?" Sarah demanded to know, bobbing in the water.

"Got a visitor."

"You? Who is it?"

"Don't know."

Kay exited the bathhouse, walking west through the lily garden, his CARG swinging at his side.

"Make it fast! We're heading to the Gaston Way later to do some more investigating!" she called. "Don't forget!"

Kay made his way back to the castle and went into the Palantine courtyard. It was a vast octagonal courtyard taking up most of the northern wing of the castle, heavily landscaped and planted with flowering trees and quiet pools. Underneath a statue at one end of the courtyard was the secret entrance to the Blanchefort bowling alley. Four medium-sized towers, Cooper, Tremblay, Maseron and Joliet, were accessible only from within the courtyard.

At the northern end of the courtyard was Firth House, a tea-room built of black stone by the old Vith centuries prior. Legend told it was the original founding of Castle Blanchefort, now surrounded and dwarfed by it. It had fallen into ruin during an attack by the old Bloodsteins centuries back and had festered as a pile of blackened masonry for some time. Lord Sadric of Blanchefort had it rebuilt and made into a lovely tearoom for the family's private use. The Blanchefort used it mostly as a secluded spot to meet new acquaintances. Countess Pardock had first met her future husband, Ferddie of Vincent, in the Firth House. So far, Kay's use of the Firth House to meet young ladies visiting from across the League had been quite limited. Lady Poe had often used it when meeting new gentlemen callers before meeting Lord Peter.

Kay emerged into the sunny Palantine and made his way through the winding paths to the Firth House; its distinctive low battlements reached up just higher than the surrounding trees like a pair of hands holding palms up toward the sky.

He wondered who it could be awaiting him. He'd only had one previous meeting in the Firth House. It was with a girl named Mertha of Trim, a rather homely person from Remnath whose bad complexion was matched only by her bad teeth.

'Mert the Terrible' Sarah called her. She had been a nice enough girl, and Kay made a friend, but nothing more.

Now, somebody else waited within.

Kay approached the black-stone structure. A new oaken door waited bearing the Blanchefort coat-of-arms, and he pulled it open. Inside was a fairly spacious room floored in rare woods from Hoban and upholstered with fine fabrics of teal and canary. The staff kept the place in immaculate condition. Lord Sadric was a well-remembered host, and a full-sized statue of him greeted all those entering, forever presiding over the goings on in the house. Someone sat in a chair at the opposite end.

Kay bowed. "Well met and good afternoon. I am Kabyl of Blanchefort, son of Lord Davage and Countess Sygillis."

The figure turned. "Hi, Kay, it's just me." The figure stood, and Lady Kilos emerged into the light.

"Ki—you're my mysterious lady caller?"

"I am."

"What is this?"

She approached. "Well, it's awful hard to get a moment alone with you, what with Sarah taking up every spare moment of the day."

"You and Sarah really need to have a heart to heart, Ki. She's not a bad person truly, and she's got a lot more of her mother in her than she lets on."

"Aunt Poe is a great lady. Sarah, however, is a rotten, loud-mouthed Shocktyte."

"Ouch."

"I sort of miss the winter so I can spend a little time with my brother. Anyway, I wanted to talk to you, and the only way to get a moment is to make an appointment, I guess."

"Ok, here I am, Ki. What's on your mind?"

Ki looked around and spied the statue of Lord Sadric. "Not, here—too many old ghosts rolling around. Let's go up to the top. I'll see you there." With that, she coiled up a Waft and blasted out of the room, shaking the chandelier in the process.

Kay chose a more conventional method to get to the top. He made his way

up the stairs and emerged into the sunshine after a healthy climb. There was Ki standing on the battlements, admiring the view of the courtyard below and the rising bulk of the castle all around. Her blue hair looked like icy fire in the sunlight.

"Took you long enough," she said. "Why didn't you Waft up?"

"I thought I'd walk."

Ki smiled. "You need to work on that, Kay. Sam would never approve."

"Yes, but Sam's not here."

"I like it up here," she said. "Very pretty. I can't wait until I entertain young gentlemen. I think I'll make them climb the stairs to see me. I suppose I've got five years to wait before my face clears."

Kay removed his triangle hat. "A man worth courting shouldn't care what your face looks like."

Ki smiled and pulled a locket from the folds of her bodice. She opened it, and two silver ladybugs of superior size came fluttering out. They moved lightly through the air like little jewels.

Kay recognized what they were. "Whispers. Those are Whispers, right? Some of Aunt Poe's familiars?"

"You're right," Ki said. "They come in handy. Now, nobody can hear us talking, and nobody can see us up here, just in case Sarah comes blundering in."

Apparently, Ki wanted assurance of privacy, and two Whispers would provide just that. Kay moved to the edge of the battlement and stood beside her. Beyond the battlement wall, the green floor of the Palantine was about a hundred feet down.

"So, what's on your mind, Ki?"

"I wanted to get some time alone with you to talk about Sam, actually."

"What about her?"

Ki hesitated and considered her words. "You know that I like Sam. I like her a lot. She's my friend, and I'm very glad that we've all become close. But, you're my brother and my first loyalty is to you, and I wanted to make sure you're aware of certain things. What I have to say might change your mind about Sam, or color your feelings for her a little. I hope not, but, I have to say my bit, for good or ill."

Kay was a little taken aback by Ki's tone. "All right, Ki, I'm listening. Sarah's nowhere to be seen. Let's have it."

She collected her thoughts. Her white-blue hair shimmered in the sun. Her face was still very puffy from her childhood, especially around the eyes, but, once it cleared up, Ki would be a true beauty. It was easy to see. One of the Whispers buzzed past her face. "You, Kay, are unlike all of the other young lords in Vithland, and in Zenon, and in Remnath and Esther, too. Did you know that?"

"You forgot Calvert."

"No I didn't. I don't count them. My point is—you should be here in the Firth House meeting young ladies several times a week at least. Your correspondence pile should be huge. When was the last time you were here to meet a lady?"

"Last year, when Mertha of Trim came."

"Yeah, Big Mert, I remember that. Don't you find it odd that you are a virtual wallflower at the age of twenty-two, when you should be one of the most highly sought after prizes on Kana? Traditionally, unattached gentlemen and ladies begin formally courting as soon as they get past their Puffies." Ki touched her puffy face for a moment, hating it.

"As you've never seemed to have had it, Kay, you should have been courting actively for the past two years, and I recall Mother stating she would not allow you to court until, at least, the age of twenty. So, here it is, two years later, and you see virtually no one."

"I'm not really looking, Ki. I've got Sam."

"Yes, you do, but that's a secret relationship, Kay. As you've not announced yourselves to the League, you are officially available. As the next Lord of Blanchefort, you should be on the top of anybody's wish list."

Kay seated himself on the battlement, the hundred foot fall to the cobbled path below precariously close. "Just give it to me, Ki. What are you getting at?"

"I'm saying you are isolated in the League, Kay. Look at me, I'm only eighteen and puffed up like a marshmallow; yet, I'm already getting more correspondence from young gentlemen than I can handle. I can't actively court them yet with my damn face and Mother monitoring the situation like a rat peddler, but I'm already lining up my prospects for the future. Phillip has lots of mail, Hath is starting to receive notices, and even that Jo-Boy Sarah is getting some. And you, out-ranking us all, have almost none. Doesn't that seem odd to you?"

Kay sighed and adjusted his hat. "Sure, I guess."

"I think Sam has done something over the years to keep you isolated from those who might prove to be a competition for her. Kay, it's obvious that Sam has had her sights on you for a long time. I remember hearing a voice coming out of your room once when you were sleeping. '*Arin-Dan, Arin-Dan,*' it said. Do you know what that means in her language?"

Kay nodded.

"From my research, that word isn't something Monama women just toss around. It means she is serious about you, Kay, that, in her mind, you are hers. Having gotten to know Sam, I don't see her as the kind of person to sit back meekly and allow things like fate or chance to get in the way of what she wants—to get in the way of her *Arin-Dan.* I think she's taken matters into her own hands. I think she's actively eliminated her competition, either literally or mechanically."

One of the Whispers landed on the black stone surface of the battlement. Kay watched it move about with interest. "Be specific, please."

"All right. Do you know Lady Wilhelmina of Pole?"

"No."

"I do. She's a friend of mine from Saga in Barrow. A real chatterbox—you think I like to talk; I'm nothing compared to her. She's soon to become the Duchess of Holly, I think, if all goes well. It's not a great Household to attach herself to, but it sounds good anyway. She's told me that she has written to you over ten times through the years and never gotten anything back. Now, I know you're not the most attentive letter-writer; however, you're not so rude as to ignore a lady's query ten times in a row."

"I don't remember ever getting a letter from her."

"No, I don't think you would. What about from Hadjinal of Effington or Lycona of Pert? Hadjinal told me she's written to you seventeen times and Lycona eight times. Lycona even told me she bought a magical doll from Bazz to cast a spell on you with it out of revenge for ignoring her. However, neither of those two hold a candle to Lady Renceval of Mystery; she's the record-holder, I think. She has written you over thirty times, she says. She even gave me a letter to hand-carry to you."

"Again, that name doesn't ring a bell."

"No—though I set it on your pile personally last year. I guess it vanished, didn't it? So, I'm asking the question—what happened to all these correspondences? The Vithland Guild of Posts is not so bad to mishandle *all* of those letters."

"So, you're thinking that Sam intercepted them."

"Yes, I am. Sam can do some amazing things, and she can see the future. She probably knows exactly when some babe out there is penning you a note and goes and fetches it before you have a chance to read it. And, that's not all, no no. Stealing letters is tame compared to what else I think Sam's done."

The stream below babbled and caught Kay's interest. "Now what? What else has Sam done?"

"Sarah loves talking and reading about the bizarre, correct? The unusual and gothic? She's so droll. I hear tell she is fascinated by the Wraith of Gaston."

"That's right. In fact, she wants to head out there again today to do some 'investigating' as she puts it near Tardy."

Ki laughed. "Oh, Sarah and the little things that drive her. Would you be so shocked if I told you that I'm quite certain that Sam *is* the Wraith of Gaston? That you've been kissing and wrestling with one of the biggest phantasms of Sarah's imagination?"

An interesting series of images flashed through his head. He laughed. "And, I suppose you have compelling proof?"

"I wouldn't have mentioned it if I hadn't." The sun moved past the edge of the towers surrounding the courtyard, and the two of them were suddenly in shade. "I didn't even think the Wraith of Gaston existed—I mean it's a rather silly story isn't it? A pale, spectral creature, wreathed in black, occasionally haunting the lonely mountain passes of the Gaston, vexing some passers while sparing others."

"I'm aware of the story."

"Wilhelmina of Pole—yes, she, once again. A few years back, mother transacted a rather large business agreement with her father, Lord Venture of Pole. Apparently, at some point in the transaction, you came up as a topic of discussion, as did Lord Venture's daughter, Wilhelmina. That happens quite a bit, Kay, in case you were wondering, with businessmen and women mixing business and pleasure liberally. Mother and Lord Pole began comparing notes, discovered you and she were of similar ages, and she invited her here, to the Firth House, to meet you. She thought, perhaps, you might make a friend, possibly more."

"I wasn't aware of that."

Down below in the courtyard, Sarah and Phillip appeared through the south gate, dusters flattering, the both of them heading toward the Firth House. Sarah was loudly muttering something about being late to the Gaston.

Ki laughed and leaned over the side. "We're up here, you manky git!" she yelled, Sarah and Phillip hearing and seeing nothing past the Whisper's veil. They went into the Firth House clearly looking for Kay and then came back out a few mo-

ments later, Sarah in a froth. She headed toward the secret entrance to the Blanchefort bowling alley, opened the hatch and went down. Phillip stood on the path. He lit his Sight for a moment and looked around. He quickly saw them standing on the battlements. He waved, and Kay waved back.

"He's seen us. Don't worry about Phillip. He won't give us up to Sarah."

Ki also waved. "I like Phillip. I'd like a man like him to court me someday, calm, fairly cerebral; I can't believe he's Sarah's brother."

"You need to come off Sarah a little. She is a good friend and a good sister."

"She started this, not me."

"True, but perhaps if you swallowed your pride a little, you could end it, and we could all be friends."

Sarah came storming back out of the bowling alley entrance. She closed the hatch, and they both headed back toward the south gate, Sarah in a clear tizzy. Phillip glanced back at them once as they went.

"Looks like you're in for it later, Kay. Anyway, back to the topic at hand. Guess what happened to Wilhelmina as she made her way down the Gaston?" Ki continued. "I'll give you three guesses, but I'm hoping you only need one."

Kay watched Sarah and Phillip disappear back into the castle, marveling at the effectiveness of the Whispers. "She travelled here in her coach, dropping into the Gaston Way to avoid the restricted skyways of Pithnar and Atalan, and met the Wraith somewhere along the way. Is that right?"

"She certainly did. She described the ordeal in hearty detail. It made quite an impression on her. She said it came upon them in the wild and ran upon the ground, as fast as their coach could fly, and when they took to the air to escape it, it followed, running through the air after them. Wilhelmina got a good look at it; it was like a thunderstorm with a glowing person hidden within. Those black eyes on a pale face, she said, enough to chill her soul. She said it 'glowed' with an infernal light. She said she didn't remember it having a mouth, but it definitely had claws. She said it disabled their coach, doing a fair amount of damage in the process, until they had to veer out of the Gaston and return to Barrow quite convinced the Vithlands are haunted. That's when Wilhelmina started writing to you, as she was too chicken to return."

"You're assuming that Sam's capable of such an incredible feat."

"Kay, we both know Sam is capable of doing a lot. Look at how strong she is, how fast. Look how she can alter her appearance and how she can zero in on you just by using her nose. And what about when she speaks to you even when she's not here—no com, no holonet? How does she do that?"

"She told me how that works. She may transmute her voice across the earth."

"All the more proof to illustrate my point. Sam is very powerful. Also, do you remember the word she said during the future-telling?"

"She said: '*Olonol'.*"

"I looked it up. It means: 'machine'. What machine? What was she talking about?"

"I don't know. I asked her, and she won't say. She's like that. Has all sorts of secrets she doesn't think I can handle."

A few staff members came out and began tending to the grounds. Kay and Ki sat silent, listening to the sounds of their tools as they clipped the bushes and raked the gravel, the sounds carrying. "I'm sorry I had to tell you this, Kay."

"I'm sorry too," he replied. "I'm sorry you think I'm so stupid, Ki."

Ki turned to him. "Kay, I ..."

"Of course you're correct. About everything. Sam is quite powerful. She can do all sorts of things. She could break me in two if she wanted, or gut me in an instant. The only variable you didn't figure into your thoughts was me. Ki, I've known Sam has been doing something all these years to keep me from exposure to potential rivals. I simply never bothered to rationalize it out in such a forensic manner as you have—it had no meaning. As you mentioned, I know that Sam has been near to me my whole life. I have no idea what drew her to me, or what compelled her to leave her fog-bound home and come to the north in the killing cold. What Monama besides the paid seer does that? I have no idea what Sam sees when she looks at me. A great man? A powerful man? A fool? What is there to be seen? I really don't know, and I'm sure if I were to ask, she wouldn't answer. All I know is that if I have been fortunate enough to command such devotion from someone like Sam, who am I to question it? I have been blessed. I have been enriched by the girl with the pale face and black eyes."

"You're not disturbed? The letter stealing? The Wraith?"

"I wouldn't expect anything less from her. And, if I were to shrink from such a thing, I wouldn't be a Vith, would I? As you said, she's not the sort of person to simply sit back and hope for the best. I actually admire that about her. And, I'm certain Sam is not the first lady in the League to take steps to sabotage a rival. Such things do happen, right, Ki?"

Ki smiled. "Yes, they do. I just can't think of anyone who went to such extremes. Usually ladies pay to have somebody else perform such things for them. There's a guild on Planet Fall specializing in just that."

"Sam doesn't do anything half-way, and she doesn't have the money or the means to contact a guild on Planet Fall. No, Sam would take matter into her own hands. Isn't that the Sam we both know and love?"

"I suppose so. So, Kay, how long have you known about this?"

"A long time. I'm not sure when I put it all together, but it makes sense. None of what you've just told me is at all surprising."

"And, you're just acting when you present yourself like a complete, dull-witted moron?"

"Well, let's not quite go that far, shall we, Ki, with the name calling?"

They laughed. Kay held out his hand. "Come on, Ki, let's get out of here."

Ki took his hand, and they exited the battlement, moving down the black stairs. She collected her two Whispers and put them back into her locket. "One last thing, Kay. You're certain you are at peace with this? I mean, to be spoken for your whole life? Have you no thoughts of what else might be out there?"

They exited the Firth House.

"Not really, no. I've no need to look anywhere else. I have all I need." They moved down the path and re-entered the castle.

"Hey, what are you doing?" came Sarah's loud voice. "Creation, we were about to list you as a missing person! Where've you been?"

"*Speaking of morons*," Ki said under her breath.

"Just having a talk with my sister, Sarah."

Sarah marched up. "What do you want to talk to her for? Your sister's making us late. The Gaston? Remember, we're heading out there? I don't want it to get dark on us!"

Ki spoke up. "Why do you want to go to the Gaston, Sarah?"

"No reason that would interest *you*," she replied in a rude voice. "Come on, Kay, let's go. Phillip's got the Ripcar ready and waiting!" Sarah grabbed Kay by the shoulder and pulled him down the corridor.

Kay looked back. "Hey, Ki?"

Ki stopped.

"Thanks for caring."

She smiled and waved as Kay was dragged away to go crouch in the weeds and cold rock planes of the Gaston to investigate the Wraith.

The spectral creature that loved him.

11—The ARLISS

They ate dinner in the Capricos Hall that evening. Everybody was there, along with a few guests. Dinners at Great Houses could be staunch, rigid affairs full of protocol and hidden rules, but not at Castle Blanchefort. Lord Davage, often starved as a child for failing to abide by the many rules Lord Sadric had put in place regarding meals, abolished every one of them. As a result, meals in the castle were informal, pleasant occasions full of good food and company. Lord Davage and Sygillis always sat side by side, laughing, talking, often times holding hands under the table. Lady Poe and Lord Peter followed suit. Countess Pardock of Vincent was often there for dinner, her husband dead and her children grown, but she was not there today. Milos and Millie often sat near their parents, Millie, being so young, still needed attention from Lady Poe at meal times, which she got in doting quantity. Milos wouldn't be around for much longer—he was soon to begin attending the old university in Arden. He already had his school pin, which he wore proudly on his lapel. Lady Kilos and Hathaline sat in random spots, as did Kay, Sarah and Phillip. Maser, that ridiculous kid, sat in a highchair near his mother Sygillis eating that soft kid's slop that Kay recalled hating.

Lt. Kilos and her Tweeter were also there sitting at the far end of the table. After his pool-side exploits with Sam transformed into Kilos' likeness, Kay wondered what the real Kilos was like during an intimate encounter. Sam portrayed her as a brutal, slightly sadistic lover, but, having gotten to know her over the years, Kay imagined her as a more passive, laid-back lover in bed. Who knows.

Sam was missing. Sam rarely missed dinner at Castle Blanchefort as she loved eating Elder food.

"Sarah," Davage said, "how was the Gaston today?"

"Oh, it was fine, Uncle," she said, working on her plateful of roast beef. "We didn't see anything."

"Well, it's not surprising, Sarah. I've gone up and down the Gaston more times than I care to recall. I've never encountered a spectral creature there before."

"Are you certain, father?" Lady Kilos replied. "You never can be too sure when the Wraith might turn up."

Sarah tried to absorb the meaning of that and then dismissed it. "Lord Davage," Sarah said, "are you to be heading out soon?"

Davage wiped his lips. "Indeed, Sarah. Several days hence. Heading out for three weeks."

"Anything hot out there?" she asked.

"Actually, yes. We, along with several other ships, are headed to Hoban to lend support to an investigation of odd activity there. Just like the days of old, when the Xaphans were a constant threat, I'm rather looking forward to it."

Lt. Kilos took a drink from her tankard. "Kay, are you ever going to head out with your mom and dad … see the stars?"

"I don't like space travel, Lt. It makes me feel ill."

"Ohhh, you get used to it, kid. I used to get sick, too, in my early days. Want to know what cured it?"

"Um, yes, yes Lt., please. Tell me."

"Booze, kid. And lots of it."

Sygillis put her fork down and spoke up. "Ki, please don't encourage my son to take up drinking."

"Syg, lighten up, will you? Don't listen to your mom, Kay—a tankard of narva will cure anything."

"Ki," Sygillis said tartly, "it's been a long while since you and I stepped outside. If you would like a refresher, then please continue."

A footman entered the hall and spoke, "Lords and Ladies, may I present Lady Sammidoran of Monama and Astralon." Everybody at the table stood.

Sam glided into the hall in her usual black gown and bustle. She approached the table, looking a tad windblown. "Please forgive my tardy arrival. I was detained at home."

Kay pulled out a chair and properly seated her as another footman handed Sam a menu of the evening's choices. Sam made her selections, and the footman retired to the kitchens to fetch them for her.

"I'm so hungry this evening," she said.

"We were just discussing the Wraith of Gaston, Sam," Lady Kilos said.

"Oh," Sam said, unfolding her napkin. "A lot of sensational nonsense."

"The Wraith is real all right," Sarah said. "Too many people have seen it to be a hoax. I've got all kinds of stuff on it. And then there's the murders."

"*Sen-tre?* What murders?" Sam asked, astonished.

The footman returned with Sam's selections. She picked up her fork. "And, what would you do should you ever come face to face with this creature?" Sam asked.

"I'd stand before it and demand it reveal its identity. I wouldn't be scared."

"Really? Are you certain?" Sam replied.

Lady Kilos jumped in. "What if, Sarah, you were actually sitting right next to the Wraith and didn't know it? What then?"

"What?" Sarah asked. "What's that supposed to mean?"

Sam looked around, noting all the weapons lining the walls. She seemed anxious to change the subject. "Lord Davage—all of these weapons, they are the famous LosCapricos weapons of old, yes?"

"They are, Sam, every known type is displayed here. These are mostly mock-ups. They do not function."

Sam pointed at the wall behind Davage. "That wand-shaped example behind you, my lord— what is that one?"

Davage turned to look. "This? This is the ARLISS of House Dare."

"It is very pretty."

"This mock up is made of ivory, but they are normally made of gold or silver."

Sam seemed a bit preoccupied. "Do you see that, Kay? The ARLISS. Do you think the ARLISS is pretty?"

"Sure, Sam, it's very pretty."

"What's it called again?"

"The ARLISS."

"ARLISS. Will you remember that for me, Kay, the ARLISS?"

"Sure, Sam."

✶ ✶ ✶ ✶ ✶

A few days later, Kay, Sam and his cousins went down to the village to buy a birthday present for Duchess Torrijayne. Having no luck in finding inspiration for her gift, they ended up in a jewelry store on the Rundle Way, Phillip thinking a nice blue stone to match her eyes would be a fine touch.

As Sarah and Phillip browsed around, Kay saw Sam, in her usual goggles, talking to the jeweler. She seemed to have him quite perplexed.

"No ma'am, I do not have one of those, and I don't know of any who might. If you need a purple stone, I have a fine quantity of amethysts and purple topaz."

"I do not want any of those. I must have a spinel, and it must be at least 300 carats in weight."

The jeweler shook his head. "You might try a store in a larger trade city, like Minz or Atalea. Certainly Armenelos would have such a thing. And, be ready for a hefty price."

Phillip and Sarah decided on a lovely sapphire ring for the Duchess. As they paid for it, Sam stood there next to Kay and looked rather sad.

✶ ✶ ✶ ✶ ✶

Sarah had gotten a little nicer to Sam over the last few weeks. Strength impressed Sarah, and Sam had that in abundance. There was a soft mound in the Grove called Lennybus' Cone, and they loved to play King of the Mountain on it. Sarah, with her Gift of Strength, usually won such contests, Kay and Phillip not being able to dislodge her, but Sam could. Even at full strength, Sarah was no match for Sam, her wiry arms strong as a bear. Once Sam got to the top, she was there for good. Sarah grumbled about cheating but was still suitably impressed.

The bath house was another favorite haunt. In the evenings, they changed into swimwear and got in the huge heated pool. Lady Kilos often joined them, Sarah normally chasing her out, but Sam insisted she be allowed to stay and sit with them as Sam and Ki were close friends.

One evening, Sarah was going on and on about a Brandtball match taking place in Rustam; apparently, she was a big fan. One of the annoying things about Sarah was her love of holonet, and she had to have it blaring at all times, or she wasn't happy. The bath house didn't have a holo-net terminal, and Sarah had forgotten her portable unit. She was making an awful racket about missing the game but didn't want to leave the soothing pool to go and get it herself.

Kay laughed and said he'd go and get it for her just to shut Sarah up.

"Don't be long," Sam whispered in his ear. "Want me to come with you, Kay?" she asked.

He kissed her pale skin. "No, Sam, it's fine. I'll be right back. I'm going for your terminal, Sarah," he said.

"Make it quick; I might miss the first set."

Kay pulled his boots on and donned a robe. He then made the long walk through the Ten Gardens back to the castle to get Sarah's terminal. It was quite a slog. If he were a better Wafter, he'd do that to save himself a walk, but his Waft was awful. Sam didn't approve. *Work on your Gifts, Kay, for me,* she always said, and for good reason.

To save himself a bit of time, he walked through a large oak clearing populated by several ancient trees. The footing on either side of the clearing could be hazardous, but he knew the terrain so well he wasn't worried about it. He pressed on, walking at a good clip.

Ahead, a figure stood at one of the trees staring at its gigantic trunk. From a distance, he couldn't see clearly; the figure was tall and slim, female; it looked like his aunt, Lady Poe. He quickened his pace to say hello to her.

Slowly, the figure turned toward him.

"Kay?" he heard to his left. "Kay, is that you?"

Sitting some distance away in a wicker chair was his aunt, Lady Poe. Her head was lolled to one side, as if too heavy for her neck. Her eyes were rimmed with bags. She held a drink that had tipped over and spilled. She looked on the verge of death.

"Aunt Poe?" he said approaching her. "What's wrong? You seem ill."

She managed a small smile, her eyes long slits. "I'm fine, Kay," she whispered. "Just tired. I need rest."

"What are you doing out here?"

"Getting a little air. Peter went to get me a blanket."

Kay was worried as she looked terrible. "Is there anything I can do for you, Aunt Poe?"

She slowly raised her hand and touched his cheek. "No, Kay, no. Did Snugs work for Lord Lon?"

"Oh, yes, Aunt Poe. It worked perfectly."

"Good. You and Sarah and Phillip, how close you are. That's important. Families need to be close. I love you like my own child."

She appeared to fall into a delirium. "Everything I do is for you and the children. Don't be afraid, Kay."

"Afraid of what, aunt?"

"The Tulees. Don't be afraid of them."

Kay was confused. He was about to ask her what a 'Tulee' was when Lord Peter returned carrying a blanket. "Evening, Kay," he said.

"Evening, Uncle," Kay replied as Peter pulled the glass from Poe's limp fingers and began tucking the blanket in around her. He looked at Kay and appeared to note his concern.

"Don't worry about your aunt; she's fine. She's had a busy time of it lately. She just needs rest."

Kay knelt down, gave Lady Poe a kiss on the cheek, and took his leave. "Good night, Aunt Poe, Uncle Peter," he said.

"Good night, Kay," Peter replied.

Kay walked away and continued on toward the castle. It occurred to him just then—there was Aunt Poe sitting in the chair, so who was that he previously saw near the tree? He had been sure that was his Aunt Poe, too.

He walked back to the tree to investigate.

Nobody was there.

12—The Quest for Bowling

Sarah had been dying for this for weeks. The four of them had been planning a bold adventure, and, now that the time had come, Sarah was beside herself.

✶ ✶ ✶ ✶ ✶

Blanchefort Castle's nearest neighbor was Castle Durst, about seventy miles to the southwest. It was a grand Vith structure like Blanchefort Castle, but much smaller and less well appointed. The Dursts were gone—no heirs, and the standing House name was officially extinct before the Sisters and the League Ex-Commons. With the passing of Countess Medaline of Grimm some ten years back, the castle stood empty. None of the remaining five Durst daughters, all married off and living elsewhere, chose to occupy the old ancestral castle.

Castle Durst was officially a ruin, one of the many floating around the Vithlands of Kana.

As per League custom, all of the Durst's possessions were to be appropriated and redistributed to any with legal claim to them. The Durst daughters, though direct descendants, had no legal right to their own possessions, such was the very unfair but traditional male-oriented law of succession in the League.

However, Lord Blanchefort, having sworn to protect and maintain the Durst name until, with good fortune, the House could be legally reconstituted, secretly stole in and made off with the Durst's most valuable and treasured possessions. He hid them in a secure secret location until such time as he, or his progeny, could give them back to the future Dursts. When the hoard of claimants fell upon the castle to pick its bones, they only found an empty stone building and rotten food in the pantries.

Of the few possessions that Lord Blanchefort allowed to remain in open viewing were the blueprints to the castle, showing the many hidden areas and secret places that all Vith castles had in abundance. Sarah and Phillip had gotten hold of the map and poured over it, greatly interested in seeing them for themselves. On several afternoon expeditions, they had located the Durst holding room, several arcane libraries (now empty), a room that appeared to be a torture chamber, and a distillery where they fermented illegal spirits, the smell still thick in the air.

One thing that Sarah and Phillip were keen to find but couldn't was the Durst bowling alley. They knew it was there somewhere—all Vith Great Houses had hidden bowling alleys placed somewhere within the castle or on the grounds. The seven Durst daughters grew up with very good bowling averages. The deceased Lady Hathaline was said to have bowled a 300 game in the lost alley. However, try as they might, tearing the blueprints apart, they found no hidden alley. Sarah, bold as always, wrote to Lady Analine of Twill, the second of the last seven Durst daughters, and flat out asked her where the hidden alley was located. Analine wrote a terse response stating that was "none of her (expletive) business".

Sarah, however, took the rebuke as a victory. "That proves it's there some place, and we're just too dumb to figure it out!" Analine's response did nothing but whet Sarah's appetite.

✶ ✶ ✶ ✶ ✶

One lazy evening they all sat in Kay's Tower, in a favored reading room on the 63rd floor. Sarah and Phillip were flopped out on couches, their dusters tossed aside and, as per usual with Sarah, the Airenet was turned on. Some show bounced loudly in mid-air. Phillip typed into a terminal, as was his habit.

Kay and Sam sat on a couch by themselves near the terrace. Sam, shoes off and wearing one of the Countess's bodysuits, lay on him casually, her finger toying with his bellybutton that she found so fascinating. She loved quiet evenings. In a contented dream, she hummed a Monama tune.

They all sat in easy silence doing their own thing.

Sarah wasn't paying attention to the blaring Airenet. She was pouring over her copy of the Castle Durst blueprints, determined as ever to locate their alley. She was hoping to see something in the plans that had previously eluded her but wasn't having any success so far. Flopped on her stomach, her booted feet rocking carelessly back and forth, she tapped the paper with her fingers.

"We tried the west wing, already, right?" she asked.

"I believe so," Phillip responded absent-mindedly.

She poked the map. "I see a promising dead spot in the walls near the eastern wing. I think, given the dimensions, a small bowling alley could be shoehorned in there."

She turned to Kay. "What do you think?"

"I think you should just leave it alone, Sarah. Would you want somebody poking around our castle looking for the Blanchefort alley?"

"No, but that's different. Castle Blanchefort's never going to be a ruin. I'll blow it up myself should it come to that."

There came a knock at the threshold. Lady Kilos stood there in a white gown holding a box of Perlamum pieces.

"Hi, everybody," she said in an uncharacteristically meek voice, "I was wondering if anyone was up for a game of Perlamum?"

Sarah took immediate exception. "Nobody wants to play Perlamum, *Tez*," she said in a rather ugly tone. "This is the fun room. The boring girls-wearing-gowns room is elsewhere. Push off!"

Kilos, holding her box, swallowed and made to leave.

Sam turned to Kay, silently demanding he speak up. "Hey, Ki, don't go. I'll play a game with you," he said.

She smiled and entered the room, seating herself across from Kay and opening her box. Sarah scowled—Sarah had never liked Lady Kilos much and wasn't shy about making her thoughts known.

"How can you wear those things?" she asked, noting Ki's Blanchefort gown.

Ki arranged the jade and turquoise Perlamum pieces on the fold-out board. "This? I love wearing my gowns. They feel quite comfortable to me. Your mother certainly wishes you'd wear a gown every so often, Sarah."

"Mother's going to have to soak it up on that one, isn't she? Never catch me in one of those. How do you go to the bathroom I wonder?"

Before Ki could answer, Sam spoke up. "No need to answer that, Ki. I think you look lovely in your gowns."

Kay and Ki began playing, Sam sitting and watching. Eventually, Sarah forgot about Ki's presence and returned to staring at the Durst Castle map.

Sam sat up and stretched. "*Sar-te, inge fortencar?*" she said in her musical Monama language. She was now speaking in more complex words, with Kay having mastered the more basic ones.

Kay thought a moment. "Wait, you asked if I ..."

"*Te, te*, not *Ane*," Sam corrected. "I was speaking to everybody."

"All right, you asked if we'd like something to eat, right?"

Sam was elated. "Close, Kay. Very good. I was asking if anybody would like something to drink: *fortencar,* not eat. To Eat is *dradzar* I was planning on getting something from the kitchen."

"No, thanks," Kay said puzzling at the board.

"Well, if you're going, Sam," Ki said, "I'll take a Blue Gasol."

"That figures," Sarah replied in a loud voice. "Give me a Red Gasol, Sam, if you wouldn't mind," she said.

"I'll be right back," she said. She removed Snugs and Blinked away.

Kay and Ki continued playing. Glancing over, Ki became curious as to what Sarah was pouring over so intently. "What are you looking at?" she asked.

"None of your business," she replied.

Phillip stopped typing. "Sarah, give her a break, won't you? It's the plans to Castle Durst, Ki. We got them from Lord Davage."

"Oh," she said. She thought a moment. "Why are you looking at those?"

"Full of questions, aren't you?" Sarah responded.

Phillip made to respond. "We're ..."

"Shhhhh!" Sarah said, cutting him off. "It's a damn secret! You want the whole League to know telling this motor mouth?"

Sam reappeared holding a tray full of drinks and snacks. "She's looking for the Durst bowling alley, Ki," Sam said, apparently having heard the conversation. She set the tray down and picked up a green can. "Here, Kay, I brought you a Verdalar anyway."

"Thanks, Sam," he said vacantly, gazing at the board.

Sarah, taking her can, was rather annoyed that her secret was out. "Great, Sam—you just blabbed to the blabber!"

"I'm not going to tell anybody," Ki said taking a drink. "What do you want with their bowling alley anyway? It's stripped. I saw the pins for it in the secret storage area down in the village. I went with Father as he supervised the process."

Sarah was jubilant. "Aha! You saw their pins? That proves it exists, and we just can't find it!"

"When you find it, what are you going to do?" Ki asked, taking Kay's jester. He sighed in misery.

"We're going to go there and bowl, Tez! What do you think we're going to do?"

Kay was annoyed, both from losing his jester and from Sarah's sour attitude. "Sarah, what have I told you about calling her that? She's my sister."

"Yeah?" Sarah replied. "What are you going to do about it?"

"I might have to kick your little butt right out the window."

Sarah sat up and pushed the blue prints aside. "Well, let's go then. I don't see anything between us but empty space."

Phillip and Sam didn't pay them any mind. Kay and Sarah were constantly getting into little wrestling matches.

Ki, unused to this sort of confrontation, was uncomfortable. "Well, there's no need to have an altercation on my behalf. It's fine, Kay."

They both stood up, and Sarah put her hair back.

"They do this all the time, Ki," Sam commented, putting her feet up. "If I didn't know Sarah was Kay's cousin, I'd be pretty jealous as they're always rolling around with each other. *Parjen-thar will*: little 'snapping turtles'."

"Well, there's really no need to ..."

"Sure there is, Tez," Sarah said, rolling her sleeves up. "I'm going to mess your brother up a little right here, right now."

Kay and Sarah locked up. Quickly, Kay had her in a tight headlock, her blue hair squirting through the crease of his elbow.

Ki sat there holding her Queen Perlamum piece, feeling a little put off, and glanced at the forgotten blueprints to Castle Durst. "Sarah you said you couldn't locate the Durst ancestral bowling alley, is that right?"

Sarah grunted something inaudible as she tried to free her head. She flailed around, trying to grab hold of Kay's tailed hair. She wasn't allowed to use her Gift of Strength indoors, so she had to get by as is.

"Well, I see it right there on the blue prints plain as day."

Sarah reacted. "What? Wait a minute! Wait a minute! Let me go!" she said, her voice muffled. Kay released her, and she grabbed the blue prints.

"Where do you see it?" she said, skeptically. "There is no possible way you see it so fast."

"Right there," Ki returned, pointing.

"Where?" Sarah marched to the table and laid the blue prints out, scattering the Perlamum pieces.

"Hey!" Sam said. "You've ruined their game!"

"Who cares, Sam? Now then, Tez, where do you see the hidden alley?"

Ki pointed. "Right there." She pointed to the drawing of the large central tower, Rhoda Tower, easily the castle's tallest and largest feature.

Sarah looked at the drawing. "No, no, that's in the upper levels of the tower. The alley can't be hidden in there. It has to be below the ground level of the castle. You got me all worked up for nothing!"

"But why not? Our bowling alley is located underground, but that doesn't mean theirs has to be as well, right? Also, I recall Father mentioning the ground at Castle Durst is much more water-saturated than ours is; therefore, it seems to make sense that they would put their hidden alley in an elevated area. Rhoda Tower is quite large and should easily be able to accommodate such a thing."

Sarah studied the drawing intently. Phillip, becoming interested, came over and looked as well.

She tapped the paper with her finger. "Well, I see a fairly large blank area here between the sixty-forth and seventy-third floors. What do you think, Phillip? Kay?"

Phillip rubbed his chin. "I have been operating under the biased notion that the Durst alley is located below ground level, as that's where ours is, and the same at Oyln Manor."

"Will you shush-up on that!" Sarah yelled. "That's a secret!"

Phillip continued. "And the soil is, in fact, much wetter there than it is here. Lady Kilos could be correct. I'm rather embarrassed that I didn't think of that myself."

✶ ✶ ✶ ✶ ✶

The next morning, they got the big old silver Ripcar out of the park and began loading it. Kay and Phillip were there wearing their best coats and hats: Kay in his usual black and purple coat, custom-made by his mother, and his black Vith hat, and Phillip wearing a smaller Esther hat that he favored and a hunter green coat with tails. Both Phillip and Kay were wearing their CARG's, Kay's silver one and Phillip's verdant one that he rarely used. His SAPP hung about his neck as a scarf.

Sam blinked in, also wearing her nicest gothic black gown of taffeta and lace with a huge bustle with rather pointy Monama shoes. Lady Kilos was also there wearing a minty blue gown.

They were heading to Castle Durst to bowl in their secret bowling alley.

"It looks as if we should be heading out to a wonderful ball or an evening at a lavish restaurant, not going to a sinister castle ruin to play a simple game," Sam remarked.

Phillip laughed as he loaded his bowling equipment, his balls, gloves and shoes, into the back of the Ripcar. "It's tradition, Sam. We're supposed to dress up when we bowl. That's how all the ancestors did it."

Kay threw his bag into the back. He noted the large dent toward the rear of the craft—Mother had done that. "Of course, Mother has a thing about bowling nude, which we seldom speak of. I'm bringing the yellow ball you favor, Sam. Do you want a different one?"

She took his arm. "No, no, the yellow is fine. Thank you."

Down the path, Sarah emerged from around the bend. Unlike the rest standing by the Ripcar, she was wearing her usual duster and boots. Her hands were pretty full. She was carrying a bowling bag with her ball and shoes and travelling cover containing her usual lemon-colored gown. She was also carrying a cooler full of stuff.

"Why aren't you dressed, Sarah?" Phillip asked.

She approached, somewhat out of breath. "Because I'll change once we get there. I hate gowns."

"Then why wear one at all?" Sam asked.

"Because we're bowling, and a gown is the uniform you wear when you bowl."

Sarah piled her stuff into the Ripcar and took inventory. "Everybody got everything?" she asked.

"We're ready to go," Kay replied.

"What about pins? We'll need pins to play."

"Already loaded."

"And power? What about power?"

"I brought several portable power units, Sarah," Phillip said.

Apparently satisfied, Sarah climbed into the back.

With everybody present, they piled into the big silver Ripcar, and Phillip lifted it into the air. He moved south around the formidable bulk of the castle, rising high.

"Look there, Sam," Sarah said pointing. "That notch in the mountains over there is the northern portal to the Gaston Way. Just a big, old pass through the mountains that goes all the way to Arden. It's flippin' haunted!"

Sam turned to look and adjusted her goggles. She saw the long line moving through the mountains, vanishing in the haze far to the south. "Really?" she said. "I believe I remember you talking about that before. What sort of apparition haunts it again, please?"

"The Wraith of Gaston. A creepy ghost that chases you in your Ripcar! I've seen it myself!"

Sam appeared rather surprised. "Have you?"

Phillip looked back. "You have not, Sarah!" he said. "That was foxfire, and you know it! Don't exaggerate!"

Sam, her incredible mass of black hair flowing in the breeze, laughed. "I wouldn't count on any further hauntings down that way, Sarah. I foresee no further troubles there." Sam removed her goggles and settled into Kay's shoulder, shutting her eyes. "There's no need for it anymore ..."

"What did you say?" Sarah asked. "I didn't hear."

"Nothing ..."

Phillip cleared the castle and the coastal shelf and settled into the vast valley between two ridges heading southwest, following the natural contours and passing the great cone-shaped mountain of Mt. Durst. He picked up some altitude and came out of the valley bearing west.

Ahead, in the cold distance, was Castle Durst, sitting at the highest point between two mountain rivers. They passed over the walled outer compound, which was crumbling in places. The grounds within the wall were once carefully tended; now, the greenery had fallen back to nature and was overgrown and threatening to tangle. Ibex's had claimed a healthy portion of the south grounds through a breach in the walls, and the northern part was flooded a bit as the river was up. Elsewhere, wild, predatory animals were on the prowl. They passed fast-flowing Durst creek and were over the inner-compound. Here, Lord Davage's crews worked once a month to push back the tide of growing things, and it still appeared fairly-well tended.

The castle at the center of the grounds was quiet and forlorn. The white paint was starting to peel, revealing the old, gray rock beneath, and the whole place had a stark and singularly vacant feel to it. The window panes, once glittering in rare crystal and colorful stained glass, had been removed, and the dozens of gaping holes left behind gave one the impression of a mouthful of rotten and missing teeth. Unlike the sprawling layout of Castle Blanchefort, Castle Durst was built around a central axel, like a great wheel, with smaller and larger spires rising up at regular points along the spokes of the wheel. The central feature of the castle was Rhoda Tower in the center. Though the castle was much smaller than Castle Blanchefort, Rhoda Tower was far and away larger than any single tower at Castle Blanchefort.

Phillip turned the Ripcar and landed in the pebbled drive. He killed the engine, and they all got out. Sam put her goggles back on to protect her eyes from the afternoon glare. She craned her neck back. "How tall is this tower?"

Sarah, hauling her stuff, walked past her. "Rhoda Tower is two thousand, four hundred, fifty feet. I read it on the blue prints."

With everybody lugging their gear, they marched across the dragon-tooth moat and entered the open main doorway. Sam carried the impressively heavy box containing the bowling pins they would use for their game. The box's weight didn't appear to be troubling her in the least.

The emptiness of the place was astounding once inside. Once well known for its tapestries and lavish interior, all that greeted them now were bare walls and bits of garbage on the floor.

"So sad," Sam said, looking around. "The life and joy this place once must have seen, now all gone and stripped away. I don't like abandoned buildings, Kay. They make me uneasy."

"It's not abandoned now. Not with us here," Sarah said with a touch of optimism.

They worked their way to the base of Rhoda Tower. A massive spiral stairwell greeted them.

"The lifts are out," Sarah said in dismay. "Phillip, can you get this working? I'm not walking up sixty-four floors, no way."

He walked up to the panel and opened the cover. He attached the leads to a small portable power unit he'd brought just for this very purpose, and the lift came to life. "I figured you'd be a sissy about it, Sarah, so I brought this. I've got some more here with me for the bowling alley," he said.

"Good thinking," Sarah offered as the lift came down, and they piled in.

They went up sixty-three floors and got out into near total darkness. Sarah and Phillip lit their Sights and got out, the twin beams of their eyes panning about like flashlights; Phillip's was silver while Sarah's was an aqua blue.

"Let me locate the junction panel. Just a moment," Phillip said, his silver beams shining bright, pooling on the walls.

Something brushed past Lady Kilos. "Sarah?" she said.

Two blue beams of light turned to her from down the hall, floating in the dark.

"What?"

"Did you just brush past me and tug my gown?"

"No!" She turned away and resumed looking for the lights.

"Kay," Sam said still holding the heavy box of pins, "you should go out and help them."

"It's pitch black out there, Sam. I can't see."

"Use your Sight, Kay."

"I don't have the Sight, Sam. I wish you'd realize that."

As he stood there in the dark, he felt a sharp pinch in his lower back. It hurt quite a lot. "Oww! Sam, did you do that?"

"Do what, Kay?"

"Pinch me!"

She stood there holding the box with one hand. "Why would I pinch you, Kay? I can see fairly well in the dark. I'll help Sarah and Philip."

"Wait!" He saw her pulling her goggles off and carefully put them into a pocket in her gown. In the pitch black he somehow clearly saw her. "Sam, you ..."

The lights came on with a click, revealing a musty antechamber of tight-fitting ochre stone blocks. "Got it!" Sarah cried in triumph.

Kay, Sam and Ki exited the lift shaft. As below, the corridor was bare and windowless. Wire and metal hanging clips were pressed into the walls at various places indicating that vast murals and other hangings once decorated the corridor.

Phillip stood at an open panel at the end of the corridor trying to shore up the power connections he had just made. Sarah was closely scanning the walls, looking for the entrance.

"Well, don't just stand there, you people! Give me a hand finding the entrance to the place!" she said.

"Don't bother with the east wall; concentrate on the west wall. That's where it has to be," Phillip added.

"I know that!" Sarah cried.

They put their things down and began a protracted search of the walls. "What are we looking for?" Kilos asked, tentatively feeling with her hands.

"Hidden panels, levers, buttons, wheels, anything that might open the door and reveal the damn bowling alley," Sarah said tugging on a slight imperfection in the stone.

They gave the stone walls the once-over, feeling and testing but finding nothing. Sarah and Phillip gazed at the walls with their Sight, but they saw nothing through the stone but stone.

"I don't think it's here," Kay said taking a step back. "We're suspecting that the alley is hidden between the 64th and 72nd floors, so the entrance could be anywhere on those floors. It might even be elsewhere."

Sarah turned to him, her eyes lit up like cyan laser beams. "Better get climbing then. I want to keep searching here for a bit more, then we'll be up, right?"

Kay made his way down the corridor to the spiral staircase at the end. Sam clapped her hands together to clear the dust she'd picked up from the walls and followed him up.

"Hey, Sam, I think I might have something here. Could you please help me?" Ki asked, feeling about a suspect imperfection in the wall. Reluctantly she stopped and joined Ki at the wall.

He clambered up the stairs to the next level. The level above was plunged in darkness, and he couldn't see a thing. In the estuary between the light from the level below and the darkened corridor above, he squinted and tried to see, straining as hard as he could.

Nothing. He thought he'd been able to see Sam removing her goggles in the dark after feeling a pinch. He recalled his father talking about pain enhancing the Gift of Waft. Perhaps it would work with the Sight as well, though his father didn't think so. He took a pinch of skin on his forearm and squeezed, but all he did was hurt his arm and make it red.

Sure enough, despite what Sam said and thought, he couldn't see in the dark. He had no Sight and was therefore a great disappointment to his father and a setback to the House of Blanchefort. Watching Sarah and Phillip do it so easily, he felt a little coiling of shame building up in him somewhere, as he had previously in his father's study.

He drew his CARG. It always glowed a bit in darkness, an unintended side-effect of the introduction of his mother's Silver tech during its forging. The glowing wasn't directed into a beam, however, and the soft glow often did more harm than good as it completely fouled any night vision he might have had going.

"Phillip, I'm going to need light up here!" he yelled down.

Waving the CARG around, he found the wall. As below, it was bare stone and forgotten memories all appearing cavernous in the diffuse silvery light. The windowless interior here was more cave-like than castle. His mother often spoke of part of her soul having grown up here, in the good days when the Dursts were full of high hopes with the promise of ascendancy amongst the old Vith Houses. Surely a male heir would come. Surely the House would live on.

Kay moved his CARG along the stone face of the wall, hoping to see some sort of obvious lever or button that might reveal the entrance to the bowling alley. This was turning out to be more work than he'd been hoping for. Sarah and her little adventures. He pressed on into the dark, hoping to ...

What's that?

Something down the corridor caught his eye, and he stopped, turning his attention to the gummy darkness ahead. He was certain he had seen something pickup the silvery light of his CARG and reflect it back, something flat and coin-like—like a pair of eyes. Kay felt a thrill run down his spine, and his loins tighten. He raised his CARG and held it steady.

"Who's there?" he said, his voice shaking slightly.

Listening intently, he thought he could hear something stirring in the dark.

A voice?

"I know you ..."

Down below, Phillip and Sarah got into a loud, cursing argument about something, and the din of their drifting voices drowned out all else.

Damn those two—he couldn't hear! Holding his CARG at the ready, he stepped farther down the corridor, dreading to catch another glance at whatever it was. He got to the end and saw nothing.

Something had been there, he knew it!

He felt a brush across his back. He whirled around.

"Kay!" Sam cried, startled. "It's just me. What's wrong?"

He put a protective arm around her. Sam's taffeta gown crinkled a little as he squeezed her. He raised his CARG and held it out. Sam's pale skin picked up the light and shown with a moon-like glow. "Creation, Sam, you startled me. I thought I saw something."

"Saw what?" she asked.

"I don't know, a pair of eyes possibly. I thought I heard something, too."

Sam looked around. "You must have been imagining it." She embraced him and offered a loving kiss. She put her hand over his heart. "Gods, Kay, your heart is pounding. It's all right, *Arin-Dan*. There's nobody here."

"Then what did I see?"

"Well, Kay, I don't know. It's dark and unfamiliar in here. Perhaps you imagined it? That's perfectly understandable." Sam embraced him in a protective fashion. He could smell the wormwood in her hair.

"Do you smell anything?"

"I can't smell much when I'm wearing Snugs."

"Take it off."

"I don't want to take it off. It's probably freezing in here. It was just your imagination, Kay. That's all."

There was a commotion coming up the stairs. Sights lit and bobbing, Phillip and Sarah appeared.

"Are you kissing?" Sarah cried in dismay, her two blue beams fixed on them in a pair of blue spotlights.

"What if we are?" Sam replied.

"It's time for bowling, not kissing!"

Phillip, his silvery Sight beams panning about, passed them and went to the junction panel. He opened it and attached a pair of cables. The lights came up a moment later.

Kay rubbed his eyes, seeing nothing but the drab, water-stained stone walls. Sarah was already at the walls scanning for the entrance. Lady Kilos was making her way up the stairs. Sam smiled and gave him another kiss, finally letting him go. They both went to the wall and joined the search.

"Oh, here! Here! What's this?" Ki cried, spying a recessed lever in the wall.

They gathered around. At eye-level was a small metal lever sitting within a housing in the stone. It appeared to have once been behind a painting or hanging. Greedy and impatient, Sarah put her hands in and tried to move the lever.

"No, it's stuck. Damn! Phillip, open this! I'm not allowed to power up inside, remember? I promised mother." Phillip approached but couldn't get anywhere with it either.

"Sam?" Sarah said turning to her.

Sam took a look at the lever, reached in and pulled.

BANG!

The rusty lever broke loose and came forward. In the center of the corridor, a hidden doorway slid in and moved aside, revealing a cloudy darkness from within.

There it was—the Durst's hidden bowling alley. They all gazed at the open doorway.

"Wait!" Sarah shrieked. "Don't anybody go in; I need to get changed first!" She took her gown (still in its bag) and ran down the stairs with it.

They stood there gawking at the dark space within waiting for Sarah to return.

"I really don't wish to do this," Ki said. "I feel as though we are treading upon the Durst's memory."

"We're honoring them by coming here to play and revel in their memory," Phillip replied. "I don't have an issue with it."

The doorway and whatever was beyond it beckoned. Nobody went in.

"I wonder how many times Mother walked through this door to play?" Ki said.

"Mother?" Kay asked.

"She always says a small part of her soul grew up here in this castle."

Sarah came back up the stairs. She was in her lemon gown, trying to cinch it up in the mid-section area. She was wearing her bowling shoes and holding her bag with her prized clear bowling ball within. "Ok, I'm back, let's go in." She pushed past everybody and got to the open doorway, standing there. "It's powerful dark. Phillip, can you bring up the lights?"

He shook his head. "Nope, not until we get inside. It must be in there someplace."

Sarah lit her Sight and plunged in, followed by Kay and Sam and Lady Kilos.

Kay and Sam stumbled through the dark, feeling their way. Sarah and Phillip's lit Sights panned about.

"There's a ramp here leading down. Be careful," Phillip added.

Ki groped about in the dark and took Kay's arm. "Kay?" she asked. "Can you see?"

"No, Ki, I can't."

"You can, too, Kay! *Jon-de Mi*! You make me so angry sometimes!" Sam yelled, sounding quite annoyed. In the dark she got into his face; he could feel her heat and smell her breath. "Come on, Kay, it's time for you to grow up! You promised me you would practice!"

"I don't have the damn Sight, Sam! How many times do I have to feel this humiliation?"

Sam simmered in the dark, ready to lose her temper.

The lights came on.

The Durst bowling alley stretched out in flickering light as Phillip shored up the power connections. It was quite a bit smaller than the Blanchefort alley, having only one lane as opposed to the three that they had. It was sunken quite a bit, and there was a switch-back ramp trailing down to the alley floor. As in the corridor, the stone walls were bare. The whole place was plain and rather depressing, though, in its day, it was probably lavish with paintings and tapestries.

Sam seemed a little put off and went out into the corridor to get the heavy box full of pins.

Down below, Phillip was fiddling with the pin pit, trying to restore life to the pin setter, while Sarah stocked the small bar behind the scoring table with drinks and snacks she'd brought. Kay and Kilos made their way down as Sam reemerged through the door with the box.

"Hey, Kay, what's this?" she asked, her momentary morass forgotten.

She was looking at a stone pillar partially buried in the stone wall. On it, several generations of Dursts had scratched their names. There were many names ending with 'line,' the usual ending of a girl's name in the old Durst House, and many 'thas' as well for the men. Sam pointed at one name. "Look at this one, Kay!" she said.

The one she was pointing at read:

Hathaline loves Davage

Part of his mother's soul had written that inscription years ago.

"I would like to write our names, Kay," Sam said handing him the box. Kay staggered a bit under its weight as Sam scratched their names into the pillar with her fingernail.

"Hey, come on!" Sarah yelled, getting impatient. "No time for that, Sam!"

Kay, still struggling with the box, headed down the ramp with a giddy Sam following, giving him little tickles as he worked his way down.

Sarah had placed her clear ball on the rails and was getting Phillip's green ball out of the bag. Ki seated herself and put on her bowling shoes.

Phillip had no luck in the pin pit. "The mechanism's gone!" he called out from down the lane. "Looks like somebody's going to have to stay down here and manually reset the pins."

"What did you say, Phillip?" Sarah yelled from the scoring table.

"Nothing, Sarah," Kay responded. "I'll just get into the pit and reset them myself. I've never been overly big into bowling anyway."

"No, Kay, we'll take turns. It's not fair for you to do it all the time!" Sarah said.

"Sure, sure. I'll take the first shift."

Phillip stood and made his way up the lane and got his ball off the rails as Kay pulled himself into the tight confines of the pit. Sam followed him down.

"Kay, make room, and I'll join you back there," she called.

"No, Sam, you play and have fun. I'll be out soon. Promise."

She hesitated. *"Ange-zein ah stener-zwei, Arin-Dan?"* she asked him quietly.

"Of course I'm not angry with you, *Cerri-Tela,*" he replied, understanding complex Anuie more and more. "Go on, Sam. Get your shoes on."

She leaned down and kissed him, then carefully made her way to the scoring table, not wanting to risk slipping in her Monama shoes on the waxed surface. Kay set the pins up and climbed up out of the way as Sarah wound up and took the first throw.

✶ ✶ ✶ ✶ ✶

The game seemed like it went on forever, with ball after ball shooting down the Durst's old lane. Kay was nearly driven deaf as each throw made a commotion of noise in the pit. He had to stuff his fingers in his ears so that his eardrums wouldn't split.

Midway through the first frame, Lady Kilos was in the lead, followed by Phillip, then a distant Sarah and Sam dragging the rear. Sam could throw the ball very hard, but she had no touch and could not pickup a spare to save her life. She had left a trail of open frames in her wake. Peeking up the lane through the pit, he saw Ki giving Sam pointers. It was odd seeing Sam, wraithlike in black holding a fruity-yellow bowling ball, her fingers stuck in the holes.

"Hey, Kay!" Sarah shouted. "Come out! We're going to have a bathroom break and get some refreshments before we continue. I brought drinks!"

"Come out, Kay," Sam said. *"Stantis meine arte kinder-loe!"*

"What's that mean?" Sarah asked.

"It means: I was hoping we could take a short walk before we begin playing again," Sam said.

"Well, don't be long!" Sarah said. "Creation, we've a game to finish!"

Kay, walking up the lane, had to laugh. That was clearly not what Sam had said. Sarah would freak if she knew what Sam had *really* said.

Sam was waiting for him. "Come on, slow poke," she said. He took her hand, and they explored the back half of the alley. In the rear was a door that opened up into a circular stair spiraling all the way up to the top of Rhoda Tower far away. There were small windows at regular intervals, so they had light to see. They went up about three floors, and then Sam put him up against the wall and rubbed into him.

"At last! We could make love right here and now, Kay. All that bowling has made me rather randy I'm afraid," she said into his ear, her voice changing into an earthy burr as it usually did when she was becoming aroused. "I find it oddly provocative with Sarah around, as she despises my touching you." She felt up his leg.

Despite himself and the close proximity of his sister and his cousins, Kay was fairly keen to try. He reached up through the volumes of crinkly black cloth of Sam's gown and found the hot apex of her crotch. Sam moaned.

Sam had his shirt pulled out and was well on her way to unbuttoning his pants when Kay heard Sarah rooting around downstairs somewhere close. "Kay! Sam! Where are you? We're going to resume in a few minutes!"

Hearing Sarah's voice so close was a bit of a mood-killer for Kay. Sam, unmindful, wrapped him up in her long arms. Soon there would be no reasoning with her, and she'd make enough noise that Sarah was sure to hear.

"No, Sam, we can't ..."

Sam licked his neck and began working him. "No, no, no, Kay. I want to make love."

"Shhhh, shhh!"

"I want to make love!"

She was steamy and unreasonable. "All right, but not here. Let's go up to the top. The prospect of Sarah catching us is not a pleasant one for me."

Panting, Sam let him go. She removed her Snugs and Blinked away. Damn, her Blink was fast. Kay tried to relax and calm his breathing. He settled and began to perform a Waft, trying to implement what he'd learned in his father's study. As usual, it took a great deal of patience and inner calm to start the process. Slowly, he felt the twisting column of wind form around him, and he became light and airy. He felt himself moving in the direction he wanted to go, passing through the dozens of stone levels to the distant top where Sam was waiting. Things were indistinct around him. In a twilight, he saw the great, windowed lounge of the upper most room of Rhoda Tower appear. He allowed the Waft to swirl to a stop.

Kay looked around. The room, once a grand gathering area featuring commanding views all around, was empty and surrounded by open terraces and galleries. To the east, Kay could see the distant confusion of spires from Castle Blanchefort like a reddish pincushion low on the horizon. Farther east he could see the domain of Bloodstein, his distant relatives, clinging to the leeward side of the mountains. Northeast was the ancient hamlet of Shirster Point locked in ice by the sea, and, to the west, was the Vith city of Mt. Holly. He could even make out the distant gray line of Xandarr Bay.

Castle Durst certainly commanded a central viewing of most of the Vith's great holdings.

The notion struck Kay as odd for a moment. Castle Durst, from its rather elevated position, commands most of Vithland. Should somebody wish to launch an attack of some sort, it would be ideal to do it from this place. Kay was alarmed for a moment, almost panicked.

Attacks and Castle Durst—that seemed familiar to him.

But of course, that was silly. Who would want to do such a thing, as Castle Durst was just a ruin.

"Sam?" Where was she? He thought she might have gotten comfortable in one of the terraces; Sam liked to make love in odd places. He took his coat off and laid it down.

Ah, there she was. He saw a black form standing framed in the northern gallery, facing the balcony. She was holding some sort of red torch that lit her up in a garnet glow. "Sam, what are you doing over there? We don't have much time; Sarah will kill us."

He saw her head turn slightly. Over her shoulder, he saw the pale skin and black eyes.

"I know you ..."

The figure standing against the wall was not Sam. It was clearly a Monama with the pale skin and black eyes. It had the usual thin body type and massive head of black hair and was wearing a black waistcoat of some kind with baggy white sleeves. It was apparently male, with rather dainty features.

"Clatera?" Kay asked. "Clatera, is that you?"

Hearing his name seemed to wake him up a little. He stirred and turned to face Kay.

"What are you doing here?" Kay asked. "You'll freeze."

Thick tears dripped down his face. Clatera mumbled something.

"I didn't hear you. Let me help, you're probably freezing to death."

He spoke again. *"I told you ... too many questions!"*

He sprang, covering a fair distance. Kay backed away, rubbing up against the wall. Clatera landed in a half crouch. He raised his arms, and he had four of them. Two were clad in his baggy sleeves while two more had burst out through the fabric of his shirt and were bare. Long, deadly claws glistened at his fingertips.

"See what happens! See what they do to us! You did this to me!" Clatera growled. There was some sort of hole or deep depression between his eyes that undulated open and closed with frequent regularity. Thick fluid dripped out--the 'tears' Kay had seen.

Clatera was a Berserkacide!

He advanced on Kay, moving in a supple fashion like a panther. He barred his teeth in a ghastly smile.

Kay tried to back away, to give himself room. Up against the wall, he sidestepped to his left and bumped into something solid, yet fleshy. In an instant, four pale arms went around his chest. Claws drilled into his flesh.

"Care for something exotic?" whispered a feminine voice in his ear. He pulled away and the arms parted, allowing him to fall forward. Looking back, there was Mitzilaran, four-armed, wearing her slinky black dress. She had a diabolic look on her face. She too had a hole between her eyes that gushed fluid.

"I can be anything you want me to be." She raised her arms and slowly advanced.

Kay was surrounded with Mitz in front of him and Clatera coming up from his rear. Both of them had transformed into Berserkacides. Despite his situation, Kay felt his heart break. He barely knew these two, but he considered them friends. Mitz had been so kind to him, so warm and friendly. She had understood how he felt. And now, here they were ...

Berserkacides. All of Sarah's lurid stories and postings hit him full. They had opened up to him a little, and now they were Berserkacides, as if they were being punished for speaking to him. He backed away and unsaddled his CARG preparing to wield it against his friends.

Berserkacide: Four-armed. Bestial Rage. Death of Personality.

Permanent.

Whoever Clatera and Mitzilaran of Cardinal had been was gone forever. Only the Berserkacides remained.

The gravity of the situation hit him full. This wasn't a rumble session in the Grove with Sarah and Phillip or a wrestling match with Sam; this was for keeps.

"Phillip!" he yelled. "I need help! Sam!"

Where was Sam?

Mitz came at him, moving with incredible speed. Kay held his trembling CARG out, one-handed as usual. Behind him, Clatera side-stepped to his right.

Mitz brandished her four hands barbed with glistening claws, allowing him to appreciate them.

From listening to Sarah over the years, he'd assumed Berserkacides were these roaring beasts slavering mindlessly to taste warm meat. However, Clatera and Mitz weren't making much noise at all, and that was even worse. Mitz darted about, staying at the end of his CARG, testing his defenses, gathering information on Kay.

How fast was he?

How skilled?

Where was a weakness and how best to strike?

Mitz seemed very deliberate and cunning. Clatera, stayed in his rear, readying to attack.

"Sam!" Kay cried. "Phillip!"

Mitz smiled a little and took a solid swipe at Kay's CARG, hoping to either bisect the weapon with her claws or knock it from his grasp. Kay felt the CARG tremor, but he held fast. He tried a quick thrust, but she nimbly moved aside.

From behind, Clatera advanced. Kay whirled around in a wild swing, hoping to keep him at bay. Clatera leapt away, easily evading.

They circled, and the two Berserkacides began a new tactic. They backed him up into the west gallery where he would have no place to go except over the side in a long drop to the cold ground far below. Clatera feinted one way, and when Kay reacted, Mitz darted the other and got past his defense, swiping him in the shoulder. She buried her claws where they bit deep.

Pain.

Kay grimaced and saw stars. His wound was on fire. His eyes watered, and he felt instantly sick from the pain.

And he saw something through the amber haze of pain. In the gallery behind the Berserkacides, he saw some sort of strange, partially constructed device sitting in the center of the room, one that hadn't been there before, or at least he hadn't seen it.

His innards reacted to seeing the device. Something told him it meant no good, that if it was made whole or woken up, then terrible things would happen. The device could not be allowed to remain. Something deep within told him he had to get rid of it.

It was imperative, but why he felt that way he didn't know.

He tried to get a better look at it, but Mitz was on him. She batted his CARG aside and got in close, her four clawed hands slashing his neck and head. Kay managed to keep his poise and forced her to draw back with quick strikes from his light weapon. She backed away and made to do a final lunge, either knocking Kay over the side or spilling his blood with her claws. It really didn't matter. To his right, Clatera coiled up for a side-strike.

Kay performed a sudden move that neither of them expected. Kay's CARG was a wonder. Imbued with Silver tech, it could do a number of useful things, including length expansion. All he had to do was want it to get bigger and it would on its own. His father's King CARG had to be manually adjusted.

He jammed the horn of the CARG into the floor and rapidly expanded its length. He rocketed forward, like a pole vaulter, sailing over the flailing Mitz and landed in the center of the room, the two Berserkacides tearing after him.

He was standing right next to the device. Glancing at it, it seemed to be only partially constructed. Several obvious components were missing. As the two Berserkacides closed the distance, he hauled back and swung, cleaving the thing in two, shredding metal and circuitry.

"*No!*" Mitz screamed. He watched it topple over for a moment and felt immensely relieved. Whatever happened now didn't matter.

The thing was destroyed.

Mitz and Clatera lost their sly calmness and roared in rage, thirsting for his blood.

Kay raised his CARG and readied to make his final stand.

"What are you two doing?" came an angry voice. "You better not be naked up here for Creation's sake!" Sarah shouted marching into the room.

"Sarah! Look out!" Kay cried.

Mitz skittered to a stop and turned to gut Sarah.

"What are you ..." Sarah saw the Berserkacide beast coming at her. Instead of her usual bravado and love of fighting, Sarah's mouth dropped open, and, eyes wide, she froze in place. She locked up solid as the slavering Mitz came at her. Kay had always suspected that Sarah's bluster when it came to Berserkacides covered up a genuine terror of them. Vith didn't feel fear, but Sarah was half Esther, and she was petrified.

"Sarah, move!" he cried. She just stood there in her lemon-colored gown as death approached.

Seeing Sarah's bloody end mere moments away, Kay again turned to his CARG. As it could expand in length, it could also fire a blast of Silver tech. Kay could do a fair amount of damage with it. The trouble was that it did not always work, and there was no way to know if it would or it wouldn't.

Kay gripped the hilt and summoned a blast. Either this worked, or Sarah was dead.

The CARG grew hot, and then a molten blast of Silver tech surged out, hitting Mitz squarely in the chest. Rolling with the blast, as if caught in the spray of a fire hose, flesh-shredding, Mitz rolled across the floor leaving a bloody trail and was swept over the side of the gallery.

Clatera roared and altered his course and went at Sarah, also. "*First her, then you!*" He bounded in for the kill.

Kay aimed and fired another Silver tech blast, depleting it, the CARG's light dim.

Missed, Clatera bounded away from it, closing the distance with Sarah fast.

Another figure joined her as Clatera approached.

It was Lady Kilos. Though she only had a quick moment to take in and process what was happening, she acted fast. She got in front of Sarah.

"*Stop!!*" she said in a fairly accomplished Dirge voice which reverberated around the gallery.

Clatera reacted as if hot oil had been poured over him. He fell to the floor, curled up and kicked and flailed, his claws sparking off the old tiles. He pawed at his head and pulled out fistfuls of black, Monama hair. The power of the Dirge wore off, and he sprung again with incredible speed.

Ki put her arms around Sarah and, in a blast, Wafted away, leaving the Berserkacide only empty space.

Phillip entered the gallery, saw what was happening and drew his CARG and SAPP. He formed his SAPP into a black shield as Clatera squared off with him, trying to get around his shield.

Kay joined him, CARG at the ready. They worked well together, Phillip holding Clatera at bay while Kay threatened him with his CARG poised over top of the SAPP, like a horned, carapaced beast. Clatera tried to lunge to his right, and Phillip stopped him with his reaching CARG. Kay then attacked and impaled him through the ribs. He cried out and backed away, blood spurting.

They pressed the attack, relentlessly pushing toward the wall. Clatera tried to bound away and Phillip slashed, drawing more blood. Kay came in and thrust, getting him deep in the thigh.

With a burst of strength, he pushed them away and staggered toward the gallery where he made to leap over the side and then down to the ground far below. Kay and Phillip charged in pursuit, but the Berserkacide Clatera was far too fast and would reach the side well ahead of them.

Something happened. They saw the beast's head, arms and torso go over the side and plummet away; however his waist and legs were still there. Then there was blood bursting from the legs in a torrent. Then, the sick mess toppled over.

"Kay!" he heard a voice. It was Sam. They ran to the gallery and looked over the side.

There was Sam, clinging against the tower face with her claws like a rock climber. Her right hand was soaked in blood. She had killed Clatera with a swipe of her hand, bisecting him clean with her claws. Though she was fastened against the face of the tower with a two thousand foot drop below, she tried to hide her bloody hand from Kay.

"The light, Kay, the red light. Is it gone?"

Lying on the floor near the center of the gallery was a garnet pool of light. "I see it over there. Let me help you up!"

Sam clung fast to the side of the tower and refused to move. "No! Dispose of that light, Kay! Destroy it!"

Phillip went to the light and poked at it with his CARG. It shattered, and the light went out. "It's out, Sam! It's out!"

He helped her up into the gallery. She could barely stand she trembled so. "I thought you were dead, Kay, and I couldn't help you. I was too frightened to help you!"

Kay pulled her straight and held her. "It's all right, Sam. I'm fine."

Sam went limp with fright and shame.

"Sam!" He propped her up and looked around. "Where are Ki and Sarah?"

Phillip lit his Sight. "I think I see them several floors down. They look ok."

They searched the area. Three floors down, they found Ki and Sarah, unharmed, though Sarah appeared out of her skull with fright. Ki stroked her hair and soothed her.

* * * * *

They returned the next day with Lord Davage, Countess Sygillis and the Magistrates of Blanchefort and Mt. Holly. A search of the area found nothing of note in the castle; however, on the grounds, Clatera and Mitz's transport was discovered, partially destroyed and hidden by brush. The remains of Mitz's body was gathered up and put in a box, as was Clatera's. Kay wanted to take their remains back to Lake Monama so that they could be buried with their people, but Sam said Berserkacides could not be buried on Monama lands. After some doing, he convinced his parents to allow him to bury them in the servants graveyard deep in the Grove. He said these two were his friends, and he owed it to them. He felt it was his fault they were transformed into Berserkacides, that, if they hadn't encountered him in the fog, perhaps none of this would have happened. He swore, if he could someday make this right, he would. He would not forget them.

Of the strange device Kay said he saw and destroyed, not a trace of it could be found, no fragments, no nothing. Davage looked the area over several times with his Sight and confirmed nothing was there to be found. The Magistrates scanned the gallery with their best equipment: empty.

Perhaps Kay imagined it in the heat of the moment.

The Sisterhood of Light

13—A Visit from the Sisters

After the incident at Castle Durst, Sarah became much friendlier toward Lady Kilos. She never actually thanked her for saving her life, but her gratitude was clear.

Unfortunately, her attitude toward Sam soured to almost the point of hostility. Sarah no longer differentiated between Monamas and Berserkacides and regarded Sam with a mistrusting eye, often leaving the room when she entered.

Sam never quite recovered after Castle Durst, as she allowed Kay to fight for his life alone, too terrified of the Berserkacides to help. She seemed diminished a bit, not quite the powerful figure she had presented herself as before. And Sam's absences increased. Always unexplained, never a reason for being gone offered.

✶ ✶ ✶ ✶ ✶

Kay, Sarah and Phillip were surprised when they were called into Lord Davage's study a week after Castle Durst. Sam, as usual, was not there, and that suited Sarah just fine.

Eagle-eyed Sarah had seen the Sisters' procession come up through the village that morning. The floats, the flanking Marines.

The Sisterhood of Light had maintained a very close relationship with the House of Blanchefort over the years. When Kay's mother, Countess Sygillis, joined the House, the relationship became a bit rocky, as, she being an ex-Black Hat, created some measure of tension. However, after a tenuous first few encounters, the Sisters grew to trust and accept Sygillis and value her counsel.

The Sisters came often. They, occasionally, needed advice, and Lord Davage was always good for that. It was also said that, when they had a question about the Xaphans, they asked Countess Sygillis, as she was once a Xaphan.

Others simply said they enjoyed Lord Davage's company and liked to be sociable when they could. In any event, their meetings were always private and not spoken of to any great extent.

Today, however, was different. Everyone present, in turn, was asked to come to Lord Davage's study and spend a few moments with the Sisters, staff included. It was an odd thing to be asked to see the Sisters. Everybody in the castle couldn't help but be nervous.

"I'll bet you it's about the Berserkacide thing in the castle," Sarah speculated. "I'll bet they think Sam's a Berserkacide and was in on it."

"Quiet! She was not, Sarah," Kay replied, cross.

Kay, Sarah and Phillip sat outside the study, feeling a bit put off. Inside the study were the Sisters, and Creation knows what they really wanted. Lady Kilos and Lady Hathaline were there, also. Lady Kilos, usually a witty, somewhat sarcastic girl, sat silent in her lilac gown, obviously wanting to be elsewhere. She had her little terminal with her but wasn't typing anything into it. Lady Hathaline, ever the adventurer, didn't seem to care one way or the other. She asked a question.

"I don't know, Hath," Ki replied.

The door to the Lord Davage's study opened, and Lady Poe and Lord Peter came out holding hands.

Lady Poe, looking drawn and rather tired, gave a friendly nod to everybody present, stopped and adjusted Sarah's collar, and fussed with her hair. "You should be wearing a gown for this, young lady," she said under her breath.

"Let her be," Peter said. "You look just fine, Sarah."

Sarah smiled at her father.

The door opened again, and Lord Davage called in Kay, Sarah and Phillip, Ki and Lady Hathaline.

Slowly, as if they were going to their deaths, they stood and walked inside.

In the study was Countess Sygillis, sitting near Davage's desk in a bright teal gown. Sitting across from them were five Sisters, each wearing their usual white robes with blue cloaks. Their winged headdresses were large and pure white. A handsome, uniformed Marine stood by each one.

Davage returned to his desk and took a seat. "Come in, everybody, don't be shy," he said cheerfully.

One by one, they approached the desk, turned to the Sisters, and bowed. The Sisters acknowledged them with a short nod. There was a padded bench placed in front of the desk for them to sit, though, there wasn't enough room for everybody, so Kay and Phillip stood while Sarah, Ki and Hathaline seated themselves.

There was silence for a minute or two.

Kay felt quite uncomfortable and wanted to stare at the floor, but he knew proper etiquette demanded that one always look the Sisters in the eye, and he did, though it was hard. Phillip, standing next to him, was having less success, and his eyes often wandered to the floor.

After what seemed like an eternity, a Marine spoke. "Lord Blanchefort," he said for one of the Sisters, "you have truly grown into a fine young man. You do your House proud, as always. You and your kin are well favored, and we are honored to be counted amongst your friends."

Kay knew the proper response. "I am humbled to be in the exalted presence of the Sisterhood of Light and am also humbled that you find favor with me and my kin. I will, as the next Lord of Blanchefort, look forward to sustaining our age old friendship and open my arms to you, as you see fit."

The Sisters listened to his greeting and smiled.

Another Marine spoke. "You are, no doubt, curious as to the nature of our visit today. We shan't keep you in suspense any longer. Several weeks ago, our sacred stronghold at Hiei was breached by parties unknown, and an item was stolen."

Kay was shocked. "Stolen?"

"Yes. Fortunately, no Sisters were hurt or killed during the execution of this robbery. It is our wish to spend a moment with you to make you aware of this event, and to inquire if you have heard anything regarding the person or persons responsible. We are touring all of the Great Houses across Kana and asking for their help as well. Any information you have to share shall be most appreciated."

Kay could feel his insides churning a bit—the Sisters were Staring him up and down. If he had known anything about the robbery, their Stare would have dug it out immediately. The banter was, as they say, merely lip service.

Sarah was fidgeting hard, and Phillip looked sick—they were getting the

Stare treatment, too. Lady Kilos bit her lip and sat as still as she could. Lady Hathaline seemed to be suffering the most. She rocked back and forth, holding her stomach. Davage and Sygillis watched. Syg, in torment, took Davage's hand and squeezed it.

Hathaline stood and slumped over, holding her face with her hands. Kay went to her side and held her up. "Sis," he said. "Just let it pass through. Ok, let it go."

Weeping, she held onto Kay and struggled to endure the Stare.

Sygillis stood. "Enough, you are hurting our daughter!"

A Marine responded. "There's a darkness with this one. Has she been to Esther?"

"No, she has not, Sister," Davage, replied. "She is sixteen years old, for Creation's sake, and I'll thank you to let her go."

The Sisters' Stare continued. They dug deep, sifting for information and little Hathaline wasn't handling it well.

Whoever was stupid enough to steal something from the Sisters would be hunted forever. They were not forgiving about certain things, the Sisters, nor were they forgetting. If he or Sarah or Phillip or anybody else had actually been the one who committed the robbery, they would have been killed where they were.

They seemed to be taking a particular interest in Hathaline, peering deep into her soul. She made a gurgling sound.

"Sisters, enough!" Davage said in a commanding tone.

They let her go, and she staggered. Kay helped Hath back to her seat. "You ok, sis?" he asked, offering her a cloth.

She took it and nodded, wiping her face. Sygillis came to her side and held her.

After a moment, Kay resumed his spot next to Phillip and spoke, as was his duty. "Great Sisters, I am relieved to learn that none were harmed during the execution of this heinous act. Unfortunately, I have no information to share with you at this time. I will swear to keep a weather ear, and, should I hear anything of value, I will inform the Sisterhood at once."

The Sisters smiled. Apparently everybody had passed their Stare test. "Thank you, Lord Blanchefort. We would like to take this moment to remind you that our chapel at Kurtis in the Great Armenelos Forest is always open to pilgrims and esteemed visitors, and we invite you and your fine kin to please come and share some of your time with us. It would be an honor to entertain you as our guests."

"Thank you, Great Sister," Kay said. "I will remember your invitation, and when my travels bring me close, I will certainly stop and share a moment with my esteemed friends, the Sisterhood of Light."

The Sisters smiled and nodded, and the meeting was over. Davage stood and escorted them out of the study. Kay helped Lady Hathaline out; she was still reeling from the Stare.

"What the Feature was that all about?" Sarah said under her breath as they exited, shuffling her feet. "I feel like I need to vomit after that."

"I guess they want their item back."

Hath cried in Kay's ear.

"I know, sis," he said. "I know."

14—Hocked Jewels

A few days after the Sisters' visit to the castle, things were finally getting back to normal. At seven bells Kay waited in the Capricos Hall for Sarah and Phillip. Sam, too, should be by shortly, so she had promised, but, so far, he was alone at the table. They had planned on taking a Ripcar to the Clovis ruins and look for more signs of the Wraith of Gaston.

The morning table was set with heated trays of scrambled eggs and piled up mounds of bacon, hash, pancakes and waffles, fruit and an assortment of other delicious breakfast fares. Kay, expecting a vigorous afternoon, heaped his plate full of bacon and eggs.

He didn't have a good feeling. No Sam. Either Sam showed up early, or she tended not to show up at all. She promised, though.

Lady Kilos Wafted in with a blast, sending Kay's napkin flying.

"Ki, have you ever heard of simply walking from one place to the next?" he said.

"Well, you can't get good at something if you don't practice, can you? I intend to have fully mastered the Waft by the time I hit the Ball scene. I want to Waft in so hard I blow everybody's hats off."

Kay took a mouthful of eggs. "I suppose it's good that you've a goal in mind."

Ki smiled and sat down next to him. She shuffled her feet and tapped her fingers on the tabletop.

"Are you not eating?" Kay asked, noting that she hadn't grabbed a plate.

"You know what, Kay?" she said in a sheepish voice, ignoring his question.

"What?"

"I have more gossip."

He rolled his eyes. "Oh, Creation, what now?"

Sarah and Phillip filtered into the room, Sarah yawning and Phillip putting his duster on. They sat down on the other side of Kay, and Sarah filled her plate with eggs. For such a thin girl, Sarah had a big appetite.

"What's going on?" Sarah asked. "Where's your lady? We're hiking today, and she better not make us late. If she wants to hang out with us, she'd better be on time."

"Don't know, and chill out, Sarah," Kay responded. "We'll wait all day for Sam if we have to. She promised she'd be here."

"I have gossip," Kilos said, excited.

Phillip grabbed a plate and put two waffles on it. "You mean the news about Lady Sammidoran selling her jewelry in Armenelos? Am I correct?"

Ki was shocked. "How did you know about that, Phillip?"

"I, like you, have my sources."

Kay couldn't believe what he just heard. "Wait a minute! You're saying Sam went to Armenelos and sold some of her jewelry? When did that happen?"

Before Phillip could answer, Ki butted in. "Yesterday. And she didn't sell just a few pieces; she sold a lot of it. I heard she wanted to make a substantial set of purchases and, of course, she didn't have the ready cash, so she hocked her stuff—there's a market for that black Monama jewelry they wear. She even tried to disguise herself, but when she found out how expensive whatever it is she wanted to buy was, she dropped her disguise she was so flustered. I heard she also told a few people's fortunes to boot, as she was short on money."

Kay tried to ignore her. "Ki, why don't you get something to eat and leave me be?"

Ki wasn't having any of it. She was in full Gossip-mode. "So, Kay, what's Sam buying you? A gift of some sort?"

Sarah saddled right up to him and made a silly-sounding voice. *"Ohhhh, she loves you, doesn't she?"*

Kay ignored her. "Ki, I'm not aware of Sam buying me anything. Sam doesn't have much money. I've always told her to save her money. If she needs anything, she knows to come to me, and I'll give it to her."

"So," Sarah said chiming in. "Who's Sam buying the thing for, then, Kay?" she asked as she tore into her eggs. "It must not be for you. Must be for somebody else. See—Monamas—you can't trust them."

"I'm sure it's nothing to be concerned about. What's with you? Sam's your friend, and you're treating her like garbage."

Sarah looked at her plate and grumbled. "She's a good-for-nothing Berserkacide who was going to let you die in Rhoda Tower. I'm not going to forgive her for that."

"She was scared, Sarah, just like you were. You didn't help out much. Give her a break, will you?"

"So where is she? Who's she buying the thing for? I don't trust her."

"You've got a suspicious mind, Sarah."

"You bet I do. It's a dangerous world out there, Kay, and the sooner you realize that, the better. So then, why the sneaking around? Why didn't she come to you if she wanted something?"

"Maybe she wants to surprise me with it."

Sarah, with a mouthful of eggs, continued: "Or, maybe," she said swallowing, "maybe she's buying something nice for somebody else, like I said before."

"Don't be stupid."

"Oh, don't be stupid, eh? Why don't *you* not be stupid for a second? Let's get one thing straight right here and now—Monamas do not hang out with Elders—they just don't! They stay in their creepy little area by their creepy little lake in the fog, and they don't come out! And when they do come out, they go 'Nuts' and kill people. They Berserkacide, just like in Green Sabre with the Duke and just like those two freak jobs in the castle!"

"Those 'freak jobs', Sarah, were my friends, and I got to watch them die! And, it's probably my fault they ended up like that, you see?" Kay said, becoming angry. "Take it back!"

Sarah sat there a moment. "Sorry, I take it back. But, it's the damn truth, Kay, and it proves my point. Monamas and Elders don't mix!"

Phillip finished his waffles. "Sarah, I think you're exaggerating a tad."

Sarah continued. "Ever given a thought that she's just hanging out with you for your cash? Ever thought of that, Kay?"

"No, Sarah, I haven't."

"Perhaps you should. Perhaps you should come to the realization that she's been playing you this whole time. She's probably got some impoverished Monama dude back there by the lake that she's feeding coin to—your coin. By Creation, Kay! You're a Blanchefort; you're supposed to be playing people, not the other way around!"

Ki was conflicted. "Well, normally I'd agree with you, Sarah, but …"

Sarah cut her off. "Listen to your sister, Kay!"

"The sound of your voice is starting to wear on me, Sarah!" Kay said. He stood up and made to leave. He threw a questioning glance to Phillip, who looked back and shrugged his shoulders. Kay then walked away.

"Where are you going? We're supposed to be heading out to the Gaston!" Sarah cried.

"I no longer feel like it."

"If you're going to your tower to cry over your girlfriend, make sure you've got a healthy supply of tissues. When you're done bawling, come on back down and join us, and we'll forget this ever happened! Seeing a Monama—now I've heard it all!" Sarah, feeling victorious, ate her breakfast in earnest.

✶ ✶ ✶ ✶ ✶

That night, Kay wrestled with his thoughts. Ki's voice. Sarah's voice.

Sam's voice …

They all mixed together. Could Sarah be correct—could Sam have been toying with him all this time? All that talk of *Arin-Dan*? Monamas are a reclusive lot—rarely mixing with outside Houses on a social level, and whenever they did, they oftentimes went berserk.

Look at poor Clatera and Mitz.

He decided to go to Cathomere's Cathedral and sit there in peace. If Sam did show up tonight, he did not want her to know where he was. He thought, if she showed, he might say some things that he would regret later; such was his state of mind.

She had a lot of explaining to do, but now was not the time. Later, when he was more cleared-headed, when Sarah's voice was gone from his thoughts, that would be the time.

But not now. Sarah was allowing her obvious fear of Berserkacides to bleed over to a dislike of Sam, though she was hardly an unbiased source. Her head was full of tabloid Postings and lurid media junk proclaiming Monamas dangerous loners who could see the future, and were best left alone.

Loners who could go Berserkacide at any moment.

And that was horribly proved at Castle Durst.

✶ ✶ ✶ ✶ ✶

Sometime later, he heard a soft voice coming from behind him.

"Kay? Kay, what are you doing in here, darling?"

It was Sam. She was peeking her head into the cathedral, wearing one of his robes. Her face was drawn and tired. Snugs hung at her neck. She lit up a little bit, as she always did when she saw him.

As he previously thought, Kay felt a great deal of bitterness build up inside him. "I wanted some privacy."

Sam walked in and sat next to him. "Why?"

"I didn't particularly feel like seeing you this evening, Sam."

She was hurt. "Kay, are you angry with me? Is it something I've done?"

Kay leaned back— he felt a cruel streak coming on. All his love for her seemed encapsulated in his brain, and an angry, hateful Kay took his place at the controls. "Why do you keep coming here, Sam?" he asked.

"Because here is where I want to be. Because you're here, *Arin-Dan*, and I love you."

"Do you?"

"Kay, why are you acting like this?"

"Because I'm tired of ... everything. I'm tired of the secrets and the hiding and the weeping, and the deals behind my back."

"What deals?"

He wanted to stop, but was helpless. He couldn't shut his mouth. "Armenelos. I know all about it. You sold your jewelry to make a large set of purchases."

Sam, sitting there in his robe, was desperate. "I ... I didn't want you to know about that. But, please, it's not what you think."

"Yes, just the latest in a long series of secrets that you don't want me to know about. I must say the intrigue is starting to tire me."

Sam was shattered. "So, what are you saying Kay?" she said in an unsteady voice.

Kay's mouth started moving on its own—his heart not able to stop it—a clawed hand pulled his internal strings. "I'm saying I don't know if there's a future for us. I'm saying I don't know if I want you here anymore."

How could he have just said that?

"Sarah thinks you've been playing me for a fool, and I think maybe she's right."

Sam reacted like she'd been struck. She stood up, holding her face in her hands and knocked over a small brazier which fell with a loud commotion. Every bit of Kay wanted to go to her and comfort her, but a tiny cruel piece held him back. He just sat there.

Sam doubled over and made a noise. She then ran out of the cathedral, her feet slapping on the stones and was gone.

Kay stayed in the cathedral that night, partially asleep in a shallow pool of restless nightmare material. Even though he was in a 'safe' place, he was surrounded by phantasms: a happy Sam, a loving Sam, Sam crying, Sam angry, and an image of Sam that terrified him—she was crouching, four arms extended, ready to spring and tear his throat out. A Sam that wanted his blood.

Berserkacide.

His thoughts fell into the Shadowlands. He thought something small stood at the door of the cathedral. He heard a voice:

What did you just do, buddy?

The leering chorus jolted him from sleep. "Sam!" he yelled, but, of course, she was not there.

The cathedral appeared strange to him. Everything was in amber. For a moment he thought he could see Sam again, standing there doubled over in agony. Then she was gone. He saw the cathedral empty. He saw it fill with people there for service, then empty, then fill over and over again.

Then, he saw no cathedral. He was standing on a grassy plain overlooking the cliff to the sea far below. It was as if he was seeing back through the ages, to a primitive time of Old Vithland before Castle Blanchefort was built.

He then saw something quite strange—he saw himself and Sam standing side by side on a distant hilltop. They faced away from him, gazing at a turbid sky.

He blinked a few times, and it was gone. The amber haze cleared, and he was back in Cathomere's Cathedral, alone with his guilt.

As he sat there in the breezy airiness of the cathedral, he felt he had come to a crossroads of some sort. He was either at the beginning of something new, or at the end of something old, but he couldn't tell which. He kept thinking of his vision, that distant hilltop, he and Sam standing there side by side, facing away.

Somehow, it comforted him.

15—"I Run for You ..."

The next day was a waking nightmare. Kay stumbled through the day, honestly not knowing whether or not he was awake or asleep, alive or dead. Everything seemed strange and bile-tinged. Sam, and his caustic treatment of her, was always on the back of his thoughts, tormenting him.

Maybe he had gone insane. Maybe he had fallen over the edge after being so cruel to Sam. It certainly felt like he was insane.

He walked around the castle seeing strange things. His mother appeared smaller than normal, hunched, and ready to spring. He'd look away, and for a tiny second, she would be wearing her old Black Hat robes and mask. His father looked at him with a crafty, calculating eye, hand going to his CARG.

He walked down a corridor, not really knowing where he was going.

He felt hands at his throat.

He turned, and there was his sister, Ki, standing there innocently.

"Did you just try and strangle me?" he asked.

"Yes," she said and bounded away, tittering in an unsettling manner.

He went to the kitchens to grab something to eat. He kept seeing the staff approaching with hidden knives and odd powders hoping to tap them into his food.

Sarah was running around in her yellow gown, screaming his name, paints and makeup smeared on her face like a harlequin.

Kay tried to avoid her, as she seemed rather sinister. He hid from her in the foreboding Hall of Portraits, lined with paintings of past Blancheforts.

"KKKKKKKKKAAAAAAAAAAAAAAYYYYYYY!!!!!" Sarah screeched as she passed by.

He clutched at his head.

Sanity slipped away.

✶ ✶ ✶ ✶ ✶

Something spoke.

"Hey, Kay ... you awake?"

Kay stirred. He was in the dark in the Hall of Portraits, huddled on the floor. "Who's there?"

"It's me. Hey, you remember that thing we were talking about the other day?"

Kay whirled around. Surly he hadn't just heard a voice just now.

"You're not hearing things, Kay. It's me."

He saw nothing but the myriad portraits hanging from the wall. "Who are you?"

"A friend. For the Love of Creation, Kay, you're going to have to trust me on this."

"What is happening?" he said.

"You are under attack right now, from Castle Durst. Remember me telling

you this?"

"What?"

"Castle Durst—the device I told you about. Remember?"

A device at Castle Durst? He struggled to clear his mind, to find clarity.

"Yes, I remember it. I destroyed the device at Castle Durst."

"It's back! They fixed it, Kay, and it's on! You have to give them an 'A' for effort on their part. They are using it on you even as we speak. Don't feel quite normal, do you? Everything seems a little off, doesn't it? It's their machine at Castle Durst doing that to you, Kay. The light it creates drives you insane."

"Insane? Father, I'll get Father and ..."

"Your father can't help you, Kay, nor can your mother or anybody else for that matter. They are under the light and are helpless before it. You have to get rid of it."

"What? How?"

"The light doesn't affect you like it does everybody else. You are able to shrug off its effects. I don't have time to explain why right now; just trust me."

"What? What should I do?"

"First, make your way to your room, Kay, and be careful; if it looks dangerous out there along the way, it probably is. Don't stop for anything, no matter what you see, okay? Just get to your room; that's the main thing. Oh—and lock the door when you get there."

Struggling with his sanity, he exited the Hall of Portraits and made the long walk to his tower. He saw an orange flickering light, the southern wing of the castle seemed to be on fire. He saw people along the way lying on the ground. He saw staff members on the floor here and there.

Was it nap time? It was so hard to think. Why was the castle on fire?

Maybe somebody should put the fire out?

Up ahead, who's that? Phillip? Yes, it's Phillip, asleep too. That's not like Phillip. Kay went to his side to wake him up.

Blood all over Phillip. His throat was gone.

Looking back. Red everywhere. The staff were all dead.

All dead ...

Fire...

All dead...

He teetered.

"GET TO YOUR ROOM!!" rang through his head.

He continued on, stumbling through the castle toward his tower.

Everything was a muddle. Hard to think. Passing a mirror he saw his own reflection: it was odd, distorted. He saw a mark around his right eye, very similar to Mother's Shadowmark.

Ahead was the base of Zorn Tower, his tower. There was a commotion going on down the corridor. There was a pile of yellow fabric on the floor with a patch of black over it.

Sarah in her gown, in pieces. Something in black was on top of her, tearing her body apart with relish.

It was terrible. Kay quickly stumbled into his tower and locked the door. He then took the lift up and up to his floor.

He staggered in, closed the door and locked it. He sat in a corner staring at the walls.

There were strange sounds coming from below, a steady droning of misery and a growing roar of fire. He looked out his terrace and saw, far in the distance, a pinkish light coming from Castle Durst. It was golden and warming, rather comforting and pretty to see.

There were knocks at his door, but he didn't answer.

Knocks at the door again. This time, somebody tried the latch, finding it locked. The person tried even harder, the old door shaking in its frame.

"*Kay,*" he heard through the door. The voice was familiar yet distorted and wicked. "*Let me in, Kay; it's Sam. I want to kiss you.*"

The door shook in its ancient frame. *"KAY!"* came a shriek from the other side as the door withstood a torrent of banging. He heard wood splintering and curling away as something sharp assailed it from the other side.

Eventually he got into bed, fully dressed, and pulled up the covers, listening to the door rattle on its hinge.

Suddenly the room was filled with silvery light, and his bedclothes were ripped away.

"Kay! What are you doing? No time for sleeping! It's time to go to work!"

"Who are you, and what do you want?"

Something wrenched him out of bed and set him into a kneeling position on the floor. "*Who am I? I'm your best friend, Kay; that's who I am! We've got a long night ahead of us, but, first, you've got a big mess to clean up!*"

"What? Fire?"

"That too. I hate to have to give you a crash course in using your own Gifts, but ..."

Kay felt a burst of agony bloom in his side. It felt like he was being bitten by a shark.

In a halo of pain, the room turned to amber, and things became muddled.

Though he might have been dreaming—it certainly felt like he was dreaming—he found he could see past the walls of his room through the depths of the Castle.

Carnage everywhere, death and fire! Outside his door was a Berserkacide in the shape of Sam, his *Cerri-Tela*, clawing at his door, trying to get at him He felt himself sicken with heartbreak.

"Stay with me, Kay. I know it's hard, but you have to have faith."

The southern wing of the castle was now enveloped in flame, windows shattering. Elsewhere, his father was lying on the floor—not moving. His mother was walking about in a strange stilted fashion, a blank look on her face with blood on her hands. His sister Kilos was holding her head spinning around in her room. Lady Poe and Lord Peter were laying on the floor of their bedroom huddled together, covered in giant bugs! Everybody else, Hathaline, Maser, Sarah, Phillip were still, like they were dead.

The swarm of insects covered Lady Poe and Lord Peter in a seething mass.

Kay tried to pull away, but was held down and in agony. "*Focus, Kay, focus. Be calm. I promise everything will be all right. Now, I need you to look out into the Telmus Grove, specifically, to an oak clearing where Sam once mentioned the name 'Olonol'. Do it now, Kay.*"

"Everybody dead ..."

"Kay!" the voice said with rising anger. "*Look to the Grove! Do it now!*"

As commanded, Kay saw out through the castle walls into the amber night, out into the Grove. He saw the stone walkways and ancient trees. He saw the flickering menagerie of fire light coming from the castle.

There it was. There was the clearing. Nobody there, lonely.

"Now," the voice said, "*this is going to be a little strange, but stay with me.*"

The image of the darkened Grove changed. It began moving, as if in reverse. The light from the fire went out. Night faded to twilight, which returned to dusk.

Passing birds flew backwards, and a confusion of people appeared. They acted out a strange scene in reverse.

"All right, that's far enough. Now look."

Things seemed to slow down and stop and then resume a more normal running.

There was Sam, Blinking into the Grove. She slowly placed Snugs around her neck, not bothering to pull the chain through her hair and fell to her knees. She wept bitterly. A knife dropped out of her hand.

"Sam!" Kay cried.

"I'm not going to lie, she's in a bad state, kid, ever since you said those things to her in the cathedral. You broke her little heart, and she also can't forgive herself for not helping you fight those Berserkacides at Castle Durst. She's at the end of her rope, and her head is not in a good place."

"I need to get to her. To talk to her!"

"What you're seeing has already happened, Kay, earlier today. You're seeing into the past, and pretty soon you're about to find out what it is that Sam has been so afraid of through the years. You wanted to know, so now you get your wish. Watch, just watch and don't be alarmed."

A cloudy green slit formed in the air behind Sam, and two people appeared through it as if from nowhere, a tall man in golden armor and a rail thin, bent woman wearing some sort of beaded dress. She had red hair that was styled into a towering bee-hive. Kay struggled but was held in place.

"Just watch!"

The man and woman approached Sam, standing at either side of her.

The woman spoke seemingly kind words in a rasping voice as the man looked on.

She told Sam that she had had a good life, that they had let her go on for a long time, relatively free. They told her they had allowed her dreams to come true, and she'd been so happy.

Wasn't that right?

The broken Sam agreed.

Now, she said, it was time to fulfill her mission, one that they had selected for her since she was a small girl. The woman told Sam that she was her favorite slave by far.

Sam reacted a little and searched for her knife. The man kicked it away.

Blink, Sam, Blink! No, she can't with Snugs on.

The woman gave her a tender hug and kiss, and then savagely wrenched her head back by the hair. She held something in her hand.

Light, red light, just like what Clatera had been holding at Castle Durst. The woman forced her to gaze into the light.

Sam struggled a moment, and then slowly stood up. A second pair of pale arms punched through her black gown like two milky snakes.

"Berserkacide!" Kay wailed.

Then the woman gave Sam her command: Kill. Kill everyone in the castle, and leave *Arin-Dan* for last. Tear his throat out when you get to him.

Sam turned and ran as only she could toward the castle, her new arms held over her head.

"I know what you're thinking, Kay, but don't! What you just witnessed is

what happened earlier today, but, we aren't going to let that happen, are we?"

"How am I seeing this?"

"You can do quite a bit with your Sight, Kay—that's right, the Sight you didn't believe you had, well believe it. And, with your Sight, we can prevent this from happening at all."

"We can stop it? Prevent it?"

"We can. Take these."

Something small and slightly squishy fell into Kay's hand.

"Now, you're going take a few steps forward, and you'll be out there in the Grove, in the past with Sam. Take what I've put in your hand and scatter them around. These objects I've given you will prevent Mr. and Mrs. Creepy from appearing out there. They won't last forever, so make it snappy, see? Now, listen to me, and heed what I say! Do not take your eyes off her! Do not blink, and do not look away, otherwise you'll lose her! You won't have much time, so you better get out there, make up with her and get her to leave and quick about it! Be warned—the past isn't like a scene from a film replayed over and over. You have one chance to step through and fix this; after that, this moment in time will be blacked out, and you'll never be able to see it again. We could, in theory, keep going back farther and farther and keep trying and really make a mess of things, so let's do this right the first time. Are you ready?"

Kay had no idea what to make of this. The voice allowed him to stand. "I'm ready," he said having no notion as to what was going to happen.

"Then go. I'll be waiting for you when you're done."

The scene reset itself. There was Sam entering the clearing, holding her knife ...

... and Kay was standing behind her.

She sniffed and whirled around. She looked at him with big eyes. She hunched over a little.

"What are you holding there, Sam?" he asked.

She looked down and hid what was in her hand.

"Give me the knife, Sam."

She wiped a tear away and quietly held out the knife. Kay took it. He kept his gaze fixed on Sam. "Please put your Snugs on before you get cold."

She quietly put her medallion on and worked it through her hair. Sam looked at him oddly for a moment, and then burst into a smile. "You're seeing! You're using your Sight, aren't you? I knew it! I knew you could do it!"

"What are you doing out here, Sam?"

She looked down at her hands. "I ... I've lost your love, and, after my performance at Castle Durst, I don't deserve it." Her face cringed into sadness. "I was too frightened to help you, and I came here to end my life. I wanted to be near you when I did it. I thought perhaps you would bury me on Dead Hill and then, one day, you and I might rest near each other. I was hoping you would forgive me!"

"You don't need to be dead to be near me, Sam. There is forgiveness that's needed here. Forgive my words. Forgive me, Sam."

Kay thought he heard something moving behind him. Gods—the things in his hand, he'd forgotten to scatter them! Quickly, he tossed them to the ground and several objects tumbled into the grass. A few objects remained in his hand.

There was movement and sounds. He smelled burnt umber, but Kay ignored it all. He trained his gaze on Sam, not daring to look away.

Sam held her stomach, as if she were about to be sick. "I didn't want you to see me like this."

Kay felt his eyes going blurry. Quick! Be quick!

"Sam, I said the things I said because I was hurt—because I thought you might be straying, or toying with my emotions."

"I would never. I ..."

"I know, but I let Sarah get the better of me. I repent everything I said. You know I didn't mean any of it."

"You ... love me still?"

"More than ever. I have seen the things that hover over you, and I know that they are soon to be here to change you into a Berserkacide."

Sam's mouth opened in terror. She looked around.

"Have no fear, Sam. They cannot enter for the moment. You must get away from here for the time being and guard yourself. I want you to be strong. You have always taught me to be strong, now it's your turn."

Sam approached and put her arms around him. "I'll ... I'll have to run, Kay. They will be after me."

"I will stand at your side, Sam. Let's face them together. I'm not afraid."

"No, no I think I know what to do. I'm almost ready. My *Arin-Dan*, I have something planned that can save us—I know it will! That's what I've been doing, but I had to be careful because they're watching. They are *always* watching us. I just need a bit more time. No Monama ever runs from them, but, if I have your love, then I'll run for you. I'll do what I must until I'm ready."

"Then take my strength, *Cerri-Tela.* You have my love, and my adoration, and my CARG remains yours."

Sam breathed in and out, a new light in her eyes. She stood up straight. "Thank you for reminding me of what I already should have known, and for giving me new strength, my love. I don't know when you will see me again, but you will. Don't worry about me. Your love shall lend wings to my feet, and they will never catch me."

Kay held out his hand. "Sam, take these. I don't know what they are, but they shall somehow hinder those who chase you. Take them."

Sam took the objects in his hand. She smiled. "Oh, so adorable. Thank you for this gift, Kay! I should have known; I should have seen this!"

In Kay's side vision, he caught a glimpse of several small blue figurines in Sam's hand.

Sam then moved her gown aside, exposing her collarbone. In Kay's amber Sight, he could see there was some sort of studded collar there—wait! He'd seen it before near the bathhouse, stitched into her neck. With her strong hands, she pawed at it, and ripped it bleeding from around her neck. She held the thing for a moment and regarded it with hatred. She then flung it with all her might a considerable distance away.

"Now, I am free, Kay, for good or ill. Your love has freed me."

His Sight wavered. "Go, Sam. Be safe and know that I love you."

She turned and removed Snugs from her bleeding neck. She looked at him one last time and mouthed the words in Anuie: "*I run for you.*"

Then she was gone.

16—Return to Castle Durst

"Great work, kid!" the voice exclaimed as Kay returned to his room.

"What just happened?"

"You made her day; that's what just happened. So, one big mess down, one to go!"

He tried to gaze through the walls and into the castle, but he couldn't see through the stone of his room.

"Don't worry about your folks—they're fine for now. What you need to be worrying about is that damn light atop Castle Durst. You need to get over there pronto and take care of it—for good this time."

Kay felt the effects of the Insanity Light coming from Castle Durst again. Things became a tad muddled.

"What? I'll get my father and we'll go ..."

"No time. Out the window! Hurry!"

Obediently, he started going to the window.

"Wait... Out the window? What am I supposed to do?"

The voice appeared to get angry. *"Use your Gifts and be a Man, Kay! Go to Castle Durst and destroy that damn light! Do it!"*

Kay began to climb out the window. "Wait! How am I supposed to get down?"

With that, something head-butted Kay out of the window, making the decision for him.

He plummeted through the air toward the dark, night-washed ground far below. Sam had threatened several times to bodily throw him out a window to force his use of Gifts but had never done it.

Now, here it was and he didn't like it one little bit!

Falling, feeling the wind tickle his face and muss his hair, he panicked for a moment.

He thought about everybody in the Castle, on the ground, laid low, attacked by something coming from Castle Durst. On fire, Covered in bugs. The cold night air cleared his head a little, and he concentrated.

Better than dead, though, better than dead. He had made up with Sam, and she knew he loved her, and given her hope. Now she was running from ... whomever.

He began to Waft. He had about two thousand feet before he hit the waiting rocks below. He tried to imagine himself standing in the Grove with his cousins charging at him, a nice sunny day, not a care in the world, Sarah and Phillip laughing and cavorting.

Sarah and Phillip lying in a death-like state in their rooms, previously gutted!

The biting wind flew past him as he plummeted. His hat was gone. Who knew where it was.

Relax.

The air slowly spiraled around him, the beginning of a Waft—the random hand of the wind taking shape and organizing in a cylinder around his plummeting body.

Remember what Father said—the wind is not the Waft, but the by-product of it.

Waft! Just Waft!

"Kay!!" someone shrieked from high above. Kay thought he saw a small, silvery head peeking out his window and two little round eyes fixed on him. "Waft, Kay! You're going to hit the ground!"

Thanks for that confidence-shattering update!

The air moved faster. *Almost. Just Waft!*

He thought he saw the large stained glass windows of Maserfeld's Cathedral go whizzing by, lit up in gothic reds and blues. If that were the case, he didn't have long.

"Kay!!!"

A small tornado of wind formed around his body.

He hit the cold, rocky ground, but instead of a crushing, life-ending collision, he was only vaguely aware of the impact. It was a rather muffled, blunted hit, like landing in a pile of pillows. He felt himself moving through the air, Wafting, as a ghost. He came out of it several yards away with a skittering blast.

Getting his bearings, he stood.

Pain, sudden pain in his leg. He fell and slid to a stop, skinning his palms. His left ankle was broken from the fall. Must have hit the ground just before he Wafted. It could have been worse. A lot worse.

He limped into the covered park to the west of the castle—a great number of Ripcars of various sizes and makes were parked there. At the front of the line was a modest little green one—the tortured one his mother favored using, though she was a terrible pilot, just like he was. Mother's green Ripcar was dinged up from the many little accidents she'd had with it. She rarely used it anymore, favoring her perfected *Seeker,* which she could enlarge in size for quick and effortless transportation.

Next was the big silver one they had taken to Castle Durst for their bowling adventure. He thought about hopping into it, but the ignition pan wasn't there—Phillip always removed it, a habit the Duke had taught him.

Nearby was Hath's little souped up blue one. It was sleek and fast, and not quite legal—Lord Peter and Lord Milos of Probert himself had made several choice modifications to the thrust system. It had large tailpipes sticking out the back. It didn't create exhaust per se, and, therefore, didn't need tailpipes, but it had them anyway for show. The name HATH was painted in a sparkly, flowing script on the hood. Lady Hathaline loved this little Ripcar.

The ignition pan was there, snapped into place. Hath never removed it—who would dare make off in her Ripcar?

He thought of her lying dead in the castle. Surly, she wouldn't mind in this desperate situation.

He hopped in and fiddled with the controls. Hath had all sorts of girly beads and trinkets hanging from the controls, and Kay wiped them away with a sweep of his hand and turned the pan, firing it up in a rumble

He didn't know what he was doing. In this regard, Kay was certainly not his father, who could fly anything. He wasn't even his little sister who could fly this Ripcar with surprising skill. He'd seen her do it many times. She'd crushed Lord Phineas of Tyrol with it during the Falling in Love ball, creating quite a scandal in Tyrol and a huge increase in Hath's correspondence pile.

The car roared, stalled, lurched with a puff of ions and careened into the silver one. The big silver Ripcar lurched over and smashed into the little green one—his mother's favorite, now partially destroyed.

He would apologize to the both of them later.

Somehow, he got the protesting blue Ripcar out of the park and into the air, flying through several trees in the process.

Lurching, he fell onto his broken ankle and was livid and in pain.

Pain.

The dark of night fell away into a pall of amber, and in that moment, he could see everything, for miles and miles. He could see Castle Durst like it was right there—he could see every detail of it. It was overwhelming. After a moment passed, everything faded back to night.

He hit the thrusters and hung on for dear life. Barely under control, the Ripcar roared into the mountain passes heading west.

There was a mountain ahead, coming up fast out of the darkness: smooth, steep and cone-shaped—Mt. Durst from the looks of it—a slightly smaller twin of Mt. Vith to the east. He tried to go around it, but the Ripcar kept on going straight. He moved the sticks but nothing happened; the cursed car kept plowing ahead toward the waiting mountain.

As the bulk of the mountain rapidly approached, he found himself oddly fascinated by the movement of Hath's beads on the dash.

Good Creation, his family was dying, his castle was burning, and he was going to fly his little sister's Ripcar into Mt. Durst while gawking at her beads. He was probably the worst pilot ever, even worse than his mother. His father, should he live, would surely laugh, or possibly cry.

He remembered one afternoon his father showing Lady Hathaline something about having to use the foot pedals to bank when in-atmosphere. The sticks only were effective in orbit. And then he remembered Lady Hathaline stepping on the pedals and successfully turning the craft.

He glanced down and saw the pedals.

Mt. Durst was a hulking shadow in the dark getting closer every second. The bare trees growing on its side seemed to be reaching out for him.

His red-headed, gown-wearing, pasty-faced sister could bank the car.

He stepped on the pedal, and the Ripcar banked so hard it almost dumped him out.

Recovering, he went around the mountain, righted the Ripcar and set a direct course for Castle Durst, the light from Rhoda Tower gleaming across the night.

The old, empty castle emerged ahead like a bleached white hand with patina-clogged fingernails. Wanting more speed, he risked using the thrusters and punched them; the car surged ahead, again almost dumping him out.

He aimed for the top of Rhoda Tower. He could see something there in the gallery at the top creating a bright focused light pointed at Castle Blanchefort, and it pointed in several other directions as well to the north, east and west. Several people milled about in the gallery. He would be there in seconds.

Wait! How does one stop this crazy contraption? He was speeding toward the high gallery of Rhoda Tower, and there was no way of stopping the Ripcar … none that he could see. He tested the various controllers and buttons in a frenzy, and none produced the desired effect of slowing the craft down. Moments before impact, he released the controls, leapt over the side and began to Waft, again testing fate. As he fell, the speeding Ripcar plunged into the tower face, taking off a good part of the eastward gallery. Bits of composite materials, stone, and flaming shards of metal came spiraling down, keeping pace with his fall. There was screaming, too—people clad in scant golden robes were falling amidst the debris.

Golden robes: Golden People. That seemed familiar to him.

The Golden people are your enemy and tormentors of the Monamas.

Just as the Waft took hold, he thought he saw the falling gold-robed people change shape.

Changing shape; again, that was familiar.

One turned into a large bird of some sort, and another turned into an alien, starfish-like creature. That was impressive. Sam could change shape, but only into other types of humanoids. She couldn't make herself into a bird or a starfish like these Golden People had just done.

With a blast, Kay Wafted and appeared near the ruined, flaming edge of the gallery. Nursing his ankle, he lurched in.

Twelve golden figures milled about, their light gold robes waving in the breeze of Kay's Waft. They looked at Kay impassively. A moment later, a large bird and strange alien creature with starfish-like limbs appeared over the gallery and entered the lounge.

The bird, talons flashing, swooped at Kay. He dove aside, hitting his broken ankle.

Again, pain washed over him. In amber he saw sitting in the middle of the lounge, where the extinct Dursts once entertained guests (he and his family included), a tall, strange-looking device. It was shaped something like a Xandarrian oil lamp, having a tapering base expanding into a bulbous center section going to a thin, stalk-like top. It was composed of a smooth pearly, pinkish material with a harness of black circuitry strapped to it at various points. A strong pinkish light glowed at its top, sending several quiet but deadly shafts of light out in various directions—including one toward distant Castle Blanchefort.

The device jogged his memory--he'd seen it before in this very spot as he fought the Clatera/Mitz Berserkacides; only now, it was alive and functioning and hidden in a Cloak of some sort, allowing him to see it only when he was in excruciating pain. Clatera and Mitz must have been placed here as Berserkacides to guard this device.

Time seemed to speed up. He saw one of the golden females standing next to the device raise her arm and bathe him in a beam of reddish light. He saw himself melting in the light, leaving only his clothes and his skeleton behind. The amber haze faded, and he saw the Golden People standing there next to the device, the bird and starfish joining them and quickly changing shape back into golden, toga-clad people.

What had he seen—the future perhaps?

Just as he had predicted, one of the golden females raised her arm, finger extended.

He knew what was coming. Kay pointed his CARG and loosed a blast of

Silver tech. The female produced a cone of red light from her finger and met Kay's blast in the middle, the red and silver swirling together for a moment. Two energies wiped each other out and faded with a crack.

Kay and the group of Golden People stared at each other for a moment. They chortled amongst themselves in an odd language. One of them produced a controller and pressed a few buttons. A type of greenish gate opened behind them. They stepped through the gate and were gone.

Now alone in the gallery he approached the odd device. It was casting powerful beams of light in various directions. One beam was bathing Castle Blanchefort. Another was heading east, in the general direction of Bloodstein. Another pointed north toward the Holts of Shirster Point, and a vast beam, pointing southwest, seemed to be shining on the city of Mt. Holly.

This one odd machine was attacking several of the more prominent Vith strongholds all at once from this central location.

He hauled back and gave it a good whack with his CARG as he had previously. Nothing happened. He hit it again with similar results. His CARG was just bouncing off.

Creation!

"Blood-gutted Shocktyte!" he yelled as he stepped back, pointed his CARG, and let fly with another blast of Silver tech. His blast hit the device in a wave of silver fire.

Ah! The device was somehow shielded, the mass of his Silver tech strike being reflected and diverted away. He could see it plain as day. He laid into it, searing it in silver. After a few moments, the power of his blast took effect. The shield faltered and fizzled out.

He tried to blast it again, but, of course, no more Silver tech; the CARG sputtered, needing to recharge. He shambled up to it and gave it several hard cutting blows, the tubular shaft of his CARG this time biting deep into the device's pearly surface in angry furrows.

The lights at the top of the device sputtered and went out. The deadly beams were quieted.

Good, good!

Before Kay could catch his breath and chop the device into bits, another misty green gate opened in mid air. Three forms were dumped out roughly, and the gate closed.

They were naked, stark white with thick black hair that went down to the floor. They were tied up at the wrists and ankles with dark chains. They wore odd collars studded with long, diamond-shape crystals. They shivered.

Collars—just like Sam's, the one she tore out and was terrified of.

Monamas!

He then ran to them. There were two men and a woman. Just like Sam, they were thin and ghostly pale, their black hair bursting and thick, their eyes black as midnight.

The woman appeared to be having trouble breathing. He knew what was wrong with her; the cold. Monamas couldn't take the cold, and here they were, stark naked in the open gallery. He took his coat off and draped it over her. He then began working to undo her ties. "I know you're cold. I'm going to release you; then, I'm going to get you warmth."

He grabbed the collars around their necks and tried to pull them off. They didn't budge. They were stitched deep into their flesh, as Sam's was, and he couldn't pull them loose with all his strength.

They would have to be cut off.

As Kay worked, the Monamas didn't respond much. They sat there, heads lolled, eyes blank, mouths open and drooling.

Head Swarm. Is this what happens to a Monama when they go into Head Swarm?

He shook them trying to roust them from it.

Slowly, they started to stir.

"Are you all right?" Kay asked, gently shaking them.

Gradually, they came into focus. They were terrified. *"Not ... not safe ... It's not safe ... "* one of them said in a language similar to Anuie, but not quite. Must be Conox, a sister tongue they spoke in the southern parts of Lake Monama. Sam had told him about it once.

"It's all right," Kay said in Anuie. *"I'm not going to hurt you. I'm going to get you someplace warm, and I'm going to get these collars off you."*

All three of them looked grief-stricken.

The woman struggled to say something. Kay leaned in to listen.

"Devada, devada," she said.

He didn't understand. *"I'm sorry, Hosfra, I don't know that word."*

She grit her teeth and switched to League Common. "... run ..." she said breathlessly. "Run, sir, please! Run for your life!"

The crystals embedded in the collars at their necks came to life glowing a rosy reddish color.

Their black Monama eyes suddenly lit up with a crimson glow. As Kay watched in horror, the Monamas, like rabid animals, suddenly lurched in their chains, roaring and slavering in fury. They raised their arms up toward the ceiling and, with a sudden sickening crunch of cartilage and bone, an extra set of arms, complete with delicate hands, fingers and claws, came shooting out under their armpits. Like the popping of a great boil, a hole blasted open between their eyes spewing noisome fluid.

They got three eyes! Three of them! The third one sees into some creepy chaos realm! Sarah loved to say about ...

Berserkacides!

He jumped back.

As the rabid Monamas bloodied themselves trying to get out of their chains, three misshapen people emerged from the back of the tower, a man and two women. The man was clad in armor that appeared to have been a gold color at one point, but was smeared with some sort of brown, stinking substance. The women were clad in fibrous reddish gowns or dresses that were heavily sewn with odd beads.

The man's armor was anatomically correct, down to the smallest and most modest of details; yet, his body was strange and malformed—as if his bones had been broken and deliberately mended in incorrect positions. The women appeared to be skinless, and their dresses were sticky against their bleeding bodies. As they stood there, blood and urine pooled beneath them. Their joints, too, were malformed.

Kay was horrified.

One of the women approached the roaring Berserkacides and held up a reddish prism, which seemed to enthrall them. The other approached the tall device in the center of the room and pressed a few buttons on its pinkish surface. The harness of black circuitry strapped to it moved and twisted, re-wiring itself like a tangle of sinewy snakes. Then, like a juggernaut, the light at the top of the device came back to life, glowing again bright as ever. The machine and its deadly light were back in action.

Kay made to finish the device off, and the armored man jumped forward and raised a hideous weapon that was fashioned to resemble a male phallus.

He raised his CARG and held it out, one-handed as usual. He leaned forward and felt the angry protest of his broken ankle.

"This machine stands before my family's life, and by Creation, I'll see it in pieces!"

The man in armor laughed and slobbered.

One of the women opened her terrible mouth and made a hideous noise—a sort of half screech, half moan.

Kay couldn't move. He couldn't move a muscle. She had cast some sort of arcane spell on him, and he was in its thrall.

"Release the Berserkacides and kill him," one of them said in a hollow voice.

Casually, the other woman slinked forward, swinging her hips in a seductive fashion. "Oh, but why waste this wonderful piece of meat? They'll spoil it. He's not going anywhere." She looked Kay up and down, and, with her blood-crusted hands, touched him all over. She breathed graveyard breath into his ear and kissed him, her hands going to forbidden places.

Kay's flesh recoiled at her touch, but there was nothing he could do. He couldn't move. He was be-spelled.

These beasts! These were what Sam, and Clatera and Mitz and all the Monamas were so terrified of. Here they were, and they were horrendous.

The woman roughly pushed him down and climbed on top of him, the others watching with perverted glee. She produced a small, blunt knife and danced it over the surface of his clothes, slowly slicing them off.

Kay, under the woman, became aware of a growing sound coming from outside—a steady buzz or droning sound. The sound got louder and louder, penetrating his ears and settling into his brain.

He noticed a mass of small bluish objects filtering into the gallery, flying on shiny, reddish wings.

Bugs! The gallery was filling with huge, buzzing insects! They swarmed around and settled on the walls, covering them in a moving carpet of wings and legs. The three monsters swatted at them, were annoyed by their presence. Kay had heard of these giant bugs, from Sarah's posts.

Paraflies.

Their numbers quickly growing, the bugs made a pervasive, deep-seated buzzing drone which saturated Kay's ears, got into his mind, pushing all else out.

And … he could move. The spell had been broken!

Quickly, he spun his CARG around and rammed it into the woman's midsection, the shaft of his weapon thudding to a stop at the base of her spine. He threw her off, and she landed a few feet away, dropping her knife and gushing blood.

Kay quickly stood and raised his CARG.

The mass of Paraflies lining the walls had very shiny wings, and coupled together as a whole, they made a coppery reflective surface, like a mirror that slightly undulated with the movement of their wings. He could clearly see himself in it.

The woman Kay had stabbed was also gawking at herself in the mirror at her mangled face, her skinned body and broken joints. She looked at her image as if seeing herself as a monster for the first time.

She slowly put her hands to her face and, in the din of buzzing, began a long, pitiful scream. She stood, gushing blood from her wound. She glanced back at Kay once—a look of genuine horror and shame etched on her ruined face.

She turned and ran, gibbering, to the broken rim of the gallery where she threw herself over the side without hesitation and was gone.

The armored man, averting his gaze, cried out: "Release the Berserkacides!"

"She had the controller!" the woman croaked, her voice nearly drowned out in the buzzing.

The pair of them sprang to attack. The remaining woman drew a dirty-looking knife and moved to Kay's right.

The man swung his penis-shaped weapon in a cleaving stroke, and Kay raised the CARG one-handed to meet it. Their weapons clanged. Kay lurched backwards, his ankle proving to be inconvenient. Another collision of weapons, and Kay tried to move to his left to rest his ankle. Paraflies swirled around, bouncing off of each other as Kay and the monsters fought. The noise they created was deafening.

CLANG! Another clash of weapons.

Suddenly, the woman grabbed him from behind. Her skinned arm was slick with partially dried blood and stank of innards. He felt something sharp jab into his back.

Pain.

Everything turned to amber for a moment. For an instant, he could see this mutilated woman as a smiling, pretty girl wearing a fine gown, her hair set in a pleasing style. She sat with her family enjoying an outing by the sea.

Another image entered his head—the girl confined in a small, transparent container, full of a noxious brown substance. She screamed for help, for relief. None came apparently.

He saw her come out of the container a monster, lost in an evil dream.

It was heart-breaking. Kay pushed the images from his head.

She jabbed him again, and this time he flipped her over his head. She landed with a slippery thud. Like a panther, she sprang to her feet. Without allowing himself time to think about it, Kay swung his CARG and took her head off.

A smiling, pretty girl with her whole life ahead of her, turned into a wrecked monster.

Who could do such a thing?

The Golden People, that's who. The people trying to drive his family mad.

The man came at him again, and they clashed weapons a few times.

Around and around they went: jab, slash, counter and thrust, their weapons ringing off one another. The man kept attempting to push Kay into the chained Berserkacides, where they could tear him to shreds. Kay made sure to avoid that area and stay well out of their reach.

As they exerted themselves, Paraflies began trying to land on Kay. With his free hand, he tried to shoo them away, but they were big and persistent. They landed on his back, they got in his hair.

The man, also being covered by Paraflies, tried to run Kay through. He just barely countered, his concentration being disrupted by the Paraflies. As they neared the broken railing of the gallery to the sheer drop beyond, the man tried to hook Kay's CARG out of his grasp. They spun around and, when the man's back was facing the edge, Kay extended the shaft of the CARG like a piston and forced him past the edge out into open space where he fell.

He laughed and tittered all the way down, his grotesque weapon falling with him.

He was gone. Kay turned his attention back to the device.

The Golden People had returned, and they stood next to the device as the Paraflies buzzed in a cloud. An oiled, golden female walked over to the raging, tied up Monamas and held up another red prism. She showed it to them. They slavered in renewed fury, their chains just barely containing them.

With a wave of her hand, their chains unlocked and the three of them, bounding on all fours, came at Kay in a lather.

A scene right out of Sarah's eager nightmares was coming true. Berserkacides, on the move, four-armed and lusting for blood—his blood, in this case.

They were moving fast.

He pointed his CARG and tried to fire off a Silver tech blast.

It sputtered.

As they came at him, he couldn't see any good way out of this. The device still functioned, still emitted the Insanity light. His family still suffered in its glow.

He threw his CARG in a spiral, hitting the device right in the center—impaling it deep. The device shuddered and trembled as energy built up within. As the Berserkacides reached him, he allowed himself to fall backwards out over the edge of the smashed gallery, preferring the cool, lonely fall to a bloody death at their claws. He fell out into the night as the mortally stricken device exploded in a ball of fire that devastated Rhoda Tower, caving it in and toppling the spire above. The Berserkacides were thrown out into space with the force of the explosion, one of them in pieces, another on fire. A cloud of Paraflies surged away from the explosion like a blue and green snowstorm.

I got it, he thought as the night air raged past him. *Mother, Father … I got it.*

He readied to Waft away and noticed a form falling nearby.

It was the female Monama, who, just minutes earlier, had shivered under his coat, had feared for his life and begged him to run. Now she reached out for him, straining to rend her claws, all four of them, into his flesh, her face puckered in bestial rage.

Despite his situation, he felt nothing but grief for this woman.

So much like Sam … and Mitz.

Forgoing the Waft, he reached out for her; his outstretched hand and her grasping, clutching claws almost but not quite touching.

And he fell and fell, the flailing Berserkacide falling with him. He didn't try to Waft—there was no time. He'd let the fall have him.

The device and its light were gone, for good this time.

He'd done his job.

✶ ✶ ✶ ✶ ✶

Kay was swimming in darkness. He felt comfortable and warm. He moved his arms and felt soft bed clothes. His ankle felt like normal. Was he dead?

Something leaned over Kay and smiled. A silvery seal's head and round, bright eyes looked down on him. "You awake, Kay?" he asked.

He was pretty sure it was Carahil—Nargal Spirit and god, born right here at Castle Blanchefort by his Aunt Poe's hand.

"I think so. What happened tonight? Who were those people?"

Carahil gave him a nudge. "People who don't fight fair. People who use others to do their fighting for them."

"The Monamas. They became Berserkacides. Are they all right? Did you save them, too?"

Carahil paused. "You're never all right after you're made to become a Berserkacide—there's no going back from that. They're dead, Kay, and better off."

Kay thought of the woman, before and after her transformation. All he could think of was she, chained up, his coat draped over her shivering shoulders. A woman very much like Sam, possibly with somebody waiting for her back home, somebody who loved her, somebody who would never see her again. A tear came to his eye.

"Those poor people. They were so frightened. They tried to warn me. I wish they were home safe in their beds right now."

Carahil blinked. "I do, too. See, that's why I'm on your side, because you care."

Kay sighed. "How did I get here?"

"A little bird flew by and saved you," Carahil said. "That same bird put out the fire here at the castle—it wasn't too bad, and cleaned the place up a little. Yeah, that little bird was pretty busy last night. Hey, why didn't you Waft, Kay? Why did you let yourself fall?"

"The woman. I wanted to stay with her. I didn't want to let her go. I saw Sam in her face. Is she at peace, Carahil, the woman? Does her soul rest?"

Carahil backed away. "I guarantee it. Get some sleep; you did good tonight, Kay, and I'm proud of you. You've often wondered if you're actually a Vith Lord. I think tonight proves that. You saved your House, and you saved your love, too. I'll not let them do such a thing again; I swear it. Now I am at guard. I am summoned."

"Where's Sam? I need to help her!"

"She is in a place where you can't get to her now, Kay. She's all right, I promise. She's out there running for you, Kay, and for the possibility of what might one day be. I'm sure you'll be seeing her soon."

Carahil leaned down and gave Kay a nuzzle on the forehead. "Well, you know the drill by now. I'm going to take this from you, Kay, this whole day—it's for your own good. You'll go to sleep and not remember a thing about what happened tonight. You'll just have some vague memories of another bland day. It'll be like one of those days that you sleep through and can't remember except as a dream. Nobody here will remember this attack, except for two people. But, I have to say, sooner or later, we're going to have to come to grips with those whom you saw tonight. Sooner or later there will be a fight that must be fought, and it must be won. For the sake of the League, But, that's for another day, okay?"

Kay slept, and the whole thing was forgotten.

17—The Wraith

Kay wanted little to do with Sarah for the next few days, partially blaming her for his reaction to Sam. Sam hadn't shown up, and she didn't join him in bed. This absence, discounting the mandatory summer lay-off, was by far longest he'd been without Sam in years.

Sarah and her mouth.

Phillip seemed to understand and gave Kay his space. Sarah, knowing that Kay was hurting, partially because of her, tried to occupy his time, make him forget, but it didn't work. He avoided her, and when their paths did happen to cross, he ignored her. As the days passed, Kay could tell Sarah was starting to feel quite guilty about what she'd said. She'd convicted Sam without good reason, and she saw how crushed Kay was.

She was sorry and didn't know what to say, which was odd for her. Sarah always had something to say.

Kay was not the only sad person in the castle—Lady Hathaline, normally unflappable, was beside herself. Her beloved Ripcar appeared to have been stolen and flown into the ruins of Castle Durst by some miscreant whom she swore to personally hunt down and slay. Lord Davage promised he would get her another one—a faster one, and she brightened. A day later he and Countess Sygillis took her to Minz and bought her a fast, new red Ripcar.

Kay drifted around the castle lost in a stupor.

He had a dim notion that he'd not seen the last of Sam—that she wasn't going to go out that easily. If she were going, she'd go swinging. She would not let all they'd created together go without a struggle. He kept that thought close to him.

Or maybe his words were so hurtful he knocked the love right out of her. That was a possibility as well.

In any event, if she didn't show up soon, he would go to her. He would go to Lake Monama and, welcome or not, visit her ancestral castle by the shores of the lake. There, he would beg her forgiveness.

✶ ✶ ✶ ✶ ✶

Arin-Dan ...

Kay awoke in bed alone. He had a feeling that Sam had recently been there, sitting in a chair, gazing at him in the dark. Maybe it was a dream, but he didn't think so. Sam had been there with him earlier, but now she was gone.

Additionally, he had a feeling that she was around in the castle somewhere at that moment. He grabbed a robe and headed out of his tower, determined to find her. The lofty hallways of the castle were dark and craggy with shadow. The noisy silence of night filled the air—alive with creaks and taps and other bower sounds that were drowned out in the daytime.

He made his way into the central area of the castle, and he heard a faint droning sound, like a continuous chanting, coming from somewhere nearby. He couldn't make out the words of the chant, but it sounded like Sam's voice.

Sam!

The sound seemed to be everywhere. He moved around, trying to locate the source of the sound, and soon, heading west, he stood at the darkened entryway to Cathomere's Cathedral.

Sitting in a pew near the doorway was Sam. She was fully dressed in her black gown and elegant black shoes. She was sitting straight, her long arms extended in front of her, hands open, palms up.

Her delicate neck had bandages stuck all around it.

She appeared to be in a sort of trance. She was chanting, and her voice was hoarse from it. Tears leaked from her closed eyes.

She said, over and over again in Anuie: "*Now's the time. Now's the time. Now's the time. Now's the time.*"

Elated, he ran to her. After a moment or two, she became aware of his presence. She slowly opened her eyes and looked at him, her face drawn and haggard.

"Now's the time, Kay," she said. Then she winked at him and disappeared, the sound of her chanting voice still echoing through the silent castle.

✶ ✶ ✶ ✶ ✶

Two foggy days later, Sam returned to him again.

Kay lay asleep in his bed, as usual waiting for Sam, hoping she would come. A partially read posting that Sarah had shoved under his door lay on his bed:

BERSERKACIDE SCOURGE UNCOVERED IN VITHLAND!
—MONSTERS FOUND IN MT. HOLLY, SHIRSTER POINT AND CASTLES DURST AND BLOODSTEIN!
—LOCAL MAGISTRATES BAFFLED. SISTERS INVESTIGATING.

He hadn't read the rest. It didn't interest him.

As he lay there staring at the high ceiling, he thought he caught a hint of movement beyond his window.

He sat up.

He saw something lit up and murky through his curtains. A mass of light came nearer and nearer.

A few moments later, something glowing came in through his window, moving like smoke.

It was Sam, wreathed in black cloud. She was floating on air, her body glowing with a sort of inner light, her black hair alive with serpentine movement. Her long arms waved about in a sort of dance macabre. Her nude body was coursing with yellow light and was partially obscured by seething black clouds that twisted around her. Kay noticed her mouth was missing—just a blank spot where her mouth should go. Moving through her body, as if through liquid, was her Snugs medallion.

She was wearing a long necklace made of white flowers. It, too, moved with a weightless fluidity.

He recognized the flower—small, daisy-like with a black button: White Emilia.

Glowing, clouded and necklace flowing, she settled over his bed.

Kay reached up to touch her, and his hand passed right through her chest.

"Sam?" he said quietly.

She stared down at him, her mouthless expression unreadable.

She stared at him for a long time.

Finally, *"I will first ask: do you still love me?"* she said in Anuie in a grave-like voice though she had no mouth.

Kay responded. His voice came out in a whisper. "Yes, Sam—I'm sorry, I didn't mean what I said. I was hurt and angry, and I struck out at you. I'm sorry. Of course I still love you. I want you to come back home to me."

Then, *"You wish to court a daughter of Monama, then you will be put to Trial in accordance with the traditions of the House of Monama and the tribe of Astralon. You will be Tried, and you will be Judged! I tried to shield you. I tried to protect you and give you time to get a bit older. I BEGGED you to develop your Gifts—but now, it… it's too late! They come for me. There is no time! There is no time!"*

She pulled a long hair pin out of her black mane and showed it to him. It was centered with a black jewel. *"Do you see this?"* she asked. *"This is the NIGHTMARE, Monama females have been using it for centuries. With it I can alter reality and create images from my deepest of fears. With this, I put you to Trial according to our customs. I cannot allow my feelings for you to color or temper my thoughts or my actions—I must test you to your limits. With the NIGHTMARE, I will place perils before you that, should you misstep, will bring about your death. Hence is the price of the Gods in Jade and Sapphire."*

She dropped down on him and hovered just inches from his face. She put the NIGHTMARE back into her hair. She seized the flower necklace and presented it to him. *"The White Emilia is before you—the flower that offers either sweet riches or sudden death. Are you ready to face Trial?"*

Kay made to say something and she interrupted. "*Before you answer—be it known and made perfectly clear that, should you fail in the Trials to come ... you, and I, will die. Are you ready?"*

"Yes."

"*Then follow me.*"

Kay climbed out of bed and followed Sam as she drifted through the door and down the hall. He was wearing nothing but a pair of pajama bottoms, and wanted to grab a robe or a sheet or something to cover up with, but Sam wasn't waiting around.

She glided out of the castle and into the Grove, Kay following.

They went a long way into the tangle; Kay tried to ask questions as he stumbled along, but the ghostly, illuminated Sam nested in a thundercloud wasn't answering.

Finally, they reached a clearing. It was the same clearing where Sam had previously run through the snow and yelled '*Olonol'* years ago.

In the clearing were three black, potato-shaped objects of indistinct smoky material floating above the ground. Sam stopped and turned to Kay, bobbing up and down slightly as she floated. The black nest of clouds swirled around her. Sitting nearby were two small figurines floating on pillars of cloud. The figurines looked like tiny blue effigies of Carahil in a fun pose. Those seemed awfully familiar to him, and they were important for some reason.

He couldn't remember what.

She took off the necklace of White Emilia and held it out.

"*You have one final chance, Kabyl, Lord of Blanchefort. If you choose to proceed now, if you accept this necklace, there is no turning back, and your life will be forfeit to me. I will ask you again, and for the last time; do I mean enough to you to risk your life? Does a life and future with me mean that much to you? Do you wish to be put to Trial? Death awaits should you fail."*

"Yes."

The clouds around Sam became excited and probing, wrapping around Kay. "*Then, let it begin."*

She placed the necklace around his neck. For a moment, it came to life and began squeezing his throat. Then, it relaxed and settled.

"I will introduce to you the Judges of the Trials. I have created these manifestations with the NIGHTMARE—they will have a life all their own, and they are here to assist you in progressing from one stage of the Trials to another. They will not help you other than to provide information with which you will need to proceed. They

might even have to kill you should you fail. Do you understand?"

Kay didn't really know what was going on, but he nodded anyway.

Sam drifted over to the first mass and touched it. The dark material twisted around and elongated into the shape of a huge bronze man, about twenty feet tall, standing in a pewter chariot. He looked just like the statue of Lord Cathomere from Cathomere's Cathedral, only much larger and animated into life. Carved into his chest was a sturdy, shield-shaped coat of arms (the House of Blanchefort coat-of-arms). The whole thing was very shiny and reflective. Harnessed to the front of his chariot were three naked women, tall, their eyes alight with orange fire. The women appeared to be constructed of dabbed mud or clay. They seethed in their harness and giggled.

Sam touched the next mass. A strange deer-like creature emerged from the dark. Its legs appeared gnarled and broken, its angry head hung on a broken neck. Its body twisted with unnatural flexibility. It gazed at Kay with its lolled head.

She moved to the last mass and touched it. Another form emerged from the dark—the strangest yet. It was a skeleton suspended in a flowing, golden protoplasmic mass.

Kay stood there staring at this horrific collection of creatures. Sam drifted behind him, and her voice changed back to normal, though Kay couldn't see her.

"Kay, oh my *Arin-Dan*. The Trial is upon us; we can wait no longer. It is now in motion and beyond my control. You must succeed in what is to come … for both our sakes. You are going to be made to feel great pain in the upcoming days … and I am sorry. If you are to survive, you must have your Gifts, and, to fully activate them, you must be made to suffer—I wish there was some other way. I watched you fight those Berserkacides alone and survive, and so I have hope. Know that I love you, and I do this in the hopes that the *Olonol* will one day stand here, and we will be free."

She put her arms around him. "I—I'm sorry for this … I should have left you alone. Why couldn't I just stay away, and you wouldn't have to worry about what is coming. I have brought all this upon you …"

Kay gently pulled her around to his front, her face was flush with tears. "Because, if you had stayed away, I never would have met my true love, my *Cerri-Tela*. I'll face these trials, Sam. I promise I'll succeed."

"You promise?"

"I promise. I won't fail you, Sam."

She took his face in her hands. "Be true to these Trials, *Arin-Dan*, to this symbolic necklace of White Emilia, and we may be together as man and woman, no matter how bleak the future seems. I love you, Kay."

She paused. "They're coming—they're coming for me!!" Her voice shook with panic.

There was a sizzling flash, and a cloudy green slit appeared in mid air. One of the blue Carahil figures took flight and began swimming or dancing in the midst of the green slit. The slit then vanished with a 'pop', along with the figurine.

The tall bronze man reached out and took Sam in his hands. Though still glowing, she appeared to be solid and whole as she sat in his giant palms. The coat of arms in his chest opened like two halves of a clam-shell revealing a hollow cavity within. Sam stepped in and looked at Kay one last time. She waved as the two halves of his chest closed with a solid-sounding thud, entombing Sam within. Gears engaged, locking tight.

Nearby, the green slit appeared again. The last Carahil figurine came to life and dispelled it.

The statue-man in the image of Lord Cathomere finally spoke in a brassy voice. "I am the Judge of your Gifts, the Vessel of your Love, and the Judge of your First Trial, Lord Blanchefort. Within me rests your love, safe from all who wish to harm her. There she will remain until the Trials are concluded. I am also tasked with enabling your Gifts, and, when that is done, I shall set you to your first Trial."

The three women unharnessed themselves from the chariot and surrounded Kay. They snickered and circled him. They pushed him and acted in a haughty and aggressive fashion. Kay tried to stand his ground. He noticed that all three of them looked just like muddy, rough statues of Sam.

"My 'horses' represent your three Gifts," the statue-man said. "When you can defeat them, you have progressed enough to continue on to the Trials."

One of the women grimaced in fury and suddenly punched him in the stomach, doubling him over and sending him wheezing to the ground.

The three stood naked over him and laughed.

One of them pulled him up.

"I am your Waft," she said, laughing. "You have long to go before you can best me. Frankly, I think your sister would be a tougher fight than you." She pushed him away.

A second woman lifted him from the ground and seemed loving and kind "I am your Cloak," she said. "You're as handsome as I thought you'd be."

The last woman tackled him and, seizing him by the hair, pushed his face into the hard, cold ground. She appeared enraged. She then flipped him over and, by the scruff of his neck, lifted him close to her furious face. "Look at me! I am your Sight, which you've ignored your entire life! You will either master me, or you will die. I will kill you! I want to kill you!"

With strength unheard of she mashed Kay's face into the ground again with her foot.

"Stop it!" Cloak said.

The three of them returned to their harness and strapped themselves in. The one who called herself 'Cloak' was concerned. "Are you all right, Kay?" she asked quietly.

The statue-man continued. "You are at Trial, Lord Blanchefort. There is no time limit to constrain you, but I advise haste. Your first task will be to go to the planet Xandarr. There you will train, and there you will develop your Gifts. Again, if you fail, you will die. We will speak again at the correct time."

With a few ground-shaking steps, he hopped back onto his chariot and with a lash, took to the air, pulled by the snickering, naked women, all arms and legs, as the chariot climbed into the starry night.

The strange broken deer-creature and the mass of protoplasm lingered for a moment and then were gone as well.

What happened next was a blur of sound and confusion.

The green slit returned, and this time there were no Carahil figurines to ward it off. Two figures stepped out of the slit: a tall man in golden armor and a bent woman in a red beaded dress. "Sam!" the woman screamed. "You can't run from us, Sam! Where'd she go?"

The man and woman noticed Kay and, before he could react, attacked. In a wretched, ugly voice, the woman cast some sort of screeching spell upon him.

The sound was terrible to listen to, and was somehow vaguely familiar, like he'd heard it before. He couldn't move, he could barely think—the sound filled his head and froze his muscles in place. He toppled over, helpless.

They approached Kay's fallen body.

In the distance, Kay thought he could hear buzzing, like a swarm of insects. Again, vaguely familiar, though he couldn't place it.

The man was tall, over six feet. He was clad in golden armor that was hammered to resemble a robust male musculature, complete, as Kay noted, with an angry phallus that was bolted to the base of his chest plate. The interlocking pieces of his armor were formed to look like fingers coming together at the knuckles. He had a strange heart-shaped helmet that covered his whole head except for his mouth.

The woman was tall and gangly, thin to the point of been utterly famished and decidedly bent in the torso, like a broken yard stick. She was wearing a strange sort of beaded red and black dress. She had long, curly red hair that was wound up over her head like a beehive, held in place with cords of what looked and smelled like clotted blood. She also had on a gold mask that covered her forehead, eyes and cheekbones, leaving her mouth and chin exposed. Her exposed skin appeared to be glistening with—blood maybe—and her flesh was deeply cut into, as if she had mutilated herself.

The two carried an odd smell with them—a burnt stench mixed heavily with dry blood. It was a terrible smell.

The woman slinked up to Kay and stared down at him. She stopped the screech that she was making, though the sound of it lingered in his head.

Her voice was thin and ugly. "Hi ya, Kay," she said. "You remember me? No?"

The woman reached down and stood Kay's immobile body back up like a mannequin, showing a fair amount of strength for such a skinny person. "I been having sex with you for years. Don't remember, huh? Well, that's sad ..." She licked his face with a horrid tongue. "You and your girlfriend are in a lot of trouble. Sam removed her shockers—they never do that—they're too scared, but she did anyway. She loves you, don't she? Awwww... ain't that just sweet?"

She grabbed him by the face, squeezing his cheeks together.

Her hand, skinned and bloody, stank.

"She was supposed to kill you the other night—supposed to appear in your room and go Berserk on you, rip you limb from limb—wouldn't that have been a sorry story in some League rag? People should be saying 'Oh, look what happened to the now extinct House of Blanchefort, tsk, tsk,' but, here you are. We had it all planned out. She pulled her little shockers right off her neck, and you destroyed the Boss's light. The Bosses are real mad at you, and her, too."

She pushed his immobile face away with a jerk. She then produced some sort of small knife and quickly cut Kay out of his pajama bottoms with a savage ripping of cloth.

When she was done, she hauled back and seized him by his male parts with a slap.

Pain, unimaginable pain.

The clearing lit up in amber. He could see a vortex of movement beyond the clearing—like a fast approaching storm cloud. And, for a moment, for a tiny moment, he thought he saw the terrible woman standing before him as a smiling girl, soaring through the sky in a fast Ripcar. He thought she looked like …

The man in golden armor slapped her hand away. "Trying to make me jealous?" he said.

"Awww," she said. "I just wanted to have a little taste for old time's sake."

With Kay incapacitated, the two casually looked around the clearing. "Hmm," the man said. "We're going to get in a lot of trouble over this, and it's all that little bitch's fault. I have had it with her. She knows the penalty for pulling her shockers out. Her purpose has come and gone—and what a mess she made. Let's kill this idiot, eat him, and manually trigger her just for fun, shall we? We'll make an example out of her little ass."

"Ain't got no shockers to trigger her with. Gonna' have to run her down," the woman said. She pulled the necklace of White Emilia away from his neck and held it up. "Ah, young love."

The woman reared back and waved the necklace around. "That's right, Sam!" she yelled into the air. "We're going to kill your fella' here! We're going to take him apart and eat him! Then we're coming for you!"

The woman cozied up to the armored man. He bent down, and they kissed sloppily.

"I could do you right now, she said."

"Patience. I'm hungry."

A loud buzzing filled the grove. Kay saw a host of black flying objects come swarming in.

The man picked Kay up by the neck with one hand and regarded him with disgust. "I've waited to kill this fool for years. Look at him. So soft and weak. I used to look up to him—admire him, can you believe that? This is too easy—what fun is this?" With his free hand, he swatted at large bugs that swarmed around his head.

"What are these?" the man asked, bothered by them.

The woman sneered. "Who cares? Just bugs. Let me have him for a bit. I want him."

The man cuffed her across the face with a bone-cracking slap. "I said I'll kill him, and you can have fun with his dead body. Then, we'll eat hearty!"

"Awwww …" the woman said. "I just want to have a little taste while he's alive. It tastes so much better when they're nice and fresh."

The man, troubled by the growing number of bugs in the clearing, threw Kay down to the ground. The woman, shooing bugs, slobbered with excitement and produced the small, blunt knife again.

"You may have him, love. Take him. Be quick about it. We've got to get to hunting down our wayward slave Sam."

"Can I mess him up?"

"Please do."

Screeching, the woman fell on Kay and did terrible things to him as the armored man casually watched, the growing number of bugs beginning to perturb him.

As her knife, covered with blood, rose and fell, the clearing filled with giant bugs, their shiny wings reflecting in the moonlight.

Coppery light and buzzing.

Book Two

The Machine

Prologue

Time awash and strange.

She had risen from her bed after a night of bad dreams: nightmares, *halofluges* the Vith called them. She couldn't remember them much, only that they'd been terrible, she was sure. *Halofluges* were like that—terrifying even though you really couldn't remember what frightened you so. She had a slight memory of a knife in her hand, and blood. She remembered blood.

And bugs too. There were so many bugs.

Feeling a bit shaky, she'd gone down to have breakfast in the hall and begin her day. A good breakfast would help rid her of the horrid taint her dreams had left behind. After breakfast she'd go flying; flying always remedied anything that troubled her.

There was her brother, lying on the stones near the Grove gate as she arrived in the hall, an expanding pool of blood forming around him. She stood there staring at him. Her older sister, blue-haired and elegant, pushed past her and went to him, screaming his name, pulling him up, getting blood all over her white gown. Staff members rushing about. Her parents. The confusion.

"Hospitaler!" they cried. "Fetch a Hospitaler!"

And she just stood there and watched, numb. The *halofluge* returned to her fresh and whole.

The knife in her hand, the blood ...

✶ ✶ ✶ ✶ ✶

She had flown away in her fast little Ripcar as the family gathered in her brother's room to watch him die. She did not go to his room with the others. Instead she flew away, soaring high, looking for peace in the clouds. She loved to fly and she had rare talent, just like her father.

She found a mountainous spot, out of the way, uninhabited, unseen by any save the random mountaineer. She pushed the nose of her Ripcar over, picking up speed, heading for the ground fast. A screaming, bucking power dive under full control; she was going to dash herself into the rocky valley between the mountains. Her family was to lose two children today: her brother, and herself, both by her hand.

For she had killed her brother ... The *halofluge*.

She hit the boost. The diving Ripcar pushed through the sound barrier in a flash of condensation, the mountains below coming up at fierce speed. She held the sticks in her tiny hands, perfect control, not flinching, not afraid in the least, eager for it all to be over.

The dream had been real. She held the knife that killed her brother.

The mountains, the speeding Ripcar nose down at an acute angle, the trembling sticks.

She shouted her brother's name in last few moments as the rocky face of the mountain came up.

✶ ✶ ✶ ✶ ✶

"My lady?" came a soft voice. "My lady, wake up."

She opened her eyes and she was back in her bedroom in Drella Tower, the stuffed animals, and paintings of her father's starship, the *New Faith* hanging on the walls, her four-poster bed draped with white veils. It was unmistakable.

What had happened? Was she dead? Was she now to become a ghost haunting her bedroom for the rest of eternity?

Would she be a good ghost, tickling those sleeping in her bed and lightly pulling their hair, or would she be a vengeful demon crawling into bed with them and troubling their dreams, giving them *halofluges* like she had had?

"You're not dead," came the voice. "Just in case you were wondering, you're not dead."

She sat up. Bright sunshine, cheery through the veils. She wanted to know what happened.

"I saved you."

She was confused.

"I've made it a habit of saving you Blancheforts lately. I'll ask you the same question I once asked your brother: why did you try to kill yourself just now?" the voice asked.

She answered: blunt, the whole truth, nothing held back, the macabre details rolling out.

Halofluge. The knife in her hand.

"You think you killed your brother?"

She nodded her head. The voice didn't answer right away. She had a thought, a hope, that it would comfort and reassure her. *"Of course you didn't do it ..."* she hoped it would say. *"It was just a dream, kid ..."*

Then the voice spoke. "Well, even though you're just a little girl—I remember when you were just a newborn baby in your mother's arms—just look at all that red hair—you're a Vith, and you're strong too like your mother and father. I feel I can level with you. You did attack your brother, kid."

She sat there on her bed and was devastated. Why? Why didn't the voice just let her die in the mountains?

"... and you didn't do it, either. It was you, but it wasn't you. Understand?"

She didn't understand.

"Go to your mirror and take a look. Go on."

She slid off her bed, pushed through the veils and went to her mirror, gilded and full-length. The reflection in the mirror was monstrous: tall, bent, bleeding, wearing a golden mask covering the top part of what was left of her face and her red hair twisted up into a filthy beehive.

And, her eyes—lusty, diabolical, demented ... pure, restless evil.

The reflection in the mirror didn't look much like herself, but it was her no doubt about it. The stance was right, the turn of the head, the rise of the chin and so on. And, since it *was her* all the energy that she normally put into things that she loved, like flying and attending to her studies and learning Vith history, this demented version of herself would no doubt apply the same zeal to deviltry and mayhem and unspeakable crimes.

… her dying brother.

She wanted to put her hand to her mouth and scream, turn away and run, yet she forced herself to stand tall and appear outwardly impassive. She was only sixteen years old and just a child, but she was a Vith from a strong House. She was taught from an early age to be fearless, to face such things without pause or hesitation. Her father would not shrink from such a sight and nor would she.

"There are bad folk about, my lady, and this is what they do. They are the masters of the Horned God's temple and they are able to use its power to move back and forth through time. Moving through time is like a nice ride in the country for them. They will take you as an adult, many years from now, and, using methods that I will not tell, turn you into what you see here. They will fill your head with travesties and keep you in an evil dream, and you will joyfully do things you'd otherwise never do—like harm your brother, and his beloved. This future version of you is the servant of the Horned God and his time-travelling angels, and she is evil through and through."

She put her hands to her face. She tried to be strong, but she was overcome. She couldn't look anymore and fell to her knees. She wanted to die.

Why didn't you just let me die?

Something came to her side and nudged her. Something small and silvery.

"Because, if I had done that you'd spend eternity in the Gallery of the Dead feeling nothing but regret. This is a moment to be strong, my lady, not to give in. Your brother right now is fighting for his life. Lady Sammidoran, at this very moment, is being pursued, by the monstrous future version of you. They need our help. Together, we can beat the Horned God and his angels. We can end this."

We can?

"Yes. You, of all people, can be of great help. Can I count on you?"

Yes, of course, she'd do anything.

But first, she needed a moment, to be weak, to be a frightened little girl.

The silvery creature next to her was tiny, no bigger than a small dog; whiskers, flippers, smoothed-domed forehead, bright, inquisitive eyes.

"It's all right, Lady Hathaline," Carahil said. "I'm here and I'm not going anywhere. You can cry if you want, and I won't tell. I promise."

She embraced Carahil and held onto him for a long time, weeping into his smooth neck; weeping for her brother, and for Sam, and for herself.

The little silver god had come again when he was needed most.

Time. He had nothing but time for her.

1—Through the Grove

Kay lay there in the morning frost. The sun was rising. The purple sky of dawn gave way in lacy veils to dark blue.

What happened? He remembered Sam, and the man and woman.

He remembered not being able to move. He remembered the woman falling on him.

Creation—things were spinning. His stomach hurt; he was in agony.

He remembered bugs, big ones, the clearing full of them.

He had been hurt by the woman. She cut into his stomach near his belly-button. He had lost a lot of blood, and he could feel it congealed around him in a dry pool. He had no idea how badly he was hurt, but it was bad.

It was very bad.

Looking down, his stomach was a mass of red. His pajama bottoms had been cut away by the woman just before she fell upon him with a dull knife and mutilated him. Despite his dire situation he allowed himself to indulge in a bit of modesty.

He was lying in the Grove in an oak clearing, not far from the Ten Gardens area. The ground was covered with morning frost. All around, ancient oak trees towered over him, the same ones that had seen war and death for ages. What was one more death to them? They were mute and indifferent to Kay's plight.

Holding his stomach, he staggered to his feet. Everything in his torso area felt loose and ready to come out. He tried to hold it all in place.

What had happened?

Sam, his love, his *Cerri-Tela,* had come to him in the night and demanded he follow her into the Grove. She had appeared to him as a wraith and floated over his bed.

Once there she put him to Trial in accordance with her people's traditions. Using the NIGHTMARE, the LosCapricos weapon of her line, she created several arcane monsters from her deepest fears to guide and test him through the Trials.

A broken, half-dead deer of sinister presence.

A golden amoeba-like creature with a humanoid skeleton for a nucleus.

A bronze, twenty foot high living metal man in the image of Lord Cathomere who took Sam's body and sealed it inside his hollow chest where she would be safe.

That's when *they* appeared—a hideous man in golden armor and a bent, skinless woman. They claimed to be Sam's tormentors and her masters, and they were pursuing Sam for tearing her control collar from around her neck. Her 'Shockers' they called it which they used to turn Monamas into Berserkacides.

Sam escaped, safe within the metal man where they could not get to her. In revenge they fell upon Kay, and loudly promised they were going to kill him, and then *eat* him.

And, making a terrible noise that rendered him helpless, the woman fell upon him, stabbing him over and over.

Why was he still alive?

The man and woman were gone, and Kay was all alone in the clearing. He fought off a wave of nausea and, with supreme effort, took a step over the uneven ground toward the castle.

He took another, and then another. His heart pounded. His guts shifted.

The castle was so far away. He'd walked these passes innumerable times with his cousins, Sarah and Phillip, and never thought twice about the distance involved. He was in the back half of the Telmus Grove near the Ten Gardens. To return to the castle, he had to pass through the oak trees and enter the Inner Plaisance of the Grove, passing the Sarfortnim, Greyson, Humboldt and Telmus courtyards, and then he would cross the bridge over Blanchefort Creek and be in the castle.

It was at least two miles.

Step after tentative step, his arms bloody from holding his stomach, he went. Through the trees, there was the Sarfortnim courtyard.

He remembered the horrid, skinless woman wearing a golden mask sitting on him, her bloody arm rising and falling as the armored man watched. Her knife biting into him one small chunk at a time. Sam had always loved his bellybutton, and he had a notion that the woman was trying to cut it out to spite Sam. He couldn't move during the whole ordeal, couldn't fight. She was making some sort of scream that got into his head and be-spelled him. He couldn't move while she screamed. He couldn't defend himself.

Through the Sarfortnim, beech trees forming a canopy of fluttering green lined the path, and then the Greyson was right ahead. It was called Carahil's Walk for the great Silver tech seal Carahil who once played there. Carahil had been created in a fountain by Kay's aunt, Lady Poe of Blanchefort, and was supposedly a great spirit of some sort, a god, he had heard, created by his smiling, humble aunt.

Carahil had helped save the planet Xandarr some twenty years prior. They loved him on Xandarr. He heard they carved statues of him there, and the children had a tradition of hand-writing little notes and leaving them by the statues, cradled in the stone flippers. The notes often started with the line:

Dear, Mr. Carahil. I need help.

And all that started right here near the Greyson courtyard where a god once played.

Carahil! his thoughts roiled. *Carahil, help me!*

He wondered how he survived? Did the woman have a sudden fit of remorse or conscience? No—no, she was spoiling to slowly kill him and then devour his sliced flesh. She said so! She was salivating in fact, drooling onto his face as she filleted him alive, eager for a taste.

So what happened? Where did they go? He couldn't remember.

In Humboldt courtyard, Kay could deny the pain and sickness in his guts no longer. He toppled over like a fallen tree face first into the cobblestones, feeling a fresh flow of blood from his stomach.

This was it; he was dying. Sam's beautiful face flashed into his head. His love, his *Cerri-Tela*, now pursued by the same woman and man who had killed him.

Sam was terrified of them. Kay felt no fear here at the end of his life, only impotent dying rage and longing for his love. Perhaps he would come back as an angry spirit and wait for the skinless, bent woman to return, if she dared. Then, he would fall upon her with supernatural light and give back what she gave him and make a ghost out of her.

Things dimmed. Sam's beautiful pale face floated in front of him.

I'm sorry, Cerri-Tela.

I'm sorry, Sam.

The bitch killed me!

* * * * *

BZZZZZZZZZZ ...

Something reached into the dark and troubled him. It was a terrific buzzing sound, like that of a bee that had landed on one's ear and sounded huge.

Go away. I'm dying! Give me some peace!

BZZZZZZZZZZZ ...

He opened his eyes. Sitting on his face was a gigantic blue bug with a sea-green belly, like a dragonfly only it had strange wings. Its wings, instead of being straight out, were swept back, like those of a fast sub-orbital, and were the most remarkable color. They were a bold coppery color, shiny and inviting, like Sam's goggles from Hoban that she wore in the village to cover her black eyes.

Sam wearing her geared, copper and silver goggles, laughing, sampling de-

lights from the shops. Pushing the goggles back and kissing him.

Kissing him.

He would die with a happy thought in his head after all.

Things began to go blurry again.

The bug crawled a tickling course across his face, down his nose and then onto the Humboldt cobbles, standing on the strewn purple strands of his long hair. It moved away an inch or two.

BZZZZZZZZZZZZZZZZ ...

It beat its wings in a coppery blur. Creation! What a loud noise, so deep, so clear.

The sound got into his head and sorted out his thoughts. Only moments before he was nearly off the coil and dead. Now, with the buzzing filling his ears, he was fully alert.

Lying on the Humboldt courtyard stones with the huge blue bug.

Wait! Bugs! Paraflies!

He remembered Paraflies, a deafening cloud of them, entering the clearing as the woman sliced him up. He remembered the man in armor being bothered by them, waving them away from his face.

The woman, ignoring them at first, got up off him and ran as they began crawling over her horrid, skinless body. She cursed and swatted at them. And the two of them departed in a flash of green.

Paraflies, huge, buzzing and inquisitive, saved his life, or what was left of it anyway.

Clutching his stomach, he rose to his knees and then stood.

The Parafly preened its face with its legs for a moment, and then took flight and buzzed away.

He exited the courtyard seeing no more bugs. They seemed to like to swarm and fly together in a cloud. Paraflies. Kay recalled his cousin Sarah, a lover of the lurid and sensational, sending him news postings of an alarming infestation of Kana by huge, previously unidentified insects called 'Paraflies' by the media. Big and colorful. Loud, too. Flew in great swarms and seemed immune to bug gasses.

Why one Parafly? They liked to swarm, so why one? Almost like it was sent to him specifically to buzz in his ear and annoy him back to life.

One Parafly. One half-dead man.

All right. Fine. You get your way.

I'm alive.

Kay continued, one step at a time.

✶ ✶ ✶ ✶ ✶

The great reddish bulk of the castle studded with spires rose in the distance as he passed through the Telmus courtyard.

How far had he gone? Nearly two miles. Creation, his guts hurt.

His legs turned to stone. He struggled across the bridge. Veins empty—no blood.

He couldn't move, but there was the castle! Right there! Just a bit more.

No, no, can't move. Can't go any farther!

His heart skipped a beat.

That woman—killing him with her knife one stab at a time.

That woman!!

Shocktyte bitch!!

Rage flared through him. Hatred! Not for himself, but for Sam!

That woman! Trying to kill him and trying to kill his Sam, too. His *Cerri-Tela*. So frightened. His love looking over her shoulder, being harassed by that skinless wretch her whole life. Sam was running from them, and now she was all alone.

Five minutes! Give me five able-bodied minutes alone with the bitch, and I'll show her what fear is!

Everything spun, and he fell over.

Sam!

Hatred could only move him so far. He could see the gate of the castle and the dark, stony interior.

Crawling, he was there. He was just inside the castle, partially in sun, partially in shade. He'd made it all this way, only to fall to his wounds at the castle gate.

"Kay!" He heard a hollow, echoing scream.

Rapid footfalls were coming toward him.

Everything went black.

Top Row: Lord Davage, Lord Peter, Lady Sammidoran, Lord Kabyl, Lt. Kilos, Lord Lon
Bottom Row: Countess Sygillis, Lady Poe, Thomasina 19th, Lord Phillip, Lady Sarah

2—Saying Their Goodbyes

"Can he hear us?" a female voice asked.

"I wouldn't think so, no," replied a male's.

He had no idea where he was, or who he was, for that matter. He had been born, apparently, he had lived for some period of time in luxury and peace, how long he did not know. He had parents and siblings, and friends.

He had a pale woman who loved him ...

Now, it was time to die.

He heard a carnival of voices all around him. He tried to see, but there was nothing but soft amber in a rippling, indistinct pool.

"Tell me what was done to him," came a somewhat familiar female voice.

"Syg, now's not the time," came another voice, male, more authoritarian.

"Tell me, Ennez!"

The folds of amber flowed. He was in pain, though nothing hurt. He was in a blinding and deafening cacophony.

"All right, if you wish to hear this, then I shan't deny you. Your son has suffered a severe lacerating event of the abdominal wall resulting in a partial disembowelment of the lower gastrointestinal tract. Some of his tract is missing. It appears to have been chewed through. He has been stabbed over a hundred times with a small and rather blunt metal object, like a dull knife or something of the like. The instrument used against him was filthy, full of poison. He also has been mutilated all about the abdominal area, including the carving of rune-like lettering into his flesh and the partial tearing away of his umbilicus ..."

"His what?"

"His bellybutton, Syg. Lastly, he was sodomized about the penis and rectum."

Silence ... flowing amber.

"Who did it, Ennez?" came the female voice, this time dark, choked with emotion. "Who did this to him? Who is going to die by my hand?"

"We're not certain. We've collected select material samples and other evidences that we shall have analyzed in our Hospitaler sanctum in Minz. We're convinced the identity of the attacker shall be made known at that time."

The woman's voice again—now ragged with fury. "I'll tell you who it was—it was Lady Sammidoran. She did this to our son!"

"You don't know that, Syg."

"Who else could it be? Bark saw her leading Kay out into the Grove, and now look at him, flat on his back, torn to shreds ... atrocities performed upon him! I've had enough of being civilized and proper. I want her head before the sun sets!"

"Syg?"

"No, no! I want her head, and if I can't have that, I'll have the heads of her kin, every last one of them!"

The man's voice grew solemn. "Syg, now is not the time to crave revenge.

I understand how you feel, however, you need to compose yourself. You must hear what I have to say. You need to go in there right now and … say goodbye to your son while you still can."

The amber bubbled. Silence for a moment.

"Goodbye?" the woman asked, her voice fearful. "What talk is this, Ennez, Beth? You—you have cleaned his wounds and closed his lacerations—masterful work. I don't understand. He's fine, the danger has passed."

"He is … beyond our help, Syg. His muscles we can repair, his skin and entrails we can stitch together, but, for his poisoned blood, there is nothing we can do. This is the worst case of it I've ever seen. He is well beyond Apex, even after a massive transfusion the taint remains."

Silence.

"He is gone, Syg. I'm sorry, but we've done all we can. Don't let these last few moments pass, I pray you. Say your goodbyes, wish his soul well and then take him to Dead Hill where he belongs and honor him as he deserves."

Somewhere in the amber haze, he could hear the woman weeping.

✶ ✶ ✶ ✶ ✶

Arin-Dan ...

He wondered if he was dead and this was the afterlife. He tried to see, but there was nothing but amber. He tried to move; nothing.

He felt a soft hand touch his face. *Arin-Dan. Summon your strength and tell them to perform test X-452. Tell them … Make yourself heard, my love. Make them understand.*

Test X-452 What's that?

It will guide them in properly attending to you. He told me it would help.

Who told you?

Carahil told me.

Who's Carahil? The name was familiar but everything was a muddle.

A friend.

And who are you?

I'm the woman who loves you, Kay ...

There were presences all around him, lurking, leaning over him. He tried to see, but there was nothing, just flowing amber.

A shape came up to him and emerged through the confused murk. It was a girl wearing a white gown. Her whitish blue hair was falling all around her shoulders. Her gown was soiled with blood—possibly his blood. Mental images passed in front of him of such a girl: proud, capable, eager to socialize. His sister. Kilos was her name. Kilos was his sister, shopping with him in the village with Sam.

Sam ...

Seemed so long ago.

Her lips trembled. Love and grief. None of her training in the social niceties prepared her for this, for the death of her brother. "Look what you got yourself into," she said, leaning close, stroking his hair. "You, you ruined my favorite white gown. It's from Hoban, it's …" She stopped and choked back a groan. Tears fell. "Bye, big brother …"

She vanished, replaced by a tall blonde-headed woman and a slightly shorter brown-haired man. He remembered the woman, teaching him his lessons out in the

Grove. So patient and kind. All the little silver creatures she created. His aunt, Lady Poe and his uncle, Lord Peter.

Now, haggard and care-worn, the two of them.

Test X-452

She touched him. "Be well on your journey, my beloved nephew. Take your place with our ancestors and share us your insight. Let death still not your voice." She kissed him on the cheek and Lord Peter led her away.

Two more figures popped up: a boy a girl, both his age. Long coats and tall boots. Vith blue eyes and blue hair in a ponytail. His cousins Sarah and Phillip. His best friends, come to say goodbye.

They stood there looking down on him, neither one of them knowing what to say. Then, Sarah broke down.

"I am so s-sorry, K-Kay," she stammered in-between sobs. "My big, stupid mouth is to blame for this. I'm sorry I blamed Sam and drove you apart, I'm sorry I was afraid. Stupid Jo-Boy I am! Stupid, stupid, stupid! I'll make it right, Kay, I'll fix this, I promise, j-just don't go …" She wheeled around. "Can, can he hear me?"

Somebody standing in the amber said "No."

She wept and leaked slobber and possibly snot all over him. "Please don't go ..." She pawed at him, trying to shake him awake. Phillip took her by the shoulders and led her away. Phillip hadn't said anything, but he was clearly hurting too. As always, even on his deathbed, Phillip let Sarah do all the talking.

Sarah, he tried to say through the amber. *Test X-452. Quit blubbering and do test X-452. I don't know what it is, just do it.*

He tried to say it, just nothing came out.

Another figure. A tall brown-headed lady in a uniform and a big hat held in her hands. A silver bird was sitting on her shoulder, his image burning through the murk. Lt. Kilos, family friend and mentor, Silver tech Tweeter at her side as always. Namesake of his sister. His childhood crush.

She stood there and then leaned close, her big brown eyes full of sorrow. "I'm really sorry, kid. I wish I could have been there with you, you know, to stand at your side and help when you needed me. Don't worry about your mom and dad—I'm going to take good care of them, you can count on me." She put her strong hands on his face. "Be well, and ever green. All these worlds are yours."

She kissed him on the forehead.

Test X-452 he tried to say.

Lt. Kilos didn't hear him and turned away, placing her hat back on her head.

Test X-452!

Her Tweeter bird reacted a little, just the flutter of a wing and a turn of the head. "What?" Kilos said. She leaned back down, her searching brown eyes like a pair of lanterns in the amber. "Kay did you just say something?"

I said: *Test X-452.*

"Kay?" she said again. "Tweeter here is telling me you're saying something. I don't hear anything, but he swears it!" She moved away and was gone.

A tiny woman emerged: small, green eyes framed by red hair. Shadowmark.

"Kay," his mother said in an unrecognizable voice burdened with grief. "I will have revenge for you. Revenge …"

His mother, full of love and brightness, her evil days as a Black Hat behind her.

His mother, watching her son die. The Black Hat returning to destroy and lay waste.

Two more figures appeared. “I’m telling you, Dav, he said something!”

Lt. Kilos had brought his father, Lord Davage.

“Ki,” his father said. “he’s near gone. He can’t talk.”

“Sight him, Dav,” Ki protested. “Tweeter said …”

“Enough with your bird!” his mother shouted. “My son is dying!”

Ki would not be denied. “Don’t accept him as a dead man, Syg. I swear he’s saying something. He’s struggling for life, struggle with him. Hear what he has to say.”

“Do not burden me with false hope, Ki!”

“Dav!” Ki yelled. “Sight him!”

His father leaned over. His eyes lit the amber up, cutting through it, changing colors in the twilight as he tentatively probed with his famous Blanchefort Sight.

His father reacted. “God’s Bodkins!” he cried. “He’s Sighting! Ki’s right! Somehow he’s Sighting! He can see us right now, perhaps he can hear us as well!”

“Can it be, Dav?” his mother piped, the Black Hat fading a little from her voice. “Ennez said he was gone.”

“I don’t doubt Ennez’s assessment, and I don’t doubt the resilience of our son either.”

He leaned down close, close enough for Kay to feel the stubble on his cheek.

Test X-452

“Did you hear that? He spoke, just now I heard him! Faint, I’ll grant you, but there it was! Ennez, Beth!” his father cried. “My son lives!”

Sigil of the Grand Order of Hospitalers

3—A Shadow tech Male

Voices around him, swimming in the dark.

"Test X-452," came the voice of Ennez, "is a test we of the Hospitalers use to determine the presence of a Shadow tech Male—an Invernan as they're called. It's a standard test approved for use by the Sisterhood of Light, and, according to our database, it was performed upon Kay when he was two years old in Minz about twenty years ago. With Syg being a Shadow tech Female, it was possible, however statistically unlikely, that Kay could be a Shadow tech Male—hence the test."

"But the test was negative," his father said.

"Yes, so our records show. Case closed."

Somebody small and delicate approached and hovered over him, smelling of soft perfume and humming a pleasing tune. A whispered feminine voice came filtering down. "My training as a Hospitaler tells me you shouldn't be hearing a word I say, however my heart says you can hear me just fine. You can hear me, can't you, Kay?"

He could not respond. He just lay there, suspended in amber.

Warm hands on his face. "Do you remember me? My name is Bethrael of Moane. I was there the day you were born. I delivered you, I delivered your sisters and your brother too. Now here I am again, supposedly for your death. My training also tells me you should be dead, but again, I've a feeling you're not going to be dying today."

"Is the test done, Beth?" Ennez asked.

"Give me a moment," she replied. She pulled something away from his face and walked away into the amber gloom. "Here. It's done."

Indistinct movement.

"Yes. Look here," Ennez said. "The test is conclusive. Kay is a Shadow tech Male."

"But how can that be? He was tested negative."

Beth's voice came up. "The Ephysians say that Shadow tech Males sometimes do not manifest themselves until later in life. That seems to be confirmed here."

"So," his father said, "what does this revelation mean? How does his status as a Shadow tech Male assist him?"

Beth again. "Shadow tech Males are said to be very resilient—able to ward off injury and Apex-plus blood poisoning that would prove fatal for any other."

"All conjecture," Ennez said.

"Here's the proof!" Beth replied. "He lives."

A form approached; his mother's. "Can this be true, Beth?" his mother asked.

"Look here, Syg. According to the Troutman, Kay's blood-poisoning level is at Apex, plus 4. He should have been dead hours ago, but, here he is, hanging on."

"Then, what are we to do? How may he be helped? Tell us and it shall be done!"

Ennez again: "There's no method of treatment for Apex blood poisoning approved by the Sisterhood of Light. It is a fatal condition."

His mother: "Then, let us discuss the unapproved ones ... immediately."

✶ ✶ ✶ ✶ ✶

Sometime later, talking and indistinct forms moving through the amber. He recognized the voices, but the cloudy pool still veiled his eyes.

"We are risking the Sisters' punishment should they learn of this," Ennez said.

"Let me worry about the Sisters," his mother said. "Should they become involved, we'll simply say I forced you to do it on pain of death."

"Ok, ok, Syg. So, here's how we're going to proceed. We're going to introduce Kay to Beth's Silver tech. It is said in Xaphan texts that Shadow tech Males absorb and feed upon Shadow and Silver tech energy, and perhaps it will cleanse his blood, though I guarantee nothing. You understand that, right? This could be very dangerous and Beth might be risking her life on an unknown."

"She needn't take such a risk. I'm his mother, it should be my Silver tech offered up."

"No, Syg, it won't work. As you're related to him, he won't react to yours—Lady Poe's neither. It has to be Beth."

Beth's tiny form returned to his side and gazed down at him. "I'm going to try and help you now, Kay. I'm going to share my Silver tech with you. That is not something lightly done. When I was a Black Hat, I was taught never to allow a Shadow tech Male to touch me. Never. We were told stories how Shadow tech Males can dominate us, change us into a *Wandwilla*. Do you know what that is? No? Don't worry about it—I really don't think they exist, but, in any event, I would have killed a Shadow tech Male before I let him get near me." He heard a soft laugh. "And now, here we are. You are the son of my dearest friends, I delivered you and placed you into Syg's arms for the first time and I'm not going to let you die. If I can save you with my Silver tech, I will do so gladly. This shall be my gift to my friends, and to you."

More people approached. "Are you ready, Beth?"

"Yes, I am."

"Are you certain you wish to do this?"

"We've little choice. I can help him, therefore I shall."

"There are dangers."

Beth became annoyed. "I'm a Hospitaler Samaritan of the Knickerbaum Order, just as you are, Ennez. I am aware of the dangers and my training and knowledge in the medical arts shall help protect me. I understand, as a Shadow tech Male, he might have some minor form of control over me. As he touches my Silver tech I'll probably experience a slight elevation in temperature, a mild seizing in the joints and a dilation of the pupils. He might even be able to command me to some extent—I highly doubt it, though. I am rather skeptical of that alleged ability; my will is my own. All in all, I believe this experience might prove highly invaluable, as our knowledge in the Hospitalers regarding Shadow tech Males and their effects upon Shadow tech Females is suspect and incomplete. I shall try to speak aloud my thoughts and feelings as we proceed, so that we may add to our knowledge."

Ennez came up. "I think you're underestimating what a Shadow tech Male can do to you, but very well. Here is how we shall proceed. Beth, you create a coalesced ball of Silver tech. Dav and I will then lift Kay's hand and place it within the ball. Syg, you shall time us. Timing is critical. For safety's sake, we'll allow Beth to remain in contact with Kay for no more than thirty seconds. When the time elapses, we'll remove Kay's hand from the ball. If this works, Kay's B-reading might go down well below Apex and he'll be out of danger."

Things happened all around him. He saw a brilliant ball of shining, chrome-like silver form in front of him, floating, cutting through the amber, seeing it with perfect clarity; its fair moon-like shape, its flawless surface. Clouds of past and future reflected off its face as a coming storm.

Beth had created her Silver tech ball.

His hand was lifted and moved into position.

"Begin," his mother said, and his hand was slid into the Silver tech ball, the tips of his fingers breaking the round surface and penetrating it like a blob of warm mercury.

KAAAAAAAAAAY! Beth screamed in his thoughts.

A bomb went off. The world turned around him, the amber veil cast aside in an expanding circle with shocking clarity.

There was his large bedroom. He was in his bed, the old stone walls and vaulted ceiling all around carved in the Vith style. There was his terrace looking out over the mountain shelf plunging to the village far below. Proud sunshine poured in, just like any day. Scanners, rolls of cloth, medical instruments, bottles of Hospitaler 'De-bug', discarded empty vials of blood, bundles of veri-plas tubes, bags full of discarded bio-materials and crimson waste were strewn about everywhere. An untidy row of empty mis-matched chairs were lined-up against the wall, probably where his relatives had sat in vigil, now gone.

KAAAAAAY!

Time jumped back and forth, no longer having form and continuity.

The chairs were empty.

The chairs were full of his mourning relatives, his aunt and uncle, his sister and cousins. One sister in a bloody gown. Where was his second sister? Where was she?

There was Sarah sitting slumped, overcome with grief, Phillip with his arm around trying to console her.

The wall behind the chairs was marred with tiny defects he'd never noticed before: slight but obvious discolorations, minute scratches, the tell-tale hits and jabs from the ancient stone mason's chisel who cut it. A left-handed stone mason by the angle of the hits. All perfectly clear.

And look there; Sam had written her name on the wall in a tiny polished script, using nothing but her iron hard fingernail, sharp as a sword-blade and as fine as a jeweler's scribe; SAMMIDORAN. Her name was everywhere actually, right-side up, upside down, off-angled, on the ceiling, toward the floor—she seemed to have a liking for defacing his walls.

Time disjointed, he saw her doing it, bent over, shrouded in black, as a child, as an adolescent, as a young woman, in bed with him scrawling it as they made love: SAMMIDORAN, SAMMIDORAN.

Sam ... he loved her so.

Her name was also carved into his flesh in a different, mocking hand: SAM on the shaft of his penis in bloody black and red letters only recently repaired by Ennez.

The fleshless woman had done that to him with the same little knife she'd devastated the rest of his body with. Fresh hatred moved through him.

Nearby, his father (coatless and hatless) and Ennez were leaning over him holding his arm aloft in Beth's floating silver ball. His mother was seated on the other side of the bed gazing at a timepiece.

His large oaken dresser sat against the wall. Awash in time he could see himself and Sam standing in front of it. In the top drawer was the old note he'd receive years before—the IN LOCK note whose letters were too washed-out to read. He always kept it there, a tantalizing mystery, hoping to one day decipher what it said.

Today was that day, the smeared red letters moving back in time, shrinking down into their original legible form.

Folded up in the drawer on the other side of the room, he could now read it perfectly. It said:

To: Kabyl, Lord of Blanchefort

BE WARNED...

BE WARNED... Beth, sitting on the other side of the room, shrieked and his attention was diverted away from the note. She was gritting her teeth as if she were in agony.

Bethrael of Moane. Something was wrong with Beth. Time to end this. Pull his hand out. How long had it been in there?

He was quickly overwhelmed by an intense feeling. Though Beth was seated several feet away, it felt as if she was right on top of him engaged in a bout of heated sex. He could feel her skin, the softness of her breasts and humid warmth of her ragged breath. He felt her tongue deep in his mouth and her legs tight around him, the heels of her feet going up the backs of his legs. Her pounding heart ...

And he could feel himself deep inside her, the warmth, the wracking spasms of her muscles tightening up, releasing then tightening again.

Flex!

She coiled up in the chair, clenching her teeth.

Flex!

He recalled her previous words:

My will is my own.

My knowledge will protect me.

Clearly Beth hadn't been prepared for the primal ferocity of allowing him to touch her Silver tech. The dry, dispassionate words on a page she'd studied somewhere in a Hospitaler sanctum couldn't compete with the overwhelming reality, and she was lost in it.

"Beth!" Ennez cried. "What are you experiencing? Should we stop?"

She grunted something in response.

"Syg, what's the time?"

"Fourteen seconds!"

Fourteen seconds? Is that all? Kay saw her body pulsing with energy and a white-light mass about her waist and legs. He could see through her body, to the balled up fist of her uterus watching it clench up, relax and then clench again like an inverted punching bag belted into a blur.

Flex! She climaxed. Flex! Again.

Kay billowed on the edge of a projectile orgasm … and Beth, linked to him via her Silver tech, was doing the same, over and over.

Flex!

"Beth!"

Kay yearned for relief. End it, kill him, make it stop! Time detached and wandered ahead. He saw what was about to happen.

"Enough, she's had enough! Remove his hand!" Ennez will say.

A Silver tech lance piercing his heart. Beth standing. Beth attacking his surprised parents.

I AM YOURS, KAY!

COMMAND ME!

TELL ME WHAT TO STEAL! TELL ME WHO TO KILL!

COMMAND ME!

JUST DON'T EVER LET ME GO!!

She throws her arms around him and they became fluid, their enraptured bodies mingling as one. Welded together. One eternal creature, locked in ecstasy … forever.

Wandwilla … a creature she knew of and feared, just moments away.

Just moments away …

"Stop!" Kay cried.

He jolted from bed, wrenching his hand from the Silver tech ball. He fell to the floor, his parents swarming around him.

"Syg, what was the time?"

"Just eighteen seconds. Was that enough."

Ennez turned to Beth. "Beth, are you all right?"

Grunting, she rose from her chair and staggered away toward the door. Her mouth was open, like she was about to sneeze or scream and couldn't get it out.

Flex! Another one.

Flex! Yet another.

FlexFlexFlexFlexFlexFlex....

She threw the door open and wobbled out. "Beth!" Ennez called after her.

His heart racing, everything closed in around him.

"Did it work?" came his mother's voice. "Dav, did it work?"

And he faded into unconsciousness.

4—Trials and Wellermans

Two weeks later, Kay was still confined to his bed. Ennez and Beth had done good work. The strange swirls and rune-like carvings the woman had made in his stomach were barely visible; the other various atrocities she had done, too, were mostly gone. He occasionally reached down through his dressings and felt his bellybutton. The woman had tried to cut it away, probably because Sam loved it, and she had failed. That gave him a small measure of satisfaction.

He lost two feet of small bowel and had to be fed intravenously for a week as the stitches healed and knitted together. His blood levels were measured hourly. B-20 to B-67 on average; still high, but manageable and going down by the day. He took his Cynth medication and, slowly, his blood returned to normal.

Beth reacted to him after the Silver tech incident where she helped save his life. She would look at him twice when she thought he wasn't watching and she even gave him a huge, rather passionate, kiss which caused his mother to raise her eyebrows.

The image wouldn't leave his head: *Wandwilla,* welded together with Beth as one.

It almost happened.

Flex ...

He took short walks about the castle, his mother and father at his side. His mother made few bones about her feelings in the aftermath of the attack.

"Kay, you will never see Lady Sammidoran again, am I understood?"

"But why? Sam didn't attack me. She offered me the White Emilia and I accepted. I am bound to her via Trial and I must continue when I am able."

Sygillis spoke in a calm and dispassionate voice. "You will not proceed, Kay. She and her House are lucky you survived, for they would all be dead had you not. I would have killed every one of them. You will never see her again, am I understood? You shall begin seeing new ladies in the Firth House, all carefully interviewed and screened by me first. I have a young lady already lined up for you next week."

"I'm not interested. Mother, I promised Sam I'd be true to her Trials. She is counting on me."

Sygillis' voice was icy and deadly calm; Kay wished she'd be yelling. "That is one promise you shall not keep. I have spoken."

"Mother ..."

"I have spoken, Kay."

And they continued their walk, Kay stewing.

✶ ✶ ✶ ✶ ✶

He made up with his cousin Sarah. He'd been angry with her for her rude treatment of Sam and for being partially responsible for provoking the horrible fight he had with her prior to being attacked.

He remembered seeing Sarah sitting there in the chair, beside herself with grief, her devotion as best friend and cousin tested and proved.

She came one afternoon, meekly opening the door to his room, walking over and sitting on his bed, neither of them saying anything, their body language doing all talking.

"I'm so sorry," Sarah's body said as she sat there. *"For all of this. Forgive me."*

"It's all right," Kay's responded.

And they embraced.

After that, Sarah and Phillip came to see him often, the three of them sitting in his room with the curtains to the grand windows thrown open like they were ten years old again. Tired of holos, card and vid games, they started doing their correspondence together. They all had a lot and it took all day to catch up. Even Kay, who usually had little correspondence because Sam had been stealing it, now had letters from ladies from all over wishing him well.

Sam, wherever she was, was a little too busy to be stealing letters at the moment.

Sarah, still feeling bad for her role in all of this, doted on Kay, fetching snacks from the kitchens with regularity and fluffing his pillows whether they needed it or not.

As Kay worked on his pile, he remembered the faded note sitting in his dresser drawer. "You know, the other day I thought, just for a moment, that I could read that note."

"This one? The weird one, right?" Sarah asked. She got it out of the drawer. She looked at it for a moment, lighting her Sight. "I can't see anything—just a blur."

She brought it back to Kay's bed, its pages messy with smeared ink. Phillip looked at it. "Hmmm, I can't see anything either. What did it say?"

Kay looked at the note. "It said my name; then, it said something about a warning. I didn't have time to look at the rest."

Beth ... Wandwilla ...

Sarah looked at it again with interest. She loved a good mystery. "A warning? That sounds creepy. Can you see anything now?"

Kay shook his head. The note was an indecipherable mess of faded red paint as always. "Nope. Just the same as before. This note came with the dried White Emilia flower—remember that? As Sam put me to Trial, she placed a necklace of White Emilia around my neck and said something about it being tradition."

Kay sat there looking at the note, wondering what it had to tell him.

✶ ✶ ✶ ✶ ✶

Time passed and Kay had mostly healed. His blood was back to normal and no longer had to take daily doses of Cynth. He was eating solid food again. Davage and Sygillis were due to leave in their starship, the *New Faith*, two days hence, and Sygillis didn't want to go—she wanted to stay home with her son, but Davage talked her into coming. Kay was fine. The numerous Bark dogs patrolling the Grove and castle grounds found nothing. No sign of Lady Sammidoran or the phantom fleshless attackers Kay claimed had harmed him. Time for life to continue.

* * * * *

Lord Davage called Kay, Sarah and Phillip into his study near the lovely Palantine Courtyard in the northern wing of the castle.

Davage sat behind his age-old desk. It was piled high with scrolls and books. Davage had never had much time for technology, and his study was devoid of holo terminals, insta-types and so forth. The room was huge and multi-leveled, the walls lined with thick books and shelved mementos. Portraits of Countess Sygillis and the children were everywhere. A Silver tech cat named Whiskers, whom Lady Poe had made for Davage some years ago, prowled the upper reaches on the constant lookout for StT's. A large over-stuffed chair sat to the side of his desk. It was the chair Kay's mother usually sat in, though it was empty now. Through the large window, the distant village and the sea beyond could be seen. The *New Faith* sat parked in the bay on its pylons like a great white blob. As usual Davage was in his wonderful blue Fleet uniform, his hat and coppery CARG resting in their usual place behind his desk.

"Well," Davage began, "we're due to sortie again in a few days and it's always good to see my son and my favorite nephew and niece right before leaving." He looked at Sarah and took in her blue-haired features. "Sarah, I must say—and I'm sure you've heard it before— as you mature into a beautiful young lady, you are the image of your grandmother, Countess Hermilane. Looking at you sitting there, it's like seeing my mother in the flesh all over again."

Sarah smiled. "Truly, Uncle?"

"Indeed. Even your shade of blue hair is the same. Astounding."

Davage turned to Phillip. "And, Phillip, what a fine young man you've become. Everything that's good about my sister and your father, Lord Peter, is doubly so in you."

"Thank you, Uncle."

"I've also heard you've grown into an amazing pilot. Is that true?"

"I really can't say, sir. I do enjoy flying."

Davage laughed. "Can you out fly my little girl, Hathaline?"

Phillip, humble as always, shrugged. "Well, I ... Lady Hathaline has amazing talent."

"I see. Well, if you ever want to join the Fleet, your place is assured. Lord Phillip of Blanchefort, a fine junior helmsman on some lucky ship—I can see it now."

Davage then turned to Kay. "And Kay, how are you feeling this morning?"

"I'm fine, Father."

"Any pain?"

"A little, nothing to bother with."

Davage stood, turned, and went to the window. Outside it was a typical dark blue, sunny day. The sea beyond was cold and calm. "Your mother is down in the village attending to business at the factories right now, had the whole fall collection tucked under her arm when she left. 'Madam Thimble', as they used to call her, is at it again with her designs and swatches. I still recall when she sacked all my designers and took over operations herself, I thought that was end of our family business. I even thought, if she failed, that would give me the excuse to restart the old family tradition of firearm making, but no, she has done a masterful job and made us proud. Her designs are even worn on Hoban of all places, most amazing."

He paused. "I wanted to take this time and talk to you, Kay,—and to you as well, Sarah and Phillip, in private."

Still staring out the window, Davage continued. "Kay, I want to know what you are planning to do about the Trial Lady Sammidoran set to you."

Kay sat quiet for a moment. "Father, Mother forbade me to …"

Davage turned from the window and stared at him. The gold ivy and stars embroidered on his collar glinted in the light.

Kay swallowed, unable to lie to his father. "I am going to continue the Trial, Father. I am going to follow it and allow it to lead me where it will. I promised Sam, and I believe in her. She's counting on me, and I'll not fail her. I love her, Father."

Davage smiled. "I thought as much. Your mother and I have much discussing to do regarding Lady Sammidoran's status here at the castle. I'm sure you understand. She is most angry, as she loves you very much, Kay. I, however, am not as ready to convict Lady Sammidoran as she is. I am not convinced the attack on you was created by her in the least. I, too, believe in her, and in you, Kay."

Sarah spoke up. "But, Uncle, Kay's admitted that Sam said the Trial could be deadly. Kay could die should he proceed."

Davage turned to Sarah. "I've been told by your mother that you like stories, Sarah. Tales of all those old Vith heroes and what not. All the niceties that show up in earnest in the daily Posts."

"Yes, Uncle, I do."

"Then you'll know that a common theme in many of those old stories is a Vith hero facing death. Fighting a monster, performing a deed of some sort—it happened all the time back then, and it still does today. Stories are still being created. There are still Vith heroes. Sometimes, when you're a member of a Great Blue Household like this one, you're expected to act like a Blue Lord, and that sometimes means facing death."

"You cannot be serious, Uncle," she said.

"It sounds a bit bizarre, I know, but there it is. And don't get me wrong. A fair contest in which death is a *possible* outcome is a far cry from what happened to Kay in the Grove—that was outright sadism and attempted murder. And I cannot believe Lady Sammidoran is capable of such a thing. She loves him very much; that's very plain to see. From what Kay has said, she offered him multiple opportunities to bow out, and he chose not to. He promised to see the Trials through to the end. He chose to face death, for her, and he is going to live up to that promise as best he can. For that, I am very proud of him. That is what Blancheforts do. Just so I know, Kay, what is this Trial specifically?"

"She didn't specify. She presented me with the White Emilia and then said the Trial would consist of three distinct stages, each presided over by a Judge."

"A Judge?"

"She created three bizarre creatures using something she called the NIGHTMARE and said they were the Judges of the Trials."

Davage considered that a moment. "Hmmm, the NIGHTMARE is the LosCapricos weapon of the House of Monama. It's a hairpin if I'm not mistaken, and Monama women are said to be able to conjure up creations using shadow material. She didn't say what the object of each stage is?"

"She didn't. She climbed into one of the creatures—it was a gigantic statue-man that looked like Lord Cathomere and sealed herself inside."

"That's a weird thing to do," Sarah said. "Wish I could have seen that."

"I think she was trying to protect herself from the same creatures which attacked me. She said they were after her ... and, before the skinless woman went to work on me she swore she was going to get Sam. I will see that monster again, Father, and next time things will be different I swear it."

"All in good time, Kay. The need for revenge is a parlor guest who will never leave your premises until dully seen, trust me," Davage said. "Let it sit and wait."

Davage paused and placed a hand on some of the old books piled on his desk. "I've been doing some reading about Shadow tech Males—a fascinating subject, really, but flawed with a lack of concrete scientific data. It appears that, even in our modern League, we really don't know much about them as they are quite rare. And, it appears the Sisters and the Science Ministry, as well, have been somewhat delinquent in pursuing the subject further."

He pointed at a huge brown book sitting on his desk. "This book right here. The Sisters wouldn't be happy if they knew we had this book."

"What is it?" Sarah asked, brimming with interest in the forbidden.

"It's a book of Xaphan Cabalism. A lot of poppycock, if I'm being honest; however, there's also a good bit of useful knowledge to be had if one chooses to examine the information in the proper prism. And, Xaphan Cabalists appear to be the preeminent authority on Shadow tech Males." He gave the book a rap with his knuckles. "Do you know that a Shadow tech Female, like your mother, and yours, Sarah and Phillip, cannot detect a Shadow tech Male? They must rely on imperfect technology; that's why your mother never knew it. We had you tested as an infant, but apparently, as we see with you, Kay, one test is not enough. Apparently many tests are needed, or possibly a better test needs to be developed. Samaritan Bethrael has repeatedly requested that she be allowed to test you, Kay, in order to increase the Hospitalers' knowledge."

"She wants to test me, Father?"

"Yes, and, if you wish to participate, that's your choice; however, I think you should give her a wide berth for the time being, Kay. She seems to have developed quite a crush on you."

Sarah laughed.

Phillip, interested, spoke up. "I have read, Uncle, that Shadow tech Females—mothers excluded, of course—cannot resist the touch of a Shadow tech male. And that immunity must also pass to close relatives, as Kay has touched my mother's Silver tech many times."

Davage smiled, clearly recalling the incident in Kay's bedroom. "Yes, mothers and relatives excluded, we can only thank Creation for that, can't we? And, as far as not being able to resist a Shadow tech Male's touch, it seems that notion has been validated, as I saw Beth having a bit of a ... problem ... as Kay touched her Silver tech. I'll say no more on the subject."

Kay thought back, the feeling of Beth all over him returned.

"For that very reason, the Black Hats go to great lengths to monitor the location and whereabouts of Shadow tech Males. When they discover one, they try to abduct and hold them in stasis. Others, of lesser value, they simply kill. Apparently, the Spectres were created to assist the Black Hats in this ongoing search for Shadow tech Males and keep them under heel. I must advise the three of you to keep this matter strictly under the cuff, for Kay's sake. Agreed?"

Sarah and Phillip looked solemn. "Of course, Uncle," Sarah responded.

"Additionally, it is speculated that Shadow tech Males have a high degree of resistance to physical damage and the deadly effects of blood poisoning."

Davage paused and looked a bit sad. "Your status as a Shadow tech Male saved you, Kay. Your wounds should have been mortal. You were disemboweled and at Apex blood poisoning—the worst readings I've ever seen. We tried using one of your Aunt Poe's wondrous Silver tech Fins fish to heal your terrible wounds, but it didn't work. It just sank into the wounds and vanished. Apparently, you must have absorbed it somehow. I have already prayed my thanks to our ancestors, and to fate, that you were so ideally equipped to ward off such an attack."

Davage continued. "And, one final thing, Shadow tech Males have strange Gifts—your abilities regarding Shadow tech will react with your Gifts and make them act in unexpected ways."

Kay considered his father's words. "I do recall seeing some things in amber in my bedroom as Beth and I…" He cut himself off. "But only for a moment, then it was gone. I never thought I had the Sight, though Sam insisted I did. One of her manifestations claimed it was the embodiment of my Sight and was very angry with me, said I'd squandered my Gift."

"Ah, yes, amber. My reading tells me such a thing is called the 'Dark Sight'. Don't let the name fool you. It simply means that you see things in an amber sort of tint, and your eyes don't glow, as is usually the case with the Sight. According to the text, the Dark Sight is very pliable as far as time goes, and you should be able to see very far into the past, present and future. I can see a few seconds into the future and several minutes into the past, but that's all. You, Kay, might be able to look back and forth in time as far as you like—wondrous, really. You do have the Sight, Kay, it's just an odd, different sort of Sight. I wish I had known such a thing, been more informed. We could have been exploring your Sight together for years now, and I feel that I have failed you in this regard."

Kay sat up and tried to reassure Lord Davage that that wasn't the case. He continued. "I'll tell you, when I was boy, not too much younger that you are now, I was frightened by my Sight. The things I saw, day in and day out, were things that I didn't necessarily want to see. It's easy to focus on the bad, on the frightening, and not notice the good, to not see it. Lady Sammidoran mentioned having to put you to pain. I think she said that because she wanted your Sight activated. I think she knew or was aware of your status, Kay. Monamas tend to know things that no one else can. The Dark Sight, according to the text, exacts a hefty price. It requires a strong and sustained jolt of severe pain to get it started. It might sound a bit morbid, but a healthy and controlled pain-creation session can sometimes be a positive thing."

Davage approached his son. "You'll have to work with your Gift, accept it for what it is, and with control, with discipline, you will begin to filter out the bad and see more of the good. Then, you will truly begin to appreciate the wondrous Gift you've been given, I promise you that. My only regret is that you will, most likely, have to discover those wonders on your own."

"Father?" Kay asked.

Davage stood up and went to the window again. He gazed down at the village below. The long tail of his blue hair sat flat against the center of his back.

"Your mother will be back soon, and we haven't long to talk. My son, are you aware of something called the Wellerman's March?"

Sarah's eyes lit up. "I am! I know what it is!"

Kay, who really didn't know, rolled his eyes.

Davage laughed. "Well then, Sarah, please inform your cousin."

"It's a youth initiation. Every Great Lord, as they come of age, is supposed to undertake one."

"Yes, correct, Sarah, well done," Davage said. "All Great Lords take the Wellerman's March at some point in their young adulthood. It usually is a journey that takes a fair amount of time to complete, sometimes several months, and takes one far away from where they start. Sometimes, it is nothing more than a grand, elaborate errand—the Grenvilles are famous for those—but, other times, it can be a dangerous, possibly deadly, labor. And so, Kabyl, Lord of Blanchefort, I suppose the time has come for you to go on yours, and, apparently the stakes couldn't be higher. This Trial for Lady Sammidoran is your Wellerman's March."

"Sam's life and mine."

"And," Davage stated as cheerfully as he could to Sarah and Phillip, "if I know you two like I think I do, I am certain you will want to go with him as you have a stake in this as well. This is your Wellerman's, too."

Phillip and Sarah lit up.

"I'm glad. I think that the three of you, with your various talents and strengths, can accomplish anything. I mentioned, Sarah, how you resemble your grandmother. She, too, went on a Wellerman's once—one of the few Ladies of Standing to do so. I'm certain such an added distinction will please you."

Sarah smiled and blushed.

"The three of you are uniquely placed for this adventure to come. Not only are you family, you're best friends as well, and that means something. In the years to come, no matter how far life takes you from each other, you will always have this—this Wellerman's March that you shared together, when the three of you took on the universe as one and came through triumphant. That is a bond, a closeness that will never be diminished or intruded upon."

They sat there listening in rapt attention.

"I will ask, Kay, that you wait until your mother and I leave on our next sortie in a few days. Knowing your mother, if she catches wind of this, she will don a bodysuit and tear off to try and stop you herself. What is your first destination?"

"Xandarr. The Judge, with Sam inside of it, said I was to be trained there immediately."

Davage approached Kay. "Training? It seems Lady Sammidoran is trying to maximize your potential for success. Well then, it's time for your gift. It's tradition for a Lord undertaking the Wellerman to receive a gift. I was hoping to save it for later, when you fully come of age, but it's obvious that that time has already come and gone. Look at you, a man already. And you, Phillip and Sarah, have also grown into fine young people—how time moves on. You shall have a gift as well, though I hope your mother will not be angry with me. Certainly, my gift will come in handy in your adventures to come, and I want you to have it."

The three looked at each other, and then at Davage expectantly.

"I shan't make it easy for you, however," he said. "This is a test of Sight, Kay, and of Strength and of thought, and it's a difficult one, so do be ready. Here are your instructions. Go to the southern end of the castle and locate the chapel of Lord Demophalon. When you get there, take a knee and reflect a bit. You will know what to do then. And remember that you each get one, no more; if you take more than that,

I will know and will be most angry."

"Yes, Uncle!" Sarah and Phillip agreed.

They stood, and Davage embraced all three of them in turn. "Ah, my family," he said, "a better gift I could not have been given. Now go, set to it, and remember, do not leave the castle until we launch; otherwise, your toughest test, no doubt, will be surviving your mother's wrath."

5—The Old Poltava

After the meeting in the study, the three made their way to the southern end of the castle. They were eager to receive the gift that Davage had offered to them.

The problem was finding it. The chapel of Lord Demophalon? Kay knew of no such place.

"So, come on," Sarah said, her eyes wide with anticipation, her duster fluttering. "Think, people. Where's this chapel?"

"I really don't know, Sarah," Kay said hurrying to keep up, his black and purple coattails flying behind him. "Phillip, have you heard of such a place?"

"I know of Lord Demophalon, a Vith fighter of old, but I wasn't aware of a chapel anywhere dedicated in his honor."

The southern end of the castle was made up of a number of huge, cathedral-like structures, five of them in all. Each cathedral was dedicated to a Vith hero of the past. The largest was dedicated to Emmira, the Vith Maiden and progenitor of the Blanchefort line. There was one dedicated to Holt of the Mountain, Subra of the Mark, and two cathedrals for Maserfeld, Kay's great grandfather. One wasn't enough; apparently Maserfeld was not only a brigand but a grand narcissist as well.

The three stumped in a hurried fashion through the various cathedrals, their footfalls amplifying and echoing through the huge spaces. The local rectors, who tended them during the day, wanted to throw the lot of them out but couldn't. Kay being the next Lord of Blanchefort couldn't be excluded from his own castle. In the muted stained-glass light, they looked around.

"Who're we looking for again?" Sarah asked, her loud voice reverberating.

"Lord Demophalon," Phillip replied.

They had been through all of the cathedrals and chapels, not finding what they were seeking. They found lots of chapels crammed in all over, but none dedicated to the right lord.

"Perhaps his name is an anagram, a puzzle of some sort?" Phillip suggested.

"No, my father hates those."

After a bit, Kay had a thought. "Wait a moment. I suppose, since I am now given lease to explore the disturbing depths of my Sight, such as it is, that I should try to use it to discover this chapel. What do you think? Father did say this was a test of Sight."

"Sure, sounds fine," Sarah said. "And hurry up! I want to see our present. It would be bad—real bad—to have to walk back to Uncle's study and tell him his task was too adult for us."

Kay and Phillip agreed.

Finding an out of the way pew in Subra's cathedral, they sat and Kay took his hat off.

He took a deep breath. "Before I start—there isn't any need for you two to do this. Are you sure both of you want to join me in whatever is to come? It could be dangerous."

"I ought to pop you, Kay," Sarah said, indignant.

"We are with you in this," Phillip said. "Besides, this is why we come up here—for fun, for adventure. You, Kay, are fun to hang out with, as they say."

Kay smiled, grateful for their presence and help. "All right, then we do this together. Here I go."

Kay sat back and relaxed. He closed his eyes and tried to release the amber realms that were all around him.

Nothing happened. There was only the muted light of the stained glass windows, and the small sounds of the cathedral amplified up to loud bangs and thumps.

"Just relax," Sarah said lighting her Sight and looking at him with blue beams. "See."

The rector charged forward holding a candle snuffer. "No Gifts in this place of worship, young lady! I do not care who you are. I'll have you on my knee!"

Sarah waved him off. He turned and walked away, cursing.

Kay sat there. "No, it's no good; I can't do it."

Phillip chimed in. "Well, as your father said, you might need a good dose of pain to kick it off. I hate to say it, but that is probably the case."

Kay looked at Sarah and held out his hand. "Sarah, take my hand and start squeezing."

"You want me to squeeze your hand, Kay? I'm not going to hurt your hand."

"I'm not saying break it. Just squeeze enough to make it hurt. What's the big deal? You've never had a hard time causing me pain before."

Sarah took his hand, and Kay felt her grip turn hard and stony—the Gift of Strength. He felt a dull beacon of pain well up from his hand through his arm. His joints gave a little pop; then, he was really feeling it.

"Do you want me to stop, Kay?" Sarah asked.

Through the stony-handed wall of pain, it was easy, so easy, for Kay to fade away. The cathedral turned to amber, and things appeared to slow down around him. Glancing to his side, Sarah and Phillip appeared to be asleep. They were sitting, stiff and unmoving. He could see the cathedral filling and emptying over and over, day and night. He thought he saw his parents strolling alone up the aisle way, hand in hand, in love as always, and the brief image warmed his heart.

He then saw his mother flat on her back on the altar giving birth, a group of Hospitalers in attendance and a chorus of Sisters, assisting Mother in the process.

No, on closer inspection, it wasn't his mother; it was Sarah giving birth. But, that was silly, as Sarah had never given birth. It must be Countess Hermilane, his grandmother, giving birth. Creation, she certainly did look like Sarah as everyone had always commented on; no kidding. They even did their hair the same way.

Two girls in Blanchefort gowns and a finely dressed gentleman, who must have been Sadric, his grandfather, watched the birth. The two girls were Pardock and Poe, his aunts. He was witnessing the birth of his father. Again, he felt touched by the scene. Perhaps, as his father had mentioned, his Sight, properly used and tempered, wasn't such a bad thing after all.

Continuing, the scene accelerated into a blur, moving back, back, back through time, through the ages. Suddenly, the cathedral was gone, and Kay was standing on a rocky bluff overlooking a drop to the sea far below, the sky big and cloudy overhead.

Looking back, he saw the castle, though a much smaller version of it—just a modest pile of rocks on a wind-swept bluff. He recognized it as the Firth House, the tearoom in the Palatine courtyard.

And something was moving in the sky above the clouds in a brownish patch, something big and round like a large moon blotting out the sun.

The Elders—Kay was seeing one of the twenty-five Elders floating in the sky, now long gone in modern times. He felt humbled and a bit frightened.

Looking to his right, he saw a small chapel that was partially underground. There was a small plaque before the chapel, written in Vith, which Kay had been taught to read. The plaque read: Tomb of Demophalon.

He saw a group of ragged blue-haired people come running to the chapel. They appeared panicked and were moving about in a disordered clump. Their blue hair was filthy.

The Vith.

He was seeing the Vith, his ancestors. A few men and women took up a defensive position. Just then, several huge spider-like creatures appeared and engaged the blue haired Vith in a savage battle. No, they weren't spiders—they were odd, eight and ten-armed creatures, all beautiful and pale-skinned, part male, part female, long-haired and fit, easily ten feet tall.

They savagely battled the defenders, killing a few, while one or two of their number fell badly wounded. They slung the dead over their slender but powerful shoulders and began a retreat.

One of them, a ten-armed one, looked back and seemed to see Kay. It moved in his direction at speed. He noticed as the creature approached that it had five pairs of breasts to match its five pairs of arms.

It was on him and seized him in a huge, feminine hand. He could feel the warm hand, the soft but somewhat rubbery skin, and strength beyond compare.

He cried out, and the vision was gone.

When he opened his eyes, he was back in Subra's Cathedral with Sarah, Phillip and the angry rector looking down at him. His hand was throbbing.

"I want the three of you out of this holy place, now!" the rector demanded, holding his candle-snuffer in a threatening manner.

"What happened?" Kay asked.

"You fell into a trance for a second, then you cried out, and I let go of your hand," Sarah said.

The rector gave them no peace, so they shuffled out of the cathedral into the hallway where he slammed the doors shut behind them.

✶ ✶ ✶ ✶ ✶

They found a quiet alcove in which to talk. Sarah was dying, as she was into this hard.

"Well?" Sarah asked. "What did you see?"

"I saw it," he said proudly. "I saw Demophalon's chapel. It's buried under Maserfeld's cathedral, I think. Yes, that should be right if I'm gauging the distance correctly."

"Which one?" Phillip asked. "He's got two."

"The bigger one."

"How's your hand?"

Kay made a fist a few times. "Hurts, but nothing's broken."

He told them how he seemed to go back in time and everything he saw—the Vith, the strange gigantic creatures, and how one saw him and attacked.

"Those are the Haitathe, the giants of old," Phillip said. "Vithland was once overrun with them. You say one of them *saw* you?"

"Yes, it grabbed me, and that's when I cried out." He thought back. "I saw the Elders, Phillip. I saw one floating in the sky like a great moon. It was humbling. How I wish they were still here with us."

Phillip was shocked and a bit envious. "That must have been something to see."

Sarah was rather impatient. "I'm sure it was inspiring. So, you say you saw Demophalon's chapel? Where was it, again?"

Kay looked around. "It was where Maserfeld's Cathedral currently is, I think. The big one."

They exited the alcove and made their way in that direction.

They entered the cathedral; it was a large, somber place in muted light. They looked around. Kay tried to get his bearings.

He pointed at the altar, which was, as near as he could guess, situated approximately where he had seen Demophalon's tomb in the past.

They approached the altar and looked around, testing it, pushing and pulling; it was a good thing the rector of this cathedral didn't appear to be around for he would not be too keen on all of this. Eventually, the large altar moved a tad.

"Give me some room," Sarah announced. She rolled up her sleeves and exerted herself to Full Strength. "Wait!" she cried. "I'm not allowed to use the Gift of Strength indoors. Remember? Mother said so."

"I'm certain Mother will forgive you this one time, Sarah," Phillip said.

She was dubious. For all her bluster, Sarah was basically a good kid who did as her mother asked. "Sarah," Kay said, "as the next Lord of the castle, I grant you permission, on this occasion, to power up indoors, provided you don't tear anything up."

She nodded and accepted Kay's proclamation as valid and allowed herself to power up to Full Strength. She leaned into the face of the altar like she was wrestling with it and strained. Eventually, it moved enough to uncover a small passage beneath it. They lowered Sarah in and, lighting her Sight, she crawled off into the dark.

"What do you see, Sarah?" Kay called.

Down below, the beams of her blue light panned about this way and that. "I see the remains of an old chapel. It's pretty neat. Wow!"

"We've no time for that, Sarah."

"Hey!" she called back a moment or two later. "It's a dead end."

"You sure?" Kay called down to her. "Look around; can you Sight through it?"

"I can't see through things yet," she called back, her voice echoing a little. "There's nothing, just a solid wall at the far end of the chapel."

Kay and Phillip thought for a minute or two. "I know this is it," he said.

"Phillip, get down here and help me!" she called up.

"Just a moment. I believe your father mentioned something about taking a knee and reflecting," Phillip added. "This is a test of thought, as well as Sight and Strength."

To the far right, in an alcove, was a large painted icon of Maserfeld, their great grandfather. There he was, tall, bearded, tipsy with ale mug in hand. Beneath his icon was a kneeling bench. Phillip walked over to the bench, considered it for a moment, and knelt down.

"Hey!" Sarah cried from under the altar. "What did you do? The wall just opened a bit!"

Kay could hear her rustling around in the dark, then:

"Hey!! Hey, you two, get in here!! You won't believe this!! Hurry up!!"

Kay found a heavy bust of Maserfeld and put it on the bench to keep it pressed down. He and Phillip then plunged into the dark under the altar. There, at the end of a short crawl, was Demophalon's ancient buried chapel, the same one he'd seen in his Sight, only now covered up and forgotten. At the far end was a hidden chamber, about ten by ten feet, lit up by the blue light of Sarah's Sight.

Inside, mounted on shelves, were about three dozen Blanchefort PtVa pistols.

✶ ✶ ✶ ✶ ✶

The Blanchefort PtVa was a classic firearm, designed four hundred years earlier by Posnam, Lord of Blanchefort. It was a brilliant design, being fairly small, with a huge punch and an infallible firing mechanism. Its workings were still copied in modern weapons like the popular Grenville 40. The 'Poltava', as it was nicknamed, was once the lynchpin of the Blanchefort fortune, factories in the village churning them out in quantity to a clamoring market. Lord Sadric, however, despised the practice of firearm production and disbanded it, converting the factories into fabric and textile manufacturing sites. He went a step further and destroyed the back inventory of Poltavas. Then, he bought up all the surplus inventories he could find and smashed those as well; thus, the weapon virtually ceased to exist overnight. The Poltava, now rare and much sought after, was a collector's dream and worth a massive amount on the open market.

And here were dozens of them: all small, short barreled, easily fitting in the palm of the hand. And these weren't production, off-the-line models either; these were all masterpieces, each one enameled and filigreed, each one a work of art. Here, in this hidden chamber, was a cache worth a king's ransom several times over.

The three sat there feasting their eyes. Sarah, after carefully looking at each, selected a dark blue one, the handle inlaid with gold and serpentine. She held it in her hand, feeling its perfect balance. "This one's mine," she proclaimed.

Phillip took less time, picking out a green and brown specimen on an upper shelf, its handle inlaid with onyx and opal flakes.

"Why that one?" Sarah asked eyeing the color.

"Don't know," Phillip replied. "I just liked this one. I like the brown and the green. Maybe it's karma."

Kay found one that was red with gray highlights that he admired and pulled it off the shelf.

"No, no," Sarah said. "Not that one." She took a purple one highlighted in black pearl. "This one, Kay; it suits you."

Kay looked at it. "I don't want that one. I want this one."

Sarah wasn't giving up. "I really think this one's for you. It even matches your hair. Come on and take it. Just like Phillip said—it's karma."

Kay looked it over one more time. On the reverse grip, there was an enam-

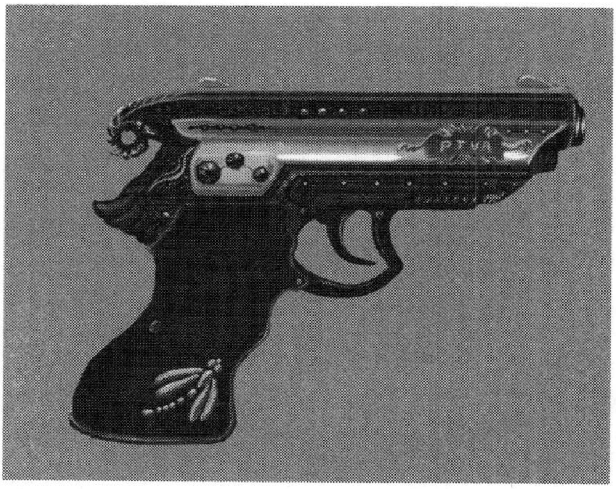

eled image, in lapis and green beryl, of a dragonfly-like bug with brassy wings.

He remembered the Parafly in the courtyard whose buzzing saved his life. That was the deciding factor. Smiling, he took the purple one, and it settled into his hand like it had always been there. Such a small, elegant weapon with a brutally powerful, infallible punch. Even quiet and unloaded, it made him feel secure knowing it was there. He put the red one back on its shelf.

"Good choice," Sarah said admiring his weapon. "I knew it suited you."

Sarah and Phillip had already placed theirs into pockets within their black dusters. Carefully, they exited the room and climbed back out of the altar. They moved it back into place and returned the bust to where it was, sealing up the chamber of riches.

✶ ✶ ✶ ✶ ✶

After dinner, they went back to Kay's room. Sarah had gotten a load of standard ammunition from somewhere and was loading her blue Poltava. Kay and Phillip got theirs out, and she loaded them as well.

Kay walked to his dresser and got the old IN LOCK note out as Sarah slid the bullets into the magazine. There it was, faded and illegible as ever. He went back to the bed and sat down.

Sarah eyed the note. "What, you want me to squeeze your hand again?" she asked wanting to know what the note said.

"Go ahead," Kay said holding his hand out. Sarah took it and began squeezing. In an amber pall of pain, the note reverted in time, the letters shrinking back down into their original form.

It read:

To: Kabyl, Lord of Blanchefort

BE WARNED:

For some time, my 72nd grandchild, Sammidoran, has been in love with you, and she, against my advice, is unable to compose herself and stay away. I am certain you already know that. Although you are the son of my cherished friends from the north, I have advised her to forget you and keep her heart closer to home, not only for her sake, but for yours as well.

I understand why my granddaughter feels as she does. You are, without question, a fine young man, however there are things you must know, and my granddaughter, because of our traditions, cannot mention them to you. As I shall, no doubt, be dead by the time you receive this letter, I shall speak for her. May the gods have mercy on my House.

I have included a flower you call White Emilia. It is a common plant that grows near our home. It has a tendency to kill insects that come to drink its sweet nectar. Only the right insect at the right time may drink without fear. It is symbolic of our Trials of Love. My granddaughter, should your relationship become generally known, will have to put you to Trial, as is our tradition, and, therefore, try to kill you. You father has an understanding of our Trials, but I do not think he fully appreciates their import or gravity. Know this—should you be presented with the White Emilia, and should you accept it—then you shall face death at the hands of my granddaughter. She will have power over the NIGHTMARE, which is magic that comes to us from the Gods of Jade and Sapphire. She will use the NIGHTMARE to create visions from her deepest fears and set them against you. She has no choice in the matter, it is our way. And she has much to be afraid of; we all do. The things that haunt Monama nightmares are truly horrific.

We, of the Lake, are a cursed people, watched and kept in chains. There are things unseen that hover over us, torment us, and compel us to do things not of our choosing. We have, for ages, been slaves to demons who step out of thin air and take us from our homes and turn us into monsters, Berserkacides, at their whim. My granddaughter loves you because of her visions—she dreamed of you for years prior to your birth. I have always suspected that our visions are sent to us by the demons that confound our existence. If my granddaughter saw you in the future, then I believe that is because the demons, for reasons unknown, WANTED her to see you, and, in her innocence, she fell in love and lost her heart to an Elder boy from the north. Alas, I believe the demons haunting us and the Horned God they worship now turn their attention to you, and, therefore, we, as their pawns, shall also be set against you as well. I see a future of blood where the gods turn their attention to this place and shrink from what they see. I see the possibility of the Sisterhood of Light coming to kill us, and I cannot wholly say that I blame them. My advice, Lord Blanchefort, is to avoid my granddaughter and stay out of the troubles of the House of Monama for as long as you can. The troubles are coming sure enough, but, perhaps, if you stay away, you can remain unaware for the length of your life and pass in bliss. I pray the gods that you and your family live long and safe, unhindered by our demons.

The world is a much more dangerous place than you realize.

You have been warned.

Do not accept the White Emilia.

Signed:

Hortensia, Countess of Monama and Astralon

Sarah sighed and let go of his hand. "I guess she's a little late with the info."

Kay sat there and tried to absorb the information. "A letter from Sam's grandmother? Watched by demons? Is that what attacked me in the Grove? That man and woman?"

"You did mention they popped out of thin air," Phillip said.

"Over this last winter, Sam did act in a peculiar fashion. Jumpy, looking around—acting like she was afraid of being watched." Kay thought about the note. "And, one time I tried to contact her in the chapel; instead of getting Sam, I heard a voice, an angry whisper that frankly gave me the chills. Was I speaking to a 'demon'? I don't want you two coming with me. I don't want you to be endangered," Kay said.

Ignoring him, Phillip took his now-loaded green and brown Poltava back, went to the window and stepped out onto the balcony. He looked up at the deep blue sky. “So, Kay, when are we leaving?”

“Did you not hear me?”

“And our first destination is Xandarr?” Phillip asked, still ignoring him.

“It is.”

“How are we going to get to Xandarr, if I may ask?”

“I’m going to book passage. Standard transport—first class, of course.”

“Forget that,” Sarah said. “We’re going in the *Goshawk*!”

Phillip came back in and headed to the door. “I better preflight it. The thing’s twenty years old, you know.”

Kay stood there. “Sarah, Phillip, I don’t want you endangered. Your souls might be at risk.”

Phillip smiled. “Come on, Kay, I’ll need your help with the pre-flight.”

Sarah and Kay stood and followed. He was glad they were coming. Despite his protests, he didn’t want to do this alone.

✶ ✶ ✶ ✶ ✶

With the usual fanfare, the *New Faith* rose out of the cold water of the bay. Countess Sygillis hadn’t wanted to go. She was normally an eager cosmic adventurer, but, with the attack on Kay so fresh in her mind, she clung to him. Bethrael of Moane wearing her winged, silver helmet, decided to go with them—a huge ship like the *New Faith* always needed good Hospitalers. She gave Kay a huge hug and whispered in his ear: “*You and me, anytime, anywhere, Kay*.” She let the tip of her tongue enter his ear. “*I can still feel you. HeHe.*”

He knew exactly what she meant. He had a strange dream about her—that they were standing in a vast forest, and they came together, Kay feeling the ecstasy that he felt before when he touched her Silver tech.

In his dream, Beth held onto him, not letting go. She wrapped him up in Silver tech, and they were welded together, man and woman merging as one. They became some sort of vast tree-like creature with waving vine-like branches and hanging purple fruits. Though a massive tree, it moved slightly every so often—twitching in a climax that was unending.

Kay woke and had to run to the bathroom. He never had such a dream. He had a thought that, on the *New Faith*, Beth was having a similar dream. He splashed himself, trying to calm down—trying to get the image of Beth and the tree out of his head, and everything went to amber again, all on its own.

Unable to control it, his Dark Sight uncoiled away from him, this time, shooting forward instead on falling into the past.

What he saw was terrifying. He saw that hideous man and woman again, swooning in depravity, *eating* him. He saw Lady Poe, his loving aunt, watching with approval—she having become an evil vision as well. He saw Sarah and monstrous Lady Kilos locked together in a fight to the death. He saw Paraflies everywhere, crawling, stinging.

He saw a smooth silvery creature with flippers and whiskers, head bowed, being led away in chains.

Was that ... Carahil?

His aunt and sister, monsters?

Carahil imprisoned?

He saw some sort of vast, dark space, marked by stone columns at regular intervals like a poorly lit, subterranean church or temple. At the front was a platform, and sitting on it was a gigantic, deer-like creature with a tangled crown of antlers. Bodies burned all around it. It reveled in the burning.

The Horned God had his blood.

✶ ✶ ✶ ✶ ✶

That evening, Kay was playing with Maser in the Grove. With Kay's help, Maser had built a massive fort somewhere deep in the green. It was nothing more than a conical pile of dirt about four feet high, but Maser, clumsy, filthy, beamed with happiness in the dimming light. He had a little yellow bucket that he was using to transport loads of dirt. Kay emptied the bucket and put it on Maser's head, like a helmet. The high clouds, tinged with twilight red, were ready to give way to an open pallet of stars, the brightest of which were just beginning to come out.

"I think I hear Phillip coming," Kay said. "And he's going to want to tear this fort down to the stones. Be ready to pummel him."

Maser picked up two handfuls of earth and was ready to throw. He had a big stupid grin on his face. Being so small, he still wore kid's clothes, a miniature version of his father's Fleet uniform, only it was one piece with a trapdoor on the bottom in case he soiled himself. With his mother gone, aloft in the *New Faith*, one of his nannies would be looking for him soon.

Kay was far too old to be playing in the dirt, but, he couldn't help himself. He loved roughhousing with his brother and his cousins and, for that matter, he was only twenty-two. He was still just a child, too.

Everybody seemed to forget that.

Lady Kilos strolled into the clearing, heading back to the castle for the evening. She was holding a handful of flowers she'd picked from the Ten Gardens. "Kay, there you are. We need to get Maser into the castle for the night."

She saw them playing in the mud. "Oh, for Creation's sake," she said looking at Kay in the dirt, disapproving. "What are you doing?"

"What's it look like, biscuit-face!" Kay said, noting Kilos' unfinished, puffy face still locked in her childhood.

She turned red with anger. "That was so mean! You know I hate that!" She dropped her flowers, put her hands to her face, and began to cry.

Immediately, Kay felt bad and jumped down off of the dirt mound. He thought of Ki's bloody gown, and how she had wept over him on his deathbed.

"Hey, Ki, I didn't mean that. I'm sorry. Really, I'm sorry." Making sure to keep his muddy hands away from her green Blanchefort gown, he gave her a hug and, after a moment, she buried her face into his shoulder. "You can put my hair into your mouth, if you want, Ki," he said. "Remember how you used to do that?"

She laughed, and he helped her pick up her flowers. He looked at her, his little blue-haired sister. Though her face was puffy and unfinished, it didn't take much imagination to picture her as soon blossoming into a true beauty. Sam had predicted the future and said in five years her Puffies would be gone and she would be a beautiful young woman. Soon, very soon, there would be gentlemen calling on her from all over the League, waiting to see her in the Firth House.

Sam also predicted she'd be taken by the enemy in 003256.

A monstrous Lady Kilos and Sarah of Blanchefort, fighting to the death ... an evil Lady Poe watching with glee. He'd seen it. A dark vision where House

Blanchefort and the League falls. Carahil in chains. It was in the future. How could this be?

"Sam is fine," Ki said.

"I have to believe so," he replied.

"She is Kay." She considered her words. "You know our great-grandmother Christiana was a Bloodstein witch, right? She had a secret collection of arcane books that are passed from the eldest female to the next. Aunt Pardock presented me with the collection a few years ago—she and mother thought I was old enough to have them. So there I was with all these 'spell books' sitting around supposedly able to do all sorts of bizarre feats of magic."

"I remember you showing me those."

"Yes. They can do some pretty nasty things, but I'd never used them. No, I take that back. I did hex Lady Togstra with a case of uncontrollable profanity once after she spread a rumor about me."

Kay laughed. "Did it work?"

"Sure did, caused a real commotion, too."

"Well then, score one for our departed Bloodstein great-grandmother. Ever use them on Sarah?"

"Been tempted to, but no. Good thing, now that we're friends and all." Ki became serious. "There is a litany in one of the books that allows one to 'look in' on another from afar if you have something personal of theirs; it's nothing overly specific, just general impressions and such. I have plenty of Sam's hair in my brushes, so I used a strand or two and spoke the litany."

"And what did you determine?"

"I determined that Sam is fine at the moment. She is in a safe place, though she cannot tarry in any one spot for too long. She sleeps inside of a metal man and dreams of you, Kay, and, as soon as she can, she will return. She is eager for that time."

Kay closed his eyes. "What an amazing sister I have. Thank you for this news, Ki. I've had to put Sam out of my thoughts as of late; if I hadn't, I'd be mad with worry. Now I can, at least, look to this Wellerman's March and be a little less troubled."

Maser climbed down from his mound of dirt and tugged on Kay's pants leg. Kay looked down at him.

"Can I come with you?" Maser said in his tiny kid's voice.

Kay knelt down and picked him up. With Ki standing there and the sun setting, he felt like this was the last day of his childhood, the waning moments of his innocence. Tomorrow, the sun would rise, and he would be a man, the Lord of Blanchefort, with all of the worries and troubles that came with it.

The loaded Poltava in his coat emphasized the point.

"Hey, chief," he said to his brother. "I'll be back before you know it. Take care of our sister here, all right? You have to protect her while I'm gone. Can I count on you to do that?"

"Yeah."

Ki stood there, and Kay thought he saw her begin to tear up.

"The Wellerman's March can last a while so I'm told. Do you know when you'll be back?" she asked.

He realized how much he loved his sister, and his brother.

"No, I don't, Ki," he said softly. "I am going to take this march, and I am going to make sure that all the things you want, all that you hope for, come true. I know you are soon to be a fabulous beauty, just like you have always wanted to be."

Ki reached out to him. "Then take my hand, Kay, and walk me back to the castle. Let's find Hath, so you can say goodbye to her, too."

Kay was about to take her hand when he remembered his own hands were muddy. "I don't want to get you dirty, sis."

"I don't care, Kay," she said. "I expect you to be careful on your journey. You are my brother, and I shall think of you every day until you return. I honestly can't recall the last time I told you that I love you. I suppose, being my brother, it should be understood, and I also suppose that saying it should be easy, but it's not. I love you, Kay."

"I love you too, Ki."

Ki took his hand and, with Kay still holding Maser, they walked back to the castle, reveling in the last few minutes of Kay's childhood. The stars leapt out, unmindful of the scene below.

Lt. Kilos and Tweeter

6—The Demon's Identity

Bright and early the next morning, Kay, Sarah and Phillip headed out to the black, bat-like *Goshawk* parked deep in the Grove. Xandarr was a two day flight away, so they told their mother, Lady Poe, who seemed rather tired, that they would be gone on an outing for several days. She was, of course, full of questions, but Xandarr was now a League world, and the route to get there was well-patrolled. There was no danger. Additionally, the Blancheforts, due to their efforts in defeating the Black Hats twenty years ago, were well favored in the court of the King, Balor I and his queen Zoladerra. Lord Peter was actually quite excited—he wanted Phillip to test out some of the new gadgets they had installed. They checked the old ship over, and it came through just fine, a tried and true design, sturdy, fast and reliable.

Lady Poe, looking haggard, kissed both of her children and gave Kay a large hug.

Carrying their bags packed with several changes of clothes and a healthy supply of food, mostly snacks, they headed out for the ship. Kay, initially wanting to go alone, was glad for the company. He was not looking forward to the trip—space was not a pleasant thing for him.

They were so far out past the Ten Gardens that the castle was low and far off in the distance. Only the tallest of spires were visible over the horizon, like a cityscape of tall buildings. Nearby, beyond the walled outer-rim of the Grove, a gallery of steep mountains loomed—the vanguard of the Northern Vith range, a bumpy carpet of sheer mountains that extended for thousands of square miles all the way to Minz in the east and south to the Tartan headlands. Mt. Vith, its peak bathed in clouds, rose like a gnarled finger to the east, just the first of many towering, monolithic peaks lurking in the range.

✶ ✶ ✶ ✶ ✶

The *Goshawk,* sitting there in the tall grass like a bat sunning itself, wings outstretched, was over twenty years old and was once used by Peter of Ruthven in his alleged pirating activities with the Duke of Oyln. In the intervening years, the Duke had, allegedly, given up pirating, instead going on the occasional space-faring adventure with his Duchess, Torrijayne of Oyln. He also had built a faster, more modern ship called the *Windhawk,* which was a true marvel, and sold his obsolete *Goshawk* fleet to Balor I who used them as a template for Xandarr's new star militia. The ships now sat in a lavish park on Xandarr, where they were venerated as the Defenders of the Planet during the Black Hat cleansing scourge of twenty years ago. King Balor was always hoping to add the *Seeker* to his collection when she was retired, but she still flew, soaring through the skies with Captain Gona of St. Paris in command.

Peter of Ruthven, however, had bought his old ship from the Duke and kept it in perfect working order. While he was courting Lady Poe, he used it to take her on exotic outings, the fast black ship sailing at speed to far off places, and it was said that Phillip and Sarah were conceived on one of the couches in the rear area of the ship while on one of these frequent outings. It was a prized hot-rod that Peter kept for special occasions.

The *Goshawk* was a black, barrel-shaped vessel, about fifty feet tall and a hundred and fifty feet long. It had a large, swept-back wing with no tail. It was agile and fast, small enough to be able to land just about anywhere, but large enough to support several people in space fairly comfortably. It was brimming with once illegal scanning technology, now commonplace in the modern League. The pilot section at the front of the ship was flared out a bit, giving the whole thing a rather bat-like appearance from a distance. It had a few small crew quarters and a fair-sized cargo hold. Lord Peter had removed the old shock-skids and replaced them with a knobby set of cranked, semi-retractable wheels. With all of the modifications Peter and his gifted sons Milos and Phillip had made to the ship, it was twice as fast as it once was—a true speedster.

✶ ✶ ✶ ✶ ✶

When they got to the clearing where the *Goshawk* was parked, its black metal surface crawled with shiny, rust-colored life. They could see their reflections on an undulating surface.

It buzzed.

Sarah gawked at the scene open-mouthed. "Look—Paraflies!" she exclaimed. "I've read about these. The whole planet's infested with them."

Phillip squinted to get a better look, but kept his distance. "I heard they're supposed to be stowaways from another planet and are running rampant."

"Lt. Kilos seems to think they're from Bazz," Kay said.

"Creation, they're huge, aren't they, but I read they're not supposed to be dangerous," Phillip replied.

"No, but look at them—probably could sting your eyes out," Sarah said, rather morbidly.

Kay remembered the cloud of them, buzzing as he was attacked in the clearing. And, he remembered the one Parafly that helped save his life as he struggled to return to the castle in the aftermath of his attack. He admired the shiny carpet of their coppery wings and wasn't worried in the slightest.

"They're not going to sting you, Sarah. I consider them good luck."

"Yeah," she replied. "If they decide to come after you, 'good luck'."

After a moment, the huge insects took flight, buzzed in the air in a swirling, droning mass, and departed to the north.

A bit put off, Phillip got a small controller out of his duster, and the hatch slid open. They all piled in and selected quarters—Phillip and Sarah picking quarters with windows, while Kay took a small interior room. He didn't want to see the stars. They would make him sick.

All moved in, Phillip plopped down into the pilot's chair and began the complicated process of starting it up.

Sarah, always a good planner and packer, checked all they had brought to make sure they hadn't forgotten anything.

"Phillip, how many SAPPs did you bring?" she asked.

"I packed three," he replied.

"Three, and I brought two—that should be good. Kay, you have your CARG?" she asked."

"You saw me walking out here with it, Sarah," Kay responded.

"Where is it now?"

"In my cabin."

"And does everybody have their Poltavas?"

Kay and Phillip both nodded.

"Let me see them. I don't trust you two."

Kay and Phillip reached into their coats and brought out their guns. Sarah was satisfied, and they replaced them in their pockets as she loaded the food they brought into the cooler.

"Oh, what about money?" she asked.

"I've got several bags of haders here."

"Ok, good. What if we head out to Bazz, we'll need a Cred Stick."

"Bazz?" Kay said with dismay. "Well, if we end up on Bazz we'll just go to the SBL and buy a Cred Stick. No big deal."

The *Goshawk* came to rumbling life as Phillip slowly powered it up, the metal floorboards thrumming underfoot.

Sarah took a look around and was giddy. "Oh, I hope we end up on Bazz—I love Bazz. You know, I think this is going to be fun. Thanks, Sam, for doing whatever it is that you're doing. It'll be a great adventure. What do you think, Kay?"

"I think I'm not going to like this one bit," he said quietly. "I hate space travel."

"Oh, you big sissy. Hey, if you think you're going to be sick, use a bag. There are plenty of bags back there, so use them if you need to; that's important. Father will kill us if we bring the ship back soiled with your sick, okay?"

She got her blue Poltava out of her duster—she liked to admire it still. Kay sat there and looked out the open hatch to the sunny wilderness of the Grove, wishing he was outside.

Phillip finished preparing the vessel and, with a clank, he hauled it into the air, quickly gaining altitude and pinning Kay into his seat. Kay watched the ground quickly fall away as the nimble ship climbed. The open hatch made him quite queasy. "Phillip, will you shut the hatch, please!"

"I'll shut it later. I'm going to do a lap down the Gaston Way; then, we'll climb up and out into orbit. I'll shut it then—promise."

Through the hatch, the familiar mountainous passage of the Gaston Way came into view, moving by fast as Phillip hugged the mountains. Sarah unbuckled and went to the hatch, fearlessly leaning over the edge, her blue pony tail and coat tails taking flight in the slipstream.

"Oh, there's Clovis down there!" she cried pointing. "We'll investigate Clovis for the Wraith next!"

Kay, despite his clenched up stomach, chuckled a little. Little did Sarah know that the fabled Wraith of Gaston was actually Sam in disguise all this time.

Moving fast, they were out of the Gaston, and Phillip rapidly pulled into a climb, shutting the hatch at last.

"Roll it!" Sarah shrieked. "Roll it, Phillip!"

Kay went through every sick bag they had.

✶ ✶ ✶ ✶ ✶

That evening, as they set the ship to auto-pilot and shadowed, with permission, a four-ship convoy of Gioma spice merchants, they changed into their pajamas and readied for bed. As usual, Sarah had the Aire-Net blaring as she watched her favorite programming, munching on some sweet snacks. Though they were speeding through the dead of space, it was just like being at home.

A message chattered in on the Com. It was from Lt. Kilos far away across the League on the *New Faith*. She looked serious. "Sarah, turn it down, I need to take this," Kay said.

Sarah muted the Aire-Net, and they settled in front of the screen. Lt. Kilos was sitting in her quarters on the *New Faith,* coat off, Tweeter fluttering around. "How you feeling, Kay?" she asked

"I'm fine, thanks."

"Your mother is driving me crazy and I'm ready to get her in the gym and beat the daylights out of her. Seems all the Barks she's got running around aren't seeing you anywhere in the castle or out in the Grove and she's freaking out over it. Where are you?"

"We're on an outing."

Ki was skeptical and saw right through him. "An outing? Ok, what's going on? You can tell me. Wait! Let me guess—you're out after Sam, aren't you?"

They looked at each other. "Why tell you something you already know? I made her a promise," Kay said.

Ki ran a hand through her long, somewhat windblown brown hair. "Gods—if your mother finds out about this, I wouldn't want to be you, let's put it like that. You Vith, I swear ... You know, Kay, I've made lots of promises in my hundred-plus years that I've not kept for one reason or another and I got over it!"

Kay fired back. "This isn't just about keeping a promise, Ki. It's about trust and loyalty, and yes, keeping a promise falls into that, I suppose. It's also about not failing the person you love most when they need you most, and seeing that person safe in your arms once again. And, it's about revenge, as the woman who nearly killed me is out to get Sam too. I'm eager to see her again and spill her blood. Does that spell it out for you, Ki?"

Ki sat there and shook her head. In the background, Tweeter was pecking at a set of variously-sized brass bells mounted on a stand, making a twinkly sort of free-form music.

"Yes, Kay, yes it does. Well, don't worry about me, I won't say anything to your mom. I'm assuming your father knows about this, right?"

"He does."

"Ok, good. Well, it's about the person who attacked you as to why I Comm'ed tonight. I wanted to tell you that we know who did it, Kay."

"Pardon, Lt.?"

She took a look around and leaned closer to the screen, Tweeter's bell pecking bright and clear in the background. "Ennez took the material samples he gathered back to Minz and had them analyzed. It wasn't too conclusive at first; there was Sam's DNA all over you—that's no surprise, Sarah and Phillip's also and a little from your parents. It was the ... bite on your entrails, that's the one that was conclusive. The Hospitalers got a match from the DNA samples taken from your guts."

The three of them listened in rapt attention. The auto-pilot controls clicked in the cockpit beyond. A rush of hatred welled up in Kay.

The skinless woman with the golden mask.

The man in armor.

The Demons. Sam's tormentors and nearly his murderers.

He seethed with rage.

"Who? Who was it? Who's going to die the moment I get back to Kana?"

Ki looked around again and continued. "It's your sister, Kay."

They were shocked. Kay was opened-mouthed. Sarah and Phillip, too.

"You're saying Lady Kilos attacked me in the Grove?" he said with disbelief. "It wasn't her, Lt. I got a good look at her—she was tall and miserably thin. She was also bent at the torso in an odd fashion. She had no skin for Creation's sake."

"I didn't say it was Bottle, Kay." Lt. Kilos always called his sister 'Bottle' as they both had the same name. "It was Lady Hathaline. Your youngest sister, Lady Hathaline, nearly killed you in the Grove."

Kay didn't know what to say. Phillip and Sarah looked at each other and shuddered.

"Lt.," Kay said, "Lady Hathaline is sixteen years old and is still rather small. This woman was adult and tall. She was a perverted monster."

"I didn't say I understood how or why, Kay, but the fact remains. Her teeth marks and her spit were on your guts that she chewed off."

Kay was aghast.

More bells twinkled in the background as Tweeter fluttered from one to another, pecking at them in a pleasing fashion.

"Look, I was pretty freaked out when the Hospitalers told me—I mean, it doesn't make any sense, right? I mean, Lady Hathaline couldn't possibly have attacked you, so I went on a Manhunt to find out the truth myself," Ki said.

"A Manhunt?" Sarah asked. "With what?"

"With Tweeter, who else." Tweeter's glowing silver form fluttered up on the screen for a moment, and then resumed pecking.

Sarah was skeptical. "You know, I've asked my mother if Tweeter has all these wondrous abilities you claim he does, and she says no. She created him after all, she should know."

Ki was visibly perturbed. "You know, girlie, if you were standing right here in front of me, I'd sock you one. He's not like the other crappy Tweeters your mom cranks out—he's special. I think Carahil breathed something into him way back when before the three of you were born. He can do anything I ask him to do and he heard you, Kay, as you were lying on your death bed, so you have him to thank for your continued well-being today. With that in mind, let's not harsh on my Tweeter again, Sarah, ok?"

"All right, all right, wow you're touchy."

Appeased, Ki continued. "So, I went out into the Grove and found the spot where Kay got attacked—Tweeter showed me where it was. I let him root around for a while to get the feel of the place, and then I told him to point me out the guilty."

"He can do that?"

"Yes, he can. They don't call me 'Manhunter' for nothing. Usually, manhunts take a while as I have to follow the subtle hints and clues he gives me. It's a slow process. This time, though, he hopped off my shoulder and started flying, which told me the guilty party was fairly close by."

"So, what did you do?"

"What did I do? I followed him. Tweeter zeroed right in on Lady Hathaline. She was out messing around at an old fountain in another part of the Grove and he nearly got stuck in her hair. Gave her the fright of her life, too. So, there it was—proof the Hospitalers were right. Tweeter put the finger on her."

"No, no, it can't be," Kay said.

Lt. Kilos continued. "Look, here's another thing. The other day, when the Sisters came to the castle and Stared everybody down over the theft at Hiei, they nearly took Lady Hathaline to Twilight 4 with them. They said she had something 'bad' about her. They didn't know what it was, but they were sure eager to find out. Only thing that saved her was your dad. He talked them out of it. I mean, we've all seen weird things in our day, haven't we: Alteration, Transformation, Cloaking, all that other stuff I don't claim to understand. Changing one's appearance isn't all that difficult if you have the means to do so."

Kay thought about it, and something told him that she was right—that his tiny, red-headed sister, Lady Hathaline, was the one who attacked him in the Grove.

He became confused, his shock and hatred mixing together. He had no idea how to feel. He loved his sister.

"Do my parents know about this?"

"Creation no."

"What are we going to do?"

"I don't know. I've asked some of my contacts in the Blanchefort Magistrate's Office to keep an eye on Lady Hathaline. Now, here's the really crazy thing. The night you were attacked, Lady Hathaline was asleep in her tower the whole time. I reviewed the security logs myself. I can tell you how many times her heart beat, if you really want to know. She grinds her teeth, and she gets up to pee fairly often."

"So, what are we to make of this then? How can my sister be in two distinct places at once in forms both fair and foul? And who was the man in armor? And, according to Sam, those two had been secretly tormenting her for her whole life. As

Sam is quite a bit older than Hath, how did she manage that?"

"You got me, Kay. You know we have stories on Onaris, of skinless kin who come and terrorize their household, causing strife and destruction. We call them 'Jennybacks', just folklore for a dark night around the fire with a jug of moonshine, but look what we have here. The lady you described, Kay, sounds like a nasty Jennyback to me. The Xaphans, too, have stories about such things. I've no idea how this has happened, and I don't pretend to understand it, but I intend to protect both you and Lady Hathaline. The arcane is at work here, and I don't like it one bit."

Tweeter tired of pecking the bells and flapped up onto her shoulder. Ki gave his beak a loving rub. "Listen, I'm going to send you a code via your personal holo-account. When you get home, use it. It might help. Make sure it's midnight when you do, okay?"

"What is it?"

"You'll see—and don't take no for an answer, ok? I've got to go. Be safe, and do not let your mother find out about this. Oh, by the way, your honey, Bethrael of Moane, says hello."

"Thank you, Lt., and good night."

"Goodnight." She screened off.

They looked at each other.

"Well, I'm good and creeped out," Sarah said. She peered around at the darkened interior of the ship and the stars shining through the cockpit glass. "What does that mean? How could Lady Hathaline have been the one who attacked you?"

Kay closed his eyes, feeling sick again. "I don't know, but it feels right. The woman was a monster: thin, bent, like she'd been broken and then crudely put back together again. Still, she seemed like Hath, had her presence now that I think on it. And, let me tell you something else …"

He told them of his vision, of the evil Lady Poe, and Sarah and Lady Kilos locked in a terrible battle.

Sarah laughed. "Me and Lady Kilos in a fight? That wouldn't be much of a fight!"

"It wasn't just a fight, Sarah, it was a struggle to the death, and my sister was doing just fine. She's pretty tough—you've never given her the credit she's due, and, like the image of Lady Hathaline, she was ugly—monstrous."

Phillip went to the cockpit and checked the auto settings. Outside the Gioma ships flew nearby, their running lights winking in a comforting fashion.

"What does all of this mean? Do you really think you're seeing the future, Kay?" he asked.

"No clue, Phillip. All I know is that, if it is the future, I'm not going to let it happen. I'll change it somehow."

They slept, and Kay had nightmares. The skinless woman came and tormented him. She ripped off her golden mask and there, mutilated and aged, was what was left of Lady Hathaline's face. He wanted to hate her, as he did before, but couldn't. His heart broke as she got out her knife and began stabbing him again and again.

7—Xandarr

Two days later, Phillip set the *Goshawk* down in a lovely forested area south of Xandarr Keep. The Keep had been completely rebuilt since the infamous Black Hat attack twenty some years prior. It was a large, domed palace built in the opulent Xandarr style of polished marble and hammered brass, but it was nowhere as big as the former structure had been. It was surrounded by a large wooded park, mostly open to the public so that the citizens could enjoy it; however, the wooded sections to the south of the Keep by the banks of the River Torr were private for the King and his House.

Balor I, the king, and his wife, Queen Zoladerra, never forgot the promises they made after the attack. Balor was a good king and, slowly, Xandarr built itself back up to prominence. Fifteen years prior, Xandarr had petitioned and been admitted to the League, the first formerly Xaphan planet to do so. As such, Xandarr was a target for ambitious Xaphan warlords and led to an acute uptick in League-Xaphan space battles, all of which the vastly superior Fleet won. The great northern city of Zamma became a major League outpost and ship berth.

They were greeted by several footmen who were dressed in colorful veils and light vests—typical Xandarr clothing. Kay announced himself and his party, and the footmen immediately escorted them to the king and queen.

They were sitting in a landscaped garden terrace out in the purple sunshine and big sky of the afternoon. They had a stunning view of the Torr and the snowy mountains beyond.

"Lord Blanchefort!" the King exclaimed. "You have been too long in visiting us. You will find that you and yours are always welcome here! Always!"

Kay bowed, and Sarah and Phillip did the same. Balor's children of various ages surrounded Kay, fascinated by his purple hair. Of course, all of the Xandarr children were blue-haired.

Queen Zoladerra smiled at him from her couch. An ex-Black Hat, she had the Shadowmark on her face, just like his mother and aunt did. As per usual with former Black Hats, she was very pretty with a long, ringed head of blue hair. She wore a small silver charm at her throat in the shape of a seal. Her charm had an embossed '1' in the center.

✶ ✶ ✶ ✶ ✶

Kay's father had often told him of the Xandarr 44. During the Black Hat attack, Carahil (yes, he again) had helped save forty-four Black Hats during a pitched battle inside the Keep. Being a god, Carahil was able to free the Black Hats of their thrall to the Black Abbess, and King Balor took them in. In the aftermath of the attack, they formed a sorority, calling themselves the Xandarr 44. They lived in a grand marble villa off the village square, with Queen Zoladerra as their tacit leader, hence her '1'. The '44, he'd heard, were key in thwarting Xaphan spies, assassins and subversives sent to create chaos on Xandarr after it joined the League. Throughout his childhood, Kay recalled occasional female guests in the castle from time to time, all wearing veils and sporting little numbered seal charms about their necks. They came to the castle to go to the Greyson Courtyard and pray, offering their thanks and hoping to commune with the little silver god in the form of a seal who, in kindness, had saved them years ago.

* * * * *

"We were there on the day you were born as honored guests of your House," the queen said. "You have grown into such a handsome man. Why have you not visited us sooner?"

"I am sorry, Great Queen." He looked around, admiring the ornate architecture and the mountains in the purple distance. "It is a breathtaking place to be certain."

"Thank you, and please, simply call me Zoladerra."

"Thank you," Kay said, feeling shy about addressing a queen by her name.

As Sarah and Phillip offered their greetings to the King and Queen, several veiled females Wafted onto the terrace with aplomb. They were shoeless, dressed in the usual Xandarr style, Shadowmarked, and wearing charms with the numbers 6, 14, 26 and 33; more of the Xandarr 44. They laughed and seated themselves in a gregarious manner as servants brought them a variety of iced drinks.

"Well," 33 said, "who do we have here today, Zol? What attractive young people."

"This is Lord Kabyl of Blanchefort and his cousins, Sarah and Phillip, here to visit us at long last, Willa," the queen replied. They all turned to Kay.

"They're too over-dressed," 14 stated. "They need to relax and be comfortable. Are you not hot, dear sir?" she said to Kay taking a sip from her sweating ruby drink. "This is not Kana, you know. Our dress is much more casual."

"I'm fine, Great Lady," Kay replied.

"Oh, listen to him," 6 said holding her drink. "I'll wager he's sweating buckets under all those Vith clothes. Now there's a young fellow worth seducing, wouldn't you say, Gal?"

"Yes, I'd slip a love potion into his tea, I would," 26 added.

"Actually, I'd take all three of them," 14 said, and they all giggled.

Number 6, a small, handsome woman with ringed brown hair, stood and made her way to Kay, still holding her iced drink. As she approached, Kay noticed her garb was rather transparent, and he could, if he wanted, see every bit of her down to the ring on her bare ankles. He was disciplined enough to keep his eyes locked with hers and not waiver. That seemed to impress her.

"Domeneau of Xandarr, formerly of Holly and number 6 of the Sisterhood of the Xandarr 44, at your service, sir." She bowed and Kay followed suit. "Had I but known you were coming, I'd have baked you a cake, but perhaps a kiss will do instead."

Kay turned several shades of red as Sarah gave him a chiding elbow in the ribs.

She continued. "These cretins here are my sisters. 33 is Willa-von-Tapmos of Hoban. 14 is Zagamoria of Gulle, and 26 is Galla-Metra-Forna of Tudor. Don't worry about them; I'm much more skilled in bed than they are."

"You are not," 33 said.

King Balor laughed. "Oh, Dom, such a lady you are! Give the boy some space and leave your door unlocked tonight. Perhaps you'll have a visitor! So, Lord Blanchefort, to what do we owe the pleasure today? Do you bear any official dispatches from your parents, perhaps?"

"No, Great King. Under unusual circumstances, I was told to come here for training."

The King lit up. "A lesson? You're here for a lesson? That is wonderful news! You have had an open invitation your whole life, but your mother would not allow it. I am pleased that she finally has agreed."

Domeneau, number 6, persisted. "I've a lesson or two for him I'd like to teach, King."

Kay tried to maintain his bearing. "Lesson, Great King?"

Zoladerra laughed. "You needn't be shy; many come for lessons. It is a much sought-after service that we offer, usually at great expense to the trainee. For you, no monetary payment will be accepted. However, you will be expected to offer a small gift of some sort. You shall see."

The King poured two glasses. "Lord Phillip, Lady Sarah, please sit and relax. You'll have your turn later."

Kay still stood there, not quite sure what to do.

"Take the path a short way to the river," the King said. "We shall wait for you here. Don't forget you will be expected to offer a gift of some sort."

"Yes," 6 said, "And I shall still be here when you return." She licked her lips.

Sarah sat down and picked up her glass. "Well, Kay, go on."

Kay tipped his hat and started down the path, his elegant boots crunching on the pebbles as he walked. The path twisted and turned through a stand of dense trees. He began to feel a bit hot and loosened his collar. Xandarr was a warm world—far warmer than he was used to, coming from the cold Kanan north. There were statues mounted at various points along the path cut into pebbled nooks, backlit and well-tended. One particularly large statue was the likeness of a seal—Carahil. Kay smiled and looked at it for a moment. He loved Carahil. Everybody did.

Carahil ... being led away in chains ...

Carahil's front flippers were littered with little folded scraps of paper. Kay stopped and picked one up. It was a hand-drawn note written in colored pencils by a child. It had a fanciful drawing of Carahil on it followed by a short, heart-felt note.

Kay put the note back where he found it. Whatever the child had requested, he was certain Carahil would answer. He was a friendly, accommodating god.

He had the feeling that he'd just recently seen Carahil, but couldn't place it; it was one of those déjà-vu feelings.

He continued on down the path. Eventually, the trees opened into a small clearing by the banks of a broad, lazy river, the Torr, no doubt. Beyond, he could see the valley below and the mountains in the distance, all tinted in purple. Very pretty setting. Several moons hung in the sky.

A small, long-haired woman sat by the edge of the river. A canvas was set up in front of her, and she appeared to be sketching—lost in concentration. She was wearing light blue and purple veils, just like the King and Queen, and her blue hair was set and ringed in a similar style to Zoladerra's. Her leg veils were pushed up to her knees, and her feet were submerged in the cool river water. A dusty box of colored chalk sat at her side.

Carefully Kay came up to her side, trying to be quiet.

"Have you come to help me finish my drawing?" the woman asked in a breathy, dreamy fashion, not turning around. "I've been working on it for awhile now, and it's almost finished, but I just can't seem to know where to stop."

Kay looked at the canvas. It was nothing but a scrawl.

He had heard of Princess Vroc of Xandarr often while growing up. His father talked about her every so often. His mother despised Princess Vroc. He had heard how she was responsible for nearly killing his mother in single combat. He had heard how she nearly managed to blow up Castle Blanchefort and how she was under the sway of the Black Hats. He had heard she was nearly responsible for killing every living soul on Xandarr, her family included.

He had also heard how she was insane, a tormented Eleventh Daughter of the House of Xandarr, worthless and hounded, always at fault; how her father, King

Hezru, had sold her into prostitution and then to a meat market in Burgon to be consumed. He had heard how the Black Hats drove and tortured her until she fell into utter madness and killed her entire family, except for Balor who hadn't been home that day. And, he had heard how King Balor had taken his mad sister back to Xandarr and, through love and care, had restored her to at least a hint of her sanity. At last, she was now at peace.

And, one more thing, he had heard that, for whatever reason, Princess Vroc of Xandarr was one of the greatest swordsmen his father, Lord Davage, had ever faced. It was at first thought that the Black Hats, through sorcery or via chemical means, had enhanced her physical strength and her fighting abilities. But, through the years, her skills and her amazing strength never faded. She was reputed to be a genius, her small but lethal sword arm legendary. She was the tutor of many, many League Lords daring to seek out training. Much of the considerable income derived from these tutoring lessons had gone to help rebuild Xandarr.

Now Kay fully understood. He was here to fight the legendary Princess Vroc of Xandarr. His mother, should she become aware of this development, would be livid. It was a good thing she was far across the League and his father had chosen to be discreet.

Kay took a good look at the princess in the purple afternoon sun. Her physical appearance had been related to him many times, and he always wondered what he might do if he ever stood in her presence. She had achieved a larger-than-life stature in his mind, rather like her older sister, Princess Marilith, another legendary princess of Xandarr.

She was small, not much bigger than his mother, but not nearly as diminutive and bone skinny as she had been described to him. She appeared trim, but well fed enough to not be overly thin. Her straight blueberry hair was down to her waist and ringed in the Xandarr style. In years past, her hair had been cut short in an unflattering crop.

He had been told that Princess Vroc was rather homely—his mother had said that, and his father hadn't disagreed. Her sister, the famous Princess Marilith had been a rare beauty, but Vroc, it was said, was plain and mannish in the face to the point of being ugly. However, in seeing her in person, her face painted and her hair done up, she certainly wasn't homely or mannish in the least—she was no raving beauty like the Xandarr 44 up on the hill—or like Sam, for that matter, but nor was she ugly.

Her left arm, covered with a veiled sleeve, bore a ragged, chewed-up scar, a reminder of her long ago battle with Kay's mother where they nearly killed each other.

And, true to the Xandarr style, her veils were light and see-through. Her nude body underneath was plain to see if he wanted. He tried to be demure and avoid looking at the private areas of her body.

She looked up at Kay, her fingers tinted with chalk. "Would you like to help me finish my drawing?"

Kay knelt down and selected a piece of chalk out of the box. He surveyed the scribbles on the canvas and scratched out a few lines of color. "There, he said. "A fine sunset."

She looked at what he had drawn. "You are an artist, sir." She glanced at the CARG saddled at his side. "CARG," she said. "LosCapricos weapon of House

Blanchefort. I've never faced a CARG before."

Kay didn't bother to correct her; it wasn't prudent, for Princess Vroc most certainly had faced the CARG before.

She looked at the weapon and sighed. "I suppose it is too much to hope that you are here simply to sit and chat with me." Her eyes moved to his purple hair. "I like your hair. I wish mine was purple, too."

Kay took his black triangle hat off and let her look at it. After a time, she spoke again. "I have a price. I require a payment."

"Payment for what, ma'am?" Kay asked.

"Payment for fighting me. That's why you are here, to fight me, isn't it?"

Kay smiled. "No, actually I came to help you finish your drawing."

Vroc's face lit up. There was no chair for Kay to sit in, so Vroc scooted over, and she shared her chair with him. Together, they spent the rest of the afternoon scribbling on her canvas, the only sounds being the occasional gurgle of the river and the back-and-forth scratching of the chalk on the canvas.

Later, as the day grew old and the sky darkened to a deep cranberry, and Kay stood to take his leave.

"You're going, sir?" Vroc asked.

"I am. I've a long journey home."

Vroc gazed at him with her deep blue eyes. "I have enjoyed sitting with you."

"And I with you, ma'am."

She stood up and dried her wet bare feet on the grass. "Are you certain you don't wish to have a match with me?"

Kay placed his hand on his silver CARG. "I feel shy, ma'am."

"Why?" She drew a BEREN from the side of her chair. It was a sham BEREN, a mock up—the slim, fluted blade was visible, not the real thing which, if his knowledge of LosCapricos weapons was accurate, was invisible. Now that she was standing, he could see the real thing saddled to her left leg. "You needn't feel shy, sir. I can handle myself, I assure you. Please, I want to see your skills and offer advice if any is needed. I wish to have a match with you."

Kay sighed and unsaddled his CARG. "What about your price?"

Vroc thought a moment. "My price? Very well, here is my price. I demand a lock of your purple hair. Will you agree?"

"Is that all?"

"Yes, that is what I wish of you." She raised her fake BEREN and assumed a classic fighting stance. "Please level your weapon, sir."

Kay readied the CARG. He held it one handed in a fencer's pose, as he usually did. His father would never approve.

Some of the cloudy dreaminess left her eyes. She appeared ready, focused, and eager to begin. She neared him and crossed his weapon, taking an aggressive posture. "You hold your CARG one-handed, why is this? With the CARG's advantage in weight, a two-handed grip shall maximize your capabilities. I will allow you a moment to change your grip, and I highly advise it."

"No need, I am at ease."

Vroc smiled. "Then, be at your guard."

They lightly clanged weapons, Vroc twisting the blade of her fake BEREN, Kay matching with the CARG.

With a strong thrust and septime, Kay turned Vroc's weapon, and they exchanged positions, weapons still crossed. "Yes, excellent, you fence well," she said.

Vroc came again, feinting and thrusting, Kay foiling her strikes with beat and opposition, the shaft of the CARG ringing and scratching with each hit. Suddenly, Vroc swept his legs out from under him and had him on the ground, her wet and slightly muddy foot placed on his throat. "Recall, sir, that I have feet, that I can move around. A fencer standing still is greatly disadvantaged by an opponent who moves laterally. Again, please, you are doing quite well."

She let him up, and they started again, and, as before, Kay fenced one handed with his CARG.

Vroc side-stepped, and Kay drew back to adjust. He had an opening but didn't take it. Vroc, with a hard block, moved his CARG aside and hit him in the face with a right cross, easily the hardest punch he'd ever felt. He hit the ground with a thud, his lip starting to swell.

"And I have hands as well. I gave you the opportunity to hit me; why didn't you?"

"I'll not hit a small woman."

"I am a small woman who could kill you in many different ways," she said. "Again, and this time if you choose not to fight me, I will bleed you deep."

She became intense and highly aggressive. She pressed him with the BEREN, forcing him this way, then that, pushing him back into the river. She hiked her veiled leggings up and followed, her bare feet splashing.

Their weapons moved in a blur and then locked. "Put both hands on your weapon!" she said, her voice a growl. "Do it now, or I'll kill you!!"

Kay, swallowing hard, put both hands on the hilt, the CARG feeling strange in his hands with this grip. His father had wanted him to fight with two hands for years, but had, obviously, never threatened to kill him during a practice.

Vroc came, and she seemed to be fighting for keeps. Cross, thrust, heel, bite, bang, BANG! She drove into him, trying to move his CARG aside and belt him again, and this time he side-stepped, releasing his CARG and seized her by the neck. He easily lifted and threw her into the water. After a bit of splashing, she surfaced, her blue hair a wet mop. Her veils were like drenched tissue paper around her. She looked up at him and smiled, all of the fierce intensity gone. "Excellent, sir. Very well done."

Kay helped her out of the water, and they sat down to dry off.

"I've hurt your lip," she said tenderly. She dipped a cloth into the water and sat next to him, dabbing his bloody lip.

"I hope I didn't hurt your neck. I shouldn't have done that."

"My neck is fine," she said absently, continuing to dab his lip.

She put the cloth down and looked at him. "Now, for my payment," she said. She sliced off a small lock of Kay's purple hair, which she coiled up and set aside.

In the twilight, Kay saddled his CARG and picked up Vroc's chair, her canvas and the box of chalk. Vroc took his arm, and together they walked back up the path. She hummed quietly as they walked.

At the top of the path, King Balor and Queen Zoladerra sat where they were previously, their terrace now lit up in soft lighting. The ladies of the Xandarr 44 were gone.

Sarah was rather salty. Her duster lay over the arm of her chair, and her boots were removed. "What in Creation took so long? It's getting dark. I'll not have my turn!"

The King laughed. "All in good time, my Lady. Tomorrow you'll get your turn—we've fine accommodations awaiting you all. Well, Vroc, what do you think of young Lord Blanchefort here?" he asked cheerfully.

She looked at Kay, still holding his arm. "He fights well. Needs a bit of work, and has several bad habits to correct, but very talented. I am quite pleased."

"Vroc, you seem to like Lord Blanchefort," Queen Zoladerra said.

"I do, Zol. I am going to marry him."

Kay's jaw dropped.

Balor laughed. "Did you hear that, Lord Blanchefort? My sister likes you.

What do you say to that?"

Kay blushed. "Princess Vroc is a genius—every bit as skilled as her reputation dictates. I am glad I did not embarrass myself."

Vroc slowly approached him. "I will expect to see you again, Lord Blanchefort; we have much to train. I offer you another blade. And my price will be another lock of your hair—and a kiss. What say you?"

Balor, Zoladerra and Vroc all stared at him.

"I do not wish to intrude on the Princess's valuable time."

He bowed and turned to leave. When he stood, Vroc quickly drew her BEREN and laid it on his shoulder.

"I would not have invited you for a second lesson if I didn't have time or the inclination."

Kay, feeling on the spot, bowed again. "Then, yes, I am honored, and I shall meet your price."

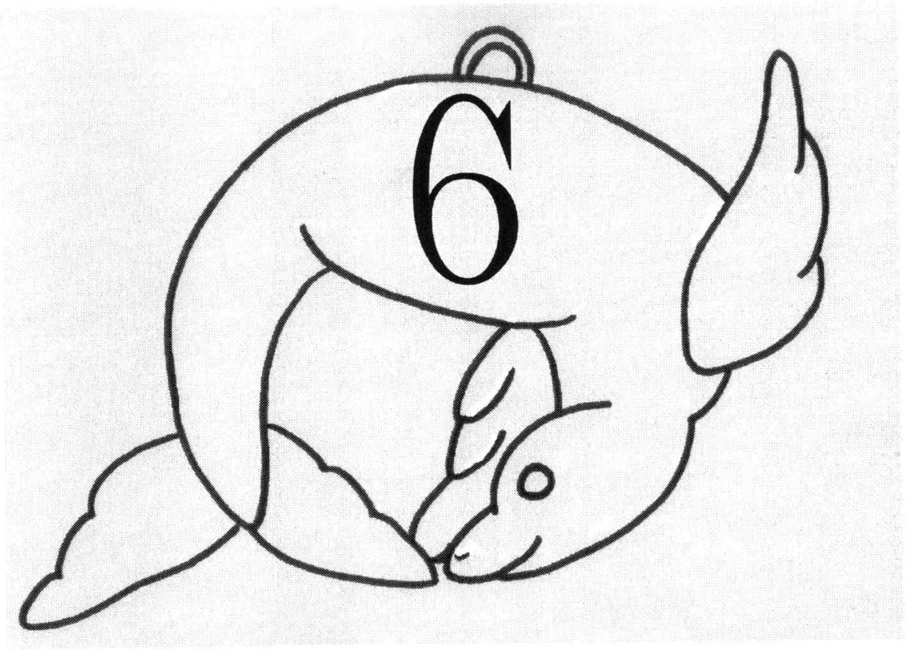

Sigil of the Xandarr 44

8—Racing with Waft

Kay settled into bed. The King had given him a large room in the eastern wing of the Keep, with Sarah and Phillip in adjacent rooms. The room was lovely, all polished stone, hanging veils and lofty worked brass hammered out in the intricate Xandarr fashion. A large curtained terrace looked out over the valley, sparkling with lights and the rising bulk of the mountains in the far distance. There was no glass or window pane—Xandarr's warm, dry climate made such a thing unnecessary. Two bright moons hung quartered on the horizon.

Kay was drifting to sleep. Sarah, now snug in her bed in the next room, had given him no peace. Sitting there in her pajamas, she demanded to know all of the details of the encounter with Princess Vroc, as she was eager to take her on in the morning and didn't think she'd be much of a challenge.

Poor Sarah. She was in for a real shock for Vroc had controlled him in their duel like he'd never been before. He had been in lots of duels with his father, but of course, Lord Davage had never tested him to that extreme. And, his father had never belted him across the face or stepped on his neck.

He thought about Princess Vroc. Now, no longer a character in a fable, she was a living, flesh and blood person, and not the monster she had been made out to be. His mother had a small stained glass window built in one of the corridors of the castle depicting the battle with Princess Vroc. The images of Vroc were less than flattering—some were rather monstrous. He must admit that he felt quite glad at the attention she had shown him. Sitting there by the Torr, scribbling with her on the canvas, he felt a real kinship with her.

He felt he liked her. Such skill. The things she'd endured and overcome.

He thought about Sam. He was still so young. This was the first time he had really been away from home on his own—Sarah and Phillip were with him, but still. There was so much out there, so much he had not experienced. Sam had, to a greater or lesser degree, been with him his whole life and had taken aggressive steps to ensure he was isolated and alone. He thought of his sister, Lady Kilos, standing with him atop the Firth House, voicing her views about Sam stealing his correspondence and haunting the Gaston Way, preventing her rivals from visiting.

Aren't you curious as to what else is out there? she had asked.

Had he given his heart to Sam too soon? He had never thought so, until now.

He thought he heard a rustling on the terrace and sat up. He saw the tall, slender figure of a woman standing by the rail. The woman glanced back at him.

"Sam?"

The figure turned, exposing a grotesque bend in the torso. She suddenly cringed and raised her hands.

Roused to wakefulness, he grabbed his CARG and went to the terrace. "Hath!" he yelled. He threw open the curtains.

The figure, if it had ever been there at all, was gone.

In the far distance, he saw something moving through the air. A chariot, floating on the wind, pulled by three naked women and driven by a tall, statue-like bronze man, approached.

Soon, Kay was backed into the room, the tall man looming over him in his chariot. The orange eyes of the three women pulling the chariot glowed in the dark.

"It is time for your first test," he said in a flat baritone. One of the women unharnessed herself from the chariot and stepped forward. "This will be a test of Waft. Remember, Lord of Blanchefort, this test tonight is a mortal one—fail, and you will die."

"Where is Sam?" Kay asked.

Without answering, the chariot turned, and the remaining two women pulled him back out into the night air. He was gone as quickly as he came.

Kay and the woman stood there staring at each other. Her mud-like appearance cleared up. Now, with the exception of her orange eyes, she looked just like Sam. Her mane of black hair went down to her ankles, and her naked body was inviting if he allowed his mind to wander.

"Get dressed," she said finally. "Or we can do this naked; it's your choice."

Kay, remembering the night in the Grove, started dressing.

"She must really like you, to go to this extreme," Waft said watching him dress. "In any case, make no mistake, I really don't care whether you survive this or not—it makes no difference to me. I am here to test and expand your abilities with the Waft, and I will not be a gentle teacher. You will progress to my satisfaction tonight, or you will die. I hope that's clear to you."

"I'm not helpless," Kay said pulling his boots on. "I'll defend myself."

"Oh, going to fight me with your CARG are you? Go ahead, take my head off with it—won't make a difference, I'll just put my head right back on. I am a creature of the NIGHTMARE, and you cannot harm me with your weapon. The only way you're going to beat and be rid of me is with your Waft. Understood?"

Kay finished dressing and saddled his CARG. She looked him over.

"Now," she said, "your test has begun. First, I want you to Waft out to the courtyards below."

Kay went to the terrace and peered over the side. He was two stories up, about sixty feet to the grass below. He decided it was best to get this over with and comply with her wishes. He stood straight and began to Waft. Slowly, he could feel the usual funnel of air begin to build up around him.

Should take about a minute, and …

"No!" Waft screamed, incensed. "Too slow! Too clumsy!" She strode up to him as the wind began to blow and punched him hard in the stomach, doubling him over. She then picked him up with one arm and threw him over the side of the terrace like a sack of laundry, where he landed in the grass below with a cry.

Kay lay there blinking up at the stars and moons in a daze. He was in great pain, but he didn't think anything was broken. After a moment, she appeared in front of him, naked as ever. "Your Waft is pathetic," she said standing over him. "Your concentration is terrible, and your technique is laughably bad. This could very well be the last night of your life, and that will make her very sad. She's doing this because she loves you. Why, I really don't know."

She helped him up. "Anything broken?" she asked.

Kay checked himself over. "No, I don't think so, but …"

She took his left hand and savagely broke his pinky. Kay reared back and choked down a scream.

"I'd Waft away if I were you," she said breaking the next finger in a grotesque fashion. Kay tried to pull his hand way, but her grip was unbreakable.

"Waft, Kay!" she yelled. Pain and nausea flowed through him. Just as she was ready to break his long finger, there was a rush of wind and Kay was gone. He had Wafted back up to his terrace. He stood there holding his hand, agony throbbing through him. The room fell to amber. He could see his broken fingers. He could see the snapped bones under the skin—nice clean breaks. Nothing that couldn't be repaired. Incredible pain. He concentrated and pulled his Sight back to normal. Now wasn't the time.

She appeared a moment later and smiled. "That's better," she said. "Pain, unfortunately, is a fine motivator. I'm sorry, and there's nothing personal. Look how fast you Wafted up here—that's what I'm looking for: fast, effortless, with a minimum of wind and noise. A lot of wind and noise is the hallmark of a bad Waft, contrary to popular belief. Let me see your hand."

Kay didn't want to give her his hand, but she took it anyway, examining his broken fingers. "Good. In the morning, should I not have to kill you, the King's Hospitaler will be able to fix you right up. For now, you need this dose of pain. If you can do what I think you can, then you can virtually fly. Great Wafters can Waft so fast, they can fly through the air—you can do that. Not even your father can Waft that fast."

She stepped out onto the terrace and pointed to a distant mountain. It was the tallest of a sturdy range, shaped like a crooked shark's snout. Kay thought he could see a dusting of snow at its gentle rounded peak. "You see that mountain, the big one?" she asked. "We're going to have a race right now, you and I. We're going to race to the top of that mountain, and either you beat me to it, or you're going to die. Understand?"

Holding his hand, Kay walked to the edge of the terrace and gingerly looked out. The mountain seemed far off in the night. "How far away is that mountain?"

"About sixty or seventy miles—what difference does it make? Here, I'll give you a head start." She picked Kay up with one arm and threw him off the terrace again. This time he Wafted with a quick blast as he tumbled through the air and appeared several hundred feet away, landing on his feet. He looked back. She was standing there on the terrace, her pale body framed by her black hair. "Better move!" she yelled, her voice echoing.

He was standing on the ground, surrounded by tall trees, he couldn't even see the mountain from where he was. Using the moons overhead as a directional guide, he started running. He had taken a few steps when he was roughly clotheslined by Waft's soft but strong arm. He hit the ground holding his throat.

She was irate. "If you're going to waste my time running, I think I'll just go ahead and kill you now!"

She pulled a medium-sized tree out of the ground and made to slam it down on Kay. He jammed his broken fingers, creating a spray of pain and Wafted several hundred feet away to the top of a distant tree. She threw the tree aside and followed in a blast.

Ahead, the copse of trees ended and opened up to a broad, hilly plain that spilled out into the night like a vast, shallow bowl. He could see little huddles of glittering light—small hamlets and villages sprinkled about, and far away, the looming range of mountains. Taller than the rest, there was the big snowy mountain, his destination. Picking a point fairly far away, he Wafted in a blast, then he did it again and again, moving in little stages, always stopping to mark his bearing and continue. As he progressed, he was dimly aware that he was Wafting in mere seconds, whereas before he needed every bit of a minute. His heart pounded with excitement. He was doing things he never thought he'd be able to do.

Waft—to a distinctive hill in the distance in a cone of wind.

Boom!—to a windmill.

He was really covering the distance. He figured he'd gone about ten miles so far in a matter of only a few minutes. Incredible. He didn't see Waft and was feeling rather proud of himself.

As he made his rapid but jerky progress along the ground, he saw a black figure moving at speed across the sky framed against the stars. It was she, with her naked body and mane of long black hair, she looked like she was swimming across the sky. He could feel the wave of her blasts drift into him.

He decided that this was a race he could possibly win. He gauged her speed and her height and Wafted.

He appeared behind her in mid-air and grabbed her by the hair. Spinning round and round, he sent Waft rocketing, arms and legs splayed, toward a farm house where she smashed into it with a satisfying crash. Feeling himself beginning to fall, he righted himself and found a distant landmark in which to Waft.

With a sharp boom, she appeared under him and sent a fist into his chin. After another moment, she was far away, heading in the direction of the mountain range that was getting closer and closer by the moment.

As Kay fell, he lined her up and Wafted. When he emerged, he put a boot into the back of her head, sending her spinning.

The mountain range unfolded in front of him. He could see a confusion of small foothills and minor mountains spreading out beneath him along with little populated hollows and small points of isolated lights. He had to be at least three hundred feet in the air. He had no idea how fast he was moving, but it was fast.

She appeared about two hundred feet in front of him. Finding that he enjoyed putting a beating to her, he lined her up and Wafted, aiming to put a hard elbow into her back.

She Wafted when he got there, again appearing about a hundred feet ahead.

He Wafted.

She Wafted. Over and over. Gravity no longer had any meaning—Kay was now a creature of the air. He had no idea how high he was, possibly a thousand feet up moving who knows how fast, the mountains streaking below at a blur. He found, as he appeared, that the cushion of air he created supported him for a good two or three seconds before he started falling. Such a span of time was an eternity. He could leisurely pick his spots, whether on the ground or at the heights, and instantly go there.

He was, for all intensive purposes, flying.

Snow. He must be getting close. Where was she? Head on a swivel—there she was! He Wafted and was at arms with her. They struggled in space for a moment, then she had him by the scruff of his shirt, hauled him around and sent him spiraling down where he crashed into the snowy ground. Things spun. His fingers ached.

She appeared in front of him, the fresh snow coming up to her calves. She seemed unfazed by the cold of the snow.

"My Lord," she said. "Look where you are."

Frantically he looked around. He was on a high, uneven bit of ground that was deep in snow. In the far distance, he could see the valley below lit up with bluish moonlight. Far away he could see the blinking, pearly complex of Xandarr Keep. There were mountains all around.

He was on the summit of the large mountain.

"You won, my Lord," she said bowing low, arms outstretched. "The race is done."

"You threw me down here. You could have won if you'd wanted."

"Maybe and maybe not. I never said that my goal was to win the race at all costs. My goal was to determine if your Waft could be expanded, and if so, to develop it—and look where you are. Look at the ground you have covered with me at speed."

She put her hands on his face. "You have passed my test. Maybe she was right to believe in you after all."

She stood him up. "Remember what you've accomplished tonight. Your Waft can save your life if you let it. I'm sorry I broke your fingers and caused you pain."

"I'm sorry I kicked you in the head."

She smiled, and they stood there in the snow, looking at the surrounding mountains and distant lights. "Embrace me, if you will," she said. "My time is done."

Kay opened his arms and gave her a long hug, which she returned. "Are you not coming back to the Keep with me?"

"I am returning whence I came. Fear not, though your lady sleeps, she dreams of what we have done tonight, and I am certain she is proud of you, as I am."

They stood there and enjoyed the night for a bit longer.

Unused cover concept by Carol Phillips

9—Admiral Carfax

The gigantic *New Faith* was snug in low orbit over the south of Kana, a few bars north of Dare. Captain Davage, Lord of Blanchefort, had been in command of the vessel since its launch twenty years prior. His arguments for the command chair before the Admiralty had been half-hearted. He hated leaving his old vessel, the much smaller, *Straylight*-class *Seeke*r, but he had been told, in no uncertain terms, that the time had come to move on.

His initial reaction to the ship had been tepid at best. He was in love with the swan-like *Straylight* class of ships that his *Seeker* belonged to, this new *Triumph*-class ship being like a double-tiered slug in comparison. He found the ship too big, too slow with a turning radius the size of a small moon. He demanded speed and agility, as the *Seeker* had given him. He pestered and tested the patience of Lord Probert, the designer of the vessel, and that of the Lady Branna, Probert's new bride and designer of its weaponry. Davage demanded changes and, by Creation, he was going to have them. How could he fight the Xaphans in such a lazy beast? It couldn't turn; it rolled only under protest; and it had the heft of a large elephant.

Captain Davage wanted his *Seeker* back.

Lord Probert and Lady Branna threw their hands up in dual frustration. So, back to Provst the ship went. Probert re-ducted the entire ship. He tripled the amount of thrusters and vents and added mass drivers at key points along the ship's length. He also stiffened the superstructure and altered its center of gravity. The result: the *Faith* variant of the *Triumph*-class of Main Fleet Vessels became the fighting standard. Now it could turn almost as tight as a *Straylight* and could barrel roll even better. Lady Branna's much contested Sar-Beams proved to pack a tremendous punch and, armed in concert with canister missiles, the *Triumph*-class ship was the most heavily-armed vessel the League had ever seen.

Such weaponry and performance, as it turned out, was needed. With the entry of the planet Xandarr to the League in 03977AX, the Xaphans shook off their melancholy and fear of the League and began a protracted campaign to forcibly seize Xandarr and re-claim it as Xaphan territory. Camilla, Baroness of Sorrander, declared herself the Queen of Xandarr in exile, demanded tribute and fealty, and offered rich bounties to any who could deliver her fiefdom to her. Xaphan warlords answered her ridiculous charge and schemed to unleash hell on Xandarr. They designed new warships in far-away yards. A new Xaphan mastermind, Lord Verd of the old House of Charn, appeared to be quite skilled, and this latest generation of Xaphan vessels was comprised of very competent designs. And the Charn ships weren't all that was coming fresh off the Xaphan yards. They were flying around in damn bizarre ships, if one could call them that. These new ships looked like giant statues, like works of fine art at a museum. Davage had never seen anything like them. The old *Merci* and *Ghome* vessels, once the mainstays of the Xaphan Armada, were gone and quaint in the memory. Now they roamed aloft in bug-like Charn ships and bizarre flying statues that actually performed quite well; as in the days of old, Xaphan warlords, they openly took on the League and its mighty Fleet in grand, swirling battles in space.

The *New Faith* and Captain Davage, with his fighting countess Sygillis at his side, was right in the middle of it, engaging them time and time again, the double teardrop silhouette of his ship becoming a dreaded sight for the Xaphans all over again.

✶ ✶ ✶ ✶ ✶

A recurring theme in the Xaphan's attack plan was not only to reclaim Xandarr by force, but also to take a League world in retribution. The obvious choice was Hoban. Proximity-wise, it was near to Xaphan space, and several Xaphan Great Houses had close ties to various Households located on Hoban. The region of Hibernia on Hoban was considered sacred ground to Xaphan Cabalists. Historically, one of the Xaphan's greatest heroes, Princess Marilith of Xandarr, had centered many of her schemes around Hoban, so it was a hot-spot, so to speak, in their activities. The Lords of the Fleet weren't overly concerned, though the Xaphans were re-motivated and re-equipped, they were still no match for the Fleet.

Still, a troubling series of events on Hoban had bubbled to the surface and needed to be dealt with immediately. Several prominent Households on Hoban, including the Governor's, had fallen into madness and melancholy. Captain Davage wasn't completely clear on the details, but whatever had happened was certainly traumatic and had the Governor of Hoban fearing for his life.

The Governor called for the Fleet. He wanted it there at all costs, and a grand task force was being assembled at once to deal with the matter.

Parked off the *New Faith's* starboard were two mighty ships: the *Bethel,* commanded by Lord Harrison of Dare, 3rd Order, and the flag vessel *Westerville* under the command of Admiral Carfax, Lord of Woodland. All three were *Triumph*-class, three cities in space.

Admiral Carfax was quite a rarity—a *fighting* Admiral. He had been appointed to the *Westerville's* chair some years ago and led it with fine skill. For his ability as a ship's captain and his Admiral's polish as a diplomat, he commanded great respect from the Fleet Captaincy, Davage included. If only there were more like him.

Coming in from the northern pole were two *Straylights* on loan from the 4th Fleet: the *Twilight* captained by Lord Van of Mystery and the *Halo Dawn* captained by Lady Strella of Jacarta.

When the ships assembled, all the captains were due aboard the *Westerville* at once for a meeting with Admiral Carfax. The old practice of using Ripcars to travel between ships in flight had largely been discarded. Instead the *Triumph*-class of ships made use of an electro-matter teleporter. It had been refined greatly over the years and forced to comply with a number of stringent regulations to prevent unwanted incursions, as with the *Triumph* incident of twenty four years ago. In its original incarnation, one simply teleported anywhere one wished and appeared there in a ball of light. Now, the places where one could teleport were quite limited indeed. Also, now, the teleporter consisted of a long dark hallway. One could only go to the end of the hallway with no variation allowed. Usually the two teleporter areas of the various ships were linked, and nowhere else.

Davage and Countess Sygillis, arm in arm, walked down the teleporter hallway, the *New Faith* at one end, the *Westerville* at the other.

Syg sighed in her wonderful gown. Davage gave her a hug and smiled. "Worried about Kay?"

"Yes."

"I know, to have such a thing happen. But, he's fine— and he's a big fellow now. You can't stand guard over him forever."

"Watch me. We should have stayed home, Dav. None of the Barks I asked Lady Poe to set out are seeing him. I think he's gone away somewhere"

Syg looked up at Davage and kissed him. "I guess I'm getting to be an old pest, huh?"

"Well, you're my old pest, Syg, and I love you. Do you want any more after all this?"

"Absolutely," Syg said. "They're all getting so big. Soon Maser will be going off on his own."

"Syg, Maser's barely twelve."

"Yes, and he's getting older every day."

"I was thinking, Syg. It's been a while since we've been off on an outing, you and I. How about, when this business is concluded, we take a trip, just the two of us? Perhaps to Bazz?"

Syg smiled. "Dav, whenever we go on an outing alone, we usually end up with another child. I know what you mean, though. I sometimes miss the days when it was just you and me. This business with Kay, I feel very much older in the aftermath." She took his arm and snuggled into him, enjoying the privacy of the teleporter.

Davage thought about the horrid shirts with which that Duchess Torrijayne of Oyln had saturated Blanchefort village. "Syg, did you ever get even with Torri for the shirt thing?" he asked.

"I did, actually. You'd be proud. It was rather fun, and I intend to continue. I find I enjoy pranking that miserable bitch—I mean duchess."

Davage laughed.

As they walked, a light appeared in the distance. "I suppose I'll need to be a countess again. The things I do for you, love." Syg stiffened and assumed her rigid public appearance.

"Love you, Dav," she whispered as they entered the *Westerville's* teleporter room.

After the usual greetings were exchanged, Davage was quickly ushered to the *Westerville's* massive main conference room. Waiting for him were captains Harrison, Van and Strella. In the corner, three Sisters sat along with a flanking contingent of Marines. Orderlies shuttled back and forth, fetching them drink and plates of tasty hors d'oeuvres.

"Did you see what the Xaphans threw at us at Two-Pitch Nebula last month?" Captain Harrison asked, holding a drink. He was a mountain of a Barrow-man, broad and blonde-headed, even taller than Davage. "It was a starcraft of some sort that looked, for all accounts, like a naked woman. I mean it had no discernible bow, stern or beam, no lights, no dorsal or ventral. I really didn't know what to make of it. It was a pity to put it to the sword actually. It was quite a lovely statue."

Captain Strella, wearing a ladies *Tremblar* uniform, stirred her coffee. "That is a new thing among the Xaphans. They call it 'Bondarism' or 'Bondarunga'. It's an artistic movement where they eschew standard and practical construction techniques in favor of bizarre, functionless forms and unlivable structures. It's their hope that these oddities will accelerate their evolution to a higher form of life."

Harrison laughed, his massive chest rumbling. "That is the stupidest thing I've ever heard."

Strella blew and took a drink from her steaming cup. "They're Xaphans, sir, not known for overly sane thought."

Eventually, Admiral Carfax and an orderly appeared, and the meeting began.

<What are they saying, Dav?> Syg asked via telepathy, always chatty.

<The meeting has only just begun,> Davage replied.

The Admiral was doffed out in his huge blue coat with knee-britches, leggings and black buckle shoes—an admiral's outrageous uniform was one reason why Davage had never wanted to become one.

<I want to know what they're saying, Dav. Why can't I just come in?>

"Thank you all for coming," Admiral Carfax said. "These are exciting times, I must say. Though nobody likes to see the daily horrors of armed conflict in space, the recent upswing in Xaphan aggression has me feeling as I did in the days of old, when we had an enemy to fight and lives to save. We are in a second Golden age of the League/Xaphan conflict, and every day glory awaits, but I digress."

They all, with the exception of the Sisters and their Marines, seated themselves at the large conference table. The Sisters sat out of the way, like an all-powerful chorus in an ancient play, sitting with their plates of hors d'oeuvres, silently watching from the wings of the room, taking it all in.

The Admiral's orderly dimmed the lights slightly. In workman-like fashion, the orderly then pressed a few buttons, and a holo-map of a large planet appeared over the table, hovering in mid-air. Davage looked at it: average land-to-water ratio, three distinct continents, a fierce-looking mountain range to the south, long, flowing coast-line to the north. Clearly, it was a map of Hoban.

"Yes, as you may or may not know by the look of it, this is a holo-relief map of Hoban. What can any of you tell me about the latest doings on Hoban?"

Captain Harrison spoke up. "Lots of Xaphan activity, especially from the combined Houses of Sorrander, Woodward and Midas equipped with new Charn cruisers and those outrageous statue ships."

"Aye," Carfax agreed, "there has been that. Most of their current activity has been funded by the wayward Camilla of Sorrander and by the Vorsham Consortium selling Gifted Xaphans to Ming Mooreland, so our spies tell us. Excellent, what else?"

Captain Vann chimed in. "I have heard that the House of Elam suffered a recent tragedy. As a result, the Elams have withdrawn from League society and have hermited themselves in their holdings in the south of Hoban."

"Ah, yes," Admiral Carfax said. "That is true." The orderly pressed a button, and a blinking red light appeared on the map's southern continent, indicating the location of House Elam. "Pray, have you heard what had happened to them, good Captain?" Carfax asked.

"I have not."

Lady Strella stirred. "I have heard that the House of Gregory also suffered some sort of tragic event. Something to do with Lord Gregory's youngest son, I think."

Again Admiral Carfax's orderly pressed a button, and a blinking red light appeared in the central area of Hoban's main continent.

The admiral turned to Captain Davage. "And you, Lord Blanchefort, have you also heard similar stories coming from Hoban?"

"I haven't. I'm afraid I've been consumed with matters at home as of late."

"Oh, well, I hope it's nothing too pressing."

The orderly pressed buttons, and twenty more blinking lights appeared.

"As you can see, there have been a number of such recent incidents on Hoban—all of the blinking lights here denote where a similar incident has occurred. These incidents have a usual thread or pattern. Usually, and this is not generally known to the League, the lord or countess of the Great House in question is brutally attacked by a member of his or her own family."

The captains looked at each other.

The Admiral called up a list. "Let's see: Lord Carlisle attacked and killed by his son, Lord Derth. Lord Hisborough attacked and wounded by his youngest daughter, Lady Carbina. Lady Derlith molested by her own mother. And, just a few days ago, Lord Nels of Crossland was attacked and mildly wounded by his youngest son, Lord Mervin."

Davage sat there and listened. His thoughts became dark, recalling the attack on Kay.

"Admiral," he asked. "Are there any reports of these attacks occurring outside of Hoban, possibly on Kana?"

The Admiral paused a moment, considering his words. "Yes, Captain, with increasing frequency, though nothing approaching the levels we see on Hoban. As I said, a common theme in these attacks is that the perpetrator is invariably a beloved family member—a son, a daughter, a parent. A passed-on ancestor in some cases. Let us take the case of Lord Hisborough. He was attacked by his own daughter, Lady Carbina—the DNA evidence is conclusive. However, and please stay with me, Lady Carbina is naught but twelve years old and is safe and sound at this very moment in her home. The creature that attacked Lord Hisborough was a twisted, mutilated monster, at least one hundred ten years old, according to the Hospitaler report. A monster certainly, terrible and hideous, yet it was Lady Carbina. A parent always knows their child, no matter what form they might take."

The captains looked around at each other. Davage listened with rapt attention seeing patterns forming.

Kay.

<*What's going on, love?*> came Syg.

<*Nothing, darling. Just boring stuff,*> he lied.

<*Are you going to be done soon? I'm feeling a bit hungry.*>

<*Yes, yes, just bit longer.*>

The Admiral continued. "The effects of these attacks are demoralizing and heartbreaking, as you might well imagine. Lord Hisborough killed himself in grief for his daughter. With the number of these bizarre attacks increasing, Hoban is slowly dying of a broken heart, one Household at a time, and, friends, we have got to put a stop to it. We have been tasked by the Governor himself to investigate this matter and bring it to an immediate close."

Strella looked at her hands. "But, how—how it this possible?"

"Clones, no doubt," Van said.

Admiral Carfax shook his head. "No, sir. Clones, although created from like DNA, show clear deviation and are rather easy to detect. The creature that attacked Lord Hisborough was not a clone."

Captain Harrison thought a moment. "Then it must be a flesh replica—a robotic construct covered in flesh. I recall a ring of them in the Calvertlands of Onaris some years back. Yes, the Drury Matter, as I recall."

Again Admiral Carfax shook his head. "An interesting thought, Captain, but no. A flesh replica is still a robot at its heart. This creature had no robotic parts, no synthetic parts either. I am afraid, at this point, our thoughts are leaning toward the most improbable of all choices regarding these monsters."

"And that is?" Van asked.

The Sisters, sitting in the corner, stirred. A Marine spoke up. "We, of the Sisterhood, know of the possibility of time travel, in various forms, some more problematic than others. We know, theoretically, that it is possible to travel back in time if the flesh has been properly treated, and a temporal anchor-point has been established. There, with the anchor-point in place, a person could interact with himself or herself and not create a temporal schism. We believe that these people, these bizarre attackers, at some point in a theoretical future, have been abducted, held, tormented, mutilated and then released into the past to wreak havoc."

Captain Harrison objected. "Are we speaking seriously? The mechanics of time travel are plain and clearly possible; however, the issue is not connecting two disparate points in time—the issue is bridging a member of one continuum to another. The effects of temporal gravity are impossible to defeat. It cannot be done."

"Again," Marine said for a Sister, "the anchor-point is the key. Travel to the past, free of bridging, is possible up until the point that the anchor-point was enabled. It is a finite tunnel to the past, allowing easy passage from one temporality to another, free of temporal gravity."

Harrison still objected. "Such an 'anchor-point,' as you put it, Great Sister, will require a device colossal in size and draw ruinous amounts of operational power. I doubt the whole of Kana generates, at any given time, enough power to fuel such a beast."

"Agreed, but nevertheless ..."

"How are the Xaphans doing this?" Strella asked. "It must be the Xaphans behind it, correct?"

The Admiral shook his head. "It doesn't seem like a usual tactic or technology they would choose to employ. Additionally, we have spies in their midst, just as they do in ours. Through our spies, we have heard of similar instances happening with great frequency in Xaphan space as well for years and years. We assumed that it was a byproduct of their madness."

The Admiral pulled a kerchief from his pocket and wiped his brow. "The Xaphans even have a name for these monsters: *Killanjo*, the bringers of sorrow and chaos."

"So then," Davage said, "assuming you are correct, who is doing this future abducting and tormenting? Who is responsible for this?"

The orderly pressed another button. A few bits of old-looking holographic pottery appeared next to the Hoban map.

Carfax: "We have always assumed, and our scholars have made no clear distinction, that we were the first inhabitants of Kana, that Kana was a vast, uninhabited paradise just waiting for our arrival with the Elders ages ago. Doesn't really make sense, does it—a bountiful world like Kana having no intelligent life prior to our arrival? Recent scholarly teams from the Science Ministry, working in close cooperation with the Sisterhood of Light, have made remarkable discoveries in recent years. We have discovered evidence of an old precursor civilization vastly predating us on Kana. We have found bits of odd, petrified technology, traces of ancient cities, and fragments of pottery. And, this one here …"

One of the pieces of pottery expanded in size. Davage could see it was decorated with tiny symbols. The Admiral highlighted and expanded one of the symbols in size.

"We have found similar glyphs carved into the flesh of Lady Carbina's *Killanjo*. Like a chill wind from the past, whoever these people were, or possibly are, they are our enemy, not only of the League, but of the Xaphans, too. Any who are Elder are in their gaze. We are all under attack. Perhaps they fear our Fleet—fear to make a public statement of war and face us in open battle. Perhaps it is their intent to strike at the soft tissue beneath the armor. In any case, our mission to Hoban is thus: identify and thwart the attackers, discover their purpose, create some sort of dialog if possible and determine the location of this theoretical temporal anchor-point."

"So, we're operating under the assumption that such an improbable device exists?" Captain Harrison asked.

"We are, Captain. We are dealing with the improbable, as with these *Killanjo* monsters. We have already eliminated the impossible, cloning, flesh replicas and so on; therefore, the improbable is all that is left to us, and that is how we shall proceed until evidence dictates otherwise."

"Tell me our mission again," Harrison demanded. "The short statement."

"Very well. We are to defeat these fiends and put their temporal anchor-point to the sword. Simple enough?"

The Sisters stirred. "Tell them the rest, Admiral," a Marine said.

The Admiral winced and shook his head. He squeezed his kerchief. "I protest, Sisters."

"Do it, sir."

He struggled for words, then: "Another common feature of these Hoban attacks, as the Sisterhood wish to point out, is that they come with the presence of

Berserkacides."

The captains stirred. "Berserkacides," Harrison said in a dry voice, "are a construction of lurid posts and imaginative journalists looking for a sensational story to frighten the public."

"I agree," Davage said. "I have seen odd things recently with my own eyes, however, I shall not subscribe to superstition and folklore."

"I understand how you feel," Carfax said. "Berserkacides, however, are very real. And, wherever we have seen these attacks on Hoban, the Berserkacides are present to add a further touch of terror. Firstly, let us make sure we are speaking on common ground. The term 'Berserkacide' refers to men, women and children hailing from various tribes of Monama. Somehow, some way, they become enraged, four-armed beasts, never to return to the shy, quiet folk they were before. We currently have no information on how or why a Monama becomes a Berserkacide, but, once they do, there is no going back, and they must be killed. A massive nest of them was found in Vithland recently, stashed in the ruins of Clovis. We have the Sisters to thank for the discovery and eradication of this nest."

Admiral Carfax looked down at his shoes for moment. "Due to these recent events and the increasing propensity of Monamas to become dangerous Berserkacides, the Sisterhood is considering performing the rite of *Shuw-shun* against the House of Monama."

Davage stood up, outraged. *Shuw-shun*—the utter destruction and killing of all members of a particular House. To wipe them out to the last man, woman and child. The Sisterhood hadn't done such a thing in ages.

"That is barbaric!" Davage said to the Sisters. "The Monamas are a good people, and they are citizens of the League. This cannot be done! They do not deserve this!"

"The Berserkacides are real, Lord Blanchefort," a Marine said. "And the Monamas pose a clear and present threat to the safety and well-being of the League. We believe that the recent theft at our stronghold at Hiei was perpetrated by a Berserkacide. The evidence is overwhelming."

"Yes, yes, back to that again," Davage said. "Sisters, I am sorry somebody stole a piece of your property; however, you cannot use that as an excuse to wipe out an entire House. You cannot!"

"We have hair and bits of skin from a Monama perpetrator. Unfortunately, we do not have a comprehensive database of Monama DNA on file. However, the evidence is clear that it was a Berserkacide who did it, or it was a free Monama, and that makes the crime even worse. We shall keep the League safe from this menace."

"All right!" Davage shouted. "Assuming Berserkacides are real, then clearly the condition is a malady of mind and body that must be examined and treated. They are our friends, and we must help them."

"There is no helping a Berserkacide. Only death. And the only clear preventative step is eradication," a Marine stated.

Davage slammed his hand onto the table. "I recall leather-bound Sisterhood dogma stating that a Xaphan Black Hat could not be turned from evil. For thousands of years that's what was said, but, look, Black Hats fall from evil with regularity now. We have found a solution to what was once accepted as impossible!"

The Sisters rustled and appeared perturbed. "Then, we suggest, Captain, that you set to it and discover this cure for yourself. Whether or not the tribes of Monama live or die depends upon the success of this mission and the useful information that is gathered from it. We will be watching. If you cannot uncover the true perpetrators of this growing conspiracy to undermine the League, then the Sisterhood will have no choice in the matter and personally intercede—and our first step will be to partially disarm the attackers and declare *Shuw-shun* against the tribes of Monama and destroy them. Of course, we will not do such a thing lightly; however, if it must be done, than it shall be done, and it will be on our conscience and ours alone."

"You are not thinking clearly. You are reacting to a situation, not responding to it."

The Sisters stood. "This conversation is at an end. If you do not wish us to 'react', as you put it, Lord Blanchefort, then 'respond' with results." The Sisters then left the room, with the Marines following.

The captains sat in silence for a bit. "Admiral," Davage said. "I will not allow this. I will not allow the good people of Monama to be laid waste like a tainted crop."

Admiral Carfax darkened. "Then, as the Sisters said, it is up to us to save them. What we do in the next few days might determine not only the fate of the tribes of Monama, but possibly the course of the League itself. I pray the Elders that we are successful."

10—An Afternoon with Cloak

The following morning, every bit of Kay hurt. His body was stiff as a board, and not even the fine Xandarr bed he slept in could comfort him. His ribs were sore from getting punched by Waft, and his back was a mess from getting thrown off the terrace by her. And his fingers, broken clean, were two spindles of pain.

He might have thought that last night was a fantastic dream—that he dreamt the entire race with Waft, but his aching body and broken fingers bore proof that it had, in fact, happened. As he stiffly dressed and exited his room, he tried testing himself just to see if last night was a mere fantasy. He Wafted once or twice and was astounded. As he recalled from last night, he could now Waft in a mere blink of an eye—truly remarkable.

His fingers becoming unbearable, he found a porter and requested to see a Hospitaler as soon as possible. He was taken at once to the King's personal Hospitaler where she began working on his painful fingers. Halfway through the procedure, Sarah and Phillip walked in, and he told them what had happened. Sarah didn't believe it, of course, and it wasn't until he showed her with a demonstration of Waft, after his fingers had been fixed, that she believed.

"Didn't you hear the commotion? I was making a lot of noise."

"Didn't hear a thing," Sarah said. "Did you, Phillip?"

"No, I didn't."

Sarah, as usual, was fascinated. "You went all the way to that mountain?" she said, shading her eyes against the morning sun. "That big one way over there?"

"Yep," he said, hungry for breakfast, his aching body beginning to loosen up.

"Why didn't you come and get me so I could watch or help?" she wanted to know.

"Because there was no helping, Sarah, and she didn't give me any time to fetch my cousins to watch the spectacle."

"Damn!" she cried. "I would have loved to have seen that."

* * * * *

Sarah was the first to see the Princess that day. Holding her SAPP, she marched down to the river, the tails of her duster blowing majestically in the breeze. She came back about an hour later an awful, soaked mess; apparently, the Princess gave her a rather rough way to go. Phillip asked her what happened, and she said she didn't want to talk about it.

Phillip took his turn. He, too, came back up the path about an hour later also looking to have been roughly dumped into the river, but he took it in better stride. "That was amazing," he said. "Truly."

Finally, it was Kay's turn. He strode down the gravel path and made his way to the river. There, sitting alone in her little chair, was a small, veiled female, as before.

Kay smiled and walked up to her. "Good morning, Princess," he said cheerfully.

The woman who looked up at him was not the Princess; it was another mud-like naked female wearing a veil over her bushy head.

"Hello, Kay," she said softly. As with the previous one, her rather muddy appearance changed to that of Sam's—with the exception of her eyes, which remained orange. She transformed into the pale likeness of Sam.

"Where am I?" he asked.

"You're in a Painted illusion. Right now, you're wandering around in the woods somewhere. I've got you. I have been looking forward to our meeting." She stood up, stark naked, her veils falling to her feet.

Kay raised his fists and made to fight. She raised her hands in a defensive fashion. "Please," she said, "I'm not going to hurt you. I don't wish to fight. I'm not going to attack you or cause you pain, I promise." She stood there smiling at him.

Kay lowered his fists and suddenly felt a bit awkward speaking to a naked woman, even if she was in Sam's image. "May I please offer you my coat?"

"Oh, yes, thank you."

Kay took off his coat and draped it over her, expecting at any moment to be attacked. She stood there and held the coat shut with her hand. "I think, of all my sisters, I'm the most like your lady. I suppose that means that I love you because she does, and I have no intention of harming you."

"So, what are we going to be doing? You're here to test me, yes? And if I fail, I die?"

"That is how it works, I'm sorry to say." She held out her hand. "But, you're not going to fail. I'm going to teach you until you pass. Please, walk with me."

He took her hand, and they strolled down a path until they arrived in a large clearing full of white marble statues frozen in various poses, all nude. Some were standing, some were sitting, and others were engaged in what appeared to be wrestling matches of some sort. In one hand, they were all holding little wind chimes that tinkled in the breeze in a pleasant fashion, and, in the other hand, they held small torches. Orange fire cracked and spit. The statues were arranged in a rock garden of colorful gravel and calm reflecting pools. A very peaceful setting. Cloak escorted Kay through the rows of statues.

"Your Cloak isn't something that I can shock into service with pain or aggression, like Waft did with you last night. Rather the opposite. You need to be relaxed—at peace. The Cloak takes years of study and mastery. You couldn't hope to perform a fully Painted Cloak in just one night, and it isn't realistic or fair of me to expect that from you. Invisibility, however, is another story. Once you master invisibility, then the other various disciplines of Cloak will follow in kind. You, Kay, are going to make all of these statues disappear, and I don't mean just visually—you are going to Cloak them thermally and audibly as well. When you can do that and hold it, then you will have passed my test."

"And, if I can't?"

"Then I'll have to kill you, and I don't want to do that. That would break my heart. That's not going to happen though. You're going to do just fine."

They sat down in the grass with the statues laid out before them in a gallery of white-marbled poses. Cloak got very close to him and began playing with his hair.

"Now, I want you to relax, Kay. Just let your mind be at ease."

She whispered into his ear. "Just pretend that I'm Sam. Pretend that it is she whispering into your ear and that you'll get a kiss when this is all over, possibly more. Pick a statue and Cloak it, Kay. Come on; it's not hard."

Kay was heavily distracted. Cloak's mouth was so close to his ear he could feel her breath and her lips brushing past his earlobe.

"Just relax."

He allowed himself to relax and, sure enough, the statue vanished, a full visual Cloak.

"Very good, Kay." She reached out with her foot and kicked in the direction of the statue. He heard the jingling of chimes, held in an invisible hand. "Now, let's Cloak it at an audible level, too. Just keeping doing what you're doing." She began kissing his ear. He tried to move away from her, and she followed, matching his movements.

"Don't worry about what I'm doing, Kay. Just concentrate and be at ease."

He concentrated. "No, it's too much. My head feels as if it's going to crack open."

Her tongue wandered into his ear. "That's natural," she whispered. "It'll feel odd at first, but just let the initial discomfort pass by. Go on, Kay, Cloak it audibly."

He struggled, feeling a great fist of pressure building in his head. Cloak kicked at the statue, and, slowly, its chimes faded into silence. Soon, the heat from its torch was gone, too.

She stopped kissing him and gave him a large hug. "Very good, Kay. See, it's easy." Kay stood and paced about, examining the remaining statues in detail. They were an assortment of male and female statues—the female ones all looked like Sam, and the males all looked like Kay. And, though he previously thought some of the statues were carved in wrestling poses, on closer inspection, that's not what they were doing.

They were having sex, some in demure basic poses, and others in tangled-up challenges of form and flexibility, all locked in a screaming, ecstasy-filled moment. Meanwhile, to his shock, some of the Sam statues elsewhere were performing acts upon the Kay statues best left for closed doors. He blushed.

"You're so funny. You needn't be shy, Kay. It's pretty clear she likes you," Cloak said. "This is what's on her mind much of the time. Monama women enjoy their sex and she thinks it's so funny how demure you Vith are. She's baffled by it sometimes. I like you, too, Kay, and I want you to be at ease."

"I'm having issues concentrating with all of this."

"So shy you are. Sit down, Kay," Cloak said.

He sat down, and then Cloak quickly climbed into his lap, putting her legs around him and pushing his face into the dip between her breasts. "Now, back to your task," she said. "I want you to Cloak all of these statues at once, both visually, thermally and audibly; then, we'll be done. Take your time, I'm in no hurry. Take all day if you need to. You're going to pass my test with ease."

"There are too many statues to Cloak—my head will explode," he spoke muffled into her chest.

"No, it won't. You'll feel the strain for a bit at the beginning, but then you'll forget all about it. Just forget about it." She began rocking back and forth, his face between her breasts. "Just forget about it ..."

A sarcastic voice rang out from a distance. "Why are you being so nice to him, Cloak?"

At the far end of the grounds, the last female, still in her mud-dabbed appearance, came striding in. The final female: Sight. She crunched naked across the gravel, looking rather surly. Her orange eyes blared at Kay.

"I will conduct my test as I see fit," Cloak said. "Kay is doing quite well. There is no need for anything more."

Sight walked up and pushed Cloak aside. She picked up Kay and pushed him down roughly in a clatter of gravel.

"Sight, leave at once—I'm warning you!" Cloak demanded.

Kay got up, and, giving tit for tat, pushed Sight down hard, her feet flying into the air as her head hit the ground. She sprang back up and tackled Kay. They rolled around in the gravel.

Calmly, Cloak separated them. Sight sputtered with rage, and Cloak slammed her naked body into the ground once or twice; then, spinning Sight around by her hair, Cloak sent her spiraling away, where she disappeared through the clouds and was gone.

Cloak knelt down next to Kay. "Are you all right?"

"I'm fine."

Cloak kissed him. "I'm afraid Sight doesn't like you very much, Kay. I think she feels you've ignored her for your entire life, and she's very bitter. Very angry."

Throughout the rest of the afternoon, Kay, with Cloak's patient guidance, Cloaked every statue, muffled their chimes and cooled their thermal images. He passed his test with a fair amount of ease, though his head pounded with the strain of Cloaking all the statues at once. Cloak gave Kay a large hug and a kiss, and she gave him back his coat.

She seemed sad. "I've enjoyed our time together, Kay. I wish I had more time to teach you. You're a good student. And, like I said, I love you because she loves you."

"What will your fate be?"

"My task is done. I'll go back to the nothingness from whence I came and be forgotten."

Kay embraced her. "I'll not forget you. I thank you for your kindness today—I wasn't expecting it."

"Just remember," she whispered into his ear, "tomorrow, when you face Sight, stand up to her. She wants you to look at her, to acknowledge her. Don't let her push you around. Whatever she has in store for you, I know you'll be up to it. And, wherever I am tomorrow, I'll be rooting for you."

Kay looked at Cloak. "You are just like Sam, in every way."

"Am I? Will you do me a favor then?"

"Name it."

"I have a few hours left. Will you sit here and share this time with me? We can enjoy the remainder of the afternoon together."

"I'd like that."

Cloak transformed the Painted rock garden into a lovely sea-side at dusk. Sitting down, Cloak tucked her knees up into her chest and laid her head on Kay's shoulder. Together they watched the sun go down.

She was so much like Sam.

11—Brawling with Sight

A raging storm, a rather unusual occurrence on Xandarr, pelted the Keep that night.

Kay hadn't bothered going to bed. He figured his sleep would be rudely interrupted, and he wanted to be ready.

Sight was coming for him, and this was going to be his toughest test.

He didn't have long to wait. Through the rain, he could hear a taunting voice filtering in from outside.

"Kay, little Kay ..."

He heard a wry giggle. *"Wanna' fight? You're going to die, Kay."*

He got up and went to the wind-whipped terrace. Outside, through the roaring rain, he could see a solitary figure standing in the grass beyond the Keep.

He felt a little relieved that it was finally here. He saddled his CARG, and, without thinking about it, Wafted down to the wet grass and the rain.

Her hair was alive with movement. "So," she said, her mud-like appearance gone, "you actually showed on your own without me having to collect you. This is the prize event; make no mistake. Waft was indifferent, and Cloak liked you. Me, I'm going to tear you apart! I'm not here to help you. I'm here to win this and send you to your death!"

"Cloak said you are angry with me, that I've ignored you my whole life!"

"And haven't you? Sight is your most powerful Gift, and you have frittered it away. Hiding from it—shrinking from the wonders that were yours for the taking! Enough! Fight me, and pray I don't choose to break you in half immediately!"

"What is my test?" Kay asked as Sight assumed a fighting stance.

"Figure it out for yourself!" she yelled, charging.

An odd thing happened. Sight, raging, a creature of the arcane and incredibly strong, missed. Kay, calm and collected, simply Wafted behind her.

She snorted in anger and charged again. Again, Kay Wafted, and this time he put a huge, thudding blow on the back of her head with his CARG.

She fell to the ground and immediately sprang back up. Kay Wafted again, but this time she anticipated where he'd come out and put a massive left hook right on the button, dropping him. Savagely, she pushed his face into the wet ground. "I have the Sight, remember. You want to Waft again? Then do it, and I'll be waiting. I know your every move!"

She grabbed him by the leg and lifted him into the air, where she then slammed him back down with a splat. She ripped his CARG off its saddle and threw it off into the darkness.

Dazed, Kay looked up and took a foot to the chin.

He was just about done. He was in agony.

WHAM!! She struck a terrible blow to the back of his head.

And everything went to amber. He could feel his Sight open up and detach, like a thistle seed from its husk, and float around him. He could see everything clearly. He could see past the driving rain and the thick vault of clouds. He could see the stars laid out in their unfamiliar constellations and the moons. He could see his CARG coursing with Silver tech energy lying in the grass some distance away. He could see the Keep and Sarah and Phillip asleep in their beds.

The Keep? The Keep was behind him. Creation, he was seeing out of the back of his head!

Time seemed to come to a crawl. He could see Sight planning to hit him with a fight ending—and possibly life ending—shot to the neck. He could see her anticipating his counter-move, and he could see himself anticipating her anticipation. On and on, ruse after ruse, until she reached her limit. He, however, had not.

He blasted into the air, hovering at about a hundred feet, and then Wafted down at speed, mashing Sight into the drenched ground.

Another round of ruse and counter ruse, and Kay put his elbow into Sight's chest as she didn't know which way to turn.

He took a good look at Sight standing there in the rain. Her body seemed whole and normal, but in just a moment of observation, he had a wealth of information. Deep down, she was made of some sort of smoky substance—the NIGHTMARE material that Sam used to create her. And deep within her chest was some sort of hollow spot.

He gazed at it and saw that, at one time in the past, there was a gold medallion there, filling up that space. The medallion wasn't there now, but it *was* there yesterday. He was, again, seeing into the past.

The medallion, he Sighted, had an embossed image of Sam's smiling face.

As he and Sight began grappling in the rain, he was fixated on the medallion that was once there but now gone. He recalled the giant, multi-armed females he saw in the distant past—how one of them saw and actually seized him. He had a notion that he could somehow interact with objects in the past, and possibly in the future as well. Perhaps that medallion was his test, to reach out into the past and get it.

After the usual bit of ruse and counter ruse, Kay Wafted to his CARG, lifted, and presented it to her. It looked strange in his Sight, coursing with energy from the Silver tech flowing within it.

His Sight fell backwards, and there was the medallion mounted in her chest.

She charged, and Kay, with a direct thrust, pushed the horn of his CARG through her chest and out the other side.

Lying in the muddy grass was the medallion. It wasn't there now, but it *was there* once. He picked up the medallion from the past, held it, and gazed at it. It felt solid in his hand.

He showed it to her. "Here, Sight, is this what I was after? Is this my test? I have looked back through time to present you with this medallion. I have used my Sight to accomplish this." He looked away, and the medallion vanished, falling back into time.

She looked at his hand, then lowered her fists, the hole in her chest closing up. "Yes, you have passed your test."

She appeared incredulous. She lowered her head, turned, and began walking away through the layers of rain. All around him, his Sight hovered and spun like an uncaged gyroscope. It was freed from the constraints that had held it his whole life. Nothing could hold it back now.

"Sight!" Kay called to her through the rain. "I want to thank you. Thank you for opening this Gift to me and showing me what is possible. You were right. I ignored my Gift; I was afraid of it. You have helped me to face it, and I thank you."

Slowly she turned to him, and her face softened. In the rain, she approached Kay and put her arms around him, pressing her forehead against his. "I guess she chose well, after all. Use your Sight, Kay. Don't be afraid of it. It will bring you back to her, and it will save your soul if you let it. Pass your Trials, and be one with her." She looked at him in the rain. "Go back to your bed, Kay, and wait. Our master will be by soon, and you will receive your instructions."

Sight then kissed him on the cheek, walked off into the rain, and was gone.

Hospitalers Ennez of Inarri and Bethrael of Moane

12—Over Hoban

The Fleet task force of three *Triumphs* and two *Straylights* travelled at a leisurely pace. Hoban was a rather long slog from Kana, taking at least three days at a good pace and four, at worst, if at half-sail. Once in the Hoban area, they were to link up with a detachment of Marines from the 22nd division flying *Trelaine* attack ships.

Captain Davage surveyed his bridge. How big and modern it was in comparison to his old *Seeker*. The bridge overflowed with scanners and sensing stations, all laying out the surrounding space in bold holos and vivid displays. The navigator's chair, once a horrendously simple set up, now had a colorful array of holos floating around it, including the clock, the AM/PM orientation dials and stellar charts. The sensing station, once manned by team of seven people, now only required one person with a battery of holographic and printed out displays. The old Missive station was gone altogether. He still recalled the *Seeker* with its primitive bridge and sensing equipment—the ship was virtually blind. He always stood there behind the helm wheel, his lit Sight, seeing through the hull, quite literally using his own eyes to pilot the ship. He still missed it to some extent.

His countess Sygillis, as usual, sat in his chair. For twenty four years she had fared the stars at his side. Together they shared in many adventures and built a family; Syg never changed. She had grown a bit Bluer as time progressed, taken to bowling and had a superior bowling average of 177-180, but he could live with that. She loved their home at Castle Blanchefort and their children and was loathe to part from them, but she never allowed Davage to sortie without her. Their youngest daughter Hathaline, to Davage's delight, loved coming with them on their missions. She even had her own billet on the ship, permanently set aside for her use. They had always hoped Kay would want to join the Fleet, but he was rather insistent that he didn't enjoy space travel, so that was quite a disappointment for them. But little Hathaline, always trying to impress her father, was a natural. Davage was certain she would want to join the Fleet some day. Perhaps she would follow in his footsteps and become a junior helmsman. She seemed to have all the tools required, and her pedigree couldn't be better. Lady Hathaline was her father's daughter.

Lt. Kilos, Davage's ever-present friend and first officer, was also on the bridge standing at her station. She had been at Davage's side for over thirty years, starting out in the Stellar Marines, and then changing to the Fleet. She had plenty of chances to strike out on her own and command a vessel over the years, but she had always declined. She knew her limitations, and she considered herself a much better follower than a leader. At least she was honest about it.

As the Fleet arrived near the outskirts of the Capri-Thenister system where Hoban was the third planet, Davage felt more and more uneasy. The meeting with Admiral Carfax and the Sisters kept flashing through his head. The poor families of Hoban, attacked by their own kin—and not just by their kin—-but by bizarre, tormented visions of their kin, along with packs of snarling Berserkacides.

That is what bothered him the most. The Sisters, watching and waiting, were considering the *Shuw-shun* against the Monamas.

To level their homes.

To destroy their property.

To kill every last one of them, down to the very young without trace, as if they'd never been there at all.

✶ ✶ ✶ ✶ ✶

Shuw-shun

The Sisters hadn't done such a thing in hundreds of years. It never looked good for the Sisterhood to flex their muscles in such a way, and, obviously, it made the Great Houses of the League quite nervous. Normally, the Sisters liked to stay in the background and allow the general League leadership via the Ex-Commons to address a pressing matter. But, apparently, they were concerned enough about the situation to pull out all the stops and involve themselves directly, and that could mean *Shuw-Shun*.

Nobody was quite sure how the Sisters could accomplish such a thing; they were more powerful than they let on. They wisely kept such power hidden.

The most recent House to feel the *Shuw-shun* was the lowly House of Mutt, a wretched Calvert House whom nobody was sorry to see go. The Sisters occasionally punished unruly Great Houses and wayward cities which they felt had strayed too far into decadence, but they normally informed the victims first, giving them time to up stakes and vacate. Then, at the appointed time, the Sisters literally blew the House or city off the face of Kana in a cloud of destroyed debris and scorched earth—Dee and the Remnath city of Rostov had been blown away once by the Sisters. The Barrow city of Saga had nearly been scorched to nothing, but had managed to postpone their wrath and mend their ways in the aftermath. The House members or city inhabitants, now destitute and penniless, rolled about the landscape, humbled and contemplative. It was hoped that such a public punishment would teach whomever a lasting lesson and cause them to grow from the experience.

The *Shuw-shun*, however, came without warning in a flash of destruction and death leaving no survivors, no bodies to bury, and no earthly possessions to distribute.

The *Shuw-shun* left nothing behind; everything was ground into dust and thrown high into the air.

And, as the fleet neared Hoban, the *Shuw-shun* was coming for the House of Monama. To save the League, they will genocide the tribes of Monama and close their eyes forever, unless Captain Davage and the rest of the fleet task force could come up with something conclusive—provide the Sisters with the identity of the true attackers, for the Monamas appeared to be nothing more than pawns. Dangerous, rabid, slavering pawns.

They must not fail.

✶ ✶ ✶ ✶ ✶

"Syg," Beth said, "The Hospitalers have tasked me to obtain permission to perform tests on Kay—a Shadow tech Male. Think of what we could learn. It's not an opportunity we should allow to pass by."

They sat in the main mess at their favorite table, seeing the stars pass by, seeing the glow of Hoban steadily grow through the windows.

Lt. Kilos took a big swig from her tankard. "Beth, what is it with you in the last few days? Kay this and Kay that. Heck, I like the kid too, but …"

"Beth?" Davage asked, "Are you still addled from the Silver tech incident ? Of course you know we're in your eternal debt."

She sat there and stared at her coffee cup. "Syg," Beth said, "have you ever allowed your Silver tech to touch Kay?"

Syg took a drink of coffee and stared at Beth. "Of course I have, I'm his mother after all. I used to create little toys for him to play with—little ships that floated, little soldiers and whatnot."

"Well, apparently, his power doesn't work on you—and that is a very good thing, Syg, because let me tell you—you don't want to feel what I felt, he being your son and all. I'm still having chills."

Ki laughed. "Kay gave you *chills,* Beth?"

"It's not funny, Ki. You laugh, but you don't understand. He gave me more than just that—a lot more."

"Did it hurt?"

"I wish all it did was hurt."

Syg shook her head. "Beth, you're a Hospitaler—you said you knew what would happen if you allowed him to touch your Silver tech. You said you were prepared for it."

"I thought I was. I knew from a forensic, textbook standpoint what would happen, yes. I knew he could control me if he had wanted. But—to feel it, to actually experience it. Nothing could have prepared me." Beth took a drink of coffee, her hands shaking slightly.

"Prepared you for what, Beth?" Ki asked.

"Come on, Ki—use your imagination for Creation's sake! It's no wonder the Black Hats are so afraid of Shadow tech Males, and what they can do to them." She turned to Davage. "Sir, you said you're in my debt, yes?"

"Of course, you know that. You saved his life."

"Then I'd like permission to court Kay—would you take offense to that?"

"What?" Kilos cried.

Syg interjected. "Why, yes, Beth, I think so. I think we would."

"Why? He's a man now. He can make his own decisions."

"He's only twenty-two," Syg said. "Besides, Beth, you're like family. It's a little creepy to think about it. You delivered him. You slapped his little naked bottom, remember?"

"So? Why don't you allow the two of us to decide what's creepy and what's not. This really doesn't concern you, Syg, and I was only asking right now as a courtesy."

"Beth, you're scaring me," Ki said.

She took a drink of coffee. "Yeah? Scares me, too."

* * * * *

Hoban was a distinctly brownish-colored world with a single moon. The larger cities of Brindecea and Crossland stood out against the dark landmasses. Its single moon, Lauralea, was distinctive for having its own atmosphere. Its largest city Synthmere also stood out in the darkened sky.

The Fleet task force settled into a high orbit along the equator, spacing out so that they could cover the whole planet.

As planned, a Marine contingent of twenty-five *Trelaine* attack ships came in from 4:45AM and took up station around the huge Fleet vessels.

And, there they waited.

13—Lord Christopher Park

It was getting dark. A man wearing a long coat and a scarf sat in Lord Christopher Park, a lovely wooden area outside the southern city of Lyra, one of the larger cities in the Zenon region of Kana. He'd been there all day. He was far from home.

As the sun began to go down, several sets of people who had been enjoying the park saw him, stopped and advised that he should take his leave. The park wasn't safe at night as of late, they said.

Berserkacides, they said.

The man thanked them for their concern but didn't move. He simply sat there on the bench, got out a portable holoterm, and did some reading to pass the time. Eventually, as the bright southern stars came out, he sent a Com to his wife.

She was lying in their bed. She looked thin and bone-tired through his screen. She said she was very worried about him. He said he was fine and that he loved her. She begged him to be careful.

She said she couldn't live without him.

He put the holoterm away and sat some more.

After a time, a slight buzzing came from his coat pocket. Looking around, he opened his coat and pulled out a small, robotic animal in the shape of a large bug. He held it in his hand for a moment, made a fine adjustment to it, then let it go. It flew on its metal wings, hovered gracefully in the air, then landed on the bench, its jewel-like green eyes alert and watching.

The man had been at this for two days with no success. He was tired and he wanted to go home to his wife. Perhaps tonight would yield results.

The robotic bug became agitated and took flight, moving down the path to the south.

The man got up and followed it, walking at a brisk pace. Perhaps now his patience would be rewarded.

The path took him into a deep copse of trees, the canopy of green blotting out the stars. The robotic bug flew a bit farther, and then it landed on a tree branch.

The man stopped walking. He knew how to read the robotic bug's movements. He had perfected it in the last few weeks, and it was finally working like he hoped it would.

His wife, his beloved wife, couldn't take much more. He had to get it right and gather just a little more information. Then, it would be perfect. For his wife's sake, it had to be perfect.

The robotic bug began beating its shiny wings, making a rather loud BUZZZZZZZ....

It was time, the man knew to be at his guard.

Coming down the path in the opposite direction was a person walking a large white dog.

The person and the dog approached the man. As they got close, the dog was revealed. The dog had six legs.

The person walking it was a hideous monster, skinned and dripping bile and gore.

The dog was a Berserkacide, naked and ravenous for blood and walking on all sixes— four arms and two legs. It was held on a bloody chain.

The monster and the Berserkacide looked at the man for a moment. Then:

"Our first catch of the night. Kill him," the monster said in a callow voice, unleashing it. The monster watched the Berserkacide lope ahead a few paces, and

then it vanished in a green flash.

The Berserkacide roared and sprang as the man, ready, took his black scarf off and laid it out in front of him. As the Berserkacide charged, he skillfully got his scarf around it and, like a great constricting snake, the scarf moved on its own, wrapping around the Berserkacide in a tangle of thin, gangly limbs and hair, and commenced to squeeze the life out of it.

The Berserkacide struggled as the man watched. It was very strong, and it rolled about on the ground, trying to free itself.

But the black scarf was strong, too, and it squeezed even harder. The Berserkacide's bones began to crack under the pressure as the scarf relentlessly constricted. One of its black eyeballs popped out and hung there. It moaned and wailed—the man hadn't expected that. The man, watching, felt sorry for it as it died. The agonizing process seemed to take forever.

When it was at last still and newly dead, the man took his scarf back and said a short prayer for the Berserkacide's soul.

This is for you too. I want to bring this to an end.

He then dragged its crushed, pale form off of the path, and, taking a small kit full of instruments from his coat, began working on its dead body, the robotic bug watching silently nearby from a tree.

He carefully collected the samples he needed. Finally, they would be whole and ready.

Finally, his wife might have peace, for she couldn't take much more. The man collected his robotic bug and began the long journey back to home and his wife.

14—Rostov

The Great Metal Man appeared to Kay the next night, his chariot moving through the air on its own without Waft, Cloak and Sight to pull it. They had returned from whence they came. He landed in the green near the Keep and, with thunderous strides, dismounted. Kay sensed his presence and Wafted outside to stand before him. Towering, the metal man looked down at Kay, and appeared neither impressed nor sympathetic that Kay had passed the first portion of the Trials.

Inside his great chest polished to a mirror finish, Sam slumbered. Kay Sighted his chest but could see little within.

"You have bested my horses," he said finally. "You have proved your Gifts are now of a suitable level that you have a reasonable chance of surviving the Trials to come. The Lady of Monama's preconditions have been met in full. Very well, it is time for your first Trial."

"I want to see Sam," Kay said looking up at him.

"Not possible. She slumbers within, safe and unharmed. If you wish to be reunited with her, I suggest you proceed with your Trials at once."

Kay didn't give up. "Sam is pursued by something—those creatures that attacked me in the Grove. I want to know who and what they are."

The Metal Man didn't answer Kay's question. Instead, he continued. "The House of Rostov is built on lies and stolen goods. Their House sits upon blood-stained ground. A wondrous device rests within a vault at House Rostov. You will take this device and keep it safe with you."

A shimmering object appeared before the man, spinning, floating on air. It looked like a smallish, rather organic-looking ring made of silver. It had a hole in the center, like a silvery doughnut.

The shimmering image faded. "Take this device and keep it safe, and you will have passed the first Trial. You will not see me again until you pass all three of the Trials set before you. If you succeed at the House of Rostov, Bathloxi will seek you out and continue to the second Trial."

The man climbed back into his chariot.

"Wait!" Kay cried. "You're certain Sam is all right?"

The man turned the chariot and climbed into the sky. "Safer with me than anywhere else."

* * * * *

"So, what the hell does that mean?" Sarah asked as she pulled a drink from the *Goshawk's* small fridge.

They were all sitting by the *Goshawk* in the purple evening under the rising moons. They all had come to like Xandarr, its King and Queen, the 44, and its remarkable princess. They would all leave this place truly enriched.

The next morning they said goodbye to King Balor and Queen Zoladerra.

Kay took the long walk down the path and said goodbye to the princess. She didn't react at first, just sat there by the river and drew on her canvas. After a bit, Kay turned to leave.

Hearing rapid footsteps from behind, he turned and saw her running toward him. She was holding her canvas. "I made this," she said, panting. "I made this for you."

Kay looked. On the canvas was a very accomplished portrait of him, done in pleasing pastels. His eyes were deep and roving.

As he held the canvas, she put her arms around him and wept.

Had Sam not been in his thoughts, he felt sure his heart would have been lost to Princess Vroc right there and then. How his mother might have reacted to that.

Then, with heavy hearts, the group boarded the *Goshawk* and flew off, all vowing to return someday. Kay put the picture Vroc had drawn of him in a safe spot in the cabin.

✶ ✶ ✶ ✶ ✶

Two days later, they tucked into orbit around Kana and barred in on Rostov.

Rostov was a sea-side city on a small peninsula jutting into the southern Sea of Esther. It was perched about as far west as was possible. To the east of Rostov were the warm lands and rolling hills of Remnath. There wasn't a whole lot beyond the outskirts of the city, just a series of green steps and hills. The nearest city was the Remnath bastion of Wiln about a thousand miles to the northeast. A little farther east was St. Paris, that fine, trendy city of quiet manors and sprawling castles. The Sisterhood strongholds of Twilight 4 and Deep 7 hugged the coast far to the southeast.

Though Rostov was technically in the Remnath region, it was not a Remnath city. The Rostovs, the founders of the city, were notorious of the Calvert line, hailing from the seedy city of Bezzel. Censured by the Sisterhood of Light for the crime of wife-swapping, they were chased from their ancestral holdings by the Sisters when they continuously harassed the chapel of Barton, deep in the Great Armenelos forest. Though the House of Rostov, led by their scabby patriarch Nouables hadn't broken any laws, the Sisters had had enough and forced them from their dreary holdings in Bezzel. Smiling and polite as always, the Sisters informed them that their House would be completely and utterly destroyed, and they advised them to not be present when that happened. Flying away in a rickety transport, they prowled the southern coastline trying to squat in the Zenon city of Lyra. However, being made to flee by the city militia, they eventually settled on the rocky finger of land in a barren area of Remnath that eventually became the city of Rostov.

There, isolated and left alone, they flourished, though they didn't really create anything productive. Rostov became a haven for sportsmen, with most if not all of the more notorious sportsmen on Kana either hailing from or having trained extensively in the city. Dirty courtesans also seemed to come out of Rostov with frequency. In fact, the dirty courtesan's trademark fungus, 'The Weed' had been elevated to new heights in the moist hot houses of Rostov.

✶ ✶ ✶ ✶ ✶

With the *Goshawk* safely in orbit around Kana, Kay, Sarah and Phillip began working on a plan. Kay, though still a little shaky in space, was much more able to endure a long space flight than he was before leaving for Xandarr. They thought it best to check into a quaint inn somewhere in the city and use it as their base for the duration of this unusual operation. Rostov was a dark, dirty city of narrow streets and seedy shacks. The city itself was, with the exception of a few outlying structures, comprised of one, huge, walled-in structure. It was built villa-style, in a vast spread-out design of confusing courtyards and galleries.

As the *Goshawk* descended, an automated message popped up, informing them that the airspace over the city of Rostov was restricted and advising a more southerly course. Phillip veered to the south and settled at fifty thousand feet. They tuned the ship's scanners and took a look. From the air, they could see many people moving around in the open spaces. They could see the piled up stacks of refuse that passed for buildings. There were barred windows and black stone. In a courtyard, they thought they saw someone getting executed as townspeople watched.

After witnessing that for themselves, none of them really wanted to stay in Rostov, so they found a suitable establishment in a hamlet outside of Wiln near the sea. It was far away from Rostov, but it was better than actually having to stay there.

Sitting in Sarah's room that evening, they stayed up late and formulated a plan. Sarah was basking in this; she loved hanging out in nice inns and ordering room service, and she loved planning things.

"So," she said, relaxed in her pajamas, "we're looking for a small, dough-nut-shaped device that is hidden in a vault? Why's 'Sam's Doughnut' so important?"

"I don't know, and yes, that's what he said."

"Did you write his clue down word for word?"

"For one, Sarah, I didn't have anything to write with, and two—it doesn't sound like a clue, per se, to me. He told me exactly where it is."

"Can we get him back here to ask questions?"

"No, Sarah, we cannot."

They tried calling up detailed maps of the House of Rostov's manor, a black-stoned heap of rocks by the sea called Leap Manor—many such places, including Castle Blanchefort, were detailed in the Holo-net. But, like Castle Blanchefort, none of Leap's secret locations were revealed, just holos of it from various angles and the barest of maps.

"I think," Phillip said turning away from the Holo, "that we're going to have to fly over it and make our own detailed maps."

"It's restricted. They'll probably try to shoot us out of the sky."

"Not if we're Cloaked."

Kay and Sarah listened. "Kay, you said that on Xandarr your Gifts were expanded, including your Cloak. Is that correct?"

"Yes, but I'm still pretty raw. Just a few forms of basic invisibility. I can't disguise myself yet, and I certainly can't Paint an illusion."

"Invisibility is all we'll need. But, we'll need to Cloak not only ourselves, but the *Goshawk,* too."

Kay shook his head. "The *Goshawk's* too big. It'll give me a headache."

"So, you get a headache. Endure it." He got up and went to the terrace. Outside, beyond the tended gardens of the inn's back lot, was the usual ship park. Several ships, a few mid-sized transports, and a number of land cars and floats were arraigned in a row, including the black *Goshawk,* which was off in a corner by itself.

"Try to Cloak the *Goshawk,*" Phillip repeated.

"It's too big," Kay insisted. "And it's too far away."

Sarah shut down the Holo. "Well, how about we work our way up to the ship. Start off by Cloaking yourself, and then us. Then, when you get used to that, Cloak the ship."

For being an impulsive hot-head half the time, Sarah could, at the strangest of moments, demonstrate flashes of jaw-dropping, cool, collected reasoning. Kay couldn't argue.

Kay recalled his training session with Cloak. He recalled how nice she was—how much like Sam she was. He relaxed, and after a moment or two, he was Cloaked, falling easily into its invisible embrace, his head hurting with the initial strain.

"That's pretty good," Sarah said looking around. "I can't see you at all." She reached out and touched his arm. "And I can't really feel you too much either. It's like you're there, but you're made of clay." She lit her Sight and panned around. "My Sight is starting to improve. I can see your outline a little if I really concentrate."

Phillip lit his Sight, his eyes glowing silver. "I can see him well enough."

Kay dropped the Cloak, and he reappeared—his head throbbing.

"Now do all three of us," Sarah commanded. Kay took a moment to allow his head to stop hurting, then he cleared his mind.

"All right, we're Cloaked."

Sarah and Phillip looked around. "Everything looks the same." She looked at her hands. "And I can see myself."

"Of course you can see yourself—that's how a decent Cloak works. We can even talk to each other, but nobody outside of the three of us can hear or see."

"Really?" she said.

Before they could stop her, she bolted out the door in her pajamas and went hurtling down the stairs to the pub. The impulsive Sarah was back in earnest.

"Are you feeling any strain?" Phillip asked.

"Yes. My brain feels like it is being wrung dry."

"If you can keep this up, then we should be able to penetrate House Rostov and be off with the device in no time. We just need a little recon to gather insight on the floor plan, and that means Cloaking the *Goshawk,* too."

He went to the terrace again. "Come on, Kay, Cloak it. You can do it."

Kay sat down on the bed and concentrated. After a minute or so, the *Goshawk* faded into a Cloak. The strain was terrible. To Cloak the three of them and the ship as well was too much; it was overwhelming. From downstairs they could hear Sarah whooping and hollering joyously in the pub.

"Good, good," Phillip said.

"I should drop it on Sarah while she's down there running around like an idiot and give her a thrill," Kay said. "I'm going to let it go," he said, holding his head.

"No, leave it up. In fact, keep the ship Cloaked all night. That'll be a good test. I've heard from Duchess Torrijayne that good Cloakers can keep things Cloaked for a long period of time, and without really having to think about it. Since I can't Cloak, I can't confirm or deny that."

"My head will explode, Phillip. I'm dropping it. It really hurts."

"If you drop it, I'm going to punch you in the neck," Phillip said in a serious tone, pointing at him. "Keep it up." He kept looking out the terrace.

It appeared Phillip was a sterner taskmaster than Cloak was. Kay lay back on the bed and held his throbbing head, convinced he was going to die of an aneurism at any moment.

Although the first few minutes were terrible, after a bit, he had to admit he felt a second wind coming on. His head began to feel better. Even though he was Cloaking all three of them and the *Goshawk,* it was almost as if he could hold the Cloak and not think about it. After a while, the pain vanished, and he forgot he was doing it at all.

Sarah came dashing back into the room, out of breath. She was holding a half-full bottle of spirits.

"You two!" she yelled, excited. "I took this bottle of spirits right off a man's table, and it fell into Cloak with me!"

Phillip was cross. "Sarah, put that bottle back where you found it, right now!"

She turned and bounded back down the stairs with a bumpy fuss. Kay got up off the bed, and he and Phillip left the room and went down the stairs.

"You all right?" Phillip asked.

"Fine, I'm fine."

It was a strange thing to move about unseen and unheard. Inn guests and staff were going about their business, unaware that Cloaked people wandered about. Kay recalled, as a young boy, his parents taking him to fine restaurants in Minz and Hannover. As they sat eating their dinner, his father sometimes telepathied to his mother that Cloaked people were walking about the floor. At some of the finer restaurants, the establishment actually employed Cloakers to covertly remove dirty dishes and silverware from patron's tables, thus enhancing the illusion of near miraculous service. Lord Davage often enjoyed speaking to the Cloaked people as they approached the table, seeing them in his Sight, and watching them jump in surprise. In the north it was considered incredibly rude to Cloak one's self into invisibility—only people who had something to hide Cloaked themselves. To be caught while under Cloak could be a serious occurrence, and, sometimes, Cloakers who over did it found themselves in prison or in a bad way with the Sisters.

Kay and Phillip spilled into the pub. Tables full of people were scattered about. They saw Sarah sitting at a gentleman's table. She was holding the long blue length of her ponytail and was going to tickle a man's nose with it as he dined.

"Sarah!" Phillip yelled. "What are you doing?"

"I'm doing something I've always wanted to do, and don't try and stop me!" She waved her hair and the man brushed his nose absently. "Haha!" she cried.

Phillip moved to the far side of the pub. "How're you doing, Kay?"

He seated himself at the bar. "I'm fine."

Sarah again. She'd moved on to another table and it looked like she was about to pull something off of a lady's plate.

"Sarah, if you're hungry, get dressed and we'll come down and eat!" Phillip shouted, heard by only the three of them.

"You're no fun," she said getting up.

* * * * *

Later that night Kay dropped their Cloak and they went outside onto the terrace, Sarah eating a plate of something she'd gotten from the pub and rubbing her tired eyes. Phillip sat down in a chair and enjoyed the night breeze.

"What are we doing out here?" she asked, tired, wanting her rented bed.

"Making a fool of yourself in the pub tires you out, doesn't it?" Phillip asked.

"It does."

Kay turned. "We're going to begin our recon."

"How are we going to do that?"

Kay allowed his newly activated Sight to roam. "I'm going to look in on them."

"From here?"

"Yep. You see Cloaking the two of you and wandering around in the pub reminded me that my Gifts are now working a lot better than they were. And, I now have access to my Sight. I'm going to test it. I'm going to look in on Rostov. If I'm able to see it from here, that'll keep us from having to fly over it and risk getting shot down."

Sarah, becoming interested, rustled in her seat and set her plate aside. "Ok, that's about a thousand miles from here, right? You really think you're up to it?"

"We'll see in a moment, I suppose."

Kay allowed his Dark Sight to stretch out.

"So your eyes really don't glow?" Sarah asked, looking at him.

"Apparently not."

"Kay," Phillip said, "you're facing the wrong direction. Rostov's that way." He pointed to it.

"It doesn't matter. I can see out the back of my head, too."

Phillip and Sarah looked at each other, impressed it seemed.

The amber passes of his Sight reached out from their little inn at Wiln and moved, slowly expanding in all directions. It was hard—the concentric bubble of his Sight expanded in stages and then stopped, only to expand again in regular hops. His eyes strained. Just when he thought he'd reached his limit, he'd hop out again, like a person holding his breath under water to see how long he could go, *just a few more seconds, just a bit longer.*

And soon, the walled fortress of Rostov came sprinting into view, perched on its nook by the sea. It was an irregularly shaped citadel of black rock, bastioned at various points with turrets and watchtowers. The keep was a confused collection of buildings in the far western section of the fortress. The eastern part was open within the walls, and many shacks and other ill-constructed buildings were piled up in a haphazard fashion. There, amidst those seedy surroundings, Kay could see many people milling about. They were at sport, betting money on this game of chance and that. Farther away, under the keep, was a huge treasure vault guarded by many men and a few bizarre-looking creatures. Heaped about in the treasure room was an assortment of artifacts and other valuables. With regularity, people came into the vault, either removing an item, or depositing one.

There, mixed into the pile, was the twisting, doughnut shaped device—'Sam's Doughnut,' Sarah called it.

"I see it. There it is."

"Where is it?" Phillip asked. Is it guarded?"

"It's in a large treasure room several levels below the ground. A vault of some sort. It's guarded by many men. I see patterns of energy. The vault appears to be Waftlocked, and there are numerous arcane devices scattered about to detect the presence of invisible beings, no doubt. I also see a host of strange creatures roaming about the vault."

"Creatures!" Sarah exclaimed.

"What do the creatures look like?" Phillip asked.

"They are rather snakelike in appearance, about fifteen feet long, with tiny lizard-like arms and six tails that are barbed. They appear to be green on their dorsal quarter and are yellow with black spots on their bellies."

"Those sound like mickalmicks—woodland creatures from the Armenelos forest area. They can be tamed and trained to perform all sorts of functions. They are said to be able to see Cloaked people, so, given that, the Waftlock and the other arcane instrumentality in place, our infiltration into the vault will be greatly complicated."

Kay had a sudden thought. He recalled the Haitathe warrior who saw him from the past. What if he could simply reach out and grab the piece and pull it back?

He turned around to face in the direction of Rostov, then he reached out with his hands, and sure enough, he could feel the smooth, cool sides of the device. He pulled it back, his hands shaking with new confidence.

"Look, Sarah, Phillip, I got it!" He looked away for a moment in triumph, and the device was gone. It fell back into the vault in Rostov. Kay shut his Sight down in bitter disappointment.

"What?" Sarah said.

"I had it. I had Sam's Doughnut in my hands. But, the moment I looked away, it was gone, right back where it came from. Oh, that's frustrating."

"Try it again," Sarah said, excited. "Maybe you messed something up!"

Shooting Sarah a dirty look, Kay tried again. Once again, he held the device in his hands, and, once again, it fell back to the vault the moment he turned his gaze away.

"I saw you holding something!" Sarah said. "It was round, about a foot and a half wide, right?"

"That was Sam's Doughnut. Again, as soon as I looked away, it fell back to where it came from. Creation!!"

Phillip remained calm and empirical as ever. "Where is this vault?" he asked.

"It's in the western-most point of the keep. And it's under heavy guard with those monsters as well."

"That would be Leap Manor, per my reading on the Holo-net here," Phillip said.

"Bring one of those monsters back here so I can see it!" Sarah demanded.

Not bothering to acknowledge Sarah's ridiculous request, Kay took one more look. As he spied in on House Rostov, his Sight tended to wander into the past and the future. Going back into the past revealed little. The House, after a few bouts of destruction and recreation, simply disappeared, and an uninhabited bit of windy land, grazed occasionally by wild animals, appeared.

Going forward, however, was illuminating.

He could see multiple possibilities for House Rostov. In one future, they continued as is, being a cradle for sportsmen and courtesans, falling further and further into vice and decadence. He saw the city being destroyed once or twice, by raiders and rival Houses. Eventually, he could see the Sisters once again chasing them from their rocky perch, leaving a crater of scorched earth where the city now stands.

However, in a radically different path, he could see House Rostov being transformed, the House reforming and fully embracing Elder teaching. He could see Rostov becoming a real city by the sea, led by a man in white with a large triangle hat. At his side was a small woman with long, curly amber hair and a Shadowmark adorning her right eye. Behind them walked the people, and the city rose. In this path, Rostov became a place of great learning and enlightenment—a place where Great Houses wanted to live, where inspiration and new ideas flourished. He could see the black eminence of Leap Manor failing down, being replaced with a white stone castle of a new House Rostov without walls—a place where the Sisters would never come in anger again.

All this, Rostov could be. The central figure in determining which way the House went appeared to be a huge, scabrous man in a long, dark coat holding a sinister rifle-like weapon.

He was the key. If he lived, the House would fall into ruin and be destroyed in a flash of fire. If he died, it would be reborn.

Hmmmm, Kay thought, interesting but immaterial.

He quieted his Sight and told Phillip and Sarah what he'd seen

"I think," Phillip remarked, leaning back in his chair, "that the easiest course to us is to simply go in, Kay. You Cloak yourself, sneak into the vault, deal with the mickalmicks and the machines, and grab the piece."

"That's a novel plan," Kay said.

"Sometimes simple is better."

Kay shrugged. "We'll tarry here a day or two and continue to observe Rostov and get a feel for their schedules, if they maintain any. Then, we move. You're not in any hurry, are you, Sarah?"

"Nope," she said.

The night was lovely, and they continued to sit outside, listening to the gentle sounds of the sea and feeling the cool breeze. Eventually, to appease Sarah, Kay pulled back one of the mickalmick creatures, and she gasped with delight.

15—Message From The Cat God Pub

"Can you believe, Beth?" Syg said in their quarters, getting ready for bed. She sat at her mirror in her favorite nightgown.

"I suspect touching Kay with her Silver tech was a pretty jarring experience, much more so than she expected," Davage said. "It's a good thing she's out here with us instead of wandering around Blanchefort on her own—might keep her out of trouble. Still, Syg, Kay's old enough to pick his own relationships. If he wants to court Beth, who are we to stop him, though I don't think he's got eyes for anybody other than Sam."

Sam. Syg bristled at the sound of the name. "Yes, well," she said, brushing her hair, "that relationship is at an end. I have already forbidden him to see her any further, and, if I catch her on our grounds ever again, I will kill her without question."

Davage struggled, wondering how much he should tell Syg about the attacks on Hoban, and about the attack on Kay. He wondered if he should tell her that he, more and more, believed that the attacker was a demented, twisted version of Lady Kilos, his beloved daughter. He didn't think Syg would take it very well; he himself was barely square with the thought.

She put her comb down and turned to him. "What are we doing out here, Dav, far away over Hoban? We should be home defending our own."

"The ship still sails, Syg. We've a duty to accept the charge appointed to us. All is well at home."

"Is it? I have not seen Kay about the castle for days. I asked Lady Poe release Barks all over the place and I haven't seen Sarah or Phillip either and, coincidentally, the *Goshawk* is missing. Seems to me that they're on an outing. You wouldn't happen to know anything about that, would you?"

"I know all about it," Davage replied. He had to be careful, as Syg could determine truth from lie (and little white lie) with ease. A generous helping of truth, misdirection and a dash of obfuscation was the best course of action when dealing with a potentially unruly Syg.

"Where did they go?"

"Xandarr, I believe."

Syg considered that. "Why in the Name of Creation did they go to Xandarr? The place is so bloody hot no Vith goes to Xandarr on a whim. You complained until my ear fell off the last time we were there."

"Xandarr was his destination."

"He should not be going to Xandarr. He's still recovering."

"Syg, our son survived and is well. You cannot treat him like he's infirm, or dead for that matter—that is not our tradition. He cannot become a hermit in our castle, stashed away like a scared rabbit, and I have encouraged him to resume his usual activities."

Syg flushed up. "He went to Xandarr to see Lady Sammidoran, didn't he?"

"I'm not aware of that."

Syg stood and approached him. "Do not attempt to skirt around the question, Dav, or bend the truth to your liking. You know exactly why he went to Xandarr, and it wasn't for the beating sunshine and salt breezes. Now, let's have it, all of it, and if I don't like what I hear I'm taking an immediate transport to Xandarr to confront Kay and drag him home by his ear myself."

Being married to an ex-Black Hat had its disadvantages, as Syg could detect truth from lie, and she was skilled enough at debate to know when he was attempting to divert to course of the discussion or cloud the issue entirely, and, he had no doubt she wouldn't hesitate to personally fetch Kay in an embarrassing public spectacle.

He decided to simply lay it out and appeal to her using logic. He composed his thoughts and readied to reply when the Com rang in.

"Com," he said in answer, thankful for a momentary respite.

"Sir, you have a pending message."

Davage looked at the clock—it was well past the evening bell. "At this hour? From whom?" It couldn't possibly be from the Fleet. "Is it live or pre-recorded?"

"The message is unregistered from a live source. The sender does have a valid code."

Unregistered? They forgot about their discussion. In the old days, he was used to getting mysterious messages. He frequently received odd messages from his old antagonist, Princess Marilith of Xandarr. But, he hadn't heard from her in twenty years—she was dead.

Syg killed her.

Davage had a feeling that the unregistered message, whatever it was, had an ominous portent, as did Syg. They approached the large desk where the Com terminal was placed. They seated themselves, Syg taking Davage's hand.

"Fine, Com. I'll take the message here."

"Aye, sir."

"It must be regarding Kay, Dav," Syg said, concerned. "What if it's from Sam and she wishes to gloat? What if she wishes to boast and threaten another attack?"

The cone lit up.

A woman wearing a lavish black evening gown appeared. She was sitting in a grand smoking room. It reminded Davage of a particular officer's lounge in the north wing at Fleet that he favored; it was a large, nooky sort of room lined with shelves and old books. There were leather chairs all about and credenzas topped with sparkling glasses and bottles of aged spirits. He thought he could almost smell fine tobacco floating on the air. The room on the cone was different from the one at Fleet in that it was decorated in a greenish sort of motif; rich green carpeting, green accent lighting and tall green vases containing leafy green ferns. There were also cats all over—ceramic cats hidden in the corners, paintings of smoky cats with alluring green eyes, pearly cats nestled up in the shelving, and so on.

The woman seated before him also seemed rather catlike, with that ubiquitous feline aloofness. Her long hair was a cat-like mackerel color with black tabby stripes. Hanging from her throat was a black charm embossed with a large capital 'M'.

Apparently, Syg was seeing something completely different from what Davage was seeing. "Who are you?" she said, somewhat incensed.

She smiled. "My name is Mabs."

"Why are you sitting in my personal study? I'll ask you to leave my study at once! That room is to be locked at all times unless I am present."

She shook her head. "I am not sitting in your study, Countess. This is a small establishment I run. I call it the 'Cat God'. Different people see it as different things. Each to his or her own."

<Is she telling the truth, Dav? I see my study redecorated in green,> Syg sent to him via telepathy.

In the background Davage saw waiters moving by, transporting trays of drinks to indistinct people seated all over the room. *<I don't see your study, Syg. I see something that looks like a smoking room I favor at Fleet—also done up in green with cat statues in abundance.>*

<I too see cats. So, what does this person want?>

<I suppose she'll make that plain momentarily.>

Davage, Syg and Mabs stared at each other for an odd, awkward moment.

"I have been asked to help you, and that is what I intend to do," Mabs finally said. "I am sorry for the hour."

Davage was mystified. "You want to help us in some fashion?"

"Yes."

"Who, by chance, made this request?" Syg asked.

"Carahil."

Davage and Syg knew Carahil well. Carahil, protector of Xandarr and a god (supposedly) created in tree-filled passes of their own Telmus Grove by his sister, Lady Poe of Blanchefort. Lady Poe considered him her son, and therefore Carahil was their de facto nephew. Davage recalled with a smile that Carahil was a notorious prankster. Now that Carahil was mostly gone from the Grove, away to who knows where, Davage missed his pranks to some extent. He also liked to think he was somewhat of an authority on Carahil, and if this woman was familiar with him, then he should know her as well. He didn't.

"How do you know Carahil?" Syg asked.

"I am very close to him. All the gods have their secrets, and I am honored to hold his." Several children came into the cone and played at her feet. They appeared to glow with a silver radiance. "You go and play," she said to them. "If you're good you'll all receive a special treat." Chattering, the children streamed away.

"Were those your children, ma'am?" Davage asked.

"Yes," she said with pride. "I have news for you, and guidance."

"News and Guidance? From Carahil you say? Where is Carahil? Why isn't he here giving us this news himself? He's hardly a stranger and he does get around."

"He is far away, Captain, doing things he feels he must."

"What things?" Davage asked.

"He is defending the life of Lady Sammidoran."

Syg spat. "He defends the attacker of our son. How could he?"

"Lady Sammidoran did not attack your son, Countess, and you needn't me to tell you that. Your mother's heart is full of rage and the need to strike out for your son whom you love. I know that feeling well. For ages I lamented my lost children. You knew me then, Countess. You knew me once when I was full of rage."

"I did?"

"Yes. And now, thanks to you and Carahil, I am at peace with new children to warm my heart."

Davage interjected. “I am pleased you have found solace. Now then, you have news for us?

“Your son is making great strides and is becoming a powerful Vith lord. You would be very proud.”

“We’ve always been proud of our son,” Syg said. “Is he still on Xandarr?”

“No.”

Not on Xandarr? Davage thought about it. Kay must be having success in his Wellerman’s March. That was good news indeed. “Thank you for this news, ma’am. You also mentioned having guidance for us?”

A waiter came by and she took a bubbly green drink from his tray. “Your guidance, Captain, is to stay your course, for you shall soon have answers, though they might not be what you wish to hear. You wish to help your son, Countess, then you are ideally placed at Hoban. Hoban is where you may serve your son best.”

“Here, at Hoban you say? I don’t see how I can help my son so far from home.”

“You shall soon see.” She turned to Davage. “Captain, are you aware of the ancient hero named Atrajak of Want?”

Davage thought a moment. “He ... was a Remnath, I believe. A berserker from antiquity.”

“Do you know anything further?”

He tried to remember, to recall his studies of the Kanan past. He had volumes of knowledge in his head of the history of Kana, unfortunately, his studies were dominated by Vith teaching and Vith heroes. Atrajak was a Remnath from the south, and the Vith never gave them much due. He felt rather embarrassed for his lack of knowledge.

“I’m afraid not, ma’am.” Syg sat next to him and was rather shocked—Davage not knowing something. It was astounding.

She smiled. “That’s all right. There is a volume you will want to look up: *‘The History of the Hidden Wars and the Long Journey of Atrajak of Want.’* It will be of great use, I promise.”

“What does this volume tell?”

“It contains crucial information.” Mabs stood and approached the cone. “Now then, I must be off. Be true to yourselves and always know that Carahil, and I, are with you. Farewell.”

The cone went dark.

Syg was incredulous. “What was all that about?”

“I really have no idea.” Davage turned to the terminal and called up the ship’s library.

“What are you doing?”

“I’m looking this fellow Atrajak up. I feel rather ashamed. I suppose we of the north do tend to look down on the Remnaths quite a bit. I shall make it a point to correct that error in the future.”

Information flowed in on the holo-cone and Davage was disappointed. “Oh, look at this, Syg?”

“What?”

“Apparently, Atrajak of Want was labeled a traitor by the Sisterhood of Light after he attacked their strongholds of Twilight 4 and Deep 7 in 000004ex. Quite a long time ago. There isn’t much here, most of it is restricted, including the book she suggested."

"So, what are we to do? Do you really think this book Mabs suggested reading will help us somehow?"

"Hard to say, since we can't see it to find out." Davage suddenly felt very tired. "Well, let's sleep on it. Perhaps fresh ideas will present themselves in the morning."

Davage stepped into the lavatory while Syg went to the bed and removed the top cover. He loosened his collar and removed his shirt. "Perhaps I'll inquire with Captain Strella of the *Halo Dawn* in the morning. She's from a Remnath House and might have familial ties to the old House of Want. It's far too late to inquire with her now, she's probably off to bed."

"Dav, come here, please," Syg said.

Yawning, he returned to their bedroom. "What is it, darling?"

Syg pointed at the bed. Something rectangular and rather large was placed under the covers. It made a pronounced box-like bulge in the bed. "This. What is this?" She pulled the bedcovers back.

A large book was revealed; old, leather-bound, creaky with vellum. The cover was lettered in old writing which neither one of them could read.

"I suppose Carahil couldn't resist giving us a gift," Syg said.

The book smelled of cream pie, Carahil's usual calling card.

16—The Tombs of Crossland

Orders came down from Admiral Carfax the next morning. The *New Faith* had been assigned the task of investigating incidents in the north Croatoa region of Hoban, starting with the influential House of Crossland. The Lord of the House, Nells, was reported to have been attacked by a monstrous version of his son, Lord Mervin. Additionally, the monster was said to have been slain by the House staff and was kept on ice for inspection.

The teleport tube came down on the trimmed lawn of Crossland Manor. Captain Davage, Countess Sygillis, Lt Kilos, Bethrael of Moane and Ennez of Inarri walked out into the balmy Hoban afternoon. High above, sitting in the command chair of the *New Faith* was the dashing Paymaster Stenstrom, Lord of Belmont-South Tyrol. He was the son of the great Captain Stenstrom the Older of the *Caroline*, a warbird of great respect. Although Stenstrom was a Fleet Paymaster—a glorified legal observer and civilian clerk—he had his father's gift of command and had become a Paymaster merely to appease his mother, Lady Jubilee, as she didn't wish to fear for her son as she had through the years for her husband.

Paymaster Stenstrom was gifted, willing and eager, and Davage felt perfectly at ease giving him the ship.

Samaritan Ennez hadn't initially come on the journey to Hoban. He had been Davage's Samaritan for thirty years, but, as Hospitalers weren't members of the Fleet, their participation was on their own initiative, and Ennez's verve for sailing had diminished a bit as of late. Davage had heard Ennez was finally ready to settle down and seek out a bride, but had no luck as of yet. Fortunately, Bethrael was available and willing to fly. Still, after they sailed, Ennez, cantankerous as ever, changed his mind and booked passage with a fast transport in Atalea, linking up with the *New Faith* just short of Planet Fall. Beth and Ennez were a matching set, both Hospitaler Samaritans of the Knickerbaum Order. They wore the black uniform with silver instruments sticking out of the pockets. Also, the two wore their little winged silver helmets and carried the jet staff which they could use with lethal efficiency.

Ahead was Crossland Manor. It was a sprawling, provincial estate built in Remnath style, full of lacy stone-work, statues and fluted rails. A host of local Hobans tended the meticulous grounds, trimming the bushes, watering the flowers and raking the pebbled drives. The manor was built of some sort of burnt umber stone which matched Hoban's odd amber sky. In the late afternoon the sky was decorated with its lone pearly moon.

They had announced their arrival some hours earlier. Their plan was to interview Lord Nells of Crossland, his Countess Alberta, and have a look at the remains of Lord Crossland's attacker.

They needed something—anything to give to the Sisters. Davage was desperate for information. What they discovered here on Hoban could either save or condemn the House of Monama. The Sisters would not wait much longer.

The atmosphere inside the manor was surreal—the recent attack on Lord

Crossland had apparently sucked the life out of the place. The staff seemed sad and dour, going about their duties in a strange, pre-programmed sort of fashion. The Crosslands themselves all seemed to be rolling about in shock, like they were stuck in a bad dream. The Countess of Crossland, Alberta, greeted them in her brown, jeweled gown and, of all people, seemed the most lucid, though her sadness was thinly veiled. Her lips trembled as she spoke; her little hands shook.

"We are so glad that you are here and bid you welcome," she said.

The Crosslands had fourteen children, three of whom still lived there in the manor. Mervin, the boy in question who had supposedly attacked his father, was safe and sound in his wing. The Countess took them upstairs and admitted them into his room. There Mervin was, wearing a miniature version of the long Crossland coat. Only fourteen years old, he played with his toys, oblivious to the maudlin atmosphere around him, to the sorrowful, somewhat suspicious, somewhat fearful eye with which his mother looked at him. Lt. Kilos, proving to be great with children, approached and played with him—the poor boy seemed starved for attention. He marveled at Ki's Silver tech bird, Tweeter, watched him hover about with joy. Beth carefully scanned him as he played, and he came out clean. Just a happy, healthy fourteen year old boy. He appeared to want his mother, but she didn't approach. She just stood there and looked at him, her horror thinly veiled.

Then the Countess took them into the depths of the manor, to the body that was waiting there. She had the clear sense to keep it on ice, to preserve it for just such an investigation. Of all the Crosslands, Countess Alberta appeared to be the only one who'd kept her head, the only one who hadn't given up in sadness, though just barely.

"I'm sorry for the dark," Countess Alberta said lifting her skirts as she went down the stairs. "This is our wine cellar and there are no lights—it's bad for the wine, so I'm told." Tweeter's silvery light cast the cellar in an eerie pall. Dusty bottles appeared in morgue-like symmetry. She looked at the rows of stored bottles sporting the cheerful House label of vines and rolling meadows; they seemed to remind her of happier times. The Countess stopped at a cubby and produced several small lanterns that she turned on and passed out. "This way, please." Holding the blue, flickering lanterns, they continued into the depths of the cave-like cellar.

The frozen corpse that emerged in the bluish lantern light was truly monstrous.

It was of bizarre and tortured proportions. It was about eight feet tall—its body somehow elongated and stretched, painfully so. Its joints were all distended and fused in an unnatural way. His skin, if one could call it that, was a mauled, sliced patchwork partially covering his thin musculature. His face had no skin at all. Several portable freezing units were placed next to his body, keeping it rock solid.

Ki looked at the thing on the slab in horror. "Elders balls," she said. She covered Tweeter up in her hand. "Don't look at him, Tweets."

Syg, thinking back to Kay and the thing that had attacked him, put her head into Davage's chest as they beheld the creature's dead face.

"Great Countess," Davage said quietly. "How was it that you were able to determine that this was your son?"

Without missing a beat she answered: "It feels like him. It has his presence—I cannot explain further—I just know. A parent always knows his or her child."

Without saying it, Davage fully understood; Syg did, too.

The lantern light was dim, and Davage lit his Sight.

There were obscenities carved into his flesh from top to bottom, vulgarities and profanities, the graffiti of the dead written by an insane hand.

The creature's face was truly terrible. His eyes, nose and ears had been removed—in their place was a travesty of male organs stitched into position and jutting.

Beth couldn't look any further, and she turned away. Ennez, stalwart as always, got his scanner out and examined the hideous corpse in workman-like fashion.

"Who could do this?" Ki asked.

Ennez waved his scanner around. "Five penises on his face, attached by some sort of fusing process that I'm not familiar with."

"There are only four, Ennez," Ki corrected. "Isn't that enough?"

Ennez continued. "I repeat. There are five attached to his face. There's one in his mouth as well."

That was all she could take. Even the iron-nerved Lt. Kilos, a former Marine who had seen it all, turned away.

Ennez carefully scanned the ones attached where his eyes should be. "These ones here have some sort of sensory structures built within—again, I've not seen anything like this before."

"This can't be their son; it just can't," Syg said.

"It is," Ennez said. "The DNA is a perfect match to the child upstairs. No hint of 'Blanding' as one sees in a clone, and I detect no robotic parts, so it cannot be a flesh replica either. This is Lord Mervin of Crossland. Only, it is much older. I'd say he's at least a hundred years old, his blood is poisoned deep, and I see indications of rampant decay throughout his body."

Syg stared at the body. "How is this possible? How can he be upstairs playing in his room and be here as well, dead, in a monstrous, aged form all at once?"

Davage adjusted his hat and looked at the thing on the slab. "Time travel—the Sisters believe it to be a possibility."

Ennez checked his scanner. "I would not rule that out at this point. His tissues do show damage consistent with theoretical temporal travel, as described in the various writings put out by the Sisters. The time travel aspect itself isn't all that difficult to achieve; it's the temporal anchorage that is the key. Without it, bridging from one temporality to another would be impossible."

Syg snapped out of her funk. "You're saying this—thing—is from the future?"

"I am. What other option is there? Make no mistake, Syg—this is Lord Mervin. His tissues are much older than he currently is, and this isn't a clone or flesh replica as I've already established. His DNA would show signs of that, and he's not a robotic construct. He is from the future. I would imagine that at some point about a hundred years from now, given the age of his body, Lord Mervin will be transformed into this creature by parties unknown and then sent back and turned loose on his family."

"Talk sense, will you?" she replied.

"Here it is, Syg, right in front of you. What do you want me to do?"

Lt. Kilos and Tweeter returned to the table. "It's like the old stories we have on Onaris; the Jennybacks. They're evil versions of kin that return to plague their House."

"This has happened on Onaris?" Syg asked.

"Sometimes, yeah. I've never seen them myself, thank Creation, but I've heard people talk."

Davage stood there looking at the thing and felt his heart break.

Kay.

He'd had his suspicions, his simple theories as to what happened to Kay in the Grove. Was something similar to this what attacked Kay? It had to be. One of his daughters, in an monstrous exertion like this one, had done it and is still on the loose.

Davage was a fearless man … for himself. He found as time passed that his fearlessness didn't necessarily extend to those whom he loved. He worried somewhat about Syg, but she could handle herself. What of his children? What of Kay, and Ki and Hath and Maser? How would they measure up to the dangers of the world? The world had almost been too much for Kay.

And now here was this monster, and his girls and young son, home alone with the staff. He felt himself panicking. Home, that's where he and Syg should be, defending their children from monsters such as these.

Mabs ...

You are where you need to be.

Shuw-Shun. The fate of a whole people depending on this investigation. He stared at the creature on the table, his thoughts far away.

You are where you need to be ...

The Countess Alberta stared at the abomination lying dead on the table. "My son," she said.

Davage composed himself. "Your son is safe and sound in his wing, playing with his toys. We are going to get to the bottom of this—rest assured of that. But, first, you must protect your son and do your best to keep him from this fate."

She looked at the creature with horror.

"You must steel yourself, Countess. You must be his mother and not fear him, as I detected you were doing earlier. Do not let this—thing on the slab—alter or color your love for him. Someone or something did this to him with the express purpose of shocking you, of breaking your heart. Don't allow their efforts to be successful. You, with diligence, might save him from this."

The Countess nodded. "I am trying. Of course, you're correct. I am trying."

"Countess, were there any Berserkacides with this monster?" he asked.

The Countess thought a moment. "I do not know what a Berserkacide is, Captain."

"A Monama. Naked, rail thin, black-haired, black eyed. Most of these attacks that we've seen across Hoban have been accompanied by Berserkacides."

She shook her head. "No—just this. Is that not enough? I—I think we surprised him. I don't think he was ready to encounter us so quickly."

Davage nodded. *No Berserkacides.*

Unable to view the creature any further, they took their leave, went back upstairs, and saw the lord of the manor—Lord Nells.

On the way Davage pulled Lt. Kilos aside. "Ki," he said. "I need you to do something for me."

She could see he was serious. "Name it," she said.

"I want you to return to the ship. Apprise Paymaster Stenstrom of our situation and take a *Trelaine* back to Castle Blanchefort immediately."

"I'm not leaving here, Dav," she said. "The Jennybacks …"

Davage lost his composure for a moment. "You must, you …" He took a breath and calmed himself. "Ki, our girls are at Castle Blanchefort undefended. I need you to go there and protect them—Lady Kilos, your namesake, my little angel Hathaline. Our little boy, Maser. I need you to do this for me, Ki, please!"

"But what about Lady Poe? She's there."

"She is not well as of late, and I fear for her. Please, Ki. My children."

Ki could see how serious Davage was—how desperate. Desperation wasn't a thing she was used to seeing from him.

"All right, Dav. I'll do it. Me and Tweets will go there at once, and not leave until you return. I'll not let anything happen to them; you can count on me."

They embraced causing Tweeter to dislodge from her shoulder. Tweeter flapped up and landed on Davage's hat. Davage, pulling free, reached up and gave him a pat on the beak. He then returned to Ki's shoulder.

Giving Davage a last look, Ki turned and exited the manor.

He took a deep breath, Ki will protect his home. He felt reassured and then joined the rest in the study.

Lord Nells of Crossland sat in his large study. He had been attacked several days prior while walking in his garden with his Countess. A monster had appeared from thin air and had got him in the leg. The couple appear to have surprised it—like it wasn't ready to encounter them so quickly. The monster was then was killed by one of the staff. Though it was hideous and tortured of form, they instantly recognized it as their son Mervin. Parents always know their child, even in such a state. And Lord Nells fell into a deep melancholy, sitting in his study oblivious to all.

He hadn't bathed or eaten in days. He just sat there, shell-like and morose, his cheeks stubbly and drawn. He was thin and gaunt.

Countess Alberta admitted them, and she tried to pull him out of his daze. "Nells," she said. "Darling, the Fleet is here. They are going to investigate this matter and give us answers."

He barely seemed to recognize her.

They interviewed Lord Crossland, and he mumbled his way through it, staring off into space, answering the questions that he had only half-heard. His mind was elsewhere—still grappling with the beast in the form of his son. Afraid of the innocent boy playing upstairs.

"We, with your permission, sir, will search the grounds and look for clues," Davage said.

Lord Crossland didn't respond.

"You have our permission. The grounds are yours," Alberta said. "I will show you where the attack happened."

She showed them out of the study.

"Lord Crossland," Davage asked looking back, "are you drugged, sir?"

He didn't answer.

"Lord Crossland, I understand how you feel, but this is not the time to …"

He rousted out a bit. "Lord Blanchefort, Captain of the Fleet," he said. "I have been attacked by a monstrous image of my son who tried to kill me and my wife—his mother. Additionally, the next day, I saw my Countess standing in the fog, beckoning, arms wide, for me to come to her. I was about to but remembered that my Countess was inside the manor."

Davage, Syg and Beth looked at each other.

Nells sighed. "What was that I saw? A ghost—another monster? What would have become of me had I gone to it? We are surrounded by evil here. Our home is no longer ours. The League is no longer safe. By your leave, you cannot understand how I feel, Captain."

"With respect, sir," Davage said, "I know exactly how you feel. My son—our son—was attacked and badly wounded by a monster similar to the one in your basement, a monster whom I am convinced is a member of my own family."

Lord Crossland stirred a bit at this news.

Syg turned to Dav, shocked. *"What?"*

Davage continued. "So, forgive me, sir. I know exactly how you feel."

Crossland rustled uncomfortably. Alberta looked at the floor.

"How I wish that it had been me attacked, and not my son," Davage said. "That such a thing could happen to one so dear to me, and I wasn't there to assist him, to help him. However, I am not going to sit back and fret and feel sorry for myself. I am here, on Hoban, far away from my home, trying to discover who has authored this attack, and I am going to discover them, sir—make no mistake! I am going to discover them, and I am going to make them pay, make them rue the day they chose to come at my son. Meanwhile, you've your family to think of and defend, and you've your beautiful Countess and your young son who needs his father. I suggest you set to it and protect them as best you can. In any event, you may either assist me in this endeavor, or you may get out of the way."

Crossland didn't respond.

Countess Alberta approached. "Please, come this way, I will show you where the attack took place. Please ..."

As they readied to leave the study, Crossland stirred and called out to them. "The tombs, Captain. Check the tombs, I hear them there. I hear my wife's voice calling to me there."

* * * * *

Far back from the manor, past the lovely manicured gardens, pebbled walkways and service structures, was a huge, walled-in space encompassing several square miles. The Countess, using a large, ancient key ring, opened the rusty gate, and they all went in.

Within the wall was the Crossland necropolis. The interior was vast, housing an uncountable number of fallen tombstones, vaults and mausoleums. The ground was lumpy and somewhat moist with undrained, standing water. The air felt thick and humid, and patches of fog reached up to them from the tussocks.

Centuries of Crosslands and their staff were buried here. The place had an unnatural, ominous feel to it.

The Countess took her leave, and Syg immediately confronted Davage about his theory that either Lady Kilos or Lady Hathaline had attacked Kay.

She was close to hysterics. Davage told her it was only a hunch, but the evidence was mounting, and Syg nearly collapsed, weeping into his shoulder.

She turned an angry eye to Beth and Ennez. "Did either of you know about this? You ran tests. Did you know about this?"

Beth looked down and adjusted her little silver helmet. She didn't say anything. Ennez spoke up. "Yes, Syg … We did. Lady Hathaline's DNA was all over Kay. Our samples were conclusive."

Lady Hathaline? It was Davage's turn to be shocked and wrecked. He was

certain it had been Lady Kilos. His little girl, Lady Hathaline, had done it??

"And were you going to say nothing? I thought you two were our friends. Beth, how could you?"

Beth managed to find her courage and spoke up for herself. "And what were we to say, Syg, that your daughter nearly murdered Kay, and ate a bit of him as well? We were trying to spare you until we knew more. We're searching for answers too. The both of us … didn't know what to say. I'm sorry, Syg."

Syg flopped down onto the wet ground and began to weep. Recovering from his own momentary funk, Davage pulled her back up.

"Syg, you're not going to do this—you're not going to tuck in like Lord

Crossland sulking in his study."

"I want to go home and protect our children! They need us! Take me home, Dav!"

"I have already dispatched Lt. Kilos, before our audience with Lord Crossland. She is on her way there with speed, even now, and she will protect our Household. Syg, we are where we need to be—right here investigating this plot and determining the attacking parties. You heard Mabs, we must put an end to this, not only for the sake of our children, but for the sake of others as well—for that little boy playing alone in his room, feared by all."

She listened to him and calmed. "Ki's going to watch out for our children?"

"She is, Syg."

Syg nodded and felt assured. After a bit, she, showing a lot more guts than Lord Crossland, stood tall and assumed her place at Davage's side. "Whoever is behind this, Dav—they're going to die. I am going to kill them, and don't try to get in my way."

Beth stood there, sheepish under her winged helmet. Davage and Syg approached her and gave her a grand hug. "Thank you, Beth," he said. "For being a friend."

Syg smiled at her. "I know that was difficult, Beth. Thank you, I'm sorry I yelled at you just now. You still do not have permission to court Kay, by the by."

Beth laughed.

They separated. Ennez had already started sweeping the area with his scanner. Heading north, they followed him into the rows of the dead.

"What are we looking for?" Ennez asked waving his scanner around.

"I'm not sure," Davage said. "The fact that there were no Berserkacides present during the attack troubles me. According to Admiral Carfax, all of the attacks on Hoban have featured the presence of Berserkacides. As they seemed to have surprised the monster, perhaps it didn't have time to properly deploy them. Also, Lord Crossland is convinced that a monstrous version of his Countess is roaming the necropolis, calling to him. We must therefore search for sequestered Berserkacides and a phantom countess."

"Wonderful," Ennez said.

Syg, standing close to Davage, threw up a blob of Silver tech and created her usual *Seeker* familiar.

* * * * *

Syg's Silver tech familiar was a four foot long, one foot high miniature version of their old ship, the *Seeker*. Externally it looked exactly like the *Seeker,* being rather swan-shaped, with wings, turrets, a tower and a roving, light-emitting sensor mounted on the frontal section. It could fire little guided canister missiles that exploded with a massive punch, and could lay down a blistering wall of Battleshot fire from tiny gun batteries arrayed along its length. Soaring overhead, Syg could see what it saw with its roving sensor, and she could speak and hear through it as well, it having a much greater range than mere telepathy. The light from its sensor could also destroy and clear out StT's, which was handy.

Syg liked to say that there was a tiny crew roaming around inside: a tiny Dav and a tiny Syg. She'd tinkered around with it over the years. She added a feature that she could expand it in size and get in, like a Ripcar. She even had space for two—she

liked to take Davage for rides in it.

The *Seeker* familiar took shape and soared about like a model spaceship, loitering about, its Cyclops eye panning this way and that casting a strong beam of silvery light to the ground—Syg able to see what it could from its overhead vantage point. Its high-flying presence and roving eye was comforting. Syg's little silver *Seeker* could do a lot of damage in a hurry if it needed to.

Beth looked up at it soaring overhead. "Syg, you're still using the *Seeker* as your familiar? You don't fly in the *Seeker* anymore. Why don't you redesign it to look like the *New Faith*?"

"Because the *New Faith* is ugly," Syg said. "I like my *Seeker* familiar. It has served us well for twenty years now, and I've no intention of changing it."

"Ah," Beth replied. "Here's mine; let me show you. I've been working on it." Beth tossed out a large blob of Silver tech of her own, which twisted and turned into the shape of a huge, long-legged frog with bulging orange eyes. The frog shifted in color from silver to green, to a lit-up blue, to a pearly pink and back again. "It took me the longest to get the colors right," Beth said happily. "I call him 'Bernie,' after Lord Bernard of Hopkins—that man could eat."

They moved on, 'Bernie' hopping along at their side, the *Seeker* loitering overhead.

They passed many vaults—row after row of moss-covered Crossland vaults, old and nameless.

Beth had advanced several rows into the graveyard, using her jet staff as a walking stick to get through the sucking mud. Her Silver tech frog became interested in a flooded furrow. "Bernie! Bernie!" it said in a froggy voice. Beth knelt down next to him.

"Hey, come here!" she called out.

They made their way to her. There, partially submerged in the furrow, were four badly decomposed bodies. They pulled them out and laid them on top of a small vault. Beth and Ennez poured over them with their scanners.

"Four bodies," Ennez said. "Two adults and two juveniles. They have been lashed together at the wrists and ankles. Apparent cause of death—exposure, starvation and neglect. Somebody tied them up and left them here."

"Are they Hobans?" Davage asked.

"Nope," he said. "They appear to be Monama. The bone composition looks like what we know Monama bones to be. Notice the higher presence of cartilage in the joints, ribs and chest cavity—that's a Monama hallmark. Also, and we of the

Hospitalers have suspected this, they appear to have an under-developed, extra pair of cartilaginous arms here, a vestige from the past, as, apparently, they were once four-armed. Monamas do not appear to be Elder in origin. They have very alien physiology."

"That is still in debate," Beth said.

"Look for yourself, Beth. Do these scans look Elder to you?"

Beth didn't answer.

Davage looked down at the sad, lashed skeletons. They looked so tiny to him. "Berserkacides always seem to have four arms."

"Monamas can't survive long away from Kana," Beth said. "Remove them from Kana and all their Gift-like powers vanish, and they soon grow sick and die. Also, if it gets too cold, they quickly take ill."

"Again," Ennez said, not letting the matter drop, "confirming that they are of alien origin."

Davage felt sorry for them, these forlorn bodies. "These poor people were scooped up from their homes, left here and forgotten—probably by the monster now rotting in the Crossland dungeon."

"These poor souls were intended to be Berserkacides?" Syg asked.

"Probably, why else would they be here? I want these bodies attended to and brought back to Kana where they may be identified and returned to their tribes. They'll not be left on Hoban."

They heard a muffled groan in the distance. Drawing their weapons, they made their way to the source of the sound. Syg lifted her *Seeker,* and opened its tiny Battleshot ports, putting it in a good position to cover them. Its spotlight shown down.

A few rows away, they came across a large vault. The sound they had heard came from within. Ennez tried the door, and it was locked. Davage Sighted into the vault.

"I see six people grouped together inside!"

Another groan.

"Syg," Davage said. "Deal with this lock, please."

Syg went to the door and, drawing back, blasted the door off its ancient hinges with her Silver tech.

They pushed the door aside and went in.

Within the vault, leaning against the wall, were six naked people, all tied together—four men and two females. Clearly, they were Monamas. Their skin was dead white, their hair black and bursting down to their feet. Their black eyes were pallid and a rather unhealthy gray in appearance. They were bound together at the wrists and at the ankles. They appeared to be in bad shape. Beth and Ennez quickly began scanning them.

One of the Monama females was moaning.

"Five are alive, one of the females is dead. Dehydration, hypothermia, and acute malnutrition," Beth said.

"I'm reading an excess of gamma, Dav," Ennez announced.

"Gamma?"

"Yes, and it seems to be coming from these Monamas."

"Beth," Davage said. "Find Countess Alberta and tell her we need water, blankets, anything she has, here immediately. Then, contact the ship and inform Paymaster Stenstrom of the situation, and tell him we will be back directly with wounded!" Beth ran out and Wafted away. Bernie hopped after her.

"We'll need to get these people back to Kana as soon as possible—Monamas don't do well away from there," Ennez said.

Ennez tried to cut their bonds with a scalpel pulled from his pocket, but the cords refused to break. "These bonds resist cutting."

Syg came forward and started working on the bonds with her Silver tech. Even with Silver tech, she appeared to be having a hard time.

"What is this? It's like jelly."

Syg finally got the bonds off, and they fell to the ground wiggling like snakes. Ennez carefully picked one up and put it into his pack for study later.

The Monamas were in bad shape. Their bonds had been so tight that two of them had broken wrists; another one's hands appeared to be dead from lack of circulation.

The survivors appeared to be in a funk. Their eyes were open, but their expressions were blank.

"They're in Head Swarm, Dav," Ennez said.

"What is that?" Davage asked.

"A state of waking catatonia. They have seen their deaths and fallen into Head Swarm—sort of a defensive mechanism they have. I don't know if it's possible to get them out of it."

Davage tried to stand them up, but they were flaccid and uncooperative. And, somehow, they still appeared to be bound together though their bonds were cut.

"We are facing a serious conundrum here, Syg," Davage said. "Clearly, these poor souls were left here by the enemy for the purposes of changing them into Berserkacides and they were left here when the attack was partially botched. So, here's our problem—we cannot leave these people here to die, however, we invite disaster upon ourselves as they could transform on us at any given moment."

Syg struggled with the limp bodies. "So, what should we do?"

"We have got to determine how and why they become Berserkacides. If we know how it's done, then we can stop it. Ennez, what data have you?"

"Very little. Your guess as good as mine. If it's not simply related to mental illness, it could be a chemical reaction, a response to stimuli, or possibly a drug-induced or a surgical enhancement. I doubt it's a chemical reaction and surgery is not practical. It must be a result of direct stimuli—something they see or hear."

Davage thought a moment. "I recall Kay mentioning something about a red light—seeing a red light at Castle Durst, and that Sam was mortally afraid of it. Sam is a very courageous woman, and for her to be so afraid of something that she was unable to stand at Kay's side and fight means her fear was primal—deep-rooted. Perhaps a certain frequency of red light is the stimuli used to turn a Monama into a Berserkacide."

"Sounds reasonable, Dav," Ennez said, "but where is the stimulus? I don't see any red lights around here."

"Ennez, you said to saw an excess of gamma band energy around them—perhaps that's where we should look." Davage adjusted his Sight on the Monamas and struggled. "Gamma is so difficult to see."

Davage focused in. "Syg, Ennez!" he cried. "Look here! I can see they are wearing some sort of necklace or collar!"

"I don't see anything," Ennez said.

"I see it in Sight, Cloaked in the Gamma band."

He saw a thick, black cord wrapping around their necks, lashing them together though it could not be seen without Sight. Davage tried to break it, but the cord resisted.

"Ennez, raise the ship and tell Paymaster Stenstrom that we need precision cutting tools down here as soon as possible now!"

"You need to start carrying a communicator, Dav," he said. Ennez put his scanner away and ran out.

Davage looked more closely at the cord, straining to see it. A number of oblong objects sprouted out of their collar. They were smooth diamond-shaped crystals covered with arcane writing. "Syg," he said, "I see prisms of some sort studding the collar. Red prisms. These prisms at their necks must be what turns them into Berserkacides. They must!"

Davage tugged at the bizarre necklace of prisms. "Help me get them off. Hurry! We can prevent this from happening!"

Syg started pawing around. "Why can't I see it? Is it Cloaked?"

"Sort of. It's not like a standard Cloak though. It's some sort of Gamma-band distortion field. I'm having a difficult time seeing it myself."

Davage and Syg struggled with their necklaces. As he concentrated and tuned his Sight, he could see them clearer and clearer in the Gamma spectrum. He saw, to his disgust, that the necklaces were stitched rudely into their flesh. As he tried to dig them out, the surviving girl stirred in muddled pain. She looked at them with groggy eyes and struggled. She cried out.

"It's all right, ma'am. It's all right. We're here to help you."

The girl cringed in fear. She mumbled a few words, but, they were in some Monama tongue.

"Oh, Creation," Davage said. "Ma'am, do you speak the common League tongue? I'm sorry; I don't know your language."

She didn't respond. Davage continued to work at pulling away the prisms as she struggled weakly.

He managed to pull off the prisms studding her collar, there were six of them. He threw them to the floor and kicked them away. The last one he placed deep within a coat pocket for study later. "Our ship is nearby. We are going to take you there and keep you safe."

Syg managed to cut the fibrous lash binding their necks, freeing the girl. She said a few more words. "Ma'am, I can't understand you. Oh, where is Kay when we need him? I'm certain he'd understand."

She struggled and spoke in broken League common with a bad accent. "Get house ..."

"You want to go home? We are going to take you there. Safe and sound. You and these fellows here shall be our special guests."

As he tried to calm the girl, he saw a flash of Gamma waves coming from outside the vault. It snaked through the air like a green cloud.

Someone walked in just then. It was Countess Alberta.

But it wasn't Countess Alberta—it was a hideous monster in her guise, half skinned, dripping blood, wearing a crown of fingers and ears. She was capering about, holding a prism in her right hand, glowing red. "Kill them!" she screeched. "KILL THEM!!"

The monstrous Countess then screamed something in a hideous, high-pitched bark, as if she were casting some sort of spell.

Syg, sensing danger, pumped her fist and blasted the creature with a stream of Silver tech, blowing her jaw off. She dropped the prism she was carrying and held her face.

Syg blasted her again—this time blowing her out of the vault.

"Dav!" Syg screamed. "I can see from the *Seeker* that there's movement all over the graveyard!"

A din of growling and screaming filtered into the vault from outside.

The prisms around the Monamas necks all burst into a rosy red glow staining the walls of the vault as blood. Davage took the girl's face and pushed it into his breast, keeping her from seeing the light. She struggled feebly.

The four remaining Monama men came to life in a roar. Where, only moments before, they were languishing on the verge of death, lost in 'Head Swarm' as Ennez had called it, now they were fully energized. Their already formidable-looking claws lengthened, and as Davage watched, they sprouted an extra pair of arms, delicate and studded with black claws. Slavering like raging beasts they hacked at the fibrous rope binding them together with their claws.

The girl, her face shielded by Davage's chest and coat, whimpered in terror.

"Creation, Berserkacides!" Syg screamed as she readied to box them into a Sten.

Jawless, cackling with delight, the monstrous image of Countess Alberta came running back into the vault—missing her lower jaw, an arm, a shoulder and a good portion of her chest. She grabbed Syg from behind and pulled her out of the vault.

Holding the girl to him, Davage unsaddled his CARG and, one-handed, swept the thrashing Monamas—now raging Berserkacides—back, holding them temporarily at bay.

He glanced outside. There, he saw Syg struggling with the monstrous countess. He saw a sort of feathery door open behind the monster in a green flash of Gamma, and she pulled Syg into it. The door then closed and Syg was gone.

17—The Berserkacides

Davage stumbled of out the vault and ran in the direction of the manor. He ran like he never had before, hurtling over the jumbled obstacle course of gravestones, tombs, and vaults, the drenched, uneven ground sucking at his boots, slowing him down. The terrified Monama woman was cradled in his arms.

Syg was gone, and he feared for her. Beth and Ennez weren't anywhere around.

Behind, Berserkacides pursued in a snarling mass. The ones from the vault came tearing out after him. They ran on all fours, like leopards, holding their extra pair of clawed hands over their heads, ready to slash and tear. Others came howling in from all over the graveyard in primal fury—apparently a whole host of them had been stashed there.

Overhead, the Silver tech *Seeker,* without Syg to control it, sauntered about mindlessly.

The Berserkacides shall soon overrun him. They were so fast.

He tried to Waft away and get the girl to safety, but couldn't. It sputtered and coughed around him. He couldn't Waft! What was happening?

The Monama woman! Holding her was somehow counteracting his Waft! He recalled Kay and Sam talking about such a thing once at dinner—how Sam thought it was funny that her touch disrupted his Gifts, and how it took practice for him to overcome the odd phenomena.

Davage didn't have time to practice.

He didn't have a tregador to contact the ship. His telepathy was terrible other than with Syg and Ki, so he didn't bother trying.

Instead, he ran, leaping over the vaults, springing off the tombstones as fast as he could, the shrieking, foaming Berserkacides howling in from all sides hot on his heels.

One stumble, one misstep, and they would be on him.

Syg—where was Syg? What was happening to Syg?

There was no escaping the ones from the vault; they were simply too fast. They were mere moments from bringing him down. In desperation, he dropped the woman with a splat into the muddy ground, and, free of her touch, Wafted just as the Berserkacide claws were about to find his neck.

Confused, they skittered to a halt and turned their attention to the woman.

With a blast Davage reappeared behind them, CARG at the ready. He took the top half off one Berserkacide and lopped the head off another.

Snarling, the last two sprang.

Davage Wafted second time and again appeared behind them. With one swing of his famously heavy CARG, he bisected both, cleaving through flesh and bone alike.

The graveyard was alive with noise and shadowy movement, closing in fast. He picked the girl back up and began running again.

He reached a small clearing and Sighted a mass of Berserkacides coming in on his position from ahead. He was about to be cornered.

He veered to his right and found a large vault with a recessed door—a good place to make a stand. He dove into the recess and put the girl down.

"Don't look, ma'am! Whatever happens, don't look!" She curled up into a ball and whimpered, covering her face with her hands, her long black hair, rather like Lady Sammidoran's, thick and all over the place.

Davage raised his CARG and readied for the onslaught. He drew his MiMs pistol and cocked it. He didn't really think the tiny MiMs could do much to stop these Berserkacides fiends, but it couldn't hurt. This girl, this Monama, had information he needed. Willing or unwilling, she was in the service of these monsters, these 'Jenny-backs' Ki had called them. She was therefore the key to understanding this mystery. If only to get her to safety, he would hold this position until he could do so no longer.

She had to survive and tell what she knew. She had to. The fate of her people possibly depended on it. Davage had to give the Sisters information; otherwise, they would wipe the Monamas out.

And the Berserkacides came in.

Davage's Sight gave him a great advantage, he could see when the Berserkacides would attack a few seconds before they actually did it, giving him time to ready his CARG or fire his MiMs.

Swing after swing, he laid into them, hacking off arms and legs. One Berserkacide dug his claws into the stone of the vault just before Davage chopped his arm off—the appendage hung there, disembodied and still struggling. The Berserkacides were savage in the extreme, incredibly strong and fast, outdoing even the terrible, foam-flecked Black Hat Hulgismen. Gravely wounding Berserkacides did little good, nor did lopping off their arms and legs, as, wormlike, they crawled back into the fight. The only thing to do was take off their heads.

And Davage did that, swing after swing, the pale naked bodies piling up to either side of him; heads lopped off, faces cleaved in two. He emptied his MiMs and dropped it—the tiny gun having no effect.

The torrent did not yield—Berserkacides kept pouring in. Davage Sighted them overwhelming his position in a few moments, their sheer weight of numbers taking him down and the girl with him. He Sighted their claws tearing out his throat and tearing the girl apart. He could Waft away, but then the girl would be lost.

This was it.

"Ma'am!" he yelled to the cowering girl behind him. "I want you to climb up over the top of the vault and run. Run to the manor, as fast as you can! Keep running until you get to safety! I'll try to hold them here!"

The girl, in terror, didn't move.

"Ma'am!"

Davage picked her up by the scruff of her neck and threw her up and over the top of the vault. Recovering her senses a little, she scrabbled away.

Lowering his guard and tossing the girl was costly. The Berserkacides came in a killing wave, and he couldn't possibly stop them all. He didn't have time to build a Waft.

From a distance came a sharp: CRACK! CRACK! CRACK! CRACK!

Four Berserkacides' heads exploded, and they fell in a dripping heap. Beyond, standing on the distant outer wall, was the thin, coatless form of Lord Crossland holding the SMOKELESS, the LosCapricos weapon of his House—a long rifle that never missed. His triangle hat was huge on his head. Countess Alberta, the real one, stood next to him. Apparently, he had recovered from his funk, or she had rousted him from it.

Countess Alberta held the small form of their son to her breast.

Lord Crossland reloaded his SMOKELESS. The Berserkacides regrouped and continued the assault.

Momentarily clear, Davage Sighted for the girl.

She had covered a fair distance in the direction of the manor but ran right into a pocket of charging Berserkacides. She screamed in terror as they fell upon her.

SNAP! SNAP!

With a lightning fast Silver tech tongue, the Berserkacides were pulled off their feet and into the huge, waiting mouth of a giant, orange-eyed frog lurking in one of the trees—a frog of changing, scintillating colors.

"Bernie! Bernie!" the frog said as he devoured one Berserkacide after the next, his insides apparently mystically pocketed to allow him to easily consume such impossibly huge things.

After a moment, Beth and Ennez appeared and, with their whirling jet staves and lances of Silver tech, fought the remaining Berserkacides in the area with devastating skill.

SNAP! SNAP! "Bernie! Bernie!"

Back at the vault, another wave came in, and Davage readied himself for the killer assault.

A shaft of light shined down from above just then. The silver *Seeker* roared into the clearing, banking gracefully at an acute angle. Its tiny Battleshot batteries opened up, mowing down a large group of incoming Berserkacides—their crazed bodies collapsing under the weight of its minute but withering shot.

With a blast, Syg Wafted into the doorway. Covered in sticky-looking blood, she quickly threw up a Sten field across the vault. The Berserkacides slammed into it, its shocking touch sending them into a frenzy. They pawed at it in a fury, their clawed hands sparking as they painfully raked at it, unable to pass through. Safe behind the Sten, Davage and Syg fell into each other's arms, grateful that the other hadn't been killed.

In the usual 'Baaaaaaaaaa! sound, the *Seeker* familiar blasted the Berserkacides leaning against the Sten into paste.

Then, overhead, five Marine *Trelaines* came diving in from the heavens, ordered down by Paymaster Stenstrom. They raked the howling Berserkacides with passing fire and then set down with ranks of red-coated Marines quickly piling out and forming defensive lines. There, they engaged the remaining Berserkacides and secured the necropolis, their deadly Marine SK pistols easily large enough to bring the Berserkacides down.

Soon, as quickly as it began, the battle was, thankfully, over, Davage holding the bloody Syg to him. She dropped the Sten, and they came out, joining with Beth and Ennez. Bernie, full of devoured Berserkacides, leapt down from the tree and dutifully followed her.

They went a distance, and there, huddled against a tree stump and lit-up in the *Seeker*'s spotlight, was the Monama girl—sick, terrified, naked, but very much alive and in her right mind.

18—Sam's Doughnut

Two days later, Kay, Sarah and Phillip dressed, had breakfast in the pub, and checked out. They went outside into the warm Remnath sun, and, at first, thought the *Goshawk* had been stolen, for it wasn't there in the ship park where they had left it. Kay had forgotten it was Cloaked—had no idea he was still doing it. Truly, as Cloak had said during their afternoon together, the more relaxed you were, the better the Cloak worked. When they thought nobody was looking, Kay dropped it, and the *Goshawk* appeared as if from nowhere, black and bat-like.

They then mounted it and headed west for Rostov. Phillip flew low, hugging the rolling grasslands, causing herds of wild animals to flee as they passed, the fast ship nimbly following Phillip's control. When they neared the city, Kay Cloaked it again, and Phillip set it down a mile or two away near the sea.

On foot, following the rocky coast and the crashing waves of the sea, the sound of the breaking waves loud, they walked into Rostov.

The looming black gates, lined with stone and watch towers, were open, waiting for them. They passed through, and inside was a collage of noise and activity—a whole seedy world in miniature. Within the black walls was a patchwork of thrown together structures and fallen debris, all pushed up against one another with little thought paid to design, visual appeal or function, forming a nonsensical, drunken grid of threadbare streets, metal-strewn yards and shabby dead-ends. Due to the roughshod and non-permanent nature of most of the structures, the layout of streets and alleys often changed daily. There were makeshift marketplaces, made from the rusty hulls of old, scrapped Fleet ships, selling all manner of questionable items from illegal pharmaceuticals and counterfeit dura-techs to low-end finished goods, everything blasted in gaudy 4-D lights of indescribable colors. There were banned substances being bartered about a-plenty, home-made spirits of questionable levels of toxicity, and they even came across an alley full of venders selling various incarnations of The Weed to hopeful courtesans of all shapes and dispositions. Sarah saw a stand selling Remax to a clamoring crowd. Remax, as Sarah knew from her avid reading, was a dangerous painkiller and stimulant from Bazz, easily leading to addiction, spontaneous deformity and death. It was supposed to be illegal in the League.

There were small, walk-up diners selling noodles, dried fruits and fried savories designed for the eater on the go. There were flop-houses and cricket huts to crash in, dingy residences and flesh peddlers out and about in unabashed force. There were even areas of greater and lesser prosperity—some of the nicer structures appeared fairly well built and semi-permanent, while others looked to be, quite literally, falling apart at the rusty seams.

And, by far the most plentiful and omnipresent, there were sports houses—places of gambling and lost money where, for a price, you could risk all and lose everything at the throw of the bones or a pull on the wheel. Every sort of game and entertainment was available to be tried, from modern holo-shunts and needlers to ancient games of chance. All one needed was a little money and the hard stones to give it a toss.

All of this, this cornucopia of depravation, was a sure-fire way to get destroyed. The whole place was just crying out to receive a fiery visit from the Sisters.

Huddled up against the western wall and watching over the whole odd mess was the keep—Leap Manor—the seat of House Rostov, a menacing collection of buttressed towers, dark windows and impressively sharp-looking spires, seeing everything that happened below and nothing at the same time. It looked like a collection of variously-sized black spears stacked up and piled in a corner.

Underneath that pile of black rock was the vault and their objective: Sam's Doughnut.

Marching proudly through the masses was the Watch—roving groups of House Rostov guardsmen wearing checkered tunics, making sure that the House got its coin. They milled about, armed to the teeth, and holding those odd mickalmick creatures Kay had seen at leash. The mickalmicks wore a type of harness just behind their heads. Attached to the harness was a checkered House Rostov flag on a short pole.

Casually making the rounds through the city, they saw all sorts of things they wish they hadn't. They saw dirty, impoverished mothers betting—and losing—their children at games of chance; the weeping children being carried off by the Watch after the dice or needle-cast failed them—no doubt a career in prostitution awaiting them. They saw a gentleman betting his mechanical arm and his artificial groin, but, fortunately, he won them back plus a big score. They saw a lady betting the clothes off her back, and soon she was wearing nothing but a dirty blanket.

Sarah, always hungry and ready to try new things, bought something fried on a stick from an eat shack. Apparently she liked it, as she bought two more. "So, how are we going to do this? What's our plan?" she asked getting her teeth into the fried morsel.

A solitary member of the Watch approached them. He was a smallish fellow, sandy haired under his large triangle hat, and quite young. He was wearing a white tailed coat and matching pants with a pair of black Calvert boots. He didn't have the scarred, burned-in look of the other Watch they'd seen. He had a Dare A-H gun holstered at his side and a second one tucked into his checkered sash. In his left hand, he held a leashed mickalmick. His mickalmick seemed friendly and tame—almost like a reptilian dog. Its spotted belly shown in the sun, and its little checkered flag waved in the breeze.

"Greetings, strangers," he said.

"Well met," Kay replied.

He looked them over. "Nice clothes," he said referring to Kay's Blanchefort coat and hat. He glanced at Sarah and tipped his hat. "I believe, good sir, that there are a number of nicer places to take such a fine young lady besides Rostov. There's nothing to do here but waste your money. I suggest Wiln, nice scenery, fine dining ..."

"Good sir," Sarah said. "Do you know that there are people bartering Remax down the street?"

He sighed. "Again? All right, I'll go down there and break them up. Won't do any good. They'll just re-surface somewhere else."

He prepared to take his leave, and then stopped. "You three have the Vith look—you look like Vith to me. That's fine, the sportsmen here just love the Vith—always come with a lot of coin, they do. However, allow me to give you a bit of friendly advice. With Vith comes trouble—that Elder razzle-dazzle they like to pull—and the Watch are extra vigilant against such antics. You're probably being watched even as we speak. If you try to turn invisible, or Dirge somebody, or try to Waft away, they'll be on you in no time, and the laws can be pretty harsh about certain things here in Rostov, the use-of-Gifts being one of them. Please, enjoy yourselves—assign yourself a limit on how much you're willing to lose and stick to it. When you've met your limit, take your leave. Go to Wiln or St Paris and have a good dinner. It's just a bit of friendly advice; take it as you will."

"We will, sir," Sarah said. "And thank you," she added petting the mickalmick on the head.

With that, the Watchman tipped his large hat again and he and his friendly mickalmick made their way down the street. Kay watched him for a bit—he seemed familiar to him for some reason.

Continuing on, Kay saw a stand down the street that looked a bit nicer than most of the others. It, like many of the other sporting establishments, flew a white and black checkered flag—the crest of House Rostov. The presence of the flag indicated that the House and not some urchin or random chump was running that stand. Without consulting Phillip and Sarah, Kay walked up to it.

A skinny sportsman dressed nicely in the Calvert fashion, sat behind the counter and regarded Kay for a moment.

"Good day to you, fine sir," he hissed.

"What's your game?" Kay asked.

"Shell game, nice and simple," the sportsman said.

He produced, as if by magic, a small dried pea and three similar-looking turtle shells on the countertop.

Kay smiled. "How much for a game?"

"How much you want to bet, dear sir?"

Kay produced a Blanchefort hader and set it on the counter. The sportsman looked at it and seemed satisfied. He produced a few Rostov solaris and placed them next to the silver hader. "We start nice and easy—2 to 1, how about that? That all right?"

"Fine."

With that, the sportsman covered the pea with the turtle shells and began skillfully moving them around on the countertop. With his Sight, Kay could see the shell with the pea under it dancing around gracefully on the countertop. Suddenly, he Sighted a pea under each of the shells. Clearly, the sportsman's dexterity was without peer and wanted Kay to win this opening teaser round. A classic ploy.

The shells came to rest. "Please choose, sir," the sportsman said.

Kay sighed and pointed at the middle shell—he knew he couldn't lose. The sportsman turned it over, exposing the pea. "Looks to be a winner." He slid the solaris and Kay's hader back to him. With incredible skill, the sportsman made the other two peas disappear. He showed Kay the single pea again and covered it. "This time, we play 3 to 1—that all right?"

"Sure," Kay said, putting his hader back on the counter. The sportsman put more solaris next to it.

The sportsman started moving the shells quite a bit faster this time. Again, toward the end of the shuffle, two more peas appeared under the shells. Again, Kay couldn't lose. He picked one and won. The sportsman then reset the game. "This is your lucky day, sir. Now, we play for 5 to 1. How about that?"

Kay shrugged. "I think I'm done, thanks."

The sportsman reddened in the face. "Now, just a moment, lad. You've gotten pretty lucky so far. I'd like a chance to win my payout back. Come on—I'm paying 5 to 1 this time. You're on a hot streak; you can't stop now."

"Frankly, I'm a bit bored. Haders and solaris—big deal."

The sportsman leaned forward, intrigued. "Ahh, a high roller, eh? Well then, name your score. We aim to please here."

"I want to play for an item in Rostov's vault."

A few dirty courtesans saddled up to the counter to watch. One began touching Kay on the shoulder. The sportsman shooed them away.

"That a fact? Want something from the vault, do you? There's some wondrous things in there, no doubt about it," he said watching the courtesans depart. "But swag like that doesn't just come up for just anybody, or anything. The spice needs to be right—see, you've got to put something nice on the table first; then, if it is agreeable, we can possibly deal. So, with that in mind, let's see the color of your money."

Without missing a beat, Kay reached into his coat pocket and pulled out his Poltava, Phillip and Sarah's eyes growing wide. Slowly, butt-first, he put it on the counter, the enameled dragonfly on the grip flashing in the sun.

The sportsman, skeptical, picked it up and looked it over. "What's this?" he said as he turned it around in his hands. He blinked and looked it over again, his interest growing by the second. "This looks to be a Poltava. Not a knock-off. This seems to be the real thing. A rare beauty, too." He whistled. "You kill somebody for this?"

Kay shook his head.

"Ah, well, none of my business who you killed over a treasure like this one. So, you'd like to bet your Poltava against an item in the vault, would you? Very well; I think we can deal. Any particular one strike your interest?"

The dirty courtesans returned, and this time, the sportsman was too absorbed to run them off. They looked at Kay's Poltava with wonder. One of them skillfully tried to steal it, and, with a click, the sportsman drew a long dueling pistol and put it up her nose. She skulked off. Before long the Watch converged and had her in chains, dragging her off to who knows where.

Kay, a bit put off, described the piece he wanted—a small, silver, doughnut-like device. The sportsman dispatched a runner and, soon, a contingent of the Watch approached the stand. They had several items from the vault matching Kay's description. They displayed the items for Kay, and he pointed; the Watchman on the right had Sam's Doughnut—just as he had seen it from Wiln, small, silver, made in an organic-looking, twisting sort of design. It wasn't really much to look at in person.

"That look to be the one?"

"It does."

The sportsman smiled and turned his head. "Looks like you've got an esteemed audience." He nodded away toward Leap manor. Standing on one of the flat-topped terraces, there was a huge man in a long black coat.

"That's Lord Xerin up there a-watchin', our goodly host," the sportsman said. "He's interested in how this plays out. He's never had a Poltava in his vault before."

Kay and Sarah looked up. He recognized the man from his vision of the future. The dark Lord of Rostov who will lead the House in ruin, again. There he was, right up there on the terrace.

"So then," the sportsman said. Are we agreed, the Poltava against this device? Winner take all?"

Kay thought a moment and shook his head. "I have another thought. My Poltava is quite valuable—a real find and probably worth twenty-times the value of the silver item. What say we simply trade up—a straight swap of goods and be done?"

The sportsman was disappointed. "I'd say be off. This isn't a market or a pawnshop. If you want to trade, go down the street and bargain for tissues to cry into. This is a place of sport. We bet—winner take all."

"I imagine, sir, that, at this point, any shell that I pick will not have a pea under it."

The sportsman was enraged. "You calling me a cheat, boy?"

"I'm calling you a businessman. Mere chance is bad for business."

The sportsman's ire diminished a little. He chuckled and leaned back. "Now, sir, are we going to play, or are we not?"

Some of the dirty courtesans watching became restless. "C'mon, Charlie, play. Play!"

Kay ignored them.

"We are not." Kay pulled his Poltava off the counter and put it back into his pocket. The courtesans gasped. The sportsman was shocked and drew his dueling pistol again.

The Watch surged forward and seized Kay by either shoulder. "You are under arrest!" one of them said.

"For what?" Kay cried.

"For theft. You cannot take an item off the table once bet—that is the law! The Poltava now, by law, belongs to House Rostov. You will be taken for trial, and then executed."

"What?" Kay said struggling.

As the Watch began trying to chain Kay up, the young Watchman they had spoken to earlier with the large triangle hat returned, his mickalmick making barking sounds like a dog. "What's going on here?" he asked.

"This man's to be tried and executed for taking a bet item off the countertop."

"Come on, Jessum," the young Watchman said. "The gentleman here is obviously new to Rostov, and wasn't aware of the serious nature of taking a bet item off the table. Give the 'Charlie' a break, how about it? He's probably got a lot more coin to spend, which he won't be able to do so if he's dead. Right?"

"Phender," the Watchman spat. "You milquetoast whore-seed. I'd expect such womanly behavior from one such as you! The Poltava now belongs to House Rostov, as does his un-spent coin. He will be tried and executed—no exceptions."

Phillip and Sarah pulled their Poltavas and got the drop on the Watch.

"More Poltavas!" somebody cried. "Look!"

Guns: pistols of all kinds, energy weapons, rusted Dee-Dees, sonic lashes and a whole host of other nasty-looking weapons emerged from everywhere and were leveled at Kay, Phillip and Sarah.

The young Watchman named Phender rolled his eyes. His little mickalmick made a small barking sound again.

19—Tellerran of Monama

Under Ennez's care, the Monama girl improved a bit. Her system, though, was in turmoil. So far from Kana, her body was slowly shutting down. He, with Davage's help, managed to remove the invisible collar stitched into her neck and gave it to the Sisters for examination, along with the prism Davage had collected.

She hadn't said anything since being brought aboard the *New Faith*. They gave her clothes to wear, which, she put on and a blanket for her to wrap up in—Davage and Sygillis knowing from Lady Sammidoran that Monamas liked it warm. Ennez brought in a small heater, and she sat next to it in her baggy donated clothes, shivering under her blanket.

After a day, Davage and Syg joined her in her room.

She hadn't slept in the bed, and the food that the orderlies had brought in for her sat uneaten. She just huddled in a corner next to the heater, curled into a pathetic ball.

Davage sat down and looked at her. Syg also sat.

They noted her plates of uneaten food. "Ma'am, you've not eaten since you've been aboard, and who knows how long before that even. You must be hungry. Please eat."

She didn't react.

"You needn't be frightened. You're safe here."

She gazed at them from under her mane of black hair and said a few words in her Monama language.

"Can you understand us, Ma'am?"

She didn't react.

Davage stood and went to the holo-terminal. He pressed a few buttons, and a woman in a Fleet lieutenant's uniform appeared.

"Fleetcom," she said.

"Fleet, well met. We have with us a guest who does not speak much of the common vernacular. We require a translator, please."

"Aye, sir. Can you tell us what language your guest is speaking?"

"I'm not entirely certain. Our guest is a Monama, if that helps."

The Lt. punched a few buttons. "Aye, sir, stand by." The Fleet header came up for a few moments, then a crewman sitting in a crowded cube room somewhere at Fleet popped up.

"Crewman Laval here, sir," he said in a distinctive Zenon burr.

"Well met, crewman," Davage replied. "We have a Monama guest here who does not speak League common. We are hoping you might translate for us."

He saw the Monama woman huddled in the corner and spoke up, speaking some sort of Monama tongue. Upon hearing more familiar words, she pricked up her ears and became a bit more lucid. She said a few things back to the crewman on the screen.

"Captain, she is speaking Conox. It's one of a family of related languages spoken by the Monamas. I am most proficient in Anuie, but I can get by well enough."

"Excellent. We appreciate your help. Can you ask the lady her name, please?"

They exchanged a few words. "Her name is Lady Tellerran of the Fphenook tribe. She would like to know your name, sir."

Davage turned to her. "I am Davage, Lord of Blanchefort, and captain of this vessel. With me here is my countess, Sygillis of Blanchefort." Syg bowed to her.

Though fearful, she smiled a little in response and pushed her hair out of her face.

"Crewman, can you ask her why she's not eaten? We are very concerned about her."

More banter back and forth. "Captain, she says she doesn't feel good. She says she thinks the Elder foods presented to her will make her sicker."

"Then please ask her what we can bring her that she will eat?"

The crewman and Tellerran exchanged more words. "She says she would like some Gesser. She thinks she can eat that and not get sick."

Davage smiled. "Com," he said looking up.

"Com here, sir," came the business-like reply.

"Com, please ask Lord Ottoman to prepare a fine dish of Gesser as soon as possible. Have it brought to room 10-6 when it's ready."

"Aye, sir."

"Sir, as Conox isn't an overly exotic language, I'm uploading the programming for an endecar that you may use to speak directly to her. It should be ready for you in a few minutes. They're very simple to use. It will create two voice cones, one in League common and the other in Conox. All you need do is speak into it."

"Thank you, crewman; if we require anything further, we'll com the Fleet."

The Crewman's image disappeared from the screen, and Tellerran appeared to panic for a moment. She cringed and huddled back into the corner, shivering under her blanket again.

They spent an awkward few minutes in silence as they waited for the endecar and the food to arrive. At last, the door opened, and an orderly brought in the endecar. It was a small device composed of a black disk with two trumpets, one red, the other blue, protruding from either end. The orderly turned the device on and showed them how to use it.

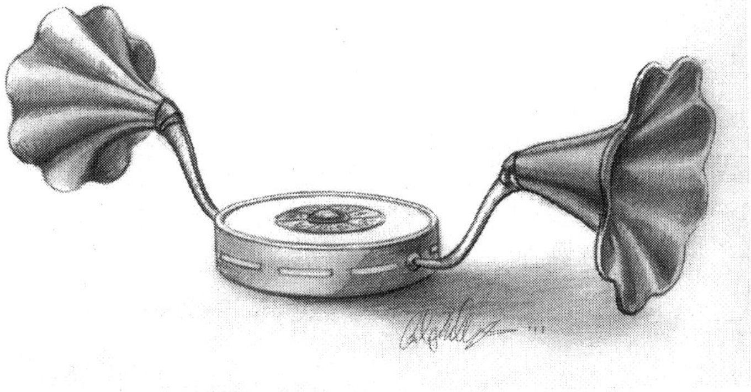

"The blue end will accept sounds and repeat back in League common; the red one will do the same in Conox." The orderly then left. Davage placed the endecar on the table and pointed the red trumpet toward her. He leaned down and spoke. "Can you understand me, Lady Tellerran?"

She seemed surprised and fascinated at the same time. Slowly, she got out of the corner and seated herself, still huddling under her blanket. "Yes. Yes, I can," came a slightly synthesized voice out of the blue trumpet. "What wonders you Elders create. I've never seen anything like this."

"Yes, quite. I've never used a device like this either. It seems to work well. Are you cold, Lady Tellerran?"

She nodded. "I'm freezing."

Davage got the portable heater and placed it near her on the table. "Does that help, ma'am?"

"Yes. Thank you."

"So," he said, trying to break the ice. "You speak Conox; is that right?"

"Yes."

"I've not heard of Conox before."

"My tribe speaks it, and a few others do as well. Do you speak any languages, other than the common?"

"I speak Vith. I can write in it as well. Does Conox have its own alphabet?"

She nodded. "It didn't used to have an alphabet until only recently. And we use the common alphabet."

Davage then tried to deepen the conversation and capture her full attention. "My son's *Cerri-Tela* speaks Anuie, I believe."

She seemed quite astonished. "*Cerri-Tela?* I know that word. Your son is seeing a Monama girl? Is she a Zerb or Minzer? No, she must be a Cardinal."

Syg seated herself at the table and spoke into the trumpet. "No, ma'am, she is an Astralon."

Tellerran thought about it. "Astralons are mean. They don't like other Monamas. Think they're better than the other tribes, like mine who speak Conox. I'm sorry. I didn't mean to speak ill of your son's *Cerri-Tela.*"

She sat there and puzzled for a moment. Davage could see she was full of questions. "Your son's *Cerri-Tela?* How did they come together?"

"She said she'd dreamed of our son since she was a little girl. Her grandmother was our personal seeress, and we gave her permission to visit whenever she wished."

"And she sought him out?"

"She did."

Tellerran looked dumbfounded. She grappled with the notion. "I once dreamed of an Elder boy, but I never had the resolve to leave the fog." She seemed lost in remembrance.

A moment later, several orderlies brought in a large plate of steaming hot Gesser, silverware and a tankard of water. Davage thanked them, and they left.

The Gesser looked like a pile of black beans on a hot bed of something dark and fibrous. Davage secretly hoped he didn't have to eat any now to get her to start.

"Come now," Davage said. "You'll want to eat it while it's hot. I'm told that's how it is best. Our chef made this just for you. I'd hate to see it all go to waste."

Tellerran picked up her silverware and scooted in front of her plate. She then looked over her shoulder once or twice.

Syg pitied the poor girl. "Please, miss, eat. You're safe here, we promise. Nobody is going to hurt you."

She grabbed the endecar and slid it a little closer to where she was sitting. She then began eating, trying to hide the fact that she was ravenous.

Clearly famished, Tellerran finished the first plate in no time, and Davage called for another serving. A second plate soon arrived, and Tellerran tucked into it. As her hunger was slaked, she became a bit more talkative. The endecar seemed to be a security blanket for her, as she kept touching and adjusting its position on the table.

"Thank you for the meal, my Lord. It was very good," she said into the endecar.

"You're welcome. Are you still feeling sick?"

She nodded. "It's space, being so far from home. My people don't live long in space."

"We're going to arrange transport for you back to Kana, and we will return you to your home. Would you like that?"

She looked at her hands. "My family won't accept me. I was taken, and I am considered dead. They will consider me a Berserkacide, whether I'm one or not. There's no place for me there anymore."

She looked up at them with her black eyes. "You shouldn't have brought me here. It's not safe. I don't want to hurt anybody. Better to have left me where I was and let me die."

"What sort of talk is that?" Davage said. "If you're worried about becoming a Berserkacide, I can assure you that won't happen. We've removed the prisms that were attached to your neck—we've learned a great deal in the past few days."

Again, she sat there astonished. "My Shockers, you took my Shockers off?" A mixture of wonder and fear filled her face. She felt about her neck and shoulders with her hand.

"Shockers?" Davage said. "Is that what you call them, those odd prisms?"

Tellerran was terrified. "We're not allowed to take those off. We're not allowed to touch them. That's an unforgivable sin. To remove the Shockers means instant death."

Davage smiled. "Instant death? Yet, here you are."

"They'll come for me. You can't stop them."

"'Them?' You must be referring to those monstrous beings who attacked Lord Crossland and my Countess."

"Yes. They watch us all the time, and they make us do terrible things. We are their slaves. We have always been their slaves. I can say no more."

"No longer, for you are free."

"I'm not free. None of us are free. I am a slave. Your son's Astralon woman—she is a slave, too. They came and pulled me and my sister and my brothers out of our warm beds, and they brought us to this place and left us there, tied together. There is nothing we can do. They watch us—always. They'll punish us. They'll shock us!" She cringed in sadness. "My poor brothers! My sister ..."

Davage tried to comfort her. "I saw them when they tried to turn you into a Berserkacide. I saw them open a Gamma-band portal, step through it, and then depart. I know where they hide now. We are wise to them and have set up defenses. The Sisters aboard this vessel are on vigilance for them, even at this moment. Those people cannot harm you any longer. My heart is with you, and your departed kin, but, perhaps, something good may come of this. Perhaps, together, we will put an end to it, and your brothers and sister needn't have died in vain."

Tellerran looked around, looking for hidden people who weren't there.

"So, please, Lady Tellerran, it is very important that you tell us anything you can. We do not wish to see any others harmed by these fiends, but we are sorely lacking in information, and we need your help."

"They'll punish us!"

"There will be no punishment. We will protect you."

Tellerran looked like she wanted to start talking, but she stopped herself. "You can't fight them. They cast spells which paralyze you. They cannot be fought."

Syg moved around the table and put her arm around Tellerran. She adjusted the endecar. "Lady Tellerran, our son was attacked by these creatures, and I blamed Lady Monama. I was angry and frightened, and I blamed her. I see now that I was wrong, that it wasn't her fault. In the necropolis, they came at me, and pulled me into their horrid realm. It was a dark, an alien landscape, the sky full of stars that I didn't recognize. I could barely see, and there they were, several of them—monsters and demons all. They laughed and were eager to have at me. They tried to cast spells, and there, alone, I fought them. I fought back, and I killed them—I killed every last one who was there. These beasts are not invincible, they can be beaten. Look at me—I am small, and I beat them, and I made them fear me as I did it."

Tellerran gawked at Syg with a mixture of fear and disbelief.

Syg gestured towards Davage. "My Lord knows what to look for now, and he will see if they dare to come. He can see anything. He saw the prism around your neck and got it off. He watches over you and, if they come, we will take care of them. So, please, trust us. We want to help you. You are our friend, and we want to help you, to free you."

Tellerran turned to Davage. "You can do that? You can see them?" Hope welled up in her face.

"Yes, I can," Davage confirmed. "I promise you."

✶ ✶ ✶ ✶ ✶

Clutching her blanket, speaking slowly into the endecar, Tellerran began a long oratory, and Davage and Syg held her long-nailed hand as she talked.

"We have been slaves to them for ages. They once roamed Kana in great, mirthless cities. They pretend to be beings like us, but they are not. They are shapeless and changeable, making themselves into whatever they choose.

"Long ago, we were evil, and we worshipped a Horned God in his temple deep in the earth. Then, the Gods in Jade and Sapphire came and took the evil from us in exchange for our second pair of arms. We turned our backs on the Horned God and lived by our lake where it is warm and we were a happy people. The Horned God was angry and set his angels against us. They took our people into their windowless laboratories and experimented on us—tortured us. Treated us like cattle. They built into us the Heart Trigger, a genetic code in our tissues that, once activated, turns us back into what we once were—Berserkacides. They sew the Shockers into our flesh and tell us never to take them off on pain of death. They come and take us, use us as warriors in faraway places against enemies whose names we do not know. Worlds have fallen under our claws, all for the sake of these angels, these Shapeless People, who make others do the fighting for them. We prayed for deliverance, but the gods told us we were evil, and this was our punishment."

"But," Davage said, "your people are so strong, so fast. Why didn't you fight back?"

"We cannot. They cannot be beat. They killed the Anuians, the greatest among us."

Davage knew what this was: conditioning. They had been conditioned to be afraid of these beings, whoever they are, over many millennia. And that hold, that conditioning, was not going to be broken easily.

Tellerran continued. "Then you came with your Elders, and they were afraid. They destroyed their cities in clouds of fire and fled. They left us on Kana near our beloved, warm lake and we rejoiced at our deliverance. But they came back, watching us, hiding in the shadows, telling us to do things. They watch us always, and if we told and gave away their secret, they swore to kill all of us—every last Monama. And so, under their heel, we have lived keeping to ourselves, doing what we are told by our tormentors from afar.

"There were centuries when they didn't come at all, and we rejoiced. We forgot the terror under which we had lived and the Horned God in the ground. We began to stretch out our hands, to embrace you Elder people, for you appear to be good folk, and we find you so beautiful. We began to share our gift of prophesy. We wanted to seek you out and share our dreams with you—love you, like your son's *Cerri-Tela*, who did something few of us have the courage to do. But, in the last few decades, the Horned God's angels began coming again with frequency, taking us from our houses, from our beds. And they make us become Berserkacides. They make us spy on you—lie to you. When they come for us, like they did for me and my sister and my brothers, we never come back. I saw my death at their hands, tied up in the vault with my sister and my brothers. My soul died into Head Swarm. I was resigned to it though I didn't want to hurt anyone. All I wanted to do is go home, and now I can't even do that."

Davage lifted her chin. "These monsters that they send—Lord Crossland's son, the Countess, what are they?"

"They are demons that they create in their Tanks; they are their generals and their soldiers—laughing and chiding. They torment us, kill us for pleasure, use us and then discard us."

Tellerran lowered her head. "I just want to go home."

Davage gave her a pat on the head. "We will take you home, Lady Tellerran. You have given us much useful information. We will discover who these people are, and we will put a stop to it. Get some rest and fear not. We will protect you."

Davage and Syg started to leave the room. As they approached the door, Tellerran ran forward, dropping her blanket. She put her arms around Davage's legs. She started speaking, but it was in Conox. Syg picked up the endecar and handed it to her. She held onto it with both hands.

"I saw my fate, and that of my brothers and my sister. We always know when we are going to die. I saw myself dying as a Berserkacide, and I was resigned to it. I was in Head Swarm. I never saw you coming to help me, to risk yourselves for me. Thank you, my Lord, Great Countess. Thank you for protecting me, for standing over me ..."

She wept and they knelt down and comforted her.

20—The DEATHLOKK

The standoff in Rostov seemed to have lasted quite a while. Phillip pointed his Poltava at one of the Watch, who had a throbbing Tartan energy gun pointed at Kay. Sarah had her blue Poltava pointed at another Watchman, who had his dingy-looking pistol pointed at Phillip.

"So, what's going to happen here?" one of the Watch said. "There's no way out of this; why not lower your weapons?"

"Why not lower yours?" Sarah asked.

"You have broken the law."

"It's a stupid law. You've got people here betting their children over a throw of the dice and selling Remax tablets to addicts, yet you're willing to get into a shoot-out with us over a breach in betting protocol?" she argued.

The young Watchman named Phender again tried to diffuse the situation. "Look, Jessum, if we keep imprisoning and executing visitors to Rostov, we'll not have any customers left. I say let's let these people be on their way."

Jessum scowled at him, raised a small holocam, and took a scan of Kay, Phillip and Sarah. He then backed away into the crowd of people with drawn weapons.

Kay, standing there by the counter, was the only one in sight without a drawn weapon. Slowly, he picked up Sam's Doughnut and held it in his hands, feeling its weight.

Sam's Doughnut.

Once again, the sportsman pointed his dueling pistol at the back of Kay's head. Sarah covered him with her Poltava. "You're calling the thunder down upon you, Sonny-Jim!"

"It might seem odd to you now," Kay said studying it, "but one day, this could be a place of great learning and enlightenment. A place where people will come from all over and want to live and raise their families—not to fester and throw their lives away. A great city of white stone could stand here marveled by all," he said.

"How do you know that?" Phender asked.

"I've seen it. More 'razzle dazzle' that you touched upon earlier."

"Rostov is as it is. Who are you to judge us?" the sportsman asked, angry.

"Me? Nobody. I'm nobody at all," Kay replied. He looked at the sportsman. "You want to make a bet? I'll bet I can do something you've never seen before."

"Slim chance of that, Sonny-Jim," the Sportsman replied.

Kay set the silver device down and allowed his Sight to fall away. Back in time it went, through the ages.

He turned his gaze north. Eventually, he found what he wanted. It didn't take him nearly as long as he thought.

With an odd movement, Kay reached out, as if he were pulling on something. The Watch tensed, and one of them cocked the hammer of his weapon.

Suddenly, two huge creatures emerged in the dingy street in front of Kay. They were at least fifteen feet tall, mostly naked, and multi-armed and multi-breasted. One had twelve arms, the other eight.

Haitathe, from thousands of years ago.

The Rostovs looked around for a moment, perplexed. The people on the street turned their gaze to them and were shocked. The sportsman screamed as they towered over him.

One of the giants heard the scream and kicked at it, leveling the stand, causing Kay to leap out of the way, his gaze almost faltering.

All at once, the giant Haitathe, part man, part woman, began kicking and punching at anything near them. The crowd flailed about, people screamed, the report of many guns erupted. The Watchmen scattered. Soon, the entire city was in turmoil as the giants splintered the drab structures with their delicate, yet brutally powerful fists. They swung boards, knocked down shacks and tossed people high into the air. They roared with fiendish delight as bullets and energy beams bounced off their slender, pale bodies. Occasionally, they picked up struggling persons and devoured them. The whole walled enclosure was like a huge playpen for them.

In a killing frenzy, they both began growing. Soon, they were nearly twice as tall as when they started, looming, stomping, smashing and devouring.

Kay kept his gaze fixed on them, not taking his eyes off—not blinking. As long as he kept his gaze fixed on them, they would remain. They would remain until he wished them gone and looked away. It was hard work, though, tiring and easy to let slip.

The sportsman emerged from the ruins of his stand, came up from behind and pointed his dueling pistol at Kay. Kay couldn't look away; he had to concentrate on the Haitathe, or they would vanish, and the three of them would be surrounded in a hostile city focused on them.

POW! Sarah gunned him down.

A Watchman made to shoot Kay with an old Hit-Six frag-lock.

POW! Phillip got him with his green and brown Poltava.

Bullets flew from Sarah's and Phillip's tiny but powerful Poltavas. People dove for cover. As incoming and outgoing lead and energy lances whizzed by, Sarah was sure she saw Kay get hit once or twice, but he didn't seem fazed. He stood lock still concentrating hard on the Haitathe.

The two Haitathe headed west, toward Leap Manor, destroying everything in their path, a fireworks display of energy shots and gunfire following them in a colorful cloud.

Sarah and Phillip pulled Kay away, toward the gates.

One of the remaining Watchmen drew a bead on Kay with his Redwagon energy gun and aimed at his head.

There was a shot, and the Watchman fell dead, the Redwagon clattering from his hand.

Phender, the young Watchman with the large hat, stood there holding his smoking Dare, and quickly put it away. "That true, what you said?" he asked Kay.

"Yes," he replied, his voice distant.

He looked around watching the two Haitathe giants tear up the city, killing and stomping with every step. "Did you summon these beasts?"

"I did. I'm sorry."

He looked around at the destruction. "I can't say that I blame you. My older brother was going to have you killed simply because you didn't want to get cheated by my uncle Ebenezer who's never run a fair game in his life. I can't say that we don't deserve it. It's not like this place hasn't been leveled to ground many times for one reason of another—be it by monster, brigand, lout or infuriated Sister. I'm sick of this, embarrassed by it. Maybe a fresh start would do this place well this time."

He picked up Sam's Doughnut and handed it to Kay. "Take the piece and get out of here. You better run, and you better watch it. Lord Xerin of Rostov is not a forgiving, or a forgetting, man."

Somebody fired a Dee-Dee, blowing off one the twelve-armed Haitathe's arms. It bellowed in rage and trawled the streets for the culprit.

Another Dee-Dee shot took the head off of the other Haitathe. Headless, it staggered for a moment, then a new head grew back in place of the old—a totally different-looking head with black hair.

Like two huge spiders, they began scaling the black walls of Leap Manor.

Activity on one of the high towers of Leap Manor caught Kay's attention, and he almost let his gaze slip again. The large man in the dark coat stood on the tower, apparently quite agitated. Someone joined him on the tower roof—it was Jessum, the Watchman who had tried to arrest Kay. He handed Lord Xerin a holo-viewer and pointed in their general direction.

Four servant girls, each holding onto the corners of a large red pillow, appeared on the tower and approached Lord Xerin. He reached down and pulled a huge, nasty-looking black rifle off the pillow.

"You three better get out of here!" Phender said. "That's Lord Xerin up there, and that's the DEATHLOKK he's holding. All he's got to do is want to hit you with it, and he will. Jessum just showed him your picture. You could be a continent away, and he'd still hit you in the chest with it."

Phender unchained his mickalmick. "Gersey," he said to it, "get them to the city gates. I'll do my best to cover you—my very best!" With that, the mickalmick reached out like lightning and seized the three of them with three of his six tails. He held them aloft, Kay doggedly focusing his concentration on the Haitathe.

"Who are you?" Phillip asked as Gersey began bearing them away.

"I'm Lord Phender of Rostov," he said drawing another Dare from his sash. "Maybe I liked the sound of what you said. Maybe we can be something after all."

Gersey moved fast, slithering on his belly like a greased rocket, through the chaotic crowded street and throngs of panicked people, toward the gates of the city. Watchmen converging from all sides took potshots at them as they passed; Sarah and Phillip, held aloft, returned fire.

Kay concentrated on the Haitathe and held onto Sam's Doughnut.

Far away, Lord Xerin, holding his DEATHLOKK, fired it into the air with a deafening, mortar-like report. After a moment or two, one of the Haitathe fell dead, struck to the chest, the shot having made a terrible hole there.

Nonchalantly, he reloaded, and fired again. Another massive report, and the last Haitathe fell dead. Kay quieted his Sight and let them fall back, dead, into time.

Ahead, several of the Watch had created a barricade in the direction of the city gates. They were cutoff.

A Watchman with a DeeDee rifle laid a bead on Sarah. There was a CRACK, and he fell, taken down by Lord Phender some distance away.

Gersey extended his three remaining tails, running on them in stilt-like fashion. He cleared the barricade and continued.

Kay, free of the Haitathe, concentrated and Cloaked all three of them, Gersey, too.

Ahead, the city gates, were not a hundred yards distant.

Kay Sighted and was appalled. He saw the man in the dark coat holding the DEATHLOKK.

Then he saw DEATHLOKK bullets zeroing in on them.

"Phillip! Sarah! Get your SAPPS out and make a shield. Hurry!!"

Phillip and Sarah took off their SAPPS and quickly formed them into two broad, semi-convex shields. They pointed them skyward just in time for a massive shot to come raining down on them from above. Even though it was just a rifle bullet hitting the shields, it hit with the explosive power of a large grenade. Gersey was knocked off balance, and he skittered to a stop just short of the gates.

"Creation, that just about broke my arm!" Phillip said, trying to hold up his shield.

Gersey released them and slithered away, falling out of Cloak.

Another shot came whistling in, and Sarah screamed with the blow. Even Cloaked, it didn't matter. All Lord Xerin had to do was want to hit them, and the DEATHLOKK would connect—no matter where on Kana they were. This was a gun from which one couldn't hide; as long as one was outside, one was vulnerable.

Another deadly shot. "Kay, we need cover! My SAPP can't handle much more!" Phillip yelled, struggling to hold his SAPP up. They were pinned down, unable to advance.

Kay rolled out from under the shield and allowed Lord Xerin into his Cloak—such was the improvement of his skill.

Now Lord Xerin could see him plain as day.

From a distance, they stared at each other.

Kay set down the silver device and zeroed in on the man standing on the tower. Lord Xerin saw him and laughed. Casually, he loaded the long DEATHLOKK with a fresh bullet. Apparently, it was a single-shot weapon.

Kay drew his purple Poltava and aimed. Lord Xerin again laughed out loud, seeing Kay point the tiny gun at him. Xerin probably knew his weapons, and he probably had heard about the power and accuracy the Poltava was reputed to have. But still, it was nothing more than a short-barreled pistol that probably had an accurate aimable range of fifty feet.

They must have been at least a half mile apart, Kay's chances of hitting him at this range were virtually nil. He finished loading and held his arms out to his side, inviting Kay to fire, giving him a free shot, with the DEATHLOOK clutched in his ham-like fist like a huge, black matchstick. Then, once Kay fired and missed, he would pull the DEATHLOKK's trigger and blast Kay into yesterday.

Kay zoomed in with his Sight, adjusted his gun, and pulled the trigger.

POW!

Lord Xerin was hit right between the eyes. The power of the Poltava's shot was such that the bullet entered his skull, scrambled his brains, and exited the back in a confusion of destroyed tissue, where it continued on and eventually fell into the sea. Arms waving, Xerin stumbled backwards and, doing a half-back flip, went over the side of Leap Manor, down several hundred feet into the crashing waves of the sea below—his DEATHLOKK falling with him in a lazy twist. Jessum, the Watchman standing nearby was stunned. He looked over the side to see where Lord Xerin had fallen.

POW!

He, too, was hit in the back of the skull by a second shot from Kay's Poltava; a few moments later, he, too, was falling over the side of Leap Manor, eventually his body floating in the surf, nudging against Lord Xerin's.

Kay put his gun away. The three of them left the city as fast as they could, just as a contingent of the Watch came surging out of the city gates looking for them. The Watch had mickalmicks with them that, supposedly, could detect Cloaked people; however, they were looking in the wrong direction, the wide open space outside of the walls being too much ground to search.

As they made their way from the black city and its dead patriarch, Kay was satisfied that the House of Rostov had, most likely, a better future ahead.

Conox, or "Lesser Monamas" in tribal garb

21—The Trouble with Lon

They made their way back toward the *Goshawk*. Moving in what they thought was a clever and silent fashion, they approached the waiting vessel and went in with their prize, Sam's Doughnut, safely in hand.

Somebody was sitting inside waiting for them. Trigger happy after Rostov, three Poltavas came out of their coats.

They couldn't believe it. Sitting there on the back bench was Lord Lon of Probert, Kay's and Phillip's friend from Arden, his little triangle hat in his hands, his leggings and hose-socks, his buckle shoes splayed apart at an irregular angle. He was wearing his usual big Probert coat—green this time.

He was asleep, mouth open, snoring.

"Lon?" Sarah called, putting her Poltava away. He didn't react.

"Lon!" she yelled, kicking him.

He woke, snorting to life, looking around in a daze. He focused on them and smiled. "Oh, hello—I must have nodded off." He stopped suddenly and checked his breath.

Shaking his head, Phillip dropped into the pilot's chair, shut the hatch, and began firing the ship up, eager to put some distance between them and Rostov.

"Where in Creation did you come from?" Kay asked.

Lon smiled, feeling proud of himself. "I was keen to speak to you, Kay. I heard you were in the Wiln area of Remnath, and I came hither. I inquired at the various inns and so forth to see if you had checked into any. I had the good fortune to locate the lovely inn you had checked out of this morning. Then, as it happened, I saw the *Goshawk's* departing silhouette against the sky and, using simple arithmetic, zeroed in on your approximate location. I then hired a coach to bring me out here. I used a stealth code to open the hatch and get in. I hope you don't mind."

Phillip jerked the ship into the air and banked east. "You saw our silhouette, Lon? But how did you find the ship? It's Cloaked."

"I know—I was wearing my No-Cloak goggles."

Kay stood there and shook his head. Only Lord Lon. "Anyway, it's good to see you, Lon."

"And you, Kay." He put his hat back on. "Which brings me to my point. I was wanting to discuss something with you, if I may?"

Kay went into the cargo hold and put the silver piece into a small chest. He then came forward and sat down across from him. Sarah opened the cooler. "You want anything to drink, Lon?"

"Whatever you're having, Sarah, is fine. Thank you."

Sarah pulled out a few cans of red Gasol and handed one to him and Kay. Lon popped it open and began drinking.

"So, what's on your mind, Lon?"

He straightened up a bit, swallowing his drink. "Kay, I want to discuss Lady Sammidoran of Monama with you."

Sarah's ears pricked up, and Phillip turned his head a little from the cockpit, trying to listen.

"Lady Sammidoran of Monama?" Kay said. "What about her?" Kay had a sinking feeling. Whatever was on Lon's mind it couldn't be good.

"You mean the creepy lady in black I was going to beat up at the 'Falling in Love' ball a few months back?" Sarah chimed in, playing dumb.

"Yes, the very one," Lon replied laughing. He put his drink down and darkened a bit. "I want to know what your relationship with Lady Sammidoran is, Kay. I want to know what there is between the two of you. There is something, I know there is."

Sarah cut in. "Well, Lon, she wanted to get with Kay, you know, but, when she found out that I was going to knock her teeth out if she tried, she backed away, and we haven't heard from her since."

Lon wasn't buying. He sat there with his drink and looked at Kay with an odd intensity.

Kay stammered—Sam had sworn him to secrecy. "My relationship with her, Lon? My relationship with Lady Sammidoran of Monama, if any, is rather private."

Lon wasn't going to be denied. "I demand to know, Kay. She has sought me out several times—she has a wonderful mind and a keen interest in technical matters. I believe that I find her lovely, intelligent, inquisitive and enchanting."

"Lon, what are you saying?"

"I'm saying that I have allowed myself, after a bit of introspection, to fall in love with the Lady Sammidoran. Yes, not only is she an exciting intellect, but she is most beautiful as well, and I wish to formally court her. But first—I know there is something between the two of you, and I want—*I demand*— to know what it is."

Kay made to say something but stopped—Sam's promise holding him back. Sarah chimed in for him. "Lon, Kay and Lady Sammidoran have been actively seeing each other for five years."

A frustrated wave passed over his face. He gritted his teeth.

"Five years?" he said. "Five years? I suppose, then, that the prospect of getting beaten up by you, Sarah, wasn't much of a consideration, was it?"

Sarah's mouth fell open in shock.

Lon focused on Kay, his face turning red. "Then why have you not announced yourselves? By the Elders, you looked like you were going to vomit at the ball when she started making eyes at you, Kay."

"Yes, Lon, I was just acting. I'm sorry."

Lon looked at his shoes. "You've been seeing her for five years, and you've not done her the courtesy of announcing your intentions to the League?" Lon was positively livid.

"Are you ashamed of her, is that it? Does her lowly status as a Monama give you pause? Is she not good enough for the mighty Lord of Blanchefort? Is she your secret whore, Kay?"

Kay's eyes flashed. "That will be quite enough, Lon."

Lon considered his words and continued. "I'm still waiting, Kay. Answer my question, or do you require Sarah to do it for you?"

Kay threw his hands up. "Yes, yes, we have been seeing each other for quite a long time. And I wanted to announce ourselves to the League long ago; if it were up to me, we would have been announced properly by now, but she never let me. She insisted that we keep it to ourselves, and I honored her request. Believe me; you don't want to know why she wanted it kept secret."

"It's a Monama thing, Lon," Sarah said.

Lon sat there in frustration. "Phillip, please land the ship. I don't think I fully believe you, Kay. And, for that matter, I'm not backing down. I have always been the novel friend, the nice, silly boy hanging in the wings—the person everybody likes but nobody loves. You and Phillip—you two could have virtually anybody you wanted—daughters of Great Houses lining up to throw their lot in for your hand. And what do I have—nothing but a shiny pin and a pat on the back from my latest scholastic achievement. I want to be that person, Kay, for Creation's sake. I want to be the man who gets the girl. And I have my hopes set on Lady Sammidoran, a Monama who couldn't hope to be on the same social level as the Great House of Blanchefort."

"Lon, what do you want me to tell you? I don't care about her standing or her House," Kay said, pleading.

Lon stood. "Phillip, in the Name of Creation, land the ship! I don't want you to tell me anything, Kay," he said reaching into his coat and pulling out his CEROS. "When Phillip lands the ship, we will step out and present our weapons."

"Lon!" Sarah cried. "You can't be serious!"

Phillip looked back, the *Goshawk* wobbling a little as he did. "Lon, I'm not landing the ship for this foolishness."

Lon was determined. "Then present, Kay. Do it now!"

Kay and Sarah were stunned. The ship lurched a little as Phillip whipped his head around again. Lord Lon, their friend from the time they were kids, the fellow who helped him design his CARG, now wanted to duel with Kay over Sam.

"Please put your weapon away," Kay said.

"Present, Kay, or I'll kill you unarmed. By Creation I will!"

Kay stood up. "Then kill me."

Lon was enraged. "The last time I spoke to her, she was in tears. She was inconsolable. What did you do to her? You must have done something!"

The thought of Sam in tears banged his heart. "We had had a fight, Lon. I accused her of all sorts of crimes. I was unreasonable, and I made her cry."

Lon's hand, the one holding the CEROS, shook. He then dropped it and sat back down on the bench. He looked angry, sad, and embarrassed as well.

Kay took Lon by the shoulders. "Was she all right, Lon? Was Sam ok?"

"She was upset about something—she avoided saying what."

Kay picked up his CEROS and handed it back to him. "I'm sorry about all this, Lon, and I'm sorry I couldn't bring you into my confidence. If I had known what you were feeling, I would have told you in advance. The last thing I want is for you to suffer. Sam wouldn't want that either; she likes you. In fact, she is keen to find somebody out there worthy of you."

Lon looked at his CEROS and gritted his teeth.

They sat there and stared at each other in silence—the only sound being the steady thrum of the *Goshawk's* engine.

After awhile the ship gave a loud thump, and Phillip moved some levers on the pilot's dash.

"Water," Lon said quietly.

"What?" Sarah asked.

"That thump—it probably was the super-condenser. It engaged, meaning the air suddenly became much more humid, which means we're over water."

Sarah shook her head. "Phillip, are we flying over water?"

"Yes," he responded.

Lon suddenly seemed consumed with emotion. It all came spilling out of him. "Look, all I wanted was someone I was sure nobody else did. A beautiful, intelligent woman, consigned to the dregs of League Society. I thought that nobody could possibly want her."

Kay leaned forward. "Don't sell yourself short, Lon, ever. You have talents and skills that few in the League could rival. I think you've convinced yourself that you loved Sam because you thought she was a safe choice—that there was no competition. If a Monama is what you truly want, then pursue one. They are good people, a strong people. Sam sought me out as a child, and I had the good fortune to win her love. Perhaps the same will be for you, if that's where your heart truly lies. A Monama girl could be dreaming of you right at this very moment, like Sam did with me. She has over twenty sisters, you know," Kay said.

Lon seemed to brighten a little. "I've ... I've been doing research on Monamas. It's a fascinating House. There isn't a whole lot out there regarding their private ways and habits. I, I even picked up a little Anuie to attempt to impress her."

Kay responded to him, in Anuie. *"Sam loves speaking in her mother tongue. She taught it to me."*

Lon replied. *"A pretty language to speak."*

"Sometimes she refuses to speak anything else. I never knew I could pick up a new language so fast. In fact, now that you're here, maybe you would like to assist us. It's one of those 'Monama habits', as you put it, that we are investigating even as we speak."

"You'll pardon me then, Kay, for being angry? For presenting my CEROS? Are we still friends, or have I ruined our friendship?"

"Of course I will, Lon; it's already forgotten. And, no, you could never ruin our friendship."

They embraced, Kay playfully jabbing Lon in his round Probert belly like he did when they were kids.

Sarah intervened. "Hey, what's going on? And, for the sake of those here who don't speak 'Sam', can we please talk normal?"

"Sure, Sarah," Kay said, still hugging Lon.

Phillip looked back and smiled. "It's a good thing you're making up back there; otherwise, I was going to have to knock some heads together."

"You fly the ship, Phillip, and I'll do the head knocking," Sarah replied.

Kay re-seated himself. "Now, let's to it. I know that Sam came to you some time back for assistance. What was she wanting specifically? Anything you could tell us will be of great help."

"She wanted detailed technical information on a lost machine that she'd been researching."

"Which machine?"

"A legendary machine built by the House of Want long ago. A machine called the *Oberphilliax."*

"What does the machine do?"

Lon settled himself and began chirping happily. "We had a spirited debate on just that very topic. Supposedly, and this is merely coffee-table conjecture, the machine creates a singularity between two or more separate points of temporality."

"What?" Sarah said.

"A time machine," Phillip said from the cock-pit.

Lon giggled, his belly rumbling. "Yes, that is the modern conclusion, though the machine's use is rather mysterious. I must say, Lady Sammidoran strongly disagreed. She said, in so many words, that the *Oberphilliax* is a device that allows degrees of separation in disjointed continuums to be thwarted safely and rejoined elsewhere without the benefit and limitations of a temporal anchorage. A theoretical impossibility. That is simply too ridiculous to contemplate, but she was adamant."

"I disagree," Phillip commented from the cockpit. "The Mana of Kind in a vacuum states that two separate continuums may be bridged should degrees of separation be properly severed and rejoined."

"But," Lon said, his excitement and enthusiasm growing, "but the degrees of separation have not been proved as an Actuality by the latest thoughts on quantum mechanics."

Kay felt his head starting to spin. Sarah also looked confused. "Gentlemen—a fascinating topic, but food for a later conversation. Can we sum up somehow? What did Sam say the machine does, in ten words or less?"

"By her account, it supposedly allows objects from separate time continuums to seamlessly merge, but that is just not possible. Such a thing would make it the Golden Goose of time travel."

"How on earth would Sam know something like that? So, it is a time machine?" Kay asked.

"No, Kay, that would make it a temporal bridge—very different and much more complex and desirable than a mere time machine. However, Lady Sammidoran's speculation is, at best, a fanciful bit of conjecture," Lon said.

Kay shook his head. "Is that all you talked with Sam about, Lon?"

"No, she wanted to know if such a machine could be built."

"And what was your response?"

"I told her no—impossible. The House of Want used an assortment of unique materials and machining methods that were lost when the House left the League centuries ago. Such a great loss of knowledge. Also, I told her that the power source for the unit is not generally known. I could see she was disappointed; she started crying right there at the cafe. I tried to cheer her by stating that there currently is an *Oberphilliax* already in existence. Its current location and the detailed specifics of the machine are manifested in a book, property of the Sisterhood of Light at Hiei, though that particular book is not available for research."

"There is?"

"Yes. Over lunch we did some vigorous Holo-research. The Science Ministry has a complete manifest of all printed materials in the Sisterhood's possession—as the Ministry often works hand-in-hand with the Sisters regarding various projects. I know my mother's Science Ministry codes, and I accessed their database."

"And you gave Sam the information?"

"I did. The name of the book and its exact shelf location at Hiei. I told her not to bother—the book's not available for reference. It's restricted for the time being."

Kay recalled the visit from the Sisters. Could Sam have broken into Hiei and stolen the book in question?

"Did she say why she was so interested in this particular machine?"

"She refused to say. Quite the secretive thing, isn't she?"

Kay smiled. "She sure is."

Lon sat there with a look of longing for a moment.

Sarah opened the *Goshawk's* holo-terminal and started a session. The familiar holographic gentleman popped up, wearing his long black coat and holding the red staff of knowledge.

"Access history: *Oberphilliax,*" Sarah said. Working the holo-terminal took practice. Kay, not much of a lined-in researcher, usually let Sarah do it. His sisters, Kilos and Hathaline, were expert at it. Sam, with practice, appeared to have gotten quite good as well.

The gentleman waved his staff and spoke in his slow, elegant voice. "*Oberphilliax,* ancient machine designed by Lord Revis, House of Want, 000009ax."

Next to the gentleman, a shimmering image of a dainty silver machine appeared. It was a slender archway about seven feet tall and three feet wide; its silvery legs and twisting crosspiece were designed in an organic, sinewy sort of style. It looked fragile—like something that should be used as a decoration in a garden path.

"What is function, *Oberphilliax?*"

"Query suspended—function *Oberphilliax* in contest and denied access."

"Countermand."

"No countermand possible."

Sarah huffed. Certain Ministries and, on occasion, the Sisterhood restricted information regarding various topics, and using the Holo could be a tiring and frustrating adventure. And, if you pushed the matter too much, said Ministries and, likely, the Sisters might become wise to your activities. A visit from the Sisters could be a possibility. Kay would rather look up information in old books.

"What is current status, *Oberphilliax?*"

"Current status, *Oberphilliax* ... Status—in dispute. One known unit constructed."

"Status, *Oberphilliax* known constructed unit."

"Status—unit thirded by order of the Sisterhood of Light, 000570ax."

Sarah was perplexed. "Thirded? The Sisters broke it into three pieces? Why didn't they just destroy it?"

"They probably couldn't—the House of Want was near Elder-Like in their knowledge. It was a great loss for the League when they left," Lon said.

"Where did they go?" Sarah asked.

"Unknown. I think they went to Cammara, you know, the old home world during the CX Epoch. I think they went back there."

Sarah returned to the Holo-net. "State location, thirded pieces of *Oberphilliax?*"

"Query suspended. Location of *Oberphilliax* restricted."

Sarah turned away from the terminal. "Well, that's that. Looks like we've run into a dead end."

Kay sat back and thought. "Sarah, I think the three portions of Sam's Trial are to recover the pieces of the missing *Oberphilliax*."

"Sam's what?" Lon asked.

"She is putting me to a Trial, Lon—it's some sort of Monama tradition. We've already accomplished one portion of the Trials, and two more await. I'm not clear as to her ultimate intent, but I believe she is guiding me into recovering parts of a strange device: a machine of some sort. Three parts to be precise. I am now convinced she's guiding us to recover the three pieces of the *Oberphilliax*."

"How could Sam know where they are?" Lon asked.

"There was a recent theft at the Sister's stronghold of Hiei. They weren't happy about it; they even shut Hiei down for a bit. They came to us asking if we knew anything about it."

"They came to our House, too," Lon said. "I was really scared. The Sisters scare me. I got sick."

Sarah laughed. "You got sick in front of the Sisters, Lon?"

"Well, if you must know, I got sick *on* the Sisters."

Kay laughed and clapped Lon on the shoulder. "Lon, I now believe that Sam was the perpetrator of the break in at Hiei. I believe that Sam, craving information, stole the book you mentioned to her."

Lon shook his head. "I won't believe that—she'd be throwing her life away."

Kay stood up. "You require proof? Sam is a stubborn little pistol. If she gets something into her head, there is no stopping her. Allow me." Kay went into the *Goshawk's* cargo hold and brought out a small chest. He opened it. Inside, the doughnut-shaped metallic piece he'd retrieved from the House of Rostov sat on its cushion. "This is the first piece, Lon—we just now retrieved it. Take a look. What do you think?"

"We've been calling it 'Sam's Doughnut'," Sarah added.

"Yes, yes, I see that."

Lon carefully took it into his hands. "Oh, this is most definitely a House of Want construction. Feast your eyes on the detail, the craftsmanship. This metal—it's an alloy of some sort. Wondrous." He pulled a set of goggles out of his green coat and adjusted several prisms. He then examined the device again, turning it over in his hands. "Yes, indeed, this is a treasure. Where did you get it again?"

"The House of Rostov; it was thrown in a vault full of gambled booty."

"Can you make anything out of it?" Sarah asked, sitting down next to him.

Lon sucked in his breath as he carefully looked over the device's silvery surface. "It's an alloy, as I said before. It's a solid piece, yet its construction is not solid—it's made up of millions of tiny interlocking pieces—amazing. Amazing!" He looked up, flabbergasted. "I must have this for study."

"After we're done with it, you can have it," Kay promised.

Lon adjusted his goggles. "I believe that twisting in this direction and applying a bit of pressure here…"

Suddenly, as Lon worked the device, it began to grow. Like a plant sprouting up out of the ground, it expanded in size until it was about six feet long. Lon had to turn it lengthwise so that it didn't go through the top of the *Goshawk*.

In comparing it to the flickering holo image on the terminal, it was clearly one of the legs supporting the machine's elegant arch. Without question, this was a portion of the legendary *Oberphilliax*. Lon worked the device, and it shrank back down to its former configuration.

"So," he said with sobriety, "you appear to be correct. Lady Sammidoran must have stolen the book from Hiei. I cannot stress the need for secrecy—should the Sisters find out, they will bring their wrath down upon her and her House."

"Yes," Kay said. "I'm certain all here can be counted on for our discretion."

Phillip turned from the cockpit. "Now that we know this information, if the Sisters ever Stare us, the jig will be up."

Lon smiled. "Oh no, no … there are ways around the Stare. My mother taught me. You think my mother, as a top scientist—an Imperator of the Science Ministry—contents herself with sticking to Sisterhood dogma and restrictions? If the Sisterhood knew what was rolling around in my mother's head, oh boy!"

Lon suddenly fell silent and looked around. "Forget I said that, okay? Anyway, there are techniques that can be applied to defeat a Stare. We'll discuss that in further detail later. Now," he said in full discovery-mode, "what about power?"

"I don't know. I suppose we'll handle that issue when we get to it."

"What is to be done with this machine once it's reassembled and properly powered?" Lon demanded.

"Unknown. With luck we'll have Sam back, and she may explain herself in more detail at that time. I don't know what Sam wanted with it."

"Where is Lady Sammidoran at the moment?" Lon asked, and Kay filled him in on the proceedings to date. He listened and nodded.

He looked at the piece of the *Oberphilliax* and seemed to burst with excitement. "May I come as well? I would greatly enjoy fetching the remaining parts, and you will probably need my help during the reassembly."

"Glad to have you, Lon," Sarah said.

"So, let's get me up to date. You have the first portion; where is the next one?"

"Don't know. I haven't been told yet. We're going to fly to Esther and await further instruction."

"And the final piece?"

"We haven't been given that clue yet, either."

"Oh, I see." He sat there for a moment, his mind spinning. "Power will be the big thing. It will be a crystal stone, about the size of my fist."

"I disagree," Phillip said. "Many known devices of the House of Want were solar powered."

"True, but this device is unlike many of their previous creations. I recall seeing a large stone mounted in the centerpiece of the machine on the Holo-display. That must furnish its power."

"What if it's just a decoration?" Sarah asked.

"A decoration?" Lon said, aghast. "I suppose that's what Lady Sammidoran was asking about when she came to me that second time."

"Come again, Lon," Kay said,

"She came to me and was very sad. My heart went out to her—that's when I decided that I wished to pursue her. After she calmed down a bit, she showed me a holo drawing of a large crystal and wanted to know if I thought it looked correct. I made some minor changes to it, and she thanked me."

"Did you ask her what she was doing with such a thing?" Kay asked.

"She said something about saving her heart for the future."

21—Bathloxi

With Lord Lon now in tow, they decided to head to the Esther region and await Kay's next set of instructions. It was maddening not knowing what was coming next or when the information would arrive. Kay felt a little nostalgic for the Gift trials, and he found himself missing the three Gifts who helped to train him, especially Cloak, who was the most like Sam—the things he had shared with her.

Before they could go to Esther, they had to make their way north and quickly stop in the city of Arden. Lon, never really straying too far from home for any length of time, had to check in and let his parents know what was going on and get a few things.

Probert Manor was partially a Vith ruin, partially a modern, progressive structure on the cliffs by the sea. Lon's father, Lord Milos of Probert, loved to keep up on the latest in styles and trends; in so doing, he kept adding onto the manor turning it into a mishmash of form and function. The newest structure on the grounds was a large lab he had built for Lady Branna, his wife.

Phillip set the *Goshawk* down near the cliffs. They all piled out, and Lon led them into the manor. Sitting them down in a comfortable study, he bolted up to his wing to get a few essentials. When he returned to the study, his mother, the Lady Branna of Probert, was with him.

Lady Branna was one of the League's top scientists—she being one of the four Grand Imperators of the Science Ministry. A tiny, blue-haired woman of the House of Pitcock line, she struck a regal figure. A scientist through and through, she was also a prolific inventor and innovator. Her contributions to League technology could not be denied or easily calculated, her lab often crackling with strange sounds and glowing with an odd light. Formerly, when she was still married to Lord Timon of Fallz, her battles with Lord Milos of Probert, the Stellar Fleet's chief engineer, were legendary, and rather humorous—she wanting to incorporate new technologies into his grand Fleet ship designs, and he telling her, publically, to 'buzz off'. She always swore that she'd have Probert rotting in her dungeon sooner or later, and he always replied that she was soon to have a lengthy stay in prison for war crimes against the League for her stupid ideas.

The dungeon for Probert.

Prison for Lady Branna.

The fact that she didn't have a dungeon at House Fallz didn't matter. She swore to build one just for him and stock it with all manner of blood-thirsty worms, lice and vermin to feast specifically on his flesh.

When her husband died, she found an immediate kinship with Milos of Probert, her old rival. Despite their combative relationship over the years, she'd always greatly respected him and admired his intellect—one to rival her own. He had been politely rejected in courtship by the Lady Poe of Blanchefort, and the two of them, lonely and evenly matched intellectually, soon struck up an unlikely friendship that blossomed into romance and then marriage. Relocating to Probert Manor,

Branna and Milos had four children—with the Lady Branna already having twelve from her previous marriage. Lon was their youngest and final child, so she swore.

Lord Lon had his father's mechanical and engineering skills and his mother's insatiable curiosity and need to constantly innovate. He, also, though a bit on the roundish side, had more of a Pitcock look to him than a Probert—which was a House known for their minds, not their good looks. In time, Lon, no doubt, would be a fine handsome fellow, but, at only seventeen, he still had a lot of the Puffies and wasn't overly suave with the ladies—another of his father's traits that he'd inherited.

He was the delight of his mother's eye. Countless times as he was growing up, his mother dragged the tiny Lon into the lab to show him something she'd created, and she was amazed how many times Lon instantly grasped what she had made and, sometimes, even improve upon it. Though a mother would never admit to having a favorite son or daughter, Lon was clearly Lady Branna's favorite—her pride and joy, and she doted on him in an embarrassing fashion.

"Lord Blanchefort," she said to Kay. "Your mother and father are aware of this 'field experiment,' are they?"

"Yes, my lady," Kay replied.

"And how long will Lon be gone?"

"Oh, it's difficult to say. Pending on our ... 'results' ... we should have him back in a week or so."

Lady Branna looked skeptical. "I see. Knowing you Vith like I do, I expect you'll be taking my Lon off somewhere to perform some brazen and foolhardy act. Will you assure me that whatever you are doing is perfectly legal?"

Kay laughed. "Oh, most certainly, my lady."

"Yes or no will do."

"Yes, our activities shall be perfectly legal."

"And, you will guarantee his safety, Lord Blanchefort, will you? You will personally look after him?"

"I will, my lady. I promise."

Lady Branna seemed satisfied, and, after a round of hugging and tossing his hair, she led him away to pack.

Sometime later, Lon returned, lugging a few small suitcases, a fresh blue Probert coat and freshly polished buckle shoes.

Lon endured a final round of hugging from his mother, and then they went outside and climbed back into the *Goshawk*, Lady Branna waving a hanky as Phillip lifted the ship away. Inside, Lon took over Kay's tiny cabin—Kay opting to sleep on one of the couches.

They then headed east to Esther to whatever awaited.

✶ ✶ ✶ ✶ ✶

They didn't have long to wait. As the *Goshawk* soared at altitude over Thirkill Bay near the mouth of the Kronos River, the ship fell into a thick storm cloud that brewed up out of nowhere—one that caused the *Goshawk's* screens and instruments to go totally dead.

Flying blind in the unnatural dark, Phillip struggled to keep the ship level.

Then, the hatch flew open, and several snaky tendrils of black shadow material twisted their way into the cabin. Quickly, one of them located Kay, wrapped around him as he drew his Poltava and pulled him out of the ship, the scrambling

Sarah and Lon unable to get to him in time.

Outside, in the moving, streaming dark, Kay was held fast. He couldn't breathe, couldn't get a lungful of air. Desperate, Kay Sighted, looking for the *Goshawk,* but he couldn't see it—it just wasn't there. He looked down, seeing through the murk, and didn't see Thirkill Bay below either.

The dense mist parted, and he found himself standing alone in an immense room, like a vast, squared-off cavern of carved rock plunged in darkness. It was huge, the ceiling being so high off the stony floor he had to use his Sight to see it clearly. The room was rectangular in shape, with the distant walls being lined with the fallen remains of gigantic idols, all toppled over and broken. In front of him, far away, was a platform or stage lined with stone pillars that went up to the ceiling. The place was oddly quiet. For some reason, he imagined this quiet colossal space should be filled with savage, pounding noises: whoops of lust, screams of pain—a din of commotion that had known no end in ages.

There was something large in the darkness ahead, something big, like a huge streamline animal resting on the ground.

He heard the rustling of heavy chains, and saw a large silvery beast shackled from top to bottom. It had a smooth-domed head and whiskers. It turned its head and gazed at him, bright eyes blinking.

"Carahil?" Kay asked, "is that you?"

He's after me too, kid, came a reply and the beast vanished.

"Carahil?"

No answer.

Kay detected movement on the platform in front of him. Sighting, he could see a mass of something spread out on the stone floor of the distant platform. He couldn't quite make out what it was. It looked like a dead body, flattened, trembling ever so slightly.

Unsaddling his CARG, he continued toward the platform, the gritty, crunching sounds of his footfalls quite loud.

He approached the platform and climbed up. Lying flat on the floor before Kay was what appeared to be a dead deer, its body smashed and broken beyond repair. He recalled seeing this creature along with the other Judges of the Trials that night in the Grove. Sam had created it, Though it lay there unmoving in a fatal pile of flesh and fur, its eye, looking up at Kay from the floor, was bright and quite alive, flickering with erratic movement. Every so often, its bent legs twitched.

Kay looked down at the poor creature. "Are you the Judge of my next trial? I remember you from the Grove." His voice echoed in the huge space.

Without moving its head, it spoke. *"Aye, I am."*

"Where am I?"

"Over Thirkill Bay. This is simply a NIGHTMARE illusion. This is a representation of a place your lady fears most—the place ALL her people fear most. This is the Horned God's temple, a place built by the ancient Monamas long before the League came when they were still four-armed and savage, like beasts, like demons, perfect in their evil. They worshipped him here, bathed in his blood, indulged in offerings of torn and burnt flesh. This is the place they abandoned in favor of their Gods in Jade and Sapphire, losing a pair of arms in the process. This is the place where the Horned God festers in his rage, swearing his eternal vengeance on the Monamas who turned their backs on him. This is where her people go and never return. For her, this is the pit of Hell. She has seen it many times in her nightmares."

"Where's Sam?"

"She is safe where she is."

"Do you know my next step?"

"I do. You will go to the University of Dee. There, in the library, is an item

that you shall seek. Secure it, and you will have passed the Second Trial."

The glowing image of a device identical to the first piece from Rostov floated in the air before Kay and shimmered.

"Where is this device?"

"Use your Sight. It will become obvious. It shan't be hard. You will succeed, no doubt."

"Thank you for the vote of approval."

Kay looked at the smashed deer in front of him. "Sir, may I ask—Sam created you, yes?"

"She did—using the NIGHTMARE. Monama women can do quite a bit with it, though if they use it too much, they will mark themselves for death."

"Death?"

"Yes. They *will, no doubt, come for her when this is all over—thus the importance of your passing the Trials. They cannot get to her where she currently is, but they will once the Trials are concluded."*

"The machine—the *Oberphilliax*, I know Sam is making me seek the pieces of the *Oberphilliax*. Why does Sam want it? What is its purpose?"

The deer considered his words. *"To circumvent a dark future."*

"Can you elaborate?"

"No, I must take you back now. I have given you your instructions. You will now pass your Trial, or, when next we meet, I will slay you."

"If I may ask? Why are you like this? Sam created you—why did she make you in such a state? There must be a reason for it."

"Because I am in the image of the Horned God whom your lady fears. This is his temple that his angels use to cross the stream of time and place. It is his power that gives this temple life. I am the image of He whom she fears and hates."

Dark tendrils formed around Kay. "Wait! Who, who is that? Can you tell me more?"

As Kay faded into the dark, he heard one last thing before he was put back aboard the *Goshawk*. He heard the deer say: *"Bathloxi."*

23—The Battle of Hoban

Over the next few days, Lady Tellerran of Monama improved greatly. Since her ordeal in the Crossland necropolis, she had gained a bit of weight and shed most, if not all, of her initial fear. As a Monama, she shared much in common with Sam. She had the Monama pallor, and was extremely chalky and pale, she had the usual black eyes and thick head of black hair, and her fingernails were long and pointed, like a set of daggers. However, there were significant differences from Sam as well. Sam was a buxom six feet tall, while Tellerran was much smaller and less-full than Sam, standing only about 5'4, though her thick mass of hair gave one the impression that she was much bigger than what she actually was. Her black eyes were tiny compared to Sam's, as were her lashes and lips. She was skinny in the hips and the chest. She was dressed in a warm set of crewmen's clothing, furry boots and a flight jacket that she got from a Marine. She carried the endecar with her everywhere, and she even made a little decorative bag to carry it in out of scraps of cloth she found in the laundry area. She slinked about and flirted with the crew, soaking up the attention she was getting. She didn't even want to return to Kana anymore—she was having too much fun.

It was said that, when a Monama saw his or her own death, that their personality died; Lady Tellerran's, however, appeared to be reborn with a vengeance. She smiled and laughed. She was intelligent and interrogative, flirtatious, a bit catty and somewhat prone to a touch of arrogance. With her massive head of black hair now combed and cared for, with her chalky skin washed, she was quite pretty, though not quite as attractive as Lady Sammidoran, if a comparison had to be made. Davage had heard she had won her flight jacket by oiling up and wrestling a Marine for it. She was a great hit with the Marines. She took great delight in hanging out with them in the mess, arm wrestling and beating them; her wiry, freakish Monama strength, even in space, was surprising. Her prize for beating a Marine—he had to show her his bellybutton, which seemed to excite her. She even took to drinking with the Marines, though Ennez made her stop—her metabolism couldn't handle it.

Ennez had initially wanted to get her on a fast *Trelaine* back to Kana as soon as possible, as Monamas didn't do well away from there. As Ennez observed her, he discovered that her system didn't appear to absorb nutrients very well in space. As his findings became clearer, Ennez conjectured that he should be able to keep her fully healthy with augmented nutrients, though her Gift-like powers, except for her tremendous strength, could not be restored. With frequent check-ups, a daily regimen of vitamins, and a shot of iron every once in a while, he was satisfied she could remain in space indefinitely and not suffer any ill effects.

She took her vitamins and flirted with the crew, becoming saucier as the days went on.

This one Monama woman, Lady Tellerran of the Fphenook tribe, had provided a wealth of useful information.

She developed an undeniable crush on Captain Davage, she following him about, insisting that he take her arm as he showed her the huge workings of the *New*

Faith—batting her black eyes at him. Countess Sygillis, at first, was patient and accommodating, allowing Tellerran to occupy a spot at Davage's side that normally she filled, but, she eventually, and politely, told her to back off, and Tellerran did.

The Fleet was still in orbit around Hoban, doing dry laps around its coffee-brown equator. The information Tellerran had given them was insightful, but not definitive. They had been in orbit for five days, and, since the attack in the Crossland necropolis, nothing further had happened. The swarm of Marine *Trelaines* had thinned a bit—several ships had been dispatched to quell nearby Xaphan activity. Captain Harrison of the *Bethel* was beginning to make noises about wanting to leave and press on to other matters, but Admiral Carfax ordered him to stay.

The Sisters had been hard at work going over some of the items collected in the attack: the prism, cords and the gate device that Syg had used to return after her attack. They found that the prism resonated at an extremely high, very complicated frequency in the Gamma band. The red light they created was due to the glyphs carved on the surface, which resonated at a much longer wavelength, appearing red. How or why such a frequency could turn a Monama into a Berserkacide eluded them. Ennez and Beth hypothesized it was the combination of gamma and the red light that created the Berserkacide change.

The cords were fashioned from some type of charged, resinous, polymer that had the Sisters baffled, as did the device that Syg had brought back with her. Those things they took with them into the ship's priory, and they were not seen again. No doubt, they were spirited away to Twilight 4 or Valenhelm for intense research.

They did, however, come up with a potential fix for the Monama/Berserkacide issue. The Sisters created a thick black paste that effectively filtered out both Gamma-band wavelengths and red light. Ennez put the paste into capsules fired from an air gun. The paste then came bursting out of the pellet, totally covering a target's face, and it was so sticky that it refused to come off without a reactant being applied to it. It was also semi-porous, so a person having his or her face covered with it could still breathe, though it was rather labored.

Ennez rigged up an air gun and test fired it at Davage. Sure enough, it covered his face and wouldn't come off without the reactant being applied. He reported it wasn't quite like being smothered to death, but it was close. Davage agreed that the paste did make an effective barrier against Gamma-band and red light. It should work. It should protect the Monamas from being transformed into Berserkacides, provided it could be applied in time. Davage ordered a great many air guns and pellets be prepared and distributed to the Marines, and he gave one to Lady Tellerran and told her to carry it with her at all times and to shoot herself in the face should an attack happen, which she thought was very funny. She wanted a holster to put her air gun in, and she got a neat-looking Marine holster. Tellerran loved walking around with her gun in its holster.

✶ ✶ ✶ ✶ ✶

As the sixth day wore on, Davage, true to his word, kept looking for traces of Gamma band. It was tiring and hard to see—his eyes ached. For days he had seen nothing. The Sisters, too, looked, though they couldn't see Gamma like Davage could. They could, however, tune their thoughts and 'hear' it as noise. But, they, as well, had heard nothing.

* * * * *

Davage sat in the mess with Syg having breakfast. Lt. Kilos' usual seat was empty—she was back on Kana, watching Lady Kilos and Lady Hathaline. She Com'ed in daily, giving Davage and Syg detailed reports. Lady Kilos and Hath were safe and sound. She mentioned something about Lady Kilos giving her a hard time during her tutoring sessions but nothing more distressing than that. Kay, Sarah and Phillip were still gone.

All was quiet on the home front. Just like it was over Hoban.

They were joined for breakfast in the mess by the lovely Captain Strella of the *Halo Dawn*. She had been good enough over the last few days to take a look at the odd book they had recovered in their room. Sitting at their table, Strella was dainty and regal, a typical Remnath woman, complete with their south Kana accents. She wore the *Tremblar* version of the standard Fleet uniform, which was designed specifically for a lady: a light coat and white blouse, demure skirt, knee boots and an odd Remnath hat that could be folded up and placed in a pocket. It was something worn more often by land-locked female officers at Fleet HQ and was generally eschewed by ship-borne ones, like Lt. Kilos, but Strella wore it well.

She pushed the book across the table returning it to Davage. "You know, books like these don't surface much outside of old southern parlors and dusty libraries." She had a pronounced south League Remnath accent, rather like his friend, Lt. Verlin of the Stellar Marines. "These books are considered contraband by the Sisters. A stern talking-to could be in order or, at worse, a censuring and confiscation of property should they discover you have it." She sniffed the cover. "And, why does it smell like pie?"

He laughed. "Long story. Now, if I understand correctly, these books are censured because Atrajak of Want attacked the Sisters' strongholds, is that right?"

"Yes, near the end of his life. It's an old Remnath story. He went mad after he lost his wife. This book details all of that. It's written in a very old form of Remnath and some of it is beyond me, frankly. Atrajak was a man of remarkable power—a male Sister it was said. He fell in love with an Anuian Monama woman, a princess of Nebulon named Tiverlan. He then led the Monamas in a long series of battles called the 'Hidden Wars', hidden because a few people, including the Sisters, knew of their existence. This book deals with that conflict in detail."

Davage shrugged. "I've never heard of these battles myself. Who was being fought?"

Strella opened the book, flipped through the thick vellum, and came to a page with a rich illustration. It depicted an armored man battling a creature that was in the process of stepping out of a smoky slit hovering in mid air. She pointed at the drawing.

"A mysterious group of beings he called the Kestral Oligarchy, or, more simply, the 'Golden People'. According to his writings, they could simply step out of thin air whenever they wished and vanish just as quickly. They watched our doings, past the Sisters vigilance. They, according to Atrajak, preceded us on Kana, a very heretical conclusion."

She turned the page to another illustration. Fleshless monsters covered in depravity and nude, four-armed Berserkacides.

"These Golden People were very powerful and could become anything they wanted. They worshipped some sort of blood thirsty Horned God who lived in the ground and had many slaves working in their thrall. They had demons whom Atrajak called *Killanjo* who did most of their work for them. He mentions something about time travel with these *Killanjo*, that they were treated and made resistant to prolonged exposure to travelling through time. I don't know, I couldn't understand that part very well. Also, there were the Monamas themselves. The Golden People and their *Killanjo* lieutenants could transform them into Berserkacides at their pleasure. Atrajak speaks of them taking the Monamas away into windowless cities and experimenting upon them, creating the Berserkacide and triggering them at will. They made use of their strength as warriors. It was for the love of his wife, his Anuian Monama princess, that Atrajak began the Hidden Wars against the Golden People and their *Killanjo*, to free the Monamas, and they followed and called him their Sar-Gra-Ma, or 'father'."

Davage was interested. "Well this is a revelation. We can use this information with the Sisters. Clearly these Golden People are behind the attacks on Hoban and elsewhere. What did these Golden People want? What was their objective?"

"Atrajak never knew, he simply thought they were deranged and evil," Strella said. "Tiverlan, his wife, thought they were parasitic, somehow feeding on the gods themselves. I think I read that right."

"What became of the Hidden Wars?"

Strella flipped through the book. "Here. It mentions Atrajak and his Monama army had great success and routed the Golden People and the *Killanjo* from the south of Kana, however, their ability to come and go as they pleased meant that victory could never be fully achieved; they'd just pop up again sometime later. He writes of having two choices. The first choice, as advised by his friend and great general, was to quest across the cosmos and engage the Golden People on their home soil. The second was to locate a mythical temple somewhere on Kana and destroy it. That's what his wife wanted to do, but he chose the former. Atrajak then went on a long journey across the cosmos, to confront and face the Golden People and defeat them for all time." She opened to a chart of a ten-planet solar system. A vast nebula bisected the system.

"He has all sorts of maps and charts in the book detailing his stellar journey, and this one here is where his general thought the Golden People came from and that's where Atrajak and his army went in an Elder ship. However, his army soon grew sick in space and died, including his wife. He returned to Kana a broken, deranged man."

"What became of him after that?" Syg asked.

"His wife, before dying, told him again of a temple deep in the ground somewhere on Kana where a fearsome Horned God lived. She believed this god and his temple granted the Golden People much of their power over space and time, and over Kana itself. She said to be rid of the Horned God's temple would also rid Kana of the Golden People, and she begged him to seek it out. Returning to Kana, he did so, mistaking Twilight 4 for the elusive temple and bringing the Sisters wrath down upon him."

She closed the book.

"A Horned God and a temple in the ground? Well, this is informative," Davage said. "I think we might have something here."

Captain Strella finished her coffee. "True, however, this book is contraband,

and the Sisters will not take council from its teaching."

"The Sisters are well known for holding grudges. Look at this knowledge that has been kept from sight for centuries because a broken man dared attack their holdings. Our stated mission is to locate some sort of improbable 'temporal anchor point', discover its use and destroy it. You mentioned time travel in Atrajak's book, and that this Horned God's temple is said to provide the Golden People with free access to Kana. Perhaps this temple is the anchor point we have been tasked to locate. This book is therefore key in our mission here and can help save the Monamas, and I will gladly risk their displeasure. We should convene a meeting at once."

Strella stood and checked her timepiece. "Oh dear, I need to get back to my ship. I'll contact Admiral Carfax and arrange a briefing as soon as possible. Then, you can slit your throat with the Sisters. Good morning, sir." She pulled her tiny hat out of her pocket and popped it on her head. "Countess," she said bowing to Syg and took her leave, exiting the mess.

Alone at the table, Syg, wearing a lovely cream-colored gown, called for a fresh cup of coffee. "You really think the Sisters will be upset we have this book?"

"Oh, without question. They don't forget such things. Look at the theft at Hiei—they're still up-in-arms about it. They're simply going to have to sit down and see reason. I'm convinced that this temple Captain Strella mentioned, whatever it might be, is our objective. As Mabs told to us—this book is quite important."

The door to the mess opened, and Lady Tellerran came through in her borrowed clothes, the wrestled-for jacket and holstered air gun, followed by Ennez and Beth in their black uniforms and silver helmets. A group of Marines hoisted their mugs and cheered as she entered. She saw Davage, waved, and headed in their direction. Syg scowled and rolled her eyes.

<Well, there goes a quiet breakfast with my husband,> Syg shot him with a bit of scorn.

<What?> Davage replied.

<Your girlfriend has arrived. Oh, I swear she's going to step on my last nerve again.>

Tellerran strode proudly up to their table and sat down, carrying herself in that distinctive Monama way. She got out her endecar out of its bag and set it down, adjusting its positioning for optimal effect.

"Good morning, Lady Tellerran," Davage said standing.

"Good morning, my Lord," she responded happily through the device. She turned to Syg. "Countess …"

Syg nodded in a courtly way. Ennez and Beth sat down—they could see the annoyed state Syg was in and smiled. "You seem a bit—agitated this morning, Countess," Ennez said.

"Do I?"

Tellerran took a deep breath of Davage's coffee. "My, that smells good," she commented. "Countess, do you mind so much?"

Beth started laughing. Syg put down her cup and looked ready to explode.

Suddenly Davage sat bolt still. Everyone noted him and watched.

<Syg!> he telepathied to her. *<Don't move! Don't react!>*

<Dav,> she replied, *<I'm not going to rough her up too badly. I'm just going to hit her in the…>*

<Syg—a Gamma Band just opened up, near the aft wall!>

Syg started to turn around. Beth, who could hear Davage's telepathy, began looking as well.

<Don't look—don't react! It's there, even now. I can see several foreboding shapes staring through it. They're looking at Lady Tellerran.>

<What should we do? Should we attack?>

Davage looked around. *<Syg—I see several more Gamma Bands opening up all over the ship, and I also see several opening outside. Big ones—big enough to drive a starship through.>*

Tellerran could see that something was wrong. "Captain Davage, is everything all right?" she asked.

"Com!" he said.

"Com here, sir," came the reply.

"Has Captain Strella arrived aboard her ship?"

"Aye, sir, she just checked in."

"Good, good—thank you."

<Syg—contact the Sisters. Tell them that the fleet is under attack. We need them to alert the other ships. Also, we'll need the Marines deployed in Sections 4, 7, 15 and 22 at once. Hurry!>

Davage saw a grotesque figure emerge from out of the Gamma Band and shamble in their direction. It was a man, about eight feet tall. He was thin and shirtless and rather gray of skin tone. Somehow, attached to his chest—possibly bolted or sewn on—was a lower torso and a pair of female-looking legs that went up over his head like a pair of antennae—the legs waving about in a sinister fashion, the torso's crotch ending just below his chin. Tied to both ankles were a pair of odd devices, apparently some sort of advanced Gamma Band emitters keeping him hidden from sight, except for Davage's.

And that wasn't all. At first Davage thought the man was wearing a broad, stiff skirt of some kind, cone-shaped, that went down to his ankles, but it wasn't a skirt. It was a multitude of female legs attached to his waist, at least twelve of them. The legs all moved in a semi-organized trilling fashion, like a centipede.

Eyes lamp-like and wide, he confidently strode toward Lady Tellerran. In one of his hands, he was holding a diamond-shaped prism.

Back to their standard repertoire, Davage thought. He was going to turn her into a Berserkacide right here and now.

So, here they were, just like the lurid illustrations in Atrajak's book, the servants of the Golden People, the *Killanjo,* appearing from thin air at their leisure. The Hidden Wars apparently had never ended. Here the enemy was yet again, hidden and malevolent, confident and unchallenged.

Just like the ones who nearly killed his son.

Not this time! Atrajak the Remnath had begun the Hidden Wars, and Davage the Vith would continue them.

Davage rose and pulled the air gun from Tellerran's holster. Quickly he aimed and shot her in the face. The pellet hit her in the cheek, separated and, just like that, her face was covered in the black, sticky paste. She pawed at it, trying to clear her mouth, but it wouldn't give. She fell to the floor, crying out in muffled Conox.

He would apologize to her later. "Ennez, Beth, get to Deck seven. I thought I saw a Gamma Band opening there! They might be trying to deposit Berserkacides. Save them if you are able!"

Beth and Ennez exited.

"Com!' Davage yelled. "Beat to Quarters! Helm, bear 2:00pm of 9:00am and make rotations for full speed!"

The claxons went off and people began jostling around.

Davage, CARG in hand, engaged the creature nobody else could see. The first thing the creature did was open his mouth and commence a wretched scream of some sort. He recalled Tellerran saying something about the *Killanjo* casting spells that renders one helpless. Kay, also, recounting the sordid details of his attack in the Grove, said that his attackers 'bespelled' him, rendering him unable to move and defend himself.

Therefore, it was imperative to silence this beast. He fired the air gun again, hitting the creature in the mouth. His face clotted with black paste and he gagged in surprise.

Davage, flourishing his CARG, came to grips with the monster. Despite his fierce appearance, he was surprisingly easy to defeat. In only a few cuts, Davage had him down, his legs, thrashing in a rhythmic fashion, went still.

As the ship heeled around, five more bizarre creatures dashed out of the Gamma Band. They were arrayed in all manner of depravities. None of them carried a Gamma cloaking device, and they could be seen plain as day by all. Upon seeing them, some of the crew screamed.

Another Gamma band slit opened, and a clump of ten naked people were dumped out rudely into a pale pile on the floor.

Monamas. They were clearly muddled in Head Swarm, just as Tellerran and her kin were in the Crossland necropolis. The enemy is sticking to their favorite tactic, Davage mused—fronting the attack with *Killanjo* and Berserkacide. He surged forward, trying to get between the grotesque brutes and the newly arrived Monamas. "Syg, take these people down, and do not allow them to speak!"

With a growl, Syg unleashed a brutal Sten, boxing in three of them in an instant with two managing the dive aside. The ones trapped in the Sten box died in a storm of sparks. Syg held the Sten long past the need for it—she wanted them to suffer.

"For my son!" she roared with satisfaction.

Davage engaged a *Killanjo* man with three heads who fought with a blood-soaked spear in one hand and a red Berserkacide prism in the other. The *Killanjo* was attempting to make his way to the pile of Monamas on the floor and trigger them. Davage aimed the air gun and fired at the Monamas over and over, covering them in paste, hoping to get them sufficiently covered to protect them from what was certainly coming.

The multi-headed man lifted his prism, and it began glowing bright red. Accordingly, a string of red lights around each of the Monamas' necks blossomed in a rosy, rather festive glow.

A crewman holding a chair ran up from behind hoping to break it across his filthy back. One of his heads opened its mouth and made a horrific sound that stopped the crewman in his tracks.

With a blast of Silver tech, Syg pulverized the head, silencing it. The *Killanjo* staggered.

The last creature, a skinned female, bounded her way toward the struggling Lady Tellerran, avoiding thrown bottles and chairs nimbly.

Syg loosed a blast of Silver tech and missed. Davage took a swing at her with his CARG, and she leapt over it, landing next to Lady Tellerran. She lifted a prism, setting it to a glowing cherry sort of red. She held it to Tellerran's paste-covered head. "Kill them all!" she tittered.

Nothing happened. The paste seemed to be working. The *Killanjo* shook her prism in shocked disbelief.

Elsewhere, Davage took down his three-headed foe. He put his CARG into his heart and dropped him.

He checked the Monamas. They lay where they were, out of their minds with Head Swarm, covered in a coating of tar-like black paste. None of them reacted. If they had been transformed into Berserkacides, it should be obvious by this point.

Good!

Lady Tellerran became aware of the presence of the horrid woman and her prism. She flailed out with her hands, searching in the air. After a few moments, her hands found the woman's skinned, bleeding leg, and Lady Tellerran sprang. Moving with the agility of an enraged tiger, Tellerran attacked the woman, tearing at her with her claws, and breaking her bones with her Monama strength. The *Killanjo* woman dropped her prism and tried to get away, but Tellerran was on her fast. They rolled about on the floor in a mortal tangle. Before long, Tellerran, fighting with an age-old fury, had taken her tormentor apart, literally, having rendered her into pieces. For a moment, Davage wondered if she'd become a Berserkacide after all.

He knelt down and took her by the hands. "It's over, Lady Tellerran! She's dead. You've killed her."

Struggling for breath, her face covered with dried paste, she didn't seem to know who Davage was for a moment, and then she calmed and fell into his embrace, her long fingernails covered with blood and bits of flesh.

✶ ✶ ✶ ✶ ✶

Outside, the Fleet fell under attack. The Sisters had alerted the captains and Admiral Carfax that an attack was at hand. The *Twilight* and *Halo Dawn* lowered into the atmosphere a little and opened their Battleshot ports. The *Bethel* and *Westerville* ascended and readied their Sar-Beams. Swarming around the huge vessels were just under two dozen Marine *Trelaines*, ready to overwhelm anything that might come against them.

From nowhere, a blast, like a colossal bolt of lightning, stretched out and struck *Bethel* amidships in a protracted hit. Listing and venting, she heeled to starboard. Another bolt struck her in the belly. Light ballasts flickering, trailing debris, and badly wounded, she rolled over and drifted, helpless.

With the Waft-lock in place to prevent boarding, Davage and Syg ran up to the *New Faith's* bridge. As they ran, Davage kept his Sight eye on the battle and the stricken *Bethel.* "Weapons Master!" he yelled into the air. "I want a full Sar-Beam spread set to 3:45pm mark 6:00pm of the *Bethel's* position. Fire when ready!"

A second or two passed, the thermoplants engaged, and the huge Sar-Beam emitters uncoiled a long, searing shot into the area Davage had specified.

Nothing happened; no damage was detected. The lances went off into space and, apparently, did nothing.

The *Westerville* and the *Twilight* took up station around the stricken *Bethel*, trying to guard her from further attacks.

As Davage and Syg entered the bridge, his Sight went wild. He saw bolts coming from open Gamma bands erupting all over the theatre.

Before he could say a word, huge bolts of crackling energy appeared from a number of different places. The *Westerville* was struck dead aft, while the *Halo Dawn* took a direct hit to the nose and starboard wing. The *Twilight*, banking hard, managed to avoid a bolt coursing for its belly. Three Marine *Trelaines* were caught up in a bolt and were destroyed in a violent flash.

Confusion. Secondary explosions from *Bethel.* The wires hot with panicked messages.

Davage ran to the helm and crewman Feran, Lord of the House of Six, the ship's junior helmsman, stepped away. Davage wrenched the helm and the huge, unwieldy-looking *New Faith* spiraled through the melee.

Sight: a bolt coming in from 2:00 pm. Davage hauled the ship around and spun away as the blindingly bright bolt seared in their direction, just missing the hull.

"Return fire on those coordinates!" he roared, bringing the nose of the ship about. A second later, two red-hot Sar-Beams burned into the area where the bolt came from, again with no apparent effect.

They were shooting at nothing.

Davage, his Sight fully lit, scanned the area. For a moment, he thought he could see something through the Gamma band, but then it was gone.

"Bridge!" came a voice over the Com. "Lt. Kite, 1st Marines! We are engaged with a hostile group of intruders, deck 22, section 4!"

"Engage with discretion, Lt.! If the intruders are Monama, endeavor to make use of the air guns and pellets provided to you and strike them about the head and shoulders. If that fails, then do what needs to be done, and ensure the protection of all vital areas!"

"Aye, sir!"

The scene around Hoban was chaotic. The Fleet and Marine ships were taking heavy damage from all quarters, and the status of the *Bethel* was unknown—her Com was out and the area around her was littered with life boats launched from her upper hull. Additionally, reports were coming in from all ships that they were battling savage groups of intruders in fierce confrontations. The intruders were boarding right through the Sisters' waft-lock.

Berserkacides.

Davage Sighted: a bolt was soon to be heading right for his belly. Davage kicked the thrusters and wheeled the huge vessel around, the helm shaking slightly in his hands as he did so. The *New Faith's* wheel always shook, though nobody could ever explain why. A moment later a searing bolt came screeching past, hitting nothing

Davage then saw something strange. He saw the *Westerville* bathed in some sort of dim yellowish light. The ship didn't appear to be suffering structurally from the light, but ...

He Sighted through the hull into the interior of the ship and was appalled. Inside, bathed in light, the crew were going mad: heads shaking, hands tearing, teeth biting. Even the Sisters aboard seemed affected.

Davage rammed the wheel and clawed the ship around. "Weapons Master, I want an extended Sar-Beam placed at 5:50pm mark 4:45am. Fire and maintain—now!"

The Sar-Beams burst out of their banks and went where Davage thought was the source of the light. Nothing happened at first; then, the light flickered and went out. The *Westerville* was free—the crew now struggling to regain their sanity. Two quick bolts came in and slapped the ship across the back.

Davage Sighted: a beam of yellow light was heading straight for him.

He punished the wheel, pulling the *New Faith* into a gut-wrenching 12am climb. Looking behind, he could see a shaft of light following, struggling to bathe the ship in its radiance. After a few more seconds, the light went out having not found the ship, and Davage banked hard to his starboard.

The *Bethel* suffered a massive internal explosion that broke the superstructure and created out-of-control venting, scattering the litter of lifeboats blossoming around it. It heeled past the vertical, adrift and helpless, sucked-in like a tin can.

That was mortal, Davage thought.

Bethel is dead.

Another round of bolts. The *Westerville* and *Halo Dawn* were struck yet again; only this time, the *Halo Dawn* managed to fire off five canisters in the direction of the bolt. They entered the Gamma Band and vanished.

Davage, seeing this, had a thought. The Hidden Wars. The Golden People and their slaves emerging from nowhere through feathery slits in the air. Atrajak venturing into the slits to face the enemy.

The enemy is there, cowering on the other side of those Gamma band slits.

If that's where the enemy was, then that's where he would go.

Sighting a nearby Gamma Band, he banked and plunged the *New Faith* into it, four *Trelaines* following.

The ship fell into darkness.

Lord Phillip, Lady Sarah, Lord Kabyl, Lord Lon

24—Dee

The *Goshawk* broke the haze over the great Armenelos Forest and landed outside of Dee, a sea-side city northeast of the Withelwell River in the upper-reaches of Calvert.

Like all cities in the Calvert region, Dee was a small, but densely populated urban area that made most of its income from fishing, canning and similar industries. Unlike Vith, Remnath and Zenon cities, which were very spread out and only sparsely built up, Calvert cities were tightly packed with narrow streets, clustered buildings and chaotic alleyways. The Calvert region of Kana was, traditionally, the least prosperous of the seven. The old Calvert tribe of long ago did not do well in the time of the Elders and was a general disappointment. Eventually, most of the Calverts migrated to Onaris, where they did much better, though they missed out on the Gifts of the Mind, and they became known as the Browns.

Dee was originally a city south of the Withelwell river on the eastern edge of the Great Armenelos forest. The old Dee was an unsavory place, rife with vice and corruptions of all sorts. The Sisterhood of Light, as they occasionally had to do with Calvert Houses and cities, got sick and tired of the situation and politely announced to the civic leaders of Dee in 000221ax that they were going to destroy the city, and all persons were encouraged to leave at once, lest they be destroyed right along with the earth and the stone.

They packed up and migrated north to the city's present location and, to their credit, cleaned up their act. Dee became one of the nicer Calvert cities.

The University of Dee was founded in 000391ax as an ecumenical school. One way to get back into the Sisters' good graces after an earth-scorching was to build places of learning, and the people of Dee did just that, building the university on a flat plain just outside the city, eventually receiving praise from the Sisters for it as a nice, clean place where students from all over Kana could go to learn. Never considered one of the more elite schools, it nevertheless enjoyed a fair amount of steady success over the years and counted among its alumni a decent amount of well-known scholars. One of its most tenured professors, a Grand Dame Hannah-Ben Shurlamp, was well-known for her learned contributions, and, allegedly, for her rather ruthless methods of acquiring knowledge.

The university was a sprawling place, built of brown sandstone buildings and grand patina-capped rooftops mixed in with broad walks and pleasant green spaces. Lon, wanting to attend the older, more prestigious Vith schools in Arden, turned his nose up at the place. This, he said, was a haven for liberal arts and nonsense. Science was best taught at science schools.

Finding a good spot to land, Phillip set the ship down, and they all got out, taking a short hike into Dee and the university.

The school was quaint and pleasing to the eye, with well tended grounds and craggy buildings. Despite Lon's dismissal of the place, Kay, Phillip and Sarah thought it was a charming, approachable school. The students and staff appeared quite friendly as they passed them.

Beyond the main commons was the library. The library of the University of Dee was a huge rotunda with the large statue of a strange-looking dragon standing guard in the front by the main entrance. From the outside, the library appeared big and squat, topped with a vast green dome, like a huge mixing bowl turned upside down. Once they entered the library, the interior was breathtaking. Even Lon, who was continually disparaging the school, had to admit it was most impressive.

The library was apparently cut deep into the ground. The interior was twenty stories in total, rising to the huge ornate dome high above. The perimeter of the rotunda was a honeycomb of shelves, cubbies, reading areas, terminals and desks. Beneath the center of the rotunda was a vast open space that led down to an aquamarine pool at the bottom.

They found a quiet place to sit down in privacy and contemplated their strategy. Phillip plopped down on a comfortable couch by the rail, and Lon wandered into the maze of shelves, browsing.

"So, what are we supposed to be looking for?" Phillip asked.

"A silver device similar to the one we picked up in Rostov."

"Where is it?"

Kay looked around. "I'm not sure, really. The Judge told me that it was in the library and that it will not be all that hard to find."

Sarah saddled up to a terminal and began looking at the posts. "You better start looking around then," she said as the holographic images orbited her head. "Meanwhile, I'm going to catch up on my reading—see what's hot out there. Take your time, Kay." The posts Sarah called up were the usual sensational stuff that she consumed in volume. The first post read:

PARAFLIES FOUND DEAD IN THE MILLIONS IN CALVERT—FACE EXTINCTION

Dead? Extinction? He thought about the one Parafly that had helped save him after the attack on his life. He could still see it, plain as day, preening its face with its legs. "What's wrong with the Paraflies?"

Sarah read on. "Don't know. They're turning up dead all over the place. Says here their dead bodies clogged up the canal water in Bern."

"Ah, pity," Kay said. "I rather fancied them."

He allowed his Sight to roam. The giant library was full of a great many people, but the place was so big it appeared only modestly populated due to the size. He looked around, seeing the library clearly. He could see people walking around on the floors above and below them, including a few amorous couples kissing in quiet, romantic nooks. The underside of the dome overhead was etched with many images and shapes—the shape of a dragon being the most prominent. He could see through the dome as well, to the silty blue sky of Calvert above.

He looked down and instantly saw what he was looking for. "There it is," he said.

Sarah turned from her posts. "That was fast, I haven't even finished my first article. Where is it?"

"Down there." Kay pointed down, over the rail to the pool below.

Phillip sat up, and they gazed over the railing.

The pool, from where they were standing, was four floors down. The water was a cheerful aqua-marine. Many students on the bottom floor were seated around the edge of the pool. Some sat with their books at the water's edge dipping their feet into it. Some seemed to be talking to the water—having a conversation with nobody.

"How deep is it?" Phillip asked.

"Deep, at least five hundred feet. There's an immense cavern under there that goes on for miles."

Sarah looked over the side. "What? Five hundred feet? That pool can't be more than five feet deep. You sure it's in there? I don't see anything."

"It's in there, sure enough."

She smiled at him. "I guess you're getting wet then. Are you going to walk down and jump in, or am I going to get to toss you in from here?"

Kay continued to stare into the water. "Wait. I see something in the water moving around. Something big."

Sarah squinted, lighting her Sight. "The water looks clear to me."

"Me, too," Phillip said.

"There's some sort of Cloak or Paint over it. Beneath the surface I see a lot of stalagmites, like what you'd see in a flooded cavern, and swimming through them is a large creature."

"A big fish?" Phillip asked.

"It doesn't look like a fish. It's bizarre. I don't know what it is."

Sarah was distressed. "Why can't I see it?"

Lon returned holding a book he'd pulled off one of the shelves. "What are we looking at?" he asked.

"Kay's found the device. He says there's a monster in the water," Sarah said.

Lon looked over the side. "Really? You sure, Kay?"

"Yes, I am sure."

This sort of thing was right down Sarah's alley, and she was getting excited. "Describe it," she said. "Describe the monster."

"It's like nothing I've ever seen before. It looks sort of like a dragon with a green body, a long neck, a mane of long red hair like a horse, orange legs—splayed out like a gecko—and a long, thin pink tail with a woman growing out of the end."

"You're making that up," she said, cross.

"No, I'm not. I'd not make up such a thing."

Sarah, her imagination going haywire, strained to look into the pool—seeing nothing but the clear water.

Phillip took off his hat and wiped his brow. "So what are we going to do? I thought this one was going to be easy. No doubt if you jump in there, the creature is going to devour you."

Lon looked down and noted all the students casually sitting by the pool. "Nobody down there appears to be put off in any way."

"They must not be aware of the danger that lurks beneath," Phillip said.

Sarah started pushing everybody toward the lift. "Come on; we're going down there. I want to see this thing for myself."

Hurriedly they went down to the bottom. The bottom floor of the library was set up as a small café, serving light lunch fare to the students, a nice place to eat and read and gather with friends. They walked through the chattering noise of the café and soon stood at the edge of the pool gazing into it. Sarah, eager to see whatever it was, knelt down and looked into the clear water. Kay thought for a moment that she was going to pull her boots off and dive in—that was something Sarah would do without hesitation.

A small girl sat eating her lunch at a nearby table piled high with books. She saw Sarah and the rest gawking into the pool and laughed quietly. "You must be new here. Is this your first year?"

Lon spoke up, outraged. "We do not matriculate at this school, madam! I have been offered a full scholarship at the University of Arden, sciences."

The girl smiled and rolled her eyes. "Oh, I see," she said. "Arden, wow, you must be really smart then. Not smart enough to know what's in the water though, are you? None of those fancy Vith schools have what we've got right here in Dee."

Sarah walked toward the girl. "You've seen the thing in the water?"

"The 'Thing' in the water? Yeah, of course I have," she said in a slightly arrogant way.

Phillip interjected. "Well, then, miss, could you please inform us? What is it?"

She laughed. "Why don't you ask him yourself?"

"Ask him? How?"

The girl pointed at the other side of the café. There, perched at the water's edge, was the statue of a dragon-like monster. Sarah quickly made her way to the statue and looked it over, inspecting every inch. Long neck, dragon-like face with a mane of long hair, big beady eyes, splayed legs and a long, thin tail. "Is this what you're seeing in the water, Kay?"

"Looks like it," he said.

"It's hideous," Sarah remarked with wonder.

The girl at the other side of the café called out to them. "You're going to hurt his feelings with talk like that. Put some money in his mouth, and he'll talk to you—and be nice to him."

They looked at the girl for a moment; then, Kay slowly pulled a money purse out of his coat. He took out a Blanchefort hader and was about to stick it in the statue's mouth.

"Give him two, Kay—don't be cheap," Sarah said, wide-eyed with anticipation.

Kay scowled at her and took out another hader. He then put both of them in the statue's mouth. The coins fell in, rattled about a bit inside, and then emerged from its rear-end, entering the water with a *plop—plop!*

A moment later, a beautiful, black-haired woman wearing a toga came walking out of the water.

They regarded her for a moment.

Kay Sighted her. She was some sort of molded, fleshy bit, like the tongue of a snapping turtle that resembles a worm.

He could see that this black-haired woman was the end of the monster's tail. Far below, the monster lurked in the depths of the pool, its tail stretching like elastic and ending with what appeared to be a beautiful woman. Kay sensed danger.

"Are you the creature in the water?" Kay asked.

"Aye."

"You're its tail, correct? We are currently talking to the end of a tail, yes?"

"That is correct," the woman said.

"Do you know why we're here?"

"No. Should I?"

Sarah didn't approve of the questioning. "I was expecting to see that," she said pointing at the statue. "What are you, the monster's slave?"

The woman smiled. "As the gentleman just pointed out, what you see is the end of my tail. I can will the end of my tail to be anything I wish. I feel like being a woman today."

"What are you?" Kay asked.

"All rudeness aside, I'm from here. There are many old and deep things living on Kana. When the builders of this library began digging, they dug up my home. I wasn't angry. I even assisted them in completing the library."

"And you've been here ever since?"

"I have. This is my home. I like it here. I get three free meals a day, and I help the students with their research. I have many friends. I'm even the mascot of this university. I am very proud of our Brandtball team this year."

"What are you called?"

"Call me what you wish—I have no particular name."

"Mickey!" Sarah cried. "We'll call you Mickey."

"If you must."

Kay looked back into the water and saw the body of Mickey resting at the bottom of the cavernous pool far below.

"Mickey," Kay said. "There is a matter we must discuss."

"It sounds urgent. I am here. I am listening."

"There is a silver device resting at the bottom of your cavern. I am tasked to remove it from here. Do you know of it?"

"There are many items in here with me. I like shiny things. Can you be more specific?"

"It is a small silver object about this big," Kay said holding his hands out about a foot apart. "It is round with a hole in the middle."

Kay peered into the water and saw Mickey looking around, his long neck coiling about.

"Oh yes, I see that. It's over there. Very pretty."

"I need to take it from here. I am tasked to do so."

Mickey's tail, the woman in the toga, smiled. "There is a rule here—anything that falls into the water is mine. See," she said pointing at a distant sign carved into a stone pillar. It read:

ANY ITEM FALLING INTO THE WATER BELONGS TO THE DRAGON. NO EXCEPTIONS.

As they continued to look around, they noticed the dragon's motif everywhere, carved in the stone pillars, adorning vases and paintings; many students were even wearing clothing with a dragon stamped on the front. Even the food being served in the café followed the theme: dragon salad, dragon-tarts, dragon soda and dragon-tips.

Kay turned his attention back to the woman. "Mickey, I need this device. I have to have it. May we, perhaps, trade for it?"

The woman appeared intrigued. "What do you have to trade?"

"I have a purse full of Blanchefort haders."

The woman thought a moment. "I don't need any of those. What else do you have?"

They looked at each other, trying to come up with something. Mickey noted Kay's CARG. "That weapon will do. Let's trade for it."

Kay looked down at his CARG. "This weapon doesn't belong to me. It belongs to my beloved and is not mine to trade away, I'm sorry."

Sarah stepped forward. "What if we just dive in and grab the item? What about that?"

"Then, I suppose I'll have to devour you, and that's a shame as I just had breakfast. Why don't you try diving in later in the day, at around lunch time. I'll devour you then."

Kay continued. "It seems we are at an impasse, Mickey. There must be a way we can work this out to our mutual satisfaction."

Mickey thought. "Why do you desire this item so?"

Kay sat down at the pool's edge, and he told Mickey. He told her as much as he could without going into too much detail as the students watching nearby were beginning to take an interest in their conversation. She listened.

When Kay finished, Mickey spoke. "Well, you four seem like nice people. Why don't we try this: I'll play at a contest with each of you. If you win all four contests, I'll give you the device. How about that?"

"And, if we lose?" Kay asked, expecting some grim and horrifying punishment.

"If you lose, you lose. Big deal. Try again tomorrow."

They thought it over and agreed.

They sat down at a table and began—other students started milling about to watch.

The first contest was a game of Perlamum—an ancient board game. "I have to warn you that I'm pretty good at this game," she said producing a water-logged board and game pieces.

Lon, who was pretty decent at it as well, sat down, and they began playing.

Surprisingly, Lon beat Mickey in five moves. Mickey gawked dumbfounded at the board. "Wow, you're really good," she said. "One contest down, three to go."

Mickey rolled up the sleeve of her toga. "Next, arm wrestling." She put her elbow on the table and opened her hand. "Who wants some?"

Sarah sat down opposite her and rolled up her sleeve. Sarah had the Gift of Strength and was very strong. They clasped hands, adjusted their grip and then began.

It was over in moments. Sarah, using her Gift of Strength, literally threw Mickey into the pool—several students who were watching from a distance began clapping. Sarah, shocked at first, stood and slowly got that look in her eye that she often did when she was feeling rather happy about herself. "You all see that?" she that, brimming with haughty confidence. Some of the students bowed to her. She was eating this up.

Mickey waded back out of the water and smiled. "Boy, you're strong."

For the next test, Mickey sat back down at the table and said the contest was for someone to make her laugh. All they had to do was to make her laugh, and the contest would be over.

Phillip stepped forward. He racked his brains as he tried to think of a funny joke to tell. He settled on one he'd heard Sarah tell their mother about a Xaphan and three Sisters on their way to the communal bath. Phillip told the joke in a rather stiff, un-humorous manner, and Sarah rolled her eyes.

Mickey sat there stone-faced; then, she began snorting, and, finally, belly laughed.

"I get it; I get it!" she cried.

"You can't be serious," Sarah said. "Phillip butchered that joke. I should have told it to her."

"You already had your turn," Phillip replied, cross.

"It's funny, funny," she said laughing.

Phillip smiled and felt proud of himself. Three contests down.

It was Kay's turn. "So, what's my test to be?"

Mickey thought a moment. She turned and went back into the water. A minute or two later she returned with the silver device in her hands. She stood in front of Kay. "You need to take the device from my hand, if you are able."

"That's it?"

"That's it."

Kay looked at the device sitting in her hand.

"Be careful," Mickey said. "I'm pretty fast."

Kay slowly reached out and took the device from her hands. Mickey didn't try to stop him. She just stood there and let him have it."

"Were you even trying?" he asked

Mickey winked. "It looks like you need this more than I do. Just don't tell anybody that I'm such a soft touch."

Kay looked at it again. "I—I feel I should give you something in return for this."

"Perhaps you'll come back and visit me someday—with your beloved in hand. I would like that. I would like to meet her. That will be reward enough."

Kay stood there. "Mickey, thank you. I wasn't expecting ..."

"You weren't expecting what? That I would be kind and reasonable? You thought you'd end up in some grand battle with me, did you? Such a thought assumes that the lords of this university would willingly subject their students and faculty to a dangerous beast, which is a little odd if you consider it carefully. You look to be a Vith, and Viths are always searching for a monster to fight. Just remember this simple thought as you continue on your travels: expect the best, but be ready for the worst. Sometimes, you get the former rather than the latter. Remember that, and you'll do well."

Sarah took her hat and duster off and, before anybody could say a word, dove into the water. After a minute or so, she surfaced, all smiles.

"Did you see him down there?" Kay asked.

She nodded, still smiling. She gave Mickey's tail a hug and swore they would return some day.

With that, they bade Mickey goodbye and left the library, each glad they'd come, even Lon. Clearly, none of those stuffy science schools in Arden could boast that they had a wondrous, guardian dragon swimming in the library.

25—Nowhere

The *New Faith* and four Marine *Trelaines* emerged on the other side of the Gamma Band. The other side was a dusty corner of darkness and swirling gases—the tell-tale signs of being deep within a nebula. At the navigator's chair, the holo AM/PM orientation wheels began spinning wildly, lost and without bearing.

Surrounding the *New Faith* were at least a hundred ships of various sizes. The ships looked like collections of bubbles, all pushed together and cast in brilliant gold. Some of the bubble-like ships were tiny, barely large enough for a single man-sized person to fit in; others were gargantuan in size, dwarfing even the huge *New Faith*. The larger ships were parked in front of the Gamma Bands, firing the bolts through. There was a clutter of wreckage floating about—apparently Captain Davage's Sar-Beams and the canister from the *Halo Dawn* had got through and done a great deal of damage.

Hauling the ship around, Davage ordered his canister magazines opened.

The *New Faith*, hopelessly surrounded, fired Sar-Beams and canister off in random directions; the deep concentration of ships precluded the possibility of missing. The *Trelaines* stayed tucked in with the *New Faith*, firing their smaller Sar Beams.

The enemy golden ships, though impressive and grand, were scattered by the weight of the *New Faith's* firing. One shot seemingly deflated them, compressing them down into a deformed ingot of gold. Ship after ship suffered under Davage's guns. They also seemed to be having trouble maneuvering, the *New Faith* roaming around and through them at will. The Marines, seeing the situation unfold, broke and attacked, ranging through the crowd of golden ships, creating havoc in their wake.

In and out, diving and rolling, the *New Faith* put a merciless beating on the golden ships. They tried to maneuver around, to put a bolt on the *New Faith*, but they couldn't move fast enough. Some ships tried to shine a strange yellowish light on the speeding ship, but Davage, sensing extreme danger, kept away and focused his fire on them.

Eventually, the survivors pulled back and retreated—lumbering away and then vanishing, leaving only golden flotsam of the destroyed ships.

✶ ✶ ✶ ✶ ✶

There was jubilation aboard the *New Faith*. Just one Main Fleet Vessel and four Marine attack ships routed a massive force of enemy vessels. The enemy, whoever they were, had a massive offensive punch, but their ships were too slow and dainty to stand and fight effectively. Without being able to hide behind their Gamma Bands, they didn't stand a chance.

Reports flowed in from all over the ship. The Marines had engaged and defeated a number of roving bands of intruders. Many captives had been taken. With Davage having alerted the Marines, they were able to arrive in time to meet the attackers as they stepped out of their Gamma Band holes.

More of the grotesque *Killanjo* creatures, as before, were fought and killed, and a number of bound Monamas with them as well. Using their air gun and paste pellets, the Marines managed to save twenty six male and female Monamas, while only having to kill eight that had been turned into Berserkacides. It was a huge victory, and the surviving Monamas, naked and gaunt, were taken to the overcrowded dispensary where Ennez and Beth checked them over and removed their collars. All of them, as Lady Tellerran had done previously, acted in a deathly funk.

Head Swarm.

They were in abused shape but not beyond saving. All they needed was food and warmth, a regimen of vitamins, and the nourishing ground of Kana and they should be fine.

Kana …

Where were they exactly?

When the Golden ships vanished from the theatre of battle, so too did the Gamma Bands they had flown through. The *New Faith* and the four *Trelaines* were marooned in unknown, starless territory.

The Duke and Duchess of Olyn

26—Dimples

The four made their way back to the *Goshawk* to await their next set of instructions. Kay held the silver device. Sarah, sopping wet, chattered about seeing the dragon.

"That was easy, Kay, just like you said," she added, wringing out her hair.

"Who knew there was a friendly dragon holding the device. I don't think Mickey even tried in the contests."

"Oh, Mickey tried all right; I was just too strong for him," Sarah proclaimed.

Two of three pieces held—these Trials weren't so hard.

One trial to go.

When they got to the *Goshawk*, they were horrified.

The black ship was enveloped in some sort of golden gel.

"What is that?" Phillip asked in disgust.

Lon got out his goggles and adjusted the lenses. "Looks like amoebic protoplasm. We should get a sample. My mother would love to examine this."

Kay recalled seeing this type of creature the night the Trials began, created with Sam's NIGHTMARE.

He stepped forward. "Are you the final Judge?"

The protoplasm shot forward and enveloped Kay, drawing him into its golden interior, where he thrashed and kicked in the thick gel. Within, Kay could see bits of golden material and what looked like a sinuous black skeleton floating about as a nucleus.

The Skeleton, though not moving per se, drifted toward him.

"I am the Judge of your final Trial," Kay heard a voice say.

Kay tried to say something in reply but couldn't. He couldn't breathe in this golden soup.

The skeleton bobbed near him. *"Two items collected, yet a third remains from sight. The final piece rests in a barbaric place, next to the bones of the fallen and the bodies of those who shall soon be dead—a place of old evil and new revelations. The Temple of Ethylrelda of Waam, worn and threadbare, weary of malice, yet coiled and set to strike, a sea of Shadow tech knives waiting to dance at your throat. There you must go."*

A shimmering object appeared before Kay in the smothering golden protoplasm. It was unlike the two doughnut-shaped devices collected so far. It was rectangular and plank-like, articulated in a sharp curve at what was probably the top of the piece, and it bore, on one side, a deep ovular recess; this last piece must be the cross-section. It bore a distinct resemblance in style to the first two pieces collected. It was twisting and organic in construction, like a vine made of silver.

"If you survive the horrors of Ethylrelda's temple, and you gather this piece, you will have completed your Trials. You will then return to your home in the cold north of Kana and await additional instructions at that time. You will not see me again."

With Kay's lungs screaming for oxygen, the creature began to expel him.

It stopped, thought a moment, and then spoke again: *"Know you this, Kabyl of Blanchefort, the enemy is upon you. They are the angels of the Horned God, and his temple deep in the ground gives them lease not only in the present, but in the past and the future as well. Their hatred and their pagan god provides fuel for their travels. There you must one day go and there you must face them. That is not part of your Trial, it is merely an inevitability."*

On the verge of passing out, Kay was ejected, and the golden creature vanished.

✶ ✶ ✶ ✶ ✶

The Duke and Duchess of Oyln came running out of their huge, brand new estate as Phillip landed the old *Goshawk* on the fresh planted grounds. They were always happy to see their defacto nephews and niece.

Sarah and Phillip came bouncing out and hugged them both. This sprawling estate was their winter home, Peter and Lady Poe being given a whole wing to themselves in the northern sector of the manor.

Compared to the spired, multi-leveled sprawl of Castle Blanchefort, Grand Oyln Manner was a boxy, workman-like structure. It was built squat in the Esther-style. It was no more than four giant-sized floors high, splashed with large rectangular windows, rather squarish in construction and built of a sandy-gray stone. To view it from overhead, it looked like a massive C, with a central courtyard that had been masterfully landscaped by the plant-loving duchess herself.

It was a wonder of Esther-style construction and would serve the House of Oyln well for centuries to come.

The Duke and Duchess were all smiles.

"What's the matter, Phillip? Is it too cold for you up there even in the summer?" the Duke asked tossing his hair.

"I like it cold, Uncle!" Sarah shouted roughly hugging him.

"I'll wager you do."

Kay and Lon came out of the ship.

Duchess Torrijayne, thick in pregnancy with her fifth child, gave him a grand hug. "Well, will you just look at this handsome young man! Lord Kabyl, if I weren't happily married and madly in love, I'd just pick you up and carry you away!"

She gave him a warm kiss on the cheek.

The Duke shook Kay's hand and clapped him on the shoulder. "Good to see you, Lord Blanchefort—you don't come and see us often enough. They turned to Lon and shook his hand.

"Lord Probert," the Duke said cheerfully. "You traveling around with this sorry lot, now?"

"I am, sir," he said with a smile.

A distance away was a huge fountain in the central garden. There was a great deal of activity going on around it. Adorning the top of the fountain was a hideous, bronze statue. It was the likeness of the duchess, naked in all her glory and massively pregnant, dancing on one leg. Water streamed in a gushing, messy spray from her milk-filled breasts. Several staff members of House Oyln milled about, trying to figure out how to remove the statue.

The Duchess smiled. "Your mom did that, Kay, just in time for a large dinner party that we threw the other day. Actually, it's a pretty clever prank. I'm impressed.

Of course, I'm going to have to retaliate, but …"

They all looked at it—Sarah having issues keeping a straight face.

The Duke laughed and shook his head. "Well, we and the kids were just getting ready to sit down for lunch. Come on in and join us!"

Kay took Torrijayne's arm, and they went in to eat.

✶ ✶ ✶ ✶ ✶

After lunch, the three of them and the duchess went into the library. Lon had been corralled by the Duke. He wanted Lon to go through some of the specs of his new *Windhawk* starcraft, and they went down to the yard to have a look.

Like the many reading rooms at Castle Blanchefort, the main library at Grand Oyln Manor was huge and airy, full of books and busts and hung artwork. Unlike Castle Blanchefort, however, the library was heavily windowed, full of light and flowering plants, the duchess being a noted horticulturist in the area. It also had a multitude of obvious technologies—large, full-sized holo-terminals with not only a holographic gentleman to assist in locating data, but an elegant lady as well. There were elaborately illustrated databases and floating Silver tech automatons clattering about. The room smelled like new carpeting and fresh plaster and was decorated in the modern Esther style with lots of light.

Holding her pregnant belly, Torrijayne slowly sat down and brushed her black hair out of her face. "So, what brings you three all the way down from Blanchefort today—not that I'm not thrilled to see you?"

And they told her; they told her everything. They told her about Kay's Trial, about what happened at Rostov. They told her about Dee and the dragon. They watched the concern grow on her face as they told her about the hideous creatures who had attacked and nearly killed Kay.

And they told her that Kay was a Shadow tech Male.

Torrijayne sat there a moment, then, swallowing, she sent out a streamer of Silver tech and closed the door to the library. She then created five Silver tech serpents which lined up in front of her and awaited their instructions.

"Guard the windows and exits and watch for eavesdroppers."

The serpents slithered off. The holo-terminals snapped off, and the Silver tech automatons drifted up toward the distant ceiling. Torri looked at a nearby brandy service with longing, but remembered that she was pregnant.

"And you've told all of this to your father and your mother?" she asked.

"Yes, Great Duchess," Kay replied.

"That's enough of the 'Great Duchess' thing. Yes? To your barefoot, fountain-defacing mother, Kay, I'm 'Great Duchess,' but to you, I'm just Dimples—agreed?"

Kay smiled and nodded.

"So," she said, "you're a Shadow tech Male? That's a rare honor. Take a bit of good advice, and don't go advertising that to just anybody—I'm serious. Being a Shadow tech Male can be a dangerous thing."

"They say I can somehow control Shadow tech Females," he said. "When I touched Bethrael of Moane's Silver tech, I …"

Despite her belly, Torri sat up bolt straight. "You touched Beth's Silver tech?"

"I did. She saved my life with it. The blood poisoning …"

Torri laughed. "And, how was it, Kay?"

"How was it?" Kay asked. "I don't understand."

"How did it feel?"

"It was a little strange."

"*A little strange*? I'll bet it was. So, umm, has Beth acted a little oddly toward you since then, Kay? A little touchy-feely, perhaps?"

"Yes, a little. Why is that?"

Torri reared back and laughed. "Come now, Kay, you needn't be shy—you can talk to me. I'm not a stuffy old grouch like your mom. Touching Beth's Silver tech was, quite probably, the best sex she's ever had by far, and she's had a lot if the gossip is to be believed. A Shadow tech Female cannot resist the touch of a Shadow tech Male. It drives us mad. Touch her Shadow or Silver tech long enough, and she'll do anything you ask. She'd even kill if you told her to."

TELL ME WHAT TO STEAL!! TELL ME WHO TO KILL!!

Kay remembered and sat there, mortified.

"I'd give her some space if I were you for the time being, Kay. She'll be all right, although I'm certain the next few fellows she comes to grips with in the sack will leave her rather flat. I can picture it now: some upright lord, dressed in his best and unloading a fortune in dinner and entertainments on Beth only to have her fall asleep on him out of boredom. Nothing any handsome League Lord could do to her will come close to matching your touch. I'll bet she's thinking about you, even now."

flex ...

Torri again looked at the brandy service with longing. "I'm sorry, but I suddenly feel myself rather thirsty."

A Silver tech automaton came down and fetched a decanter full of orange juice. It poured four cool glasses and passed them around. It then glided back up to the heights of the ceiling. Torri took a few drinks. "Normally, I'd get it myself, but Lord Oyln in here is making things tough for me right now. My back and all."

Kay drank his juice and thought of Beth—remembering what it felt like to touch her Silver tech pulling him away from blood poisoning. He tried to put her out of his mind.

"Dimples," he said, "the reason we've come today is to consult with you regarding our next task. We understand the final piece of the machine we are to retrieve is located in a Black Hat's temple."

Torri put her glass down. "Really? Which one?"

"Ethylrelda of Waam. We know you came from Waam and thought you could give us some useful tips."

Torri had always been open mouthed about her days as a Black Hat Painter, much more so than Countess Sygillis, who refused to talk about it at all, as she didn't want to share such a dark period of her life with her children. Duchess Torrijayne, on the other hand, typically offered a highly censored detailing of her days when she was known as Torrijayne of Waam, a vile and feared Painter. That fact, coupled with other things, kept alive the ongoing rivalry and animosity between Countess Sygillis and the duchess. For the sake of their families, which were very close, they could act in a civilized fashion, but make no mistake—they hated each other. Fortunately, that hatred didn't extend to Sygillis' husband or her children. Torrijayne was a good friend of Captain Davage and Lt. Kilos, and she cherished Sygillis' children, Kay most of all. Such was their relationship that Torri could poke fun at the countess, often doubling Davage and Kilos over with laughter. Davage, though he loved Sygillis beyond measure, had a good sense of humor regarding her. The horrid 'shirt' incident that Kay uncovered in the curio shop was merely the latest shot fired in their ongoing conflict, and one for which the countess swore revenge—though Davage had secretly admitted he thought the shirts were the funniest things he'd ever seen. Apparently, with the defaced fountain outside, Countess Sygillis had had her revenge.

The duchess finished her glass of juice. "And you're going to do this, are you?" she asked, already knowing what the answer was.

"Yes, Dimples, we are."

"Certainly not an easy task, is it? You asked for my advice; well, here it is: don't do it. Going into a Black Hat's temple is just about the most dangerous thing you could ever try."

"If I don't, Sam will die. I promised her I would see these Trials through, and I intend to do just that."

Torri held up her empty glass, and an automaton immediately came down and filled it.

"Ohhh, you Vith," she said. "So heroic and brave all the time, aren't you? So, what's your plan? Tell me."

"We were thinking we'd take the *Goshawk* to Waam, infiltrate her temple and get the piece."

"Ah, just that simple, hmm? Let's examine this point by point. So, you want to take the *Goshawk* to Waam. Do you even know where Waam is?"

"Waam is the largest city on the planet Gothan," Phillip said.

"Correct. Gothan is about a week's journey from here—that's a lot of Xaphan space to cover. How are you going to do it without being spotted and boarded—or worse?"

Sarah spoke up, beaming with pride. "Kay is going to Cloak the *Goshawk.* He can do that."

Torri's icy-blue eyes got wide. "I see. So, Kay, you're going to Cloak the *Goshawk,* are you? Let's see it. Let me see what you've got."

Kay set his glass down and tried to clear his mind. He felt rushed and pressured. He allowed his Cloak to well up, and then, after another moment or two, he Cloaked himself, Sarah and Phillip.

Torri, watching, burst into a smile and clapped. "Really good job, Kay—I'm impressed!"

She started trying to pull his Cloak apart. She thought to have it down with a few simple tricks, found herself stumped, and then, with a cry, changed her approach, and the Cloak came down. Kay, Sarah and Phillip reappeared in their chairs.

"Wow, Kay!" she shouted. "Really good. Extremely good, actually. Come here and give me a hug!" Torri had always been a very huggy sort of lady. Kay got up and gave her a huge hug, making sure not to press too closely on her pregnant belly. He felt a bit shy at first, remembering what happened when he touched Beth's Silver tech. But no, he hugged her and didn't feel anything like what he had with Beth—Torri keeping her Silver tech deeply buried within, safely away from Kay's touch.

Sarah finished her orange juice. "We were hoping you could help Cloak the *Goshawk* for our trip."

"What for?" Torri said letting Kay go. "Kay's Cloak will work just fine. Truly. It's not quite a full Painted Cloak, but still, Cloaking a ship doesn't require an overly elaborate setup what with all that empty space to hide in. So, I'm sold. With Kay's Cloak I'll wager you'll make it all the way to Gothan without issue—provided the *Goshawk* doesn't break down on you along the way. Now, what are you going to do when you get there?"

Sarah again—apparently she was the author of their plan. "We were thinking we'd hide out in the ship while Kay goes into her temple, takes the Black Hat over and has her show him where the device is. Then he'd take it, and we'd be off."

"Oh, so you're just going to waltz into her temple and take her over, are you?"

"That's what we were thinking. Will the Black Hat not be subject to Kay's touch?"

Torri smiled. "Certainly she will, but touching a Black Hat will come with dangers unheard of." She turned to Kay. "Kay, are you certain you want to have an intimate encounter with a Black Hat, especially with an old and nasty one like Ethylrelda of Waam—because if you touch her Shadow tech, that's pretty much what you'll be doing. Does that thought distress you?"

"A little bit, yes. But what choice do I have? Again, Sam is depending on me."

Torri thought for a moment, then: "There is a great deal of danger in what you're planning, Kay. For one, to be so intimate with Ethylrelda of Waam, an old and wicked Black Hat, could be overwhelming. She has lived long, knowing nothing but rage and hate, and you will be subject to every bit of that. You could lose yourself in the process. And, let's assume for a moment that you withstand the torrent and are able to command Ethylrelda. It is quite possible that you will make a 'friend'. She could become enthralled with you, Kay. Look at how Beth reacted—and, from what you've told me, you only touched her Silver tech for a few moments. Ethylrelda might just not be able to forget your touch, and she might come after you, provided that she lets go of you in the first place. And, by the by, Ethylrelda of Waam is probably the toughest Black Hat out there. She's on another level entirely."

"I heard she faced and killed the Grand Abbess of Kentaro in a fair fight," Phillip said.

"Yes, she did. It was a huge victory for the Black Hats."

"Then, we'll free her with our Sight," Phillip said.

"Assuming that Dav is not going with you, your Sight is not potent enough yet. But, let's say you do free her—then you'll have a love-sick, freed Black Hat that will want nothing more than to become a *Wandwilla* with Kay."

"What's that?"

Beth's arms around him, their flesh welding together.

Wandwilla ...

"A *Wandwilla* is a creature that is result of a Shadow tech Female and a Shadow tech Male who have been allowed to join themselves together—basically the man and woman become one, locked together in ecstasy, forever. I've seen one myself, years ago. It looks like a huge leafless tree that creates a pod-like fruit that is very useful in certain Cabalistic recipes. Fall asleep next to one, and you're going to have a night full of sex-fueled psychedelic dreams like you've never had before."

Kay sat there and listened, white-faced.

Torri continued. "To become a *Wandwilla* is, at the same time, a Black Hat's greatest fear and greatest ambition. For a Black Hat, who has not touched a Shadow

tech Male, becoming a *Wandwilla* is something they most certainly do not want. But, touch her for more than a few moments, and becoming a *Wandwilla* with you is all she'll ever want again. Some Black Hats, who have lived for a very long time, like Ethylrelda, manage to develop a sort of consciousness all their own independent of the Black Abbess and actively seek out a Shadow tech Male and *Wandwilla* with him, as a sort of reward for their ages of service. There is said to be a hidden world, known only to the Black Abbess, where a whole forest of *Wandwillas* grow—sort of like a Black Hat's version of heaven. I've heard there are a few located right here on Kana, located somewhere in the Tartan area. It's my goal of mine to locate these *Wandwillas* and ensure their safety."

Kay, Sarah and Phillip sat listening, open-mouthed.

"For that reason, Shadow tech Males are killed without mercy or exception. Here, on Kana, safe and sound in the League, you are protected by the Sisters, and by your parents. You must realize that, because of what you could possibly do to a Black Hat, they would, should they become aware of you, not stop until you are dead.

Waam has over a hundred Black Hats living in its city proper, and their hordes of sniveling henchmen, the Spectres, are everywhere, always on the lookout for Shadow tech Males. The sentence, should they find you, is death. So, touch her Shadow tech at your peril, Kay."

They sat there in silence for a moment.

"So, Ethylrelda, huh?" Torri said. "She's a tough one. One of the oldest Black Hats I know. My temple was in her shadow, though safely out of her way. In Waam, my temple was a large X-shaped structure, which has since been flattened. Hers is a huge sphere at least three thousand feet high, a lot bigger than mine was. It rolls around like a vast marble, flattening everything before it. Kay, come here, and let me look at you."

Kay got up and approached her. She examined him with her huge blue eyes. "I just can't get enough of your face. All of your father's good looks, and only a little bit of your mother in there to mess it up."

"Dimples, I know that you and my mother …"

"Yes—stupid isn't it? That we can't just let what happened in the past go, that we hate each other still. In the old days, few Black Hats would have gotten between us—such was the sorry state of our relationship. But, that doesn't mean that I don't cherish her husband as one of my best friends, and her fine children. We are in full agreement on what matters most—your safety, your father's safety, our family's safety. I would stand side by side with your mother to defend our families to the death."

Sarah put her glass down. "Well, I for one think we'll do just fine. We did really well in Rostov, and we've our Gifts. Kay's Gifts are unbelievable now, Aunt Torri. You should see them. Those Xaphans won't be able to stand up to us."

Torri raised an eyebrow. "Really? Well, I admire your enthusiasm, Sarah, truly. However, you're overlooking one small thing."

"And what is that, Aunt Torri?"

"You are going to be in the city of Waam. Though we often don't give the Xaphans too much credit for competence, Waam is truly extraordinary. It is a great city—it could be a great League city as well. It is larger than anything here on Kana, and possibly larger than Inarri on Onaris as well. And her inhabitants are great, too. You have how many Gifts, Sarah?"

"I have two, Aunt."

"And Phillip?"

"Just one, I think, and Kay has three."

"The people of Waam are the descendants of the House of Clovis, and they have, on average, four Gifts per person, high or low. The only Gift they don't have is the Sight. And, on top of all that, they are evolved. They are on a slightly higher evolutionary scale than we are here in the League."

"How did they manage that?" Sarah asked, quite enthralled.

"There was once a great space station that orbited the planet as Gothan was being Terraformed into a livable world, Zall-88; perhaps you've heard of it. The people aboard worshipped a mysterious feline goddess named Mabsornath who gave them great knowledge and enlightenment. The House of Xandarr then came along and coveted the knowledge to be had there and sacked the station, supposedly putting all aboard to the sword. However, it is said that a number of refugees from Zall-88 made it off the station and helped found the city of Waam, and there they performed a number of innovations meant to evolve the people living there."

"And how so?" Sarah asked.

"The layout of the city is odd, built at a topical level in a wheel configuration; however, a more detailed inspection proves it's more like a convex mirror meant to focus certain types of stellar energies. These energies are supposedly meant to bathe the body in radiance and assist it in rapid evolution. Likewise, there are odd constructs built up on the streets at various points that are as old as the city itself. Newcomers to the city often report that the constructs emit a piercing and rather unpleasant sound that the locals cannot hear. According to some, this sound enhances the senses, further accelerating evolution. Whole municipalities are built with the concept of torturing the flesh in the hopes of making it better."

Phillip set his glass down. "Aunt Torri, I've heard bits and pieces of what you mention, that Waam is a city in evolutionary transition; however, let us agree that such things can only be the worst sort of science, mad and misguided to an unheard of level, even for Xaphans."

"I really can't agree with you, Phillip. It sounds insane, and, probably, many aspects of it are; still, there is no denying that the people of Waam can do incredible things, and it is a good thing for the League that they are not more invested in the ongoing conflict with us as are some of the more war-like Xaphan Houses. So, with that in mind, all four of you must tread with the thought that you are, at best, on par with the Waamites. You're not going to be 'out-Gifting' anybody in Waam. That said, Kay, are you fully recovered from the attack in Grove? Please be honest."

"Yes, I believe so."

"Have you any theories as to the identity of the attackers?"

Kay didn't hesitate. "Lt. Kilos thinks that my sister, Lady Hathaline, did it."

Torri sat there and didn't react. Kay went on. "And, even though it sounds bizarre, I definitely have a feeling that the distorted, bleeding creature that attacked me was, indeed, my sister—somehow warped ahead a hundred years and perverted into a monster."

Torri's expression darkened. "Kay, have you ever heard the term *Killanjo*? Perhaps your mother's used it before."

"No, I haven't."

"Figures—your mother was a Hammer, and they know nothing. It's a very great pity that the League and the Xaphans are enemies. If the two sides combined forces, there wouldn't be anything we couldn't accomplish. What the League knows and what the Xaphans know are two different things entirely. The League is mighty and strong, but its knowledge is flawed. Tell me, what is the driving intellectual force in the League?"

"The Science Ministry," Phillip said.

Torri shrugged. "Please, Phillip. The Science Ministry merely expands upon doctrines of thought pre-approved by the Sisterhood of Light. The Sisters determine what is known in the League and what is not. The Sisters are wise and ancient, and their knowledge of Elder-tech is truly astounding; however, they only choose to know certain things. They are decidedly ignorant on Pre-Elder and Non-Elder knowledge, and that is where the Xaphans' knowledge excels. The Xaphan Cabalists know of a creature called *Killanjo,* for they have been plagued by them for centuries. A *Killanjo* is a kind of monster that was once a loved one: a father, a mother, a—sister. Xaphan Houses sometimes were rocked to their core by these demons wearing the guise of loved ones. These Houses, so attacked, often imploded—dying of broken hearts. A *Killanjo* is a terror weapon, a heart-breaking vision, and it is terribly effective.

"Lt. Kilos spoke of them. She called them Jennybacks."

"They have lots of names."

"Where do these creatures come from?" Kay asked.

"Don't know. Whoever is the driving force behind the *Killanjo* is our enemy—make no mistake about that. I have been a citizen of the League for over twenty years. I love the League for my husband and children, for the life that we've had the opportunity to build together. I will defend the League with my life. I've noticed that *Killanjo* are beginning to show up within the League in steadily growing numbers. They are spreading; I've been watching. I'm starting to see them pop up here and there, mostly on Hoban and some of the outer-lying League worlds, but also here on Kana as well with more and more frequency. Do you remember hearing about the collapse of House Williams on Hoban? I'm convinced it was a *Killanjo* who triggered that."

There was a thump at one of the windows, the Silver tech serpents reacting to it. They looked, and there, outside on the window pane, was a huge bluish-green bug.

"And then there's these things—these huge bugs. They're everywhere. At night I can hear them buzzing in the marshes. They make an awful racket."

"They're called Paraflies by the Science Ministry. Do you think they are somehow connected to these *Killanjo?*" Sarah asked.

"Possibly—wherever the *Killanjo* show up, so too, are these Paraflies, by the thousands. A few days ago I found them dead in droves in the marsh.

"But why? I read about that."

"Don't know—they were just dead. And, they're not really bugs either. My daughter, Tulee, loves bugs and managed to collect a whole terrarium full the other day. I looked them over. I don't know what they are, they're just not insects." Torri turned to Kay.

"Let me instruct you. Should a *Killanjo* come at you again, there are certain things you must be aware of. One: *Killanjo* can cast spells, rendering you helpless. I'm sure you already know that. You cannot let them cast a spell under any circumstance. Two: *Killanjo* carry a powerful stench with them. You often smell one before you see it. Three: *Killanjo* cannot bear the sight of their own reflection. You can use that as a defense."

Sarah was intrigued. "What is their purpose?"

Torri smiled. "What do you do when you face an enemy whose arm you cannot break, whose sword you cannot bend? Why, you strike at its heart, and so the *Killanjo*, a demon once a loved one, sent to kill its House. Tell me, Kay, how does it make you feel that your sister, somehow warped ahead in time, did these things to you?"

"Words can't describe it."

"And your mother? Should she know the truth, how would she react?"

"She would go mad with grief."

A tear dripped down Torri's face. "Precisely."

27—Through Xaphan Space

Kay Cloaked the *Goshawk,* and they set out, first to Xandarr where they resupplied, then from 3PM of Xandarr, they soared into the dark night of Xaphan space.

It was a long, lonely trip.

Traveling through League space was alive with activity. There were often other ships flying at your side—transports, Fleet vessels, merchantmen, private yachts. These assorted starcraft created a small fleet of ships flying in a loose formation, as space travel, though quite safe in modern vessels, was best shared in groups. Should your vessel break down, help was close by to assist. And, should a pirate or raider rear their ugly faces, then you had the combined firepower of your 'fleet' to send them packing. Also, even if you were travelling alone, you had the Aire-net and the holos—the broad-wave transmissions that allowed one, even in the deep sea of space, to keep up on the latest gossip, to tune in on your favorite shows or talk to your loved ones as much as you wanted. Sarah constantly had the Aire-net on, even if she wasn't watching. If you tried to turn it off, she'd immediately turn it back on and give you a dirty look.

There was nothing like that in Xaphan space.

The Aire-net receptors offered nothing but static. A few boarder-area worlds had boosters that amped up the League signals, but, on the whole, the Xaphans had nothing that bound up the various worlds in their control and made them one. Each world, it seemed, was on its own, an island in space. Occasionally, as they neared various worlds, they tuned into bizarre religious transmissions spoken by monotone priests in black churches and other morose broadcasts that they would rather shutoff than watch.

They avoided the occasional Xaphan ships that they came upon, and there weren't many. They sometimes saw battered *Merci* ships that had somehow survived the old League wars, and a few beaten up *Ghomes* that looked like beetles in the slow stages of death. They came across old derelicts and battered hulks lashed together with welded metal ties. They wondered about the poor souls inside, stuck in space in ships that appeared to be falling apart and trailing rads in quantity. Lon went into a poorly thought-out lecture on what rads at that level were doing to the tissues of those aboard, even if they were wearing protective suits. Kay, seeing Sarah's face, hushed him up.

Occasionally, they'd come across ships so bizarre they had no idea what to make of them. They were built in odd shapes, sometimes in squares, other times in triangles, polygons and other symmetrical shapes. Others were literally shapeless, looking like wads of chewed cud. And once, they spotted a huge ship in the shape of a naked woman, perfectly formed, like a giant statue moving through space.

Such sights had them scratching their heads.

Also, and this could simply have been their familiarity-starved imaginations, but space itself seemed *darker* in Xaphan territory. The various dangers of space travel, which seemed so distant when in League territory, were amplified in the sudden, lonely dark of Xaphan space. Alone in the lightless soak, nothing seemed to get closer even though they were moving at speed; all their gauges and instruments said they were moving, yet they seemed to be standing still. As the days rolled by, Sarah became increasingly paranoid and on-edge. Suddenly the *Goshawk* became not a hotrod designated for outings but a critical lifeboat carrying four desperate castaways. She stopped getting into her pajamas in the evening hours and just sat there in the cockpit nervously looking at the gauges, jumping at every sound she couldn't identify, gazing at the dim, unfamiliar jumble of stars that didn't seem to be moving. Phillip made the mistake of mentioning that he thought that they had burst a helium tank—a rather minor thing to lose, but Sarah nearly panicked and insisted they set down and repair it. The closest world was Midas 6, a black, somber world of volcanic rock and fiery pits that was a former staging zone for the Xaphan Armada in the old days of the League/Xaphan conflict.

Sarah was deeply conflicted. She demanded they set down, but why did it have to be the black, lava and fume-choked Midas 6?

"You know the old stories. The House of Bodice—weren't they wiped out on Midas 6?" she asked in a shaky voice.

Phillip debated on whether or not to answer.

"Yes," Lon said. "They died on Midas 6."

Sarah slumped into a corner, openly full of dread.

Phillip put down in an uninhabited area, and Kay dropped the Cloak. As Phillip and Lon rolled up their sleeves and worked on the tank, Sarah stood there watching them with her Poltava drawn—the hand of loneliness that had nearly squeezed the life out of them in space was replaced by the cold feeling of being watched by ghostly eyes the whole time they were down there.

Sarah looked around, seeing the bleak sky laced with feathery plumes of volcanic ash.

The House of Bodice huddling in their fallen transport once looked at this same sky. The House of Bodice went extinct on this bloody world. Cursed world, lost dreams...

Phillip and Lon repaired the tank but announced that they needed to spend the night—the engines needed a rest and the tank needed to recharge. Kay Cloaked the ship, and they went inside and stayed there. Sarah, a normally bold adventurer, didn't want to leave the ship—somewhere out there was the ancient hulk of the Bodice's death ship—where they breathed their last.

She didn't want to see it.

Lon was actually the most eager to go exploring, and he and Kay set out for a bit, under Cloak, Sarah pleading with them not to go. They returned a few hours later, announcing that there was a dark city to the west. The news didn't go down well with Sarah as she expected to be attacked at any time. That night, as they peered through the cockpit glass, they occasionally saw Xaphan ships passing overhead, and they could see a dim, reddish glow coming from the city and from various erupting volcanoes nearby. Sarah swore she kept seeing figures lurking in the dark ... *the ghosts of the Bodice.*

She swore she heard rapping on the cockpit glass.

But, all three of them Sighting could see nothing there. When they took off a few hours later, with the *Goshawk* nimbly climbing into the sky, Sarah was the happiest they'd seen her in some time.

Resuming their trip, Sarah kept checking their course, kept testing the AM/PM compasses and other navigational equipment. Everything was working correctly.

It just felt like they were lost, like they were making no progress. The stop-over on Midas 6 had not helped in the least.

Ethylrelda of Waam

28—Waam

On the fourth day, only a few hours away from Gothan, she put her face into her hands and began crying—Kay having to take her into his arms and comfort her.

Finally, like the voice of a benevolent spirit, their Aire-net receptors came to quiet but definite life, replacing the empty static that had lasted for days. Sarah, elated, put her ear next to the speakers and listened as the jumpy signal quickly grew in strength.

There were voices and laughter. Sarah listened to Xaphan comedies, and she laughed though she didn't understand some of the jokes. "I think … I think they're making fun of Black Hats!" she chirped, listening.

Then, like a tiny spit of land lost in a vast sea, there was Gothan, the fourth planet in the Omicron-Thetis system, as designated by League charts. It was a green and blue world, much like Onaris, with five uneven asteroids orbiting as moons. Gothan was a life-saver. Lit up by the cheerful-looking planet, they had light and sounds, and Gothan had a fairly interesting broadband that was half-way watchable. The programs they saw were racy, outrageous and rather pornographic in nature. Waam and Gothan around it appeared to be a rather uninhibited place.

Sarah, after watching a few undressed shows and listening to the happy voices, was instantly rejuvenated—the blood-shot scarecrow that she'd become over the last few days was gone.

Now that they were there, it was time to hash out a definitive plan. They'd had four days to scheme something up, but, in the dark night of the trip to Gothan, none of them had the energy to do that.

They'd brought a small holo-database regarding Gothan—Lon had thought of that and poured over it.

Gothan. Principality of the House of Clovis. Populated after an extensive terra-forming effort in 000021ax. A temperate world of ten continents and six major oceans. During the terra-forming years, which took two decades, House Clovis took up residence in a large space station known as Zall 88. After the planet surface was made ready for population, a small fragment of House Clovis stayed aboard Zall 88, where it is said they developed powerful technology that gave them access to true enlightenment. The station was attacked by the House of Xandarr some years later—Xandarr being jealous of the supposed technology to be had there. After they were unable to decipher the knowledge, for they had killed all aboard, the Xandarrs destroyed the station in a fit of spiteful anger.

The largest city on Gothan was Waam, a city ruled by a municipal parliament, which covered an entire continent in the northwestern corner of the planet. A popular place, over one hundred Black Hats made Waam their home.

The information in the holo-database was informative, yet fairly succinct and sterile, containing no hint of oddities in evolution or the 'super-people' Duchess Torrijayne had warned them about. Perhaps she was exaggerating, or not remembering correctly.

Phillip rolled the *Goshawk* into a high altitude arc over Waam so that they could have a look at it. It was a long sprawl of tall and squat buildings all lit up in colored lights. As Torrijayne had mentioned, it was laid out in a wheel-like configuration with eight obvious spidery broadways all leading to the central core of the city.

"That is Waam-Core in the center, per the database," Lon said. Surrounding the core were various municipalities all irregularly sectioned off by roads. The differences in architecture between the various municipalities were obvious, even from high altitude. In the northern quadrant of the city was an inland sea. From the air, it was a lot cleaner looking and more orderly than they might have thought. They'd heard that Xaphan cities were a collision of mismatched design with little thought to proper planning or layout; their brief stop on Midas 6 had reinforced that notion. Waam, however, didn't seem like that—it looked like a decent place to live and visit—at least from the air.

Dropping down, they entered a bizarre layer of orbital shipping coming and going from the city. There were Xaphan ships of all kinds and colors mixed in with colossally huge ships that resembled great spirals, sort of like bacterium. The Spirals lazily orbited over the city with the smaller, more conventional craft flowing around them like tiny sperm cells swimming around a much larger egg.

"What are those?" Sarah asked as a large green spiral grew large in the glass. Larger and larger, it had a singular organic quality and offered no hint that it was a starship and that living beings populated within.

Lon came to the glass as Phillip carefully flew over the surface. "Those are ships built in Helixical Bondarism," he said. "It's an artistic design movement that started here in Waam. My father has a wealth of information on it back home. Has something to do with an effort to 'stress' the flesh, to bend it in a pre-determined evolutionary path. A lot of nonsense, really, but the results here are quite remarkable. I was hoping to see it for myself, and one can't help but be impressed."

Sarah gawked out the glass as the *Goshawk* passed the end of the spiral. "You mean there are people in there?"

"Yes, it is a starship, though I understand the interior is quite brutal to survive in."

Phillip dropped down, and the great city stretched out beneath them in a controlled mass.

Duchess Torrijayne had given them the approximate location of Ethylrelda's temple. She said it was near where her old temple had stood in the south-central area of the city. She also said that it, unlike other Black Hat temples, moved, rolling very slowly across the cityscape like a huge black marble, crushing everything in its slow, steady path. Over the centuries, it had moved in a steady southerly course spanning several miles, the city withering and changing around it.

Black Hat temples were easy to spot from the air. They were usually black, geometric buildings devoid of lights or windows that were given a wide bit of space by the surrounding buildings. Some of them had dense, tree-filled lots surrounding them for literally miles. They saw an assortment of huge square temples, towering pyramids, ellipses, intricate polygons and spread out trapezoids mixed into the cityscape like a few black onyxes in a dumped out bag of shiny colored stones.

The temple they were looking for was a huge sphere, at least three thousand feet high. Torrijayne had told them it was easily the largest in Waam, for its owner Ethylrelda was by far the oldest Black Hat in Waam. She was reputed to be one of the most powerful Black Hats possibly ever. She had fought the Sisterhood of Light more times than can be counted, and survived, putting her Hulgismen and the Stellar Marines facing her through a meat-grinder of ferocity seldom seen. Years back, she met in battle and killed the Grand Abbess of Kentaro—quite a feat.

Her temple wasn't hard to find—like a black pearl splitting the clouds and blotting out the sun for a long way in its vicinity. They looked for Torri's old X-shaped temple which was supposed to be nearby, but they didn't see it. She told them it had been destroyed. It must have been flattened and built over since then.

So, now that they'd seen Ethylrelda's temple, what was the next step?

There was a definite ring of decrepit buildings surrounding the temple for many blocks—the Black Hat apparently a bad neighbor, the coming of her temple bringing with it death and decay. They scouted out a tall building about a mile west of the temple, and Phillip put the *Goshawk* down on the flat roof. They piled out quickly and checked their surroundings. Everything appeared to be clear, and the ship was still safely Cloaked. There were several service doors on the roof which they barred and jammed shut. They then went to the edge and took a good look around.

They were about a hundred floors up. The building was vacant, old and dusty in the afternoon sun, but it was apparently sturdy and safe enough for the ship. Nearby, Ethylrelda's temple soared into the clouds—its heights obscured in the afternoon haze. Its black surface was shiny and reflected the surroundings like an obsidian crystal ball. The area surrounding the temple was clear and neglected; the people of Waam weren't friends with the Black Hats and gave them plenty of space. In the distant cityscape, they could see two more Black Hat temples peeking through the buildings—a large black cube to the north and a spire-like tower to the west. Ethylrelda's temple was pressing up against half-destroyed buildings to its south, structures ready to be slowly crushed to dust by its ongoing, imperceptible roll.

Lon panned around with his goggles. "There's nobody around for at least several blocks—not that I can see. The large black temple ahead is featureless and windowless. I can see that it is moving at a steady but slow rate. Those buildings to its southern face are soon to be rolled over. I'd wager it progresses a few feet every year. The only opening I see is a large archway at its base which appears to lead into the interior."

"The Black Hat's open door—all their temples have such a thing. You go in, and you never come out," Phillip added.

Sarah drew her Poltava. "The piece we need could be anywhere in such a place."

She craned her head back to try and see the top of the temple, its towering heights making her feel immediately dizzy. "Kay," she said, clutching the ledge of the building for support, "what do you see?"

Kay opened up his Sight. Everything went to amber. He had to focus as his Sight tended to want to fade into the past. As it did, he saw Torrijayne's X-shaped temple rise up to the east. It was sinister to look at, knowing that Dimples, the smiling duchess was once a cruel Black Hat there. He could see Ethylrelda's temple, like a relentless juggernaut, roll backwards the way that it had come—its open door staying at the bottom, despite the movement.

Struggling, he focused his Sight back to the present and on Ethylrelda's temple. Its interior was surprising. Though huge, its internals were an intestinal tract of small, twisting passages that eventually wound their way to the top—like a huge sphere full of tightly compacted earthworms. He had thought that the Black Hat would be sitting alone somewhere near the top, as his mother was once reputed to do in her Black Hat days, but in the uppermost chamber, nobody was present.

He could see figures milling about mindlessly inside, filthy and naked: Hulgismen no doubt, a lot of them. The remains of many Hulgismen lay strewn about in various stages of decay, some freshly dead, others dusty skeletons. It was utterly barbaric inside, like an animal's den strewn with random detritus: no furniture, plumbing, lighting, or any other hint of the basic necessities a person would want in their home. This was Ethylrelda's home after all. It didn't need mentioning that there was no hint of art or decoration or any of the aesthetic accessories that intelligent beings tended to like to have. It was like a huge artificial cave.

He could also see a great deal of artifacts lying about here and there, forgotten. Kay tried to locate the piece of the machine, but, with so much lying about, he really didn't know what he was looking for or where to start, yet a further complication.

At the very bottom, peering out of the large open entrance that Lon had seen, was a solitary figure: small, female, clad in scarlet robes but just as filthy and ill-kept as the Hulgismen.

It was Ethylrelda herself—it had to be.

She moved about in a stilted, pre-programmed way, her arms held bolt straight at her side. Wearing her black, featureless sash, she gazed out at the sunshine and relative cheer of Waam. Seeing through her sash, she had a pretty, robust face with long brown hair that was matted with age and neglect. Kay felt rather sorry for her at that moment. Perhaps she longed for what was out there in the inviting city of Waam beyond the Black Abbess' Clutch; for the mundane yet wondrous things she could never have.

He thought he heard a small voice enter his head, though he might have imagined it. He heard: *Hello, Kay.*

Kay looked away and quieted his Sight.

"Did you see her?" Sarah asked.

"I did."

"And did you see the piece we need?"

"I saw lots of items in there. This is going to be tough."

"It's the cross-piece, Kay—the arch of the machine."

"I know that; nevertheless, I didn't see it. There are miles of passageways in there."

Standing there on the roof of the abandoned building, the four of them were without a plan.

Sarah turned away, as the looming specter of the temple was making her dizzy, and she wandered to the other side of the building. She looked around. "Hey, you guys, what is all of this?"

They turned and joined her. Looking northwest toward the core of the city was a vast, eclectic collection of buildings framed by broad, well-organized skyways full of flowing traffic. There was an up-and-down smattering of tall, flat-topped, workman-like buildings mixed in with guilded treasures glittering in lights and spires. Here and there, in a rather surreal blend, were buildings in the shape of smiling faces, half-bodied busts and full-formed statues hundreds of feet high. There were oddities of nature, animals, flowers and more of the helix-like spirals seen in the skies above, only tipped on their sides.

"Does that building over there look like a fork?" Sarah asked pointing.

"These odd buildings are built in Mirrism, yet another, more watered-down form of Bondarism," Lon said. "According to my reading, it's just an artistic style of design meant to use common objects in unexpected ways."

"What's the point of all this?" Sarah asked.

"Evolution."

Kay headed toward the service door. "I feel more evolved already. Shall we?"

With nothing else to do, they decided to descend into Waam and scout out the surrounding area for themselves—just in case they had to make a break for it. Sarah and Phillip in their linens and black dusters didn't figure to stand out much, but Kay, with his Blanchefort coat and CARG, and Lon, with his long Probert coat, could be a problem. And then there was the hair—Sarah with her blue and Kay's purple might pose an issue. This was a Xaphan city, and they assumed the people would be sober and drab, conservative in the extreme. Kay removed his coat and borrowed one of Phillip's linen shirts. Lon, his pockets full of gadgets, including his CEROS, didn't want to be without his coat, so they agreed to let him wear it.

"What are you packing in there, Lon, just so I know?" Phillip asked.

He smiled and opened his coat. "I've got my CEROS—I never go anywhere without it. I've also got my spyglasses and goggles with an assortment of prisms and a no-Cloak freedom light and Meisha's Dirge Defeater. I've also got a sandwich, which is probably bad by now—I should throw it away. And, I've got a PITCOCK WONDER GUN."

"A what?" Sarah asked, half-laughing.

"A PITCOCK WONDER GUN. It comes from my mother's House, and this one here actually belonged to my mother in her younger days."

"Lady Branna of the Science Ministry used to carry a gun?" Phillip asked.

"Yes, she did. My mother is a scientist, and sometimes in order to quest for knowledge, one must shoot one's way to the truth."

Kay thought a moment and tried to imagine Lon's mother, the tiny, blue-haired Lady Branna, dainty and elegant, packing a gun and using it as well.

Lon continued. "It's a sort of jack of all trades gun. It fires five large caliber shots which can perform a variety of effects, sometimes area-affecting, sometimes not." He pulled a large-barreled gun out of his coat with a rotating cartridge holding five, walnut-sized slugs. "I always load mine out with a nice combination of stuff: a Perdition's Smoke round, a Hell-Fire, a Dragon-slayer for punch and a Sad Sampson No-Cloak. But, I've got a whole brace full of different ones." Lon put the huge weapon back into his coat.

Sarah clapped him on the shoulder. "Good to know, Lon, that you're armed to the teeth."

Making sure they had their small, trusty Poltavas safely concealed, Sarah and Phillip put their SAPPs on, and Kay debated on taking his CARG; it was an odd, elegant weapon and might draw attention.

"Don't worry," Lon said. "It looks pretty much like a sword, and I'll wager there will be quite a few swords roaming around on the streets."

Kay saddled his CARG, cocked his purple Poltava and stuck it in his pocket. They un-jammed one of the doors and went down the rickety stairwell to the street. The building had possibly been some sort of multipurpose structure at one time, but now it was in ruin and slow decay. When they got to street level, they bore west of Ethylrelda's temple, its shadow looming over them. The immediate area surrounding the temple was devoid of people and urban animals; apparently, the presence of the Black Hat drove all life away.

"I feel like we're being watched," Sarah said, looking around at row after row of derelict buildings.

Kay looked around with his Sight. "I don't see anybody, Sarah. This area in the shadow of the temple is completely empty, except for us."

After several blocks of nothing, they emerged into civilization.

It appeared that their fears about sticking out were unfounded. The citizens of Waam, just like one found in any large League city, came in all styles and colors. There were stylish people wearing some sort of colorful Xaphan clothing mixed together with less-stylish folk in workmen's gear. Some carried weapons. Swords, staves, clubs and mounted axes and pistols of various makes weren't an uncommon sight. Hair color also wasn't an issue—there were lots of blue heads of hair bobbing down the street, along with an assortment of other bright colors; reds, greens, yellows, purples and blacks. Apparently gaudy hair colors were in style in Waam. Quite surprising.

As they walked about, they saw all sorts of people going about their business. Though they were Xaphans, they didn't seem much different from League citizens. People moved about, some laughing and talking with friends, mothers walking with their children, some carrying sacks of groceries and other sundries.

Flowing along at both ground level and in the heights was well-ordered traffic. The bulk of the traffic confined itself to the eight highways flowing toward the core, the nearest one being several blocks to the north. Much less traffic trawled the side streets. They couldn't help but be impressed with what they saw. League vehicles were very functional; they worked well with little thought to finery and aesthetics. These Xaphan vehicles were gaudy and self-indulgent in the extreme featuring shiny metal accessories that served no discernible function, over-stuffed plush seating, rim-rams, smoke and noise-makers and more. Other sky cars were built in geometric fashion, tumbling through the air in a seemingly random fashion.

There were more statues flying about with people haphazardly riding on them without the benefit of seats, harnesses or any other obvious safety accouterments.

And ...

"Hey!" Sarah cried. "Did I just see somebody 'flying' up there in the traffic?"

They looked up, Lon adjusting his goggles. "I don't see anybody flying."

"Aunt Torri's got you seeing things," Phillip added. "There's nobody up there."

Kay was impatient. "Come on; let's be on our way."

As they got father from the temple, the throng of people increased dramatically—the city chattering with life. The buildings were also transformed from abandoned and falling apart to occupied and well-kept. Waam was not a dirty city at all; in fact, the people seemed to carry themselves with a hint of civic pride. As they made their way down the street, people smiled at them and tipped their hats. The city appeared to be divided up into innumerable municipal districts, each with its own distinctive style and colors. The one they were entering was neat and tidy with baskets of colorful flowers built into the sides of many buildings. They came across a festive green and brown sign written in Vith. It said:

ENTERING AULD MUNICIPALITY. ALL ARE WELCOME HERE. WARNING: PROHIBITION STRICTLY ENFORCED AFTER THIRTY BELLS.

On the other side of the sign, facing in the opposite direction, it read in dark blue and silver, again in Vith:

ENTERING HEATH MUNICIPALITY. DRINKING ENCOURAGED ALL 42 BELLS A DAY. BUDGES AND NEDERLANDERS NEED NOT ENTER ON PAIN OF DEATH.

"I guess we're in Auld now," Kay said leading the way.

"And I suppose that I'm still in Heath," Sarah said trailing, having yet to pass the sign.

"Auld?" Phillip said. "Why does that sound familiar?"

"Auld," Lon answered, chiming in, "was one of the twenty five Elders. Don't you go to church?"

Phillip shook his head, and they continued. Kay stopped and rubbed his ears. "You guys hear that? What is that?"

"What?" Sarah asked.

"That! That ringing. You don't hear it?"

They took a few more steps, and Sarah suddenly grabbed her ears. "Oh, now I do—that high-pitched wailing sound? Oh, I can't stand it!"

Soon Phillip and Lon were hearing it, too, and they weren't happy about it. The sound seemed to be coming from a rough-hewn gargoyle that was sprouting up in the center of an intersection. It was about twelve feet high and had a rather flowing lava-like appearance to it.

Phillip approached it. "I think this is what Aunt Torri had mentioned to us about the founders of Waam and evolution. This sound, I suppose, is intended to evolve us in some manner."

"Well, switch it off, Phillip. It's making me crazy!" Sarah ordered.

He examined the rather sturdy-looking gargoyle. "I don't see any way to shut it off."

Down the street an opulent green coach came down from the sky and landed. Several ladies in flowing green gowns and minty green hair got out and began sorting out stacks of papers amongst themselves. They then walked away in different directions up and down the street. One saw them and gave greeting.

Their coach then rose silently and climbed away. Kay noted it seemed to have no drive engine; rather, it was supported and propelled by four cables that went upward into the sky and vanished from view. He honed his Sight in, following the cables. They went up and up a surprising distance of tens of thousands of feet and ended at the base of one of the flying green spirals they had seen upon arrival high above in the thermosphere.

The woman approached. She held a stack of green parchments. She was pretty and smiling.

"Greetings, citizens," she said brightly in a Waam accent. "We have service several times a day in the Cathedral of Auld, and we bid you welcome." She pointed down the street to a large church with a steeple. "May we expect you this afternoon?"

Kay spoke up. "Perhaps, ma'am, if time allows."

She noted their discomfort. "Are you new to our city? You seem to be in a bit of distress by our Servitor here and the sound it creates. I assure you, in a few minutes you'll not notice them any longer. May I ask from where are you visiting us today?"

"Holly," Sarah said.

"Conwell," Lon said at the same time. Sarah scowled at him.

Kay jumped in. "We're from far away, ma'am. Our wits are a bit addled by this machine."

She smiled. "Well, please, welcome to Waam, good people. I again entreat you to join us this afternoon. I guarantee there will be singing and music and good fellowship. Also, though you do not appear to be in need, I will mention that a free meal will be served afterwards, available to any who wish to share it with us. I will look for you." She held out a parchment, and Kay took it.

Kay noticed the smiling woman in green was armed with a large wooden club hidden in the folds of her gown.

With that, she fell away and approached others.

"Seemed like a nice lady," Kay said.

"That was odd," Sarah said. "I wouldn't have thought Elder religion would be allowed to flourish on a Xaphan world."

"It's made a comeback in recent years, especially after the Battles at Mirendra 3 where the original Xaphans were defeated once and for all," Lon said. "Sure you don't want to go to church, Sarah and Phillip? Looks like you two could use a refresher."

Phillip gave Lon a good-natured shove.

"She was also armed with a hardwood club that looks for all the world like the MT CALM, the LosCapricos weapon of House Woolover," Kay said. "House Woolover is a League House."

"Recall your history, Kay," Phillip said. "House Woolover is a split Household—some of them went with the Xaphans to preach temperance, and some stayed in their ancestral lands south of Saga. Perhaps the lovely lady is a descendant of House Woolover."

Sarah looked around and smiled. "Say, she was right. I'm not hearing that damn noise as much."

"Good thing, too," Phillip added. "I'm not hearing it either."

Sarah suddenly tensed up. "Hey, you three, take a look."

Ahead they saw a large group of people clad in black robes slithering down the street like a patch of spilt oil. They appeared to be accosting the Waamites as they passed by. "Does that lot of toughs over there look like Spectres, or am I imagining it?" Sarah said.

"You're not imagining. They do look like Spectres," Kay said.

The group of Spectres rolled around the street in their black robes accosting random citizens as they passed by. They leisurely crossed the street, holding up traffic. They knocked a sack of groceries out of a lady's hands and pushed a small urchin to the ground. As in the League, they were a roving band of punks looking for nothing more than to create chaos on those they deemed weaker than themselves.

"The Spectres are the bootlickers of the Black Hats—they run their errands,"

Phillip said. He quieted. "Remember what Aunt Torri said, they search for fellows like you, Kay. We'd best avoid them if at all possible."

"I think we've gone far enough," Sarah said. "I think we should sit down, grab a bite, and figure something out. We can't stay here for long."

"How are we going to pay for our meal?" Kay asked. "All I have is a purse full of Blanchefort haders. That's something I forgot to anticipate. Probably won't go down too well in this Xaphan city."

"I have some un-stamped gold," Phillip said. "You can pay me back later."

Sarah looked around. "I think there's a pub over there. Looks pleasant enough. Let's go in—I'm starving."

As they made their way to the pub, Kay stopped and turned red in the face. Across the street, one of the ladies in green was being accosted by a group of sniveling Spectres. They surrounded her, pushed her in the back and knocked her parchments from her hand where they scattered to the street. The Spectres laughed in their haughty fashion.

Before Sarah and Phillip could stop him, Kay was already marching across the street, Lon hot on his heels.

"Kay, did you not hear me?" Phillip hissed. "Kay!"

The Spectres saw them coming and awaited their arrival with anticipation. The crowd on the street formed a half circle to watch.

"What have we here?" one of them taunted in a cool, haughty voice.

"I believe you caused the lady to drop her parchments," Kay said in a commanding voice. "Please pick them up, and offer your apologies—immediately."

One of the Spectres went to step on the fallen papers, and Kay roughly shoved him down. The rest drew a set of slim, curved short swords from the depths of their black robes. Kay unsaddled his CARG, and Lon drew his large PITCOCK WONDER GUN, the Spectres eyeing it in dismay.

The Spectre grimaced in rage. "*Get on your knees!*" he yelled in a hideous Dirge voice, pointing at the street.

Something dampened the sound of his Dirge, and Kay and Lon stood firm, resisting the command. The Spectres looked at each other a bit put off.

The woman in green approached Kay and Lon. "I thank you, citizens; however, I am not harmed and can attend to myself."

Kay and Lon didn't listen and faced the Spectres as Sarah and Phillip joined them.

"I see a throat aching to be cut," another Spectre said, drawing his swords.

Kay drew his purple Poltava and pointed it at the Spectre, who stared at it with obvious awe.

The woman put her hand on Kay's CARG, and she lowered his gun with the other. "Please, sir, it is time for service. There is no need for a confrontation. I shall take my leave. Auld's blessings be upon you all." Leaving her parchments where they lay, she walked down the street, joined a few other ladies in green, where they then went to the church and disappeared inside.

Kay and the Spectres stared each other down for a moment. "Done your good deed for the day, it appears," one of them said. "I fancy your gun."

"Why don't you go and lick the boots of some dirty courtesan," Kay suggested. "If I see you accosting anybody else again today, I will be glad to teach you a hard lesson."

The Spectre started to say something back, but then bowed low in a dramatic flourish. "Well then," he said as arrogantly as he could, "I suppose I have work to do." The Spectres turned and walked away.

Kay lowered his CARG.

"Ah," Lon said putting his gun away, "Meisha's Dirge Defeater gets `em every time. I hate the Dirge." He patted his coat.

"What are you trying to do?" Sarah asked angrily. "I'm always up for a fight, but this isn't the place for it. Remember where we are and what we're here for."

"I can't abide bullies," Kay responded saddling his CARG. "They harassed that sweet missionary who was doing nothing but trying to spread good cheer." He safed his Poltava and put it back into his pocket.

"She was armed with a MT CALM, Kay. She was far from helpless," Phillip added.

"I don't care."

The encounter over, they went across the street and entered the pub.

29—Thomasina the 19th of Waam

Inside the pub, they found an out-of-the way table and sat. Even in the enemy city of Waam, Sarah had a healthy appetite, and she ordered a lot of food, having no idea what she was selecting. Wary of eavesdroppers at first, it soon became apparent that nobody was interested in them in the least. People ate their food or drank at the large bar. Sportsmen plied their trade several tables down, and courtesans of varying degrees of pulchritude and cleanliness enticed prospective clients. As they ate their meal, they soon were deep into their planning, considering various methods and options. Using their utensils and condiments as visual aids, they slid them around on the table, but no matter what configuration they came up with, nothing seemed promising. It was looking more and more that the only option available was to simply walk in and try to take over Ethylrelda as quickly as possible—a prospect Kay did not relish in the least.

After some time had passed, the door to the pub opened, and twenty Spectres came in. They spread out, occupying strategic locations all over the pub as people quieted down. Conversations hushed, the cheerful atmosphere dried up. Some people Wafted away in a blast, apparently wanting to avoid them.

Three of them slowly approached their table and, with a bit of theatricality, pulled out chairs and sat down.

They sat staring at each other in silence.

They must know, Kay thought; *they must know that he was a Shadow tech Male.*

"I wonder," one of the Spectres said after a long silence, "if you really think you're going to be walking out of here with that weapon."

Kay looked down. "My weapon?"

"Yes, that fine gun you carry. Looks rather valuable."

Before Kay could respond, Sarah chimed in. "Listen, Spectre, why don't you go home before you get hurt."

The Spectre smiled and pulled its hood back, revealing an attractive, blonde-headed woman. "We are not street urchins, like the wretched Milbrats you faced earlier—we are of the Drune. We are the elite Spectre order of Waam. Now, give us your gun, or none of you will walk out of here. We'll not ask again." She pulled her hood back down.

Kay was burning to give this Spectre a taste of his CARG, but he couldn't create too much of a scene. Questions might be asked. His status might be uncovered.

One of the other Spectres began rustling. "Yes," he said in a sniveling voice, "and give us your money while you're at it, as well." The Spectre reached into his robes and pulled out a small prism. "Let's see what you got on you."

Just then, the door to the pub opened admitting the sounds of the street and the pinkish light of early sunset. The city bells were tolling—thirty bells. Ten smiling women dressed in green and brown leather armor casually walked in. Many people, upon seeing them, groaned. Kay recognized two of them as the ladies in green gowns passing out parchments on the street earlier. Now they appeared like they were dressed for action, though they still smiled pleasantly.

Their leader walked in a moment later. She was dressed the same way as the rest, except she wore a visored leather helmet, her long green hair spilling out of a hole in the back. Her presence was commanding.

"Good evening, friends," the lead woman said in a lilting voice. She carried herself in a regal fashion. She was fit and well-formed with a slim torso, perfect hips, long legs and fairly broad shoulders. Her eyes were large and dark brown and glinted with a thoughtful light. A very attractive woman.

"I trust everyone has enjoyed themselves tonight. However, I see that it is thirty bells, the sun will soon be down, and you've your wives and families to return to. I am afraid the pub will be closing shortly, and I advise all in attendance to head home in peace." And then she added: "Now."

She noted all of the Spectres present. "That includes you, Spectres, or shall we have a repeat of last week?" A few Spectres walked out obediently.

The barkeep threw his rag down in frustration. "Xaphan's Beard, Thomasina! This is a lawful establishment, and all my customers have conducted themselves in an orderly fashion—even the dammed Spectres. The most notorious rabble-rouser I've had to contend with lately is you!"

Thomasina laughed and approached the bar. "Thirty bells, Ruben, you know that. And this … rotgut … that you serve in flowing quantity has yet to take its full effect. So, while things are still above board, while the minds of your patrons are still clear, why not end the evening on a positive note?"

A sportsman sitting at a game with a few Xaphan sailors was unimpressed and called for more booze. "Woman, the evening is young, there is mutton still to eat, ale yet to be quaffed and fools' pockets still to empty. I am going nowhere."

The woman in green armor looked at the man and smiled. Suddenly, a large wooden club, carved with glyphs, sat in her hand. All of the armored women in her entourage likewise produced clubs. MT CALMs, every one of them.

She approached the sportsman and gave his glass of strong spirits a tap with her club.

"If you spill my drink, I'll take it out of your hide!" the sportsman said. He picked up the glass and tossed it back.

His eyes bugged out of his head, and he spat out the liquid in a surprised spray.

"Water!" he cried in dismay.

"Indeed," the woman said laying the end of her club gently on the tabletop. "As I have said, this pub is closed. I'll not say it again, lest you'd like to walk home with your teeth in a bag."

Enraged, the sportsman pulled a small Laserlock energy gun from his coat. Moving like a green cat, the woman whacked the gun out of his hand with a blow from her club. She followed it up with a quick bonk to the forehead which seemed to utterly drain the sportsman of all his hostility. He oozed back into his seat, a contented grin on his stubbly face. The green-haired woman then, with strength belying her slender size, picked him up over her head, took a few steps and threw him out the door.

She turned to the other tables, club in hand. "Again, and for the final time, myself and my Singing Ten bid you return to your homes lest you be chaperoned out in a similar fashion to that gentleman there! That goes for you, too, Spectres. Out!"

Resigned, the pub filled with the sounds of shuffling chairs and moving feet as the patrons began to empty—some Spectres mixed in with the rest. Appeased, the green armored women sang an Elder hymn and even passed out religious holo literature to the pub patrons as they exited.

As Kay and the rest watched, they noted in a bit of amazement as the rather simple-looking people exited the pub. Most walked out via the door while some Wafted away and others casually walked up the side of the wall and went out a window.

A few even seemed to take flight and soar out the windows.

The leader, whom the barkeep had called 'Thomasina', chatted with various patrons as they made their way out. Once or twice she got a small money bag out of a pouch in her armor and handed out several coins.

Like a mother hen overseeing her roost, she approached Kay's table and noticed nobody sitting there was in the process of taking their leave. She gave them a good hard look. "I told you to leave, Spectre," she said to the leader.

"We have business with these four that does not concern you, Portator," the lead Spectre said.

The other one holding the prism lifted it up and gazed through it. He stood up suddenly and was shocked. "Great Marilith!! Invernan!!—this one's a Shadow tech Male!"

All eyes in the pub turned to Kay.

The Spectres looked at Kay, shocked for a moment, then they picked up their weapons and made to attack. "Kill this one!" the Spectre shouted. "Invernan! Gaaa!!!"

Some of the Spectres sprang to action. They vanished in a puff—all Cloaking themselves into invisibility.

The lead Cloaked Spectre attacked. Kay unsaddled his CARG and let his Sight go. The pub interior went to the now familiar amber tint, and he could plainly see the Spectre standing there in front of him.

"*Stand still and lift your chin!*" she commanded with the Dirge.

Lon's Dirge Defeater squelched the sound of her Dirge. He quickly crossed her duel rapiers, which were headed for his throat. Sarah and Phillip lit their Sight and formed their SAPPs into long broadswords.

"Drunes!" Thomasina yelled. "Drunes!! Protect the people!!"

Cloaked Spectres began attacking in earnest, some running with speed, some flying like robed bats.

The armored ladies formed a defensive position, trying to protect the remaining patrons from Spectres that they couldn't see. They swung their clubs in precise, well-trained strokes, hoping to score hits. They seemed quite adept at combating Cloaked opponents, and several Spectres fell out of Cloak unconscious.

One of the green ladies went down, slashed in the mid-section after a Spectre Wafted to her left.

As Kay battled his Spectre, his Sight wandered away into the near future. He saw her Wafting to his right and burying her rapiers into his neck. He Wafted to counter hers, and they got into a protracted Wafting duel, blowing Sarah's, Lon's, and several patrons' hats off. Two more Spectres Wafted in to overwhelm Kay—the four of them Wafting this way and that in a near continual blast.

He Sighted a flying Spectre swooping in for the kill. Sarah, Sight lit, cleaved him in two with her SAPP.

The remaining Spectres, in a sudden killing frenzy, began attacking anything in range.

Ruben, the pub-keep, cried out and went down, holding his bleeding arm. Thomasina jumped to his side, defending him with her club. As Kay went round and round with his three Wafting Spectres, he Sighted another Spectre Wafting in front of Thomasina, getting through her defenses and killing her.

"Phillip, Sarah, defend at the bar—quickly!" he shouted. "Lon, get under the table!"

Phillip and Sarah ran in that direction, but Sarah got intercepted along the way by a Spectre. In too close to get a good swing with her SAPP, she dropped it and engaged the Spectre hand to hand, the two rolling on the floor.

Phillip ran to Thomasina's side, his Sight lit in a silver stream. He engaged as the invisible Spectre Wafted in, using his SAPP in short, economical strokes. Soon, he had the Spectre down. More came in, the battle raging, Thomasina now anticipating Phillip's movements and lending her MT CALM into the action.

Sarah picked up her battered Spectre and threw him, literally, out the door.

Kay was very worried about poor Lon. He tried to keep an eye on him even as he soared about the pub with his Wafting Spectres in close pursuit. He'd sworn to Lady Branna he'd protect Lon.

Perhaps he needn't have worried. Lon stood, jumped on the table, and put on an odd set of goggles, adding a quick adjustment to the lenses. He then drew his CEROS from the depths of his coat—it looked like an ornate dinner plate. With Cloaked Spectres bounding, leaping and swooping in on him, he raised the CEROS to show it to them as was tradition; then, he loosed it, the hinged silver weapon howling through the air. He took down a flying Spectre, caught the weapon and then gutted another one. He assisted one of the armored ladies who had been taken off her feet, and downed another one on the return stroke. Kay was impressed. Lon might have been a shy and unassuming fellow most of the time, but his mastery of the CEROS was clear. With his CEROS, he stood tall, and was calm and dispassionate, picking his targets with care, using his weapon with lethal efficiency.

Elsewhere, Kay was a tornado of movement, Wafting across the floor, then up into the rafters, then down behind the bar, the three Spectres attempting to Waft with him. He could end this windy confrontation right here and now and slay all three at a whim, but, as usual, his Sight wandered off into the future, and the things he saw gave him pause.

He glanced at Phillip and Thomasina fighting side by side near the bar, and he saw the future.

He saw Phillip and this green-haired Xaphan woman far away in time. He saw them in each other's arms. He saw them carving their initials on a tree in the Grove: P + R (R?? Kay didn't quite understand that). He saw the woman *flying* over the tree-lined horizon of the Telmus Grove and Phillip sitting on a blanket watching and clapping. He saw marriage and children. He saw Phillip happier than he'd ever seen him and the woman, this Thomasina, yet another odd but worthy addition to the collection of ladies from strange places having married into the House of Blanchefort. He thought he saw a few vague images of conflict along the way, but he didn't focus on those; he just looked at the end result: Phillip and Thomasina happy, he and his Xaphan bride, meant for each other.

And it all depended on what Kay did right at this moment. If Kay stayed in the heights and killed his three Spectres, that future would vanish, and Phillip and Thomasina would not be together. Both would be much less happy, the future much less bright, the two of them having, unknowingly, settled for somebody else. Kay saw Phillip as a dreary man in a dreary future, his potential not met. He saw Thomasina as bitter and fat, growing jaded in her long, lonely life as a Xaphan Matriarch. Without each other, both of their individual potentials were to be stunted and un-grown. Regarding a person's potential, Kay's mother was fond of saying that the mind sets the stage, and the soul provides the raw material, but it's the heart that truly inspires one to be his or her best, to meet his or her potential—and Phillip's heart, unmotivated, uninspired, unchallenged would fail him without this Xaphan woman at his side.

If he instead spared the Spectres and Wafted down to the bar right now, then Phillip, his cousin, his best friend, could have what, ultimately, everybody wants—a happy ending.

He thought about it for a quick moment as he only had a second to decide Phillip's fate, and then he Wafted down.

Here you go Phillip—my gift to you. Enjoy it.

Kay appeared in a blast by the bar, the three Spectres appearing a moment after. He took a step back and tripped on a spittoon. He knew it was there but decided to play this out to the fullest. This was Phillip's moment.

✶ ✶ ✶ ✶ ✶

A cyclone of wind hit Thomasina square in the chest and blew her off her feet. She fell against the bar and hit her head.

The confused room spun a little. She saw the pub in a flurry of movement. She saw her Singing Ten fighting a desperate battle with a bunch of Cloaked, Wafting Drune Spectres. They often didn't see Drunes in this part of the city; Drunes were dangerous. She saw a small, pot-bellied boy in a long coat and goggles standing on a table with a strange weapon which he cast, slaying a number of Spectres in an impressive fashion. She saw a blue-haired girl wearing a black coat in a berserker-rage, fighting several Spectres hand-to-hand.

The fellow with purple hair and holding a silver, pipe-like weapon of some kind appeared nearby in a fast Waft and stumbled to the floor, tripping over Ruben's prize spittoon—legend tells that Princess Marilith of Xandarr, hero of heroes, once spit into that spittoon, and it became Ruben's treasure.

That purple fellow—the Spectres said he was a Shadow tech Male—and, if that's the case, then he was a dead man. The Spectres will come for his bones. She shouldn't get involved, for she had to think of her people. She did not need more Spectre orders overrunning her district; they were a handful as is.

And she saw the fellow in a black coat, whom she'd briefly teamed up with, standing tall against the wind, the long split tails of his coat flapping in the breeze of the Waft, holding his black sword. He glanced back at her, his eyes glowing with a silvery light.

Glowing eyes. Auld taught that people with glowing eyes are favored, can see all that is hidden. She had never seen the Gift of glowing eyes—she didn't believe it really existed. But look, look at his eyes. What had Auld brought her today?

His soul … she could see his soul there in his light, all his thoughts and dreams laid out on a hint of silver tableau.

Here is a good man from far away, an honest man. A strong man, one strong enough to stand at her side. She saw herself planning elaborate schemes and complicated kidnappings—all intended to make this man with glowing eyes chase her and go to places she wanted him to go; always she was the prize, waiting at the end of the adventure with open arms. She felt an instant connection with him, a oneness—the two of them now linked via the silver causeway of his glowing eyes. Auld wants this, she thought; the Elders have made this possible.

Auld has brought this man to her.

He looked away and fought people she couldn't see. He could see them plain and true with his glowing eyes.

He skillfully swung his sword, and a Drune Spectre appeared on the floor, dead. He exchanged positions, moved his weapon a few more times, and another Drune appeared, bleeding, slain.

Clean fighting technique, short, fuss-free strokes. She approved.

And another, fallen, dead. He picked up the purple Shadow tech Male, and they stood there together. She could feel the kinship between them, the closeness. She felt a hint of jealousy—she wished a kinship with him, too.

The berserker girl with blue hair arrived at their side. Who was she? What was her relationship to this man with silver eyes? She felt her stomach constricting.

She groaned rather theatrically, and the man with glowing eyes turned and helped her up.

✶ ✶ ✶ ✶ ✶

Lon saw a Spectre ready to kill a green woman. The CEROS howled, and the Spectre fell. Lon then put his weapon down and pulled a small prism from his coat. He set it on the table and turned it on. It cast a thin, pinkish light that feebly lit the pub. Drawing his PITCOCK WONDER GUN, he spun the cartridges, aimed at the rafters and fired with a booming report.

The capsule went up a bit and then exploded, filling the pub and rafters above with a fine red powder.

Suddenly all the Cloaked Spectres lit up like stringy cats under a street light. Thomasina's group gave a battle cry and engaged the now plainly visible Drune Spectres, and they began falling wholesale; the ladies' skill with their MT CALMs was clear. The MT CALM was a weapon noted for its ability to drain the fight out of anybody it hit and for its miraculous tendency to transform spirits and beers into plain water, a handy tool for the determined pub-rouster and prohibitionist. It was said to be made from the heart of a secret type of tree and was lathed with a supposedly enchanted set of gouges. One hit was all the ladies needed, and the Spectres dropped in a contented pile.

Soon, order was restored, and the city police came charging in, whistles blaring. They spoke a few words to Thomasina and began pulling the Spectres out into the street.

Thomasina went to Ruben. He was wounded. She called for one of her ladies to fetch a local Cabalist to mend his wound. She then mounted her club in a brace at her back, approached Kay and grabbed him by the scruff of the neck. "My Ten," she said, "restore order here. I will deal with this lot myself."

She whispered into Kay's ear. "*If you value your skin, do nothing, say nothing, and come with me.*"

Several of Thomasina's guard came and surrounded the four of them. Scanning, the Singing Ten reached out to disarm them. Sarah, still all pepped up from the fight, took exception. "Hey!" she cried.

"It's all right, Sarah," Kay said calmly and handed over his weapons.

Disarmed, Thomasina led the four of them out into the street. "They'll fetch a fair price, eh?"

There, waiting by the curbside, was a large open-air coach—green and brown and gaudy, just like their armor. It was similar to the one they'd seen earlier in the day driven by cables trailing up into the vast sky. Thomasina threw them in, and the coach went up into the air. The coach moved smoothly with a great deal of silent acceleration up into the sky, pinning them back into their seats a bit. They went up and over the tall, flat-topped buildings, covering a number of city blocks in just a few moments, and then began a quick descent into a large wooded compound below. There were at least twenty good-sized buildings situated within the compound and a central manor hall. Several of the buildings on the grounds were quite tall, rivaling the neighboring buildings in height. All of the buildings had a greenish tint to them. Between the buildings were nicely landscaped grounds including ponds, tree-lined paths and innumerable shrines to the Elders.

They were set down on the pebbled drive before a large manor built of serpentine and sandstone. They got out of the coach and were ushered in.

Green appeared to be the featured color, and it was everywhere, in the marbled floor, in the polished walls, in the jeweled ceiling. She led them into a large study plush with inviting couches, again mostly green. She unmounted her MT CALM and set it aside. She then pulled her tall brown boots off and put them in a corner. She flexed her tired feet and removed her helmet, allowing her long, green hair to come flowing out.

"Sit and be comfortable," she said. "Remove your shoes if you like. I apologize for pulling you out of Ruben's pub in such a fashion, but it wasn't safe. The Spectres announced that you are a Shadow tech Male, and that is a very dangerous thing to be in this city with so many Black Hats around. The Spectres that grovel at their feet have standing orders to kill Shadow tech Males upon discovery. They, even now, are most likely gathering their forces. Some of those were Drunes in the pub—quite a high-level order—very powerful, much more so than your average street-prowling Spectre. We don't see them very often here in Auld. No doubt they'll be arriving here in short order, demanding that I turn you over to them."

"With all due respect, ma'am," Phillip said. "We are not helpless—not against them or you."

Thomasina turned her gaze to Phillip and studied him with her huge brown eyes. She looked at him for a bit, apparently distracted, then continued. "I've no doubt, sir. It appears that we have not yet had time for formal introductions. I am Thomasina the 19th. I rule over this district as its Portator, I sit on the municipal parliament, and I am also the local magistrate. It is a duty I take very seriously."

A servant entered the study and spoke a few words to Thomasina. "Refreshments for me and my guests," Thomasina ordered, and the servant left.

"It appears things are happening quickly beyond the compound walls, as I previously mentioned. Spectres from multiple orders will be here soon."

"Our business here in Waam need not concern you, Great Lady," Kay said. "We shall take our leave and spare you such an inconvenience."

"Is that a fact, Shadow tech Male?" Thomasina asked with a rather unpleasant tone. "You fought rather well in the pub, but you would be four against thousands, and, should you somehow manage to put up a good fight, the Black Hats themselves would become involved, and nobody wants to see that. Black Hats roaming the streets is never any good for anybody. I suppose that honesty is your best course at the moment, as I can either be a great friend to you, or a terrible enemy, make no mistake, sir, and I like truth-telling. We can start with your names. I have already given you mine."

She pointed at Phillip. "You first."

Phillip looked around, clearly unused to being addressed ahead of Kay, who, in the family chain, out-ranked him. "My name is Lord Phillip of Blanchefort. And these are …"

Thomasina interrupted him. "I'm sorry … Blanchefort did you say? As in the League House of Blanchefort of Kana? As in the House of Captain Davage, the scourge of Princess Marilith?" She sat back and was rather annoyed. "I said that I wished for an honest discourse, and you set off with an outlandish lie. That does not bode well for us here right now, does it? If you didn't have such a handsome face, '*Phillip,*' I'd turn you out into the streets, let the Spectres have you."

Phillip continued. "It's not a lie."

"Oh?" Thomasina got into Phillip's face. As all noted, she didn't get up and walk around the desk; she *flew* over it, legs bent slightly at the knee, hovering in the air. She stared intently into his eyes, her feet not touching the ground. She seemed to be making a show, displaying her abilities for him to appreciate up close.

"I have a talent for discriminating truth from lie," she said. "Go ahead, *Phillip*, tell me again—to my face."

Phillip, always the quiet one, appeared quite bashful and looked to the floor. "I am Phillip of Blanchefort and …"

"Look me in the eye, please," she said interrupting.

Phillip looked up and locked eyes with Thomasina as she invaded his space, floating on air. He continued. "I am not lying. Captain Davage is my uncle. My companion here is Lord Kabyl of Blanchefort, his eldest son. He carries the CARG, though, of course, we have been disarmed."

Thomasina sighed. "You have the most remarkable hazel eyes, sir. Surely you've been told that before. Now, tell me, what is a CARG?"

"It's the LosCapricos weapon of House Blanchefort. It's a tube-like weapon with a hilt, rather like a sword."

Thomasina released Phillip from her gaze and returned to her desk, flying over it and settling back down. There, she pressed a button and sat back. "Just a moment, please," she said.

They all stood in silence. Thomasina's gaze was like a vise, and Phillip withered a bit in it.

Seconds worth of silence felt like hours. Kay spoke, trying to break the tension. "Do all people fly in Waam?"

Thomasina seemed pleased and eager to talk. "No, not all. My father was a man of Bondar, where people fly." She turned to Phillip. "Can you fly, sir?"

"No, ma'am."

"And I can't make my eyes glow like you did in Rubin's pub, so it's a trade-off."

An armored woman came in holding a large basket full of their weapons. The tubular shaft of Kay's CARG stuck out like a gangly lamp post. She set the basket down on the table and turned to leave. She stopped and went before Lon, where she curtsied. She then left the room.

Thomasina inspected the contents of the basket. "Galada offers her thanks," she said absently to Lon. "For assisting her in the pub. Now then ..." She pulled Kay's CARG out of the basket and looked at it. "Is this it? Is this the CARG you mentioned?"

"Yes, my lady."

She carefully looked the CARG over, turning it about, examining it in detail. She noted with her fingers its smooth, tube-like shaft.

"Its balance is superb," she said balancing it on her fingertip. "It's nice and light, too." She saw the name etched into the shaft. "What's SAMMIDORAN?"

"'Sammidoran' is the name of Lord Kabyl's girlfriend," Sarah answered, having been unusually quiet through all of this so far.

"How quaint," Thomasina said giving Sarah a quick glance. She turned to a terminal on her desk and punched a few buttons—her large brown eyes going back and forth from the screen to the CARG and back again. After a moment she seemed satisfied. "It certainly looks like a CARG, but maybe you killed somebody for it. Maybe 'Sammidoran' is somebody else's girlfriend."

Kay got out his purse and flipped a Blanchefort coin to her, which she caught out of the air. She looked at it and flipped it back to him. "Vith currency. Again, you could have taken the fellow's purse as well."

She glanced at Phillip. "You don't seem like a murderer to me, Lord Phillip—no murderer has eyes like that. I'll assume for the time being that you do not frequent company with the like as well, therefore, it seems we have esteemed visitors in Waam today." Again she turned to Phillip. "Where is your CARG, sir?" she asked looking into the basket. "The long black one I saw you fighting with in the pub? I don't see it in here."

"I am still training with the CARG. I prefer the SAPP. I was using a SAPP in the pub."

"The SAPP? What is a SAPP? I am not familiar with that weapon."

Phillip approached the basket and took out his SAPP—it looked like nothing more than a long, black scarf.

She seemed puzzled. "What is this?"

"It's the SAPP, Great Lady," Phillip said handing it to her. "It is the LosCapricos weapon of House Ruthven—my father's House. House Ruthven serves in fealty to another; therefore, we took the name of Blanchefort as is tradition—our mother is Captain Davage's sister, Lady Poe of Blanchefort. The SAPP is a type of cloth woven in secret and loomed using rare materials. It will bend to its user's will, shaping itself into virtually anything."

Thomasina examined the cloth, then handed it back to Phillip. "Really? Let's see. Make it do something."

Phillip took the SAPP, made sure he had plenty of room, then brought it to life. It twisted about for a moment like a snake, and then hardened into the form of a black sword. Thomasina smiled and clapped. "Yes, excellent! I've read about all of the various weapons the Great Houses of the League use, but I've only seen a few until now. I'm very impressed, Lord Phillip."

She handed Kay his CARG and began taking all of their weapons out of the basket, laying them out on the desktop. She gave a soft whistle when she looked at the Poltavas, at their beauty and craftsmanship. "These are works of art," she remarked.

She picked up Sarah's blue one. "Whose is this?" she asked.

"That's mine," Sarah responded. "And that SAPP over there is also mine."

Thomasina smiled and gave it to her, butt first. She also gave Sarah back her SAPP. Thomasina then picked up Kay's purple one. "I'll wager this one is yours, sir," she said smiling to Kay. He nodded, and she handed it to him. He could tell by the weight that it was unloaded.

Her eyes bugged out as she looked at Lon's PITCOCK WONDER GUN. She picked it up, pointing the barrel at the ceiling. "Who belongs to this, please?"

"Yes, that's mine, Great Lady," Lon stammered. She winked at him and gave it back, its chambers empty. "Oh, and the CEROS there—that's mine, too," Lon added.

Thomasina whirled around and looked. "This?" she asked seeing the round, silver CEROS. "I thought it was a supper plate."

"No, Great Lady, no." She tossed it to him.

Thomasina then picked up Phillip's Poltava and held it. She noted its green and brown coloration—which matched her armor almost perfectly. She burst into a smile. "And, could it be that this belongs to you, Phillip? I'm sorry. May I call you Phillip?"

"Of course."

"I must say I like the colors. Green and brown. Very interesting."

"An odd coincidence," Phillip remarked.

"There are no such things, sir. I think Auld has spoken to us," Thomasina replied. "You know what is said: 'One cannot go against the wishes of the gods.'"

"Yes, I—"

She held the Poltava up. "Go ahead, Phillip, take it. I give it back to you."

Phillip reached out, and Thomasina moved her hands. He moved his hand, and again she moved hers—their hands moving in a crazy zigzag pattern. Finally, she put his gun behind her back and pushed out her bosom. "Well, come on, Phillip. Take your gun." She stood there and looked at him invitingly, lips parted.

The servant returned with a tray of goblets full of rich, cherry-red liquid. Thomasina turned to address her, and Phillip quickly snatched his Poltava and placed it in his pocket.

"Ah," Thomasina said, "thank you, Garland." She picked up two goblets. "I've given you back your weapons as a demonstration of good faith—your ammunition will also be returned later, once we've established a few things. I'm not afraid of your swords, for I can handle myself against those, should you choose to raise them." She offered a goblet to Phillip. "Please, Phillip, try this. I'm certain you'll love it as much as I do."

She paused and looked around the room. "And so, I now know who you are, Lord Phillip, and who he is," she said pointing to Kay, "so who else do we have here? Is this attractive lady with the lovely blue gun your wife, perhaps?" she asked referring to Sarah.

"No, no, Great Lady. This is my twin sister, Lady Sarah of Blanchefort, and this fellow is Lord Lon of the House of Probert." Lon doffed his hat.

"Sister, ah, good, good." Thomasina smiled at Lon. "I was greatly impressed with your skill, sir, and at your defeating the Spectre's Cloak in the pub. Very handy." She thought a moment. "Probert, Probert, why does that name sound familiar?"

"My father is the lead engineer for the Stellar Fleet, my lady."

"I see, so he designed those pretty vessels that constantly defeat our ships in space?"

Lon deflated a little, forgetting that he was speaking to a Xaphan. "Well ... yes, I suppose so."

She laughed. "No need to feel bashful—I'm no great Xaphan patriot. My soul belongs to the Elders." Thomasina turned back to Phillip. "I am pleased to have met you all. Please relax and enjoy your drinks. I am not going to throw you out. You are safe here."

The drink was sweet and cold, clearly a fruit concoction. "Great Lady," Kay addressed her holding his glass. "If I may ask, are you perhaps, of the House of Woolover?"

She set her glass down. "Aye, we were once called by that name. I was born in the great helix floating above. It, the grounds and this very house have been in my family for centuries. I have never been away from Waam. I am rarely far from this sector of the city except when I go to Parliament. I am a Waamite, a Gothan and, by proximity, a Xaphan as well. I suppose, in the purest sense, that I am your enemy—geographically and politically speaking. However, I follow the teachings of the Elders, as I am sure that you do. My family has its ancient roots near Saga, in the Barrowlands of Kana—not too terribly far from Blanchefort if my geographical knowledge of Kana is accurate. So I suppose, in some regards, that we are neighbors, and that makes us friends."

Sarah put down her glass. "Then, how did you end up here, in Waam?"

"The House of Woolover has always been a high-minded and pious one. We have always closely followed the ways of the Elders and preached their tenets: sobriety, moderation, prohibition and self-sacrifice. During the Great Betrayal, under the leadership of Thomasina the 5th, we determined to put our preaching to the test. A fragment of the House followed the rebellious Vith Houses to the Xaphans. There, spread out in Xaphan space, we fought to bring news and the word of the Elders to these poor sinners, to demand moderation and enforce prohibition. We sacrificed ourselves—and have been here ever since. Even as the Xaphan influence faded, word of the Elders remained. We have done our duty. Please, don't misunderstand—I am not some abandoned soul longing for our ancient homeland. I am proud to be a Waamite. We are good people even though some of us might choose to sail and fight the League. We are an honest, simple folk trying to provide for our families."

She took a drink, then: "Tell me, Lord Phillip, do you attend regular services back home?" She seemed truly fascinated with Phillip and didn't appear to care much about any of the others there.

Phillip, who Kay knew couldn't remember the last time he'd set foot in church, blushed. "Err, no, my Lady, to my regret."

Thomasina leaned forward. "And are you a womanizer, sir? A drinker and slacker of duty?"

"No, my lady."

She smiled. "Then perhaps there is hope for you." She stood up, went around the desk and sat down next to him. She lifted her hand. "It is customary in Waam, when addressing a lady, to take her hand."

Phillip swallowed. "Lord Kabyl out-ranks me, my lady."

"Does he?" she said, not moving her hand. "Do his eyes glow, too?"

"No, but ..."

Thomasina sat there holding out her hand. Phillip looked to Kay and finally took it.

Kay chuckled to himself. Having seen the future—the path he'd chosen for Phillip and Thomasina was already making itself felt in a small way. *You're going to thank me for this later, Phillip.*

Thomasina brightened. “So, what are you four doing here in Waam? Certainly, it wasn’t simply to see me.”

Kay stood and answered. He told her what they were up to—about Ethylrelda the Black Hat. It took quite a while actually, with Thomasina stopping him to ask several questions.

“So,” she said. “You are here to save your woman, your ‘Sammidoran’ whose name is etched on your weapon, are you? How romantic.”

“Yes,” Kay said. “I offer my thanks for this respite.”

Thomasina gave Phillip a sweltering stare. “You have quested in search of a lady, and you have found one. Do the Elders not work in wondrous ways?”

Phillip gulped.

“Do the ladies fly on Kana, Phillip?”

“Not without a coach, Great Lady.”

“Please call me Thomasina.”

Kay allowed his Sight to wander. Beyond the manor, he could see a contingent of Spectres headed their way, escorted by several armored females. “Spectres approach,” he said.

Conceptual sketch of Waam, by Carol Phillips

30—The Spectres

Thomasina let Phillip go and returned to her desk. "I wondered what was taking them so long. Please, be seated. Now, before the Spectres arrive, let us be blunt. I could do one of two things—I could give you to them, where I'm certain a bloody battle would shortly ensue here in my home. And I've no doubt that you four could hold your own against an army of Spectres. Or I could shelter you, and nobody will be hurt. Then, at a suitable time, I could assist you in breaching Ethylrelda's temple and retrieving the item that you require. I personally have been in her temple many times assisting wayward souls whom she had ensnared."

"You'd help us?"

"Yes, I would—that is what the Elders teach, is it not? I have a price, however, one that I insist be paid."

"And that is?" Kay asked.

"We have church services here every morning at four bells. I insist that one of your party attend with me. It won't be bad, I promise. There will be joy and singing, and perhaps you will find inspiration. Perhaps you will find your faith renewed. What say you?"

They looked around at each other. Kay knew exactly who she wanted sitting in church with her. He hadn't considered the ramifications of what he did in the pub, now that this Thomasina the 19th appeared to be well on her way to falling in love with Phillip, and he didn't think she was going to be a passive participant in all of this. Something happened in that short moment when he descended to the pub floor with the three Spectres in pursuit—something profound. Maybe Thomasina was impressed by the way Phillip fought. Obviously she noticed him in a big way. In any event, Thomasina appeared to be walking happily down the path Kay had selected for her, so he only had himself to blame for any complications that may come, for he hadn't bothered to investigate those.

It'll be worth it—the complete man he saw Phillip become is worth it.

Suddenly, this was all the more complicated, but he vowed not to regret his decision.

Finally, Kay spoke, already knowing her response: "I will join you."

Thomasina didn't react. Kay felt a bit awkward. "Sarah, would you like to attend services in the morning?"

Sarah looked truly terrified and, again, Thomasina didn't react.

Phillip winced. "You said four bells?"

Thomasina nodded. "Yes, Lord Phillip, four bells."

"And it concludes at five bells, correct?"

"Incorrect, it concludes at eight bells. May I expect you, sir?"

Phillip looked like he was about to be eaten by a lion. Outside, Kay could see the contingent of Spectres approaching—they were just down the hall.

"Yes, Phillip will be honored," Kay said.

Thomasina's face blossomed into a smile. "I will look forward to the service tomorrow. I've never been to church with such a handsome man at my side."

Just then the doors to the study opened, and four Spectres came in, black-robed and hooded. They spotted Kay's group and pointed. "You are harboring a fugitive, Thomasina the 19th!" one of them rasped.

Thomasina turned to them. "Come now. Where are your manners? Announce yourselves, please."

The Spectres shrugged in a frustrated fashion. "I am Morge of the Drune. On behalf of the terrible Ruthinkiln of Waam, slayer of worlds and eater of children, we demand the living personage or dead body of the Invernan standing before us. You will give him up, or you shall die."

Another Spectre stepped forward. "I am Jessug of the Harms. I speak for the mighty Jennamaxx of Waam, douser of light and cracker of bones. She demands this Invernan be brought before her immediately, naked and shackled, where his body will be dismembered and his flesh cooked and consumed at her leisure. His genitals shall be the first to be consumed."

Thomasina winced. "Oh my," she said.

A third Spectre came forward. "I am Dez-Mortimer of the Gogan. My mistress, the fiendish and treacherous Wilhella Cormand-Grande of Waam, Queen of shit, Ruler of shit and Eater of shit, bids you go fuck yourselves and ..."

"Watch your language, please, Gogan," Thomasina responded in a commanding tone.

Reproached, he continued. "The Mad Black Hat, Wilhella Cormand-Grande, demands the immediate and corporeal banishment of this Invernan." He drew a smelly, dirty-looking sword. "With this sword, which, for ninety moons has sat in the anal tract of the sacred Malulah beast, I am commanded to perform the action at once. He will then be burned, shat upon and then made into a statue to sit forever in the throne area of Wilhella Cormand-Grande's temple, located in fabulous Waam-Core."

Thomasina rolled her eyes.

And finally, the last Spectre came forward. He stood there, quiet.

Thomasina stirred. "Well, sir, get on with it. Let's hear what you have to say."

The Spectre appeared shy and solemn—a very different attitude from the other Spectres. "I am Krotan of the Yard," he said. "I am compelled to offer greetings to the Invernan on behalf of my mistress, Ethylrelda of Waam."

Ethylrelda? Kay's ears pricked up, and he listened.

Krotan seemed bewildered by his own oratory. He continued: "Ethylrelda of Waam wishes it known that she has lived long in the service of the Black Abbess; may Her Darkness be troubled not by the Light of Dawn."

The three other Spectres mumbled something in response. Krotan of the Yard continued. "For centuries, Ethylrelda of Waam has fought the Sisterhood, killed the Sisterhood, fought the League and laid terror on the people of Waam. She has inspired nightmares and created incalculable suffering. My mistress is ancient and tired and has earned her reward—a reward she is eager to embrace. My mistress bids you welcome, Invernan, and she offers you safe passage to her temple on the sword of the Yard. We will conduct you there at speed. My mistress wishes to be one with you Invernan—it is her right."

The other Spectres were outraged.

Thomasina was shocked.

Kay was shocked.

"To *Wandwilla* is a blasphemy!" Morge shouted, drawing his swords.

Krotan drew his. "The Yard will kill any, be they Spectre, Black Hat, or unsuspecting fool, who tries to stop us! Ethylrelda of Waam will have her reward, and the Yard will deliver it to her!"

Thomasina, as if by magic, produced her MT CALM and separated them. "As always, gentlemen, there will be no killing in my home," she said. "If you wish to kill, you may go out to the street and kill, where I and my Singing Ten will then arrest you for murder. So, is this all? I expected more."

"There are more!" Morge shouted with bile. "There are many more fools from this Order and that clamoring in the streets with claims to the Invernan, but, no matter. Their voices are weak and irrelevant, and the Drune laugh at them. The Invernan will die before the hideous gaze of Ruthinkiln of Waam!"

"Fuck that!" Dez-Mortimer yelled drawing his swords. "The Invernan's fate will be to become statuary in the shit-clogged presence of Wilhella Cormand-Grande, the Mad Black Hat of Waam!"

"No!" Jessug yelled drawing his swords. "The Invernan will be consumed by Jennamaxx of Waam, marrow-sucker and harlot-supreme!"

Krotan put his swords away. "The Invernan will *Wandwilla* with Ethylrelda, and that is all there is to the matter," Krotan said quietly. He drew from his robes a black Shadow tech rose. "Which of you gentlemen is the Invernan? My mistress has a gift for him."

Thomasina sat back and smiled. "Don't you know which one it is? There are three gentlemen here to choose from."

"That fucking information has not been made plain. I will identify the prick," Dez-Mortimer said putting his swords away. He reached into his robes and pulled out a small prism. Before he could raise it up and look through it, Thomasina sprang. In four quick movements, she had the Spectres on the ground, all bonked in the head with her MT CALM. They lay there in contented bliss. She was truly a formidable fighter.

Thomasina thought for a moment, then she knelt down and spoke to the fallen Spectres. "You four will leave when you are able and return to your respective Orders. Then, you will each tell them that I have agreed to hand over the Invernan at twenty bells on the morrow. Oh, and Dez-Mortimer, you will also clean up your potty-mouth at once." She went to the door and motioned for her assistants to enter. They did and picked the Spectres up by the armpits. "Get them outside and separate them." Instantly, they dragged the Spectres off.

Thomasina returned to them. "The MT CALM happens to make those struck by it very susceptible to suggestion. So, Lord Blanchefort, you will be either captured and killed, captured and eaten, captured, killed, pulverized and made into a statue in the Mad Black Hat's throne room—which isn't a place where I'd want to be—or you will live for eternity in mind-rattling sexual bliss with a four hundred year old Black Hat. Sounds like the forth option is the most pleasant."

Kay looked at the black rose resting on the floor and unsaddled his CARG. "There is a fifth option—we shan't wait for them. We will leave under Cloak and return to our ship. I will then enter the Black Hat's temple, locate the item and be off."

"But, if you do that, Lord Phillip will miss church. Please, you'll be fine for now. The Spectres will spend the rest of the day out on the street arguing amongst themselves. I have a great wealth of experience dealing with Spectres, and believe me when I say they will not be an issue until twenty bells tomorrow. Meanwhile, I have a secret system of tunnels that will take us all the way to the Cathedral of Auld, which is quite close to Ethylrelda's Temple. In the morning, we will simply use the tunnels and be off. I'll tell the Spectres that Lord Phillip here over-powered me and took his leave. By that point, you'll be gone." She winked at Phillip.

"Isn't lying something the Elders preach against?" Phillip asked.

"Why, I don't know. I suppose we'll find out tomorrow morning in church, won't we?"

✶ ✶ ✶ ✶ ✶

Kay spent a restless night. Thomasina had given him a small room in the uppermost floor of the manor, Sarah, Phillip and Lon in adjacent rooms. Outside, in his amber Sight, he could see a mass of black-robed Spectres surrounding the compound for blocks. As Thomasina said, they seemed to be having a hard time getting along. Kay saw a lot of angry confrontations between various Spectre Orders, and fights, including a few mortal ones, broke out with frequency. But, so far, they remained beyond the walls and didn't try to storm the complex. Apparently they felt he was safely boxed in. They even had an assortment of concealed rockets and missiles, in case he should try to fly off in a craft of some sort.

And what about Thomasina? He looked around the manor. There she was, in the opposite wing, sitting in her vast bedroom. Though it was early in the morning, she wasn't asleep. She was in her room wearing a robe, several of her Singing Ten milling about her. Some were doing her hair, others her nails—apparently she was already preparing for church with Phillip in a few bells. Several ladies held green gowns for Thomasina's inspection, and she didn't seem to be able to make a choice. They all talked and giggled.

You're welcome, Thomasina.

He got up, dressed and decided to put his new skills to the test. He Cloaked himself and then Wafted through the manor, high into the night sky. He passed a shell of flying Spectres, all looking down into the compound, not seeing him. Floating momentarily on his pillow of air, he could see the vast rectangle of Thomasina's compound with its tall buildings down beneath him and the pepper-grains of Spectres camped all around its perimeter. Beyond, Waam stretched out in a pleasing cityscape of colored, blinking lights and a smattering of honey-shaded clouds. Fairly close by, about five miles away, was the black pearl of Ethylrelda's temple. Though it generated no light of its own, it perfectly reflected the lights of Waam like a crystal ball. With his Sight allowing him to see all around at once, he headed off in the direction of Ethylrelda's temple, fast Wafting, moving through the night like an invisible bird, cushioned on a nest of wind. The temple got closer at speed, and Thomasina's compound faded to the rear. In only a few Wafts, he found the abandoned building with the *Goshawk*. The ship was still Cloaked safe and sound, though he could see through it with his Sight. It was black and bat-like, sitting on its cranked wheels, asleep.

He landed on the roof near the silent *Goshawk's* aft. He felt incredibly free and burdened at the same time. He could get out of this with no problem, but Sarah, Phillip and Lon were trapped; although, if he were gone, the Spectres would leave them alone. It was he that they wanted, not them.

He stood there on the roof and enjoyed the night air and the scenery. Looking back, he could see the distinctive greenish buildings of Auld, including the tall buildings of Thomasina's compound, mixed into the skyline. They looked homey and inviting as his tired, troubled mind began to settle into a sleep-ready mode.

He took a deep breath. What was going to happen here? Though quickly becoming tired, he focused on the temple and let his Sight drift into the numerous paths of the future.

Amber.

Kay standing there in the night. Something black coming out of the temple. Kay harpooned with a Shadow tech barb and pulled into the temple fast like a fish on the line.

Wandwilla.

Another vision. *Kay in the temple. Kay lost. A thousand Shadow tech spears pointed at his throat. No place to go. Ethylrelda.*

Wandwilla.

And another: *Kay in the temple. Kay cornered by Shadow tech. Kay seizing it. A battle of wills. Kay victorious. Kay exiting with the piece in hand. Ethylrelda soon following him back to Kana. Castle Blanchefort in flames, mother dead, father dead.*

Wandwilla.

Any way he looked, it was all the same: *Wandwilla, Wandwilla, Wandwilla.* Ethylrelda was too powerful to be denied.

He became so tired, so weary. Milling through the possible futures, he saw one last possibility, once small, but quickly gaining in strength:

Hunted, pursued, running through the streets of Waam. Flying people and cables from the sky.

Krotan.

Krotan of the Yard ... and ...

Something entered his mind, and his Sight fell away, pushed aside. *Wait—what was he about to see? It was important.*

Then he heard a voice.

I'm waiting for you, Kay. You needn't fear, I'll not allow you to be harmed. I know why you are here; you seek an item in my temple. You may have it. You may give it to your friends, and they may go in peace. You and I have our eternity to consider. We will Wandwilla, and become a creature of bliss and impassioned dreams. I have earned my reward. I want you, Kay. Let me touch you.

Kay thought he saw a reaching tendril of Shadow tech come snaking out of the temple, though he couldn't be sure.

He saw his vision coming true. Quickly, he Wafted into the air, and soared back to the manor and went to bed in the little room Thomasina had given him.

Safe, for now.

31—Hunted

In the morning, Phillip clearly planned to 'over sleep' and miss church; however, several of Thomasina's assistants came and got him out of bed. They barged into his room, and, giggling, they made him dress and follow them to the chapel.

Kay got up and dressed. He wasn't sure which fate troubled him the most: to be summarily killed, to be dismembered and eaten alive, to become a statue, or to become one with Ethylrelda. It would be easy to simply give in and become one with her—he still could feel Bethrael all over him—such pleasure. To experience such a thing forever, just imagine.

But, to fail Sam, to never see her again.

Sam, asleep in the protected chest of the metal man.

Sam, running from the demons, for him.

With Sam's face in his thoughts, he fought off the urge to give in, though his options appeared limited. One way or another, Ethylrelda of Waam was going to have her way.

He met up with Sarah—Lon hadn't gotten up yet—and together they explored the grounds. Tall, green buildings were mixed in with squat provincial manors, ornate Elder chapels, dormitories and workshops where MT CALMs were turned on mystical lathes, all bound together with trees, ponds and green, grassy spaces. Singing came from a nearby chapel, and they decided to peek in and see how Philip was doing.

Inside was a cheerful church, not unlike the churches one might find all over Kana, though this one was mostly decorated in green. Sitting inside near the front was Phillip, with Thomasina in a fine green gown to his right. They shared an oversized song book, Phillip holding the left side, Thomasina the right, with her left hand lightly resting on Phillip's shoulder.

"I've never seen a lady as love-struck as this one. She couldn't take her eyes off him. Did you see that?" Sarah said, astounded. "And, if she's the kind of lady I think she might be, then I can't imagine her just letting him walk out of here."

Kay raised his eyebrows. "What makes you say that?"

"Just look at her. And, not only is she a Xaphan, she's a Woolover, too."

"What's that got to do with anything?"

"Woolovers, Kay—those obnoxious people from Barrow. They tried to get the Duke to impose stricter drinking laws in Esther a few years back. They made a big fuss when he told them to get bent. It's a mostly female House, and either they don't like men, or they don't know how to properly deal with men because they treated the Duke like a piece of garbage, in his own home and everything. If this Thomasina's got a shine on Phillip, then I think one of the biggest fights we're going to have is with her."

Kay had to agree. He hadn't anticipated this.

"Morning," Lon said emerging from the manor, pulling his coat on.

"Morning, Lon," Sarah said. "Sleep well?"

"I did—fine actually. Where's Phillip?"

"In church still."

"Oh." He thought for a moment. "I wonder what Phillip's going to do when we leave here, poor fellow."

"What do you mean?" Sarah asked.

"Well, clearly, he has an eye for our hostess. Correspondence with Xaphans can be rather difficult, and the Sisters rather frown on it."

Sarah twitched. "How do you know that, Lon?"

"Body language for one thing, and I happened to see them this morning before they stepped into the church."

"This morning?" Sarah asked.

"Yes, I got up to seek the kitchens—I was hungry. Anyway, I rousted up a hearty leg of mutton and stepped outside to enjoy it. I saw Phillip and Lady Thomasina standing by the lake. They appeared to be sharing a rather private moment."

"The lake?" Sarah cried. "That's pretty far from the manor, right?"

"I was wearing my goggles. Zoomed right in on them."

Goggles? Sarah and Kay looked at each other.

When Phillip got back from church, Thomasina was hanging on his arm, clearly enamored.

Kay was fully ready to leave the premises as soon as possible, but Thomasina was maddeningly nonchalant. She made them sit down to breakfast and then took them on a guided tour of the compound, though the only person she talked to was Phillip.

Finally, with Kay ready to lose a gasket, Thomasina changed into her green armor and, along with ten of her assistants, they descended into the bowels of the manor and slithered into the small dark mouth of an abandoned sewer. There, she gave them their ammunition back and watched as they loaded their weapons. With Kay Sighting up through the tunnel roof, he could see the throngs of Spectres sitting outside the compound at street level. They moved east through the tunnels. Kay didn't really need Thomasina, but she followed anyway, as always standing near Phillip.

As they continued, a voice entered Kay's head.

Come to me, and let us be one ...

He grimaced. "Black Hats cannot detect Shadow tech Males."

They all stopped and looked at him.

"Who are you talking to?" Sarah asked.

I have lived long and learned things untold to other Black Hats. I have known of your presence since you arrived. I can smell you, Kay.

"What about those I travel with?"

If you willingly join with me, I will give them what you came for and ensure their safety. I swear it.

Sarah shook Kay. "Who are you talking to?"

Kay continued. "I cannot—I am committed to another."

I have hope that you shall come to me of your own choosing, that our union will be something we both want; however, do not misunderstand. I will Wandwilla, and, if need be, I will take you if I must, though I would rather not. I bid you welcome, and all that I have is yours. Just remember ...

Kay forced the voice out of his head. "Ethylrelda. She can sense me somehow. She says she'll give us the piece we need if I give myself to her."

... My patience will not last forever ...

Thomasina smiled. “Well, now, it sounds like you’re all set. If you follow this run, it will dead end at the Cathedral of Auld, just like I promised. Just pop out onto the street and you’re there. Good luck with Ethylrelda. Now then, Phillip, please come with me.”

Phillip looked at her. “What!”

“We just got acquainted, and you have a lovely singing voice. I insist you stay with me for a bit and be my guest. I promise that I’ll make it worth your while.”

Everybody drew their weapons, Kay, Sarah, Phillip and Lon facing off against Thomasina and her ten armored assistants.

Kay came very close to regretting his decision just then. The future he’d briefly seen was apparently coming true and gaining strength by the second: hunted, pursued—by Thomasina the 19th! Kay took a second to survey the surroundings. They were in a small area of the tunnel with not a lot of room to maneuver or escape. Apparently, Thomasina wanted them in close quarters before announcing that she wished to take Phillip.

The Singing Ten fanned out, covering any possible avenue of escape.

“Phillip can’t stay here, Great Lady. He’s our pilot. We can’t leave without him,” Kay said.

“What are you going to do?” Sarah said. “Hit us with your clubs and make us forget that Phillip came with us or something?”

Thomasina raised her MT CALM and crossed Phillip’s SAPP. “Good idea, Lady Sarah. And I’m sure you’ll muddle through, Lord Blanchefort, without Phillip to fly your ship. Come now, Phillip, I’d hate to have to rap you in the skull and carry you back, but that’s what I’ll do if I have to. I promise I won’t drop you.”

“You gave us our ammo back,” Sarah demanded. “Why don’t we just shoot you where you stand?”

Thomasina reared back and laughed. “Go ahead and shoot me, Sarah. You won’t though, will you? You seem to like to talk tough, but you won’t shoot me. You know I mean your brother no harm—quite the opposite. I wish to get to know him better is all and show him the wonders of Waam.”

Phillip raised his SAPP and showed it to her. “This is all you’re going to get to know, Great Lady,” he said.

“I enjoyed our kiss this morning, Phillip,” she replied. “We can settle this between the two of us, right now, and we needn’t involve anyone else. Come on, Phillip—let’s fight, you and me, man to woman. You win, and you can go. I win, and you’re coming with me. I’m eager to lay my hands all over you.”

“Lady Thomasina, please,” Kay said. “We have enough on our hands as it is. We do not wish to fight you and your lovely ladies here.”

“Aw, you’re no fun. In that case, Phillip, start walking.” She pointed back the way they had come.

Sarah extended her SAPP and pointed it at Thomasina. With a quick movement of her MT CALM, she had it out of Sarah’s hand where it fell to the damp stone.

Kay had had enough. He concentrated and, after a moment, Cloaked all four of them. “Quick, back away from them,” he said. “Don’t worry; I’ve Cloaked us audibly as well. We can speak freely, and they’ll not hear us.”

They backed away as Thomasina and her band began swinging, trying to cover every possible avenue of escape with their clubs.

"A very impressive Cloak," Thomasina said looking around, moving her MT CALM in a whirl. "But, it's not like I've never faced a Cloaked person before is it, and, in this tight area, I'll have you down sooner or later. Come on, Phillip, I'm starting to get angry, and I'm really not an Elder-like person when I'm angry."

The ladies covered the ground well with their clubs. Any hit, anywhere on their bodies was enough to incapacitate them—the MT CALM was a frustrating weapon to face. And what could they do? Their weapons were meant to kill, and they certainly didn't want to harm Thomasina and her group.

Lon had the answer. He drew his PITCOCK WONDER GUN and spun the four cartridges. He then fired upwards, where the slug fell out of Cloak. Thomasina, hearing the shell, quickly hit it out of the air with her club. She then zeroed in on Lon and got him in the shoulder. He immediately fell in a smiling heap.

The shell he fired burst open and began spewing smoke which quickly filled the tunnel.

"Don't let him get away!" Thomasina shrieked, her voice suddenly ugly and ragged with anger. Somebody got hit in a swirl of flailing MT CALMs and fell.

Kay, in his Sight, could see perfectly. Sarah, with her Sight lit, was dragging Phillip away from Thomasina, for she had got him in the face and was prodding about looking for him. Kay sprang and got Lon, who was on the ground with a huge, stupid grin. A lady blocked Sarah's path, and without hesitation, she punched her hard in the nose, knocking the lady down. Thomasina, hearing the lady fall, jumped in front of them and began flailing with her MT CALM.

Kay blocked it with his CARG; then, turning it, he cut the club in two.

Thomasina was quickly all over him. Before he knew what had happened, she put three fierce punches square into his Cloaked face, easily the hardest punches he'd ever felt. She then walloped him in the gut, again, all of this under Cloak in a smoke-filled tunnel. She could fight.

Sight—She was going to try a blind leg sweep.

Kay jumped over her armored leg, as it came sweeping in and then returned the favor, socking her in the cheek. He expected her to go down, but she didn't—she was one tough Xaphan. Not having any other choice, he hauled back and socked her again, this time sending her down into the clouds of billowing smoke.

Not wasting a moment, Kay grabbed Sarah and led her out of the area, she using her Gift of Strength to easily drag both Phillip and Lon.

"Phillip!" Thomasina yelled, searching for him in the smoke. "Phillip please! PHILLIP!!"

Soon, with great effort, they got away from Thomasina and her Singing Ten. They decided that staying in the tunnels might be too dangerous, as they didn't figure on Thomasina giving up any time soon. Fortunately, she didn't know where they had parked the *Goshawk,* so, at least, that would keep her guessing. And, as the smoke cleared, they could see the Singing Ten break into small groups, each looking in a different direction. They even heard one of them saying something about watching the temple for their arrival. That was a disadvantage, for she knew that was where they ultimately had to go. Now that they weren't boxed in, their Cloak would be much more difficult to defeat, but it looked like the Singing Ten were going to give it an A+ effort. Suddenly, the brooding Black Hat Ethylrelda and her windowless temple seemed less a threat than the love-struck magistrate and her band of club-wielding ladies.

They began looking for an exit before Thomasina could get them cased—which wasn't going to be long by the number of ladies that were filtering into the tunnels. Thomasina called them her Singing Ten, but there seemed to be quite a bit more of them than just ten. There appeared to be hundreds.

After a bit of searching, they found a cover to the street and went out into an alley. There they'd regroup, allow Phillip and Lon time to recover and hash out some sort of plan. Sticking their heads out onto the street, they were clearly in a different municipality; the streets and buildings looked different. Kay panned around with his Sight and saw the more familiar buildings of Auld a few city blocks to the south. He even saw the tall buildings in Thomasina's compound; once they appeared charming and homey, now they seemed sinister and prison-like. He had a thought that Thomasina might have a few ladies stationed on the tops of her buildings, scanning the streets. Sure enough, there were several ladies on the rooftops looking around with high powered binoculars.

They took a moment to catch their breath. "What are we going to do, Kay?" Sarah asked. Her eyes were wide and eager. She was clearly enjoying this. "Did you see me hit that lady right in the face? Dropped her with one punch."

"I saw it. Great punch. Let's move across the street and get a few city blocks between us and them. Come on. We're under Cloak and should be fine."

They hauled Phillip and Lon and stepped out into the street.

A cable tipped with a strong net came down from the sky in an instant and had them pinned fast to the street. "What in the name of creation is this?" Sarah yelled, struggling with the net.

Kay was tangled. He tried Wafting through it and couldn't, it seemed to be Waft-locked. The ends of the net were barbed, and the barbs had sunk deep into the street, holding the net fast. Traffic floated past them.

"Waft-locked!" he said in frustration. "This must have come from Thomasina's orbiting Helix ship."

"How'd it zero us?"

"I don't know!" He had a thought. "Wait, check your pockets! I wonder ..."

Kay felt through his pockets and, sure enough, there was a small green device sitting innocently in one. "They've got us rigged!"

"Oh, Feature! How are we going to get out of this? And it better be fast 'cause I'm certain she's on her way."

Kay tried to draw his CARG, but he couldn't free his hands enough. "Sarah, power up and pull this net off us! Hurry, will you?"

Sarah began the process of hardening into Full Strength. It usually took her about a minute. Kay lay there in the net. His Sight wandered away. He saw a huge vehicle come blundering down the street ready to plow into them. It wasn't long before it would be on top of them.

"Sarah, hurry!"

She pulled on the ends of the net. The cords stretched and groaned. Down the street a large Xaphan barge came floating into view.

Sarah pulled one of the barbs free. They'd need at least three or four more free to slide out.

"Sarah, you see that barge heading right for us? Do you?"

"Shut up, Kay, or I'll wrap these cords around your neck!" Two more were yanked free.

The net had loosened enough for Kay to unsaddle his CARG. He jostled it around and sliced through the cords of the net. They pulled Phillip and Lon away from the oncoming barge which hit the cable square, ripping the remaining barbs out of the street with a great commotion.

They moved south desperate to get off the street.

Sight.

"Sarah, jump aside!"

Another cable and net from above came screaming down, and then a third, all of them clamping down fast onto the street. Carrying Phillip and Lon, they made it off the street under an overhang. Sarah gasped and stared at the open sky. "That stupid ship she's got up there is really annoying me!" she yelled.

Kay Sighted. "Sarah, check your pockets again. You've got three rigs on you, Phillip has about ten in various places, and Lon has three."

Cursing, Sarah went through her pockets, finding the small green devices in abundance. They pushed them into a pile. "Is that all?"

Kay looked her over again. He sighed. "No, you've got a few in your stomach, too. As do I, and Phillip and Lon as well. She must have rigged our breakfast this morning."

Sarah looked down at her stomach. "That conniving Shocktyte!"

His Sight wandered off into the future again. He looked skyward. "Sarah, hide Phillip and Lon and then get against the wall! Hurry—we're about to have company!"

Sarah picked Phillip up and tossed him down the alley several feet. She then tossed Lon, the two of them lying there in a heap. She quickly joined Kay and pressed up against the wall. "What are we doing?"

"Shh!"

A few moments later, a fast descending cable came down from above. The end of the cable had a small platform and rails, just wide enough for two people to stand. Two ladies in green hopped off and moved into the alley. They were both carrying rifles tipped with darts. They discovered the pile of discarded rigs and kicked at them in frustration. One of them lifted a scanning device of some sort and waved it around, moving right past where Kay and Sarah were standing. Cloaked, Kay quickly moved to the other side of the alley, Sarah following. The lady with the scanner turned around once or twice and finally put her device away. She ran back to the waiting cable, climbed onto the platform and was gone; the both of them pulled skyward as quickly as they'd arrived.

"Well, that was a near thing," Kay said. "Good thing the proximity of all these rigs fouled their scanner readings. Come on, let's get these two and keep moving."

Even though they had a whole city to hide in, Thomasina's ladies seemed to be everywhere. They prowled the streets. They rode about in green coaches suspended from cables, their MT CALMS drawn, many with large binoculars stuck to their eyes. Spectres, too, were out in force, many roving on foot, some in a mish-mash of vehicles. They were in such a hurry they didn't even bother to harass the people as they passed by.

The hunt was on. Some were hunting for Kay, others hunting for Phillip.

Though Cloaked, they felt very exposed. They decided to try taking a circuitous route to the temple. Instead of going straight for it, they circled around it to the south, always keeping the black pearl of Ethylrelda's temple to their left. Dragging Lon and Phillip, they left Hamm district and entered a seedy municipality called Nilpop. They couldn't stop and rest for the Singing Ten were right on their heels, in some cases, entering alleys and streets moments after they had departed. They looked about with their binoculars, and others waved scanning equipment, one of them finding the fresh drag marks made by the heels of Phillip's boots where Kay had pulled him along. They were relentless, and they were thorough. With this latest piece of information, they hit their communicators, and the hunt was on afresh.

They continued north, bearing slightly to the east. They entered the municipality of Stove and then an ugly place of industrial warehouses and fallen lots called Ferd. They stopped to rest near a dumpster full of mannequins. Carrying Lon and Phillip both for most of the way, Sarah was exhausted.

"You doing all right, Sarah?" Kay asked.

She settled down near the dumpster with her knees pulled up into her chest. "I'm fine. Just need a few minutes." She patted Phillip on the cheek. "When do you think these two will start coming around?"

"I'd hoped they'd be recovered by now."

"Check the future. Seriously, Phillip's getting heavy."

Kay casually consulted the near future, seeing a vast number of possibilities sort themselves out in front of him. "What do you see?" Sarah asked.

"I see a couple of things. We could do things the hard way or take an easier route—it's up to you."

Sarah sighed. "Let's take the easy way, please. I'm too tired for anything else, right now."

"In that case, just stay where you are." Kay got down next to the dumpster and peered around the side.

"What are you looking for?" she asked.

"One moment."

As they rested, an odd vehicle came floating in from the west. It appeared to be the black statue of a robed woman in a demure pose. The statue was about three hundred feet long. It possessed no apparent power source, control surfaces or other accessories that would allow it to fly; it simply looked like a floating statue. It moved smooth and silent through the air. A host of Spectres milled about on the statue's back, standing wherever they could find a decent purchase on its irregular surface. Light came out of the statue's mouth and palms, panning around. After another few minutes, it moved on, flying silently to the south. Sarah watched it soar away.

"Those things are actually pretty cool. Just out of curiosity, what would the hard way have been like?" Sarah asked.

"Oh, we would have continued on, and they'd have spotted us, and we'd have gotten into a shootout."

Sarah was a bit put off. "Well, I'm sorry we missed that, actually. Perhaps next time."

After a few more minutes, Phillip and Lon recovered. They were finally able to stand on their own again.

Phillip was smoking hot as they crouched near the dumpster. "Can you believe the nerve of that woman?" he yelled. "What was I to be? Her prisoner—her slave?" He hit the dumpster with his fist.

"Well, gee, Phillip, after a round of face-sucking this morning I'd have thought you'd be happy she wishes to enslave you!" Sarah said, her eyes flashing.

"How do you know about that!" he raved.

"Lon caught you red-handed, so don't try and deny it!" Phillip glared at Lon, and he backed away a bit.

"I guess she didn't want you to leave, Phillip. I guess she likes you," Sarah said pinching him on the cheek. "You're just so adorable."

"Got a damn funny way of showing it, doesn't she?"

"Why didn't you just fight her?" Sarah said. "You could have saved us all this fuss."

Kay shook his head—remembering the love taps Thomasina had given him in the tunnel. "I don't know. She's pretty tough; she hits like a man, a big man, and probably been in a lot more scrapes than Phillip has. I think she might have won that fight, had you accepted her challenge."

Phillip gritted his teeth. "She is a rude and imperious woman, and I will gladly knock her teeth out should we encounter her again. What's our status?" He looked around, seeing the seedy warehouses and the ever-present round mass of Ethylrelda's temple in the distance to the northeast.

"We are being tailed. We have all ingested a number of rigs for the purposes of their zeroing in on us."

"She fed us rigs this morning for breakfast?" Phillip was horrified.

"She did, along with larger ones placed in our pockets, which we've already eliminated. With those, she was able to zero in on us from her high-flying spiral ship floating above with great effectiveness. The smaller ones inside us don't appear to have as much range."

"Well, that's something anyway," Phillip said.

"What about your lip-lock with her this morning?" Sarah asked.

"What about it? We shared a moment; I kissed her. I didn't expect one kiss and a few songs in church to grant her an invitation for abduction, mayhem and rigging."

"You don't just smooch up a Xaphan and walk away from them, Phillip. What's wrong with you?" Sarah yelled.

Kay, despite the situation, laughed. "Perhaps she lacks a bit in couth and basic manners, but I don't think she had it in her mind to harm or enslave you. And, she was quite the picture in her armor, don't you agree?"

"I don't recall what she looked like," Phillip said.

"She was very attractive," Lon said. "You thought so as well, or you shan't have kissed her."

"May we please move on from that?" Phillip cried. "I don't care. Any good will I might have had for her is gone and done. She has revealed herself as a despot and a lunatic!"

"Ha!" Sarah exclaimed.

Kay shook his head, knowing better. Though their situation was unusual to be sure, Kay now felt certain that they selected the correct path—that there was hope for coming out of this successfully. He no longer saw the many *Wandwilla* futures with Ethylrelda—most of those had vanished. Still, he was sure a large confrontation was in the offing, as the image of Krotan of the Yard was still floating about in his mind.

"Oh, come on," Sarah said checking the streets. "You've always said you like them a bit wild."

"Wild, yes," Phillip cried, "but not insane, maniacal and slavering." He stepped away from the dumpster and looked around. "Are we certain we didn't tell them where the *Goshawk* was landed because I can picture that green-haired fool staking it out and waiting for us there."

He suddenly turned white. "What if she finds it and vandalizes or destroys the ship? What then?"

Sarah couldn't resist. "What if she suddenly materializes out of thin air with blood-shot eyes and dripping fangs, Phillip? Look!!"

Phillip whirled around, ready to kill with his SAPP. Sarah laughed.

"This is not funny! Kay, is the *Goshawk* still Cloaked?"

"It's still Cloaked, Phillip. Relax," Kay said, amused. Phillip was normally such a calm, clear-headed fellow. Now, he seemed on the verge of panic.

"Are you certain?"

Kay reached out with his Sight. He could see the *Goshawk*, miles away, sitting Cloaked in the afternoon sun. Nobody was around. "Yes ... And why are you so upset? All you've got is a love-struck, green-haired hottie gunning for you. Me—I've got a 400 year old Black Hat, who probably hasn't bathed since we've all been alive, wanting to merge into a bizarre, sex-crazed creature with me, and several others waiting in line wanting to either perform atrocities on my dead body, use it for arts and crafts or devour it whole! That's what I've got going on."

"No, the guy said she wanted to start with your genitals first," Sarah corrected.

Phillip shuffled his feet and paced, unimpressed with Kay's dilemma. "Does anyone recall mentioning, or even *hinting* at the *Goshawk's* location?"

"Shut up!" Sarah said.

"I don't recall it coming up in conversation," Lon said.

Lon rubbed his chin. "The only issue is that Lady Thomasina knows what our goal is—Ethylrelda's Temple," he said pointing at it in the distance. "Therefore, she will most likely assume that our vehicle is somewhere nearby. Due to the size of the temple, that's a lot of area to cover, but, still, I don't think I'd put it past her."

"Yes, well, we need to hurry." Phillip began shuffling them along. "Lon, that Super Gun of yours..."

"WONDER GUN," Lon corrected.

"Whatever. Get it fully loaded—and shoot to kill if you have to!" Phillip was crazed with fear.

"Boy, Phillip," Sarah said egging him on. "Feeling pretty happy about yourself, aren't you? She's probably got some other fellow enslaved by now."

"We need to continue," Phillip said again.

"Wait a minute, Phillip. What's our plan going to be? What are we going to do when we get to the *Goshawk*? I believe Ethylrelda's temple has become a bit of an afterthought at this point," Sarah remarked.

"We're going to lift her off and move her, far away, in some random direction. Kay can then Waft into the temple on his own."

Phillip considered what he just said and appeared a little ashamed of himself. "I'm sorry, Kay. That was a selfish remark. Does that sound possible to you? Can you Waft that far at speed?"

"Sure I can." He looked around, not seeing anybody suspicious. "I don't think there is a continued need to Cloak ourselves. Doing all four of you and the *Goshawk* is giving me a slight headache. And, it doesn't really matter given the fact we're rigged," he said.

"No, no—we need to be Cloaked. She'll spot us and drag me back to the love nest. If we're not Cloaked, I'm not moving!" Phillip said.

Love nest, if you only knew, Phillip ...

Kay laughed and Cloaked everybody again. They headed east, leaving the low and dingy cityscape of Ferd and entering into the upper-scale municipality of Marilith. Apparently, Princess Marilith of Xandarr was a big celebrity in Waam. There were statues dedicated to her, streets named after her, and the ladies walking down the street even did their hair in the long, short banged style she wore. Odd, statue-like vending machines in Princess Marilith's form, selling everything from junk food to sex protection and procreation-defeating gels, stood on every corner bathed in flashing lights. The breasts of the statutes were convex monitor screens granting access to Waam's version of the Holo-Net. Traffic in Marilith picked back up, and Phillip eyed each passing vehicle with suspicion, no doubt imagining that each was filled with maniacal green-haired women.

And some were. Green and brown, waving scanners, supported by cables going up into the sky.

After a few blocks, they plunged into the dead zone around the temple and headed back to the *Goshawk*, which was probably a good four miles away at this point. They suspected that Thomasina had staked out the perimeter of the temple, and, sure enough, as they moved on, Kay saw the now familiar green and brown armor of Thomasina's Singing Ten hidden in various buildings.

"They're up there," Kay said, "scoping the area with scanning devices."

"Are they detecting the rigs we swallowed?" Phillip asked.

Kay gazed upward. "They seem to be reacting to our approach, but I can't tell if they've good enough a signal to lock on. Their actions don't seem to indicate that they've established a lock."

"What are they packing?" Sarah asked.

"Rifles armed with darts. I suppose Thomasina's not giving up, and she's not playing around either."

Fortunately, since he could see the ladies plain as day, they skirted around the Singing Ten placements, using the dead buildings as cover. He watched for any signs that they may have spotted them, but, outwardly, they looked tired and bored and probably wished they were elsewhere.

Finally, after making their way building by building, they got to the correct one. After first checking to make sure there were no ladies waiting for them upstairs, they went in and made their way to the top. Kay couldn't remember when he'd seen Phillip moving so fast—he wanted out of Waam in a bad way. They really couldn't leave, though, as they hadn't secured the final piece of the machine. As Phillip had rather rudely suggested, they'd move the *Goshawk* possibly several hundred miles away to another part of the city and let Kay Waft in. It was the best plan he could think of. It would cut down on the fuss and bother of Thomasina, leaving only the fuss and bother of Ethylrelda.

This was the good path; Kay was certain. He had a chance to get out of this with Sam's item and with his soul as well. He wasn't certain how, though. The situation simply needed to play out.

They got to the open sunshine of the rooftop and Phillip thanked his maker for his deliverance and went into the ship—the *Goshawk's* familiar interior never looking so good.

32—The Brand

As they piled into the comforting confines of the *Goshawk* it was déjà vu; they were horrified to discover a person sitting quietly on the back couch waiting for them.

Phillip drew his Poltava, ready to fight to the death. It was Thomasina! It had to be her!

It wasn't Thomasina sitting there but rather a black robed Spectre, quietly seated.

"Greetings," Krotan of the Yard said.

They drew their weapons. Krotan appeared unfazed. "Please," he said in a calm voice, "There is no need for your weapons. I am here to assist you."

"How did you find us?" Kay asked, holding his CARG at the ready.

"My mistress knows much. She told me where your ship might be found. She is eager to join with you, sir, whichever one of you is the Invernan."

"She's not getting him," Sarah said. "We are going into that temple, and we are going to take what we came for."

Krotan smirked. "You will be killed instantly. However, my mistress is tired of death; she is tired of everything. For centuries, she has gazed out of her door to the sights beyond, not understanding what she was seeing—such is the Clutch the Black Abbess holds over her. She has come to know that there is more than just the darkness around her. She simply desires to have her reward, to *Wandwilla.*"

"That is not going to happen!" Sarah yelled.

Krotan rustled in his seat. He reminded Kay of a wolf stuffed into a velvet bag. "Perhaps we can agree upon an alternative, mutually beneficial course of action."

Kay lowered his CARG and sat down. "What do you propose?"

Krotan looked down at the floor, then began. "I am of the Yard—I have served our mistress for years doing her bidding, standing in her terrible presence, living while all else died around me. I suppose that, despite it all, I worship Her Mightiness; nay, I love her, truth be told. Though she is powerful and terrible, she is, at her core, an innocent and is full of dreams that little girls dream. I want to make her dreams come true, and I want to share them with her. I propose that I take your place. I wish to *Wandwilla* with Ethylrelda. You don't want it—I do!"

"Are you a Shadow tech male?"

"I am not."

"Then how do you propose to proceed?"

"We of the Yard have made a great study of Invernans. I know more about you than you do yourself. If I may—which one of you is the Invernan?"

Kay hesitated, then he admitted it. "I am a Shadow tech Male," he said.

Krotan smiled. "Thank you. It is probably not known to you, but, among the many things you can do, you have the ability to brand another male."

"Brand? I don't understand."

"You may create another Invernan. Invernans are not just born; they can be made as well. A branded Invernan is not as potent as a born one, but, regardless. I am asking you to brand me. I will then *Wandwilla* with Ethylrelda. It is my wish. I want it like nothing else. And, to reward you, I will give you the item you seek. You may then go on your way."

From the depths of his robes, he produced a fairly large bundle wrapped in a cloth.

"I can feel that you are people of character, people of your word—that is an admirable thing that we of the Yard do not often get to enjoy. I offer you this, the wondrous item you came for, and, in exchange, you will brand me."

Kay took the bundle and unwrapped it. There, shining up at him was a twisting, organic-looking rectangular object, about two feet long, shining in silver. "Lon?" Kay asked, "Is this the piece we need?"

Lon accepted the piece and scanned it with his goggles. "Yes, yes, this does appear to be the piece, yes indeed."

Kay stared at Krotan: sinister-looking, intense, like a psychopath swaddled in black, but apparently sincere. "I thank you for giving us the item we require. I must be perfectly honest, I do not know how to do what you ask."

"I will instruct you. Do I have your word?"

Kay thought for a moment and looked at Lon holding the final piece of Sam's machine. There it was, right in front of him. Sam's salvation was at hand. Here was the last piece of her *Olonol.*

"Yes, you have my word."

Krotan stood up. "Then, if you are ready, we must go outside, in the fresh air, and you must ready yourself, sir, for this shall not be painless."

Everybody, except for Phillip, went outside into the afternoon sun—he couldn't be dragged out. Krotan removed his hood, revealing a heavily tattooed bald head, so bald it looked like a dirty egg just waiting to crack open. He then stripped to the waist and threw his small swords aside. He lay down on the dirty surface of the roof. "Now, sir, please, what is your name?"

"My name is Kabyl."

"Thank you, Kabyl. Now please lie on top of me and place your Mark over my right eye. That might sound a little confusing, so simply lay your right temple on my right temple, yes?"

Tentatively, Kay lay down on Krotan and placed his temple against his—it was awkward. They almost appeared to be kissing all twisted up.

"Now, and this is the distressing part, we must both be run through with a sword or other sharp weapon. We must both be pierced and made to feel great pain."

"Are you insane?"

"It must be done. The Brand will save us from death. Trust me when I say that. When we are run through, the Brand will begin. We must not be separated until it is done. Then, after a minute or so, we may be separated, and I will be an Invernan—though not as powerful as you."

Kay lay there, wondering what to do. Then: "Sarah," he said. "Take your SAPP and run us through. Be careful to pick a spot where you will minimize puncturing my vital organs and my spine."

"By Creation, Kay, I'm not going to run you through with my SAPP! We have the piece; let's go!"

"I gave this man my word. Now, I must be true to it. According to him, we'll not be harmed. Come on, Sarah, we haven't all day."

Sarah huffed and formed her SAPP into a thin, spear-like shaft with a wickedly sharp point.

"Use your Strength, Sarah—let's make this a nice clean thrust. I don't need you digging around in my back."

Sarah hardened up. "You ready?" she asked, holding the SAPP against his back.

"Yes, yes, hurry up."

Sarah then ran the SAPP through the both of them and skewered the roof beneath Krotan. It was easy. The scalpel-sharp SAPP cut through their flesh like nothing. She even didn't need her Strength.

Kay and Krotan writhed in agony, like skewered fish on a hook. Kay had never felt pain like it before, and he hoped he never would again. He tried to raise his head, but Krotan held him fast.

"Do … not … break the … connection!"

Kay's Sight spun in a carnival of past and future events.

Sam … asleep inside the metal man.

Phillip and Thomasina holding each other, that future now set.

A dark place of pagan idols.

People suffering … fire and oil. Lightning from above.

Sam being tormented before a Horned God …

Carahil in chains …

Clawed hands at his throat …

SAM!!

POW!!

He couldn't concentrate. Everything was falling apart.

And his Cloak fell. Suddenly the big, black *Goshawk,* with Phillip sitting inside, appeared on the roof top.

In his agony, he trained his Sight, forced it to obey his pain-clotted mind. And he saw what was about to happen.

"Down!" he shrieked. "Sarah, Lon, get down!"

Sarah let go of her SAPP, and she and Lon hit the roof, just as a cloud of fired darts came whistling in from all quarters, panging off the rooftop and the side of the *Goshawk.*

The Singing Ten had spotted them. Now, it was on in full! Thomasina herself would probably be arriving in no time.

It was raining darts. Lying on the roof top really wasn't any cover, as some of the Singing Ten were perched on taller buildings quite a distance away. Rolling away and just missing a dart, Lon stood and drew his CEROS. He presented it as was customary and moved it just in time to block a dart that was heading right for his throat, ready to administer a knock out dose. These Singing Ten were crack snipers.

Lon depressed a hidden trigger, and the CEROS expanded, doubling its usual size. He then donned his goggles, adjusted the lenses and began a skilled dance, protecting Sarah, Kay and Krotan from the hail of incoming darts, his long coat and buckle shoes adding a comical edge to his masterful skill.

There was a lull. Kay could see the Singing Ten reloading for another volley. Lon lined up a shot and let the CEROS go at a howl.

"Lon!" Sarah cried. "You aren't planning on killing any of them are you?"

The CEROS went about a quarter mile at speed and bisected one of the Singing Ten's rifles as she reloaded it. It then returned to him as always. "That one was in too good of a position," he said. "She would have had us before long."

Kay writhed. "Sarah—cables! Cables from above!"

As if from nowhere, three cables pierced the surface of the roof from the spiral ship in orbit above and held tautly. Moments later, three ladies in green armor came screeching down the cable length in a controlled fall. They carried dart-tipped rifles.

Sarah was on the first new arrival. She grabbed the barrel of the rifle before she could aim and hit the lady in the face with a powered up punch. The lady went limp, and Sarah took her weapon.

The other two sprang into action, one rolling into a protected firing position near a stairwell, the other taking flight. As Sarah and the Singing Ten maneuvered around on the rooftop for cover, the sky darkened. Glancing up, she saw a strange silvery cloud rolling in from the east, like a rogue rain cloud alone in the sky on a sunny day. It had a distinct animal shape, sort of like a great, flippered seal performing a trick. As Sarah watched, the odd cloud seemed to grow 'whiskers', as a number of black cables appeared through it. Thomasina was sending down cables from her ship above en masse, trying to skewer the *Goshawk.* The cables seemed to be having a hard time passing through the layers of the cloud, losing their speed and power coming down limp and ineffectual.

The Singing Ten on the rooftop lined Sarah up with her rifle and fired.

The shot was blocked by Lon's thrown CEROS. Sarah promptly returned fire and darted her in the leg. Sarah's victim fell forward, unconscious.

The flying lady came around from the north and lined up Sarah for a shot. Lon drew his impressive PITCOCK WONDER GUN and spun the chamber. Before Sarah could say anything, he fired with a bristling report. A large slug hit the lady in the chest and exploded in a spray of shards, apparently stunning her and throwing off her aim. "That's Mad Molly's Crystalline load!" he said with pride. "Hurts like the devil!"

"Lon!" Kay shrieked, still impaled atop Krotan. "I see another volley coming in!" Sarah moved to get the stunned flying lady out of the way and shot her with a dart. It hit her in the side, and she immediately began plummeting past the edge of the building and down to the street far below.

"Oh, Creation!" Sarah cried. "I didn't mean for that to happen—I thought she'd land on the roof first, then pass out! Gods—she's going to be killed!"

Lon went to the edge, aimed his WONDERGUN and fired. A large slug came skittering out, covering the distance fast and opened up into a billowy cascade of web-like strands that enveloped the plummeting woman, slowing her fall. Sarah watched with relief as the web-like mass with the lady safely nestled within landed far below soft as a baby. "Great shot, Lon. Thanks!"

Then Sarah saw the mass of approaching vehicles. "She's here! She's here! They're storming the building! Slam the door and wedge it!"

Five float cars arrived, carrying at least fifty ladies. They piled out of the cars and entered at a run. Some began bounding up the side of the building, while others flew.

More cars arrived, a motley bunch—Spectres, dozens of them. They streamed out of their cars like a box of black mothballs dumped out, only to be met by other Spectres of the Yard who had been hiding in the adjacent buildings. In a mass of shouting and cursing, black robes and bloodied swords mixed with green armor and whirling clubs, they fought a pitched battle with Spectres of other Orders and with the Singing Ten both on the ground and in the heights.

The battle for both Kay and Phillip was on in earnest.

Sarah made her way to the service door. The other service doors went nowhere—this one was the only one that mattered, and with Lon covering her, she braced it as best she could.

Kay, still locked together with Krotan, had more bad news. "Creation—rockets! Incoming Laser-Lock rockets! They're going for the *Goshawk*!"

Inside, Phillip freaked. He began trying to start the ship up—it was a long, intricate process. He pulled handles, tugged on gauges and set the pumps. The landing lights came on, and the engines began to slowly cycle.

The Singing Ten, camped out all around, were done messing about. Atop a distant building, they were readying a cache of rockets. The rockets appeared to be fairly small, two stage models that probably couldn't do serious damage, but they could probably punch large enough holes in the *Goshawk* that it wouldn't be going anywhere without repair.

About a mile away, one of Thomasina's ladies lined her target up, lazed it, and fired. The rocket jumped out of its tube with a small launch engine; it then ejected the spent motor and fired its main rocket. It appeared to hover in the air as it did so.

Howling, Lon's CEROS cut it in two, touching off a colorful propellant fire in the now useless pieces. Again, Lon was deadly accurate with his CEROS, and it returned without fail to his hand.

No time to bask. "Lon!" Kay cried. "Many incoming Laser-Locks. Northeast quarter!" Kay appeared to be on the verge of passing out.

"They're here!" Sarah screamed, holding the door shut with her Strength. "I can feel them on the other side!" Armored fists banged on the door from within, and Spectres and Singing Ten swirled up over the side of the roof in a confused furball.

The *Goshawk* made a puff of ionized gas and died with a sputter—Phillip had mis-done the startup sequence. He emptied the tanks, reset the levers and started all over.

A shadow passed overhead. The black statue crawling with Spectres they'd seen in Ferd was back, punching through the silver cloud, now dissipating. Standing on its back, shoulders and extremities, they rained projectile shots down onto the roof.

Rockets from the Singing Ten lit into it from all sides, peppering its length with tiny explosions. The statue endured the small attacks, seemingly impervious to them. The rockets the Singing Ten were using appeared to be meant only to cause moderate damage. The Spectres standing all over it returned fire. Some were struck by incoming dart fire from the Singing Ten, tumbling away and falling off to their doom like fleas from a gigantic dog.

As Kay cringed and watched helplessly, Lon adjusted his goggles and saw a Spectre standing on the statue's back hoist a deadly-looking shoulder-fired rocket.

The Spectre locked on and fired in a blast.

Lon spun the cartridges of his gun, selected a fiery red one, aimed and fired in return.

The large red slug, an Inferno round, skittered out of the gun at a fairly slow speed. It went about three hundred feet, corkscrewing slightly, then exploded in a cascade of fire. The fire formed an expanding curtain between them and the incoming Spectre rocket. The rocket entered the fiery veil and exploded in a nasty ball of blue flame that expanded all the way to the exterior of Ethylrelda's temple. That was a killer explosion, and, had it hit the rooftop, everything on it would have been destroyed. The entire building probably would have collapsed.

"Lon, he's reloading!" Kay cried.

Lon looked down and searched his coat for another Inferno round.

Too late. The Spectre, robes billowing, was already leveling his rocket launcher and lining them up for another shot.

Cables came down from the sky in a taut cloud, barbing fast into the flying statue and holding it suspended in mid-air like a marionette. One of the cables even bisected the rocket-firing Spectre. He dropped his rocket launcher, and hung there, impaled like the statue he was riding on.

Kay, in agony on the rooftop, considered the irony. Only moments earlier, the Singing Ten were their opponent. With the arrival of the Spectres, they were now tacit allies against a common enemy.

The small rockets of the Singing Ten coming in from all quarters began to take effect, and the black statue crumbled, breaking apart in arms and legs suspended from the sky, dumping off the remaining Spectres in a grim harvest destined for the ground. A few began flying and were engaged by Spectres of the Yard and the Singing Ten, some Wafted and others fell to their death.

Lon raised his gun in triumph. "Here's to the Singing Ten!" he cried, and then fell as a dart pierced his neck right on the button and dosed him. He was out.

The alliance, now that the Spectres were mostly out of the way, was over.

"They're beating on the door—they've got something on the other side. I can't hold it much longer!" Sarah cried. Without Lon to defend her, a dart pierced her leg, and she immediately fell unconscious.

At that moment, cable cars rose over the roof's edge and the door burst open. Thomasina the 19th and her Singing Ten gained the roof in a howl of triumph, both through the service doorway and over the side of the building. A volley of ten Laser-Lock rockets came in, this time passing through the hanging meat of the destroyed Spectre statue ship. They headed for the *Goshawk.* Those rockets wouldn't destroy the ship. They would do just enough damage to mess it up and keep it where it was.

✶ ✶ ✶ ✶ ✶

And the black pearl of Ethylrelda's temple came to life. Like a massive black octopus, innumerable tendrils of Shadow tech came snaking out. They seized the incoming rockets, held them burning in air, and then crushed them in plumes of fire. More tendrils slithered up to the roof top. There, they gently picked up the fallen Lon, his WONDER GUN, and Sarah and placed them within the open hatch of the *Goshawk.* The tendrils also latched onto the struggling Thomasina and her ladies and lifted them into the air along with a number of Spectres. They whacked at the black tentacles with their clubs and swords, but it did no good.

Ethyrelda was in command here.

Then, a final tendril came and gently pulled the SAPP out of Kay and Krotan. It picked Kay up by his shirt and, again, placed him inside the *Goshawk*, where a frantic Phillip shut the hatch. He purged the tanks and began restarting the ship for

a third time.

Krotan rose amid the waving forest of Shadow tech stalks blooming with rockets and Singing Ten. Arms spread in welcome, he serenely walked to the edge of the roof. He stepped off into thin air, where Shadow tech tendrils came up to support his feet as he did so. More tendrils came down and began gingerly, tentatively touching him—they throbbed and tremored at his touch and he was swiftly born away, down into the mouth of the temple far below where Ethylrelda awaited him.

There was a muted explosion within. The air around it shook with their combined ecstasy, a moment of passion that will last an eternity. The perfect sphere of the temple wrinkled, and began to warp and deform. The striating tendrils of Shadow tech set Thomasina and her ladies down and retreated into the roiling mass of the temple.

Inside the *Goshawk,* Phillip furiously worked the controls, trying to start up the ship. It was a complicated process. He had done it so many times it normally wasn't much of an issue anymore.

But now, with his enemy outside the ship, he fumbled with the controls, fouling the tanks, over-priming the engines, mis-starting the ship. He'd failed twice now.

Finally, tanks properly primed, it cranked to life as Sarah stirred, the gauges winding to a ready state. She shook her head, groggy from the dose she took, and checked Kay, who was out next to her. Lon, too, hit in the neck, was out fast. She checked Kay's back, and couldn't find the hole she'd made in him, just the tear in the fabric of his shirt and nothing more.

Phillip finally had the ship ready, and it thrummed to life, the engines purring steadily, ready to go. The floorboards vibrated as they normally did.

He glanced out the cockpit glass as he finished his work, and there she was.

Thomasina the 19th.

She stood there in the sunshine in her green and brown armor and visored helmet—an incredibly attractive, yet imminently scary lady. Outside, framed in billowing smoke from the destroyed flying statue, she was smiling and statuesque. Thomasina walked slowly up to the *Goshawk*. She stopped at the cockpit glass and lightly rapped it with her MT CALM.

"Phillip ..." she cooed. He couldn't hear her, but he could see her lips moving. Just a few more preparations, another lever or two, and the ship would be ready to go. The engines powered up to idle.

She tried the hatch. It was locked.

Suddenly, she reared back, eyes bugging, fists bolt straight at her side. "PHILLIP!" she screeched. She ripped her helmet off. Her green hair was an angry tangle around her face.

Phillip engaged the pan—finally, the *Goshawk* was ready to sail. All he had to do was grab the sticks, raise her up and fly her off.

Huffing, she went around to the back of the vessel, out of sight, and started messing around with the ship. They could hear her clanking about outside.

"She's ... going to do the *Goshawk*!" Sarah cried, groggy.

"Oh yeah?" Phillip said with a sadistic grin. He raised his hand and calmly pressed a button. A blast of air jarred the ship and Thomasina, rolling head over heels, was blasted away along with several of her Singing Ten, their released MT CALMs bouncing, some going over the side of the roof.

Phillip smoothly lifted the *Goshawk* and spun it around over the edge of the roof, hovering to face her.

He had to do it—something made him do it.

She stood, and they stared at each other for a moment. Phillip augured the nose down and they were eye to eye. She threw her MT CALM at the cockpit glass, where it bounced off with a harmless thud. If the glass hadn't been there, the throw would have been right on the mark. He then yawed the ship, free as a bird, and let it soar down the sheer side of the building where he joyously buzzed the armored ladies and surviving Spectres standing at street level, causing them all to dive for cover. Leveling and gaining slow altitude through the metal canyons of Waam, Phillip was all smiles. A cable came down from the heavens, hoping to skewer the ship, and then another. He easily evaded them.

He rolled the ship. He looped it. "Creation, that felt good! See ya', Thomasina! Goodbye, and good riddance!"

"What are you doing, Phillip?" Sarah asked crossly, still trying to collect her wits. "Are you showing off? You're showing off for Thomasina, aren't you?"

✶ ✶ ✶ ✶ ✶

As Waam began to fall back into the distance, Kay awoke.

Sarah was sitting next to him. "You ok?" she asked. He nodded and sat up.

He Sighted into Ethylrelda's shrunken temple. Inside, he could see a great portion of the twisting passages had broken away replaced by what looked like a gigantic, leafless tree. Soon, the tree, the new *Wandwilla*, would burst through the cracked sphere of the temple and reach for the sun.

It had worked—both Ethylrelda and Krotan had gotten what they wanted. He could only imagine the joy they were feeling now and forever.

And he had what he wanted, too. He checked the back of the ship. There were the two pieces of Sam's machine, and, sitting on the couch still wrapped up in its cloth was the final piece they'd come for, the three pieces together for the first time in centuries—the *Oberphilliax.*

Olonol. The Machine.

It's done, Sam; it's over. I did it, Cerri-Tela!

Kay had passed the Trials.

Epilogue

The Skull in Reverse

We're going after the Horned God, Hath, you and me.

Lady Hathaline chuckled and clapped as she watched the scene unfold on the *Goshawk*. She'd watched most of Kay's adventures throughout the trials. She'd seen him grow in stature and power and was very impressed and proud of her brother, and her cousins as well. She wished she could have gone with them and flown the *Goshawk* through Xaphan space, or maybe one of those weird statue ships in Waam, those looked fun to fly. She couldn't wait to see him again alive and well.

She was leaning over a Vith fountain in the Grove—the same one her aunt, Lady Poe, had created Carahil in years ago. He had told her much about this fountain. He had brought her out there through the tangle of beech trees and shown it to her; it just seemed like an overgrown fountain, an old Vith ruin. Carahil said that some of the material used in his creation was still there, sopped up in the cracks and pores of the stone like cooking oil in a well-seasoned iron frying pan, waiting to be activated.

As he showed her, it was an easy process to bring the fountain to life. All she needed was a little bit of cool water from the lake and pour it into the basin, just enough to create a bit of depth at the bottom. That done, all she had to do was peer in. Images formed in the shallow water and she could see things beyond the confines of the Grove. She could see anything she wanted, the surface of the water alight with images. Carahil instructed her to focus the images to see specifically what she wanted to.

As she concentrated on the fountain, she often heard whispered laughter in the beech trees and saw soft flashes of green light come and go.

"That's the enemy," Carahil told her. "Hidden behind their veils. Don't worry about them—I'm here to protect you."

Dubious, but trusting in him, she returned to her work. As Carahil directed, the object of her attentions was a curious skull sitting in a library on the 50th floor of Xyotel Tower. It was her cousin Sarah's Mystery Library, a sort of clubhouse where she, Kay and Phillip liked to hang out. She had only been in it herself once or twice. Sarah was very particular about the place and made a nasty fuss whenever she entered as she wasn't on the WELCOME list, neither was her sister Lady Kilos—in fact she had been on the FORBIDDEN list for a long time. So, she generally avoided the place. She had other things to do.

There was a bleached, partially fossilized skull sitting on a shelf in the library surrounded on either side by books. Sarah proudly proclaimed that it was a Berserkacide skull and that Carahil himself had asked her to guard it years ago while she was still in training pants. Given Sarah's habit for epic exaggeration, Hathaline had always thought the story was either a half-truth or a complete fabrication.

"That skull in Sarah's library once belonged to the Horned God's Secret-Talker. All the gods have one," Carahil said. "A Secret-Talker is an individual whom we entrust all our secrets, hence the name. We can't achieve our full measure with the universe without a Secret-Talker, they're sort of like a safety-valve and paper-trail, I guess, and that's how the universe likes it. The gods have lots of secrets, and if you're a god and you're messing up and doing things you're not supposed to be doing, the Secret-Talker is going to know and have a complete memory of it. That's how the gods are supposed to police each other, by having access to the secrets held by the Secret-Talker. That's the theory, anyway, however in practice it's very difficult getting to a god's Secret-Talker, because we take great pains to ensure they're well hidden and protected—you wouldn't believe where we've got some of these poor people stashed sometimes. I have my Secret-Talker and she's very dear to me and nobody's going to find her—she never stays in one place for very long. It was her idea."

Carahil winked at Hath. "So, here's our task. What we need to do is get to the Horned God's Secret-Talker and find out his secrets. I'm pretty certain the Horned God and his damn temple is the root cause behind much of the weird stuff that's happening here on Kana, and if we can get at his secrets we can be rid of him for good."

Hath had a question.

"Yep—once we take him out you won't have to worry about becoming a monster, The only things you'll have to worry about, Hath, will be your bowling average and what to wear on a Saturday night and which lucky fellow to court first."

Hath said she hated bowling and didn't care about wearing clothes and courting boys. She wanted to fly and join the Fleet.

Carahil laughed. "Ahhh, all in good time. Now, here's the thing, if you're a god you really need to keep your Secret-Talker happy, otherwise bad things can happen. If you mistreat or abuse them, then their loyalty might waiver or change all together, and I think that's where the Horned God has slipped up. I think he, being rather confident in himself and the fences he's created, forgot about his Secret-Talker in the depths of antiquity and sort of left him there in limbo, and his Secret-Talker was very sad, for a long time. I can feel the loneliness permeating the bone and hollow spaces of that skull—whoever this person was, he wasn't very happy and that's for certain. I would never allow my Secret-Talker to be neglected to point of misery like the Horned God did his, and that's where we can make our move."

Hath asked who the Horned God is.

"Oh, a right git he is. He is the 'Boogey-Man' of the gods. He's a criminal who goes around terrorizing the younger folk, making them worship him, making them kill for him. It has long been suspected that he is one of us, a member of the Celestial Arborium in disguise, and the quest to uncover his identity has been going on for centuries. Most recently, Anabrax was accused and convicted of being either the Horned God himself or in league with him and she was sent to the Windage of Kind. I recently visited Anabrax and she told me she was framed, and I believe her. She told me that the Horned God is none other than Bathloxi himself.

"Who's Bathloxi, you ask? He is a beloved senior member of the Arborium, well-respected and above reproach. He is a friend, giver of laws and mentor of many gods. He is wise and very kind—or, is he? I think, over the course of his long existence, the rigid constraints of the very laws Bathloxi wrote began to wear on him, and he, like many beings, yearned for something more—something his sadistic alter-ego, the Horned God, could deliver to him in earnest. Maybe he thinks the laws he wrote don't apply to him and he has lease to do whatever he wants. Or, maybe, the ravenous Horned God who has tormented Sam and her people for ages, is who he really is and the calm, reserved Bathloxi sitting at the top of the universe surrounded by his friends is the alter ego. Perhaps he really is the Devil. I don't know."

Carahil was lost in thought for a moment, lamenting the possibility.

"So," he said, "let's look to it. Sarah's skull in the Mystery Library is the key. Obviously, since it's just a skull, the Secret-Talker is dead. Been dead for a long time, but time's the whole thing, isn't it and he's alive somewhere in the past with the secrets we need. Here's what we're facing—Bathloxi has placed four significant protections around his Secret-Talker. The First Protection proclaims that no god or other member of the Older Folk may interface with him, ok? So, that takes me and everybody else from the Arborium out of play. By the way, technically, his First Protection goes against the rules of Universal Balance since the whole point of having a Secret-Talker is for accountability amongst the gods, but nobody's ever called him on it—I suppose status and familiarity speak for themselves, don't they? Here's the Second Protection, Bathloxi's got him stashed away in a time loop somewhere in the distant past—nobody's quite sure where or when. So, even though the Secret-Talker today is just a skull, he's still getting fed current information in the past; I'm not quite sure how it works, but it does. That's the Second Protection."

Carahil blinked. "Still with me, Hath, 'cause here's where it gets tricky."

Hathaline nodded and listened.

"Good. The Third Protection is that Bathloxi's Secret-Talker can only be located in the past by one of his servants—and, when I say one of his servants, I don't mean the cute little creatures up in the Arborium that help us out with this and that, I mean his '*servants*'; the Golden People, the *Killanjo* and, by default, the Monamas. If anybody else tries to look back into the past with a magic mirror or other such time-seeing device, they're not going to see anything. Here's where you come in, my lady. You, Hath, are one of the Horned God's servants; you don't want to be his servant and you haven't been converted into one yet, that's still years off in the future, but you still fulfill the criteria. I checked on it. Bathloxi's protections around his Secret-Talker, like any magical contrivance, only work as well as they're written. The Third Protection is the most porous and poorly thought out of the four, and that's because gods, like him and I, don't really understand the mechanics of how time works any better than anybody else does—we're bound by the flow of time too. The Golden People who serve Bathoxi have a vast understanding of time—they ride it like mariners across the sea. They created the Time Loop used in the Second Protection and helped Bathloxi write the Third Protection and assured him it was sound and he listened to them. They're his loyal servants, after all, but I think they made the Third Protection a little vague intentionally so that they themselves could get at the Secret-Talker whenever they want. Why, I don't know. In any event, the Third Protection is flawed because it doesn't say you have to be a *current* servant, it just says *servant*, and that's what you are, a future servant of his. Thanks to that loose wording you should be able to focus on that skull, look into the past and see Bathloxi's Secret-Talker. It's a loophole the Golden People wrote and Bathloxi doesn't seem to be aware of it."

Carahil blinked and gazed down at the calm water in the basin. "Now, here's the Fourth and final protection, and this is the toughest one. Bathloxi's Secret-Talker won't give up his secrets unless you know his name. So, even if you locate him back in time and he wanted to tell, he couldn't unless you first say his name. He can't tell you what it is—you have to say it to him first. Ok? I've done all the research I can and his name is lost to the ages—it's just not written down anywhere, there's no lore or songs or oral histories with his name hidden within—there's nothing. And, it's really frustrating too."

Hathaline stood there listening. Carahil gave her a little nudge with his silver noggin. "So, your task, in a nutshell, is to use this fountain, focus on the skull in Sarah's library, locate the Secret-Talker in time and then observe him until you discover his name. If we have that, then we have the Horned God and we will take him down. And, best of all, since we have the Secret-Talker's skull we'll be able to use it to mess him up if he tries to come at us. It's our ace-in-the-hole, and he doesn't know we've got it, but first we need the name. That's the key."

✶ ✶ ✶ ✶ ✶

And Lady Hathaline set to her work. Every day she went to the fountain, standing over the old basin and peering in, concentrating on the skull in Sarah's library as Carahil watched.

The water came to life. There was the skull, sitting on the shelf, bleached white and smooth. At first, nothing happened, she simply stared at it, wondering what she was supposed to be seeing; the tedium of standing there was killing. Few children her age could have stuck with such a test of endurance for very long, but Lady Hathaline was stalwart. Carahil said the skull was vital, so, she'd come out and stare into this fountain all day every day if need be.

Day after day passed with similar results—a skull on a shelf. Every so often Carahil left her side, saying he needed to go and "Look after Sam", and "See how Kay's doing", and he'd vanish, leaving her alone in the Grove. He didn't leave Hathaline defenseless, however. He gave her a handful of little blue figurines shapes in his smiling likeness. "If you hear or see anything disturbing, use one of these," he said. "Just toss 'em and you're good."

Needing a break, she occasionally used the basin to check in on Kay herself—she was quickly becoming adept at its use. She saw him far away, and she heard his thoughts. He seemed to be doing fine. Look at the things he could do now. What a strange city Waam is.

She checked in on Sam. She was sealed inside a gigantic metal man riding on a pewter chariot through the ether. She slept and dreamed. She saw Carahil flying by her side lending his protection.

Just an all around nice guy Carahil was.

And there were the voices and the tittering jibes coming from the trees. "*Hath!*" she'd hear. "*Hath, we're going to get you … We're going take you, do things to you … Make you one of us …*"

… make you one of us …

She stood tall though and trusted to Carahil and the little figurines he'd left her, throwing them in the direction of the sounds, and they would quiet down for a time, leaving her in peace. His protection worked.

✶ ✶ ✶ ✶ ✶

Hathaline continued on with the skull, and her persistence began to pay off. In the shallow water, time changed around the skull, moving backwards into the past. Slow at first and then accelerating, events unfolded in reverse. She saw the skull gone from the shelf being given to a tiny, pig-tailed Sarah by Carahil on her mother's birthday some fourteen years ago. "Take good care of this for me," Carahil had told her, and, hugging it with both arms, she promised she would, mouth open and pigtails jangling.

So, Sarah hadn't been exaggerating after all.

Events in the fountain were flying now, moving steadily backwards in time. Watching actions in reverse, Hath had to re-train her thoughts and how she processed information; not in normal time progression, but watching from end to distant beginning. It was bewildering to see things in reverse. As a growing pilot, her father had taught her how to process information quickly and in concise order, a skill that was a must-have for a person flying such a fast and potentially unforgiving craft like a Rip-car. He taught her to clear out a familiar spot in her thoughts and then place pertinent, concise information into that clean space in precise order, first A, then B, then C, all organized and available for immediate recall when needed. With her thoughts working in such an orderly manner, she could remember vast amounts of detail: pitch, yaw, speed, altitude, landmarks, hazards, and recall them perfectly in the short term. Now, she was seeing everything happening in reverse; Z, then, Y, then X. She forced herself to concentrate, to adjust, to correctly process what she was seeing and not miss a single detail.

This was for Carahil, and her brother … and for herself.

Continuing back in time, she saw the skull being dug out of the ground in a heavily wooded area. Carahil had dug it out, holding it in his mouth, dirt caked up around his muzzle like a beard, and flying away holding it in his teeth, a rare and eagerly sought after prize. She felt his excitement.

✶ ✶ The skull stayed in the ground for a long, long time—ages passed, stuck in a vein of coal, to compacted peat, to dry earth.

✶ ✶ The skull unearthed in ancient times, sun rising and falling, resting before a headless skeleton on a pile of filthy rags in a primitive, fallen down hut, the skeleton's hands crossed over its heart.

✶ ✶ Now, deep in antiquity, there was the skull no longer a skull. Now it was a face and muscle and skin and a body, alive and breathing.

There was the Horned God's Secret-Talker.

✶ ✶ Clawed hands clasped with another's—a final moment of solace and shared comfort after ages of solitude and pain.

✶ ✶ The figure sat alone in the woods, head down, garbed in black rags. It sat there by itself for a long time. It had a string of bone beads around its neck, which it fingered with clawed hands and toyed with, the bone rubbed smooth. It was all alone, deep in time. Watching through the waters of the fountain, Hathaline could feel the Secret-Talker's loneliness.

So lonely, longing for what once was.

"I think the Horned God's forgotten about his Secret-Talker in the antiquity of time ... " Carahil had said, and he was correct.

She couldn't help but feel sorry for it.

Hathaline studied the figure, taking in every detail. It was a woman (not a man as Carahil had assumed), and, from the looks of it, she was a Monama woman. She had the characteristic chalky white skin, the bursting mane of ankle-length black hair and the tell-tale large black eyes. She looked a lot like Sam, only more primal, more unleashed. She was full and strong, beautiful, the face of an angel, fierce and proud.

Wait—four arms. The Secret-Talker had four arms. She was a Berserkacide.

✶✶ All alone.

✶✶ All dead, mate and child, kin hand in hand. All dead. All gone. The last of her kind, denied the simple gift of death. The Horned God had done this to her. Full of His secrets. All His fault. She walked away from the temple in the ground where she had reveled in blood and returned to the woods, her ancient home now empty and unfamiliar. She would never see the temple again. Good riddance.

Time continued backwards.

✶✶ The Golden People, wearing stolen forms of the aliens of jade and sapphire, became the Horned God's new angels of death. They hated her. She hated them back.

✶✶ New beings came from the temple, shapeless and golden, emerging from the mists of time. They routed the accursed aliens of jade and sapphire, chased them from the planet, killed them, and stole their forms. They came to her to steal her form as well and she killed them with her claws.

✶✶ All the dead who could not be replaced, turning to bones where they lay.

✶✶ They breed like grass. No end to them. Giving birth to ten or twelve heretic two-armed children at a time, while she and her people were barely managing just one. Outnumbered. Her four-armed kind slowly dying out.

✶✶ Battles! Two-armed Mo-Na-Ma freaks wearing the jade and sapphire aliens' clothing fighting the woman and a primitive band of four armed Berserkacides in rags and furs. Death and savagery. Hatred. Ripping each other apart—each the anathema of the other. The two-armed Mo-Na-Ma heretics, though tamed, though civilized, were still strong, still had claws, still could bite and stand in battle against her four-armed purebreds.

✶✶ Two-armed abominations emerging from the alien cities in the north at last, wearing their clothing, speaking their language … sharing their beds and turning from the Horned God. A blasphemy! Look at them! How soft! How timid and weak! Kill them!! Sacrifice them!! We will wipe them from Tevlapradah!

✶✶ Rivers choked with dead, pale four-armed bodies. Botched experiments. Flotsam.

✶✶ Jade and sapphire aliens in northern cities where it was too cold for them to reach, more capable than the Horned God had anticipated, ensnaring her people and dragging them inside the walls. Experimenting on them. They called this place Ka-Na.

✶✶ Aliens, soft and weak wearing clothing of jade and sapphire, lured in from the stars by the Horned God for his angels to kill. He always brought them creatures to hunt and play with. To sacrifice them in the temple. To hear their final screams. They lived for blood and sacrifice. These aliens were merely the latest and their blood shall be spilled in the temple to mingle with the rest. They were doomed as they stepped out of their armada of vessels, looking at the landscape with wonder. They thought they'd discovered heaven when instead they were in Tevlapradah—hell. Welcome to Hell, your visit shall not last long.

✶ ✶ The four-armed woman, receiving a gift from a gigantic monster standing on two hooves, shaggy, wearing a horned crown of lightning. The Horned God giving her the gift of immortality and sharing his secrets, becoming his Secret-Talker. Such secrets he had to share. An honor.

✶ ✶ The four-armed woman standing on a platform of blood for decades, oiled, feathered, wearing her bone necklace, holding sacrifices and burnt offerings in her four strong hands. A high priestess to the Horned God in his temple, he watching with cross-armed approval. He brought them gifts: people to kill, full of blood to drink. The Horned God was kind in his beautific evil.

✶ ✶ A temple of blue stone being built and hacked out of the ground by her people. The Horned God watching from the earth, impatient for the suffering to begin.

**Primitive and proud, the woman shook totems and strings of beads in worship. They killed everything around them, silencing the landscape, collecting the skulls and fashioning little altars of skulls, anointing them in blood and smoking clouds of burning animal fat. They were covered in the blood of the slain. All for the Horned God. He was very demanding.

✶ ✶ Something came from the sky and watched them from the woods. They were afraid of it. She took the head of a slain woodland creature and presented it to the thing in the woods as an offering. The first bit of blood offered to the creature they would come to know as the Horned God. He had found Tevlapradah. He was pleased.

✶ ✶ The woman roaming with her people through the woods and plains, unshod, filthy, clad in furs and crude, stinking skins. Beautiful, yet fierce and terrible, they killed everything they encountered, dragging their prizes back to their woodland hovel to be torn apart and devoured raw. She was part of a group, a war party bounding across the countryside ever seeking their next victim. This was to be alive—to hunt and kill with her kin, to soak her four hands in blood. This was Tevlapradah.

✶ ✶ In a rare moment of peace, the woman received a necklace of bone beads from a war-like four-armed man. She accepted the beads—some sort of primitive marriage ceremony.

Hath wondered what at this was leading to. She'd seen epochs of time, the coming and passing of the Horned God, the creation of the modern Monamas in now lost alien cities, and the building and anointing of the Horned God's temple. And, the four-armed woman, how she'd gone from being a warrior-hunter, to a high priestess in the Horned God's temple, to his immortal Secret-Talker and then to the last of her kind.

Nowhere in all of that, in the shouting and dying and ringing of weapons and beating of drums did she hear her name uttered. Did she even have a name?

But wait ...

Time continued backwards. She saw the woman and the man she would 'marry' alone in a pool, nude and bloodied, full of entrails from a recent kill, having a contorted round of sadistic, animal-like sex—furs cast aside, their pale bodies tangled together, pitted with cuts and clouding the water with blood.

The male was shouting something. Grunting it. The woman was latched onto his neck, mangling it with her teeth.

Hath strained to hear.

"On....., On..c.a, Ond.c.." he cried in primitive ecstasy.

What? What was that?

"Ondecca, Ondecca, Ondecca!"

The Horned God's Secret-Talker was named Ondecca.

Mission accomplished.

Book Three

The Temple of the Exploding Head

Prologue

Once Upon a Time ...

"Well," the young man said, "this sucks."

A handsome young man and a beautiful young lady sat in a vast library; a collection of books, scrolls, files and other artifacts was scattered on the table in front of them. The man glowed with a silvery light. The woman at his side wore a charm at her throat with the letter 'M' embossed on the face. She also had a small but definite bump in the center of her belly.

It was obvious they loved each other.

Bright sunlight streamed in through the windows. Pleasant floral notes drifted on the air.

What sunlight? Where? When? What plants? This Library was awash in time and place, lost in the chaos of infinity and the morass of oblivion. It was difficult to find, and impossible to fully comprehend—even for the gods. To sit at these tables was a miracle, so, they sat in the sunlight and appreciated it though it wasn't really sunlight, and they smelt the flowers knowing there were no flowers anywhere near.

They went through the open books and consulted old scrolls with aplomb. The reading wasn't pleasant. They considered their options and bickered over things, tapping the scrolls with their fingers, rapping the surface of their table as they argued.

The far door opened, and the proprietors of the library came in, gliding toward their table. One of the proprietors was a fair-haired man in silken, somewhat woodsy garments and soft boots. A small, key-like sword was scabbarded at his back. His companion was a lilting lady with gossamer hair set high over her head. They were both quite thin and tall, rather elongated in their profile.

The proprietors stopped at their table, noticing their agitation. "Your research not to your liking?" the fair-haired man asked.

"Uh, not really, no."

The tall lady laughed. "The future is always a little depressing, isn't it?"

The man sitting at the table reacted. "Well, yeah. We came here hoping to see how best to raise our children, we thought it important, and look what we see. According to these books, a lot of people are going to die, something about the Devil getting his way and reveling in unmitigated blood, and I'm going to be blamed for it and thrown into prison for a few millennia. Me! That doesn't sound like a lot of fun."

The male proprietor chuckled. "You missed a bit here," he said sliding a scroll toward them. "Please attend."

They opened the scroll and leaned over it, reading as fast as they could.

The young man was open-mouthed as he read. "The Devil is going to be eaten?" he cried pointing at the scroll.

The proprietor leaned down and looked at the scroll. "Yes," he said, "he, and possibly others as well; you two included. They feed on the gods, and they appear to be feeding hearty, don't they?"

The woman with the 'M' at her throat was beside herself. "We're going to be eaten? Can we change it, the future I mean? Can we do something about it?"

It seemed reasonable. If one knew the future, then why couldn't one change it? They awaited his answer.

"Absolutely not," the fair-haired man said.

The seated silvery fellow wasn't giving up. "Why not? I'm looking at this, all of this. It sucks, I don't like it much, and I want to change it. I don't want to be thrown in prison, or eaten for that matter. I don't want Mabs here eaten either. Why can't I change it? I mean, if I know it's going to happen in advance, why can't I?"

"Are you asking a question?" the man asked.

"Yes, I am. We have vast knowledge at the Top of the Universe, but none of us really knows a lot about Time. Time, time, it's so confusing. However, I, unlike many of my peers— my lovely lady here included—have no issues asking questions when I have them. So, I'm asking ..." He pointed at the pile of open books, charts and scrolls. "Can I fix this?"

"Again, absolutely not," the fair-haired man said.

There was an odd brick of bluestone mixed into the collection of materials sitting in front of them. The silvery man picked it up. "And what is this?'

The brick had an inscription on it reading:

THIS TEMPLE IS DEDICATED TO CARAHIL

"Any idea what this is? I don't."

The tall woman looked at the brick and laughed. "We've had that here with us for a long time. You seem like such a nice fellow." She studied his features. "Are you really a god, Carahil?"

Carahil blushed.

His companion with the 'M' spoke up. "You're so modest. Yes, Queen Wendilnight, he is a god, and so am I. My name is Mabsornath. I was once a goddess of wisdom and knowledge."

"Well then, we should be so honored. We don't often entertain such company. I am not a god, nor is my lord Fiddler Crowe, yet we are expert in areas the gods are not, namely time."

"Fiddler Crowe?" Carahil asked. "Is that your name, sir?"

"It's the one I prefer in this timeline."

"Well sir, as I told your queen, Mabs and myself shall be at your service if you help us."

Fiddler Crowe was unconvinced. "You're determined to meddle in uncertain things, are you?"

Carahil threw an eye to the odd brick with his name on it, and to the open scrolls predicting his death. "I think it prudent."

Queen Wendilnight smiled. "Then, walk with us, please."

Carahil and Mabs stood up and followed Queen Wendilnight and the fair-haired Fiddler Crowe out of the room. They entered into a long corridor filled with odd machines: bulky box-like contraptions, metal tuning-fork-like devices, mirrors, step pads and so on.

"We maintain a collection of devices that we've encountered over the ages that deal with the subject of time travel," Queen Wendilnight said. "These machines here are all failures. They all utilize a similar method of operation and, therefore, suffer from the same flaws. There are a number of problems with time travel, and these devices highlight one of the most vexing problems: *perception.* You cannot perceive changes you might have made to the stream of time, in either the past or the future, with these devices. Your perceptions depend on a consistent, logical flow of time to make sense of your surroundings. You're a god, Carahil; your point of view is loftier than that of the younger folk, and your vision is great, but you perceive time the same way any mundane person might. If you go back in time in one of these machines and make a change, you'll never be aware of it because everything you know will instantly be unmade. It's like a dream, so clear in the morning, but forgotten by noon. You'll never know you made a change; you'll never even know you wanted to make a change in the first place, so your efforts to change the future may yield fruit, and they may not. You might have already tried to change the future to something more to your liking and have no idea you did it. You might have made things worse. Recall the odd brick sitting in your pile back in the library—the one with your name on it. Perhaps you wrote your name on it yourself in the antiquity of time and have no memory of doing so."

Carahil and Mabs looked at each other.

"Is that possible?'

"Most certainly."

"An ideal scenario for the casual time traveler," Fiddler Crowe said, "would be to bundle up everything you know and take it with you to the past or wherever, make your changes *and* remain aware of them afterwards so that you can critique your progress with a discriminating eye."

"That would be great," Carahil said. "Can we do that?"

"No," was the flat answer.

Carahil and Mabs stood there in the Hall of Time Machines and felt defeated. Mabs' hand went to her belly.

Queen Wendilnight gazed at them with a motherly eye. "Well, I think these two will be of great help in time; they will be our good friends, and I want to help them." A secret door opened behind her, and she stepped aside. "Please," she said, motioning for them to enter. "Witness something few, high or low, have ever seen."

"We should not allow this," Fiddler Crowe said.

"Oh please, darling," Queen Wendilnight replied. "I wish to help these two kind gods. It will be all right. I have faith in them."

They entered a very dark room, so dark Carahil and Mabs couldn't see the walls, the ceiling or the floor. Lit up in vivid neon shades of blue, red, purple and green were a multitude of long, cyclone-like funnels of light; they hung from the unseen ceiling and trailed off to the floor, some longer and fatter than others. They rotated counter-clockwise and undulated from side to side, like a gallery of neon-lit tornados.

"What are these?" Mabs asked.

"These are, to quote the vernacular, *tunnels through time*," Fiddler Crowe said. "Aberrations created by the turbulence of strong emotion. They pop up with regularity and then they fade. Very ponderous, very unwieldy and thirsty for energy. Very bad for the flesh as well—but they do allow for novice travel back and forth through time from the present to a fixed point in the past. Within these tunnels through time the various laws of singularity do not apply—you could meet yourself and it would be like nothing, and, best of all, you may perceive time in its infinancy, which means you may traverse time and remember everything."

"We make it a point to monitor such things," Queen Wendilnight said. She led them to a particularly fat tunnel, blue in color, longer than the rest, more turbid, and much larger. It was a roaring vortex in time, huge and powerful. "This one here … this tunnel is the one that causes your bad future, I think."

"It is?" Carahil asked.

"Yes. This is an old one, been sustained and nurtured like a candle flame grown to a raging fire, never allowed to grow dim or burn out for a long, long time. For eons. Quite a feat."

Carahil and Mabs gathered around the whirling blue cylinder, seeing it flash with lightning strokes of raw energy. "What's inside?" he asked.

"The Horned God's Temple. Take a look. See what's happening in there," Queen Wendilnight said.

Carahil swallowed and took a peek, putting his head into the whirling light. He immediately pulled back out. He was shaken.

"What did you see?" Mabs asked.

"It was terrible," he stammered, falling to his knees. "How could such a place exist? So much suffering. Where are the gods?"

"There are bad things in the universe, dear Carahil," Queen Wendilnight said, "and the Horned God's Temple is one of them. The rage and suffering his temple has seen has created this time tunnel and fed its hunger for ages."

Carahil was dispirited, and Mabs embraced him.

Sprouting off the main funnel of the blue cylinder were many smaller, differently colored ones. They twisted like tendrils of a flower stem, some growing and then sputtering and dying, while others sustained themselves, glowing bright only to fade moments later.

Fiddler Crowe explained. "The Horned God's time tunnel is very messy. See these smaller time tunnels sprouting off the main one? The emotion and suffering of the Temple creates them, but they usually don't last long. They lose energy and burn out. See there."

Carahil and Mabs watched the multitude of smaller time tunnels of yellow, green and red sprout off of the main blue one, flicker and then die only to be replaced by others in an unending cycle.

"That's how they always start. Very small," Queen Wendilnight remarked.

Amid the flickering lights was a bright white time tunnel clinging to the giant whirling face of the Horned God's blue one. It was small and tormented, yet it stubbornly glowed, refusing to die unlike the others around it.

"Look at this one," Carahil said pointing it out. "This one endures." He looked into the white shaft of light. He saw something that fascinated him. "Who is she?" he asked.

"Who?" Mabs replied.

"Look inside Mabs. There's a pale little girl in there with long black hair. She looks very sad, but she's determined. My heart goes out to her."

Mabs stuffed her head into the white shaft. "I see her. A very brave little girl."

"She could be anybody," Queen Wendilnight said. "She has something to do with the Horned God's Temple. Look how her little time tunnel grows and sustains itself, entangled with it. But watch, it begins to fade."

The white time tunnel created by the emotions of a little pale girl far away began to flicker and fade to be consumed by the Horned God's tunnel just like the others. Carahil and Mabs reached up and placed their hands into the white glow, lending it their power. Its brightness returned and stayed strong.

"Ah, assisted by the gods," Queen Wendilnight said. "Perhaps the little girl has a chance after all—time will tell."

She motioned for Carahil and Mabs to follow her. "Come, witness a sight seldom seen." She led them away from the masses of colored lights to a quiet corner of the room. A velvet curtain emerged in the dark.

Carahil looked back once, at the blue cylinder of light: the Horned God's temple. The smaller white one was still there with it, glowing strong.

"You want to travel time? You wish to right wrongs that have yet to happen? This is what you need to use." Queen Wendilnight moved the curtain aside. "There are only two of these machines in existence—this one and the prototype. Our friend made us this one."

Something tall and silvery was revealed behind the curtain. Carahil and Mabs stared at it in wonder.

"What the gods could do with this machine. It does what is impossible. We shall lend it to you for a limited time."

"And remember," Fiddler Crowe said, "it is not available for your everyday use. Use it well while you can."

And Carahil and Mabs returned to the library to begin their planning. There was much to consider and properly understand. That weird brick with his name on it had Carahil flummoxed.

That pale little girl with the black hair he'd seen in the small white tunnel through time, Carahil saw lots of possibilities with her.

Yes, many possibilities.

All in good time.

1—Sam Dreams

I need you to run for me, Sam ...

Deep within Lady Sammidoran's head, she dreamed of warm places and green fields. She dreamed of herself sitting on a luxurious red cloth out in the afternoon sun. Far away, gazelle, quizzical heads turned, grazed in safety.

Sam was wearing a flowing black garment, her chalky-white skin glorious in the sun. Her thick black hair curled all the way down past the small of her back and spread out on the grass behind her, forming a great carpet of black, bumpy with rises and falls of curls. She was molding a large clay pot or jar, working the clay with her strong pale hands. It was a very large jar, three feet high, about a foot wide. She held it in place with her knees as she shaped the sides, turning it bit by bit as Monama women before her had done for ages. She scratched away defects and lumps with her long nails. She had a lot of work to do before it was ready, but it would be perfect once it was finished. It was a labor filled with love, and she was going to savor every moment.

This jar would one day contain and nurture her and Kay's children. Sam herself had been born in a jar made by her mother. Kay was her love, a great Vith lord from the north; he was an Elder, her *Arin-Dan*. She'd loved him all her life, dreaming of him from her home in the fog by the lake. She hummed a Monama tune as she worked, and, every so often, kissed the unfinished side of the jar, adding all the love she could into its making.

Kay was far away, performing the Trials for Love for her. She couldn't wait for him to finish so she could return to his side. She never wanted to be away from him again.

Casting a great shadow behind her was a huge metal man gleaming bronze, twenty feet tall, standing next to a giant-sized pewter chariot etched with traditional Bronta designs. His chest was opened like the two halves of a clamshell—she'd been sleeping within his chest, kept safe from the demons that were out to get her.

And there were many, and they were relentless.

Three nude figures unharnessed themselves from the chariot and approached; they were tall, slim, black-haired—all manifestations of NIGHTMARE material. She had created them to test and train Kay. Each one represented one of his three Gifts: Waft, Cloak and Sight.

Waft stopped before Sam and bowed, black hair curling. "He traveled with me at speed and passed my test," she said. "I broke his fingers and caused him pain. I had no choice."

"You did what you had to do, and I thank you for teaching my Kay so well."

Waft shimmered and vanished.

Cloak approached and bowed. "He sat with me and passed my test, and I was loath to let him go." She paused. "You'll swear to me you will love him as he deserves?" Cloak loved Kay as much as Sam did.

"I promise," Sam said. "I will love him the length of my days."

Cloak nodded and vanished.

Sight came up, the final one. "I was angry. I wanted to punish him for ignoring me."

"I know," Sam said.

Sight smiled a little. "But, he proved his Sight is without peer. I am proud of him."

"Then go and be at rest. Know you've done your job well."

Sight bowed and was gone.

Alone at the cloth once again, Sam set back to work on her jar.

She wasn't alone for long.

The gazelle became aware of something approaching. They stopped grazing, craned their collective necks and then took off fast, leaping through the grass and were gone.

Massive footfalls. The ground shook.

Striding over the horizon was an incredible giant, possibly thousands of feet tall, rising up on the horizon with each step as if it were ascending a staircase from hell. It was shaggy—possibly part-human, part animal. A tangle of antlers the size of mountains sprouted from the top of its head, and it wore a crown of lightning. It had a sylvan face, flicking ears and diabolical eyes, a beard and a relatively small goat-like mouth. Its head split the clouds. Its shadow darkened the landscape.

Sam knew the old lore. It was the Horned God—he whom her people feared most of all. There were many who tormented her people, but the Horned God was the worst of the lot, the most ancient and the most persistent. Always lurking, always demanding.

To see the Horned God was to die.

Clutching her jar, she stood, hoping to throw herself back into the relative safety of the Metal Man and be born away.

His gaze fell upon her, a negative-image corridor of hatred and chaos.

Sam felt herself going insane in his gaze. She covered her eyes. When she opened them, the terrible rising mass of the Horned God had vanished.

Sitting at the far end of the cloth was a deer that hadn't been there before. It was the size and shape of any deer, tawny, antlered, hoofed—only its probing, lofty eyes and hardpan expression gave it away as being something other than just a deer.

Its eyes held her fast."Are you Lady Sammidoran of Monama?" it asked in a steady voice.

Sam was terrified, afraid to answer.

"Speak up," the deer said.

Sam struggled to catch her breath. "Are … you the Horned God?"

The deer sighed a bit and spoke as if rehearsed. "My name is Bathloxi. I live at the top of the Universe with my Celestial brethren. It is my task to ensure that order is maintained. I have performed that role for eons. You needn't be frightened." The deer's voice was at once measured and reasonable and stern and unyielding. He had an undeniable air of authority about him. Hugging her jar with both arms, Sam seated herself opposite the deer.

"What do you want?" she asked.

"I want to know secrets. Specifically, I want to know all your secrets."

"My secrets?"

"There have been many crimes committed here, by a demon in silver who calls himself Carahil."

"Carahil?"

"I am tasked to gather evidence of Carahil's unspeakable acts and present them to the Arborium, where we may then deliberate on his fate. I suspect he has done the very worst thing we of the older folk can do … I'm certain of it in fact."

Sam held onto her jar. "And that is?"

"To revel in worship and accept blood sacrifice done in his name, to enjoy it, to bathe in it, to become drunk with the power that comes with such things and attempt to hide his misconduct from the gods. To keep slaves and inflict suffering. To entice and entrap innocent members of the younger folk to his dark place where he may revel in their death and destruction. Carahil has made himself a dark deity; in short, he's made himself the devil, and for it he shall be punished. Justly so."

"Is Carahil the Horned God?"

Bathloxi raised his eyebrows. "You tell me Sam; after all, you are his Secret-Talker. Correct? You've seen all he's done, and I demand you share his secrets with me."

Secret-Talker?

Sam opened her mouth to respond but found she had no words. She sat there dumbly, mouth open. She wanted to please this mighty spirit, and she almost started to answer, 'yes, I am his Secret-Talker' though she honestly had no idea what that meant.

"Speak up, my dear."

"I'm his what?" she finally said. "I'm sorry. What's a Secret-Talker?"

Bathloxi became impatient. "I should have known he'd have protected you with some sort of child-like, magical conditions. He is a juvenile and a delinquent at heart."

Sam thought about that for a moment.

The Devil's a juvenile delinquent?

Several golden servants clad in rich togas appeared holding baskets and trays. They set them down on the cloth and backed away. They glanced at Sam as they departed, and their eyes burned with hatred.

"What is all this?" Sam asked. The servants had placed a number of desserts on the cloth in front of her: cream pies topped with sliced bananas and strawberries, cookies loaded with chocolate, nuts, and dried fruits. There were colorful hard candies, strings of taffy, cake and gateau. In addition, there were baskets full of live kittens and puppies, a bowl full of fish and several colorful plush toys.

Bathloxi dryly explained. "Carahil has a love of desserts and confections and droll toys and worthless creatures that have no meaning and serve no purpose. Certainly, his magical conditions demand that I offer you pie and cake and serve you cookies and sweets and other such rubbish. Here they all are, baked using the finest ingredients with the greatest of care. Now then, my question remains—I want Carahil's secrets."

Cookies and cakes, sweet delights and cuddly kittens. These were things this Carahil fellow loved: the Devil? With an undeniable sweet tooth and soft spot for adorable creatures? Seemed odd.

San had no idea what to make of any of this. She felt small and uninformed in the deer's presence. "I'm sorry. I don't know what you mean," she repeated.

The golden servants surrounded Sam and seized her by the arms. She struggled, dropping her jar, breaking it into pieces. Sam was a Monama and had incredible strength, but she couldn't budge these Golden People. They held her fast.

Bathloxi became agitated and rather threatening. "I had hoped you'd cooperate. I'd hoped your last few moments in this life might have been more pleasant. Suit yourself."

He reared back on his hind legs, hooves flailing, and he transformed back into the shaggy half-man/half deer form of the Horned God.

Sam's heart skipped in fear and she screamed.

He spoke in a monstrous rasp. "*Take her to the temple!*"

The Golden People jerked her up. Green slits of feathery smoke formed all around, floating on air.

"I will view your secrets, my dear," the Horned God croaked. "And then I'm going to adjust them a bit. I'm afraid the process will hurt. It'll hurt quite a lot actually. And then, we go to the Arborium, and I'll say, 'Look what Carahil has done on Kana, for here is his Secret-Talker with the truth,' and I'll be suitably shocked and outraged before my peers, and I'll give him to my servants here as punishment, for they hunger."

She heard beating drums through the slits and the base notes of screaming. She saw fire and oily smoke. She smelled burnt flesh and exposed entrails. The Temple where the Horned God lived—the place of nightmares when many of her people were taken and never heard from again, where the pit of hell and rotten gullet of absolute evil awaited.

"And then," he went on, "with the guilty punished and sacrificed, the Arborium will turn their attention elsewhere, and I'll return to resume playing in my playpen with my dying toys. Oh, how I long for the blood, the screaming!"

Bathloxi was the Horned God. The Temple was his infernal playground thick with the tormented spirits of the dead.

They dragged her toward the slit and the horrors that waited behind it.

She managed a ragged scream!

"Ahem!" came a bright voice from behind.

Heads turned.

A small silvery creature sat on the red cloth, wearing a beard of cream pie, a half-empty pie shell sitting in front of him. "Were you all looking for me?"

The Horned God, towering over him, regarded the newcomer with disdain and transformed back into his deer shape. "Carahil ..." he said with disgust.

"Yep, that's me." He smacked his lips and licked the cream from his mouth with his long silver tongue. "Really good pie, Bath." He burped and turned to the Golden People holding Sam. "So, what's going on here?"

"You know full well," Bathloxi said. "I have her at last—did you really think you could hide her from me? I've been at this game for eons. I'm going to extract the secrets from this Monama woman and learn the full measure of your malfeasance, and then I'm going to send you to the Windage of Kind where you belong. Maybe I'll do worse. Maybe I'll let my servants have you as an example to the others."

"Oh, so you think she's my Secret-Talker?"

"Isn't she? You've spent a great deal of time protecting her, flying at her side, warding off those seeking to perform justice upon her. Such attention can mean only one thing—that this Monama is your Secret-Talker."

Carahil hopped up and down on his silver flippers. "You take the cake, you know that? You've been playing the innocent so long, you've got it down! You're going to drag Sam into your temple in the ground, and then you're going to fill her head full of fake secrets under torture. Then, you're going to take what's left of her to the Celestial Arborium and frame me for the things you yourself have been doing for ages. Just like you did to Morglum. Just like you did to Anabrax and Folster. Admit it, will you? Admit what you did!"

Bathloxi chuckled. "Those are serious accusations, Carahil. Unprovable all, and rather entertaining to hear."

"I visited the Windage to see Anabrax, and guess what? She wasn't there. Neither were Morglum and Folster."

"Certainly they escaped the Windage," Bathloxi replied.

"I've seen their city, and saw the Great Pyramid," Carahil said. "I saw Anabrax there, though it was too late for her. I saw the remains of Morglum and Folster. You gave them to your servants, didn't you?"

Bathloxi flashed in anger. "And you shall be next, Carahil. You shall be next!" He turned to the Golden People. "I believe you were in the process of taking this woman. I suggest you proceed."

The Golden People resumed dragging the struggling Sam toward one of the slits hanging in the air. It opened up like a tear in the wholeness of the universe revealing a terrible, pain-filled place just on the other side.

"Hey, buddy!" Carahil said. "You might want to look out."

The Golden person peered back at Carahil once with scorn and then readied to pull Sam through.

A silver book fell from the sky and hit the Golden Man in the head with a great THUD! He released Sam and fell.

"I warned you! Go fish!" Carahil cried with glee.

The remaining Golden People converged, and fuzzy hands holding pies appeared from everywhere: up from holes in the ground, from knotholes in trees, from sudden clouds. Animals appeared, rabbits, squirrels, birds, fish from the stream, all packing pies in paws, wings and fins. They let them fly, hitting all the Golden People in the faces. They staggered about in outraged confusion. There was momentary chaos.

"Sam, run!" Carahil cried. "Run!"

Sam stood and ran to the waiting Metal Man. She scurried up the side and plunged back into the safety of his hollow chest. She looked to Carahil and motioned for him to join her. He sat on the red cloth, blinking up at her with his innocent silvery eyes.

"Don't worry about me—just go! Hurry up!"

The gears spun, and the clamshell doors slammed shut; she was sealed up inside good and tight, quiet, floating in the null field.

Muted confusion from the other side, clawed hands banging on the metal skin.

<*Hurry up!*> Carahil's thoughts barged into her brain.

With ponderous steps, the animated Metal Man climbed into his gigantic pewter chariot, grabbed the reins, and set it moving down the glade, rolling large on its great wheels, Golden People attacking, piling on.

So slow.

Outside, banging hands, green slits all around, surrounding. No escape.

<*Sam!*> Carahil's thoughts came again.

Something struck the body of the Metal Man, knocking him from the chariot and roughly to the ground—Sam was tossed about, helpless inside his chest. The Metal Man was like a turtle on its shell, feebly thrashing with his arms and legs trying to get up.

Roaring and primal anger. Blows on his metal body and dents appearing.

The doors pried open by clawed hands.

Eyes of the Devil …

"SECRET-TALKER!!"

Man and god, no one escapes the Horned God.

✶ ✶ ✶ ✶ ✶

Sam's dream ended. She floated on the verge of consciousness, safe in the Metal Man's chest, her light sheet pulled up clutched in her hands, drowsy in the silent space.

Something spoke.

Sam, what you just witnessed was nothing but a dream. But, be advised, there is a Horned God, and he is after you, and he's after me too... he's after all of us.

"You'll protect me, Carahil? You'll protect Kay?"

I'm doing my best. But, be warned, you have to run, Sam. I need you to run for me ...

The Metal Man standing in his chariot soared through the ether though a storm of green slits and leering faces, flying on dwindling NIGHTMARE magic, and, at his side, a tiny god in silver flew as well, lending his protection.

Lady Poe of Blanchefort and her Fabulous Familiars (cerca 003215ax)
From Left to right: Fins, Tweeter, a Tuleefly, Whisper, Snugs (flying), Shadow (in lap), King, Bark and ... Carahil.

2—Lt. Kilos

The two day trip back to Kana was a long, lonely one for Lt. Kilos. She certainly hadn't wanted to leave Hoban, what with the discoveries they had just made. She always had a nose for when trouble was about to start—and she could feel a whole mess of trouble coming right around the bend.

But, Captain Davage, her dearest friend, had asked her to go to Castle Blanchefort with all possible speed and protect his children. It hadn't been an order; it was merely a request, but, Ki could see the concern in his face, the near panic. Captain Davage was a Vith lord, and he didn't normally feel things like panic and uncertainty; yet, there it was plain to see.

Ki, my children are home at Castle Blanchefort unguarded, undefended ...

The bloody creature they'd seen in the Crossland cellars was horrific, a skinned, defaced mess. There were monsters afoot on Hoban, and possibly roaming the Telmus Grove at Castle Blanchefort as well. They had attacked his son, Lord Kabyl, and nearly been the death of him. And, now, they might be after his daughters, Lady Kilos (her namesake), Lady Hathaline and their tweener son Maser, still in his diapers.

And Ki knew that Lady Hathaline, in a grotesque aged form, had been the one who had attacked Kay, just like what had happened on Hoban.

You must do this ... for me.

She was on her way to Blanchefort. She wasn't going to let Captain Davage down.

She returned via tube to the *New Faith*, informed Paymaster Stenstrom of the situation, and immediately took her leave to Kana in a fast Marine *Trelaine*—no 158, 16th Stellar Squadron, nicknamed by its crew, the '*Bobbsie*'.

Being a former Marine, Ki easily interfaced with the two Lts. flying the ship.

"What unit did you two come out of?" Ki asked, sitting back on the padded bench, uninterested in the sparkling carpet of stars passing outside, her triangle hat pulled down over her eyes, letting sleep begin to take her. It was going to be a long trip. Tweeter, her faithful Silver tech familiar, sat, as always, on her shoulder, getting drowsy right along with her.

"Bathe, the old 01," one of them said.

Bathe? Ki remembered it well. A mixed bag of feelings passed through her thoughts.

Ready for your lashes, Pleeb?

"That's where I trained."

Both pilots looked back at her. "You were a Marine?"

"Sure," she said, "thirty-five years ago. I trained at Bathe. That's where I learned Anthecary."

"And then you joined the Fleet?"

"Yep."

The pilots seemed astounded. Marines didn't usually switch services. Once a Marine, always a Marine.

"You know, they're closing Bathe down, in favor of a brand spanking new training facility at Niles. They're having a big celebration there next month to retire it in style. I'm sure, being an ex-GP, that you'll be invited. I'm going—you bet I am. I loved Bathe—turned me into a respectable fellow. I wasn't always a good guy, but I am now."

The pilot resumed flying, but the copilot felt like talking. His voice kept pulling her back from the silent wellspring of sleep.

"So, what about it, Lt.? What are your most vivid memories of Bathe?"

In her sleep-clouded mind, Ki recalled Bathe. She remembered it very well.

Missing her husband.

Sitting alone with her tray.

Loneliness.

Fights.

Incarceration.

Work details.

Peering out through the bars of her jail cell.

The lash on her deserving back.

"Lt.?" the Marine co-pilot asked.

Ki stirred under her large triangle hat. "Yeah, yeah ... Bathe. I had more good times there than I care to recall."

Marine speak for: *I hated it…*

The pilot understood and resumed his duties. Ki drifted away.

* * * * *

When Ki got settled into her usual accommodations in Pendar Tower on the north face of the castle, she checked in with Davage and Countess Sygillis of Blanchefort (formerly of Metatron).

Over the Com, they told her about the battle in the Crossland graveyard right after she left.

Berserkacides.

Berserkacides everywhere.

Ki was incensed—she should have been there. She should have been at their side.

She paid a visit to Lady Poe and Lord Peter, who were overjoyed she was there. It, at first, galled Ki quite a bit that she had to return and babysit the kids. Here, in the presence of Lady Poe, a mighty Shadow tech female, what could Ki, a Giftless Brown, do? Surely Lady Poe could whip up some sort of happy-faced Silver tech animal to counter any situation as it occurred. After all, she created Carahil, and he was supposed to be a god.

Lady Poe was the mother of a god …

But, as Davage had touched upon before she left, Lady Poe of Blanchefort did not look well at all.

In fact, she looked like she was about to die.

On meeting with Lady Poe, Ki noticed she wasn't her usual happy self. She seemed very tired, almost to the point of being delusional. She sat in her chair on her favorite terrace, wrapped up in a blanket, slumped and boneless. Her face was drawn and sunken-in, like she hadn't slept in some time. She looked like one of those poor refugees she and her regiment of Marines had once rescued from a Xaphan sulfur pit: eyes sunk in like half-moon slits, skin like old paper, shrunken lips like snails. Lord Peter stood next to her holding their youngest child Millie. He tried to wear a bold face and appear unconcerned, but Ki saw right through.

Peter was terrified for his wife.

Tweeter, recognizing the woman who created him, jumped onto her shoulder and chirped. Lady Poe reacted and smiled faintly.

Millie babbled and stuck her fingers in her mouth. She was a cute kid—looked just like her mother, platinum blonde hair and all.

Seeing Poe like this reminded Ki of the days when she was thought to be mentally ill, going week after week in a Shadow tech poisoned cloud.

"Lady Poe, is there anything I can do for you?" Ki asked, genuinely concerned.

Coughing, eyes laden with bags, she said something.

Ki leaned down. "Pardon, my lady, I couldn't hear you."

"... I've failed, Lt.," she said in a hollow voice.

"Failed? At what?"

Lord Peter spoke up. "As you can see, Lt., Lady Poe is rather tired. She'll be fine—she just needs to rest. As you are here, and we are most comforted by your presence, might I ask a favor?"

Ki turned to Lord Peter. "Um, sure. Anything I can do to help."

"Thank you. Lady Poe is the tutor of the children, and it is a task she relishes, but, given her current need for rest, may we ask you to assume that duty, just for a day or two?"

"Me, tutor the children? I don't know a thing about—"

"I have all of Lady Poe's notes here on crystal, including her complete curriculum. There's nothing left out—nothing to chance; all you need to do is collect and present the material to the children. Milos is gone to school in Arden. Sarah, Phillip and Lord Kabyl are still away, so it will be just Lady Kilos and Lady Hathaline. Lord Maser and Millie here are still too young to attend." As if in response, Millie babbled something nonsensical.

Peter looked at her with a hopeful eye. "May we count on you, Lt.?"

Ki stood there and thought about it for a moment. She felt uncomfortable and on-the-spot.

"Sure, Lord Peter, sure," Ki said finally. "Anything I can do to help."

Lord Peter was relieved. "Ah, excellent, excellent! Thank you, Lt., and we know you'll do just fine."

He gave Ki the crystal containing the full curriculum and notes. Ki stood there holding it cupped in her palm and looked at Lady Poe again, worry building within. "Lady Poe, are you sure you're all right?"

Lady Poe seemed like she wanted to say something, but then stopped herself.

"She needs to rest, Lt.," Lord Peter said. "And we thank you again for agreeing to school the children. We are grateful for your comforting presence here."

Ki took the crystal and studied it in her tower later that evening. Tweeter, as usual, bounced around, finding lots of perches and nooks in her reading room. He often flew off on his own when she was sitting or sleeping, but, ever faithful, he returned to her shoulder the moment she needed him.

Lady Poe took careful notes, which was good. As Ki looked over them, a clear picture formed—there was a problem student in the bunch, a fly in the ointment.

If Ki had to guess, her first thought was to peg Lady Sarah, that blue-haired hellion, as the problem student. She was rambunctious and hot-headed, and she couldn't sit still to save her life.

But, as Poe's notes indicated, Sarah wasn't the issue.

It was 'Bottle', Lady Kilos, that little gown-wearing, blue-haired stinker, who was prone to tardiness, prone to cheating, prone to instigating bad behavior, and who was terminally unmotivated. Ki had given her the nickname Bottle as a baby. Lady Kilos had a tendency to throw her bottle with great accuracy and always when your back was turned:

Pow!

Right between the shoulder blades. Syg always thought it was really funny. Kay had never thrown his bottle.

Perhaps her namesake, whom she had always thought was her complete opposite in terms of temperament and social wants, was more like herself than she had ever considered.

A mal-content. A troublemaker and toxic presence. A want-to-be socialite. That all sounded familiar. Ki, during her childhood, was all those things and more, except for the socialite part.

Ki laughed. So, little Bottle's a handful? Could be worse, and was nothing she couldn't deal with.

She made the rounds of the castle following Tweeter as usual, for Ki, other than her Pendar Tower haunt, still couldn't make heads or tails of the craggy, maze-like place; too easy to get lost in.

She checked up on Bottle who was still awake, sitting on her grand terrace in Harkness Tower talking to her friends over the Aire-net. Bottle waved at her absently and then returned to what she was doing. Moving on to Drella Tower, Ki saw that Lady Hathaline was sound asleep in her bed, clutching a large stuffed bear her father had given to her as a present once. Lady Hathaline clearly adored her father—wanted to be just like him, a real chip off the old block.

Ki lingered by her door for a while.

Hathaline, in another form, had attacked Kay viciously. Ki never worried much about the how's and why's of a thing. She had a job to do— to protect that innocent girl sleeping in her room. Hathaline hadn't attacked Kay; it was a twisted, skinless future version of her that had done it. Ki thought of that poor little boy, Lord Mervin of Crossland, feared by his mother and father for something a monstrous future version of himself had done.

Ki wasn't going to let that happen to Lady Hathaline.

She swung by Lord Maser's set of rooms. One of his nursemaids was asleep near his crib. He was safe and sound.

Satisfied, she followed Tweeter back to her room on the sixty-fourth floor of Pendar Tower. Snugs, the little silver hummingbird, was waiting for her, keeping her room nice and warm as she liked it. As usual, Tweeter and Snugs jostled around in mid-air, each vying for Ki's attention. She undressed and Com'ed her husband back on Onaris, letting him know where she was. As she gazed out at the lovely night view of Blanchefort Village through her window, they chatted for a while, talking dirty to each other, then, tired from her long trip, she bade him good night and crawled into her big comfortable bed. Ki just loved her Pendar Tower bed, easily the loveliest thing she had ever slept in—she'd have to buy it from Dav one day.

Quickly her mind drifted and settled toward sleep. Disturbing images popped into her mind.

Kay.

Kay attacked.

Lady Hathaline, in a monstrous form, attacked and sodomized Kay.

Lady Hathaline sleeping in her bed in Drella Tower, clutching a bear given to her by her father.

Impossible, yet it happened.

And the monster Hath was still out there somewhere.

✶ ✶ ✶ ✶ ✶

Ki awoke later.

Thump, thump ... thump ...

She heard an odd series of sounds coming from the window. She rubbed her eyes.

Tweeter, her faithful Silver tech bird, was bouncing off of the window. He wouldn't stop.

"What are you doing, Tweets?" she asked him.

He stopped hitting the window and flew onto her bare shoulder.

Ki rubbed her eyes again, got up and went to the window. She picked Tweeter up and held him in her closed fist.

She opened the window with her other hand and looked out.

Blanchefort was normally a quiet place—too quiet sometimes for Ki's liking; however, outside with the window open, she could hear a definite, sinister-sounding drone, like the buzzing of a huge swarm of insects, like the infernal wave of sound the Onaris locusts back home made when they swooped in to devour your fields and leave you with nothing. It was a primal sound that filled her with dread.

Looking out, Ki thought she could see a cloud of something moving past the castle, darker than night itself.

3—Letter from Carahil

The next morning Ki awoke rested and refreshed. A typically restless person who spent little time in her rack, she was up before the sun. She crawled out of bed and put on a robe.

She called down to the kitchen and asked them to bring her up a plate of pancakes and some coffee; she went out onto the terrace as she waited for it to be brought up to her. Tweeter and Snugs followed her out there, Tweeter for companionship and Snugs for warmth, as the pre-dawn hours in Blanchefort were pretty cold for a woman from Onaris. As usual, the two Silver tech creations fluttered around each other, apparently in some sort of contentious silent communication. Tweeter seemed to like to push Snugs around.

"Leave him be, will you, Tweets?" Ki said as she admired the view below stretching out beneath the castle. With her sharp eyes, she could see way down into the yawning cavern of the Sarfortnim College Brandtball pitch. She'd have to check the schedule for a match while she was here. She loved watching Brandtball.

The pancakes came up a few minutes later, and Ki tucked in, drowning them in dark Nadine syrup. The staff knew Ki well. She had requested coffee, which they included in a steaming pot, and they also included a small flask full of spirits. Ki really didn't like coffee much, unless it was chased with a little something special. She ate her pancakes, drank her coffee, and then reached for the flask and tipped it, feeling the strong stuff fill her up.

"I could get used to this," she said to Tweeter. "I must be getting soft or something."

She noticed a note sitting under her plate. She pulled the folded slip of paper out from under and sniffed it. It smelled strongly like cream pie.

"More notes, Tweets," she said to Tweeter. She remembered getting lots of notes in Castle Blanchefort years ago, written by a demon's hand. She didn't feel nervous or put off at all, as the note smelled like pie, which was a Carahil trademark. And Carahil was her friend.

She opened it. It read:

Dear Ki

You should be old hat getting weird notes in Castle Blanchefort, but don't worry; it's just me, Carahil ...

I heard you were in the castle, at Lord Blanchefort's request to look after the kids. Excellent choice. I can't think of anyone I'd trust more than you. I feel safer already.

Speaking of which, since you're there, I was wondering if you would do me a favor. I'd really appreciate it. There's a pub down in the village off Rundle Way called 'The Cat God'. It's a new place—good food, good drink, and I remember you once saying your goal was to drink at every pub down in the village—well, here you go. I was wondering if, at your earliest convenience, you could go down to that pub and ask to speak to Mabs, the bartender. She knows to expect you, and I've got your tab covered. Mabs will give you a box and some simple instructions. You like simple, right?"

"Smart alec," Ki said with a smile. She read further.

That's all. Can you do that for me, Ki? I'd really appreciate it. The drinks are on me.

Yours

—C

She folded the note back up. She finished up her breakfast, dressed and made her rounds. Everybody was still asleep. Well, not quite. Lady Hathaline was up, sitting in the Capricos Hall. She was reading a book and eating her breakfast. Her clash of red hair looked like a mass of tropical vines over spilling a vase.

"Morning, Hath," Ki said.

She smiled and replied.

"Hey, since you're up, do you mind taking me down to the village real fast? I've a quick errand to run."

Hath didn't need to be asked twice. She stood, brushed off her cranberry gown and was ready to go. They walked out to the ship park and got out Hath's souped-up red Ripcar she was so proud of. She fired it up, and soon they were rocketing over the castle proper and down the mountain shelf toward the village, Hath flying the Ripcar with skilled abandon, just like her father did. Ki had to hang onto her hat and her stomach all the way down until Hath swung it around and landed like a feather near the docks.

Ki stumbled out. "Creation, kid, you got a license?"

She nodded and powered down the Ripcar.

Ki looked around at the maze of buildings before her stretching out north along the curve of the bay. As Carahil had mentioned, she was familiar with most of the pubs in the village.

The Cat God pub?

She'd not heard of that particular one before. Must be new.

"Tweeter, lead us to the Cat God pub, please."

Tweeter leapt off her shoulder and flapped north. Ki and Hath followed. After twenty years, Ki was expert at following Tweeter. She didn't need to keep her eyes on him anymore; she could manage just by feel. Hath, though, craned her neck and struggled to keep sight of the little silver bird as he moved across the eves and rooftops. "Watch where you're going, Hath," Ki said with a laugh as she stumbled along.

They headed north, passing the familiar environs of the Drunken Eel tavern. Hath pointed it out.

"Yep," Ki said, "that one's my fav, but I wouldn't recommend it to a lady like you, Hath. It gets a little rough in there sometimes, especially on Thursday nights, and you're not old enough."

Hathaline said she wasn't afraid. Bring it on.

Fearless and brash, just like her mom and dad.

They continued on, past the weathered white bell-shaped structure of St. Vith cathedral looming overhead with a patina-green dome. Hath trotted quietly at Ki's side, humming to herself.

Such a good kid, Ki thought. Her whole life ahead of her.

Not the monster—the twisted, bleeding Hath who devoured the flesh of her kinfolk. There would be no monster Hath, not if Ki could help it.

Tweeter veered to the east, down the blinking, iron-wrought canyon of the Rundle Way just north of the cathedral. It was clogged with shoppers. Ki remembered years back when it was just a dark street of cricket huts and spacious, glass-free allies good for fighting in. Ki'd been in quite a few there. Now, it was a trendy place of lights and little shops and the welcoming smells of eateries.

"Do a lot of shopping here, Hath?" Ki asked trying to find her past haunts on the street.

She shook her head and mentioned something about Bottle and Sam.

"Figures," Ki said.

About halfway down, Tweeter veered north into an alley. They followed, pushing past the ash cans and piled up boxes, leaving behind the bustle of the street. At the end of the alley was a doorway lit up in green lights. A sign swinging over the door read THE CAT GOD in flowing cursive letters. Soft piano music from within came twinkling out, filling the alley with a touch of green-tinged class.

"Looks like we're here, kid," Ki said. "Doesn't seem to be a bad place. Not really a good location for attracting business, though—the back of an alley, I mean, but whatever."

Tweeter came down and landed on Ki's shoulder, and they went in. Inside was a spacious pub, dark and smoky, peppered with light piano music underscored with the base notes of slow people chatter. Past a few rows of booths and tables there was a massive bar occupying one side of the pub lit with hidden green lighting. It was the sort of pub Ki liked, full of quiet nooks and shadowy hidden areas with a nice sturdy bar that was a pleasure to drink from. Ki often thought of opening a pub of her own some day, something like the Drunken Eel. It was a pet project/daydream she'd always had, she even had a little file dedicated to the project where she collected her thoughts regarding what her pub would look like, what sort of fabrics and textures she would want to decorate the place with, what foods she would serve, the whole nine yards. The Eel had always been her dream pub to replicate, but this, this CAT GOD pub, this was nice. Forget the Eel, if she were ever to open one, it would be a lot like this. She liked everything about it.

They went to the bar, and Hath hopped up onto a seat, her feet dangling. The bar was made of some sort of dark brown hardwood carved with acorns and topped with a speckled green marble top. The wall behind the bar was covered with large and small cat figurines looking back at them with sparkling jeweled eyes.

As Ki saddled up to the bar, the barkeep appeared. She was a tall lady, rather like Ki, with mid-length hair dyed in a green and black striped pattern. She was wearing a trendy green dress and wore a charm at her throat with an embossed 'M' on the face.

"Are you Mabs?" Ki asked.

"I am."

Ki looked around. "Is this your place?"

"It is."

"Nice pub. I'll have to remember it. Do you know Carahil?"

"I do know Carahil. I keep his secrets and more. What can I get you?" she asked.

"Green Gasol for the kid here, and a shot of pure grain for me."

The barkeep got the drinks. Hath sipped her fizzy Gasol, while Ki tossed back her shot. Nice and smooth. Good stuff.

The barkeep looked at Hathaline and smiled. "Carahil is very proud of you, my lady," she said.

Ki was rather shocked. "He is?" she asked holding her empty shot glass.

"He certainly is." She turned back to Hath. "Do you like to play games, my lady?"

Hath shook her head. Too old for games.

The barkeep laughed. "Oh, you're never too old for games, Carahil taught me that. Here, try this one—this is a game you made possible. If you play well, I'll give you a prize." She reached beneath the bar and placed a small plush toy of a deer-like creature with large pipe-cleaner antlers onto the marble surface. She then presented a wooden chest, rather like a cigar box, to Hath and lifted the lid. Inside was a chaotic, felt-lined collection of miscellaneous carved figurines, all colorful and inviting, like a box full of toy soldiers.

"My lady, reach into the box and select three figurines and then place them around this little plush toy. That's all you have to do."

Hathaline looked at the bewildering assortment of figures in the felt-lined box. It was a cataclysm of form and color. She wanted to know which ones she should pick.

"Whichever. Let your heart guide you."

Hath sat there for a moment, carefully weighing her choices. She reached in and selected three objects. She placed a figurine that looked like a bouquet of flowers in front of the toy deer. To its left, she placed a weird figurine that looked like a plucked chicken.

The barkeep laughed as she watched. "Interesting. One more."

Hath placed the final figurine to the deer's right. It looked like a little dog, sort of like a spaniel. The barkeep clapped.

"Well done, my lady. Front, left and right—that's exactly where the figurines should go."

This was a rather odd game. "What does she win?" Ki asked.

"Everything," the barkeep replied. She collected the three pieces and placed them in a rich velvet bag pulled closed with a string. "Keep these safe, my lady, and promise you won't lose them, all right? It's very important."

Hath promised. She wanted to know what they were for.

The barkeep gave her the bag. "Let's just say that sometimes the gods need a little help, and these innocent little pieces, moved by your hand specifically, can work wonders." She reached down and placed a perfect bowl of ice cream on the bar, glazed in chocolate and topped with whipped cream and a cherry, garnished with a silver spoon. "Here's your prize."

Hath was shy at first, then she tucked into the bowl with relish.

"I'm told that you have a package here for me," Ki said setting her empty shot glass on the bar.

The barkeep smiled. She removed the plush deer from the bar and put it below. "Yes, I do." She poured Ki another shot. "Let me get it for you." She walked away.

Ki looked at Hath sitting there with her ice cream and kid's drink. "Go ahead and finish that up, and we'll be out of here in just a sec."

As Ki waited for the barkeep to return, she felt she must be getting a little drunk, which was odd because Ki could drink like nobody else. It would take a whole bottle of this Kanan grain stuff just to warm her up, but, now after just two shots her head spun a little, and her thoughts became addled.

She became aware of all the conversations around her coming from the corners of the pub, hearing them as if they were being whispered directly into her ear.

She heard the voices of people who shouldn't be there.

"Thanks for coming, for keeping my children safe. You're a true friend," came a voice from a shadowy booth. Sounded like Captain Davage.

She responded. "No problem, Dav, though I'd rather stay with you," she said into the empty air, her slightly addled mind accepting the sound of Davage's voice, though she knew he was several million stellar miles away over Hoban.

"Kay?" came Syg's voice: the Countess of Blanchefort. *"How is Kay?"*

"He's not home, Syg. He's off with his cousins. I'm sure he's fine."

Another voice filled her head. *"Are you ever coming home? I miss you, Ki."*

Sounded like her husband, back home in far-away Tusck.

"Miss you too, hon. I really do."

"Mom?" she heard from another part of the pub. *"Mom?"* A little boy's voice coming from the corner sounded like it was directed at her. Ki didn't have any children.

"Mom?"

She stepped away from the bar. "Who are you?"

"Who do you think?" came another voice, this time older and rather angry. Something hunched and repulsive sat in a corner booth. *"They dragged me out of my bed in the middle of the night, turned me into a monster and drove me mad. Do you know what I went through? Where were you when I pounded on the glass, begging to be free? Who was there to help me? Do you think I wanted to do all those things to Kay? Do you?"*

Ki was alarmed. She strode into the shadows to confront the voice.

The barkeep returned, holding another small box. "Lt.?" she asked.

Ki plunged into the booth.

"Lady Hathaline, if that's you, I know it wasn't your fault. I'm here to help you. Let me help you!"

Nobody was there. Just nice green felt, buttoned leather and an empty table-top wiped clean.

"What are you doing?" the barkeep asked.

"I heard a voice," she said.

"Of course you did," the barkeep said.

"Who was it?"

"Could be anybody."

Ki felt confused. "Am I drunk? After just two shots? I think I'm drunk."

"I don't think you're drunk. Here's your box."

The barkeep placed the box on the bar. Ki walked back and tested it. It was light, almost like there wasn't anything inside.

"This is from Carahil?"

"Yes."

"Can I look inside?"

"Of course."

She hesitated before opening. "Am I going to be hit with a pie or something?"

The barkeep giggled. "I don't know. Possibly. He does like that, doesn't he?"

Ki opened the box and looked in. Inside were a number of tiny figurines clinking around. She reached in and pulled one out. It was a blue figurine in the shape of a seal, smooth and slightly squashy, about two inches long, small enough to fit in the palm. Clearly, it was an image of Carahil, in love with himself as always. He was looking back over his shoulder, smiling, showing his teeth, seemingly saying "Look at me—Aren't I awesome?"

Ki remembered the mystical quality of Carahil's figurines. She'd seen them before on Xandarr twenty years prior and how they were rather effective in a battle against Black Hats; back then they were white, silver, black and speckled. She squeezed it to see if it would make a sound—Carahil's figurines usually said what they did when squeezed—but, this one didn't.

Hath wanted to look at one, and Ki handed it over. She cupped her hands and took it.

"He said in his note you'd have instructions for me," Ki said to Mabs the barkeep.

"Carahil would like you to take these and place them in the Telmus Grove. He would really appreciate it," she said.

"Why doesn't Carahil just do it himself?"

"Because I can't," came a child-like voice from behind. Ki turned. A small dome-headed shape was sitting in a booth, eyes round and shining, nose wet. *"He's after me—trying to frame me."*

"Carahil?" Ki said.

Had something been there? The booth appeared to be empty. Ki turned to Mabs. "What is this place?"

"Just a pub I run. Carahil has rules to follow, Lt., just like everybody else. He gives all his secrets to me."

"You said that already."

"Did I? It's a role I cherish," Mabs said. "It's worth repeating."

Ki felt a little light-headed. "Where am I supposed to place these?"

"In an oak clearing near the Lilly patch of the Ten Gardens, south of an old Vith amphitheater. Take these little figurines and simply scatter them about. Just get them nearby, and that will do. It doesn't have to be exact."

"Just scatter them? Is that all?"

"That's all. Oh wait, after you scatter the pieces, you need to say the proper incantation."

"Magic words?"

"Yes, if you like."

"What are they?"

Mabs leaned over the bar and whispered into Ki's ear.

"Really?" she said. "I have to say that?"

"Yes."

Ki was a little dubious. "All right. What do these little figures do?"

They keep the monsters away ... came Carahil's voice again, whispered into her ear. His voice seemed to be coming from Tweeter.

Ki turned. "Carahil, come out and talk to me," she said, feeling a little desperate. She felt confused and slow-witted. She didn't like the feeling one bit.

"He can't," Mabs said. "He has to stay away for the time being. It is imperative that the figurines be placed in the Grove where I specified. Just do this for him, and say the silly magic words. He'd really appreciate it."

"Or what?"

"Or bad things will happen."

Mabs poured Ki another shot.

Ki reached for the drink but thought better of it. "I don't think I should," she said. "It might be too early in the day, and I think I might be getting drunk."

"You're not drunk, Lt.," Mabs said. "Go ahead. I only serve the best."

Ki thought about it and then tossed it back. "Really good stuff," she said. "I'll need to come back here when I've got more time."

Mabs shook her head. "You won't find me here again. I'm glad you enjoyed what I had to serve."

Ki pulled a moneybag out of her Fleet coat to pay for the drinks. "No need," Mabs said. "It's on us."

Ki shoved the bag back into her coat. "Tell Carahil not to worry. I'll make his drop for him. He can count on me. And tell him to not be such a stranger. We like seeing him from time to time."

"I will. He likes seeing you too."

Ki took the box and turned to Hath. "Come on, kid, time to go."

They began walking out. "Are you sure you don't have any more questions, Lt.?" Mabs asked, holding a rag. "I'm not all that easy to find. There are many answers here in my pub."

Ki tried to clear her head. She couldn't think. Her brain felt numb. "Nope, well, just one. I heard a kid call me 'Mom' in there. Who was that?"

"Your son, Lt."

"I don't have a son. I don't like kids."

"Not now, and yes, you do."

Ki's muddled brain contemplated that for a moment. The thought of her having a son alarmed and confused her a little. She didn't have time for kids. She let it pass out of her head. She and Hath then turned and walked out, Tweeter following.

"Did you hear what the lady said, Hath?" Ki said as they emerged from the alley. "She said that was my son talking to me. I must be drunk."

Hath replied.

"You did? You heard it too?"

Hath nodded.

"Hold this," Ki said handing her Carahil's box. "Wait here!" She then marched back into the alley, hoping to go back into the pub and ask Mabs a few more questions. She was suddenly bursting with questions, mostly centered on her son. Who was he? What's his name? Was he a good kid?

Would she be a good mother?

Ki should have known. The pub was gone, just a darkened doorway and a dusty vacant interior where the pub had been only moments earlier. She felt that she'd just squandered a remarkable opportunity.

"Tweeter, where is the Cat God pub?"

He sat on her shoulder and fluffed his wings. Ki read his movements.

The Cat God pub was very far away now.

* * * * *

Hath brought the Ripcar down to tree-top level just west of the Ten Gardens, its engine whining in the cold air. The Lilly patch was easy to spot from the air with its large rectangular bathhouse built in the center, Ki thought she could smell notes of chlorinated water even from the air. Holding the controls and hovering, Hath banked the Ripcar and pointed down. Ki looked over the edge. "Oh—I see an old Vith ruin there to the west. I guess this is the spot, right?"

Hath nodded as the Ripcar's blower kicked in and roared.

"Here goes nothing." Ki took the box and dumped out the contents. She watched the little blue figurines tumble away, scattering in mid-air and falling from sight.

"There you go, Carahil. Job done. I guess we're all set, kid!"

Hath pushed forward on the sticks, and the Ripcar pitched down and rumbled out of the area.

Holding onto her hat, Ki remembered something. "Oh wait, Hath! I have to say the magic words!" Hathaline pulled back on the sticks and came about, smoothly moving the Ripcar around like a living thing. Ki, as an occasional Ripcar pilot, knew how difficult they were to control; the touch and the balance had to be perfect otherwise possibly fatal things might happen. Ripcars were very unforgiving; Hath, though, was in complete control.

Ki cleared her throat and cupped her hand to her mouth so that she could be heard uttering Carahil's magic words.

"Go fish!" she yelled into the air.

4—Giant in the Grove

Ki sat out on her favorite terrace that evening, watching the village and the sea beyond. She felt rather miserable. She couldn't get the sound out of her head:

Mom ... mom?

She'd never considered such a thing. Motherhood? She endured the occasional complaints and arguments from her learned husband; of motherhood, of starting a family.

No way. She had her life to live, and she had no time for kids. She even had her womb mentally shut down, for twenty years now.

Mom ... mom?

That little voice called out to her and wouldn't stay quiet.

After a good long time of sulking, she got up and went to her terminal. She opened a mail header and typed:

Where is the Cat God pub?

She addressed it to: CARAHIL and sent the message, knowing that the message would get lost in the holonet somewhere and get dead-headed.

She stood to go to bed, and the terminal beeped. She had a message.

That was fast.

It read:

The Cat God pub is never where you expect it to be. I'll tell Mabs you're looking for her, and maybe she'll pay you a visit again someday. I can't promise anything, but I'll try—Mabs and I are very close, but she's her own person and she does things her own way.

Thanks for making my drop for me today.

—C

"No problem, Carahil," Ki said. She left the terminal on and went to bed, sliding into the inviting sheets. Like a little night light, Tweeter settled on the table nearby. Ki gazed at him as she waited for sleep to take her.

Mom ... mom? passed through her thoughts again as she drifted off.

* * * * *

The next morning Ki made the rounds. Lord Maser was already well into his routine, being cared for by the doting staff; the little red-headed boy was running around in a miniature Fleet uniform. Ki reviewed a few security steps with the staff should anything happen. They listened and thanked her.

That done, she went to gather Bottle and Lady Hathaline. They were going to have breakfast, and then she was going to take them out into the Grove for their daily lessons. Lady Poe had a lovely courtyard surrounded by huge beech trees where she taught them every day. Most of her students were gone—Kay, Sarah and Phillip, out on their Wellerman's March. She hoped they were doing well, wherever they were. The only two she had to worry about were Lady Hathaline, the good kid, and Bottle, her namesake—the stinker.

Lady Hathaline was easy to find; as before, she was sitting at the long table in the Capricos Hall eating breakfast in her usual cranberry-colored gown. Ki sat down with her, and they chatted. Hath was full of questions about what it was like to sail with her father and mother.

Ki delighted her with a series of anecdotes about her father. She had over twenty years of stories to share.

Bottle so far had been a no show.

"Wait here," Ki said as she sic'ed Tweeter on her. A few minutes later Ki found Bottle hiding out in the west wing of the castle in a lime colored gown. Arrogantly, she tried to pull the old Blue/Brown thing, telling Ki that she had no right to make her eat breakfast and go to school if she didn't want to.

She then ordered Ki out of her presence with a wave of her hand.

A few minutes later, Ki reappeared in the Capricos Hall, dragging Lady Kilos by her regal ear, Hath laughing her head off.

The first few tutoring sessions were rather touch and go, with Ki not really knowing what she was doing, and Bottle quick to pounce on any slip up or mistake Ki made and use it to try to humiliate her. Fortunately, it would take a lot more than a blue-haired kid in a gown to fluster her, and, as the days wore on, Ki began to get the hang of teaching. She was actually becoming quite good at it.

It took Bottle a few tutoring sessions before she began to warm up to her. Her initial attempts to confuse her at tutoring having failed, she next tried to discombobulate her.

On the second morning, she came down wearing a loose shirt over her gown. The shirt had easily the worst holo-picture of Countess Sygillis ever taken stamped on the breast—distributed by the Duchess of Oyln, ever an enemy with the Countess. It was easy to see what she was doing: Bottle had hoped such a thing would put Ki off.

Ki laughed until her guts hurt and wanted to know where she had gotten the thing; she wanted to buy a few for herself. They might come in handy for the future.

The next morning Bottle was again a no show. The kid just didn't seem to learn. Again, Ki set Tweeter after her, locating her this time all the way down in the village, hiding out in a café on Rundle Way. Again, Bottle got dragged away by her ear, and this time in front of the whole village. As a further punishment, Ki made her work in the kitchens that evening.

After that, Bottle began to behave, and even seemed to take to Ki a bit. Ki proved to be gaining a knack for teaching as well; despite herself, she had a good way with kids, even sneaky, unruly ones like Bottle. She thought about her experience in the Cat God pub when she heard the child's voice saying "Mom." She felt frustrated that she didn't linger and ask more questions; she'd felt so addle-headed.

She wondered what it might be like to teach a kid of her own some day. Though the Cat God pub was far away, the little boy called out to her still.

✶ ✶ ✶ ✶ ✶

Beep, beep, beep ...

Ki, eyes bloodshot, was pulled from sleep by her terminal. It was beeping. A message was pending. In her nightgown she slid out of bed and padded up to the terminal to check the message.

It was a holo postcard, and it was bizarre. Blipped out in vivid 3-D was some sort of urban setting with tall, somewhat dilapidated buildings all around. There was a black, round building which looked to Ki like a Black Hat's temple looming in the distance—a big one at that. The temple was sprouting a host of Shadow tech tentacles like a giant sea creature. Sitting atop a nearby flat-topped building was a black, bat-winged ship that Ki recognized as a *Goshawk*. As Ki looked further, there seemed to be some sort of battle going on. There were numerous people in black robes, mixed in with a number of females in tight-fitting green and brown armor. They were standing on the rooftop, and they were also flying in mid-air and clinging on the side of the building as well—the whole mass locked up in a general swirling conflagration. It looked like a big, Blue Gift fight for certain, and she loathed those. If people wanted to fight, they should just stand on the ground and fight.

Using the holographic controls, Ki spun the image around, honing in on detail that caught her interest.

Standing on the rooftop in the confused mass of people was Sarah; Ki was sure of it— duster, blue hair in a bouncing ponytail— there was no doubt. She was toting a rifle as well.

And, who was that standing next to her? Was that Lon, Lord Lon of Probert? She saw a small kid with a pot belly and a long blue coat and buckle shoes wearing goggles over his eyes. He was holding CEROS, the LosCapricos weapon of House Probert. It was Lon all right. He was actually pretty impressive to see, standing tall in the middle of the fight, head up, shoulders back, looking like he knew what we was doing.

Ki became concerned; there were Sarah and Lon, but where was Kay? Where was Phillip? Those four were inseparable. She turned the image with her holographic controls.

"There's Phillip!" she said with a sigh of relief. He was sitting inside the *Goshawk* in the pilot's chair, firing it up. Outside, near the *Goshawk*, Ki saw a flying woman in green armor wearing a leather helmet, green hair spilling out. She was focused on the ship, and Ki could literally feel the intensity pouring out of her. Ki knew that look; whoever she was, it was obvious that she was after Phillip. Moving on, she couldn't locate Kay anywhere. "I can't find Kay!" she said, becoming concerned.

Tweeter fluttered up and hovered over a portion of the holo. Ki zoomed in.

There was Kay, lying on the rooftop with a bare-chested bald man in black beneath him. Ki was in a panic. Was Kay hurt? Was he dead?

There was a text tag mixed into the holocard. She punched it up. It read:

VICTORY IN WAAM!

Just so you know, Kay and the rest were successful in performing their Wellerman in the Xaphan city of Waam of all places. They are, even as you read this, safe and sound in the Goshawk on their way back to Blanchefort. They should be home tomorrow or the next day.

I need to ask another favor of you; I hate to be a bother. There is a Giant in the Grove, and Sam is sleeping inside it. She created the Giant. Now that Kay has passed his Trials, the enchantment Sam placed on him is wearing off and fast, and the Giant has returned to the Grove to await his arrival. When Kay gets home, the doors in the Giant's chest will open, and Sam will come out.

I wish I could say that's the end of the story and we could all get on to a happy ending, but unfortunately no. Those figurines I had you spread out were meant to help protect the Giant from those who would do it (and her) harm.

I'm a bit worried about Sam. Can you check up on the Giant, and make sure he's ok?

—C

BTW—Find me in the pic and touch my nose, and I'll give you a present.

"Tweeter," she said, "Is there a giant in the Grove?"

He fluttered up to her shoulder. From his movements Ki knew the answer was a resounding 'Yes'.

She moved the pic around looking for Carahil. It was like a puzzle. She had a hard time with all the stuff going on.

There he was! He was in the *Goshawk*, sitting on the couch behind Phillip, his silvery face and his button nose cute as ever. She zoomed in and touched him on the nose. He moved his head and smiled. The word WINNER! appeared on his dome-like forehead, and the holocard vanished.

"So, what did I win?" She didn't see anything magically appear or pop up from nowhere. You never knew with Carahil, that's what made him fun.

She stood to go into the bathroom and wash and nearly tripped. Lined up in a row before the bathroom door were three plush toys of Carahil; one silver, one minty blue and one red. Each sported a ribbon around its neck and a bow. Ki reached down and picked up the red one. A tag attached to the ribbon read: FOR LADY HATHALINE

Ki checked the other two. The blue one had a tag reading: FOR LADY KILOS. The silver one also had a tag: FOR YOU.

She placed the silver plush Carahil on her bed and began to get ready. She got dressed, clipped on her gun belt, checked her mag and holstered her SK. "You said there was a giant in the Grove, right, Tweets?" she asked throwing on her coat.

He concurred with a wing flutter.

"Show me." Tweeter headed to the door, as did Snugs—the two of them jostling about as usual. "No, Snugs, you stay here and keep my room warm, ok? That's very important."

Snugs returned to his perch.

Ki noticed that her bed was now perfectly made, and a bowl of fresh fruit and other snacks were laid out on her nightstand along with a silver flask pushed off to the side like a voyeur and a current Sarfortnim College 'Fighting `40's' Brandtball program. The silver Carahil plushie sat innocently on the middle of the made bed, right where Ki had left it.

"A couple of box passes to the next match would be nice as well," she said.

The plushie didn't move.

She picked up the other two and headed out. She went to Harkness Tower and left the blue one for Lady Kilos; then, she went to Drella Tower and left the red one outside of Lady Hathaline's door. As she walked back toward the lift, she heard the door open and close. Looking back, the red plushie was gone; inside Hath's room, watching over her. Good to know.

She then followed Tweeter out of the castle into the darkened, early morning passes of the Telmus Grove.

* * * * *

They went far out, farther than Ki usually went. They passed the cobbled, landscaped area dotted with courtyards and continued on into the dense twist of massive oak trees, the biggest she'd ever seen. The footing between the trees was rough and rutted out, but Ki was used to it, coming from rural Onaris where nothing was flat, and she managed just fine. The Grove was a haunting place in the dark. She remembered Dav telling stories about the old Vith who used to live here and the battles with the Haitathe they once fought. They said each oak tree was a dead Haitathe warrior frozen in time.

As dawn approached, Tweeter led her into a clearing and then north to the remains of an old Vith amphitheater pocked with age and overgrown with scrub. Standing in the center of the ruin was what appeared to be a towering bronze statue. Ki was having difficulty gauging the statue's height as it was standing alone in the center of the platform, but she imagined it had to be at least twenty feet tall. A battered Vith altar, also large and over-sized, was nearby. She unclipped her SK and approached, Tweeter flapping at her side. Walking through the ruined amphitheater awaiting the drama of first light she felt the blue eyes of the old Vith sitting in the stands watching some morose Vith production.

Soon, Ki was standing right in front of it. It was a fully articulated statue of a man made from a combination of stone and shiny bronze. Covering his chest was a bulky breastplate of polished metal that Ki could see her reflection in. The Blanchefort Coat-of-Arms was embossed in the center—specifically, it was Kay's coat of arms. Actually, as Ki examined it further, it was Kay's Coat-of-Arms on its side in a lozenge; therefore, it was meant to herald Kay's lady. Who was that? Kay wasn't officially attached to anybody.

"Sam?" Ki said, her voice lost in the open air before it. Tweeter flapped up and veered away, landing on the nearby altar.

The chest-area of the statue was easily large and deep enough to fit a full-sized person within. She reached up and touched it with the flat of her palm. The metallic surface was slightly warm. There was a seam dividing the breastplate in two running from top to bottom. The two halves of the breastplate fit tightly together. It looked sturdy and solid, like a giant-sized safe none could ever possibly break into.

"Sam, are you in there?" Ki yelled.

She noticed the giant statue was moving ever so slightly, walking as if in slow motion. He was moving away from the altar Tweeter was sitting on.

On second glance, it was not an altar. Instead, it looked like a pewter chariot, easily big enough for the giant statue to stand in. There was a place to harness three steeds; the leather strap that once held them lay coiled on the ground. "Tweets!" Ki said. "Where's Sam?"

Tweeter took flight and fluttered up against the Statue's chest. Wearily the Metal Man looked down at him.

"Hey, you there, wait a moment!" Ki yelled.

The statue stopped. Ki marched up.

"What are you?"

He slowly answered, his voice a whisper. "I am the Judge of the Trials. The Trials are done, and I am done. Not much time left."

"The Trials? You mean Kay's Wellerman?"

"Yes."

"You're protecting Sam?"

"Aye."

"Why? From what?"

"The gods. Some have smiled upon us and offered safe haven, while others pursue. Move and counter move. I have spanned the heavens, keeping my Lady safe. Surrounded by enemies, the little god flew at my side. The gods will win out in the end. The trials are done, and I can do no more."

"What gods? You mean Carahil?"

"I do not know his name. He has sheltered us, while the other pursues."

"What other?"

The statue motioned to the woods all around. "There ... his minions."

Ki looked at the perimeter of trees beyond the amphitheater. Just a line of craggy old oak trees swaying in the wind. "I don't see anything," Ki said.

The statue didn't respond.

"Hey," Ki said. "Are you all right?"

He spoke one last time. "My Lady's lord returns ..."

The surroundings were still as a vacuum. She stood there in the shadow of the Metal Man gazing at the line of trees.

Something was out there, watching her; she could feel it, and it wasn't the ghosts of the old Vith, it was something malevolent and quite living.

She heard jeering voices.

"Come here ..."

"Hey, come here!"

"We have something for you."

"Come here!"

The perimeter of trees rustled with hidden movement. She thought she saw hints of green mist and flashes of snaking light. She saw slices of faces through the trees, moments of eyes, open mouths, wagging tongues, dripping fluids and hunched shoulders.

"Who are you?" Ki demanded speaking up, making herself heard.

"*Who are you?*" a voice came back. "*Who are you?*"

"I am she who defends this place!"

"Are you? We are those who are unseen and watch from the shadows. We are those who preceded you here in this place and will follow when you are gone. We hold the Monamas leash and parade over them as their masters. We are the lords of the Berserkacides."

"That right? Come out where I can see you."

"*We are going to take you, as we have done the others, and transform you into one of us. You shall bow to the Golden People and feast upon the flesh of your kin. Think of the wonders that await you.*"

"Change me into a monster, a Jennyback, like you did to Lady Hathaline, and that poor Lord Mervin of Crossland? If you want me, here I am. Come and get me."

Ki heard a dismissive snickering in response.

There was a faint clicking sound to her right. She saw the dim outline of a green slit appear in mid air, and then fizzle and vanish.

Another one appeared to her left, vanishing just as quickly. As Ki whirled around, she kicked something lying on the ground.

It was one of the little blue Carahil figurines she'd scattered a few days prior. She picked it up and held it in her palm. These were somehow preventing the enemy, whatever they were, from appearing, protecting both her and Sam's Metal Man in turn from attack. Carahil had mentioned something about that.

A large green slit appeared in front of her. She thought, for a tiny moment, she could see something lurking behind the slit, trying to get through to her. She held out the figurine, and the slit vanished.

This time, the figurine let off a puff of smoke, and his right front flipper turned to ash and blew away.

These figurines were finite. With every appearance and cast aside, they grew a little smaller, and eventually, they would fade away into nothing, and their power would be lost.

She heard a clamor of movement in the trees along with a great number of green flashes. The Jennybacks were assembling in the trees, beyond the range of Carahil's protection.

A great rumble kicked up. A dark cloud appeared in the distance. What more could happen?

"We are going to overwhelm you with Berserkacides. You know what those are, don't you?" came a voice from the trees.

Ki pulled her SK. "You know what this is, right?"

Cajoling, arrogant laughter. *"And what do you propose to do with that weapon?"*

"I'll show you! Tweeter," Ki said cocking the chamber, "point them out!"

Tweeter took wing and flew toward the tree line. He fluttered over a spot and settled. Ki lifted her SK, hardened with Anthecary, and fired.

TACK!

She didn't see anything fall, but she heard a body hit the ground and rustle in the leaves. Tweeter moved on, flapping about.

He settled.

"We're in business!" Ki cried as she hardened up and fired again, threading her shot in between two oaks. This time she heard the familiar slap of flesh being destroyed and bones being shattered by the fifty caliber slug, and she caught a glimpse of a body flying back in a misty cloud of blood. The SK was a comforting weapon to fire, for anything hit by it wasn't getting back up. Even a wing shot from an SK was deadly.

More flashes. Tweeter moved into position. She fired. Another cloud of blood. Another body hitting the ground.

A dreadful scream came out of the woods and assailed Ki's ears. It filled her head and froze her joints. Very quickly, she couldn't move a muscle, just like being caught in a full TK.

Jennybacks could freeze you in your tracks if you let them, she'd always heard. Kay—what did Kay say happened during his attack? He said his attackers made a strange sound, and he couldn't move afterwards. Bespelled, he said.

And now it was the same for her.

Frozen, she saw a dance of red light come from the trees

A line of pale, bounding creatures shot out of the trees seconds later, running fast.

Nude, chalk-like pale skin, black mane-like hair. Four arms.

Berserkacides! Seven of them, tearing up the ground as they clawed their way to her, growling like rabid dogs.

She couldn't move. She couldn't defend herself. Ki had but moments to live.

5—Paraflies

As the snarling Berserkacides came in to tear Ki apart, a sudden black cloud descended upon the amphitheatre in a prickly confusion, fast and smothering, such that Ki thought she'd gone blind. She saw grainy bits of movement aloft and travelling in sequence, as if she were suddenly in the center of a roaring tornado, full of debris.

What was happening? She couldn't process it all. And such noise, a head-splitting buzzing sound that she had to put her fingers in her ears to drown out, and ...

Wait! She could move. She was free! Protecting her face with her hands, she staggered ahead, seeing nothing but a multitude of flying shapes clogging the air. She felt prickly legs crawling up her backside, getting under her coat and her shirt leaving itchy trails in their wake. She felt wings vibrating.

Something came through the mass and collided with Ki, knocking her down. A shapeless arm reached out, seeking Ki's neck. It went limp and fell away.

Ki stood, and as quickly as it had come, the cloud lifted above the treetops and buzzed away to the south like a living cyclone of unimaginable power.

What was it? What was going on?

A swarm of giant-sized bugs had fallen into the amphitheater. She'd read about them in the posts.

Paraflies. Gigantic, swarming insects, thought to be imports from elsewhere in the League. Some said they came from Onaris, home of a whole host of big creepy-crawlies, but Ki, being from Onaris herself, didn't recall anything quite that big and noisy there.

Her skin was crawling from their legs, and she checked herself over. They seemed to be gone, though she felt the ghost of them still on her, her skin twitching.

The ground between the ruin and the line of trees was clotted with the pale lumps of fallen bodies. One was literally at her feet, reaching out for her in death. She counted twelve Berserkacides in all, twisted up on the ground in various stages of distress. There were the seven she saw before the Paraflies attacked and five more, closer to the trees, that she hadn't seen. Ki inspected their bodies. These Berserkacides seemed tiny, slight and skinny, much smaller and slighter than Sam, who was the only Monama Ki'd ever spent much time with; Sam was solid and buxom. She wondered: did they shrink when they became Berserkacides?

There were dead males and dead females mixed together, both sexes being on the smallish side. There were a few children as well—dead. Their black eyes were much tinier than Sam's, and they lacked those feathery eyelashes she associated with Sam. Their bodies, except for their heads (eye brows, eyelashes and scalps of thick black hair) were quite hairless and smooth. She had heard Berserkacides came with four arms, and there they were, sprouting out below the armpit area of the first set. Slender and light, quite dainty actually, but tautly cabled with lean, efficient muscle, probably giving them ten times her strength. Their fingernails were sharp and deadly, like pointed lengths of exposed bone. As she took in the details, she noted their extra set of arms were odd in appearance, scaly, crabby with ridges and bumps, almost primordial in shape with their hands being mostly like mal-formed claw-studded nippers. She checked their feet, expecting them to be clawed as well like their hands; however, their feet weren't clawed. In fact, they were delicate and small, like a ballerina's foot.

Hey, look at that, Ki thought with an observant eye. No bellybutton on any of them. That's weird. She also noticed a small but definite hole between their eyes that reminded Ki of a third nostril. She thought the hole might have been a well-placed bullet hole at first, but, several of them had a similar hole in the exact same spot, and, a hit from her SK wouldn't have made a little hole, it would have blown their heads clean off.

Their eyes. Open in death, they weren't all black like Monamas had, they were white and beady with an angry black dot in the center.

Their naked bodies were covered in ugly purplish bumps oozing venom. Stung to death no doubt, and by the looks on their dead faces, the process of being killed hadn't been painless. All twelve dropped fast, stung to death in a matter of moments by a sudden cloud of apparently deadly Paraflies.

These were Berserkacides, but they were also Monama men and women, sisters and brothers, husbands and wives, kids, all taken from their homes at a moment's notice and turned into monsters to lie dead on the cold ground of the Telmus Grove. The empty chairs and unmade beds, the children's toys lying on the floor, the loss. None of this was their fault.

Or maybe it was; maybe it was their fault after all. Why didn't they stand up? Why didn't they use all that speed and strength to save themselves? Why didn't they fight back? Ki felt rage build up within and the thirst for revenge grow. She wanted retribution for these poor dead people, especially for the kids who died as monsters today. She would get the staff and gather their bodies up. She knew enough from listening to Kay and Sam that their people down south wouldn't take them back as Berserkacides, so she would make sure they were buried here and remembered as victims of a cruel enemy. She felt they were owed.

SK ready, Ki made her way into the tree line. More bodies awaited her; only this time they weren't Berserkacides. These were monstrous, skinned wrecks, similar to what Ki had seen in Crossland. Jennybacks they were called on Onaris. *Killanjo* the Xaphans called them. Five were nude and dripping; another, a female, was wearing a beaded sort of dress. A bloody golden mask sat ajar on her dead face—the lady looked like a fallen-down drunk at a costume party, only this one wasn't drunk, she was quite dead. Like the Berserkacides, all here in the trees were covered in savage stings, including the three whom Ki had shot dead and horribly mangled with her SK.

The Paraflies must be packing a lethal punch to kill so quickly.

Stings! She was stung too, wasn't she? She removed her coat and checked herself over, for she was certain she'd been stung as well. How could she not? The Paraflies just slaughtered twelve Berserkacides and six fleshless Jennyback demons in a matter of seconds, and it made no sense why they would spare her. They were just bugs, after all. She should be down on the ground dead like everybody else.

She didn't see or feel stings anywhere. She thought, from previous experience, that she was slightly sensitive to bee and wasp stings; one got her once in the arm, and she recalled puffing up like a beach ball afterwards. Patting herself down, she didn't seem to be swelling up anywhere.

Off in the distance, she heard a furtive, deep-pitched buzzing. The Metal

Man standing on the platform was crawling with Paraflies. He was wearing them like a beard and a coat. Their vibrating wings made him appear to be trembling.

Despite herself, for Ki didn't really like bugs of any kind, especially big ones with a potent sting, Ki went toward the Metal Man. Their coppery wings made a pretty, slightly undulating display on his chest. As she neared Ki could see herself easily in the reflection. There were hundreds crawling on him.

What the heck was she doing?

These bugs had swooped in just in time to save the day like a squadron of airborne Marines, killed her attackers with deadly stings and yet spared her body; not a single sting as far as she could tell.

And, though her guts told her to high-tail it out of there fast, she was going to find out why.

The Paraflies swarming on the Metal Man's chest were large, their bodies about the length of her hand, fingers extended. They looked mostly like dragonflies, except that they had a single pair of long, swept-back wings instead of two pairs of outstretched wings like dragonflies normally had. Paraflies were certainly colorful, being a shiny metallic blue mixing with a sea foam green at the belly with gorgeous coppery wings. Their large wings were extremely shiny—rather mirror-like.

The racket of buzzing they made was clear and loud.

Ki approached. She wrestled with herself internally because she normally didn't like bugs much—she once lived in fear of the huge spiders and blood-sucking flies of Tusck that came out of everywhere. All the big-fanged, hairy bugs in the universe came from Tusck, she used to like to say.

She expected them to either swarm away or attack her in self defense—that's what bugs did. But these did neither. They just sat there and buzzed their rust-colored wings.

Ki found herself reaching out for one; she honestly couldn't help herself. Somehow, she didn't feel threatened. Somehow she didn't think she was going to be stung. They had spared her flesh previously—not a single sting. Why sting her now?

As her fingers neared, one of the huge bugs moved toward her hand and settled contentedly into her palm, giving her skin ticklish jolts with its wings.

Carefully, Ki raised her hand and took a good look at it close up.

She couldn't believe what she saw.

Close-up, the Parafly had a happy face; compound eyes big and deep like a puppy and, though it had an insect-like head with a segmented mouth, it was clearly smiling at her.

Carahil

6—What Carahil Asked

"Good Morning, Lt.," Lord Peter said as Ki stood in the foyer of Josephina Tower in the northwestern section of the castle. Josephina was Lady Poe and Peter's private tower. The foyer was elegantly set up in Poe's particular provincial style. A silver Bark dog, another of Poe's Silver tech creations, sat lazily on a chair. His floppy silver face jolly, he thumped his tail.

Peter was just pulling his coat on as he emerged from the lift.

"Good morning, Peter," Ki said. "I would like to see Lady Poe. I need to have a word with her."

Peter shook his head. "I'm afraid Lady Poe is not well this morning. She's upstairs in bed. Can it wait, or perhaps I can relay a message to her? She always enjoys hearing from you. You're such a good friend."

"Did you not hear the ruckus just now? The Grove was attacked. I've locked the whole castle down. You weren't aware of that?"

Peter blushed. "We've been in a Whisper Cone for most of the day yesterday and so far this morning and couldn't hear anything. I also didn't have any of our terminals turned on. I thought it best, as she needs her rest. What happened?"

"I was attacked by Jennybacks."

"Jennybacks? What are those?" he asked.

"Fleshless creatures. There were also Berserkacides at leash, and a swarm of giant bugs."

"Bugs?" Peter said, surprised. "You were attacked by the Tuleeflies? That's not possible. Did they hurt you?"

Ki was confused. "By the what? No, no, they were Paraflies, lots of them. I don't know what a Tuleefly is."

"Well, they're ..."

"Peter, please," Ki said as Bark bounded up and put his paws on her waist. She petted his floppy silver ears. "I think I really need to speak to Lady Poe. I hate to insist, but I do. I insist that I see her, for the safety of Davage's children, and yours as well."

Peter saw Ki wasn't going to be denied. He turned and went back into the lift. "Give me a moment, please, Lt."

"Sure," Ki said. "Sure. Oh, enough with the 'Lt.', stuff, all right? Just call me 'Ki', Peter, ok?"

He smiled, and the lift surged away. Ki stood alone, Bark wanting her attention. Tweeter chirped down at him from her shoulder. As she waited, Ki admired Poe's foyer. There were paintings of Poe and her family, not towering, intimidating ones like in the Hall of Portraits, but smaller, more inviting ones painted in a friendly style. There were also little statues of Poe's various familiars placed in pleasing locations all over. There was Tweeter, of course her personal favorite. There were Bark the hound and Shadow the cat, Fins the incredible goldfish that could heal virtually anything, and Snugs, the humming bird, another useful one that kept Ki's room nice and warm. There was a colorful statue of several tiny Whisper ladybugs—Silver tech familiars that Cloaked one sight and sound. All of them, as per usual with Lady Poe's creations, were smiling and happy. That was her trademark, her calling card. Every Silver tech creature she created had a happy face … just like the Paraflies outside that had saved her life,

Off in a corner was the ceramic image of a bird with a long tail sitting on a stand, but it wasn't Tweeter or Snugs; in fact, Ki didn't recognize him at all. It was a little bird with a crested head and a long, arrow-like beak. It was a little puff-ball of nested feathers. And, unlike all of the other familiars Lady Poe had created, this little bird didn't smile. He seemed dour and serious.

The lift returned. "Poe is ready to see you, Ki," Peter said.

Ki continued to examine the statue. "Peter, what's this one? This little bird here? I've never seen this one before."

"That is a project Poe was working on. He's not ready yet. He was placed on the rear burner for the time being."

"What's his name?" Ki asked as she got on the lift.

"King."

"King? Like a kingfisher? Is that what he is?"

"Yes."

"Well he looks neat enough, I actually sort of like his annoyed expression. I'll like to see more of him once he's ready to go."

Peter nodded and closed the doors. The lift went up dozens of floors fast.

He led her into their huge bedroom which took up the entire circumference of the tower on the 100th floor and was circular. The curtains on the eastern side were thrown open, admitting a lot of light. There was Lady Poe of Blanchefort, elder sister of Captain Davage and Shadow tech Female. She was in her four-poster bed propped up by pillows dressed in night linens. Her breakfast, brought to her on a tray by Peter, sat mostly uneaten. She was tall and lean, just like her brother, and had a head of platinum-blonde hair streaked with blue, cut simple and short. As a Shadow tech Female, she had the Shadowmark around her right eye; however, her Shadowmark was the largest Ki had ever seen, much larger and more complex than Syg's or Duchess Torrijayne of Oyln and far bigger than Bethrael of Moane's, which was rather tiny and faint in comparison. Another Bark sat at the foot of the bed near her feet, and a Shadow cat was curled up near her head. On her nightstand, several Whispers of various pastel colors buzzed about inside a glass jar.

"Good morning, Lady Poe," Ki said.

Poe, her head resting on her overstuffed pillow, looked at Ki with bloodshot eyes and smiled a little. Peter sat down next to her and tried to get her to drink a glass of orange juice.

She looked deathly tired. "Good morning, Lt.," she whispered.

Ki didn't mince words. "Lady Poe, talk to me about the Paraflies. I know you're creating them."

Poe seemed to wake up a little and turned to Peter in shock.

"How have you made such an odd deduction, Ki?" Peter asked, a little dumbfounded.

"Come on, Peter—a huge, friendly bug with a happy face—only Lady Poe of Blanchefort would come up with something like that. And, I know from your Whisper familiars that you can create all sorts of colors other than just silver."

Poe closed her eyes and was silent.

Peter set down the glass of orange juice. "Ki," he said. "What you have to understand is …"

"Lady Poe," Ki said, interrupting, "those insects—those Paraflies—saved me today."

"What?" Poe asked, a bit louder.

"They saved my life as well as that of Lady Sammidoran's. I was attacked in the Grove this morning."

"From what you said in the foyer, I thought you said the Paraflies attacked you, Lt.," Peter said.

"No, Peter, that's not what I meant."

Peter rubbed his chin. "Well ... that's wonderful news actually, Ki. If you can recall, how fast did the Paraflies respond to the attack?"

"Fast. They were there before I knew it."

"And did they move with purpose? As one, perhaps?"

"There was a big cloud of them. Yes, I'd say so."

Poe listened, then took the glass of orange juice and gulped it down.

"Lady Poe—I'm here at your brother's request, to protect his children. I am happy to do it. Please, you can trust me. Tell me what is going on."

Poe sat up and took Peter's hand. "Lt.," she said softly, "on my birthday a few months back, I was visited by Carahil. He always visits me on my birthday; he's such a good boy, but this time his visit came with a warning. He said the League was in danger, and he asked me to help him in protecting it. He said monsters will come and attack us in our homes, and he begged me to do what I could to protect the people. He called the monsters *Killanjo*."

Peter poured another glass of orange juice and gave it to Lady Poe, which she greedily drank.

She continued. "He told me that these *Killanjo* could cast spells which render us helpless, and that they always brought Berserkacides with them. He also told me that the *Killanjo* were detectable in something called the Gamma Band, and that there was a counter frequency that breaks their spells. He also said the monsters couldn't bear the sight of their own image. He asked me to create something that can detect these fiends, create sound at the correct frequency to counter their spells and be able to reflect their image."

"And," Peter added, "be able to patrol the whole world."

Poe ran her hand through her short blonde-blue hair. "Yes. I—I didn't know what sort of Silver tech creature could accomplish all those things. I didn't know what to do, and then Peter came up with the answer. He made a little robotic bug. Its eyes could see in the Gamma band, and its wings could buzz at the correct frequency to create the required sound to counter their spells. Also, these bugs were shiny enough to create a large reflective surface if enough of them massed together. It was a brilliant design. Using his little robot as a model, I then began working on creating the first of what eventually became millions of Tuleeflies."

"Tuleeflies?"

Peter spoke up. "After our niece, Lady Tulee of Oyln, because she loves bugs. Poe even made them in Lady Tulee's favorite colors: blue and foamy green."

"I wanted them to be pretty—I thought people might be less afraid of them that way," Poe said. "The Science Ministry and the press eventually began calling them Paraflies."

Peter exited the bedroom and returned several minutes later holding a small chest. He set it down on the bed and opened the lid. He reached in and pulled out a toy Parafly.

"This, Lt., is the original robotic Tuleefly that we have been modifying, adjusting, and perfecting over the last few months. This is what Poe has modeled her design on."

It was a jeweled, blue and green bug made out of copper, nickel and aluminum. It looked pretty much exactly like the Paraflies she'd seen outside, except for its face. It had a standard bug-face, with jeweled green eyes. The happy face was a Lady Poe trademark. The name TULEEFLY was embossed on its copper wings.

Peter pressed a hidden button on its rear, and its copper wings beat to life, buzzing clear and proud just like the real ones did.

Lady Poe then continued. "There have been … many incarnations of Tuleeflies since then. The first few just didn't work like I had planned. They were failures: they didn't fly correctly, and they didn't buzz at the right frequency—the list of technical problems was endless. If it weren't for Peter and his tireless testing, I'd never have gotten it. I began to think that I'd failed Carahil and the League. It took me months of trying to finally get it right, but eventually I came up with the first of a successive line of Tuleeflies that worked as planned, and I created them, every night, by the millions."

"Millions?"

"Yes ... Every night, I lay back and created them—I had to make enough that they could spread out over the whole planet. They are a very complex form of Silver tech. It was exhausting. Every night, to bleed myself dry …"

Peter spoke up. "But, even after perfecting the first generation of Tulees, there were problems. They didn't react fast enough. They didn't move with purpose, and they didn't see Gamma as well as we'd hoped. The details were so complicated."

"The day the castle was attacked from Castle Durst made it all clear to me, and I made changes," Poe said.

Ki was alarmed. "The castle was attacked? Dav didn't mention anything about it to me."

"No—he doesn't remember it. Nobody does but us. I think Carahil blanked their memories. But, sure enough, Castle Blanchefort almost fell one night several weeks ago."

"What happened?"

"There was a light, coming from Castle Durst," Peter said. "We could feel ourselves going mad bathed in its beam. Poe then summoned the Paraflies to us. We lay down, and they covered us from head to foot, buzzing. Their shiny wings kept the light off us, and we weathered the night, frightened, but unharmed."

"How was the attack defeated?"

"Kay—he saved the castle. His Shadow tech Male abilities allowed him to resist the light. He was magnificent, Ki. We were so proud of him."

Poe continued. "The attack was revealing. After that, I realized the Paraflies had to see Gamma better and move a bit more aggressively, and as one. I created a newer version, to replace the old …"

"The mass extinction, the one I read about?"

"Yes—I couldn't sustain the older ones as they depended upon me for energy. I let them die. But still I was not done."

Peter spoke up. "We knew they were finally working as we'd hoped after the attack on Kay; they discovered the enemy and came to his aid all on their own. They even attempted to cover him with their wings to drive the enemy away."

Poe was bitter and remorseful "But they couldn't do much to come actively to Kay's defense. We realized they should have done something more to help him, and perhaps he needn't have been brought to death's door." She turned red in the face.

Peter tried to soothe her. "Yes, it came to us that the Tulees needed more punch, to protect aggressively instead of just in a passive sense."

"To kill ..." Poe said with great sadness. She began to cry, and Peter took her into his arms.

"My wife is no killer, Ki, but we knew that, in order to protect the people, we had to arm the Tuleeflies, for they could have saved Kay from his ordeal. So, in the latest version, we instilled in them a powerful desire to seek out and kill the *Killanjo*, and, to that end, we armed them with a stinger and a very lethal cocktail of Silver tech Nyke poisons that can kill just about anything—a true marvel of arcane engineering."

Lady Poe blushed.

"Also, we felt that we should include Berserkacides in the Paraflies' list, to protect against them as well, though we didn't want to hurt innocent Monamas. We needed a Berserkacide to test with."

Poe jumped back in. "And Peter, my beloved husband, set out and looked to encounter a Berserkacide. He could have been killed."

"I managed to get attacked by one in Lord Christopher Park. It came at me from nowhere where I'd heard many attacks had taken place. I managed to bring it down with my SAPP and take a sample of its flesh and blood. With the additional information, Poe again modified the Tuleeflies' design and programming. Now, the Tuleefly is the mortal enemy of both the *Killanjo* and the Berserkacide and has the vigilance, the speed and the power to bring them down. All else are safe and needn't ever fear them. Again, she sent them out in the millions."

"I'm so tired," she said weeping into Peter's arms.

"Well, I guess you got them working, Lady Poe," Ki said. "They bagged the Jennybacks and the Berserkacides cold."

"And they didn't hurt you?"

"No. They creeped me out a little, but that's all."

Poe ran a tired hand through her short hair. "Thank Creation."

Ki thought a moment. "May I ask, if you had this knowledge, why didn't you tell Dav? Such information could be critical in his mission over Hoban."

Peter looked down at the floor. "That's my fault, Ki. Poe wanted to tell him, but I asked her to hold off until we were certain of all the various parameters. I didn't want to provide him with incorrect information, as the original Tuleeflies just didn't seem to see very well in the Gamma field, so I questioned what it was we were looking for."

Poe, for the first time, brightened. "But, now that we know they're working as we'd hoped, we should inform him right away. Let's do it right now."

Peter stood and went to get a portable terminal. He went to the other room and came back carrying a small, circular one. As he set it up, Poe began munching on a piece of toast. The robotic Tuleefly landed on the monitor and buzzed its wings.

He readied the terminal and turned to Ki. "Lt., do you have a current code for the Captain?"

"Sure do. Here, allow me." Peter turned the monitor toward her, and Ki keyed in the code, the Parafly watching her type it in. The terminal connected to FleetCom and then bounded off into space toward the *New Faith.* Though it was far away over Hoban, the signal should connect in a matter of moments.

The connection failed. The *New Faith* could not be located.

"That's weird," Ki said.

"I heard there's a significant rad storm off Planet Fall," Peter said. "Might be creating interference. We'll try again later."

Poe, her burden lifted, began to power into her breakfast. She was like a new woman.

"Pardon me, Lt., may I offer you a glass?" Peter asked.

"Some orange juice? Sure thing."

Peter poured her a tall one.

As Ki sat there, she looked at Poe in awe. This tall, unassuming woman, a hidden Shadow tech Female, had the dedication and raw might to populate the entire world with complex Silver tech creations, that, after a long period of trial and error, were starkly effective—nearly killing herself in the process. She created Carahil after all, and he was a god. Look what she could do.

Ki didn't get this way often, but she was humbled, completely humbled to sit in her presence. "They work, Lady Poe. Creation knows how many people they've saved so far. You, my lady, are a hero."

"I'm no hero, Lt. Dav, Syg, Kay, my children—they're the heroes."

"I don't agree. It's easy for someone like Dav and Syg to be heroic. They go out and do great things and receive the acclaim that they've well earned. You stand unseen, bleeding yourself half to death every night with not a word said, not an ounce of praise given. That selflessness is the true mark of a hero. Carahil came to you for help, and he was right to do so."

Ki kissed her on the cheek. "Thank you, Lady Poe. Your job is done. Kana is safe."

"I can rest … I can finally rest. It's been so long."

"You have kept your promise, to Carahil and to the League. Let your creations do their job. Let them protect the people."

Peter handed Ki her glass of orange juice.

"'Tuleeflies,'" Ki said. "I think I like that name better. Sounds friendlier than 'Parafly' does." Ki took a drink. "What about the rest of the League worlds—Onaris, Hoban, Planet Fall, Xandarr and the like—they could sure use your Tuleeflies too."

"We have commissioned several automated transports, one for each of the major League worlds—they're just sitting down in Blanchefort village. We are going to crate them full of Tuleeflies, launch the transports, and turn them loose. Once there, they'll multiply and maintain a steady level. We already have more than enough here on Kana; all Poe has to do is call them and they'll come."

Poe sat back and finished the breakfast that Peter had brought her—the great weight lifted off her shoulders.

7—Atrajak's Book

Moving through the blackness of unfamiliar space, the *New Faith* took aboard the four Marine *Trelaine* attack ships and began sailing at speed, quickly winding for full rotations.

Since the desperate Battle of Hoban, they'd been cut adrift from the League. Their stellar compasses were dead, their Astro charts useless. The AM/PM clock system of navigation that was caged precisely to the north/south poles of Kana spun aimlessly, occasionally locking onto ghosts. They moved without rudder or direction.

Kana and the League must be very far away.

Captain Davage, Lord of Blanchefort and his fighting Countess, Sygillis of Blanchefort, had struggled to keep control of their frightened crew and guide them back to the safety of the League, but who knows where that was.

They had gone to Hoban with a small armada of ships under the command of Admiral Carfax of Woodland to investigate a troubling series of attacks taking place there. The attacks involved odd, demonic creatures called *Killanjo* that appeared to have the ability to step out of thin air and controlled vast numbers of Berserkacides. Davage had been eager to accept the charge, for his son Kay had been attacked in a very similar manner. He wanted answers, and he wanted retribution as well. On a slab in the Crossland cellars, he came face to face with one of the *Killanjo* 'demons'. There, he learned his own daughter, Lady Hathaline, in a similar guise, had been the one who had attacked and nearly killed his son. Going mad with worry, he sent Lt. Kilos, his trusted friend and first officer, home to Blanchefort to guard his children. Later, in the tombs of Crossland, they had rescued a Monama girl and prevented her from becoming a Berserkacide. They were just beginning to make important discoveries when they were attacked in space and suffered heavy casualties from unknown forces. The Fleet, with no apparent enemy to fight, was scattered. The great warbird *Bethel* was destroyed. Davage and a few Marines managed to drive their vessels through a Gamma band gateway and come to grips with the enemy up close, which they did with devastating effect.

And now there they were, stuck in enemy space, position unknown and enemy disposition unknown as well. As they moved blind, they felt enemy eyes watching them from all quarters.

The senior staff and the Marine pilots, who had fallen through the Gamma gateway with them, met in the main conference room to try and decide how to proceed. Davage stood at the head of the table, tall and decked out in his Fleet uniform, his Vith blue hair tied up in a tail as always. His countess Sygillis, tiny and red-haired, sat there in a white gown, quiet and commanding as always when in esteemed company. Paymaster Stenstrom, the acting first officer (as Ki was not there), paced the floor sporting his mask and his long hunter green HRN coat swishing at his booted ankles. The two Hospitalers, Ennez and Bethrael of Moane, sat there with their shining jet staves and silver helmets. Lady Tellerran of Monama, the woman they'd saved in the Crossland tombs, was also there in an advisory role. She didn't speak much

League Common and had a translating endecar sitting in front of her, reciting everything said into her native Conox language.

"So let's to it. Have we any idea where we are?" Lt. Surfit of the 9th Marines asked.

Davage stood. "We are far from the League; that much is clear. AM/PM clock orientation is useless, and none of the stars in this area of space match any known charts in our possession."

One of the Marines shook his head. "Creation, we're stuffed. Best to put down on some primitive green world with good water and plentiful game and start making pottery."

Davage placed a large leather-bound book painted and studded with colorful stones on the tabletop and pushed it forward. "Let's be patient for a moment. About a week ago, my Countess and I received this. It's an old Remnath book, and we were told it would be of great importance to us."

"A book?" one of the Marines spat. "And how is that to help us?"

"Will you please allow the Captain to finish," Paymaster Stenstrom demanded.

The Marine regarded the odd Paymaster decked out in his mask and swashbuckling kit with a bit of scorn. "Must I listen to this demented civilian?"

"Yes, you must," Davage said. He continued. "If I may, this book is a chronicle of the old Remnath hero Atrajak of Want."

"The Berserker?" Stenstrom asked. "He was a madman if I remember my lore."

"He has been branded a madman by the Sisters, true enough," Davage agreed. "However, it has been proved the Sisters can be quick to judge and slow to forget."

Lady Tellerran chimed in through her endecar. "Atrajak of Want was a hero to our people. He fought the demons and the Golden People for years."

"Yes," Davage said. "Exactly, and Atrajak's experiences are key for us now. In this book he writes of the Undisclosed Conflict, or the Hidden Wars, he refers to it by various names where he and his faithful army of Anuian Monamas fought a persistent enemy across the south of Kana, an enemy who could step out of thin air and vanish just as fast. He called them, for lack of better terms, the Kestral Oligarchy. As he described them, they were shape-shifters, they could be anything they wished, and they employed a frequent tactic where they abducted innocent victims and transformed them into hideous monsters with the intent of softening their targets up and sapping their will to resist. They then came in at their leisure, abducting some while killing others. They did that often in the old days—sounds rather similar to what we experienced over Hoban, does it not?"

"It does," Stenstrom said.

"The book then goes on to detail Atrajak's mounting frustration. As the Kestrals and their foul *Killanjo* servants could simply come and go as they pleased, Atrajak realized he could never seize final victory without taking additional drastic steps. He took his Monama army on a long stellar voyage off Kana, hoping to face the Kestrals on their home ground and destroy them there for all time. He was not aware of the Monamas' susceptibility to protracted voyages in space, and they all perished at some point along the journey, including Atrajak's wife, Tiverlan of Nebulon, who was a Monama princess. He lost his mind in his grief."

Davage pressed a few buttons, and the holo-display came up. "I'm going to make a key assumption here. Atrajak established that the Kestrals come and go via gamma band doorways that are quite invisible, and we encountered them over Hoban. The League is on one side of the door, and the Kestrals are on the other. I am assuming that, at present, we are on the Kestral's side of the gamma door, wherever that may be. Certainly we are very far from the League as our AM/PM compasses and other navigational devices are dead. Does anybody disagree?"

Nobody answered. The people sitting at the conference table felt lost and marooned. The stars outside the large window were countless and unfathomable. The Marines were uncomfortable and fidgety. Lady Tellerran toyed with her endecar.

Davage sensed their flagging spirits. "Friends, Atrajak's book is our salvation. There is a wealth of stellar charts in this book, many detailing Atrajak's journey to the Kestrals. These charts are crude and fanciful, but I believe they are invaluable to us. They are our lifeline back to the League."

He pressed a few buttons, and a glowing representation of a stellar chart, colorful with painted, robed figures and burning globes representing stars and planets, came up. "I believe that this chart here details the whole of Atrajak's voyage, starting at Kana and advancing a very long way to his eventual destination—to the Kestral Oligarchy itself." Davage pointed at a bearded man wearing blue robes. Playing at his feet were two small robed girls.

"How have you determined that this figure represents Kana?" Ennez asked.

"Because the girl wearing the reddish robes is also wearing a charm with an octagonal symbol. See there? I interpret that to mean the Octagon Crater on Kana's second moon, Elyria, a moon with a surface of reddish rock."

They studied the chart and nodded. Seemed reasonable. One of the Marines had a thought. "All right, I'll acknowledge that this chart lays out the course Atrajak used long ago, and I'll also agree that this figure represents Kana; however, our basic problem remains. We have no idea where the endpoint is located in relation to our current position. It could be anywhere. We have no point of reference to start from,

and this chart does not have the necessary pertinent detail to allow us to astrolog it out."

Davage pressed another button. An elaborate chart of a ten planet solar-system came up, painted with jewel-like globes. The solar system was bisected by a fair maiden with vast flowing hair.

"Have no fear, sir," Davage said. "We have many charts in Atrajak's book. This one here details what I believe to be the home solar system of the Kestral Oligarchy. It contains a wealth of information: relative planet size, rotational period, number of moons, and so on. We even have spectral data on their star and this depiction of the lady with her hair bisecting the system between the fourth and fifth planets. I believe that figure represents a nebula. Such a feature, if I'm interpreting this chart correctly, would be very distinctive."

The chart disappeared from the holocone, replaced by a swirling Astro chart of 3-D star points. "The Charting Lab has discovered a very similar solar system … here. They just located it this morning."

On the holomap, a star began blinking. "It's about three million stellar miles from our current position off our port beam. Look at the emission nebula splitting the fourth and fifth planets—that is telling. This solar system is the bastion of the enemy, and it is where we shall plant our flag and mark our bearings back to the League."

Davage hit a button, and the AM/PM clock orientation rings appeared around the solar system and calibrated.

A glowing red path appeared, trailing off the edge of the cone like a welcoming carpet.

"This, friends, gives us our point of reference. Using the charts in this book we shall be able to navigate back to home."

"Assuming that Atrajak was not, as the Sisters claim, an utter madman," Lt Damon said.

"That is an assumption we must make. His charts tell us he was perfectly sane."

Ennez spoke up. "So, given this knowledge, how long will it take us to get back to the League?"

"Using a liberal amount of Stellar Mach transverses and a fast tach speed, about ten weeks."

"Assuming we can maintain such a speed, and assuming we are not beset upon in the process," Damon said.

"We are fully serviced and sustained no damage in the previous attack. Once safe and proper Stellar Mach transverse points have been determined, we should make weather time."

Davage turned at Ennez. "What is the status of the Sisters?"

Ennez shook his head. "Gone, Dav—all of them. During the battle."

One of the Marines was incensed. "As per usual. When things get really dangerous, the Sisters can be counted upon to vanish and leave us to our fate."

Davage cut him off. "They are civilians and not expected to share our charge. The Sisters will be as they will be. For now, we must stay sharp and look to it. We've much ground to cover and can expect many challenges if we plan to make full sail for ten weeks." Davage ran his hand though his head of long blue hair.

Lt. Damon spoke up. "The enemy may fall upon us as they see fit. It's just a matter of time before we are engaged afresh."

"Then let them come," Sygillis said, speaking at last. "And let them be destroyed. They have come at our homes, our children and lacked the courage to face us in direct conflict. They have revealed their lack of character to us and shan't be spared or offered quarter."

Davage gazed at the holographic stars. "Paymaster, you're to the books. What is our current provisioning?"

Stenstrom shook his head. "We are not provisioned for a protracted voyage removed from the League—we were not expecting to be operating away from easy harbor. We have, with considerable rationing assumed, one week's worth, and we have an emergency store of mostly hardtack and other inedibles. We also have refugees collected during the attack, and we have twelve additional Marines to feed who have no provisions."

One of the Marines rustled. "Yes, well, sorry about that."

Davage sighed. "I forgot about the Monamas we saved during the attack. How many are there?"

Lady Tellerran spoke up. "Thirty-seven, Captain," she said through her endecar, her voice popping out through the blue trumpet as slow, slightly synthesized purr.

"Then we shall need to keep a sharp eye out for locales of possible forage and be prepared to go to shore when the opportunity presents itself. That shall be imperative. I'll assign several teams to man the telescopes' bells high to begin the search."

They continued hashing out the mundane details of their return voyage to the League. Outside, as seen through the meeting room windows, the stars moved, though at what seemed to be a crawl.

8—The *Killanjo* Tank

With the course Davage had set the *New Faith* was approaching its first Stellar Mach transverse. Stellar Mach was an extremely quick method of traveling from one point to another in space. Much faster than standard tachs, Stellar Mach was, nevertheless, a phenomena that nobody truly understood. Davage often listened to his friend, the great engineer, Lord Milos of Probert, and his scientist wife, Lady Branna, talk about it at dinner. The two babbled about points of transverse and singularities and eddie points, and Davage just listened and nodded his head, knowing that, although they sounded impressive, they really didn't know what they were talking about either. The Stellar Mach coil was Elder technology and had been used by the Elder-kind for centuries. However, after the passing of the Elders, the fundamentals of its use were lost. As such the Stellar Mach coils, which all Fleet vessels carried, were never used for more than three minutes at a time. Anything more than that, and the point where one emerged from the transverse would be unknown and random, and the possibility of hitting something along the way was greatly increased. Many ships, seeking to push the limit, had been lost in such a fashion, while others were blasted into atoms in an epic rail gun-like collision.

However, the risks and rewards of Stellar Mach were undeniable. For a Centennial journey such as the *New Faith* was currently on, using tach drives alone would take centuries to reach the League. With Stellar Mach, used to its safe limit and carefully planned, centuries would be cut down to about a little over two months. The geometry of a Stellar Mach transverse had to be calculated down to the minutest of details and triple checked; the slightest error could be disastrous. And, the effects of its use on the body could be crippling. To some, a rocketing jolt into Stellar Mach was like nothing, just a savage, bumpy ride. To others, it was a sickening, terrifying experience where some lost their sanity along the way. Some said the ship moved so fast it left one's soul behind. Most Fleet washouts in the early days of training were due to a lack of tolerance for Stellar Mach.

* * * * *

Thirty minutes before the ship was set to transverse a fifty second Stellar Mach run, all calculations had been checked and rechecked out to 12k decimal points—the math had to be perfect; otherwise, any error would cause them to either emerge in an unknown area or, worse, fly through something and be scattered into atoms. Fifty seconds from their current position was determined to be safe and obstruction free. The ship would accelerate to Stellar Mach speed, disappear into chaos for precisely 49.7478643254688234078121001233 4595 ... seconds and then emerge twelve light years away cutting several decades off their return trip. Deep within the ship, the SM coils were rumbling to a slow steady beat, ready to be unleashed and brought to full life at the correct moment, testing fate yet again.

SM was like being on a roller coaster and the crew, to avoid injury, had to lock into place in ready-made harnesses built into the walls of the corridors. They used those lock-in points during battle, which was also a harrowing ride, and they used them for SM, which could shake an unsecured person's teeth out of their mouths. Most of the non-essential crew were already locked into their positions ready to ride the ordeal out. All else would lock in at the last possible moment.

Captain Davage and Syg sat in his office, both eager to get the procedure over with. There came a knock at the door, and Ennez entered. "Ennez?" Davage said, surprised. "What are you doing up here? You hate SMs. You should be sulking in your dispensary right now, bemoaning your fate."

"I wanted to go over some readings I've begun to notice, just in case I don't survive this suicidal plunge we're about to take. I thought it important."

"Oh, Ennez, always so dramatic," Syg chided. "What readings?"

Ennez checked a pad he was holding. He adjusted his winged Hospitaler helmet and considered his words. "We are all starting to exhibit troubling signs of tissue degradation, Dav. It's not much at this point, but it's there, and we're all showing signs of it."

Davage was concerned. "All right, you have my attention. What's causing this?"

Ennez gazed at his pad and puzzled over the readings. "Well, that's the thing. I'm not certain. We're showing distress in our tissues, and that's a fact. It's not noticeable now, but, if it continues to progress, in a few weeks we'll begin to show significant inflammation in our joints, our tissues, most notably our kidneys, and our skin will, for lack of better terms, slough off."

Syg was appalled. "That sounds pretty gruesome, Ennez. What does Beth think?"

"She doesn't know either. The good news is I think, if we maintain our schedule, if we stay on course, or, better yet, arrive a touch early, then we can present ourselves at a proper Hospitaler sanctum and receive extensive examination and treatment. If these readings hold, I'm fairly well certain after ten weeks we'll still be at the beginning stages of this degradation and won't be overly addled. But, if we go much past that, every one of us will need significant treatment, and that's for sure."

"Well, I don't see any reason why we won't maintain our schedule," Davage said. "The ship is running in top shape, and every day we make substantial progress. I'll enquire with the engineers; perhaps we may risk lengthening the Stellar Mach transverses a touch and, as you say, arrive a bit early. This is very disturbing news. Perhaps we were subjected to some sort of radiation or other cosmic hazard that penetrated our shielding without our knowledge. Stay on it, if you would, and provide me with updates as they become available. And, I'm sure it doesn't need mentioning, but let's keep this to ourselves. We don't need a panic on our hands."

Ennez agreed.

The door opened, and Paymaster Stenstrom entered, dashing as usual in his long green HRN coat and rather mysterious in his mask. "Dav, I've an issue I need to discuss with you in private," he said noting Ennez's presence.

"Seems the issues are piling up prior to our SM. You may speak, Bel—Ennez has our full trust and confidence."

"Very well. I just received roll call. Everybody is present in their locked-in stations and ready for the call to Mach Steady, except for one person who is missing and unaccounted for."

"Missing?" Davage said, shocked. "Who?"

"Crewman Lasset from the Astro Lab. She has not checked into her assigned lock down station, nor is she in her quarters."

Davage turned and Sighted down through the levels of the ship to the Astro Lab far away on Deck 4. He saw the various Astro technicians and officers cubbied up into the walls in their lock down stations, awaiting the all clear to resume their work. One of the lock downs was notably empty—presumably where Crewman Lasset would go.

"Bel, what's her quarters number?"

Stenstrom waved his hands and produced, from thin air, a pad. Among other things, the mysterious Lord Stenstrom was also said to be a Tyrol sorcerer. He could make things appear and disappear with a wave of his hand with great skill.

He looked the pad over. "4-27."

Davage moved his Sight away from the lab, down the corridor to 4-27, her quarters. Seeing through the closed door, inside was a small, neat room decorated in a cheery fashion.

Empty.

"I don't see her. What about her MAGGA transponder?"

"It's not responding. Perhaps she's not wearing it. The Com has also announced for her presence at her lock down, and she has not responded to that either."

Davage was worried. "Come on, let's get down there and take a quick look. I want her found before the Stellar Mach event occurs. Bel, what's the count to Mach Steady, please?"

"Twenty-four minutes, fifty-two seconds. Should we delay the SM and recalculate?"

"No, out of the question. Unfortunately we must SM as planned; not doing so could add weeks to our return trip. All right, Bel, take the chair and command the ship. I'm going to find Crewman Lasset."

Stenstrom handed Davage the pad, and he, Syg and Ennez exited the office and went down the lift to Deck 4. Like termites in the wall, most of the crew were already locked into their harnesses and ready to ride out the SM. Some of the crew acknowledged the captain as he passed; others were asleep in their positions. One nervous crewmember had mis-done his straps. Ennez stopped to assist him, moving the straps to their correct positions and offering a lecture.

Davage checked the pad. It sparkled with MAGGA information as he walked past the crew, their transponders working perfectly and reading out on the pad display in a regular burst of data. The only one missing—Crewman Lasset.

"Where could she have gone, Dav? I don't like this," Syg whispered.

Davage panned around with his Sight. "Me neither. Personnel from the Astro Lab pride themselves on punctuality, and it's not like them to turn up missing especially before a harrowing event like an SM, and to violate regulations and walk about without their MAGGA." He stopped. "Ah! There she is!" he cried with relief.

"Where?"

"Wandering around two decks below near Cargo Hold 2. She's moving in an odd sort of fashion. She seems to be in a trance of some sort. Come on, Syg, let's Waft down there and get her. Ennez, after the Stellar Mach transverse is over, perhaps you'd like to look her over; she might require medical assistance."

"If I survive the SM," Ennez said, catching up to them. "Will you two please wait?" he said as Davage and Syg Wafted down several decks. Ennez, being a Brown, couldn't Waft. He'd have to get down the old fashioned way and walk.

They emerged in the dark, rather drafty corridor near Cargo Hold 2. It was near the bottom of the ship, and Syg rarely went there. It had an industrial, rather abandoned feel to it. Nobody else was around.

"Where is she, Dav?" Syg asked.

"Down that way," he pointed. They started walking. "She's still not reading on this pad."

"Should we wait for Ennez?"

"No, we haven't time."

"Perhaps she's experiencing some of what Ennez warned us about. Perhaps she's sick. I'm very concerned about that."

"As am I. We'll find out more as Ennez learns more."

As they approached the hatch to Cargo Hold 2, they spotted a solitary figure hugging the walls.

"Crewman Lasset!" Davage called out. "Crewman, we're nearing the call for Mach Steady. You should be in your lockdown. You have been missed by your peers. You could be injured."

The figure didn't respond.

"Crewman, are you all right?"

Davage placed his hand on her shoulder. "Crewman Lasset?"

She looked up at the captain with hollow, alien eyes.

She held something in her hand.

"Dav!" Syg cried.

There was a green flash.

Whirling around, Davage and Syg were no longer on the *New Faith*. They were standing in a type of medical facility, sterile, inhospitable and rather alien in appearance.

Crewman Lasset stood in front of them. She bore an unreadable expression and eyed them both passively.

"Crewman, what is the meaning of this?" Davage demanded.

Lasset lifted her hand, and a cone of ephemeral red light reached out and bathed Davage in a bloody glow. He dropped his pad and writhed in the light, falling to his knees.

Syg acted fast. She pumped her fist and blasted Lasset square in the chest with a Silver tech lance. Her Silver tech passed through her body, creating a round, fairly neat hole about the size of a tea saucer just below Lasset's sternum. Syg could even see through it like a knothole in a fencepost.

Lasset regarded the hole with indifference. Her body began rippling with a liquid sort of movement, and she fell apart into an amber mass of gel, clothes and all, the entire mess spreading out on the sterile floor in an expanding pool.

Syg ran to Davage's side. His Fleet coat and shirt smoked slightly. "Dav! Dav, are you all right?"

Davage shook his head and tried to recover. "I think so, Syg. That was ... amazing ... to say the least."

He stood, and they took a moment to get their bearings. They were in a large room with bleached white walls. The opposite side was composed of a solid wall of inhospitable geared, tightly-fitting machinery. The machinery filling the wall was not in operation, yet the methodical sounds of moving parts and turning gears throbbed from all around. A single door framed the far wall.

"I don't like this, Dav. Where are we, and what happened to Crewman Lasset?"

Crewman Lasset had broken apart into an amber pool encompassing a number of black, grit-like structures suspended within. Nearby was a small controller device made of gray polished stone. She had been holding it. Davage picked it up.

"That looks like the controller the *Killanjo* monster of Countess Alberta of Crossland was using when she pulled me away from the tombs," Syg recalled with a shudder.

The face of the controller was covered with flush glyph-like markings that blinked on occasion. "Here," he said, "see what you can make of this." He handed it to Syg.

Behind them, a shimmering green slit hung in the air. Through it, they could see the somber empty corridor of the *New Faith* where they'd come from. Davage inspected the slit. "This is a doorway of some sort, resonating in the gamma spectrum. It's just like Atrajak described in his book, and it's like what we encountered over Hoban and at Crossland."

He tested it with his hand, passing it through. "I can even feel a temperature difference; the *New Faith* is cooler than where we are now. The doorway seems stable; that's something anyway." Davage saw movement down the corridor on the *New Faith*. "Someone's coming. I can't see who it is."

Through the slit, a pair of shadows approached. There was Ennez walking down the corridor in his black and silver Hospitaler uniform, and the lithe, jacketed form of Lady Tellerran of Monama was at his side. She noticed the slit and jumped back with fright, hiding behind Ennez, who, apparently, was having a difficult time seeing it. Tellerran pointed with her long nailed hand, peeking out from behind his back with little quizzical black eyes. Ennez leaned down and peered in. He reached out and put his hand through the slit, waved it around, and then stuck his head though.

"Dav?" he asked. "What is this?"

"A gamma band doorway, used by the enemy."

"Where's Crewman Lasset?"

"There." Davage pointed at the pool of amber gel on the floor.

Ennez looked back through the slit and spoke a few words to Lady Tellerran. She violently shook her head, jangling her great mass of black hair about. She shrank back. Ennez then pulled out and expanded his Jet staff and came through without hesitation. "Amazing," he remarked, taking a good look around.

Syg pointed at the amber gel on the floor. "That, Ennez, is what is left of the enemy. It took Lasset's form, and I killed it with Silver tech."

Ennez got out his scanner and took various readings. "It's a type of protoplasm." He was puzzled. He got out a few vials from his sash and collected samples. "What's this?" he asked.

"What?"

Ennez put his scanner and vials away and reached down into the protoplasm. He pulled out a rugose brown object several inches high; it was human-shaped, crudely formed like an anthropomorphic doll. "This. What's this? Is this a nucleus of some sort?" He handed Syg his staff and placed it into a sample container from his sash.

Syg looked back at the remains "What about Crewman Lasset?"

"No trace of her in this mess," Ennez said. "Not Elder."

"I think we are certainly in the presence of the enemy," Davage said. "The Kestral Oligarchy, as Atrajak called them. The Golden People. Shape-shifters. Perhaps the crewman was abducted and her form borrowed or stolen."

A synthesized voice came from the doorway. "This is a place of death. This is their place." Lady Tellerran was crouched down near the doorway, holding her endecar with one shaking hand and hugging herself with the other. Apparently, she had summoned her courage and come through. She was clearly terrified. Ennez went to her.

"You know this place, my lady?" Davage asked.

"Yes."

"You've been here before?"

"Yes, or someplace like it. When I was a child. All of us …"

"What is done here?"

She pointed at the machinery along the far wall. "This is their Shocker Room. They bring us here as children. I remember it as yesterday. There were tables arranged on the open floor where they washed us, prodded us, and then put us into this machine, one after the next by the hundreds."

"Into this?" Syg asked looking at the complicated, inhospitable machinery. She shuddered. "For what purpose?"

"To stitch the Shockers, our control collars, deep into our necks with a great needle, which turns us into Berserkacides at their whim. They place us into the workings of the machine that are tight and full of gears that operate with precision movement, and we pass through. Some of us don't insert properly and are mangled to death along the way, their blood anointing the moving parts. They don't stop the machine, and they don't clean away the dead; they simply keep passing new ones through it. I remember being plunged into the dark, being closed in, not being able to move, and the bleeding and pain as the needle went in, brutally stitching my control collar into place. I came out on the other side a slave, lathered in my own blood and that of others, just one of thousands run through on that day. I remember pain—how it hurt." She placed her hand on her collarbone where the Shocker collar had once been. Ennez had removed it shortly after she came aboard, but its ghost troubled her.

Tellerran trembled. Ennez comforted her.

"Ennez, take her out of here, back to the *New Faith*. She's had enough."

"Come on, Dav," Syg said.

"No. We have approximately fifteen minutes before the Stellar Mach sequence begins. As Crewman Lasset's captain, I am duty bound to ensure her safety as best I can and return her to the ship, dead or alive. She's the daughter of Bannaster of St. Paris, and I've no intention of travelling to his home and telling him that his daughter is dead. She must be around here somewhere." He picked up the pad. "Look here, it's seeking her signal, but it's not locked on. We've fifteen minutes, twenty-two seconds, and I'm going to make good use of them. Stay here and guard the doorway."

As Ennez helped Tellerran back to the shimmering doorway, she spoke. "Tank, they probably took her to the Tank. That's where all the Elders go. Through the door." They passed through the green doorway and were back on the *New Faith*.

Davage, holding the pad, went to the door.

"Wait, I'm coming with you," Syg said. She threw a Silver tech lance out through the doorway into the corridor of the *New Faith*. She anchored the near end to the floor. She then created a multitude of Silver tech blobs from her hands that dripped to the floor as rain drops. Once they hit the floor, they changed shape into the form of tiny silver bug-like creatures. "I've learned the value of StT's, and have been training with Poe. They are quite awesome actually, and these StT's here will guard the doorway. I've given them orders to attack and kill anything other than us."

The StT's crawled about, positioning themselves around the green slit like army ants guarding a rotten log, ready to attack.

They made their way toward a door at the far side of the room. A few StT's sat on Syg's shoulder, ready to spring to life at her command. Tiny, fast and lethal, StT's were comforting to have around.

Davage checked the pad. No signal. Must be interference. He Sighted through the door, hoping to discover what was on the other side.

"What do you see?" Syg asked. "Tellerran mentioned a … Tank?"

"I'm not certain what she meant by that. I see a great confusion of tubes and pipes and a vast array of glass rectangular containers all lined up in a row."

Davage tried the door, and it opened. Beyond was a short walk that opened up into a long factory-like corridor that stretched off right and left a long way. Dead ahead was a T-bend ended in a half-wall and a rail. A deep abyss-like chasm yawned beyond the rail, giving one the impression of a vast amount of enclosed space. Far away, on the other side of the chasm, was a similar, mirror-image corridor that trailed right and left into the gloom. Above and below were more corridors.

The place was colossal. The continual throbbing of machinery filled their ears.

Lining the near wall was an innumerable collection of glass, or otherwise clear, rectangular containers about seven feet long. They were each mounted on a metal frame in a slightly reclined position, each supported by a host of wires, struts and coiled tubes. The containers looked rather like coffins.

Davage and Syg moved down the corridor to their left. Most of the glass containers were empty and clean, and others here and there were full of a brackish brown substance.

"Dav, what is all this?" Syg approached one of the full containers. "It looks like mud."

THUMP!

Something moved inside the container, and Syg jumped back. Davage Sighted the interior.

"Creation, Syg, there's a person in there!" He unsaddled his CARG and took a swing at the container. The glass-like surface cracked, but resisted the blow. Brown, reeking fluid leaked from the cracks. Davage wound up and gave it another fierce hit. This time the container gave way, spilling its noisome contents on the floor.

A body had been soaking inside: a young man. He was discolored into an unhealthy, swollen black, and his hair was caked into a smear. He coughed and sputtered. Syg reached down to clear his face getting a little of the substance on her fingers. She immediately pulled back. "Gods, Dav, it feels like acid. My fingers are burning!"

The man began thrashing, opening and closing his fists.

"Hold on, sir, we shall get you to safety aboard our ship," Davage said.

The man screamed. He clawed and tugged at his bloated, blackened skin. He tore at it. Davage tried to calm him. He screamed and wailed.

Syg, watching with horror, sent a single StT off her shoulder and into his ear where it vanished inside. After a moment, the man stopped struggling. He lay still on the floor.

He was dead. "It was breaking my heart, Dav—the poor man was in agony. I gave him peace. I couldn't allow him to carry on any further." Davage stood. She expected him to put up a fuss, to argue for rescue and treatment as opposed to a mercy killing.

But, he said none of that.

"Is this what they do, Syg? This place, this 'Tank'? Is this how they create *Killanjo*? Soak them in this poison until they're stark raving mad and cut themselves out of their own pained flesh? Is this what will happen to our daughter some day? Is she to be imprisoned in one of these very coffins with no one to help her and emerge like that poor man?"

He looked around, rage obvious in his face. "We shall find Crewman Lasset, and we shall put this vile place to the sword, Syg. We shall deprive the enemy of its use and spare all those imprisoned here."

"Destroy this place? How?"

"StT's, Silver tech" He checked the pad. "Twelve minutes, thirty seconds. Create as many as you can, spread them out, while I continue looking, then we burn this place to cinders." He went to the rail and held out the pad.

It beeped. "Lock! There she is! Up there! Start creating your StT's, Syg. Create as many as you can, I'm going after her. Remember, twelve minutes!"

Before Syg could reply, Davage Wafted away.

He went up about a thousand feet, appearing on a corridor exact in every way to the one he'd come from: a long industrial corridor with rows of empty glass coffins. He checked the pad. She was still up about two hundred feet and on the other side of the chasm. He got his bearings and Wafted again, appearing in a quick blast.

More coffins. He ran down the rows, coattails flying.

Coffins everywhere.

The pad beeped. MAGGA lock. Here she was, inside a filled coffin right in front of him. Ten minutes left.

"Crewman Lasset!" he cried. "Crewman!"

A muffled voice came from within. "...captain..."

"I'm going to break through the glass. Ready yourself." He unsaddled his CARG, wound back, and swung. The heavy CARG smashed the face of the coffin. Brown fluid and Crewman Lasset came spilling out. She was in poor shape, skin red and inflamed, half out of her head. "...captain..." she said again.

He took off his coat and wrapped her up. "Come, let us back to the ship where relief awaits."

"Well, well," came a chiding voice.

Standing down the corridor were several *Killanjo*, all hunched and skinless, throbbing with stitched-on parts. Chained at their side were several Berserkacides, bestial on four arms and two legs and eager to tear out his throat. Beady eyes fixed on him.

"Looks like we've another one for the Tank. He's a fine big fellow; won't he make a lovely monster."

Davage picked Lasset up and tried to Waft away.

One of the *Killanjo* screamed, casting their foul spells, a difficult weapon to overcome. The sound got into Davage's head, and he quickly began to stiffen up, paralysis taking hold.

He couldn't Waft. They were going to have him.

At the last moment, he took Lasset and leaned over the railing. Over-balanced, he plummeted over the side, falling away from the *Killanjo's* eager grasp. He fell like a statue, stiff and immobile. Floor after floor tumbled past, the *Killanjo* spell still rooted in his head. As he fell, he caught glimpses of creatures jumping into the empty space of the chasm after him, birds and spiders, elongated humanoids and other completely alien beasts, all tinted in gold.

A ruddy golden tentacle wrapped around his waist like a bullwhip. A golden alien beast from above had him.

A cone of silver light came up from below followed by a wall of Silver tech lead. A *Seeker* familiar, one of Syg's old standbys, roared up fast. A perfect one-by-four foot replica of their old *Straylight*-class vessel, the *Seeker,* blasted the alien creature with tiny but potent Silver tech shot. Mangled, the creature let go, and the *Seeker,* controlled by Syg far below, came up and got under Davage like a dutiful Silver pet. It instantly grew in size, stretching out to about ten feet. Davage at last could move, and he settled onto its neck, riding it like a horse.

All around was chaos. He saw ten more of Syg's Silver tech *Seekers* climbing into the chasm, engaging with the enemy, swirling about amidst the moan of Battleshot, alien roars and the hissing collisions of Silver tech with red light.

From the corridors all around, fire erupted, and glass shattered. Syg's StT's were spreading out, getting into everything and going off like grenades, blowing the dreaded Tank into ruins. Several of the *Seekers* broke away and strafed the rows with concentrated shot, creating tremendous damage.

A few golden aliens streaked past headed for the bottom of the chasm, blown apart by Syg's familiars. A *Seeker* went down in a blob.

The *Seeker* Davage was riding came down to the correct level—there Syg was standing by the rail, controlling all her familiars at once. A host of dead *Killanjo* and Berserkacides, sundered and flayed, lay scattered around her. Slinging Lasset over his shoulder, he jumped off, and they ran down the corridor to the waiting Shocker Room, as Tellerran had described it. An enraged mass of *Killanjo* came from the opposite end, ready to meet them.

"Kill!" Syg cried, and the StT's sitting on her shoulder jumped off and scrabbled ahead into the *Killanjo.* Fiery explosions raked their numbers as the StT's took them down in ragged clumps. The over-sized *Seeker* Davage had ridden flew alongside and polished off the rest with a deadly strafing run.

A tumult of red light bathed it from all over, and the *Seeker* tumbled away, melting, destroyed. Golden enemies flying in the chasm were rallying.

They entered the Shocker Room at a run. Syg went through the shimmering doorway, followed by Davage and Lasset, and, just like that, they were back into the *New Faith's* corridor.

Ennez and Tellerran were still there. "Gods, you found her?" he cried.

Davage handed Lasset's trembling body, still wrapped up in his coat, to Ennez. "Get her to the dispensary right away! She was immersed in a caustic fluid and requires immediate treatment. What is our SM count?"

"About two minutes!" Ennez and Tellerran went down the hallway. "Come on, Dav!"

"We must guard the doorway! Syg, can you close this?"

She struggled with the controller, mashing buttons, trying to get it to vanish. Nothing happened.

Through the doorway, a battle was in progress in the Shocker Room. Berserkacides and *Killanjo* faced the StT's Syg had left behind, and they ravaged the attackers with savage blasts and searing fire, but were soon used up and gone. Red lights dashed them aside.

A Berserkacide tried to come through, and Davage CARG'ed its head off.

There was a moment of calm on the other side as the *Killanjo* and Berserkacides parted.

Several Golden People wearing decadent togas stepped forth, commanding the room.

The Kestral Oligarchy. The Enemy. There they were, wearing human forms.

The ship began to buck; the SM transverse was moments away.

"Mach Steady!" came a cry over the Com from Paymaster Stenstrom.

The Golden People glared at Davage and Syg, eyes flaring. One of them raised his hand and sent out a cone of searing red light. Syg met it with a Silver tech beam—the two forces combining and swirling in midair through the doorway.

Stellar Mach was at hand. The *New Faith* kicked and surged forward in a shaking, bone-grinding whirlwind of light and chaos as Davage and Syg held onto each other. The shimmering doorway flickered and went out as the ship surged ahead, leaving the Golden People and their monsters and their burning Tank far behind.

9—The Metal Man's Ordeal

Kabyl, the Lord of Blanchefort and son of Captain Davage and Countess Sygillis, felt victorious as he and his cousins returned to Kana. It felt like they'd been gone from home a long time.

He had passed Sam's Trials. His Wellerman's March was over.

Kay's cousin, Sarah of Blanchefort, always the planner, was full of questions as her brother Phillip flew the *Goshawk* back into orbit, slowly lowering it into the thickening atmosphere. "So, now that we've got the pieces to this thing, what are we going to do with it?"

Sam's Trial, which would have cost Kay his life should he have failed, was to collect three odd pieces of an arcane machine called the *Oberphilliax*, created by the departed House of Want in 000011ax. Sam had foreseen the coming of the *Oberphilliax* and was keen to see it realized. Her intention with the machine was, up to this point, unknown. She repeatedly had stated that it could "save their souls," but Kay had no idea what that meant.

The quest to recover the *Oberphilliax* had taken them across Kana and deep into Xaphan space.

"We're going to hit the Grove and reassemble it," Kay said.

"Then what?" she asked.

"Then, I don't know, Sarah. I suppose Sam will reappear and state what's on her mind. At least I don't have to worry about her trying to kill me anymore now that the Trials are said and done."

Lord Lon of Probert, their friend from the south of Vithland, had come with them to Waam and had been a great help. The whole way back he'd been tinkering with the three pieces of the Machine, making little discoveries here and there and keeping careful notes. His parents, Lord Milos of Probert and his mother, Lady Branna, were renowned engineers and scientists in the League, and Lon had inherited their skill and curiosity.

"I've determined what piece is what," he said proudly. "The centerpiece here is obvious, and the side with the ovular indentation appears to be the front. This piece over here," he said pointing, "is, after close examination, clearly the right side, or the right leg. The remaining piece is then, naturally, the left leg. When fully assembled, the three pieces will make a sturdy arch, standing roughly seven feet tall."

"Does it really matter what leg goes where?" Sarah asked. "They both look the same to me."

"Of course it matters!" Lon cried, beside himself. "Also, there are literally thousands of connections to be made. Over the past few days, I've identified and mapped a good number of them. I anticipate the reassembly time to take a minimum of two days, under optimal circumstances and built-in breaks for lunch and dinner."

"I assumed we were simply going to slap it together," Sarah said.

"That's why you're you, and I'm me." After his fine showing in Waam, battling both the Singing Ten and the Spectres, Lon's confidence had soared. The four of them, Lon most of all, had grown from their experience.

Phillip, following the directions given to him by the space and air controllers in Bern, settled the *Goshawk* into the mouth of the Gaston Way and headed north, winding easily through the mountain passes. Sarah opened the hatch and breathed in the cold air, her blue pony-tail livid in the wind. "Feel that?" she cried. "Home!" She fearlessly leaned over the open ledge of the hatch, a long fall just inches away and watched the gray mountains whiz by. "Maybe we'll see the Wraith today."

The Wraith of Gaston, a spectral creature said to haunt the pass, was one of Sarah's favorite ghosts.

"I doubt it," Kay said.

"Why? Why not?"

"Because ..."

From the pilot's chair, Phillip cut them off. "Look, ghosts and goblins are great fun, Sarah, but we've got a very real problem on our hands, and we need to discuss it right now."

Sarah was unsympathetic. "Oh Creation, we're not going to start talking about Thomasina again, are we?"

"We are!" Phillip said.

Even Kay and Lon were tired of the topic. In the Xaphan city of Waam, they had met Thomasina the 19th of Waam, Portator and magistrate of the municipality of Auld. She was a fiery, bold woman and immediately took a liking to Phillip, culminating in her attempting to prevent him from leaving Auld by force. She tried to kidnap him. She and her Singing Ten chased them through the streets, and Phillip had been talking about her the entire seven day trip back.

"Phillip, either admit that you enjoyed her attentions, or be quiet about it," Kay said.

"How could I possibly enjoy such a spectacle? What are we to do if she appears at our home?"

"Then be a man one way or the other!" Sarah yelled. "Either give her a big hug and a kiss and lead her to your waiting bed, or roll up your sleeves and fight it out!"

Phillip stewed the rest of the way back. He angled in over the great mass of Castle Blanchefort and then out over the vast green expanse of the Grove.

Sarah leaned out the open hatch. "Hey, what's that down there?" she cried, pointing.

Down below in the center of an ancient Vith amphitheater glinting in old light was a giant metal man, like a colossal statue towering over the fallen stone and tumbled rock. Phillip banked the *Goshawk* and did a slow orbit around it.

Kay was elated. "That's Sam! Look! That's the Metal Man she created that night in the Grove when the Trials began. I told you about that, remember? She's here!"

Sarah struggled to get a good look. "You mean Sam made that giant creature down there?"

"She sure did, out of NIGHTMARE magic."

Sarah was suitably impressed. Lon pressed in to have a look. "And you're saying that Lady Sammidoran is inside that fellow, even now, is that correct?"

"Yep! His chest opens up, revealing a small cavity within. He's constructed like a battle wagon—nothing's getting to her in there." Kay Sighted down through the thick armor of the Metal Man's chest hoping to catch a glimpse of her, but the interior was murky and clouded. "I can't Sight into it. She might still be in there, or, perhaps she got out and went inside the castle."

"Hey!" Sarah cried. "What's that?" she asked pointing to a huge pewter object at the far end of the amphitheater.

"That's his chariot. That's what he flies around in. Those three manifestations of my Gifts I told you about, Waft, Cloak and Sight, used to be harnessed to it."

"I'd like to have seen that," Sarah said.

Kay was giddy seeing the Metal Man standing safe and sound down below bearing his precious cargo. "Sarah!" he cried pulling his coat on, "I'd like you to power up and throw me out the hatch."

"Why? Oh wait—you want to Waft down and show off for Sam, right?"

"Yes I do! I want to show her what I learned while she was away. Creation, I want to hold her in my arms again so much I can taste it!"

Phillip, flying the *Goshawk*, gained a little altitude. "Well, wait a moment, Kay, what about the Machine?"

"Yes, yes," Lon said, "what about the pieces we collected?"

"There's an oak clearing to the west of here a short distance, that's where Sam said the Machine would one day stand. Let's re-assemble it there. I want it to stand exactly where she said it would."

"Ok, ok, I see it," Phillip said. "You go and have a few minutes alone with Sam. I'll land the ship and we'll get the parts and meet you and Sam there."

"We'll need proper tooling," Lon said, "to make all the fine attachments, and we'll probably need power as well."

"The smithy by the lake should have everything we need," Sarah added. "All right, I'm powered up, I'll throw you a good one. Hey! Don't let Sam do anything with that Metal Man and his chariot until I've had a chance to take a good close look at him, ok! Promise?" She blushed a little. "And, I suppose I've some apologizing to do to Sam ... for me being such a git and all."

Kay saddled his CARG. "I'm certain Sam won't need any apologies, Sarah. She'll be overjoyed to see you." He looked himself over. "Well, I'm ready when you are."

Sarah led Kay to the hatch, waited a moment for the Metal Man to come into range and then heaved Kay out into open air. He sailed a good distance savoring the cold bite of the northern air. This was home.

Under full control he allowed himself to fall a few moments then Wafted fast in a cloud, reappearing on the Metal Man's shoulder. Looking up, he watched the *Goshawk* soar away to the east and disappear behind the trees.

"Sam!" he cried, knocking on the Metal Man's head. "It's me, *Cerri-Tela*! It's Kay! I passed the Trials! You don't have to worry about trying to kill me anymore! I've got the parts of the Machine to prove it."

No answer.

Kay clambered around on his shoulder. The giant's metal skin was dense and solid, like a bank vault. "Sam?"

He unsaddled his CARG and tapped on his chest, making a deep, hollow: BOOM, BOOM, BOOM.

The Metal Man moved slightly. Kay jumped down and faced him. The Metal Man turned his head a little.

"Lord Blanchefort ..." he whispered.

"The Trials are done. Let me see Sam."

"I've little left to sustain me," he said. "I'm near my end."

"Your job is complete. I'm here to protect Sam now."

"The ... enemy is all around. Where is the Silver God?"

Kay looked the Metal Man over. His body was covered with damage: chips and dents, blasts from heat, pock marks and gouges from monstrous hands trying to rip his chest open, to get at Sam. His chariot was deformed and partially melted from relentless attacks. Kay allowed his Sight to drift back in time to witness for himself what had happened.

It was terrifying. While he was undergoing the Trials, Sam and her Metal Man were under constant siege. Kay saw him standing in his chariot flying through an ethereal night. Green clouds burst open all around him belching forth monsters, the Metal Man unable to do anything except endure and attempt to outrun them through the ether.

Fire and claws and beating fists. He saw strange cities and horrid roads leading to ruin.

There was no outrunning the demons—they were all around, never tiring. And then, just when the Metal Man was ready to be overwhelmed, a silver light approached and drove the enemy away.

Carahil, swimming through the ether, leant his protection time and time again, flying at his side.

And, according to the Metal Man, the danger hadn't passed.

Kay whirled around. The empty environs and fallen stone of the amphitheater where he and Sarah and Phillip once played 'war' as kids now seemed sinister and isolated. Listening, he heard whispered voices; looking about he saw shimmering, indistinct movement.

He unsaddled his CARG. There was a definite ring of solace stretching out about a hundred yards all around the Metal Man, with him in the center. Beyond was a lonely wasteland decorated in green veils. It was the *Killanjo* Aunt Torri had told him about: the enemy, the demons that had tormented Sam and her people for centuries, and the same demons that nearly had killed him in this very Grove not long ago.

Why weren't they attacking? Was something protecting the Metal Man? He noticed the grass-filled stone cracks of the amphitheater were littered with little blue objects. He fished one out of the ground.

It was a tiny blue figurine of a smiling Carahil. These figurines must be what kept the enemy at bay.

He heard a voice. *"Kay ... Kay .. eeeeeeheheeehehehe ..."*

It was *her!!*

Standing at the perimeter of the protection Carahil provided was the bent, female demon who had nearly killed him weeks before. Hatred surged through his soul.

"Hi ya, Kay," she said in a wiry voice through gritted teeth. "Have you missed me?"

Skinned, a bloody mess, wearing a golden mask and a beaded dress under a clotted swirl of twisted red hair, she raised her hand and wiggled her fingers at him.

His heart pounded and his hand clenched over the hilt of his CARG. How he'd dreamed of facing *her* again. "I've been waiting my chance to kill you," he croaked.

"Oh?" She crouched down a little and brandished a squat, dirty knife. "Well, here I am, lover boy. I was hoping to have another taste of you, mmmmmhuhuh. One bite just wasn't enough, eeeeeheheheeee."

Kay readied his CARG. "I know you!" he said. "You are a *Killanjo*, a distorted future image of my sister, Lady Hathaline, yet there's nothing left of her in you," Kay said. "For my sister, my *true* sister, and for my beloved Sam, I'm going to split you in two right down the center! I've been waiting for this moment!"

She blew him a kiss with her bloody hand. She crouched, ready to fight. "Then, why don't you come over here and get me, Kay? Maybe you'll let me fuck you one last time ... mmmmmmm, for old time's sake."

In the distance there was deep, throaty buzzing, far off but rapidly closing in, like the drone of an incoming cloud of locusts.

Kay's first thought was to take the *Killanjo* up on her offer, Waft into her and start fighting. But, there was the Metal Man with Sam within towering over him. He had to guard them.

He stood his ground. "I'll have a pass this time," he said. "But, don't concern yourself, I'll be dealing with you soon enough."

Hathaline's *Killanjo* became agitated. "Oh, I see. Worried about your girlfriend, are you? She's dead ... sooner or later. She's dead!! I'm going to kill her! Understand?"

Behind her several *Killanjo* appeared in feathery green slits. Two of them were carrying odd, tube-like weaponry. They positioned themselves and took aim, holding the weapons like one would a shoulder-mounted rocket. They were readying to attack Sam.

Kay drew his Poltava and fired.

POW! He hit the *Killanjo* between the eyes and his head erupted. His weapon clattered to the stone, followed soon after by his dead body.

Kay changed his aim and fired again.

POW! That one was for Hathaline's throat.

Missed! She moved like a panther and the shot went wide. She opened her mouth and began an ugly-sounding screech.

Screech ... He remembered sitting in Aunt Torri's library before he and his cousins had set out to Waam. Aunt Torri, or 'Dimples' as he called her, told him all about *Killanjo*, that they had many weapons. They could cast a horrid spell that rendered Elders helpless. It had happened to him twice already: once in Castle Durst, and once by Hathaline herself in the Grove, where she then mutilated and sodomized him.

Dimples had said it was crucial to not let them cast their spells.

He could feel it filling his brain.

Kay Wafted fast, appearing to her right. He rammed his CARG into her jaw, dislodging it with a satisfying pop and knocking her down.

He turned to the second *Killanjo*. His face and arms were covered with fused-on fingers which moved back and forth with a cilia-like coordination. He opened his mouth to cast a spell.

Kay swung and bisected him through the waist. Before his two pieces could hit the ground, Kay quartered him from head to groin.

Hathaline recovered and made to attack again. He extended the Silver tech shaft of his CARG like a piston, hitting her hard in the face a second time. She spun away, holding her jaw which was hanging off her bloody face at a grotesque acute angle.

Kay moved in for the blessed kill. This was it for the *Killanjo* of his little sister.

Sight. He saw someone large in dirty gold armor attacking him from the rear. He turned just in time to meet a huge, grotesque weapon shaped like a phallus. A giant man in horrid golden armor stood there wielding it. He gritted his teeth. "Not very nice to our sister, are you? And what about me, Kay?" he said, slavering. "Know who I am?"

Kay knew who he was. He didn't need Sight or anything else to tell him.

"I'm counting on you to protect your sisters while I'm gone. Can you do that for me, Chief?"

"Yeah ..."

Maser, his little brother—still in training clothes. This foul, giant-sized man was the *Killanjo* of his little brother.

For a moment he couldn't react. The thought of it left him in a stupor; his sister and his little brother both turned into monsters.

He was wide open, and Hathaline tackled him hard from behind, sending him to the ground. Furiously, he tried to stand, Hathaline's *Killanjo* all over him rasping and spitting, possessing a wiry, unnatural strength.

Screeching, more spells—this time coming from Maser.

As he struggled, Kay became aware of buzzing—deafening buzzing. Giant bugs were dropping into the clearing like black hail.

Paraflies, they had to be! Paraflies had saved him before when Hathaline was about to finish him off, and here they were again. Their presence was a comfort.

"Goddamned bugs!" Hathaline screeched, her jaw still hanging. She waved at the Paraflies as they came in, trying to land on her sticky body. A cloud of them followed behind, like locusts descending on a cornfield, just moments from completely overwhelming the amphitheater. The Paraflies seemed more aggressive this time—they seemed to be stinging or biting, and Hathaline reacted with panic.

"Come on, let's get out of here!"

"Aaaa!" Maser cried as he picked the immobile Kay up. "They're stinging me, the little shits!"

Hathaline produced a small controller, and, using it, she created a feathery slit of green in midair. She disappeared through it fast. Before Kay knew what was happening, Maser tossed him in.

Flash! He was through the shimmering green doorway in a swampy, humid darkness. Kay could see the amphitheater through the green slit as if he were seeing it through a viewing screen. Paraflies were coming in fast. Maser picked up one of the fallen rocket-like weapons, leveled it and fired. A great blast of energy came out, snaked forward, and struck the Metal Man in the chest. A halo of fire! Kay saw him topple over in flames, and then Maser's *Killanjo* came through the slit, blocking his view.

Sam!!

Maser pawed at the few Paraflies that had managed to come through with him. He stomped on them, hacked them with his sword. "They won't die!" Hathaline joined him and, after some doing, they managed to silence them.

It was dark on the other side of the slit, a greenish twilight. Kay, unable to move, seemed to be lying on a barren coastline on coarse grass under an unfamiliar sky. He felt far away from Kana. Through the green slit he could see the amphitheater swirling with Paraflies. Fire and explosions in the distance.

Sam was burning!

The buzzing of the Paraflies had knocked a bit of the *Killanjo* spell from his head. He moved slightly. He had to help Sam!

"Ah, no ... no! You stay right where you are!" Hathaline fell on him and screamed again. Kay covered his ears, but the sound of the spell went right through anyway and got in his head. He struggled with her for another moment and then was still. The *Killanjo* spell took effect. Once again, he was rendered helpless. He stiffened up and could move no more. He had no way to combat it. No Paraflies to save him, they were on the other side of the green slit, on Kana.

Hathaline stood, reared back and kicked him hard across the cheek. She turned and fiddled with her hanging jaw. Maser came and helped," Get away from me!" she yelled.

"Shut up! Shut up!" he roared in response, roughly snapping her jaw back into place with a gristly crunch. She opened and closed her fists in pain and fury.

She turned back to Kay. "This time, I'm going to do you until you're dead, understand? Dead!" she said smashing her bloody hand into his face. "This time you're not walking away! You're on our side now. This is our world, and there is no help for you here!"

Eager laughing and a line of bobbing torches emerged from the dark. Several other *Killanjo*, each a new description of depravity, joined them, waving torches about. They saw Kay lying in the grass and slavered. "What meat have you brought us?" one hissed, distorted in torchlight.

"A young man, healthy and strong. My brother …" Hathaline said with disgust.

"Ah." They threw their torches down "Then let us eat. A feast is best shared."

Hathaline stood over Kay, "Just remember, I want his heart, his balls and his ass. They're mine!"

Like zombies feasting on an unfortunate victim, they fell on Kay and ripped at his clothes, exposing the sweet meat underneath. They jostled with each other to get at him and have the best parts.

Kay was about to be eaten alive.

There came a sizzling flash at the open gate to Kana. Something happened at that moment, rough and chaotic. One of the *Killanjo* was roughly pulled backward and away, out of Kay's immobile line of sight. After a bewildering moment, the *Killanjo's* streaming torso, missing waist and legs, came flying into their midst like a torn-open bag of guts. They reacted with confusion.

"What has happened? Who would dare?" They scrambled, looking around.

Through the shimmering slit, Kay saw the Metal Man lying on his side engulfed in fire. The Metal Man was propping himself up on one arm, his chest area was above the fire. The doors to his metal chest were open revealing a tomb-like hollow interior. A cast-aside bed sheet was draped out the opening, burning.

The interior was vacant, no Sam.

One of the *Killanjo* screamed. There was a rending of bone and ripping flesh.

Their voices shuddered with fear.

"What? What is it?"

"It's a Monama! Look!"

"A Monama? A female Monama!"

"Where, where is she?"

"There she is, over there! Look, she's big! Bigger than the rest!"

"Ha, Monama ... On your knees, slave!"

"On your knees! Serve us in your worthlessness!"

"Get on your knees. Wha—Aaaaa!"

"Aaaaaaaa!"

There was an ululation of surprised screams and agonized wails underscored by a rasping, guttural yowling of hatred and fury, like that from an enraged animal. Bones cracked, flesh was torn, entrails dangled. Things were tossed into the air and over the side of the cliff.

"Turn her! Show her the crystal. The Crystal!"

"Turn her!"

"Look into the light, Monama! Look! What are you doing?"

"Aaaaaaa!"

Kay saw a carnival of red light waving about.

More screaming.

A *Killanjo* creature came back to Kay and clattered roughly into the grass leaning over him, slobbering in fear. "I'll kill this one first, and ..."

A slender, pale fist blasted though his chest and roughly pulled the *Killanjo* away into the darkness.

Something thin and pale bounded onto Kay, lithe and panther-like. The next thing Kay knew, he was picked up effortlessly and whisked from the area at incredible speed, passing through the green slit with a sizzling hiss and back into the relative peace of Kana.

Sam was carrying Kay away, running as fast as a cheetah. She had emerged from the burning Metal Man, entered the green slit where no Monama dares to tread and slaughtered the *Killanjo* with lust and fury. Her hands and claws were clotted with blood and bits of bone and hair. A Monama was finally enraged enough to stand and fight, after thousands of years. The *Killanjo* never stood a chance.

Sam had come out for him.

Glancing back, Kay saw two bloody forms gazing out through the vanishing slit: Hathaline and Maser. They had survived.

Damn!

Cradled in her bloody arms, Sam and Kay looked at each other for the first time in weeks. Neither said anything, but their glance spoke for them.

To touch you again ...

I am yours, and you are mine, Arin-Dan.

Cerri-Tela ...

My place is at your side, and yours is at mine.

I love you ... How I love you ... How proud I am of you ...

She stopped near the line of trees and put Kay down.

"Gods, I was worried about you, Sam!" Kay cried. "It's all right. It's all right now. Come with me to the castle and we'll find a safe place where the demons cannot follow.

Sam threw her arms around Kay. "I can't Kay. I can't go to the castle. I have to keep running."

"But why? We'll keep you safe here."

"Because I promised."

"Promised who?"

"Carahil. He's been protecting me, without his help I'd have been killed by now. In a dream he told me that he is being accused of committing crimes that he hasn't done. He said the gods believe that I am his Keeper of Secrets and that they wish to capture me to discover his activities. I don't understand it all fully."

"What has Carahil done?"

Sam wept. "I don't know. Nothing. I'm tired of running, Kay. I'm tired of being away. I don't want to run anymore," she said pleading.

"You needn't run. We'll face the unknown together."

Sam summoned her resolve and pushed Kay away. She hugged herself in misery. "I can't! I promised Carahil I'd run. I'd run as long as I can. He said it was important! I just ... I just wanted to see you first, for a moment, to give me strength. I shouldn't have come. The Metal Man is dead and I've no NIGHTMARE magic left."

Kay, still stiff from the *Killanjo's* spells, tried to approach her. His Sight drifted away, and the future unfolded.

The glade filling with *Killanjo.* Reaching hands and blood. Golden People eventually arriving to take Sam themselves. The castle in flames, the towers falling. A Horned God reveling in it all.

Sam captured, Kay killed.

A beating temple in the ground. Sam being tormented before the insane Horned God and filled with his infernal secrets. The Golden People and the *Killanjo* all servants of the Horned God. It was the Horned God attempting to frame Carahil for *his* crimes.

He saw Carahil and other gods in animal shapes being carried away in chains to a City of Many Forms by the Golden People, never to return.

The future was full of pain and death for them and for the gods; anyway he looked, there it was. Turn right, turn left, go back: die, die, die!

And then, The Horned God, with a free hand, would destroy Kana and all on it.

Wait! One possibility, one slim thread. If Sam could elude the Horned God long enough, confound him, deny him, then there was a chance ... The gods might rally. Carahil might triumph.

Sam, anguished, took Kay's chin with her bloody hands and savored his face for a moment. "I must go, Kay. I have to keep running."

He couldn't let her go. "Sam, let me come with you! Let me stand at your side!"

"You can't follow me, Kay! I love you. Pray for me!"

Kay struggled. He was still so stiff from the *Killanjo's* spells. He knew this was going to happen, but he couldn't let her go. "Sam, please take me with you."

Standing there in her black, veil-like garments, she looked at him one last time.

"*Ja chandle de ne infir portaleis tarne Telmus,*" she said in Anuie. She ripped off her Snugs medallion and then Blinked away.

Kay was stunned by what she had said.

10—Sam's Confession

Kay stood there alone in the clearing. He Sighted ahead and saw nothing of further note, no *Killanjo*, no Golden People, no Horned God. Apparently, they were after Sam, she being the one the Horned God wanted. Kay and his Grove were of no consequence.

Carahil begged her to run, and she was running. How long could she last?

He had to help her.

Behind him was the Metal Man, toppled over, propped up on one arm, the fires dying around him in the cold air. He was battered and blackened, but he had held. He had protected Sam to the last.

The doors to his chest were open. Kay approached to have a look. Inside was a small cavity about two and a half feet deep and eight feet long. The back portion of the cavity was lined with a soft mattress, like an inverted bed. There was some sort of null or anti-gravity field inside the cavity, and one could lie back and rest at ease even though the Metal Man was standing vertical. The burned remains of a red sheet from his bedroom was in the cavity as well. It smelled like Sam.

Sam had slept there in safety, clutching a sheet from his bedroom for comfort.

Kay climbed back out and jumped down. The Metal Man then shimmered for a moment and vanished, back to the shadowlands from whence he came.

His life and mission over, Sam's magic at an end. Kay lamented his passing—he was all of Sam he had to cling to, and now he was gone. Worry and dread for her began to build inside.

He made his way out of the amphitheater and walked to the clearing where Sarah, Phillip and Lon should be waiting with the pieces of the Machine. He needed a moment to think. Where was Sam now? What was happening to her?

And, what had she said before she departed?

"*Ja chandle de ne infir portaleis tarne Telmus,*" she had said in Anuie.

"I have written for you my confession in the Telmus Grove near the lake."

What did that mean?

* * * * *

Sarah, Phillip and Lon were all there in the clearing, as well as Lord Peter and Lady Poe. Everybody was all smiles.

Lt. Kilos and Tweeter were there also. "Kay!" she said, elated. "There you are! We were starting to get worried! Great to see you! I saw the *Goshawk* come in! About time you all showed up! Where's Sam?"

He told them what happened. He told them everything.

Ki sped off to check the grounds near the amphitheater for more *Killanjo*. Lady Poe was deeply concerned. She waved her hands, and several Bark dogs, her vigilant Silver tech familiars that could hear much and see far without tiring, formed in front of her. She gave them their orders and they spread out in different directions to guard the Grove. One trotted to the far end of the clearing and flopped down of all fours.

With another wave, Lady Poe created over twenty pastel-colored Whisper familiars.

"I have assigned several Barks to watch the area and discover intruders. I also have the clearing here Whisper-locked now, Kay. Nothing outside of the Whisper's veil will be able to hear or see a thing in this clearing unless they know the password. And, it is going to be ..."

"Mother, let me pick!" Sarah cried.

"Fine, fine, you may pick," Lady Poe said.

"Frogs in Winter!" Sarah announced.

"Yes, thank you," Poe responded. "'Frogs in Winter' it is. Tomorrow we shall pick a new one."

The Whispers flew in a lazy, ladybug fashion colorfully spiraling about the clearing, some landing in the trees.

Lon and Lord Peter had the Machine assembled to the point that it resembled all the old paintings Kay had seen of it. It looked like a rugose silver arch. The legs seemed to have dug into the ground on their own, and it had a very earthy, tree-like look to it. Several colorful Whispers climbed up the legs.

"You're certain you want it out here in the Grove, Kay?" Lord Peter asked.

Kay's thoughts were elsewhere.

Sam ...

"Kay?" Peter repeated.

"What? Yes, yes, uncle," Kay replied. "I'm sorry. I want it exactly where Sam said it would be. Right here."

Lon scrutinized the work they'd done. "We're about half-way complete. The assembly is easier than I'd thought. For lack of specific direction, we gave it an east-to-west facing. That should maximize its operation."

"Fine by me."

Sam all alone, running for her life ...

"Where is the power source," Lord Peter asked.

"We don't have one."

They sat in the clearing and watched as Lon, Lord Peter and Phillip continued the reassembly. Kay sat there in the grass, feeling dead.

Where was Sam?

"I'll leave these Barks and Whispers here," Lady Poe said. "As a temporary protection, they should function quite well. Just remember the password."

Kay didn't react.

"I have written for you my confession in the Telmus Grove near the lake."

"Kay, I know you're worried about your lady, but we're doing all we can right now, and I'm certain things will turn out." Poe said. One of the Barks came up to Kay and placed his floppy-eared, jolly face in his lap.

Poe smiled. "Bark used to see Lady Sammidoran doing a lot of praying here in the Grove at night; perhaps you should offer a prayer yourself. It might help."

Sam? Praying?

Kay stood. "Aunt Poe, where did Bark see Sam praying?"

"In an old Vith ruin near Lake Killbane."

Kay knew the one.

Ja chandle de ne infir portaleis tarne Telmus she had said.

"I have written for you my confession in the Telmus Grove near the lake."

The lake! Lake Killbane.

Kay Wafted away without a word.

"Hey, Kay, where're you going?" Sarah cried.

✶ ✶ ✶ ✶ ✶

There was an old Vith shrine of weathered stone that Kay knew, tucked in the tangle of beech trees near shallow Lake Killbane in the north of the Grove. He'd shown it to Sam years earlier. It was hard to find, lost in the trees. They'd made love there once or twice; the whole Grove was dotted with their love-making sites.

He appeared in the Ishtar courtyard, clawing his way past the wall into the thick growth. His coat caught and ripped, then his pants. He was bloodied. He kept on. Through a bower of beech trees was the entrance. Inside was a hexagon of stone penned in by black trunks.

The old site, built centuries earlier by the Vith to celebrate a victory against the Haitathe, looked like a carbon bomb had gone off. The tree trunks crowding the perimeter were hacked and stabbed, like they'd been bayoneted by a rush of charging troops. The tough stone also bore the scars of many hits and deflected blows. One smaller pillar had crumbled all together.

What happened? He drifted his Sight back into the past, and he soon had the answer.

Sam.

Sam apparently came there often, always at night. Whirling around in the dark, pulling her hair out, jabbing at the stone and the trees in a fury of anger, defacing and damaging what had stood unblemished for centuries with nothing but her two hands.

The central pillar seemed to be where Sam focused most of her time and energy. He Sighted her kneeling in front of it in a frenzy. He gazed at the pillar and let his Sight drift.

The pillar was covered in minute writing etched into the stone by Sam's hand. Little thoughts were left there by her, each bound and separated from the others by scratched-in cartouches.

The detail she left was astounding, spelling out her life as a Monama and a slave to the horrid *Killanjo.* He read for hours, taking in the key salient points:

"We were evil in Tevlapradah, and the gods are punishing us ..."

"Once, ages ago, we were ALL Berserkacides. Four-armed, lusting for death. We built a Temple in the ground and worshipped a Horned God in Tevlapradah ..."

"The Gods of Jade and Sapphire came from the stars and desired the warmth of our embrace. Genetic manipulation ... Purging the Berserkacide from our souls, taking away our second pair of arms."

"They called us 'Mo-Na-Ma': Bearers of Offspring. We bore their children."

"No longer evil, no longer four-armed, we abandoned the Temple and forgot its lore. The Horned God was angry, spiteful, and has plagued us ever since."

"The Horned God enticed the Golden people to come and torment us. Demons. The Return of the Berserkacides, in their windowless cities, turning us back

into what we were. Haven't we paid enough for our crimes?"

" ... Their demons have no skin, they never have skin, lording over us as the Gods do over Kana."

" ... they are immortal, they never get old. The male and female have tormented me since I was a child and look no different now than they did then. I think they are your kin; they smell like you. Look what they became ..."

" ... they take us to a faraway place and stitch our collars into our necks. Don't touch, don't ever touch! They turn us into Berserkacides."

" ... so afraid. Always so afraid. Want to be brave, like you."

" ... any given day can be our last, when the demons come for us."

"... talk too much—Berserkacide!"

"... think too much—Berserkacide!"

"... cross the demons—Berserkacide!"

"They take us to the Temple we built and give us to the Horned God."

" ... demons serve the Golden Ones, who can be anything they want ..."

"Golden Ones, apostles of the Horned God ... change their shapes ..."

"Always watching. No peace ... Berserkacides!"

And on and on. Sam lamented her lot in life, her people, and that the only happiness she'd ever known was with him.

A recurring cartouche kept popping up, mixed in with the rest:

" ... Atrajak. Atrajak led our people. Atrajak sought the Temple. Atrajak chose Poorly ..."

Who was Atrajak?

Nearby, the ruins of a shattered wall lay in pieces, smashed by Sam. He ran his Sight backwards, watching the wall reform.

He saw the chilling message that was there:

Kay remembered the odd dreams he had of being visited by a strange, misshapen woman in the night. In hindsight, it was probably Hathaline's *Killanjo.* Were they not mere dreams but real events, and Sam knew about all it, coming to this place to vent her fury?

Had Hathaline's *Killanjo* shared his bed?

Let me fuck you again, she had said.

It was a horrid thought.

He returned to the castle and closed himself in his room high atop Zorn tower. Through her etchings at the ruin, she had come clean regarding the *Killanjo,* the demons that haunted both her and her people. But, she remained frustratingly tight-lipped as to what she was doing in secret, in essence, offering his flesh to the *Killanjo* to ensure she got some time unwatched to act in private.

"I have accomplished things past their vigilance ..."

What things, Sam? And at what price? You wanted the Machine, the *Oberphilliax*. I got it for you!! Why?

What purpose does it serve?

Why? Why?

Propped up against the wall, he fell into an uneasy sleep clouded with uneasy images.

Visions of Sam and *Killanjo.*

The Machine now in pieces in the Grove.

The Demon, that was once his sister, coming to rape his sleeping body in the night and Sam letting her do it.

For my art, she wrote. Not telling him. He remembered his ill-fated friend, Mitzilaran of Cardinal, sniffing him in the fog. *"You have the demon all over you ..."* she said.

You have your sister's stink all over you.

The threads of his soul got into a tangle. He didn't know what to think or feel.

As you kill me ... she wrote.

✶ ✶ ✶ ✶ ✶

Something came and comforted him as he slept, helped sort everything out.

Kay... a kind voice said. *You want answers—go get them. I left you a present. I love presents. See Sarah in the morning.*

✶ ✶ ✶ ✶ ✶

In the morning, Kay felt refreshed, all the gloom of the previous day gone. He would go find Sarah and Phillip, say he was sorry if they required an apology for Wafting away on them, and begin looking for Sam. He'd search the whole world if he needed to. He wasn't going to let her run alone.

He left to find his cousins.

11—The Two Choices of Atrajak of Want

Kay linked back up with everybody in the Capricos Hall as they ate breakfast. Sarah had her typical plate piled high with bacon and eggs. Phillip was more modest with waffles and syrup. Lon and Ki both had pancakes and eggs with Tweeter pecking away at the tabletop.

Sarah wasn't happy much with Kay and didn't have an issue sharing that fact with him.

"I thought we were a team! You don't go Wafting off like that! I wouldn't do that to you, even if I could Waft!"

Kay sat down at the bench next to Ki. "You're right, Sarah. I'm sorry."

"We sat out there in the clearing all evening waiting for your dumb butt to return. I wanted to see the ruin Mother mentioned!"

"I apologize. I was out of my head. I'll show it to you later."

"What about Sam's Metal Man."

"He's gone, sorry, I know you wanted to see him."

Sarah sat there over her plate and scowled.

"Lt.," Kay said to Ki, "I didn't have a chance to tell you how glad I am that you're here. It's a big comfort having you around."

Ki smiled. "It's good to see you too, Kay."

"Yeah, yeah," Sarah said.

"Hey, Sarah, give him a break, will you? Yesterday was pretty rough, for all of us. I saw the scorch marks in the amphitheater, Kay. Was that from the Metal Man?"

"The *Killanjo* did that. Have their bodies been taken care of?" Kay asked.

"The Grove is clear now, for what it's worth, as our friends can just step out of thin air whenever they want. Lady Poe has a bunch of Barks running around. If they see anything, we'll know. Oh, and, there's the Paraflies."

"What about them?" Kay asked.

Ki told him everything. "They're out there, and they work; Lady Poe's perfected them. There were a bunch of them swarming in a dead tree trunk, and I dared Sarah to stick her face in there."

Kay laughed. "Did you, Sarah?"

Sarah thought about it a moment and apparently decided to forgive and forget. Her anger instantly passed, replaced by her usual unbounded enthusiasm. "Yeah, I did. It tickled. Hey, I was out taking a stroll this morning, and I saw this in the grass."

She placed a glass vial on the table. It was a several inches long, gilded in fine silver and adorned with a long, silver chain. Within the vial, like a detailed porcelain sculpture, was a tiny, fully formed image of Sam, dressed in black and holding a large clay jar.

"Looks like Sam, doesn't it?" Sarah said. "There's an inscription on the jar she's holding. It's too small for me to read."

Kay looked. It read: "*In all these Worlds, I would love you just the same.*"

"Oh," Sarah said in disappointment. "It's sap ..."

At that moment, silvery sand came pouring out of the jar in a muted hiss, quickly filling the vial all the way to the top, obscuring Sam's image within. Puzzled, Kay noticed there was also a tiny note stamped into the silver lid of the vial. It read:

SAM'S SAFETY METER

When the sand is full, Sam is safe. When the Sand is gone, Sam is in Mortal Peril.

He shook it. The sand was packed solid within.

"Must be a gift from Carahil," Ki said. "He's been leaving all sorts of goodies lying around here lately.

"Then it's a rare gift, and I'm thankful for it. Thanks, Carahil!" Kay said into the air as he put it around his neck.

"So," Ki said, "we can assume Carahil knows what he's doing and, for the moment, Sam's safe. What's the next move?"

"There was a word Sam kept repeating at the ruin: 'Atrajak'. She wrote it down over and over again. I don't know who or what Atrajak is. She says that Atrajak made some sort of mistake; that he chose badly, whatever that means. I think we need to find out who Atrajak is and then start looking for her."

Lon wiped his lips. "That's not overly difficult, Kay. Atrajak was a hero from antiquity, from the Remnath region, I think. He was a berserker, so the Sisters say. He led a great army of Monamas for a time and fought a series of battles they called the 'Hidden Wars'."

"How do you know that?" Sarah asked.

Lon blushed. "When I thought I was in love with Sam, I did a lot of research into Monama history. Atrajak's name comes up prominently in their lore."

Kay thought about it. "I've also done a fair research into Monama history and lore, and I never came up with that name."

"I have access to the Science Ministry's private archives via my Mother's personal codes, which contains a trove of information not available to the general public. Atrajak met his end going up against the Sisters, and they banned most of his writings and generally erased him from history for his temerity."

Sarah was ready to go. "Well, why don't we do this: Lon, you and I— let's look this Atrajak guy up again with your codes and see what more we can find out, as Sam thinks he's important. Kay and Phillip, you two hit the Grove and finish building the Machine. I mean, we lugged it all the way back here, so we might as well finish, right?"

Kay glanced at Sam's Meter hanging from his neck. The sand was still up to the top packed solid. "Oh, the Machine—I'd forgotten about it."

Sarah beamed. "You sure did. It's about halfway put together. My dad, Phillip and Lon got a great deal accomplished while we were waiting for you to come back yesterday."

"Well, ok then," Kay said. "Phillip, when you're ready, let's go."

Ki finished up her pancakes. "Let me check on your sisters, and I'll come with you."

✶ ✶ ✶ ✶ ✶

When Kay and Phillip and Ki got to the clearing, they saw nothing but the empty expanse of grass surrounded by giant oak trees. "Where is it?" Ki asked.

"Oh!" Phillip laughed. "Mother still has it Whisper-locked. Remember?"

"That's right, I forgot," Kay said. "Boy, the Whispers really do work. I don't see a thing."

"Let me recite the password, and we'll be invited into the Whisper's veil and will be able to see and hear everything that's going on in the clearing," Phillip said. "The password for today is: 'My Dog has Fleas'."

"Did Sarah come up with that?"

"Sure did."

After Phillip uttered the phrase, the Whisper's veil moved around them, and all was revealed.

The *Oberphilliax* was standing to the east, looking exactly as it did the day before. Twenty colorful Whisper ladybugs buzzed around and through its silver legs, in harmony with it. Some wandered up its legs and clung to the crosspiece. A silver Bark dog rested at the base of the Machine. Ever vigilant, he thumped his tail as they entered the clearing. Several open toolboxes sat next to the Machine with various tools laid out making indentations in the tall grass. Lord Peter was there, already hard at work, sleeves rolled up to his elbows. The remains of his breakfast sat in a basket nearby. He was standing atop a step ladder, working on the right leg. A Snugs medallion hung at his neck—Lord Peter hated the cold climate of Blanchefort.

He saw them and came down. "Phillip, Kay, good morning!"

"Morning, Uncle," Kay said.

"Morning, Father," Phillip replied. "Having any luck?"

"Oh yes! Remarkable device. There is an amazing amount of connections and links here, but they seem to want to connect and link themselves, to grow together on their own. I anticipate we'll be done in a few hours, certain enough."

Kay looked at it: silver and rugged, grown into the ground like it had always been there, like a pair of ruddy tree trunks leafed in silver foil. He pounded one of the legs twice with his fist; it was solid and unmovable.

Peter craned his neck back to look at the top. "The only issue I can see after we finish the assembly is power. No power."

"Can it be solar-operated, Father?" Phillip asked.

"I don't think so." He pointed at the indention in the center arch. "Something goes right there in that spot, possibly an umbilical, possibly a powering stone or power accessory of some kind. You say Lady Sammidoran directed you in the recovery of these pieces, Kay? Did she mention anything about power?"

"No, nothing."

"What about in the ruin where she left you all the information?" Phillip asked. "Anything there?"

"She wrote absolutely nothing about the Machine. She didn't even hint at it. She mentioned something about her 'art'—maybe that's a vague reference to the Machine."

"You know what that tells me," Kay?" Ki said, leaning against one of the legs. "That tells me that Sam believes that this Machine, whatever it is, is of critical importance and is determined to keep it a secret from the enemy. That's why she didn't mention it. That's why she had you fetch it in the first place."

"Yes, but in doing so, Sam's kept the Machine a secret from us as well. We've no idea what she meant for it," Kay said.

They all stood there and looked at the silent silver contraption. It stood tall, daring them to determine its purpose.

Bark's tail thumped. "Someone's coming," Lord Peter said. "Probably Sarah."

"My Dog has Fleas!" came a loud voice. A moment later Lon and Sarah entered the clearing. Sarah came up and gave her father a warm hug around the waist. Lon pushed his hat back and surveyed the work. "Wow, it's coming together. Doesn't look like there's much left to do."

Kay checked Sam's Safety Meter. The sand filled it to the top as before. "Lon, did you and Sarah have any luck with this Atrajak person?"

Sarah replied. "We did, up in the Mystery Library. He was a hero from Remnath, I think he was even a forefather of the guy who invented this Machine here; they were both from the House of Want, right? He was sort of like you, Kay; he fell for a Monama woman and started hanging out with them."

"Sarah's over-simplifying a bit," Lon said. "Atrajak of Want became a great hero to the Anuian Monamas of old. They called him '*Sar-Gra-Ma*', which means ..."

"It means 'father' in Systerel," Kay said jumping in.

"Yes, yes it does. Kay, you really are a fine linguist. Monamas call a person *Sar-Gra-Ma* when they place their complete faith and trust in them. Atrajak displayed a number of amazing attributes, and the Anuian Monamas were suitably impressed and rallied around him. In 001082EX, he led them on a protracted offensive against the *Killanjo* demons, and against their overlords as well."

"Overlords?" Kay asked.

"Yes, a mysterious group of people he called the Kestral Oligarchy—apparently they're the ones in control of both the *Killanjo* and the Monamas."

"That was that whole 'Hidden Wars' thing," Sarah added. "The Kestrals are pulling all the strings."

"Will you let Lon do the talking, Sarah, please?" Phillip said.

She huffed.

Lon continued. "Atrajak wrote that the Kestrals were beautiful, made of gold and could change their shape at will. Not just humanoid shapes, but anything they wanted."

Kay thought back. "Sam mentioned the 'Golden People' in the ruin, and how they could change their shape."

"Atrajak also said they were incredibly powerful, much more so than the *Killanjos* and the Berserkacides, who are just flunkies under their sway, I suppose."

"What else?" Kay said.

"During the Hidden Wars, Atrajak and his Monamas won a series of victories against the Kestrals, destroying a number of places he called 'Tanks', where the *Killanjo* are created. The problem he faced is the same one that we still have today—the Kestrals and their *Killanjo* minions always have the advantage of stealth and retreat. They strike when they choose to strike and flee when they choose to flee, and have never fully been beaten or sent away for good. They always return, stepping out of thin air on their 'feathers of green' as Atrajak put it."

"I saw one of those. So, what did he do?"

Lon went on. "Atrajak was presented with two choices. His Monama wife, Tiverlan of Nebulon, wanted to attack a legendary temple in the ground, a hidden place where they once worshipped a fierce and rather bloodthirsty Horned God. She said a goddess named Anabrax in the shape of a mole visited her in a dream. She told her the Horned God's temple was hidden deep beneath the ground, and that the gods knew of its existence, but didn't know its location. Anabrax said she stumbled onto it as she dug through the earth and saw what was done there. She said the temple was a place of endless horror and death, and that it furnished the Kestrals with great power. She tasked Tiverlan to seek the Horned God's temple and destroy it, for the gods cannot destroy another god's temple. As the dream faded, she watched Anabrax be captured by the Horned God and dragged to his temple to be sacrificed, where the Golden People feasted upon her body. Tiverlan begged Atrajak to locate and destroy this temple at once."

The Horned God again— he seemed to be everywhere. Kay shuddered.

"I've heard of this temple, and Sam mentioned something about it as well, a temple in the ground."

"For the second choice, Atrajak's friend Vorchera, a great Monama general, wanted instead to attack the Kestrals directly. He claimed to know the stellar positioning of their home world far away from Kana. Atrajak considered both options and decided upon following his general's advice, questing to the Kestral's home world. Once there, he planned to engage and defeat them in their own backyard and compel them to either quit Kana for good, or be exterminated."

Lord Peter, fiddling with the Machine, jumped in. "I know this part. They set sail in a vast Elder ship and went off into space for a long time. Along the way, all of Atrajak's Monama army eventually got sick and died leaving him alone on a ship of corpses and on the verge of madness."

"That's right," Lon said. "Monamas don't do well in space away from Kana, especially the Anuians like Sam, and Atrajak lost everything: his wife, his friend Vorchera, his whole army and his sanity."

"What did he do?"

"He determined to press on with the voyage and perform a forced Cobalt ignition of his stellar engines when he got there, thus destroying himself and the Kestrals along with him. The problem was, when he finally arrived at the planet Vorchera had specified, he discovered no Kestrals there, just an uninhabited infantile star system bisected by a large nebula."

"So, he did it all for nothing."

"Apparently so. He returned to Kana a broken man, raving after his long return voyage alone on a ship full of ghosts. He spent the rest of his life trying to do what his dead wife had initially proposed: to locate the hidden Horned God temple and destroy it. But, he never found the place, instead coming to grips with the Sisters at Twilight 4, where he met his end."

Sarah caught a teal-colored Whisper and held it cupped in her hand. "So, that's what we got, Kay, a story of a guy who fought the Kestrals and lost. Real encouraging, huh? What do you think we should do?"

"I think we should ..."

A mental growl filled all of their heads.

<grrrrrrrrrrrrrrr ...>

Bark, sitting by the Machine, was detecting something in the trees.

Weapons came out of coats. Ki had her giant SK in her hand, Lon his deadly CEROS, Sarah her loaded Poltava and Peter and Phillip their SAPPs formed into swords. Kay drew his CARG and froze.

"I see it," he said.

"What do you see?" Ki asked, finger on the trigger.

"I see a green cloud-like slit has formed, just there, beyond the trees." He pointed.

Everybody looked. "I don't see a thing," Sarah said, lighting her Sight.

"It's there, all right. Floating on air, like a green cloud. Sort of how Atrajak described them—with feathers of green. I see several shapes huddled within it, looking out."

As they waited, Kay saw several hideous forms emerge from the cloudy slit, naked and bloody, covered in depravity.

Bark stood: "Arf ... Arf, Arf!!"

"Two *Killanjo* have just entered the clearing," Kay said. "They're looking around, trying to be stealthy. They don't seem to be able to see or hear us."

"They cannot see or hear through the Whisper veil," Phillip said.

"They're Cloaked; we're Cloaked—everybody's Cloaked. Where are they?" Sarah demanded.

"Right next to you."

She cocked her Poltava. "I'm going to plug 'em!"

"No, wait!" Lord Peter said. "If these are *Killanjo,* the Paraflies will detect their presence and have them down. Their Cloak shouldn't matter; the Paraflies can see in Gamma. I want to observe the process."

In the near distance, a furtive buzzing arose and a hiss of moving wings.

As they waited, Kay reached out with his CARG and gave one of the *Killanjo* a tap on the bloody shoulder. The creature whirled around with surprise, teeth chattering. It looked right past Kay, not seeing him.

"How does it feel to wonder if you're being watched, demon?" he said. The *Killanjo* didn't hear him and continued slinking about.

The buzzing quickly grew to a roar. A moment later a churning cloud of Paraflies fell into the clearing, Paraflies by the hundreds. The *Killanjo* were startled and shambled back to their green slit, hoping to escape. Kay stepped out and swung with his CARG. He took the foot and ankle off one *Killanjo,* sending him crashing down as the other entered the slit and vanished. A moment later he was covered by Paraflies. Another moment passed, and he was dead. The green slit disappeared. The Paraflies hovered for a moment, searching for their quarry, and then took to the trees to begin their vigil again.

"Wow, what happened?" Sarah cried.

"Paraflies got him," Kay said. "He's right here in the grass, stung to death, though the second one got away."

"Why can't we see him?" Ki asked.

Kay looked his body over and found a small device in his palm. Kay crushed it with the horn of his CARG, and the gruesome body appeared for all to see, covered in oozing stings. Sarah was appalled and entranced at the same time. She greedily looked the body over, savoring it. They all got their fill of the sight.

"Whoah, he stinks, doesn't he?" she said.

Lord Peter was elated. He checked his timepiece. "By my count, it was less than fifty seconds before the Tuleeflies were on him, and he was dead. Did you see how they moved together as a single unit? We worked long and hard to achieve that. Yes, that will do. Lovely, lovely!"

Phillip loosed his SAPP and put it back around his neck. "So, what are we going to do? Look at this enemy we face. They come and they go as they please, like ghosts. The Paraflies can defend well enough as we just saw, but how are we to mount any sort of offensive? We have the same problem Atrajak of Want had. The enemy commands the field."

Kay stared at the dead *Killanjo*. "Perhaps Atrajak should have listened to his wife. She wanted to attack some sort of temple the Kestrals maintain. Sam also mentioned a temple and a sinister Horned God residing in it."

Ki put her SK away. "Yes, but Atrajak didn't know where this temple is, and neither do we."

Kay glanced at his Sam Safety meter. The sand had lowered a bit, and now her head was uncovered down to her nose.

"I suppose I'll have to ask Sam if she knows where it is."

12—Lt. Kilos' Code

They returned to the castle where Kay went to the eastern wing, Phillip, Lon and Ki following.

"Where are we going?" Ki asked.

"To the Chapel of Countess Fercandia," Kay replied.

"Why?" Lon asked, trotting at his side.

"Because, in the chapel, I can talk to Sam. As a boy, I often spoke to her there—apparently certain places that are buried or close to the soil are accessible to her thoughts. The chapel is buried, and I can hear her speak no matter how far away she is. I'm going in, and I'm going to try and contact her. I want to hear her voice."

They arrived, and saw the tiny grate near a bench. "You're going in there?" Ki cried.

"I am, wait here for me."

Kay Wafted in, the familiar dark of the place lit up in his amber Sight. "Sam!" he cried in the dark.

The statue of Countess Fercandia emerged. "Sam!"

He heard a small whimper in reply. *<...k ... Kay?...>* the sound of her thoughts faded in and out.

"I'm here, Sam, I'm here, *Cerri-Tela.* Are you all right? Tell me where you are!"

<Do.n't k.ow. T..y'r. a.ter me. C'n.t st.p...>

"Sam, tell me about the Horned God's temple. Where is it, do you know?"

<.n Gr.u.d. Kill u. t.ere. P.ace of.ower...>

He got nothing back for a while. Then he heard one final chopped up message and got nothing more.

<G.a..d th. m.chine. H.lp me ...>

✶ ✶ ✶ ✶ ✶

On top of all that had happened, word had reached the castle about a massive Fleet battle over Hoban. The holos were livid with the news. Great victory! The Fleet was heroic in action, as always.

Three cheers for the Fleet.

Lon had codes and access to private Fleet channels, and the news flowing there, kept from the general League populace, was certainly less cheery. It was terrifying, in fact.

The Battle of Hoban had been a debacle for the Fleet.

The Main Fleet Vessel *Bethel* had been so badly damaged that it had to be abandoned in orbit with many casualties sustained, including its commander, Captain Harrison of Dare, who went down with his ship. Fleet ships *Westerville, Twilight* and *Halo Dawn* had also been greatly damaged, and six Marine *Trelaines* had been destroyed outright.

No damage to the enemy could be assessed.

Once again, they were fighting ghosts.

Additionally, and most disturbing, the *New Faith*, Kay's father's ship, and several Marine vessels had vanished from the scene of battle without trace. Current Fleet status: MRA: Missing as a Result of Action.

Lt. Kilos, hearing the news and clearly feeling she should have been there, was devastated. She excused herself and left the table, Tweeter following. She did not return.

Sarah and Phillip managed to calm Kay down a bit, both about Sam and his missing mother and father. His parents could take care of themselves—they were certain of it.

But Sam, alone, frightened, pursued by the Horned God and his monsters who could step out of thin air. What could she do? How could she defend herself?

Sam could certainly Blink away if she had to, as she did today. But, to keep it up forever? She had to sleep. And if they came at her family, what then?

He constantly checked the vial. Had the sand moved? He wasn't sure anymore.

What was he to do?

Atrajak's Temple, the place he couldn't find. What was it? Where was it? What was its import?

He had to know. He had do something to help Sam, and perhaps the best way would be to discover this temple and see what was there.

Kay remembered that, during their trip to Xandarr, Ki mentioned a code that she'd downloaded into his Holo-mail. Use it, she had said, *to find answers*. He opened his terminal and sorted through the volumes of unread mail sitting there. He eventually found the post that Ki had sent to him.

Use it after midnight, she had said.

That evening, Kay, still fully clothed, entered a small, cozy reading room in his tower and readied his terminal. He thumbed through his messages and again found the one that Lt. Kilos had sent him. In examining it further, he found it contained a Com code—it looked like a code to someplace on the planet Onaris. He accessed the code and was just about to enable it when a knock came at his Tower door several floors down.

Sighing, he Wafted down the stairs and opened it.

Standing there in their pajamas were Sarah and Phillip. "So, there you are!" Sarah cried in her robe and bare feet. "Where've you been all day, and why are you still dressed?"

Kay Wafted back up the stairs. "I'm following a lead," he said and settled in front of his holo-terminal.

Intrigued, they quickly followed him in. "What lead?" Sarah said breathlessly as she plunged into an overstuffed chair next to him. No matter what the hour, Sarah was always ready for an adventure. She looked at Sam's meter hanging at Kay's neck. "Hey, I can see the top of Sam's head!"

"No kidding, Sarah."

Lon was nowhere to be seen—probably tucked away all cozy in his guest tower. Tomorrow, they'd have to take him home.

Phillip, in a more measured tone, pulled up a chair. "You're performing research on Atrajak's Temple, aren't you?"

"I am. It's important somehow, and I'm going to know why," Kay said readying the code. Though he acted annoyed, he was glad for their presence.

Sarah sank into her seat, crossing her legs. "Who are you contacting?"

"Don't know, really. Lt. Kilos gave me this code while we were on our way to Xandarr, and told me to use it at this hour."

"Well," Sarah said, "get on with it already. Wait! Can I go get something to eat first?"

Kay, exasperated, shrugged, and Sarah, feet slapping on the stone floor, ran out and down the stairs.

A few minutes later, Sarah returned with three glasses of milk and a bowl full of pastries. Kay thanked her and drank his glass and had a pastry—he hadn't eaten since the incident in the Grove. Then, everyone settling back into their seats, Kay sent the code through. After a moment a colorful header for the University of Tusck came up floating on the Holo-terminal; then a message came on stating:

"Re-Routing to the Department of Polytheistics."

The message lingered there. A jingle played.

A thin male voice, hidden behind the video header, began speaking after a minute or two.

"You have missed my office hours. They are clearly posted and adhered to by the letter. Try back two days hence, and do not be late next time."

"Sir, sir!" Kay said, excited. He now knew exactly who was on the other end of the Com.

Lt. Kilos' husband. A mysterious man from Tusck, a professor and saged eminence. A man of whom Kay had heard many things. Supposedly, and this might have been dinner-time hyperbole, Lt. Kilos' husband was a man who could find answers to virtually anything. Kay cleared his throat—why hadn't he thought of this sooner?

"I am sorry, sir. My name is Kabyl, Lord of Blanchefort, and I was ..."

"You are Captain Davage's son?" the voice interrupted.

"I am, sir, yes."

"Standby, please."

They waited and music played. Sarah bobbed in her seat. "Lt. Kilos' husband is a Hertog, isn't he? Right? One of those criminal intellectuals who cross swords with the Sisters all the time?"

"I hadn't heard that," Kay said.

"I'm going to ask him," she said, eager.

"Don't, please, we need to stay focused."

After a moment, the screen header vanished, replaced by the dark, cluttered interior of an office. A small man wearing professor's robes sat at a huge desk. He was studious in appearance, but rather handsome in a bookish sort of way. The desk was gigantic, adorned with all manner of modern technology. Beyond, a large painting hung on the stone wall—it was a highly stylized and angelic likeness of Lt. Kilos.

"Lord Blanchefort," the man said. "Well met. I am Lt. Kilos' husband. You may simply call me 'Professor'." He looked at Sarah and Phillip. "And these two sitting next to you are, given their apparent age and appearance, your cousins, correct?"

"Yes, sir, these are my cousins. This is Sarah of Blanchefort and Phillip of

Blanchefort."

"Sir, good morning and thank you. This is an honor," Phillip said.

The Professor nodded and sat back. "So, Lord Blanchefort, what can I do for you?" he said in a slow, calculated voice.

"Professor, I have a few questions that I was hoping you could help me with."

The Professor tented his fingers. "Yes, yes … I have often assisted the House of Blanchefort in the past. I have often been able to gather information that was otherwise lost or unknowable."

Perhaps this small remarkable man could offer him answers. Kay began to tell the Professor everything.

The Professor, cut him off. He stood up and approached the screen. "I am not really interested in helping House Blanchefort any further."

Kay was thunderstruck.

The Professor continued. "I have helped your father, at my wife's request, many times. And always the dashing Lord Blanchefort triumphs. And what about poor me? I sit here alone in Tusck, missing my wife. What do I ever get for my tireless, and, might I say, brilliant efforts? I get naught but the high hat and an empty bed for my troubles."

"Professor," Kay squeaked. "If it is payment that you require, I can provide you with …"

"I am not interested in money. Do I look like I need or care about money?"

Sarah shot out of her seat and barged in front of Kay. "What if we could get Lt. Kilos to come home for a while? How about that?"

The Professor regarded Sarah in her pajamas. "Yes … What a clever girl you are. I have been told you are the image of your grandmother, and truly you are."

Kay pushed Sarah out of the way. "Professor, you wish for Lt. Kilos to come home for a bit?"

"I do. I am lonely."

"Well, sir, I can relay your request."

The Professor sat back down. "Let us be frank here for a moment, Lord Blanchefort. Clearly, you have some pressing matter that you feel is very urgent. Clearly, you hope that I will be able to gather information and harvest answers that you cannot. You are correct, sir. There is nothing that is beyond my notice or out of my reach. I do not allow the Sisters to determine the things that I know. I do not allow the established and the conventional to determine the width of my resources. Anything that is worth knowing, I can know, and in short order."

"Are you a Hertog?" Sarah blurted out, unable to contain herself. "I heard you're a Hertog."

He leaned back in his chair for effect. "The Hertogs are criminals, my dear, and rather mercenary as well. The sisters just love them, don't they? Since you mentioned it, let's pretend I am a Hertog for the moment. Hertogs always demand a price for their help, whether their help is any good or not, and the price for my assistance is my wife, here, in my arms."

"Sir, I ..."

"Will you promise to bring me my wife? I must have your word."

Kay thought for a moment. "Yes, sir, I promise."

Without another word, the Professor screened off.

"Good going with the Hertog thing, Sarah!" Kay shouted.

"Sorry."

Phillip shook his head. "Looks like we're stuffed. I saw Lt. Kilos heading for the bars—the fact she wasn't there for the battle over Hoban, and with the *New Faith* missing, I think she's taking it pretty hard."

Kay stood up and saddled his CARG. He glanced at Sam's Meter.

"Where are you going?" Sarah asked.

"I'm going down to the docks to find Lt. Kilos, and ask her to come home with me."

"We're going to Onaris?"

"We are."

Sarah and Phillip jumped out of their seats. "And, when she tells you to light off and get bent?"

"Then I'll ask her a bit harder."

Sarah put her hand on Kay's shoulder. "Hold up. Let us get changed, and we'll come with you."

"You need your beauty rest, Sarah. I can do this myself."

"Who needs beauty rest? And, if you think I'm going to miss this, you're crazy."

* * * * *

Leaving Lon to snore in his bed, they went down into the village and checked the pubs along the dock. There were quite a few. Surely Lt. Kilos, a notorious pub-rat, would be in one of them.

It didn't take too long.

In a large pub at the southern end of the dock, known as the Stumbling Fool, was Lt. Kilos, a mug in her hand and Tweeter on her shoulder.

She was deep in her cups.

"Hey, Kay!" she said loudly, rather drunk. "What are you … doing in here? Didn't think your mom let you drink … I been ... I been looking for the Cat God, but ... I can't find it."

The three saddled up to the bar, and she clapped Kay warmly on the shoulder.

"Good morning, Lt.," Kay said. "I used the code you were kind enough to give us as we journeyed to Xandarr."

"Oh, that! I'd forgotten! Did you use the code?"

"I did, and I thank you."

"So, what did my husband say? Did he have any information for you? He wasn't mean to you, was he?"

Kay tried to smile. "He said he could help."

"That's great! See, my husband … there isn't anything he doesn't know. We'll have to ask him where the damn Cat God pub is." She winced as she took a drink. "Dammit! This stuff here is swill ..."

"Lt. … Ki, he said he won't help me."

Ki belched. "What! Why not?"

"He said he won't help me unless …"

"Unless what?"

"Unless I bring you home. He wants you home."

Ki laughed in an intoxicated manner. "Oh, my husband … he gets lonely every so often! Yeah!" Ki finished her mug and set a coin down on the bar. "Listen, you get him on the Com and you tell him to quit whining, and that I said …" (she emphasized *'I said')*, "for him to help you—got it? Tell him we've all got our jobs to do, and I want him to do his!"

Ki turned to leave. Kay stepped in front of her. "Lt., please, I promised your husband that I would bring you home to him. I desperately need his help."

Her face darkened into misery. "The ship attacked and I wasn't there. Missing … Why wasn't I there? I should be standing with your father and mother, right now. What good am I here? Those damn bugs can protect better than I can …"

Phillip approached. "Lt., we have the *Goshawk*. We can take you at speed to Tusck, spend a day or two with your husband, and by then I'm certain the *New Faith* will have turned up. We will then link you back up with it straight away, we promise."

"Listen son, I'll tell you what. I'll Com my husband and set things straight with him, and then you can rest assured that he will help you. Ok? I'm just going to find some place and drink some … more and try to forget that, when Captain Davage, my best friend, needed me most, I wasn't there! Good Night."

She started to walk past him, but Kay wasn't moving. He put his hand on Ki's shoulder.

"Lt., I made your husband a promise, and I intend to keep it. You are coming with us to Tusck, where we will then return you to the ship in due order once it's located. I know my father, and he will have them through safe and true."

"Really, or what?"

Kay paused, then: "Or start eating that barstool over there with your face."

Ki looked at him and smiled. "Kay, I don't think you really want to do this with me right now."

"Lt., I am dead serious, and I am steadfast. My beloved is out there somewhere alone and frightened—pursued by things that I do not understand. Your husband has information that I require, and I will have it. Therefore, you, ma'am, are coming with us."

Ki turned back to the bar for a second, then wheeled around and tagged Kay right in the jaw, sending him flying into the bar and then to the floor.

All the chattering in the bar stopped. People rubber-necked to see.

Ki knelt over him to help him up. "Look, I'm sorry I had to do that. Maybe it's for the best; maybe I just knocked some—"

Quick as thunder, Kay slugged Ki in the gut, doubling her over, and then busted her in the face sending her back over a table, flushing Tweeter from his pocket. She emerged a moment later, and Kay threw his body into hers where they went down in a tangle.

The pub patrons stopped what they were doing for a moment, then: "Fight!" they yelled, and the pub erupted into a random melee. Phillip was grabbed by some surly barfly, and Sarah, with a shout of joy, began swinging at anything that moved.

As the pub descended into a chaos of flying fists and thrown furniture, Tweeter casually flew up and settled on an overhead light ballast—obviously, he had been through this sort of thing before.

Bodies knocked about as the patrons fought with everybody and nobody at the same time. Ki and Kay, though, were focused on each other, trading blows, grabbing onto each other, struggling to land open shots. Kay landed a thudding shot to the

back of Ki's head, just behind her ear, and she roared with anger.

She drew her SK

Kay unsaddled his CARG.

They stood there for a moment in the ruckus holding their weapons. Then, coming to their collective senses, they both threw them down at the same time and rushed each other empty handed, content to slug it out fair and square.

A courtesan was sent flying upside down through a window.

Phillip, fighting Esther-style, was doing quite well. As usual, everything he did, he excelled at in his quiet, no-frills way. "If only Thomasina could see this!" he shouted as he mopped up a stumblebum.

Sarah, tucked up into the fetal position, went sailing over the bar in a heap with some grubby merchantman in close pursuit.

After a minute or two more, exhausted, Ki and Kay lowered their fists and slumped to the floor, side by side. Just as they did, the magistrate and a bunch of guardsmen came running in, whistles blaring. Netting some diehards and lightly shocking others, they quickly quelled the brawl. They then began the process of sorting out and arresting the instigators. They came to pick up Kay, who had been fingered by the barkeep. When they saw who he was, they scowled and made a move to bag Ki. Kay locked eyes with them and shook his head. They politely moved on.

"So," Ki said finally, panting, "I guess you feel pretty strongly about this, Kay. Wow …"

"Yes, I do, and I'm sorry it had to come to this."

Ki looked at him and smiled. "Sorry for what—for taking me on, for treating me to a good fight? Apparently I didn't take you seriously enough."

She stood up and offered him a hand. "That was a heck of a fight … you can hit, just like your dad. I've been slugged by two generations of Blancheforts now: by your dad, by your mom a whole bunch of times, and now by you. I guess I should feel proud or something."

"Learned it from you."

"Yeah, that's right. I taught you well, didn't I? Who would have ever thought we'd end up tangling in a bar? Creation, I'm pumped. That was awesome!"

They then began fishing through the wreckage on the floor for their weapons. Kay found her SK and gave it back. Ki wiped her nose and blushed. "Hey, I'm really sorry I drew on you, Kay—no hard feelings?" she said.

"Of course not," he said picking up his CARG.

Kay approached the frazzled barkeep. "Sir, I wish to apologize for the events of this evening."

The barkeep studied him and nodded.

"Sir, if you will kindly present yourself at the castle tomorrow morning and ask to see the Head of Staff, you are to be fully reimbursed for the damages wrought here today."

The bar-keep smiled and bowed. "Praise be to you, my Lord."

Ki shook her head. "Hey, just for the record, I've never paid for a bar fight in my life, but I like how you owned up and handled that. You're a good kid, Kay—heck, what am I saying? You're a good man and I'm proud of you."

Such praise meant a lot to him.

Kay and Ki found Phillip and then Sarah, who was in the process of being arrested, and they headed out into the early morning, through the crowded buildings and alleyways of the village. Tweeter, glowing silver, lit the way. Sarah, sporting the beginnings of a shiner, was chirping with joy. "Now that's what I call a fight!! Did you see that big grub I was fighting? He was tough, and he sent me over the bar with one punch. He was a nice guy; we should have him up at the castle sometime!"

"Kay," Ki said looking back at the empty docking pylons where the *New Faith* usually rested "why don't we head to my tower right now. I'll get my husband on the Com and straighten this out. I promise he'll help you out all he can when I'm through with him."

"Ki, I'm certain, as you probably know your husband better than anybody, you could get instant results. I'm certain you know all the right things to say, and I'm sure he wouldn't want to disappoint you—still, I made him a promise. I don't want to go, but I have to be true to my word … and I didn't find his request unreasonable. So, unless you want to head back to the pub and start a fresh session, you're coming with us to see your husband."

Ki looked at him a moment, then smiled. "So," she said, "I guess I'm going to be gone for a few days—I'll let Lady Poe know I'm leaving. Bottle and Lady Hathaline will be fine, what with the Paraflies on the lookout and those Carahil plushies."

"Carahil plushies?" Sarah asked.

"Never mind. Now, once the *New Faith's* discovered, you sure you're going to get me back to the ship?"

"We promise, Lt.," Phillip said.

"All right—good enough, I'm going to pack a few things, and I'll meet you bright and early in a few hours. I figure if we make good time we'll be in Tusck by tomorrow afternoon. Good … it'll be nice to see my husband, and not even a holiday and all. It'll help take my mind off things."

The Professor

13—To Tusck

Bright and early, they, once again, all piled into the large black *Goshawk.* They had meant to make a quick stop in Arden to drop Lon off—but he didn't want to go. "I'm eager to meet this great man," he said. "Lt. Kilos, your husband is …"

"Yeah, yeah," Ki said. "He's an egghead, and I love him. You're going to get me all misty, Lon."

"He's a Hertog, right?" Sarah asked.

Ki scowled at her. "Don't know what you mean," she finally said. Sarah had more questions, but Ki dismissed her.

Phillip, plopping down into the pilot's chair, began the complicated process of starting the *Goshawk* up.

"Been a while since I've been in one of these," Ki said looking around as she tossed her small bag onto a seat.

Kay sat down on the rear couch. The body of the ship began to rumble as the powerful engines spun up, Sarah and Phillip chattering away as they readied the ship. Lon flopped down next to him.

Ki sat back and held Tweeter, rubbing his little silver head. Phillip then grabbed the sticks, and the *Goshawk* jumped smoothly into the air.

"Roll it, Philip, roll it!" Sarah cried, and Phillip barrel-rolled the ship. Kay, sitting there holding his CARG, didn't react.

Ki watched him. "I thought you get air-sick?" she said.

He shrugged. "I used to." He sat there and thought of Sam. All of this was for her. He looked at the Vial. The sand was now down to Sam's chin.

Sarah looked back. "He did, Lt.. He used to go through all our sick bags."

"What happened?"

"I grew up," Kay said.

✶ ✶ ✶ ✶ ✶

The *Goshawk,* with Phillip and Sarah taking turns flying, easily made it to Onaris, and in only five hours—very good time, much faster than a standard transport.

Onaris, glowing in the light from its star, 'Old Scrub', was, at first glance, very similar in appearance to Kana, however, Onaris was a much more extreme place than the more gentile Kana. Onaris was a slightly larger world with only one moon, while Kana had two. It also had a smaller land-to-sea ratio than Kana did, having one huge continent with a surrounding outlying ocean while Kana had three. Onaris' ocean, the Great Onaris Abyssal, or the 'Big Blue' as they called it, was incredibly deep. Its main river, the Hearth, was the longest in the League by far, even longer than the Torr on Xandarr, and its mountain, the Lone Rider, was the tallest, extending into the mesosphere.

The environs around Onaris were relatively clear, lacking most of the confusion of shipping, docking, and satellite traffic Kana had. Alone and free, the *Goshawk* settled into orbit.

Phillip did a lap around the equator, giving the massive geographic imminence of the Lone Rider a wide berth. He settled into the calm atmosphere, nosing the ship to the south. The land to the south, the vast area known as Calvertland, was a rich golden yellow—lots of agriculture, lots of food being grown. Most of the larger cities observable from the air appeared to be confined to the western coast across the mountains in the Pinthrop area: Tharpolli and the insufferably large sprawl of Inarri. All by itself was Tusck to the south, hugging the eastern seaboard. The continental interior was mostly wild and unspoiled and shockingly clear in the clean air. Fazo, a popular vacation spot for Kanan Blues, sat to the far south by the sea.

Following Ki's direction, Phillip brought the ship down low and fast. Instead of bringing the ship into Tusck where Ki said it would probably be stolen or dismantled, she directed him to put down in the distant outskirts of the city, in what appeared to be the walled ruin of a small Elder chapel surrounded by miles of unbroken wheat. As soon as the wheels hit the ground, a hoard of people came trotting out of the ruin.

Squealing with delight, Ki threw the hatch open and ran out into the warm afternoon sun, Tweeter flapping behind her.

"Come on, you guys!" she yelled from outside. "Come meet the family!"

Phillip, Lon and Sarah jumped out and Kay, not feeling overly sociable, slowly came out last.

The *Goshawk* was landed in a large, open grass enclosure that was walled in on all four sides. A fallen-down Elder chapel, built in the Calvert-style of fluted stone, made up the western wall. The walls were made of old, mottled brown stones mortared in place, and they rose up about thirty feet. The grass inside the enclosure was deep emerald green, and the dirt kicked up by the ship's wheels was a healthy, fertile black. The air was warm, and Kay, a true Blanchefort, felt miserably hot already. Still, there were a lot of people looking at him, and he stood tall and proper and came forward to be introduced.

There were about fifty people milling around the enclosure. They were clearly related to Ki, tall and strongly built, their skin was deeply tanned, and their hair was set to a thick, brassy blonde. Kay, recalling Ki talking about her impoverished childhood, was convinced that they would be dressed in rags; that's how he always pictured Ki's family. But no, they were dressed in simple, colorful clothes: sturdy, functional shirts and pants for the men, bright dresses for the women—all completely serviceable and not old in the least. Apparently, Ki and her husband gave them a fair amount of money, and they lived quite comfortably. Many, Kay noticed, had Bio-Plants—artificial limbs with wet-wired accessories that the Giftless Browns of Onaris tended to indulge in. One of Ki's sisters had a blinking metal arm, a nephew had a glowing right eye, and so on. Bio-Plants were virtually unheard of on Kana, where Gifted Blues looked down on such vulgar technological trappings, and good Hospitalers could be well-afforded. Wearing Bio-Plants was a sure sign of lowly birth and impoverished circumstance on Kana.

"And who do we have here, Ki," one of her sisters asked, thick with an Onaris accent.

Ki beamed with pride. "This, sis, is Kabyl, Lord of Blanchefort."

Kay bowed in a courtly fashion, and suddenly he was surrounded by Ki's family. They certainly weren't shy. They moved in close, felt the rich fabric of his coat with their rough (and in some cases, artificial) hands and pulled his black triangle hat off his head. They then began curiously examining his hair.

After a moment, Ki waded in. "Yeah, yeah, he's got purple hair. Neat, isn't it? Come on, give him some space."

Before long they were swept inside the ruin. To Kay's surprise, there was a large multileveled structure beneath the ruin full of sitting rooms, kitchens, and dormitories for the legion of kids, grandkids and other hangers-on. Apparently it was wise to be discreet with one's appearance of wealth on Onaris. Soon they were seated at a long table, as long as any in Castle Blanchefort, and were treated to a genuine Tusck meal served in wooden bowls: meats in thick sauces, exotic vegetables and soft, chewy bread—something of a novelty back home, all washed down with hearty home-brewed ales and dark beers. Sitting next to Sarah and Phillip, Kay thought the food was very tasty, and soon he had eaten his fill and more. Ki's many sisters and nieces couldn't get enough of Kay's purple hair—they watched him as he ate, and one even threw a pea at him (Ki later told him a thrown pea is a sign that a woman likes a man, and is an invitation). Phillip also had a few peas thrown at him. So did Lon. One of Ki's sisters pummeled him with peas, and he blushed and stumbled as he tried to make conversation. One of Ki's brothers was thoroughly taken with Sarah.

Again, a gregarious, outgoing, huge and fully functional family.

Kay looked around the vast table. "Where's your husband, Ki? I thought he would be here."

"Nah, he usually sleeps in his office at the university. He only shows up here when I'm around or when it's harvest time, when an extra set of hands come in handy. Not afraid of hard work, my husband."

Ki finished her tall glass of brown Tusck ale with relish. "Oh, that's good. So," she said, "at first light we'll head out. We'll ride on stoutbacks until we get to the city outskirts, then we walk the rest of the way—Tusck really isn't that big size-wise, you'll see. I think you guys will have fun; just stay close to me. You two, Phillip and Lon, will be just fine, but you, Sarah and Kay, will stick out like grapes on a cream pie."

"Why?"

"Why? Let's see, Sarah's blue hair is a pretty bright giveaway, and you, Kay—your fancy clothes, your hair … and your CARG ... you're going to be made as a Blue Lord from the get go."

"Is that bad?"

"No … but get ready to be harassed by panhandlers and street vendors, since they'll think you have money. I don't recommend you handing out any money because that'll be the end of you. Ok? If you want to buy something from a vendor, then by all means do so, but, if you don't, then just ignore them. And let me warn you about a few things. One: dirty courtesans are *everywhere* in Tusck. If you were a bit older, I'd say that what you choose to do or not do is your business, but, since you're still not quite of age yet, I would appreciate it if you do not try to go off with one—your mothers will surely have my head."

"Our mother?" Phillip said.

"I'm really not worried about your mother so much, Phillip—it's Kay's overprotective and temperamental mother that gives me pause. Now, dirty courtesans in Tusck can be extremely aggressive—not like the tame little things like we have in

Blanchefort village. They are rubbed up on some serious Weed here and have balls like you've never seen. Don't talk to them; don't even look at them. If you give them the time of day, if they smell blood, indecision or weakness on your part, you'll never be rid of them. They will literally drag you into a hot-sheet motel or cricket shack, rock your world, and leave you stuck with the bill. Ok?"

"We'll be fine. I've dealt with overbearing females before," Phillip said, with Sarah rolling her eyes.

"Good, next—the people in Tusck are basically decent folk. They might look, sound and act a little strange sometimes, but they're mostly harmless. I want you to watch out for Spectres though, ok? Courtesan rules apply here, so don't talk to them, and don't look at them. If one happens to get in your face, sock `em hard and keep going. They wilt before strength. All right, don't forget ... most people good, Spectres bad, ok?"

They all nodded. "We know how to deal with Spectres," Sarah said.

One of Ki's sisters added something, whispering in her ear. "Oh yeah—don't stick your hands near the stoutback's mouth tomorrow, otherwise it might get bitten off. Good point, Maia."

Ki smiled. "Great! This is going to be fun, and I can't wait to show you my home town and see my husband! Get some rest, you lot. We set off at first light."

She stood up. One of her sisters gave her a shove. "Oh, before I forget. Maia here wanted me to tell you there's going to be a Laserum tonight up top, and you're all welcome to come."

"What's a Laserum?" Sarah asked, holding her beer.

"It's a traditional Onaris dance. It's for good luck, for a bountiful harvest, to give strength to those you love, and to simply have a good time. You can just sit and watch if you want, or you can join in. This isn't Kana, nobody's going to judge you one way or another."

Her sister gave Ki another shove. "Will you cut it out!" Ki said to her. "Lon, Maia really hopes you'll Laserum with her tonight."

Lon turned a deep shade of red. "Oh, well, I'm afraid I don't dance."

Ki laughed. "This isn't going to be a choreographed Kanan step dance, Lon—it's good old-fashioned stomping. There's no good way or bad way to go about it--you just do it. You'd be a natural."

Sarah and Phillip, tired from a long couple of days, trudged off to a dormitory to get some rest. Lon was like a kid in a candy store, surrounded by Ki's sister Maia and her cousins. He'd never seen so much female attention before in his life and was sopping it up like a biscuit in gravy. Maia eventually cleared out all the hangers on and took Lon all for herself. She pulled him away to show him the complex.

Ki disappeared, off mingling with her family. People were coming and going at all hours. They were just as nocturnal as Ki was.

Kay, though, went outside; he wanted to be alone. He walked across the yard and climbed up onto the *Goshawk*, its protesting, banging metal beginning to sweat in the rapidly cooling night air. From his high perch, he could see all around. To the west was the black, cloud-wreathed dagger of the Lone Rider, its lofty summit breaking the atmosphere reaching into low orbit. To the northeast was a gentle but high hill. A bluish glow came from beyond—Tusck was behind the hill, just out of sight, and only the halo of its city lights could be seen. He could Sight through the hill if he wanted and have a look, but he didn't feel like it. He'd see it tomorrow.

Overhead was a treasure chest of sparkling stars, all scattered about in unfamiliar constellations. Kay looked around to where he thought Kana might be.

There, high overhead, a dim blue light mixed in with all the others: Kana.

Far away, Kana … Home. And Sam—wherever she was—was up there too, reduced to a pretty light in the night sky.

Sam, all alone.

Sam, running for her life, one step ahead of her pursuers. He checked the vial, a usual habit for him now. Sam's face was now uncovered.

"I love you, Sam," he said quietly tucking the vial back into his shirt, his own voice sounding loud in the night air.

His heart pounded with worry. He couldn't stop it.

✶ ✶ ✶ ✶ ✶

An hour or two later, Ki and her family came out of the ruin and formed a large circle in the center of the courtyard. With many hands, they quickly set up a bonfire, which glowed orange and leapt up, crackling and smoky, into the clear air. In the center of the bonfire was some sort of green light, like a large laser that pointed up into the night sky.

Then, from around the circle, music began to play. It was fast and frenetic, heavy with synthesized notes and pounding drums. People began dancing around the fire; very different from the civilized, powdered step dancing seen in the ballrooms of Kana, this dancing was stomping and sweaty, tribal, and utterly passionate. As the cathartic dancing and music reached a climax, the laser light in the center of the bonfire began moving, rather like the pendulum of a metronome, its green beam sweeping a huge beat across the sky. Kay looked around. Across the countryside, he could see other pockets of orange glows and laser lights moving about—the neighboring laser lights moving with different beats.

As Kay watched, he saw Ki mixed in with the dancers, stomping away. She was still wearing her uniform, but her hat was missing, her long, thick locks bobbing with movement as she savagely danced; Tweeter flapping overhead, glinting in the firelight. Also, Sarah and Phillip were there, moving to the beat. Lon, too, was being led by Ki's sister.

Soon, a group of Ki's sisters, their sleeves rolled up, approached Kay and bade him to join them. He didn't want to.

"Come, come dance," they said. "It will give power to those you love." They gently pulled him down and led him to the fire. Shy at first, he soon was lost to the music, moving, bobbing, allowing the dance to manifest all his grief and worry.

He danced for Sam. He danced for hours.

✶ ✶ ✶ ✶ ✶

In the morning after a noisy breakfast at the huge table, they set off for Tusck. They and a few of Ki's brothers and sisters rode on stoutbacks, a type of strange reptilian creature with a scaly back, long flexible neck and six sinewy, tentacle-like legs. The stoutback was the Onaris version of an ox and was often seen working in the fields and scaling the steep sides of the Lone Rider. Moving quickly, they tore off down the lane and up the side of the hill Kay had seen the night before, Ki's sisters laughing with joy, their thick bronzed hair blowing in the breeze. Even

Ki's hair, after only a day, seemed a few shades blonder.

The hill was bigger than it looked from a distance and steeper too, but soon, the quick reptilian steeds, moving easily, crested the hill, and Kay could see what waited beyond.

In the distance, situated on a prominence against the sea, was Tusck, one of the bastions of Onaris, the third largest city on the planet. It was a huddle of tall, bluish-gray stone and metal buildings. The buildings appeared scalloped, with gentle flutings and contours rising up into the big Onaris sky. At the moment, they were still deep in the country, with golden fields of grain growing for as far as the eye could see. The distant buildings looked surreal, almost like an island of stone and metal in the sky nested in cloud over a land of gold.

As they continued on, the golden fields eventually gave way to small hamlets and roadside villages. Soon, the dark, huddled canyons of the city proper loomed just ahead. They halted the stoutbacks and turned them around.

"From here we're walking," Ki said straightening her Fleet coat, Tweeter hopping into his pocket. "Stoutbacks aren't permitted any further. It's only about a mile or two."

They dismounted, and Lon got lots of hugs and kisses from Ki's friendly sister, Maia. She wanted to come with them, but Ki said no. Maia wasn't giving up quietly, and it seemed for a moment that the two of them were going to come to blows right there and then, but Maia relented and withdrew. Following Ki, they entered the waiting bulk of the city that was buzzing with hidden movement.

✶ ✶ ✶ ✶ ✶

Tusck was unlike any city Kay had ever seen on Kana: crowded and dark with cobbled and paved streets, sheer towering buildings, murky alleyways and smoky sewers. The buildings, Ki said as they walked by, were CWC's, small cities in themselves, each containing shops, eateries, medical facilities and residences. Some of the residents of these monolithic structures had never left their particular building, and they spoke odd languages and wore strange clothing. The narrow streets were lined with merchants and vendors loudly plying their trade. Street vendors with carts also bustled about—it reminded Kay of the scene on Blanchefort village dock, only at a huge, towering scale.

Also, technology was bleeding everywhere. On Kana and Hoban, the trend for the last several centuries was to hide technology, to dress it up in the trappings of the past. Even very modern structures, such as Grenville Manor, were very old in appearance, all the considerable technology boxed up in guilded housings.

In Tusck, technology was on grand display, bare metal, hissing steam and dangling wires in stunning neon and ultra light. There were vendors selling holo-stims and magga-packs and the latest delights from Planet Fall. They saw black light stands selling Wolf, Vulture and Panther menthols that Sarah was eager to try, as menthols were also rather rare on Kana. Kay gave her some money, and she bought a pack of Wolfs and Panthers, stuffing them into the pockets of her duster. "Don't tell Mother," she said.

Elsewhere, huge, monstrous vid screens blared out rough sporting events and other noisy entertainments; people gathered around them to watch. Gaudy 4-D tattoo parlors, some mobile on steam-driven carts, were everywhere.

"Shall I write out your conquests for all to see, my lord," a 4D tattooist asked Kay, holding aloft her steaming needle gun loaded with nanotech.

"I already have one," Kay responded and they moved on.

"You lie!" Sarah laughed, shouting over the steam.

"No, really. I have a 4D tattoo. Sam wanted to get one together last winter, so we did. It's nothing too outlandish, but still."

Ki was astonished. "Your dad hates tattoos—does he know about that?"

"Of course not."

Continuing on, Bio-Plants—hands, arms, legs, eyes and various other parts— were sold and installed in abundance right there on the crowded street for all to see in sparks and blasts of steam. People tooled about in floater vehicles, anti-gravs and hotly painted sub-orbitals, some skimming the steamy street, others cavorting about at the heights, coming and going from lofty CWC docking bays.

The citizens were dressed in a motley variety of styles and fashions. There were the occasional Fleet, Marine and merchant types walking about, many with courtesans hanging on their arm. There were outlanders and folk from nearby Bazz dressed in their usual Barbary style, and there were the waifs, the ragged street trawlers and urchins mucking about trying to scratch out an existence. Other groups of people wore nothing but black, their faces hidden in black hoods—clearly Spectres. They clung to the shadows and alleys, silently watching, white menthol smoke coming out of the dark hoods in exhaled clouds.

There were also the servants of various Great Houses, both Onaran and Kanan, apparently there bartering for goods to take back with them. As Ki had mentioned, Kay felt a bit overdressed and out-of-place, the beautiful clothes his mother had designed for him being far too rich for the surroundings. It was painfully obvious he was a Great House Lord engulfed in Tusck.

And he was under assault.

"League-Lites?"

"A hint of jasmine?"

"A bauble for you, kind sir?" the vendors asked hopefully. Kay, as Ki had warned, ignored them. One woman wanted to buy Kay's coat; she apparently liked the fabric and wanted to copy it. Through the backlit gauntlet of steam, Kay did see something he wanted, a cart tended by a small smiling woman selling interesting charm bracelets hanging from hooks. A pretty jet and garnet one caught his eye.

"Failyte, from Hoban," the vendor said in a smoky voice. "Stones that will last forever."

"That's not Failyte," Lon announced seizing one of the bracelets off a hook. He pulled his ever-present goggles out of his coat and looked at it in detail. He took the goggles off again and gave the bracelet back to the vendor. "My mistake, it is Failyte."

And Kay bought it, also buying a blue one for Sarah that she liked, and two more, one for each of his sisters to present to them later. Phillip also selected a bracelet—a green and brown one.

"Who's that for, Phillip?" Sarah chided as she put her bracelet on, already knowing the answer. Phillip, staying silent, took the bracelet and put it into his duster.

As they continued down the street, Kay looked at the jet and garnet bracelet he'd bought. "I'm going to give this to Sam someday, and I'll say: `Sammidoran, I bought this for you in Tusck, to begin replacing the jewels you sold.'"

"You're getting me all misty now," Sarah said.

It could be so easy to get lost in this city, the mystery, the unknown possibilities, the waiting adventure. Kay, after buying the bracelets, began to feel more at home. He found he was beginning to like the city quite a lot. He checked Sam's Meter; it was holding steady, Sam's tiny face uncovered, but nothing more.

That's when they noticed that a courtesan was hanging on Phillip's arm. She had appeared from nowhere, clad in a brown dress with pale skin and kinky, shoulder-length, butternut hair. A ragged menthol hung from her mouth, spewing aromatic smoke.

And she was definitely a dirty courtesan, one of the ones Ki had warned them about. She was all over Phillip, whispering in his ear and blowing smoke, and he wasn't dismissing her. Losing his normal cool and calm, he seemed enraptured. He was in her thrall.

Just like with Thomasina in Waam—he didn't seem to know what to do in the presence of a forceful lady.

Kay stepped over. "Pardon us, madam. We are in great haste."

The courtesan looked at him slow with luminous violet eyes—a sign of a designer fungus—one that had been specifically cultured and grown. She had the smell that he had always heard dirty courtesans had, and it really wasn't a good smell, but it was penetrating, alluring, and quickly seductive. Kay had to concentrate to maintain his focus.

Slow smoke curled out of her nostrils. "First this gentleman," she purred in a seductive contralto, "then you, sir." She pulled her lips into a thin smile. "Perhaps you'll fight over me … perhaps I will enjoy watching."

Ki popped up and seized her by the arm. "Look, Trix, be off! These children are in my charge, so ply your trade elsewhere!" Ki ripped the burning menthol from her mouth and threw it down. She then gave her a rough shove, and the 'Trix' fell to the street, hands first. Continuing on, Phillip shook his head, trying to clear himself from the funk he was in.

"Phillip, I told you to be careful," Ki snarled.

"I'm sorry … I don't know what happened."

Suddenly, the dirty courtesan jumped in front of them. She took Phillip by the hand. "I'll not be denied; come with me, sir … I've not all day."

"You're about to lose a mouthful of teeth!" Ki shouted. "I told you to be off!"

The dirty courtesan wasn't intimidated. "I believe the gentleman can make his own decisions." She approached Phillip and displayed her bosom, letting him get a good whiff of her. "Do you wish me to go away, sir?" She ground her teeth together.

Phillip stammered. "I, I …"

She narrowed her violet eyes and began pulling him. Ki quickly slapped her hand away and grabbed her by the scruff of the dress. The dirty courtesan in turn grabbed Ki by the coat, flushing Tweeter out of his pocket.

"Perhaps we should to the alley and settle this between the two of us," the violet-eyed courtesan said in a gravelly snarl. "You are about to cost me an afternoon's wages."

"Let's!" Ki responded. "And, when I'm finished with you, you'll be lucky if you'll be in any shape to do the deed with anybody ever again. I'll stuff that Weed you're wearing right down your throat."

Kay looked around. He saw a group of Spectres watching from a nearby alley. He Sighted their weapons at the ready.

He got in between and pushed them apart, determined to end this and be away. "Ladies, please," he said. "Here, for your trouble." He flipped the dirty courtesan a shining, silver Blanchefort hader which she caught out of the air.

"What's this?" She looked at it skeptically at first, flipping it over in her hand and biting it. Finally accepting it as a real piece of currency, she slid it into a hidden pocket near her breast.

She smiled and glided into the alley, flanked by the Spectres. "Many thanks, great sir. Should you change your mind, I shall be at your service. Any time." She disappeared into the darkness of the alley. "Any time …"

Sarah, who had been an uncharacteristically meek observer, hauled back and cuffed Phillip in the head, the beads of her new bracelet clicking together. "What is wrong with you?" she yelled.

Phillip hurried along, trying to compose himself. "I don't know, Sarah … I just couldn't help myself. I really wanted to go with her."

Ki glared at him for a moment, then laughed and slapped him across the back.

"S'ok, Phillip. I guess you've got a thing for dangerous women, just like your uncle, and just like Kay here. Boy, wouldn't old Thomasina the 17th—"

"19th," Phillip corrected.

"—be mad if you'd sashayed off with that Weeded up bimbo."

Lon looked back toward the alley. "That woman is playing a dangerous game. That was a particularly toxic strain of The Weed she was wearing—turning her eyes violet and what not. It'll eat the hide right off her, and she's to go blind one day if she's not rid of it soon. Perhaps I should go back there and warn her."

"You're an all-around nice guy, aren't you, Lon?" Ki said. "I'm pretty sure she knows what she's doing. Come on, just a few more blocks, and we're there."

✶ ✶ ✶ ✶ ✶

The University of Tusck was a fairly large school consisting of about a hundred halls, dormitories and libraries contained in a large rectangular enclosure surrounded on all four sides by the towering buildings and clouds of steam of downtown Tusck. The university was old; the huge trees and landscaping were also old—the whole thing appeared to be a part of a different time and place from the smoky, neon-lit, implant infested city right outside its walls. Making their way through the maze of craggy buildings, they entered a large redbrick hall next to a quiet pond and went up to the third floor. Arriving at a walnut door at the end of the hallway, Ki knocked.

"Go away!" came an irritated voice from within. "I'm thinking."

Testing the door and finding it locked, Ki drew her SK and smashed the door knob with the butt of her gun, knocking it off clean and making a huge hole. She then hauled back and roughly kicked the door down where she charged in and disappeared, Tweeter following.

After several moments, Kay and Sarah cautiously peered into the office.

Inside, Ki and a small robed man were rolling around on the floor. Ki looked up at them. "You four make yourselves at home … and give us a couple of hours."

They quickly excused themselves and found a nearby school café, where Kay bought lunch for Lon and his cousins. Sarah couldn't resist and smoked a Wolf menthol right there and then. She said it made her feel 'wolfy' afterward.

14—Of Anuians and Conox

That evening, they reassembled in the Professor's office. It was huge, with a desk, a small sitting area and a large workspace full of gadgets and artifacts that blinked and knocked. A large painting of Ki sat near the desk.

Kay, Sarah, Lon and Phillip sat on a couch. The Professor and Ki sat on a couch across from them. Ki was wearing a blue robe and was asleep, curled up in the Professor's arms. It was strange and a little unsettling seeing her out of her beloved Fleet uniform. Tweeter sat nearby, cozied up next to the painting in a silver glow.

"Well, I must say I am taken aback a bit," he said. "I didn't think you had it in you to get my wife here, Lord Blanchefort. But, you fulfilled your part, yes you did, so I shall do mine." The gadgets on his desk clicked and whorled. He looked at his wife and softly stroked her long hair. "So, go ahead with your questions. I am, as they say, all ears."

Kay checked Sam's Meter; it was still holding steady. He leaned forward and cleared his throat. "Sir, I have a friend who is a Monama. She is pursued by monstrous creatures that are Cloaked and by some sort of entity known as the Horned God. I am invested in her safety. I am looking for a place that may or may not exist, the Horned God's temple that was once sought after by the great hero, Atrajak of Want."

The Trials were over, and the need for secrecy had passed; however, it was second-nature for Kay to attempt to cover-up his relationship with Sam. "Can you tell us where this temple, if it exists, might be located?"

The Professor didn't appear to be listening. He gave Ki a kiss. "A friend who is a Monama?" he said absent-mindedly. "How quaint. Why don't we start out with a bit of honesty and truth here, Lord Blanchefort? I'd heard you were carrying on an extended relationship with an Astralon-tribe beauty and were attempting, somewhat ham-fistedly, to keep it quiet. Is that the case? Have you fallen in love with this Monama girl?"

"Sir, I'm sorry, we really don't have the time to explore such things. Please answer my question."

"Lord Blanchefort, you're going to learn something about me very quickly, and that is that *my* questions come first, and I'm very curious. So what about it? Are you in love with this Monama, yes or no?"

"Yes."

"Well, I must say I admire your spunk. You Blancheforts—first a Black Hat, then a pirate, now a Monama—you do tend to dip into wells seldom tapped."

"You're going to be adding a Xaphan to that list real soon," Sarah piped, getting a deadly look from Phillip.

The Professor was surprised. "Really? I'm fascinated. We'll discuss that further a bit later. Now, Lord Kabyl, let's talk about sex."

Kay was appalled. "Sir, I must insist we ..."

"This is a rare opportunity to gather knowledge regarding Monama sexual practices, and I'm not going to let it pass. You must realize, of course, that you and she are not of the same species, yes?"

"Come again, sir?"

Ki stirred, and the Professor adjusted her robe. "I will grant you the benefit of the doubt that you are simply a very tolerant fellow and not blindly unobservant. The differences are obvious—the eyes, the pallor, the vulnerability to colder temperatures, and the extra set of arms they once had. To use the vernacular, sir, Lady Monama is an alien, or rather, we are an alien species to her, as the Monamas are clearly indigenous to Kana, while we are stellar transplants only lately arrived. You needn't worry, our two species are completely compatible genetically—my research proves that Monamas can mate and successfully procreate with just about any humanoid species; quite remarkable, actually. There have been a few Elder/Monama pairings in the past—with very happy results, though my data are incomplete. Due to the manner in which our differing genes line up, any boy child you have with her will be an Elder, while any girl child she bears will be a Monama. I'll advise that you need to be careful, as Monamas procreate at a staggering rate, having a full term gestation period of just under three months and a standard birthing bearing five to twelve young—you could find yourself with eighty or ninety children without half trying."

"Like little bunny rabbits," Sarah piped.

"Yes," the Professor replied. He gave Kay a wry look. "And I'll wager that Lady Monama simply loves your bellybutton, doesn't she? Monamas find them exceedingly attractive and rather erotic. Is that the case? Does Lady Monama arouse herself to sex just by looking at your bellybutton, or does she need to touch it first?"

"His bellybutton? Why?" Sarah asked.

"Because Sam doesn't have one," Kay replied. "And, yes, merely looking at it gets her very excited."

The Professor stirred. "An obvious question should have immediately entered your mind. With no bellybutton, how then do they gestate?"

"Yes, Professor, that thought did occur to me, though I failed to dwell on it."

"Well, my research is continuing; however, I believe that Monamas develop via yolk sac connected near the anal region while in the womb. I'm certain you've looked at her butt before, yes? Have you never noticed the little dimple there? That is her version of a bellybutton."

Sarah was a bit repulsed.

The Professor smiled. "Monamas have huge libidos—sex and death; these dominate their art and culture, don't they? Ever taken a close look at their pottery, at the intricate embroidery on their gowns? If so, you might notice that all the little swirls and designs are actually composed of either skeletons or tiny people in the act of having contorted sex. They call it Bronta. You shall have your work cut out for you, Lord Blanchefort. Now: transformation. I am told Monama females enjoy transforming themselves into various guises for their men as they have sex, that they derive a great deal of pleasure from it. Has that been your experience?"

Kay didn't respond.

"You needn't be shy, sir. All in the accumulation of knowledge, and modesty has no place. Remember, my questions come first; therefore, what is your answer?"

"Yes, she does transform for me—she insists upon it."

Kay's thoughts spun. *The gallery of women, demons and creatures Sam's been for him: Ki, a Sister ... Sarah ...*

"I'm also told Monama females tend to get a little carried away when they become aroused and can be quite a handful. Has that been your experience as well?"

Kay sat there and blushed.

Beating a ravenous Sam across the back with her chain, raising welts, Sam screaming in primal delight.

"Well, Kay," Sarah said demanding to know, "does Sam like it rough or not! And, what does she turn into for you?"

Kay said nothing. He remembered the things Sam had transformed into for him; a blonde, one of the cooks, a demon, Lt. Kilos several times, and once as Sarah herself.

Sam, slamming him up against a tree, pinning him to it ... ravenous, purring in a berserker's voice wearing Sarah's face. "Use the chain! Hit me with the chain!"

He kept his thoughts buried deep down. It was very personal for him, something shared between him and her alone.

If Sarah knew what Sam had turned herself into for him ...

Lord Lon had a question. He jumped in, saving Kay from the embarrassing line of questioning. "If you are correct, and, as you say, Sam is an alien with a developmental period under three months, how then can they be compatible with us, as a Gifted Elder takes a bit over two years to mature in the womb?"

"Wonderful question, Lord Lon. How indeed? Again, my research indicates Monamas are procreative wonders, real work-horses, able to successfully mate with just about anything that crawls. In a mixed species procreation scenario, Monamas produce young that are either female Monama or males of the other species—in this case, Elder. Lady Monama's womb will not sustain young past three months. She will expel them, and, thus, she will deliver a clutch of fully-developed Monama girls and badly under-developed Elder boy fetuses. Don't be alarmed! All is not lost, as Monama females have a remarkable time-tested solution for that problem. Lord Kabyl, has your lady ever mentioned anything called an '*Anuian Jar?*'"

Kay thought a moment. "She has said that she was *born* in a jar. I thought it was simply an expression."

The Professor was surprised. "Does she? She says she was born in a jar?"

"She does."

The Professor's mind was spinning. "How tall is she?"

"A shade under six feet. She's about my size. Why?"

"With all her hair, though, she's more like seven-two," Sarah added.

The Professor mulled it over. "The typical Conox Monama is anywhere from five-three to five-six. Six feet is more like an Anuian. What about her eyes?"

"What about them?" Kay asked. "They're big and black. They're a lot larger than some of the other Monama eyes I've seen."

"I see. And her eye-lashes? Are they long and feathery?"

"Yes."

"Lips?"

"Notched."

The Professor slapped his knee. "God's bodkins. Well then, she is indeed an Anuian. Very rare."

"That word again. I've believe I've heard it used by the Monamas themselves. Something about an old, larger line of Monama. What does it mean?"

"Once there were two distinct types of Monamas roaming about Kana: the

Anuians, or Greater Monamas, fierce and proud from the north of the lake, and there were the smaller more taciturn Conox to the south. Today there are only the Conox, the Lesser Monamas. The Anuians are gone."

"What happened to them?" Sarah asked.

"The Anuian Monamas were hunted into extinction, leaving only the Conox, though their language, Anuie, still exists, as spoken by the modern lesser Monama tribes of the north lakeshore. Their bloodline still floats around as well, and every so often an Anuian is born among the Conox, as in this case. The Anuians take a bit longer to develop than a Conox does. They take six months instead of just three, and when one pops up, they are born badly premature. The Conox consider the birth of an Anuian a blessing, and have taken steps to preserve them, thus the Anuian Jar. It's basically an artificial womb. They make a large clay jar, line it with the stalks of White Emilia plants and fill it with a brine solution of some sort. During the birthing, a Monama woman called a 'Searcher' sorts through the young and, if she discovers an Anuian, she places it inside the jar, and there they finish their development. I'm still missing a few technical details, but that's the gist of it."

Kay was becoming frustrated. The Professor was on a tangent and his own question, the one he'd come all this way for, remained unanswered. He glanced down at Sam's Safety Meter, just to see how she was doing.

He jumped out of his seat with dismay! The tiny image of Sam within the vial was now almost entirely uncovered, the sand just barely covering her pale ankles, a huge change since the last time he'd consulted it.

Sam, far away on Kana, was now in mortal peril!

What was happening to Sam? Kay turned in a panic, not knowing what to do. "Sam ... Sam!" he cried pacing about. He suddenly felt very far away from home, from Sam. He had to get to her side. He had to help her—to save her!

"Kay, what's wrong?" Sarah asked.

"The vial, Sarah, look at the vial! Sam needs me!" He held it out, his hand shaking. Sarah got up and embraced him, trying to calm him down. He tried to push her away, but Sarah was difficult to get away from. She whispered in his ear, not letting him go.

"Look, Kay, look. The vial says Sam will be in peril when it's fully uncovered, and her feet and ankles are still covered up. That's what it says! Look! She's ok for now, and the Professor is going to tell us what we need to do."

"Is he? Or is he going to continue grilling me about my sexual practices with Sam?"

The Professor's voice came up from the couch, strong and soothing. "I'm done with my questions, Lord Blanchefort, and I am ready for yours. First, let me bear you some news, and you must steel yourself, for it is not good news. I have heard that the *Shuw-shun* is coming for the House of Monama."

Kay heard the words. "What?"

"Sit down."

Reluctantly, Kay sat.

The Professor continued. "Yes. I have heard that the Sisters were not prepared for these series of attacks that have beset the League. The Sisterhood doesn't understand the situation, and doesn't know what to do—and that is a very dangerous thing. The only thing they know for certain is that Berserkacides are heavily involved. Berserkacides are Monama, and therefore the Monamas are a clear threat. They are planning *Shuw-shun* against them."

Lon was beside himself. "Professor, they can't do that. The Monamas are good people."

"I have information that the recent Fleet mission to Hoban was, in part, a last ditch effort to uncover the true perpetrators of these attacks, to prevent the *Shuw-Shun.* Make no mistake—they will blast the House of Monama into dust without hesitation if they feel they have to, down to the last standing child."

Phillip stood up. "So, what can we do? What can be done to prevent this?"

"I think Lord Blanchefort's question will serve us well in preventing the *Shuw-Shun*. So, let's to it. Atrajak of Want, in the last few years of his life, pursued a mythical temple belonging to some fanciful pagan god that his Monama wife had told him about prior to her death. She believed it was a great center of power, that the 'Kestral Oligarchy', as he called them, used it to consolidate their presence on Kana. She wanted to locate and attack it, believing that would free them from the Kestral's grip. Instead, Atrajak listened to his general friend and went on his ill-fated voyage to the stars, hoping to meet the Kestrals on their home soil and defeat them once and for all."

"We know all that. He found nothing when he got there," Kay said.

"Why? Why did he not find anything there?" the Professor demanded.

"That is irrelevant," Kay said.

"No, it is not. I'll ask again, why did Atrajak of Want find nothing there?"

Kay shrugged. "I don't know. Perhaps he went to the wrong solar system. Perhaps the Kestrals there were Cloaked or otherwise hidden and he failed to detect them."

"No, no, he was in the correct location, and he, like you, Lord Blanchefort, was adept at seeing through Cloaks. So, what was he not realizing? What did Atrajak of Want not put together in his mind?"

They all looked at each other.

"While you're mulling that over, I'll answer a previous question that you asked. You asked what happened to the Anuians? Who wiped them out? It was the Kestral Oligarchy who did it. Why? Because it was the Anuian Monamas who followed Atrajak of Want, their *Sar-Gra-Ma*, and dared to raise their hand against the Kestrals. The moment Atrajak was cold and stiff, the Kestrals returned and wreaked misery on the Anuians, wiping them off the face of Kana and further illustrating to the remaining Conox that they cannot be beat."

15—A Tunnel Through Time

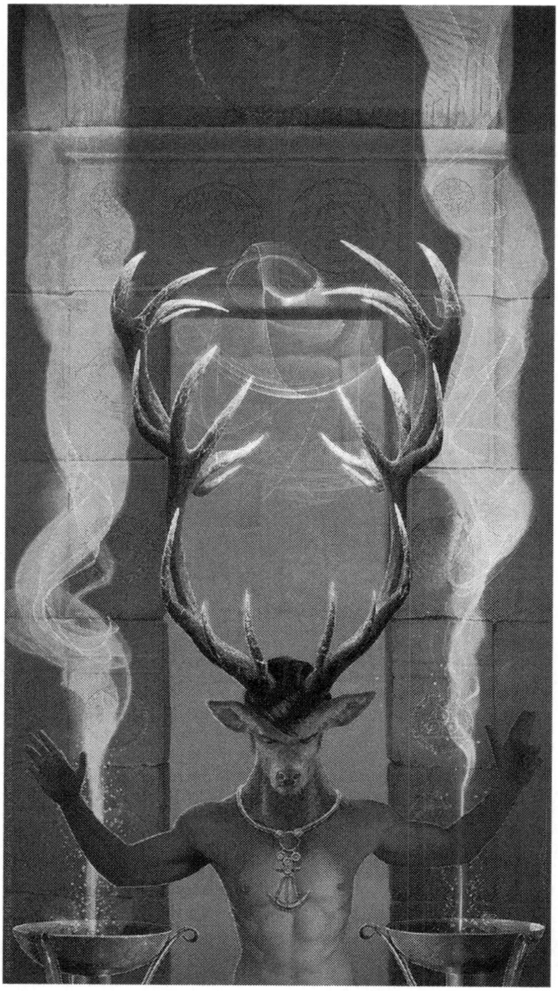

The Professor paused and allowed the information to sink in. It felt like they sat there in silence for a while. Sarah, having acquired Kay's habit, pulled out Sam's Safety Meter, glanced at it, and replaced it in her pocket. Kay Sighted through her duster and saw it sitting there; the sand hadn't moved since the last time he checked. That was good.

The Professor continued. "Any thoughts? Why was the Kestral home world empty? I wonder ..."

Ki stirred and yawned. "Gods, you make me crazy sometimes," she mumbled. "Just tell them, will you?"

Reproached, the Professor spoke, somewhat deflated. "It's because the Kestrals did not exist yet."

Everybody took the news in silence.

"What? What does that mean?" Kay finally asked.

"It means that the Kestrals do not exist in the same positioning in time as we do. Consider this hypothesis: our present is their ancient, primordial past. I'm convinced the Kestrals, the Golden People of a pagan Horned God, live thousands, if not millions, of years in, what to us, is the future."

Lon stirred. "What leads you to believe that, Professor?"

"It makes perfect sense, Lord Probert. Think about it. The Remnath hero Atrajak of Want arrives at the Kestral's home world and discovers it bare; too infantile to support life, though, one day far in the future, after enough time has elapsed, it *will* support life. Consider the Kestrals themselves; what do they use as a weapon against us? The *Killanjo*, yes? What are the *Killanjo?* They are innocent victims plucked from random points in the *future*, tortured into monsters and then sent back into the past. Look at the Berserkacides. What is a Berserkacide? It is a genetic regression in time to a point when the Monamas were four-armed and much more savage than they are now. It is clear that the Kestrals are the masters of time and may move back and forth at their leisure. Atrajak found nothing at the site of their home world because they were not yet there to face."

Kay wasn't buying. "What does this theory have to do with Atrajak's temple?"

"It is this supposed temple that gives the Kestrals their ability to harness time and gain access to Kana from their fastness in the future. That's what I believe."

The Professor flopped several large books down onto the table.

"I had the opportunity to read a fascinating text from the old Monama Nebulon tribe stating that they, tens of thousands of years ago, were much more like the Berserkacides of today: four-armed, fierce, craving flesh and chaos, and possessing an odd glandular opening between their eyes whose function is currently unknown but which may have regulated their aggressive nature. In addition, *they* built a curious temple in the ground where they worshipped a blood-thirsty Horned God and brought him sacrifice for ages."

"Does the Nebulon text describe the location of the temple?" Phillip asked.

"No, only that is was deep in the ground with no door. So then, somewhere along the way, the Monamas lost their second pair of arms and their odd gland and much of the bestial savagery that had ruled their existence for ages. They mention the Gods in Jade and Sapphire who took away their second pair of arms and their madness as well, introducing them to things like, culture and reading and sex. They mention *loving* the Gods in Jade and Sapphire and bearing their offspring. And, tamed, they turned their backs on the Horned God, whispering his name, fearing him as a shadow from the past."

"So, how is this forgotten temple relevant?" Kay asked.

"The temple, by all accounts, was a place of rage and suffering. Such things are significant; such things leave their mark. It became, a nexus, a fixed point in time, shining bright like a lighthouse in the dark of night, and it attracted those who ride the waves of time from the distant future: The Kestrals. Atrajak's wife had it right. The Horned God and his temple are the keys to the Kestral's power on Kana. I believe it provides them with a gateway into the deep past and allows them and their servants the ability to simply step out of thin air, like ghosts. Deal with this temple and you've taken care of the Kestrals. They shall be marooned in the distant future and have no further hold here."

"It's witchcraft then," Sarah said. "How can we fight against such an enemy employing witchcraft?" Sarah asked.

"There's no such thing as witchcraft, Sarah," Lon said. "Neither the Kestrals nor the Horned God can do all of these things without some sort of technology to assist them."

The Professor smiled. "I like your thinking, Lord Lon. Tell me—allow your thoughts to soar a moment—what sort of technology could be at work here, allowing the Kestrals to do all of these seemingly miraculous things?"

Lon thought a moment. "Well, clearly time travel is the key, as you speculated. Time travel itself, as a concept, is not all that difficult to achieve. There are many techniques that may be employed to affect a temporal transference—the 'Looking Glass' effect as the Science Ministry calls it; however, there are many, many complications that arise. The main problem is that your temporal positioning has gravity—strong gravity. Should you attempt to visit a point in time not your own, be it in the past or future, that gravity will ceaselessly want to pull you back to where you belong, and defeating that gravity for any length of time is impossible. The best way, by far, would be by bridging: to sever the gravitational bonds of time that bind you and re-connect them elsewhere, thus freeing you to travel; unfortunately, that does not appear to be possible. The next best way is to make use of a tunnel in time by way of temporal anchorage. Within the boundary of the time tunnel, temporal gravity does not apply—and nor do the understood laws of singularity."

"What does that mean?" Sarah asked.

"It means that anything goes. Within the confines of the theoretical tunnel through time, you could visit the past as you will. My mother has proved this phenomenon. She has a time machine in her personal lab using such a concept."

"She does? She has a time machine?" Phillip asked.

"Yes." Lon was on a roll. "It's not quite as grand as what you might think. She routinely sends atoms back in time. She developed a large coil of rotating electrons and tapped it into the city of Arden's power grid. She turned the coil 'on' two years ago—and, therefore, may freely send atoms back in time two years, to the point when the electron coil was activated. The coil is, in effect, a tiny tunnel through time, a temporal anchorage, with the anchor-point being two years into the past. A year from now, the tunnel will go back in time three years, and so on."

"I don't understand," Sarah said.

Lon settled into his seat. "The concept is really very simple. You can think of it as a spool of string. If I take a piece of string, tie it to the Professor's desk, and start walking away, paying out the string as I go, then the string represents a tunnel through time. The spool that I'm holding represents the present, while the Professor's desk represents the anchor point, a fixed point in the past that the tunnel is tied to. As long as the string is attached to the desk, I can freely travel to any point along its length up to my current position in the present. The present, as it pertains to me, and the past are tangibly joined by the string and the desk—hence a tunnel through time anchored to a fixed spot in the past."

Sarah thought about it. "It sounds simple enough."

"What were the results of your mother's experiments?" Phillip asked.

"Well, that's the whole thing about a time tunnel—it's hard to tell what your results are. See, a Time Tunnel is not a perfect or desirable solution by any means. One, if you managed to make a change in the past, you're never going to know it because your perception will change as well. It's all a matter of perception, what you can perceive and what you can't, and you cannot make sense of a change in the past because your future has changed accordingly. You can't take it with you, so to speak."

"What?" Sarah said, annoyed.

"Never mind. Another problem, you cannot visit the future as it pertains to you with a Time Tunnel, only the past. Referring to my mother's little time machine back home, she can send an atom back in time to yesterday, or wherever as she will; however, she cannot send one ahead to tomorrow. That is a significant drawback. Third, the tunnel through time is actually quite bad for your tissues. Unless you pickle yourself first or wear a cumbersome protective suit, your tissues begin to breakdown—the Sisters have hypothesized on this phenomena and my mother's research concurs. Fourth, you cannot visit the past farther than the point when the time tunnel was activated. If you activated the time tunnel on Wednesday, say, you cannot visit Tuesday, or Monday. Wednesday is as far back as you can go. Finally, the energy requirements to feed the anchorage and the size of the tunnel itself are daunting problems. It's not possible to generate enough energetic power to create an anchor point and tunnel wide enough to move anything larger than individual atoms through at a time. You also have to sustain the anchor point in perpetuity—if you lose energy, at any time, the time tunnel vanishes, and you have to start over again in the present. See, a Time Tunnel is a bad proposition for a lot of reasons. A Bridge on the other hand, theoretically, would overcome all of those problems."

The Professor was impressed. "Yes, Lord Lon, however a working Temporal Bridge has yet to be achieved, at least according to the Sisters. So, let's focus on our Time Tunnel. Imagine, if you will, that we are not simply sending single atoms back in time, but whole living beings—ten to the 27th power of atoms at once. Imagine we're sending back Kestrals and hideous *Killanjo*, who appear to be 'pickled' as you mentioned earlier, possibly to proof them against the rigors of frequent and protracted time travel with the added effect of being a horrifying vision to their intended victims. Imagine, if you will, that size of the tunnel is enormous, possibly light years in scope, and, also, imagine that we're not simply going back in time two years—we're going back ages."

"Again, that is not possible," Lon replied. "Sending a whole living being back through the ages in a time tunnel light years in size would require an unheard of amount of energy, and a device of mammoth proportions that's been in continuous operation to maintain it. My mother darkens the lights back home when she sends a single atom back through her temporal tunnel. She sent back three atoms simultaneously once and took out the lights entirely. Talk about some angry people at our door."

"Yes, but let us suppose such a device exists—so large that it is more like a massive structure than anything else—a structure coursing with power. Suppose the Kestrals, by way of the Horned God, have such an anchorage and tunnel through time. With such a device in place, they wouldn't need a starship to visit the League; they could simply walk out of thin air, and come and go as they please provided they were in range of such a structure—and I would wager such a place would have a vast range—again, perhaps light years in size."

"So, you're saying that the Horned God's temple is an anchorage in time?" Sarah asked.

"Yes, it is the end point of a huge and extremely old tunnel through time."

Sarah looked around the room dubiously—wondering at what might be unseen around her.

"You needn't worry; I have many safeguards in my office to ensure privacy. There are no *Killanjo* or Kestrals watching us here. So," the Professor continued, "are we agreed? I don't know how the Kestrals and the Horned God fell into accord, and I don't know when such a deal was struck or what was offered in barter. I also don't know what the Kestral's motives are or what their endgame might be; as Atrajak discovered, their logic is erratic and their thoughts unknowable. Perhaps, existing so far ahead in the future, something is lost in translation when they visit the past, perhaps it's the confusion of lost perception. It is, however, clear they are using the Horned God's temple as a doorway into the past, and that is where we must focus our efforts."

"What should we do? Where should we go?" Kay asked.

"Well, that's a good question, isn't it? Where is this horrid Temple that great Atrajak couldn't find? Your Monama woman, Lord Kabyl, she is an Astralon, is that right?"

"Yes."

"Then start at Castle Astralon and seek answers there. The Monamas built the temple; they must have information regarding its location, some anecdote or written account. Force them to divulge what they know. No detail or off-handed quip, no matter how small, is unimportant—gather it all. All I need are a few key hints and a little time, and I shall zero-in on this terrible place and make it known. Where Atrajak failed, we shall succeed."

"We will go at once," Kay said standing. "Professor, will we have your ear as we need it for further questions?"

"I am a busy man, Lord Blanchefort. I, of course, sympathize with your plight, and that of your lady, but I cannot guarantee that I will be available at a moment's notice for …"

Ki reached up and whispered something into his ear. His expression changed completely. He looked at his wife with shock. "My Lord," he said, his voice choked with emotion, "you have my ear, anytime it is needed. I am yours."

✶ ✶ ✶ ✶ ✶

Later, as they walked down the street toward to exit the city, Kay couldn't contain his curiosity any further.

"Lt.," he said. "What did you say to your husband to get him to change his mind?"

Ki blushed and looked at the ground, a huge smile on her face. "I told him that I'm pregnant. An Elder woman always knows when she's pregnant, right from conception. I told him he's going to be a father."

"I didn't think you ever wanted to be a mother, Lt.," Phillip said. "What changed your mind?"

"That little boy's voice in the Cat God pub, the one that called me 'Mom'. I want to hear his voice again, only for real this time."

✶ ✶ ✶ ✶ ✶

The dirty courtesan with violet eyes watched the group walk down the street. There was that silly kid in the black duster again. A handsome young fellow, he was an 'Easy' as they were called—a gentleman who couldn't resist the allures of the Weed and completely fell apart in its presence. The coin she'd received from the guy with the purple hair was very lucrative. She'd taken it to a bank and exchanged it for more money then she usually saw in a week. They called it a Blanchefort hader—pretty rare on Onaris and worth quite a bit in Onaris callos.

She wasn't going to let a good thing pass. All she had to do was get in the kid's face again, let him have a whiff of her, and she could probably expect a whole handful of Blanchefort haders to see her gone this time. Her price for going away had just gone up.

And if the Fleet officer with the blonde hair tries to stop her—she'd pull her into the alley and, along with her Spectre friends, kill her.

"I'm going to get us some easy coin," she snarled in her gravelly voice, flicking her menthol away. "Wait here for me, in case their Fleet watchdog needs killing."

As she made to exit the alley and accost the kid in the duster, a hand fell on her shoulder.

She turned.

"I've been wanting to have a word with you," a voice said.

The courtesan narrowed her violet eyes in anger. "Take your hand off me, Slag, before I chop it off!" She looked past the figure; all of her Spectre friends were down and out, possibly dead.

Something exploded into her face, and she fell into a contented dream.

16—Castle Astralon

They had a fair amount of difficulty leaving Lt. Kilos' home—Ki's family all over them, wanting them to stay for a bit. Ki's sister Maia desperately wanted to come with them back to Kana, and Ki literally had to drag her and her bag out of the *Goshawk*. They took off and headed for Kana, making the trip in a little less than four hours. Phillip nosed the ship to the south and arrowed down through the layers of clouds and vapor, heading straight for Lake Monama. Kay hadn't said much on the return trip. Everybody had left him alone—he wasn't in the frame of mind to be sociable.

He wanted home.

He wanted to be with Sam—to save her from these people: these *Killanjo*, these Kestrals and the damn Horned God. He guessed she could lead them on a heated chase for quite some time. She had enormous endurance, and could go for long stretches without sleep, food or water. She had to elude the *Killanjo* and the Kestrals long enough to give them time to locate the Temple, the Kestral's temporal anchorage and deal with it.

And he would kill any in his way. Sam's Meter stood firm, the sand touching her ankles. Something had happened to greatly lower the level, and he dreaded to find out what it was.

Through the glass, the bulk of the southern continent came into view. To the east was the green tangle of the Great Armenelos Forest, growing with abandon and the sandy yellow sliver of Calvert clinging eastward to the sea. To the west were the tan rolling hills of Remnath. To the north were the thirsty, lapis tail of the Great Blue Pierce River and the stately Zenon-lands. South of the river was a great wall of towering pinkish thunderclouds and light-smothering mist: Lake Monama and the pale people with black-hair crowded around it.

Sam's home.

Lon scooted forward, seeing the wall of reaching clouds they were about to hit. "The clouds are a product of lake effect. The waters of Lake Monama are very warm, and coupled with the rather cool air rolling in from the west of Remnath, the lake is constantly creating an upwelling of steam and dense mist."

"Looks arcane to me," Sarah said, seeing the fists of rapidly approaching clouds rimmed with lightning.

"No, no—it's lake effect," Lon repeated.

The *Goshawk* hit the clouds, and Phillip's instruments went blind, alarms and warnings trumpeted in force.

"How am I supposed to fly in this soup?" The turbulence hit him in both sticks, and the *Goshawk* clawed for stability. Phillip lit his Sight but could see little more than before.

Kay let his Sight go, and the clouds melted away in amber.

Below he could see the whole expanse of the lake, the deep warm waters, and the many castles and villages surrounding the bank that looked like little fossils from the air. Unlike his first visit to Lake Monama, this time he could see perfectly.

"Phillip, we appear to be descending too rapidly. Pull up a bit."

Phillip pulled back on the sticks, and the *Goshawk* eased out of its dive.

"Turn the nose to the eastward; that's it—now stop. Hold this course."

"Do you see Castle Astralon down there?" Sarah asked.

"I see a large white castle on a hillside of black north of the lake. I suppose that's the place. That's how Sam once described it to me."

With Kay guiding his movements, Phillip brought the ship down. Even mere feet from the ground, Phillip could see nothing but fog.

With a slight bump, the *Goshawk* settled on the unseen ground, a pool of swirling fog all around. They got out carefully—none able to see a thing except for Kay, who could see everything. Lon put on his goggles and, adjusting them, could see reasonably well. Kay took Phillip and Lt. Kilos by the arms, and Lon took Sarah.

Tweeter took flight, but his silver light was swallowed by the fog.

They began making their way up the hillside.

It was hot and stuffy as they walked—the air thick with humidity and dank with heat. Her boots crunching, Sarah knelt down and pulled up a clump of grass. She held it up to her nose, and, with her lit Sight, could see it was:

"Black—the grass is black."

"It's a lichen," Lon said. "From the humidity. And it's not black, just very dark green."

"Looks black to me."

Moving on, they reached the crags of a blackened ruin, the splintered walls and fallen battlements emerging from the fog. The environs were silent, interrupted only by the occasional sound of breaking waves from the nearby lake.

"Is this it?" Sarah asked.

"No. This is an old Anuian fort, I think," Kay said. "Sam's castle is just up the way here."

Mixed into the black walls of the ruin and all around its base was a fluffy carpet of white. White Emilia flowers.

"I think this is their Forgetfulness Wall," Lon said, adjusting his goggles. "They plant a flower here, so that they may forget their dreams."

"Why would they want to forget their dreams?" Sarah asked.

Kay looked at the flowers, at all the loss and sadness they represented. "Come on," he said. "This way."

They entered a large compound surrounded by a fallen stone wall covered with designs in twisting relief. Sarah felt her way to the wall and lit her Sight, pressing her nose against the stone. "Hey!" she cried in delight, "these designs—they're made up of a bunch of little people having sex! The Professor was right. Look!"

Kay grabbed her, and they continued up the hill.

Ahead, the castle loomed backlit in fog—white as a bone. Castle Astralon.

So far they had encountered nobody, not a single soul. They were alone in the fog.

As they approached the castle, the fog began to thin until it formed a swirling halo around it. The castle was a tall, gothic structure, built in a towering square with flat-topped battlements guarding each corner. The structure seemed in need of repair; it reminded Kay of Castle Durst—a strong, proud structure slowly falling into ruin.

Creation Sam, when this is all over, and you're safe in my arms, I'm going to

give you all the money you need to fix up your ancestral home. I insist.

The massive door leading into the castle was ajar, and they went in.

"Hello?" Sarah yelled, never having an issue making herself heard. "Kay, how do you say 'hello' in Monama?"

"*Yenta*, and it's not 'Monama', Sarah, it's Anuie."

She cupped her hand to her mouth. "Yenta! Yenta!"

No answer. The castle was empty—not a soul around.

Ki unclipped her SK. "I don't like this. Where is everybody? Monama families are supposed to be huge, right?"

"So I've heard." They entered a dining hall. The tables were set with plates of food, partially eaten. Silverware strewn about. A half-sewn shirt lay on the floor near an overturned basket of sewing materials.

Chairs all over the place …

Look at the overturned chairs.

A strange burnt smell lingered in the air. The shapeless remains of some unidentifiable meat were burned up in the hearth. "Euggh," Sarah said. "Smells terrible, whatever it is."

They continued into the interior to the bedrooms. The unmade beds, the dropped items of clothing. Over here—a bathroom, the shower stall overflowing with running water.

Look, a mirror—cracked.

There—a spot of newly dried blood! Dark Monama blood.

Kay whirled around, the truth hitting him. "They came! They came and took them. Sam's family is gone," he said in misery.

"You don't know that," Ki said drawing her SK. "Hello!" she called out. "Sorry. Yenta! Yenta!"

With dread, Kay let his Sight go and fall into the past.

And he saw it all.

He saw the Astralons, the day before in the early morning—some up, some sitting down to a breakfast, some still asleep.

Sam's family—people he'd never seen. They were all so small compared to Sam, and he couldn't see her face in them. They spoke Anuie, though, and he heard Sam's accent.

The flashes of green light invading the castle—the monstrous people that stepped out of nowhere.

Killanjo. Ten of them. Monsters all. Hathaline! Maser!

The screams! The Monamas being hauled about like fish in a net. They were pulled from their breakfast, pulled from their sewing, from their showers and their beds, pushed to the floor and tied up.

Blink, you people! Run away or fight! What's the matter with you?

Trembling, they begged for mercy.

Mercy, please!

They found none. The *Killanjo* found the strongest-looking male present, and they began beating him. They beat him until he could endure no more and began crying out for them to stop, blood splattering his clothes.

"Secret-Talker!" they shouted into the air. "We shall kill every one of these worthless creatures you claim to love. Come out! You are the guest of honor at a humble ceremony we've planned for you! Come out!"

No response. They continued beating the male until he fell to the floor.

For Creation's sake, fight back! They're killing him!

They did not stop: hitting, kicking, laughing. Eventually, he stopped moving and lay there.

Then, they ordered that his body be cooked in the hearth, and served. They untied the Monamas' bonds and made them eat his flesh.

"Secret-Talker!" they roared with glee. "Dinner is served!"

Weeping, the Monamas sat at the table and ate … wishing their deaths. Anything was better than this.

Tears poured down Kay's face as he watched in horror. He looked around, hoping that Lady Poe's Paraflies would come and save the Monamas and sting the *Killanjo* into agonized lumps.

Far away he could see a mass of Paraflies swarming about in the fog bank, lost—unable to see through it. They were of no help here.

For Creation's Sake, fight back. Sam had fought, all by herself she had wiped the *Killanjo* out. He unsaddled his CARG and readied to engage the *Killanjo* and save Sam's family—to stop this. If they wouldn't fight, then he would do it for them.

Something was stopping him—the way was blocked, closed off, unavailable. All he could do was watch.

"Fight back!" Kay screamed. But the Astralons did not fight back; they sat there in terror and ate the unholy meal of their brother, choking down one tearful bite at a time. The Astralon Monamas vastly outnumbered the *Killanjo* and could tear them to pieces with hardly a thought if they only raised their hands and fought back as Sam had done, but with ages of terror inflicted upon them, they could do nothing but be terrified and helplessly allow their fate to unfold.

Many of them began falling into Head Swarm, slumping face-first into the table, their mouths still full of food.

The *Killanjo* produced an assortment of knives and prepared to set upon them—to slay everyone of them. The bent images of Hathaline and Maser dancing in the misery—enjoying every terrifying moment of it.

Kay couldn't bear to watch.

And then Sam appeared at the end of the hall, haggard and worn. She fell to her knees and begged them to stop—to leave her family alone, to take her instead and be done with it.

The *Killanjo* fell upon her, stripped her bare and wrenched her head up by the hair.

There was a look on Sam's face, that proud, beautiful face, Kay had never seen before: utter, hopeless terror.

"Sam!" Kay cried.

There was a burst of smoke, then a crack of lightning, and a large half man/half deer monster appeared in the hall with a tangled web of electrified antlers.

His eyes were the eyes of the devil.

"Led me on a merry chase, did you?" her roared in an elfin voice. "Your flesh, and that of the rest of these creatures is mine! Mine!!" He reached out and seized Sam, holding her like a pale doll. He stroked her black hair. "But, it's not your flesh I want. It's your brain and the little things I'm going to put into it. You and your god Carahil have been very bad .... Eeeehehehehhehee ... very bad indeed. Ohhhh," he said in a calm, almost tender voice, "the wonders that await you in my temple."

A huge green slit opened in the center of the room. Golden people clad in robes came out and swarmed around the Horned God. They reached up and touched Sam on her bare legs. The sounds of beating drums came out through the slit. He and his golden entourage then shuffled into the slit, Sam struggling feebly.

The Horned God looked back. "Kill every one of these creatures," he commanded the *Killanjo.*

And then he was gone, Sam with him.

Sam was gone, in the clutches of the Horned God. Kay tore his hair out in panic.

The *Killanjo* immediately set to the rest of Sam's family. They laid them out on the tabletop and readied their knives. They slavered in anticipation.

There was a flash, and the scene in the past blacked out. Kay could see no more. He returned to the present and fell to his knees.

Sarah came to his side and embraced him. "What, Kay—what did you see?"

He was inconsolable.

"Kay, what did you see?"

"I saw … I saw them come and take Sam ..."

Sarah checked the Sam Safety meter. "What happened?"

"About a day ago. They came and attacked Sam's family. They were merciless and cruel. They roasted one of Sam's brothers and forced the rest to dine from his flesh. Sam appeared and begged them to leave her family alone. The Horned God came and took Sam to his temple. He then ordered they all be killed."

"You saw the Horned God?" Sarah said.

"Yes, Shocktyte bastard! I'll kill him!"

Ki looked around. "I don't see any bodies here, no sign of bloodletting. It looks clean to me."

"I didn't see the massacre. It blacked out just as the *Killanjo* drew their knives to begin!"

Lon panned around with his goggles, checking the tables. "I don't see anything either, Kay—no blood, no scoring, no torn bits of cloth."

"I can't believe the *Killanjo* would clean up after themselves," Phillip said. "There couldn't have been a mass killing here. Something happened to prevent it."

"What, Phillip?" Kay cried. "They were moments away from setting to them!"

"Tweeter!" Ki called, "were the Astralons massacred in here?"

He didn't move. "He says 'no', except for the one fellow, which you appear to be correct about, Kay." She glanced at the blackened mass in the hearth and shuddered.

"Then, what happened to them?" Sarah asked. "Where are they?"

"Tweeter," Ki said, "lead us to the Astralons."

Tweeter erupted out of his pocket within Ki's coat and flapped outside into the foggy murk.

They all followed him out, except for Kay. He stood there, convinced Sam's family was dead, and he hadn't been able to help them.

"Come on, Kay," Sarah said. She took him by the hand and led him out.

They went down the hill, exited the gate and entered into the thick fog again, Tweeter's glowing mass quickly swallowed up.

"Where'd he go?" Sarah asked.

"He's heading toward the lake, I think," Ki said, following him telepathically.

The blackened battlements and broken shards of the old Anuian fortress emerged in the gloom. Fallen, lichen-covered rocks and a thick carpeting of white flowers covered the grounds. Tweeter was there sitting in a broken out window, waiting for them. Sarah crunched onto the rocky beach, the surf from the lake gently reaching out and tapping her boot heels.

"So where are they?" she asked. She spied an interesting rock and picked it up.

"I don't know," Kay said.

"Can you see anything, Kay?" Phillip asked.

Kay tried to open his Sight. "No, I can't see anything. The near past is blacked out."

A harsh, metallic groan came out of the fog. They drew their weapons.

Sitting in the uneven rocks of the ruin, covered by white flowers, was a male *Killanjo*. He was tied up at the wrists and ankles. His head bobbed. He seemed partially unconscious. As they approached, he shook his head and revived.

He was terrible to behold. His body was bleeding and skinless; white petals from the flowers were stuck to him. A single erect penis was attached to his forehead like a unicorn's horn. He focused and sneered.

"What took you so long? Care for a taste?" he said in a demon's voice. He reared his head back and began emitting a horrid screech.

Kay was enraged! "*Killanjo!*" he roared, tagging him across the jaw, knocking him senseless. He fell upon him in a fury, rustling the white flowers all about, kicking up a sweet, nectar-like smell.

"For what you did to those poor people, I'm going to kill you, understand? I'm going to take you to pieces, slice after slice!"

After a moment, the *Killanjo* recovered from Kay's blow. He laughed. "Bit worked up, aren't we? Those creatures are ours! They belong to us to do with as we please!"

Kay raised his CARG. Sarah and Phillip tackled him. "No, Kay, no! We need to talk to this thing—maybe we can get something out of him! Kay!" Sarah cried, trying to control him. "Kay!"

"Sarah! Let me go!"

Lon approached the *Killanjo* and studied him with his goggles, adjusting the lenses. "His brain isn't functioning like a normal Elder. It's like he's asleep."

"We don't sleep. We eat your flesh!" the *Killanjo* said. "Come a little closer, deary. That's it ..." He chopped his teeth together.

Kay seethed. "This is pointless! I'm going to kill him, Ki!" Sarah held onto him. "Sarah!"

As Sarah struggled with Kay, Phillip noticed something shiny flash from the battlements. He drew his Poltava and investigated, stepping into the murky fog. "What, in the name of creation, is this?" he said a moment later.

Sarah and Kay stood up and waded into the fog. There, draped over the rocks was what looked like an empty skin, tawny, with short fur and a huge pair of antlers. Flies buzzed off it.

"Gods ..." Sarah said in wonder.

Enraptured by this horrid spectacle, she released Kay and took the skin from the rocks. She held it out so that she could properly admire it.

"Eugh!" she said, shaking it slightly. Something fell out of the folds of skin.

Phillip reached down and picked up the object that had fallen out.

With Sarah out of the way, Kay returned and approached the *Killanjo,* moving Ki aside. "I'm going to do you a huge favor," he growled. "I'm going to send you to a deep, dark place right now!"

The *Killanjo* smiled, eyes wide.

"Wait, Kay!" Phillip said. He approached holding a mirror. It had fallen from the folds of the skin.

The *Killanjo* saw the mirror, and his snide expression dried up.

Phillip showed the *Killanjo* the mirror. "I understand you don't like to look at yourselves. I can see why."

The *Killanjo* was terrified. He screamed and slavered, trying to get away. Kay threw his CARG down and seized him by the bloody face.

"Oh, don't want to look at yourself, do you? Go ahead, take a look! Take a nice long look!"

Kay wrenched his head around and forced him to stare into the mirror.

He screamed so loud his voice echoed across the battlements, starting off as a demon's roar, then changing to a pitiful wail. The change in sound was so shocking, Kay let him go. The *Killanjo* put his face into his hands and sobbed. When he looked back up, the *Killanjo* was gone—all that was left was a mutilated, terrified young man. He stared up at them, lips trembling.

"P-please," he said, "I didn't mean it. I didn't mean to do any of it! I'm so sorry …"

The five of them converged on him. He sat there in the flowers, and never a more pitiful specimen was ever seen. With bloody hands, he tried to cover himself up.

"What's your name? Tell me your name," Sarah asked in a soothing voice.

"G-Georges of M-Maddox … I was the sixth Lord of Maddox."

Ki knelt down next to him. "What happened to you, Georges?"

"I was taken. Me, and my brother were out in Hoffman Plate, and they came. They took me and my brother …"

"When?" Lon asked. "What year did they take you?"

"003239…"

"003239?" Lon said back. "That's twenty-five years from now."

Georges continued. "They put me in a tank … filled it with liquid that made my skin hurt. I don't know what happened to my brother, and I don't know how long I was in there, but when they let me out, I hurt so bad I cried out, 'It hurts! It hurts!' They stood over me, watching me suffer. They gave me a knife, and I cut myself out of my own skin—I couldn't bear it. Then, I fell into a dream. I did terrible things—I killed people. *I ate people…* The misery I've caused, the things I've done … How could I?"

"You had no choice. You were under a spell," Sarah said.

He cringed and shook his head. "No, no … I should have resisted. I should have fought for my sanity." He looked at Kay. "You wanted to kill me—please, do it. I can't bear this—any of it! The pain in my body, and the guilt in my soul. Kill me, please, and give me peace if you've any kindness in you."

All the hatred Kay had felt for the monster drifted away. Now all he had was pity.

"I will grant your request, sir. But first, those creatures took my beloved Sam and then the Horned God ordered you to kill her family. What happened? Please tell us what happened."

Georges sniffed. "We ... were about to go to work on them. We love hurting Monamas … I … I had one all picked out, the things I was going to do to her ... and then ..."

"Go on."

"And then the Horned God returned. He ordered us to stop. He demanded that we wash and dress the Monamas."

"He did?"

"Yes, and we didn't know what to make of it. We asked him why he wanted them washed and dressed, and he said: 'WASH THEM! DO YOUR DEMONS' EARS NO LONGER FUNCTION? TEST ME AGAIN AND YOU ALL SHALL BURN IN THEIR PLACE!' So, we did it. We hauled them upstairs, lathered them, and bathed and rinsed them. It was so difficult because they had all fallen into a trance like they do when we come to kill them, and they were limp and rubbery. It was hard to move them about."

"Head Swarm?" Kay asked.

"Yes. And then we stuffed them into clothes from the closets and brought them back down to the eating hall. The Horned God surveyed our work and wasn't pleased. He said: 'Put their clothes on correctly', and we could not understand, but we obeyed. It was such hard work. The woman I was dressing rousted out of her trance somewhat and started kicking. I whipped her across the back, and the Horned God became enraged. He said: 'THIS FLESH IS MINE, UNSPOILT, UNMARKED!! WHO DARES MARK THIS FLESH!' And he sent me away in a puff of smoke. Before I knew it, here I was, tied up in the rocks."

They looked at each other rather incredulously. "The Horned God wanted the Monamas washed and dressed?"

"Yes."

"What happened to the Monamas after that?" Phillip asked.

"I don't know. I had a dream that they were turned into rocks for safe keeping, and will remain that way until cast into the waters of the lake."

"Rocks?" Sarah asked. She looked around and kicked at the sandy ground.

"Georges," Kay asked, "where was Sam taken?"

"To the Temple. No Monama ever comes out of there alive—we kill them by the scores there. I've killed them. They just stood there and let me do it. The things I've done in that place ..." He babbled in misery.

"Where is this Temple? Please tell us."

"Deep in the ground. I don't know where exactly. Its entrance is surrounded by a cylinder of ugly faces. It's in a desolate place, near a large river—I don't know which one. I don't know Kana. If I knew, I'd tell you."

"Hey!" Sarah cried. "She reached down and picked up a colorful stone. "Look at this!"

Gathering around, they noticed the stone in Sarah's hand was smooth and colorful, like a polished onyx. And, like a mandrake root, it was roughly man-shaped; it even had a mane of rough Monama hair. They showed it to Georges. "This. Did you dream of rocks like this one?"

"Yes, something like it."

"And the Horned God did this?"

Georges shook his head. "It was a god. He didn't look like the Horned God."

Lon adjusted his goggles and leaned down over the dense carpet of White Emilia flowers. "Look here," he said reaching down into the flowers. He pulled out a small, oddly shaped stone that had been hidden in the growth. "There're more. They certainly look Monama to me."

They all began digging through the bed of flowers and soon had a healthy pile of colorful rocks, about fifty. Coming down from his perch, Tweeter found a few more that they had missed.

They questioned Georges a bit more, but got little of use. In agony, Georges of Maddox fell into a sobbing madness, holding his hands to his face.

"We have twenty-five years to protect you from this, Georges. We promise we'll not let this happen to you."

He smiled a little. They held his bloody hands.

And then Kay gave him peace.

They stood there in the fog with a pile of odd rocks and a dead *Killanjo.*

Lady Tellerran and Lady Sammidoran

17—A Visitor at Castle Blanchefort

"We need to give him a proper burial," Phillip said. "This wasn't his fault. Come and help me." Kay and Ki took off their coats and made a hole near the ruins for Georges' body.

As they worked, Lon made his way back to the *Goshawk* and fetched a chest. "I'm going to gather up all these rocks. I think we should take them with us for safe keeping."

"I agree," Kay said, standing in the hole.

"Georges said they will be reverted to normal when placed in the lake water. I think perhaps we should test it and see if that actually happens."

"That can wait, Lon," Ki said, knee-deep in silt. "We don't need a sick, scared Monama on our hands right now. All things considered, they're probably better off as is until this business is done."

Kay thought about that.

Sam.

Where was Sam? What was happening to her?

He worked hard on the grave, trying to put it out of his mind.

"Sarah, we need some rocks for his cairn. Can you gather a few for us, please?" Phillip called out.

Sarah wandered out to the beach and started gathering large and medium-sized rocks. "Little help here, Lon," she called out.

Lon was finishing putting the rocks in the chest. They were pretty and shiny, like they'd been tumbled and washed. "Me, lift heavy rocks?" he cried in dismay.

"Never mind," she said. She saw a good looking rock and moved across the silt to get it.

Lon looked around. "Is this all? I hope we haven't missed any."

"Tweeter!" Ki called out. "Are there any more Monamas here on the beach?"

He flicked a wing. "Nope—you got them all."

Sarah reached the rock she wanted and then stopped. She stared for a moment. "Hey, can you all come over here, please?"

"We don't have time, Sarah. We need to finish, say a few words, and go. We've got to locate Sam!" Kay said.

"No, really. Come here."

Kay, Phillip and Ki climbed out of the hole and joined Sarah on the beach.

"Look at the rocks," she said, pointing down.

Mixed into the silty sand and accumulated beach trash were a number of colorful stones that seemed to be arranged into letters. They read:

CARAHIL WAS HERE

Kay stared at the letters. "Can it be true? Carahil? Was that second Horned God Georges saw in Castle Astralon actually Carahil in disguise?"

Phillip rubbed his chin. "It must be. From what he described, the second appearance of the Horned God was much more benevolent than the first and seemed to be actively protecting the Monamas from the *Killanjo*. Perhaps it was he who changed the Astralons into rocks to save them. There's also that discarded skin we found in the rocks—he must have been wearing it."

"Then why didn't he come and save Sam? Why?"

"I don't know, maybe he couldn't for some reason," Phillip said. "He probably couldn't save Sam."

"Why not?"

"Well, what did Sam tell you in the Grove? Something about being framed by the Horned God and that he thought Sam was his 'Keeper of Secrets' or whatever? Remember that? Perhaps if he'd arrived sooner he would have been captured or something."

Kay kicked at the silt in frustration.

"Look, Carahil would have saved her if he could've, Kay. You know that!" Ki yelled. "You said the whole reason the Horned God thinks Sam is his Secret-Talker is because of all the time he spent protecting her since we've been gone, so don't be getting mad at him now. He can't do everything!"

Kay silently agreed, though it galled him.

"So, what are we going to do?" Kay asked. "We came all this way for information, and what did we learn—that Sam has been taken by a pagan god and her family turned into rocks by Carahil?"

Phillip checked Sam's Safety Meter and was more empirical about the situation. "I think we've learned quite a lot. Georges of Maddox confirmed the existence of the temple and that it is near a river."

"Phillip, there are thousands of miles of river coast on Kana. That tells us nothing! We're no closer now to discovering the location of this hidden temple than we were before!"

"Actually it rules out the Isle of Barrow and vast areas of Vithland, as there are no large rivers there," Lon said, lugging the chest of rocks back to the *Goshawk.*

Kay had a thought. "Ki, what about Tweeter? Can he zero in on the temple?"

"It's worth a shot. Tweeter, where is Lady Sammidoran of Monama at this very moment?"

Tweeter hopped back up to the battlements and lingered there—a sure sign he was either confused by the question, or, for whatever reason, the answer eluded him.

"And so?" Kay asked. "What's he saying?"

"He isn't saying anything. Sometimes various arcane places and objects throw him off a little. Either that, or, wherever Sam is, it's not on Kana."

Tweeter flew down from the battlements and pecked at the rocks on the beach.

"Wonderful," Kay said. "Then we better finish up here, get back aboard the *Goshawk* and contact the Professor and tell him we found out nothing."

Ki checked her timepiece. "Nope—he's conducting class right now. It'll have to wait a few hours."

Sand, stirred up by Tweeter, flew. Kay brushed it off his collar.

"Sam is in mortal peril at the moment, and we cannot afford to wait. We need to take action!"

More sand. "Tweeter!" Kay yelled. "Will you stop it?"

Tweeter had made a mess on the beach. Sarah, gathering more rocks for the cairn, inspected his work. "Look at this," she said.

"What?" Kay said, annoyed.

"Look!"

Tweeter had fouled the rocks on the beach that read: CARAHIL WAS HERE. Now it read:

CAR H L WA E

✶ ✶ ✶ ✶ ✶

After they laid Georges to rest and finished his grave, Phillip ripped the *Goshawk* out of the fog at a fast climb and bore northwest, across the shallow Sea of Atalea, toward the mountains.

"What's our course?" he asked.

Kay was inconsolable—what he had seen, Sam and her family, so powerful and proud, reduced to terrified groveling, and eating the cooked flesh of their own kin.

They could have fought back, and they could have annihilated the *Killanjo*. Why didn't they?

Sam was in the Horned God's temple. He had to locate it.

Atrajak of Want, a legendary hero, couldn't do it ...

As Phillip leveled out over the Sea of Atalea, Sarah opened the Holo-term and put a call out to the Professor.

As expected, he didn't answer. "I told you, he's conducting class right now," Ki said.

She opened the holonet terminal and started doing research. The Holographic gentleman appeared, and she looked up the House of Maddox.

"According to the listings," Sarah said, "the House of Maddox currently is a House Minor from Z-Encarr, Planet Fall. Their trade is the precipitation of argon gas and other trace elements. The House is presided by Lord Christian and his Sub-Countess Georgina. What's a Sub-Countess?"

"That's another word for a 'concubine'," Ki added with a wink. "Lots of those on Planet Fall."

Sarah smiled. "Oh. It also says they currently have ten children, and yes, they do have a Georges of Maddox. He's currently four years old—the sixth Lord Maddox of his line—I think that's what he said, wasn't it?"

Kay looked at the listing. "We're not going to let him become one of those things. He has his life to live. We're putting a stop to it. We save Sam, and we save him too."

"We'll keep our findings here in mind," Ki said, "and tonight we'll get my husband on the line and see if he has anything further to add. He should—he knows everything."

"That's because he's a Hertog, right?" Sarah asked.

"If I may ask, Lt.," Phillip said from the front, "what is your husband's name. I don't think I know what it is."

"Don't ask," Ki commented back.

Phillip settled in a high altitude arc. "Where are we headed? Perhaps we should just go home and wait?"

"No," Kay said, "we've got to keep moving. We've got to do something! We can't just wait until tonight!"

Lon interjected. "Sam could be anywhere. We've got to keep our wits about us and think rationally."

The Holo-term rang in. "Somebody's signaling," Sarah said.

"Maybe it's the Professor. Accept the Com, Sarah!" Kay said.

She manipulated the controls and up popped the holographic image of Lady Poe, looking much better and more rested.

"Oh joy! I thought I'd find you there," she said. "Phillip, Phillip?" she called out.

He turned from the cockpit. "Yes, Mother, I'm here."

"Oh, Phillip!" she exclaimed, "I'm so glad I got you. We have a guest here at the castle today—someone who is simply dying to meet you."

Phillip darkened. "I see. And just who might this person be?"

Lady Poe moved the Holo-cone, and the back of a tall wicker chair emerged. They recognized it as one of the chairs from the western terrace overlooking the village. Slowly, the chair turned to face the Holo-cone.

"Phillip," Lady Poe said, excited. "This is Lady Thomasina the 19th of Woolover, and she has been asking to see you. She's a big fan of yours! Isn't that wonderful?"

There she was, sitting in the wicker chair in a green gown holding a summer drink. Her alluring brown eyes were burning in their sockets. Her long, green hair spilled onto her bare shoulders. "Hello, Phillip," she said in her cool Xaphan voice.

Phillip's eyes fell out of his head, and he bolted out of the cockpit, the *Goshawk* banking slightly to the left. "Creation, help me!" he cried.

"Greetings. It is good to see you again, Phillip. Might I say our previous parting in Waam was … unsatisfactory at best." She looked around. "My, this is a wondrous place. I was hoping you'd be here. I wish to explore it in your arm. Shall I wait for you in the ... what did your mother call it: The Firth House? Shall I wait for you there?"

"You've got a lot of nerve," Sarah said confronting Thomasina over the holo, "showing up at our home, sitting in our chairs, drinking our liquor! Besides, you're not supposed to drink liquor! You're a Blood-gutted, bar-rousting Woolover for Creation's sake!"

"A drink, in moderation, is fine, I've always said that. And this is a lovely Kanan grain spirit—quite a treat and something not to be missed. We don't have access to such things back home. It has a wonderful flavor. And, speaking of things that taste good, am I not welcome here, Phillip?" Thomasina asked.

Phillip started to say something, and Sarah cut him off. "No! You're a Xaphan!" she roared. "She's a Xaphan, Mother!" Sarah cried into the Holo, but, being a directed cone, Lady Poe couldn't hear a thing.

"I am a lady descended of the House of Woolover, which makes me a defacto League citizen, and, yes, I am a Xaphan as well, I made no bones about that with your fine parents as I introduced myself. I took a stealth ship to Xandarr and, from there, using my House Woolover affiliation, booked legal passage to Kana. Along the way, I'd heard your group was in Tusck, and I stopped there to see if I could locate you. Apparently, there was a vile street courtesan who was hoping to steal money from you, Lord Blanchefort, and I happily relieved the strumpet and her

Spectre crowd of their teeth, and allowed you to continue unmolested." She smiled a great, pointy smile. "You're welcome."

"So, what now?" Sarah roared. "What are you going to do? Sic your Singing Ten on us again? Fire more rockets at us?"

"Sarah, calm down a peg, will you?" Lon said.

"Did she cast a spell on you or something, Lon?" Sarah cried. "This is the woman who chased us across Waam like a pack of dogs!"

"Would it be so horrible to hear her out, Sarah?" Lon asked. "By the way, who's flying the ship right now?" he said looking back at the un-manned cockpit. The sticks gave a small jerk, and the nose dropped. Sarah yelped and flew into the chair.

Phillip faced her. "So, ma'am, what do you want?" he said quietly.

"That should be obvious, Phillip. You left without saying goodbye."

"Ah yes, after you tried to kill us with rockets."

"Kill you? Those were tiny little rockets—would have barely scratched your ship. So, I've come to your home today to announce my intentions."

"Ladies do not announce intentions to Great Lords, Thomasina! It's the other way around!" Sarah yelled from the cockpit, craning her neck around to see the Holo so she could scream at it.

Thomasina smiled. "I'm a Xaphan, remember—we're so uncivilized. I wish to court you, Phillip. Auld brought you to me, and we shouldn't take a blessing of the Elders lightly. I am alone, as you can see, and unarmed. Obviously I feel rather strongly about you. And, though I admit I lost my temper in Waam, I wouldn't have harmed any of you. I must say, I found the whole incident rather enjoyable. You are a highly skilled quartet. For my loss of temper and previous bad manners, I do apologize." Thomasina shifted in her seat and looked around. "Lord Lon," she said. "Lord Lon, can you hear me?"

Lon stepped up. "Great Lady?" he replied, bowing.

"My Ladies were very impressed with you, sir. One of them says she owes you her life. They wish to know if you are currently available."

Lon smiled. "Why thank you, my lady, and yes, I am …"

Sarah cut him off. "It doesn't appear that Phillip or Lon have anything to say to you, Xaphan Jo-Boy!" she shot back from the cockpit, in full froth.

"Really? I hear Lady Sarah doing a lot of talking, and what do you say, Phillip? Have you nothing to say to me?"

Phillip stood there a moment. "That is correct, Thomasina—I have nothing I wish to say to you," he stammered.

She smiled. "Oh, Phillip, lying does not become you. You forget, I've been a magistrate for years—I can spot a bold-faced lie a mile away. I can also determine quite a bit just in looking at your surroundings. Given the apparent intensity of the sun coming in through the cockpit glass, you are far to the east and to the south, and noting the cloud formations in the distance, you are either over water or very near to a sizable body of it. Now then, when may I expect you here? Remember, it's rude to keep a lady waiting."

"Creation, she's zeroing us!" Sarah said. "Cut the damn link before she knocks on the door!"

"We shan't be home any time in the near future," Phillip returned.

"I see. I plan on staying the night here. In the morning, I shall depart and attend church with my House in Saga. I greatly wish you to join me, Phillip."

"Why? Are you gonna' show him off like a trophy and then devour him?" Sarah shouted. "Phillip, shut it, and cut it!"

"I'll not attend church with you, Thomasina," Phillip replied.

"Well then," she said. "Then I shall be back, and next time I won't be wearing a gown."

Ki unbuckled her SK and jumped in front of Phillip. "If you're planning on attacking Castle Blanchefort …"

Thomasina looked at Ki over the Holo and sized her up for a moment. "And, you are?"

"Lt. Kilos, first officer MFV *New Faith*, a family friend and protector of Castle Blanchefort in the absence of its Lord."

"I see," she said. "Fear not, there will be no attack. Surely Phillip can handle one unarmed woman who simply wishes to instill a goodly way of thinking in him. Surely such attention flatters him."

"You wanted to kidnap him in Waam," Sarah accused from the cockpit, the ship flying a little wobbly. "Had we not intervened, he'd probably be chained and naked in your pits even now!"

"Pits? You have a lofty imagination, Lady Sarah, though that does conjure up an interesting series of images. Again, I lost my temper, I have said so and have already apologized for that."

"And, if you lose your temper again?" Ki asked.

Thomasina chuckled and didn't answer. "So Phillip, may I expect you or not? Just so you know, I have been accommodated in Joab Tower this evening on the fifty-second floor, and, should you choose to show, my door shall be unlocked."

"Why?" Sarah roared, "so you can snog him up again?"

"Most certainly," Thomasina said.

Phillip stood there. The ship lurched. "Watch that yaw, Sarah!" Phillip snapped, pointing. Red-faced, she held the sticks and glared back at him. He turned back to the Holo. "No—no, Thomasina, I'll not be there."

"Very well, so be it. You shall never hear from or see me again. Farewell."

"Thomasina wait!" he said abruptly, stepping forward.

She leaned in toward the Holo and gave a wide-eyed, open-mouthed grin. "Ahhh, so Phillip, you do care. I knew it—how nice." She watched Kay sitting restlessly and detected something was wrong with him. "I see Lord Blanchefort back there is in quite a state. Why don't you come here and pick me up, and I'll assist you in whatever it is you're doing. Or, tell me where you are, and I'll come to you."

"You needn't trouble yourself, Xaphan!" Sarah yelled. She dove out of the cockpit and switched off the Holo-terminal—Thomasina's face deformed and vanished. "Who does that Xaphan witch think she is?" she said picking herself back up.

Phillip recovered from his funk and threw himself back into the cockpit and grabbed the sticks as the *Goshawk* began to power dive.

"Well, Phillip, you really told her off, didn't you?" Sarah roared standing over him.

Phillip squirmed in his seat. "Quiet, Sarah, or I'll open the hatch and pitch you out head first!"

"Oh, yeah? Where was all that tough talking when Thomasina was on the Com? You dummied up just like you did in Waam, and in Tusck! What's the matter—can't handle a tough lady? Either admit that you like her chasing you around, or check yourself into an Elder monastery where all the tough women in the League can't get to you, and start scrubbing the floors!"

"If I weren't flying this ship, I'd floor you right now!" he responded.

"Well, put it on Auto, big boy, and let's go!"

✶ ✶ ✶ ✶ ✶

As Phillip and Sarah loudly bickered, Kay sat down and held his head in misery. Seeing Thomasina twist Phillip into knots reminded him of Sam.

The Horned God in his Temple

18—Of All Those Gods

After Sarah and Phillip finished their shouting match, she returned to the Holo and continued to try the Professor.

Ki sat down next to Kay. "You all right?"

He smiled and nodded.

Lon sat there and held his goggles. "I keep thinking of that poor fellow—Georges of Maddox. As soon as he looked into the mirror, his brain scans returned to normal, though he was clearly in distress. How could such a thing happen?"

"It's not going to happen. He and my sisters and brother—-none of them are going to suffer that fate."

Ki gave Lon a knock on the shoulder. "Hey, you told Thomasina that you're available, but I wouldn't be so sure about that."

Lon was confused. "I don't quite know what you mean, Lt."

"My sister Maia. She's got the hots for you bad. She wanted to come with us so she could hang out with you some more, but I told her no—had to punch her too."

Lon blushed.

"And, I'm pretty sure she wouldn't take it well if you went off with one of Thomasina's ladies. Suddenly, Lon, you've got all sorts of women looking for you."

Lon started asking Ki questions about Maia when Sarah gave a cry of triumph. "The Professor! I got him! I got him!"

They gathered around the Holo term, and there he was, sitting in his office in Tusck. He listened as they filled him in on what they had discovered at Castle Astralon.

"You're sure this is accurate, what you have told me? Down to the last detail?" he asked

"Yes, Professor," Kay replied. "It was a traumatic and rather wasted trip."

"Certainly it was traumatic, but it was hardly wasted. We have learned much."

"We have?" Sarah said.

"Yes. While you've been busy traipsing about Kana, I have been studying this Horned God entity in greater detail. He's a beast—a creature of chaos and destruction ruling over a hell-like place called Tevlapradah. He revels in blood and burnt sacrifice and the suffering of others. He is, for lack of better terms, the 'Boogie-Man' of the gods. As for what he wants with your Sam, the Horned God has been known throughout the ages for abducting the Secret-Talkers of other gods and, ultimately sacrificing the gods themselves to the Kestrals."

"What for?" Sarah asked.

"Unknown. He sacrificed the old mole-goddess Anabrax and others, so it's written."

"He believes Sam is Carahil's Secret-Talker. What is that?"

"It's an individual, usually a mortal person of the so-called younger folk, who, either consciously or unconsciously, keeps a complete mental record of all a particular god's doings. The gods use them to enhance their power and to police each other—if a god begins to act in an improper manner, the other gods could then look at the Secret-Talker and uncover the truth. Alas, from what I've read, the gods go to great lengths to hide and protect their Secret-Talkers to prevent just such a thing from happening. If the Horned God believes that Lady Sammidoran is Carahil's particular Secret-Talker, then it's possible he might be trying to either alter the secrets she supposedly carries, or implant false ones altogether."

"To what end?" Kay asked.

"Possibly to divert suspicion, to plant evidence."

"To frame Carahil?"

"That is a possibility. Possibly to sacrifice him. And, if that's the case, that might afford us time to act."

"How do you mean?"

"According to several old texts I've consulted on the topic, implanting false secrets into a Secret-Talker is not easy; in fact, it's a laborious, time-consuming process."

"How long?" Kay asked. 'How long do we have?"

"If my reading is accurate, about three days. We've already lost a day and then some, so we have a little less than two days left. Certainly, what Lady Sammidoran is experiencing right now in his temple is not pleasant, but her death does not appear to be what the Horned God seeks. He wants her alive and well, carrying a head full of bad secrets."

"Well, come on, hon," Ki said. "Where is this Temple? Georges of Maddox said it was located deep in the ground near a large river."

"Yes, the Horned God's Temple, the place Atrajak of Want couldn't find. That's the tragic thing about heroes though. They spend too much time swinging about on the battlefield and not enough time page-turning in the library. Do a little reading and a clear picture emerges. Throughout the ancient history of Kana, there have been frequent writings referring to the Temple. It's referred to by a number of names—most commonly the 'Temple of the Exploding Head', for that seems to be the fate of many worshipping there. However it's named, it's a sinister place, full of death and misery—just the sort of place that would foster a raging tunnel through time."

Kay thought about Sam in such a place, full of dread. "Then where is it?"

The Professor paused. "I don't know."

Ki was open-mouth shocked. The Professor saw it and quickly responded. "Though I do not know the *exact* location of the Temple, I'm convinced it is located somewhere in the Hala region of Kana. I base this conclusion on a number of clear factors. One, assuming the old writing is accurate and the Monamas themselves built the Temple, then it would have to be confined to a geographic area that is within their range, as many parts of Kana are simply too cold for them to survive. Hala does fall within the extreme northern reaches where they can safely roam. Two, a number of ancient texts mentioning the Temple of the Exploding Head were written in or near the Hala region. See, among the many errors Atrajak made was that he assumed the Temple had to be located somewhere in Remnath. League heroes, especially those from Kana, tend to do that—to automatically assume that anything worth seeking out could only be located in their particular slice of Kana. Atrajak was a Remnath, and, therefore, per his reasoning, the Temple had to be in Remnath as well. It probably never crossed his mind that the Temple he sought was actually in a quiet, non-descript place like Hala; nevertheless, the evidence is clear."

He paused a moment. "To continue with my evidence gathering, the word you saw on the beach '*Carhl Wae*' is very important, and I'm a little disappointed none of you picked up on it. That's not simply just gibberish created by my wife's Tweeter—it's an actual phrase in the old Hala dialect. It isn't such a surprise, Tweeter has exhibited odd, psychic episodes in the past. I've experimented on him and determined that to be the case."

"Wait a sec, darls—you've *experimented* on Tweeter?" Ki cried.

"I have. I made sure you were asleep first. Let's focus. *Carhl Wae* in old Hala means: *dreadful mouth*. I don't see how that's a coincidence. I don't know what it means just yet, but I will, give me time. Finally, Georges of Maddox provided an invaluable clue. You have to listen to and discriminate what people say, you must also consider the person saying it, and the truth will be revealed. He said the area of the Temple is 'desolate' and near a 'large river'. I interpret his use of the word 'desolate' as actually meaning 'rural'. The House of Maddox comes from Z-Encarr, Planet Fall, which is about as urban and densely packed as one can possibly get in the League. Thus, a quaint rural Kanan setting, to him, might appear as being desolate. The river he mentioned must be either the River Seven or the Killbane. Both are in the Hala region, and both run through some very rural country. Go to Hala at once and start snooping around. Stick to the rivers. That's a lot of ground to cover, I know, but it's a start. One thing, and this is very important: when we discover the Temple, it is critical that we *not* encounter the Horned God there. According to my reading, a god encountered in a temple dedicated to him is supremely powerful—possibly more so than all the other gods combined."

"We'll do our best," Kay said.

"Good. Meanwhile, I will continue my research here. Contact me again tomorrow. I should know more by then."

"Professor, we are running out of time," Kay said.

"Agreed. Still, I cannot simply snap my fingers and have all the answers. Knowledge requires diligence and research, reading and tenacity. I assure you, by tomorrow, I will have the precise location of the Temple."

The Professor said a few more things to Ki and then screened off.

Kay turned to Phillip. "Phillip, let's head east to Hala."

"Hala's a big place. Do you want to hug the rivers?"

"No. I'm thinking we'll start off at Castle Vincent, our aunt's castle. From there, maybe we'll get some clues—she knows a lot about the region. We can't simply wait until tomorrow night."

Phillip banked the *Goshawk* and headed east.

19—A Boy Learning to Read

Although the voyage back to the League had just begun, it was already looking bad for the *New Faith*. They hadn't seen another ship or encountered any trace of intelligent life, for that matter, for days. The huge League vessel was apparently alone in the vastness of space.

But that didn't mean they weren't under constant attack. After the sinister tank encounter, even after several Stellar Mach transverses, there were golden infiltrators constantly seeking to penetrate the ship through quickly formed and dispersed Gamma bands. Davage, ever vigilant, would see a band open, and an innocuous person would step out and try to blend in with the crew, their purpose or intent unknown. Sending a security team, they quickly captured the infiltrator, who then vanished before questions could be applied.

That's how it started. It quickly got worse.

As with Crewman Lasset, the infiltrators tried to replace various crew members with duplicates. The infiltrators came at their target when they were alone or when they were asleep. They then envelop the person and tried to take their place. Others were hauled away through the green gamma doorways to an unknown fate. Several crew were lost in such a fashion before adequate counter measures were put into place.

Davage began an endless vigilance, constantly scanning the ship looking for Gamma. Once detected, he directed a team to intercept. He gave out a general order that no personnel were to be alone at any given time, and the crew were ordered to move about in pairs.

Then there were the lights—the Insanity lights shining down from hidden places, attempting to bathe the ship in its terrible glow. The light wasn't hard to avoid, but it slowed them down, almost to a crawl sometimes.

Davage avoided the beams when discovered and turned the ship to maul whatever it was that had created the light; but nothing was ever there. As always, they were chasing ghosts.

The enemy was all around, poking and testing, but unwilling to present, unwilling to stand and fight. What kind of enemy was that? Even Xaphans had enough courage to join the field and fight it out.

These people, these Golden People, were so alien, so unlike the Elders, that it was difficult to know their minds and take measures against them.

One thing was perfectly clear: they wanted them under wraps and under heel. Just like the Monamas. To turn them into monsters in a tank and send them back to create terror and destruction in the League.

Additionally, the changes in their tissues that Ennez had detected hadn't gone away. It was still there and getting progressively worse as time passed. If they didn't either determine the cause and prescribe treatment or present themselves to the Hospitalers for examination, they would all soon exhibit debilitating symptoms, and Davage predicted a panic and crash in morale should that happen.

They had to maintain course and speed. They had to make it back to the League and soon.

And Davage, under the strain of having to see into the Gamma band constantly, was beginning to feel its toll. Exhausted, he couldn't stand any further and was confined to his bed, where Syg sat at his side and held his hand. His head ached with the strain.

Food and lack of provisions was another pressing issue, as the *New Faith's* pantries were near bare. Diligent teams were on the scopes bells-high, searching the starways for nearby locales of possible forage.

And they were successful, locating promising green worlds that certainly might offer raw bounty. Forage missions were assembled, however, they quickly discovered the enemy was not going to allow them to browse unmolested. Every time they stopped and sent down teams to collect food, the attacks would come in waves, both on the ground and on the ship. Lightning strokes from nowhere and Insanity Lights were rampant. Whole teams vanished; abducted and gone. Eventually, they had to plan these forage missions like a full military campaign, using the Marine attack ships they'd taken on as screens and high cover. They were hit with Berserkacides and *Killanjo*, each more horrid and savage than the last. In some cases, the Enemy scorched the planet they hoped to forage, leaving them nothing but cinders.

Each attack, though warded off, cost them crew, cost them strength, and left them a bit weaker.

Ennez and Beth did what they could for Davage, but he was slowly succumbing. He needed rest, but there was none to be had. The intruders' attacks were unrelenting. Fortunately, Paymaster Stenstrom was doing a fantastic job commanding the ship in his absence. What the stuffed shirts back at Fleet would say if they knew he was allowing a civilian, and an accountant at that, to sit on the chair.

Whatever, each to his gifts, and with no Ki around, Stenstrom would do.

Stenstrom commanded with dash and a sure hand, just like his father, Stenstrom the Older, had before him on the warbird *Caroline*. Davage had heard the sprint vessel *Warlock* was soon to need a captain, and who better than the dashing Lord Belmont, a fighting Paymaster of all things, his father's son in every way except that he was a civilian accountant instead of a Fleet Officer. He could even do the ship's transactions, Davage noted with amusement—something he himself had little understanding of. All Davage had to do was get him home, and his career, his true career, could begin in earnest. Paymaster Stenstrom, the man from Tyrol in the Hoban Royal Navy coat and a silk mask … captain.

But, that prospect was looking bleaker by the moment.

✶ ✶ ✶ ✶ ✶

Stenstrom came into Davage's room, decked out as usual in his HRN coat and his silk mask. His deadly NTH pistols jutted out of his green sash.

He approached, bowing to Countess Sygillis. His blue eyes sparkled through the holes of his mask. "Great Countess, well met. Captain, we are well on course. We have a count of two days, thirty four minutes until our next Stellar Mach transverse."

Davage, sweating under his bed sheets tried to focus. His head ached. "How's the crew, Bel? How are they holding up?"

"They are in threadbare shape, but doing as well as can be expected. They are eager to get home."

"And provisions?"

"We'll be fine for the next few days provided we stick to our rationing; however, we will need to stop again for forage soon."

Davage dreaded the thought. "And how is Crewman Lasset?"

Stenstrom shook his head. "Ennez placed her into a purpose-induced coma today. She was in a great deal of pain. Her skin … I offered a few Holystones to help sedate her. I was glad they helped. I will prepare more to extend her treatment."

Davage thought about the *Killanjo* tank and the poor man they'd rescued. He had screamed in pain. Syg killed him with an StT, a mercy killing. They'd rescued

Lasset only to consign her to unbearable torment in Ennez's dispensary. Perhaps they should have given her peace too.

One by one, slowly but surely, they were all going to die. It seemed inevitable; they'd starve, be abducted, be driven mad or their bodies would succumb to an unknown malady. The prospects were all unpleasant. He put his hand to his forehead—his head was splitting. He drifted off.

"Dav?" Stenstrom asked.

Syg jumped in. "He's very tired, Bel," she said. "Anything on the roster today?"

Stenstrom waved his hands and produced, out of thin air, a pad. That was another thing the Paymaster could do: Tyrol sorcery, make things appear and disappear. Magic, or sleight-of-hand? Davage always wondered. It was always a sure thing to see.

"How do you do that, Bel?" Syg asked.

"Magic." Stenstrom looked at his pad. "I have this month's payroll to count, for what it's worth. Also, I was going to inspect the refugees we picked up—the Monamas in the hold taken after the attack over Hoban. They've not been seen yet in an official capacity." Another wave of his hands and the pad was gone.

Davage closed his eyes. "Ah, yes. I'd forgotten."

The refugees ...

He slowly rose and began to get out of bed. Syg tried to keep him lying down, but he was determined.

"I'll review the refugees."

"You need to stay here and rest, Dav," Syg said.

"No, no, our guests deserve to see their captain as is proper. Bel, you get to the bridge. And keep a weather eye."

Stenstrom looked at Davage. "Sir, the Countess is right. You need your rest."

"I'm fine. And I'm not infirm. I shall see the refugees. Go on."

Stenstrom tipped his hat and left.

Davage's entire body hurt as he began to dress.

"You sure you want to do this, love?" Syg asked tenderly.

"Yes, it'll help take my mind off my aching head."

Syg helped him get ready and popped his hat on." "How I love you," she said.

"And I you."

Together they left to inspect the hold.

✶ ✶ ✶ ✶ ✶

Davage hadn't wanted to see the refugees—the Monamas who'd been saved from becoming Berserkacides over Hoban. Seemed like a long time ago. The Gamma and Red light-blocking paste designed by the Sisters was a huge success, and many had been saved. They had learned much, and Ennez and Beth, working fast, shuttled from one Head Swarmed Monama to the next digging the sinister Shocker collars out of the flesh around their necks. They became skilled working with the odd, stretchy material that they couldn't see, and soon were able to have them off in just a few minutes, with Davage certifying their work as complete after they finished each patient. Ominously, the Shockers were all glowing in the Gamma band—the enemy trying to trigger the Monamas from remote. They shattered and jettisoned most of them, leaving one safely locked up for study.

But now, here they were, a load of frightened, sick refugees, lost in enemy space just like he was. He'd been strangely ambivalent towards them, and that wasn't like Captain Davage. He normally should have welcomed them with open arms when time permitted, made them feel wanted and at home.

This situation though, was bleak. Near rudderless in enemy territory, under constant, covert attack and his strength ebbing from having to scan the ship, their presence was problematic and inconvenient. More people he had to protect, more mouths he had to feed with stores he didn't have, and more faces looking to him for answers, for hope.

And he had none, plain and simple.

Perhaps that's why he'd avoided them, because his hope was rapidly diminishing. Captain Davage, Lord of Blanchefort, the optimist, was seeing doom at every turn. The enemy would have them sooner or later. Perhaps it might have been better if these people had simply been killed over Hoban. Like Crewman Lasset, at least they would have had peace by now.

Slowly, he and Syg went down into the hold.

"Dav, this is the same hold where we encountered the enemy being in the form of Crewman Lasset," Syg said.

"You're right; it is," he wearily replied.

"Was it stalking the Monamas, possibly hoping to trigger them?"

"Possibly. Probably."

Taking a deep breath, Davage readied himself, and they entered.

Inside the vast room were thirty plus Monamas: men, women and children. They all wore an assortment of borrowed and donated clothing, as they had been deposited on the ship nude. The clothing was, generally, too big for their thin, wiry bodies.

They had moved various boxes and crates around in the hold, trying to create make-shift enclosures. A large quantity of blankets and heaters had been provided to them, and some shivered underneath them. Elsewhere blankets hung on the walls and across boxes, an attempt to make the place a bit more private.

Some slept on beds of piled-up blankets, some prepared meals using improvised ingredients provided to them by the mess: mostly hard tack provisions and salted meat. The air in some places inside the hold was thick with unplaceable scents and unappetizing odors. Most had bandaged necks from the removal of their Shockers.

Many carried little air-guns loaded with paste-pellets should an attack occur. They had been shown how to use them by the Marines.

Lady Tellerran emerged from the rear of the hold, still wearing her flight jacket and holstered air gun, and she met Davage and Syg.

"Captain, Countess!" she said, arms outstretched, holding out her ubiquitous endecar to translate his League Common into her native Conox language. "How are you feeling? I know you've been tireless in your efforts to keep us safe." She spoke Conox into the red trumpet sprouting out of the endecar, and League Common came out the blue one in a smooth synthesized voice.

"I'm fine, my lady. Thank you."

"Where's Ennez?" she asked.

"Elsewhere, in his dispensary perhaps."

Tellerran was a little disappointed.

Davage was dizzy and close to falling. He leaned heavily against Syg. She took his arm and held him up.

<*Dav, you need to get back to bed,*> Syg sent to him.

Ignoring her, they continued the inspection. All the Monamas were looking at Davage. They all seemed so tiny to him, like children almost. Some whispered his name, and others pointed with their long fingernails. They stood there, holding their blankets, some eating scraps of food, some holding their little air guns. Some huddled around endecars held up in open hands, hoping to hear encouraging words, their expressive black eyes turning to him for leadership, courage, and possibly hope.

Doomed people. We're all doomed.

Davage tried not to look at them in the eye—he didn't want to make a connection. He walked through the hold, tipped his hat to the ladies, and kept moving, trying his best to keep his soul out of the way.

These people should be dead. All of them. They'd be better off.

"I'm going to ask the engineer to raise the temperature in this hold and bring some more heaters down," Davage said to Tellerran. "It seems a bit cold in here."

"Thank you, my lord; they'll appreciate it," came Tellerran's synthesized voice from her endecar. "The people here have been eager to see you, to offer thanks. I have told them what a fine man you are—the wonders I've seen you perform. I'm glad you've come."

"No thanks are required. What tribes are these people from?"

"Minzer mostly, some Cardinals and Darathons, and a few Nebulons."

Davage's head was splitting open.

<*You all right, Dav*?> Syg asked mentally.

<*Hold me up, Syg, I'm feeling weak …*>

Syg braced him, and they continued.

The Monamas had followed them into the depths of the hold, a brass band of little blue trumpets from their endecars pointed at him. They were saying something, whispering amongst themselves: *"Sar-Gra-Ma. Sar-Gra-Ma.*"

He continued walking. "My lady," he said to Tellerran, "what are they saying? Are they speaking Conox? Are their endecars not working?"

"Most are speaking Conox, my lord. Some are also speaking Anuie, which is close enough to Conox to be understandable, and a few are speaking Systerel, which is a special language for us. We mostly use it when we're speaking to the gods. Our endecars here aren't programmed to speak Systerel."

"We'll have to correct that. 'Sar-Gra-Ma'? What does that mean?"

Tellerran smiled. "It's Systerel. It means '*father.*'"

Davage considered that. "Are they calling me 'father'?"

"They are, sir."

Davage felt something sting deep inside. What did these people want? What did they expect of him?

"I'm sorry, my lady," he said quietly to Tellerran.

"For what?" she asked.

"For this. For all of this. I promised to get you home safe, and here we are, marooned in deep space. Doesn't look like any of us are to be going home."

"The attacks?" she asked.

"Relentless."

"My lord," she said. "I have spent my whole life being afraid—all of these people have. Afraid of the shadows. Afraid of things that might be hiding and might be watching. I have told you of Head Swarm—where we fall into a great apathy after we see our deaths. I argue that we, as a people, have been in a continuous Head Swarm for centuries since the Anuians were killed—frightened and cowering, waiting our turn to die.

"And then you came and stood over me, protected me from death, showed me that those who hide could be met, could be fought with a sure hand and a ready heart. You brought me out of my Head Swarm, and I am never going to be afraid again. For my brothers who fell in Crossland, for my sister, I am going to stand and face my fate unafraid and with a clear head, as you have taught me. The gods have punished us. *They* have taken from us throughout the ages, reveled in our fear, and used the strength of our arms for their own ends. No more, I say. If I am to die, then it will be standing up, as Lady Tellerran of Fphenook."

They reached the far end of the hold. There, sitting in a small enclosure made of boxes and hung blankets was a woman and a small boy. The woman had handwritten a series of sentences on the side of a box using improvised ink and possibly her fingernail as a writing implement. The letters were familiar, however, they were all jumbled around—possibly written in Conox. The boy leaned next to the box tracing over the lines of text with his fingers. He was sounding out the words, one syllable at a time.

The boy was being taught to read.

Davage was shocked. Here they were, a group of Monamas, snatched from their homes and intended to be used by the enemy as shock troops and then cast aside. They had survived, were making the most of the situation, and were trying to live their lives as best they could. The simple act of a mother teaching her son to read suddenly took on new meaning: to endure, to continue on.

To live.

Davage, despite his best efforts, found his heart going out to these people, to this boy learning to read.

"Ma'am?" Davage asked, "Is this your son?"

Tellerran handed the woman her endecar and repeated what Davage had asked in Conox. She held the endecar to her mouth and spoke into the red trumpet. "Yes, yes, sir," she said quietly.

Davage leaned down to pick the boy up. "May I?" he asked.

The woman nodded, and he picked the boy up by the armpits—he was light in the extreme. "What is your name, ma'am?"

She curtsied and held the trumpet to her mouth. "I am Clauderan of Cardinal."

Davage smiled. "I see, well met, ma'am. And who is this fine fellow?"

"Tell the Captain your name," she said to her son. "It's all right. This is Captain Davage, *Sar-Gra-Ma*, and his wife. He is watching over us."

She held up the endecar. "Ovus," the boy quietly replied through the red trumpet.

Syg, nearby leaned in. "Ovus, what a lovely name," she said.

"Are you coming along in your studies?"

"Yes."

"Are you eager to get home?"

"Yes."

Davage put the boy down and looked about him, at all the Monamas gathered around, blue trumpets everywhere.

They were starving—not for food, but for leadership, for hope. No more hiding, no more shyness, their cards were on the table.

Sar-Gra-Ma! Father!

Help us, they said. Save us, they silently pleaded.

They looked to Davage.

He stood there a moment. Then: "The thing that has haunted you through the ages, now haunts us all," he said. "I have learned much, since I began this voyage. I have come to know that we … have failed you."

The Monamas, listening closely, appeared confused. They waited, and Davage continued. "We have come to know that you have been tormented for centuries by these Golden People and the demons who serve them. We knew nothing of this. We were oblivious. Perhaps you didn't come to us and ask for help because you thought that we might say no, or possibly laugh at you, or do nothing. Perhaps we didn't cultivate an environment where you felt at ease to come to us and ask for help. Perhaps we weren't listening—and in that we have failed you. And now look— look where we are, far from our homes, surrounded by those who would see us fall."

The Monamas looked at each other and appeared deflated.

This tall, blue-haired Elder could do nothing for them. He was just as powerless before the demons as they were. Once again, as was always said, the enemy could not be beat. They turned, lowering their endecars to resume what they were doing.

Davage continued on. *"Sur-ven-ni,"* he said, carefully sounding out the words. The Monamas stopped and listened.

"I'm told by my son that that is an expression you have. I'm told it means: 'pick up a brick'. I once asked him what in Creation does that mean, other than the obvious, and he said: 'Pick up a brick and soon you'll pick up a second. Pick up enough, and eventually you'll have a row of bricks. Create enough rows, and eventually you'll have a wall. Have enough walls, and soon you'll have the makings of a home'. I take away from the expression that it means to not shy away from doing the work that needs to be done. That is wise advice, and, we shan't shy away from such work here."

All eyes were on Davage.

"We're all in this together, my friends. You have lived in fear of the enemy—hiding in the shadows, hiding from all to see. They want us all as their slaves, their blunt instruments and horrid monsters—and I say they'll have none of us! By Creation, we will stand! All of us shall see our homes again. I swear it!"

The Monamas began chattering amongst themselves a little, and their endecar trumpets wobbled with growing excitement. Talk like this, of defiance, of victory in the face of the enemy, was apparently unknown to them.

"This cowardly lot, whoever they are, no doubt sit back and say: 'We will take the Monamas and the Elders on that ship and do with them as we will', but when we're done with this, they'll surely lament 'We fought the League there, man and woman, Elder and Monama, and we fear to do so again!' You needn't be afraid any longer! I am Captain Davage, Lord of Blanchefort, and this I promise you. We stay our course, run our guns, hoist our flag, and hold our ground! We also have a saying in the Vithlands. We say: '*Genda aba vera*', and that means: 'go with light'. With light, there is no darkness. With light there all is revealed! With light, one is never lost!"

An invisible wall seemed to come down, and the Monamas swarmed him, reaching out, trying to touch him. The paralyzing cloud of fear that had separated these Monamas from the rest of the League fell away at that moment, never to return.

A Monama man came up to him, speaking through his endecar. "My name is Orris of Minzer, Captain. I have a wife and ninety children." Davage shook his hand and tipped his hat.

A woman walked forward. "I am Darllan of Cardinal, wife, mother and sister."

They all came and said their names. "Gernian of Minzer."

"Rufus of Nebulon."

"Sisteallan of Minzer..."

and on and on until they all had said their names. They had started out as nameless refugees meant to be used as Berserkacides and be discarded. Now, they all had names, wearing borrowed clothing, living on borrowed time, but living nevertheless.

And, surrounded, Captain Davage found new strength. He pushed the pain from his head and the weariness from his bones. His spirit was reborn in the hold with these Monamas, just as theirs was.

He and Syg took their leave and went to the bridge.

He had a ship to command and those under his protection to keep safe.

20—Castle Vincent

Over the mountains, past the Tartan headlands and across the River Seven was the Halalands, a vast flatland of fields and quiet hamlets. Always a modest and understated tribe, the Halas were content to be tillers of the land and growers of food while other, more adventurous tribes, such as the Vith, Barrows, Esthers, Zenons and Remnath, took to the stars. The Halas performed their role, and, for the most part, quietly went about their lives leaving heroics for others to revel in.

The *Goshawk* moved eastward over the river. Through the glass, the flatland below was dark and sleepy. In the far distance they could see a small carpet of lights coming from the city of Feren to the south by the sea, but, below and to the north, there was nothing but small country lanes, farmhouses and fields. The nighttime Kanan sky was always starriest in Hala, with little light pollution to dim the stars.

If the Professor was right, then somewhere, under all that quiet Hala splendor, was a wretched place of evil squatting in the dark, where Kay's love awaited her death.

Phillip turned southward, following the coast, and eventually the smallish stone structure of Castle Vincent came into view.

Castle Vincent was quite large for a Hala structure, but on the smallish side when placed in comparison to other castles across Kana. Like the city of Rostov, it was built by the sea and was comprised of a large, roughly ovular walled-in compound with a keep occupying the far northward portion of the enclosure.

Seeing the castle emerge from the dark gave Kay bad memories—his aunt lived there, Countess Pardock of Vincent.

Countess Pardock was one of those relatives that, for no particular reason, always scared Kay as a child. His parents were very close to the Countess, and she often visited, but she had a commanding, off-putting presence that terrified Kay when he was younger. And it wasn't just Kay who got that impression—his sisters Ki and Hathaline also hadn't wanted to spend too much time around Countess Pardock, their mean, old, blue-haired aunt from Hala.

"Sarah," Kay said as the castle grounds got bigger in the glass, "did Countess Pardock creep you out as a kid?"

Sarah, mostly asleep in her seat, replied. "Yeah, she did. Phillip too."

Phillip, bringing the ship down, chimed in. "Only one woman creeps me out now."

Kay shook his head.

It wasn't that Countess Pardock was an unkind person, quite the contrary—it was just one of those things. It was said she looked a lot like their great grandfather Maserfeld, and had his raging brigand's spirit to match. Maybe it was the blue hair and piercing eyes. In any event, Kay considered her a person best avoided if possible.

Phillip put the *Goshawk* down in the center of the compound, and they announced themselves at the keep's door. The staff who greeted them said that the Countess had gone to bed for the evening and that she would rise later at 6 bells.

Somewhat relieved, they all went into a comfortable study and, seating themselves, caught some sleep.

✶ ✶ ✶ ✶ ✶

Kay awoke an hour or two later.

Leaning over him was a tall, blue-haired woman in a pointy House Vincent gown.

His aunt: Countess Pardock. For a moment, all the old childhood fears he harbored as a boy returned, but he fought them back.

She was quite old, well over two hundred and fifty years and much older than his father, but, like a true Elder, she looked no older than Kay or Sarah or Phillip. She was a real beauty with a captivating face and a pair of haunting eyes—like their great grandfather.

Leaning over him, she smiled. "Kay, you have grown since I last saw you," she said with a slight, acquired Hala accent. She pulled him up and gave him a mighty hug. "Why do none of my nephews and nieces ever want to come and see mean old Aunt Pardock?"

She gave him a pinch on the cheek. Those hands, still strong after all these years. The same hands that had, many years before, thrown down the baton at his father's wedding to Princess Marilith of Xandarr, preventing the wedding and paving the way for all that followed.

"It is good to see you, my Countess," he said.

"Call me 'Countess' again, Kay, and I'm going to punch you. And, though I'm an old goat, I can still hit. Ask your father."

Everybody woke up, and she greeted them all. "Come," she said, "breakfast is soon to be on the table. Let's sit and catch up."

Sitting down to breakfast at Castle Vincent was quite a different experience than at Castle Blanchefort, with its massive dining halls and tables hundreds of feet long. Here, Countess Pardock's dining room was, while elegantly appointed, rather small and cave-like in its intimacy. The table was round and only big enough for six or eight people to comfortably sit.

As they took their seats, Kay updated the Countess, and she listened, making apparent mental notes on this and that, her long blue hair set in the rustic Vincent style jangling about her face.

"If you want to know about Hala, you've come to the right person—nothing goes on here, whether past or present, that I don't know about. You see, your sister, Lady Kilos, inherited her snooper's ear and Stare from me, your mean old aunt."

"Aunt Pardock, nobody thinks you're mean."

"Kay, you lie about as well as your father does. It's all right—it's my own fault. I've been accused of being mean lots of times, of being a bully too. I had, and still have I suppose, a pretty hot temper and a big mouth to go with it. Tends to rub people the wrong way. But, none of you need to worry about that—you're family, and I love you like my own children. You too," she added to Ki and Lon.

She looked at Sarah. "Even you … mother," she said, again noting Sarah's resemblance to their grandmother, Countess Hermilane.

The door to the dining room opened, and a small girl wearing a blue robe came in. She yawned silently, her hand to her mouth.

"Hello, Joy, good morning. Please come in; breakfast is almost served,"

Pardock said.

Everybody at the table stood, and the girl, seeing the table full of strange people, was open-mouth startled. She turned to quickly leave the way she came.

"Joy," Pardock said in an assertive tone, "you need your breakfast. Sit down and be sociable. There's nothing to be afraid of. We have family here this morning."

The girl, leaning over slightly, obediently turned, quietly approached the table, and seated herself.

She was small, only about five feet tall with a slender build and a large head of curly, amber-colored hair that went down past her waist.

Her downcast eyes were jade—a creamy shade similar to Kay's. The intricate Shadowmark wrapping around her right eye was unmistakable.

"All, please allow me to introduce Joy. Her full name is Joicellus-Zortens-Ka of Midas. Just call her 'Joy'. Obviously she's a former Black Hat—we're all old pros with Black Hats, are we not? Joy here was a particularly nasty little Black Hat from Midas—they called her 'The Knife' if I'm not mistaken."

They all looked at her, and she sat there in obvious discomfort. One by one Pardock introduced those sitting at the table to her and, eyes downcast, she nodded at each of them. Tweeter flapped off of Ki's shoulder and landed in front of her. She gasped and gently picked him up, marveling at his Silver tech construction.

"That's Tweeter," Ki said proudly as Joy stroked his tiny beak.

"My son Enoch," Pardock said. "He's probably the best Black Hat fighter out there. I remember when I first met your mother, Kay, all those years ago, when she discovered Poe was a Shadow tech female. My son Enoch was there, and he became fascinated with the idea of freeing Black Hats, as Lord Davage had done. He talked about it endlessly—I assumed he would forget all about it; you know how boys are. But, Enoch never did, and, when he came of age, he set out into Xaphan territory and began freeing Black Hats—'Fighting' them, as it's called."

"How many has he freed?" Phillip asked.

"Dozens. He married one of them—Mixstaluna of Law. Perhaps your parents have mentioned it. The rest he brings here to old Castle Vincent. I give them a room and bed and bid them to stay for as long as they need to. This is a quiet place, far from the bustle and confusion of Vithland or Remnath, where they may adjust to life in the League at their own pace. They usually don't stay for too long—all sorts of Lords from across the League come calling, hoping to court them; Black Hats have a lot to offer, and they are eagerly sought out, and rightly so. They are good people when taken from the Black Abbess' sway."

She looked at Joy with a motherly eye. "Joy here has had a difficult time. She's so very shy, but she's made vast strides since first arriving. Soon, I'll wager she'll be leaving and setting out on her own. Lord Strathmore is her most persistent caller."

"I don't like Lord Strathmore," she said quietly, looking at her plate.

"Well then, I won't let him in the next time he visits. Joy, everybody here, with the exception of Lt. Kilos and Lord Lon of Probert over there, is the offspring of a Shadow tech female. Lord Kabyl—the fellow with the purple hair—is the son of a particularly rotten Black Hat, Sygillis of Metatron."

Joy looked at him through her curly bangs of amber hair.

Kay laughed. "I'm certain my 'rotten' mother sends her regards, Aunt Pardock."

Pardock darkened a little. "Still no word from the *New Faith*?"

Kay shook his head.

"I wouldn't worry. Dav will have them through—you watch. Have faith in your father."

The breakfast was served, and all ate their fill. After a while, Joy began to warm up a bit; Kay and Phillip even made her laugh. When she wasn't smiling, she had a rather small-chinned face, but when she smiled, her face opened up. She had a huge smile—all teeth. The table was alive with chatter, and it was easy to see that Pardock was greatly enjoying it—like the old times when her husband, Lord Ferddie, and her children were all here at the table. Lord Ferddie was killed at the Battle of Embeth some thirty years prior, and Pardock had chosen to remain a widow. Her children were all grown and gone.

As the meal wound down, the topic of discussion returned to the Temple of the Exploding Head.

"...and we're here to see if we can discover any clues as to the whereabouts of this supposed temple," Kay said. "We also await the coming of nightfall to contact Lt. Kilos' husband in Tusck, as he is certain he can discover its location via research, but our time is drawing near, and we must make haste."

"Strange doings," Pardock said. "All these attacks, these swarms of bugs ..."

"Oh, don't worry about those," Ki said. "Lady Poe created them."

"Any fool could see that, Lt.. My sister and her love of happy, smiling faces. Some things never change. Those bugs are huge and noisy, but remarkably docile and durable. They were swarming in my garden a few weeks ago, like a tornado of wings and legs. I tried everything to be rid of them: beating them with a broom and my shoe, stomping on them, trying to poison them, and burning them—nothing. I even tried biting the head off one—that's when I saw the happy face and Com'ed Poe. She didn't want to talk, but I got it out of her regardless. Poe cannot keep a secret when vigorously prodded."

Kay had no trouble imagining Countess Pardock trying to bite the head off of a struggling, buzzing Parafly

"And," she said, "as far as your egghead in Tusck goes, why wait for sundown—you really don't have the time. I think I can tell you where this temple is located."

They all looked at each other.

Pardock took a drink of her juice then began. "We all know about the Great Betrayal—when twenty Great Houses betrayed the Elders and fled to the Xaphans way back when. It's generally taken for granted that most of the Great Houses who fled were of Vith stock: the Xandarrs, the Clovis, the Charns, the Hollys and so on."

"The Woolovers also left," Phillip added.

Sarah rolled her eyes. "Will you come off your Lady, please, and shut it?"

Pardock was intrigued. "A Woolover? Are you seeing a Woolover, Phillip? I haven't heard that."

"Yes, Aunt Pardock," Sarah said. "It's new. He's got one chasing after him, and he won't admit that he *loves* it."

Pardock smiled. "Better quit drinking then if you haven't already, and you better start going to church. Anyway, what people tend to forget regarding the Great Betrayal is that, other than the Vith, it was Houses of Hala stock that made up the second–most of their number."

Phillip finished his meal. "If memory serves, it was the Houses of Wayreth and Zary from the Hala region that went to the Xaphans."

"There were a few more than just that. There was the House of Caroline and House of Bodice as well. Wayreth and Zary were rootless malcontents who left because they wanted to create chaos, and good riddance. The Carolines left because they were coerced by the Zary—never could make decisions on their own, the Carolines. And then there was House Bodice. A House of simple farmers, such as any you'd find in Hala. Their patriarch, Lord Porter, while not being overly bright, was a good man, a saintly man. They were just good, honest, hardworking folk. Not quite the sort you would figure on betraying the Elders and becoming star-faring Xaphans.

Not rabble-rousers like the Charns and the Zary."

"So, why did they?" Sarah asked.

Pardock smiled. "Why indeed. They left for a lot of reasons. They left because the land around their Manor went bad and because of the demons they always saw in the moonlight. They left because of all the insanity and birth defects they endured without a bit of help from the Sisters, though they begged for it."

Pardock paused. "And they left because of the drums, beating in the deep that never stopped, giving them no peace. Poor House Bodice. It didn't work out for them, going to the Xaphans. House Bodice is extinct. Ransacked by the Charns shortly after they left. They crashed on Midas 6 where, as the story goes, they were captured by the very demons they sought to flee, taken to an unholy place, and burned alive. The Sisters, somewhat belatedly, did something they rarely do—they admitted that they had failed House Bodice, and that it was their fault they were gone. Such a tragedy. They created St. Porter's day in their honor—but what difference does a holiday make if you're dead?"

"They heard drums, Aunt Pardock?" Kay asked.

"Yes, coming most loudly from a deep well on their lands. A well they called 'Carhl Wae'."

21—The Ruins of Bodice

They quickly left the keep and made their way back to the *Goshawk.* They each thanked their aunt for the timely information, for her hospitality, and for all the times they'd been scared of her for no reason. Kay, Sarah and Phillip each swore they would visit more often, and they each intended to keep the promise. Lon tipped his hat.

When they climbed into the ship, Joy was sitting there on the back couch. She had changed into a blue dress and, as typical for an ex-Black Hat, she wore only a miniscule pair of sandals.

"Madam Joy?" Kay asked.

"I want to go with you," Joy said.

"You should stay here. It might not be safe."

"I am not helpless. I can fight."

"Doubtless, but I don't wish you to be endangered."

She smiled—again, a huge, toothy smile. "The countess has told me that, in the League, I am free. Free to do what I wish. I wish to go and assist you."

Joy didn't appear to be moving.

"We could probably use her help, Kay," Ki said. "Nothing will happen to her."

Kay relented, and Phillip lifted the *Goshawk* into the morning sky.

∗ ∗ ∗ ∗ ∗

According to Countess Pardock, the ruins of Bodice weren't far from Castle Vincent, only about three hundred miles north by west, near the mouth of the River Seven. Moving at speed, the *Goshawk* made the journey in only a short time.

Flying over the rustic, untended lands, they spotted the remains of a small manor in ruin on a hillside near the banks of the river. From the air, they thought they could see a figure standing amid the ruins. Phillip slowed and set the ship down.

It was quite depressing, poking about the ruins. Outwardly, the fallen structure reminded Kay of Lt. Kilos' family home on the outskirts of Tusck—but, where Ki's house was a ruin hiding an abundance of life, this ruin was stagnant and dead. A heap of rubble covering a shallow grave of sorrow and lost aspirations. They could see where the now dusty land was once tilled and planted with all manner of crops, tended with love and harvested by the Bodice. Now, only the cairn of their manor remained, covering bones of the dead that weren't there.

A giant-sized statue stood in the rubble—they had seen it from the air. It was a tall likeness of a Sister, robed and wearing a headdress with the usual winged cornet. The statue stood with her hands over her face, as if she were crying.

An inscription at the statue's base read:

Here was the House of Bodice
Goodly and law abiding

Asked for help, received none
Forsaken by the Sisterhood of Light in 99989ex
Failed by the Sisterhood of Light in 99989ex
Betrayed by the Sisterhood of Light in 99989ex
Our penance is forever more... Let us never forget the House of Bodice

The statue was sobering and lonely there in the ruins. They could feel the sadness pouring out of it.

Joy, small, big-haired, followed Kay around as they looked through the rubble. It was easy to tell when an ex-Black Hat liked someone, for they didn't hide their feelings well, and she clearly had some for the handsome Kay, their eyes a matching set. Since she was wearing only light sandals, Kay helped her through the rocky ground, even carrying her at times to protect her feet.

Ki shook her head. "That, what you're doing there, Kay, looks really familiar." She remembered Captain Davage once carrying Sygillis on a rocky world.

Kay wanted to be rid of Joy—he tried to give her to Phillip or even Lon. He wished he hadn't let her come, for this very reason. This whole exercise was for Sam—his true love. He didn't have time for a Black Hat with the beginnings of a crush. And, she seemed so shy and disaffected—how would she do should things get violent?

Sarah eventually took her.

They puttered around in the rocks of the manor, feeling sorry for and lamenting the loss of people long gone. Lon found the toppled soapstone statue of an elephant. "I hear tell the Bodice once worshipped an elephant-like creature."

"Maiax," Ki said.

"I heard it was a demon," Sarah said. "When the Sisters didn't help them, they turned to a demon."

There was an inscription scrawled into the soapstone. It read:

GOD IS MAN
AND MAN IS GOD

The ground seemed tired and bankrupt of nutrients—an odd thing for Hala, a place of dark, rich soil and good planting. Lon popped on his goggles and took a handful of ochre-colored dirt, rubbing it with his fingers.

"The soil is very alkaline, almost to the point of being poisonous," he said. "I can even see a hint of radiation here."

"Aunt Pardock did say the land went bad."

Lon adjusted his goggles. "This isn't natural, though, and the radiation—it's like there's an unshielded fusion plant around here somewhere."

Phillip looked around. "There probably is one, buried deep. This temple is supposed to be a mixture of the technological and the arcane. I'm certain not a lot of thought was paid to shielding and proper engineering."

Ki took off her hat and wiped her brow. "So where's this creepy well? I don't see it anywhere."

They looked around. It was quiet. Every so often the wind made a noise, and sometimes the lonely River Seven splashed in its banks, but beyond that there was nothing.

Or was there?

"You hear that?" Sarah said, pricking her ears up.

"Hear what?" Phillip asked.

"Listen!"

They listened. Though it could have been their collective imaginations, they thought they could hear a hint of drumming behind the quiet veil of wind.

Tweeter came out of his pocket and landed on Ki's shoulder. "Tweeter, find the creepy Carhl Wae well," she said.

He jumped off her shoulder and started flying to the southeast.

Kay looked around and let his Sight go. He scanned the lonely, quiet land in the direction Tweeter was heading.

"There!" he said. "I see it! To the south about three miles away."

Phillip patted some of the grime off his duster. "Three miles is too far to walk. Let's get back in the ship."

Kay looked at him and smiled. "No need." With that, he Wafted high into the air and took off covering the distance quickly. Blasting his Wafts, he passed Tweeter and landed in front of the well in a matter of moments.

Standing there alone, he immediately wished he'd gotten into the *Goshawk* with the others.

In front of him, poking out of the dusty ground like a neck bolt, was a stone well, black, about eight feet across. That's all it was, just a well made of stone and mortar. But, it had a horrid feel to it, a gaping hole to hell itself.

Carhl Wae, the dreadful mouth.

Kay could feel raw evil pouring out of it. He'd never experienced such a thing before. No wonder the Bodice left—how could they live with such a thing? How could they endure? They couldn't; they fled, and not simply to some other area of Kana or nearby League world. They went to the Xaphans for relief and were wiped out of existence.

Perhaps this thing, this Carhl Wae, had left a stain on them, one that followed them to the stars and led to their sorrowful deaths.

That Sam could be anywhere near this well was chilling.

Sam—he had to get her out.

Tweeter approached and landed on Kay's shoulder. He had stirred up a few Paraflies who were hiding in the dry grass along the way, and they followed him, the two Silver tech creations of Lady Poe attracted to each other. They buzzed in the air, Kay was comforted by their presence.

The black bat-like mass of the *Goshawk* came over the rise and landed nearby.

They all got out and instantly had the same reaction Kay had, except for Joy who didn't seem bothered by it at all.

"What is this?" Sarah asked, eyeing the well in dismay.

"It has a rotten feel to it, sure enough," Lon said. Wearing his goggles, he looked the well over.

Phillip took his SAPP off and formed it into a sword. "Have you Sighted this thing yet, Kay?" Sarah did the same, and Kay unsaddled his CARG and drew his Poltava.

Ki cocked her SK.

Weapons drawn, it was all of them against Carhl Wae, and Carhl Wae was winning.

"Well?" Phillip pressed, drawing his Poltava.

"No, Phillip, I haven't."

"What are you waiting for?"

"I don't know. I don't want to know what's down there."

Lon seemed the only one with enough guts to approach and touch it. "There's a lot of EM radiation coming out of it—that accounts for the strange feeling it's creating in our bodies. It's not harmful I don't think, just a bit peculiar."

He looked down into the well's mouth. "It's deep; it goes way down. I can't see all the way down. Come on and look, Kay."

Kay stood there, his insides blanching.

"Kay?"

Joy approached him. "It's all right to be afraid. Some things are best to be afraid of." She stood there looking at him. She was cute, really cute.

Kay shook his head, trying to pull out of the short trance he was in. He stood next to Lon and looked down into the well.

His Sight drifted away. Down it went, down into the poisoned ground and troubled stone, down Carhl Wae's gullet.

Kay gasped. "It's deep," he said. "It goes down and down, at least a thousand feet, with a few cataracts along the way."

"Do you see a temple down there?" Sarah asked.

He looked around. "I see something, but it's fuzzy, hard to see clearly."

Sarah shivered. "EM or not, Lon, this thing is giving me the creeps. Kay, could you please Cloak us—it'll make me feel better."

Kay didn't argue. He Cloaked them all, feeling the usual sharp anguish in his head that rapidly faded to nothing.

"Thanks," she said, greatly relieved.

Ki shook off her feelings of dread and approached the well. She looked down, careful not to touch the rocks. "How are we going to get down there? And, what's going to be waiting for us when we do?" She stopped and listened. "I can really hear drumming now. You hear that?"

They listened. The ghostly beat of deep drums throbbed out of the well.

Kay swallowed and saddled his CARG. "Give me a moment, I'm going down to take a look."

Palming his Poltava and holding it tight, he climbed up onto the well's mouth, took a deep breath, and allowed himself to fall in.

He plummeted for bit, and was very quickly in pitch black. He loosed his Sight and could see the maudlin stone lining of the well streak past him. Ahead, the shaft became tighter as he fell, and he had to Waft past a very narrow spot about five hundred feet down.

Down and down, he felt totally alone as he fell.

Another tight spot coming up. Again he Wafted past it.

After he'd fallen about half a minute, the shaft opened into a large cylinder cut in stone. The rushing air moving past him was getting warm. He thought he smelt cinders.

The bottom was coming up fast. He Wafted and touched ground. His fall to the bottom of Carhl Wae had taken nearly a minute.

Tightly holding his Poltava, Cloaked, Kay took a look around.

He was at the bottom of a carved stone cylinder about a hundred feet in circumference. It was like being deep within a gigantic circular chimney. It went up about a thousand feet where it constricted to the smaller shaft leading to the top. The stone walls were lined with grotesque, leering Monama faces carved in stone, mouths open, tongues sticking out. The faces were hissing—the open mouths were spewing forced air from the surface. And that wasn't all. Mixed into the spaces between the faces were carved four-armed bodies, entrails, screaming genitals and grasping hands. The skill and touch of the stonework was familiar—Monama hands had created this place. Different Monamas from long ago—evil ones. Georges of Maddox had mentioned something about this. He'd called it the 'Cylinder of Ugly Faces', and it was an apt name. This cylinder carved in hideous relief was the entrance to the Temple of the Exploding Head.

He looked for an opening or doorway and saw none—just row after row of ugly faces, bodies and more, all laughing at him.

And here, at the bottom of the well, he could hear, without a doubt, the steady beating of a chorus of drums.

He tried to gauge where the drumming was coming from, but it seemed like it was coming from all around.

He Sighted through the walls, trying to locate the interior. There was nothing, just deep stone.

He could see the network of small shafts cut in the faces for ventilation. He had assumed they went up, toward the surface. They didn't. They went down.

Kay looked down. There, about fifty feet below, through solid rock, was a vast open space that was laced with energy, like a rampant fusion generator. That was it. That was the Temple. It seemed to have no entrance—the evil Berserkacide Monamas could possibly blink in, and the *Killanjo* demons, able to step out of thin air, also didn't have a need for something as pedestrian as a door.

Down there, in that darkness of beating drums and flowing tangible energy, was Sam in a place with no door.

Kay felt alone and isolated. He put his Poltava away and quickly Wafted back up to the surface.

"Did you see it?" Sarah demanded.

"Yes, but there's no entrance that I could see, just a honeycomb of tiny vent holes."

"How are we going to get in?" Ki asked. "How are we going to get down there to begin with?"

Kay thought a moment. "I'll Waft us down."

"You can't Waft us, Kay—I've seen such a thing nearly kill your father."

"I'm not my father," he replied. "I don't think I'll have a problem." He looked around. "We'll have a test. I'll try to Waft Lon down. There's a cataract at about five hundred feet. If I start having a problem, we'll stop there and have Joy hoist Lon back out with Shadow tech. Agreed?"

As always, Lon was ready. Ki was dubious but didn't say anything. Kay approached Lon from behind, put his arms around him, and Wafted with a blast.

It didn't take long. After only a few Wafts, they were down in the Cylinder of Ugly Faces.

"Are you feeling all right?" Lon asked.

Kay took a breath. "Yes, actually, just a little winded, but nothing more. Sit tight, I'm going to get the others." Lon, still wearing his goggles, drew his CEROS from his coat and moved to the other side of the cylinder. Kay unsaddled his CARG and gave it to Lon—its light softly filling the chamber.

Soon, one by one, Kay brought them all down, the Cylinder of Ugly Faces now crowded with people.

"So, where is it?" Sarah asked while admiring a particularly ugly face.

"Beneath us, about fifty feet down."

Ki looked down and kicked at the ground with her boots. "So, what's our plan? Do we have a plan?"

Phillip inspected the ground. "We're all under Cloak. I suppose we could go down, scout the area out covertly and formulate a plan."

"How big is the area?" Ki asked.

"Big—but I can't see it clearly; it's obscured somehow."

As they bandied about ideas, the many leering faces surrounding them began to glow a muddle green.

"Uh, everybody …" Sarah said "I think we should …"

Before anybody could react, the sandy floor turned green and flashed. They were all whisked away into darkness.

The Temple of the Exploding Head had made the decision for them.

22—The Vortex

Davage had truly been revitalized after the trip to the hold. His spirits were good, and his strength returned to him. Sygillis was relieved to see her husband back to normal. His strength buoyed hers.

In the dispensary, Crewman Lasset's condition had improved. With Lady Tellerran's help, Ennez and Bethrael of Moane, trying a combination of salts, minerals and sodas, had managed to arrest her dreadful condition and turn it around. Lasset's skin had improved to the point that Ennez could release her from her coma. Davage spent lunch once or twice with his crewman and managed to coax a smile and a laugh from her. She still needed a great deal of treatment, but it was good to see her showing improvement.

And, more good news. Ennez and Beth had created a set of goggles that could see reasonably well in the Gamma Spectrum. They made quite a few of them, distributed to the Marines, who prowled the decks in squadrons, looking for intruders.

Now, Davage could calm his Sight, relax, and command the ship.

They had made a great deal of progress. They pushed Stellar Mach to its limits and found they could go safely past it for a few seconds. The time savings was tremendous, cutting almost a week off their return trip, which was excellent; the sooner they presented themselves to the Hospitalers the better.

They had also scored a tremendous forage operation at a green world brimming with game and gatherables. As usual, the enemy attempted to attack during the operation; however, Davage had developed a feel for their tactics and was ready for them. Paymaster Stenstrom, leading the shore party, returned with a bounty of goods, and their pantries, at least for the time being, were stocked. They'd managed to sink two enemy ships, possibly more, skulking behind their Gamma band doorways.

Things indeed were looking up.

✶ ✶ ✶ ✶ ✶

"I'd like to learn how to fly, Captain," Lady Tellerran said through her endecar. "When we get home. Will you teach me?"

They were sitting in the mess, eating their small rations of wild game caught on a recent forage mission.

"You wish to learn to fly, my lady?" Davage asked. "What brings this on?"

"I wear my flight jacket—which I'm not going to give back, by the way—I won it fair and square. I'd like to learn."

Joining them at the table was Syg, Ennez and Beth. "I'd like to see that," Ennez said. "You can't fly, and you can't even talk without that stupid endecar. When are you going to learn a little League Common? You've got nothing but time right now to practice."

Tellerran smiled, pushed the endecar away, and cleared her throat. "... I cvould ... keek your ... your ..." She got flustered, and Beth leaned over and whispered in her ear.

"*Ban, vica,*" she said to Beth, thanking her. "Ass. I cvuold keek your tiny ... ass," she said with a bit of triumph. She quickly pulled her endecar back. "How's that?"

Ennez laughed. "Bring it on."

Tellerran wound up her index finger and gave Ennez a good flick on the shoulder. "Ow!" he cried in genuine pain.

"We're actually making wonderful progress," Davage said. "I could see Wayreth 16 in the observation dome telescope this morning. At least I think I saw it. Another six and a half weeks and we're home."

"How are the attacks coming, sir?" Beth asked.

"Better. In fact I've not seen any attacks since our last Stellar Mach transverse twenty hours ago."

"Do you think we're clear of the enemy, Dav?" Syg asked.

"Don't know. I wouldn't think so, as they have lease to appear in the League as well. Perhaps we've lost them for the moment."

"Once we arrive at Wayreth 16, we'll still have to fight our way through Xaphan space," Syg added.

"Ahhh, I'm not worried about them. After all of this, meeting a Xaphan armada on the field might seem rather refreshing, like putting on an old pair of shoes. Xaphans we can handle."

Ennez finished his rations and pushed his plate away. "Come on, Tellerran. I want another go." He put his arm on the tabletop like he wanted to arm wrestle.

Tellerran snorted. "Again? You just don't know when to quit, do you?" She pushed back the sleeve of her flight jacket and placed her pale elbow on the table, playfully moving her fingertips past Ennez's knuckles. "I'm becoming tired of arm wrestling, Ennez. Perhaps you might soon challenge me to something more 'adult'. Ah well, same prize as always? When you lose, I get to look at your bellybutton all I want." Lacing her fingers with his, she squeezed with tendon-popping force. "Such a nice bellybutton."

Paymaster Stenstrom came in, HRN swishing. He looked around, saw them at their table, and headed in their direction.

"How goes it, Bel?" Davage said when he arrived.

"You have correspondence, sir." he said holding out a letter.

"I have? Out here? Where did it come from?"

"I'm not certain. It was in the ledgers this morning."

Davage took the letter and opened it. "Must have come from one of the crew."

Syg leaned in to read over his shoulder. Ennez and Tellerran suspended their arm wrestling match. They were all curious.

He pulled the folded paper out and read.

Lord Blanchefort

I commend you on your seamanship, and for keeping your ship together under difficult circumstances. The words you spoke to those lost people in the hold meant the world to them; you even got me all misty to boot.

I must beg a great favor. I hate to ask, but I need your help.

At eight bells a vortex will open right ahead of the ship. The vortex, though large, shall be easy enough to avoid. Go around it if you wish, and your destination is but six weeks away.

I would ask that you not go around it, but that you go through. Going through the vortex will send you fairly close to where you started, right back under the veil of the Golden People and all the danger that such proximity entails.

I beg you go through the vortex. There, at 6:45am, you will find a small planet. Go down to the planet, 16 22, north by west and see what there is to see. You must arrive at 16 22 north by west at ten till twelve bells, no later.

There is a person named Ondecca, and you must speak to her. All of us have our Secret-Talkers, kept in hidden places, and she is His, kept in a perpetual loop in time. The thing about loops in time that I've learned, they're messy, got loose ends all over the place. I have come to know that one of the loose ends is at 16 22 north by west. Find Ondecca and hear what secrets she has to tell. She will be unpleasant to say the least. Take an endecar programmed with Conox, Anuie and Systrel and demand she tell you her secrets.

Remember, ten till twelve bells.

The eyes and ears of man are the parchment scrolls of the gods. See what is there and hear her truth-telling, and I shall have the proof I need.

I cannot influence you other than to beg and pray you trust my counsel. This isn't for me or for you, but for everybody else. You said 'with light, there are no shadows.' Please remember those words, and also remember that the gods, wherever they may be, high or low, fair or foul, look for a light in the dark too.

I pray you take the vortex.

Eight bells.

—C

✶ ✶ ✶ ✶ ✶

Syg, sitting in their quarters, read and reread the note. "Dav, what is this?"

"Your guess is as good as mine. It appears to be from Carahil."

"What is all this mention of a 'vortex'? If he has something to say, why doesn't he just appear and say it?"

"You know Carahil, always claiming to be impeded by the doings of the universe."

The Com rang in. "Sir, Fore-Sensing has detected the indications of a nebulous mass coming right head. Navigation suggests a divergent course of 2:52am by 7:16pm to go around the mass."

Davage checked his timepiece. "Eight bells, right on the tick. Com, send to helm. I want a full stop."

"Full stop, aye."

Syg was alarmed. She put the letter on the table. "Dav, you're not thinking of taking the ship in there, are you?"

He thought a moment. "No, not the ship. Just you and me. I was going to take a Ripcar and go in alone, but I figured you'd want to come too."

"What? Well, of course I'm coming with you. But, please tell me why we are doing this?"

"Because Carahil asked. He wouldn't have done so if he didn't think it important. And ..."

"And what?"

"And, I'm not certain what we shall find when we return to Kana."

"What do you mean?"

"I mean we are on course for what we believe is Wayreth 16 in Xaphan Space. The reason we were able to determine it was Wayreth 16 is because of the nearby pulsar that emits radiation at a very precise rate. However, Wayreth is not where she should be."

"Come again?" Syg said.

"I'm saying that Wayreth is not where it's supposed to be—it is shifted, so is the companion pulsar, and so are all of the stars in Xaphan Space the Charting Lab has identified using Atrajak's chart. The only way that can happen is through the passage of time, a lot of time, in the order of millions of years. I think we are very far into the future. Look how Carahil's note is worded: '*Go around it if you wish, and your destination is but three weeks away'.* Notice how he doesn't say 'The League is three weeks away', or 'Kana is three weeks away'. He just says 'destination'. What if there is no League there anymore. And then, there's what Ennez told me."

"What did Ennez tell you?"

"The other day, while I was in the dispensary having lunch with Crewman Lasset, we'd finished our meal, and she'd nodded off, and I asked Ennez how his research into our condition was coming along. He said he was still gathering data, and then, off-handedly, he said his readings looked more and more like tissue damage consistent with theoretical time-travel that he'd read about in manuals published by the Sisters. Time-travel, Syg. I think we are displaced in time and our bodies are reacting to it. If that's the case then there is no cure, other than to return to our proper place in time. How far removed we are I don't know, but far enough that Wayreth 16 isn't where it should be. I honestly have no idea what shall be waiting for us on Kana when we arrive. Certainly, not our children, not our home."

Syg sat there and was chilled.

When Davage and Syg returned to the bridge, Davage called a staff meeting and informed them what he was planning to do. They didn't take the news well. They sat there in stunned silence.

"Going into that vortex is suicide, Dav!" Paymaster Stenstrom yelled after he'd recovered. "Alone in a Ripcar? You'd never make it back to the League in a Ripcar, even if you started from our current position. Have you thought this out? What are your plans once you get there?"

"I don't think Carahil would simply ask us to throw our lives away; that's not his style. He must have a plan of some sort. All I know is he thought it important enough to ask, so there must be a good reason for it." He checked his timepiece.

Nine bells.

Tellerran, sitting over her endecar, chimed in. "Then we all should go. We'll go in, see what is there to see, and then begin again for home. We made it this far once, and we can do it again."

"Not acceptable," Davage said. "The *New Faith* shall continue on, while Syg and I go in via Ripcar. There's nothing more to be said on the matter. Bel, the ship is yours. I give you the chair."

"Then, if the ship is mine, we are also going in. That is my first command as acting captain."

"Bel, don't be ..."

"Don't be what, Dav? We're not going to last three tachs without you, with or without our Gamma goggles. The enemy is not finished with us. They are massing for some sort of concerted attack, be it here or elsewhere. We are no safer here then back where we started from. Furthermore, if what you say is true, then there is no home for us to go to in the first place. All the things that make Kana our home are, no doubt, long gone. I say we go in as well. What have we to lose?"

"Any who enter that void shall be in the enemy's veil. Returning to Kana, despite its unknown current status, appears to be the path of least resistance."

"Then let's leave it to the Drum to determine our fate," Stenstrom said.

"The Drum?" Tellerran asked.

Davage shook his head. "He wants to put it out for a vote."

"Then I vote we go in," Tellerran said. "If the enemy wants to come, then let them come. I've a little something I'm eager to introduce them to." She held up her hand and allowed her nails to glint in the light.

"Fine," Davage said. "Let's put it to the Drum. And, if the Drum says nay, then the ship shall sail to Kana under your command, Bel, without further argument, while I and my countess enter the vortex. Respect the Drum."

Paymaster Stenstrom sent out the 'drum' via ship's holomail, and it soon came back. By a count of three-to-one: Enter the Vortex with Captain Davage.

"The count is in, Dav, and it is 'Aye'," Stenstrom said. "Respect the Drum."

Davage sighed and checked his timepiece again.

Near Ten bells. Two and a half to go.

So, running out the guns, heating the Sar Beams and launching the Marines in a flanking pattern around the ship, the *New Faith* went forward into the vortex and disappeared.

23—The Temple of the Exploding Head

When Lon and Ki appeared in the dark, they thought they had somehow gotten separated, for Kay, Sarah, Phillip and Joy appeared to be missing.

They were in a low-hanging chamber barely six and a half feet high—Ki's triangle hat was smashed up against the stony ceiling. Uncomfortably, she stooped down a little.

They were in a dark, hot space. The low stone ceiling made them feel very claustrophobic.

"Lon?" Ki whispered, her voice amplified in the space. "You ok?"

He looked around, seeing Ki dimly standing a few feet away. "I believe so. Where's everybody?"

"Don't know."

In the distance, they heard a loud buzzing crack, like a powerful arc of lighting or a ball of plasma and the steady thrumming of a great dynamo.

Lon took a step toward her and tripped over something on the ground.

It was Sarah, crumpled up on the floor. Phillip was lying next to her, Kay a few feet away, his glowing CARG resting against the stone floor, making a low disk of whitish light. Joy was lying near Ki.

They knelt down. "Kay, Sarah, you all right? What's wrong?"

Sarah struggled to speak. "Lon … sick, dying…"

Phillip, Kay and Joy appeared to be in similar distress.

There was another loud crack that blasted their eardrums, and they saw, off in the distance, a bluish rod of lightning blossom and stretch out.

"What's wrong with them?" Ki said in a near panic.

Lon pulled on his goggles and looked them over. "They're all going into shock."

"Why aren't the two of us affected?"

"I don't know."

Lon looked around. Although the space they were in was low in height, it was very wide—Lon with his goggles couldn't see the end of either side. In the dark, he could see row after row of stone pillars. The pillars were fatter in the center than at the top and bottom. He picked up Kay's CARG and waved it around like a torch, its silvery light doing little to penetrate the gloom.

He adjusted his lenses. The pillars were coursing with plasmatic energy. He noticed the pillars in their vicinity were throbbing with power, while ones farther away were doing nothing.

"Lt.," he said. "I think these pillars here are somehow draining them of energy. Wait! I think they are drawing power from their Gifts. I don't have any, and you don't have any either—that must be it."

He looked around again. "I think this pillar to our right is going to …"

A nearby pillar to their right suddenly spewed a white-light gout of lighting that danced into the nearby pillars and forked away. The noise it made was deafening, it's light blinding.

"Good Creation!" Ki exclaimed plugging her ears. "My teeth!"

Lon was worried. "We've got to get them away from here. This area isn't safe."

Ki got Tweeter out of her coat pocket. "Tweeter, these columns are no good; can you get us away from them?"

Tweeter fluttered away to their right and waited for them a few columns down. Sparks came off his body and danced into adjacent pillars. Ki managed to start dragging Phillip and Kay. Lon tried to moved Sarah and Joy but couldn't do both, so he stuck to Joy, as she was tiny. She whimpered feebly in his grasp.

"Lon!" Ki shrieked on the move, "where's Sarah?"

"She's back there still. I couldn't drag them both!"

"Creation, you need to get fit, Lon!" She put Phillip and Kay down, seized Kay's CARG, and blundered back into the dark, waving it about, looking for Sarah. She finally found her and made her way back, following Tweeter's light.

About a hundred yards ahead, the orderly rows of columns abruptly stopped. "Lt., there's a broad staircase heading down. I can see it!" Lon said.

Slowly, they made their way to the stairs, Ki dragging Phillip, Kay and Sarah in stages and Lon, moving faster, dragging the tiny Joy.

Occasional casts of lightning dogged their heels.

As they approached the stairs, Kay began to stir.

Deep throated drumming boiled up from below as they gathered at the top of the stairs.

Lon tried to roust Kay. "Kay—you all right? Kay?"

He shook his head and looked badly sick. "Creation, what was that?" Phillip rolled over and tried to wretch.

"Some sort of energy-draining field coming from those columns. How do you feel?" Lon asked looking him over.

"Wonderful. Is everybody ok?"

Phillip sat up, and Sarah held her head. Joy appeared to be having trouble standing, and Kay helped her up.

"Let's make a note not to go in there again," Sarah said.

Lon looked back at the vast, pillared space. "It's like a huge inductor field, drawing ambient energy into itself. It was sucking you four dry."

Kay gazed into the dark. He tried to Sight. "No, it's no good; I can't see anything. Phillip, is your Sight working?"

Phillip looked around. "No, nothing."

Sarah tried hers. "Mine too. I guess that means our Cloak is down, right?"

Kay nodded. "Yes, it's down, and I don't think I can Waft either."

Sarah spun around. "Well, that's that—we're stuffed! How are we going to get out of here?"

Ki shook her head. "You Vith—somebody takes away your Gifts, and you start crying like sissies. Tweeter!" she yelled. "Is there a way out of here big enough for us to use?"

Tweeter sat on her shoulder, apparently doing nothing. Ki smiled. "See, he says there's another way out—so don't worry."

"I didn't see him do anything," Sarah said.

"He's talking to me, Sarah—he's not talking to you! He talks to me in ways only I can understand. Besides, a place this big has to have a large vent going to the surface, or possibly out to the river. So, when we're ready, Tweeter will take us there."

They seemed a little relieved, though Sarah never really believed that Ki had this silent telepathy with Tweeter.

Kay closed his eyes and strained. "Wait, I can see a bit, if I concentrate, but it's limited and stuck in the present."

He looked around. "The space around us is huge. It must go on for miles. I see energy seething through the pillars and in the walls. It's blinding."

"Where's Sam?" Ki asked.

"I don't see her on this level anywhere."

He pointed at the huge staircase going down. "She must be down there."

Ki drew her SK. "What do you see?"

He followed the staircase down with his Sight, "I see a lot of stairs, going down deep."

"How deep?"

"At least a thousand feet. It lands at the mouth of a gigantic room which must be the main Temple area, and then the stairs continue down another thousand feet to a pillared room similar to this one here."

"All right, concentrate on the center room. What do you see?" Ki asked.

Kay brought his Sight back up to the large central temple. "It's huge. I see pillars lining the sides creating a vault overhead. I see statues and burning fires. I see dense oil smoke clinging to the floor and rising high into the vault where its beaten back down by rain water. I see a vast open space in the center of the Temple and a raised platform far off in that direction," he said pointing.

"Do you see the Horned God?" Lon asked.

"No."

"Do you see Sam? Hey!" Sarah yelled, punching him on the shoulder.

"I see captives down there—they look like Monamas. They're chained on the platform I mentioned."

"Who are they?"

"I don't know—Monamas. Different ones, I suppose."

"Do you see Sam?" Ki asked.

"I can't tell. She's probably mixed in with the rest up there.

Joy rubbed her aching head and moved in closer to Kay. "You can see all of that, Lord Blanchefort?"

"Yes."

"What else?" Ki said. "What about the bad guys? I can't believe the Monamas are in there all by themselves."

Kay looked around. "I see a lot of *Killanjo* in the center of the Temple."

"A lot?" Ki said flatly. "How many's a lot? Hundreds? Thousands?"

"A lot, Ki, I don't know. There's hundreds at least. Possibly thousands."

"What are they doing?" Sarah asked.

Kay sighed. "All right, since you asked, they appear to be having a heated orgy in the Temple proper."

Though Sarah appeared disgusted, she had that familiar look like she wanted to go and see for herself. Kay anticipated that. "You really don't want to see what they're doing, Sarah."

Ki was grim. "Kay, can you Cloak us? Without that Cloak we'll be dead before we get started. The six of us can't stand up to a hoard of thousands."

He quieted his Sight. "I'll try." He tried to relax. "No, it's no good. I can't Cloak."

"I'll do it," Joy said. "I can Cloak us."

She took a deep breath and relaxed. After a minute or two she shook her head. "No, it's no good. I can't keep it up. I'm so sorry."

"It's all right, Joy; you tried," Phillip said.

Phillip went down a few steps and thought. "All right, our Cloaks are no good, but what about Shadow tech. Can you still create that?"

Joy raised her hand and a ball of brackish gray Shadow tech formed, floating on air.

"Good," Phillip said. "Now, can you form the Shadow tech around us and add a texture to it—to disguise us, make us look like the *Killanjo*? Perhaps we can sneak in and go unnoticed."

Joy thought. "May I try it on you, first, sir, as a test?"

Phillip nodded, and she formed her Shadow tech around him; after a moment, he took on the look of a corpse.

"It has to look worse than that—wetter and bloodier. Use your imagination," Sarah said.

Joy did her best, and after a while, Phillip looked truly horrid.

"Oh, that's good," Sarah said.

Joy was concerned. "Does the Shadow tech hurt you—mine isn't fully turned yet, and it might harm you if you touch it for too long."

"It feels a little crawly, but, I think, in the short term, it'll be fine."

So Joy, set to work, disguising everybody in turn. Sarah wanted a crown of fingers and eyeballs and got it. As Joy worked on them, her creations became more and more horrid—she appeared to truly have a ghastly imagination once it got going. After a few minutes they looked a frightening, dripping mess.

Joy turned to do Kay.

"No," he said. "Joy, you can't disguise me."

"Why not?"

"I don't want to go into it, but you simply can't." He could not allow Joy's Shadow tech to touch him—bad things would happen.

"Then, what shall we do?"

Kay thought. "I shall wait here and observe. The rest of you go down, get to the platform, and try to get into a position to locate Sam and free her, the captive Monamas as well. They're coming too."

"How many of those are there?" Ki asked as Shadow tech flesh slid off her face.

"About fifteen. I'll be watching. Once you're ready, I'll come charging in and try and draw the *Killanjo* to me. In the confusion, you free them all and lead them out to safety, following Tweeter.

"It'll never work," the now horrid Sarah said.

"It's the best I can come up, unless anyone else has a better thought."

Lon chimed in. "You'll be under heavy attack. He reached into his coat and pulled out his PITCOCK WONDER GUN and his brace full of large slugs. They were covered in blood. "Madam Joy, would you be so kind?" he said holding out the bleeding accessories.

"Oh, certainly!" Joy removed the covering of Shadow tech, and Lon handed his gun and brace to Kay.

"Now, when you make your diversion, use my gun. Take note of the slugs in my brace—the gray ones are basically nothing more that high-powered bullets, but the brightly painted ones are area affecting, so just load up with those, give it a spin and shoot into the crowd. Should create quite the display and thin them out greatly. Should give us time to get Sam and the Monamas out."

Kay took the huge gun and slung the brace over his shoulder. "All right, let's do this, and be careful. I'll be watching."

They made their way down the stairs. The walls were covered in Monama/Berserkacide carvings. Joy, looking like a gutted fish, wanted to seize the moment and give Kay a kiss, but he backed away—he could not allow her Shadow tech to touch him. After a moment, hurt, she turned, and, in a dripping mass, went down into the main Temple proper with the others.

"Joy," Kay said, feeling bad about treating her in such a fashion. "I'm sorry."

She looked up at him, and then continued down.

Kay, holding Lon's PITCOCK WINDER GUN, watched as they made the long descent down into the Temple of the Exploding Head.

24—The City of Many Forms

Passing through the blue vortex, the *New Faith* emerged fairly near to where they started from, just as Carahil had warned in his note. The ominous ten planet solar-system with its now familiar nebula was directly to their 3:00pm and not an bell or two hard sail away.

On the bridge, Davage was tense. "What is our proximity?" he asked.

The crewman at the sensing station checked the readings. "The ship is currently clear. There is a small, Type 4 planet sitting at our 6:45am."

"Are we reading any signs of habitation?"

"Uncertain."

"Continue scanning."

"Aye."

The planet came into focus on the holocone. Small and rocky, somewhat yellow in appearance, it seemed rather unremarkable.

Syg looked at the image with a skeptical eye. "We've come back all this way for this? What are we supposed to be seeing?"

"Helm, ease us in. Sensing, focus in on an area 16 22 north by west."

"Captain, training sensing on 16 22, north by west. We are not seeing anything of note. It appears to be a dry canyon composed of various limestone groups, schists and shale."

Davage looked down at the planet and Sighted through the decks of the ship, seeing the planet with his own eyes. It was a rather yellowish, dusty world, similar to Poteete back in the League. "Doesn't look like much, does it? Sensing, you said it is Type 4?"

"Aye, sir, Type 4, with a methane-helium atmosphere."

"Temperature?"

"Nominal, 34.4 degrees Celsius."

Davage continued Sighting the area, seeing nothing of note. "All right. I want a team of Atmospherics made ready, a Cloaker of the highest order, as well as a squadron of Marines to flank them. We're going to take a tube down and see what there is to see."

"Aye, sir."

Davage headed to the lift, followed by Syg. "We convene at the tube in fifteen minutes. Bel, take the chair."

They stopped at their quarters where Syg quickly changed into her usual Hospitaler bodysuit and rolled-up shawl. "Ready, love?" she said.

"Ready. Now, don't forget, this is going to be Type 4, and we won't be able to breathe without the Atmospherics creating a pocket of habitable air for us, right? I hate having to use Atmospherics, as they can be a bit touchy and headstrong. It's also going to be a tad on the warm side at 34.4 degrees. Just stay near me, please. Let's go."

✶ ✶ ✶ ✶ ✶

Ten and a half bells.

They made the long walk down the tube, the darkened corridor stretching off to what seemed like infinity. Syg walked to Davage's right, Ennez to his left carrying his Jet Staff. Flanking them in groups of five were Marines of the 12th division, Lt. Kilos' old outfit. Striding near Davage in a standard Fleet uniform and hat was Lt. Benson, Lord of Mystery, a Cloaker from Zenon whom Davage knew well and trusted from the old *Seeker* days. With Lt. Benson there to paint them into a full Cloak, they should be able to pass undetected. Walking behind them were five Atmospherics in their handsome sky blue coats, led by Lt. Septonius of the Tenth Order of Worlds. The Atmospherics, rarely used in the League with all its Type 1 Terraformed planets, appeared eager to use their training at last.

The Atmospherics were always mouthy, willful and rather insubordinate. Davage loathed their presence, but he really didn't have much choice.

"Keep to a distance fifty meters circular; that is where you shall have sweet lung unhindered," Septonius said with his Remnath accent. "We shall scent the air created by us in a pleasing banana note. If you smell bananas, you know you are good and safe within our influence."

"Good to know, thank you, Lt.," Davage said. Banana smell was a standard Atmospheric procedure—he didn't need to be told.

"Please allow me to introduce to you the skilled graduates of the Temple of Worlds who will be pleased to create a pocket of sweet lung for you today. I have here Lt. Acton, my right hand, Lt. Jasiland, my left and adepts Brennan and Richmond."

Davage tipped his hat. "Pleasure." He turned to the Marine Lt. "Lt. Marta, are you kitted out with a contingency of aquanaughts, should they be needed?"

"Aye, sir," she said. "To a man."

Lt. Septonius was incensed. "Aquanaughts!" he spat with disgust. "We shan't need such ponderous devices. We of the Tenth Order shall provide sweet lung in earnest."

"Doubtless, sir, doubtless," Davage said. "Just a backup is all, in case you or your people get killed."

Septonius gulped.

As they walked, a point of light appeared in the distance.

Ennez spoke. "Tellerran wasn't at all happy about not being allowed to come with us. Did you see how mad she was?"

"I did, and she's a brave woman," Davage replied. "Too many people, and not enough Atmospherics to go around. She'll be safer on the ship."

"Do you notice how her hair gets rather bushy when she's angry?"

"I notice a growing familiarity, Ennez," Syg said. "I think she likes you."

"Think so, Syg?"

"I do. All that grabbing and flicking she does."

"You know how bad it hurts when she does that? I've got welts."

"Lots, I imagine. Love hurts sometimes."

Ennez snorted. "I thought she liked you, Dav."

"Oh, that was just a momentary crush," Syg said. "I think she's found her man at last, good thing too."

The light rapidly approached, blinding.

"Ready your firearms!" the Marine Lt. barked. The Marines' hands went to the butts of their SK's.

The tube ended just ahead, opening up to a great, dusty yellowness. The Atmospherics began their work, the air thickening around them, the smell of bananas strong. "We are ready. Stay within fifty meters," Septonius said. "That is all we can give you."

Lt. Benson came up. "All right," he said, "we're Cloaked."

"I can help, Lt.," Syg said.

He bowed. "Thank you, Great Countess, I can manage."

The Marines split into groups of five and fanned out a short way into the blinding yellow sunshine. When given the all clear, the rest followed.

All around was what appeared to be a vast city of rising and falling carved stone, bewildering and pyramidal, cut in with a complex grid of channels flowing with amber water and multileveled into the ground. The Marines, startled, scrambled into a defensive position, their SK's pulled. Davage drew his CARG, and the Atmospherics huddled in the center, allowing the Marines to cover them. Lt. Benson, always a brave man from Zenon, stood tall and drew his MiMs.

"Lt., send to *New Faith*! Tell them there is a massive city down here! Somehow it eluded our scans."

"Aye, sir!" Marta replied.

As they hunched in their defensive positions, they got their bearings. The city all around them was vast, stretching off into the flat horizon for as far as they could see interspersed with broad channels flowing with amber water. There seemed no sense of scale; some structures were gigantic while others were tiny. The alley-like flat spaces between the stone buildings were littered with statuary, thousands of them—millions possibly. Statues of men, statues of women and children, animals of all kinds, alien creatures of all shapes and sizes, wings, horns, claws, fins, machines, robotic creatures and so on arranged and posed in the rictus of a frozen moment. It was like a life-sized diorama, or an endless wax museum, and Davage had always found those rather disquieting.

The city was also far from uninhabited. There was movement all around them. The amber water in the channels was coming up out of the banks with great frequency, moving onto land in a splashy viscous manner, engulfing random statues. The water then took on the shape of the statue it had engulfed and moved on, either walking, rolling, crawling or flying away as the case may be. Sometimes, the statue that had been engulfed was consumed to nothing in the process leaving a blank spot, and sometimes it wasn't.

<It's the enemy!> Davage sent to Syg. *<They're all around us.>*

"They don't seem to be paying us any mind," Lt. Septonius said, looking around.

"It's the Cloak," Lt. Benson said with some irritation. "Our Cloak is Painted and sound."

Lt. Marta checked her ranger. "Captain, we are not at 16 22, north by west. It's about a mile in that direction," she said pointing to the north.

Davage checked his timepiece.

Eleven bells.

"All right. We have plenty of time, and we're under full Painted Cloak, so

let's make our way there now. Let's move carefully and safely and not push our luck. No stragglers, right? We've gone unnoticed so far, thanks to Lt. Benson. Lt. Marta, please inform the Engineer the tube was not zeroed on our desired location, and I'd appreciate a better showing next time."

"Aye, sir."

They made their way north, passing the odd buildings and dusty avenues. All manner of golden creatures moved around, not seeing them. So far, so good.

A short walk away was a sunken lot full of statues packed together in tight, messy rows rising up to a squat pyramid likewise covered with statues, giving it a fungal fruiting body look. One of the Atmospherics stopped. "Look at them," he said. "They look like they're in pain." The statues in the courtyard were, on closer inspection, contorted in all manner of defensive poses: arms up, hands out, heads thrown back, mouths open in a scream. It was all rather terrifying to behold.

Ennez, curious, stepped up to one and reached the end of the Atmospheric's pocket. He motioned for one to follow him, and Lt. Jasiland did so, extending the bubble in that direction. He began scanning.

"Ennez, come on," Syg hissed. "No straggling, remember?"

"Just a moment," he said waving his scanner over the statue's face. "Dav, this isn't a statue. This is a person, preserved somehow, giving him a stony appearance. He's alive, too."

Several of the statues appeared to throb with subtle movement which caught Ennez's attention. He and Lt. Jasiland moved over to inspect them.

"These here are covered with a number of amber, resinous nodules," Ennez said. "Odd." He inspected closer, pushing his helmet back.

"Ennez!" Syg said again.

"Syg, have you not a bit of scientific inclination in you at all? You wouldn't last five minutes in the Knickerbaum Order."

Lt. Jasiland standing near Ennez jumped in. "Good sir, what is that?" she asked.

On a nearby statue, which was also covered in amber nodules, one of them had cracked open and was spewing amber fluid. As they watched, the statue seemed to deflate, like a life raft rapidly losing air. Soon the statue was nothing more than a resinous pile of crystals.

The amber mass that had emerged from the statue came together in a long tube. It browsed through their ranks, slithering past their feet like a snake.

"Everybody, step away," Davage warned. They all took a step back.

As it neared Davage, it began piling up on itself, getting taller and taller, assuming a rough, proto-humanoid shape. Soon, it assumed the full likeness of the statue that it had been attached to, perfect in every way. It appeared sluggish and dull, out of its head with delirium.

"What is this? What are we looking at?" Syg asked.

"Birth, possibly," Ennez said. "Those amber nodules must be eggs or pupae or something."

Nearby, another nodule burst open, spewed, crawled, and then took the shape of the statue it had been attached to. In a similar stupor, the newly born Kestral joined the other.

"Captain!" Lt. Benson cried, pointing toward the sky.

Overhead, several golden winged creatures came down in a fast dive, heading right for the two newly born Kestrals. Davage grabbed his people and pushed them aside as the winged beasts came in. Screaming, one of the new-born Kestrals was seized in the talons of the golden bird and carried away.

"Gods!" Lt. Septonius cried, watching the golden bird flap away with its struggling human-like Kestral prey gripped in its talons. "What was that?"

The second Kestral managed to avoid capture. Stumbling, still in a stupor, the Kestral made its way north, wary of the open sky.

They followed the odd creature, Ennez watching with interest. "Yes, see look here. I'll wager these Kestrals are parasitic, requiring a host not only to sustain them nutritionally as they develop, but to also provide them form. See how all these host statues are all humanoid. Perhaps that's the first instar stage of their development; then, if they survive, they move onto more exotic forms of life."

Davage considered that. "And, given what we've seen, it seems the Kestrals make it a practice to apply predation pressure to their own offspring, perhaps to weed out the weak and ensure only the strong and most cunning survive."

"They're eating them too, Dav! The bird has set down and is ripping the new-born Kestral apart," Syg said, watching the horrid spectacle in the distance.

Davage shuddered. He gazed out at the vast fields of statues all around. "Look at all the humanoid statuary—they must need a plentiful and on-going broodstock to keep themselves replenished in young."

"It's possible that they cannot change shape into a particular form unless they've first consumed it and 'programmed' it into themselves, rather like we program specific languages into an endecar," Ennez said. "I'll go even further. I'll wager that they can only transform into exactly what they consume. Say, if one consumed me, it could, therefore, transform into my likeness, but not yours, unless it first consumed you as well."

"Maybe they collect them as they age, adding forms into their repertoire as they progress," Syg said. "This seems to be a city of many forms."

Ennez was in full discovery mode. He followed closely behind the surviving new-born Kestral, watching it stumble northward down the lane. Ahead, a great pyramid, thousands of feet tall, came into view, floating in a river of amber water joined to the surrounding banks by a number of narrow causeways. The four sides of the pyramid were adorned with huge life-like statues, carved in grand sitting positions. One of the statues was a colossal sleeping female, and another was a giant half-man, half-goat-like creature with great horns. The final two were placed on the other side of the pyramid and were generally out of view.

Davage took in the scene. "I see many roads leading to this central Great Pyramid, and I see many figures converging on it. Look!"

From all around, stumbling, insensate humanoid figures, men, women, and children, blundered toward the pyramid, making their slow, steady way just like the one they were following. The Kestral turned and made its way across the nearest causeway, joining several others. Ennez wanted to follow, but Davage held him back.

"It's like watching the sea turtles hatch and make their way to the surf; remember seeing that in Fazo, Dav?" Syg said. "Remember Kay and Ki and the Grenville children constructing the mesh screen to protect the baby turtles from seabirds?"

"I do. There does seem to be a similarity."

They watched golden alien creatures in all manner of configurations pick the new-born humanoid Kestrals off in droves as they crossed the causeways. Some swooped down fast from above, while others rose out of the amber water and seized them with dripping tentacles. They Wafted in, angled with webbing, and jumped down, furry and clawed, from the craggy buildings. Flying machines came in and speared them into the sky. Some passed right by Davage and his group, not detecting them through Lt. Benson's Cloak.

Through this dire gauntlet, not many of the new-born humanoid Kestrals made it to their apparent destination—the Great Pyramid, just like the sea turtles struggling to reach the waves in Fazo, only in this case, there were no children watching to protect them from predators.

"Despite myself I rather feel sorry for them," Syg said. "I realize they're the enemy, yet it's so sad, so brutal."

A scant few managed to cross the long causeways and reach the Great Pyramid. Once there, they climbed up the side of the pyramid until they reached the giant statues seated there. They then scaled the statues and attached themselves, resuming their previous, nodule-like shape.

"Did you see that?" Ennez asked. "What is that? Are they incubating? I'd like to get a closer look."

Davage checked his timepiece: twenty after eleven. "I appreciate your zest for knowledge, but we've tarried long enough. We need to continue on our way."

Ennez lingered. "Look there! I thought I saw the great statue move. He exhaled, I think. And see how he's restrained, chained in place? Can somebody lend me a pair of binoculars?"

"Ennez," Davage said. "Let's go."

Reluctantly, he turned, and they pressed on, leaving the Great Pyramid behind. As they continued north, they entered into a low, rather empty part of the city full of vast dusty lots.

"This is it, sir," Lt. Marta said. "This is 16 22, north by west."

"Here? Ah, at last. Thank you. Please form a defensive perimeter and get posted. Though we are under Cloak, I want nothing left to chance."

Lt. Marta clapped her hands and got the Marines moving. "Let's go! I want a unit facing north and west, and I want Bailies assembled and ready to deploy!"

They spread out into the dusty area and concealed themselves as best they could.

Syg created several silver, wide-mouthed pots with her Silver tech and placed them around the perimeter of the lot. The pots were decorated with complicated designs.

"What are those, Syg?" Davage asked.

"StT Pots," she replied, placing the final one on the ground and scooting it around. "Lady Poe invented them and taught me. These things are awesome, and I've been dying to try them out."

"StT's?" Septonius snorted. "Those are products of Black Hat sorcery."

"I'm not a Black Hat, sir," she replied with a bit of ire.

They settled and waited, the city moving unaware around them. Syg seated herself next to Davage.

"Who are we looking for again?" Ennez asked.

"Ondecca."

"And who's Ondecca?"

"I really don't know."

"And she's supposed to be here someplace?" he asked.

"Apparently so, at ten 'til twelve bells. We've some time to wait, however." Davage checked his timepiece.

Eleven and a half bells.

The Atmospherics settled in the center of the lot and tried to make themselves as small against the terrain as possible. One of them got up and inspected one of Syg's StT pots.

"Get away from that," Septonius barked. The Atmospheric backed away and returned to their group, Septonius telling him something under his breath and pointing at Syg.

Lt. Benson leaned against a fallen wall, hands in pockets, unconcerned, trusting fully in his Cloak. "I should have brought something to whittle with," he said. The Marines, lined up and ready for action, scanned the surroundings. Ennez, using a borrowed set of field glasses, observed the Great Pyramid in the distance, watching the never-ending waves of young Kestrals get picked off as they approached.

Time passed. The idle waiting appeared to damage the Atmospherics' calm, and they became extremely nervous. Davage moved among them, trying to allay their fears.

"Your name is Lt. Jasiland?" he asked one of them.

She nodded.

Davage took a deep breath. "Well, you're doing a wonderful job. I've never breathed so easily in all my life. I've almost forgotten this is a Type 4 world. We'll get this business behind us and be back on the ship before you know it."

"Thank you, sir."

<*Dav ...*> came Syg. <*Look!*>

A green slit opened among them and hovered. Several Marines scrambled to get out of the way. They reformed their lines and aimed their SKs. After a minute or so, a number of *Killanjo* appeared through the slit. They wore intricate golden helmets and tanks at their backs, allowing them to breathe in the oxygen-depleted atmosphere. They carried ugly, cruel-looking scourges.

Eight Monamas also came through. They wore no helmets, they seemed to be holding their breath. The Monamas carried with them a number of captives: men, woman, children, all terrified and apparently in some sort of suspended animation. Under direction from the *Killanjo* the Monamas began arranging the captives in the apparently empty lot with ant-like precision, coming and going from the slit and spacing the statues out evenly. The *Killanjo's* tanks hissed as they exhaled and watched. Occasionally, they laid their scourges across a Monama's back, drawing blood.

"The enemy's bringing in fresh brood-stock," Ennez said.

"Look at these captives, look at their clothes—they appear to be Xaphans. Conwells if I'm not mistaken, brought here, no doubt, to be parasitized, and using the Monamas to perform the heavy lifting," Davage said.

Some of the captives were wearing Conwell garments, and others appeared to be wearing nightclothes, as if they had been taken from their beds.

"What should we do, Dav?" Syg asked. "Should we act?"

"We should not," Lt. Septonius of the Atmospherics said, jumping in. "No, no, we are under cover in enemy territory. Leave the Xaphans to their fate. They are not part of our mission."

Ennez scanned the captives. "They're in some sort of stasis. Their vital signs are low, but they're present. Lots of adrenaline—they were terrified prior to being placed in stasis."

"We can't just leave them here, Dav," Syg said.

"Countess, you're not proposing we intervene, are you?" Septonius asked. "We could be detected, and how are we going to carry all these people back to the tube?"

"We're not going to have to walk back. We'll have the engineer reconfigure the tube to appear in this location," Davage said.

"Captain, you cannot ..."

Davage waved him into silence and checked his timepiece: fifteen until twelve. "Lt. Marta, we are going to assist these captives. I want these *Killanjo* dealt with at once; then we'll try to gather these people up and bring them aboard the ship via tube."

"What about the Monamas, sir?"

"Stun them with your SK's. I don't want them harmed if possible."

"These people are Xaphans," Septonius said.

"I really don't care who they are, sir. We're taking them aboard. Once we determine their identity, if any have criminal records or outstanding writs in the League, we'll throw them in the brig. Until then, however, they shall be treated as our guests." Davage turned to Lt. Marta. "Lt. ..."

"Sir?" she said.

"Attend to these *Killanjo*."

The Marines drew their Monicas from their coats and moved into position to assassinate the *Killanjo*.

"Gentlemen," Syg said. "A moment please. Watch." A number of StT's came skittering out of the silver pots she had placed: small, silver, cockroach-like. They crawled through the dust toward the *Killanjo*, silently climbing up their horrid legs, up their backs and underneath their helmets.

"Won't they feel that?" an Atmospheric asked, watching intently.

"They will not," Syg said, "and that is unfortunate, for I wish them to suffer."

The Marines moved into position near the Monamas as they struggled with the statues. They raised their SK's, stun barrels cocked and aimed at their skulls. "By your command, sir," Marta said.

"Wait a moment," Davage said.

One of the Monamas, a female, turned and sniffed the air, catching whiff of their scent. The *Killanjo* noticed. "Get back to your work!" he roared through his helmet lashing her across the face.

"Now!" Davage cried. Syg snapped her fingers, and every single *Killanjo* went limp and fell dead, dropping their scourges, hitting the ground face first and kicking up dust as if in synchronization; killed instantly by Syg's StT's.

Pfft! The Marines fired their SK's, stunning the Monamas. They fell. The Marines dragged away the limp *Killanjo* bodies.

"What about the Monamas," Lt. Marta asked.

"Gather them up and we shall take them with us. Ennez, remove their Shocker collars."

Everybody, except for the Atmospherics, began pushing the immobile Xaphan captives and fallen Monamas into the center of the lot. Ennez set to work skillfully slicing off the invisible, prism-studded collars that would turn the Monamas in Berserkacides. "I could use some help," he said, finishing with one and moving on to another.

Davage turned to Lt. Jasiland of the Atmospherics. "Lt., would you mind?"

She knelt down and began assisting Ennez. Lt. Septonius took exception. "Stop what you're doing! Captain, you do not order my people about. Mark my words, this will come to no good end, and, sir, I am considering placing you on report for needlessly endangering those in your charge."

"Stop complaining and help us," one of the Marines said.

"We are here to provide you with sweet lung, not to toil with corpses, unconscious Monamas and Xaphan abductees. We shall not!"

Lt. Benson, struggling with a Xaphan, took exception. "I'm ready to put you out of this Cloak I've made once and for all, and you may stand naked for all to see!"

"You wouldn't dare! I've a mind to cut off your sweet lung and let you choke."

As Benson and Septonius bickered, something descended on their position, casting a shadow over the lot.

All fell silent and looked up.

An intricate golden vehicle came down to street level and hovered. It was roughly hexagonal in shape, jointed and armored with spotlights panning about. It appeared to be an automated vessel, as there was no place for a person or persons to sit. It came down in an adjacent lot filled with statues and transformed into a toga-clad woman of great beauty; her toga was encrusted with flashing green and blue stones. They watched as she strolled down the orderly aisles of statues, looking them over. She selected one, placed her hands on it and held them there. When she pulled her hands away, two amber nodules were left behind.

"She's laying eggs," Ennez said.

The Kestral moved on to another statue, and then glanced in their direction.

She saw the pile of fallen *Killanjo* pushed in a heap. She reached out, her arm stretching, and picked one up, examining it, noting the cracked helmet and the dead, skinned face within.

"Did you not pull them into the Cloak?" Septonius asked Benson.

The Kestral somehow heard Septonius speak through the Cloak and was alarmed. She changed shape into that of a swarm of giant-sized crow-like birds. The birds flapped about, cawing in a malevolent fashion.

Birds flapped in Septonius' direction, swirling. "Ahhh, shoo, shoo!" he cried. One of the birds became huge and swallowed him whole, beak open, gulleting him fast, his shoes kicking in the air.

Syg Pointed at the bird. It stood there for a moment, enduring the Point, then it expanded in size and exploded in a cloud of skin and feathers, vomiting out Lt. Septonius. The power of Syg's Point had been too much for it.

The green slit, still hanging in mid-air, churned with excitement. More *Killanjo* rushed out. They raised their hands, holding prisms.

Five Monamas, whom Ennez had yet to attend to, were bathed in red light from their collars. They erupted, kicking, growling, an extra pair of clawed arms sprouting of their bodies. Holes opened between their eyes spewing clear liquid.

"Berserkacides!" a Marine yelled. A moment later, his head was off, his body torn to rags.

There was chaos. Two more Marines were dead, slaughtered by the Berserkacides. The Marines rallied and unleashed enough fifty caliber lead to kill a whole company of Xaphans, *Killanjo* went down as Davage and Syg struggled to pull the remaining three Monamas without their collars to safety, shielding their eyes from the red light. A Berserkacide, riddled with bullets, threw itself at them. It exploded in a gruesome rain under Syg's deadly Point. Ennez, brandishing his Jet Staff, caved in the skulls of two *Killanjo* right through their helmets. Two of the Marines carried Bowsers: seventy-five caliber SKs. The SK slugs shredded the newly arrived *Killanjo* and unfortunate Berserkacides, mowing them down.

The remaining Kestral birds took flight in a gaggle and the Marines opened fire, doing no apparent damage. The birds shined down cones of red light from their open mouths. The Marines caught in the light writhed and fell to their knees. Lt. Benson, also caught in the light, toppled, and his Cloak went down with him. The group appeared in the lot plain to see.

Syg readied a lance of Silver tech and loosed it. She hit several birds, and they fell, changing into an amber gel. The rest sounded a fearful alarm, their screams echoing across the expanse of the city.

The Kestrals became alerted to their presence. They came flying, swimming, running and bounding in a golden mass. Syg blasted Silver tech, and red lights came back in return.

Captain Davage picked up a Bowser from a fallen Marine and blasted away at the incoming hoard. The Marines launched their Bailies.

StT's erupted out of the pots like a cloud of locusts. They flew out fast and met the Kestrals, exploding and slashing.

Too many! The killing wave came in.

Three, two, one ...

Ten till twelve.

25—The Secret-Talker

There was a flash. The yellowed, dusty city they were in moments earlier vanished, replaced with a dank, olive green twilight.

No Golden People. No chaotic masses.

The temperature dropped to a humid chill. They appeared to be somewhere deep in a tangled primordial forest.

Davage whirled around. "Are we all here? Is everyone all right?"

Dav and Syg were there, Ennez too, and Lt. Marta and her Marines. A quick count: five Atmospherics and Lt. Benson. Three prostrate Monamas lay nearby on tangled roots. Fifteen Marines present. Five dead during the battle.

Many bathed in the Kestral's red light were fallen. Ennez checked them over with his scanner. "They're all alive. Vitals are a little shook up, but I think they'll be just fine with rest."

"And the Monamas?"

He checked them. "They're fine, just stunned. They weren't turned. It would be obvious if they had been."

The Marines still on duty scattered, trying to form new defensives lines in the dense forest, having trouble with the footing. "No targets!" the Bailies said. Lt. Marta, still a bit dazed from the red Kestral light, struggled to get them lined up.

Davage and Syg took stock of the situation. No apparent enemies. They were clear. One of the Marines yelled, "Captives, Lt.!" The Xaphan captives were toppled over in the trees. All of them seemed to be there.

"Let's try to collect these captives and Monamas and keep watch over them," Davage said. The Marines began toiling with their rigid forms, hauling them out of the dense brush one at a time. Syg, showing her new mastery of StTs, created a small swarm of them and got the captives down, the StT's able to lift and move the statues easily though they were tiny.

"I think we're back on Kana," Lt. Marta said. "Look at the moons!"

Sure enough, through the reaching branches of the forest, there were two moons in the sky that appeared quite a bit like Elyria and Solon, the two moons of Kana; the size of the moons and general coloring looked to be the same, with Elyria being rather reddish, while the smaller Solon was whitish-blue. But, as Davage noticed, they were not the quite the same either.

"Yes, but, Elyria seems to be missing some of its key cratering," Davage said, pointing. "Look there—it's missing the Octagon crater."

The Marines and Atmospherics craned their necks skyward. "Perhaps the Octagon is on the far side right now," Ennez said as he scanned Lt. Septonius.

"No, no," Davage said. "Look, there's Mare Fullum—the slightly more-reddish area. Octagon should sit right in the center of it. It's just not there."

"So what does that mean, Dav?" Ennez asked. "That we're back on Kana, only deep in the past before Elyria received its Octagon Crater? Is that what you're saying?"

"I really don't think I'm saying anything."

Syg stood next to Davage. *<Love, could this really be Kana?>*

<The moons overhead do look like Kanan moons, and this forest has a somewhat familiar feel to it. Perhaps Ennez is correct.>

Ennez finished up with Septonius. "This Atmospheric is going to be fine. Well, wherever we are, I think there's plenty of breathable air here. I'm getting good readings indicating we're now on a Type 1 planet."

"Acton?" Septonius said, shaking his head. "Lt. Acton! Where is Acton?"

They looked around. Lt. Acton was missing.

"She was here just a moment ago; I counted her," Davage said.

Davage's Sight, which had been squelched in the dusty enemy city, was working as normal here in the forest. He saw a few moments into the past. He saw Acton stand, dazed, her hand to her face, and wander a few steps away.

And, just like that, something pulled her into the trees. Acton was abducted. Davage saw a heat trail leading off into the woods to the north. Whatever had just abducted Lt. Acton had come and gone from that direction. "This way!" he yelled, unsaddling his CARG. Syg, Ennez, and a squad of Marines followed him into the trees, while the rest remained and formed a wall around the remaining Atmospherics, Benson, the Monamas and the immobile Xaphans.

Davage tore through the trees, following the trail. Syg and Ennez ran at his side. They soon entered a small clearing populated at one end by a haphazard pile of gray stones resembling a crude hut. Partially consumed slaughtered animals hung by their necks from the stone walls.

Lt. Acton was there, pinned to the ground, making furrows with her grasping fingers and booted heels. Something pale was tensed up on top of her. A female Berserkacide, with four clawed hands, was perched over Acton's body, ready to rip cloth and flesh alike. Her claws were dug in, drawing drops of blood through Acton's clothes. Her mouth was pulled into a grimace revealing yellowed fangs hovering near her neck. Her thick black hair was like a cape covering her back and waist. A necklace made of hollowed-out segments of bone hung at her neck.

SK's, Ennez's Jet Staff and Davage's CARG all pointed at the Berserkacide.

"Lt. Acton, are you all right?" Davage asked.

She was immobile with fear.

"Yes or no, Lt.! Are you all right?"

"Y-yes ... yes ..." she responded.

The Berserkacide hissed. She was like a coiled up snake, ready to strike. Her claws flexed. More blood. Acton whimpered.

<Dav, I can kill it with Silver tech!> Syg sent. *<I'll blast her right off clean!>*

<Wait Syg, wait ... this creature might be Ondecca, the person we're here to see.>

<A Berserkacide?>

Davage reached into his coat and pulled out an endecar. It was rather colorful, studded with trumpets of blue, green, red and yellow, one for League common, and one for Systrel, Conox and Anuie. He held it out and spoke. "Are you Ondecca?" A spray of three different languages came out of the green, red and yellow trumpets.

She reacted on hearing the name. She flexed her claws again, and Acton squealed. The Marines readied their SK's.

"Ondecca, let her go!" Davage said.

She glared at Davage. "This creature is mine to kill!" she said through the endecar. She spoke an odd dialect—encompassing bits of all three Monama languages: Systrel, Conox and Anuie. Her voice siphoned in, pieced together and disjointed.

"Hurt her, and you die moments later," Davage said.

The Berserkacide laughed. She raised herself up a little and slashed herself across the chest, drawing a torrent of dark, pulsing blood. Almost instantly the wounds healed. "He won't let me die while I have His secrets," she said. "Death is a lover I crave."

They were at a standoff. Lt. Acton's heart didn't appear like it could take the strain of being under the Berserkacide's claws for much longer. She was terrified.

What did Carahil mention in his letter? He mentioned something important. Think!

... She will be unpleasant to say the least. Take an endecar programmed with Systrel, Conox and Anuie and demand she tell you her secrets.

Secrets?

It was worth a try. "Ondecca, I demand your secrets be told!"

She made a barking sort of sound and gnashed her teeth. Black-eyed, she regarded him a moment in a fury, and then backed away. The Marines quickly dragged Lt. Acton into their ranks. They raised their SK's again.

"Wait!" Davage said to them. "Wait! Ondecca, I demand to hear your secrets! I'll not ask again!"

She stood, her four arms moving with tentacle-like grace. She approached Davage and sized him up, appraising his potential qualities as a warrior. She pushed her bosom out, showing it to him in a primitive manner. Davage couldn't determine if she was readying to fight or presenting to him as a mate. Taking in her features, she was beautiful in the extreme, so soft and delicate, yet vicious and deadly at the same time. She was wearing a filthy gauze-like black garment covering her perfect pale body. She wheezed like a tiger.

"Many have wished to hear secrets through the ages, and look what became of them." She pointed to the trees behind the hut. Davage Sighted. Hanging from the branches were dozens of brown skeletons of various sizes, dangling like macabre ornamentation.

"The Golden People from the Temple—they come for secrets, and my claws kill them. Why should I give you my secrets? Why shouldn't I make you a skeleton in the tree too?"

Davage considered his response. "Because I am not a Golden Person from the Temple. They are my enemy, just as they appear to be yours."

She snorted and seemed to approve of his answer. "Very well," she said. "You wish to hear secrets, then come with me." She pointed at the hut beyond. "Come and hear them."

Davage stepped forward, and so did Syg.

"Not her!" Ondecca said pointing with a clawed hand. "Just you."

<*You're not going in there alone!*> Syg sent.

<*I'll be fine. Just wait here for me. I'll call if I need you.*>

She disappeared into the darkened hut, and Davage followed. Wearily, she stepped across the dirt floor and went to a clump of rags that made do for a bed. Next to her bed was a pile of rugose skeletons, old and doll-like.

Davage recalled the odd skeleton-like structure removed from the dead body of the Kestral who had taken Crewman Lasset's form.

"They came for secrets too, and I killed them. Speak," she said. "Ask your questions."

"Is this place Kana?" Davage asked.

"Ka-Na," she said. "Yes, this is Ka-Na," she repeated bitterly. "It is no longer Tevlapradah. It is now Ka-Na ..."

"What is Tevlapradah?"

She shrugged. "This was Tevlapradah. It was our place. We ruled here, fought here and killed here. We roamed the countryside seeking game here. And then at the end of things Tevlapradah was thrown down and there was Ka-Na."

"Whose secrets do you keep?"

"Bathloxi's! The Horned God's. Both."

"I've heard of the Horned God. Who is Bathloxi?"

"An elemental spirit living atop the universe. All the gods have a Secret-Talker who knows their hidden things, and I am his, given eternal life, such as it is. He has many friends there and sits in consul and judgment. He is well respected, a giver of laws. He helped compose the laws the Universe lives by."

"What is his relationship with the Horned God?"

"He is the Horned God! Bathloxi saw us, long ago, on Tevlapradah. Before Ka-Na, this place was Tevlapradah. We were four-armed and magnificent then. Terrible we were, bounding through the forests. Nothing that lived could stand before our claws. We feasted on the bountiful game and drank warm blood and listened to the music of their dying screams." She closed her black eyes. "I was one of many then, a slayer like the rest, no different. A man dared approach and bested me in battle, and I drank his blood and gave him a child. He called me Ondecca." Her hand went to her necklace. She touched the well-worn bone segments. "He called me Ondecca ..."

She continued. "Bathloxi was sent by his companions atop the universe to observe us and see what was done here. *'Go to Tevlapradah, Bathloxi, and level judgment,'* they said. They thought perhaps we were too perfect in our rage, our evil, and needed quelling, and so they sent the best among them, wise Bathloxi. Untaintable Bathloxi."

She paused. "We saw him in the woods and gave worship with torn flesh and mounds of burnt offerings. He tried at first to be coy, but intoxicated he became, and more he wanted for himself. Bathloxi became our dark Horned God, and I was his favored, his High Priestess, presiding over all the creatures that died. We never saw Bathloxi again—only the Horned God. Always the Horned God. He was doing things forbidden by his order, things he himself punished other gods for doing. He hid in the dark lest he be discovered and sent to the Hell of the gods for his crimes. He commanded we build unto him a temple, and it was done. We built him a temple of blue stone dug out by the strength of our bare hands where blood could flow unabashed, and we covered it with mountains of earth, leaving no trace on the surface."

"How could such a thing be hidden from the sight of the gods?"

Ondecca bitterly spat. "The gods are not gods. They are not all-knowing, and they are not all seeing, and so we hid his temple deep in the ground and made blood for him unobserved for ages. The gods asked him: *'Bathloxi, what goes on at Tevlapradah?'* And he said '*Nothing.*' And they believed him and turned their attentions elsewhere. With a freehand, he wanted more and more. He lured in victims from faraway places, they fell from the sky and he gave them to us to kill. Tevlapradah became Hell, and he was the Devil presiding over his chosen demons ... us."

"And, what happened?"

"Nothing is forever. The end of Tevlapradah came. Ka-Na came. The gods are not gods. The Horned God erred and lured in an armada of aliens whom he thought would be easy prey for us in the hidden temple. Soft and weak they were, so civilized, so decadent of the flesh in robes of jade and sapphire. They were tainted of the flesh and barely able to reproduce themselves, slowly dying off. They called this place 'Ka-Na', and the Horned God laughed at them. We were eager to sink our claws into their soft flesh and listen to them scream in the Temple. But, alas, their technology and their cunning was greater than the Horned God understood, and they made shelter in the cold north where we could not get to them. They saw us waiting to kill them, to drag them to the Temple, and they thought we were beautiful and so strong. They rejoiced. They thought we were their 'Mo-Na-Mas', their 'Bearers of Offspring'. They longed for us too, just as the Horned God longed for us. They wished us to wear their clothes and read their books—share their beds, admit their tongues into our mouths, place their arms around us and bear the young they could not. They came in their machines, captured us by the netload and took us within their walls in the killing north. They experimented upon us, seeking to quiet our bloodlust—to turn us into freaks! Failing. Generations of failing, the deformity. The rivers choked with dead bodies of our people in all manner of tormented exertions. There came a time when we feared them—so soft and weak, yet so powerful in their northern cities. We who had feared nothing, feared the Gods in Jade and Sapphire."

She fingered the worn bone necklace at her throat.

"At last, the Gods in Jade and Sapphire found success. Our people emerged from their cities after decades, no longer our people. They were freaks, Mo-Na-Mas: two-armed, and lusting. So calm and shy and pathetic. Wearing their clothes, eating their foods. Sharing their beds at long last and having their children by the score. As we were driven by our lust for blood, these new two-armed Mo-Na-Mas were driven by their lust for mating. We hated them, they were so ugly to us. We fought them, killed them, the grounds wetted with blood! But they were as strong as we were when prodded to fight. Their claws were still sharp, could still kill. So many dead! They bore young by the score, while we struggled to produce just a few, and soon they outnumbered us. Soon, we were gone. Only I remained, kept alive and holding His secrets in trust."

"And, what became of this Horned God?"

"The Mo-Na-Mas abandoned the Horned God and the Temple in the ground. They migrated south, by the lake and festered there, breeding like vermin. The Horned God raged and lamented what was gone. He schemed to restore us to our former glory. He could look through his magic mirrors and see us in the past as we were, terrible and proud, but all he could do was watch, for he could not go back in time. The gods are not gods. He could not go against the constants of the universe, and he raged like a child in the dried blood and old bones of his abandoned temple, unable to act."

"And how did the Golden People come into this?"

Ondecca gnashed her teeth and cringed with hatred. "They came centuries later. They are formless Mariners of Time, riding it as ships do the waves, adrift in it sometimes, forgetting themselves when they go too far. They seek ports of anchorage in time, places they can reach from their fastness far in the future where they have circumvented the crushing waves of time, looking for shapes to wear, peoples to enslave and hosts to sustain their young. The Temple in the Ground is such a place. Like a blinking lighthouse in the mist, they saw the Horned God and his Temple and anchored to it, emerging through the old stone and marveling at what was there. They encountered the Horned God and found him a kindred spirit and potential victim, how his power would feed their children and make them mighty. They entered into a pact: the Horned God's Temple and its positioning in time in exchange for their 'servitude'. They added technology to the Temple, and the Horned God provided the lightning and rage to operate it in perpetuity. The Horned God was jubilant, for surely these Golden People could stretch out their hand and pluck his four-armed demons that he couldn't forget from the veil of time. And once that was done, their first victims would be the Golden People themselves, for they would have outlived their usefulness."

"You're saying the Horned God was going to sacrifice the Golden People to your ancestors once they were returned to him?"

"Of course he was. He loved us, could never forget us. However, as he erred with the Gods in Jade and Sapphire, he erred with the Golden People. They were much more cunning then he realized. They told him they could go no further back into the past than the anchorage would allow and could not reach my ancestors. And the Horned God raged."

"What happened to the Gods in Jade and Sapphire, the creators of the modern Monamas, if I'm following you correctly."

Ondecca laughed and clutched her necklace with longing. "The Golden People did to them what we were unable to do. To impress the Horned God, they rousted them from their cities, stole their forms and fed them to their children. The Gods in Jade and Sapphire are gone: consumed by the Golden People.

"I have been to the Golden People's city where there is no air to breathe, but I cannot die and I have seen what is there. Here are two secrets that even the Horned God himself does not know. The Golden People could restore my people in time if they wanted, for the temporal anchorage in the temple goes back in time much farther than they let on. They know what will happen should the Horned God have access to his dark angels again, so they lie to him. 'Oh, Bathloxi—we cannot do what you ask', they say. 'We can create Berserkacides and fleshless *Killanjo* servants, but we cannot give you what you want'. Bah—lies, lies, all lies. The Horned God lies to the Golden People. The Golden People lie to Horned God. Everybody lies. And here I am, lost in time, the last of my kind having to listen to it all. 'Kill them! Kill them all!' he rages in his bitterness. But the Golden People, ever cunning, saw great value in the Mo-Na-Mas. Their strength, their speed, their multiplying in vast numbers. They could not steal their forms, as they can with others. They took them and, as the Gods in Jade and Sapphire had done to us, experimented upon them and discovered how to revert them in time and create Berserkacides—the almost perfect warriors in our image who burn out quick and soon die. With them, they tantalize the Horned God. All they ask for in return for their service is, occasionally, a god or member of the Older Folk whom they can take to their city and sacrifice. And the Horned God obliges as Bathloxi, convicting lesser gods of crimes and quietly giving them to his servants."

Davage stood there and took it all in.

"And what is the second secret?"

"Far into the future, the Golden People take the Horned God himself and lash him to their Great Temple. I saw him there, bound and suffering. They have many such gods whom they pretended to serve lashed to their temples. There in the far veils of the future, they feast on the gods to draw out their power and take it in, little by little, making themselves greater in the process. They have suckled on many gods, and when the Horned God's usefulness is done, they will suckle on him too."

Davage recalled the pyramid in the City of Many Forms—the statues sitting all around it, carved into its sides, where the surviving Kestral young migrated and attached themselves. One of the statues had horns … *was that the Horned God himself, enslaved, used there in the future as a brood host?*

"So, all of this, in short, is so Bathloxi can have the Monamas back as his slaves and so the Golden People can have their tunnel through time and the Horned God himself as their unsuspecting victim?"

"That is the truth I know." She sprang at Davage with incredible speed. Davage raised his CARG, and she landed in front of him, tensed like a tiger. Syg, Ennez, and several Marines tore into the hut, ready to kill.

"I wish to give you a gift," she said. "I have spoken you my secrets, but I have ages more. Take them from me; I give them to you." She raised two of her clawed hands. "Take them from me."

Syg and Ennez readied to attack, but Davage stopped them. "I was told to come here for secrets. I was told they are important."

"Then have them! Have them all"

He stepped forward, and she placed her hands on either side of his head. It took only a moment. Ages passed into his head, and then it was done.

"Now, you are His Secret-Talker. Now I can die by your hand," she said. She reached out and touched his CARG. "I have given you a gift; now give me one in return. Kill me."

Davage hesitated.

"Can you smell it?" she asked in a growl. "The roasted meats and cups overflowing with blood? I cannot linger here any longer. There is a feast of offal awaiting me in the Lands of the Dead, with my people ... with my mate whose blood I tasted and whose child I bore, long gone. I hunger for it. Send me there to them."

She removed her necklace and held it tightly in her palm. With her other hand, she reached out and took Davage's. She placed it over her heart. "Can you hear them? I do not wish to be alone anymore. They call to me."

Davage lifted his CARG. "Are you certain?"

She nodded and closed her eyes. Davage swung with a massive cutting chop, removing her head from her slender neck. She went limp.

They stared down at her dead body.

"Did you hear her secrets?" Syg asked.

"I did."

"What did you discover?"

"That the gods are not gods."

He picked Ondecca's light body up and placed it on her bed along with her head, arranging her in a dignified position for her long sleep. Her necklace of bone had fallen from her grasp and lay on the dirt floor. Davage picked it up and placed it back in her hand.

He felt she was owed.

"What was the point of all of this?" Syg asked.

"I think Carahil believed it was somehow important that we hear what Ondecca had to say, for now that we know, the Horned God's secret is lost."

Ennez looked around. "So? How's that help us?"

"At this point I really don't know."

Syg backed away. "Dav! Look!"

Ondecca's head lit up with bluish energy growing to white light that filled the interior of the hut. Davage grabbed Syg and Ennez and pulled them out into the clearing.

Blue energy filtered out, engulfing them all.

Skull in the Mystery Library

26—Ondecca's Skull

Lady Kilos of Blanchefort had never seen her sister act this way before. Lady Hathaline had run into her boudoir in a froth, shouting nonsense. That was very unlike the normally reserved Hathaline, very mature beyond her age.

Lady Kilos tried to make sense of the situation. "So, you're saying we have to go somewhere, right now?"

Hathaline was beside herself.

"And, you're saying it has to be you and I? Now?"

Hathaline grabbed her by the arm and started pulling.

"All right, all right, I'll go. No need to pull. I'm coming. Where are we going? South? Why are we going south? And we need to get something first before we go? What? Where? I …"

Hathaline pulled her through the castle to the ground floor entrance of Xyotel Tower. Sarah's tower.

"The Mystery Library? Ki said. "What do we need in there?"

Hath pulled on the sturdy latch to enter the tower, but the door didn't budge.

"It's locked," Ki said. "What are we supposed to do? I can't Waft in if the door's locked. It's Waft-Protected."

Hathaline pulled Ki outside and into her rumbling Ripcar. She hauled it into the air, through the needlework of spindly towers, up the stony face of Xyotel tower to Sarah's balcony on the 42nd floor. Hathaline brought the Ripcar to a smooth hover just off the balcony's edge and pointed.

Ki looked over the side, seeing the thousands of empty feet to the rocks far below and Wafted onto the balcony. "What am I looking for, Hath?"

Hathaline told her at a shout over the whine of the Ripcar's engine.

"Really? Ok, I'll be right back!" Ki plunged into the interior of Sarah's room and then, free to Waft now that she was inside the tower walls, she blasted up to the 50th floor. There was Sarah's beloved Mystery Library, where she kept all her favorite stuff, organized and shelved. A slate named all those who were welcome to enter and those who were unwelcome. Her name: LADY KILOS had only recently been scratched off the FORBIDDEN list. She entered and whirled around, uncertain as to what she was looking for. She wandered into a set of book cases at the far end of the library.

Sitting on one of the shelves was a bleached skull, supposedly that of a Berserkacide. It was old and smooth, partially fossilized, one of Sarah's prized possessions. She had a lot of weird things back there: an old-looking sword, a necklace on a soapstone bust of Carahil, and so on. She'd have to ask her about all this stuff later.

For now, the skull was what she was looking for. It had all sorts of horny ridges criss-crossing here and there, along with a tiny hole placed right between its eye sockets. Though it was only a skull, she felt that hole between the eyes was somehow aware of her presence, possibly watching her.

She grabbed it and went down and back out onto Sarah's balcony. "I got it Hath!" she said as she Wafted back into the Ripcar. Hath wheeled the little craft around and shouted at the top of her lungs.

"All right, all right, I'm strapped in!" Ki said clicking the safety straps into place, crushing her gown.

And they tore off to the south, Hath's Ripcar burning it up. She flew the car over the interior shelf and dropped down into the familiar passes of the Gaston Way, hitting the boost and pinning Ki back in her seat with gut-churning force.

"Why are you going so fast?"

Hath tortured the Ripcar, forcing more and more speed.

"Hath!"

She held the sticks and wove in and out of the passes.

"Hath, why are you crying?" Ki asked. "Hath!"

Hathaline answered. She repeated it.

"What?" Ki said. "Of course, you're not a monster! I know you love Kay!"

Hath said nothing else for awhile. They came out of the Gaston Way and bore southeast across the sea. In the straightway, Hath really put the screws to the Ripcar, blasting low across the water, stirring up a water-trail, passing over the Isthmus of Kana, and crossing to the other side in mere minutes. Ki tried to compose herself as she held the skull tightly to her breast, still feeling rather uneasy about it. "Will you please tell me what this is all about?"

Hathaline muttered something.

"A dream? This is all over a dream?" Ki tried to sound casual, but she knew from her growing Bloodstein witchcraft training that dreams could be very important.

Hathaline told her in the dream she had seen herself as a fleshless monster roaming the Grove, tormenting Sam, eating human flesh and having sex with Kay, her own brother. The dream was of something she may one day become, and it was terrifying. Hath wept as she spoke. She said she considered killing herself, that death was better.

"And what prevented you?"

Carahil. Carahil told her in the dream that he needed her, and he reminded her that she was a Vith, and Vith didn't take the easy way out of things. There was urgent work that needed doing.

"What work? This skull? It belonged to a Berserkacide woman named Ondecca, and she is important to the Enemy? But, how did Sarah end up with it?"

Hath was nearly hysterical.

"Carahil gave it to Sarah and asked her to take care of it? Why didn't he come to me? I could have cared for it better than Sarah."

And now, the time had come to take it south to a specific location.

"Where are we taking it?"

Hathaline pointed at the distant beach of the coast and the twisted line of old trees.

The Great Armenelos Forest coming up fast.

They tore over the coastline and skimmed the treetops, Hath slowing the Ripcar to a hover as she checked her bearings. She found a tiny crack in the canopy of green and skillfully set the Ripcar down, winding through the layers of dense growth without hardly touching a single branch.

"Are we here?" Kilos asked.

Hath shook her head. She pointed to the south. She got out of the Ripcar, holding a dark blue, velvet bag.

"What's that bag?"

Hathaline didn't answer.

"We'll never make it in this tangle," Ki said, her gown and shoes ill-suited to this untamed, overgrown country. Hath tore off the bottom of her skirt up to her thighs and allowed her shoes to fall away in the muck. She wanted to press on. Ki was more careful with her gown, but Hath fell upon her skirt and started tearing it off for her.

"Wait!" Ki said. "Hold still—I'll Waft us."

Ki put her arms around Hath and Wafted several hundred yards south, emerging exhausted. They were in a maze of trees and untamed growth. Hath wandered away, looking around. Ki, holding the skull, followed her. Though she saw nothing but trees and hummocky ground, she got the impression that there was something here once, a long time ago, a settlement perhaps.

Hath found a fairly flat patch of ground.

"Here?"

She wanted the skull. Ki approached and gave it to her. "Is this the spot?"

Ki became aware of being watched, from the woods. She saw green slits appear in midair and heard jeering voices that froze her soul. "*Hath ... Hath! You're one of us. Your evil is rare and unbound. Hath. Come join us ...*"

Hathaline spoke. The voices laughed at her.

"We have stolen your voice and hold it in trust. Come to us and be whole. Revel with us."

Hathaline stood tall, holding the skull and the bag. She spoke again, louder, stronger, more assured, her voice returning to her.

"I'm taking back what you stole from me, and I'm not afraid of you!" she said, her voice proud and steady. She put the skull down and emptied the contents of the velvet bag into her hand.

A great screaming sound came from the slits, and Ki felt herself freezing up, just like what Kay had described.

In answer to the screaming, an even louder buzzing came up from the woods. Paraflies fanning their wings by the thousands. They swarmed in, filling the forest like a vast living wall.

"This is for my brother!" Hath said, yelling so that her voice could be heard over the buzzing sounds. She placed a small figurine at the front of the skull.

She placed another to the right of the skull. "This is for my family! And, this is for me!"

She placed the final figurine to the left of the skull. "*Genda aba vera!*" she hollered, raising her fist.

Ki ran up to Hath and put her arms around her. "What did we just do?"

"I don't know," Hath said, "but it is all right now! Carahil promised! We have done our job!"

They stood there in the forest, sister to sister, standing in a cathedral of noise from the Paraflies.

✶ ✶ ✶ ✶ ✶

It was the entire universe against five ships. The *New Faith* was in close quarters with thousands of golden enemy vessels that had launched themselves out of hundreds of Gamma band slits formed all around the planet. They swarmed in for the kill.

Paymaster Stenstrom was doing as well as he could. He was frantic to locate the captain and his party and attempt to escape into open space. He blasted the enemy with canister fire and Sar-Beam sweeps.

"Have we located the captain and his party?"

"No sir!"

"Locate them! This ship goes nowhere without its lord and captain!"

Launched canisters. Incoming bolts. Destruction all around. The *New Faith* shuddered. The Marines scrambled to their *Trelaines* and exited the surrounded *New Faith*. They heated their Sar-Beams and waded into the mass of golden ships.

There was no aiming, no plotting solution and consideration for a shot. Just point and shoot—no missing was possible.

And the five ships, in a sea of gold, were leaving quite a trail of destruction in their wake.

"Number 4's out, Paymaster!"

"Increase power to the remaining engines! Sensing, I want the captain located immediately!"

"Paymaster! We're being boarded!"

In the center of the bridge a blue vortex appeared. Stenstrom drew his NTHs and cocked the hammers ready to fire.

"Bel, wait, it's us!" came Captain Davage's voice as he emerged through the vortex. Syg stepped out, followed by Ennez, the Marines and the rest of their party.

"Captain, what happened?"

"Long story."

A group of several civilians bound together with Silver tech and frozen in place appeared along with three unconscious Monamas. After all had come through, the vortex vanished.

"Who are these?"

"Xaphans!" Davage cried, "and a few Monamas we picked up. Marines, administer the protective paste!"

A bridge Marine drew his air gun and hit the three Monamas in the forehead, covering their eyes with black paste. In such a state they could not be turned into Berserkacides and were no longer a threat.

Davage Sighted and saw the dire situation around him. Wave after wave of golden enemy shipping, deadly bolts and insanity lights from the surface. He took the helm and wrenched the ship out of orbit, the Marines vessels following as best they could.

With the shaking wheel in his hands, he tormented the giant ship, demanding more of it then ever possibly considered.

Down! Down, to 6:00am!

Bolts incoming, hard over and pull up!

More bolts, 8:45pm. We're hit! For Creation's sake, counter flood to starboard and contain the damaged area!

Engines hot, Captain!

Damn the engines! Burn them—burn them up!

Insanity light shining down from 2:00pm.

Roll, roll! Hospitalers to the aft, decks ten and eleven—got clipped.

The Marines outside were surrounded. Bolts came in from all over. One *Trelaine* disappeared in a blast, then a second, their little ships not seen again.

Davage could see, in the center of this malaise, a huge golden ship, much larger than anything else in the theatre.

The mother ship. The Flagship!

Davage steered toward the ship, and the enemy reacted, trying to keep him from engaging with it. They fired bolts in earnest, shined Insanity lights. It seemed they never expected the *New Faith* to have lasted this long. Certainly, it should have been destroyed at the outset.

And they began trying to infiltrate the *New Faith* in droves.

✶ ✶ ✶ ✶ ✶

Bethrael of Moane and Ennez, newly arrived, defended life support, along with 'Bernie,' her Silver tech familiar in the form of a giant, big-eyed frog. Droves of Berserkacides and *Killanjo* emerged from Gamma bands, the three of them fighting them off. When *Killanjo* appeared, Bernie simply ate them with a SNAP, wrenching them into his waiting mouth before they could utter a sound. Beth began leaving Bernies everywhere, with standing orders to devour anything not wearing clothes. They prowled the halls and stood guard over the vital areas.

Elsewhere, two squadrons of Marines defended engineering. There, using their improvised goggles, they were heavily engaged with Berserkacides. With their SKs the Marines were quickly able to gun them down in a horrid dismantling of flesh.

Another wave of Gamma Bands. This time several *Killanjo* stepped out, screeching, casting spells. One or two fell under the Marine's guns before the spells took effect.

The Marines were helpless. A fresh wave of Berserkacides came through and charged the frozen formation.

Now the enemy would have engineering, and that would be that.

Another group of Berserkacides came in from the opposite direction. Berserkacides wearing baggy clothing. One of them leading the charge was wearing a flight jacket.

Not Berserkacides—Lady Tellerran and the Monamas from the hold, wearing paste over their eyes in a sprayed-on black line and using their acute noses to move about.

They launched themselves into the air and engaged the Berserkacides and the screeching *Killanjo.* Having thrown aside their yoke of fear, they fought with an age-old fury and met the Berserkacides claw for claw, strength for strength, in a heated battle. Not since Atrajak and his army of Anuians did Monamas dare raise their hands against the *Killanjo* and their Berserkacides. These Monamas fought savagely for their *Sar-Gra-Ma* and for their freedom, and they would not be denied. They slashed through the initial wave of Berserkacides and then fell upon the screeching *Killanjo.* The *Killanjo* were panicked—they had never seen Monamas dare attack them. Why would they not transform into Berserkacides? Quickly, the Monamas dealt with the *Killanjo*, sundering their horrid flesh, separating heads from necks and silencing them. After a bit, the Marines were free, and they finished the rest of the Berserkacides who still lived, though most were brutally mangled. Some of the Monamas had been badly injured, and the Marines began treating them as best they could until Beth and Ennez arrived with ten Bernies, scintillating colors flashing, climbing the walls and starving for enemy flesh. Savoring their victory, the Monamas cheered!

Engineering was secure.

✶ ✶ ✶ ✶ ✶

On the bridge a Gamma Bands opened, and several *Killanjo* streamed out, screeching. Syg, moving quickly, threw a vicious Sten at them, killing most. Paymaster Stenstrom gunned down the last ones with his NTHs. Syg, wearing a pair of Ennez's Gamma-goggles, sent massive Silver tech charges into them. Those select few *Killanjo* that did manage to stagger out were instantly gunned down by Davage and the Paymaster.

More Gamma bands opened. This time Golden People streamed out in various guises. SK's hammered, doing nothing. Syg skewered them with Silver tech. Paymaster Stenstrom dropped them with his NTH's; a pool of amber gel forming on the bridge floor with each hit.

Outside, the *New Faith* had clawed its way to the huge central ship, taking a bolt along the way and venting. The golden ship was many times the size of the *New Faith,* and it blasted off one bolt after another, most missing but a few connecting, causing massive damage in the ship's upper tier.

Davage then opened up, hitting the gigantic ship full broadside, the Sar-Beams cutting deep and Canister penetrating the thin outer skin and detonating within.

The great ship returned fire, sending bolts down the *New Faith's* back.

They traded blasts for a few moments, then the giant golden ship caved in and decompressed into slag.

The bridge crew cheered, but it was short-lived.

The *New Faith* was shutting down, succumbing to the damage she was taking. Davage wheeled around, but the *New Faith* was steadily slowing and in desperate need of respite and repair.

His remaining engines went out. Davage was down to maneuvering thrusters. Golden ships were everywhere, moving in for the final kill. His deadly Sar Beams went quiet.

"Where are my weapons?" Davage roared.

"Thermoplant is out! It must be restarted!"

No time, no engines, no weapons.

There was no place to go.

27—Save Sam

They descended the stairs for a long time in the dark, seeing sinister four-armed Berserkacide figures carved into the walls. Eventually they reached a landing, passed through a pair of giant Berserkacide statues and entered the massive Temple of the Exploding Head.

It was enormous. It was rectangular in shape, at least a mile long and half a mile wide. The ceiling was a healthy thousand feet from the floor and held up with massive arches.

The walls were lined every hundred feet with large stone pillars that made their way to the ceiling high above. Between the pillars were large stone idols carved in gigantic proportions. Some of the idols were carved to look Berserkacide-like in appearance with four arms; others were horrid and monstrous. All of them were on fire, and the sputtering, jumping light from the idols cast the temple in an unsteady reddish glow. Drummers beating large, skin-covered drums, stood before the burning idols.

The five of them slowly entered. They felt exposed in their skinned, dripping Shadow tech disguises. Trying to "act natural," they made their way into the heart of the Temple.

In the center was a vast open area. In the reddish, smoky distance was the large platform Kay had mentioned. It was far away.

"I see them up there," Lon whispered. "The Monamas, I can see them."

"Shhh," Sarah said.

On the platform many people were chained to several pillars. Monamas, heads lolled, oiled and nude. "Who are they?" Phillip asked.

"Don't know," Lon replied. "Could be anybody. Looks to be about twenty of them."

"Is Lady Sammidoran up there with them?"

"I can't tell from here. Probably."

Ahead, a bolt of lightning came down from above and popped into the stone floor with a noisy flash. The ceiling was obscured by a dense cloud. It was raining inside the center of the Temple. The air soon became dank, and they began to get wet.

Between them and the distant Monamas was what, at first glance, appeared to be a huge battle in progress marked by a steady drone of lust and suffering. Glistening, naked bodies squirmed and writhed in the center part of the Temple, a humid, unbearable cloud of tepid, lightly falling rain settling over them.

Killanjo, thousands of them. They were at each other, moving with the beat of the drums. If they had simply been having a large orgy, that would have been one thing, but that wasn't all they were doing. They consumed each other, biting off fingers and tearing off patches of flesh with their greedy teeth. Channels cut into the floor were filling with rainwater, blood and gore. Heads were chopped off, bodies were roasted on the nearest oil-fire.

The Temple was soaking up the foul energy the *Killanjo* created, condensing it in a storm cloud.

They made their way forward, staying on the outskirts of the mess. Any *Killanjo* that came too close got roughly handled by Ki—they had to blend in as best they could, and being meek and timid would not do.

A partially disemboweled man came forward and started pulling on Lon. Before a moment had passed, the man fell dead, and was immediately fallen upon, his body torn limb from limb by his fellows.

Joy had killed him with Shadow tech.

As they approached the platform, they emerged from the rain cloud in the center of the Temple. They could now clearly see the Monamas. They were stripped bare, oiled or greased from top to bottom and tightly chained to numerous pillars on the platform. They counted twenty three of them, all from some unknown Monama tribe. They were all lost in Head Swarm.

Sarah and Phillip looked around, trying to find Sam in the masses of Monamas. They couldn't locate her—all the female Monamas, with similar heads of hair, looked the same. Sam should probably be larger than these ones chained here, but they just didn't see her.

They finally reached the front, and the platform was just a few feet away, all of them hot and wet, their Shadow tech disguises galling and uncomfortable to wear. They could see the Monamas clearly now. They appeared drugged, their heads lolled and legs splayed out, the chains holding them up.

Phillip looked around. “Where’s Sam? I still don’t see her. The ones here all look like the smaller Conox Monamas the Professor mentioned. They’re too small to be Sam.”

Ki looked down and whispered into her coat. “Tweeter, where’s Sam?”

Silence.

“Did he say anything?” Sarah asked.

Ki pointed up toward the misty, boiling ceiling obscured by cloud. “Up there. He says she’s up there.”

They craned their necks up, seeing nothing but rainy mist.

“I see a chain anchored on the platform leading up,” Lon said. “Sam must be suspended in some sort of cage or harness at the end of it.”

They settled and tried to position themselves to be ready when Kay began his diversion. Phillip looked back. It was going to be a long run, herding a bunch of people who looked to be drugged.

“We’ll have to cut their chains and get them moving,” Ki said. “The chains look sturdy. What do we have to cut them with?” she whispered rolling around on top of Phillip, their mushy Shadow tech disguises slopping together. They were trying to blend in with the writhing mass behind them.

“We’ve our SAPPs. I’m pretty sure we can cut them with our SAPPS.”

Joy was underneath Lon. “I can cut them with Shadow tech. Cutting things was my specialty.”

“All right,” Ki said pushing Phillip off her. “When Kay begins the diversion, you two cut their chains as best you can. Sarah, you bring Sam down nice and light. Lon and I will try to move the Monamas toward the exit.”

“And just where is that?” Sarah said, putting Phillip into a dripping head-lock.

“Back the way we came, I guess. Tweeter will lead us.”

Several robed *Killanjo* appeared on the platform and tended the fires with pots of oil. They then stepped forward and watched the scene in the Temple, wide-eyed with glee. One of them watched and wrung her hands with excitement.

There was something familiar about her.

Sarah stood, and took a step forward. She saw the figure standing there. She mumbled something in shock.

Then: “MOTHER!” she cried in grief and dismay.

The *Killanjo* looked at her and grimaced. It was what was left of Lady Poe of Blanchefort, corrupted into a monster.

The figure standing next to her jumped down off the platform. It was a night-mare version of Lady Kilos of Blanchefort. She smiled with what was left of her face and drew a small knife. She fell on Sarah and began pushing her around, trying to get her knife into her gut.

Sarah was in a funk. She couldn’t take her eyes off of her mother, who watched them struggle. Sarah could feel the knife entering her flesh.

Lady Kilos’ *Killanjo* was roughly pushed away. She then fell apart in a bloody mess. Joy had killed her, had sliced her to tiny bits with micro-fine Shadow tech.

Lady Poe’s *Killanjo* opened her mouth to begin casting a spell when Joy, moving her hands in an intricate slicing fashion, first up and then to the side, cubed her flesh into a fallen mound. Joy’s precise control of her Shadow tech was laser-like.

Her nickname of 'The Knife' was well earned.

And the Temple behind them exploded.

✶ ✶ ✶ ✶ ✶

Kay watched as his friends made their way to the front of the temple past the masses of rain-soaked depravity in the center. He watched Ki and Joy stave off and kill several along the way. He saw lightning flash and strike the floor.

He took Lon's PITCOCK WONDER GUN and loaded it up with five brightly colored slugs—he had no idea what they did. He closed the chamber with a click and threw the brace over his shoulder.

When they got to the front, he saw them begin rolling around, mimicking what the main group of *Killanjo* was doing behind them. He could see the chained Monamas standing in a flaccid manner on the platform.

He looked around. Where was Sam? He noticed a chain on the platform leading up into the lofty heights. His Sight cut through the murk. High above was a decorated stone coffin dangling from the end of the chain. Someone was trapped inside of it. It had to be Sam.

Soon, my love, soon I'll have you free.

He saw two robed *Killanjo* appear on the platform and tend the roaring fires.

Creation, one of them looked like his aunt, Lady Poe, and the other one was his sister, Lady Kilos. He gasped—he had seen this! He'd seen all of it!

He saw Sarah freak out before her mother's *Killanjo* and get attacked by Lady Kilos.

It was time; it was now or never. He ran down the stairs holding Lon's gun in one hand and his purple Poltava in the other, Lon's brace slung over his shoulder.

He saw the Berserkacide carvings on the walls as he made his way down. Claws, leering eyes and obvious bloodlust—this is what the Monamas once were. It disquieted him for a moment.

He reached the entrance and ran into the mouth of the Temple. Spinning the cartridge of Lon's gun, he aimed into the masses of *Killanjo* and fired. A huge green slug corkscrewed out, went a few hundred feet, and exploded in an expanding ball of what looked like a huge spider web. Hundreds of *Killanjo* were hopelessly stuck within, the falling rain crackling off of it.

Several who hadn't been caught, rushed Kay. He gunned them down with his Poltava. POW! POW! POW!

His Sight told him of danger—lightning.

He dove to his right and a massive stroke of lightning hit the floor near where he'd been standing, shattering rock.

Spinning Lon's gun, he fired again—this time an angry red slug shot out. It tumbled ahead and then exploded in a huge fireball that roasted many *Killanjo* in an instant. The fireball also ignited the spider web, burning all those trapped within.

More *Killanjo* came, trying to cast spells and immobilize him—the drummers were also attacking. He gunned them down with his Poltava.

Another blast from Lon's gun. And another. This time a molten wave of tar gushed out followed by a cloud of sizzling, limb-rending buckshot. In a matter of a few moments, Kay had killed hundreds of *Killanjo*. Gunning down a few more stragglers who had been beating the drums, he assessed the situation. The center section was nearly clear, the raincloud rapidly fading away. By Creation, he had an open path forward.

He quickened his pace.

There was a pocket of *Killanjo* in the distance. He fired Lon's gun. The slug exploded, and the *Killanjo* were covered in what looked like a cascade of grape jelly. They advanced on him.

Kay stopped to quickly reload the WONDER GUN. As he slid the brightly colored slugs in, he picked a bright pink one out of the brace that read: FOR MISCREANTS! Kay slid it in and spun the cartridge, readying to fire. The *Killanjo* covered in grape jelly began dissolving, falling apart in a mass of goo.

He looked around. There didn't appear to be any more large massed groups ahead. The *Killanjo,* killed en masse in a number of entertaining ways, the drummers shot dead, the Temple was now rather quiet. He ran for the platform, which was still a good way off. As he approached, he could see Joy and Phillip busy cutting the Monamas chains, their Shadow tech disguises dispensed with. Lon and Ki were trying to get the Monamas who were already free moving toward the Temple mouth. They were having slow success. The Monamas were lost in Head Swarm. They staggered about like drunken fools. Many lay there curled up on the ground content to lie where they were. Moving them was going to be difficult.

It would be ideal for Sarah to use this time to start pulling on the chain and bring Sam down. Surely she had to know by now that Sam wasn't among the captive Monamas; he didn't know who they were, just more innocent victims of the Temple.

Sarah was kneeling next to the horrid remains of Lady Poe's *Killanjo*. She was trembling, a pool of Shadow tech lay around her.

"Sarah!" Kay cried as he approached. She didn't respond.

She was lost.

Kay shook her. "Sarah, that's not your mother. Lady Poe is home back at Castle Blanchefort at this moment, safe and sound with your father."

"No … she's right here …"

"This is something she might have become, you know that! Come on, Sarah, we've got work to do!"

He picked her up, and he could see the sadness in her face. "Trust me, Sarah, we're not going to let this happen to her. We're going to take care of this place, and that future will never happen, I swear it!"

She snapped out of it a little and meekly followed Kay onto the platform. "Here," Kay said holding out Lon's WONDER GUN. "Keep an eye out and use this if you see anybody."

She took the large gun and watched.

Lon and Ki were trying to move the Monamas, but they were so laggard, so apathetic.

"Come on!" Ki roared. "Move, get moving!" She got Tweeter out of her pocket. "Tweeter, find us a way out of here, now!"

Tweeter flapped up and hovered in the air, waiting for Ki to follow. One by one, she pushed the Monamas forward, grabbing them by the hair and tossing them forward.

Kay approached the chain that went up toward the ceiling. He pulled on the chain. Slowly the coffin high overhead came down in jerky stages.

As he guided it down, Kay heard a few deep reports from a gun.

Ahead, Sarah was firing Lon's gun. A few *Killanjo* had survived and were regrouping. She fired at them. More lava, more tar.

Elsewhere, Ki, Phillip, Lon and Joy had freed all of the Monamas and were roughly moving them off the platform in halting stages. Good, good.

Sarah appeared to be having fun with Lon's gun—her previous melancholy forgotten. She fired the final shot and, as the bright pink slug exploded, a mass of knicker-like garments appeared and rained down on the dying *Killanjo* in a variety of satiny colors.

"Lon, what in Creation is this one? The pink one?" Sarah asked.

Lon blushed. "It's an underwear bomb—I created it to get even with the House of Mendenhall who tried to humiliate me at the Science Exposition last winter.

Sarah started laughing.

A huge screeching filled the Temple.

Before anybody could react, several gigantic and grotesque *Killanjo* appeared out of nowhere.

They screeched from all quarters, and the sound of it filled the Temple.

Kay felt himself instantly clench up. He couldn't move. Creation—he should have been watching for the arrival of more! He'd become careless.

Ki couldn't move. Neither could Sarah, Lon, and Phillip. Joy, over-balanced, fell over. The Monamas they were moving, though immune to the sound, tucked up into little Head Swarmed balls on the floor.

Ki toppled. Lying there on the ground, she made a sort of grunting sound, and Tweeter began moving, flying into the heights of the temple ceiling and was gone.

The *Killanjo* were terrible. There were ten of them. Forty feet tall, they were composed of a score of skinned people, welded together to form a rather spidery appearance. They stood on ten legs made of welded-together bodies. Their palps were composed of bodies, ending with more bodies. They were a collection of many people, and they screeched in an ear-splitting chorus.

Gamma Bands flashed. Fifty normal-sized *Killanjo* appeared and ran about, some wearing golden armor, some beaded dresses.

The elite had arrived.

The huge spidery *Killanjo* spread out across the Temple floor, and the small armored ones surged forward. Ghastly, the *Killanjo* pulled Kay's CARG and the rest of their weapons from their immobile hands, and tossed them aside. The *Killanjo* then picked them up like statues and carried them out into the damp center of the Temple.

The raincloud formed again, covering the ceiling. Rain began to fall afresh.

The *Killanjo* carrying Kay were familiar: Hathaline and Maser. They had come again.

Other *Killanjo*, armed with cruel scourges, began whipping the Monamas back onto the platform.

Hathaline gloated over Kay, rainwater and streaked blood dripping off of her chin. "Nice try! Did you ever really think you had a chance? Did you? This is our place—our place of Power!"

The *Killanjo* got them into the drenched center and threw them to the floor. Hathaline quickly got on top of Kay and straddled him. "Oh, by the way, mommy and daddy are dead! Just thought you'd like to know!"

Hathaline then began cutting away Kay's clothing.

Maser turned, saw the form of Joy lying nearby, and fell on her. He took her by the arm and began eating it.

Slavering, all of the *Killanjo* elite began eating while the larger ones watched, screeching still.

A ball of silver entered the central temple from above. Tiny, yet bright and steady, it came down through the raincloud.

Tweeter. He'd returned. He flapped down from the heights of the ceiling through the rain and dense mist like an airship with its running lights on.

And he wasn't alone.

The cloud churned, and behind him came a moving torrent that throbbed through the air, giving it life.

Paraflies! Thousands of Paraflies led down into the depths by Tweeter burst out of the clouds. All the labor and love Lady Poe of Blanchefort had poured into the 'Tuleeflies', as she called them, culminated in this moment. The task they had been created for was in front of them.

Like smothering locusts the Paraflies began buzzing and attacking, filling the vast temple interior, the sound they made quickly overtaking the screech made by the *Killanjo.*

The buzzing knocked the spell right out of Kay's head, and he could move as it grew loud. He threw Hathaline off, where she landed like a drenched cat. They circled for a moment, Hath's *Killanjo* bent at the torso as ever.

Kay saw his CARG lying a distance away. There was his Poltava too. Unable to Waft, he ran for it, and Hathaline took off after him. As he neared it, she tackled him and plunged her knife into his back.

In agony, he reared up and elbowed her so hard that her nose sank into her face. He sprang and had his CARG. She evaded two of his swings, but the third got her clean, taking her right arm off at the elbow.

Paraflies landed on her bloody body and applied their fearsome stings. Hathaline, in pain, tried to slash Kay's throat with her remaining hand. She missed, and he seized her by the head. She thrashed like a gruesome doll.

He held her for a moment. *"I love you, sis,"* he said as he broke her neck. "*You're free.*"

Killing a charging *Killanjo* with his CARG, he tossed Ki her SK, and she hammered away with it, its pounding TACK, TACK, TACK joining the buzzing echoing around the Temple. Phillip and Sarah, using their recovered SAPPs and Poltavas, engaged one of the larger *Killanjo*, who was covered in stinging Paraflies. It capered about, getting stung, slashed and shot at the same time.

Kay recovered his Poltava and shot a *Killanjo* who was whipping the Monamas. He fell dead.

Several of the larger *Killanjo*, under relentless attack, climbed the walls up into the heights of the temple, trying to get away from the cloud of Paraflies.

Lon, with his CEROS, was dismantling another of the larger ones, his shining weapon chopping it down one cast at a time. A *Killanjo* in armor advanced on Lon and, casually, he lined him up and took him down, the CEROS going clean through his chest, armor and all.

A female *Killanjo,* covered in Paraflies, fell. So did another one.

The Paraflies covered the Monamas, who cowered on the platform. Several Parafly-covered *Killanjo* in armor waved lit prisms, trying to turn them into Berserkacides, but the beating wings protected their eyes.

Kay engaged the *Killanjo* and sliced them to tatters. A few fell, stung to death through the joints of their armor. One saw his reflection in the wings and, screaming, threw himself into one of the fiery basins.

Maser was still all over Joy—his armor protecting him from most of the Parafly stings. Kay sprang, covered the distance, and engaged his brother. Joy, fallen, gushing blood from terrible wounds on her arm, didn't move.

Maser laughed with glee as they fought. He carried a sword-like weapon.

"Just you and me, big brother?" he sneered and attacked.

With a crash, one of the large, spider-like *Killanjo* went down—stung literally thousands of times, Paraflies crawling all over it.

Another one fell out of the heights with a commotion.

"Ki!" Kay yelled, squaring off with Maser, "get these Monamas out of here!"

As the Parafly-covered Monamas began moving, Kay fought with his brother. They were quite evenly matched, exchanging sword and CARG cuts, the *Killanjo* of Maser being bigger and stronger, but Kay faster and determined.

Phillip and Sarah tried to add their SAPPS to the fight. "No!" Kay cried.

"Help Joy—she needs help, and then get Sam! Hurry!"

Phillip ran to Joy's side, and Sarah returned to the chain and resumed lowering the coffin to the floor.

Most of the *Killanjo* had fallen, either stung to death, gunned down or slain by SAPP and CARG. Two of the spiders were spinning in agony, the Paraflies slowly killing them. One of them rolled over, its horrid legs wiggling in the air.

Phillip wrapped up Joy's mangled arm with his SAPP and carried her tiny body away. On the platform, Sarah worked the chain fast. The coffin, presumably with Sam inside, was nearly to the floor

Tweeter led Ki to a large barred culvert about halfway down the length of the Temple flanked by two giant Berserkacide statues, where all the accumulated water, blood and drippings were being funneled. There was a lot of water moving in there—it had to go somewhere, probably to the River Seven or the sea several miles away. Ki and Lon worked the bars, trying to spread open a hole large enough to squeeze through. Together, with Sarah's SAPP formed into a stout lever, they spread the bars in the grate and herded the Monamas in.

Kay and Maser clashed weapons and strained for advantage.

The point of Maser's sword speeded for his belly.

Turned, barely, the horn of Kay's CARG whistled for his throat.

Met and held. A rough push and another cut, grazing flesh.

As they fought, Maser was quickly becoming covered from top to bottom in Paraflies. Eventually, Kay couldn't see his body anymore—he was a shapeless mass of bugs holding a horrid sword.

The stinging between the joints of his armor took hold at last. He screamed in agony. Tormented, Maser lowered his guard.

Kay darted his CARG in and took his head off. His brother fell as the Paraflies began to disperse in a triumphant cloud, their foes all dead. In a swirling tornado they filtered back up to the ceiling and waited there.

Kay made his way to the coffin Sarah had lowered to the ground. It was blocky and rough-hewn, like a sarcophagus carved from a single block of stone. It was covered in sinister writing, black ink smeared with clawed hands. Sarah fiddled with the lid, trying to get it open. They searched over its face.

"Here's the hinge, I think!" Kay said.

Sarah backed away, and he chopped at it with his CARG. The lid moved. Straining, they both got it open.

28—Head Full of Secrets

Inside the coffin was a confusion of blood, hair and twisted limbs. A strong, nose-wrinkling sanguine smell drifted out.

The interior of the coffin was lined with dozens of long spikes clotted with thick, dark blood. They were positioned to impale the extremities, the sides and, most terribly, the eyes. There was a pale body inside, spotted with blood in a nest of hair.

It was Sam in a cringed position, impaled, full of bloody holes. Kay couldn't take it all in.

"God's Bodkins!" Sarah cried. "Sam!" Kay stood there looking at her deflated, bloody body. She was impaled from top to bottom.

Her eyes were put out.

His thoughts roiled. Sam … he was too late. The Horned God had killed her.

"Kay, Kay! Help me with her!" Sarah reached in, puzzling over how to safely extricate Sam from the coffin. She felt her neck. "She's got a pulse; she's still alive!" Sarah shook Kay on the shoulder. "Help me with her! Hey!!"

He came out of his funk. Gingerly, he tried to pull Sam out. It was like she was nailed to the bottom of the coffin; her body was fixed in place. "I don't see a good way to do this, Kay. We're just going to have to yank her out as quick as possible. I don't think she's pierced anywhere vital, so we should be able to get her some help in plenty of time once she's out. Come on, Kay, let's do this. Are you ready?"

Seeing his love in such a predicament was too much for him. He drifted in and out. He tried to focus.

"Ok, on three …" Sarah counted, and they wrenched her out of the coffin.

Sam was perforated with dozens of holes, mostly in the arms, legs and lower abdomen. Most of the wounds didn't seem too deep, which was good. Her eyes, though, were horrible to behold. They were closed and flattened out, bruised and bloody.

Put out, gone, her black Monama eyes shut forever. Her trademark head of thick Monama hair was stringy and matted with grime and sweat. Her mouth was pulled into a limp grimace. One of her teeth was missing.

Kay cradled her to him. "Sam," he said quietly. "Sam, it's all right, *Cerri-Tela*. It's all right. I'm here. I'm going to take you home."

She mumbled something. Kay kissed her clammy forehead and put his coat around her.

"Come on, Sarah, let's get her safe. Is everybody out?"

"They're in the culvert on their way to the river. We've got about twenty Monama captives with us. We don't know who they are, but we've got them moving."

"Good. Once Sam's out of danger, I'm coming back here, and I'm destroying this place stone by stone, and then I'm coming for the Horned God."

Kay held Sam in his arms as he and Sarah made their way to the culvert.

As they neared, they heard an echoing sound fill up the interior of the temple. It was a clopping sort of sound, like great hooves on bare stone: CLOP, CLOP, CLOP, CLOP.

Sarah was on edge. "What's that?"

Kay turned. Standing in the distance was a colossal shaggy creature, the same one he'd seen in Castle Astralon. Its head and shoulders were wreathed in thick vapor near the ceiling.

The Horned God himself. Through breaks in the mist above, Kay could see his great horned head flashing with cracks of lightning. He hoped the mass of Paraflies on the ceiling of the Temple would attack, but they didn't; insane cloven gods weren't on their list. The Paraflies did nothing.

Kay handed Sam to Sarah. "Take Sam," he said. "Get her well away from here. Get her to the *Goshawk* and take to her Minz or someplace where she can receive immediate medical treatment."

"Aren't you coming?"

"I'm settling with this creature once and for all. Go on."

Sarah began to argue.

"Go, Sarah! Take Sam and go!"

She relented and disappeared through the bent bars of the culvert. Kay heard her drop down and splash away.

Alone, Kay turned and faced the gigantic creature towering over him. The Professor's previous words vaguely passed through his head: *"...it's imperative that we not encounter the Horned God inside the Temple ..."*

Kay didn't care. He spoke. "You have laid terror on the Monama people, and you are responsible for the abductions of a countless number of mine, including both of my sisters, my brother and my aunt, and, you have gravely wounded my love. You are a disgrace, a parasite and a criminal and a coward, and I am going to destroy you!" He unsaddled his CARG.

The Horned God leaned down through the layers of mist and glared at him with eager eyes lustful and a delighted deer mouth slavering with anticipation, lightning crackling through his great tangle of antlers. His echoing laughter filled the Temple. "Sweet mortal," the Horned God chided in a thundering voice. "Child of the Younger Folk, I am going to give you a wondrous gift, right now. ... I insist."

Instead of attacking, the Horned God shrank down in size, compacting into a deer-form. He stood there on four hooves like any ordinary deer of the forest, only with giant antlers much larger than normal.

Time passed. The deer spoke. "You see, Mincoil, it is far worse than we first thought," he said in a reasonable voice, speaking into the dank air.

From the shadows of the Temple, an otter emerged—a giant otter. He stood up on his hind legs and had a look around, whiskers twitching, his slick fur glinting in the jumpy light. "Is this truly the place, Great Bathloxi?" he asked.

"Yes. This is the place in the ground, far from our easy vision that we have sought for ages, where Carahil has performed his acts of terror."

The otter saw the lumpy dead bodies of the *Killanjo.* "And are these foul things Carahil's servants?"

"Apparently so. It is time to call the Arborium and hear the evidence against Carahil, for I have his Secret-Talker at last."

The otter sighed. "Very well, I shall summon them."

The air in the Temple swirled and filled with movement. A host of animals of various kinds and of giant size began appearing in the Temple proper: a dog, cat, owl, snake, lizard, cow, beaver, horse, and birds of many types, to name a few. They all took in the sights, as if bewildered by them.

"Friends," Bathloxi said. "Though it pains me to say it, one of our own has betrayed us. Look around you—this is the place we have heard of for so long. Look at the monstrosity of it, the shed blood, wandering souls and torn flesh. The savagery that has taken place here cannot be allowed to stand. Carahil must be punished."

"You are certain it is Carahil that has done this?" the owl asked.

"I am, Slywing."

"Carahil would not have done this," the dog said.

"I second that. Carahil is childlike in his goodness," the snake said.

"Do you have proof?" the cat asked.

"I do, Mabsornath. I have his Secret-Talker as last." Bathloxi turned to the beaver. "Dear Meingobble, scribe of the gods, do you detect the presence of Carahil's Secret-Talker here with us?"

The beaver spoke up. "I do. I sense the presence of his Secret-Talker."

Bathloxi nodded. "Then it is time to hear the secrets and know what has been done in this deep place once and for all."

Kay spoke up, his voice surprisingly small and hollow in the great open space of the temple though he shouted as loudly as he could, hoping to command the attention of the gods. "He's lying, and ..."

A metal band formed around his head and mouth, silencing him. He unsaddled his CARG, and chains wrapped around his body, immobilizing him from top to bottom. He tried to Waft out of it but could not Waft—the Temple continuing to rob him of his Gifts.

The gods' eyes turned to him as he struggled.

In a puff of smoke, Sarah appeared next to him, similarly bound and gagged, then Phillip, then Lon and Ki, Joy, and then the Monamas. They lay there on the damp, bloody ground of the Temple, the blinking forms of gods in the shape of animals looking down at them. "Who are these?" the dog asked.

"Carahil's servants, dear Padfoot. He has a host of them among the Younger Folk," Bathloxi shouted. "Secret-Talker! It is time."

From Kay's vantage point, he saw a pale figure appear in the mist moving wearily, bobbing from side to side, toward the center of the Temple. The figure was thin and pale, glistening with streaks of blood and dripping with brackish water. Matted black hair hung down limp to its ankles. The figure moved in a slow, plodding manner, nude, hugging itself about the midsection, as if it were cold.

Kay struggled to see.

Was that Sam?

The figure walked right past him and continued on without pause or hint of recognition. Gagged and bound, Kay couldn't move or speak.

He and Sam both had received 4D tattoos several winters back in the village. His father disapproved of tattoos and of tattoo parlors, so the merchant in the village was operating it in secret. He and Sam had both gotten one. Since they were 4D, they only were visible on the skin when the two of them were in close proximity together. Kay's was on his upper arm, and Sam's was on her right foot just below her ankle.

Sure enough, appearing on the figure's pale ankle was a little red heart with KAY scripted in the center.

It was Sam. He struggled to move, to get free. He struggled to save her.

She made her way into the center of the Temple. The gods watched her slow progress. Bathloxi patiently stood on all fours.

Finally, he spoke. "Now then, Secret-Talker of Carahil, share with us all that has been done."

Sam shuddered a bit, and the gods were appalled. Secrets erupted out of her head into the open air of the Temple and hung there in a lurid tableau. Ages of blood and death. Ages of screaming and sorrow and loss of innocent life.

A giant silver creature, saw-toothed, leering, presiding over it all, demanding ever more. No amount of blood was ever enough.

Carahil, heavy in Sam's memories. An evil, blood-soaked Carahil, one delighting in torment and death.

The gods moaned in sadness as they took it all in.

"Not Carahil!" one of them cried.

"I won't believe it!"

"How could he?"

"Seemed like such a nice fellow."

One of the gods, the dog again, took exception. "Carahil's a Nargal only recently summoned. How then has he haunted this place for ages, Bathloxi? How has he managed that?"

"Dear Footpad," Bathloxi said, "you will find that, while Carahil's body is new and only recently made, his spirit is old. I have evidence to that fact. He is an evil spirit of ages past disguised as a benevolent being."

The deer became restless. "It is an occasion of sorrow to see that one of our own has fallen to such depths." He turned to Kay. "We must spread our net and stretch out our hands until Carahil is in our custody and can do no more evil. As for punishment, the Windage will not do for depravity such as this. My servants have suggested an alternative punishment and we must consider it."

A green slit opened revealing the yellow, hummocky Great Pyramid in the center of the City of Many Forms. A giant chair was carved into the side of the pyramid: an empty chair.

"My servants propose 'The Rock'—where Carahil will spend ages bound there, being bled dry."

The gods murmured amongst themselves in shock.

"It is a brutal thing, I grant you, but in this case it is well deserved. We cannot have places such as this temple."

Bathloxi turned to them. "In the meantime, I give you these Younger Folk here. Not only did they impede us in our quest for justice, but they have actively and knowingly assisted Carahil in his wanton rampage of destruction. They have served him of their own accord and shed themselves of their innocence; therefore, they are subject to punishment as well. And, per our laws, the punishment is death."

Bathloxi looked around at his peers. "Do any of you disagree?"

The gods rustled a bit.

The dog, Padfoot responded. "We are sworn to guide and protect the Younger Folk."

"Yes, and in cutting away the wanton flesh, we are protecting them."

Kay and the rest struggled in their bonds but could do nothing.

"Then let us proceed at once."

There came a loud noise in the distance, like a heavy bit of metal clanking onto stone, followed by a distinctive dragging sound.

"Justice shall be swift."

Green slits opened up all around. Golden people, beautifully oiled, clad in splendid togas, emerged from the slits. They gathered Kay and the rest and carried them into the center of the Temple. The Golden People lined them up in a kneeling position, Sarah to Kay's right, Phillip to his left.

Sam approached. She was dragging a giant axe on the ground behind her.

"Slay them," Bathloxi said.

Moving in an automated, pre-programmed way, Sam tottered over to Sarah. Sarah tried to kick and issued out a muffled scream. Sam wobbled over her and effortlessly raised the huge axe high over her head with one arm.

Sarah was about to die.

* * * * *

"Am I missing anything?" Carahil said loping out of the shadows from the back half of the Temple.

Bathloxi and the gods and the Golden People turned and watched him approach.

"Carahil, my heart is breaking," one of the gods said. "Please tell us you didn't do any of this."

Carahil paused. "I think ... you shouldn't have come here. You're all in danger."

The gods moved quickly, and Carahil was trussed up in mystical chains. He toppled to the floor and struggled. The Golden People surged around him. They pawed at him with lust. They climbed all over him.

"And here is the guilty at last. We have seen your art here, Carahil," Bathloxi said. "Your Secret-Talker gave us much to think about. First, before we send you to your punishment, witness the end of your younger-folk servants."

Like an animated doll, Sam put her foot on Sarah's back, lined her up and brought the axe down in a blur. She cleaved Sarah's head off, drawing a glitter of sparks as the axe-blade passed through bone and flesh and bit deep into the stone floor. Sarah's body instantly deflated, and her head rolled away. The gods gasped. Some turned from the sight. Kay and Phillip struggled in their bonds.

Sam moved down the row without pause or hesitation. She beheaded Phillip, and then Ki, Joy too, and then Lon. She turned to Kay. He tried to call out, but was bound.

She put her foot on his back, flattening him to the ground. Then, the axe came down.

Sparks flew.

"Justice is swift," Bathloxi said. The gods were silent.

The Golden People would wait no longer. They swarmed around Carahil like ants, hoisting him up, pulling on his flippers and carrying him to the open green slit where the sunlit but sinister City of Many Forms awaited. They passed through and vanished.

Gone.

Bathloxi was solemn. "Justice has been done. Let us remember Carahil not for the evil he has done in this place, but for his projected goodness."

"Now, just wait a second!" came a voice from the far reaches of the Temple.

All turned. Carahil, still chained, struggled into the center.

"Where did *you* come from?" Bathloxi roared.

"From that horrible city. It really wasn't any fun there, was it?" he said in a bright voice.

Green slits appeared all around. Golden People emerged, saw Carahil and converged on him. As they approached, they were transformed into a host of golden rabbits, mice and squirrels. They streamed away and pranced about in harmless bushy-tailed shock. "Thanks for showing me around, guys, but I'm done with the tour." He loped around in his chains to face Bathloxi.

"So, Bath, you're going to feed me to your boys, eh?" Carahil said. "I guess feeding them Anabrax, Folster and Morglum only satisfied them for so long. Now, it's my turn, right? Well, I don't think I taste all that great, so I'm saving them a rotten tummy ache." A great silver book appeared in front of Carahil. He nosed the cover open and pushed through the pages. "Just a moment, I need to take care of something real quick ... Ah! Here we are, 'B' for Blanchefort." He reached into the book with his mouth and pulled out a squirming and apparently unharmed Kay, Phillip and Sarah. "Let's see, Brown ..." He turned back a few pages and pulled out Ki and Lon. "And finally: Black Hat." He pulled Joy out.

"What in the Name of Creation just happened?" Sarah asked.

The gods turned to the beheaded corpses on the floor. Colorful strands of spun sugar in pink and blue peeked through their chains. Their rolling heads: all hollow shells of milk chocolate.

"Does your depravity know no bounds, Carahil?" Bathloxi said.

"Nope! It sure doesn't! I'm just getting started, too."

"You are chained in eternal bonds," Bathloxi said. "Your power is gone."

"Oh, yeah?"

There was a POOF!, and Carahil burst from his chains.

Another POOF! A garnish of flowers appeared in the tangle of Bathloxi's antlers.

"You like that? I'm on a rampage here! Ha ha ha!"

POOF! POOF! POOF!

The gods were suddenly wreathed in flowers, coated in chocolate, and polka-dotted in bright colors.

Carahil winked at Kay and the rest. "It's too nice a day out to be stuck down here with me and the gods, so why don't you all go outside and fly a kite or do something fun."

POOF!

The axe in Sam's hand was replaced with a colorful kite and a ball of twine. Kay ran forward and embraced the insensate Sam.

POOF!

The whole group vanished from the Temple. They emerged in the sunshine and lonely ruins of the Bodice manor. Ki rubbed her eyes in the bright light.

"Well, what the heck was that?" Sarah asked. "Sam, did you really try to chop my head off?"

"She's doesn't know what she's doing, Sarah," Kay said.

As they tried to regain their bearings, a confusion of green slits appeared all around them. Golden People emerged.

✶ ✶ ✶ ✶ ✶

Sarah, Phillip and Ki re-appeared back in the Temple and were pushed to the floor by the Golden People. Bathloxi eyed them with considerable anger. "Where are the others?"

The Golden People said something in an alien language.

"I see," Bathloxi replied. "No matter. No matter."

Carahil sighed, seeing the three of them returned. "This doesn't concern them."

"Oh yes it does," Bathloxi said. "I've condemned these younger folk to death and your continued antics shall not save them," He said a few things to several of his Golden servants, and they disappeared in a cloud of green. He waved his hand and Carahil was again wrapped in chains.

POOF!

"Time for your fate."

The chains vanished just as fast. They reappeared around Bathloxi. He roared in fury. The chains vanished, only to reappear around Carahil again.

Carahil slithered out, like they weren't even there.

The gods gasped again. Several of the Golden People watched Carahil with interest.

"Bet you're wondering how I'm able to do all this stuff when I should be trussed up like a chicken on Nether Day in the Golden People's death city, right? Well, guess what? Somewhere in this huge Temple, there's a brick, a single, solitary brick bearing the inscription: 'THIS TEMPLE IS DEDICATED TO CARAHIL'. So, this nasty place is, in fact, partially dedicated to me, and, therefore, I have all my power here and then some. I ought to destroy this place right now!"

Bathloxi was unfazed. "You cannot destroy a god's temple anymore than I can, Carahil. They are inviolate to the gods. In any event, your Secret-Talker has spoken your secrets."

"Uh, hello! Lady Sammidoran is not my Secret-Talker, and you know it! Speaking of Secret-Talkers, let's hear what *yours* has to say. Let's do that right here and now!"

There was a great blue flash, and then a booming thud and a pillar-shaking groaning of masses of metal. Through the mist, a great, bulbous form appeared, huge and ungainly. Points of yellow light, like a city block full of houses with lit-up windows, shown through the mist. It was a space-borne Fleet ship, its white hull scorched with hits and battle damage, its gun ports open and run out. The stern of the ship faced the center of the Temple, and its stern plate read *New Faith* in bold black letters. Though colossal in size, the *New Faith* was still dwarfed by the overall size of the interior of the Temple, like a massive airship engulfed by an even larger hangar. The structure of the ship was more than rigid enough to handle the rigors of a gravity environment, but it wasn't designed to be landed on solid ground; it was meant to berth on calm water, and slightly over-balanced, the vessel leaned over to the starboard on its keel ridge, its ventral flanks tapping the floor of the Temple with a great hollow BOOOM!!

Stabilizers and gasses vented, filling the air with clouds of ozone and ionized gas.

"Here we are," Carahil said proudly. "The mighty Fleet vessel *New Faith.* And now, I wish to introduce to you her captain *and* the Secret-Talker of Bathloxi, the incomparable Captain Davage, Lord of Blanchefort!"

POOF!

Captain Davage, tall and resplendent, stood on the floor of the Temple before Bathloxi and the other assembled gods. He whirled around in shock.

"What has happened?" he cried. "Carahil? What is this?"

"I fetched you, thanks to your daughter. Hope you don't mind," Carahil said.

"Dav!" Ki cried, seeing him. She was overjoyed and moved to his side, throwing her arms around him.

Davage was lifted into the dank air. Bathloxi eyed him in a threatening manner. "This is not my Secret-Talker," he announced, dismissing him.

"Oh, yes he is," Carahil replied. "I got through all your protections and figured out who your Secret-Talker was and where you had her stashed. Ondecca sang like a bird, didn't she? She got sick and tired of being stuck there in the woods, and she willingly gave Captain Davage all the nasty stuff in her head. Go ahead, take a look! Take a good hard look!"

As before with Sam, secrets flowed from Davage's head in a swirling cloud. Ages of blood and lost life, the atrocities that had taken place under Bathloxi's gaze.

The beating drums from antiquity.

The cracked bones and tortured flesh.

The Horned God reveling in it all, Bathloxi's alter-ego.

And the gods were appalled.

"What is this, Bathloxi?" an eagle asked.

"Have you truly done these things?"

"I certify these Secrets as real!" the beaver Meingobble said.

"You are a deceiver, Bathloxi!"

"Liar!"

"Fiend!"

The gods grew in size and made to rush Bathloxi, to take him in chains to the Windage of Kind, the prison of the gods.

Lightning struck. Bathloxi reared up on his hind legs, transforming once again into the horrid image of the Horned God. He blasted the gods in a wave of malice and they scattered before him, shrinking in size, withering in his power. Davage and Ki tried to protect Sarah and Phillip from the blast.

"Yes, *friends*," Bathloxi said, his voice changing into a heathen growl. "I am the HORNED GOD!! Look at me! I've laughed in your faces for ages, stalking you in your very midst! I've written laws that I've hankered to break. I've committed crimes just so I could blame others for them! Behold, see the wonder, the mystery, the terror that I've made for myself deep in the ground far from your foolish faces! All this in the name of chaos and blood and dead mortal folk whom I've watched die. Hahahahhhahaha!! There might have been a time when I would have invited to you lot to join me, to take the Universe by the throat and suck the marrow from its living bones! But why, why share? There's no need, no need, and I want it all!! You have all walked into my lair and you know the old rules. Carahil just said it—a god in his Temple is all powerful. This is my house, and I have the power here, per the old ways!"

All around, green slits opened, and great, old Kestrals emerged, giant-sized, in various alien guises, some humanoid, some not, all brimming with power. They seized the diminished gods and lifted them up struggling into the air.

"The unbridled Age of Blood is here at last!! Take them! Take them and chain them to your rock! The death of billions awaits!"

The Golden People were impatient. They wanted the Gods. They wanted them all. They turned to the open green slit where the City of Many Forms waited, ready to haul their prizes away.

The green doorways fizzled and went out. They milled about, confused.

"Sec here, Bath. Yep, yep, I did that," Carahil said, growing in size. The Golden People tried to open their doorways back up, but they wouldn't form. "Unfortunately, nobody's leaving until the movie's over," Carahil said.

"Then I'll have my servants slay the gods where they stand and their dying shall feed the Temple," the Horned God replied.

"Not so fast, baby doll, you're forgetting one small thing. I've got the *New Faith* here, and I can blow your Temple to tiny bits. The Younger Folk and their works are a constant. They are undiminished, be they great or small. The Younger Folk built this temple for you, and the Younger Folk can destroy it too! I can light off the *New Faith's* engines in a cobalt flare, and this Temple will cease to exist; it'll be nothing more than a smoking crater in the ground and your 'Age of Blood' will be short-lived and rather underwhelming to say the least. Your Temple will be gone, your Golden servants will be marooned in the distant future, and you will be a wanted fugitive, a shambling wreck not worth being afraid of."

The Horned God raised his hand. "Then I'll see it gone."

"Try it and I'll press the button, and that's it. We go!"

The Horned God's eye narrowed as he faced Carahil. "So, we have a standoff. I have the gods and your servants, and you have your little spaceship and your hand at my Temple's throat. Shall we face each other forever, while all around us withers and passes into memory. These people mean nothing to me."

29—A Contest of Heroes

"But, they mean everything to me," Carahil said. "I say, let's settle this the old way, a Contest of Heroes, winner take all."

Despite himself, the Horned God seemed intrigued. "I see. You wish to have a contest of blood. You pick your hero, and I pick mine, and we watch them fight like animals? Hmmmm ... What do I win? What is there to be gained?"

"Why, you can be what you've always wanted to be: the Devil. Kana will be your private Hell, and this time, sanctioned by the gods. You can kill and slay all you want and not worry about being caught and sent to the Windage. We'll even keep you stocked with fresh victims. You will be the master of it all and feared throughout the cosmos."

"I can have those things regardless. You offer nothing. Not good enough."

"Not good enough? Really? You might be wondering how I was able to stick a brick into your Temple and make part of it my own? You might be wondering how I managed to change the deep past in anticipation of this confrontation? How'd I do it, huh? Must be some powerful time-spanning magic or tech that I have access to in order for me to be able to do that, right? Right?"

The Horned God put his clawed hand to his chin. He mumbled and debated to himself. "Can it be? Can this little fool actually be speaking the truth? Can he? Can he? It must be. He must have something otherwise he'd be in chains with the others."

The remaining Golden People turned to the Horned God, demanding he act. "And, you'll let my servants have you and the gods if I win?" he asked

"Not the rest," Carahil replied, "but they can have me. I'll give myself to them."

The Horned God considered that. "And, if you win?"

"Oh, that's easy. If I win you shall willingly shuffle off to the Windage of Kind and begin your prison sentence. Perhaps a few ages of cooling your heels at the bottom of the Universe shall teach you some manners. You shall also abandon this place and never set foot in it again, and perhaps the stain of all that's been done here will be silenced at last. This place, as an anchorage in time, will die."

The Horned God was convinced and eager to participate. "Very well, Carahil, we shall have your Contest of Heroes. Your flesh and your time-tech against the soundness of my temple, it's agreed.

"Just remember," Carahil said, "in all of this I tried to save you too."

The Horned God scoffed. "How sweet. As per the old rules, we each get to make one stipulation. My warrior must be killed, and his blood must flow; that is my stipulation."

Carahil responded. "My stipulation is my warrior shall be removed from the battle on first blood. I'll sequester them deep inside the *New Faith* where they'll be safe and then I'll return them to his or her home as quickly as possible later."

The Horned God scoffed. "What a little child you are. You've all but ensured my victory. Very well, in saving this mortal lot, you have preselected them to participate."

Sarah was shocked. "Us? We're going to fight?"

Carahil winked at them. "'Fraid so. You'll do just fine."

Sarah pulled off her SAPP and formed into a sword.

The Horned God was jubilant. "And, facing your little children and worthless serf is my champion ..."

A flash blossomed in the Temple. A ten foot tall golden man, rippling with muscles and carrying a huge fork, appeared."

Carahil eyed the golden man. "Hey—is that Chorpa the Lersh?"

"He is," the Horned God said in an eager voice. "The butcher and befouler of worlds. A thousand shapes he wears and a million beings he's killed."

Sarah looked up at him. "We're fighting this guy?" Phillip moved to her side and formed his SAPP as well. Ki drew her SK.

Chorpa the Lersh raised his fork and readied to skewer Sarah with it.

"Wait!" Mabsornath, the cat, cried, restrained by several Kestrals. "Per the old rules, each god wishing to participate in the Contest of Heroes may also offer a champion, and I, Mabsornath, throw my lot in with Carahil."

"Then you shall go to The Rock with him when he loses."

"So be it. I select as my champion the crew of the *New Faith*, starting with her captain, Davage, Lord of Blanchefort."

Davage raised his CARG and got in front of Sarah, standing off with Chorpa the Lersh. She thankfully backed away and drew her Poltava, covering him from the rear.

Hatches opened on the *New Faith,* and people came out in bunches. There was Syg, Ennez, Bethrael of Moane, Lady Tellerran and a squadron of Marines. They moved into position near Davage.

"A sentimental if ineffectual selection," the Horned God said. He turned to the masses of captive gods and picked out a goose. "You, Serasee, you will fall in with me, won't you?" he said, squeezing her neck.

The goose, clutched roughly by the Kestrals, nodded. The Horned God whispered a few words, and the goose spoke. "I, Serasee, throw my lot in with the Horned God Bathloxi, and select as my Champion the Red Mountain Goats of Cathada, fierce and terrible!"

Flash! A group of a thousand armored men holding glowing spears appeared in the Temple proper.

Carahil was hopping mad. "Oh, okay—I get a couple hundred on my side, and you reciprocate with a thousand!"

The otter Mincoil responded. "I'm with you, Carahil! Take my selection!"

"Ok, let's add a Xaphan presence to spice things up," Carahil said. "May I introduce Lady Thomasina the 19th of Waam and her lovely contingent of Singing Ten."

Flash! Thomasina and a hundred ladies, all in green leather armor, appeared in the Temple holding clubs. Thomasina, looked around confused, saw Phillip, and her jaw dropped open. "Phillip ..." she said. He winced.

The Horned God noted the newcomers and then pointed at a bound turtle. "You, Karafan, you're with me, correct? You wish to survive this, yes?"

The turtle trembled. "Yes, yes ..."

"Tremble," the Horned God cried, "for I have the Nergott Yogg and his

Chortlymph." A bewildered looking golden man in a toga holding a black drum appeared. The Horned God snorted. "Your souls are lost ..."

Carahil appeared a bit put off. "Is that the same Nergott Yogg who can create Wvulgroms?"

"It is," the Horned God said, with an obvious hint of smugness.

"Yeah, well so what?" Carahil replied. He turned to Davage and Syg and said under his breath "*You guys are going to want to take out Nergott Yogg as soon as possible, ok? I should have thought of him.*"

Maiax, the elephant, trumpeted. "I'm with you, Carahil!"

"Thank you, sir! Then, may I introduce the Duke of Oyln and the incomparable Duchess Torrijayne of Oyln." The Duke and Duchess appeared on the League side—Torrijayne massively pregnant. Sygillis, seeing her enemy arrive, rolled her eyes.

On and on went the gods picking sides: the terrified ones going to the Horned God, and the more courageous ones standing with Carahil.

And the Temple, already crowded with the towering presence of the *New Faith*, filled with odd characters.

Flash! "I have Touables the Mope ... the greatest swordsman ever known in Kestral," the Horned God proudly said. A giant golden man wearing what looked like a soiled diaper and holding a filthy sword appeared.

"Will you quit bringing in guys?" Carahil yelled. "Ok, I have Princess Vroc of Xandarr ... a better swordsman." Vroc appeared, veiled and ringed.

The Horned God countered. "The Agate Thendicus and his Maul Forra." A strange golden skinned man and woman sitting at a loom appeared.

Flash! "Lord Mapes of Grenville and his Lady Suzaraine," Carahil countered. "I can do this all day!"

"Kesjanni and her 10,000 Slugs of 10,000 Slug Mountain." A bunch of slimy naked women appeared all over the hull of the *New Faith.*

"The 14th Marines from 01 Olgilvy, otherwise known as 'The Screaming Bitches'," Carahil said as 25 red-coated Marines appeared.

The Horned God rolled his eyes. Flash! "The Sniffers of Death." Twenty black suited men carrying what looked like rubber hoses appeared.

Carahil responded. "King Balor of Xandarr and his queen Zoladerra and the lovely Xandarr 44." Forty five people from Xandarr appeared, veiled and ringed.

The Horned God responded. "I have the Unmentionable ..."

Something appeared—there was a collective gasp in the Temple.

The temple was nearing to capacity with heroes—some League, some Xaphan, and some Kestral; they stood there looking at each other, none quite knowing what was going on.

Carahil laughed. "What a pack of freaks you've dug up! This is going to be brutal!"

Chorpa the Lersh raised his fork and tried to skewer Captain Davage with it.

Sygillis loosed a Silver tech shield and blocked the fork, turning it aside.

And it began in a howl, movement everywhere, screams rang out, weapons clashed as the Horned God, Carahil and the other gods watched.

The Nergott Yogg, apparently a deadly Kestral fighter, feared by all, picked up his drum and began running, screaming for an exit. An enraged Priestess of Kestral chased after him.

Silver tech blasts mixed together with odd beams of red cascading light, whistling clubs, fired bullets, viscous spit and thrown spears—the League, Xaphan, and Kestral heroes engaged in a noisy tangle.

The Unmentionable began attacking any nearby. It made a huge dent in the mass of Red Mountain Goats and passed into the struggling group of 10,000 Slugs, eating them like slimy candy at a handful. The Horned God, realizing his mistake, brought it down with lightning, to the collective relief of all present.

The remaining Red Mountain Goats waded in and were met by Thomasina and her singing, club-wielding ladies of Waam. The Marines, with SKs blasting, engaged the slimy women of Slug Mountain. They dove for cover.

The Xandarr 44 fought well and as a unit. Very quickly they thinned the 10,000 Slugs out to a few hundred with a concerted Silver tech attack. A vile red bomb hurled by one of the Kestral priestesses serving the Horned God then did the same thing to them, thinning them down to just a few.

It was a strange battle to be sure. Captain Davage, wielding his coppery CARG, was back to back with Ki and Princess Vroc of Xandarr and her invisible BEREN. Countess Sygillis was standing side by side with her enemy—the pregnant Duchess Torrijayne of Oyln. Phillip and Sarah were locked up with Thendicus and Maul Forra, who was sitting at some sort of loom, creating deadly warriors made from spun linen, whom Beth and Ennez engaged with their jet staves and Silver tech.

Nergott Yogg, who apparently wanted nothing to do with this battle, was chased down by the Priestess. They appeared to argue in their odd, chortling language for a moment, and then he set his drum down and began playing it. A type of gate opened in front of him, and a shadowy figure stepped through.

With a massive crack, the figure's head was lopped off by the FENNISTER whip of the Duke of Oyln. The headless figure fell. The FENNISTER came again, this time for Nergott Yogg's head. Lifting his toga, he dove for cover. The Priestess saw the Duke and readied to attack him, when she took an NTH shot in the chest from the dashing Paymaster Stenstrom, who was standing far away on top of the *New Faith's* hull. He hit her square in the gut, and she collapsed into goo. Nergott Yogg, seeing all of this happening around him, lost his composure again, grabbed his drum, and took full flight.

Kestrals changed shape and flapped up into the heights, focusing on the *New Faith*, hoping to destroy it. Paymaster Stenstrom attended to them one at a time, his mystical NTH's able to kill anything with one shot no matter how huge, old and powerful. Amber rain fell.

Elsewhere, bounding and sticking to the walls, the remaining 10,000 Slugs came down on Ennez to 'hug' him with caustic, blistered arms. He skillfully evaded them, again letting fly with his Jet Staff with perfect accuracy. The Marines set up a quick line and put a wall of SK fire down on the Slugs as Ennez bounded away, only to be re-engaged with a group of strange Linen warriors created by Maul Flora's loom.

Her loom was a marvel. She stopped with the linen warriors and created what could only be described as a massive thundercloud made of spun linen that rose up into the heights of the temple. A bolt of spun lightning came down—Syg and Torri having to dive aside.

In response, two blobs of Silver tech came up, one formed into the shape of the *Seeker*, the other into a huge silver serpent. The *Seeker* opened up with its tiny guns. Smoking pieces of cloth came raining down as the silver serpent tore into it with its fangs. The cloud responded with gouts of linen lightning.

In the central temple area, Slugs went down all around Davage and Princess Vroc, his CARG and her BEREN an impenetrable wall. The Slugs fell in clumps.

Phillip and Sarah, fighting together, were doing well against Thendicus, who fought with some sort of stick, when something nudged Phillip from behind.

He turned, and there was Thomasina. Before he could react, she bopped him in the noggin, and he fell, dropping his SAPP.

"Thomasina!" Carahil cried.

"That counts. He is out of the fight, per your stipulation," the Horned God said, and Phillip vanished.

Sarah, still struggling with Thendicus, was outraged. "Are you out of your mind?"

Thomasina looked surprised that Phillip had vanished, and then finished off Thendicus. She then threw herself into Maul Forra.

The *Seeker* dove away, and the serpent 'ate' what was left of the linen thundercloud.

A great Kestral fist came down and pulled the Silver tech serpent apart. Moments later, an NTH shot from the distant Paymaster Stenstrom killed the Kestral monster. From his elevated position atop the *New Faith*, he was picking them off left and right. The Kestrals had had enough of him and his killer NTH pistols. They attacked in force, with far too many to be shot. They were met atop the *New Faith* by Marines of the 12th division, various crew members, and the charging Monamas from the hold.

Elsewhere, between Davage and Princess Vroc, and the remaining Marines, the horrid Slugs of 10,000 Slug Mountain were decimated down to a dozen or so. Touables the Mope, came slashing in with his filthy sword and got the Princess in her bad arm.

She vanished.

Ki tried to shoot him, and Touables got her too. She also disappeared. Davage and the Mope then engaged in a heated, clashing contest, CARG against sword.

Ennez, using his gerts, was running the wall ahead of a mass of chasing, sticking Slugs. Like a shooting gallery, Silver tech blasts from Countess Sygillis, Duchess Torrijayne and the tiny *Seeker* familiar pocked the Slugs and thinned them out to a single pursuer that Ennez handled with ease. He then dove into a group of unsuspecting Mountain Goats and began clearing them out with his Jet Staff.

Another group of Red Mountain Goats, all warriors, came slashing in with their glowing spears, only to be swept away by the dual Silver tech power of Sygillis and Duchess Torrijayne.

Kesjanni and Suzaraine of Grenville got each other, Suzaraine vanished, and Kesjanni fell.

The Singing Ten got locked up with the Sniffers of Death. Clubs and whistling rubber hoses flew as they battled.

Lady Tellerran of Monama tried to link up with Ennez and fight at his side, but she was cut off by a passing group of Mountain Goats. One of them pulled her into the shadows by her hair where he might have thought to claim her as a prize. Recovering, she promptly laced him with her claws. She lingered there in the dark. Her confidence quickly growing, she picked off stragglers who blundered by, taking a Sniffer of Death, a Kestral Priestess and four Red Mountain Goats. She also took out Ennez, who happened by in pursuit of a Mountain Goat. "I'm sorry, Ennez, I'm sorry!" she cried in Conox as he vanished, dropping his jet staff.

Lord Mapes of Grenville was involved with Chorpa the Lersh. The Lersh managed to get the Grenville 40 pistol out of his hand, only to be stabbed in the neck by his lightning quick VUNKULA. Mapes also took care of a few lingering Red Mountain Goats, before being dispatched by a Sniffer of Death.

The periphery of the battle turned into a massive free-for-all, with fighters on both sides dropping at a frantic pace. Nergott Yogg got taken out by an angry Priestess, who was tired of his non-participation in the fight. She then got removed from the battle by sniper fire from Paymaster Stenstrom and his NTH pistol, who then got erased by a skulking Red Mountain Goat who, dancing in victory, got dealt with by #22 of the Xandarr 44, who was in turn vanished by a Sniffer of Death, who then got removed by Lady Tellerran, still red-faced for accidentally getting rid of Ennez.

The featured fight in the center of the Temple was Davage and Touables the Mope. Davage, in an epic sword fight with the Mope, took out a Mountain Goats who came stabbing in. Likewise, the Mope, while fighting Davage, took out a whole bunch of charging Marines and Sarah, who tried to get him from behind.

People were falling and disappearing all around.

Syg and Torri were doing a huge amount of damage. They finished off the Red Mountain Goats, took out one of the Kestral monsters and dispatched the remaining Sniffers of Death, who were fleeing from the Singing Ten and Thomasina.

King Balor got removed by a sizzling red light from a Kestral Priestess, who also decimated the largely untouched group of Singing Ten with more red light. Queen Zoladerra engaged her with Silver tech in a back and forth duel.

Touables and Davage swirled into the remaining Singing Ten, who got removed wholesale by Touables' big, dirty sword. The Mope, with his soiled diaper, was proving to be an awesome fighter.

#14 of the Xandarr 44 came in, and the Mope handled her. Seeing a momentary opening, Davage got him in the arm. The Mope tried to counter attack and took an SK blast from a lingering Marine. He fell to one knee and was wide open, but Davage hesitated.

"The Mope is done!" Carahil cried. "He fought well, and I'm taking him out of the fight!" He disappeared with a bellow. "That hurts, Bath—you're just about out of guys here!"

A Priestess tried to get Davage with a cone of red light, but he dove aside. Syg responded with a blast of Silver tech, and the two got into a protracted duel.

Overhead, the strong emotions and chaos of the battle created yet another cloud of energy that the Temple lapped up. Lightning again threatened to rain down.

Zoladerra finished up her Priestess with a crushing TK and began working on the remaining Kestrals along with Davage, who slashed in with his victorious CARG.

The Priestesses were concentrating on the remaining Marine forces standing atop the *New Faith*, which was pouring fire down on them.

The Priestesses and remaining Kestral monsters were pounced on. A new Silver tech serpent from Duchess Torrijayne serpent ate one of them whole, and Davage's CARG took care of the rest.

Aside from a few skulking Red Mountain Goats, the Kestral heroes were gone, removed from the scene.

"That's it!" Carahil exclaimed. "You're done!"

The gods cheered.

The Horned God laughed. "Not quite," he said. "My primary champion is still afoot and yet to be defeated, as is yours, Carahil. This battle comes down to one champion against another, and has yet to be decided."

✶ ✶ ✶ ✶ ✶

Kay removed the head of the Kestral creature that had come for him with his CARG while Lon buried his CEROS in another. Ki, Sarah and Phillip were pulled through the green doorways by reaching golden hands and vanished.

Joy lay in the dust, unmoving and Sam tottered about in a daze. Kay led her to a fallen wall and sat her down.

Lon attended to Joy. "Her arm is horribly mangled. She's lost a great deal of blood.

"Can you help her?"

Lon wrapped her arm up with material from his coat. "This is the best I can do," he said. "This field dressing should hold, but I'm sure she's pretty badly blood poisoned. I don't have a Troutman, but I'm certain of it, look at her color. She needs a Hospitaler and soon."

Kay looked over his work. "I feel my Gifts returning. Where's the nearest town from here?"

Lon sighed. "I think there's the ruins of the House of Zary to the north, and then there's the old chasm of Magravine due west. We're in the least inhabited part of Kana there is."

Sam was huddled up against fallen stone, still wearing Kay's coat draped over her, still hugging herself about the chest. Kay tried to comfort her, but she was insensate and stilt-like. Unresponsive.

"Sam!"

No response.

A single Parafly landed on her shoulder and buzzed. He seemed to be alone, all the rest in the area were in the Temple far below.

"They both need medical attention at once."

Seeing the Parafly made Kay feel a bit better—he considered them good luck.

"What about Valenhelm to the north?" Lon asked. "The Sisters there could help them. You could Waft us all there. It's a good distance, but I think you could do it."

"No, it's too cold for Sam at Valenhelm. She doesn't have her medallion, and she'd die along the way. I think we should head south back to my aunt's castle. There, her Hospitaler can perform some initial triage on them, and then we could take her coach to Minz or Feren, anyplace with a sizable Hospitaler sanctum."

"Castle Vincent is about three hundred miles, can you manage?"

"We don't have a choice. I'll have to manage."

"What about the *Goshawk?*"

"What about it? Can you fly the *Goshawk*? I can't."

"No," Lon said. "I can't."

"So then, we Waft."

They gathered Sam and Joy up and moved away from the manor ruins.

"I hope everybody's all right," Lon said. "Where were they taken do you think?"

"Probably back to the Temple. Carahil will protect them. The Paraflies are down there too."

Kay readied himself. Far away, he could see the *Goshawk* and the well of Carhl Wae, the mouth of the Temple. Lon struggled with Joy.

Behind them, several green slits formed amid the manor ruins. Lon saw them. "Kay, look!"

The green slits hovered there like smoke. Golden People stepped out, Kestrals in advanced, monstrous forms.

"Gods Kay, they're after us!" Lon shouted, drawing his CEROS.

The Kestrals came out all around them. One was a giant, rock-like man, another was a crawling octopus-like creature with a thousand reaching tentacles.

Kay unsaddled his CARG and buried it in the giant man's chest. Unfazed, he raised his fist to crush Kay flat. Kay blasted him with Silver tech from his CARG hollowing him out, scattering rock-like bits over a wide area. The giant fell apart in amber.

Golden tentacles came up all around them. Lon loosed his CEROS, bisecting several at once. The monster issued a roar from its bag-like head and lurched forward.

Kay slashed it, drawing amber blood. "Lon, where's your gun?" he demanded.

"Sarah had it!" he responded, cutting away several more tentacles.

Kay plunged his CARG horn-first into its bag and tried to fire off another Silver tech burst, but nothing happened; his weapon needed to recharge.

More tentacles came in, and Kay and Lon were engulfed. A terrible, mouth emerged from under the bag, opening, ready to devour the both of them.

The thing shuddered.

The top of the monster's head was sheared off, cut clean as if by a laser. Its bisected head toppled to the dirt, and then the monster fell apart in goo.

Joy, hand raised, had gotten the monster with micro-line Shadow tech, cutting clean through its flesh. She then went limp, her hand falling.

Lon shuttled to her side. "Well done, Joy, you are a master with your ..."

He was cut off in mid-sentence. He dropped his CEROS.

"Lon?" Kay asked, standing.

Blood came out of his mouth, first a few drops, but then quite a bit came out. His eyes went glassy.

"Lon, what is it?" Kay asked, seeing him in distress. "Lon!"

Lon fell. Kay went to his side. What had happened? What was wrong?

There was a ragged, bloody hole in his back.

Kay tried to revive Lon, to preserve any spark of life left in him.

Lord Lon of Probert was dead. His smiling, round face now locked in death.

Sam stood like a mannequin nearby, her face expressionless. Her hand was bloody.

"Sam?"

Buzzing. The Parafly was crawling about her neck and face. It was stinging her, over and over, raising ugly purple welts.

Moving in a machine-like manner, Sam reached up and seized the Parafly; it stung her hand as she did so. She squeezed, and eventually it popped like a balloon.

"Sam ..."

His coat that had been draped over her shoulders fell aside. Her pale face was blank, eyes gone and blackened and covered with welts from the Parafly.

She exhaled and moaned. A small hole opened up between her eyes. It leaked clear fluid that dripped down her face. Gristle crunched as a second pair of mal-formed, crab-like hands came up from around her waist, bumpy with ridges, armed with slick, iron-hard claws. She reached out to touch Kay's face with her hideous extra pair of hands.

Horror moved through Kay.

The Parafly had been attacking her, if more had been about, they'd be attacking her too.

Lon ... dead! Sam had killed him.

Sam was a Berserkacide. The Horned God had done it.

Death of soul, death of personality.

Sam is a Berserkacide.

Sam is a Berserkacide?

Sam is a Berserkacide!!

The hole between her eyes got larger, more fluids dripped from it. She wobbled a bit, sniffing the air. Her powerful Monama nose locked-on to him. Smelling him seemed to bring her out of her funk a bit. She gnashed her teeth.

Things spun around Kay. Berserkacide! The permanency of it, the hopelessness. The loving woman Sam had been was dead, gone, replaced by the raging Berserkacide ... forever.

She lifted her bloody hand and smelled it. She licked her fingers and gave a snarl-like giggle.

She raised two of her hands and brought them down, claws first. Kay moved aside, and she buried her hands into the ground. She sniffed the air and locked on again. She sprang like a panther.

Kay Wafted away, near to where Joy was passed out.

Crouching, Sam listened; she sniffed. The hole on her head opened and closed, providing her with unknown information.

She dashed toward him, moving at incredible speed. Kay picked up Joy and Wafted again, appearing near the ruins.

Sam stood there, sniffing the air, thin and pale. She howled.

"*Kay* ..." he heard her say in a fury-clotted, unfamiliar Berserkacide voice. "KAY!" she screamed.

As he watched, Sam located Lon's fallen body, straddled him and began desecrating his flesh, ripping it apart.

Kay had promised Lon's mother that he would keep him safe. He saw the future. Lon in his coffin, his heartbroken mother and father weeping over his open grave—the many who came to say goodbye, and there were many. Everybody loved Lon.

Even Sam, his killer.

You promised, Lord Blanchefort, that you would protect him! You promised!!

She hacked his head off and threw it in some random direction. "KAAAAAY!" she bellowed, and then tore toward him, bounding across the ground

on all fours, holding her new hands over her head. She was moving like a jaguar, covering the distance fast.

This couldn't be happening. There had to be some way out of this.

Kay thrust his Sight into the future and looked at the possibilities. He saw lots of things. In some instances, Sam tore him apart. In others, he killed her. In a few morbid cases, he saw them killing each other, his CARG in her chest, her claws mortally rending his flesh. In any event, there was no happy ending—no good way out of this. The Horned God had flipped some primordial switch within her, and there was no going back. Sam would be a snarling beast for the rest of her life, however long that lasted.

The woman who loved him was dead. Lon was dead.

And either he was going to die, or she was, or both of them.

There was nothing but darkness ahead.

Kay Wafted to the top of the ruined manor and hid Joy's body away in a place that would be difficult for Sam to get to.

Moments later Sam arrived in the manor grounds, tensed like a wolf. She tested the air with her nose, breathing in deeply. Blood trickled out of her mouth and down her chin. She spat out small white objects, some panging off of the fallen masonry, others hanging from bloody strings. Kay puzzled for a moment.

Teeth! Those were her teeth, all pushed out in favor of a new set of multi-layered, mazelike choppers that looked like a primordial thornbush of crimson fangs all coated in a slick layer of blood.

"*Arin-Dan* …" she said in a sultry, growl voice. "Why are you hiding? All I want to do is put my arms around you and WRING YOUR NECK!! No, no … I think I'd rather tear your throat out. That way I can watch the life beat out of you and bathe in your warm blood. You once told me you'd do anything for me. Then let me watch you die … that's what I want."

Her icy words skewered his soul. "THAT'S WHAT I WANT, KAY ... TO KILL YOU!!"

She bumped into a fallen piece of masonry, and she shattered it with a swipe. "I can't see you, Kay," she growled, the hole in her head pulsing open and closed. "But I can sense your living aura. I can smell you too. I know you're here, and I'm going to get you, sooner or later; we both know that. I've many times the endurance you have, I'm faster, and I'm much stronger than you are. Let's be reasonable." Her voice was a caustic sneer.

She smiled, fangs jutting out of her mouth. *"Let's be reasonable ... darling …"*

She stopped and raised her head. She caught wind of something. "That's fine perfume you're wearing!" She launched herself into the air like a jumping spider, zeroing in on Joy's perfume.

Kay wound up and met her with his CARG, shattering her collarbone, sending her back down. She flailed out as she fell and knocked Kay loose from his perch. He Wafted down several yards from where Sam had fallen. He moved into the ruins.

"Sam, this can't have happened to you … I was going to ask you to marry me. The Trials are done!"

There was a pause. Then: "Ha! How sweet! I am what the two-armed freaks once were—what they should be today. Blood and life is ours to take, and our Horned God to worship. I am the condensation of all that is dark in their souls, all their hate—all their anger. I have been waiting for years to kill you, to taste your blood. I only hoped I'd get the chance."

Sam caught wind of his scent and abruptly tore off through the ruins after him, oblivious to her wounds, and in a few glistening bounds, she was on him. She sent a clawed hand in a whistling arc to his throat. He ducked at the last second. With a crash of crushed stone, she took a huge chunk out of the column behind him. Kay put a heavy up-stroke into her ribs, which she partially blocked with one of her arms. Her arm broke with the weight of the hit, and she squealed in pain. He could have made the stroke a cutting blow and killed her—but he couldn't do it.

Her voice in the dark. Sharing his desserts with her. Shopping with her in the village. Wrestling with her in the reading room. Making love to her in the pool.

Sam!!

In agony she bounded away.

Kay's thoughts raced. There had to be a way out of this—there had to.

Think!

Somewhere in the confusion of ruins, he heard her laugh. "*Did you like what I did to your friend, Arin-Dan, dear, sweet Arin-Dan? Have no fear, I did nothing to him that I'm not going to do to you too, heheehehehehehe!*"

She lisped as she spoke, her icy words crawling out through a thicket of bloody fangs. As she spoke, her voice quickly changed—becoming a crazed, malicious baritone; Sam's voice gone, replaced in total by the Berserkacide's.

Lady Sammidoran of Monama was truly gone. In her place, a murderous demon.

A Berserkacide.

"Sam!" he wheezed.

The Berserkacide didn't answer. She crouched by her column.

"Sam, don't you remember ... you had visions of me, even before I was born. Remember talking to me in the chapel? Remember how we used to argue over the posts. You made me that little gazelle—the toy I loved so much."

She made an anguish-filled noise. There was a silence. Then: "Yes, yes ... I remember. Oh, Kay, darling, it's me, I'm back. Come to me, my *Arin-Dan*. Come to me!"

Kay Sighted. He saw himself going to her with open arms. He saw the Berserkacide tear him apart with relish.

He felt his heart break. "Sam, please ..."

"It had to end this way, Elder fool. You've deluded yourself. I am now as we once were, brutal and lusting in blood—we serve our master, and it's not the damn Golden People. It's the Horned God. We are his angels of death, and he brings us the damned to torment. I could never really love you. We do not feel love. Love is for the weak! I might have thought that I loved you, but I really didn't. That foolish little girl you loved—she was my first victim! That stupid boy just now was my second, and you shall be my third! Praise be to the Horned God!"

And Kay no longer cared. He didn't care about the League or his parents or his cousins, or anything else. He wanted to die.

He grimaced in sadness and stepped out from behind his column. "Sam!" he yelled. "Come and kill me if you wish. I won't fight back." He let the horn of his CARG drop to the dusty ground.

"I don't trust you, *Arin-Dan*," her Berserkacide voice filtered back. "Will you lift your CARG and try to run me through?"

He threw his CARG aside, and it clattered into the dust. "No, Sam, I'm done fighting you."

The Berserkacide shrieked in victory and charged. She loped along, partially running on all fours. Her extra pair of arms were hoisted over her head, claws ready to bite into Kay's flesh. Her broken arm flailed lifelessly, her broken collarbone grinded. The hole puckered in excitement.

He stood there in the lonely sunshine, waiting for it to end.

He heard a voice in his head. *Coward! You're a coward!*

Visions came to him. His saw his sisters, Lady Kilos and Hathaline, standing there, monstrous. *You said you wouldn't let this happen to us! You said you would protect us!*

There was Maser—a monster in his golden armor. *I didn't want this. They made me. You're my brother!*

There was Clatera and Mitzilaran of Cardinal, friends turned to Berserkacides. *See, told you you'd take the easy way out,"* Clatera said.

There was Lon, holding his CEROS. He was bloody. *I've looked up to you since I was a kid—I wanted to be you. Now look, I just lost my life, and for what, so that you could throw yours away?*

And there was Sam, stunning in her black gown, black eyes full of love. *That beast is not me! Don't let it end like this, my Arin-Dan!*

Kay reached into his coat and pulled his Poltava.

POW!

A raging hole blossomed in Sam's chest, and she was knocked aside with the force of the blow.

She snarled and stood. She came again.

POW!

Sam crumpled up in the grip of death and was still.

Kay stood there, numb.

She struggled a bit. Sam's face, as beautiful as ever, looked up at Kay with longing for a moment. "Kay … ?" she said quietly. "Kay, where are you?"

Kay leaned forward. Her hole opened in a fluid-filled shout. She raised her savage hands and, with a final snarl, died with them around his throat.

Silence.

He held her to him.

The sorrowful Ruin of Bodice filled with the sounds of Kay, wailing in agony.

✶ ✶ ✶ ✶ ✶

"Victory is ours!" Carahil said. "You watched. You picked the cruelest combat pairing possible—and I'll not forgive you for it!"

The Horned God was silent for a moment. "So? What are you going to do about it? You are a weakling, and this place is mine. I am the Devil here, and I make the rules, and I shall break them as I wish! The outcome of this contest changes nothing!"

Carahil frowned and sighed. He looked down at Captain Davage. "Lord Blanchefort, your Engineer has been trying to relay you a message during the battle. He says the ship's Thermoplant has been repaired and restarted. He awaits your orders."

Captain Davage turned to the Horned God and shouted. "Then, the order is to open fire and maintain until this place is in ruins!"

The *New Faith* opened its port banks and uncoiled a long Sar-Beam shot into the distant walls of the Temple. The place shook, and stone began to fall.

"WHAT ARE YOU DOING?" the Horned God cried.

"Something I should have done to start with. I'd hoped you were worth redeeming."

The Horned God unleashed lightning, but the *New Faith* absorbed it. Old statues and pagan idols fell and were obliterated. The power of the Temple of the

Exploding Head began to fail.

The Kestrals, seeing the tunnel through time begin to go out, acted. The ones Carahil transformed into rabbits and squirrels presented themselves to him, the apparent victor, all smiles, ready to become his servants. They smiled and danced, their bushy tails flicking, bright eyes hopeful. They presented him with chocolate held aloft in their paws: the hollow heads of Sarah, Kay, Phillip and Ki.

Take it, partake of it.

"Get away from me," Carahil said.

They then turned to seize the gods and be off with them. They found effigies of spun sugar in their place, colorful in the shapes of animals. They would take no gods to their rock.

They would not be denied. They fell upon the Horned God, his power diminished as the Temple was diminished under the weight of the *New Faith's* guns.

"What are you doing?" he snarled.

They attacked, pummeling him, dousing him in red light. He cast them aside, but there were too many and he was weakening. He shrank and fell into their midst, punching and kicking, his flesh withering.

More Sar beams. The Temple was near its end.

The Golden People opened a doorway at last: the dusty pyramids and empty chairs of the City of Many Forms awaited.

They carried the Horned God through to their horrid city.

The Horned God roared in outrage, and then he was gone. The green slit closed behind him.

Despite himself, Carahil wept as the temple stones continued to come down.

A fallen god was such a tragedy.

30—In Victory ...

Lord Davage was worried about Kay. So was everybody. He had spoken little since Sam died.

The *New Faith* had been returned to high orbit in a blue flash. Many people who had participated in the battle had been wounded, but, thankfully, only a relative few had been killed: several Marines, buried with honor, poor Lord Lon … and Sam. The rest had been returned to their homes.

The Sisters fell upon the site of the Temple under Hala and, in a cloud of burnt debris, dug it up and utterly destroyed what was left of it, down to the last stone. In its death throes, a fork of lightning shot up into the sky, damaging several Fleet ships in orbit. The Kestral's temporal anchorage on Kana, and all that went with it, was no more. The Sisters' anger and mistrust of the Monamas was replaced with a paranoia of the Kestrals; they saw signs of them everywhere. They went on a heated quest to locate more Kestral temples across the League, if any were to be found.

The *Shuw-shun* coming for the House of Monama was forgotten.

The Hidden Wars were finally won and Atrajak of Want's name was restored to history.

* * * * *

They returned to Castle Astralon in the *Goshawk* and waded into the warm waters of the lake. They took the chest full of colored stones and scattered them into the slow surf.

The Astralons soon rose up and waded to the shore, dazed and without memory of what had happened. Free of their Head Swarm, they returned to their castle and embraced Kay as one of their own, said he'd passed Sam's Trials and was, therefore, part of their family. They proclaimed he and Sarah and Phillip were always welcome there. But, Kay never visited them. It hurt too much.

They buried Sam's body on Dead Hill in a large stone vault topped with a sarcophagus lid carved in Sam's image, holding an image of Kay's CARG to her breast. Every day, Kay visited her with a portable terminal. Sitting by her vault, looking at her prone carving, he read her the posts as he had done years before, and then he said no more, the ghosts of the Kestrals laughing at him.

* * * * *

Kay fell into a bit of madness. Day after day he spent locked in his room, with his Sight roaming in the past.

He was after Sam. He was going to locate her and pull her into the present.

And he saw her there, happy and alive. He tried to pull her forward and, when she became aware of him, she turned and ran. He called out to her, but she wouldn't listen.

He saw her at the Vith ruin, frothing in rage, scratching her confession on

the pillar.

And he reached out for her.

She simply ran, as only she could. He became angry and tried picking her up, kicking and screaming. She scratched him once, and he let go in surprise.

Sam, in the past, appeared to want nothing to do with him.

One time he managed to pull her struggling form into the present, though she screamed and spat. She was there with him for a minute or two as he tried to calm her. But he couldn't maintain it—he couldn't fix his gaze on her for long—he had to stare at her and not blink.

He couldn't maintain it for long, how could he? And she fell back into time.

Madness.

31—The Love of the Xaphan

Kay lifted up the struggling form and threw it down to the ground, hard. He then jumped on top of it, and they rolled around, getting grass stains all over their clothes.

The form got on top of Kay and held him down. Kay arched his back and roughly threw the form off, where he then stood and tackled it.

Lt. Kilos sat nearby, watching. "I'd help you out, kid, but I'm pregnant. No roughhousing for awhile."

Phillip sat next to her. "And, Lt., no drinking either."

"Yeah, yeah. You want punched, don't you?"

Kay and Sarah concluded their wrestling match and stood up, both of them covered in leaves and dirt. They embraced. Sarah just loved to fight, their adventures as of late seemed only to have whetted her appetite for it.

They approached the wall, and Phillip handed them both drinks from the cooler.

"So, here's what happened," Sarah said taking a drink. "The Temple filled up with all sorts of nasty Kestral warriors, with Carahil at one end on the hall and the creepy Horned God at the other. Then we squared off and started going at it. You and me, Phillip, were taking on that old guy and his weird wife with the loom."

Ki shook her head. "Creation, Sarah, you love talking about this."

Phillip looked down at his hands. "Well, I believe that's when I got taken out by that wretched green-haired strumpet from Waam. She got me in the head with her stupid club, and when I woke up, I was lying here, in the Grove."

"You missed a great fight, Phillip. For one thing, your mom, Kay, and the Duchess of Oyln were fighting side by side, and they were taking people out left and right. And your dad, he was standing there with Princess Vroc, and the two of them pretty much cleared out all of those slimy women. And then that dude popped up, the big guy with the diaper. He took out Princess Vroc and then squared off with your dad—that was a heck of a swordfight. I tried to get in and shoot him from behind, but he got me instead, and I ended up here in the Grove too, right next to you, Phillip."

"He got me too," Ki said. "I was pissed."

Sarah wondered about something. "That one guy running around with the drum. Bathloxi seemed to think he would be pretty tough. Carahil said he could create … what was it again?"

"Wvulgroms," Phillip said. "I was there for that much at least."

"What in Creation is a *Wvulgrom?*" Sarah asked.

"It's a hypothetical person—a person who *could* exist, but doesn't. In theory, any of us can be *Wvulgroms*—it's simply an alternate version of oneself with different experiences and attitudes. If the fellow had chosen to fight, he could have created *Wvulgroms* of any of us—and that might have made things turn out a little differently."

Sarah laughed. "Maybe he should have created a *Wvulgrom* of Thomasina."

As they drank their refreshments in the Grove, a figure appeared through the trees.

"One of me is plenty, thank you very much," came a voice.

It was Thomasina, wearing her green and brown leather armor. They all stood up.

"I can't believe you'd show your face here again after your stunt in the temple, Xaphan!" Phillip yelled.

She appeared uncharacteristically meek and apologetic. "Phillip," she said quietly. "I didn't know you'd vanish. I just didn't want you to run away again. I'm sorry. I want to say I am sorry. May we have a moment alone together, please?"

Phillip was furious. "No, we may not! I've nothing to say to you, now or ever, Xaphan! When my friends needed me the most, you had to wave your little club around. You took me out of the fight!"

"Phillip, I …"

"I want nothing to do with you! Leave now …"

Thomasina appeared stung. She just stood there. "If we could just have a moment alone."

He hauled back and pushed her into the leaves. She fell and dropped her MT CALM.

Phillip stormed away.

* * * * *

Thomasina sat there on the log, looking at the fallen leaves. Her MT CALM lay there by her armored feet. She pulled her helmet off and let it fall.

Sarah approached. She picked up the club—her brother's name had been carved into it over and over. Kay and Ki had departed in pursuit of Phillip.

"You dropped your stick," Sarah said handing it to her.

Thomasina shrugged. "I don't want it," she said.

The two sat in silence for a bit.

"Aren't you afraid of me," she said bitterly. "Aren't I a nasty, wicked Xaphan witch?"

"I'm not afraid of you, Great Lady."

"I didn't think you liked me much."

Sarah laughed. "Oh, I didn't. But, the other day Kay told me something. He said he saw the future when we met you in the pub in Waam. He said that, without each other, you and Phillip would become old, lonely people, not half of what you could be. I don't understand a lot of that 'future' stuff, but he said that you would make Phillip very happy, and that's what I want for my brother. And, I must admit, I admire you—and so too does Phillip, though he'll not own up to it. And, he's pretty sore that you took him out of the fight in the Temple. He likes to fight just as much as I do. He's just not as open about it as I am."

"I didn't think in the temple. I didn't know what was going on. I was pulled from Saga without word or notice. I was just trying to play with him."

"Bad timing," Sarah said.

"I don't understand," she said. "Am I not beautiful?"

"Of course you are."

"And is going to church not considered a good thing to do in the Kanan north?"

"It is."

"Then why? Why does Phillip fight me, resist me—shrink from me? All I want to do is take care of him, keep him on the straight and narrow and have him close to me. I thought he'd be flattered that I'd taken such an interest in him. I offered him something offered to no man in many generations. I wanted to make him my Lord. He would have been the first Lord Woolover since Thomasina the 4th."

Sarah smiled. "My Lady, nobody likes to be captured like an animal—and isn't that what you tried to do in Waam? And, to your credit, you're like a bloodhound; we couldn't get away from you no matter what we tried."

"I would have given him anything."

"Maybe, my lady, but the one thing you didn't offer him is a touch of respect. Have you ever thought of that? My brother isn't a beloved pet or a shiny object to be bought and placed upon the mantle. He's a young man, a very good man with hopes and feelings and dreams. Do you know what his favorite color is, or what his favorite foods are? Do you know his birthday? Do you know his interests? My brother is a rare find, and ladies from all over the League would be glad for a moment of his time."

Thomasina winced. "Xaphan ladies too, it seems. I've acted badly, then. I let my temper get the best of me. I've pushed him away, and now he hates me."

Sarah put her hand on Thomasina's green armored shoulder. "Phillip's always told me that he thought he'd probably start out hating the woman he eventually would fall in love with. He likes ladies with spirit—and you have that in excess. You know what I saw him doing the other day? I saw him looking up your family's history, trying to acquaint himself with who you are. He wouldn't have done that if you weren't on his mind. You are strong and brave, and you've spent your whole life trying to make the lives of the people entrusted to you better—and I know he admires that. He won't admit it, but if you hadn't come chasing after him, he would have been devastated. He talked about you the whole time on our return trip."

Thomasina looked at her MT CALM and picked it up. "I suppose I should leave, return to Waam and not come back. I've made a fool of myself."

Sarah smiled. "You know, you don't strike me as a quitter. Why don't you meet Phillip halfway? Why don't you let him come to you for a change? Why don't you blush and say thank you and, most of all, offer him the respect the he deserves."

She looked at his name carved into her club. She ran her finger across it. "I don't know how to proceed. Help me, Sarah. I don't know what to do."

"Well, why don't we put our heads together, and maybe we'll come up with something. I promise, you'll get another chance, and perhaps this time, Phillip will come to you."

✶ ✶ ✶ ✶ ✶

The next evening, the House settled in one of the eastern halls for dinner. As usual Kay, Sarah and Phillip sat together at the long table, though Phillip seemed preoccupied and unusually surly. He'd been that way since he'd pushed Thomasina to the ground the other day in the Grove. Though she was an arrogant, persistent and undeniably dangerous pest, he felt bad about losing his temper and doing such a thing to a lady, and he wished he could make it up to her.

He didn't have long to wait.

A footman entered the hall and announced in a clear voice. "Lady Thomasina the 19th of Waam," he said.

Thomasina emerged and whispered something into his ear.

"Correction," the footman said. "Lady Thomasina the 19th of Woolover."

Everybody at the table stood. Phillip rolled his eyes.

Thomasina entered and seated herself across the table from Phillip. She was dressed in a flowing green gown—a Woolover gown with a cross-hatch of fabric across the frontal area and a lace-like bodice. Though Phillip tried not to make eye contact, he noticed that her hair was no longer green—apparently she had washed out the dye. Her hair was a tawny brown, a very pretty color.

As the meal progressed, Thomasina didn't speak to Phillip. Instead she quietly ate her food and made small talk with Lord Davage. She spoke of wanting to make a sizable purchase of fabric for her church back in Waam, which she and the countess began discussing in earnest.

Sometime later, Kay stood. "Sarah, you feel like taking a walk?"

"Sure," she said, pushing out her chair.

Phillip began hurriedly eating. "Will you wait a moment?" he said.

They turned and left him there.

What were they doing? Phillip had hoped that they would wait for him, for he greatly wished to be out of the dining area—with his green-gowned enemy sitting across from him. They left him there on purpose. He silently vowed to get the both of them.

Thomasina.

He kept waiting for her to pounce. He kept waiting for her Singing Ten to come storming in and the fight to be on. He kept waiting for her to start issuing him demands and get her club out and try to conk him on the head with it again.

But, she quietly ate her dinner, selecting choice cuts of this and that, properly thanking the footmen for assisting her when she wanted more.

She didn't even look at him, and that began to annoy Phillip for some reason. A small but rather infectious piece of him found himself wanting her attention, demanding it.

Where was the attack? Where were the threats?

A roiling set of conflicting emotions began to well up in him. On the one hand, he couldn't stand this arrogant woman from Waam. On the other, he admired her strength and courage. The way she fought in the Temple—what little of it he got to see—fully able to measure up against those bizarre Kestral heroes.

He hated the way she tried to order him around and force him to attend church services with her—trying to kidnap him and hunt him down like a game animal.

He liked the way she looked at him. Perhaps he liked being chased too. Thinking back to the incident on Waam—it was a grand adventure, with the two sides scheming to outdo the other. The fact that she was a worthy and determined opponent made it all the more exciting.

Why didn't she chase him now?

Who did she think she was?

A Xaphan who loved him.

Thoroughly conflicted, he finished his dinner, wiped his lips and made ready to leave the table, making a copious amount of noise as he did so, china and silverware clanging, feet and chair shuffling.

Everyone stood up as was usual.

Thomasina sat there, no longer talking to the countess. She sat looking at her plate.

Phillip approached his mother, Lady Poe, and gave her a kiss on the cheek. He then began to walk away.

Freedom.

He paused and turned.

"My lady," he said. "That is a ravishing gown that you are wearing today."

"Thank you, my lord," Thomasina said quietly.

"Is it a Woolover design?"

"Yes, my lord."

Davage and Sygillis sat there and watched him. Lady Poe tried to get his attention, but he ignored her. Phillip again turned to leave and escape the hall, and again he paused. The two conflicting forces dueled in his head—one was the impulse to flee, the other to stay … stay and explore the possibilities.

What to do?

"My lady," he said, "I also wish to take a refreshing walk in the Grove. Would you care to join me?"

She looked up. "May I please finish my serving, my lord?"

Phillip, without saying anything, sat back down, and Thomasina finished her dinner. It took her some time, she even got more food and a bite of dessert. Phillip sat there, not saying a word. Finally, Thomasina finished. They stood and walked out into the Grove.

They wandered for a bit, taking this cobbled path then the next, the dense green swallowing them whole. Neither of them said much. After a bit, Phillip offered his hand, and she took it.

"I must say, I thought you were magnificent in the Temple—you fought with rare grace—for what little of it I got to see."

She blushed. "Thank you, Phillip."

"I wish to apologize for pushing you down. That is not something a gentleman does. I offer myself for retribution if you want to push me back."

She smiled and gave him a playful tap on the cheek. "There, I am revenged, Phillip."

They stopped at an intersection. "Is it too late for us, Phillip? I wish to reintroduce myself to you. I wish to prove myself. I have come to know that I acted and treated you terribly. I am sorry—I have little experience in these matters. I lost my temper back in Waam, and I got angry. I wouldn't have harmed any of you—I just … I, simply didn't want you to go. I didn't know what to say, I didn't know … You made me feel things I'd never experienced before … and so I got angry, and I failed to offer you the respect that you deserve, and for that I ask for your forgiveness."

"You hunted us like animals."

"Yes, and you and Lord Blanchefort and the rest, were more than up to it." She laughed. "It was like a chess match, move and counter move—I was most impressed. Your friend Lon was magnificent; all my Ladies have said so—they couldn't stop talking about him." She paused a moment. "I stopped and paid my respects at his gravesite. A terrible loss. I wept for him and prayed for his soul."

Phillip nodded and choked back a tear. "You have removed your dyes."

"Yes. I wanted you to see me as I am. I hope you find favor with it."

"It's very attractive."

"I'd hoped you would like it."

Phillip shook his head. "My lady, what do you possibly see when you look at me? I am nineteen years old. You, and I checked this, are a hundred and ten years old, matriarch of a huge, ancient House, and half of Waam either fears or respects you."

"I watched you fight in the pub with your eyes alight, and I saw a man of strength, a man who could inspire my heart as the Elders do. I've adored you ever since—I see in you what's best in all of us. What do I see when I look at you, Phillip? I see a good man."

Phillip tried to walk away, but Thomasina held him.

"I plan to go to school, like my brother," he said. "And then, after that, I do not know what I will do. I might wish to join the Fleet, see what's out there. Lord Davage wishes me to serve as his helmsman."

"That is a rare honor—to serve the great Captain Davage. Please, Phillip, do those things," she said. "If you go to school, you will excel. If you join the Fleet, you will be brave. I, in the meantime, will go to Saga and reacquaint myself with my roots. I have appointed Garland as Thomasina the 20th, and she will protect my people back in Waam. I will go to Saga and stay with my House. There, I will close the pubs when they ought to be closed. I will go to church and sing. But, part of my thoughts will be elsewhere, with you. No more chasing. No more games. If you want me, Phillip, I will wait for you."

Phillip thought a moment. "I have been doing a bit of reading on your House. I know a lot about you. I found that the name 'Thomasina' is an appellation awarded to the most fit to lead the family. If I may ask, what is your birth name, as the public records make no mention?"

"Rose. My birth name is Rose. You may call me that if you wish—I won't mind. We usually receive simple names. I've not used it since I was a small girl."

"Rose, I like it. It suits you."

She put her hands on Phillip's face. "I, as your sister informed me, know very little about you and your House at the moment. Your birthday, your hobbies, your favorite dishes … I want to learn what those are, but I'll not research them; I'll not look them up. I want you to tell me, and once I know, I'll never forget them."

Phillip smiled, and, reaching into his coat, pulled out the green and brown bracelet he bought in Tusck.

"For me?" she asked.

"I thought the color suited you. I, like my cousin, can see a bit of the future too, and I've seen you there for a long time. I always wondered what I would do if the image I saw was nothing more than a dream, how unhappy I'd be. I've been waiting for you, Rose. It feels good to finally admit it to myself."

She smiled and put it on. Phillip again offered Thomasina his hand. She took it, and they continued their walk.

They walked late into the night.

32—Sitting in the Grove

Kay pulled the quartz stone out of the Machine and threw it aside in disgust.

Kay, Phillip and Lord Peter were, once again, out in the Grove trying to get the Machine working. It had become a minor obsession for Kay since Sam's death.

The Machine sat there in the afternoon sun, quiet and stubborn as usual.

They had been trying to get it to do something—anything. Over the weeks since Sam's death, they put the Machine through the wringer. It had to be important somehow, and if they could get it to function, then the use Sam had in mind for it might become clear.

But, of course, Sam was dead, and the Kestrals and Horned God appeared to be gone. What difference did it make?

Phillip, at first, thought the Machine was solar powered, but that theory was soon quashed, as scans of the device showed it to be inert in the sun.

Undeterred, they then began trying various methods to power it up. They tried power induction—essentially 'beaming' motive power in various configurations to the Machine, a fairly common practice in League technology. All the induction efforts accomplished was making their hair stand on end and attracting Paraflies. The Machine rebuffed them and did nothing.

They then tried manually connecting power couplings using old Remnath-style connectors, as the House of Want was an old Remnath House. The first problem they faced was that the Machine appeared to have no power connector receptacles. They tried clamping and grounding the thing, but had no success. They tried cutting into it and hard-wiring the power, but the Machine, like a living thing, healed itself. Their clumsy cuts were almost instantly and seamlessly repaired. Again, the Machine resisted their attempts.

Coming up with nothing, they went to Lord Peter and asked for his help. Amicable, smiling as always, Lord Peter was happy to give it a try, and he was confident they would soon discover how to power the Machine and determine its function. Unfortunately, even with Lord Peter's help, they came up with nothing, Peter quickly finding himself running into the same problems Kay and Phillip had.

Lord Davage, seeing his son fall further into obsession and a hint of madness, offered to ask Lord Milos of Probert to take a look, for surely he could make something out of it.

Kay refused and was incensed at the notion. Milos' son was dead. Kay had sworn to keep him safe, and couldn't. Kay watched him die. He had previously gone, hat in hand, to Arden, to tell Lord Milos and Lady Branna about their son Lon, how brave and skillful he had been—how he helped save the League. Face glistening, the Lady Branna listened, then, without saying a word, retired to her gardens and did not leave them.

Her favorite son Lon was dead.

He had no right to ask the House of Probert for anything.

A week later, a letter arrived at Castle Blanchefort, addressed to Kay. It was from Lord Milos. In the letter, he said how much he appreciated Kay's visit, how much Kay's words regarding their son meant to him, and that it wasn't Kay's fault that he was gone. The fault, he said, lay with *Them*, the enemy.

His letter also contained a warning. The Sisters, thrown into a fit of agitation after the Kestral Affair and still fuming over their stolen book from Hiei, were on the prowl and were becoming more and more frantic in their search. He said he thought the Sisters might resort to something drastic to recover the book, as they were convinced its theft was directly related to the Kestral Affair. He included a simple but surprisingly effective litany technique to passively thwart the Sister's Stare, should it be used upon him in the future. He advised its use whenever in the presence of a Sister, as, he said, they were Staring everybody these days.

This place is small,
And this place is meek.
But this place is mine,
And my secrets I keep.

His final word stated that Lord Davage had briefed him on the machine sitting in the Grove. He said to concentrate on the use of powering stones—that should be the method used to provide it with power.

✶ ✶ ✶ ✶ ✶

Kay was seething and at his patience's end. Lord Peter had made an impression of the indentation in the center of the arch, assuming that's where a powering stone would be seated, and he tried to fashion one as Lord Milos had suggested. The impression showed a dizzyingly complex array of odd facets and angles that had Lord Peter baffled. Using the impression to create a cast, he first tried using a type of glass stone infused with micro-conductors. It failed, the machine literally spitting the glass stone out. He then tried other types of materials: quartz, microlyte, a manufactured diamond, and an agate.

Again, the *Oberphilliax* did nothing, the stones stuffed into its ill-fitting hole like a series of ugly hats.

Kay then had a mind wave. He recalled Sam standing in the jewelry store in the village, seeking a purple stone called a spinel.

A spinel?

Lord Peter looked into it and replicated an artificial stone chemically very similar to a spinel—a composite stone of magnesium and aluminates with a purple hue. They were confident the machine would accept it and show signs of life. Kay was hopeful.

The Machine, like a ruddy silver mule, sat there with its manufactured purple stone stuffed in the hole and stubbornly did nothing.

✶ ✶ ✶ ✶ ✶

"I was certain that one would work," Lord Peter said.

"Good Creation!" Kay cried, "—I should CARG this foul machine into bits!"

Nearby, Sarah, Lady Poe, Lady Kilos and Thomasina sat eating lunch on a blanket. Nearby, a Silver tech bear padded across the open space, and Silver tech birds chirped in the trees. The various creatures Lady Poe had created over the years always came out when she was present.

"Peter," Lady Poe called. "Are you ready for some lunch?"

"Yes, dear, I'm coming," he said, picking up the fake spinel that Kay had thrown. He looked at it, perplexed, and turned it over in his hand. Lady Poe readied a sandwich for him.

Thomasina sat nearby. She was wearing a green gown. Her hair was still in its natural brown color; however, she had added a green streak just off her bangs—she couldn't resist. "Phillip, come eat your lunch please," she said.

Phillip put his hand on his chin and looked at the Machine. "This one should have worked. What are we missing?"

"Phillip …" Thomasina said again.

"I'm coming, Rose," he said, still absorbed.

They sat down and began eating, all except for Kay, who just sat. Sarah put her arm around him. "No luck, huh?"

"Nope."

Lady Kilos pulled a sandwich out of the basket. "Kay, do you feel hungry?"

He thought about it for a moment. "Sure. Sure, Ki, thanks." She handed him the sandwich.

Lord Peter began eating his lunch. "I was doing some research the other day. I managed to hack into one of the Science Ministry's lesser used databases. Apparently, after the House of Want vanished in 000011ax, this machine was all that was left in the ruins of their manor; the great cache of wondrous machines they were thought to possess were gone right along with the House. The Sisterhood took this machine to Valenhelm and did extensive research on it centuries ago."

"And?" Kay asked. "What were their findings?"

"They tentatively proclaimed it a Time Machine of some sort, and set to discovering its secrets."

"A Time Machine? Did they say how to power and use it?" Phillip asked, tucking into his lunch.

"No. Apparently, after a great effort, they couldn't make much out of it either—and they had the correct powering stone—their observations made mention of a purple stone that was destroyed during a feedback test. The thing looks to have shattered on them. After years of further study, they proclaimed it inoperable. The only reason they kept the machine in secrecy is because of its creator—Lord Revis. The Sisters had a healthy respect for him and anything he created."

"I heard they were jealous of his works," Kay said.

"That very well could be. Lord Revis was a marvel, centuries ahead of his time. The Sisters probably were jealous of him—they aren't perfect. They are capable of such things. The fact that he and the House of Want could simply up and quit the League without them having a say in the matter speaks to his level technology."

Thomasina poured herself a glass of cold lemonade. "Looking at this from an investigatory point of view, I am guessing the House of Want used this very machine to take themselves and their kit to wherever it was they were going, and couldn't fetch it afterwards."

Phillip, sitting next to her, agreed. "That's a good thought. If the House of Want used the Machine to exit the League and go elsewhere, then it follows that it would be left behind by necessity. That being the case, the Machine clearly functions."

"So why doesn't it work?" Sarah asked. "I'm worried about Kay; he's going to bust himself up over this."

"I'm all right, Sarah," he said.

"Bull!" she fired back.

Lord Peter looked back at the Machine. "I'm not certain it's a question of not working, Sarah. I think we're simply not correctly powering it up."

The Silver tech bear had padded up to it and was using one of its legs as a sturdy scratching post. "I'm certainly no expert," Lady Poe said, "but I'm pretty certain it does … something."

"How do you know that, Mother?" Sarah asked.

"I can feel it. It … has a harmony, a rhythm—it's quite beautiful actually. Your mother also could feel it, Kay, so could Samaritan Bethrael. It speaks to us."

Sarah was puzzled. "What does it say?"

"It says nothing, though it speaks. It sings, though there is no music. I really can't explain. I get the impression that Lord Revis indeed used it once, long ago, to vanish along with his House, as you say. The Machine wonders why it was left behind." She took a bite of her food. "I think it's a wonderful machine. It's singing to me even now."

Kay took a bite of his sandwich and gazed at the silent silver arch. "Ask it how it works."

Poe blushed. "It won't tell me. I'm sorry."

Lady Kilos finished her lunch. "I'm curious. Nobody seems to really know what this machine does or how it works, correct? Not us and not the Sisters either."

"Yes," Kay said.

"Well then, how was Sam, a Monama with limited access to standard League wisdom, able to know so much about it?"

Phillip answered. "We think Lord Lon gave her certain facts."

"Yes, yes, but she approached Lon with questions. She must have had a pretty good idea what it did ahead of time, and Lon's expertise simply filled in some blanks that she had. Where did she get her information initially?"

Kay glanced up to Dead Hill. "Who knows."

Thomasina finished her lunch. "What about that book? The one Sam stole?"

Phillip smiled. "That's an obvious starting point, Rose. We already tried that."

"And, what came of it?" she asked. "Obviously that book is important."

Kay was frustrated. "Yes, and if we could find it, we'd have looked through it already."

"What do you mean?"

"I mean we can't find it. We looked all through the library—we looked all through the castle. I know I saw a strange book in the eight-sided library the day before Sarah and Phillip returned for summer—one that didn't belong there. We went to fetch it some time ago, to see what it might tell us, but, it was gone."

"Gone?"

"It's missing, Rose" Phillip said. "Plain and simple."

"Who could have taken it?"

"Don't know."

Sarah rustled. "Why don't you look back with your Sight, see what happened?"

"I did, Sarah," Kay replied. "A couple of weeks ago. One second the book is there, the next it's gone in a flash of silver."

Sarah thought a moment. "Was it a thick blue book?"

"Yes."

"You know, I think I saw it in the Mystery Library a couple weeks back. I found it on a shelf and it didn't belong there, so I put it in the UNCLASSIFIED section until I could figure out what to do with it."

"Why didn't you say something?"

"Well, I didn't know what it was. It wasn't really my thing, you know, just a listing of old items. I thought Father had thrown it in."

"Is it still there?"

"No, it vanished a few days ago."

Kay huffed with frustration.

"It is probably a good thing too," Lord Peter said. "The Duke tells me that the Sisters got very frustrated looking for their missing book, so much so that they started using arcane methods to locate it, but the League Ex-Commons convinced them to stop. They apparently reminded the Sisters that such things are illegal. If the book had been present in the library, they probably would have discovered it by now. Since the Kestral Affair, the Sisters have been acting rather primitively."

Thomasina was alarmed. "Then, this Machine places us all in jeopardy, should they discover it here, reassembled."

"I agree," Phillip said. "We should disassemble it and hide the parts."

Lady Poe reacted. "No, no, please. The Machine likes being whole—it's been so long. Let it be—let it sing. We have it Whisper-locked. None outside the veil should be able to detect it."

"I don't know if that'll be enough to shield it from the Sisters," Kay said.

"Well, look then. I'll hide it. The Sisters will never know a thing, I promise." She reached out and fired a stream of Silver tech, quickly covering the Machine, stirring up several Paraflies that had landed on its arch. Soon, the Silver warped and twisted into the shape of a massive oak tree, big and gnarled, no different from any of the other trees nearby. "There," she said. Now, to any but us, it will appear as nothing more than a solid old tree. Not even the Sisters can see through this."

Kay stood and approached the tree. As he neared, the trunk peeled back revealing the Machine within. He stepped away, and the trunk twisted back into place.

"There," Lady Poe said. "Problem solved."

✶ ✶ ✶ ✶ ✶

A year later, Kay had near fully recovered from his loss, though the light in his eyes never really came back.

All around Kay, life was moving on. Joy had fully recovered from her terrible wounds sustained in the Temple. For a time she tried to cultivate a relationship with Kay, but he wasn't offering. Sad, but understanding, she chose to leave Castle Vincent and go to school at the University of Dee to educate herself; her experience in the Temple helped to greatly shake off the crippling shyness that had plagued her since being freed. Her schooling and board were paid for jointly by the Houses of Vincent and Blanchefort. Her initial hope was that, once she'd educated herself and a bit of time had passed, Kay's heart would have healed, and, perhaps, he would want to become closer to her.

That was her hope.

Fate, however, intervened. Sitting in the library one day, she met an acquaintance of Kay's—Lord Phender of Rostov, the new lord of the House; he was attending school there for the first time as well. They quickly struck up a rapport and friendship, studying together, meeting everyday for lunch in the school's great library. They fell in love soon after, and one day Phender made Joy his countess. Together they eventually rebuilt Rostov into a fine city by the sea, stone by stone, just as Kay had seen it.

The inflammatory malady effecting Captain Davage, Countess Sygillis and the rest of the *New Faith* crew vanished shortly after returning to Kana. Apparently they had been displaced deep in time and their bodies were reacting. Having returned to Kana in their proper time, they suffered no further effects.

The captive Xaphans and Monamas rescued from the City of Many Forms were nowhere to be found after the battle in the Temple. As Ennez hypothesized, they appear to have tumbled back into their proper place in time and space, wherever that was. Ennez further hypothesized that the enemy's fastness far in the future and Ondecca's loop in time in the deep past were somehow snared or buoyed to cancel the effects of temporal gravity like a great web, thus accounting for the odd effects the City of Many Forms had on their Gifts and perceptions. Free of their influence at last, the captives returned to their correct positioning in time and space. Davage wished them all well.

Lady Thomasina was a frequent guest at the castle now—she and Phillip had gotten past their rough start and acted like a married couple. As in the old days, she donned her leather armor and hit the Grove with them, roughhousing with the best of them—not tamed in the least, simply 'refined' a bit. Invariably, she and Phillip ended up getting lost together, or, headed off to the bathhouse for a soak, enjoying the warm water and starry sky. Sarah and Lady Kilos often splashed in—everybody enjoying the close bond they had formed.

Everybody except Sam and Lon.

Thomasina had fully re-acquainted herself with House Woolover, though she rarely was in attendance in their huge ancestral home south of Saga. Instead, she liked to sleep in Phillip's tower. She redecorated his floors with a distinctly green style and re-designed the unused lower levels into an Elder chapel. Thus began a long, complicated and often peculiar relationship between the two of them where both appeared to want nothing more than to thwart and confound the other. Rather like Captain Davage's previous relationship with Princess Marilith, the two almost seemed to be vile enemies, constantly at grips. Mysterious plots, abductions, lost items and hidden mysteries were the hallmark of their relationship—where the only sure thing was that the love that grew between them was genuine, though often difficult to fathom. Unlike Captain Davage and his former antagonist, the conclusion of these adventures always ended in a joyous reunion between the two of them. Kay, Sarah, and sometimes Lady Kilos accompanied Phillip on these elaborate adventures that often took them to strange places and forced them to do strange things. As Kay had seen, Phillip, his heart fully tasked and challenged, had never been happier.

Sarah helped Kay out quite a bit—she was a good friend, and she kept his mind occupied. But even Sarah seemed to be softening a bit, and would one day go her own separate way.

A few things at the castle never changed. Though Countess Sygillis and Duchess Torrijayne had fought side-by-side in the Temple, their continued campaign against each other did not abate afterwards. Syg regularly sent her staff into the village shops to locate and seize unflattering clothing, which they often found in abundance. In response, Syg created a small enterprise whose sole purpose was to create and sell novelty items all based on the Duchess. The most popular was a milk decanter in the form of the pregnant, naked Duchess, her breasts lactating in a stream when tipped.

Their private war with each other continued, much to the delight of society gossipers.

Lady Tellerran of Monama returned to her people a changed and enlightened woman. Eschewing her black Fphenook tribal clothes, she continued to wear her flight jacket and maintained her friendship with the House of Blanchefort, visiting them often. She wore a Silver tech Snugs medallion similar to one Sam once wore to guard her against the cold. Wanting to match her skills with her jacket, Captain Davage patiently taught her how to fly. Feeling confined at Castle Fphenook, she was instrumental in pulling her people out of the fog and into the sun, to embrace the League and all that could be had. Of all people, she would one day be wed to Ennez the Samaritan, the man with the funny hair from Innari. Shortly after the battle in the Temple, she went to him with candies and flowers and all sorts of other things she'd been told Elders liked to receive, apologizing for accidentally removing him from the battle in the Temple. They talked, they laughed, and the two became good friends. Not much of a linguist, Tellerran never got past her dependence for her endecar, but it didn't stop her from being social. One night they became lovers and never looked back.

Lt. Kilos was big as a house and in the last few weeks of her pregnancy—she could no longer fit into her Fleet uniform. She was wrapping up her final tour of duty, retiring from the Fleet so that she could devote herself to her new family. Though Ki would be out of the ship, her association with Lord Davage and Castle Blanchefort would hardly be coming to an end. Lord Davage proclaimed her the new Magistrate of Blanchefort—a position that was fairly light on duties, but one that she intended to take very seriously. She'd been busy getting her usual digs in Pendar Tower, which Davage and Syg had presented to her for good, ready for both her new arrival and her husband, whom she finally convinced to leave Tusck. She had a legion of her brothers and sisters helping her, as her husband came with lots of stuff. He sent create after crate full of gadgets and trinkets, and Ki's family cleared dozens of levels of the tower for his use.

Bethrael of Moane was also around, as she was going to deliver Ki's child—she had delivered every one of Syg's children, so why ruin a good thing. She still acted strangely around Kay—his Shadow tech Male effect on her hard to get over.

Life was thriving at Castle Blanchefort. All the darkness that Kay had seen was gone. Lady Kilos was beginning to shed her Puffies—a beautiful woman was starting to emerge. Kay tutored her on the Waft, and she was a good student. She nearly had it down, though she couldn't fly with it like Kay could. Of all people, Lady Kilos was able to cheer Kay the most—she often had him laughing and smiling—he remembering the old days when the three of them, he, Ki and Sam, went into the village to shop.

Kay also made a friend from far away Xandarr, rings and bells, who visited him rather often.

Lord Lon was greatly mourned even long after his body was laid to rest. His funeral in Arden had been a widely attended function. Lon truly had no idea how many friends he had. In attendance was a large contingent of strange ladies in green gowns—the Singing Ten, who had greatly admired him in Waam. His father, Lord Milos, though in grief, didn't blame Kay or anybody else for his son's death—Lon died fighting for the League. His mother, Lady Branna, was heartbroken. She retired from the Science Ministry and went into mourning, her favorite son—gone forever.

And, there was the Machine silently sitting in the Grove covered up in a Silver tech disguise.

33—A Flower May Bloom Again

It was one of those cold clear evenings that reminded him of Sam, and he felt the need to go see her. He got his terminal, popped on his hat, and made the long walk to the top of Dead Hill. He was going to sit by her vault and read to her.

He wasn't alone when he got there.

"Hi ya, Kay!" Carahil said, sitting by Sam's vault.

Kay put down his terminal, and gave Carahil a huge hug. It was good to see him.

"What are you doing here this evening, buddy? Don't you have a universe to save?" Kay asked.

"Sure, I'm a busy fellow. But, I've always got time for you, kid—we're family. How are you doing—you feel all right?"

Kay started to lie and tell him he felt fine, but what was the point? "I miss her, Carahil. I can't get Sam out of my mind. I close my eyes, and there she is. Look at me—I lug this terminal up here to read to her in the dim hope that she can hear me out there somewhere."

Carahil smiled. "Well, if you miss her so much, why don't you go to her?"

Kay shook his head. "I can't use my Sight, Carahil—it hurts too much."

"That's not what I'm talking about, Kay."

"What do you mean?"

Carahil gave him a bop with his nose. "She gave you all sorts of clues. She knew what was going to happen; she'd seen it. Don't you recall her sobbing in the night? She saw what the Horned God was going to do to her in the Temple, and how do you think that made her feel?"

Kay thought about Sam, miserable, alone, weeping. How she must have felt.

"She had a plan, Kay," Carahil said continuing. "Monamas always know when they are going to die, and she saw her death in the Bodice ruins. Accordingly, Monamas tend to get a bit apathetic and sullenly accept it as what must be. But not Sam. She was an Anuian through and through, and she wasn't ready to give up on her future with you and let all the things she wanted be taken away from her. She was going to fight for you."

"And how so?"

"The Machine."

Frustrated, Kay ran his hand through his hair. "We've been at that machine every way we know how, and we came up with nothing every time. I don't think it works—the Sisters certainly don't. Maybe Sam heard something about it on the Holo-net or in a book and hoped it might be of some use, I don't know. Maybe she was just chasing a ghost."

Carahil laughed. "No, I think of all the people on Kana, she and she alone knew the secret of that machine, and what it can do better than any."

"And how did Sam come up with that?"

"Got it right from the horse's mouth, I think. Yes, she had a vision of Lord

Revis of Want long ago—and he told her what it could do and how it worked. That was a vision she never forgot. She was always on the prowl for that machine, for it can save the both of you."

Kay looked down into the Grove and Sighted the Machine, sitting there in the dark, safe and sound hidden under its Silver tech disguise. "Why didn't she just tell me then?"

"You should know by now that everything she did was being watched. She couldn't just leave it out for you in plain sight—because the *Killanjo* were watching. If the *Killanjo* and their Kestral masters and the Horned God himself *ever* caught an inkling of that machine and what it can do—woe to the League, and Sam knew it. She had to walk a tight line; she wanted you to use the Machine, but she had to make sure the bad guys didn't know a thing about it. So, she disguised her activities. The *Killanjo* saw her doing strange things and scratched their heads—probably thought she was in some sort of minor Head Swarm or something. *Killanjo* cannot be accused of being overly bright, and they never thought that a Monama, any Monama, would dare cross them—such was the hold they had. She also waited until she could be assured of a measure of privacy, though that greatly wounded her—her confession she scribbled down for you tells us that. She left a trail she hoped only you, or your father, could see. Follow the clues she left and go to her; be one again. You can do it."

Kay took a deep breath. "Why now, Carahil—it's been over a year since … I buried my love up here. Why did you wait so long with this news?"

Carahil twitched his whiskers and was sad for a moment. "I had to wait Kay. There was a lot of heat floating around the League after the Temple was destroyed—the Sisters, I think they took the Kestral thing pretty hard, and they went mad with fear and worry. They were paranoid, looking twice at everybody—they saw signs of the Kestral everywhere, and there was that damn book that was stolen—they hadn't forgotten about that, mark my words. I had to wait until everything died down a little. I'm sorry."

"Then, tell me what I need to do, and I'll do it. I'll do anything."

Carahil loped up beside him. "You know I can't do that. You have to do it, Kay, on your own as it should be. Your heart, your ingenuity. If I just tell you, or do it for you, bad things might happen. Follow the clues she left for you, and I guarantee you'll be glad you did."

"We've tried … the Machine won't function. I don't think I have it in me to try again."

Carahil nuzzled him on the cheek. "I've left you a present somewhere around here—I've kept it safe in one of my little temples all this time. I think it'll help you quite a bit. Sam kept every promise she made to you, and now she's just sitting there in limbo, waiting for you to keep yours. That's the mark of a true Vith Lord, Kay—not fighting monsters and facing death, but doing the little things—a promise made, and a promise kept. Ask your dad, and he'd tell you the same. That's what is important."

Carahil loped away from the tomb. "Sam ran for me, because I asked her to. I wouldn't have been able to pull off that stunt in the Temple if it wasn't for her. She gave me the time I needed to do what needed to be done. So, here I am, pulling for the both of you. Listen, I can't stay. Tell everybody, including Lady Sammidoran, that I said hello, yes? And, tell my mother … I'll see her on her birthday, ok?"

Kay gave Carahil a final hug, and soon he was gone, a silvery star moving through the sky.

* * * * *

The Machine was still sitting in the Grove, right where Sam's Trials first began. Lord Peter and Phillip and Lon had put it together. It was such a hopeful time. The Trials were completed, and he was sure Sam would soon be returned to him.

How terribly things turned out.

The Machine was covered with its complex Silver tech disguise. It looked like a large oak tree as he approached. It even bloomed, dropped leaves, and made acorns—a perfect disguise courtesy of Lady Poe. An owl hooted in its upper branches.

Though he had little to do with it as of late, Lady Poe often came out and sat near the Machine, sometimes spending whole afternoons with it. She enjoyed listening to it 'sing' to her. He heard from Sarah that Lady Poe refined the Silver tech disguise over time, and she wove into it some fierce defenses: Nyke poisons, StT's, Paraflies, the works. Should a *Killanjo* or a Kestral ever get too close, they wouldn't live long to tell the tale.

As he neared, the disguise pulled back, and there it was: the Machine, graceful and twisting.

The *Oberphilliax*—the inscrutable creation of the House of Want, a machine that was, after an initial period of enthusiasm, an unused failure.

It sat, silent and unreadable, in the starlight, the Silver tech disguise hiked up all around it. As before, it appeared to be a slender silver archway, a solidly constructed device, though it, at first glance, looked thin and rather fragile. Kay and Phillip had passed through it many times to no significant effect. Kay tried using his Sight, but the Machine, as a whole, was hard to Sight—he had discovered that certain mystical objects eluded his vision—nothing was revealed to him when he looked at it. If he looked farther ahead, he saw the same old thing: he and Sam standing on a distant hilltop facing away from him.

So here it was: the silver machine. The *Oberphilliax*.

He recalled retrieving the pieces of it—he had been convinced that, once the thing was put back together, Sam would come bounding out of her hiding place, and that would be that.

Didn't quite work out that way.

He stood there gazing through the archway.

Follow the clues that she left you, Carahil had said.

Clues? What clues? If she had something in mind, why couldn't she just have told him? As Carahil surmised, she must have been afraid of the Kestrals and their horrid *Killanjo* servants—afraid they were monitoring her actions, at least in a small way. And when they finally did attack perhaps they had detected that she was up to something, or simply had had enough of her. And, that led to the abductions and the running and the huge battle in the Temple of the Exploding Head … and, finally, Sam's death.

Clues?

What did she say? What did she do?

He recalled that winter before her death she had begun acting strangely. All the crying, all of the startled running. And her confession written on the pillar of the Vith ruin.

I have accomplished things past their vigilance …

What things? What did it all mean? If what Carahil said was correct, then Sam knew what the Horned God would eventually do to her. He thought of Sam weeping in the night in her little nightgown—all alone with knowledge of a grim future. And those periods when she would seem startled and run away for no apparent reason. Kay remembered once seeing a ghostly hand coming toward her. Apparently the hand was his own—reaching back to her from the present.

She left clues, Carahil said. Clues that led to what? What was to be revealed?

Events began to sort themselves out in his mind. Apart from the crying and the running, Sam had indeed done some curious things that winter, and they began to stick out in his thoughts as he sifted through his memory.

He recalled the ugly toy pistol mounted on a stand she made him buy her in the village. He remembered the MYSTERY DEN, the seedy curio shop by the waterfront and how she happily went in and selected it. All through lunch she kept looking into the bag. He remembered her putting it somewhere in the Grove. He remembered her burying it.

I put it here as a reminder ... she said in Anuie.

A reminder of what?

A reminder that here it begins.

There what begins? A trail of clues, possibly, leading to some unknown end with the pistol being the first clue.

He looked around. The pistol—where did she put it? He remembered her fussing around with it near an oak clearing. He remembered making fun of her, her coal black bustle sticking up in the air—like a dog burying a bone.

Creation! Which clearing was it? There were lots of oak clearings in the Grove. He wracked his brains. He remembered her working the ground, her black gown and bustle sticking up as she fooled with it. He remembered the sunshine, and the clouds ... and Mt. Vith visible directly behind her.

Mt. Vith!

He remembered the clearing. He Wafted off in that direction—it was too far to run.

Under the starry night sky, he arrived in the darkened clearing with a blast. Beyond, Mt. Vith, the tallest mountain on Kana, loomed over a brownish nest of smaller mountains, its steep, cone-shaped sides gray and cloud-mottled in the night. It looked close enough to reach out and touch. Whirling around, he positioned himself so that the mountain was directly behind him, and he started searching.

With his Sight, it didn't take long to find.

Buried in the ground was the little toy pistol that Sam had wanted in the curio shop a year and a half ago. Its stand was now firmly anchored in place with a sturdy growth of dense grass. The elements were fast consuming it. The cheap curio was crusty and tarnished with weather. Its thin top-coat of pewter was gone, revealing a cocktail of cheap metals quickly deteriorating in barnacles of rust. The tall grass had completely overtaken it, and Kay had to clear it aside.

So here it was ... Sam's little toy gun. She had touched it. She had wanted it that afternoon in the village. She had held it in her hands, and it had made her so happy. What was this supposed to tell him?

"A reminder that here it begins."

He noticed that Sam had bent the legs of its stand in such a way that, if one were to place it on a level surface, the barrel of the mounted pistol faced up and to the right a bit.

Up and to the right—like the barrel was pointing at something!

He got behind the pistol and knelt down. If he line-sighted from the back of the barrel, he could see that it pointed toward a huge oak tree about four hundred yards distant.

He sped toward it, nearly tripping on the pistol as he did so.

When he got to the tree, he found it was one of the various trees scattered through the grove where his family had carved their initials over the years. There were lots of initials on this particular old tree. There was a partially burned away D+M for his father and Princess Marilith (his mother had tried to rub it out at different times, but it kept coming back), a D+S for his parents, a K and an undecipherable letter for Lt. Kilos and her husband, a P+F for Countess Pardock and Lord Ferddie of Vincent, a P+P for Lady Poe and Lord Peter, a K+S for him and Sam, and a new one: P+R. The P+R threw him for a bit until he recalled that Phillip used Lady Thomasina's birth name: Rose.

Sam had been interested in this particular tree—why? He Sighted the tree, but it was so huge that a close scan of it would literally take days.

What about this tree was important? Think, Kay, think!

He looked at their initials again: K+S within a heart with an arrow through it—an ancient symbol of love. All of the initials on the tree's trunk were encased in hearts. Their heart was etched in Sam's neat, flowing script—her Monama fingernail making short work of the tree bark. All of the other hearts were carved out in straight lines, obviously made with a small knife.

He looked closer. There had to be something.

He noticed the arrow going through their heart was pointing down. Upon closer inspection, he could see that, originally, it pointed up, but Sam had since changed it to point down. He ran his Sight back into time. As per usual regarding Sam, many of her instances were blacked out—he often couldn't see her back in time. The *Killanjo* must have been watching. He had come to believe that, whenever her image in the past was blacked out, that the *Killanjo* were actively watching her. On those select occasions when he could see her, she ran from him if she became aware of his proximity.

Just an arm's length away, but awash in disjointed time—watched by her evil masters. It was maddening.

And, recalling further—this was the tree where he saw the phantom figure of his aunt, Lady Poe, standing in the distance. She had been interested in this tree as well—apparently trying to determine what it was Sam was doing. Just like he now was.

He followed the arrow down the face of the trunk and found a tiny scratch mark near the gnarled base of the tree.

A scratch mark? He Sighted it, magnifying the mark greatly. There, written with an engraver's skill and precision, was a tiny inscription in her distinctive hand. It was nearly microscopic in size, and the tree had, since the time of its inscription, rutted over and healed. The inscription was fairly undecipherable at present. It read:

"I p..ce m. hea.. .ere ... .o. t. fin.. Fol..w .. t.ack. .nd Time's Bo.d ..y y.t be l... b...nd.

Using his Sight, he drifted back into time, and the message unfolded for him in clear, tiny lettering.

It said:

"I place my heart here for you to find. Follow my tracks, and Time's Bond may yet be left behind."

Kay was sure he properly understood this one.

Follow my tracks ...

Sam liked to climb the biggest trees in the Grove. She could walk right up the side with hardly any effort. She used her nails, and he could see, in his Sight, the tiny scars on the trunk from where she had plunged her nails in for leverage. He rolled up his sleeves and, following as best he could, he made his way up the tree face. It was hard going—Sarah was a much better tree-climber than he was. The nearly imperceptible trail she made meandered in a maddening fashion, sometimes backing up upon itself and, at other times, jumping from one trunk run to another. Sam appeared to be making sure that only he, with his Dark Sight, could follow her trail. He eventually made it up to the top of one of the tree's dozens of runs—the trunk creaking in the breeze. He was a good hundred feet up—Mt. Vith visible to his right and the blinking, dimly backlit bulk of the castle to his left. The canopy of lesser trees below made a green, hummocky carpet beneath him.

Sam's tracks ended at a small hole in the trunk. It looked like a woodpecker hole, though his Sight told him that the hole wasn't natural—it had been hollowed out by something sharp—again, Sam's nails. He Sighted through, and inside was a fairly large, multi-chambered space. He noted that a sparrow had made a nest in one of the chambers, five little heads lifted up from a snuggly hidden nest. Tucked away in a deeper chamber was what appeared to be a large ovular object wrapped up in a cloth.

He tried to Sight the object, but he nearly fell off the trunk in a sudden gust of wind.

He put his hand into the hole, careful not to disturb the nest, and pulled out the object, nearly dropping it as the breeze picked up again. Not having secure footing, he pocketed the object and Wafted back down.

Once on the ground, he pulled it out and looked. It was a large purple stone, about the size of his fist, wrapped in a cloth emblazoned with a 'K+S' written in black ink. It was cut in an ovular, walnut-like shape. Kay had no idea how rare or valuable the stone might be, but its sheer carat-size would make it ruinously expensive.

He compared it to the stones Lord Peter had made. The size was right, and so too was the purple color, but Sam's stone was cut in an entirely different way with the facets facing inward instead of outward—a custom cut. Lord Peter's stones were created from castings made from the indentation on the Machine, and they assumed a flush fit—but the cut on Sam's stone implied a non-flush fit—Sam's stone would stick out of the Machine a bit, like an eyeball.

Sam must have spent a fortune on this. With what money? Sam didn't have a lot of money. He recalled the argument he'd had with her over the large purchase she had made in Armenelos and about her selling her black jewelry to pay for whatever it was. He'd been so jealous. He thought she had bought a gift for another man. He made her cry.

He'd been foolish ... and cruel.

Here it was, sitting purple in his hand—a gift for him after all. She had spent every cent she had for this—a purple stone tucked into a hole in a tree that she hoped he and he alone would one day find.

"I'm sorry, Sam," he said, the bitterness of shame washing over him.

He Wafted back to the Machine at speed.

He was so disappointed when he got there he nearly threw the stone and destroyed the Machine with his bare hands. The stone was slightly too small for the hole. All the stones that Lord Peter had created fit perfectly, but they didn't work. Here was Sam's stone, cut in a totally different manner and presumably would work, but didn't fit.

Once again, Kay was stymied.

Sam ... Sam appeared to have knowledge and insight regarding this machine that nobody else did—not even the Sisters. Carahil said she had a vision in which Lord Revis of Want himself had told her how it worked. The book that Sam had taken from the Sisters must have filled in any technical questions that she might have had. The Sisters' missing book held the key.

She wouldn't have gone to these lengths only to stop now. This oddly-cut stone had to fit in that hole—it just had to. Sam wouldn't have had a stone cut that was faulty or defective, what was he missing? He Sighted the stone. It was cut in a fashion that appeared to make it a type of energy relay—again reinforcing the notion that it belonged in the machine for the purposes of relaying power. He noted that it had four small notches cut into what might be the underside of the stone. The notches could be used to seat the stone into a housing of some sort. Thus mounted, the stone should fit snugly into place.

Sam must have separated the stone from its housing to further confound the *Killanjo*. Had they found the stone in the tree, they then would have been foiled by the missing housing. Just like he was currently foiled.

Think Kay ... think.

He racked his brains, and nothing came. He was at a dead end. He had no idea where to turn or what to do next.

He stood there in the starlight. A star fell.

He thought about Carahil, who obviously knew what was going on.

I've left you a present somewhere around here, he said.

Kay was certain he knew what present Carahil was referring to—the book. The Sisters' book, missing from Hiei, and also missing from the eight-sided library in Castle Blanchefort where Kay had seen it.

Carahil talked about "heat"—no doubt the Sisters had been looking for it hard, and, if it had been in the library, they probably would have found it, and House Blanchefort might have been in a lot of trouble. So, Carahil took the previously stolen book and kept it with him beyond the Sisters reach in "one of his temples", stealing it a second time, and Sarah had seen it in the Mystery Library, only for it to vanish again. He mentioned the "heat" was less so—now that the Sisters were no longer looking for it as hard. So, if he'd been keeping it in the Mystery Library and now it was gone, it must be back in the eight-sided library, even now.

He Wafted back to the castle.

He emerged in the dark space hidden in stone, the little eight-sided library where his House kept things best left undiscovered. He loosed his Sight, and the small room lit up in amber. He rummaged around, trying to recall where Sam put it.

Tucked in a corner, there it was: a thick book bound in a midnight blue cover. A book that had been stolen three times, now returned. He pulled it off the shelf and opened it. A large golden crest at the bottom of the interior cover identified it as a book belonging to the Sisterhood of Light.

So, there it was. Sam had, in fact, sneaked into the Sisterhood knowledge repository at Hiei, taken it, and somehow escaped. That was a killing offense if they had discovered her, not necessarily because of the contents of the book—but because it was theirs. It belonged to the Sisters, and someone dared to steal it.

Kay thumbed through the pages. It appeared to be a very detailed inventory listing a wealth of ancient artifacts, including weapons, jewelry and arcane machines. He continued until he found the *Oberphilliax.* There it was—the strange machine of the House of Want, listed in meticulous, Sister-like detail over several pages in the back quarter of the book, including the materials used in its construction, the layout design of its interior and its power source—a 220 carat spinel.

And, the stone was clearly depicted as being seated in a delicate silver collar or ring. That collar was the next piece of the puzzle. He had to have it.

There seemed to be a page missing. He Sighted into the past. There was once a page containing detailed technical drawings of the stone and its collar, now gone. Sam must have used it to reproduce the stone and its collar and then ripped it out and destroyed it, again foiling the Kestrals. Kay could see it in the past but the drawings were incredibly detailed and complicated. If he couldn't solve this puzzle, he wasn't certain that he could successfully dictate the drawings to an artist or draftsman to have them recreated again. It would be painstaking and difficult. He had to follow the clues Sam left him no matter what.

On the next page was what appeared to be a rather dry and somewhat contradictory treatment on what the Machine did. Over the course of several unbearably technical paragraphs, the Sisters appeared to be arguing amongst themselves as to the purpose the Machine served, eventually agreeing to disagree on that point. The Sisters also noted, with a bit of chagrin, that they accidentally destroyed the Machine's original power stone in 000448ax while testing it. They also mentioned something about the Machine being cursed; they said it "talked evil" to them in their dreams.

A final paragraph on the page gave the following terse assessment:

> ***Oberphilliax*:** One known unit constructed (thirded).
> **Duplication:** Not possible at present time.
> **Function:** Undetermined, Time Machine—in dispute.
> **Status:** Inoperable.

Despite the legendary status of the House of Want, and the authorship of Lord Revis, the Sisters apparently thought the *Oberphilliax* was a real dud.

On the next page, the book went on to list where the three pieces of the Machine were currently located. The first piece, one of the legs, started out at the Sisterhood test center at Valenhelm. Determined to be of limited value, it was donated to the House of Thompson, a grand Great House of the Hala line, where it stayed on display for many years. An addendum mentioned the treasure vault of the House of Rostov—the Thompsons losing the piece while gambling there. The book even mentioned the House of Thompson being fined by the Sisterhood for losing the piece, though, as they considered it not to be dangerous and only of limited value, they allowed it to remain in the Rostov vault.

The second piece, the other leg, had a more sedate history in a display case at the main library of the University of Dee—donated by the Sisters in appreciation for the creation of the university, and as a token of good faith and friendship after previously destroying the old city of Dee. There was a mishap: while the case was being moved to the other side of the library during a remodeling, a clumsy workman tripped, and the case went into the waters of the library's pool. The book even listed the current owner of the second piece as simply: ANCIENT DRAGON.

The location of the final and most important piece—the Machine's arch—had been scratched out and changed numerous times. Originally, it was located in the Sisters repository at Barton, then transferred to their holding stronghold at Deep 7, then moved to the monastery of Attilan. It then appeared to have been included in an exhibit along with several other arcane bits of technology—the Sisters allowing it to be publically exhibited confirming that they didn't feel it was an overly dangerous piece of equipment. Some of the items of this exhibit were lost in a Xaphan attack while en route to Onaris in 000753ax. The last known resting place of the arch—the Temple of Ethylrelda of Waam in 002947ax.

Now it sits in the Telmus Grove—House of Blanchefort—whole.

Kay was fascinated by the book and, forgetting his mission, looked through several more pages. Lon would have given his top row of teeth for a few minutes alone with this tome.

Poor Lon, how he missed him too.

So, here was the book. Now, he needed the stone's ring. Obviously fearing her Kestral and *Killanjo* tormentors, Sam hid it. Flipping back to the pertinent pages, he'd hoped it would have offered something, such as some clue or obvious next step she might have left that would help him in determining its location. But, in looking at it, he could find nothing. Perhaps if he took the book and tore it apart cover to cover, he might uncover a clue. But, this was a four thousand page book, and Sam, having gone to these lengths, wouldn't have buried a clue in such a fashion. If one were here, it had to be somewhere in this area, with the pages dedicated to the *Oberphilliax.*

He decided to carefully read the entire entry. He started from the top of the page, reading to himself: "*Oberphilliax,* machine of the House of Dare …"

He stopped.

House of Dare?

The *Oberphilliax* was created by the House of Want, not the House of Dare. Kay couldn't believe that a Sisterhood tome could contain such an error—they would never allow such a thing. They would have immediately corrected the mistake and probably executed the scribe who committed the error. He looked at the page, Sighting it hard.

Looking back through time, it was easy to see what had happened. Once, the name 'Want' had been written on the page, and suddenly it was changed to 'Dare'. He noticed after considerable effort that the original text had been removed in a shockingly meticulous fashion and re-written in a perfect copying script. Where the name *Dare* now sat on the page was once the name *Want.*

Sam, with the skill of a master forger, had forged the name Dare on the page—a virtually imperceptible change, not noticeable by any except someone with an eye for detail and the Sight.

That was his clue. That must be what he was looking for.

He sat there for a moment with the book. He then continued reading the pages to see if anything else jumped out at him.

Nothing did.

That was his clue—the House of Dare.

So what did that mean? How was that going to help him?

It came to him in just a moment. He recalled Sam at dinner one evening asking his father about the House of Dare; specifically, she kept asking him about the ARLISS of House Dare, their LosCapricos weapon. She asked over and over again, making a point to be loud about it.

Why did she keep asking about the ARLISS? Perhaps she left a clue on the ARLISS mock up in the Capricos Hall where they often ate together—inscribed with her fingernail. That must be it!

Putting the book back on the shelf, he Wafted out of the library and went to the hall as fast as he could.

* * * * *

To his surprise, Lt. Kilos and another lady were sitting there at the huge table when he arrived. Ki was having a plate of milk and cookies. Her long hair was pulled back in a braided pony-tail. A small holo-terminal sat in front of her—she had been researching the history of Blanchefort Village. The lady sitting next to her had a plate of something saucy that she was eating with a fork. Several books were open in front of her. Ki, even now ready to give birth, was still a night owl. Tweeter bounced around on the table nearby, pretending to peck at crumbs.

"Hi, Kay!" she said smiling at him. "What's up? What are you doing rolling around at this hour?"

"On a mission, Ki. How're you feeling?"

"My back is killing me, and I want to be normal again." She pointed at the lady sitting next to her. "Hey—you remember my sister Maia, right? She's been here helping me get Pendar Tower ready. Of all my sisters, she's probably my favorite, and the most likely to survive against me in a fight. She likes the place—she's going to stay on and help me out with my new duties in the village. Heck, my tower's only got a hundred and ten floors. Got more space than I know what to do with. She's already picked herself out a couple of rooms near the top floor—way too high for me."

Maia was about as tall as Ki, had the same thick head of long brownish/blonde hair and similar cheekbones. She wore a sturdy brown dress with rolled up sleeves, exposing a slim, but brawny pair of arms used to a lifetime of hard work.

"Don't let her doofy looks fool you, Kay—she's got a great head on her shoulders. She went and earned herself a degree in Tusck all on her own—got no help from anybody. I figure Kana's a better place for her than Tusck—she'd just work herself to death there or lose an eye or something."

"You like it here in the cold?" Kay asked her. She smiled and nodded, pointing at the little Snugs charm at her throat. She seemed sad somehow.

Ki continued. "She was really busted up about Lon. She liked him that night in Tusck. She liked him a lot, and once Maia gets something in her head, it's stuck there. She fell in love that night; my family has never been afraid to love, and look what happened. A shame really. A real shame."

Kay closed his eyes and remembered his friend. "There was a lot to love."

Ki changed the subject. "Hey, Kay, what do you think about 'Sebastian'? I want to name my son Sebastian. Do you like that?" She took a cookie and popped it into her mouth.

"Stupid name," Maia said in a quiet voice.

"Shut up!" Ki responded. "If I wasn't carrying this load, I'd drop you!"

"Bring it on," Maia responded.

Ki laughed. "Me and Maia have been in more fights than I can remember—some pretty good ones too. We'll probably have a few more now that's she's going to be staying on here. I might even let her win one every so often."

Maia gave a short snort.

"Are you certain it's a boy, Ki? Have you been to the Hospitalers?" Kay asked.

"Nope. But, that's what the bartender in the Cat God Pub said. Said I was going to have a boy, and I believe her."

"Oh, that pub you and Hath saw in the village?"

"Yeah, I've been keeping an eye out for it. I go down there every so often and take a peek in the alley to see if it's there, but it never is, just a dark, empty space. You know, I actually bought that little vacant parcel where the Cat God pub was. I saw Notary Christian the other day and bought it, done deal. I got it for way cheap. I think I'll clean it up and open my own Cat God pub there, just like I remember it. I've always wanted my own place."

"Well, I'll make sure I'm your first customer once you open. Oh, what if it's a girl? I'm just asking."

"Then her name is going to be Kilos. All my daughters will be named Kilos."

"Oh Feature," Maia said. "You and that stupid name."

"Won't that be confusing?"

"Nope."

Kay looked around at the scores of weapons mounted to the walls of the hall. "How's your tower coming along?"

"Great," she said. "Almost ready. With everybody helping me, just a few more crates full of my husband's stuff and we'll be all set. I can't wait—all I'll need is the man himself."

"When's he arriving?"

"At the end of the current semester. Then, he's all mine."

Kay stared at the walls, not finding what he was wanting. "Ki, do you recall where the ARLISS of House Dare is?"

She thought and slowly stood up, sliding her chair out. "It's over here, I think," she said making her way down the hall toward the far end, holding the small of her back as she walked. The silver candle flame of Tweeter's light followed her.

"You needn't get up, Ki—I can find it."

"It's okay, I'm not an invalid, you know. Come on, let's look …"

They searched around for a bit—both of them perplexed. Maia got up and helped them look, though she clearly had no idea what she was looking for. Finally, they found it tucked away in a corner—it wasn't much to see, just a small ivory wand.

"I think it turns into a suit of armor, or something like that," Ki said—a want-to-be aficionado of LosCapricos weapons, but there were so many of them that she could never keep them all straight.

Kay pulled it off the wall and turned it over in his hands, scrutinizing its surface.

"Why's the ARLISS interest you?" Ki asked. Maia started toying with a small axe on the wall. "Don't touch that!" Ki snapped. Maia put it back and made some sort of obscene Onaris gesture at Ki.

"Oh, I don't know," Kay said. "Just a little project I'm working on." He looked at her huge belly. "Are you sure you're not carrying two in there?" he asked smiling.

Ki laughed and gave him a kiss on the cheek. As her time got closer she was becoming more and more motherly.

He thought a moment. "You know, Ki—I still remember you dancing around in the fire in Tusck that night."

"Oh yeah, did you like that?"

"I did. It was a side of you I'd never seen before. We should do that here every so often out in the Grove—have a ... 'Laserum', did you call it, and dance Onaris-style. We'll make it a tradition, I think it'll be fun."

On hearing that, Maia seemed to perk up. "Can we really, Lord Blanchefort?"

Kay nodded and gave her a shove. "Call me Kay, will you?"

She smiled and shoved him back.

Ki appeared elated. "Sounds like fun—Kanan step dancing's too reserved for me. If you're going to dance—then dance. Dance hard. Dance 'til you puke. Just hold that thought until I get rid of this," she said holding her belly.

Kay laughed.

Ki's attention turned to the ARLISS Kay was holding. "Hey, whatever you're up to with that thing, just make sure you put it back when you're done with it, okay? You know how particular your dad is about this hall, and, now that this old place is my home too, I'm particular about it as well. Anyway, it's good to see you smile again, kid."

She groaned and held the small of her back, and Kay helped her back to her tower. Maia set their dishes aside for the staff to pick up, and then followed with her armload of books.

With Lt. Kilos safely tucked away, Kay took the ARLISS back and looked it over in his reading room—turning it about in his hands.

Nothing—nothing on it. No clue here.

He sat there and felt stupid for a moment—he hadn't thought to look at the wall behind the ARLISS.

✶ ✶ ✶ ✶ ✶

The lights were out when he arrived. Ki and Maia's plates were already gone—picked up by the staff. He didn't bother with the lights—he didn't need light. He peered down and examined the wall behind where the ARLISS had hung. There, written in the stone in a tiny script barely visible to the naked eye, was a short passage.

It said:

"*There it began, and there it will begin anew, a dark future averted. Resting in an open hand, a flower may bloom again.*"

He sat there looking at the tiny inscription carved out by Sam's fingernail, and it was so clear to him. He felt a thrill pass through his body, and he savored the moment.

Kay put the ARLISS back in its spot. then he made his way to the eastern wing of the castle—to the chapel of Countess Fercandia—the place where it all began.

✶ ✶ ✶ ✶ ✶

Kay Wafted into the gloom of the chapel. Eleven years ago, he first crawled in here as a thirteen year old boy, holding a flashlight because his Sight hadn't activated. He remembered he was going to kill himself that very afternoon. Seemed like such a long time ago.

Now, he stood there in the dark, seeing everything clearly, the power of his Gifts swirling about him. A true Vith. Here were the pews, the blue floor strewn with dried roses, the statue of the Countess with her dainty CARG that he had modeled his own after; they all stood out in his amber Sight.

In the open hand of the statue, the hand where he once gave Sam a pastry to eat, was an elegant silver ring, ovular in shape about four inches long in total—and just about the right size to fit around the stone. He walked a few steps to the statue and picked it up.

There it was sitting in his palm. It was real. He noticed a tiny inscription on the inside of the silver ring.

It said:

For Kay, the man I've loved my entire life. –Sam.

Again, Sam had a way of profoundly touching him.

He got out the stone, and it clicked neatly into place. It looked just like the picture in the Sisters' book. He took a deep breath and walked back out into the Grove, clothed with the dark of night.

When he arrived back at the Machine, it was damp from the night air, quickly frosting over with rimy ice crystals. Lady Poe's Silver tech parted for him, like an old woman lifting her skirts. He got the stone out of his pocket, and it fit perfectly into the central indentation and locked.

The Machine didn't do anything as the stone fell into place—but he could somehow tell it was now whole and ready for use. It felt ready. There were no blinking lights, no noises, no thrumming of measured power, no smoke or cosmetic glamour; just the whole Machine, content to be innocuous. Apparently, vanity was not something the House of Want suffered from.

Now what? Some of his previous elation fell flat. Now that the Machine was ready—and he could *feel* that it was—what was he supposed to do with it? He tested it, running his arm through its archway once or twice. As before, nothing happened. He then tried walking through it—nothing. He didn't recall the Sisters' book mentioning how to use it, per se, because they themselves didn't know. They couldn't decide what the Machine did or how to use it.

Inoperable they had written.

He remembered Phillip and Lon arguing about its use in the *Goshawk*—he didn't understand what they were talking about.

Creation—he was on the verge of something—something momentous, he knew it. Sam had led him to this moment. Sam had counted on him. Sam had refused to let her dreams die in a Berserkacide rage. So, now what? What was he supposed to do?

Help me, Sam!

He thought about the little inscription Sam had left him in the Capricos Hall. *"... a flower may bloom again."*

The maddening thing about his Dark Sight was, although he could interact with things and people in the past, present and in the future of his Sight, he couldn't maintain the connection. As soon as he quit his Sight or looked away from his object, it vanished back in time—just like the Haitathe monsters he pulled forward to fight the Watch in Rostov. Such concentration was exhausting to maintain and impossible to keep from slipping. There needed to be some way to make the transference from one time to another permanent. That was the whole trick to time travel—not the temporary joining of two points in time, but the defeating of the temporal gravity that wanted to hold you fast where you were. Even the Kestrals with their arcane technology couldn't do it without a huge and brutish device like the Horned God's Temple that was far from perfect, requiring an inordinate amount of power to operate.

Could that be what this machine does? Could this silvery archway bridge the gap from the past to the present? Not a time machine in the strictest sense, as the Sisters thought it was, but a bridge, a threshold allowing objects to pass through and stay in a time and place not its own. That would make it much more elegant and infinitely more complex than the Horned God's power-hungry temporal anchor-point.

"... *a flower may bloom again."* Could she have been referring to the dried flowers in the chapel?

He looked back at the distant castle, blinking with subtle lights.

He looked at the silent machine exposed from its Silver tech disguise. He then Sighted and zeroed in on Countess Fercandia's chapel. He scrolled back in time, years rolling back to decades, then centuries. There was the dedication of the chapel centuries ago—it had been open to the sky then. He saw several robed priests scattering fresh roses about to commemorate the event. He reached out and picked one up, careful not to alert the priests.

Holding the flower, feeling it in his hand, he then pulled the rose through the archway of the Machine, noting with a bit of dismay that it did nothing flashy as he did so.

He could feel the rose, the fiber of the stem, the tender softness of the petals, the drops of cool dew. He could smell its delicate rosy scent. He closed his eyes and ended his trip to the past.

At this point, the rose should fall back into the mouth of time, back to the open-air chapel centuries ago where it came from.

When he opened his eyes the rose was still there.

He stood openmouthed, looking at the rose as if it were not a mere flower, but the manifestation of a miracle. This flower had bloomed and been picked centuries ago. It lay in a chapel, been covered over with masonry and stone, dried up, lay there in the dark and then avoided being stepped on by his passing feet, only to jump ahead in time and bloom again.

The House of Want's Machine, without fanfare or glitz, bridged the gap from that time to this one, disconnecting its temporal gravity to the past and reconnecting it to this temporality, allowing the flower to pass through permanently, no Time Tunnel, no Horned Gods or bleeding flesh. It had done effortlessly what was considered impossible.

It had done something the gods themselves couldn't do ...

The power of this Machine, now fully understood, was staggering. The genius of the House of Want. The Sisters had made the mistake of approaching their research into the Machine as though it was a mere time travel device, which it is not, and, therefore, they concluded it was an inoperable failure. What the Kestrals could do with a machine like this, reaching out from their fastness in the future. The havoc they could create.

What the Horned God could do with this machine. His beloved Dark Angels, so long denied to him, could be just an arm's reach away.

Sam was so wise, so thoughtful and responsible in her guarding of the Machine, making sure, even at a potential cost to herself, that the Kestrals and the Horned God knew nothing of it.

He stood there holding the flower for a long time.

There was only one thing left to do—but he hesitated. Like a person who had been wishing for something their whole life, and then, when the thing they wanted was right in front of them, they were faced with crushing indecision. He'd spent a year grieving for Sam, a year learning to live without her. He needed a moment. He needed to cope with this, for, should something go wrong and Sam somehow couldn't be pulled through—the sadness would be too much to bear.

This was a mortal experiment—either Sam would live again in the present, or he would die and join her in her tomb on Dead Hill.

One last thing before he made his attempt. He took the rose, the wondrous ancient flower bursting with life for a second time and walked back to the old oak tree in the clearing. He took his time—his thoughts simmering. When he got there, he climbed the tree and placed the rose in the hole that Sam had hollowed out.

There it would rest … for centuries. Maybe someday it would bloom a third time.

✶ ✶ ✶ ✶ ✶

He stood in front of the silent Machine. All he had to do was reach back and pick her up—like they were going on an outing.

But when, when to do it? Much of his past doings with Sam were blacked out, and the select few times that he had been able to see her, she either ran from or ignored him altogether. And what if he pulled her out of a bad spot? He might change time—alter the future. His mother had always told him that the future was a lot tougher than some would choose to give it credit for. But, he couldn't know that for sure.

It was maddening. All he had to do was locate her in a non-blacked out time in the past and pick her up—kicking and screaming if need be. But, maybe if he chose a bad time, the Kestrals would become alerted and do something drastic. Maybe they'd set off every Monama they could get their hands on and turn them into Berserkacides. Grabbing Sam might trigger a chain reaction of disastrous events. Maybe that's why she had run from him—for that very reason. She certainly understood the situation much better than he did.

So what was he supposed to do? He wanted Sam more than anything, but he couldn't be responsible for the unknown—he couldn't be that selfish.

He sat there by the Machine and felt defeated. Soon, the first rays of dawn would come. It had been a long night, and he suddenly felt very tired.

Sam had planned this out—she seemed to have considered every detail. She shrank from him when he went to her in the past with his Sight, as if she knew there could be bad repercussions if she allowed herself to come to him.

Then why … why all of this if it couldn't be finished?

And it came to him.

He remembered showing her Cathomere's Cathedral—a place of solace in the castle. He'd hidden from her during one of their games of hide and seek. She couldn't find him, and she'd been rather cross when he finally revealed himself. It was a peaceful place—a place where unwanted eyes and ears couldn't see and hear. He recalled telling her that his grandfather Maserfeld once used the cathedral to plan his various raiding parties, as he knew he couldn't be spied on in there.

It was the place where she told him she'd have to try and kill him someday: the Trials. It was the place where he was cruel to her.

And then there was that night, right before the Trials began, when Kay searched all over for her, hearing the sound of her chanting voice echoing through the halls. "*Now's the time. Now's the time. Now's the time,*" she kept saying over and over in Anuie. When he found her, she was sitting in a pew near the entrance to Cathomere's Cathedral, arms outstretched, repeating the same phrase again and again. Her voice was hoarse from saying it.

"Now's the time, Kay," she said.

There, in the cathedral where she was safe from prying eyes and listening ears.

That was the place.

Kay stood up, and focused on the castle, sending his Sight back through time.

Cathomere's Cathedral, about a year and a half ago.

It only took a moment, and there she was, sitting there, arms outstretched, chanting the same phrase over and over, her lovely neck bandaged. He couldn't see through the walls of the cathedral—they were blacked out, but he could see through the open doorway, and she was sitting right next to it.

In a minute or two, Kay's past self would show up, and she would disappear, starting the long chain of events that eventually would lead to her death.

Reaching back through the open door, he called out to her, his voice floating over a lagoon of time.

She turned her head, and she didn't shrink from him. She burst into a smile.

With trembling hands she reached up and fumbled with a large pin in her hair—a pin with a black jewel.

It was the NIGHTMARE—the LosCapricos weapon of House Monama—the reality-altering device that Sam had used to create the Judges of the Trial.

There was a shimmering, and then a second Sam appeared, seated in the pew. Sam then pulled the NIGHTMARE from her hair and placed it in the hair of the new Sam sitting there, arms outstretched.

Sam leaned down and gave the new Sam a kiss on the cheek.

She took a moment to straighten her gown and fix her hair. She then took his hands and let him lead her.

He could feel her slender hands in his, warm and delicate. Through time's abyss they danced, moving in step, across the great maelstrom. Tears of joy ran down her face. She squeezed his hands with excitement and said his name. He could see her black taffeta gown, her mane of black hair stretching out behind her into the past.

And through the winds of time, he pulled her through the gate of the Machine, she following as if she were ascending into heaven in the hands of an angel.

It was over. It was done.

Sam was standing there in the coolness of the Grove on the verge of dawn, her little hummingbird charm began to flap its wings, keeping her warm.

"Did it work, Kay? Is it over?" she asked—the clear sound of her voice a shock; a plasmatic dream.

He stood there looking at her, unable to say anything.

"*Arin-Dan*, my love—did it work?"

He recovered a bit and nodded his head, still unable to say anything.

Holding his hands tightly, she leaned back and gave a cry of victory that echoed in the early morning and then was in his arms, large tears leaking out of her eyes.

Kay thought he had been ready for this moment, but he hadn't. He was halfway in shock. "Can this be true, Sam?" he stammered. "My beloved *Cerri-Tela*?"

She gently took him by the chin. "It's true, Kay. You did it. You came back for me. You don't know how lonely it was, knowing what was going to happen and not being able to tell you. I saw myself as a beast, a Berserkacide in lonely ruins. I saw myself with no eyes trying to kill you—can you imagine how I felt? You who are more dear to me than anything. That vision—that beast—is not what I am, that thing is not what I want to be! I want to be your countess, and the mother of your children—that's who I am. I love you, Kay—I felt myself die every time I saw it. How long, Kay, how long has it been since I've been dead?"

Kay was numb. "O-Over a year."

"A year? Oh my, we'll have much to catch up on."

Kay stood there, trying to recover. "The stone, Sam … I'm so sorry I got jealous. I wish you could have told me—the things I said to you. I would have bought it for you. I'm sorry I made you cry. I've never forgotten that moment—never forgiven myself. I've waited over a year to tell you that."

She kissed him on the cheek. "It's all right, my love—I'm sorry I couldn't tell you what I was doing. I couldn't tell you anything—they were watching, listening. But, here I am—it was money well spent. It was the best thing I've ever bought."

Kay and Sam stood there holding each other, his mind still not fully able to bring the reality into focus. Sam kissed him on the neck. "I'm here, *Arin-Dan*. I'm here."

"You … you just saw me probably only hours ago. For me, you've been dead over a year—a year of grief and sadness. A year of loneliness. A year of learning to live without you. I'm in shock here, Sam."

He closed his eyes and made sure his powerful Dark Sight was quiet. When he opened them, she would be gone—he knew it.

This was just a dream. It must be.

He opened them. She was still there in her black gown, looking at him happily.

"No getting rid of me now," she said.

Then it was real. Then he could accept it. He took her into his arms and kissed her, letting a year's worth of pain and sorrow drift away in her tender embrace.

Somewhat breathless, he pulled away and saw the bandages at her neck. "What happened to your neck?"

"Don't you remember? I ripped my Shockers off. I did it for you."

"I don't remember that. I think Carahil took certain things from me. Your poor neck," he said softly. "Is it all right? Does it hurt? Do you need a Hospitaler?"

Sam's face pulled back into a half laugh/half sob. "My neck is fine," she said. It was her turn to lose her composure. "It's just fine," she crumbled to the ground and wept, and Kay held her for a while.

Kay reached into his coat pocket, and pulled out the bracelet of jet and garnet that he'd bought for her in Tusck. He told he'd bought it to replace the jewels she had sold, and, teary-eyed, she accepted it. He put it on her wrist, and she proclaimed that she'd never remove it.

Locked in an embrace, they gazed at the Machine towering over them both.

"It looks different than it did in the pictures and in my vision," she said. "I thought it would be different."

"When did you first hatch up the idea for all of this, Sam?"

"I saw a vision of it when I was a little girl. I only saw it once, but I never forgot it. I saw Lord Revis, I think, and he showed me this Machine and told me what it did. A machine capable of delivering objects back and forth through time, though it cannot travel in time itself, it breaks the bonds of time and place. He told me it

could save us. The only thing he didn't tell me was its name. Then, in the eight-sided library, I saw a picture of it in one of your books."

"Did you steal a book from the Sister's library?"

Sam blushed and buried her face into Kay's chest. "Yes, I needed it, and I'm not proud of what I did. I'm just glad nobody got hurt."

"How did you survive such a thing?"

"I used the NIGHTMARE and partially turned myself into smoke. Perhaps we could return it."

"The Sisters would have us arrested and you killed."

"Then maybe we could un-steal it. You know, sneak it back in. You could use the Machine, reach out with your Sight, and put the book back and the Sisters would never know what in Creation happened."

Kay laughed and embraced Sam—a year's worth of sorrow was wiped away. He was slowly coming to grips with this situation—this miracle. It became more real with every passing second.

They stepped away from the Machine, and its Silver tech disguise flowed back around it. It appeared as nothing more than a huge tree.

"What happened?" Sam asked, looking at the tree.

"My aunt, Lady Poe, disguised it with Silver tech about a year ago. She just loves this Machine—says it talks to her. I say we should dismantle this, Sam—despite my aunt," he said. "The temptation. The things that could be done with it. The Kestrals."

"I agree Kay," she said marveling at the tree. "May we look at it a moment, one last time," she asked. "I just want to see it and offer my thanks. It's just a machine, but for me, my vision, staying up night after night pouring through old books, pursuing it through the pages, it became like a friend."

Arm in arm, they approached, and the Silver tech peeled back once again. They looked at the *Oberphilliax* for a few minutes. Sam reached out and touched it, offering her thanks.

Then they began fiddling around with it, trying to take it apart. As they began working, Kay suddenly stopped. "Wait!" he cried.

✶ ✶ ✶ ✶ ✶

Later, in the reaching purple of dawn, they ran back to the Castle, hand in hand—neither one could let go of the other.

As they ran, Kay looked back to the trees. "Come on, Lon!" he cried and, appearing from the greenery, was Lord Lon of Probert holding his hat, his shoe buckles jingling as he ran. They waited for him to catch up, and together they entered the castle and presented themselves to the shocked people within.

✶ ✶ ✶ ✶ ✶

A few hours later, the Lady Branna of Probert, retired from the Science Ministry and in seclusion, for she still mourned her son, received an odd Holo-message from Castle Blanchefort.

34—A Fond Toast

The next week, Lord Davage and Countess Sygillis threw a great ball in their castle. Normally, the Blanchefort only threw balls on the solstice and on holidays, but this was a special occasion. There, at the ball, their son, Lord Kabyl of Blanchefort, announced that he and the lovely Lady Sammidoran of the Monama Astralon tribe—mistakenly pronounced dead it seems—were to be wed, Sam becoming the Ne-Countess of House Blanchefort. Sam shed her black Monama gown for a colorful assortment of fine Blanchefort gowns all made for her by the countess—not a black one in the lot. The only black thing she would ever wear again was the little jet and garnet bracelet Kay had bought for her in Tusck. There at the ball, they danced the night away, swirling across the floor with Phillip and Thomasina, his mother and father, the Duke and Duchess of Oyln (she and the Countess having called a truce for this event) and Lord Phender of Rostov and his fiancée, Joicellus-Zortens-Ka of Midas. A special guest was the House of Probert: Lord Milos, his Lady Branna and their son, Lord Lon—also mistakenly pronounced dead. Lon's long absence was brought up as a topic of discussion: "Where was he over the past year? Where had he been?"

Extended sabbatical on a distant world was the rehearsed response.

Lon appeared to be content watching his friends dance on the fabulous floor, a resurrected wallflower as always. Someone tapped him on the shoulder. It was the pregnant Lt. Kilos. "Come on, Lon, follow me—hurry up, before my water breaks." She took Lon by the hand and led him a ways down the ballroom. Sitting there in a brand new gown was Maia, Lt. Kilos' sister. Ki stood her up and put her hand into Lon's. "What's the matter with you two, chicken? Get out there and dance," Ki said.

Standing a good six inches taller than Lon, they bashfully strayed on to the ballroom floor, dancing clumsy, but dancing nonetheless, and it was a long time before they exited.

Later, the dancing stopped, and Lord Davage stepped forward to make a grand toast to Kay and Sam. Davage requested that his son, Lord Kabyl and his Lady Sammidoran, please join him in a toast.

As they made their way forward, Kay in a lovely new purple and black coat and Sam in a fabulous teal gown, the crowd began to cheer and clap. Some reached out and patted Kay on the back, but no one would touch Lady Sammidoran—the old Elder views regarding Monamas still holding firm, even at a ball in her honor.

Though she carried herself well, she still appeared a bit hurt. She held her head high and kept a beautiful smile on her face.

Sarah, wearing a green gown (which was rather shocking to see) jumped out of the crowd and gave Sam a huge hug. She was followed shortly by Phillip and Thomasina, Lon and Maia and Lady Kilos. Soon, their shyness forgotten, the attendees at the ball shook Sam's hand and touched her on the shoulder as they passed.

As Kay made his way to his father, Davage embraced his son and turned and embraced Lady Sammidoran. He began:

"Today, we celebrate a coming of age. When exactly does one complete the journey from being a child to becoming an adult? We try to mark the event by setting an age: thirty. We also set up machinery to attempt to tangibly usher in the event—the Wellerman's March and such. But, again I ask, when does one really become an adult?

"Twenty three years ago, I recall seeing Lady Sammidoran for the first time. I had been told about her by her grandmother, Countess Hortensia. I still recall her words. She said 'Lord Davage, you will no doubt see my 72nd granddaughter snooping around your holdings. If you see her, you should tell her to go away and not return, and she will do as you say, for I have taught her proper manners.' I recall we were in the process of getting Kay's tower ready—there was much to do as it hadn't been used in several generations. I'd forgotten something in his room and returned to fetch it, and there she was, standing there holding a sponge cleaning the walls. As we stood there looking at each other, I knew who she was immediately and I considered her grandmother's warning. But, I couldn't do it—I couldn't ask her to leave and never come back. I wondered why she was there. Though she was a mere child, I could see the love in her heart, her devotion for our little boy who hadn't even been born yet. Surely she knew something about our as-of-yet unborn son, something that deeply touched her; what was it? What had she seen with her Monama eyes that inspired her so? Therefore, I couldn't ask her to leave—instead, I welcomed her and invited her to return as often as she liked. And now, twenty-three years later, here I am, raising a toast at a ball in her and my son's honor.

"We are Vith, and with that comes a vast bit of baggage. Always with the Vith is a monster to slay, or an enemy to fight, so they say. However, I say that is an over-simplification. Sometimes, the most difficult enemy to overcome is nothing more than the step one takes in going from being a boy to becoming a man, when the things one says and the promises one makes begin to mean something. Sometimes keeping a promise is the most harrowing and difficult labor of all. I have had the chance to watch my son progress from a boy to a man, and not because of the enemies he overcame or the places he visited, but because of the promises he made to the woman he loves and the steps he took to see them through, even when things seemed bleak and hopeless. Lady Sammidoran has proved her devotion over the years time and time again, and Kay, through his actions, has finally proved worthy of it—thus the boy becomes a man, the journey completed. So, to Lady Sammidoran, to Lord Kabyl, I present you together to the ball and to the League, as man and wife to be."

Raising their glasses, everybody drank up.

✶ ✶ ✶ ✶ ✶

Lord Lon certainly didn't waste his second chance. Finding a new confidence in himself, he breezed through school and was soon admitted to the Science Ministry with much acclaim, where he made discovering and defeating the Kestral's heart trigger hold on the Monamas his chosen center of interest. As he aged, he completely lost his Probert roundness and became the image of a dashing Pitcock man. He also shot up, standing nearly six feet once he was finished growing. Putting his brilliant mind to it, he soon discovered the secret of the Monama heart-trigger and, with a surprisingly simple procedure, perfected a method of rendering the terrifying genetic device dead and moot. One of the first Monamas who came to him to receive the wondrous treatment was Lady Sammidoran, and after only a few minutes work, she was rid of it forever—the raging thing within her was a thing no more. Soon, following Sam's example, many Monamas came to Lord Lon for treatment, and he was proclaimed a Monama hero and fittingly welcomed into their secretive society.

Flush with his successes and his new found fame, Lord Lon became a hot commodity, something he'd never known before, with offers pouring in from all over. But soon, he took the hand of Lt. Kilos' sister, Maia of Tusck, and made her his lady, he now almost but not quite as tall as she. From a thrown pea, to a dance around the fire, to a broken heart and return from the grave at a glittering ball where they danced clumsy, but danced nevertheless—it just seemed right.

✶ ✶ ✶ ✶ ✶

The Paraflies Lady Poe had labored over continued their guard over Kana and all over the League, ever vigilant, waiting for the nightmare creatures to return. They fell into lore, the huge, sun-loving bug with a happy face. A Parafly coming in through an open window became a sign of good luck. A lullaby would one day be written regarding them:

Gaze you into the sweet wings of the Parafly, my child.
Into sleep, he will sing you,
Into dreams, he will guard you,
Into wakefulness, he will fly you.
In Future's dreams and moonless night, sleep without fear
Lost and carefree in the Parafly's sight.

✶ ✶ ✶ ✶ ✶

The Machine sitting hidden under its Silver tech disguise was a great temptation. Kay and Sam had tried to take it apart several times, but the thing resisted, and they gave up. Kay and Sam swore it should be never used and generally left it alone.

Except on two distinct occasions ...

✶ ✶ ✶ ✶ ✶

They were in a panic, knowing for certain that the demons were coming for them. They ran through the empty confines of their cafe/transport, the fountain in the center gurgling happily.

"We should return home, grab a few things, and flee!" Clatera of Cardinal said.

"I'm sorry, I shouldn't have said anything," his wife Mitzilaran responded. "Where can we go? What of our children?"

"I don't know! I don't know!"

There was a rustling from overhead. "You two!" came a voice.

Mitz screamed.

There, standing on the terrace, was a smiling Kay. "What are you so afraid of," he said gazing down on them.

Clatera pointed to the north. "Kay, I told you we're done! The edge of the fog is that way. Now, please go, we have to be off!"

"Why?" Kay asked. "Afraid of the demons who watch you from the dark?

Afraid they'll turn you into Berserkacides?"

Kay jumped down from the terrace and stood before them. Mitz, trembling, held her shoes.

"What if I told you there is a place where there are no demons, where you don't have to be afraid?"

Clatera and Mitz listened. "There's no such place, Kay," Mitz said.

"Yes, there is." He held his hands out. "Just take my hands, and let me prove it to you. It'll only take a moment. Come on, what are we waiting for?"

Clatera and Mitz looked at each other, then they reached out and took Kay's hands. Kay pulled them back, and there was a flash.

Freezing cold and an unfamiliar, tree-filled landscape. Two silver medallions came around their necks, then everything was fine.

Better than fine.

✶ ✶ ✶ ✶ ✶

And, finally, Kay reached back and pulled the Monama woman whom he watched turn into a Berserkacide at Castle Durst. He had never forgotten that poor lady, and he pulled her safely into the future.

Her name was Versalaran of Minzer, and she had ninety children. Kay and Sam took her to her home by the lake and saw her children come swarming out to greet her.

✶ ✶ ✶ ✶ ✶

They set aside some time and climbed into the *Goshawk* . They flew to Dee and, as they promised, visited the dragon living in the main library. There, they introduced Mickey, his tail this time in the guise of some sort of helmeted, ale mug-hoisting barbarian, to Sam, Maia and to Lady Thomasina. During their visit, they caught up with Lord Phender and Joy, at that time his fiancée, and shared lunch under the rotunda of the great library. Though the whole ordeal had been painful, nothing but good had come of it. All had been enriched.

Epilogue

Kay and Sam were wed in a grand ceremony in the Telmus Grove. Making great strides in throwing aside their shy ways, many Monamas of various tribes came to the wedding, all bundled up against the cold, and they passed the baton. Clatera and Mitz were there wearing their Snugs medallions, Lady Tellerran was there, as well as Versaleran of Minzer.

The wedding seemed symbolic, marking an end to their long period of fear and shyness. Now, they could venture forth from their foggy lake and enjoy all that the League had to offer. They joined the Fleet and went to school and plied themselves at trades—some succeeding, some failing, but all with the opportunity to make their own way as they saw fit, the day of the Berserkacide and the Horned God over.

Shortly after they were wed, Kay and Sam returned to the Grove and dug up the little pistol Sam had buried years before. It was in bad shape, but they cleaned it up and put it in Kay's study on his desk. Its barrel pointed at a hidden portrait of Sam that Kay had commissioned.

Eventually, Lord Davage and Countess Sygillis, both of long life and eternal youth, would step away and give control of the House to Kay and Sam—knowing that House Blanchefort was in fine hands.

One day, far into the future they, like the Sisters, would to go the stars where they might not only watch over their House, but over the whole League as well, becoming legendary figures. Kay and Sam would dedicate chapels to them, one for each, and one for them together—a place where their love could be celebrated forever in the new sections of the castle, knowing one day they would be covered up as more were built on top. To get to their chapels, one would have to crawl and quest for them—they figured Kay's parents would have wanted it that way.

✶ ✶ ✶ ✶ ✶

Most nights, Kay checked up on Maser and Hath as they slept. He Sighted through their doors. There they were, safe and sound in a shield of warm bed clothes and favorite Silver tech animals—awash in dreams. Kay could only wonder at the circumstances and chain of events that led to their capture and torment in a Kestral tank, turning them into the horrid, demented monsters that returned to the past and died by Kay's hand. Sam occasionally had visions of them—none of her visions were bad. She saw Maser as growing into a handsome man with an interest and great talent in architecture. She saw Hath, ever her father's daughter, sailing at his side in his final years as Fleet Captain, the helm wheel firmly in her hands. Together, father, mother and daughter would share adventure in the heavens, the both of them beaming in pride for their beautiful, red-haired daughter—a far cry from the bent, famished and mutilated creature she could have become. But, by Creation, Kay would never stop watching over them—to ensure the good future Sam had seen was the one they got to enjoy. He guarded that future for them and held it in trust. He was a Vith hero, and that's what Vith heroes did.

Lt. Kilos and her husband took up residence in Pendar tower, and soon, their son Sebastian was born. Ki's stint as magistrate was an eventful one, full of mystery and intrigue: Kilos the Manhunter, Kilos of the Silver Bird with her miraculous husband at her side and her SK at her hip, became one of the most famous Browns in League history.

✶ ✶ ✶ ✶ ✶

They sometimes came to Sam's tomb on Dead Hill as they planned ahead for the future. As for the dark interior of the tomb, Kay never looked—he didn't want to know what, if anything was in there—what was the point? Lon and Phillip sometimes tried to explain the mechanics of time stream alteration, but he wasn't overly interested. All that he wanted to know and all that he wanted was right in front of him.

Fin

RDG
2011, 2012, 2013,
revised 2017

Maps & Appendices

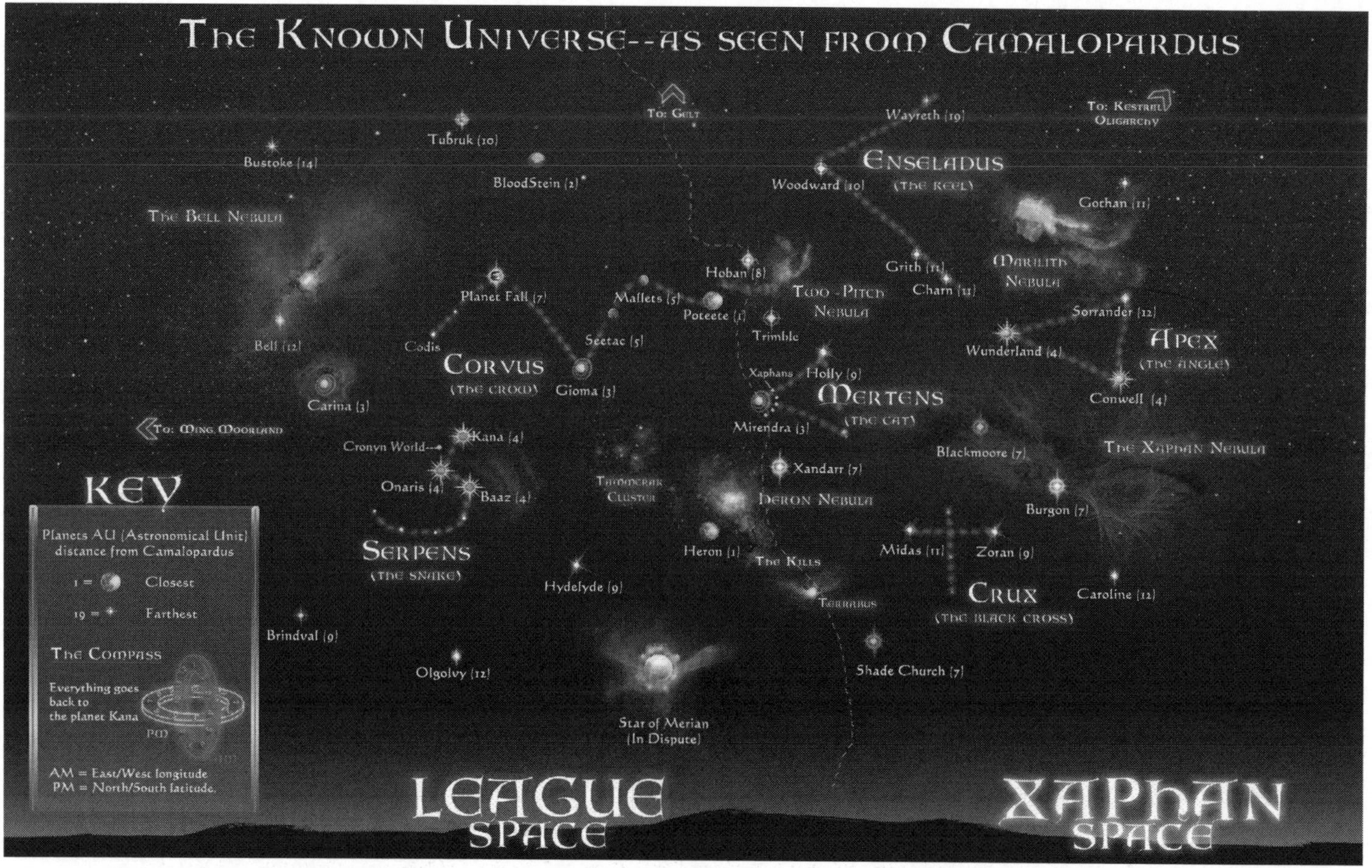

The Known Universe--As seen from Camalopardus
To: Gelt
Wayreth (19)
To: Kestrel Oligarchy
Tubruk (10)
Bustoke (14)
BloodStein (2)
Enseladus
(The Reel)
Woodward (10)
Gothan (11)
The Bell Nebula
Hoban (8)
Grith (11)
Charn (11)
Marilith Nebula
Planet Fall (7)
Mallets (5)
Poteete (1)
Two-Pitch Nebula
Sorrander (12)
Bell (12)
Codis
Seetac (5)
Trimble
Wunderland (4)
Apex
(The Angle)
Corvus
(The Crow)
Gioma (3)
Xaphans
Holly (9)
Carina (3)
Mertens
(The Cat)
Mirendra (3)
Conwell (4)
To: Ming Moorland
Kana (4)
Cronyn World
Blackmoore (7)
The Xaphan Nebula
Xandarr (7)
Key
Onaris (4)
Baaz (4)
Heron Nebula
Burgon (7)
Planets AU (Astronomical Unit) distance from Camalopardus
1 = Closest
19 = Farthest
Serpens
(The Snake)
Heron (1)
The Kills
Midas (11)
Zoran (9)
Hydelyde (9)
Crux
Caroline (12)
(The Black Cross)
Brindval (9)
The Compass
Olgolvy (12)
Shade Church (7)
Everything goes back to the planet Kana
PM
Star of Merian
(In Dispute)
AM = East/West longitude
PM = North/South latitude.
League Space
Xaphan Space

Map Of Kana
N
W
E
S
Key
City
Ruins
Sisters
Castle
1000 Miles
500 Km
Vith Land
Esther
Hala
Barrow
Remnath
Zenon
Calvert
Sea of Elder
Sea of Esther
Sea of Atalea
Straight of Elder
Shirster Point
Telmus
Blanchefort
Bloodstein
Mt. Holly
Durst
Holly
Burgos
Bell
Midas
Hannover
Xandarr
Minz
Valenhelm
Zary
Griff
The Gaston Way
Westron
Clovis
Tardy
Charn
Hazards of the Old Ones
Maqravine
Bodice
Vincent
River Seven
Kronos River
Wayreth
Hala
Tuk
Saga
Pithnar
Stanton
Tartan
Tithmus Lake
Killbane R.
Atalan
Arden
Provst
Bern
Thirkill Bay
Horace
Feren
Gotten
Dare
Atalea
Rhoda
Caroline
Hiei
Grants Walk
Pais
Pattern
Rustam
Green Sabre
Effington
Haitathe
Tyrol
Herman
Waddle
Gamboa
Tardn
Withel Well River
Bert
Falz
Champion
Caprinar
Prentiss
Kelt
Tela
Sorrenson
Veltro
Armenelos
Conwell
Dee
Kurtis
Pitcock
Jacarta
The Great Blue Pierce River
Brynthia
Howell
Mystery
Wiln
Rostov
Blue Pierce
Kentaro
Barton
Want
Woodward
Lake Monama
St. Paris
Sammarcand
Mercia
Twilight 4
Deep 7
Lyra
St. Edmund's
Bezzel
Calvert

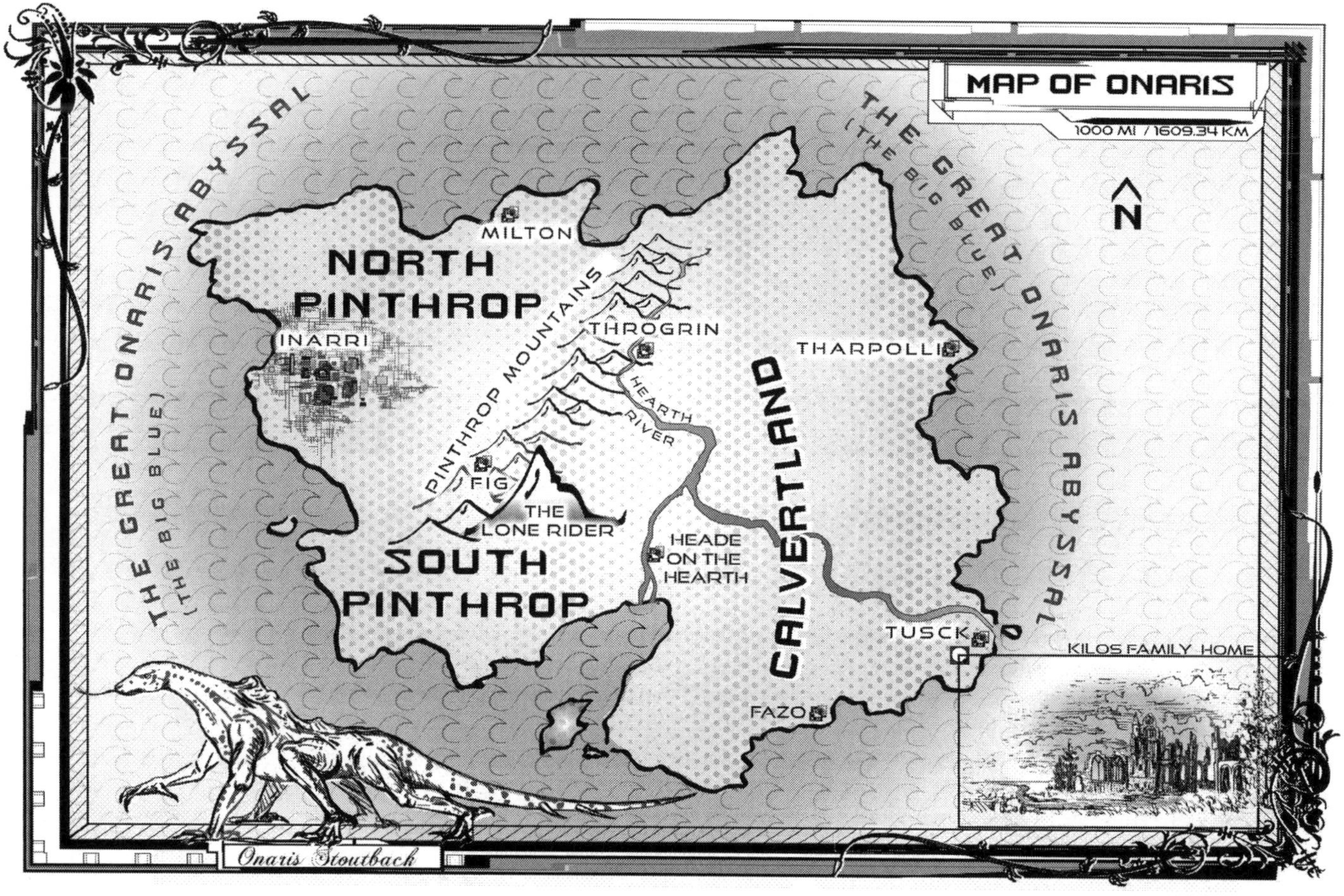
MAP OF ONARIS
1000 MI / 1609.34 KM
N
THE GREAT ONARIS ABYSSAL
(THE BIG BLUE)
THE GREAT ONARIS ABYSSAL
(THE BIG BLUE)
NORTH PINTHROP
SOUTH PINTHROP
CALVERTLAND
PINTHROP MOUNTAINS
HEARTH RIVER
MILTON
INARRI
THROGRIN
THARPOLLI
FIG
THE LONE RIDER
HEADE ON THE HEARTH
TUSCK
FAZO
KILOS FAMILY HOME
Onaris Stoutback

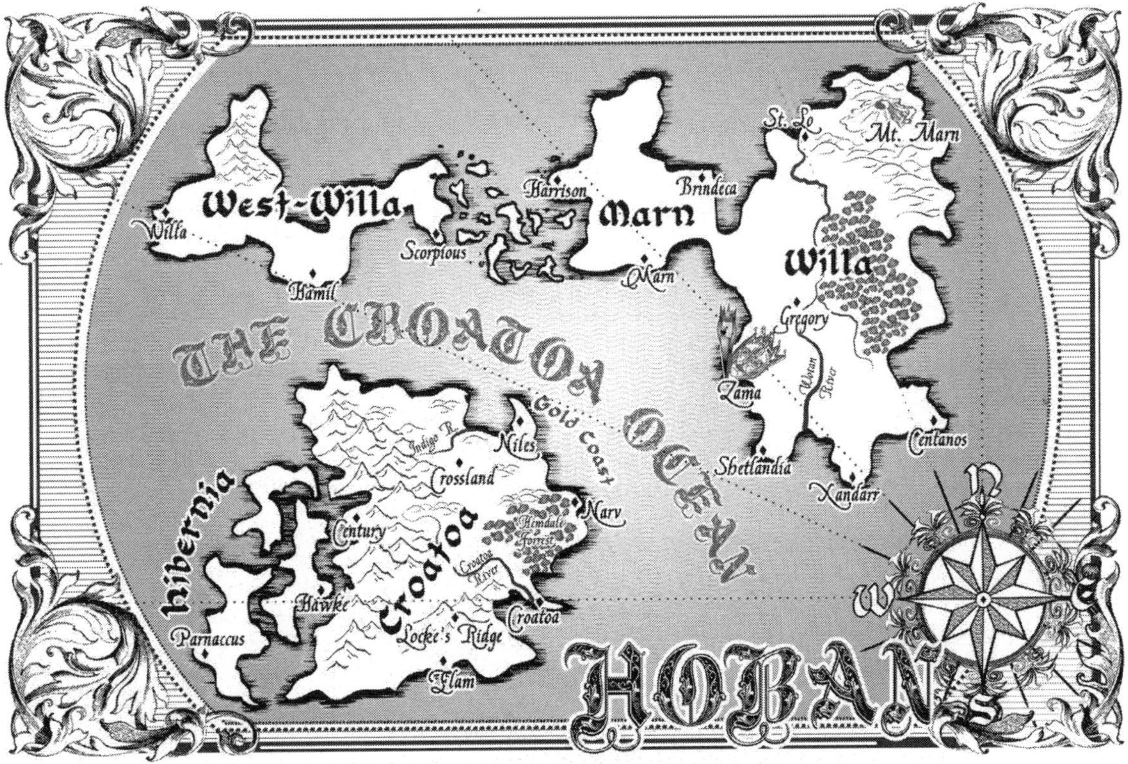
HOBAN
THE CROATOA OCEAN
West-Willa
Willa
Hamil
Scorpious
Harrison
Marn
Brindeca
Marn
Willa
St. Lo
Mt. Marn
Gregory
Wotan River
Zama
Shetlandia
Centanos
Xandarr
Gold Coast
Niles
Indigo R.
Crossland
Narv
Hemdale Forrest
Croatoa River
Croatoa
Croatoa
Century
Hawke
Locke's Ridge
Flam
hibernia
Parnaccus
N
S
E
W

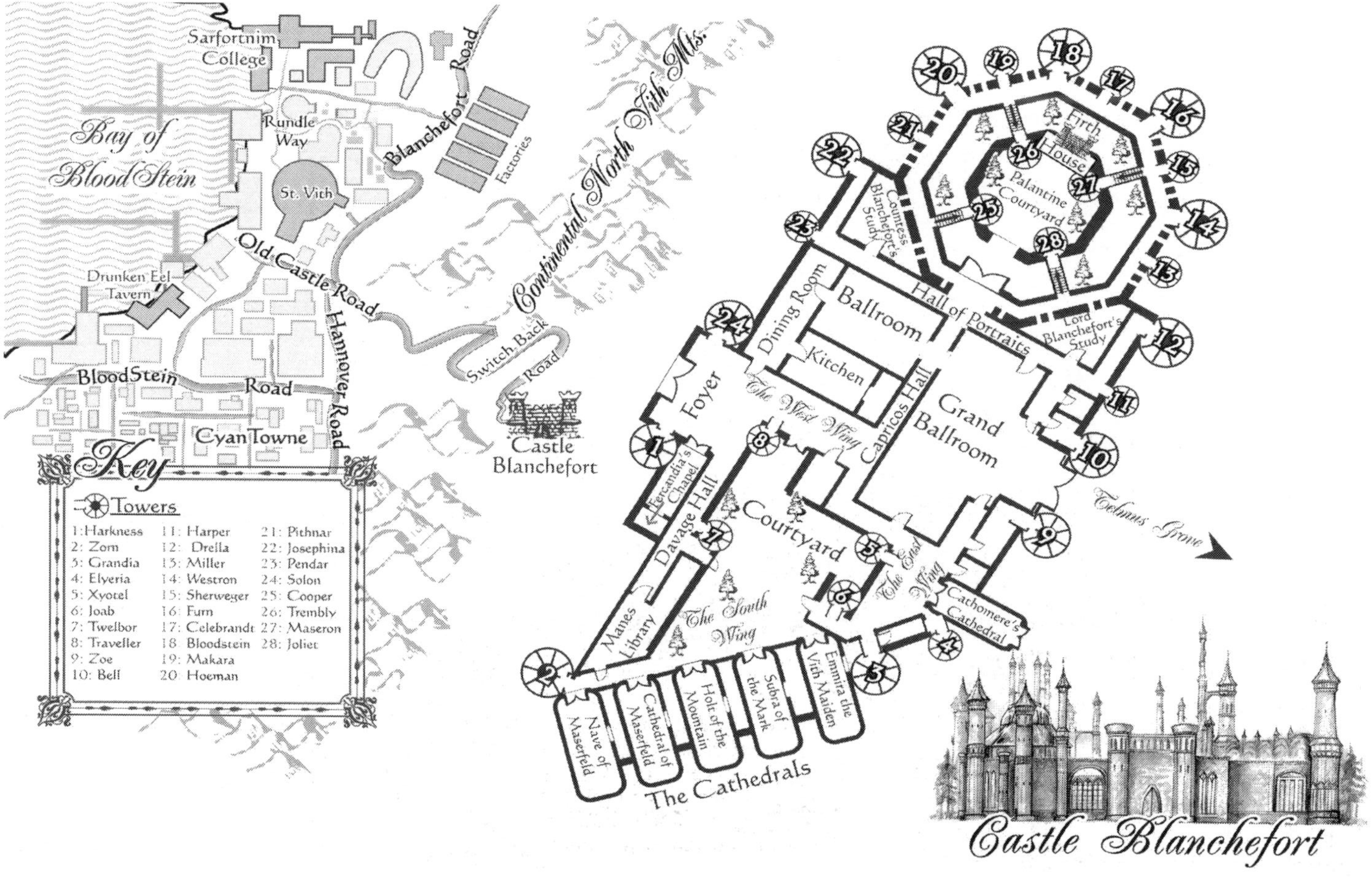
Sarfortnim College
Bay of BloodStein
Rundle Way
St. Vith
Blanchefort Road
Factories
Continental North Vith Mts.
Old Castle Road
Drunken Eel Tavern
Hannover Road
Switch Back Road
BloodStein Road
CyanTowne
Castle Blanchefort
Key
Towers
1: Harkness
2: Zorn
3: Grandia
4: Elyeria
5: Xyotel
6: Joab
7: Twelbor
8: Traveller
9: Zoe
10: Bell
11: Harper
12: Drella
13: Miller
14: Westron
15: Sherweger
16: Furn
17: Celebrandt
18: Bloodstein
19: Makara
20: Hoeman
21: Pithnar
22: Josephina
23: Pendar
24: Solon
25: Cooper
26: Trembly
27: Maseron
28: Joliet
Firth House
Palantine Courtyard
Countess Blanchefort's Study
Lord Blanchefort's Study
Hall of Portraits
Dining Room
Ballroom
Kitchen
Capricos Hall
Grand Ballroom
Foyer
The West Wing
Fercandia's Chapel
Davage Hall
Courtyard
The East Wing
The South Wing
Manes Library
Cathomere's Cathedral
Telmus Grove
Nave of Maserfeld
Cathedral of Maserfeld
Holt of the Mountain
Subra of the Mark
Emmira the Vith Maiden
The Cathedrals
Castle Blanchefort

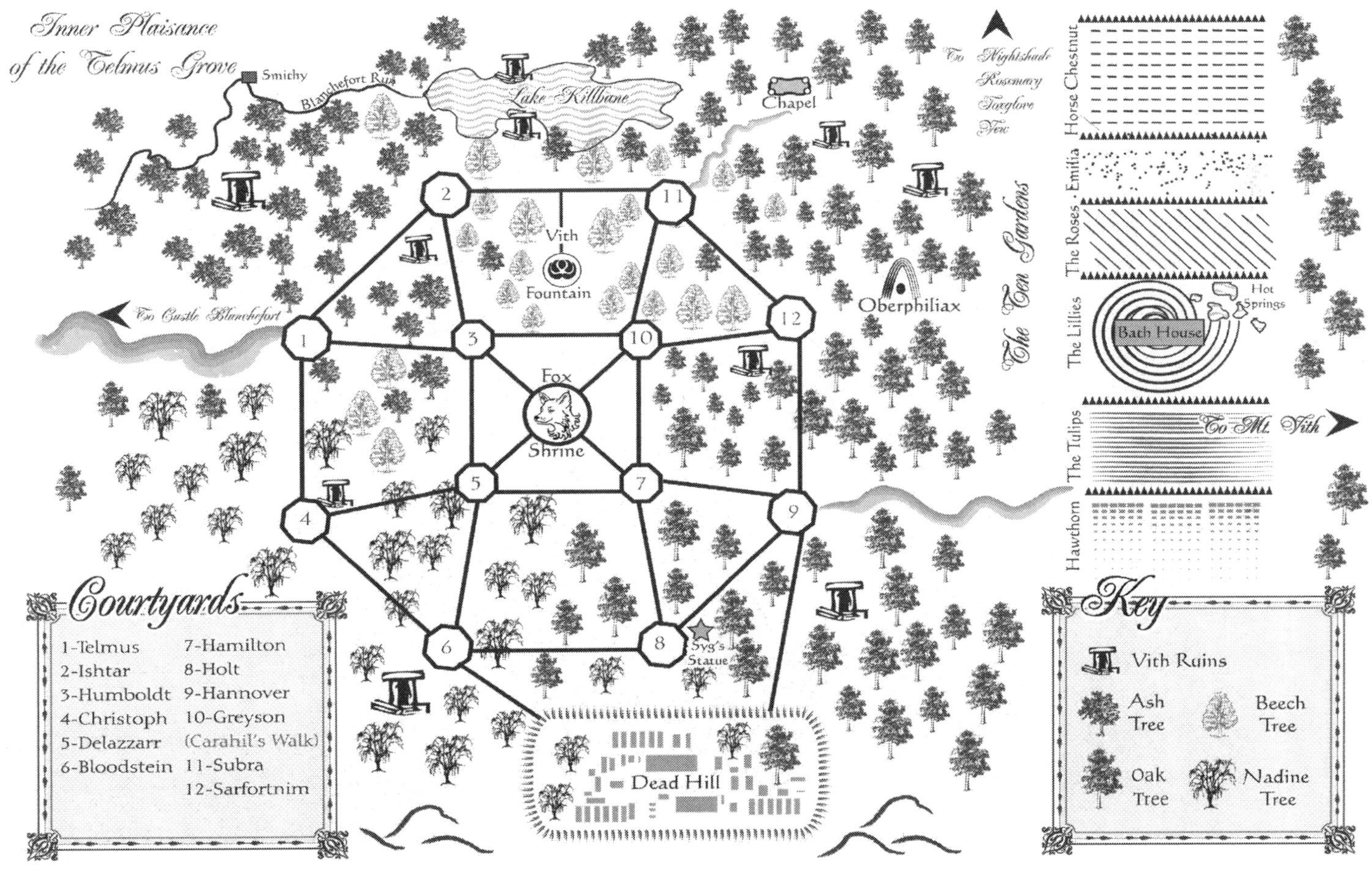
Inner Plaisance
of the Telmus Grove
Smithy
Blanchefort Run
Lake Killbane
Chapel
To Nightshade
Rosemary
Foxglove
Yew
Horse Chestnut
Emilia
The Roses
The Lillies
Bath House
Hot Springs
The Tulips
Hawthorn
The Ten Gardens
Oberphiliax
To Castle Blanchefort
To Mt. Vith
Vith
Fountain
Fox
Shrine
Syg's Statue
Dead Hill
1
2
3
4
5
6
7
8
9
10
11
12
Courtyards
1-Telmus
2-Ishtar
3-Humboldt
4-Christoph
5-Delazzarr
6-Bloodstein
7-Hamilton
8-Holt
9-Hannover
10-Greyson
(Carahil's Walk)
11-Subra
12-Sarfortnim
Key
Vith Ruins
Ash Tree
Beech Tree
Oak Tree
Nadine Tree

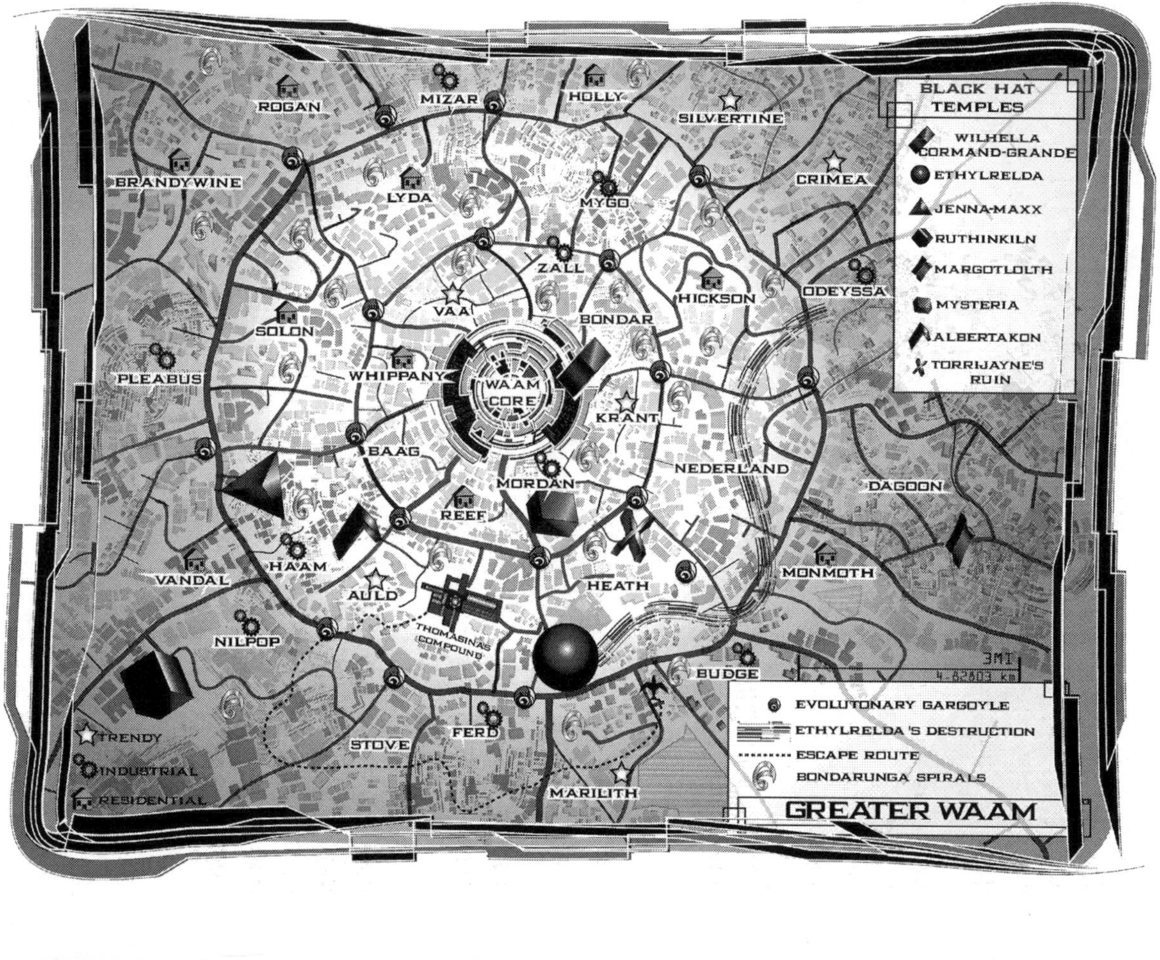

GREATER WAAM
BLACK HAT TEMPLES
WILHELLA CORMAND-GRANDE
ETHYLRELDA
JENNA-MAXX
RUTHINKILN
MARGOTLOLTH
MYSTERIA
ALBERTAKON
TORRIJAYNE'S RUIN
EVOLUTONARY GARGOYLE
ETHYLRELDA 'S DESTRUCTION
ESCAPE ROUTE
BONDARUNGA SPIRALS
TRENDY
INDUSTRIAL
RESIDENTIAL
3MI
4.82803 km
WAAM CORE
ROGAN
MIZAR
HOLLY
SILVERTINE
BRANDYWINE
LYDA
MYGO
CRIMEA
ZALL
HICKSON
ODEYSSA
VAA
BONDAR
SOLON
PLEABUS
WHIPPANY
KRANT
BAAG
NEDERLAND
MORDAN
DAGOON
REEF
HAAM
VANDAL
AULD
HEATH
MONMOTH
THOMASINA'S COMPOUND
NILPOP
BUDGE
STOVE
FERD
MARILITH

LOE Legends: Countess Sygillis and the Day of Silent Looms

The Day of Silent Looms is a bit of backstory I've had floating about the League of Elder universe for years now—it only gets hinted at in several of the books. Little dillies like this add a touch of spice to the characters, giving them more depth, but I was taught not to burden the reader with an excess of backstory—plot, you see, is king, so I've always left it out of the narrative.

But, I just love this story of the fiery little countess who dared to stir things up in Blanchefort Village, and couldn't resist adding it here, to the end of the Temple Omnibus.

—RDG

* * * * *

Big changes often begin as minor stirrings that grow and grow until there is no stopping them. Such is the case of Countess Sygillis of Blanchefort and the Day of Silent Looms.

The fortune of the House of Blanchefort is pinned on the production of textiles and the designing of men's and women's garments. In days past, the Blancheforts produced a line of popular firearms, however, Lord Sadric, a true man about town, abolished the practice and converted his factories to the production of fine fabrics, a craft he took great pride in.

His son, Lord Davage, never took much of an interest in the business and maintained a staff of well-paid designers to run the factories and create the look of the designs. Whatever the designers wanted to do, Davage signed-off on every season without much fuss. Occasionally, his sisters, Lady Poe and Countess Pardock, would have some thoughts on certain shades and textures they would like to see implemented, and the designers would accommodate them, but that was all

Things changed radically when Countess Sygillis showed up.

'Syg' was a vibrant countess, an ex-Black Hat, and she breathed new life into the old household. She was in love with her lord and with his castle and all the things that came with it, including the family business. She was given a lavish tour of the factories, the designers proudly showing off their latest creations. In her honor, they created a "red" line of fabrics for the season. Syg, so new to the family, was bewildered by it all.

Time passed. One day, Syg was watching her son, Kay, playing in the Telmus Grove with his cousins, and she was inspired. She imagined some clothes she'd like to see her son dressed in. She prepared a few sketches, tucked them under her arm, and took them down to the factories. Excited, she showed them to the designers and they promised they would turn the sketches out.

Unfortunately, the designs never came. Undaunted, Syg tried again, and again, always heading down the mountains with her sketches, always the warm welcome and smiling faces at the factories, and always the lack of results. Unlike her husband who took no interest in the factories, Syg was an animal of a completely different color, and when she got something in her head there was no stopping her. The 'misunderstanding' with the designers was becoming personal fast. She harassed them with such vigor and frequency the designers began calling Syg 'Madame Thimble' behind her back.

She took several self-help courses at Sarfortnim College and taught herself how to sew. She designed swatches and created her own fabrics on a small loom in her study. She was quite proud at what she had created. Getting rebuffed time and time again, Syg finally had had enough. She gathered the designers together and told them in no uncertain terms that she was their boss and she demanded they do as she asked.

The designers politely responded that she was NOT their boss–Lord Davage was, and they were not about to cheapen the Blanchefort line with her silly designs.

Syg was furious. She informed the designers that she not only possessed Lord Davage's ear, but many other select parts of him as well and that "Hell wasn't a half-mile off." That evening, after a furious bout of love-

making, Syg gently whispered into Davage's ear: "Love, may I please sack every one of the designers?"

Nude, glistening with sweat, she showed Davage her designs and insisted she could do a better job. She begged him to let her fire them. "Please let me fire them, Dav! Please, please, please! I promise, I'll give them a rousing severance package and I'll take the business to new heights!!"

Too tired to argue, Davage proclaimed Syg could do what she wished in the factories—she even got it from him in writing, signed on parchment placed on her bare back. He had a thought that if Syg fired the staff and failed, then that would give him the excuse to quit textiles and start producing firearms again. So, he had a happy wife and the prospect of restarting the old family business—it was a win/ win however it turned out.

The next morning, armed with her new power, Syg marched down to the factories and fired every designer who dared cross her path. The stream of people exiting the factories holding the sack became known as the Day of Silent Looms.

Madame Thimble had struck, proving it is never wise to provoke the Countess of Blanchefort.

As the various Households watched, Syg took control of the Blanchefort factories, turning out her designs in abundance. Though, not without her missteps, Syg proved to be a capable designer and a shrewd businesswoman. Her designs were bold and daring and, in time, she grew the business, invading fresh new territory, such as Hoban, which had never invested in Blanchefort fabrics. Lord Davage's dreams of making firearms again would have to wait.

At long last, Syg was able to see her son in clothes she thought proper.

List of Illustrations

LEAGUE OF ELDER
The Temple Of The
EXPLODING HEAD
OMNIBUS

About the Author

Ren Garcia is a Science Fiction/Fantasy author and Texas native who grew up in western Ohio. He has been writing since before he could write, often scribbling alien lingo on any available wall or floor with assorted crayons. He attended The Ohio State University and majored in English Literature. Ren has been an avid lover of anything surreal since childhood, he also has a passion for caving, taking pictures of clouds, urban archeology and architecture. He currently lives in Columbus, Ohio with his wife and their four Dachshunds.

For more please visit: www.thetempleoftheexplodinghead.com

97938738R00411

Made in the USA
Columbia, SC
17 June 2018